BENSON and HEDGES

CRICKET YEAR

FOURTH EDITION

VODKA
INSURANCE
FLY
GILLETTE Blue II
Cornhill Insurance

BENSON and HEDGES

CRICKET YEAR

FOURTH EDITION

SEPTEMBER 1984 TO SEPTEMBER 1985

EDITOR DAVID LEMMON
ASSOCIATE EDITOR TONY LEWIS

PELHAM BOOKS

First published in Great Britain by
Pelham Books Ltd
44 Bedford Square
London WC1B 3DP
1985

British Library Cataloguing in Publication Data
Benson and Hedges cricket year. – 1984–1985
1. Cricket – Periodicals
796.358′05 GV911

ISBN 0-7207-1599-7

Filmset in Times and Univers by MS Filmsetting Limited, Frome, Somerset
Printed and bound in Italy by Arnoldo Mondadori

Editor's Note

The aim of *Benson and Hedges Cricket Year* is that the cricket enthusiast shall be able to read through the happenings in world cricket, from each October until the following September (the end of the English season). Form charts are printed and a player's every appearance will be given on these charts, and date and place allow these appearances to be readily found in the text.

The symbol * indicates 'not out' or 'wicket-keeper' according to the context and the symbol † indicates captain.

The editor wishes to express his deepest thanks to Brian Croudy, Brian Heald, Anthony Lalley, Les Hatton, Qamar Ahmed, Victor Isaacs and Barry MacAuley whose advice and help over statistics have been invaluable.

Unless otherwise stated, all the comments and written material in the book are the work of the editor who also compiles the statistics.

Sponsor's message

Cricket boomed in England during the 1985 season despite the vagaries of the weather which did its best to ensure everyone stayed in the pavilion. Not only were the Ashes regained but we were treated to one of the most pulsating finishes ever in the final of the Benson and Hedges Cup. Leicestershire's Peter Willey led his County's charge to beat the favourites Essex after even the staunchest Leicester supporter must have given up all hope.

This match is detailed in the *Benson and Hedges Cricket Year* now in its fourth edition which provides an authoratitive report on first class cricket played around the world during the past twelve months. Published just two months after the close of the English season the book offers a winter reminder of the game's memorable moments to enthusiasts and professional players alike.

PAUL RUTHERFORD
Director, Benson and Hedges

The 1985 Australians

Tony Lewis

It became clear, from the luxurious position called 'hind-sight', that the Australians came to England in the summer of 1985, without the appropriate weapons to win the war. In an armchair game, you might have picked one England-Australian side, and only Allan Border and Craig McDermott would have been certainties, with Wayne Phillips a possibility.

There was much talk as the series went on about Border's wisdom in going into Tests with four bowlers instead of the more balanced five. He argued that he was short of runs. The one chance to see five bowlers in action was at Old Trafford when Border did not go short of runs, 257 and 340 for 5, but his side did concede a massive 482 for 9 declared by England. So, the truth was, it did not matter which way Border played it. He did not have either batsmen or bowlers, of sufficient ability.

Australia lost the series by three Tests to one, and two of those defeats were by an innings.

At one time, the Australian captain, taut and bearded, did resemble Samson in the temple, because his own heroic strength with the bat was surrounded by crumbling pillars. Where were the long, gritty innings from Wessels? Where the venomous speed of Lawson? Surely the experience of Thomson would winkle a few out; was it not time for Wood to stamp an indelible mark on Test cricket? And what about the surprise item Holland, the leg-spinner. When I spoke to Border in the nets at Lord's before the season began, he had expressed serious hopes that leg-spin would succeed because of its rarity in the English County Championship. It did not.

It cannot be argued that Australia were deprived of key players who chose to contract themselves to South Africa rather then play for their country. Alderman might have been the only one missed. His whippy action, his understanding of English conditions, and his ability to swing the ball and hit the seam more often then most, would have helped. However, five of the six Test pitches were sluggish and there is no reason to imagine Alderman having a harvest of wickets. Only the Oval offered the fast bowler bounce and pace, but even then, with Lawson and McDermot taking four wickets each, England reached 464 and won by an innings.

The disappointment of the 1985 Australians was that they did not play like Australians at all. Historically, the Aussie cricketer, bound to the native instinct for both loving and hating the mother-country, is one helluva guy to play against; never beaten until the last ounce of strength and the final twist of cunning is extracted. Here was a side which looked shockingly unprofessional at times. They appeared to give up.

The lack of professional application was demonstrated by the vice-captain and opening bat, Hilditch. I saw him play first at Somerset, before the Tests. Ian Botham sent down a number of short-pitched balls and Hilditch obliged by hooking one of them for a catch at fine leg. In the Tests, Hilditch not only got out hooking with two men set at long-leg in an obvious trap, but he did it at Lord's, Edgbaston and at the Oval. Botham might be seen as the tormentor, but truly it was self-destruction. Wood, his opening partner was about similar business. He rarely curbed the spontaneous hook, and so Botham fed the bait. The dismal habit of these two was made even more ludicrous by the Test century each of them scored. They proved that they could handle the England attack over long sessions at the crease, so it was unbelievable suicide. And, just to make the point that they were not exactly up against Lillee and Thomson, Roberts and Holding, Marshall and Garner or other famed demolishers of confidence, England's selectors had to grope for a sharp, penetrative new-ball attack. They had tried Allott, Cowans, Sidebotham, Foster, Agnew, Ellison and Taylor by the end.

Also unprofessional was the Australian habit of wearing rubber-soled shoes on moist, grassy fields. The pitches themselves were always dry and covered, but the surrounds had them slipping about. Both Gilbert and Ritchie, skidded and fell while running between the wickets at the Oval. In Manchester, Boon dropped two important catches at slip. On both occasions his rubber-soled shoes slid one way as he tried to move off in the other. Wayne Phillips too kept wickets in rubbers. Downton started the series for England in his sand shoes but quickly turned to spikes. However, Phillips was still in soft shoes in the sixth Test where he once let four byes through without laying a glove on the ball. He went quickly down the leg side, saw the ball bounce and then swing suddenly back straight again, but he skidded and never got back in line at all.

Allan Border found it increasingly difficult to hold a side of brittle talents together, although he batted magnificently, fielded well at slip and generally plotted sensibly. However, he gave a clue in his end-of-tour press interview that his side had not attacked the tour with the toughness and durability he wanted. He inferred that some had claimed to have been travel-weary, homesick and less than enthusiastic for the hard slog of a full county fixture card as well as six Tests.

Yet, out of every tour comes the good news. Border said before the tour began 'I'm confident the future of Australian cricket is here in England. It may not emerge quite as I hope on this tour but I'm sure in twelve months time we will be a major force again.'

So, for the moment, we recall Border's own form, his 196 in the Lord's Test which set up Australia's one win; his 146 not out which surely saved his team from another defeat in the rain-influenced draw at Manchester. His approach to batting is more mature these days. He is not so dour. He never shirks playing his best attacking strokes, the square cut, the pull, the drive, and he showed many an English spinner how they can be hit for fours and sixes by a batsman who uses his feet down the pitch and is not afraid to hit over the in-field.

Boon will come again; he still wrestles with the nerves of starting a Test innings. O'Donnell has a lot of work to do, but a batting place higher up the order may bring a stronger performance. Wayne Phillips was an attractive sight with the bat. He too could come on quickly if he bats in the first five and not with the tail.

The best news for Australia was the batting of Ritchie and the bowling of McDermott. Ritchie's batting in the middle order was both full of guts and yet elegant. His major innings were 94 in the second Test, 146 in the third, and a comfortable 64 not out in the fifth when the rest of the side were sinking to an innings defeat.

Of the bowlers, only Craig McDermott looked the part. He stayed fit – a huge bonus to Border. He took 8 wickets in an innings at Old Trafford. Although he showed that he could nip the ball smartly past anyone's helmet, he obeyed the old adage of keeping the ball well up to the bat on off-stump and got his rewards. Quite a few English counties were trying to attract him to a career in county cricket.

And there is one glowing memory. It was a sporting tour, and the mood was struck by the two captains. They imposed on the series the rich feeling of all-out competition on the field but a beer shared at close of play. Border, serious of countenance demonstrated this unforgettably on the balcony of the Oval pavilion when he was about the painful business of surrendering the Ashes. He heard the crowd cheer him, he turned and gave a dazzling smile which lit up the whole cricket world and did Australia proud.

Contents

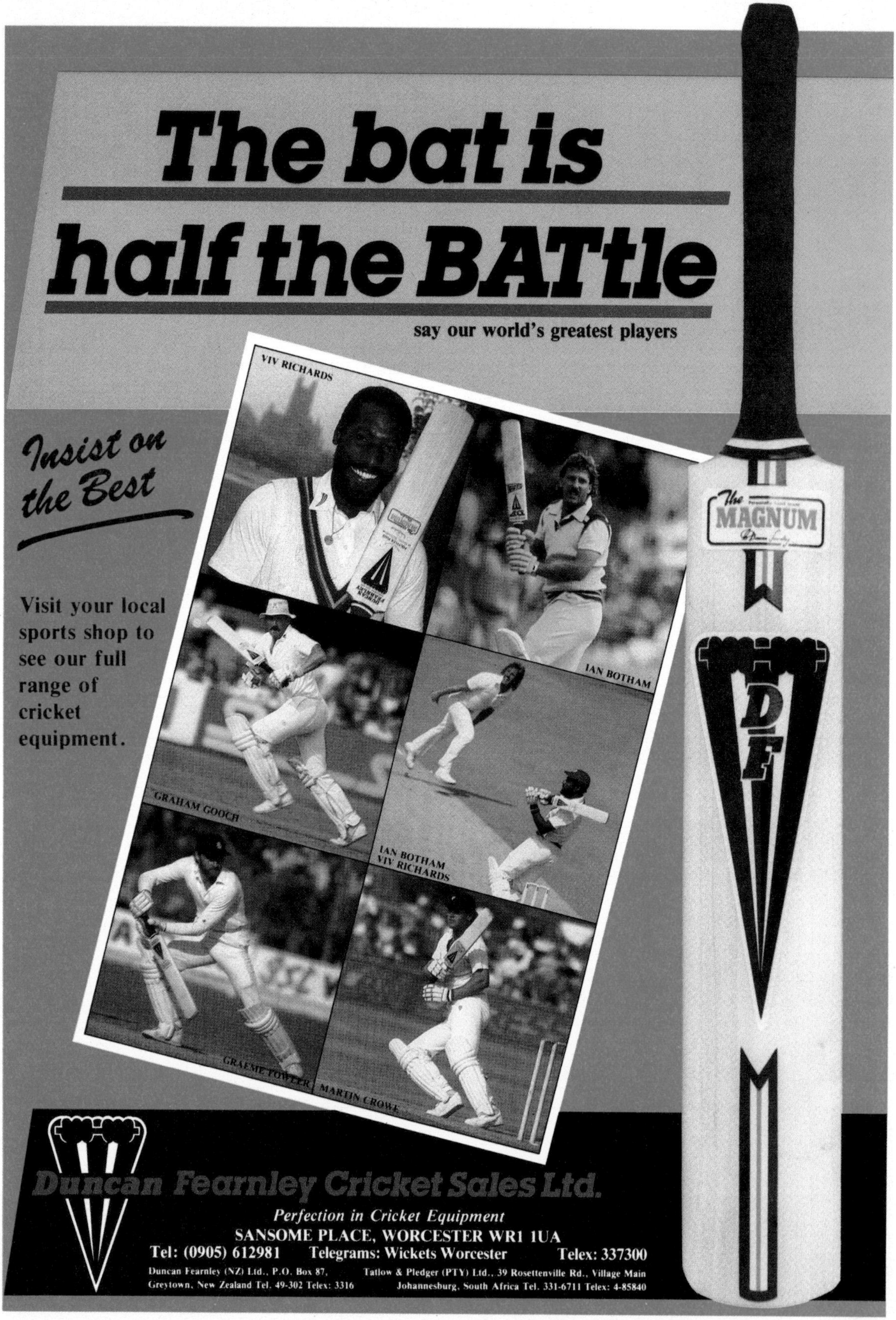
The bat is
half the BATtle
say our world's greatest players
Insist on the Best
Visit your local sports shop to see our full range of cricket equipment.
VIV RICHARDS
IAN BOTHAM
GRAHAM GOOCH
IAN BOTHAM
VIV RICHARDS
GRAEME FOWLER
MARTIN CROWE
The MAGNUM
DF
Duncan Fearnley Cricket Sales Ltd.
Perfection in Cricket Equipment
SANSOME PLACE, WORCESTER WR1 1UA
Tel: (0905) 612981
Telegrams: Wickets Worcester
Telex: 337300
Duncan Fearnley (NZ) Ltd., P.O. Box 87, Greytown, New Zealand Tel. 49-302 Telex: 3316
Tatlow & Pledger (PTY) Ltd., 39 Rosettenville Rd., Village Main Johannesburg, South Africa Tel. 331-6711 Telex: 4-85840

SECTION A

Sad Jubilee

The season in India.
One-Day International series *v.* Australia.
Test series and one-day international series *v.* England.
Irani Cup. Ranji Trophy. Duleep Trophy. Averages.
Managing by Tony Brown.

Statistics supplied by Sudhir Vaidya.

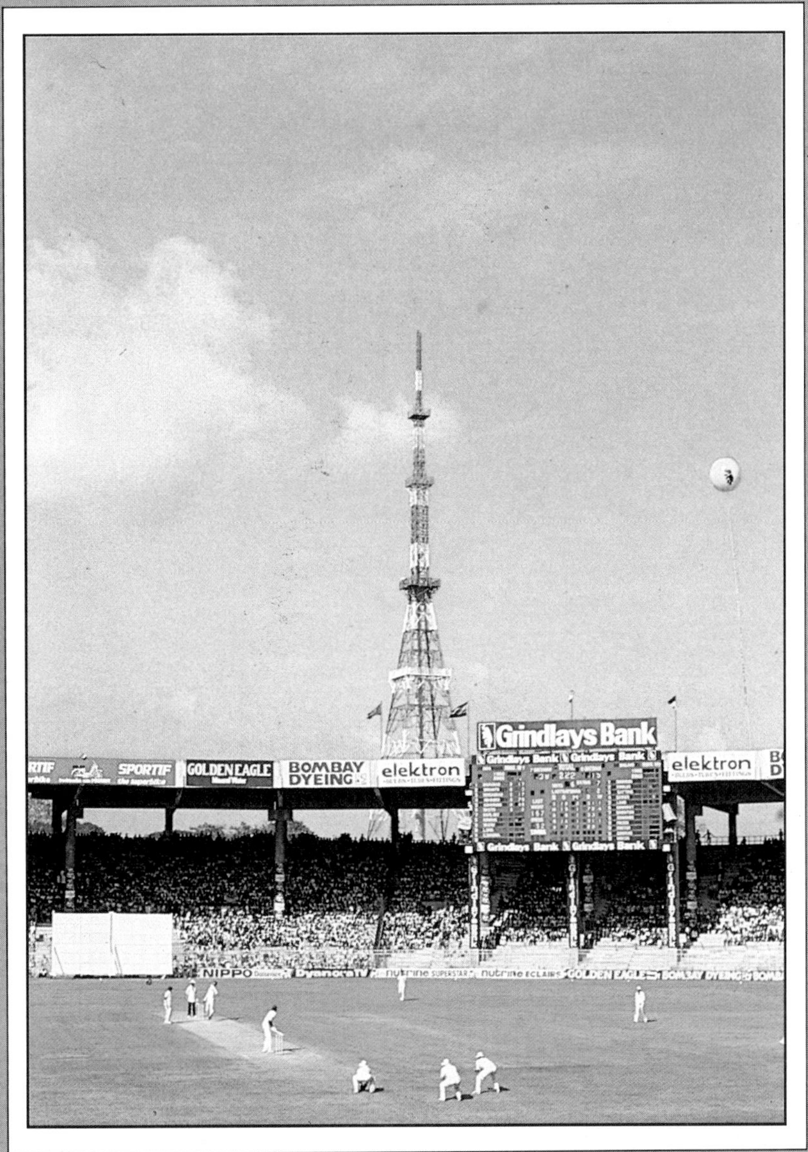

Madras – scene of the fourth Test match when England gained a famous victory. (Adrian Murrell).

In the minds of many, cricket is still able to shape a code of conduct, a fabric of social well being, but it cannot escape the tragedies and dilemmas of the modern world. For Indian cricket, 1984–85 was to have been a time of celebration and rejoicing to acclaim the golden jubilee of the Ranji Trophy, but those celebrations were overshadowed by the tragic events which surrounded the murder of Mrs Ghandi and the disaster at Bhopal. It was hard to speak of joy and celebration against this backdrop and it was not until the new year that cricket could really shake itself free from the traumas which encompassed it, but by then Australia and England had been and gone and left wounds to accompany those which had been inflicted by internal division and strange selection.

The season began with the Irani Trophy match at Ferozeshah Kotla ground, Delhi. This game, played at the start of the season, always creates problems in that the wickets are invariably under-prepared and the Delhi ground, hampered by a week of rain prior to the match, was no exception.

Kapil Dev won the toss for the Rest of India and, to the surprise of many, asked Bombay to bat. That his decision was justified was due as much to inept batting by Bombay as to any potency in the Rest of India attack. Although Rest of India got off to a brisk start, 45 for the first wicket off 34 balls, their batting showed little improvement on Bombay's and it was not until Kapil Dev's 48 that they asserted an authority over an attack which, Nayak apart, had been very wayward.

If Bombay had batted poorly in the first innings, then their second innings lacked the necessary virtues of dedication and application and there seemed an eagerness to surrender which was degrading to the fixture. Kapil Dev and Chetan Sharma made the early inroads and Maninder Singh, exploiting the potential of the wicket far better than Shastri or Baindoor had done, brought the innings to a close. Needing 107 to win, Rest of India closed the third day at 69 for 2, and when the sides reassembled on the Tuesday, Mohammad Azharuddin batted brightly and confidently for the best innings of the match.

Following the Irani Trophy match, matches were played between a side chosen from the party that had won the Asia Cup in Sharjah and the rest. The idea behind these matches was to help the selectors in choosing the team to tour Pakistan, but the futility of such an exercise, considering one-day performances in order to select a Test side, was recognised. There were some good individual performances from Khanna, who had not played well in the Irani Trophy game, Patil, Prabhakar, who had a 4 for 0 spell in one match, Shastri and More, who looked the best of the wicket-keeper-batsmen on view. He was to find no place in the Indian side for the one-day series against the Australians, however, a series which had been arranged to commemorate the golden jubilee of the Ranji Trophy.

First One-Day International
INDIA *v.* AUSTRALIA

Having had only one hour's practice since their arrival in

LEFT: *Dilip Vengsarkar, 200 not out against the tourists at Rajkot, but he condemned the game to a draw. (Adrian Murrell)*

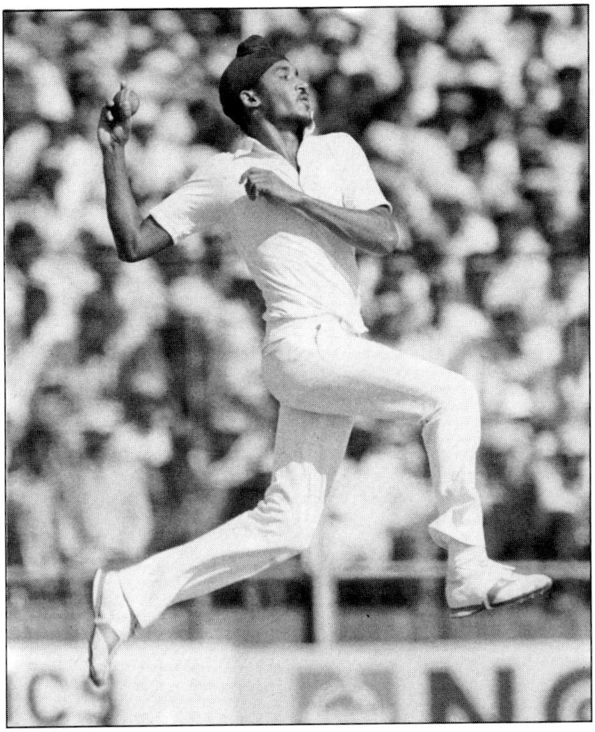

Ghai bowled well in all the matches he played against the England side and was in fine form for Punjab, but he was ignored by the Test selectors. (Adrian Murrell)

Kiran More (Baroda) made a bright start to the season, but his batting fell away and he could not win a place in the national side. (Adrian Murrell)

IRANI TROPHY – BOMBAY *v.* REST OF INDIA

7, 8, 9 and 11 September 1984 at Ferozeshah Kotla, Delhi

BOMBAY

	FIRST INNINGS		SECOND INNINGS	
G.A.H.M. Parkar	c Dev, b Maninder	33	(2) b Maninder	55
L.S. Rajput	c Khanna, b C. Sharma	5	(1) b C. Sharma	1
D.B. Vengsarkar	c Dev, b Maninder	23	lbw, b Kapil Dev	1
S.M. Patil	c Dev, b Azad	32	c and b Dev	2
S.M. Gavaskar†	c Azharuddin, b Prabhakar	13	(7) b Maninder	14
R.J. Shastri	lbw, b Dev	58	(5) c and b Maninder	15
C.S. Pandit*	c and b Binny	37	(6) b Kapil Dev	12
R. Baindoor	c Gaekwad, b Dev	0	c Azharuddin, b Maninder	6
S.V. Nayak	b C. Sharma	0	not out	24
B.S. Sandhu	not out	4	run out	6
R.R. Kulkarni	lbw, b C. Sharma	0	b C. Sharma	7
Extras	b 19, lb 8, nb 4	31	b 8, lb 4, w 1, nb 7	20
		236		163

	O	M	R	W	O	M	R	W
Chetan Sharma	17.4	4	50	3	12.4	1	47	2
Kapil Dev	16	5	25	2	11	3	17	3
Binny	7	3	23	1	7	3	26	—
Prabhakar	16	3	41	1	5	2	7	—
Maninder Singh	28	10	55	2	22	9	34	4
Kirti Azad	10	3	17	1	6	2	20	—

FALL OF WICKETS

1- 6, 2- 53, 3- 80, 4- 106, 5- 157, 6- 225, 7- 225, 8- 229, 9- 236

1- 10, 2- 12, 3- 24, 4- 70, 5- 98, 6- 99, 7- 120, 8- 129, 9- 141

REST OF INDIA

	FIRST INNINGS		SECOND INNINGS	
A.D. Gaekwad	c sub, b Sandhu	14		
S.C. Khanna*	c Parkar, b Sandhu	34	(1) c Pandit, b Sandhu	23
M. Azharuddin	b Sandhu	0	not out	51
A.O. Malhotra	c Pandit, b Shastri	34	c and b Shastri	16
Yashpal Sharma	c Pandit, b Nayak	25	st Pandit, b Shastri	1
Kirti Azad	b Baindoor	30	lbw, b Sandhu	1
R.M.H. Binny	c Pandit, b Rajput	30	lbw, b Sandhu	0
R.N. Kapil Dev†	c Parkar, b Nayak	48	not out	2
M. Prabhakar	lbw, b Kulkarni	18	(2) c Rajput, b Sandhu	4
Chetan Sharma	not out	24		
Maninder Singh	c Pandit, b Kulkarni	7		
Extras	penalty runs	4		
		25		9
		293	(for 6 wickets)	107

	O	M	R	W	O	M	R	W
Kulkarni	19.2	2	97	2	5	—	32	—
Sandhu	18	1	75	3	13	3	41	4
Nayak	20	8	23	2	4	—	15	—
Shastri	18	5	45	1	8.5	3	14	2
Baindoor	11	—	34	1				
Rajput	2	—	3	1				

FALL OF WICKETS

1- 45, 2- 45, 3- 68, 4- 115, 5- 123, 6- 167, 7- 197, 8- 240, 9- 274

1- 28, 2- 33, 3- 93, 4- 99, 5- 104, 6- 104

Rest of India won by 4 wickets

FIRST ONE-DAY INTERNATIONAL – INDIA *v.* AUSTRALIA
28 September 1984 at Jawaharlal Stadium, Delhi

AUSTRALIA

K.C. Wessels	c Parkar, b Madan Lal	107
G.M. Wood	c Khanna, b Sharma	0
K.J. Hughes†	c Parkar, b Patel	72
G.N. Yallop	st Khanna, b Kirti Azad	22
A.R. Border	st Khanna, b Kirti Azad	0
W.B. Phillips*	run out	1
T.G. Hogan	lbw, b Madan Lal	6
G.F. Lawson	c Vengsarkar, b Kapil Dev	2
C.G. Rackemann	run out	2
R.M. Hogg	not out	0
J.N. Maguire		
Extras	b 3, lb 4, nb 1	8
(48 overs)	(for 9 wickets)	220

	O	M	R	W
Kapil Dev	9	1	43	1
Chetan Sharma	9	—	49	1
Madan Lal	7	2	23	2
Patel	10	2	27	1
Shastri	3	—	23	—
Kirti Azad	10	1	48	2

FALL OF WICKETS
1- 14, 2- 142, 3- 200, 4- 200, 5- 203, 6- 213, 7- 216, 8- 220, 9- 220

INDIA

S.C. Khanna*	c Phillips, b Rackemann	13
G.A.H.M. Parkar	c Lawson, b Rackemann	16
D.B. Vengsarkar	c Yallop, b Maguire	33
S.M. Patil	lbw, b Hogg	22
S.M. Gavaskar†	c Wood, b Rackemann	25
Kirti Azad	c Phillips, b Maguire	0
R.N. Kapil Dev	b Hogan	39
R.J. Shastri	st Phillips, b Hogan	5
U.S. Madan Lal	c Lawson, b Rackemann	1
C. Sharma	not out	9
A. Patel	c Phillips, b Hogan	0
Extras	lb 2, nb 7	9
(40.5 overs)		172

	O	M	R	W
Lawson	5	—	23	—
Rackemann	10	1	41	4
Hogg	6	1	21	1
Maguire	10	1	41	2
Hogan	9.5	1	44	3

FALL OF WICKETS
1- 17, 2- 44, 3- 76, 4- 96, 5- 97, 6- 148, 7- 160, 8- 161, 9- 172

Australia won by 48 runs

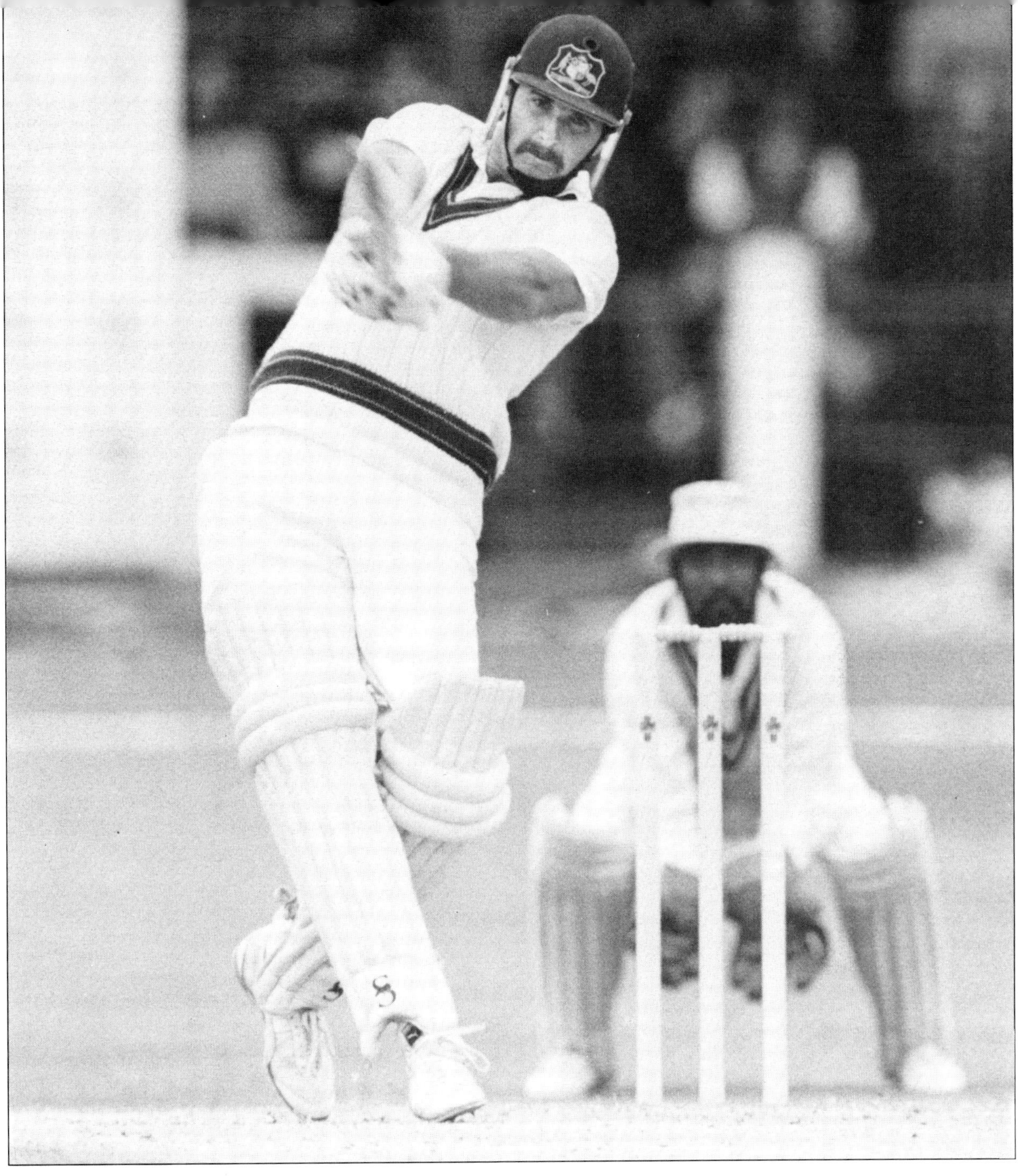

ABOVE LEFT: *Kepler Wessels. A most impressive start to Australia's brief tour, 107 at Delhi in the first one-day international. (Adrian Murrell)*
ABOVE: *Graham Yallop showed a welcome return to fitness. Kirmani behind the stumps. (Steve Powell)*

India, the Australians were expected to be slow into their stride, but Kepler Wessels dispelled Indian optimism with a fine century. He and Hughes added 128 brisk runs for the second wicket, but rash batting saw Australia lose their last seven wickets for 20 runs. The best of the Indian bowlers was Ashok Patel who was making his international debut.

Khanna kept wicket well, but he and Parkar went quickly at the beginning of the Indian innings and although Kapil Dev struck some lusty blows to give the 35,000 crowd hopes of an Indian victory, the later batsmen posed no real threat to the Australian supremacy.

Second One-Day International
INDIA *v.* AUSTRALIA

The match was reduced to 37 overs an innings after overnight rain had delayed the start by 40 minutes. Kim Hughes again won the toss, but this time he asked India to bat first

SECOND ONE-DAY INTERNATIONAL – INDIA *v.* AUSTRALIA
1 October 1984 at Trivandrum

INDIA				AUSTRALIA		
	S.C. Khanna*	c Phillips, b Rackemann	4	G.M. Wood	not out	7
	G.A.H.M. Parkar	c Phillips, b Rackemann	3	K.C. Wessels	lbw, b Kapil Dev	12
	D.B. Vengsarkar	b Hogan	78	A.R. Border	not out	4
	S.M. Patil	c Yallop, b Rackemann	16	K.J. Hughes†		
	R.N. Kapil Dev	b Wessels	12	G.N. Yallop		
	Kirti Azad	c and b Hogan	6	S.B. Smith		
	S.M. Gavaskar†	c Wood, b Hogan	14	W.B. Phillips*		
	R.J. Shastri	c Rackemann, b Hogan	2	T.G. Hogan		
	U.S. Madan Lal	b Border	9	G.F. Lawson		
	C. Sharma	not out	13	J.N. Maguire		
	A. Patel	c Hughes, b Border	6	C.G. Rackemann		
	Extras	b 5, lb 5, nb 2	12	Extras	b 1, lb 4, w 1	6
	(37 overs)		175	(7.4 overs)	(for 1 wicket)	29

	O	M	R	W
Lawson	7	—	29	—
Rackemann	8	4	7	3
Maguire	5	—	38	—
Wessels	7	—	45	1
Hogan	8	—	33	4
Border	2	—	13	2

	O	M	R	W
Kapil Dev	4	1	14	1
Chetan Sharma	3.4	1	10	—

FALL OF WICKETS
1- 7, 2- 10, 3- 53, 4- 78, 5- 103, 6- 136, 7- 146, 8- 146, 9- 166

FALL OF WICKETS
1- 24

Match abandoned

Martyn Moxon wearing an England cap for the first time, 4th One-Day International at Nagpur. (Adrian Murrell)

and the home side struggled, initially against the pace and movement of Carl Rackemann and later against some assorted slow bowling. Vengsarkar, with seven fours and three sixes, hit cleanly to help India to 175, but the Australian innings was cut short by the return of torrential rain, and, to the disappointment of 15,000 spectators, the match was abandoned.

Third One-Day International
INDIA *v.* AUSTRALIA

Rain caused the abandonment of the third one-day international after only 5.1 overs had been bowled, but by that time the game had already been reduced to farce. The match began four hours later and was scaled down from 50 to 24 overs because the Australian kit, for which no travel arrangements had been made, arrived some three hours after the match was due to start. This fiasco, and other chaotic travel

THIRD ONE-DAY INTERNATIONAL – INDIA *v.* AUSTRALIA
3 October 1984 at Jamshedpur

INDIA

S.C. Khanna*	c Border, b Rackemann	3
G.A.H.M. Parkar	b Rackemann	12
D.B. Vengsarkar	not out	1
R.N. Kapil Dev	not out	0
S.M. Gavaskar†		
R.J. Shastri		
R.M.H. Binny		
A. Patel		
U.S. Madan Lal		
Kirti Azad		
C. Sharma		
Extras	lb 4, nb 1	5
(5.1 overs)	(for 2 wickets)	21

	O	M	R	W
Lawson	3	—	14	—
Rackemann	2.1	—	3	2

FALL OF WICKETS
1- 6, 2- 21

AUSTRALIA

G.M. Wood
K.C. Wessels
K.J. Hughes†
A.R. Border
G.N. Yallop
S.B. Smith
W.B. Phillips*
R.M. Hogg
G.F. Lawson
J.N. Maguire
C.G. Rackemann

Match abandoned

and hotel arrangements, caused many to ponder what will happen if India and Pakistan stage the 1987 World Cup as is planned at present. The criticism and scepticism came from within India itself.

Fourth One-Day International
INDIA *v.* AUSTRALIA

Hughes won the toss for the fourth time in the series and asked India to bat. The new opening pair of Shastri and Binny gave India a most promising start with a stand of 104. The innings then became slowed by some good bowling by Wessels whose gentle off-breaks seem, bewilderingly, well suited to limited-over cricket. Kirti Azad, with four sixes, raised Indian hopes at the close of their innings, the last two overs producing 37 runs.

Australia, who were without Hogg who had returned home ill, batted solidly. Border and Hughes raised the tempo of the innings by adding 73 in 10 overs and Australia moved easily to victory with two overs to spare.

FOURTH ONE-DAY INTERNATIONAL – INDIA *v.* AUSTRALIA
5 October 1984 at Ahmedabad

INDIA

R.J. Shastri	st Phillips, b Hogan	45
R.M.H. Binny	st Phillips, b Hogan	57
D.B. Vengsarkar	b Lawson	14
S.M. Patil	c Hughes, b Wessels	3
R.N. Kapil Dev	b Lawson	28
S.M. Gavaskar†	b Lawson	4
Kirti Azad	not out	39
U.S. Madan Lal	not out	6
S.M.H. Kirmani*		
C. Sharma		
A. Patel		
Extras	b 1, lb 5, w 1, nb 3	10
(46 overs)	(for 6 wickets)	206

	O	M	R	W
Rackemann	8	—	50	—
Lawson	10	2	25	3
Maguire	8	—	56	—
Wessels	10	—	29	1
Hogan	10	2	40	2

FALL OF WICKETS
1- 104, 2- 111, 3- 122, 4- 132, 5- 144, 6- 160

AUSTRALIA

K.C. Wessels	c Kirmani, b Patel	42
G.M. Wood	run out	32
A.R. Border	not out	62
K.J. Hughes†	lbw, b Kapil Dev	29
G.N. Yallop	not out	32
S.B. Smith		
W.B. Phillips*		
T.G. Hogan		
J.N. Maguire		
G.F. Lawson		
C.G. Rackemann		
Extras	b 1, lb 10, nb 2	13
(44 overs)	(for 3 wickets)	210

	O	M	R	W
Kapil Dev	8	1	27	1
Chetan Sharma	7	1	21	—
Binny	2	—	21	—
Madan Lal	8	—	35	—
Patel	10	—	44	1
Kirti Azad	9	—	51	—

FALL OF WICKETS
1- 67, 2- 89, 3- 162

Australia won by 7 wickets

Fifth One-Day International
INDIA *v.* AUSTRALIA

Australia won the toss for the fifth time in the series, gave places in the side to those who had not had a game on the tour and strolled to a comfortable victory to give them the series by three matches to nil, two games having been abandoned.

Ravi Shastri became the second Indian to hit a century in a limited-over international. He hit a six and eleven fours and shared a third wicket partnership of 115 with Gavaskar which provided the foundation for a good score by the Indians. Australia again batted calmly and paced their innings well after a splendid opening stand of 53 in the first seven overs from Smith and Phillips.

The series, intended as an Indian celebration of the Golden Jubilee of the Ranji Trophy, was completely dominated by Australia. Their batting was sound, their bowling tight, their fielding good and their running between the wickets outstanding. Kim Hughes was delighted with his side's performance which, he said, heralded a new era for Australian cricket. India, bitterly disappointing in that they were outclassed in all departments of the game, took some consolation from the batting of Shastri and the controlled off-spin of Ashok Patel.

8 October 1984

at Bombay

Bombay 190 for 6 (L.S. Rajput 66)
Australians 191 for 5 (S.B. Smith 81 retired hurt, A.R. Border 70)
Australians won by 5 wickets

The last match of the Australian tour, against Ranji Trophy holders Bombay, resulted in an easy win for the tourists who reached their target with 7.2 of their 47 overs still remaining. Allan Border, with 70 and 3 for 33, had an outstanding match.

13, 14 and 15 November 1984

at Jaipur

President's XI 198 for 5 dec (A.O. Malhotra 102 not out) and 117 for 3 (M. Azharuddin 52 not out)
England XI 444 for 8 dec (R.M. Ellison 83 not out, D.I. Gower 82, R.T. Robinson 81, V.J. Marks 66)
Match drawn

The England tour of India at last began, in the pink city of Jaipur. There was more sadness as Moxon had had to return to England because of the death of his father.

Gower won the toss and asked the home side to bat. Ashok Malhotra hit a fine century in a placid Indian innings which was ended on the second morning after which England batted enterprisingly and Robinson consolidated his position as a likely Test opener. Ellison and Marks hit lustily on

LEFT: *Laxman Sivaramakrishnan, England's tormentor, 12 for 181, and the main reason for India's victory. (Adrian Murrell)*

the last morning before the game moved, inevitably, to a draw.

17, 18 and 19 November 1984

at Ahmedabad

England XI 216 (M.W. Gatting 52, R.S. Ghai 4 for 42) and 117 (L. Sivaramakrishnan 4 for 27, Gopal Sharma 4 for 22)
India Under-25 392 for 6 dec (M. Azharuddin 151, R. Madhavan 103 not out, K. Srikkanth 92)
India Under-25 won by an innings and 59 runs

Bowled out in under four hours after Gower had won the toss, England never recovered from the first day disaster and were completely outplayed by an eager side well led by Ravi Shastri. Ghai and Prabhakar appeared to trouble the batsmen with their late swing, but leg-spinner Sivaramakrishnan looked the most formidable of the young Indian bowlers.

On the second day England toiled as Srikkanth and Azharuddin put on 176 for the second wicket. Srikkanth was at his most eventful best and Azharuddin, enjoying some luck, reached his century in 5¼ hours and continued with growing confidence to show that here was a young man of considerable talent. On the last morning he took his stand with the left-handed Madhavan to 240 for the fourth wicket before falling to Marks.

Shastri declared as soon as Madhavan reached his hundred and then, inexplicably, England collapsed in under three hours, victims of a blend of off and leg spin provided by Gopal Sharma and Sivaramakrishnan. It was delight for India and chastening for England whose performance in the field had been as miserable as their performance with the bat.

21, 22, 23 and 24 November 1984

at Rajkot

England XI 458 for 3 dec (M.W. Gatting 136 not out, G. Fowler 116, R.T. Robinson 103, D.I. Gower 57) and 138 for 7 dec (A. Patel 5 for 42)
West Zone 393 for 7 dec (D.B. Vengsarkar 200 not out, L.S. Rajput 79, P.H. Edmonds 4 for 99)
Match drawn

An opening stand of 190 by Fowler and Robinson set the pattern for a match which dragged through four days to a draw. Gatting provided the brightest entertainment with six sixes in his 136 off 133 deliveries. The declaration was anticipated by Vengsarkar employing occasional bowlers and the West Zone captain then reached a double century in spite of some fine bowling from Edmonds before Ashok Patel embarrassed England on the last day.

First Test Match
INDIA *v.* ENGLAND

Few Test matches can have begun in such an atmosphere of uncertainty and unhappiness. The England party had originally arrived in India some three hours before the assassination of Mrs Gandhi. Having made their short detour to Sri Lanka, they had returned to India in an attempt to re-establish the tour. In the days leading up to the first Test they were entertained by the British Deputy High Commissioner to Western India, Mr Percy Norris, and his wife. The following morning Mr Norris was murdered.

India was in the middle of weeks of agony and there were rumours that the tour would be cancelled and the party

FIFTH ONE-DAY INTERNATIONAL – INDIA *v.* AUSTRALIA
6 October 1984 at Indore

INDIA			
	G.A.H.M. Parkar	b Rackemann	6
	R.J. Shastri	b Maguire	102
	R.M.H. Binny	c Ritchie, b Maguire	37
	S.M. Gavaskar†	b Maguire	40
	Kirti Azad	c Smith, b Rackemann	11
	R.N. Kapil Dev	not out	22
	S.C. Khanna*	not out	1
	U.S. Madan Lal		
	M. Prabhakar		
	B.S. Sandhu		
	A. Patel		
	Extras	b 5, lb 3, w 4, nb 4	16
	(43 overs)	(for 5 wickets)	235

	O	M	R	W
Lawson	9	2	48	—
Rackemann	8	1	37	2
Maguire	10	—	61	3
Bennett	10	—	37	—
Wessels	6	—	44	—

FALL OF WICKETS
1- 23, 2- 83, 3- 198, 4- 207, 5- 217

AUSTRALIA			
	S.B. Smith	c Kapel Dev, b Patel	56
	W.B. Phillips*	c Patel, b Kapil Dev	33
	G.N. Yallop	b Patel	42
	G.M. Ritchie	not out	59
	K.J. Hughes†	c Prabhakar, b Patel	6
	K.C. Wessels	not out	35
	G.F. Lawson		
	M.J. Bennett		
	G.M. Wood		
	C.G. Rackemann		
	J.N. Maguire		
	Extras	lb 4, nb 1	5
	(40.1 overs)	(for 4 wickets)	236

	O	M	R	W
Kapil Dev	8	—	62	1
Prabhakar	2	—	15	—
Sandhu	6	—	38	—
Madan Lal	6	—	19	—
Patel	10	—	43	3
Kirti Azad	2	—	16	—
Shastri	6	—	35	—
Gavaskar	0.1	—	4	—

FALL OF WICKETS
1- 53, 2- 122, 3- 153, 4- 163

Australia won by 6 wickets

ABOVE: *The beginning of England's problems. Fowler hits a full toss straight back to Sivaramakrishnan. (Adrian Murrell)*

BELOW: *A sad start to the Test series. England and India observe a minute's silence in memory of Mrs Ghandi and Mr Percy Norris. (Adrian Murrell)*

ABOVE: *The leg-spinner strikes again. Tim Robinson is caught sweeping. Kirmani and Kapil Dev leap in appeal as the bowler turns to the umpire. (Adrian Murrell)*

would return home. In the event, they decided to do what they had gone to India to do, play cricket, but the first day at least must have been shrouded in sadness.

To his credit, Gower offered the happenings of recent weeks as no excuse for England's lamentable showing on the opening day. Allott, about whose fitness there was doubt, was omitted from the England twelve which meant Test debuts for Cowdrey and Robinson although many still wondered why Cowdrey was on the tour at all, for he is clearly not a player of international standard either as a batsmen or as a bowler.

Gower won the toss and Fowler and Robinson, without suggesting longevity, looked mainly untroubled. The complexion of the game changed when Laxman Sivaramakrishnan came on to bowl the twenty-third over of the match. The leg-spinner's fourth ball was a full toss which Fowler swatted straight back to him. At the second ball of Sivaramakrishnan's second over Robinson attempted a sweep and was caught behind on the leg-side. This heralded some dreadful England batting. Gower was bewildered by Sivaramakrishnan and, having been dropped off him, stayed only long enough to be bowled by Kapil Dev. Unfortunately Gatting, who had looked more substantial, had driven a hard return catch to Sivaramakrishnan the ball before.

The England innings now disintegrated. Lamb scooped to mid-on. Cowdrey, having lived precariously, was caught behind and Ellison, to whom the bowling of Sivaramakrishnan was a source of deepest mystery, was bowled by a googly. At tea, the score was 138 for 7.

Some brave, bold hitting by Edmonds and solid partnering by Downton took the score to 190 for 8 at the close. Only five runs were added the next day and the last two wickets fell to

FIRST TEST MATCH – INDIA *v.* ENGLAND
28, 29 November, 1, 2 and 3 December 1984 at Wankhede Stadium, Bombay

ENGLAND

	FIRST INNINGS		SECOND INNINGS	
G. Fowler	c and b Sivara	28	lbw, b Sivara	55
R.T. Robinson	c Kirmani, b Sivara	22	lbw, b Kapil Dev	1
M.W. Gatting	c and b Sivara	15	c Patil, b Sivara	136
D.I. Gower†	b Kapil Dev	13	c Vengsarkar, b Shastri	2
A.J. Lamb	c Shastri, b Kapil Dev	9	st Kirmani, b Sivara	1
C.S. Cowdrey	c Kirmani, b Yadav	13	c Vengsarkar, b Yadav	14
R.M. Ellison	b Sivara	1	(8) c Vengsarkar, b Yadav	0
P.R. Downton*	not out	37	(7) lbw, b Sivara	62
P.H. Edmonds	c Gaekwad, b Shastri	48	c Kapil Dev, b Sivara	8
P.I. Pocock	c Kirmani, b Sivara	8	not out	22
N.G. Cowans	c Shastri, b Sivara	0	c Vengsarkar, b Sivara	0
Extras	b 1	1	b 4, lb 8, nb 4	16
		195		317

	O	M	R	W	O	M	R	W
Kapil Dev	22	8	44	2	21	8	34	1
Chetan Sharma	11	4	28	—	9	2	39	—
Shastri	17	8	23	1	29	8	50	1
Sivaramakrishnan	31.2	10	64	6	46	10	117	6
Yadav	12	2	34	1	29	9	64	2
Gaekwad					1	—	1	—
Amarnath	3	2	1	—				

FALL OF WICKETS
1- 46, 2- 51, 3- 78, 4- 78, 5- 93, 6- 94, 7- 114, 8- 175, 9- 193
1- 3, 2- 138, 3- 145, 4- 152, 5- 199, 6- 222, 7- 228, 8- 255, 9- 317

INDIA

	FIRST INNINGS		SECOND INNINGS	
S.M. Gavaskar†	c Downton, b Cowans	27	c Gower, b Cowans	5
A.D. Gaekwad	run out	24	st Downton, b Edmonds	1
D.B. Vengsarkar	c Lamb, b Cowans	34	not out	21
M.B. Amarnath	c Cowdrey, b Pocock	49	not out	22
S.M. Patil	c Gower, b Edmonds	20		
R.J. Shastri	c Lamb, b Pocock	142		
R.N. Kapil Dev	b Cowdrey	42		
S.M.H. Kirmani*	c Lamb, b Pocock	102		
Chetan Sharma	not out	5		
S.N. Yadav	not out	7		
L. Sivarama-krishnan				
Extras	b 4, lb 2, nb 7	13	b 2	2
	(for 8 wkts dec)	465	(for 2 wickets)	51

	O	M	R	W	O	M	R	W
Ellison	18	3	85	—				
Cowans	28	6	109	2	5	2	18	1
Edmonds	33	6	82	1	8	3	21	1
Pocock	46	10	133	3	2.1	—	10	—
Cowdrey	5	—	30	1				
Gatting	7	—	20	—				

FALL OF WICKETS
1- 47, 2- 59, 3- 116, 4- 156, 5- 156, 6- 218, 7- 453, 8- 453
1- 5, 2- 7

Umpires: Swaroop Kishen and B. Ganguli

India won by 8 wickets

LEFT: *Chris Cowdrey bowls Kapil Dev to take his first wicket in Test cricket. (Adrian Murrell)*

BELOW: *Umpires Swaroop Kishen, with ball, and B. Ganguli. (Adrian Murrell)*

ABOVE: *Gower pads the ball away and Indian fielders cluster. (Adrian Murrell)*

BELOW: *Edmonds makes a bold reply for England. He hits Sivaramakrishnan for six. Firmani and the bowler follow the flight of the ball. (Adrian Murrell)*

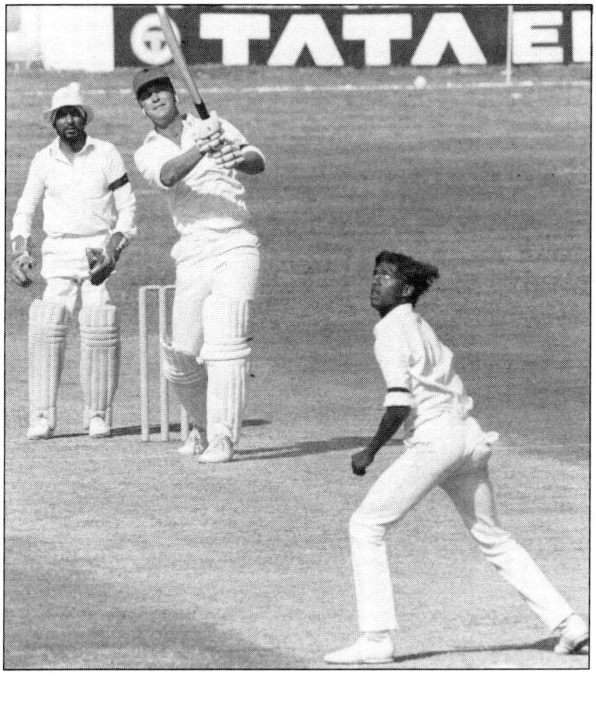

the eighteen-year old leg-spinner who had suddenly emerged as the great threat to England for this and many a season.

India batted consistently and boldly. They passed the England total in 45 overs. It had taken England 96 overs to amass. Cowdrey bowled Kapil Dev as he was threatening to tear England apart and the day ended with India 268 for 6 and England still in touch.

Kirmani and Shastri, in their differing ways, put the game out of England's reach on the third day. They extended their seventh wicket stand to 235 and both recorded their first Test centuries against England. Shastri has developed into a composed, quietly stylish batsman of unrelenting concentration. Kirmani, benefitting from a miss by Downton whose keeping was not of a high class, was all courage and determination. Shastri hit seventeen fours and a six in an innings which lasted 389 minutes. Kirmani hit ten fours in his 319-minute stay. Their stand was a record.

Lamb took one spectacular catch and missed another as India pressed for quick runs and a declaration and before the close they had captured Robinson and missed Gatting.

It was Gatting who became England's one hero on the fourth day. At the fifty-fourth attempt he at last revealed that he could do at Test level what he does weekly at county level, dominate an attack and play with a certainty and pugnacity that few can equal. His maiden Test hundred had been long overdue and even then was tinged with the disappointment that he did not bat out the day. He faced 255 balls in 310 minutes and hit twenty-one fours.

Sadly, he had little support until the phlegmatic Downton. Ellison stayed 50 minutes without scoring and without suggesting that he knew which way the ball would turn from Sivaramakrishnan who was again England's destroyer.

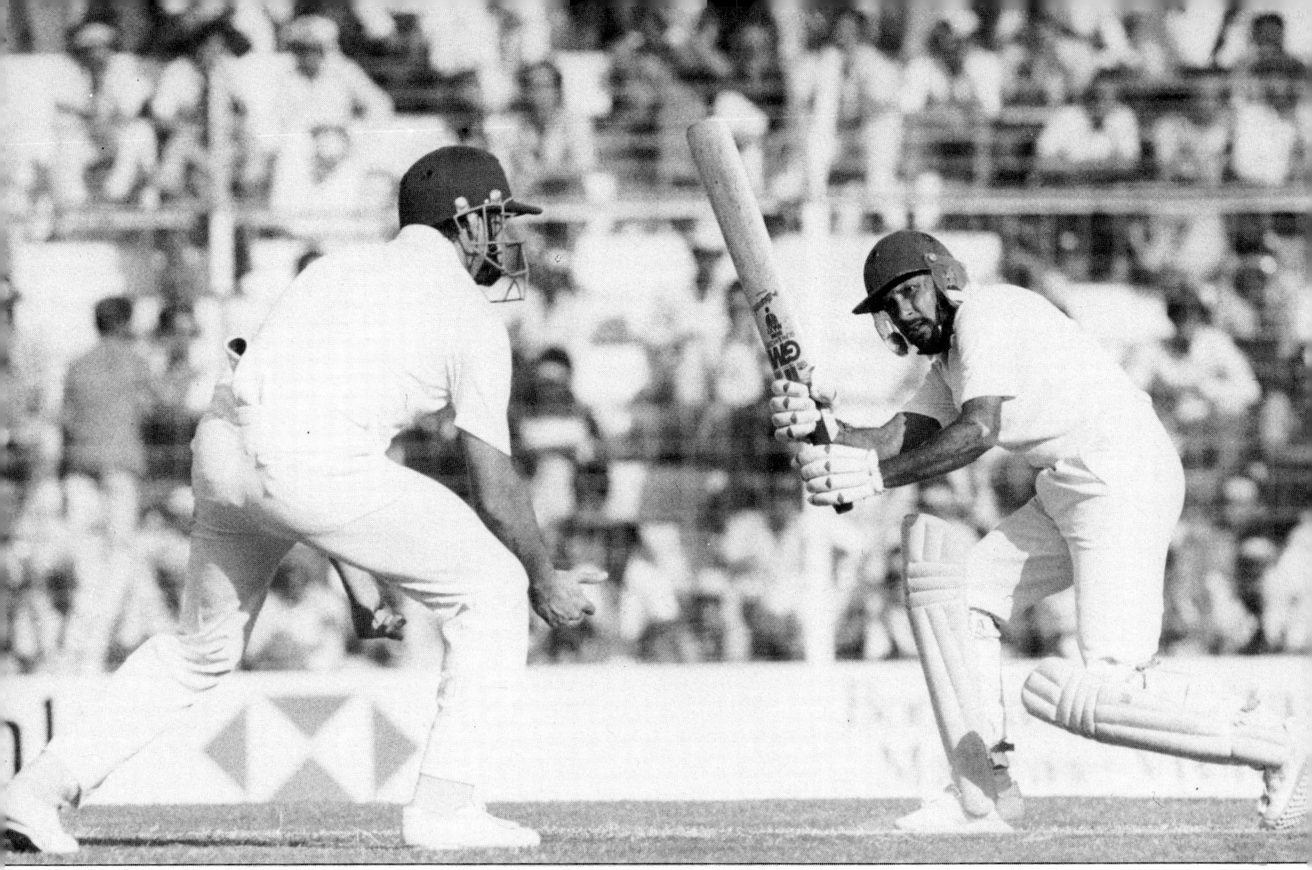

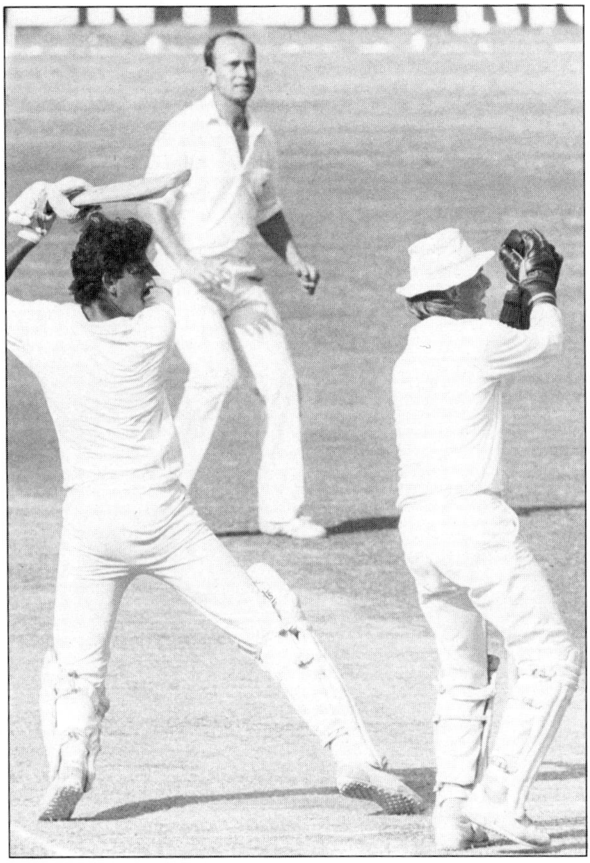

ABOVE: *Syed Kirmani, the Indian hero, who hit 102 and shared a record stand with Shatsri. (Adrian Murrell)*

LEFT: *Ravi Shastri square drives Edmonds in his innings of 142. (Adrian Murrell)*

It was the leg-spinner who finished the England innings on the last morning and India moved to a comfortable win, but not before Cowans and Edmonds had hinted at better things.

There was much criticism of the umpiring, Swaroop Kishen in particular, which was said to have favoured the Indians dramatically. Perhaps, it was time for players on both sides to reflect that an umpire only gives a batsman out

BELOW: *At last a Test hundred. Mike Gatting sweeps on his way to his 136. (Adrian Murrell)*

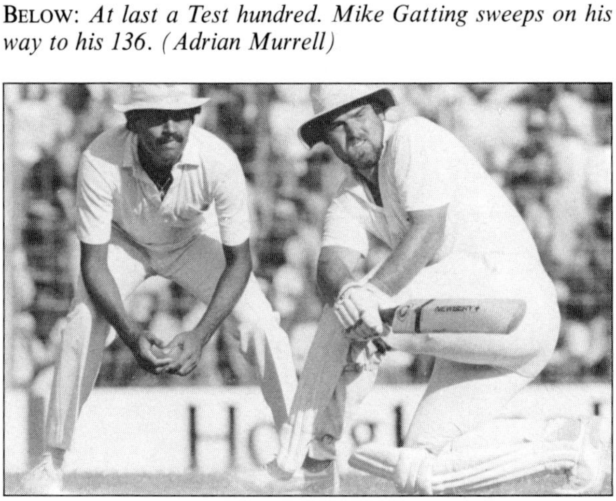

Allan Lamb is brilliantly stumped in England's second innings. (Adrian Murrell)

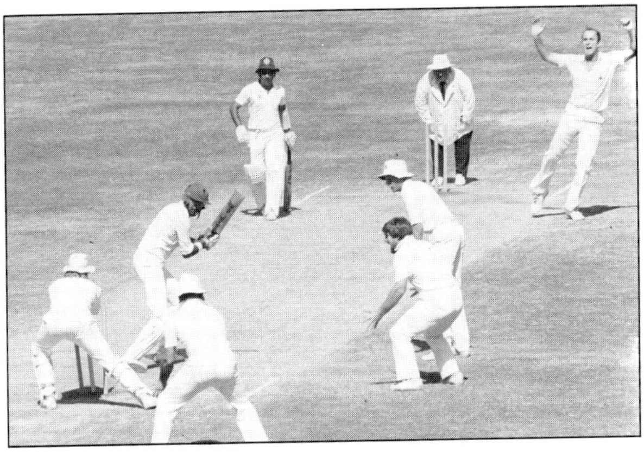

Gaekwad is stumped by Downton off Edmonds, but India win with ease. (Adrian Murrell)

in answer to an appeal and that if the umpire has erred, the initial culprits are the fielders in Tests throughout the world who take it as policy to appeal whenever the ball hits the pads and loops to short-leg or when a batsman plays and misses. Some self-questioning on the part of players would seem to be the order for it is in their hands, and attitudes, that the game rests.

First One-Day International
INDIA *v.* ENGLAND

A ground that groaned at the seams in an effort to accommodate all those who wanted to watch the match and an easy paced wicket were the setting for a welcome England victory. Gower won the toss and asked India to bat. Gavaskar chopped Foster's first delivery on to his wicket to give England needed encouragement, but Vengsarkar and Srikkanth shared a second wicket stand of 118. Vengsarkar profited from dropped catches in successive overs to reach his hundred out of 179 in 188 balls, but the Indian batsmen failed to maintain a brisk scoring rate after the stimulation had been provided by the second wicket stand.

England were troubled when Gower was hit in the face as he fielded the ball in the deep. He was led from the field and had to drop down the order. At 129 for 6, England looked to have little chance of victory but Gatting, in splendid form again, found an intelligent partner in Downton and they added 86, a seventh wicket record for a one-day international for England, and stroked their side to victory disturbed only by a riot which halted play for twenty minutes.

FIRST ONE-DAY INTERNATIONAL – INDIA *v.* ENGLAND
5 December 1984 at Pune

INDIA		
K. Srikkanth	b Edmonds	50
S.M. Gavaskar†	b Foster	0
D.B. Vengsarkar	b Ellison	105
S.M. Patil	run out	2
Yashpal Sharma	c Ellison, b Foster	37
R.J. Shastri	c Ellison, b Foster	11
R.M.H. Binny	not out	0
K.S. More*		
M. Prabhakar		
R.S. Ghai		
Chetan Sharma		
Extras	lb 2, w 7	9
(45 overs)	(for 6 wickets)	214

	O	M	R	W
Cowans	8	—	32	—
Foster	10	—	44	3
Ellison	7	—	44	1
Marks	10	—	49	—
Edmonds	10	—	43	1

FALL OF WICKETS
1- 1, 2- 119, 3- 126, 4- 189, 5- 212, 6- 214

ENGLAND		
G. Fowler	c Yashpal Sharma, b Chetan Sharma	5
R.T. Robinson	lbw, b Ghai	15
M.W. Gatting	not out	115
A.J. Lamb	c and b Prabhakar	3
V.J. Marks	run out	31
D.I. Gower†	c Shastri, b Binny	3
R.M. Ellison	run out	4
P.R. Downton*	not out	27
P.H. Edmonds		
N.A. Foster		
N.G. Cowans		
Extras	lb 8, nb 4	12
(43.2 overs)	(for 6 wickets)	215

	O	M	R	W
Chetan Sharma	8.2	—	50	1
Prabhakar	10	1	27	1
Ghai	9	—	38	1
Shastri	8	—	49	—
Binny	8	—	43	1

FALL OF WICKETS
1- 14, 2- 43, 3- 47, 4- 114, 5- 117, 6- 129

England won by 4 wickets

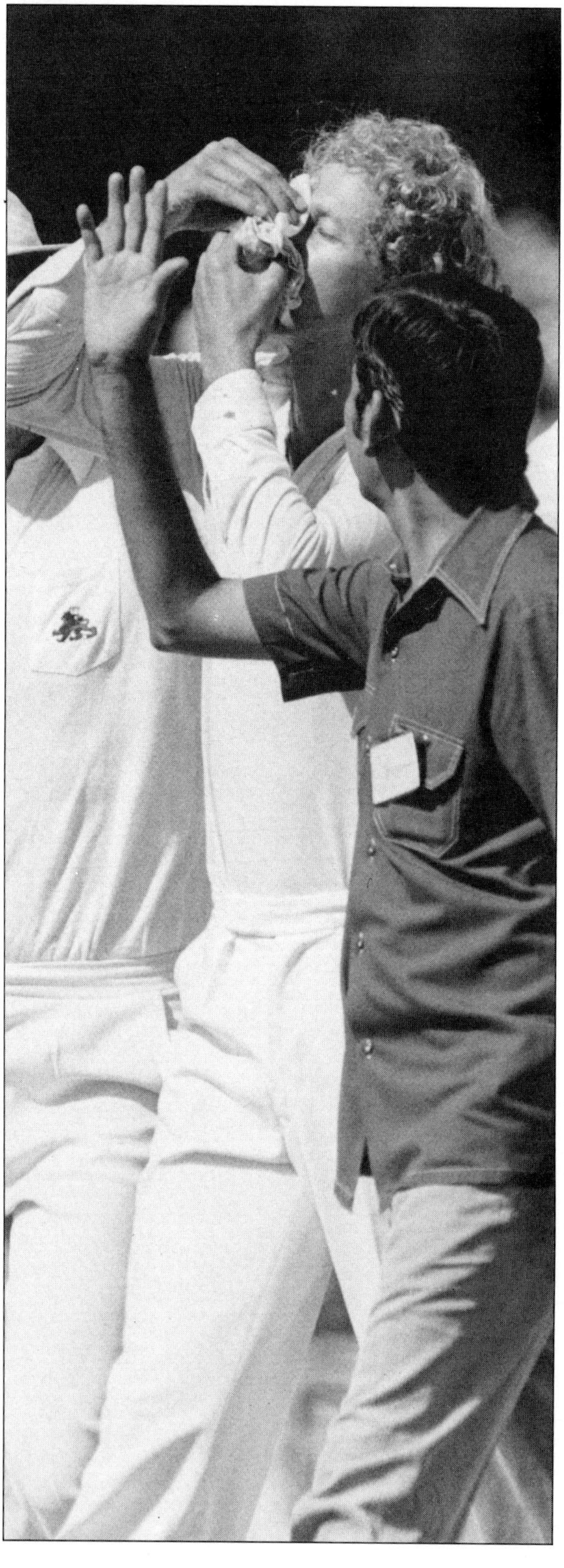

RIGHT: *Pune, the scene of the first one-day international, India v England. (Adrian Murrell)*

LEFT: *Gower leaves the field with an injured nose. Gatting is at his shoulder. Ellison and Cowdrey look concerned. (Adrian Murrell)*

Gatting's runs came from 125 balls and included ten fours and forty-four singles, a credit to the fine running and judgement of the two Middlesex players. Ghai and More made their international debuts in this match.

7, 8 and 9 December 1984

at Bombay

North Zone 186 and 176 for 3 (Gursharan Singh 53, A.O. Malhotra 50 not out)
England XI 377 (R.T. Robinson 138, C.S. Cowdrey 70, R.S. Ghai 7 for 110)
Match drawn

Commendably accurate bowling restricted North Zone on the opening day and they owed much to Madan Lal and Prabhakar who added 68 for the eighth wicket. Gower won the toss and decided to ask the home side, who fielded a strong eleven, to bat first and the England bowlers exploited the conditions well. Moxon, in his first match of the tour, scored 42 and shared a second wicket stand of 101 with Tim Robinson who batted with maturity and authority. Cowdrey gave a welcome sign of form, but neither Gower nor Lamb could find their touch. The outstanding performance was by medium-pace bowler Rajinder Singh Ghai who, though he bowled some loose deliveries which were punished, always troubled the batsmen. The match meandered to a draw on the third day.

Second Test Match
INDIA *v.* ENGLAND

When Gavaskar won the toss and took first innings on a wicket that threatened to deteriorate it seemed that England's chance of maintaining a challenge in the series was gone. There was early encouragement when Ellison had Gavaskar caught behind off an outswinger in his second over, and although Gaekwad and Vengsarkar put on 53 and in the afternoon session Amarnath and Patil added 61, the innings was never given a sense of longevity. There were some strange shots. Gaekwad wandered down the wicket, as did Vengsarkar. Patil edged a sweep and Shastri, bewilderingly, slogged the ball to mid-wicket. Shortly before tea India were 140 for 6 and in trouble, but Kapil Dev, in typically cavalier mood, and the intelligent Kirmani saw them safely to the close at 208. Pocock and Edmonds had bowled splendidly, but chances had been missed and although Kapil Dev went immediately on the second morning, the last four wickets produced 167 runs and India were in a sound position.

They seemed in no danger at the end of the second day when England were 107 for 2, Robinson having batted two and a half hours to reach his first Test fifty.

SECOND TEST MATCH – INDIA *v.* ENGLAND

12, 13, 15, 16 and 17 December 1984 at Ferozshah Stadium, Delhi

INDIA

	FIRST INNINGS		SECOND INNINGS	
S.M. Gavaskar†	c Downton, b Ellison	1	b Pocock	65
A.D. Gaekwad	b Pocock	28	(8) c Downton, b Edmonds	0
D.B. Vengsarkar	st Downton, b Edmonds	24	b Cowans	1
M.B. Amarnath	c Gower, b Pocock	42	b Edmonds	64
S.M. Patil	c Pocock, b Edmonds	30	c Lamb, b Edmonds	41
R.J. Shastri	c Fowler, b Pocock	2	not out	25
R.N. Kapil Dev	c Downton, b Ellison	60	c Lamb, b Pocock	7
S.M.H. Kirmani*	c Gatting, b Ellison	27	(9) b Pocock	6
M. Prabhakar	c Downton, b Ellison	25	(2) c Downton, b Cowans	5
S.N. Yadav	not out	28	c Lamb, b Edmonds	1
L. Sivarama-krishnan	run out	25	c and b Pocock	0
Extras	b 1, lb 12, nb 2	15	b 6, lb 10, w 1, nb 3	20
		307		235

	O	M	R	W	O	M	R	W
Cowans	20	5	70	—	13	2	43	2
Ellison	26	6	66	4	7	1	20	—
Edmonds	44.2	16	83	2	44	24	60	4
Pocock	33	8	70	3	38.4	9	93	4
Gatting	2	—	5	—	1	—	3	—

FALL OF WICKETS

1- 3, 2- 56, 3- 68, 4- 129, 5- 131, 6- 140, 7- 208, 8- 235, 9- 258

1- 12, 2- 15, 3- 136, 4- 172, 5- 207, 6- 214, 7- 216, 8- 225, 9- 234

ENGLAND

	FIRST INNINGS		SECOND INNINGS	
G. Fowler	c Gaekwad, b Prabhakar	5	c Vengsarkar, b Sivara	29
R.T. Robinson	c Gavaskar, b Kapil Dev	160	run out	18
M.W. Gatting	b Yadav	26	not out	30
A.J. Lamb	c Vengsarkar, b Yadav	52	not out	37
D.I. Gower†	lbw, b Sivara	5		
C.S. Cowdrey	c Gavaskar, b Sivara	38		
P.R. Downton*	c Kapil Dev, b Sivara	74		
P.H. Edmonds	c Shastri, b Sivara	26		
R.M. Ellison	b Sivara	10		
P.I. Pocock	b Sivara	0		
N.G. Cowans	not out	0		
Extras	b 6, lb 13, nb 3	22	b 4, lb 7, nb 2	13
		418	(for 2 wickets)	127

	O	M	R	W	O	M	R	W
Kapil Dev	32	5	87	1	6	—	20	—
Prabhakar	21	3	68	1	3	—	18	—
Sivaramakrishnan	49.1	17	99	6	8	—	41	1
Yadav	36	6	95	2	2	—	7	—
Shastri	29	4	44	—	4	—	20	—
Amarnath	2	—	6	—				
Gavaskar					0.4	—	10	—

FALL OF WICKETS

1- 15, 2- 60, 3- 170, 4- 181, 5- 237, 6- 343, 7- 398, 8- 411, 9- 416

1- 41, 2- 68

Umpires: D.N. Dotiwala and P.D. Reporter

England won by 8 wickets

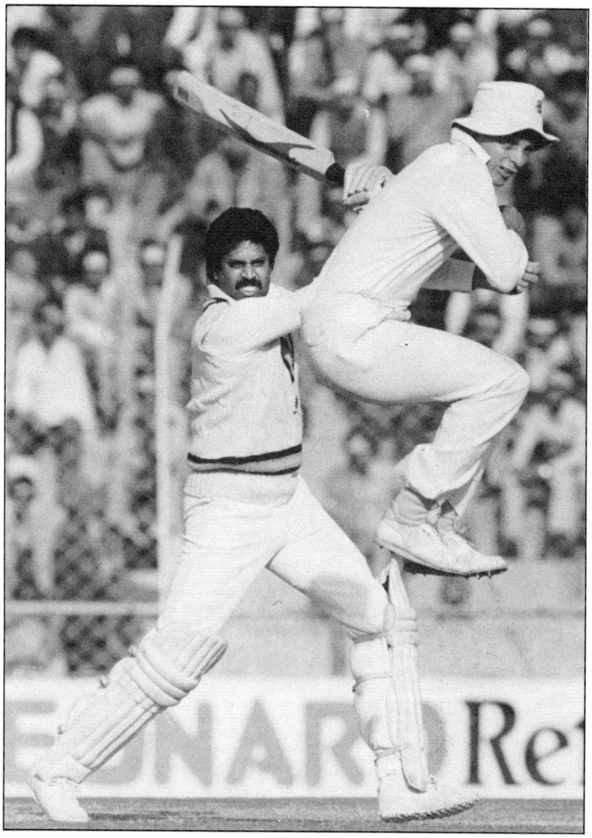

ABOVE: *Gower leaps for his life as Kapil Dev hits out in his violent innings of 60. (Adrian Murrell)*

BELOW: *Pat Pocock bowls Sunil Gavaskar and England sense victory. (Adrian Murrell)*

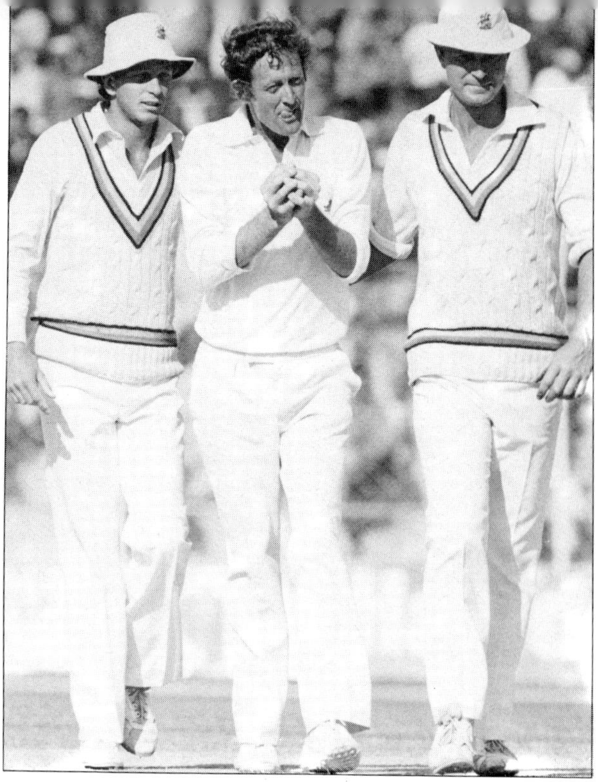

Pocock catches Sivaramakrishnan off his own bowling. Gower congratulates him and the other England spin hero, Phil Edmonds. (Adrian Murrell)

Following the rest day, the game moved in favour of England. There was another spate of decisions with which the batsmen did not agree and England were 237 for 5 with Sivaramakrishnan again threatening to demolish them, but throughout the histrionics of his more experienced colleagues, Tim Robinson stood firm, massively defiant. By the close England were 337 for 5 and Robinson was 157 not out, one of the most praiseworthy of maiden Test hundreds.

His 508-minute innings came to an end early on the fourth day. He faced 390 balls and hit seventeen fours. It was a masterpiece of concentration at a time when England were desperately in need of solidity. Downton, in spite of a limited range of strokes, played commendably although the rate of scoring was never as brisk as England could have wished. Sivaramakrishnan perplexed the tail, but England led by 111 and when Cowans removed emergency opener Prabhakar and Vengsarkar with only 15 scored England scented victory. The spinners could make no headway, however, and for the fourth day not a wicket fell after tea so that Gavaskar and Amarnath had both reached fifties by the close and India, 128 for 2, seemed to be moving sedately to a draw.

On 17 December 1984 England ended the most barren period in their Test history, thirteen matches without a win, when they beat India by eight wickets. The combined spin of Pocock and Edmonds brought about the victory. At one time, three wickets fell in five overs, and the last six Indian wickets produced only 28 runs.

Amarnath had been bowled in the second over and although Gavaskar survived a torrid time from Cowans and lasted another 70 minutes, he was suddenly bowled by Pocock. This gave England the lift they had needed and they

LEFT: *Paul Downton hits to leg during his invaluable innings of 74. (Adrian Murrell)*

BELOW LEFT: *Tim Robinson smiles delightedly after reaching a fine maiden Test century. (Adrian Murrell)*

were aided by some rash shots from Kapil Dev and Patil. Needing 125 to win, England had ample time and the situation demanded only that they keep their heads. Gatting and Lamb allayed any fears and Gower had won a Test match for the first time.

India were in some disarray and disagreement between Gavaskar and Kapil Dev became public so that the all-rounder who had led India to World Cup success was dropped, as was Patil.

19, 20 and 21 December 1984

at Gauhati

England XI 290 (G. Fowler 114, A. Kumar 5 for 81)
East Zone 117 (V.J. Marks 4 for 48) and 52 (P.H. Edmonds 4 for 13)

England XI won by an innings and 121 runs

The weakest of the zones were quietly extinguished by England in just over two days. Fowler, asserting his right to stay as England's opener, hit a six and eleven fours in the one solid contribution to England's first day 277 for 8. The second day produced only 131 runs in five hours, 94 overs. In the afternoon session, the East Zone scored 45 runs off 44 overs. They were tantalised and bemused by Edmonds and Marks who had 3 for 0 in 9 deliveries. Following-on, East Zone were in trouble against the lively Foster and then Edmonds completed their demoralisation in spite of five catches being put down. It was England's first win over a zone side for twenty years.

Second One-Day International
INDIA *v.* ENGLAND

England took a two–nil lead in the one-day series with a professional, rather than dashing win in Cuttack. Gower won the toss and aided by some poor catching and missed stumpings, Srikkanth and Shastri put on 188 in 37 overs for

SECOND ONE-DAY INTERNATIONAL – INDIA *v.* ENGLAND
27 December 1984 at Cuttack

INDIA		
K. Srikkanth	lbw, b Gatting	99
R.J. Shastri	b Gatting	102
D.B. Vengsarkar	c Gower, b Marks	23
Yashpal Sharma	lbw, b Marks	4
M.B. Amarnath	not out	6
R.M.H. Binny	b Marks	2
S.M. Gavaskar†	not out	1
K.S. More*		
M. Prabhakar		
R.S. Ghai		
A. Patel		
Extras	b 5, lb 5, w 3, nb 2	15
(49 overs)	(for 5 wickets)	252

	O	M	R	W
Foster	5	—	26	—
Cowans	10	—	39	—
Ellison	6	—	31	—
Edmonds	10	—	47	—
Marks	8	—	50	3
Gatting	10	—	49	2

FALL OF WICKETS
1- 188, 2- 235, 3- 243, 4- 243, 5- 246

ENGLAND		
G. Fowler	c Shastri, b Binny	15
R.T. Robinson	b Prabhakar	1
M.W. Gatting	b Patel	59
D.I. Gower†	c Prabhakar, b Binny	21
A.J. Lamb	run out	28
V.J. Marks	run out	44
P.R. Downton*	not out	44
R.M. Ellison	not out	14
P.H. Edmonds		
N.A. Foster		
N.G. Cowans		
Extras	lb 9, w 1, nb 5	15
(46 overs)	(for 6 wickets)	241

	O	M	R	W
Ghai	8	—	40	—
Prabhakar	10	1	34	1
Binny	7	—	48	2
Patel	10	—	53	1
Shastri	10	—	48	—
Amarnath	1	—	9	—

FALL OF WICKETS
1- 3, 2- 50, 3- 93, 4- 128, 5- 145, 6- 203

England won on faster scoring rate

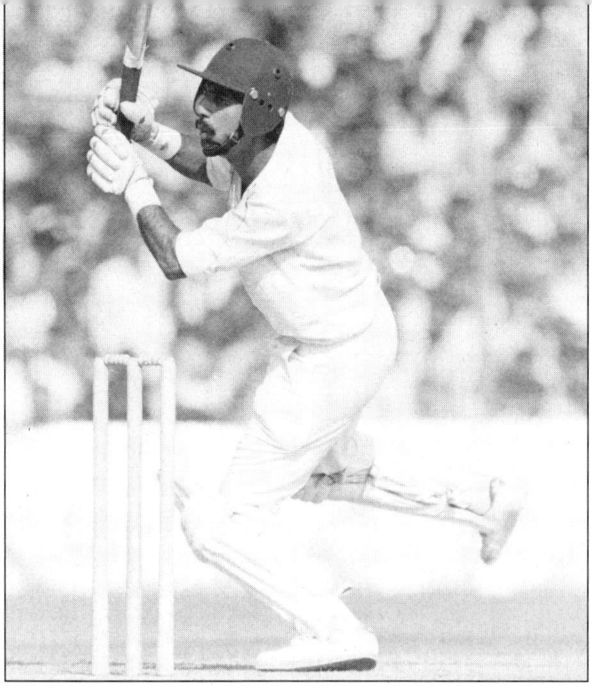

LEFT: *Srikkanth. A most exciting batsman. An opening stand of 188 in the second one-day international of which he scored 99. (Adrian Murrell)*
RIGHT: *Mohammad Azharuddin. A century on his Test debut and a century in each of his first three Tests, a feat unparalleled in Test match history. (Adrian Murrell)*

India's first wicket. This created a new record for the first wicket by any country, beating the 182 of McCosker and Turner and of Greenidge and Haynes.

To break the stand, England turned to Gatting who had Srikkanth lbw as he attempted to pull when one short of his century. He hit three sixes. Gatting bowled the majestic Shastri and after England had begun badly he scored briskly for his 59. At 145 for 5, however, England looked to be heading for defeat, but quick running in the gathering gloom by Marks and Downton, and later by Downton and Ellison took England closer to their target at the required rate.

It became so dark that the umpires offered Ellison and Downton the chance to leave the field at the end of the 46th over and the batsmen accepted. The England run rate was 5.23 to India's 5.14 and so England had won. There was a feeling, even among England supporters, that Srikkanth and Shastri had batted too well to end on the losing side, but Downton and Marks, in particular, had shown that running short singles, even in the dark, can be as important as big hitting.

Third Test Match
INDIA *v.* ENGLAND

In spite of rumoured intervention at ministerial level, Kapil Dev was not included in the Indian side. In retrospect, he was

THIRD TEST MATCH – INDIA *v.* ENGLAND
31 December 1984, 1, 3, 4 and 5 January 1985 at Eden Gardens, Calcutta

INDIA

	FIRST INNINGS		SECOND INNINGS	
S.M. Gavaskar†	c Gatting, b Edmonds	13		
A.D. Gaekwad	c Downton, b Cowans	18		
D.B. Vengsarkar	b Edmonds	48		
M.B. Amarnath	c Cowdrey, b Edmonds	42		
M. Azharuddin	c Gower, b Cowans	110		
R.J. Shastri	b Cowans	111	(1) not out	7
S.M.H. Kirmani	c Fowler, b Pocock	35		
M. Prabhakar	not out	35	(2) lbw, b Lamb	21
Chetan Sharma	not out	13		
S.N. Yadav			(3) not out	0
L. Sivaramakrishnan				
Extras	lb 8, w 1, nb 3	12	nb 1	1
	(for 7 wkts dec)	437	(for 1 wkt)	29

	O	M	R	W	O	M	R	W
Ellison	53	14	117	—	1	—	1	—
Cowans	41	12	103	3	4	1	6	—
Edmonds	47	22	72	3	4	3	2	—
Pocock	52	14	108	1	2	1	4	—
Cowdrey	2	—	15	—	4	—	10	—
Gatting	2	1	1	—				
Gower	3	—	13	—				
Lamb					1	—	6	1
Robinson					1	1	0	—
Fowler					1	1	0	—

FALL OF WICKETS
1- 28, 2- 35, 3- 126, 4- 127, 5- 341, 6- 356, 7- 407
1- 29

ENGLAND

	FIRST INNINGS	
G. Fowler	c Vengsarkar, b Sivaramakrishnan	49
R.T. Robinson	b Yadav	36
D.I. Gower†	c Shastri, b Yadav	19
P.I. Pocock	c Azharuddin, b Sivaramakrishnan	5
M.W. Gatting	b Yadav	48
A.J. Lamb	c Kirmani, b Chetan Sharma	67
C.S. Cowdrey	lbw, b Yadav	27
P.R. Downton*	not out	6
P.H. Edmonds	c Gavaskar, b Chetan Sharma	8
R.M. Ellison	c and b Chetan Sharma	1
N.G. Cowans	b Chetan Sharma	1
Extras	lb 2, nb 7	9
		276

	O	M	R	W
Chetan Sharma	12.3	—	38	4
Prabhakar	5	1	16	—
Sivaramakrishnan	28	7	90	2
Yadav	32	10	86	4
Shastri	23	6	44	—

FALL OF WICKETS
1- 71, 2- 98, 3- 110, 4- 162, 5- 163, 6- 229, 7- 269, 8- 270, 9- 273

Umpires: B. Ganguli and Vikran Raju

Match drawn

LEFT: *Shivlav Yadav, 4 wickets at Calcutta. (Adrian Murrell)*

the fortunate one. India gave a Test debut to Azharuddin and he was to provide the lasting memory of the match.

Mohammad Azharuddin came to the wicket on the first afternoon when India were 126 for 3. He lost Vengsarkar, sweeping, immediately after tea and then began his long record stand with Shastri. There were only four overs bowled on a gloomy second day by which time India were 176 for 4.

The partnership between Azharuddin and Shastri lasted until ten minutes remained of the third day. It had produced 214 runs and ended when Azharuddin cocked a short ball to Gower in the gully, a simple lobbed catch. He had scored 110 and his century in his first Test innings was received with massive acclaim by the large crowd. His hundred was reached in 382 minutes with eight fours and at the age of 21 he displayed a technique and temperament which mark him as a very fine player indeed. Like Shastri, he was aided by some poor catching and wicket-keeping, but nothing should detract from his magnificent performance.

Overall, however, the third day realised only 172 runs from 82 overs and the crawl was as inexplicable as it was unforgivable. Shastri's hundred came off 330 balls in 422 minutes, the second slowest ever made for India, nor was there to be a respite as India groped into the fourth day. Shastri was bowled after 7½ hours by the 354th ball that he faced. The week before he had scored 102 off 139 balls delivered by the same attack. Still Gavaskar did not declare. Kirmani alone showed some enterprise, but it was not until the fourth afternoon, by which time the crowd was close to riot, justifiably, that Gavaskar declared, and there were even suggestions later that the declaration came only on the advice of the police.

His rift with Kapil Dev public and his refusal to declare earlier a source of Indian anger, Gavaskar had become the focus of his country's cricketing discontent. A year earlier, in eclipsing Bradman, he had been the national hero.

England closed at 99 for 2 with Gower again unable to negotiate the Indian spinners, being bemused by Sivaramakrishnan and dismissed by the less potent Yadav.

On the last day, Gatting and Lamb entertained excitingly. Chetan Sharma took 4 wickets for 11 runs in 5 overs to hint as to why we had considered him an able opening partner for Kapil Dev a year earlier, and then the game ended in farce. A huge, enthusiastic and knowledgeable crowd had deserved more.

7, 8, 9 and 10 January 1985

at Hyderabad

South Zone 306 (K. Srikkanth 90, Arshad Ayub 58, J.P. Agnew 5 for 102) and 259 for 8 dec (M. Azharuddin 52)
England XI 334 (M.D. Moxon 153, M.W. Gatting 50, W.V. Raman 5 for 59) and 132 for 5

Match drawn

With Paul Allott having returned to England with a back injury, Jonathan Agnew, his replacement, bowled a lively spell against South Zone which brought him five wickets, but at a cost of nearly a run a ball. Srikkanth displayed his usual uninhibited strength, savaging Agnew's loose deliveries, but having more respect for the accurate and brisk Foster.

305 for 8 overnight, the South Zone added only one on the second morning. Moxon then asserted his right to a Test place with a patient and watchful 97 not out which, on the third morning, he increased to equal the highest score of his career. Three wickets by Cowdrey and a good opening burst from Foster and Agnew suggested England might snatch victory, but South Zone, with the increasingly impressive Azharuddin prominent, recovered and set the visitors a target of 232 at nearly six an over. There was a brave flourish after Moxon had gone for nought, but a draw was agreed with 10 overs remaining.

Fourth Test Match
INDIA *v.* ENGLAND

The criticism of Gavaskar was still severe when the fourth Test match began. India welcomed back Kapil Dev from his one-Test 'suspension' and included Srikkanth. England brought in Foster for the out of form and not fully fit Ellison, and many considered that Cowdrey was most fortunate to keep his place against the challenge of Moxon.

On the eve of the Test, it was remarkable to consider the change in fortunes of the two sides. From a dispirited and much criticised side, England had been transformed into a winning combination cemented by an excellent team spirit;

RIGHT: *Fowler drives Kapil Dev through the covers on his way to his double century. (Adrian Murrell)*

India, on the other hand, had descended from the heights of victory in the first Test to a team ravaged by rumours of dissension within the team and disenchantment with Gavaskar's captaincy. The India captain did much to rehabilitate himself by winning the toss and taking first innings on a wicket that looked full of runs.

Gavaskar began quite frenziedly and set the tone for the rest of the day. He hit Foster for two fours in his first over, the second of the match, and after he had hit Foster for 4 in the fast bowler's next over he played across the line and was bowled. Srikkanth drove at the first ball of the next over from Cowans and was caught behind, 17 for 2.

Vengsarkar began crisply and Amarnath immediately suggested the authority that was to produce the innings of the day. Vengsarkar played a majestic cover drive and was missed at slip before Foster bounced one steeply at him and the ball went straight and fast to Lamb at second slip, 45 for 3 off 12 overs. By lunch, the score had moved to 102. It was scintillating stuff and Calcutta had become a faded memory.

In the afternoon, Amarnath and Azharuddin threatened to take control of the match for India. In the sixth over of the afternoon Amarnath hit Edmonds to the boundary four times in succession, but England did not wilt. Cowdrey compensated for lack of true international ability by unflinching endeavour and brilliance in the field, once almost running out Amarnath.

The return of Foster brought about the end of Amarnath's beautiful innings. The batsman chased a ball outside the off-stump, got a faint touch and walked, thereby setting a model which others would do well to follow. Three overs later, Cowdrey bowled Azharuddin middle and leg and the next over Foster had Shastri caught behind, the batsman again walking and aiding the umpire in a difficult decision.

Kapil Dev and Kirmani now hit lustily, for Kapil Dev there is no other way. He is a totally uninhibited cricketer

BELOW: *A costly miss. Fowler escapes a stumping chance off Shastri when Kirmani fumbles the ball. Fowler went on to score 201. It was a rare lapse by the Indian wicket-keeper who has maintained a consistent standard of excellence over the years. (Adrian Murrell)*

FOURTH TEST MATCH – INDIA *v.* ENGLAND
13, 14, 15, 17 and 18 January 1985 at Madras

INDIA

	FIRST INNINGS		SECOND INNINGS	
S.M. Gavaskar†	b Foster	17	c Gatting, b Foster	3
K. Srikkanth	c Downton, b Cowans	0	c Cowdrey, b Foster	16
D.B. Vengsarkar	c Lamb, b Foster	17	c Downton, b Foster	2
M.B. Amarnath	c Downton, b Foster	78	c Cowans, b Foster	95
M. Azharuddin	b Cowdrey	48	c Gower, b Pocock	105
R.J. Shastri	c Downton, b Foster	2	c Cowdrey, b Edmonds	33
R.N. Kapil Dev	c Cowans, b Cowdrey	53	c Gatting, b Cowans	49
S.M.H. Kirmani*	not out	30	c Lamb, b Edmonds	75
S.N. Yadav	b Foster	2	(10) c Downton, b Cowans	5
L. Sivarama-krishnan	c Cowdrey, b Foster	13	(9) lbw, b Foster	5
Chetan Sharma	c Lamb, b Cowans	5	not out	17
Extras	lb 3, nb 4	7	b 1, lb 4, nb 2	7
		272		412

	O	M	R	W	O	M	R	W
Cowans	12.5	3	39	2	15	1	73	2
Foster	23	2	104	6	28	8	59	5
Edmonds	6	1	33	—	41.5	13	119	2
Cowdrey	19	1	65	2	5	—	26	—
Pocock	7	2	28	—	33	8	130	1

FALL OF WICKETS
1- 17, 2- 17, 3- 45, 4- 155, 5- 167, 6- 167, 7- 241, 8- 243, 9- 263
1- 11, 2- 19, 3- 22, 4- 212, 5- 259, 6- 259, 7- 341, 8- 350, 9- 361

ENGLAND

	FIRST INNINGS		SECOND INNINGS	
G. Fowler	c Kirmani, b Kapil Dev	201	c. Kirmani, b Sivara	2
R.T. Robinson	c Kirmani, b Sivara	74	not out	21
M.W. Gatting	c sub (Gopal Sharma) b Shastri	207	not out	10
A.J. Lamb	b Amarnath	62		
P.H. Edmonds	lbw, b Shastri	36		
N.A. Foster	b Amarnath	5		
D.I. Gower†	b Kapil Dev	18		
P.R. Downton*	not out	3		
C.S. Cowdrey	not out	3		
P.I. Pocock				
N.G. Cowans				
Extras	b 7, lb 19, nb 17	43	lb 1, w 1	2
	(for 7 wkts dec)	652	(for 1 wkt)	35

	O	M	R	W	O	M	R	W
Kapril Dev	36	5	131	2	3	—	20	—
Chetan Sharma	18	—	95	—				
Yadav	23	4	76	—				
Sivaramakrishnan	44	6	145	1	4	—	12	1
Shastri	42	7	143	2	1	—	2	—
Amarnath	12	1	36	2				

FALL OF WICKETS
1- 178, 2- 419, 3- 563, 4- 599, 5- 604, 6- 640, 7- 646
1- 7

Umpires: M.Y. Gupta and K.V. Ramaswamy

England won by 9 wickets

Gatting sweeps during his partnership with Fowler. (Adrian Murrell)

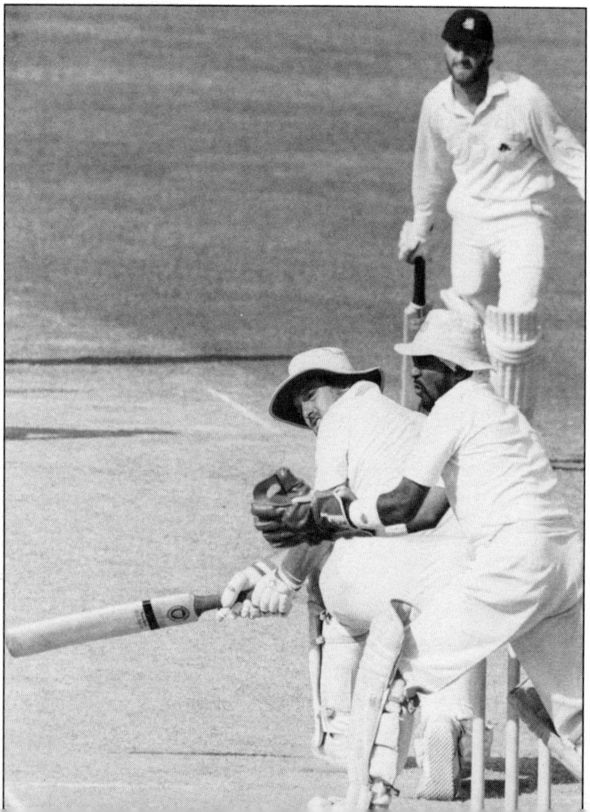

and we should be grateful for the fact. He was well caught at long-off by Cowans off Cowdrey, and the last three Indian wickets fell in 10 overs, two of them to Foster who had bowled with pace and aggression throughout to earn his best figures for England and give his country every chance of success.

Fowler and Robinson moved a little uneasily through the last 10 overs of the day, but on the following morning, they consolidated the fine work of Foster's with an opening stand of 178. They enjoyed some luck. The Indian catching was poor and their bowling, Kapil Dev and Sivaramakrishnan apart, very moderate. It was Sivaramakrishnan who took the only wicket of the day to fall when Robinson pushed forward at a leg-break and was caught behind. It was some reward for Kirmani who had a bad match and missed vital, costly chances, none of them very difficult. Fowler, showing sensible caution, reached his hundred and although Gatting did not begin well, England closed at a commanding 293 for 1.

On the third day, India were routed by the determination and ultimate magnificence of Fowler and Gatting. They became the sixth pair of batsmen to score double centuries in a Test innings and took their second wicket stand to 241. Lamb and Gatting then added 144 so that England reached 563 before their third wicket fell. No praise can be too high for Fowler and Gatting who batted a little over nine hours and eight hours respectively. Fowler, tiredly, edged to the wicket-keeper and Gatting, punishing India more and more as the hours passed, was caught on the long-on boundary.

TOP: *Tim Robinson clips the ball to leg during his fine opening partnership with Fowler. (Adrian Murrell)*

TOP RIGHT: *Another Foster victim. Vengsarkar is magnificently caught down the leg side by Downton. (Adrian Murrell)*

MIDDLE: *Neil Foster bowls Gavaskar for 17 and England are on the road to victory. (Adrian Murrell)*

BOTTOM: *Gavaskar falls to Foster a second time, caught at slip by Gatting. (Adrian Murrell)*

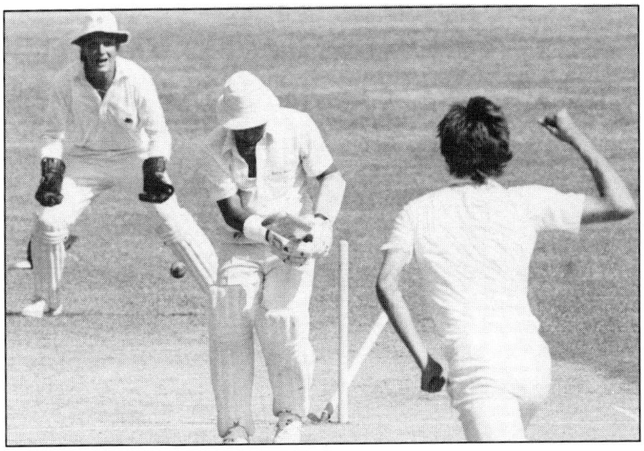

Gower, after some strange changes of batting order, declared on the fourth morning and with an hour to go before lunch, Neil Foster shattered the Indian batting with another blistering spell which accounted for Gavaskar at first slip, Vengsarkar well taken low down on the leg side by Downton and Srikkanth hooking. Gavaskar, who had desperately needed runs, and Vengsarkar were given hostile receptions by the crowd and India were 22 for 3. Mohammad Azharuddin and Amarnath revived Indian hopes of saving the match and restored the nation's pride. Between lunch and tea they scored 101 in 32 overs.

It seemed that they would bat well into the last day and India would be safe, but just before the final drinks interval of the day, Amarnath hooked Foster to Cowans who took a fine catch. Twenty-five minutes before the close, Azharuddin reached his second century in his second Test match and was now firmly established as India's new hero. At the close he was 103 and India were 246 for 4, still 134 runs in arrears.

India suffered a bitter disappointment when both Azharuddin and Shastri were out in the first half hour on the final day, victims of the spinners. Azharuddin was caught at silly point and so quickly has he established his personality on Test cricket that his dismissal is a major event. With

Grindlays Bank
Grindlays Bank
INDIA
RUNS . WT
1 INGS 272 10
2 INGS
GAVASKAR
SRIKANTH
VENSARKAR
MOHINDER
AZHARUDIN
SASTRI
KAPIL DEV
KIRMANI
YADAV
L.SIVA
C.SHARMA
7 BATSMAN
03
TOTAL
652
6 BATSMAN
03
WKTS 7
EXTRAS 43
LASTBATSMAN 36
LAST WKTAT
646
OVERS
96
T.OVERS
175
B O M R W
ENGLAND
RUNS.
1 INGS 6
2 INGS
1 FOWLER C 20
2 ROBINSON C 7
3 GATTING C 20
4 LAMB B 6
5 GOWER B 1
6 COWDREY
7 DOWNTON
8 EDMONDS LB 3
9 POCOCK
10 FOSTER B
11 COWANS
12 MOXON
Grindlays Bank
Grindlays Bank

ABOVE: *The score-board displays England's massive total and records the innings of Gatting and Fowler, 207 and 201 respectively. (Adrian Murrell)*

LEFT: *Double centurions – Fowler and Gatting. (Adrian Murrell)*

BELOW: *The decisive wicket. Azharuddin is caught by Gower (obscured by the bowler) and Pocock lifts his arms in triumph as Downton runs to congratulate him. (Adrian Murrell)*

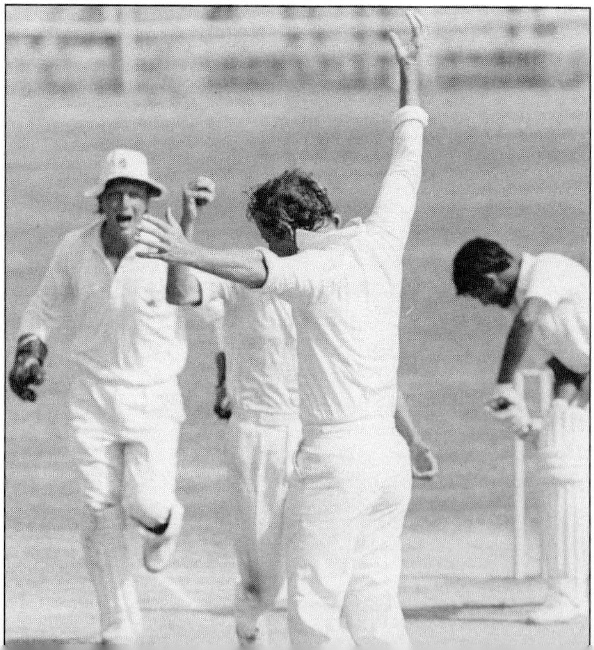

Saleem Malik of Pakistan he is the most exciting batting prospect to have emerged in the past two years. He is one who could rewrite the record books.

India were still not beaten. There was a characteristic flourish from Kapil Dev and a brave defiance from Kirmani with whom Chetan Sharma, a bitterly disapointing bowler, added 51 for the last wicket. Foster finished with 11 for 163, a career best and decisive in winning the match for England.

India survived well into the afternoon, but England needed only 33 to win for a famous victory.

Third One-Day International
INDIA *v.* ENGLAND

At a crest of success and confidence, England took the one-day series with their third win in as many matches. The game was marred by crowd disturbances which culminated in a twenty-minute stoppage when Gavaskar led his team from the field. The future of Gavaskar as India's captain was still a point of debate and Shastri and Amarnath were being tipped as likely candidates to lead the side to Australia for the mini world cup although, with that sense of the bewildering which is common to selectors, Amarnath had been omitted from the Indian side for the remaining one-day matches.

Gower won the toss and asked India to bat. Gavaskar, certainly a focus of the crowd's discontent, began well against some tight bowling, Cowans opening with a ten-over spell and performing creditably. After 25 overs, India were 90 for 2, but in the next ten overs, they panicked a little, losing three more wickets for the addition of 37 runs. It was in their last eleven overs that they were at their best, Shastri and Azharuddin showing the charm and authority that they had done against England earlier in the tour. In his first one-day international, Azharuddin continued to display the

Gatting positive in appeal at Bangalore. (Adrian Murrell)

THIRD ONE-DAY INTERNATIONAL – INDIA *v.* ENGLAND
20 January 1985 at Bangalore

INDIA

S.M. Gavaskar†	c Gatting, b Marks	40
K. Srikkanth	b Cowans	29
D.B. Vengsarkar	st Downton, b Marks	23
R.N. Kapil Dev	c Gower, b Marks	8
Yashpal Sharma	run out	8
R.J. Shastri	b Edmonds	33
M. Azharuddin	not out	47
S. Viswanath*	not out	6
A. Patel		
R.S. Ghai		
T.A. Sekhar		
Extras	b 4, lb 6, w 1	11
(46 overs)	(for 6 wickets)	205

	O	M	R	W
Cowans	10	1	31	1
Foster	6	—	33	—
Ellison	6	—	25	—
Marks	10	1	35	3
Edmonds	10	—	44	1
Gatting	4	—	27	—

FALL OF WICKETS
1- 60, 2- 70, 3- 90, 4- 108, 5- 119, 5- 185

ENGLAND

G. Fowler	run out	45
R.T. Robinson	c Viswanath, b Kapil Dev	2
M.W. Gatting	run out	3
D.I. Gower†	b Shastri	38
A.J. Lamb	not out	59
V.J. Marks	c Gavaskar, b Patel	17
P.R. Downton*	c Shastri, b Kapil Dev	12
P.H. Edmonds	c Viswanath, b Kapil Dev	7
R.M. Ellison	not out	1
N.A. Foster		
N.G. Cowans		
Extras	lb 10, w 7, nb 5	22
(45 overs)	(for 7 wickets)	206

	O	M	R	W
Kapil Dev	10	—	38	3
Sekhar	9	—	36	—
Patel	10	1	42	1
Ghai	4	—	37	—
Shastri	10	2	29	1
Yashpal Sharma	2	—	14	—

FALL OF WICKETS
1- 15, 2- 21, 3- 91, 4- 103, 5- 144, 6- 186, 7- 204

England won by 3 wickets

The crowd at Bangalore for the one-day international (Adrian Murrell)

richest of talents. His repertoire of shots seems endless and the ball was always struck with clean, decisive command. No doubt remained. Here is one of the very great batsmen and what the future holds for him one dare not prophesy, but many bowlers will suffer.

Robinson went quickly and Gatting was run out in the seventh over. Fowler and Gower added 70 in 13 overs as missiles were thrown at wilting Indian fieldsmen, Srikkanth and Yashpal Sharma were glorious exceptions, and at Ghai after he had conceded 13 runs in an over. Fowler was out in the 20th over and Gower was bowled by Shastri in the 24th. Lamb and Marks nudged and pushed England to 144 when Marks was superbly caught at square-leg in the 36th over.

India now sensed victory, but Lamb launched a savage attack on Ghai and the crowd became restive, incited by Yashpal Sharma's reaction when he had an appeal for lbw against Lamb rejected. At 178 for 5 the players left the field. They returned for Lamb to complete England's victory and take the individual award, but the game had lost its flavour and degenerated into chaos.

One was left wondering once again how the World Cup will fare in 1987.

Fourth One-Day International
INDIA *v.* ENGLAND

England gave opportunities to Moxon, Agnew and Cowdrey. All three were new to limited-over international cricket and for Moxon it was an international debut. He batted with composure and technical soundness when England were put in by Gavaskar. Cowdrey built on the foundation of Moxon's 70 off 131 balls with a violent assault and England must have been quite satisfied with their 240.

The satisfaction was doubled when Cowans and Agnew,

FOURTH ONE-DAY INTERNATIONAL – INDIA *v.* ENGLAND
23 January 1985 at Nagpur

ENGLAND			INDIA		
G. Fowler	b Shastri	37	K. Srikkanth	b Cowans	6
M.D. Moxon	c Srikkanth, b Kapil Dev	70	L.S. Rajput	c Downton, b Cowans	0
M.W. Gatting	b Shastri	1	D.B. Vengsarkar	c Downton, b Agnew	11
D.I. Gower†	c and b Shastri	11	M. Azharuddin	b Cowdrey	47
A.J. Lamb	st Viswanath, b Shastri	30	S.M. Gavaskar†	b Agnew	52
C.S. Cowdrey	not out	46	R.N. Kapil Dev	c Gatting, b Cowans	54
V.J. Marks	b Sekhar	4	R.J. Shastri	not out	24
P.R. Downton*	c Rajput, b Sekhar	13	M. Prabhakar	b Agnew	4
P.H. Edmonds	not out	8	S. Viswanath*	not out	23
J.P. Agnew			A. Patel		
N.G. Cowans			T.A. Sekhar		
Extras	b 3, lb 15, w 1, nb 1	20	Extras	b 3, lb 14, w 1, nb 2	20
(50 overs)	(for 7 wickets)	240	(47.4 overs)	(for 7 wickets)	241

	O	M	R	W
Kapil Dev	10	1	42	1
Prabhakar	10	1	36	—
Sekhar	10	—	50	2
Patel	10	1	54	—
Shastri	10	1	40	4

	O	M	R	W
Cowans	10	—	44	3
Agnew	10	—	38	3
Marks	6	—	32	—
Edmonds	10	—	44	—
Gatting	4	—	14	—
Cowdrey	7.4	—	52	1

FALL OF WICKETS
1- 70, 2- 78, 3- 100, 4- 154, 5- 176, 6- 199, 7- 221

FALL OF WICKETS
1- 5, 2- 11, 3- 31, 4- 90, 5- 166, 6- 197, 7- 204

India won by 3 wickets

who bowled well, reduced India to 31 for 3. Azharuddin, inevitably, and Gavaskar restored India's fortunes with patient and intelligent batting, and with Kapil Dev in typically aggressive form, the two central figures in India's recent disharmony added 76 in 11 overs. It was a match-winning stand brought about by contrasting styles.

Kapil Dev's 54 off 40 balls won him the individual award, but Gavaskar's more patient innings was equally praiseworthy and when he was out India needed 44 from 13 overs, a task they accomplished with 14 balls to spare.

Fifth One-Day International
INDIA *v.* ENGLAND

Overnight rain left the pitch in such a state that even the fifteen-over match that was played was conducted in conditions that were hardly fair to the contestants, but a crowd of 25,000 deserved a game for some of them had paid much money and waited patiently for five hours to see some cricket.

England were put in and, inspired by Gatting and Lamb about whose fitness there had been a doubt, they set India a formidable task by scoring at eight runs an over. Foster bowled well and accurately to frustrate India at the start and Srikkanth was run out by Gatting's direct throw as he backed up too far. Kapil Dev, in his home town, was well caught at deep square leg, but Gatting's two overs cost 29 runs, ten of them wides and India glimpsed victory especially as Shastri was batting confidently.

On the last ball of the penultimate over Shastri unwisely went for a second run and was run out by Cowdrey who was then entrusted with the final over. A better player in limited-over cricket than the first-class game, Cowdrey responded with an admirably accurate over, bowling Yashpal Sharma

In accord. Gower and Gatting, captain and vice-captain together at the wicket in the one-day international at Chandigarh. (Adrian Murrell)

FIFTH ONE-DAY INTERNATIONAL – INDIA *v.* ENGLAND
27 January 1985 at Chandigarh

ENGLAND

G. Fowler	run out	17
M.W. Gatting	c Azharuddin, b Sekhar	31
D.I. Gower†	b Sekhar	19
A.J. Lamb	not out	33
C.S. Cowdrey	c Rajput, b Shastri	5
P.H. Edmonds	c Azharuddin, b Sekhar	5
V.J. Marks	run out	2
R.M. Ellison	not out	5
J.P. Agnew		
N.A. Foster		
B.N. French*		
Extras	lb 4	4
(15 overs)	(for 6 wickets)	121

	O	M	R	W
Kapil Dev	3	—	17	—
Prabhakar	3	—	26	—
Chetan Sharma	3	—	20	—
Sekhar	3	—	24	3
Shastri	3	—	30	1

FALL OF WICKETS
1- 31, 2- 71, 3- 74, 4- 86, 5- 93, 6- 104

INDIA

R.J. Shastri	run out	53
K. Srikkanth	run out	9
R.N. Kapil Dev	c Agnew, b Edmonds	17
M. Azharuddin	c Gatting, b Edmonds	12
Yashpal Sharma	b Cowdrey	6
S.M. Gavaskar†	not out	2
L.S. Rajput	not out	1
S. Viswanath*		
M. Prabhakar		
T.A. Sekhar		
Chetan Sharma		
Extras	lb 2, w 12	14
(15 overs)	(for 5 wickets)	114

	O	M	R	W
Agnew	3	—	23	—
Foster	3	—	17	—
Ellison	3	—	20	—
Edmonds	3	—	20	2
Gatting	2	—	29	—
Cowdrey	1	—	3	1

FALL OF WICKETS
1- 22, 2- 49, 3- 83, 4- 111, 5- 112

England won by 7 runs

ABOVE: *Gatting turns the ball to the leg. More than a thousand runs on the tour. (Adrian Murrell)*

LEFT: *Edmonds congratulates Azharuddin on reaching his third century in three Test matches. (Adrian Murrell)*

with his third delivery and restricting Gavaskar and Rajput to give England victory.

Shastri was named Man of the Match and Bruce French, having played his first international match, must have felt he deserved something better.

Fifth Test Match
INDIA *v.* ENGLAND

To save the series India had to beat England in the final Test match so that the choice of an extra batsman at the expense of an opening bowler came as a great surprise. Gavaskar won the toss, but once again he was an early victim, playing back to Cowans who brought the ball in off the seam. India's dismay was soon dispelled as Srikkanth and Azharuddin engaged in an exhilarating stand of 150 in 37 overs. Srikkanth was all eagerness and belligerence. He is an unquenchably exciting player and if he enjoys much luck, it is luck that is deserved for the entertainment he gives. Azharuddin was no less entertaining, attacking the bowling from the start, scoring 20 in his first four overs at the crease and stroking the ball languidly to all parts of the ground. The hook alone seems his uncertain, unauthoritative shot.

Pocock, in particular, was dealt with severely, but the return of Foster accounted for Srikkanth. Amarnath looked in total command until he was bowled by Cowans in much

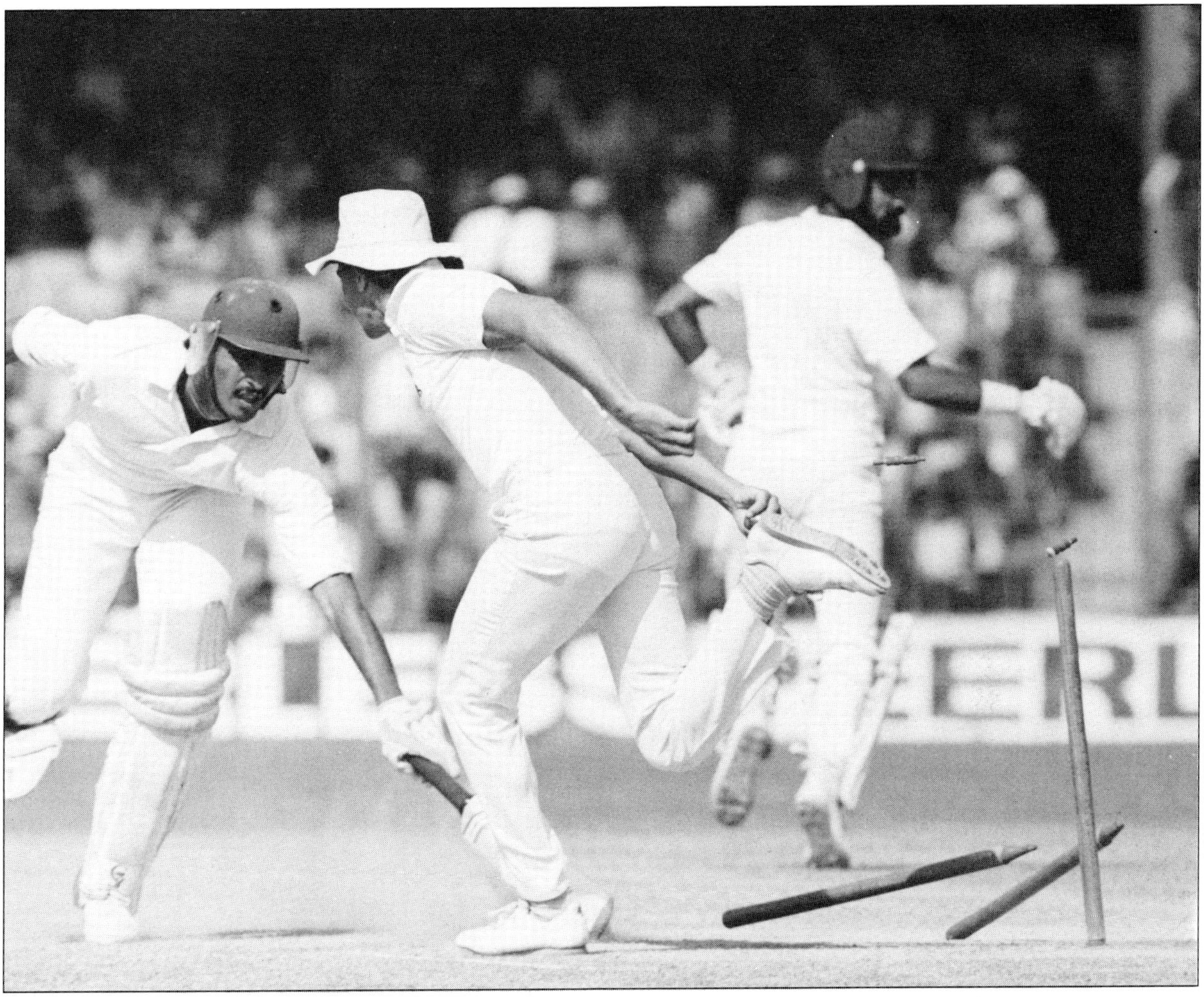

Robinson runs out Shastri in India's hectic second innings. (Adrian Murrell)

the same manner as Gavaskar had been and now the runs became scarcer as Edmonds and Foster bowled to a nagging length and Azharuddin, in sight of a record third century, went into his shell. India closed the first day at 228 for 3 and England were relieved it was not more.

Azharuddin reached his hundred on the second morning and so became the first batsman in Test history to score a century in each of his first three Test matches. It was a mighty achievement and all eyes will now be on this talented young man to see how he fares against a different attack in a foreign land.

In spite of some very loose bowling by Cowdrey, India were restricted to 180 off 57 overs before tea. Vengsarkar had completed his ninth Test match century, but for most of the time he was searching for lost form and the innings failed to gain the momentum that was needed. That momentum was supplied in the final session by Shastri and Kapil Dev who hit 50 from 79 balls and 41 from 29 respectively.

India closed at 525 for 7 and when play restarted on the third day they advanced the score by 28 in half an hour and declared. England had no chance of winning the match and to win the series they had no option but to bat for a draw. Amarnath shared the new ball with Kapil Dev, but it was the spinners, Sivaramakrishnan and Gopal Sharma, the off-break bowler who was the first Uttar Pradesh player to represent India for 48 years, in whom Gavaskar placed his trust. Sivaramakrishnan, in particular, bowled splendidly, but he was matched by determination and concentration of the highest quality from Fowler and Robinson. Fowler had been unwell and had not fielded on the second day, but his resolution was admirable. He reached fifty in three and three quarter hours, a testament to the way in which he curtailed his natural tendency to attack in the cause of defending what England had won by hard work. Robinson, playing like one who had fifty Tests behind him rather than four, was immaculate in defence, powerful on the off-side and completely balanced in temperament. They put on 156 before Fowler was caught behind off Shastri who relies on accuracy rather than spin. England could not have wished for a better start.

Robinson seemed in sight of a well deserved and hard earned century when, on the fourth morning, a ball from Kapil Dev kept low and had him lbw. It was an important

FIFTH TEST MATCH – INDIA *v.* ENGLAND
31 January, 1, 3, 4 and 5 February 1985 at Kanpur

INDIA

	FIRST INNINGS		SECOND INNINGS	
S.M. Gavaskar†	b Cowans	9		
K. Srikkanth	c Downton, b Foster	84	not out	41
M. Azharuddin	c sub (Ellison), b Cowdrey	122	not out	54
M.B. Amarnath	b Cowans	15		
D.B. Vengsarkar	c Downton, b Foster	137		
A.O. Malhotra	lbw, b Pocock	27		
R.J. Shastri	b Edmonds	59	(1) run out	2
R.N. Kapil Dev	c Gower, b Foster	42		
S.M.H. Kirmani*	not out	16		
L. Sivaramakrishnan	not out	16		
Gopal Sharma				
Extras	b 9, lb 12, w 5	26		0
	(for 8 wkts dec)	553	(for 1 wkt dec)	97

	O	M	R	W	O	M	R	W
Cowans	39	9	115	2	7	—	51	—
Foster	36	8	123	3				
Pocock	24	2	79	1				
Edmonds	48	16	112	1				
Cowdrey	21	1	103	1	5	—	39	—
Gatting					1	—	7	—

FALL OF WICKETS
1- 19, 2- 169, 3- 209, 4- 277, 5- 362, 6- 457, 7- 511, 8- 533
1- 2

ENGLAND

	FIRST INNINGS		SECOND INNINGS	
R.T. Robinson	lbw, b Kapil Dev	96	(2) retired hurt	16
G. Fowler	c Kirmani, b Shastri	69		
M.W. Gatting	c and b Sharma	62	not out	41
A.J. Lamb	c Srikkanth, b Shastri	13		
D.I. Gower†	lbw, b Shastri	78	(1) not out	32
C.S. Cowdrey	c Kirmani, b Sharma	1		
P.R. Downton*	b Sharma	1		
P.H. Edmonds	lbw, b Kapil Dev	49		
N.A. Foster	c Kirmani, b Kapil Dev	8		
P.I. Pocock	not out	4		
N.G. Cowans	b Kapil Dev	9		
Extras	b 10, lb 17	27	lb 2	2
		417	(for no wkt)	91

	O	M	R	W	O	M	R	W
Kapil Dev	36.5	7	81	4	5	—	19	—
Armanath	4	1	6	—				
Shastri	32	13	52	3	7	2	12	—
Sivaramakrishnan	53	11	133	—	10	2	22	—
Gopal Sharma	60	16	115	3	11	4	17	—
Malhotra	2	—	3	—				
Srikkanth					2	—	11	—
Azharuddin					1	—	8	—

FALL OF WICKETS
1- 156, 2- 196, 3- 222, 4- 276, 5- 278, 6- 286, 7- 386, 8- 402, 9- 404

Umpires: P.D. Reporter and V.K. Ramaswamy

Match drawn

Kanpur – the Fifth Test match. (Adrian Murrell)

LEFT: *The spoils of victory. Gower is held aloft as England win the series. (Adrian Murrell)*

blow for India for the Nottinghamshire batsman had become one of the most solid pillars of the England side and suggested a permanence which was heartening to his colleagues and distressing to his opponents.

In mid-afternoon England were 276 for 3, but Gopal Sharma, on his Test debut, then took the wickets of Gatting, Cowdrey and Downton at a personal cost of 4 runs in 29 deliveries and there was a chance that India could bowl England out for under 350 and so enforce the follow-on. They were denied by Edmonds and Gower who chose the right moment to return to form and so save the series. He and Edmonds added 100 and batted into the final day. It was fitting that Edmonds should be the part saviour for he had had a magnificent tour and had contributed hugely to England's success.

Srikkanth and Azharuddin thrashed 95 in just over twelve overs in a bid to get England at the wicket again, but Gower was not to let his hour of glory pass. He batted with confidence and solidity. Gatting, coming in when Robinson lost a contact lens, passed a thousand runs for the tour and England drew so taking the series by 2–1.

It was only the fourth time in Test match history that England had won a series abroad after being one down. It

India *v.* England – Test Match Averages

INDIA BATTING

	M	Inns	NOs	Runs	HS	Av	100s	50s
M. Azharuddin	3	5	1	439	122	109.75	3	1
S.M.H. Kirmani	5	7	2	291	102	58.20		
M.B. Amarnath	5	8	1	407	95	58.14		
R.J. Shastri	5	9	2	383	142	54.71	2	1
K. Srikkanth	2	4	1	141	84	47.00		1
R.N. Kapil Dev	4	6		253	60	42.16		2
D.B. Vengsarkar	5	8	1	284	137	40.57	1	
Chetan Sharma	3	4	3	40	17*	40.00		
S.M. Patil	2	3		91	41	30.33		
M. Prabhakar	2	4	1	86	35*	28.66		
S.M. Gavaskar	5	8		140	65	17.50		1
L. Sivaramakrishnan	5	5	1	59	25	14.75		
S.N. Yadav	4	6	3	43	28*	14.33		
A.D. Gaekwad	3	5		71	28	14.20		

Played in one Test: A.O. Malhotra 27, Gopal Sharma did not bat

ENGLAND BATTING

	M	Inns	NOs	Runs	HS	Av	100s	50s
M.W. Gatting	5	9	3	575	207	95.83	2	1
R.T. Robinson	5	9	2	444	160	63.42	1	2
P.R. Downton	5	6	3	183	74	61.00		2
G. Fowler	5	8		438	201	54.75	1	2
A.J. Lamb	5	7	1	241	67	40.16		3
P.H. Edmonds	5	6		175	49	29.16		
D.I. Gower	5	7	1	167	78	27.83		1
C.S. Cowdrey	5	6	1	96	38	19.20		
P.I. Pocock	5	5	2	39	22*	13.00		
N.A. Foster	2	2		13	8	6.50		
R.M. Ellison	3	4		12	10	3.00		
N.G. Cowans	5	5	1	10	9	2.50		

INDIA BOWLING

	Overs	Mds	Runs	Wkts	Av	Best	10/m	5/inn
M.B. Amarnath	21	4	49	2	24.50	2/36		
L. Sivaramakrishnan	273.3	63	723	23	31.43	6/64	1	3
S.N. Yadav	134	31	362	9	40.22	4/86		
R.N. Kapil Dev	161.5	52	436	10	43.60	4/81		
Chetan Sharma	50.3	6	200	4	50.00	4/38		
R.J. Shastri	184	48	390	7	55.71	3/52		
M. Prabhakar	29	4	102	1	102.00	1/68		

Also bowled: A.D. Gaekwad 1–0–1–0; Gopal Sharma 71–20–132–3; S.M. Gavaskar 0.4–0–10–0; M. Azharuddin 1–0–8–0; A.O. Malhotra 2–0–3–0; K. Srikkanth 1–0–11–0

INDIA CATCHES

11–S.M.H. Kirmani (ct 10/st 1); 7–D.B. Vengsarkar; 4–R.J. Shastri; 3–S.M. Gavaskar; 2–A.D. Gaekwad, R.N. Kapil Dev and L. Sivaramakrishnan; 1–S.M. Patil, Chetan Sharma, M. Azharuddin, Gopal Sharma, K. Srikkanth and sub.

ENGLAND BOWLING

	Overs	Mds	Runs	Wkts	Av	Best	10/m	5/inn
N.A. Foster	87	18	286	14	20.42	6/104	1	2
P.H. Edmonds	276.1	104	584	14	41.71	4/60		
N.G. Cowans	184.5	41	627	14	44.57	3/103		
P.I. Pocock	237.5	54	655	13	50.38	4/93		
C.S. Cowdrey	61	2	288	4	72.00	2/65		
R.M. Ellison	105	24	289	4	72.25	4/66		

Also bowled: M.W. Gatting 13–1–36–0; D.I. Gower 3–0–13–0; A.J. Lamb 1–0–6–1; R.T. Robinson 1–1–0–0; G. Fowler 1–1–0–0

ENGLAND CATCHES

16–P.R. Downton (ct 14/st 2); 9–A.J. Lamb; 6–D.I. Gower; 5–C.S. Cowdrey; 4–M.W. Gatting; 2–G. Fowler, P.I. Pocock and N.G. Cowans; 1–sub.

England in India and Sri Lanka 1984–85

First Class Matches

BATTING	*v.* President's XI (Colombo) 7–9 November 1984		*v.* President's XI (Jaipur) 13–15 Nov. 1984		*v.* *India Under-25* (Ahmedabad) 17–19 Nov. 1984		*v.* West Zone (Rajket) 21–24 Nov. 1984		First Test Match (Bombay) 28 Nov.–3 Dec. 1984		*v.* North Zone (Bombay) 7–9 December 1984		Second Test Match (Delhi) 12–17 December 1984		*v.* East Zone (Gauhati) 19–21 Dec. 1984		Third Test Match (Calcutta) 31 December 1984–5 January 1985		*v.* South Zone (Hyderabad) 7–10 January 1985		Fourth Test Match (Madras) 13–18 January 1985	
G. Fowler	1	—	28	—	19	9	116	2	28	55			5	29	114	—	49	—			201	2
R.T. Robinson	2	—	81	—	11	3	103	34*	22	1	138	—	160	18			36	—	13	32	74	21*
M.W. Gatting	97	—	36	—	52	16	136*	—	15	136			26	30*	37	—	48	—	50	30*	207	10*
D.I. Gower	86	—	82	—	21	8	57	—	13	2	7	—	5	—			19	—	13	41	18	—
A.J. Lamb	53	—			18	34	30*	22	9	1	20	—	52	37*	23	—	67	—			62	—
R.M. Ellison	14	—	83*	—	5	3	—	25	1	0	10	—	10	—			1	—				
P.H. Edmonds	2	—	6	—			—	8	48	8	15	—	26	—	6	—	8	—	29	—	36	—
P.R. Downton	0	—			11	6	—	35	37*	62			74	—	3	—	6*	—			3*	—
N.A. Foster	7*	—			11	20*					22*	—			26*	—			29	—	5	—
N.G. Cowans	0*	—	—	—			—	10	0	0			0*	—	1	—	1	—	0	—	—	—
P.I. Pocock	5	—			2*	0			8	22*	2	—	0	—			5	—			—	—
C.S. Cowdrey			8	—					13	14	70	—	38	—	9	—	27	—	22	6	3*	—
V.J. Marks			66	—	37	2	—	0			19	—			7	—			0	11*		
B.N. French			19	—							19	—			13	—			1	11		
P.J.W. Allott			5*	—	14	10	—	—														
M.D. Moxon											42	—			36	—			153	0		
J.P. Agnew																			12*	—		
Byes			5		4	1	2	1	1	4	3		6	4	5						7	
Leg-byes	3		15		4	2	8	1		8	6		13	7	5		2		5		19	1
Wides			4		1		1								3							1
No-balls	3		6		6	3	5			4	4		3	2	2		7		7	1	17	
Total	273		444		216	117	458	138	195	317	377		418	127	290		276		334	132	652	45
Wickets	9		8		10	10	3	7	10	10	10		10	2	10		10		10	5	7	1
Result	D		D		L		D		L		D		W		W		D		D		W	

Catches 23 – P.R. Downton (ct 16/st 3)
15 – B.N. French (ct 13/st 2)
13 – A.J. Lamb
10 – D.I. Gower and M.W. Gatting
9 – C.S. Cowdrey
5 – P.H. Edmonds
3 – N.G. Cowans, G. Fowler and subs
2 – P.I. Pocock, R. M. Ellison, M.D. Moxon and N.A. Foster
1 – R.T. Robinson and V.J. Marks

BOWLING	N.G. Cowans	N.A. Foster	R.M. Ellison	P.H. Edmunds	P.I. Pocock	P.J.W. Allott	V.J. Marks	M.W. Gatting	C.S. Cowdrey
v. President's XI (Sri Lanka)	15–3–59–3	15.3–6–37–2	11–1–45–1	33–10–93–1	19–6–62–2				
(Colombo) 7–9 November 1984	9–0–31–0	7–1–25–0	7–2–12–1	6–3–9–2	19–5–57–4				
v. President's XI (Jaipur)	12–4–29–2		14–3–42–1	30–9–48–2		12.3–4–33–0	15–3–41–0	1–0–5–0	
13–15 November 1984	6–1–35–1			11–5–15–1		9–1–29–0	9–1–30–0		4–1–6–1
v. India Under-25 (Ahmedabad)		22–5–59–0	34–10–86–0		22.2–2–94–2	27–4–99–2	10–3–34–1	5–0–10–0	
17–19 November 1984									
v. West Zone (Rajkot)	19–4–76–1		12–5–28–1	49–18–99–4		14–2–48–0	39.2–5–120–0	5–0–19–0	
21–24 November 1984									
First Test Match (Bombay)	28–6–109–2		18–3–85–0	33–6–82–1	46–10–133–3			7–0–20–0	5–0–30–1
28 November–3 December 1984	5–2–18–1			8–3–21–1	2.1–0–10–0				
v. North Zone (Bombay)		22–4–58–2	19.1–9–29–3	14–4–34–1	15–4–36–2				9–3–24–0
7–9 December 1984		8–0–50–2	8–3–19–0	13–2–37–0	9–3–30–0		10–3–14–1		7–0–19–0
Second Test Match (Delhi)	20–5–70–0		26–6–66–4	44.2–16–83–2	33–8–70–3			2–0–5–0	
12–17 December 1984	13–2–43–2		7–1–20–0	44–24–60–4	38.4–9–93–4			1–0–3–0	
v. East Zone (Gauhati)	9–2–18–2	10–4–14–1		33–16–25–2			29–11–48–4	4–1–4–1	
19–21 December 1984	6–3–4–1	15–6–32–3		9–3–13–4			0.4–0–2–1		
Third Test Match (Calcutta)	41–12–103–3		53–14–117–0	47–22–72–3	52–14–108–1			2–1–1–0	2–0–15–0
31 Dec. 1984–5 Jan. 1985	4–1–6–0		1–0–1–0	4–3–2–0	2–1–4–0				4–0–10–0
v. South Zone (Hyderabad)	9–2–37–1	19.4–6–45–3		13–7–28–0			7–2–27–0	3–0–13–0	11–1–44–1
7–10 January 1985		24–8–49–2		10–3–32–1			1–0–5–0	3–0–3–0	22–5–61–3
Fourth Test Match	12.5–3–39–2	23–2–104–6		6–1–33–0	7–2–28–0				19–1–65–2
13–18 January 1985	15–1–73–2	28–8–59–5		41.5–13–119–2	33–8–130–1				5–0–26–0
Fifth Test Match (Kanpur)	39–9–115–2	36–8–123–3		48–16–112–1	24–2–79–1				21–1–103–1
31 Jan.–5 Feb. 1985	7–0–51–0							1–0–7–0	5–0–39–0
	269.5–60–916–25 *av.* 36.64	230.1–58–655–29 *av.* 22.58	210.1–57–550–11 *av.* 50.00	497.1–184–1017–32 *av.* 31.78	322.1–74–934–23 *av.* 40.60	62.3–11–209–2 *av.* 104.50	121–28–321–7 *av.* 45.85	34–2–90–1 *av.* 90.00	114–12–442–9 *av.* 49.11

a G. Fowler 1–1–0–0; R.T. Robinson 1–1–0–0

Fifth Test Match (Kanpur) 31 Jan.–5 Feb. 1985		M	Inns	NOs	Runs	HS	Av
69	—	10	15	—	727	201	48.46
96	16*	11	18	3	861	160	57.40
62	41*	11	17	5	1029	207	85.75
78	32*	11	15	1	482	86	34.42
13	—	10	14	2	441	67	36.75
		8	10	1	152	83*	16.88
49	—	11	12	—	241	49	20.08
1	—	9	11	3	238	74	29.75
8	—	7	8	4	128	29	32.00
9	—	10	9	2	21	10	3.00
4*	—	8	9	3	48	22*	8.00
1	—	9	11	1	211	70	21.10
		6	8	1	142	66	20.28
		4	5	—	63	19	12.60
		3	3	1	29	14	14.50
		3	4	—	231	153	57.75
		1	1	1	12	12*	—
10							
17	2						
417	91						
	D						

A.J. Lamb	D.I. Gower	J.P. Agnew	Byes	Leg-byes	Wides	No-balls	Total	Wkts
				2			298	9
							134	7
					5		198	5
			1	1			117	3
			1	9	2	2	392	6
				3			393	7
			4	2		7	465	8
			2				51	2
			3	2			186	10
1–1–0–0			1	6	1		176	3
			1	12		2	307	10
			6	10	1	3	235	10
			4	4	1		117	10
			1				52	10
	3–0–13–0			8	1	3	437	7
1–0–6–1						1	29	1a
		19–1–102–5		10		12	306	10
		26–3–103–2	4	2		19	259	8
				3		4	272	10
			1	4		2	412	10
			9	12	5		553	8
2–1–6–1 av. 6.00	3–0–13–0 —	45–4–205–7 av. 29.28						

ABOVE: *Chetan Sharma, 4 wickets in a late order collapse. (Adrian Murrell)*

BELOW: *Mohinder Amarnath looks anxious as he hits to leg. Downton and Gower are eager. (Adrian Murrell)*

was England's first overseas triumph for six years. From sadness and adversity a fine spirit had been forged and a happy side deserved all the praise that was showered upon them even if there was a feeling that the opposing attack had not been of the strongest.

Duleep Trophy

Once again the Duleep Trophy had to find a place squeezed in between the abundance of international matches and once again several of the leading players were engaged in playing for India so that the tournament lacked the stature that it deserved.

Quarter Final

20, 21, 22 and 23 October 1984

at Bombay

East Zone 256 (A. Mitra 115, R.S. Hans 5 for 28) and 152
Central Zone 352 (S.M. Mudkavi 184) and 57 for 1

Central Zone won by 9 wickets

A century on the opening day by Avik Mitra rescued East Zone who were sorely troubled by the slow left arm bowling of Rajinder Singh Hans and the medium pace of Sunderam and R.P. Singh. At the close of play on the second day with Central Zone 187 for 6, the game was evenly balanced. Central had begun dreadfully, losing Sashikant Khandkar, Sunil Chaturvedi and Sanjeev Rao to the medium pace of Randhir Singh and Somnath Sahu for 17. It was due almost entirely to the efforts of Sanju Mudkavi that Central Zone effected a recovery. Coming in at 17 for 3, he was 95 not out at the close and next day completed his first hundred in the Duleep Trophy. He was last out, caught at long-on, having hit 184 off 363 balls in 372 minutes with ten fours. East Zone were handicapped by the absence of Doshi who retired with a hairline fracture of a finger sustained while fielding to his own bowling.

By the end of the third day, Central Zone were in total command, having captured the first five East wickets for 99. The remaining four fell in 80 minutes the next morning and Central Zone moved to the easiest of victories.

Semi-Finals

27, 28, 29 and 30 October 1984

at Wankhede Stadium, Bombay

West Zone 228 (R.B. Bhalekar 75) and 491 for 6 (C.S. Pandit 126, M.D. Gunjal 117 not out, R. Poonawala 56, L.S. Rajput 51, S. Keshwala 50 not out)
South Zone 593 (R. Khanwilkar 156, K. Srikkant 101, R. Madhaven 95, S. Viswanath 74, Khalid Abdul Qayyum 61 not out, R.C. Thakkar 4 for 158)

Match drawn
South Zone won on first innings

OPPOSITE: *Ravi Shastri – six sixes in an over, the fastest double century in first-class cricket – the outstanding cricketer of India's season. (Adrian Murrell)*

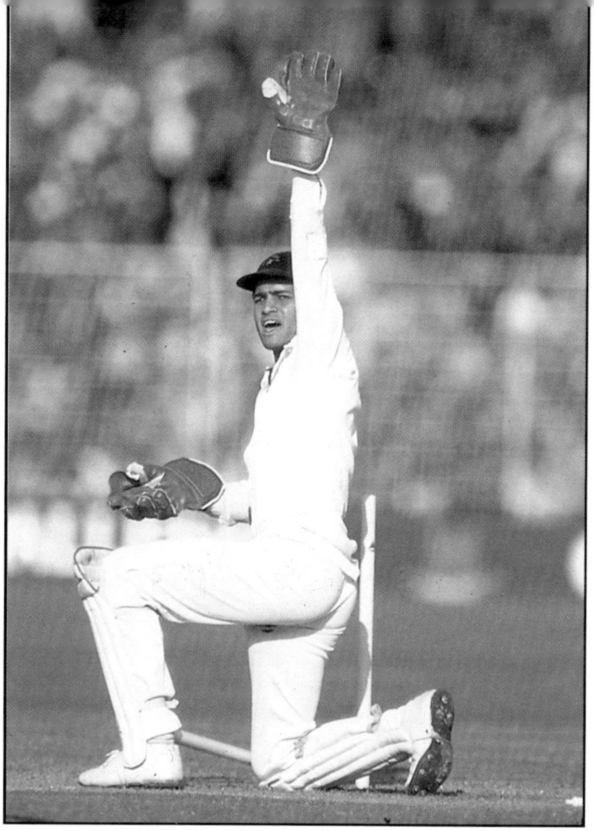

Sadanand Viswanath had a splendid season for Karnataka as wicket-keeper and opening batsman and won a place in India's team for the Benson and Hedges World Championship in Australia. (Adrian Murrell)

at Nehru Stadium, Pune

Central Zone 100 (M. Prabhakar 5 for 28, R.S. Ghai 5 for 33) and 326 (S. Khandkar 80, S. Chaturvedi 66 not out, Padam Shastri 60, S. Valson 4 for 84)
North Zone 407 (Yashpal Sharma 100, C.P.S. Chauhan 98, Gursharan Singh 63, M. Prabhakar 54) and 20 for 0

North Zone won by 10 wickets

Gaekwad's Test career is probably at an end, but he continued to score heavily for Baroda. (Adrian Murrell)

Duleep Trophy debutant Lalchand Rajput was bowled by Sekhar on the fourth ball of the match at Bombay. The other debutant opener, Riaz Poonawalla, was bowled by Khanwilkar with the first ball of the next over so that West Zone were 0 for 2. In spite of some lax fielding, South maintained the pressure throughout most of the day and the home side were bowled out for 228. The next two days were mostly occupied by South Zone building their massive score even though Azharuddin was unable to bat through injury. Srikkant and Viswanath gave them a splendid start and runs were plundered throughout the innings. An innings victory for the South seemed a formality, but the final day lapsed into farce as Srikkant chose not to try to force a win. Chandrakant Pandit hit a fine hundred on his Duleep Trophy debut and later Milind Gunjal completed a century, but much interest in the game had been lost by then.

At Pune, a fine spell by Manoj Prabhakar which brought him 5 for 28 in 19 overs and a later burst from Ghai shattered Central Zone after Sanjeev Rao had won the toss and decided to bat first. Collapsing from 38 for 0 to 100 all out, Central Zone passed their lowest ever total in the competition, 90 eighteen years previously, only because they gained 12 penalty points from the slow over-rate.

North Zone began listlessly in return, Sidhu taking 127 balls to make 35, but on the second day, aided by dropped catches, they took a lead of 307. Yashpal Sharma made a solid 100 off 179 balls in 211 minutes and he and Prabhakar added 88 in 19.4 overs for the sixth wicket. Veteran Chetan Chauhan had provided the foundation which made the later violence on the bowling possible.

Central Zone regained pride when Padam Shastri and Skashikant Khandkar enjoyed a record opening stand of 137, but again the side collapsed, the last 9 wickets falling for 167 and they were saved from an innings defeat only by courtesy of 24 penalty runs. Just 23 balls were needed on the final morning to complete the match.

Duleep Trophy Final
NORTH ZONE *v.* SOUTH ZONE

With the Indian party having departed for Australia for the World Championship of Cricket, the Duleep Trophy Final was deprived of some of its leading contestants. To make matters worse the match was played on a wicket that was under-prepared and this resulted in four batsmen being hurt and the game, scheduled for four days, ending with 80 minutes of the third day still remaining.

Put in to bat, the visitors struggled against the pace attack of Ghai, Valson and Jha and it was only a splendid innings from Syed Kirmani and the addition of twenty penalty runs that helped the South to any respectability. Kirmani hit fourteen fours before falling to Maninder Singh who took three wickets with his left-arm spin to close the innings.

The North Zone were disturbed by Khanwilkar who was replacing the unwell Sekhar, but they closed at 101 for 3 with Gursharan Singh in command and it looked as if they were

DULEEP TROPHY FINAL – NORTH ZONE *v.* SOUTH ZONE
9, 10 and 11 February 1985 at Delhi (Kotla)

SOUTH ZONE

	FIRST INNINGS		SECOND INNINGS	
V. Sivaramakrishnan	c Khanna, b Ghai	26	c sub, b Jha	19
M.R. Srinivasa Prasad	c Khanna, b Valson	0	(7) c sub, b Maninder	0
R. Madhavan	c Khanna, b Valson	0	(3) c Yashpal, b Maninder	14
R. Khanwilkar	c Khanna, b Jha	9	(6) c Yashpal, b Maninder	4
A. Jabbar	c Yashpal, b Ghai	17	(4) c Azad, b Ghai	68
S.M.H. Kirmani*†	c Sidhu, b Maninder	82	(8) c Azad, b Jha	50
K.A. Qayyum	lbw, b Ghai	0	(5) c and b Maninder	19
Arshad Ayub	c Ghai, b Jha	20	c Azad, b Jha	30
S.N. Yadav	c and b Maninder	15	lbw, b Jha	15
A.R.B. Bhat	b Maninder	5	not out	0
B. Arun	not out	1	(2) b Jha	1
Extras	b 4, lb 6, nb 7	17	b 2, lb 6, w 5, nb 3	16
	penalty runs	20		
		212		236

	O	M	R	W	O	M	R	W
Ghai	20	4	72	3	16	2	35	1
Valson	10	1	47	2	5	1	13	—
Jha	12	2	41	2	25.1	1	76	5
Maninder Singh	6.5	1	22	3	28	7	95	4
Kirti Azad	1	1	0	—	1	—	9	—

FALL OF WICKETS
1- 1, 2- 12, 3- 38, 4- 44, 5- 79, 6- 79, 7- 128, 8- 173, 9- 184
1- 5, 2- 22, 3- 54, 4- 96, 5- 102, 6- 102, 7- 154, 8- 205, 9- 233

NORTH ZONE

	FIRST INNINGS		SECOND INNINGS	
C.P.S. Chauhan	c Jabbar, b Khanwilkar	17	b Arun	23
N.S. Sidhu	lbw, b Khanwilkar	1	absent hurt	0
Gursharan Singh	lbw, b Khanwilkar	68	b Bhat	15
B. Pillai	c Madhavan, b Khanwilkar	11	c Madhavan, b Yadav	47
Yashpal Sharma	c Bhat, b Arun	32	lbw, b Arun	0
S.C. Khanna*	c Madhavan, b Bhat	12	(2) lbw, b Arun	20
Kirti Azad†	lbw, b Arun	9	(6) b Bhat	4
R.S. Ghai	c sub, b Bhat	1	(7) b Khanwilkar	54
A. Jha	not out	1	(8) lbw, b Arun	23
Maninder Singh	lbw, b Bhat	3	(9) not out	2
S. Valson	b Bhat	0	(10) lbw, b Arun	0
Extras	lb 4, nb 1	5	b 12, lb 6, nb 1	19
	penalty runs	4	penalty runs	4
		164		211

	O	M	R	W	O	M	R	W
Khanwilkar	26	5	73	4	11	1	40	1
Arun	10	—	41	2	19.5	2	84	5
Bhat	23	8	42	4	19	5	51	2
Yadav	1	1	0	—	3	1	14	1

FALL OF WICKETS
1- 16, 2- 29, 3- 71, 4- 124, 5- 137, 6- 154, 7- 155, 8- 155, 9- 160
1- 36, 2- 72, 3- 72, 4- 76, 5- 76, 6- 161, 7- 187, 8- 207, 9- 207

Umpires: R.S. Rathore and R.R. Kadam

South Zone won by 73 runs

Manoj Prabhakar. Fine all round cricket for North Zone in the Duleep Trophy. (Adrian Murrell)

Surinder Khanna (North Zone) who caught the first four batsmen in the Duleep Trophy Final in Delhi. (Adrian Murrell)

destined for a useful lead. They were bowled out in under two hours on the second morning, however, falling mainly to the guile of left-arm spinner Raghuram Bhat. In all, fourteen wickets fell on the second day. It was the combined talents of the tall, ungainly medium-paced Ajai Jha and the slow left-arm of Maninder Singh that troubled South Zone in their second innings. Kirmani and Abdul Jabbar revived the visitors' hopes and they ended the day 227 ahead with 3 wickets standing.

They added another 57 on the third morning and North Zone, with Navjot Singh Sidhu unfit to bat, were left the very difficult task of scoring 285 to win. They were 76 for 5 before Rajinder Ghai and Bhaskar Pillai added 85 in a courageous stand. Once the quietly composed Pillai had fallen to Yadav, a debatable decision, Bharat Arun, who displayed a smooth action, a good physique and a zestful pace finished off the innings to give South Zone the trophy for the first time for nine years.

Ranji Trophy

East Zone

24, 25 and 26 November 1984

at Nowgong

Assam 139 (K. Das 66) and 93 (D.R. Doshi 4 for 35)
Bengal 112 (S. Uzir 5 for 29) and 11 for 0

Match drawn
Bengal 6 pts, Assam 4 pts

at Ranchi

Bihar 307 for 6 dec (B.S. Gosain 84, H. Gidwani 78, D. Augustus 73 not out, H. Praharaj 4 for 100) and 293 (U. Das 73, H Praharaj 6 for 86)
Orissa 304 for 6 dec (A. Jayaprakash 102 not out, S. Sahu 71) and 59 for 1

Match drawn
Bihar 9 pts, Orissa 9 pts

Rain hindered the match in Assam, but Bengal's failure in the match against a side who had lost all three matches by an innings in the previous season and had gained only six points made the East Zone competition a very open one. Das and new skipper Uzir were Assam's heroes. Doshi and Shukla bowled well for Bengal in conditions which aided them.

A third wicket partnership of 143 between Gidwani and Gosain revived Bihar and Augustus sustained the recovery. Orissa came to parity with a century from Jayaprakash who shared a stand of 118 for the sixth wicket with skipper Sahu. A draw seemed inevitable, but Praharaj put in another good spell of bowling to finish with match figures of 10 for 186.

OPPOSITE: *Gopal Sharma – excellent off-spin for Uttar Pradesh brought him a Test place. (Adrian Murrell)*

1, 2 and 3 December 1984

at Eden Gardens, Calcutta

Bengal 301 for 6 dec (J. Arun Lal 157 not out, R.C. Shukla 81) and 156 for 9 dec (J. Arun Lal 54)
Bihar 172 and 157 for 4 (H. Gidwani 84, R. Deora 55)

Match drawn
Bengal 11 pts, Bihar 9 pts

at Nowgong

Assam 145 (A. Jayaprakash 6 for 66) and 123
Orissa 383 for 7 dec (H. Praharaj 197, A. Jayaprakash 88, H. Baroah 5 for 52)

Orissa won by an innings and 115 runs
Orissa 31 pts, Assam 3 pts

After Doshi had decided to bat Bengal lost 4 wickets for 48, but Arun Lal and Shukla added 161 to take the full batting points. Bihar struggled against Doshi, Burman and Mukherjee, but Satish Singh and Venkatram batted doggedly to save the follow-on. In an effort to force a win, Bengal scored briskly and left themselves 63 overs in which to bowl out the visitors, but they were thwarted by Deora and Gidwani who put on 132 after S. Das had fallen to Burman at 17.

At Nowgong, Assam won the toss and batted, but the spin of Asjig Jayaprakash soon had them in trouble. Jayaprakash then shared a second wicket stand of 295 with Praharaj who hit a career best 197. Assam collapsed a second time to spin and Orissa were assured of a place in the final stages of the competition.

6, 7 and 8 December 1984

at Nowgong

Bihar 247 (N. Kanwar 6 for 64) and 179 for 3 dec (R. Deora 52)
Assam 114 (A. Kumar 6 for 27) and 231 (A. Das 85, A. Kumar 6 for 72)

Bihar won by 81 runs
Bihar 28 pts, Assam 7 pts

8, 9 and 10 December 1984

at Calcutta

Orissa 206 (K. Dubey 60, S. Mitra 56, B. Burman 4 for 47) and 307 for 7 dec (K. Dubey 127, A. Bharadwaj 125 not out, D.R. Doshi 4 for 79)
Bengal 169 (L. Mahapatra 4 for 18) and 144 for 2 (P. Roy 60 not out)

Match drawn
Orissa 8 pts, Bengal 8 pts

Bengal failed to qualify for the quarter-finals for the first time in 25 years when they drew with the new East Zone champions Orissa. All went well for them on the first day when Doshi's decision to ask Orissa to bat seemed justified as the seam of Barun Burman and Gantam Shome shot them out before the close for 206. Roy fell to a full toss that night and next day the spin of 17-year-old Lalitendu Mahapatra in his second Ranji Trophy game destroyed all hopes that Bengal had, the last five wickets falling for 23 after Dhab and Arun Lal had hit 80 in 95 minutes for the 3rd wicket. Orissa

Roger Binny, an inspiring captain for Karnataka. (Adrian Murrell)

celebrated as Karun Dubey and Anil Bhardawaj hit centuries and added 199 for the fourth wicket in 210 minutes, a record for the contests between these two states.

Meanwhile Bihar joined Orissa in the quarter-finals by trouncing Assam. Kumar's spin on a wicket where most batsmen struggled was decisive. He had match figures of 12 for 99.

East Zone Final Table

	P	*W*	*L*	*D*	*Pts*
Orissa	3	1	—	2	48
Bihar	3	1	—	2	46
Bengal	3	—	—	3	25
Assam	3	—	2	1	14

South Zone

13, 14 and 15 November 1984

at Secunderabad

Tamil Nadu 421 (A. Jabbar 143, R. Madhavan 103, S.N. Yadav 6 for 166) and 191 for 9 dec (Arshad Ayub 4 for 63)
Hyderabad 258 for 8 dec (M.V. Narasimha Rao 72 not out, T.A. Sekhar 4 for 81) and 30 for 1

Match drawn
Tamil Nadu 9 pts, Hyderabad 7 pts

A third wicket stand of 198 between Jabbar and Madhavan took Tamil Nadu to an impregnable position, and the visitors batted brightly on the second morning, adding 122 before being all out 21 minutes before lunch. Shivlal Yadav bore the burden of the Hyderabad attack sending down 54.2 overs for his 6 for 166. The home side were 210 for 5 at the close and the one batsman to show real application was skipper Narasimha Rao who declared once the follow-on had been avoided and the 300-mark appeared out of reach. The rest was mainly academic apart from some varied off-spin from Arshad Ayub and Yadav.

18, 19 and 20 November 1984

at Bangalore

Karnataka 245 (R.M.H. Binny 87, Sudhakar Rao 57, Jugal Kishore Ghia 5 for 66) and 210 for 7 dec (B.P. Patel 50)
Andhra 151 (A.R.B. Bhat 5 for 72) and 136 (A.R.B. Bhat 4 for 41)

Karnataka won by an innings and 167 runs
Karnataka 29 pts, Andhra 9 pts

Karnataka, winners of the Ranji Trophy in 1983 but denied a place in the quarter-finals in 1984 by Hyderabad and Tamil Nadu, began the new campaign uncertainly. Put in to bat by Ravi Kumar, they struggled against the left-arm spin of Jugal Kishore who exploited the uneven bounce of the wicket. Binny and the experienced Sudhakar Rao who, like Jayaprakash, was saying farewell to the competition in this match, were the only batsmen to cope with the conditions on a disappointing first day. On the resumption, however, Karnataka took complete command. Andhra, 31 for 2 overnight, crashed to 98 for 7 and were bowled out for 151, another left-arm spinner, Bhat, revelling in the conditions. Increasing their lead to more than 300 by the close, Karnataka left themselves a day in which to bowl out their opponents. Andhra sank to 85 for 7, but Karnataka could not take another wicket before the 43rd over and so forfeited a bonus point. They were held up by Jugal Kishore and Krishna Mohan, but the end came in early afternoon.

1, 2 and 3 December 1984

at Trivandrum

Karnataka 354 for 2 dec (M.R. Srinivasaprasad 166 not out, G.R. Viswanath 129) and 223 for 2 dec (M.R. Srinivasaprasad 79, S. Viswanath 60)
Kerala 207 (S. Santosh 54, K. Jayaram 75, R.M.H. Binny 5 for 74) and 147 (A.R.B. Bhat 4 for 34)

Karnataka won by 223 runs
Karnataka 31 pts, Kerala 5 pts

Roger Binny declared at tea on the first day with Karnataka, maximum batting points long since theirs, having reached 354 off 65 overs. Sadanand Viswanath was caught behind off Hariharan without a run scored, but Srinivasaprasad and Gundappa Viswanath added 297 for the second wicket at a blistering pace. The elder Viswanath was run out, Binny hit a violent 40 and declared, leaving Srinivasaprasad with a career best.

Kerala made a brave reply, closing at 134 for 3 in 28 overs, but the next day their last 7 wickets fell for 50. Again Karnataka batted aggressively. The openers, Sadanand Viswanath and Srinivasaprasad, enjoying some luck, put on 146. On the last morning Kerala succumbed to the left-arm spinners.

Sandeep Patil. His innings of 165 for Bombay against Tamil Nadu in the Ranji Trophy semi-final proved to be decisive in taking his side through to the final. (Adrian Murrell)

15, 16 and 17 December 1984

at Tellichery

Tamil Nadu 281 (K. Srikkanth 50, T.S. Mahadevan 5 for 81) and 263 for 8 dec (V. Sivaramakrishnan 100 not out)
Kerala 235 (K. Jayaram 58, Arun Kumar 5 for 59) and 144 (T.A. Sekhar 5 for 65, Arun Kumar 4 for 44)

Tamil Nadu won by 165 runs
Tamil Nadu 31 pts, Kerala 11 pts

Kerala delighted home supporters with a spirited display on the first day. After they had asked Tamil Nadu to bat, they bowled steadily and fielded excellently. Srikkanth disturbed them with two sixes and seven fours, but thereafter the innings declined. Kerala's batting matched their outcricket in determination as they crept close to Tamil Nadu's score in front of a big holiday crowd. Left-hander Venkataraman Sivaramakrishnan was pressed into opening service and completed a fine hundred on the last morning. The visitors declared and, in an atmosphere grown heavy, Sekhar revelled, and he was splendidly supported by debutant Arum Kumar who gave a fiery display so that Kerala were bowled out in 30.1 overs. Arun Kumar's 8 for 103 was a most impressive debut performance.

21, 22 and 23 December 1984

at Salem

Tamil Nadu 154 (P. Rathod 4 for 38, A.R.B. Bhat 4 for 59) and 194 (A. Jabbar 77, A.R.B. Bhat 7 for 82)
Karnataka 186 (S. Viswanath 69, S. Venkataraghavan 7 for 69) and 163 for 6 (R.D. Khanwilkar 74)

Karnataka won by 4 wickets
Karnataka 24 pts, Tamil Nadu 8 pts

22, 23 and 24 December 1984

at Machalipatnam

Andhra 289 (K.S.B. Ramamurthy 67, Rajesh Yadav 4 for 65) and 239 (K.V.S.D. Kamaraju 81, Rajesh Yadav 7 for 64)
Hyderabad 305 for 3 dec (M. Azharuddin 121, Abdul Azeem 81, K.A. Qayyum 59 not out) and 228 for 2 (M. Azharuddin 105 not out, Abdul Azeem 68)

Hyderabad won by 8 wickets
Hyderabad 32 pts, Andhra 9 pts

A fine match, with excellent organisation and good crowds at Salem saw Karnataka, whose left-arm spinners demoralised Tamil Nadu on the opening day, qualify for the quarter-finals. Tamil Nadu showed neither application nor enterprise after winning the toss and they were bundled out in 55 overs, Bhat turning the ball appreciably. By the close, Karnataka, at 129 for 2, were in a commanding position. The Viswanaths added 105 for the second wicket, but Venkataraghavan ran through the rest of the batting on the second day. He enjoyed the bounce and turn with which the wicket helped him and the last 8 batsmen fell for 73 runs. Not to be outdone, Bhat produced a brilliant spell of 23 overs unchanged and only the meticulous Jabbar could withstand him. Karnataka were left the whole of the last day to score 163, but they needed only until an hour after lunch, Khanwilkar hitting nine fours.

Winning the toss, Andhra became victims of a fine spell by medium-pace newcomer Rajesh Yadav. A stand of 99 in 93 minutes for the sixth wicket between Ramamurthy and M.S. Kumar revived them, and a last wicket stand of 51 further embarrassed Hyderabad, but they finished the day well placed at 62 for 1. Next day they took total command. Azharuddin clinched his Test place with a three-hour innings which included a six and twelve fours. He and Abdul Azeem added 135 for the second wicket. Rajesh Yadav was once more a potent force when Andhra batted again and only violent hitting by Kamaraju at number 9 and 36 penalty runs lifted the home side. Staging its first Ranji Trophy match, Machalipatnam witnessed Azharuddin become the first South Zone batsman to score a century in each innings of a match in the competition. His hundred came in 150 minutes with ten fours. He and Abdul Azeem put on 111 in 78 minutes for the second wicket.

30, 31 December 1984, and 1 January 1985

at Secunderabad

Kerala 178 (K. Jayaraman 56, Rajesh Yadav 6 for 55) and 243 for 6 (K. Jayaraman 71, S. Santosh 61)
Hyderabad 511 for 6 dec (M.V. Narasimha Rao 160 not out, Abdul Azeem 103, Arshad Ayub 62, K.A. Qayyum 61)

Match drawn
Hyderabad 9 pts, Kerala 4 pts

Hyderabad's failure to force victory over bottom of the table Kerala jeopardised their chances of reaching the play-offs and they entered the last game level on points with Tamil Nadu. All went well at first with Rajesh Yadav again in fine form. Skipper Narasimha Rao hit a career best and there were three century partnerships, but Kerala held out for a draw.

4, 5 and 6 January 1985

at Vijayawada

Andhra 262 (Jugal Kishore Ghia 61 not out, G.A. Pratap Kumar 57, A. Verma 4 for 65)
Kerala 95 (Jugal Kishore Ghia 4 for 27) and 117 (K.B. Ramamurthy 6 for 4)

Andhra won by an innings and 50 runs
Andhra 29 pts, Kerala 4 pts

Andhra kept alive their hopes of qualifying for the quarter-finals with a convincing win in a low-scoring match. On a doubtful wicket Andhra owed much to a third wicket stand of 100 between Meher Baba and Pratap Kumar. Skipper Ramamurthy finished the match with a devastating spell of 7.2 overs.

Madan Lal. An outstanding season for Delhi won him back his place in the national side. (Adrian Murrell)

Raju Kulkarni. His opening spell left Delhi in disarray in the Ranji Trophy Final. (Adrian Murrell)

2, 3 and 4 February 1985

at Hassan

Karnataka 208 (S.N. Yadav 5 for 84) and 436 for 7 (B.P. Patel 130 not out, J. Abhiram 81, R.M.H. Binny 61)
Hyderabad 305 (A. Ayub 71, Ehteshamuddin 67, P. Rathod 4 for 74)

Match drawn
Hyderabad 9 pts, Karnataka 7 pts

at Madras

Tamil Nadu 331 for 6 dec (R. Madhavan 153 not out) and 178 for 2 dec (V. Sivaramakrishnan 99, S. Srinivasan 59 not out)
Andhra 136 (T.A. Sekhar 5 for 36) and 223 (S. Venkataraghavan 5 for 81)

Tamil Nadu won by 150 runs
Tamil Nadu 30 pts, Andhra 5 pts

While Hyderabad floundered on the matting at Hassan Tamil Nadu won easily in Madras to clinch the second qualifying spot. Shivlal Yadav bowled well on the opening day, but Hyderabad were lifted in their batting only by a seventh wicket stand of 137 between Ayub and Ehteshamuddin. Century stands between Patel and Abhiram and Patel and Binny assured the match would be drawn.

In Madras, Madhavan took Tamil Nadu to a commanding position on the first day. Andhra wilted before Sekhar, but Jabbar did not enforce the follow-on. Venkataraman Sivaramakrishnan and Srinivasan added 144 for the second wicket and the stand ended when Sivaramakrishnan was run out one short of his century. Andhra never looked like avoiding defeat when they batted again.

South Zone Final Table

	P	*W*	*L*	*D*	*Pts*
Karnataka	4	3	—	1	91
Tamil Nadu	4	2	1	1	78
Hyderabad	4	1	—	3	57
Andhra	4	1	3	—	52
Kerala	4	—	3	1	24

West Zone

7, 8 and 9 December 1984

at Ahmedabad

Saurashtra 335 for 9 dec (A. Pandya 113, K. Chauhan 60, K.D. Ghavri 59) and 219 for 8 dec (B. Mistry 4 for 43)
Gujarat 325 (S. Talati 82, A. Saheba 60, B. Mistry 56, A. Patel 5 for 95) and 113 for 5 (B. Mistry 66)

Match drawn
Saurashtra 12 pts, Gujarat 9 pts

at Pune

Bombay 310 for 6 dec (L.S. Rajput 94, S.S. Hattangadi 72, S. Jadhav 4 for 47) and 330 for 9 dec (B.S. Sandhu 83, S.M. Gavaskar 73 not out, S.S. Hattangadi 51, S.C. Gudge 4 for 93)
Maharashtra 318 for 8 dec (R. Poonawala 65, S. Kalyani 55, S.V. Nayak 4 for 83) and 212 for 6 (S.C. Gudge 59, M.D. Gunjal 51 not out)

Match drawn
Bombay 14 pts, Maharashtra 13 pts

Neither of the opening matches could produce a result. A maiden century by Aful Pandya, in his second season with Saurashtra, saved his side after 4 wickets had fallen for 37 runs to leave Saurashtra at 123 for 4. Gujarat were badly let down by their fielding and Saurashtra closed at 326 for 7. Having taken the last 3 wickets quickly on the second day, Gujarat were given a good start, 123 in 132 minutes by Talati, who hit fifteen fours, and Pathak, but the momentum was lost and a draw became inevitable.

Inspired by a 2nd wicket partnership of 142 in 127 minutes between Lalchand Rajput and Shiskit Hattangadi, Bombay easily moved to four batting points on the opening day at Pune in spite of the absence of the injured Vengsarkar and Shastri. Riaz Poonawala shattered the visitors at the close with 65 off 54 balls, including two sixes and eleven fours, but he fell straight away on the second morning. After Maharashtra had taken a first innings lead it seemed that they might snatch a surprise win, but Sandhu hit fiercely in support of Gavaskar and eventually the home side were happy to draw.

20, 21 and 22 December 1984

at Baroda

Maharashtra 305 for 8 dec (S. Jadhav 123 not out, P. Pradhan 78, S. Kalyani 69) and 238 for 5 dec (R. Poonawala 84, S. Jadhav 67 not out)
Baroda 340 for 9 dec (A.D. Gaekwad 108, M.B. Amarnath 73 not out, R.Y. Deshmukh 50) and 45 for 0

Match drawn
Baroda 9 pts, Maharashtra 8 pts

21, 22 and 23 December 1984

at Bombay

Bombay 309 for 4 dec (L.S. Rajput 110, G.A.H.M. Parkar 67) and 266 for 3 dec (C.S. Pandit 106 not out, S.M. Gavaskar 62 not out, G.A.H.M. Parkar 51)
Gujarat 297 (B. Mistry 70, S. Talati 55) and 139 for 8 (B.S. Sandhu 4 for 60)

Match drawn
Bombay 15 pts, Gujarat 7 pts

A pugnacious maiden century by Shreekant Jadhav changed the complexion of the game at Baroda on the first day and enabled Maharashtra, at one time struggling at 130 for 5, to declare with four batting points achieved. Gaekwad and Deshmukh began Baroda's reply with a stand of 107 and Gaekwad, weak after his bout of food poisoning, went on to reach his 11th Ranji Trophy century with ten fours. Mohinder Amarnath batted well, but when Poonawala and Dixit put on 113 for Maharashtra's first wicket in the second innings and Jadhav bolstered after 5 wickets had gone for 32 at one stage the game was destined to be drawn.

Rajput batted with authority and class to reach a fine hundred in Bombay and shared an opening stand of 180 with Parkar. The day had begun unhappily for Bombay when Gavaskar dropped Shastri and Raju Kulkarni for arriving late. Gujarat had problems too when opening bowler Dhanrukh Patel was called for throwing. They batted gallantly to stay in contention, but Pandit reached his third hundred in the competition on the last day and Bombay left themselves three hours in which to bowl out the visitors. They failed because of stubborn resistance from the Gujarat tail, Natu Patel and Joy Zinto in particular.

8, 9 and 10 January 1985

at Jamnagar

Saurashtra 335 for 8 dec (B. Pujara 93, A. Pandya 76, A. Patel 67, S. Oak 4 for 54) and 158 (A. Pandya 51)
Maharashtra 301 for 7 dec (S. Kalyani 103, M.D. Gunjal 82) and 143 for 4 (S. Kalyani 64 not out, R. Jadeja 4 for 57)

Match drawn
Maharashtra 13 pts, Saurashtra 10 pts

at Bombay

Bombay 371 for 4 dec (G.A.H.M. Parkar 170 retired hurt, S.S. Hattangadi 83, L.S. Rajput 66) and 457 for 5 dec (R.J. Shastri 200 not out, L.S. Rajput 136)
Baroda 330 for 8 dec (S. Keshwala 100 not out, M.B. Amarnath 88, Tilak Raj 55) and 81 for 7 (B.S. Sandhu 4 for 43)

Match drawn
Bombay 14 pts, Baroda 6 pts

Hemani Talwalkar returned to the Maharashtra side after an absence of five years and bowled Bipin Pujara who played an aggressive innings. Srikanth Kalyani hit a maiden century and Maharashtra moved to a position of parity. Saurashtra collapsed on the last day, but Maharashtra found the task of scoring 193 at five and a half an over beyond their capabilities.

The Wankhede Stadium was the scene of one of the most remarkable innings in cricket history when, on the last day, Ravi Shastri hit a career best 200 not out.

Coming to the wicket at 201 for 4, Shastri reached 50 in 38 minutes off 42 balls, 100 in 71 minutes off 80 balls, and, in 113 minutes, having faced only 123 deliveries, he reached the fastest double century in first-class cricket. He hit thirteen sixes and thirteen fours. His 6th wicket stand with Parkar produced 204 and Parkar scored 33. He equalled Sobers' record when he hit occasional left-arm spinner Tilak Raj for six sixes in an over. His first was straight, his next two wide over long-on as was the fifth, the fourth having been swung over mid-wicket. He drove the last ball straight.

Shastri's innings overwhelmed what had gone before. Vengsarkar was dropped for arriving late and Parkar who was to have stood down hit a career best before retiring with a pulled muscle. He and Rajput, jostling for a place in the Indian side, put on 153 for the first wicket.

On the second day Suresh Keshwala hit an unbeaten century and put Baroda in contention. Rajput then continued his splendid form before Shastri's arrival. Eventually Baroda endured an unhappy 18 overs.

27, 28 and 29 January 1985

at Baroda

Saurashtra 344 for 9 dec (K. Chauhan 122, D. Pardeshi 7 for 76) and 219 (K.D. Ghavri 56, B. Pujara 54, D. Pardeshi 6 for 84)
Baroda 307 (M.B. Amarnath 70, B. Quereshi 6 for 87) and 169 for 6

Match drawn
Saurashtra 13 pts, Baroda 12 pts

at Pune

Gujarat 183 (B. Mistry 75, Azim Khan 4 for 31) and 373 (P. Desai 112, S. Pathak 74, S.C. Gudge 5 for 101)
Maharashtra 290 (R.B. Bhalekar 78, S. Kalyani 51) and 153 for 6

Match drawn
Maharashtra 11 pts, Gujarat 10 pts

Eager for points in their bid to qualify for the play-offs, Saurashtra were aided by dropped catches at Baroda on the opening day which was highlighted by Kirit Chauhan's century and Pandya being given out 'handled ball'. Daskrath Padeshi had a fine match with his spin and it was left-arm spinner Baskir Quereshi who posed problems for the home side. It was only his second game in the competition. In a desperate bid for points Baroda hit 169 in 22 overs on the last afternoon, but their chances of qualifying looked slim.

A green wicket with uneven bounce provided encouragement for the Maharashtra at the Nehru Stadium. They strove to build a match-winning lead, Bhalekar taking 206 minutes for a valuable 78, but Gujarat batted nobly at the second attempt and skipper Desai hit a fine century. Maharashtra were let down by some sloppy fielding.

9, 10 and 11 February 1985

at Surat

Gujarat 370 for 7 dec (S. Talati 83, J. Saigal 85, A. Saheba 74) and 278 for 8 dec (B. Patel 70, V. Wadkar 5 for 89)
Baroda 288 (R.Y. Deshmukh 91, B. Mistry 4 for 44, N. Patel 4 for 69) and 189 for 3 (A.D. Gaekwad 103, R. Parikh 72)

Match drawn
Baroda 12 pts, Gujarat 11 pts

at Gandhidham

Saurashtra 302 (B. Jadeja 56 not out, R.R. Kulkarni 5 for 96) and 239 (B. Jadeja 71)
Bombay 339 for 9 dec (S.M. Patil 90, G.A.H.M. Parkar 90, B.S. Sandhu 56 not out) and 204 for 4 (S. Mandle 76 not out, S.S. Hattangadi 53)

Bombay won by 6 wickets
Bombay 31 pts, Saurashtra 14 pts

With every match in the zone having been drawn, and Maharashtra having finished on 45 points, the final round of games began with qualifying places wide open. A placid pitch provided by the matting at Surat saw 414 runs scored on the first day for the loss of seven wickets. In spite of Deshmukh's fine knock, Baroda could not match the Gujarat score, but fought back when Wadkar and Keshwala captured 4 for 83 before the end of the second day. The success was not maintained, however, and Baroda had to be content with Gaekwad's second century of the season and his opening stand of 185 with Parikh as consolation for a poor season.

On the matting at Ganhidham, Raju Kulkarni reduced the home side to 146 for 6, but late resistance, including a spirited last wicket stand of 81 by Jadeja and Quereshi, lifted them to 302. Bombay batted unevenly. Thanks to Parkar they reached 162 for 2 and then lost 5 wickets for 68 runs, but Patil and Sandhu took them to a lead. Saurashtra, 39 for 4, recovered through Bimal Jadeja, but Bombay were not to be denied and swept to victory and the retention of the Talim Shield, the symbol of supremacy in the West Zone. Saurashtra, however, had amassed enough points to climb into second place and qualify even though they were the only side in the zone to have lost a match.

West Zone Final Table

	P	*W*	*L*	*D*	*Pts*
Bombay	4	1	—	3	74
Saurashtra	4	—	1	3	49
Maharashtra	4	—	—	4	45
Baroda	4	—	—	4	39
Gujarat	4	—	—	4	37

Central Zone

15, 16 and 17 December 1984

at Nagpur

Vidarbha 207 (M. Kaore 56, R.S. Hans 6 for 38) and 262 (M. Kaore 70, R.S. Hans 4 for 59)
Uttar Pradesh 349 (S. Chaturvedi 62, Yusuf Ali Khan 61, A. Bambi 78, H. Wasu 7 for 102) and 121 for 7

Uttar Pradesh won by 3 wickets
Uttar Pradesh 26 pts, Vidarbha 11 pts

at Bhilai

Madhya Pradesh 392 for 5 dec (M. Hassan 116 not out, R. Talwar 93, A. Laghate 61) and 153 for 5

Maninder Singh (Delhi) 46 wickets in the season, but no place in the Test side. (Adrian Murrell)

Rajasthan 344 (Padam Shastri 93, A. Asawa 89 not out, N. Hirwani 5 for 101)

Match drawn
Madhya Pradesh 8 pts, Rajasthan 5 pts

The Central Zone season began with Uttar Pradesh, the favourites to win the zone, having to score at six runs an over to beat Vidarbha. They gave a good all-round performance and were always in command, but it was the slow left-arm of the consistent Rajendrasingh Hans which troubled Vidarbha most as he took more than five wickets in an innings for the 21st time.

At Bhilai, the bat always dominated and a draw was inevitable.

20, 21 and 22 December 1984

at Akola

Vidarbha 299 (R. Pankule 69, P. Sundaram 4 for 108) and 233 for 9 dec (S. Hedaoo 66 not out, P. Shetty 58, V. Mathur 4 for 39)
Rajasthan 277 for 7 dec (P. Sharma 94, Padam Shastri 87, H. Wasu 4 for 82) and 104 for 3.

Match drawn
Rajasthan 10 pts, Vidarbha 9 pts

21, 22 and 23 December 1984

at Jhansi

Railways 274 for 8 dec (P. Bhatnagar 75) and 323 (P. Karkera 81, H. Mathur 68, N. Churi 57, Gulrez Ali 5 for 94)
Madhya Pradesh 286 (S. Ansari 87, Sanjeeva Rao 58, A. Laghate 50, S. Khan 4 for 85) and 129 for 3 (S. Ansari 55)

Match drawn
Railways 11 pts, Madhya Pradesh 10 pts

The failure of any side to force victory on the matting wickets at Akola and Jhansi left Uttar Pradesh in sight of the quarter-finals without playing. Solidity was the key to Vidarbha's 299, and Rajasthan's reply was sparked by a 5th wicket stand of 109 between Sharma and Shastri. The curiosity of Vidarbha's second innings was that Wasu, who had bowled well, was given out 'obstructing the field'.

The match in Jhansi followed a similar pattern, with the side batting second set an impossible target.

26, 27 and 28 December 1984

at Kanpur

Uttar Pradesh 396 (R. Sapru 114, R.B. Kala 88, Gopal Rao 4 for 75) and 89 for 4
Madhya Pradesh 125 (A.G. Mathur 4 for 34, R.S. Hans 4 for 7) and 359 (S. Ansari 200, Gopal Sharma 4 for 107)

Uttar Pradesh won by 6 wickets
Uttar Pradesh 24 pts, Madhya Pradesh 8 pts

at Kota

Rajasthan 349 for 7 dec (Padam Shastri 159, A. Asawa 75) and 183 for 4 dec (Padam Shastri 101)
Railways 266 (N. Churi 85, S. Mudkavi 8 for 60) and 23 for 5

Match drawn
Rajasthan 7 pts, Railways 6 pts

A 4th wicket stand of 157 between Sapru and Kala was the basis of Uttar Pradesh's victory at Kanpur. Hans in both innings and Gopal Sharma in the second perplexed Madhya Pradesh with their spin, but Sunhail Ansari played magnificently to record the first double hundred ever hit for Madhya Pradesh, a brave innings which could not save his side.

At Kota, Rajasthan made slow progress after winning the toss and gained only 2 batting points. Their innings was held together by Padam Shastri who dominated a 3rd wicket stand of 111 with A. Mudkavi. A career best spin bowling performance from S. Mudkavi overwhelmed Railways and Padam Shastri reached his second hundred of the match, only the second Rajasthan batsman to achieve this feat in the Ranji Trophy. Sharma left only 18 overs for his bowlers to bowl out Railways and the match was drawn.

11, 12 and 13 January 1985

at Sehore

Vidarbha 376 (V. Gawate 68, Asad Khan 4 for 99) and 253 (V. Shesh 77, A. Sabnis 4 for 70)
Madhya Pradesh 293 for 6 dec (R. Talwar 85, Sanjeeva Rao 56) and 248 for 8 (S. Phadkar 4 for 56)

Match drawn
Madhya Pradesh 13 pts, Vidarbha 10 pts

at Moradabad

Uttar Pradesh 497 for 3 dec (S.S. Khandkar 261 not out, Yusuf Ali Khan 122, S. Chaturvedi 50)
Railways 147 (R.P. Singh 7 for 67) and 282 (S. Mehra 50, R.P. Singh 4 for 79)

Uttar Pradesh won by an innings and 68 runs
Uttar Pradesh 30 pts, Railways 4 pts

Some remarkable late order batting by Gawate, Shesh and Takle salvaged both Vidarbha's innings. The last three wickets added 137 in the first innings and 155 in the second to thwart Madhya Pradesh who were thankful to draw after a bold bid for victory floundered.

On the matting at Moradabad Chaturvedi and Khandkar began Uttar Pradesh's innings with a stand of 148 and Khandkar and Yusuf Ali Khan then added 189 for the second. The 23-year old Khandkar reached the highest score ever made for Uttar Pradesh and reasserted his right for consideration by the Indian selectors as his runs came at four an over. Railways offered little resistance and twice fell to R.P. Singh.

4, 5 and 6 February 1985

at Nagpur

Vidarbha 283 for 9 dec (S. Hedaoo 64, A. Sharma 4 for 66) and 184
Railways 324 for 9 dec (Hyder Ali 121, R. Jadhav 79) and 144 for 3 (R. Vats 69)

Railways won by 7 wickets
Railways 27 pts, Vidarbha 9 pts

Railways clinched second place in the Central Zone table with a win over Vidarbha, scoring at nearly 7 runs an over on the last afternoon. This was the culmination of a marvellous recovery. Facing Vidarbha's 283, they were 116 for 7 when Hyder Ali joined Jadhav. They added 202, a Railways record, and Hyder Ali recorded a ferocious maiden century. From that point the match belonged to Railways.

8, 9 and 10 February 1985

at Jaipur

Uttar Pradesh 467 for 6 dec (S. Chaturvedi 182, R. Sapru 120) and 173 for 3 (Yusuf Ali Khan 83 not out, S. Chaturvedi 62)
Rajasthan 328 (Padam Shastri 79, Amit Asawa 63, S. Mudkavi 51, R.S. Hans 4 for 43)

Match drawn
Uttar Pradesh 10 pts, Rajasthan 6 pts

In the final zonal match a 3rd wicket stand of 241 between Chaturvedi and Sapru dominated the opening day and took the Central Zone champions to an impregnable position. Rajasthan batted solidly in reply and ensured a draw.

Central Zone Final Table

	P	*W*	*L*	*D*	*Pts*
Uttar Pradesh	4	3	—	1	90
Railways	4	1	1	2	48
Vidarbha	4	—	2	2	39
Madhya Pradesh	4	—	1	3	39
Rajasthan	4	—	—	4	28

North Zone

25, 26 and 27 November 1984

at Air Force Ground, Delhi

Jammu and Kashmir 274 (S. Chowdhary 67, Parvez Kaiser 55) and 225 (S. Chowdhary 66, Ravi Pandit 51)
Services 508 (A.K. Seth 130 not out, N. Gadkari 116 not out, Srikant 80, Ratan Das 77)

Services won by an innings and 9 runs
Services 29 pts, Jammu and Kashmir 7 pts

A 4th wicket stand of 95 between Chowdhary and Kaiser bolstered the visitors to a creditable 274 on the opening day, but Services took a firm grip on the match on the second day which they closed at 385 for 5. Ratan Das and Srikant began with a stand of 153, but the innings was dominated by Niton Gadkari and Avinash Seth who added an unbeaten 234 for the 6th wicket. Gadkari hit nine fours and batted for 175 minutes. The adventurous Seth hit two sixes and twelve fours in his 137-minute innings. Jammu and Kashmir still looked as if they might save the game, but their last 6 wickets fell for 79 runs.

29, 30 November and 1 December 1984

at Rohtak

Jammu and Kashmir 101 (R. Goel 7 for 36) and 152 (R. Goel 7 for 38)
Haryana 324 for 9 dec (R. Chadha 53, Nissar Khanday 4 for 59)

Haryana won by an innings and 71 runs
Haryana 30 pts, Jammu and Kashmir 3 pts

30 November, 1 and 2 December 1984

at Ferozeshah Kotla, Delhi

Delhi 335 (S.C. Khanna 114, C.P.S. Chauhan 57, D. Chopra 4 for 92) and 137 for 6 dec
Punjab 228 (Kirti Azad 5 for 80, U.S. Madan Lal 4 for 37) and 54 for 5

Match drawn
Delhi 11 pts, Punjab 8 pts

Having decided not to retire, Rajinder Goel took ten wickets or more in a match for the 17th time and his 14 for 74 routed Jammu and Kashmir who were beaten inside two days.

In Delhi, Khanna and Chauhan began with a stand of 146, but the middle order failed to capitalise on this start. Sustained spells by Kirti Azad and skipper Madan Lal put Delhi on top and Punjab finished the second day on 184 for 8, still 2 short of saving the follow-on. Yograj Singh and Arun Sharma saved the game, however, and Delhi's lead was restricted to 107. They floundered in their second innings until rescued by Kirti Azad and Madan Lal. Punjab had 45 minutes and 20 overs in which to score 245 to win, but they were thankful for dour defence by Yashpal and Arun Sharma for saving them from embarrassment.

4, 5 and 6 December 1984

at Roshanara Ground, Delhi

Jammu and Kashmir 88 (S. Valson 4 for 34) and 111 (U.S. Madan Lal 9 for 50)
Delhi 244 (Gursharan Singh 64, Maninder Singh 61 not out, Ravi Pandit 4 for 46)

Delhi won by an innings and 45 runs
Delhi 30 pts, Jammu and Kashmir 5 pts

at Air Force Ground, Delhi

Punjab 464 for 4 dec (Amarjeet Kaypee 167, D. Chopra 120 not out, Balkar Singh 63, Navot Singh Sidhu 61) and 81 for 5
Services 504 (A.S. Bajwa 132, Bhaskar Ghosh 151 not out, Sudhakar Rao 71, R. Das 54)

Match drawn
Services 6 pts, Punjab 5 pts

Madan Lal won the toss and asked Jammu and Kashmir to bat. Combining with Valson and Sanjeev Sharma in a three-pronged medium-pace attack, he saw Jammu bowled out 10 minutes before lunch. Delhi fared badly against the Jammu medium-pacers, the brothers Ravi and Deepak Pandit, and Nissar, and they were 44 for 5 and later 146 for 9. A remarkable last wicket stand of 98 by Maninder Singh and Valson took Delhi's innings into the second day. Jammu lost two second innings wickets before a run was scored, Ravi Pandit being run out. The control and movement of Madan Lal proved too much for Jammu and he finished with match figures of 12 for 75 as the game was over in two days.

Three days of run feasting at the Air Force Ground ended, predictably, in stalemate. Balkar and Navjot began the match with a stand of 126, but the highlight of the Punjab innings was a 4th wicket partnership of 265 between Amarjeet Kaypee and Deepak Chopra, an association record. Services' reply was founded on a 2nd wicket stand of 169 between Rattan Das and Amardeep Bajwa who hit a six and fifteen fours in a spirited century. Bhaskar Ghosh played a dogged innings on the last day.

8 and 9 December 1984

at Chandigarh

Jammu and Kashmir 83 and 70 (D. Chopra 4 for 14)
Punjab 322 (Satish Kumar 108, Arun Sharma 62 not out, Nissar Khandy 4 for 97)

Punjab won by an innings and 169 runs
Punjab 31 pts, Jammu and Kashmir 2 pts

Jammu and Kashmir finished their Ranji Trophy programme in familiarly dismal manner. Electing to bat, they were all out 24 minutes after lunch. Punjab quickly moved into the lead for the loss of one wicket and Satish Kumar put them in an invincible position. Wicket-keeper Arun Sharma hit lustily at the close of the innings before Jammu gave another abject batting display to be beaten with more than a day to spare.

11, 12 and 13 December 1984

at Air Force Ground, Delhi

Services 189 (Sudhakar Rao 52, S. Talwar 6 for 68) and 227 (Bhaskar Ghosh 90, R. Goel 5 for 75)
Haryana 440 (A.O. Malhotra 132, R. Jolly 86, A. Jha 6 for 179)

Haryana won by an innings and 24 runs
Haryana 29 pts, Services 4 pts

An inept batting display on a perfect wicket against the off-spin of Sarkar Talwar and the left-arm spin of Rajinder Goel left Services struggling for survival from the start of the match. The visitors began sedately but soon exposed the limitations of the Services' out-cricket with some aggressive batting. Ashok Malhotra, twice missed, hit seventeen fours in his 243-minute innings and later Rakesh Jolly hammered three sixes and seven fours in a brisk 80. In four hours on the last day Services again fell to the spinners and their hopes of a place in the play-offs vanished.

15, 16 and 17 December 1984

at Rohtak

Delhi 459 for 5 dec (Bhaskar Pillai 149 not out, C.P.S. Chauhan 115, S.C. Khanna 58) and 175 for 3 (Gursharan Singh 57, C.P.S. Chauhan 53)
Haryana 337 (R. Chadha 83, Aman Kumar 55)

Match drawn
Delhi 10 pts, Haryana 5 pts

The match between the two strongest sides in the North Zone ended in a predictable draw. Chauhan and Khanna began the match with a stand of 128 and Pillai and Rajinder Singh shared an unbroken partnership of 121. Haryana were 90 for 4, but Chadha and Aman Kumar added 146 and some solid batting followed as the match dwindled to its close. The end was brightened by some hard hitting from Chauhan and Gursharan Singh who hit 104 for the 2nd wicket at 5 an over.

21, 22 and 23 December 1984

at Ferozeshah Kotla, Delhi

Services 191 (B. Ghosh 69) and 81 (S. Srivastava 5 for 21)
Delhi 233 (K.P. Bhaskar 135, A. Jha 5 for 80) and 40 for 1

Delhi won by 9 wickets
Delhi 25 pts, Services 5 pts

Delhi won the North Zone championship in convincing style, the game ending after only 40 minutes on the last day. It was a remarkably easy victory after an uncertain start on the Friday. The combination of slow left-arm Maninder Singh and medium pace Valson had bowled out Services for 191, but Services' skipper Ajay Jha bowled his side into a good position and Delhi ended the day on 77 for 7. Jha, tall and lean, bowled a brisk medium pace and swung the ball appreciably. He took the wickets of Madan Lal, Rajinder Singh and Prabhakat in one over. The next day the game moved dramatically in favour of Delhi as Bhaskar Pillai, just 25 years old, hit a six and twenty-one fours in a bold innings. He and Maninder Singh added 108 for the 8th wicket. Young leg-spinner Srivastava then teased Services to destruction.

21, 22 and 23 December 1984

at Patiala

Haryana 299 (Chetan Sharma 53, D. Chopra 4 for 79) and 190 for 6
Punjab 264 for 9 dec (N.S. Sidhu 124, S. Talwar 5 for 129)

Match drawn
Punjab 6 pts, Haryana 4 pts

The points that Haryana took from this match meant that, as expected, they qualified for the play-offs, but it was a dull affair. The outstanding performance came from Navjot Singh Sidhu who hit his first Ranji Trophy century on a wicket which aided Talwar and Goel. He reached his hundred with a six off Talwar.

North Zone Final Table

	P	*W*	*L*	*D*	*Pts*
Delhi	4	2	—	2	76
Haryana	4	2	—	2	68
Punjab	4	1	—	3	50
Services	4	1	2	1	44
Jammu and Kashmir	4	—	4	—	17

Pre-Quarter Finals

22, 23, 24 and 25 February 1985

at Delhi

Haryana 342 (Aman Kumar 100, Satya Dev 72) and 335 for 9 dec (R. Dogra 83, R. Chadha 71, Satya Dev 69)
Railways 213 (P. Karkera 57, R. Goel 4 for 71) and 168 for 2 (P. Karkera 75 not out)

Match drawn
Haryana won on first innings

at Agra

Uttar Pradesh 157 (S.S. Khandkar 54, A. Patel 6 for 30) and 176 (B. Quereshi 4 for 51)
Saurashtra 176 (Rajendra Jadeja 60, Gopal Sharma 5 for 60, R.S. Hans 5 for 63) and 102 (Gopal Sharma 6 for 26, R.S. Hans 4 for 45)

Uttar Pradesh won by 55 runs

Haryana recovered from the indignity of 49 for 3 through some solid middle order batting led by Aman Kumar. At 104 for 1, Railways were in a good position, but wickets then fell steadily and with a commanding first innings lead Haryana were never likely to relinquish their hold on the match.

At Agra, Uttar Pradesh, who won the toss, came from behind to win a thrilling contest. Ashok Patel spun his side to a good position and the Saurashtra lead should have been a big one, but they lost their last 6 wickets for 17 runs. Once again Uttar Pradesh did not find runs easy to get, and Saurashtra needed only 158 to win. Gopal Sharma and Hans were introduced into the attack after only three overs with the new ball. Both openers fell at 40 and thereafter the spinners dominated, 9 wickets falling for 41 runs.

Quarter-Finals

7, 8, 9 and 10 March 1985

at Delhi

Uttar Pradesh 124 (D.K. Jain 4 for 35) and 179 (K.B. Kala 52, Maninder Singh 4 for 54)
Delhi 404 (R. Lamba 84, Kirti Azad 69, A. Sharma 64, R.P. Singh 4 for 75)

Delhi won by an innings and 101 runs

at Madras

Bihar 297 (V. Venkatram 50 not out, S. Venkataraghavan 6 for 90) and 261 (S. Vasudevan 4 for 90)
Tamil Nadu 362 (A. Jabbar 72, S. Srinivasan 56, V. Venkatrum 8 for 130) and 197 for 0 (V. Sivaramakrishnan 108 not out, C.S. Suresh Kumar 76 not out)

Tamil Nadu won by 10 wickets

at Bangalore

Karnataka 489 (B.P. Patel 159, C. Saldanha 63, S.M.H. Kirmani 61, L.K. Mahapatra 5 for 123, H. Praharaj 4 for 140) and 261 for 1 dec (R.D. Khanwilkar 125 not out, C. Saldanha 118 not out)
Orissa 276 (K. Dubey 53, S. Sahu 52, D. Mahanty 51, P. Rathod 4 for 44) and 231 (A. Jayaprakash 63, K. Dubey 60, S. Mitra 54 not out)

Karnataka won by 243 runs

at Faridabad

Haryana 223 (Ashwini Kumar 56, Satya Dev 50, K.D. Mokashi 6 for 66) and 148 (S.M. Patil 4 for 31, R.C. Thakar 4 for 32)
Bombay 195 (S.V. Manjrekar 57, S. Talwar 7 for 107) and 177 for 2 (S.M. Patil 59 not out)

Bombay won by 8 wickets

At one time on the opening day in Delhi, Uttar Pradesh were 22 for 6 and they never totally recovered from the damage inflicted upon them by Valson and Jain, making his first appearance. Delhi batted consistently after losing 2 for 48 and a 6th wicket stand of 123 between Lamba and Sharma assured them of a semi-final place. Uttar Pradesh again batted poorly.

A magnificent all-round effort by skipper Venkatram could not save Bihar in Madras. They faltered against veteran off-spinner Venkataraghavan, but when Tamil Nadu were 189 for 6 it looked as if they might snatch a first innings lead. The last three Tamil Nadu wickets added 102, however, and Bihar had lost their grip on the match. Set to make 197 to win, Tamil Nadu won by ten wickets, Venkataraman Sivaramakrishnan dominating the partnership.

At Bangalore, Karnataka took charge of the game on the first day and never relinquished their hold. Brijesh Patel and Syed Kirmani put on 145 for the 6th wicket and there was a stand of 87 for the last between Bhat and Sharad Rao. Orissa slipped from 105 for 1 to 111 for 5, three wickets falling at that score, but recovered bravely. A stunning unfinished partnership of 240 at nearly five an over placed Karnataka in an impregnable position and Orissa were well beaten in spite of a late burst from Mitra.

Haryana surprisingly led Bombay on the first innings, but they failed miserably to consolidate their position, losing 6 second innings wickets for 46 so wasting the splendid effort of Sarkar Talwar. Talwar was unable to repeat his form in the second innings and Goel was blunted by solid defence so that Bombay moved to a surprisingly easy win in a match in which they were trailing for the first two days.

Semi-Finals

23, 24, 25 and 26 March 1985

at Bombay

Tamil Nadu 409 (V. Sivaramakrishnan 117, C.S. Suresh Kumar 106, B. Arun 83) and 276 for 8 dec (N.P. Madhavan 104, R. Madhavan 73)
Bombay 548 (S.M. Patil 165, G.A.H.M. Parkar 91, B.S. Sandhu 98, S.S. Hattangadi 61, A. Sippy 50, B. Arun 4 for 123)

Match drawn
Bombay won on first innings

at Bangalore

Karnataka 189 (B.P. Patel 55, Maninder Singh 6 for 62) and 307 for 8 (G.R. Viswanath 136 not out, Maninder Singh 5 for 86)
Delhi 376 (Bhaskar Pillai 91, M. Prabhakar 87, A. Sharma 50, H. Surendra 5 for 126)

Match drawn
Delhi won on first innings

When Reddy won the toss, chose to bat first and saw his openers put on 182 for the first wicket he could have been forgiven for believing that he was to lead Tamil Nadu into the Ranji Trophy Final, but the visitors threw away the fine opportunity that they had been given and they lost their last 7 wickets for 69 runs. Boosted by 24 penalty points, the Tamil Nadu score still looked impressive, but Parkar and Patil lifted Bombay from 43 for 2 to 250 before Parkar fell to Raman. When Patil was stumped after a typically free-hitting innings Bombay were still in danger of trailing on the first innings, but Sandhu launched a fierce attack on the bowling and he and Sippy added 103 for the 7th wicket to take their side into the lead and inevitably into the final.

Viswanath's decision to bat first at Bangalore did not appear justified as Maninder Singh exploited conditions and the home side were bowled out for 189. This never seemed a score likely to trouble Delhi even though they made heavy weather early on. Prabhakar and Bhaskar Pillai put on 163 for the 6th wicket and Sharma and Maninder Singh made useful contributions to ensure a Bombay–Delhi final.

Ranji Trophy Final
BOMBAY *v.* DELHI

With both sides strengthened by the return of heroes fresh from triumphs in Australia, the Ranji Trophy Final produced one of the best contests that the competition has seen. It was the fifth time in nine seasons that Bombay and Delhi had met in the final, and it was the fourth occasion that Bombay became the winners so retaining the Trophy.

Gavaskar won the toss, but Bombay began uneasily

RANJI TROPHY – BOMBAY *v.* DELHI
1, 2, 3, 5 and 6 April 1985 at Bombay

BOMBAY

	FIRST INNINGS		SECOND INNINGS	
L.S. Rajput	c Chauhan, b Prabhakar	0	st Khanna, b Maninder	63
G.A.H.M. Parkar	c Khanna, b Madan Lal	23	b Madan Lal	14
S.S. Hattangadi	c Khanna, b Valson	7	c Sharma, b Madan Lal	5
S.M. Patil	c Pillai, b Maninder	54	c Kirti, b Maninder	57
S.M. Gavaskar†	b Madan Lal	106	b Maninder	64
R.J. Shastri	b Maninder	29	c Prabhakar, b Maninder	76
C.S. Pandit*	lbw, b Prabhakar	49	c Maninder, b Kirti	44
A. Sippy	c Sharma, b Madan Lal	16		
K.D. Mokashi	b Maninder	14		
R.R. Kulkarni	c Srivasta b Madan Lal	15	(8) not out	17
R.V. Kulkarni	not out	2		
Extras	lb 2, w 1, nb 7	10	b 7, lb 6, w 1, nb 2	16
	penalty runs	8	penalty runs	8
		333	(for 7 wkts dec)	364

	O	M	R	W	O	M	R	W
Madan Lal	25	8	42	4	19	3	57	2
Prabhakar	17	3	69	2	10	3	39	—
Valson	12	—	50	1	2	—	33	—
Maninder Singh	29.5	7	75	3	34	6	132	4
Srivastava	9	—	37	—	8	1	28	—
Kirti Azad	6	—	35	—	18.3	1	54	1
Sharma	4	1	15	—				

FALL OF WICKETS
1- 1, 2- 27, 3- 42, 4- 142, 5- 194, 6- 274, 7- 276, 8- 300, 9- 318
1- 13, 2- 31, 3- 129, 4- 160, 5- 275, 6- 306, 7- 356

DELHI

	FIRST INNINGS		SECOND INNINGS	
C.P.S. Chauhan	c Hattangadi, b Shastri	98	c Pandit, b Shastri	54
S.C. Khanna*	lbw, b R.R. Kulkarni	13	st Pandit, b Shastri	27
Gursharan Singh	b R.R. Kulkarni	10	lbw, b Mokashi	2
Kirti Azad	c Pandit, b R.R. Kulkarni	9	b Shastri	0
Bhaskar Pillai	c Pandit, b R.R. Kulkarni	0	c sub, b Shastri	60
M. Prabhakar	c R.R. Kulkarni, b Shastri	21	c Rajput, b Shastri	44
U.S. Madan Lal†	c Pandit, b Shastri	78	run out	6
A. Sharma	c Hattangadi, b Mokashi	131	b Shastri	10
Maninder Singh	lbw, b R.R. Kulkarni	3	lbw, b Shastri	0
S. Srivastava	c Hattangadi, b Shastri	7	b Shastri	3
S. Valson	not out	21	not out	0
Extras	lb 7	7	b 1, lb 2	3
		398		209

	O	M	R	W	O	M	R	W
R.R. Kulkarni	32	4	106	5	7	—	28	—
R.V. Kulkarni	21	4	55	—	4	—	15	—
Shastri	48	18	91	4	39.5	17	91	8
Sippy	3	—	20	—				
Mokashi	16	3	63	1	32	10	63	1
Rajput	15	2	40	—	3	—	9	—
Patil	2	—	9	—				
Gavaskar	1	—	7	—				

FALL OF WICKETS
1- 27, 2- 41, 3- 52, 4- 65, 5- 87, 6- 191, 7- 268, 8- 311, 9- 330
1- 95, 2- 100, 3- 100, 4- 122, 5- 171, 6- 187, 7- 198, 8- 198, 9- 206

Umpires: B. Ganguly and V.K. Ramaswamy

Bombay won by 90 runs

against the Delhi medium pace attack. Their innings was righted by a 4th wicket stand of 100 between Patil and Gavaskar. Gavaskar went on to reach his twentieth century in the Ranji Trophy and he now stands only one behind Roy and two behind A.V. Mankad and V.S. Hazare so that yet another record is within his grasp. Pandit helped him to a stand of 80, but Bombay must have been disappointed with their final total.

Delhi began badly, Raju Kulkarni tearing through the early batsmen to leave the visitors in disarray at 87 for 5. Throughout the tumble of wickets the experienced Chetan Chauhan had remained calm and now he found an equally calm and experienced partner in skipper Madan Lal and they added 104. Madan Lal found another good partner in Sharma who hit his first hundred and steered his side to a valuable lead.

Trailing by 65, Bombay lost Parkar and Hattangadi before the arrears were cleared and when Gavaskar and Shastri came together 4 wickets were down and the lead was only 95. They added 115 and this was the decisive partnership of the match. Pandit and Raju Kulkarni hit well and Gavaskar declared, leaving Delhi to make 300 on a wicket that was showing signs of wear.

It seemed that his judgement had erred when Chauhan and Khanna put on 95 before Khanna was stumped off Shastri. Three more wickets fell for the addition of only 27 runs, but Bhaskar Pillai and Prabhakar, in aggressive mood, seemed set to swing the advantage back towards Delhi. Shastri dismissed them both. Madan Lal was run out as the last five wickets fell for 22 runs. Shastri finished with 8 for 91, his best performance in the Ranji Trophy. Unquestionably he had been India's cricketer of the year and this remarkable finale was an apt conclusion to all that had gone before.

First Class Averages

BATTING	M	Inns	NOs	Runs	HS	Av	100s	50s
M.V. Narasimha Rao	4	4	3	275	160*	275.00	1	1
A. Asawa	4	5	3	244	89*	122.00		3
M. Azharuddin	9	14	4	991	151	99.10	6	4
S. Jadhav	4	7	4	278	123*	92.66	1	1
C. Saldanha	4	5	2	244	118*	81.33	1	1
Bhaskar Ghosh	4	6	1	359	151*	71.80	1	2
Padam Shastri	7	12	2	711	159	71.10	2	4
R.J. Shastri	9	14	3	761	200*	69.18	3	3
M.B. Amarnath	8	13	3	687	95	68.70		6
B.P. Patel	6	10	3	460	159	65.71	2	2
Satish Kumar	3	3	1	131	108	65.50	1	
Bhaskar Pillai	7	11	2	576	149*	64.00	2	2
D. Chopra	4	4	1	178	120*	59.33	1	
Abdul Azeem	4	6	1	290	103	58.00	1	2
G.A.H.M. Parkar	8	15	2	748	170*	57.53	1	5
S. Ansari	4	8		459	200	57.37	1	2
V. Venkatram	4	6	3	169	50*	56.33		1
Ajay Sharma	4	5		278	131	55.60	1	2
G.R. Viswanath	6	11	2	491	136*	54.55	2	
M. Hassan	4	8	3	272	116*	54.40	1	
A.O. Malhotra	9	12	2	542	132	54.20	2	1
V. Gawate	3	6	3	162	68	54.00		1
V. Sivaramakrishnan	7	14	2	639	117	53.25	3	1
K. Srikkanth	8	14	1	674	101	51.84	1	4
R. Madhavan	10	17	3	720	153*	51.42	3	2
D.B. Vengsarkar	8	12	2	509	200*	50.90	2	
Chetan Sharma	6	8	5	152	53	50.66		1
B.S. Sandhu	8	7	2	251	98	50.20		3
B. Mistry	4	8		398	75	49.75		4
K.A. Qayyum	7	10	3	341	61*	48.71		3
A. Jabbar	8	13	1	581	143	48.41	1	3
J. Arun Lal	5	9	1	386	157*	48.25	1	1
S. Kalyani	5	9	1	386	103	48.25	1	4
Satya Dev	3	5		240	79	48.00		3
Aman Kumar	6	9	2	331	100	47.28	1	1
H. Praharaj	4	6		283	197	47.16	1	
S. Keshwala	6	9	2	321	100*	45.85	1	1
S.S. Hattangadi	7	12	2	458	83	45.80		5
S.M.H. Kirmani	9	13	2	502	102	45.63	1	4
C.P.S. Chauhan	9	15	1	629	115	44.92	1	5
M.D. Gunjal	5	10	2	358	117*	44.75	1	2
C.S. Pandit	9	16	2	610	126	43.51	2	
K. Jayaram	4	8		348	75	43.50		4
H. Gidwani	4	8	1	304	84	43.42		2
R.N. Kapil Dev	5	8	1	303	60	43.28		2
R. Parikh	3	4		173	72	43.25		1
Arshad Ayub	7	8	1	301	71	43.00		3
S.M. Patil	11	18	2	682	165	42.62	1	4
P. Karkera	5	10	1	382	81	42.44		3
L.S. Rajput	10	18		737	136	40.94	2	5
R. Khanwilkar	9	14	1	526	156	40.46	2	1
S. Mudkavi	7	11	2	364	184	40.44	1	1
S.M. Gavaskar	10	17	3	566	106	40.42	1	4
Amarjeet Kaypee	4	6		242	167	40.33	1	
S. Takle	4	8	3	201	40	40.20		
S.S. Khandkar	8	15	1	557	261*	39.78	1	2
Shrikant	4	6		231	80	38.50		1
A.K. Seth	4	6	1	192	130*	38.40	1	
P. Sharma	4	5		192	94	38.40		1
A. Jayaprakash	6	11	2	345	102*	38.33	1	2
S. Hedaoo	4	8	1	267	66*	38.14		2
R. Chadha	6	9		343	83	38.11		3
P. Pradhan	4	7	1	228	78	38.00		1
R.Y. Deshmukh	4	7	1	228	91	38.00		2
R. Sapru	6	11	1	379	120	37.90	2	
C.S. Suresh Kumar	5	9	1	303	106	37.87	1	1
N.P. Madhavan	2	3		113	104	37.66	1	
P. Desai	4	7		261	112	37.28	1	
K. Dubey	6	11	1	372	127	37.20	1	3
A.S. Bajwa	4	6		222	132	37.00	1	
A.D. Gaekwad	8	13	1	437	108	36.41	2	
S. Talati	4	8		289	83	36.12		3
S. Viswanath	6	10		359	74	35.90		3
A. Pandya	5	10		348	113	34.80	1	2
S. Chaturvedi	8	15	1	480	182	34.78	1	4
R. Talwar	4	8	1	241	93	34.42		2
U.S. Madan Lal	6	9	2	240	78	34.28		1
Yusuf Ali Khan	7	13	1	411	122	34.25	1	2
A. Saheba	4	8		274	74	34.25		2
N.S. Sidhu	6	7		238	124	34.00	1	1
Bimal Jadeja	6	11	1	334	71	33.40		2
D. Augustus	4	7	2	166	73*	33.20		1
A. Bambi	6	9	2	228	78	32.57		1
R. Poonawala	5	10		321	84	32.10		2
R.B. Kala	6	11	2	288	88	32.00		2
N. Gadkari	4	6	1	160	116*	32.00	1	
M.R. Srinivasaprasad	8	16	1	479	166*	31.93	1	1
A. Bharadwaj	5	8	1	222	125*	31.71	1	
S. Mitra	4	6	1	158	56	31.60		2
R. Sudhakar Rao	4	6		187	71	31.16		2
R. Jolly	5	7	1	185	86	30.83		1
Rattan Das	4	6		184	77	30.66		2
Yashpal Sharma	6	10	2	244	100	30.50	1	
A. Laghate	4	8		242	61	30.25		2
R.M.H. Binny	6	11	1	301	87	30.10		2
V. Shesh	3	6		179	77	29.83		1
M. Prabhakar	9	15	2	387	87	29.76		2
N. Churi	6	12		357	85	29.75		2
Rajendra Jadeja	5	8	2	178	60	29.66		1
S. Santosh	4	8		236	61	29.50		2
Gursharan Singh	12	18	1	501	68	29.47		5
G.A. Pratap Kumar	4	7		205	57	29.28		1
M. Satokar	4	4		117	41	29.25		
S.C. Khanna	10	15		437	114	29.13	1	1
Tilak Raj	4	7	1	174	55	29.00		1
R. Vats	3	5		145	69	29.00		1
Balkar Singh	4	6		173	63	28.83		1
S. Srinivasan	4	7	1	173	59*	28.83		2
K. Chauhan	5	10		286	122	28.60	1	1
Arun Sharma	5	8	4	113	62*	28.25		1
R.B. Bhalekar	5	10		282	78	28.20		2
A. Nandi	3	6	2	112	40	28.00		
M. Kaore	4	8		222	70	27.75		2
J. Abhiram	5	9	3	165	81	27.50		1
V. Manohar	4	6	1	137	42	27.40		
B. Arun	3	6	1	137	83	27.40		1
J. Saigal	4	8	1	191	85	27.28		1
S. Sahu	5	6		160	71	26.66		2
A. Mudkavi	3	5		133	46	26.60		
R. Dogra	3	6		158	83	26.33		1
Salim Ahmed	6	8		208	49	26.00		
L. Rajan	2	4		104	43	26.00		
B.S. Gosain	4	8		208	84	26.00		1
A. Mitra	5	9	1	207	115	25.87	1	
R. Pankule	4	8		207	69	25.87		1
S.C. Gudge	5	6	1	125	59	25.00		1
R. Deora	5	10		249	55	24.90		2
A. Das	3	6	1	123	85*	24.60		1
M.S. Kumar	3	5		123	35	24.60		
Maninder Singh	9	10	4	146	61*	24.33		1
K.D. Ghavri	5	10		241	59	24.10		2
S. Ramesh	4	8	3	119	40	23.80		
Jugal Kishore Ghia	4	7	1	142	61*	23.66		1
Sanjeeva Chowdhary	4	8		188	67	23.50		2
K. Das	3	6		141	66	23.50		1
S. Mehra	4	8	1	164	50	23.42		1
K.S.V.D. Kamaraju	4	7		164	81	23.42		1
B. Pujara	4	8		187	93	23.37		2
R. Shukla	4	6		140	81	23.33		1
Hyder Ali	5	7		163	121	23.28	1	
R. Lamba	4	5		114	84	22.80		1
P. Bhatnagar	3	6		135	75	22.50		1
P. Shetty	4	8		179	58	22.37		1
A. Patel	7	10	1	200	67	22.22		1
W.V. Raman	6	11	4	152	22*	21.74		
R. Bora	3	6		130	29	21.66		
Ashwini Kumar	6	9		190	56	21.11		1
Sunil Phatak	4	8		166	74	20.75		1
S. Das	4	8		166	45	20.75		

R. Badiyani	5	10		204	42	20.40	
K.B. Ramamurthy	4	7		142	67	20.28	1
Sanjeeva Rao	5	9		182	58	20.22	2
U. Dastane	5	10	4	120	28	20.00	
Pervez Kaiser	4	8		159	55	19.87	1
Dalbir Singh	4	6		119	46	19.83	
Deepak Sharma	6	9		177	43	19.66	
Gopal Sharma	9	10	1	173	46	19.22	
L. Sivaramakrishnan	8	8	1	134	37	19.14	
Mukesh Arya	6	9	1	147	36*	18.37	
Bharat Patel	4	8		146	70	18.25	1
Zahoor Bhatt	4	8		145	29	18.12	
S. Phadkar	5	9		160	34	17.77	
D. Meher Baba	4	7		124	39	17.71	
P. Kalita	3	6		106	38	17.66	
S. Gulrez Ali	4	6		105	41	17.50	
Thomas Mathew	4	8		140	38	17.50	
N. Parsana	5	10	1	145	39	16.11	
R.R. Kulkarni	10	9	2	106	40	15.16	
P. Hingnikar	4	8		120	37	15.00	
R. Krishna Mohan	4	7		105	33	15.00	
Ravi Pandit	4	8		119	51	14.87	1
T.A. Sekhar	7	10	3	104	38*	14.85	
R.P. Singh	8	10	1	128	30	14.22	
S. Rajesh	4	8		113	34	14.12	
Kirti Azad	9	13		183	69	14.07	1
B.P.B.V. Reddy	5	9		118	31	13.11	
K.S. More	6	10	2	101	34	12.62	

(Qualification – 100 runs, average 10.00)
S. Mandle 76* and 29, R. Jadhav 79 and 22.

Dilip Doshi – still bowling effectively for Bengal in the Ranji Trophy. (Adrian Murrell)

BOWLING	Overs	Mds	Runs	Wkts	Av	Best	10/m	5/in
U.S. Madan Lal	145	43	318	27	11.77	9/50	1	1
R.S. Hans	320.4	93	617	42	14.69	6/38	1	4
Galtan Shome	90	30	175	11	15.90	3/22		
R. Goel	388	133	652	39	16.71	7/36	1	3
P. Rathod	170	40	420	23	18.26	4/38		
Rajesh Yadav	69.5	5	324	17	19.05	7/62	1	2
Yograj Singh	63.3	6	214	11	19.45	3/13		
Maninder Singh	395.3	120	904	46	19.65	6/62	1	2
D. Chopra	135.1	29	358	18	19.88	4/14		
Arun Kumar	90.1	13	323	16	20.18	5/59		1
A.R.B. Bhat	363.3	86	952	47	20.25	7/82	1	2
R. Shukla	105.5	22	264	13	20.30	3/25		
R.S. Ghai	151.4	26	534	26	20.53	7/110		2
A. Jayaprakash	99.3	7	330	16	20.62	6/66		1
S. Venkataraghavan	260.5	54	632	30	21.06	7/69	1	3
A. Kumar	208.4	40	509	22	23.13	6/27	1	3
S. Srivastava	96.1	23	289	12	24.08	5/21		1
R.P. Singh	223	31	735	30	24.50	7/67	1	1
N. Khandee	65	4	248	10	24.80	4/59		
D. Pardeshi	182.4	35	521	21	24.81	7/76	1	2
S. Mudkavi	210.5	44	525	21	25.00	8/60		1
D.R. Doshi	181.5	46	378	15	25.20	4/35		
S. Oak	82.1	9	332	13	25.53	6/55	1	1
R.M.H. Binny	98	22	358	14	25.57	5/74		1
A. Patel	277.5	50	829	32	25.90	6/32		3
T.A. Sekhar	168.4	17	625	24	26.04	5/36		2
H. Wasu	118	15	448	17	26.35	7/102		1
M. Prabhakar	185.4	41	554	21	26.38	5/28		1
S. Gulrez Ali	178.3	53	424	16	26.50	5/94		1
R.J. Shastri	348.4	107	742	28	26.50	8/91	1	1
B. Arun	65.5	2	293	11	26.63	5/84		1
N. Patel	117	19	401	15	26.73	4/69		
S. Talwar	258.1	39	776	29	26.75	7/107		3
Gopal Sharma	357	80	906	33	27.45	6/26	1	1
B. Quereshi	137.2	21	443	16	27.68	6/87		1
A. Jha	189.4	19	669	24	27.87	6/179		3
S. Valson	190.3	19	630	22	28.63	4/34		
S.V. Nayak	147	29	468	15	28.66	4/83		
L. Sivaramakrishnan	361.3	81	998	34	29.35	6/64	1	3
H. Praharaj	137.3	18	500	17	29.41	6/86	1	1
Rajendra Jadeja	81.4	10	327	11	29.72	4/57		
A. Sabnis	119	16	417	14	29.78	4/70		
S.N. Yadav	293.2	61	883	29	30.44	6/166		2
V. Venkatram	124.4	15	430	14	30.71	8/130		1
V. Wadkar	80	9	375	12	31.25	5/89		1
A.G. Mathur	98	12	345	11	31.36	4/34		
B.S. Sandhu	225	43	760	24	31.66	4/41		
R.N. Kapil Dev	188.5	60	479	15	31.93	4/81		
K.D. Mokashi	262	51	780	24	32.50	6/66		1
Arshad Ayub	265	47	821	24	34.20	4/63		
Jugal Kishore Ghia	136.2	16	445	13	34.23	5/66		1
R.R. Kulkarni	272.3	32	1050	30	35.00	5/96		2
N. Parsana	128.5	17	465	13	35.76	3/43		
P. Sundaram	226.3	46	683	19	35.94	4/108		
K.K. Gohil	148.2	29	400	11	36.36	3/47		
R. Khanwilkar	123	19	432	11	39.27	4/73		
N. Hirwani	151.1	20	526	13	40.46	5/101		1
Kirti Azad	150	29	432	10	43.20	5/80		1
S.C. Gudge	159	18	630	14	45.00	5/101		1
Randhir Singh	175.2	28	514	11	46.72	3/83		
P. Banerjee	164.3	19	616	12	51.33	3/72		

FIELDING

28–C.S. Pandit (ct 21/st 7); 18–S.C. Khanna (ct 16/st 2) and S. Chaturvedi (ct 13/st 5); 17–S.M.H. Kirmani (ct 13/st 4); 16–B.P.B.V. Reddy (ct 13/st 3) and K.S. More (ct 10/st 6); 15–R. Deora (ct 12/st 3); 14–Arun Sharma (ct 7/st 7); 13–Ved Raj (ct 7/st 6) and S.S. Hattangadi; 12–L.S. Rajput, M. Satokar (ct 8/st 4), P. Bose (ct 10/st 2) and Bharat Patel (ct 9/st 3); 11–S. Mudkavi, A. Jabbar and Salim Ahmed (ct 7/st 4); 10–P. Hingnikar (ct 6/st 4), Sunil Phillips and S. Viswanath (ct 7/st 3); 9–S. S. Khandkar, R. Khanwilkar, Rattan Das, C.P.S. Chauhan and G.A.H.M. Parkar; 8–I. Pathan (ct 6/st 2), K. Chauhan, R. Sapru, M.R. Srinivasaprasad, K. Srikkanth, R. Madhavan, Maninder Singh, R.J. Shastri and Mahesh Inder Singh

(Qualification – 10 wickets)

MANAGING
By Tony Brown

Cricket has been my life. I was a fortnight past my seventeeth birthday when I first played for Gloucestershire in 1953 and I was to play for them for the next twenty-four years. When I retired from first-class cricket in 1976 I became Secretary for Gloucestershire and stayed with them in that capacity until 1982 when I moved to Somerset in a similar position.

My playing days with Gloucestershire were good days and twice we finished second in the County Championship (1959 and 1969) but the highlight was obviously the winning of the Gillette Cup in 1973; the first honour the County had won in nearly a century.

No England tours (there were numerous good bowlers about at that time), but there were compensations. The Captaincy of the County for eight seasons, minor tours to Zambia, Malawi and Zimbabwe and the cameraderie that goes with twenty-odd years on the County circuit.

Naturally there is a reluctance to leave such a happy environment so I was more than pleased to continue in the game as an administrator. The job is demanding, for one is concerned with the requirements of members, public, players, the press and media, the financial state of the Club and the realisation that the success which everyone seeks is dependant on so many integral parts, any one of which if it goes wrong can upset the best laid plans.

The invitation to manage the England side in India in 1984/85 came as a surprise and as a great honour. It brought me even closer to cricket at the highest level and presented me with challenges different to those which I had encountered before. There was much advice and encouragement forthcoming, and there were many warnings about the difficulties that would be encountered in India from those who had travelled there previously. None foresaw the tragedy that we would walk into.

The tragic death of Mrs Ghandi and the disaster at Bohpal cast a dreadful gloom over the first part of our tour, but we never felt ourselves to be in personal danger or under threat. I read at one stage that we were 'incarcerated', but if we were it was hardly a harrowing experience to be confined to a luxury hotel with excellent food, service and facilities. There are many who would have welcomed that inconvenience.

The problem that confronted us of course was that we had come to India to play cricket and none was being played because of Mrs Ghandi's assassination. The side was fit and eager to play and the inactivity they suffered was their greatest frustration. The efforts of the diplomatic corps and the co-operation and kindness of the Indian and Sri Lankan authorities finally enabled us to fly to Sri Lanka to get some much-needed match practice, and this was the tonic that was needed, for we had been restricted to practising on a concrete

Tony Brown. (Adrian Murrell)

pitch within the British High Commission itself, a great courtesy which had been accorded to us in a time of crisis. The saddest part of the whole trip however awaited us on our return to India.

We lost Martin Moxon for a time when he returned to England because of the sad death of his father. It was a terrible blow for a young man making his first tour with an England party and hoping to force his way into the Test side, and we all felt for him, for we had already become very much a united party, our companionship cemented by external events.

Then on the eve of the First Test we suffered a further shock. We were entertained by the British Deputy High Commissioner for western India at his home in Bombay. Mr Percy Norris was a delightful host and he and his charming wife gave the lads a most happy time. There are many social occasions on a lengthy tour and not all of them are welcomed by the cricketers, but this function was one which gave us much pleasure. Then, the following morning, Mr Norris was murdered. I've never seen a group of men so visibly affected by a piece of news. It was such a senseless act of violence. This was the low point of the tour and it would be right to say that not many of the party had much stomach for the idea of cricket.

It was reported in the Press that we considered abandoning the tour there and then, but I don't think we ever gave that idea serious consideration. We had come to play cricket and heavy of heart as the lads must have been they took the field for the first Test having received great encouragement from Mrs Norris to do so.

It is now history that we were perplexed by the leg-spin of Sivaramakrishnan and well beaten in the first encounter, but the lads sat down and talked about the problems he posed and by the end of the tour, as the results show, they had mastered him. It was this togetherness in the side which helped overcome most of our problems and which developed a team spirit second to none. It enabled us not only to beat India in India, a great achievement, but it helped us to surmount the numerous problems including establishing a better understanding with the Press! It was no secret that the relations between the England team and the Press had become strained in the past few years but David Gower's boys in India healed that bridge in splendid fashion.

One of the most memorable social occasions of the Tour was the Christmas party in Calcutta. Players (in fancy dress) and the Press combined to provide splendid entertainment. The highlights being Cowdrey, Marks, Fowler and Ellison, with their version of the Selection Committee meeting that chose the Tour party; David Gower doing a brilliant impersonation of Nawab of Patuadi; and messrs Carey and Baxter for the Press writing and singing splendid original lyrics to some popular tunes. It was an hilarious interlude.

So, in spite of the arrival of Azharuddin, a most exciting young batsman, the series was won after a splendid performance in Madras and I think, and hope, it marked the turning point for David Gower and for English cricket which is being continued against Australia this summer.

Now for the West Indies in the Carribbean.

SECTION B

A Very Full Season

The season in Australia.
The Sheffield Shield and McDonald's Cup.
Australia *v.* West Indies Test series. Benson & Hedges World Series.
Benson & Hedges World Championship of Cricket.
Form Charts and Averages. Review of the season by Frank Tyson.

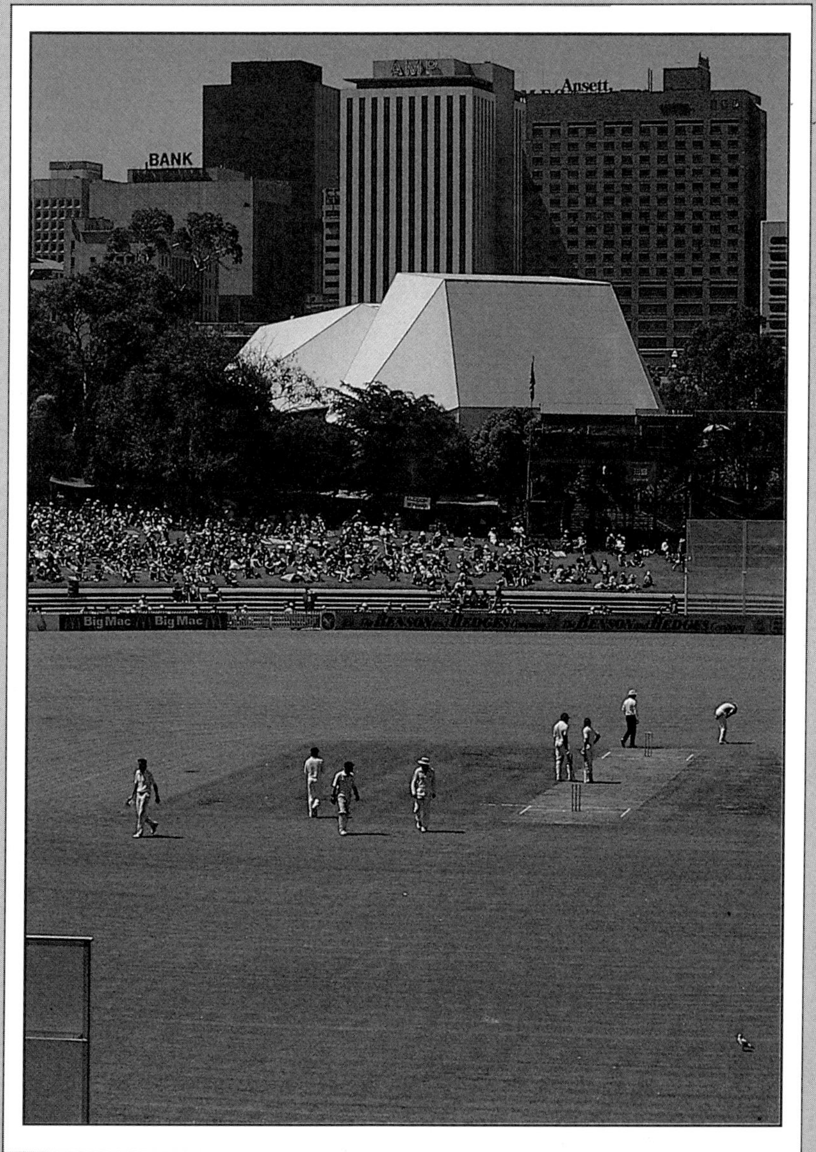

Adelaide Oval. (Philip Tyson)

Following the triumph of the Australian side in the one-day tournament with India, Kim Hughes predicted a new era for Australian cricket. Certainly an old era had ended with the departure of players like Greg Chappell, Rod Marsh, Dennis Lillee, Rick McCosker, Peter Sleep and Peter Toohey, but the Australian fan faced another crowded season with the anticipation of indigestion for not only were there the Test series, the Benson and Hedges World Series, the McDonald's Cup and the Sheffield Shield, but there was the World Championship of Cricket, a mini world cup, scheduled for Melbourne and Sydney in February and March.

There was the usual pre-season movement with Peter Clough leaving Tasmania for Western Australia and Rod McCurdy joining his third state, South Australia, having previously played for Tasmania and Victoria. The most significant move, however, was that of Rodney Hogg who left South Australia to return to the state of his birth, Victoria, who had named Dean Jones as Bright's vice-captain and could find no place for former skipper, Dav Whatmore, in their squad.

McDonald's Cup

13 October 1984

at Perth

Western Australia 218 for 5 (G.R. Marsh 104 not out)
Tasmania 172 (D.C. Boon 50, K.H. MacLeay 5 for 30)

Western Australia won by 46 runs

Wayne Clark, 4 for 70 for Western Australia in their opening Shield game in Perth. (Philip Tyson)

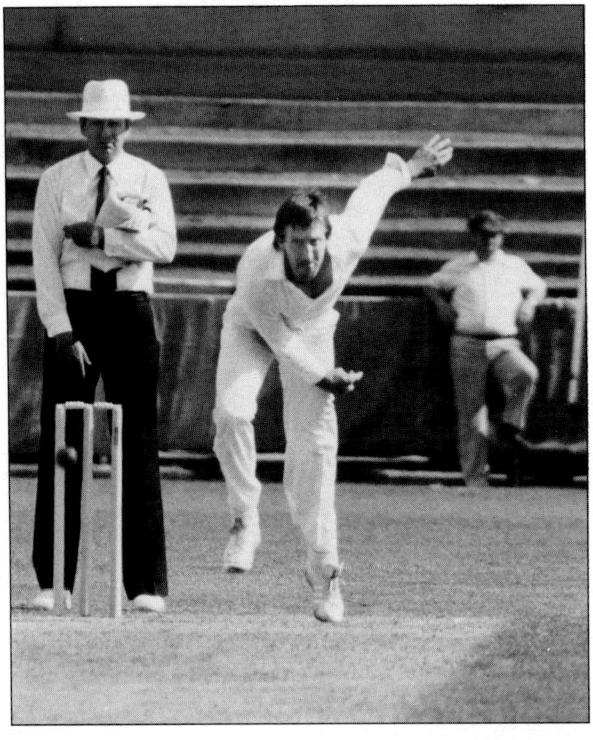

at Brisbane

Victoria 202 (D.M.J. Jones 61, K.C. Wessels 4 for 24)
Queensland 203 for 3 (R.B. Kerr 92 not out, K.C. Wessels 73)

Queensland won by 7 wickets

Still jostling for a place in the cricket calendar the McDonald's Cup provided the curtain-raiser to the season with results as would have been predicted. Wessels, with a remarkable all-round performance which again emphasised his usefulness as a bowler in limited-over cricket, took the individual honours in Brisbane while Geoff Marsh's century won him the accolade in Perth.

14 October 1984

at Perth

New South Wales 203 (S.B. Smith 73, D.M. Wellham 54)
Western Australia 189 (T.M. Chappell 4 for 41)

New South Wales won by 14 runs

at Brisbane

Queensland 219 for 5 (G.M. Ritchie 65 not out, R.B. Kerr 50)
South Australia 223 for 4 (A.M.J. Hilditch 92 not out, M.D. Haysman 87 not out)

South Australia won by 6 wickets

After two rounds of matches four sides each had one victory to throw the competition wide open. The one disturbing factor was the aggravation to a knee injury which Yallop suffered on the Saturday. Following his record-breaking season in the Sheffield Shield, he had been hampered by injury which kept him out of the tour to the West Indies and troubled him at the end of the short tour to India. With the first Test match less than a month away, he found himself again in trouble.

19, 20, 21 and 22 October 1984

at Perth

Western Australia 504 (K.J. Hughes 183, G.M. Wood 94, S.C. Clements 51) and 170 for 4 dec (K.J. Hughes 67 not out)
Tasmania 359 (R.D. Woolley 144, G.W. Goodman 57, W.M. Clark 4 for 70) and 212 for 7 (B.F. Davison 98 not out, R.D. Woolley 61, K.H. MacLeay 5 for 54)

Match drawn
Western Australia 4 pts, Tasmania 0 pts

at Adelaide

New South Wales 447 for 7 dec (P.S. Clifford 125, G.R.J. Matthews 86, D.M. Wellham 80, J. Dyson 70, R.J. Inverarity 5 for 94) and 144 (G.R. Geise 84, R.J. McCurdy 7 for 55)
South Australia 313 for 9 dec (A.M.J. Hilditch 184, R.G. Holland 4 for 86) and 144 (A.M.J. Hilditch 56, R.G. Holland 4 for 48)

New South Wales won by 134 runs
New South Wales 16 pts, South Australia 0 pts

at Brisbane

Queensland 180 (J. Garner 4 for 19) and 10 for 1
West Indians 177 (R.B. Richardson 65, J.N. Maguire 6 for 48)

Match drawn

The West Indian tour opened with a blank day. When play was possible Garner had Wessels caught at slip with the third ball of the tour, a quick assertion of authority, and Queens-

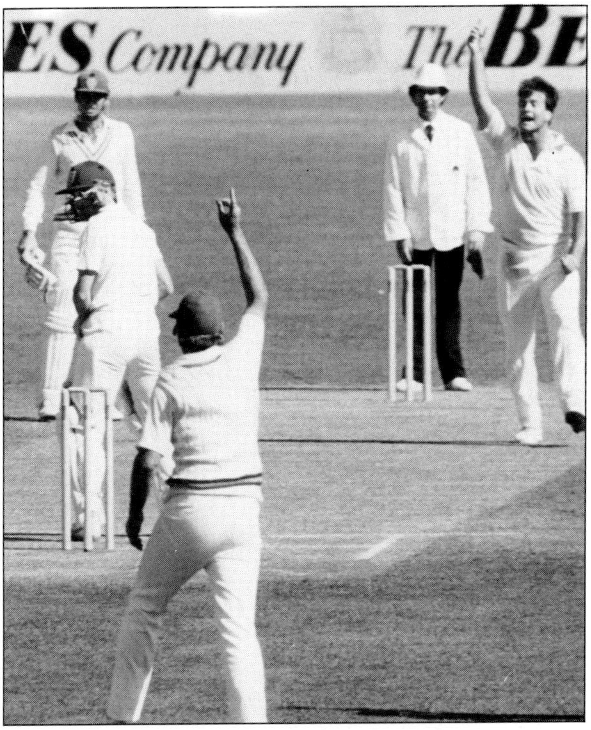

ABOVE: *Andrew Hilditch on his way to 184 for South Australia against New South Wales, an innings that did much to regain him his place in the Test side. Rixon is behind the stumps. (Philip Tyson)*
RIGHT: *Rod McCurdy returned career best figures of 7 for 55 for South Australia* v. *New South Wales at Adelaide but still finished on the losing side. He appeals successfully as Wellham is caught down the leg side by Wayne Phillips. (Philip Tyson)*
BELOW RIGHT: *Robbie Kerr, 106 for Queensland and a third wicket stand of 181 with Greg Ritchie. (Adrian Murrell)*

land finished the day on 173 for 8. The tourists seemed to be moving to a big lead when a ferocious assault by Richie Richardson, who hit Thomson out of the ground, took them to 111 for 2 by the close. They collapsed to Maguire on the last day and Australia had a surge of confidence.

In Perth, there were first-class debuts for Brown and Bradshaw of Tasmania, but the honours went to Test cricketers. Hughes asserted his form and confidence with innings of 183 and 67 not out, and Graeme Wood also batted well. Leg-spinner Stuart Saunders bowled well, but Jamaican Patrick Patterson who made his debut for Lancashire earlier in the year took 2 for 211 in his first match for Tasmania. Roger Woolley, omitted from the Australian side as an inferior batsman although the best wicket-keeper, rallied his side splendidly and in the second innings he and Davison put on 134 after 4 wickets had fallen for 41 and so saved Tasmania from defeat.

South Australia gave a first-class debut to off-spinner Tim May, a player of great promise, but he was overshadowed by the veterans Inverarity and Holland. Clifford, challenging strongly for a Test place, and Matthews led New South Wales to a formidable total with a 5th wicket stand of 184, and the home side's reply was inspired totally by a sure and forceful innings from Andrew Hilditch. Rod McCurdy then took a career best 7 for 55 on his South Australian debut, but Holland bowled New South Wales to the season's first victory, Clifford having already claimed the season's first century.

24 October 1984

at Loxton

South Australian Country XI 165 for 8
West Indians 230 for 5 (R.B. Richardson 87 not out)

West Indians won by 7 wickets

26, 27, 28 and 29 October 1984

at Brisbane

Victoria 201 (M.D. Taylor 57, C.J. McDermott 4 for 55) and 319 (A.I.C. Dodemaide 74, M.B. Quinn 54, S.P. O'Donnell 54)
Queensland 467 (G.M. Ritchie 136, R.B. Kerr 106, G.S. Trimble 90, K.C. Wessels 60) and 56 for 1

Queensland won by 9 wickets
Queensland 16 pts, Victoria 0 pts

at Canberra

New South Wales 156 and 218 for 9 dec (J. Dyson 76, T.M. Alderman 4 for 62, W.M. Clark 4 for 75)
Western Australia 171 (G.M. Wood 61, G.F. Lawson 4 for 42) and 26 for 1.

Match drawn
Western Australia 4 pts, New South Wales 0 pts

at Adelaide

West Indians 242 (I.V.A. Richards 80) and 514 for 5 dec (P.J. Dujon 151 not out, I.V.A. Richards 102, D.L. Haynes 94, C.G. Greenidge 79, C.H. Lloyd 63)
South Australia 295 (M.D. Haysman 91, D.F. O'Connor 51, M.D. Marshall 4 for 75) and 200 for 6

Match drawn

In a rather bizarre match at Adelaide, the West Indians revealed their batting strength for the first time. The tourists batted in whirlwind manner in their first innings, and South Australia, with O'Connor and Haysman adding 103 for the 5th wicket, replied more steadily. The second innings developed into farce as South Australia were eventually forced to field four substitutes, one of them West Indian. Haynes and Greenidge began with 135, and there were century stands involving Richards, Lloyd and Dujon. The state's problems had not ended for Wayne Phillips was hit on the helmet and had to retire hurt when they batted again.

The important confrontation between New South Wales and Western Australia was marred by rain. Bowlers dominated on an uncertain wicket and Western Australia lost their last eight wickets for 39 runs.

Queensland's pace attack bowled their side into a strong position over Victoria and with an opening stand of 91, Kerr and Wessels quickly consolidated the superiority. Kerr then shared a third wicket stand of 181 with Ritchie, another batsman seeking a recall to the Australian side, and with Trimble maintaining a brisk scoring rate, Queensland moved to maximum points without worry. Victoria's consolation was in the all-round cricket of O'Donnell and Dodemaide.

31 October 1984

at Corrigin

West Indians 235 for 8 (A.L. Logie 85)
West Australia Country XI 154 for 9

West Indians won by 81 runs

A forty-over match which was notable for Logic hitting 85 off 66 balls with ten fours and three sixes. He also took two wickets.

2, 3, 4 and 5 November 1984

at Perth

Western Australia 317 for 3 dec (G.M. Wood 141, G. Shipperd 97 retired hurt) and 111 (C.A. Walsh 5 for 60)
West Indians 302 (C.H. Lloyd 95, W.W. Davis 50, K.H. MacLeay 5 for 115, T.M. Alderman 4 for 52) and 129 for 1 (D.L. Haynes 60 not out, R.B. Richardson 50 not out)

West Indians won by 9 wickets

Put in to bat in humid conditions, Western Australia lost Veletta at 40, but Wood and Shipperd batted soundly and aggressively. Wood, who gave only one chance, when 94, batted for 268 minutes, and Shipperd seemed set for a century until he was hit on the helmet by a ball from Holding and forced to retire. Hughes declared and Alderman and MacLeay troubled the tourists so that they slumped to 153 for 6, but Clive Lloyd batted splendidly and Davis produced an innings reminiscent of his Old Trafford performance earlier in the year. Walsh and Holding routed Western Australia in 38 overs in the second innings and Haynes and Richardson stroked the tourists to a comfortable victory which had looked unlikely on the opening day.

McDonald's Cup

3 November 1984

at Devonport

New South Wales 170 (D.M. Wellham 58, S.J. Rixon 52, B.P. Patterson 4 for 23)
Tasmania 80

New South Wales won by 90 runs

4 November 1984

at Adelaide

South Australia 206 for 6 (D.W. Hookes 78)
Victoria 209 for 4 (P.A. Hibbert 56, M.D. Taylor 54 not out)

Victoria won by 6 wickets

New South Wales overwhelmed Tasmania to become the only side with two wins, but Victoria's win over South Australia gave them a late place in the semi-finals at the expense of Queensland who had an inferior run-rate.

McPhee, Western Australia, is caught behind by Dimattina off Hughes for 85 in the match against Victoria at Princes Park, Melbourne. (Philip Tyson)

Qualifying Tables

Group A	*P*	*W*	*L*	*Pts*
New South Wales	2	2	–	4
Western Australia	2	1	1	2
Tasmania	2	–	2	0

Group B	*P*	*W*	*L*	*Pts*
South Australia	2	1	1	2
Victoria	2	1	1	2
Queensland	2	1	1	2

9, 10, 11 and 12 November 1984

at Launceston

New South Wales 333 (P.H. Marks 75, S.B. Smith 54) and 262 for 7 dec (D.M. Wellham 115, G.R.J. Matthews 66, B.P. Patterson 4 for 68)
Tasmania 313 (D.C. Boon 138, R.D. Woolley 55) and 93 for 1 (G.W. Goodman 53)
Match drawn
New South Wales 4 pts, Tasmania 0 pts

at Princes Park, Melbourne

Western Australia 389 (M.R.J. Veletta 100, M. McPhee 85, S.C. Clements 58, K.H. MacLeay 52)
Victoria 310 for 9 (G.W. Richardson 80, P.A. Hibbert 61, W.M. Clark 4 for 89)
Match abandoned
Western Australia 2 pts, Victoria 2 pts

With the Test match depriving sides of key players and weather curtailing play to such an extent that no decision was possible in Melbourne, New South Wales lost the opportunity of building a lead in the Sheffield Shield when they were held by Tasmania for whom Boon, on the verge of the Test side, played a fine innings. The most encouraging sign for Tasmania in what threatened to be a disappointing season was the form of Patterson who took 7 for 180 in the match.

At Princes Park, there was a maiden first-class century for Mike Veletta and impressive first-class debuts by McPhee with 85 for the visitors and Dimattina who had four catches behind the stumps.

First Test Match
AUSTRALIA *v.* WEST INDIES

The new spirit of Australian cricket which had been promised before the first Test match against the West Indies was quickly dispelled by a side which completed a record ninth successive Test match victory and left the Australians shattered and demoralised.

In spite of his fine bowling against the tourists in the opening match, Maguire was the player omitted from the Australian twelve while Walsh was preferred to the magnificent Harper in the West Indian side thereby decreeing that the match would be almost totally without spin.

Greenidge and Haynes gave West Indies a brisk and efficient start after Hughes had put them in on a bumpy and under-prepared wicket. Rackemann, in particular, and Lawson were disappointing and it was Alderman who broke through when he had Greenidge caught at mid-off off his slower ball. In 47 minutes in the afternoon session, inspired by Alderman who took 4 for 5 in 26 balls, West Indies lost 5

FIRST TEST MATCH – AUSTRALIA *v.* WEST INDIES
9, 10, 11 and 12 November 1984 at Perth

WEST INDIES

	FIRST INNINGS	
C.G. Greenidge	c Rackemann, b Alderman	30
D.L. Haynes	c Yallop, b Hogg	56
R.B. Richardson	b Alderman	0
H.A. Gomes	b Hogg	127
I.V.A. Richards	c Phillips, b Alderman	10
C.H. Lloyd†	c Phillips, b Alderman	0
P.J. Dujon*	c Phillips, b Alderman	139
M.D. Marshall	c Hughes, b Hogg	21
M.A. Holding	c Wood, b Alderman	1
J. Garner	c Phillips, b Hogg	17
C.A. Walsh	not out	9
Extras	b 1, lb 1, nb 4	6
		416

	O	M	R	W
Lawson	24	3	79	—
Rackemann	28	3	106	—
Alderman	39	12	128	6
Hogg	32	6	101	4

FALL OF WICKETS
1- 83, 2- 83, 3- 89, 4- 104, 5- 104, 6- 186, 7- 335, 8- 337, 9- 416

AUSTRALIA

	FIRST INNINGS		SECOND INNINGS	
K.C. Wessels	c Holding, b Garner	13	(2) c Lloyd, b Garner	0
J. Dyson	c Lloyd, b Marshall	0	(1) b Marshall	30
G.M. Wood	c Lloyd, b Garner	6	c Richardson, b Walsh	56
A.R. Border	c Dujon, b Holding	15	c Haynes, b Marshall	6
K.J. Hughes†	c Marshall, b Holding	4	lbw, b Marshall	37
G.N. Yallop	c Greenidge, b Holding	2	c Haynes, b Walsh	1
W.B. Phillips*	c Marshall, b Holding	22	c Dujon, b Garner	16
G.F. Lawson	c Dujon, b Marshall	1	not out	38
R.M. Hogg	b Holding	0	b Marshall	0
C.G. Rackemann	c Richardson, b Holding	0	b Garner	0
T.M. Alderman	not out	0	c Richardson, b Holding	23
Extras	b 4, lb 2, nb 7	13	lb 7, nb 14	21
		76		228

	O	M	R	W	O	M	R	W
Marshall	15	5	25	2	21	4	68	4
Garner	7	—	24	2	16	5	52	3
Holding	9.2	3	21	6	11.3	1	53	1
Walsh					20	4	43	2
Gomes					1	—	1	—
Richards					1	—	4	—

FALL OF WICKETS
1- 1, 2- 18, 3- 28, 4- 40, 5- 46, 6- 55, 7- 58, 8- 63, 9- 63
1- 4, 2- 94, 3- 107, 4- 107, 5- 124, 6- 166, 7- 168, 8- 168, 9- 169

Umpires: A.R. Crafter and P.J. McConnell

West Indies won by an innings and 112 runs

Above: *West Indian centurion Jeff Dujon. (George Herringshaw)*

Right: *Michael Holding, wrecker of Australia. (Adrian Murrell)*

wickets for 21 runs and Australia were on top. Phillips, a controversial choice as wicket-keeper, held fine catches to dismiss Lloyd and Richards.

Dujon and Gomes were both hit and Dujon was forced to retire hurt when he had scored 33, returning at the fall of the sixth wicket. West Indies closed the first day at 211 for 6.

The second day saw the total disintegration of the Australian side. Gomes and Dujon reached patient centuries. Gomes, continuing in the role he had patented in England, hit nine fours in a stay lasting 472 minutes and Dujon, looking more elegant and accomplished every time he goes to the wicket, batted for 240 minutes and hit twenty-one fours. The Australian fielding was quite dreadful. Nine catches were put down, none of them particularly difficult, and the ground fielding was slovenly. The side seemed without inspiration and Kim Hughes appeared to lose control of the situation.

Australia had seventy-five minutes batting before the close. Dyson was splendidly caught low down at first slip off the third ball of the innings. Wood and Wessels fell to Garner so that Australia were 36 for 3 at the close.

The Australians had attempted a bumper war against Gomes and Dujon, an unwise tactic, and on the third morning, they suffered the consequences, shot out before lunch for their lowest ever score against the West Indies, victims of furious pace and their own ineptitude and lack of application. There were some unforgivable shots, Hughes' hooking into Marshall's hands being one of them.

Wessels was out before lunch and although Wood and Dyson batted doggedly throughout the afternoon session both they and Border and Yallop fell before the close.

Hughes, lbw without playing a shot, and Phillips were soon out on the fourth morning. Alderman and Lawson added a brave 59 for the last wicket, but the issue had long since been decided. Holding, the destroyer of Australia, was named Man of the Match.

15, 16, 17 and 18 November 1984

at Princes Park, Melbourne

Tasmania 368 (D.C. Boon 104, D.J. Buckingham 71, M. Ray 60) and 43 for 3
Victoria 491 (M.D. Taylor 118, G.W. Richardson 87, D.M.J. Jones 67)

Match drawn
Victoria 4 pts, Tasmania 0 pts

16, 17, 18 and 19 November 1984

at Brisbane

South Australia 277 (G.A. Bishop 87, D.F. O'Connor 53, T.V. Hohns 5 for 56) and 375 for 9 dec (D.W. Hookes 79, M.D. Haysman 72, D.F. O'Connor 55)
Queensland 283 for 8 dec (G.M. Ritchie 84, K.C. Wessels 64) and 370 for 5 (K.C. Wessels 144, G.S. Trimble 67 not out, W.B. Phillips 56 not out)

Queensland won by 5 wickets
Queensland 16 pts, South Australia 0 pts

Bishop, South Australia, career best 170 against Tasmania at Adelaide, 22–25 November. (Philip Tyson)

at Sydney

New South Wales 287 (J. Dyson 98) and 129 (R.A. Harper 5 for 72, I.V.A. Richards 4 for 18)
West Indians 212 (C.H. Lloyd 64 not out, R.G. Holland 4 for 81) and 133 (M.J. Bennett 6 for 32)

New South Wales won by 71 runs

After the dreadful mauling that they had received in the first Test match, the Australians were revived by New South Wales' surprise victory over the West Indians, a victory brought about by the spin bowling of Holland and Bennett. New South Wales included Imran Khan in their side and he showed an encouraging spell of bowling.

Dyson earned a Test reprieve with a solid innings on the opening day which was the foundation of New South Wales' win. He was run out two short of his century, but led his side to a good score on a wicket which showed signs of assisting the spinners. West Indies struggled in reply and it was not until Lloyd, coming in at 112 for 5, played with sense and aggression that their innings had any semblance of solidity. After Garner had dismissed Smith the West Indian bowling was entrusted to Harper and Richards and the state side were bowled out for 129. Needing 201 to win, the visitors were soon toiling against Holland's leg-spin and Bennett's slow left-arm and in spite of another fine knock by Clive Lloyd, they were well beaten. Holland, at the age of 38, and Bennett were immediately called into the Australian squad for the second Test. Bennett's 6 for 32 was a career best performance.

West Indian centurion Larry Gomes. (George Herringshaw)

Dimatinna, the new Victorian wicket-keeper, continued his impressive start in first-class cricket with five catches against Tasmania, but Victoria had to be content with first innings points in a match where both attacks lacked penetration. The most significant event was Boon's second century in successive matches, an innings which confirmed his readiness for the Test side.

Queensland, owing much to the spin of Hohns and Border, snatched maximum points against South Australia and

Faulkner bowls Dimattina for 10, Tasmania v. *Victoria, Melbourne, 15–18 November. (Philip Tyson)*

placed themselves firmly at the top of the Sheffield Shield. Queensland, needing 370 to win in 6¼ hours, were given a firm foundation by Wessels, in need of runs to keep his Test place, but it was an unbroken sixth wicket stand of 115 between Phillips and Trimble which finally won the match.

ABOVE: *Bob Holland, 10 for 113 as New South Wales gain an historic victory over the West Indians and later to be Australia's hero at Sydney in the fifth Test. (Adrian Murrell)*

22, 23, 24 and 25 November 1984

at Adelaide

Tasmania 487 for 8 dec (R. Bennett 89, B.F. Davison 66, R.S. Hyatt 56 not out, S.L. Saunders 53, R.D. Woolley 51)
South Australia 289 (D.W. Hookes 151, M.D. Haysman 53, R. Brown 4 for 46) and 383 (G.A. Bishop 170, A.M.J. Hilditch 86)

Match drawn
Tasmania 4 pts, South Australia 0 pts

23, 24, 25 and 26 November 1984

at Perth

New South Wales 386 (D.M. Wellham 86, Imran Khan 70, P.S. Clifford 51, P.H. Marks 51) and 245 for 3 (P.S. Clifford 102 not out, T.M. Chappell 65)
Western Australia 387 for 9 dec (G.R. Marsh 73, G. Shipperd 61, T.J. Zoehrer 50, G.R.J. Matthews 4 for 92)

Match drawn
Western Australia 4 pts, New South Wales 0 pts

Solid batting throughout the innings put Tasmania in a strong position at Adelaide, and, in spite of a fifth wicket

BELOW: *Bowler Hyatt and wicket-keeper Woolley appeal for lbw against Mick Taylor during his innings of 118 for Victoria against Tasmania. Boon is at slip. (Philip Tyson)*

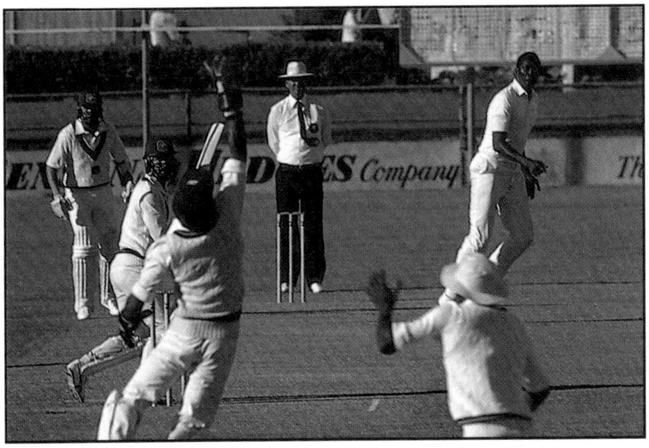

Holland, caught Dujon, bowled Garner. The fast bowler's two hundredth Test wicket.

Haynes appeals for hit wicket, but Lawson is given not out, an appeal and a decision which caused animosity between the two players. (Philip Tyson)

stand of 174 between Hookes and Haysman, dominated by the gloriously aggressive Hookes, South Australia were forced to follow-on. Hilditch, very much in form, gave the second innings substance and Bishop hit a career best 170 to put the match out of Tasmania's reach.

New South Wales failed to make any impression on Queensland's lead in the Sheffield Shield when they surrendered first innings points to Western Australia who were still 46 short of the visitors' total when the last two batsmen, Clough and Clark, came together. Clark had enjoyed a good season with the ball and he now proceded to hit 46 not out and give his side four points.

Second Test Match
AUSTRALIA *v.* WEST INDIES

West Indies fielded the side that had won at Perth; Australia

SECOND TEST MATCH – AUSTRALIA *v.* WEST INDIES
23, 24, 25 and 26 November 1984 at Brisbane

AUSTRALIA

	FIRST INNINGS		SECOND INNINGS	
J. Dyson	c Dujon, b Holding	13	(2) c Dujon, b Marshall	21
K.C. Wessels	b Garner	0	(1) c Gomes, b Walsh	61
G.M. Wood	c Marshall, b Walsh	20	c Richardson, b Holding	3
A.R. Border	c Lloyd, b Marshall	17	c sub (Harper), b Holding	24
K.J. Hughes†	c Marshall, b Garner	34	lbw, b Holding	4
D.C. Boon	c Richardson, b Marshall	11	c Holding, b Marshall	51
W.B. Phillips*	c Dujon, b Walsh	44	(8) c sub (Harper), b Holding	54
G.F. Lawson	b Garner	14	(9) c Richards, b Marshall	14
T.M. Alderman	c Lloyd, b Walsh	0	(7) c Richardson, b Marshall	1
R.G. Holland	c Dujon, b Garner	6	b Marshall	0
R.M. Hogg	not out	0	not out	21
Extras	b 4, lb 1, nb 11	16	b 4, lb 5, nb 8	17
		175		271

	O	M	R	W	O	M	R	W
Garner	18.4	5	67	4	20	4	80	—
Marshall	14.4	5	39	2	34	7	82	5
Holding	6.2	2	9	1	30	7	92	4
Walsh	16	5	55	3	5	2	7	1
Richards					1	—	1	—

FALL OF WICKETS
1- 1, 2- 33, 3-, 33, 4- 81, 5- 97, 6- 102, 7- 122, 8- 136, 9- 173
1- 88, 2- 88, 3- 99, 4- 106, 5- 131, 6- 212, 7- 236, 8- 236, 9- 271

WEST INDIES

	FIRST INNINGS		SECOND INNINGS	
C.G. Greenidge	c Border, b Lawson	44		
D.L. Haynes	b Alderman	21	(1) b Lawson	7
R.B. Richardson	c Phillips, b Alderman	138	(2) c Alderman, b Hogg	5
H.A. Gomes	b Holland	13	(3) not out	9
I.V.A. Richards	c Boon, b Lawson	6	(4) not out	3
P.J. Dujon*	c Phillips, b Holland	14		
C.H. Lloyd†	c Hughes, b Alderman	114		
M.D. Marshall	b Lawson	57		
M.A. Holding	b Lawson	1		
J. Garner	not out	0		
C.A. Walsh	c Phillips, b Lawson	0		
Extras	b 2, lb 6, nb 8	16	lb 2	2
		424	(for 2 wickets)	26

	O	M	R	W	O	M	R	W
Lawson	30.4	8	116	5	5	—	10	1
Alderman	29	10	107	3				
Hogg	21	3	71	—	4.1	—	14	1
Holland	27	5	97	2				
Border	5	—	25	—				

FALL OF WICKETS
1- 36, 2- 99, 3- 129, 4- 142, 5- 184, 6- 336, 7- 414, 8- 423, 9- 424
1- 6, 2- 18

Umpires: M.W. Johnson and R.A. French

West Indies won by 8 wickets

worth

GES

brought in Boon and Holland for Test match debuts at the expense of the luckless Yallop and Rackemann.

West Indies won the toss and asked Australia to bat. Wessels offered no stroke at the last ball of Garner's first over and was bowled by a leg-cutter. This set the pattern for a dreadfully dismal batting display which had Australia out just after tea and West Indies already 65 for the loss of Haynes before the close. Phillips alone of the Australian batsmen had shown any sense of application in what, on a good wicket, was a batting performance worse than their first innings in Perth.

There was a hint of success for the Australian bowlers on the second day when Bob Holland's leg-spin troubled the West Indians. Greenidge, Gomes, Richards and Dujon fell to injudicious shots and Richardson was dropped at mid-off by Hughes, a straight-forward chance. Richardson was 40 at the time and playing well, and he continued to bat with crisp elegance. He and Lloyd put on 152 in 124 minutes before

LEFT: *Richardson sweeps his way to his century (Philip Tyson)*

LEFT BELOW: *Lawson appeals unsuccessfully for lbw against Haynes. (Philip Tyson)*

BELOW: *Lawson claims his hundredth Test wicket. Walsh is caught behind. (Philip Tyson)*

Richardson fell to the second new ball. He had batted for 331 minutes and hit twenty-four fours. Lloyd, who was out on the third morning, made his 114 off 154 deliveries and he hit fourteen fours and three sixes. His power remains ageless. Certainly it was his attack on Holland which turned aside the threat of the leg-spinner repeating his Sydney triumph.

Australia for whom Geoff Lawson took the last three wickets in nine balls to reach 100 wickets in 25 Tests batted again 249 runs in arrears. Dyson was studiously correct and Wessels, in contrast, adopted an aggressive approach. They were both out at 88 and the pace attack gradually wore down the Australian batting. Boon and Phillips were defiant and Border also batted doggedly until brilliantly caught by substitute Harper. Hughes was lbw to a shooter; in the first innings he had again perished hooking.

If Hughes was without luck, Lawson, incredibly, was twice given not out after treading on his stumps. Eventually, West Indies needed 23 to win, a feat they accomplished after the loss of two wickets and an angry exchange between Haynes and Lawson which degraded the game.

Sadder still, Kim Hughes read a prepared statement at the end of the match in which he announced his resignation of the Australian captaincy. He broke down and was unable to continue. One could have nothing but sympathy for a likeable young man who was miscast and never supported in certain quarters as he should have been. His failure is more a

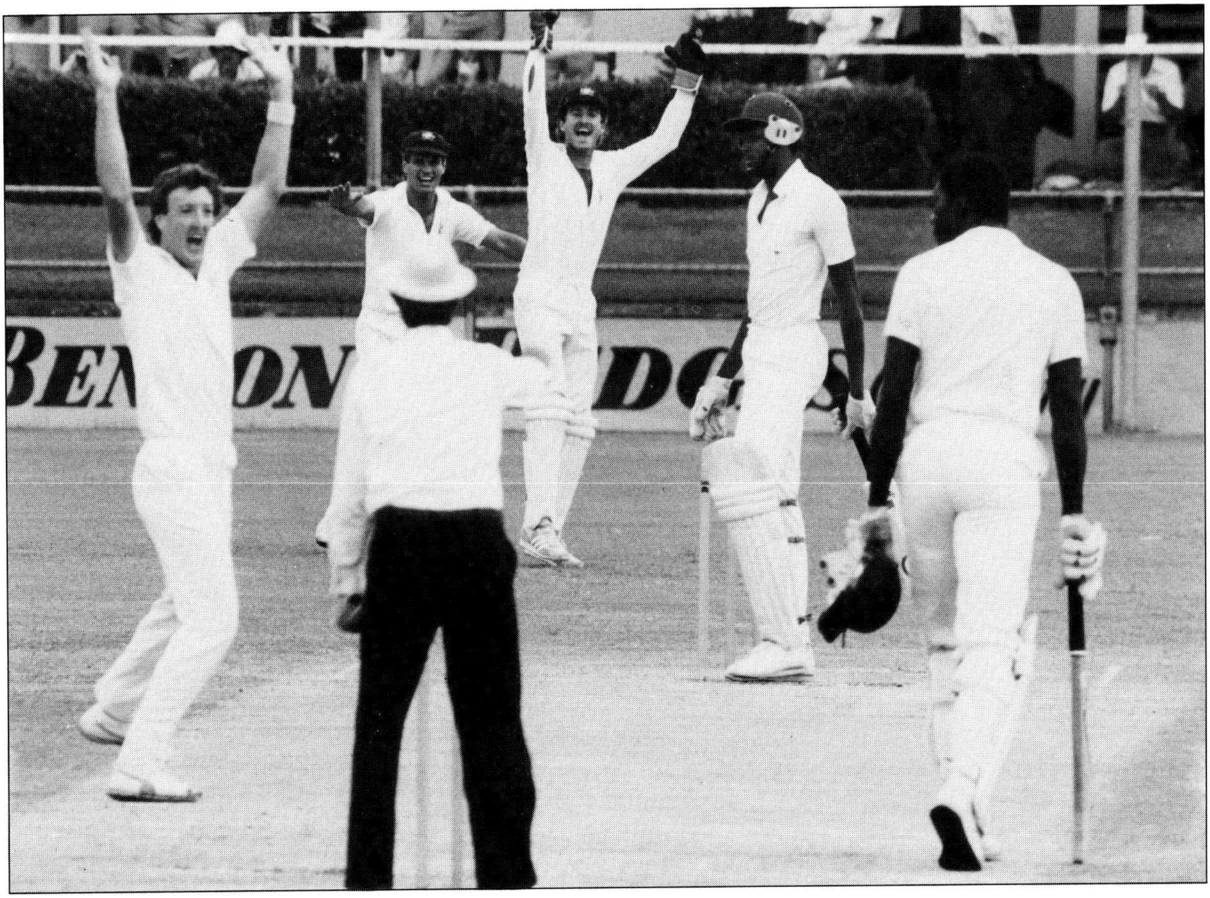

condemnation of attitudes in the game than of his own lack of qualities of leadership.

30 November–3 December 1984

at Sydney

New South Wales 370 (D.M. Wellham 89, P.S. Clifford 64, S.J.

ABOVE: *Border is caught in the slips by Lloyd off Marshall. The bowler celebrates. (Philip Tyson)*

RIGHT: *Clive Lloyd on his way to his last Test hundred.*

BELOW: *Dujon is caught by Phillips off Holland. (Philip Tyson)*

Ray Bright bowls Richie Richardson for 145, Victoria v. *West Indians at Melbourne. (Philip Tyson)*

Rixon 58, R.J. McCurdy 5 for 109) and 223 for 4 dec (S.J. Rixon 115 not out, J. Dyson 72)
South Australia 260 (A.M.J. Hilditch 80, G.F. Lawson 4 for 30) and 221 (R.G. Holland 9 for 83)

New South Wales won by 112 runs
New South Wales 16 pts, South Australia 0 pts

at Launceston

Tasmania 200 (C.J. McDermott 6 for 45) and 237 (R.D. Woolley 93)
Queensland 542 (A.R. Border 144 not out, T.V. Hohns 90, J.N. Maguire 61, G.M. Ritchie 59)

Queensland won by an innings and 105 runs
Queensland 16 pts, Tasmania 0 pts

at Melbourne

West Indians 558 for 7 dec (D.L. Haynes 155, R.B. Richardson 145, C.G. Greenidge 78)
Victoria 601 for 7 (M.D. Taylor 234 not out, S.P. O'Donnell 78, D.M.J. Jones 71, W.G. Whiteside 57, D. Robinson 52, C.A. Walsh 4 for 141)

Match drawn

The first match of the season at the Melbourne Cricket Ground produced 1159 runs and only 14 wickets in four days' play. Haynes, recovering from influenza, hit twenty-four fours on the opening day and he and Greenidge began the match with a stand of 187. As runs continued to flow Taylor encouraged speculation that he might be included in the side to tour England by batting 507 minutes, facing 405 balls and hitting sixteen fours in his mammoth innings, but the West Indians had by then lost interest. The fielding was poor and a record number of extras, 58, was conceded.

More importantly, New South Wales and Queensland maintained their clear lead at the top of the Sheffield Shield with maximum-point victories. Queensland, with Allan Border hitting his first century of the season, overwhelmed Tasmania. Craig McDermott bowled splendidly to emphasise his promise as Australia's next fast bowling hope and when Tasmania batted again only the determination of skipper Roger Woolley saved them from humiliation.

New South Wales, with Wellham and Clifford adding 122 for the third wicket, batted with assurance to reach 370 against South Australia in Sydney. The visitors began well in reply, but lost 5 wickets for 8 runs in their middle order before the wise old head of Inverarity restored some sanity. Rixon was promoted to open the New South Wales second innings and he and Dyson began at a blistering pace, their stand of 173 coming at more than four an over. The momentum was sustained and Wellham declared leaving South Australia to make 334 to win.

Rixon's century was the sixth of his career and a timely one, for the withdrawal of Phillips from the Australian side through injury left the wicket-keeping spot vacant and Rixon was to fill it.

Hilditch and Inverarity began solidly for South Australia, but both fell to Bob Holland's leg-spin. Holland then dismissed O'Connor and Bishop and 7 wickets fell for 51 runs. There was late resistance, but Holland was not to be denied. His 9 for 83 was the best performance of his career and the sixth best in the history of New South Wales. At the age of 38, Bob Holland was enjoying a wonderful year.

7, 8, 9 and 10 December 1984

at Brisbane

New South Wales 357 (P.S. Clifford 98, G.R.J. Matthews 97, C.J.

McDermott 4 for 78) and 16 for 0
Queensland 315 (G.M. Ritchie 71, B.A. Courtice 64, R.B. Phillips 56, C.B. Smart 54, G.R.J. Matthews 4 for 81)

Match drawn
New South Wales 4 pts, Queensland 0 pts

Forced to make changes for the first time in the season, Courtice and Smart replacing Test men Border and Wessels, Queensland failed to win a Sheffield Shield after three successive victories. McDermott, again in most impressive bowling form, helped to reduce New South Wales to 59 for 3, but Clifford, so exciting a prospect for international cricket, and Matthews added 131 and a late flourish by Waugh, on his debut, and reserve keeper Dyer helped the visitors to 357. In reply, Queensland batted with much consistency until the last six wickets fell for 35 runs to surrender the first innings points which bad weather deemed the only points to be won.

Third Test Match
AUSTRALIA *v.* WEST INDIES

A hundred years of Test cricket at Adelaide was 'celebrated' without a South Australian in the side, with slow over-rates, with continued acrimony between the two teams, especially Lawson versus Richards and Dujon, and with a sparse attendance.

Border had replaced Hughes as Australia's captain and Rixon had come in to the side to replace the injured Phillips. Harper replaced the injured Holding in the West Indian side.

Lloyd won the toss, but Australia had immediate success when Haynes was caught in the gully by Hughes. There should have been more joy for Australia, but once again catches were dropped in abundance, Greenidge, in particular, profiting from the errors. Richardson was out after 40 minutes, falling to Lawson who was celebrating his 27th birthday. It was Lawson who kept the Australians in contention, his career best 8 for 112 being a well deserved reward for some splendid bowling.

Gomes and Greenidge for the third wicket, and Lloyd and Dujon later rescued West Indies from disaster, but it was the Australian fielding, Rixon's keeping apart, which was their great disappointment.

Australia closed the second day at 91 for 1 with Wessels having retired hurt after being hit on the arm by a ball from Walsh. He returned the next day to bat with courage and more panache than usual and to share a seventh wicket stand of 87 with Lawson which helped Australia to some dignity

Hogg traps Richardson lbw for 3. (Philip Tyson)

after the middle order had wilted to the West Indian pace. Poor Kim Hughes was caught at slip first ball at a time when he needed every bit of luck and encouragement.

Gomes, in his customary unfussy, unadventurous way, led West Indies to a position of command with his ninth Test century, six of them have been against Australia, and he had good support from Haynes, Richards and Dujon. Lawson again bowled well for Australia and gave them something to celebrate, particularly as Alderman had been troubled for most of the match by a strain.

There never seemed any likely prospect of Australia avoiding defeat. Dyson left at 22, Wessels and Border then added 48 which, it transpired, was the highest stand of the innings. Marshall, who took ten wickets in a Test match for the first time, and Harper displayed his abounding talent so that West Indies moved to their eleventh successive Test victory. It was Clive Lloyd's 72nd match as captain and his 36th victory in that role for the West Indies.

14, 15, 16 and 17 December 1984

at Hobart

West Indians 184 (E.A.E. Baptiste 54, R. Brown 4 for 72) and 364 (A.L. Logie 134, H.A. Gomes 85, T.R.O. Payne 55)
Tasmania 387 (G.W. Goodman 123, M. Ray 59, C.A. Walsh 6 for 119) and 110 for 6 (E.A.E. Baptiste 4 for 67)

Match drawn

at Melbourne

South Australia 146 for 4 dec (D.F. O'Connor 59 not out) and 378 for 5 dec (A.M.J. Hilditch 88, D.W. Hookes 62, W.M. Darling 58 not out, R. Zadow 55, D.F. O'Connor 50)
Victoria 147 for 2 dec (D.M.J. Jones 58 not out) and 210

South Australia won by 168 runs
South Australia 12 pts, Victoria 4 pts

at Brisbane

Queensland 366 for 9 dec (K.C. Wessels 137, G.M. Ritchie 65) and 15 for 0
Western Australia 156 (M.R.J. Veletta 58, G.R. Marsh 55, J.R. Thomson 7 for 27) and 224 (M.R.J. Veletta 59, C.G. Rackemann 4 for 57)

Queensland won by 10 wickets
Queensland 16 pts, Western Australia 0 pts

If there were any lingering doubts as to whether or not the superiority in Australian cricket had moved from west to north-east, they were quickly dispelled in Brisbane where the once all-conquering Western Australia were overwhelmed by the new power of Queensland. There was little play possible on the first day when Queensland closed at 124 for 1, and an outright win still seemed improbable at the end of the second day by which time Wessels' tenacious hundred had taken the home side to 366 and Thomson had sent back Clements and night-watchman Clough with the score at 20. The third day

Wood, caught Greenidge, bowled Harper 41. (Philip Tyson)

THIRD TEST MATCH – AUSTRALIA v. WEST INDIES
7, 8, 9, 10 and 11 December 1984 at Adelaide Oval

WEST INDIES

	FIRST INNINGS		SECOND INNINGS	
C.G. Greenidge	c Hogg, b Lawson	95	lbw, b Lawson	4
D.L. Haynes	c Hughes, b Hogg	0	c Wood, b Lawson	50
R.B. Richardson	c Border, b Lawson	8	(4) lbw, b Hogg	3
H.A. Gomes	c Rixon, b Lawson	60	(5) not out	120
I.V.A. Richards	c Rixon, b Lawson	0	(6) c Rixon, b Hogg	42
C.H. Lloyd†	b Lawson	78	(7) c Rixon, b Lawson	6
P.J. Dujon*	lbw, b Lawson	77	(8) c Boon, b Holland	32
M.D. Marshall	c Rixon, b Lawson	9		
R.A. Harper	c Rixon, b Lawson	9	(3) c Rixon, b Hogg	26
J. Garner	not out	8		
C.A. Walsh	b Holland	0		
Extras	b 5, lb 4, nb 3	12	lb 2, nb 7	9
		356	(for 7 wkts dec)	292

	O	M	R	W	O	M	R	W
Lawson	40	7	112	8	24	6	69	3
Hogg	28	7	75	1	21	2	77	3
Alderman	19	8	38	—	12	1	66	—
Holland	30.2	5	109	1	18.1	1	54	1
Wessels	5	—	13	—				
Border					4	—	24	—

FALL OF WICKETS
1- 4, 2- 25, 3- 157, 4- 157, 5- 172, 6- 322, 7- 331, 8- 348, 9- 355
1- 4, 2- 39, 3- 45, 4- 121, 5- 218, 6- 225, 7- 292

AUSTRALIA

	FIRST INNINGS		SECOND INNINGS	
G.M. Wood	c Greenidge, b Harper	41	(7) c Dujon, b Harper	19
J. Dyson	c Dujon, b Walsh	8	lbw, b Marshall	5
K.C. Wessels	b Marshall	98	(1) c Dujon, b Harper	70
S.J. Rixon*	c Richards, b Marshall	0	(6) lbw, b Harper	16
K.J. Hughes	c Dujon, b Garner	0	(4) b Marshall	2
A.R. Border†	c Garner, b Marshall	21	(3) b Marshall	18
D.C. Boon	c Dujon, b Marshall	12	(5) c Harper, b Garner	9
G.F. Lawson	c Dujon, b Garner	49	c Dujon, b Garner	2
R.G. Holland	c Haynes, b Walsh	2	not out	7
R.M. Hogg	not out	7	b Harper	7
T.M. Alderman	c Richardson, b Marshall	10	b Marshall	0
Extras	b 2, lb 8, nb 26	36	b 7, lb 7, nb 4	18
		284		173

	O	M	R	W	O	M	R	W
Marshall	26	8	69	5	15.5	4	38	5
Garner	26	5	61	2	16	2	58	1
Walsh	24	8	88	2	4	—	20	—
Harper	21	4	56	1	15	6	43	4

FALL OF WICKETS
1- 28, 2- 91, 3- 91, 4- 122, 5- 138, 6- 145, 7- 232, 8- 241, 9- 265
1- 22, 2- 70, 3- 78, 4- 97, 5- 126, 6- 150, 7- 153, 8- 153, 9- 170

Umpires: M.W. Johnson and A.R. Crafter

West Indies won by 191 runs

belonged entirely to Jeff Thomson. He took his tally to a career best 7 for 27 and finished the Western Australian innings with a hat-trick. The visitors were forced to follow-on and Clements, Veletta, Shipperd and Hughes were all out before the close. There was no respite from the strong Queensland attack on the last day and the home state swept to their fourth win of the season with ease.

South Australia took their first points of the season in a rain interrupted match in Melbourne. They sacrificed first innings points and a consistently aggressive batting performance in the second innings brought runs at nearly four an over and enabled Hookes to declare. The South Australian bowling proved as consistent as their batting and in five hours Victoria were bowled out for 210, a third wicket stand of 55 between Richardson and Taylor providing the only resistance of substance.

The colder weather in Tasmania and the pace bowling of Roger Brown, a Launceston player in his first season, shattered the West Indians. Lloyd and Baptiste added 80 for the fifth wicket, but with Gomes, Holding and Davis all suffering injuries, the tourists had a thoroughly miserable time. On the second day, Goodman and Ray took their first wicket stand to 150 and Goodman went on to reach a maiden first-class hundred. Logie, who batted splendidly, led the West Indian recovery and eventually Tasmania, who had had a poor season, were left to make 162 in 100 minutes, a task which was just beyond them when they lost Boon retired hurt.

19 December 1984

at Echuca

West Indians 279 for 9 (E.A.E. Baptiste 75)
Victorian Country XI 215 for 4 (S. Bray 96 not out)

West Indians won by 64 runs

Hilditch is bowled by Davis for 47. South Australia v. *Victoria at Melbourne. (Philip Tyson)*

Jeff Thomson, a career best 7 for 27 including the hat-trick for Queensland against Western Australia, 14–17 December. (David Munden)

20, 21, 22 and 23 December 1984

at Hobart

Tasmania 188 for 3 dec (M. Ray 82, R. Bennett 60) and 193 (R.S. Hyatt 50)
South Australia 205 for 2 dec (G.A. Bishop 88, D.F. O'Connor 72 not out) and 180 for 8 (G.A. Bishop 60, B.P. Patterson 5 for 67)

South Australia won by 2 wickets
South Australia 16 pts, Tasmania 0 pts

at Perth

Victoria 405 (D.M.J. Jones 243, T.G. Hogan 5 for 106) and 231 for 6 dec (S.P. O'Donnell 129 not out, P.M. Clough 4 for 59)
Western Australia 280 (G. Shipperd 131 not out, R.J. Bright 4 for 62) and 245 for 9 (G.R. Marsh 143 not out)

Match drawn
Victoria 4 pts, Western Australia 0 pts

South Australia won their second match in a week to move into third place in the Sheffield Shield, twelve points behind New South Wales. Weather again marred the game in Hobart and the contest revolved around the second innings. Tasmania were 83 for 5, but Bradshaw and Hyatt added 72 before the last five wickets fell for 38. In search of 177 for victory, South Australia strolled to 107 for 1, but Patterson ripped apart the middle order and 6 wickets fell for 26 runs. Hookes and Zesers then added 38 which took the visitors within sight of a very narrow victory, finally accomplished by McCurdy and Zesers.

Robinson, the Victorian opener, is caught behind by Kelly off McCurdy of South Australia. (Philip Tyson)

O'Connor cuts to the boundary, South Australia v. *Victoria at Melbourne. He hit two fifties in the match. Dimattina is the wicket-keeper. (Philip Tyson)*

Dean Jones reminded the selectors of his quality with the first double century of his career. Victoria lost their last 5 wickets for 36 runs, but they retained a commanding position when Ray Bright took four middle-order wickets to reduce Western Australia to 218 for 7. Shipperd batted throughout the innings, however, to save his side and emphasise again that he has been the most underrated of Australian cricketers. The game swung in favour of the home state when Clark and Clough had Victoria at 47 for 5 in their second innings, but Simon O'Donnell hit the second century of his career in blistering style, dominating a partnership of 158 with Dodemaide. Bright declared and Victoria sensed victory, but they were thwarted by Marsh who hit 143 out of

225 and ultimately by the defiance of last man Clough.

At the end of the year, Queensland, with 64 points, had a 24-point lead over New South Wales at the top of the Sheffield Shield table.

Fourth Test Match
AUSTRALIA *v.* WEST INDIES

Craig McDermott became the youngest player to be capped by Australia for more than twenty years and he was joined by another debutant, Murray Bennett. Andrew Hilditch returned to Test cricket after an absence of five years, a reward for consistent batting in the Sheffield Shield.

Border won the toss and put West Indies in to bat. He had early success when Lawson took two wickets in six balls and West Indies were 30 for 2. Richardson and Gomes effected a recovery, adding 123 in $2\frac{1}{2}$ hours before McDermott, whose first five overs had cost 27 runs, took 3 for 1 in 7 balls. Richardson played on to a full toss, Gomes lofted to mid-off off a front edge and Dujon was beaten for pace. Lloyd stayed for a while until he swept Matthews to square leg, but Richards continued pounding away and he was 82 not out at the end of the first day when West Indies were 280 for 6.

Viv Richards had been having a lean time and he was obviously worried about his form, but his cares disappeared on the second day when he reached 208 in 376 minutes, hitting three sixes and twenty-two fours before being caught on the long-on boundary. It was an innings of power and splendour and Richards was on his throne again.

Australia responded well after losing Wood at 38. Hilditch batted with confidence and authority and Wessels whose Test career had looked in tatters only a few weeks before gave good support so that Australia were 115 for 1 at the close.

The batting became rather laborious on Christmas Eve,

Hilditch during his valiant hundred. (Philip Tyson)

ABOVE: *Wessels in aggressive mood in his innings of 90. (Philip Tyson)*

BELOW: *Richards in full flow. (Philip Tyson)*

FOURTH TEST MATCH – AUSTRALIA *v.* WEST INDIES
22, 23, 24, 26 and 27 December 1984 at Melbourne

WEST INDIES

	FIRST INNINGS		SECOND INNINGS	
C.G. Greenidge	c Bennett, b Lawson	10	lbw, b Lawson	1
D.L. Haynes	c Border, b Lawson	13	b McDermott	63
R.B. Richardson	b McDermott	51	b Lawson	3
H.A. Gomes	c Matthews, b McDermott	68	c Bennett, b McDermott	18
I.V.A. Richards	c Hughes, b Matthews	208	lbw, b McDermott	0
P.J. Dujon*	b McDermott	0	not out	49
C.H. Lloyd†	c Lawson, b Matthews	19	not out	34
M.D. Marshall	c Rixon, b Hogg	55		
R.A. Harper	c and b Hogg	5		
J. Garner	lbw, b Lawson	8		
C.A. Walsh	not out	18		
Extras	b 1, lb 11, nb 12	24	b 4, lb 9, nb 5	18
		479	(for 5 wkts dec)	186

	O	M	R	W	O	M	R	W
Lawson	37	9	108	3	19	4	54	2
Hogg	27	2	96	2	14	3	40	—
McDermott	27	2	118	3	21	6	65	3
Bennett	20	—	78	—	3	—	12	—
Matthews	14.3	2	67	2				
Wessels					1	—	2	—

FALL OF WICKETS
1- 27, 2- 30, 3- 153, 4- 154, 5- 154, 6- 223, 7- 362, 8- 376, 9- 426
1- 2, 2- 12, 3- 63, 4- 63, 5- 100

AUSTRALIA

	FIRST INNINGS		SECOND INNINGS	
A.M.J. Hilditch	b Harper	70	b Gomes	113
G.M. Wood	lbw, b Garner	12	c Dujon, b Garner	5
K.C. Wessels	c Dujon, b Marshall	90	b Garner	0
K.J. Hughes	c Dujon, b Walsh	0	lbw, b Garner	0
A.R. Border†	c Richards, b Walsh	35	c Dujon, b Richards	41
G.R.J. Matthews	b Marshall	5	b Harper	2
S.J. Rixon*	c Richardson b Marshall	0	c Richardson b Harper	17
M.J. Bennett	not out	22	not out	3
G.F. Lawson	c Walsh, b Garner	8	b Walsh	0
C.J. McDermott	b Marshall	0		
R.M. Hogg	b Marshall	19		
Extras	b 5, lb 7, w 1, nb 22	35	b 6, lb 2, nb 9	17
		296	(for 8 wkts)	198

	O	M	R	W	O	M	R	W
Marshall	31.5	6	86	5	20	4	36	—
Garner	24	6	74	2	19	1	49	3
Walsh	21	5	57	2	18	4	44	1
Harper	14	1	58	1	22	4	54	2
Richards	1	—	9	—	6	2	7	1
Gomes					2	2	0	1

FALL OF WICKETS
1- 38, 2- 161, 3- 163, 4- 220, 5- 238, 6- 238, 7- 240, 8- 253, 9- 253
1- 17, 2- 17, 3- 17, 4- 128, 5- 131, 6- 162, 7- 198, 8- 198

Umpires: P.J. McConnell and S.J. Randell

Match drawn

but the follow-on was avoided although there was a middle order slump. The fourth day was delayed by rain after which the Australian innings was ended in fifteen minutes. The wicket was now deteriorating and the West Indies, with a lead of 183 on the first innings, took their score to 163 for 5. Australia bowled well, fielded indifferently and caught badly, but their out-cricket was marred by the behaviour of Lawson, behaviour about which the West Indies lodged an official complaint after the match.

To the bewilderment of all, Lloyd decided to bat on for fifteen minutes on the last morning. In effect, this meant that Australia were spared 25 minutes batting against the fearsome attack on a wicket where the bounce was variable. It seemed not to matter when Wood, Wessels and Hughes were victims of Joel Garner in the space of five balls. It was Hughes' second 'duck' of the match and he was omitted from the side for the last Test. The gods of cricket had been most cruel to him.

His successor as Australia's captain, Allan Border, gave the steadfast Hilditch the support that was needed. Hilditch, who received more solid support from Rixon, batted for 339

ABOVE RIGHT: *The Australian plague. Walsh is dropped by Wessels off Murray Bennett. Rixon looks on. (Philip Tyson)*

RIGHT: *The misery of Kim Hughes continues, caught behind off Walsh for 0. (Philip Tyson)*

BELOW: *Viv Richards cuts on his way to his double century. (Philip Tyson)*

minutes and hit seven fours in his maiden Test century, an innings of great character which earned him the Man of the Match award. He was seventh out when he played on to a shooter from Garner, but he had shown that the West Indian attack could be defied. Lloyd took the second new ball with two overs remaining, but Lawson and Bennett stayed until the final delivery which accounted for Lawson.

So the West Indian run of victories was halted, but it was their 27th successive Test without defeat. There was some courage and joy for Australia, but it was tempered by the disappointingly low attendances and by the silly, bad manners of Geoff Lawson.

McDonald's Cup – Semi-Final

29 December 1984

at Melbourne

Victoria 181 for 7

New South Wales 185 for 3 (J. Dyson 84 not out, Imran Khan 73 not out)

New South Wales won by 7 wickets

Facing a target of 182 in 50 overs, New South Wales were indebted to a blazing innings of 73 not out from Imran Khan who joined Dyson when the score was 38 for 3. Dyson batted with great common sense, but Imran's cavalier innings allied to his earlier economic bowling brought him the individual award as New South Wales passed into the final.

Fifth Test Match
AUSTRALIA *v.* WEST INDIES

On a wicket which groundsman Leroy predicted would take spin, Australia recalled Bob Holland and coupled him with his New South Wales spinning partner Murray Bennett. Perversely, West Indies left out Harper in order to play four pace bowlers, a move they later regretted.

Border won the toss, but Australia began uneasily. The hero of the previous Test, Andrew Hilditch, was caught behind in the fifth over and both Wood and Wessels were dropped while Wessels was also lucky to escape being run out. Wood and Wessels enjoyed their luck and batted on for nearly $2\frac{3}{4}$ hours to add 114. The stand was broken when Haynes held a spectacular diving catch off Gomes. Wessels was hit several times on the body, but survived. Ritchie was less fortunate, having to retire hurt on his return to Test cricket when he was hit on the face by a ball from Walsh with his score on 30 after 90 minutes at the crease. Border stayed with Wessels to the close when the score was 235 for 2. Wessels had batted with great courage and determination. Not the most elegant of batsmen, he had, nevertheless, hit thirteen boundaries in reaching 120 after $5\frac{1}{4}$ hours and shown his rehabilitation in Test cricket complete.

Australia took complete command of the game on the second day which they closed at 414 for 6. Border, Boon, Rixon and Bennett all gave Wessels good support and Border finally declared when three wickets fell on the third morning. The Australian innings lasted just under $11\frac{1}{2}$ hours and Wessels batted for 482 minutes, hitting fourteen fours.

Few could have believed when Haynes and Greenidge began the West Indies innings before lunch on the third day that they would be starting the second innings the same evening, but, after young McDermott had made the initial breakthrough, the leg-spin of Bob Holland and the slow left-arm of Murray Bennett put the West Indians into total disorder, the last five wickets falling for 3 runs.

West Indies followed-on and McDermott had Haynes lbw at 7. Next day Lloyd, in his last Test innings, batted masterfully and Richards, his heir apparent, gave equally masterful support, but Holland and Bennett were not to be denied in spite of Australia's continued lapses in the field. It was estimated that they dropped 26 catches in the series, most of them straightforward.

The two spinners, encouraged by success on their own ground, bowled with eagerness and guile and deserved all that came their way. They bowled Australia to a memorable and deserved victory which was duly acclaimed. It was Lloyd's 74th and last Test as West Indies captain and it was only his twelfth defeat against 36 victories.

LEFT: *Australian hero – Murray Bennett (David Munden)*

RIGHT: *Australian hero – Kepler Wessels. (Adrian Murrell)*

Sadly, the game was once more marred by some disgraceful behaviour. Lawson was fined £1500 for his lapses in the fourth Test and it appeared that Border tried to organise a protest against the fine. Later Richards, Rixon and Border were engaged in exchanges of bad language which distressed the umpires. We still search for a sense of responsibility and maturity among some of our finest players. Cricket is about something more than ability; it is about bearing and character and one hopes that those who are lucky enough to be paid large sums to play the game will learn this before the game is sullied irreparably as tennis has been.

31 December 1984, 1 and 2 January 1985

at Perth

Western Australia 245 for 7 dec (T.J. Zoehrer 69 not out, S.C. Clements 60) and 79 (V.B. John 5 for 28)
Sri Lankans 217 for 8 dec (L.R.D. Mendis 67) and 108 for 3 (R.L. Dias 54)

Sri Lankans won by 7 wickets

In their one first-class match as a prelude to the Benson and Hedges World Series, the Sri Lankans gained a commendable victory over an experimental Western Australian side. The home side, who gave first-class debuts to five players, were troubled by the bowling of de Mel on the opening day, but scored briskly enough to reach a point of declaration. Sri Lanka started their reply uncertainly and were 87 for 4 before the exciting young Aravinda de Silva joined skipper Mendis in a spectacular stand of 98 in 50 minutes. Mendis, whose 67 came in just over the hour, declared 28 runs in arrears, but Vinothen John, ably supported by Ravi Ratnayeke and de Mel routed the state side in $2\frac{1}{4}$ hours. Needing only 108 to win, the tourists were 67 for 2 at the close and Roy Dias saw them to a comfortable win on the last morning.

2 January 1985

at Perth

Sri Lankans 113 (D. Smith 4 for 24)
Western Australia 114 for 1

Western Australia won by 9 wickets

5 January 1985

at Brisbane

Queensland 212 for 5 (G.S. Trimble 100 not out)
Sri Lankans 213 for 5 (L.R.D. Mendis 72 not out)

Sri Lankans won by 5 wickets

McDonald's Cup – Semi-Final

5 January 1985

at Adelaide

South Australia 296 for 6 (D.W. Hookes 101, M.D. Haysman 100 not out)
Western Australia 173 (R.J. McCurdy 5 for 23)

South Australia won by 123 runs

South Australia qualified to meet New South Wales in the McDonald's Cup Final in the grand manner. First David Hookes launched a fierce attack on the Western Australia

FIFTH TEST MATCH – AUSTRALIA *v.* WEST INDIES
30, 31 December 1984, 1 and 2 January 1985 at Sydney

AUSTRALIA

	FIRST INNINGS	
A.M.J. Hilditch	c Dujon, b Holding	2
G.M. Wood	c Haynes, b Gomes	45
K.C. Wessels	b Holding	173
G.M. Ritchie	run out	37
A.R. Border†	c Greenidge, b Walsh	69
D.C. Boon	b Garner	49
S.J. Rixon*	c Garner, b Holding	20
M.J. Bennett	c Greenidge, b Garner	23
G.F. Lawson	not out	5
C.J. McDermott	c Greenidge, b Walsh	4
R.G. Holland		
Extras	b 7, lb 20, nb 17	44
	(for 9 wkts dec)	471

	O	M	R	W
Marshall	37	2	111	—
Garner	31	5	101	2
Holding	31	7	74	3
Walsh	38.2	1	118	2
Gomes	12	2	29	1
Richards	7	2	11	—

FALL OF WICKETS
1- 12, 2- 126, 3- 338, 4- 342, 5- 350, 6- 392, 7- 450, 8- 463, 9- 471

Umpires: M.W. Johnson and R.C. Isherwood

Australia won by an innings and 55 runs

WEST INDIES

	FIRST INNINGS		SECOND INNINGS	
C.G. Greenidge	c Rixon, b McDermott	18	b Holland	12
D.L. Haynes	c Wessels, b Holland	34	lbw, b McDermott	3
R.B. Richardson	b McDermott	2	c Wood, b Bennett	26
H.A. Gomes	c Bennett, b Holland	28	c Wood, b Lawson	8
I.V.A. Richards	c Wessels, b Holland	15	b Bennett	58
C.H. Lloyd†	c Wood, b Holland	33	c Border, b McDermott	72
P.J. Dujon*	c Hilditch, b Bennett	22	c and b Holland	8
M.D. Marshall	st Rixon, b Holland	0	not out	32
M.A. Holding	c McDermott, b Bennett	0	c Wessels, b Holland	0
J. Garner	c Rixon, b Holland	0	c Rixon, b Bennett	8
C.A. Walsh	not out	1	c Bennett, b Holland	4
Extras	lb 3, nb 7	10	b 2, lb 12, nb 8	22
		163		253

	O	M	R	W	O	M	R	W
Lawson	9	1	27	—	6	1	14	1
McDermott	9	—	34	2	12	—	56	2
Bennett	22.4	7	45	2	33	9	79	3
Holland	22	7	54	6	33	8	90	4

FALL OF WICKETS
1- 26, 2- 34, 3- 72, 4- 103, 5- 106, 6- 160, 7- 160, 8- 160, 9- 160
1- 7, 2- 31, 3- 46, 4- 93, 5- 153, 6- 180, 7- 231, 8- 231, 9- 244

Australia *v.* West Indies – Test Match Averages

AUSTRALIA BATTING

	M	Inns	NOs	Runs	HS	Av	100s	50s
A.M.J. Hilditch	2	3		185	113	61.66	1	1
K.C. Wessels	5	9		505	173	56.11	1	4
M.J. Bennett	2	3	2	48	23	48.00		
W.B. Phillips	2	4		136	54	34.00		1
A.R. Border	5	9		246	69	27.33		1
D.C. Boon	3	5		132	51	26.40		1
G.M. Wood	5	9		207	56	23.00		1
G.F. Lawson	5	9	2	131	49	18.71		
R.M. Hogg	4	7	3	54	21*	13.50		
J. Dyson	3	6		77	30	12.83		
S.J. Rixon	3	5		53	20	10.60		
K.J. Hughes	4	8		81	37	10.12		
T.M. Alderman	3	6	1	34	23	6.80		
R.G. Holland	3	4	1	15	7*	5.00		

Played in two Tests: C.J. McDermott 0 and 4
Played in one Test – G.N. Yallop 2 and 1; C.G. Rackemann 0 and 0; G.R.J. Matthews 5 and 2; G.M. Ritchie 37

WEST INDIES BATTING

	M	Inns	NOs	Runs	HS	Av	100s	50s
H.A. Gomes	5	9	2	451	127	64.42	2	2
C.H. Lloyd	5	8	1	356	114	50.85	1	2
P.J. Dujon	5	8	1	341	139	48.71	1	1
I.V.A. Richards	5	9	1	342	208	42.75	1	1
M.D. Marshall	5	6	1	174	57	34.80		2
D.L. Haynes	5	9		247	63	27.44		3
C.G. Greenidge	5	8		214	95	26.75		1
R.B. Richardson	5	9		236	138	26.22	1	1
R.A. Harper	2	3		40	26	13.33		
C.A. Walsh	5	6	3	32	18*	10.66		
J. Garner	5	6	2	41	17	10.25		
M.A. Holding	3	4		2	1	0.50		

AUSTRALIA BOWLING

	Overs	Mds	Runs	Wkts	Av	Best	5/inn	10/m
G.F. Lawson	194.4	39	589	23	25.60	8/112	2	1
C.J. McDermott	69	8	273	10	27.30	3/65		
R.G. Holland	130.3	26	404	14	28.85	6/54	1	1
T.M. Alderman	99	31	339	9	37.66	6/128		1
G.R.J. Matthews	14.3	2	67	2	38.50	2/67		
M.J. Bennett	78.4	13	214	5	42.80	3/79		
R.M. Hogg	147.1	23	474	11	43.09	4/101		

Also bowled: C.G. Rackemann 28–3–106–0; A.R. Border 9–0–49–0; K.C. Wessels 6–0–15–0

WEST INDIES BOWLING

	Overs	Mds	Runs	Wkts	Av	Best	5/inn	10/m
H.A. Gomes	15	4	30	2	15.00	1/0		
M.A. Holding	88.1	20	249	15	16.60	6/21	1	
M.D. Marshall	215.2	45	554	28	19.78	5/38	4	1
R.A. Harper	72	15	211	8	26.37	4/43		
J. Garner	177.4	33	566	19	29.78	4/67		
C.A. Walsh	146.2	29	432	13	33.23	3/55		
I.V.A. Richards	16	4	32	0	—	0/1		

AUSTRALIA CATCHES

12–S.J. Rixon (ct 11/st 1); 7–W.B. Phillips; 5–G.M. Wood; 4–A.R. Border, K.J. Hughes and M.J. Bennett; 3–K.C. Wessels; 2–R.M. Hogg and D.C. Boon; 1–G.N. Yallop, G.F. Lawson, C.G. Rackemann, T.M. Alderman, R.G. Holland, A.M.J. Hilditch, G.R.J. Matthews and C.J. McDermott

WEST INDIES CATCHES

19–P.J. Dujon; 8–R.B. Richardson; 5–C.G. Greenidge and C.H. Lloyd; 4–D.L. Haynes and M.D. Marshall; 3–I.V.A. Richards and R.A. Harper (2 as sub); 2–M.A. Holding and J. Garner; 1–C.A. Walsh and H.A. Gomes

bowling and then Mike Haysman continued the onslaught. With so many runs at which to bowl, the home side's attack enjoyed themselves and McCurdy pillaged the late order to return his best figures in limited-over cricket.

6 January 1985

at Brisbane

Sri Lankans 240 for 6 (R.L. Dias 110 not out)
Queensland 153 for 0 (R.B. Kerr 87 not out, B.A. Courtice 55 not out)
Sri Lankans won on faster scoring rate

Roy Dias hit a sparkling century, but Kerr and Courtice gave Queensland a splendid start which was halted by rain after 30.1 overs.

Benson and Hedges World Series

First One-Day International
AUSTRALIA *v.* WEST INDIES

The fire of the Test series was still smouldering when the Benson and Hedges World Series began, but Australia's hopes that they would continue in the vein that brought them victory in the final Test were soon dashed. Lloyd won the toss and put Australia in to bat and almost immediately Wood was caught off Garner. There was no dramatic improvement

The world in the evening. Steve Smith of Australia ducks under a Garner bouncer. (Adrian Murrell)

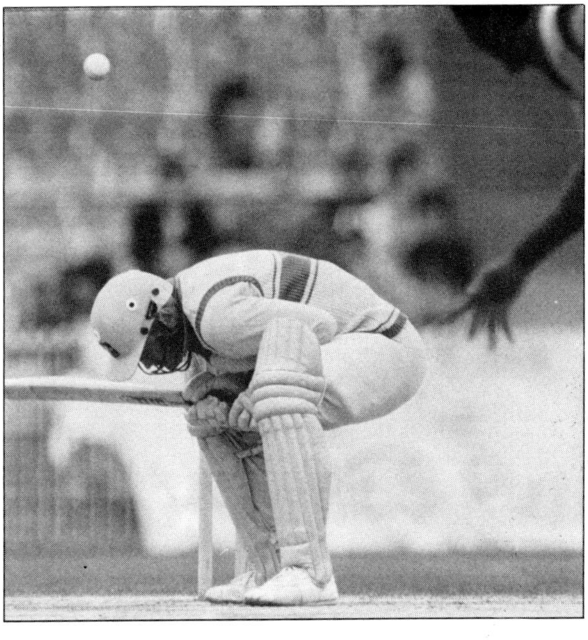

FIRST ONE DAY INTERNATIONAL – AUSTRALIA *v.* WEST INDIES
6 January 1985 at Melbourne

AUSTRALIA			
G.M. Wood	c Holding, b Garner	0	
A.M.J. Hilditch	c Holding, b Baptiste	27	
K.C. Wessels	run out	33	
A.R. Border†	c Baptiste, b Garner	73	
D.C. Boon	b Marshall	55	
W.B. Phillips*	c Greenidge, b Garner	23	
S.P. O'Donnell	not out	7	
G.F. Lawson	not out	8	
M.J. Bennett			
C.J. McDermott			
R.M. Hogg			
Extras	lb 7, w 4, nb 3	14	
(50 overs)	(for 6 wickets)	240	

	O	M	R	W
Garner	10	2	41	3
Marshall	10	—	32	1
Baptiste	9	—	73	1
Holding	10	1	41	—
Richards	10	1	37	—
Gomes	1	—	9	—

FALL OF WICKETS
1- 0, 2- 48, 3- 78, 4- 193, 5- 220, 6- 224

WEST INDIES		
C.G. Greenidge	b Bennett	12
D.L. Haynes	not out	123
R.B. Richardson	c Boon, b Lawson	34
I.V.A. Richards	c Phillips, b McDermott	47
H.A. Gomes	not out	2
C.H. Lloyd†		
P.J. Dujon*		
E.A.E. Baptiste		
M.D. Marshall		
M.A. Holding		
J. Garner		
Extras	b 1, lb 17, w 5	23
(44.5 overs)	(for 3 wickets)	241

	O	M	R	W
Lawson	10	—	45	1
McDermott	9.5	—	52	1
Hogg	8	—	43	—
O'Donnell	3	—	24	—
Bennett	10	2	23	1
Wessels	2	—	18	—
Border	2	—	18	—

FALL OF WICKETS
1- 69, 2- 140, 3- 234

West Indies won by 7 wickets

in Australia's fortunes until Border and Boon came together at 78 for 3. Benefitting from some poor fielding and catching, they added 115 in 21 overs and led Australia to a commendable score.

Their efforts seemed as nothing, however, once Desmond Haynes got into his stride. He was in devastating form, so much so that Greenidge scored only 12 of a first wicket stand of 69. Newcomer O'Donnell was dealt with severely, but none escaped Haynes' aggression. He and Richards added 94 off 81 deliveries for the 3rd wicket. Haynes hit fifteen fours and his runs were made off 130 balls to bring victory with 5.1 overs to spare.

Benson and Hedges World Series

Second One-Day International
AUSTRALIA *v.* SRI LANKA

Playing a day/night match for the first time, Sri Lanka gave a good account of themselves, but, as expected, their batting proved stronger and more reliable than their bowling.

Mendis decided to bat first when he won the toss and Wettimuny and Silva gave the Sri Lankans a firm start. The left-hander Amal Silva played some crisp drives and batted attractively although he tended to lose his way once he had reached fifty, and this was at a time when Sri Lanka needed to increase the scoring rate to press home their early advantage.

Roy Dias, that most elegant of batsmen, scored 60 off 59 deliveries although he hit only one boundary, but the Sri

Masterminds. Lloyd and Holding direct operations. (Adrian Murrell)

SECOND ONE-DAY INTERNATIONAL – AUSTRALIA *v.* SRI LANKA
8 January 1985 at Sydney

SRI LANKA

S. Wettimuny	c Phillips, b Rackemann	20
S.A.R. Silva*	c Bennett, b Hogg	68
D.S.B.P. Kuruppu	c Wood, b Bennett	22
R.L. Dias	c Border, b O'Donnell	60
L.R.D. Mendis†	b Hogg	16
P.A. de Silva	b Hogg	17
A.L.F. de Mel	b Hogg	0
J.R. Ratnayeke	not out	8
R.J. Ratnayake	not out	4
D.S. de Silva		
V.B. John		
Extras	b 5, lb 5, w 13, nb 1	24
(49 overs)	(for 7 wickets)	239

	O	M	R	W
Hogg	10	—	47	4
O'Donnell	9	2	39	1
McDermott	10	1	49	—
Bennett	10	1	44	1
Rackemann	10	—	50	1

FALL OF WICKETS
1- 66, 2- 104, 3- 160, 4- 181, 5- 214, 6- 214, 7- 229

AUSTRALIA

A.M.J. Hilditch	run out	23
G.M. Wood	retired hurt	52
K.C. Wessels	c Silva, b J.R. Ratnayeke	1
A.R. Border†	not out	79
D.C. Boon	c sub, b de Mel	44
W.B. Phillips*	c Silva, b de Mel	3
S.P. O'Donnell	not out	20
M.J. Bennett		
R.M. Hogg		
C.J. McDermott		
C.G. Rackemann		
Extras	b 4, lb 4, w 4, nb 6	18
(46.2 overs)	(for 4 wickets)	240

	O	M	R	W
de Mel	9.3	—	59	2
John	9	1	40	—
R.J. Ratnayake	8.5	—	32	—
J.R. Ratnayeke	9	—	69	1
D.S. de Silva	10	1	32	—

FALL OF WICKETS
1- 68, 2- 70, 3- 171, 4- 176

Australia won by 6 wickets

Lankans could have hoped for some twenty more runs than they finally achieved.

Wood and Hilditch gave Australia a good start, but Hilditch was run out and Wessels caught behind two balls later. Wood retired hurt with cramp and as the run rate had sagged, Australia seemed in trouble. It was Boon and Border who revived their hopes with a stand of 84 which ended when Boon was caught at deep mid-wicket when he pulled de Mel. Phillips was caught behind the same over and Australia needed 64 from the last ten overs, having been checked by accurate leg-spin from Somachandra de Silva.

It was Border who bludgeoned Australia to success and his innings won him the individual award. He was well supported by O'Donnell, but the Australians were also aided by some wayward bowling, particularly from Ravi Ratnayeke whose run up problems produced a crop of no-balls.

Benson and Hedges World Series

Third One-Day International
WEST INDIES *v.* SRI LANKA

In the first international match to be played in Tasmania, Sri Lanka again batted bravely, after a wretched start, but their bowling failed to make any impression on the West Indian batsmen who were aided by some sloppy fielding.

The Sri Lankan innings was revived by Dias and Mendis who again demonstrated what a fine player he is. There was also a very useful flourish at the close of the innings by Karnain and Rumesh Ratnayake, but, on a small ground, a target of 198 was never likely to worry the West Indians.

Wood takes evasive action. (Adrian Murrell)

THIRD ONE-DAY INTERNATIONAL – WEST INDIES v. SRI LANKA
10 January 1985 at Hobart

SRI LANKA		
S. Wettimuny	c Richards, b Garner	8
S.A.R. Silva*	c Dujon, b Garner	4
D.S.B.P. Kuruppu	c Richardson, b Holding	8
R.L. Dias	c Dujon, b Walsh	27
L.R.D. Mendis†	run out	56
P.A. de Silva	c sub, b Richards	8
J.R. Ratnayeke	b Richards	8
U.S.H. Karnain	not out	20
R.J. Ratnayake	not out	23
D.S. de Silva		
V.B. John		
Extras	b 12, lb 10, w 12, nb 1	35
(50 overs)	(for 7 wickets)	197

	O	M	R	W
Marshall	10	1	37	—
Garner	10	1	19	2
Holding	10	1	25	1
Walsh	10	1	47	1
Richards	10	2	47	2

FALL OF WICKETS
1- 19, 2- 24, 3- 39, 4- 115, 5- 127, 6- 142

WEST INDIES		
C.G. Greenidge	c Kuruppu, b D.S. de Silva	61
D.L. Haynes	c Silva, b R.J. Ratnayake	32
R.B. Richardson	not out	52
A.L. Logie	not out	34
I.V.A. Richards†		
H.A. Gomes		
P.J. Dujon*		
M.D. Marshall		
M.A. Holding		
J. Garner		
C.A. Walsh		
Extras	lb 11, w 5, nb 3	19
(40.4 overs)	(for 2 wickets)	198

	O	M	R	W
John	6.4	2	30	—
J.R. Ratnayeke	7	—	41	—
R.J. Ratnayake	7	—	31	1
D.S. de Silva	10	3	29	1
Karnain	8	—	41	—
P.A. de Silva	2	—	15	—

FALL OF WICKETS
1- 50, 2- 144

West Indies won by 8 wickets

Richardson is caught by Wayne Phillips off Simon O'Donnell in the ninth match of the series. (Philip Tyson)

Once more there was some wayward bowling and once more it was only the accurate leg-spin of Somachandra de Silva that kept the score in bounds, but when Richie Richardson turned Vinothen John to leg West Indies had won with 9.2 overs to spare.

10, 11, 12 and 13 January 1985

at Perth

Western Australia 409 for 8 dec (G. Shipperd 139, M.W. McPhee 135) and 241 (K.J. Hughes 111, R.J. McCurdy 5 for 109)
South Australia 408 (M.D. Haysman 172, R.J. Inverarity 69, T.M. Alderman 6 for 109) and 221 (D.W. Hookes 73, D.F. O'Connor 52, E. Spalding 4 for 37)

Western Australia won by 21 runs
Western Australia 16 pts, South Australia 0 pts

11, 12, 13 and 14 January 1985

at Melbourne

Queensland 301 (B.A. Courtice 69, S.P. Davis 4 for 106) and 260 for 7 dec (B.A. Courtice 70, C.B. Smart 50)
Victoria 101 (J.N. Maguire 4 for 36) and 383 for 7 (D.M.J. Jones 136)

Match drawn
Queensland 4 pts, Victoria 0 pts

Western Australia gained their first victory of the season when they beat South Australia in an exciting match in Perth. The home side were given a fine start by Mark McPhee who, losing Veletta at 56, hit a maiden century, 135 out of 189 in 223 minutes with eighteen fours. Greg Shipperd then provided the solidity and Hughes declared on 409. At 134 for 5, South Australia looked well beaten, but Mike Haysman, with twenty-six fours, and John Inverarity added 172 in 408 minutes to effect a splendid recovery. It seemed that the visitors would even snatch first innings points, but Terry Alderman, back at his best, had Zesers caught by Hogan when South Australia were still one run behind. As all about him fell to McCurdy and Zesers, Kim Hughes hit a splendid hundred, but the target of 243 looked well within the visitors reach. They began confidently and with Hookes and O'Connor in command, they reached 164 for 3, but the pace of young Earl Spalding in only his second first-class match and the spin of Tom Hogan saw the last 6 wickets fall for 37 runs.

Solid batting by the middle order complemented the efforts of Andrew Courtice, one of the replacements for those on international duty, and helped to take Queensland to 301 at Melbourne. On an easy paced wicket this looked a moderate score, but Victoria were soon in great trouble. Hibbert was forced to retire hurt at 6 and Jones fell to Rackemann without scoring. The last 9 wickets fell to the Queensland pace trio for 68 runs, but, surprisingly, Thomson failed to enforce the follow-on even though Hibbert was injured and Victoria 200 in arrears. He chose instead to grind

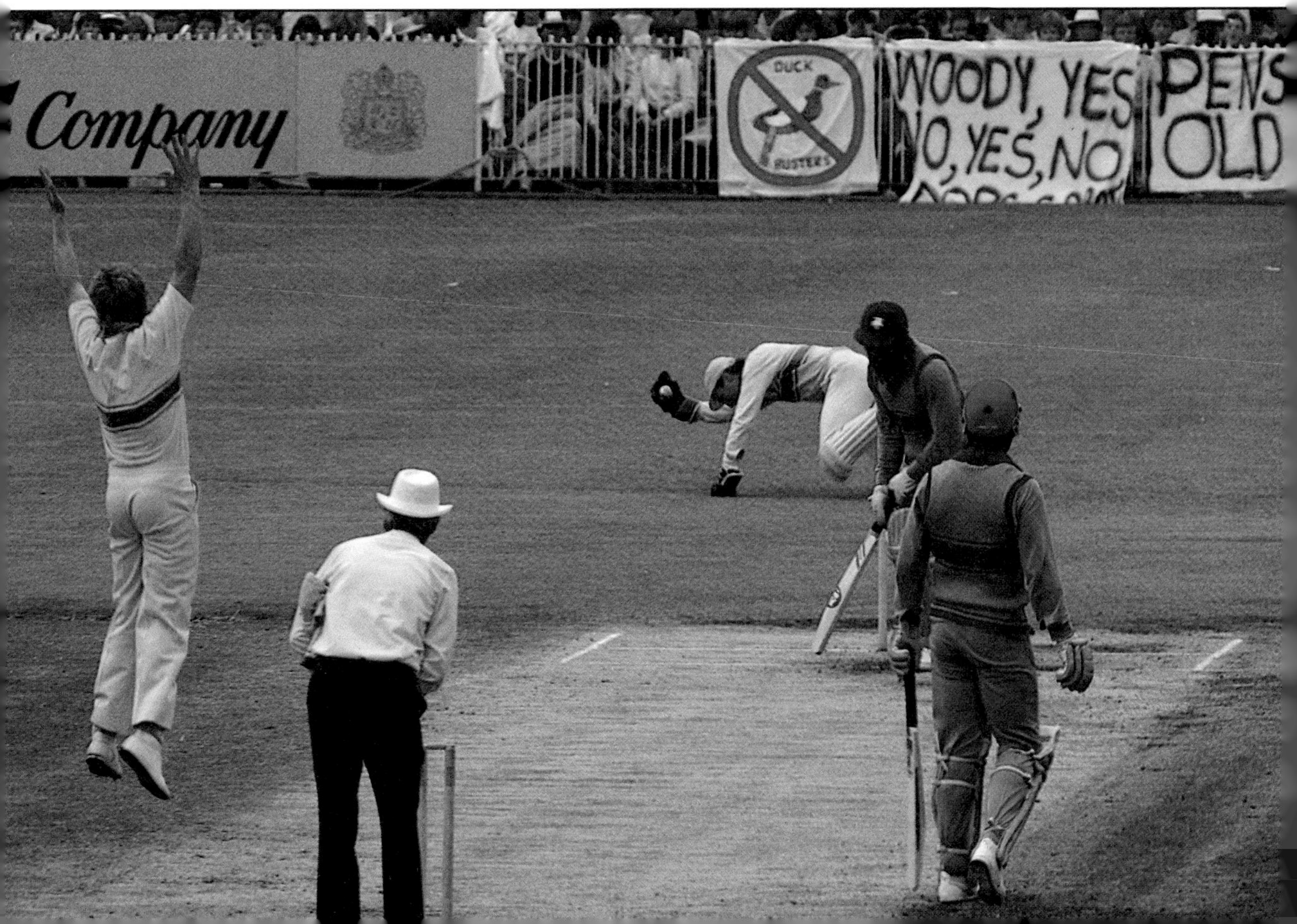

Greenidge is caught by Phillips off Hogg in the ninth match. (Philip Tyson)

FOURTH ONE-DAY INTERNATIONAL – WEST INDIES v. SRI LANKA
12 January 1985 at Brisbane

WEST INDIES

R.B. Richardson	c Silva, b John	1
T.R.O. Payne	c John, b Karnain	20
H.A. Gomes	c Silva, b Karnain	28
I.V.A. Richards	c Silva, b John	98
A.L. Logie	c P.A. de Silva, b D.S. de Silva	10
C.H. Lloyd†	not out	89
P.J. Dujon*	c Mendis, b R.J. Ratnayake	11
M.D. Marshall	not out	1
M.A. Holding		
J. Garner		
W.W. Davis		
Extras	b 1, lb 5, w 4, nb 2	12
(50 overs)	(for 6 wickets)	270

	O	M	R	W
G. de Silva	10	—	42	—
John	10	2	52	2
R.J. Ratnayake	10	—	39	1
Karnain	10	—	55	2
D.S. de Silva	8	—	57	1
Dias	2	—	19	—

FALL OF WICKETS
1- 7, 2- 45, 3- 73, 4- 92, 5- 244, 6- 269

SRI LANKA

S. Wettimuny	c Dujon, b Garner	2
S.A.R. Silva*	b Davis	20
D.S.B.P. Kuruppu	c Payne, b Holding	4
R.L. Dias	c Dujon, b Holding	80
L.R.D. Mendis†	b Holding	14
P.A. de Silva	c Richards, b Davis	13
U.S.H. Karnain	st Dujon, b Richards	9
R.J. Ratnayake	st Dujon, b Richards	19
D.S. de Silva	b Lloyd	9
V.B. John	c Logie, b Gomes	0
G. de Silva	not out	2
Extras	lb 3, w 3, nb 2	8
(48.1 overs)		180

	O	M	R	W
Marshall	5	2	9	—
Garner	5	2	14	1
Holding	10	—	38	3
Davis	10	—	29	2
Richards	10	—	45	2
Gomes	8	—	42	1
Lloyd	0.1	—	0	1

FALL OF WICKETS
1- 4, 2- 29, 3- 35, 4- 59, 5- 88, 6- 114, 7- 144, 8- 176, 9-177

West Indies won by 90 runs

to a massive lead and give Victoria no option but to bat for a draw. At 93 for 3, the home side seemed doomed, but Dean Jones hit twenty fours in a fine innings and with good support from the middle order, the match was saved. Victoria welcomed back Yallop after his season of injury and gave a first opportunity to Shaun Graf since his return from the west.

FIFTH ONE-DAY INTERNATIONAL – AUSTRALIA v. WEST INDIES
13 January 1985 at Brisbane

AUSTRALIA

G.M. Wood	c Dujon, b Richards	38
A.M.J. Hilditch	c Garner, b Davis	19
K.C. Wessels	c Logie, b Richards	47
A.R. Border†	run out	7
D.C. Boon	lbw, b Richards	4
S.P. O'Donnell	run out	25
S.J. Rixon*	run out	3
M.J. Bennett	c Logie, b Marshall	3
G.F. Lawson	c Dujon, b Garner	7
C.J. McDermott	run out	13
R.M. Hogg	not out	6
Extras	lb 10, w 4, nb 5	19
(50 overs)		191

	O	M	R	W
Marshall	10	2	42	1
Garner	10	1	33	1
Holding	10	—	31	—
Davis	10	—	37	1
Richards	10	—	38	3

FALL OF WICKETS
1- 49, 2- 77, 3- 97, 4- 107, 5- 153, 6- 160, 7- 162, 8- 171, 9- 175

WEST INDIES

D.L. Haynes	c Hogg, b O'Donnell	46
R.B. Richardson	b McDermott	16
H.A. Gomes	b McDermott	0
I.V.A. Richards	c Border, b Hogg	49
C.H. Lloyd†	not out	52
A.L. Logie	c Rixon, b O'Donnell	7
P.J. Dujon*	not out	6
M.D. Marshall		
M.A. Holding		
J. Garner		
W.W. Davis		
Extras	b 5, lb 8, w 5, nb 1	19
(37.4 overs)	(for 5 wickets)	195

	O	M	R	W
Lawson	10	1	35	—
Hogg	8	1	41	1
O'Donnell	9	—	47	2
McDermott	7	1	33	2
Bennett	3	—	21	—
Boon	0.4	—	5	—

FALL OF WICKETS
1- 50, 2- 50, 3- 74, 4-, 172, 5- 188

West Indies won by 5 wickets

Benson and Hedges World Series

Fourth One-Day International
WEST INDIES *v.* SRI LANKA

West Indies, lacking Haynes and Greenidge, stood at 95 for 4 off 25 overs against Sri Lanka in the second meeting of the two sides, and it looked possible for the Cinderellas of international cricket to spring a surprise, but Richards and Lloyd engaged in a ferocious stand of 152 at a run a ball to put the game way beyond Sri Lanka's reach. Richards hit three sixes and six fours and Lloyd hit three sixes and seven fours as the West Indies moved to the highest score recorded in a one-day match in Brisbane.

In reply, Sri Lanka began wretchedly and were 88 for 5, but Roy Dias restored dignity with an exciting and elegant 80 in 106 minutes. He hit nine fours. He gained limited support and with Richards claiming two wickets and the individual award and Lloyd bowling Somachandra de Silva with his one and only delivery, West Indies won in a leisurely manner.

Benson and Hedges World Series

Fifth One-Day International
AUSTRALIA *v.* WEST INDIES

For the second time in the week-end Richards and Lloyd paced West Indies to victory. The veteran Lloyd was in magnificent form. Wood and Hilditch gave Australia a solid start, but once Wood was out wickets fell regularly and only the determined, unorthodox Wessels offered any resistance. It was the West Indian fielding which posed the greatest threat to Australian batsmen who became frustrated by the accurate attack. Clive Lloyd ran out Border and O'Donnell and then beat McDermott with his throw to the bowler's end on the last ball of the innings.

Craig McDermott gave Australia hope with two wickets in his first over, but Richards and Lloyd were soon into the attack and added 98 to make possible a West Indian victory with 12.2 overs to spare, entertaining, if disappointing, for a capacity crowd.

Benson and Hedges World Series

Sixth One-Day International
AUSTRALIA *v.* WEST INDIES

Australia brought in Bob Holland in the hope that the leg-spinner could do in one-day cricket what he had done in the fifth Test match and bring victory over West Indies, but the visitors swept to their fifth win in five matches with 6.3 overs to spare and so left Australia and Sri Lanka to contest who would meet them in the final.

Australia won the toss and batted first and although they had a good start, they could never score at a rate that was going to trouble the West Indies. Wessels seemed more intent on personal survival than in maintaining a brisk run rate and took 39 overs to make 63, which put great pressure on the other batsmen.

Australia's 200 seemed a winning score when Lawson and McDermott had West Indies at 25 for 3 after 8 overs, but Richards and Lloyd again rallied the side. They began circumspectly, but Richards greeted O'Donnell by hitting him into the crowd at square-leg for six and taking three fours in the rest of the over. This began the acceleration and Lloyd and Richards put on 90 in 18 overs before Lloyd fell as soon as McDermott returned. Logie opened his scoring by driving Holland straight for six and with Richards now at his most regal, West Indies once more emphasised the gap between themselves and the rest of the world.

SIXTH ONE-DAY INTERNATIONAL – AUSTRALIA *v.* WEST INDIES
15 January 1985 at Sydney

AUSTRALIA			
	G.M. Wood	c Holding, b Davis	21
	K.C. Wessels	st Dujon, b Richards	63
	D.C. Boon	run out	20
	A.R. Border†	run out	24
	G.M. Ritchie	not out	30
	S.P. O'Donnell	b Marshall	17
	S.J. Rixon*	not out	2
	M.J. Bennett		
	G.F. Lawson		
	C.J. McDermott		
	R.G. Holland		
	Extras	lb 10, w 3, nb 10	23
	(50 overs)	(for 5 wickets)	200

	O	M	R	W
Marshall	10	—	38	1
Garner	10	1	44	—
Holding	10	1	36	—
Davis	10	2	31	1
Richards	10	—	41	1

FALL OF WICKETS
1- 42, 2- 103, 3- 137, 4- 161, 5- 197

WEST INDIES			
	D.L. Haynes	c O'Donnell, b McDermott	13
	R.B. Richardson	lbw, b Lawson	9
	H.A. Gomes	c Wessels, b McDermott	0
	I.V.A. Richards	not out	103
	C.H. Lloyd†	c Rixon, b McDermott	38
	A.L. Logie	c Rixon, b Lawson	12
	P.J. Dujon*	not out	15
	M.D. Marshall		
	M.A. Holding		
	W.W. Davis		
	J. Garner		
	Extras	b 1, lb 5, w 2, nb 3	11
	(43.3 overs)	(for 5 wickets)	201

	O	M	R	W
Lawson	10	1	32	2
McDermott	10	—	30	3
Bennett	6	—	40	—
O'Donnell	7.3	—	43	—
Holland	10	—	50	—

FALL OF WICKETS
1- 23, 2- 23, 3- 25, 4- 115, 5- 138

West Indies won by 5 wickets

Benson and Hedges World Series

Seventh One-Day International
WEST INDIES *v.* SRI LANKA

A Sri Lankan side troubled by injuries put up a brave, but futile struggle against the West Indies in the third of the day/night matches at Sydney. Haynes and Greenidge began in the customary remorseless manner, savaging a limp attack. Somachandra de Silva was again the pick of the bowlers and it was he who bowled Greenidge at 128. Uvaisal Karnain ran out Haynes at the same score, but Richardson and Richards, in a pensive mood, added 58, and Gus Logie came in to hit lustily so that West Indies reached their highest score of the competition so far.

The Sri Lankan innings was soon in shreds, Holding taking two wickets and becoming the highest wicket-taker in limited-over internationals, but Dias batted with his usual authority to reach 1000 runs in one-day internationals. Karnain gave a good account of himself and Sri Lanka died bravely.

17, 18, 19 and 20 January 1985

at Adelaide

Victoria 197 (A.K. Zesers 5 for 51) and 150 (R.J. McCurdy 4 for 52, R.J. Inverarity 4 for 63)
South Australia 441 (D.F. O'Connor 118, D.J. Kelly 72, A.K. Zesers 85)

South Australia won by an innings and 94 runs
South Australia 16 pts, Victoria 0 pts

at Newcastle

Tasmania 409 for 8 dec (S.L. Saunders 107, K. Bradshaw 78, G.W. Goodman 50, P.H. Marks 4 for 83) and 321 (D.J. Buckingham 78, K. Bradshaw 63, Imran Khan 4 for 44)
New South Wales 519 (P.S. Clifford 143, D.M. Wellham 113, S.J. Rixon 94, J. Dyson 87, M.P. Tame 5 for 74) and 152 for 7 (S.B. Smith 62)

Match drawn
New South Wales 4 pts, Tasmania 0 pts

at Perth

Queensland 310 (T.J. Barsby 133, B. Reid 4 for 88, T.M. Alderman 4 for 102) and 171 (T.V. Hohns 103, T.M. Alderman 6 for 42)
Western Australia 281 (M.W. McPhee 67, T.J. Zoehrer 58, J.N. Maguire 6 for 84) and 201 for 8 (G. Shipperd 69 not out)

Western Australia won by 2 wickets
Western Australia 12 pts, Queensland 4 pts

The slow-medium swing bowling of Andrew Zesers accounted for Victoria on the opening day at Adelaide. Victoria gave another limp batting performance, losing their last 7 wickets for 62 runs. South Australia were 29 for 1 at the close and the next morning, night-watchman wicket-keeper Kelly took his score to 72. South Australia reached 277 for 7 in a shortened day, but the third morning provided a remarkable transformation as O'Connor and Zesers took their 8th wicket stand to 174. O'Connor reached a maiden century and Zesers hit a career best. For Zesers, in his fifth first-class game, it was a remarkable occasion and he took the wicket of top-scorer Siddons in the second innings as Victoria crumpled to 150 against the fiery pace of Rod McCurdy and the left-arm spin of the veteran Inverarity. Lifted to 44 points by this win, South Australia were challenging strongly for a place in the Sheffield Shield Final.

The leaders, Queensland, suffered their first defeat of the season in spite of leading on the first innings in Perth. In his second match for the state Trevor Barsby hit a maiden century, finishing the first day on 120 not out. It was his 21st birthday. Western Australia finished the second day 106 in arrears with 4 wickets standing, but the tail wagged well on

SEVENTH ONE-DAY INTERNATIONAL – WEST INDIES *v.* SRI LANKA
17 January 1985 at Sydney

WEST INDIES			
	C.G. Greenidge	b D.S. de Silva	67
	D.L. Haynes	run out	54
	R.B. Richardson	not out	57
	I.V.A. Richards†	b de Mel	30
	A.L. Logie	not out	47
	P.J. Dujon*		
	R.A. Harper		
	M.D. Marshall		
	M.A. Holding		
	W.W. Davis		
	C.A. Walsh		
	Extras	lb 5, w 5, nb 2	12
	(50 overs)	(for 3 wickets)	267

	O	M	R	W
de Mel	10	1	50	1
John	10	—	53	—
J.R. Ratnayeke	3	—	19	—
R.J. Ratnayake	10	—	58	—
D.S. de Silva	10	1	48	1
Karnain	7	1	34	—

FALL OF WICKETS
1- 128, 2- 128, 3- 186

SRI LANKA			
	J.R. Ratnayeke	c Dujon, b Davis	17
	S.A.R. Silva*	c Greenidge, b Marshall	5
	P.A. de Silva	c Dujon, b Holding	21
	R.L. Dias	not out	65
	L.R.D. Mendis†	c Dujon, b Holding	2
	R.S. Madugalle	b Harper	25
	U.S.H. Karnain	not out	41
	R.J. Ratnayake		
	A.L.F. de Mel		
	D.S. de Silva		
	V.B. John		
	Extras	b 2, lb 7, w 4, nb 13	26
	(50 overs)	(for 5 wickets)	202

	O	M	R	W
Marshall	10	1	33	1
Walsh	10	1	45	—
Davis	10	–	52	1
Holding	10	2	32	2
Harper	10	—	31	1

FALL OF WICKETS
1- 12, 2- 54, 3- 54, 4- 64, 5- 124

West Indies won by 65 runs

EIGHTH ONE-DAY INTERNATIONAL – AUSTRALIA *v.* SRI LANKA
19 January 1985 at Melbourne

AUSTRALIA			
	G.M. Wood	b R.J. Ratnayake	42
	K.C. Wessels	b R.J. Ratnayake	28
	G.M. Ritchie	c Madugalle, b Karnain	13
	A.R. Border†	st Silva, b D.S. de Silva	1
	D.C. Boon	c Wettimuny, b Dias	34
	W.B. Phillips*	c de Mel, b Dias	67
	S.P. O'Donnell	b R.J. Ratnayake	7
	G.F. Lawson	c Madugalle, b Dias	11
	M.J. Bennett	not out	6
	C.J. McDermott	b R.J. Ratnayake	0
	R.M. Hogg	not out	5
	Extras	lb 9, w 3	12
	(50 overs	(for 9 wickets)	226

	O	M	R	W
de Mel	7	1	45	—
John	10	1	32	—
R.J. Ratnayake	10	3	37	4
D.S. de Silva	10	—	33	1
Karnain	9	—	45	1
Dias	4	—	25	3

FALL OF WICKETS
1- 68, 2- 73, 3- 74, 4- 88, 5- 160, 6- 191, 7- 204, 8- 220, 9- 220

SRI LANKA			
	S. Wettimuny	lbw, b Hogg	17
	S.A.R. Silva*	c Hogg, b O'Donnell	23
	R.S. Madugalle	c Border, b O'Donnell	24
	R.L. Dias	run out	48
	L.R.D. Mendis†	c Wessels, b Hoff	35
	P.A. de Silva	not out	46
	U.S.H. Karnain	b Lawson	16
	R.J. Ratnayake	not out	5
	A.L.F. de Mel		
	D.S. de Silva		
	V.B. John		
	Extras	b 1, lb 14, nb 1	16
	(49.2 overs)	(for 6 wickets)	230

	O	M	R	W
Lawson	10	—	51	1
McDermott	9.2	1	36	—
Hogg	10	1	31	2
O'Donnell	10	1	43	2
Bennett	9	1	48	—
Wessels	1	—	6	—

FALL OF WICKETS
1- 38, 2- 52, 3- 86, 4- 150, 5- 161, 6- 196

Sri Lanka won by 4 wickets

the third morning to keep them in touch in spite of fine bowling by Maguire and Rackemann. In their second innings, Queensland were shattered by Terry Alderman who, in harness with 6' 7" pace man Bruce Reid, reduced them to 7 for 3 and 30 for 5. A valiant hundred by Trevor Hohns took the visitors to 171 so leaving Western Australia to make 201 to win. Held together by the ever-reliable Shipperd, they reached the target with 4.1 overs and 2 wickets remaining and gave Western Australia hope of retaining the Shield.

Tasmania left out fast bowler Patterson as a disciplinary measure and joined in a run feast at Newcastle. There was a hard-hit innings from Danny Buckingham and a fine century from Stuart Saunders at number seven so that Tasmania recovered massively from 96 for 4. Dyson and Wellham put on 175 for New South Wales' second wicket and Rixon and Clifford 132 for the 4th. Clifford, with his third century of the season, reasserted his claim for a place in the side to tour England. There was a career best 5 for 74 from Mike Tame and after an early blast from Imran, Tasmania recovered and left the home state 21 overs in which to score 212, a task that they found a little too difficult.

Benson and Hedges World Series

Eighth One-Day International
AUSTRALIA *v.* SRI LANKA

Sri Lanka gave themselves a good opportunity of reaching the final with their first victory of the series, achieved in sensational manner over Australia at Melbourne.

The Sri Lankan bowling was more disciplined and accurate than it had been at any other time in the competition and Australia were restricted to 88 for 4 in 25 overs. Rumesh Ratnayake, later named Man of the Match, was particularly effective, but it was Somachandra de Silva who captured the vital wicket when he had Border stumped for 1. Phillips, back after his finger injury, and Boon added 72 off 98 balls, but the

Craig McDermott, youthful aggression. (Adrian Murrell)

NINTH ONE-DAY INTERNATIONAL – AUSTRALIA *v.* WEST INDIES
20 January 1985 at Melbourne

WEST INDIES			
	C.G. Greenidge	c Phillips, b Hogg	33
	D.L. Haynes	c and b O'Donnell	23
	R.B. Richardson	c Phillips, b O'Donnell	21
	I.V.A. Richards	c Boon, b McDermott	74
	C.H. Lloyd†	run out	16
	A.L. Logie	c Border, b Wessels	72
	P.J. Dujon*	c Phillips, b Hogg	23
	M.A. Holding	not out	2
	M.D. Marshall	not out	2
	J. Garner		
	W.W. Davis		
	Extras	b 1, lb 3, w 1	5
	(50 overs)	(for 7 wickets)	271

	O	M	R	W
Lawson	10	—	47	—
McDermott	10	—	50	1
Hogg	10	1	56	2
O'Donnell	10	—	40	2
Wessels	8	—	58	1
Border	2	—	16	—

FALL OF WICKETS
1- 56, 2- 58, 3- 103, 4- 138, 5- 201, 6- 252, 7- 268

AUSTRALIA			
	G.M. Wood	c Dujon, b Marshall	9
	W.B. Phillips*	c Greenidge, b Garner	4
	D.M.J. Jones	c Haynes, b Marshall	0
	S.P. O'Donnell	run out	11
	A.R. Border†	c Richards, b Holding	61
	D.C. Boon	b Richards	34
	G.M. Ritchie	b Davis	6
	K.C. Wessels	b Richards	21
	G.F. Lawson	not out	18
	C.J. McDermott	run out	19
	R.M. Hogg		
	Extras	b 6, lb 12, w 1, nb 4	23
	(50 overs)	(for 9 wickets)	206

	O	M	R	W
Marshall	9	1	29	2
Garner	9	2	17	1
Holding	10	1	36	1
Davis	10	1	52	1
Richards	10	—	43	2
Logie	1	—	10	—
Richardson	1	—	1	—

FALL OF WICKETS
1- 14, 2- 15, 3- 21, 4- 34, 5- 115, 6- 126, 7- 163, 8- 169, 9- 206

West Indies won by 65 runs

Australian score of 226 looked to be within reach of Sri Lanka's enterprising batsmen.

The visitors were given a sound start and increased momentum was supplied by Dias, who had a splendid all-round match, and Mendis. Dias was run out in the 39th over, but Aravinda de Silva and Karnain maintained the bid for victory. Thirty runs were needed off five overs and then Karnain was yorked by Hogg. When the last over began four were needed. Ratnayake scrambled a single off the first ball and de Silva swung at the second. The ball soared over the wicket-keeper's head off the top-edge and went for six, a bizarre winning hit.

Benson and Hedges World Series

Ninth One-Day International
AUSTRALIA *v.* WEST INDIES

Australia completed a thoroughly miserable week-end in Melbourne when they were crushed by West Indies on the Sunday. It was West Indies seventh win in as many matches and left Australia level with Sri Lanka who had played a game less.

Once again the Australian catching was dreadful and Richards, Man of the Match, was dropped twice before he reached double figures and twice later in his innings. Four other chances were missed. Logie batted brightly and West Indies again moved to a formidable total.

Border shuffled his batting order in an effort to revitalise his side, Wessels dropping to number seven, but Australia were 34 for 4 after 11 overs and the issue was decided. One of those to fall in the initial onslaught was Dean Jones, recalled to the Australian side after his recent successes in the Sheffield Shield.

Benson and Hedges World Series

Tenth One-Day International
AUSTRALIA *v.* SRI LANKA

Put in to bat, Sri Lanka had a wretched start against an accurate and hostile Australian pace attack, and they slipped to 55 for 4, Wessels taking two for 2 in his first over with his gentle off-spin. It was the pace men, however, who had created the frustration. Madugalle impetuously hooked at Hogg's first ball and skied to the wicket-keeper and earlier Silva had been narrowly run out by Dean Jones.

Mendis and Aravinda de Silva, the young man who excites more promise with every innings, then added 139 in 25 overs, a truly splendid performance and a 5th wicket record for the competition.

Sri Lanka must have been well pleased with their 240 and when the recalled Smith was second out in the 8th over with the score at 29, there were signs of a Sri Lankan victory, but Wessels, whose last nine overs had cost 59 runs, made amends with a resolute innings which won him the individual award and Border reached fifty off 55 balls. Their stand realised 90 in 20 overs and was ended when Border was victim of a slick leg-side stumping by the improved Silva. Dean Jones continued the hammering of the wayward attack, however, and Australia coasted to a good victory which restored their pride.

22 January 1985

at Canberra

West Indians 284 for 8 (H.A. Gomes 91 not out, C.H. Lloyd 50)
Prime Minister's XI 269 for 7 (A.R. Border 114, P.I. Faulkner 59 not out)

West Indians won by 15 runs

TENTH ONE-DAY INTERNATIONAL – AUSTRALIA *v.* SRI LANKA
23 January 1985 at Sydney

SRI LANKA			
	S.A.R. Silva*	run out	2
	S. Wettimuny	b Wessels	21
	R.S. Madugalle	c Phillips, b Hogg	7
	R.L. Dias	c Phillips, b Wessels	19
	L.R.D. Mendis†	c Phillips, b Lawson	80
	P.A. de Silva	not out	81
	R.J. Ratnayake	b McDermott	7
	U.S.H. Karnain	not out	10
	D.S. de Silva		
	A.L.F. de Mel		
	V.B. John		
	Extras	lb 9, w 1, nb 3	13
	(50 overs)	(for 6 wickets)	240

	O	M	R	W
Lawson	10	2	32	1
McDermott	10	1	59	1
Hogg	10	2	33	1
O'Donnell	10	—	46	—
Wessels	10	—	61	2

FALL OF WICKETS
1- 3, 2- 23, 3- 54, 4- 55, 5- 194, 6- 204

AUSTRALIA			
	G.M. Wood	c R.J. Ratnayake, b de Mel	0
	S.B. Smith	c Silva, b John	4
	K.C. Wessels	c Mendis, b Karnain	82
	A.R. Border†	st Silva, b D.S. de Silva	57
	D.M.J. Jones	not out	62
	D.C. Boon	lbw, b John	3
	W.B. Phillips*	b R.J. Ratnayake	19
	S.P. O'Donnell	c Karnain, b de Mel	2
	G.F. Lawson	not out	0
	C.J. McDermott		
	R.M. Hogg		
	Extras	lb 10, w 3	13
	(47.1 overs)	(for 7 wickets)	242

	O	M	R	W
de Mel	8	—	53	2
John	10	1	35	2
D.S. de Silva	10	—	62	1
Karnain	10	—	38	1
R.J. Ratnayake	8.1	—	37	1
Dias	1	—	7	—

FALL OF WICKETS
1- 0, 2- 29, 3- 119, 4- 187, 5- 195, 6- 231, 7- 238

Australia won by 3 wickets

A fine innings by Border who shared a 7th wicket stand of 104 with Faulkner and the fiery bowling of Rod McCurdy, 3 for 36 in 10 overs, were encouraging aspects of this match for Australia. McCurdy was called to join the international squad.

23 January 1985

at Canberra

A.C.T. 212 (P. Woods 58)
West Indians 213 for 2 (D.L. Haynes 86, T.R.O. Payne 67 not out)

West Indians won by 8 wickets

John Abrahams, the Lancashire captain, was in the Territories' side.

25, 26, 27 and 28 January 1985

at Brisbane

Queensland 384 (T.J. Barsby 137, R.B. Kerr 60, R.B. Phillips 59, C.B. Smart 50, B.P. Patterson 5 for 93) and 369 for 1 (R.B. Kerr 201 not out, B.A. Courtice 135)
Tasmania 507 for 9 dec (K. Bradshaw 121, P.I. Faulkner 100, G.W. Goodman 88, R.D. Woolley 67, T.V. Hohns 4 for 129)

Match drawn
Tasmania 4 pts, Queensland 0 pts

at Melbourne

Victoria 438 (R.J. Bright 84, M.D. Taylor 77, D.F. Whatmore 63, G.N. Yallop 58, P. Young 55, R.G. Holland 4 for 111) and 236 for 4 (G.N. Yallop 125 not out, J. Siddons 68)
New South Wales 442 for 9 dec (W.J.S. Seabrook 165, J. Dyson 97, R.J. Bright 5 for 139)

Match drawn
New South Wales 4 pts, Victoria 0 pts

Trevor Barsby hit his second century in successive matches, but a maiden century by Peter Faulkner and a good innings by the reinstated Keith Bradshaw who followed his 78 and 63 against New South with his maiden century took Tasmania to a record 507 and first innings points, only the second time they had achieved that mark in 8 matches in the season. When Queensland batted again, Kerr and Courtice began with a stand of 331 in 349 minutes, only 59 runs short of the record for the competition. Kerr reached the first double century of his career.

In Melbourne, where Holland and Bright bowled 115 overs between them, there was a welcome reappearance for Dav Whatmore and an equally welcome return to full form and fitness by Yallop. The honours were stolen, however, by a twenty-three year old right-handed opener Wayne Seabrook who, in his first innings for New South Wales, hit 165 off 289 deliveries with twenty-six fours. He and John Dyson put on 265 for the first wicket.

The end of January saw Queensland leading the table with 72 points. The four points that New South Wales gained in Melbourne moved them into second place with 48, followed by South Australia with 44 and Western Australia with 42. Victoria, 14, and Tasmania, 8, had no hope of qualifying for the Final.

Benson and Hedges World Series

Eleventh One-Day International
WEST INDIES *v.* SRI LANKA

Sri Lanka's hopes of reaching the final of the competition diminished when they lost to West Indies in Adelaide, the match following a familiar pattern. Once more it was Dias and Mendis who rescued Sri Lanka after a dreadful start, and Ranatunga bolstered them to 204 with 31 off 50 deliveries. Ranatunga was deputising for the injured Aravinda de Silva.

ELEVENTH ONE-DAY INTERNATIONAL – WEST INDIES v. SRI LANKA
26 January 1985 at Adelaide

SRI LANKA			
	S.A.R. Silva*	c Garner, b Davis	5
	D.S.B.P. Kuruppu	c Dujon, b Walsh	7
	R.S. Madugalle	b Davis	1
	R.L. Dias	b Holding	66
	L.R.D. Mendis†	c Richards, b Davis	45
	A. Ranatunga	c sub (Richardson), b Holding	31
	U.S.H. Karnain	not out	20
	R.J. Ratnayake	not out	12
	A.L.F. de Mel		
	D.S. de Silva		
	G. de Silva		
	Extras	b 2, lb 9, w 2, nb 4	17
	(50 overs)	(for 6 wickets)	204

	O	M	R	W
Garner	10	2	27	—
Davis	10	5	21	3
Walsh	10	—	54	1
Holding	10	—	46	2
Richards	10	—	45	—

FALL OF WICKETS
1- 5, 2- 13, 3- 22, 4- 115, 5- 164, 6- 181

WEST INDIES			
	C.G. Greenidge	not out	110
	D.L. Haynes	b D.S. de Silva	51
	H.A. Gomes	c and b Ranatunga	24
	A.L. Logie	not out	7
	I.V.A. Richards		
	C.H. Lloyd†		
	P.J. Dujon*		
	M.A. Holding		
	J. Garner		
	W.W. Davis		
	C.A. Walsh		
	Extras	lb 4, w 1, nb 8	13
	(37.2 overs)	(for 2 wickets)	205

	O	M	R	W
de Mel	4	—	34	—
G. de Silva	8.2	1	56	—
R.J. Ratnayake	10	—	41	—
D.S. de Silva	7	—	36	1
Ranatunga	8	1	34	1

FALL OF WICKETS
1- 133, 2- 178

West Indies won by 8 wickets

The West Indies made light work of scoring the runs. Greenidge, Man of the Match, hit a fierce century and dominated an opening stand of 133 with Haynes. The Sri Lankan bowling was again a disappointment, de Mel appearing to have lost the fire and accuracy that made him a threat in the recent past.

Benson and Hedges World Series

Twelfth One-Day International
AUSTRALIA v. WEST INDIES

A devastating opening spell by Garner which won the individual award set the West Indies on course for their usual victory. Wessels ran himself out in the fourth over, Border offered no shot to Marshall and Jones played on. Phillips and Wood revived Australian morale with a stand of 81 in 14 overs, but Wood earned the wrath of the Adelaide crowd when he ran out his partner. The anger increased when he later did the same thing to Rod McCurdy who had an impressive international debut. In spite of these lapses, Wood batted as well as any Australian had done against the West Indies to finish 104 not out off 142 deliveries.

The Australian score was meagre, however, and their fielding proved to be inept as catches were spilled liberally. A crowd of nearly 31,000 began to show their displeasure and as West Indies moved to another easy win the whole proceedings seemed ludicrous. Allan Border admitted as much afterwards when he gave his personal view that he was sick of playing against the same side time and again. It was the seventeenth one-day match between the sides within the space of a year during which time they have also engaged in ten Test matches against each other. How can one take seriously a competition which demands that to find two finalists out of three teams, the sides must play each other five times, and all at the expense of the domestic competition, the Sheffield Shield?

Benson and Hedges World Series

Thirteenth One-Day International
AUSTRALIA V. SRI LANKA

Australia lost their second wicket in the 24th over with the score at 99. In the remaining 26 overs, Border and Jones added 224, a record stand for any wicket in a limited-over international. The Australian total of 323 for 2 was the highest score made in the competition. Border hit three sixes and ten fours and his 118 came off 88 balls. Jones hit three sixes and four fours in his 99 which came off 77 balls. It was a splendid way to celebrate Australia Day, but it emphasised the gap between Sri Lanka's fine batsmen and bowlers who erred in basic principles throughout the tournament.

A demoralised Sri Lankan side surrendered to an eager attack in which McCurdy was again prominent and Australia moved into the final with the biggest run margin victory in the history of limited-over internationals.

29 January 1985

at Albany

West Indians 237 for 9 (R.B. Richardson 75)
West Australian Country XI 226 for 7 (T. Waldron 72)

West Indians won by 11 runs

Against a make-shift attack, Terry Waldron hit four sixes and seven fours to win the Man of the Match award.

TWELFTH ONE-DAY INTERNATIONAL – AUSTRALIA *v.* WEST INDIES
27 January 1985 at Adelaide

AUSTRALIA		
K.C. Wessels	run out	1
G.M. Wood	not out	104
A.R. Border†	lbw, b Marshall	0
D.M.J. Jones	b Garner	11
S.B. Smith	c Dujon, b Davis	21
W.B. Phillips*	run out	36
S.P. O'Donnell	c Dujon, b Garner	9
G.F. Lawson	hit wkt, b Marshall	4
C.J. McDermott	c Logie, b Garner	2
R.J. McCurdy	run out	1
R.M. Hogg	not out	3
Extras	lb 5, nb 3	8
(50 overs)	(for 9 wickets)	200

	O	M	R	W
Garner	10	3	17	3
Marshall	10	1	35	2
Davis	10	—	53	1
Holding	10	—	51	—
Richards	10	—	39	—

FALL OF WICKETS
1- 4, 2- 4, 3- 19, 4- 72, 5- 154, 6- 167, 7- 178, 8- 181, 9- 184

WEST INDIES		
C.G. Greenidge	lbw, b McDermott	39
D.L. Haynes	b McCurdy	14
R.B. Richardson	c Smith, b McDermott	34
I.V.A. Richards	c Border, b McCurdy	51
C.H. Lloyd†	not out	47
A.L. Logie	not out	2
P.J. Dujon*		
M.D. Marshall		
M.A. Holding		
J. Garner		
W.W. Davis		
Extras	b 2, lb 8, w 1, nb 3	14
(43.4 overs)	(for 4 wickets)	201

	O	M	R	W
Lawson	9	—	32	—
McCurdy	9.4	2	38	2
McDermott	7	—	37	2
Hogg	8	—	46	—
O'Donnell	10	1	38	—

FALL OF WICKETS
1- 31, 2- 93, 3- 103, 4- 199

West Indies won by 6 wickets

THIRTEENTH ONE-DAY INTERNATIONAL – AUSTRALIA *v.* SRI LANKA
28 January 1985 at Adelaide

AUSTRALIA		
G.M. Wood	c D.S. de Silva, b Karnain	30
S.B. Smith	c Silva, b Karnain	55
D.M.J. Jones	not out	99
A.R. Border†	not out	118
K.C. Wessels		
D.C. Boon		
W.B. Phillips*		
S.P. O'Donnell		
G.F. Lawson		
R.M. Hogg		
R.J. McCurdy		
Extras	b 6, lb 8, w 3, nb 4	21
(50 overs)	(for 2 wickets)	323

	O	M	R	W
R.J. Ratnayake	10	1	51	—
John	10	1	64	—
G. de Silva	10	—	50	—
D.S. de Silva	5	—	42	—
Karnain	8	—	56	2
Ranatunga	6	—	36	—
Dias	1	—	10	—

FALL OF WICKETS
1- 94, 2- 99

SRI LANKA		
S.A.R. Silva*	lbw, b McCurdy	0
A. Ranatunga	c Phillips, b McCurdy	5
P.A. de Silva	lbw, b Lawson	6
R.L. Dias	c Smith, b Lawson	3
L.R.D. Mendis†	c Boon, b McCurdy	7
R.S. Madugalle	lbw, b O'Donnell	8
U.S.H. Karnain	c Wessels, b O'Donnell	21
R.J. Ratnayake	c Jones, b Hogg	2
D.S. de Silva	st Phillips, b Wessels	7
V.B. John	c Hogg, b Wessels	8
G. de Silva	not out	15
Extras	b 1, lb 5, w 3	9
(33.5 overs)		91

	O	M	R	W
Lawson	7	5	5	2
McCurdy	5	1	19	3
Hogg	8	1	18	1
O'Donnell	9	1	19	2
Wessels	4.5	—	16	2
Boon	2	—	8	—

FALL OF WICKETS
1- 3, 2- 12, 3- 14, 4- 23, 5- 25, 6- 45, 7- 52, 8- 66, 9- 75

Australia won by 232 runs

30 and 31 January 1985

at Perth (Stevens Reserve)

Western Australian Colts 225 for 4 dec (P. Gonnella 100 not out) and 166 for 5 dec (R. Gartrell 52)

Sri Lankans 190 for 7 dec and 192 for 8 (L.R.D. Mendis 50, B. Mulder 4 for 74)

Match drawn

Mendis hit 50 off 23 balls in an effort to win the game.

FOURTEENTH ONE-DAY INTERNATIONAL – WEST INDIES *v.* SRI LANKA
2 February 1985 at Perth

WEST INDIES

C.G. Greenidge	b R.J. Ratnayake	42
D.L. Haynes	c Silva, b John	27
H.A. Gomes	c Dias, b de Mel	101
I.V.A. Richards	b John	46
A.L. Logie	run out	6
C.H. Lloyd†	not out	54
P.J. Dujon*	c P.A. de Silva, b de Mel	13
M.D. Marshall	not out	2
J. Garner		
W.W. Davis		
C.A. Walsh		
Extras	lb 10, w 6, nb 2	18
(50 overs)	(for 6 wickets)	309

	O	M	R	W
de Mel	10	—	67	2
John	10	—	44	2
R.J. Ratnayake	10	—	58	1
J.R. Ratnayeke	10	—	48	—
Karnain	6	—	35	—
Ranatunga	3	—	39	—
Dias	1	—	8	—

FALL OF WICKETS
1- 47, 2- 99, 3- 216, 4- 223, 5- 241, 6- 280

SRI LANKA

S. Wettimuny	run out	0
S.A.R. Silva*	c Dujon, b Walsh	85
J.R. Ratnayeke	b Richards	24
R.L. Dias	run out	1
L.R.D. Mendis†	c Dujon, b Walsh	8
P.A. de Silva	c Dujon, b Richards	5
A. Ranatunga	not out	63
U.S.H. Karnain	not out	28
R.J. Ratnayake		
A.L.F. de Mel		
V.B. John		
Extras	lb 6, w 5, nb 2	13
(50 overs)	(for 6 wickets)	227

	O	M	R	W
Garner	6	3	6	—
Davis	6	1	34	—
Marshall	6	—	17	—
Walsh	10	—	52	2
Richards	10	—	47	2
Gomes	7	—	41	—
Haynes	5	—	24	—

FALL OF WICKETS
1- 0, 2- 100, 3- 102, 4- 120, 5- 133, 6- 137

West Indies won by 82 runs

FIFTEENTH ONE-DAY INTERNATIONAL – AUSTRALIA *v.* SRI LANKA
3 February 1985 at Perth

SRI LANKA

S.A.R. Silva*	c Phillips, b O'Donnell	51
M.D. Vonhagt	c Wessels, b Alderman	8
L.R.D. Mendis†	c Wood, b Lawson	2
R.L. Dias	c Alderman, b Lawson	4
P.A. de Silva	st Phillips, b Wessels	52
A. Ranatunga	c Phillips, b Hogg	10
U.S.H. Karnain	c Border, b Hogg	8
J.R. Ratnayeke	run out	1
R.J. Ratnayake	c Phillips, b O'Donnell	16
A.L.F. de Mel	not out	11
V.B. John	b McCurdy	0
Extras	lb 2, w 5, nb 1	8
(44.3 overs)		271

	O	M	R	W
Lawson	7	1	24	2
Alderman	10	—	41	1
McCurdy	5.3	—	15	1
O'Donnell	10	—	42	2
Hogg	10	1	40	2
Wessels	2	—	7	1

FALL OF WICKETS
1- 16, 2- 19, 3- 26, 4- 94, 5- 110, 6- 123, 7- 126, 8- 147, 9- 166

AUSTRALIA

S.B. Smith	not out	73
K.C. Wessels	c Silva, b John	8
W.B. Phillips*	not out	75
A.R. Border†		
G.M. Wood		
D.M.J. Jones		
S.P. O'Donnell		
G.F. Lawson		
R.J. McCurdy		
R.M. Hogg		
T.M. Alderman		
Extras	lb 8, w 6, nb 2	16
(23.5 overs)	(for 1 wicket)	172

	O	M	R	W
de Mel	8	—	45	—
John	6.5	—	43	1
R.J. Ratnayake	5	—	40	—
J.R. Ratnayeke	4	—	36	—

FALL OF WICKET
1- 15

Australia won by 9 wickets

Benson and Hedges World Series

Fourteenth One-Day International
WEST INDIES *v.* SRI LANKA

The West Indians completed a hundred percent record in the qualifying competition with their tenth win. Larry Gomes hit 101 in 130 minutes, his first century in a limited-over international, with three sixes and six fours. Once again the Sri Lankan bowling was moderate and, sadly, their fielding was well below standard. Clive Lloyd benefited from poor fielding when he hit 54 off 29 deliveries.

Sri Lanka began disastrously when Wettimuny, who had had an unhappy series, was run out without a run scored, but Silva hit 85 off 96 balls and shared a century stand with Ravi Ratnayeke for the second wicket. There was some spirited hitting from Ranatunga at the close, but the issue had long since been decided before he and Karnain added 90.

Benson and Hedges World Series

Fifteenth One-Day International
AUSTRALIA *v.* SRI LANKA

The Sri Lankans completed a miserable week-end in Perth and disappointing series when they were totally outplayed by Australia in the last of the qualifying matches. Silva and Aravinda de Silva were the only batsmen to show any substance in a poor display, but it was the Sri Lankan out-cricket which was of the poorest quality. They gained an early breakthrough when John had Wessels caught behind, but thereafter bowling and fielding wilted as Steve Smith and Wayne Phillips added 157 in 93 minutes and Australia raced to victory with 26.1 overs to spare.

Benson and Hedges World Series Qualifying Table

	P	*W*	*L*	*Pts*
West Indies	10	10	–	20
Australia	10	4	6	8
Sri Lanka	10	1	9	2

Benson and Hedges World Series

First Final
AUSTRALIA *v.* WEST INDIES

Having carried all before them throughout the tournament, the West Indians found themselves one down in the three-leg final after losing by 26 runs to Australia before a crowd of 29,568 in Sydney.

There seemed no possibility of an Australian victory when, following a familiar pattern, Garner dismissed Smith and Wood in his first two overs, and Wessels and Jones were out in the 17th and 18th overs of the innings with the score at 58 and 64. Australia were lifted by a brilliant innings from Allan Border who came in in the third over at 7 for 2 and stayed to the end to finish on 127 not out. Although he should have been run out by Richards when he was on 66, Border was in total command, driving and cutting with power and fluency. He and Phillips added 105 in 21 overs, Phillips' 50 coming off 71 balls. O'Donnell and Lawson helped Border to add 68 in the last ten overs and with the help of some wayward bowling from Davis and Richards, Australia had moved to a commendable 247.

West Indies were without the injured Greenidge and they began disastrously. Haynes took 10 from Lawson's first over, but Richardson was lbw to McCurdy when he played back in the second over. Haynes swung at Lawson and was bowled. Gomes also played back to McCurdy and was lbw and West Indies were 20 for 3.

At 82, Lloyd was caught when he attempted to square cut McDermott. Logie and Dujon failed to make the required impact and Richards, having hit 68 off 88 balls, was bowled as he made room to square-cut. After Holding had been bowled with West Indies still 100 short of Australia's total it seemed that the local heroes would win easily, but Garner and Marshall, who had to call for a runner after slipping, put

FIRST BENSON AND HEDGES WORLD SERIES FINAL – AUSTRALIA *v.* WEST INDIES
6 February 1985 at Sydney

AUSTRALIA			
S.B. Smith	c Richardson, b Garner	6	
G.M. Wood	c Richards, b Garner	0	
K.C. Wessels	c Dujon, b Marshall	11	
A.R. Border†	not out	127	
D.M.J. Jones	b Davis	3	
W.B. Phillips*	c Garner, b Holding	50	
S.P. O'Donnell	lbw, b Garner	17	
G.F. Lawson	not out	14	
C.J. McDermott			
R.J. McCurdy			
R.M. Hogg			
Extras	b 2, lb 6, nb 11	19	
(50 overs)	(for 6 wickets)	247	

	O	M	R	W
Garner	10	3	29	3
Holding	10	—	40	1
Marshall	10	1	55	1
Davis	10	—	57	1
Richards	10	—	58	—

FALL OF WICKETS
1- 2, 2- 7, 3- 58, 4- 64, 5- 169, 6- 205

WEST INDIES		
D.L. Haynes	b Lawson	11
R.B. Richardson	lbw, b McCurdy	0
H.A. Gomes	lbw, b McCurdy	9
I.V.A. Richards	b McDermott	68
C.H. Lloyd†	c Wessels, b McDermott	20
A.L. Logie	c Wood, b Hogg	12
P.J. Dujon*	b McDermott	14
M.D. Marshall	b McCurdy	43
M.A. Holding	b O'Donnell	1
J. Garner	run out	27
W.W. Davis	not out	8
Extras	lb 7, nb 1	8
(47.3 overs)		221

	O	M	R	W
Lawson	9	1	41	1
McCurdy	9.3	1	40	3
Hogg	10	—	35	1
McDermott	10	—	44	3
O'Donnell	9	—	54	1

FALL OF WICKETS
1- 10, 2- 20, 3- 20, 4- 82, 5- 107, 6- 137, 7- 140, 8- 147, 9- 210

Australia won by 26 runs

SECOND BENSON AND HEDGES WORLD SERIES FINAL – AUSTRALIA *v.* WEST INDIES
10 February 1985 at Melbourne

AUSTRALIA

S.B. Smith	b Davis	54
G.M. Wood	c Richards, b Holding	81
A.R. Border†	c Dujon, b Marshall	39
W.B. Phillips*	not out	56
D.M.J. Jones	not out	13
K.C. Wessels		
S.P. O'Donnell		
G.F. Lawson		
R.J. McCurdy		
C.J. McDermott		
R.M. Hogg		
Extras	b 2, lb 10, w 7, nb 9	28
(50 overs)	(for 3 wickets)	271

	O	M	R	W
Garner	10	1	60	—
Marshall	10	—	64	1
Holding	10	1	41	1
Davis	10	—	43	1
Richards	10	—	51	—

FALL OF WICKETS
1- 135, 2- 186, 3- 203

WEST INDIES

D.L. Haynes	c Wessels, b Hogg	44
R.B. Richardson	c Wessels, b O'Donnell	50
H.A. Gomes	b O'Donnell	47
I.V.A. Richards	lbw, b Lawson	9
C.H. Lloyd†	c O'Donnell, b Lawson	13
A.L. Logie	b McCurdy	60
P.J. Dujon	not out	39
M.D. Marshall	not out	0
M.A. Holding		
J. Garner		
W.W. Davis		
Extras	b 2, lb 8, nb 1	11
(49.2 overs)	(for 6 wickets)	273

	O	M	R	W
Lawson	10	—	34	2
McCurdy	10	—	69	1
McDermott	10	—	56	—
Hogg	9.2	—	58	1
O'Donnell	10	—	46	2

FALL OF WICKETS
1- 78, 2- 137, 3- 154, 4- 158, 5- 179, 6- 265

West Indies won by 4 wickets

on 63 in 10 overs and made a West Indian victory possible.

Marshall was bowled swinging at a full toss, however, and Garner was run out to give Australia victory by 26 runs.

Benson and Hedges World Series

Second Final
AUSTRALIA *v.* WEST INDIES

Lloyd won the toss and asked Australia to bat. Smith and Wood took full advantage of batting first on a perfect wicket and rarely can Marshall and Garner have been treated with such contempt. The Australian openers put on 135 in 30 overs and so gave their side the necessary firm and briskly achieved foundation for a big total.

Smith was the first to leave and Wood, looking more assured in the later stages of this competition, was caught by Richards, not at his best in the field, in the 40th over. Border maintained the quick scoring that the openers had heralded with a lusty 39 off 48 balls, and Wayne Phillips, much at ease in the limited-over game, hit 56 off 37 balls. Phillips' innings included 15 off the last over, bowled by Joel Garner, an over which also produced a leg-bye. Australia were proudly satisfied with their 271 which looked to be a winning score.

The West Indies had looked jaded in the field, but there was nothing tired about the batting of openers Haynes and Richardson who hit 78 in 15.1 overs before Haynes fell to Hogg. In McCurdy's fifth over Haynes had hit four boundaries, a revenge for the restrictions that Lawson had imposed.

Richardson and Gomes took the score to 137 in the next 12 overs, but the game then swung totally in favour of Australia as 4 wickets fell for 42 runs in 9.4 overs to make West Indies 179 for 5 in 36.5 overs and only Logie and Dujon of the recognised batsmen remaining.

Gus Logie played an explosive innings which snatched a marvellous victory for the West Indies. From 56 deliveries he hit 60 runs and he and Dujon savaged 77 runs off 9.2 overs from Hogg and McCurdy. Logie was badly dropped by McDermott and more excusably by Lawson, but he was finally bowled by McCurdy. West Indies needed only 7 for victory with one over left. The complete over was not needed. Dujon drove the first two balls of Hogg's over through the covers for fours with majestic ease and West Indies had won a great victory.

Benson and Hedges World Series

Third Final
AUSTRALIA *v.* WEST INDIES

The Australians began at a disadvantage. Smith was unable to play because he had broken a finger when fielding in the second final and his replacement, Kim Hughes, sprained an ankle jogging so that Kerr was brought in to a side which was very dejected after the stunning defeat that West Indies had inflicted upon them at Melbourne.

There were further troubles for Australia who were put in and were doing reasonably well until Wood had his left forefinger broken by a lifting ball from Davis in the 13th over with the score on 37. Twenty overs later Australia were 89 for 7 and the game was as good as over. The damage had been done by Michael Holding who took 5 for 9 in 34 balls. It was more Holding's deceptive movement that disturbed the batsmen than his sheer pace. He was also indebted to one outstanding catch by Garner who flung himself to his considerable full length in the covers to hold a drive from Border one-handed.

O'Donnell, whose batting had been unimpressive in the series, restored Australia's pride with a sturdy 69. In 16.1

THIRD BENSON AND HEDGES WORLD SERIES FINAL – AUSTRALIA *v.* WEST INDIES
12 February 1985 at Sydney

AUSTRALIA			
	G.M. Wood	not out	36
	K.C. Wessels	c Richards, b Holding	17
	R.B. Kerr	c Logie, b Davis	4
	A.R. Border†	c Garner, b Holding	4
	D.M.J. Jones	b Richards	16
	W.B. Phillips*	c Dujon, b Holding	3
	S.P. O'Donnell	c and b Garner	69
	G.F. Lawson	c Richards, b Holding	4
	C.J. McDermott	c Dujon, b Holding	0
	R.J. McCurdy	run out	12
	R.M. Hogg	c Richards, b Garner	1
	Extras	b 2, lb 4, w 4, nb 2	12
	(50 overs)		178

	O	M	R	W
Garner	10	–	34	2
Marshall	10	1	37	—
Davis	10	1	23	1
Holding	10	1	26	5
Richards	10	—	52	1

FALL OF WICKETS
1- 47, 2- 51, 3- 57, 4- 64, 5- 80, 6- 89, 7- 89, 8- 125, 9- 176

WEST INDIES			
	D.L. Haynes	not out	76
	R.B. Richardson	run out	3
	H.A. Gomes	c Border, b McDermott	3
	I.V.A. Richards	c sub, b McDermott	76
	A.L. Logie	not out	11
	C.H. Lloyd†		
	P.J. Dujon*		
	M.D. Marshall		
	M.A. Holding		
	J. Garner		
	W.W. Davis		
	Extras	b 4, lb 2, nb 4	10
	(47 overs)	(for 3 wickets)	179

	O	M	R	W
Lawson	10	1	22	—
McCurdy	10	2	31	—
McDermott	10	2	36	2
Hogg	9	—	42	—
O'Donnell	8	—	42	—

FALL OF WICKETS
1- 14, 2- 34, 3- 161

West Indies won by 7 wickets

overs, first with McCurdy and then with the courageous Wood, he saw the score increase by 87.

The Australian total never seemed likely to trouble the West Indians, but there were moments of hope when Richardson was run out and Gomes fell cheaply. Once more, however, the Australians failed to accept the chances that were offered to them. It was estimated that they dropped forty catches in the Tests and one-day internationals against the West Indies. Richards, who had had a miserable match in Melbourne and had been booed as he walked to the wicket there, refound his touch and shared a blistering stand of 127 in 29.2 overs with Haynes.

The rest was easy for Haynes and Logie and West Indies won the arduous and over-long competition for the fourth time in four appearances.

6 February 1985

at Maryborough

Sri Lankans 318 for 8 (R.S. Madugalle 71, L.R.D. Mendis 71, D.S.B.P. Kuruppu 72)
Victorian Country XI 205
Sri Lankans won by 113 runs

8 February 1985

at Shepperton

Sri Lankans 279 for 8 (S.A.R. Silva 105, R.S. Madugalle 80)
Victorian Country XI 179
Sri Lankans won by 100 runs

Benson and Hedges World Series – Averages

SRI LANKA BATTING

	M	Inns	NOs	Runs	HS	Av	100s	50s
U.S.H. Karnain	9	9	5	173	41*	43.25		
R.L. Dias	10	10	1	373	80	41.44		4
A. Ranatunga	4	4	1	109	63*	36.33		1
P.A. de Silva	9	9	2	249	81*	35.57		2
L.R.D. Mendis	10	10		265	80	26.50		2
S.A.R. Silva	10	10		263	85	26.30		3
R.J. Ratnayake	10	8	4	88	23*	22.00		
J.R. Ratnayeke	5	5	1	58	24	14.50		
R.S. Madugalle	5	5		65	25	13.00		
S. Wettimuny	6	6		68	21	11.33		
A.L.F. de Mel	7	2	1	11	11*	11.00		
D.S.B.P. Kuruppa	4	4		41	22	10.25		
D.S. de Silva	8	2		16	9	8.00		
V.B. John	9	3		8	8	2.66		

Played in three matches: G. de Silva 2* and 15*
Played in one match: M.D. Vonhagt 8

SRI LANKA BOWLING

	Overs	Mds	Runs	Wkts	Av	Best
R.L. Dias	9	–	69	3	23.00	3/25
A.L.F. de Mel	56.3	2	353	7	50.42	2/53
U.S.H. Karnain	58	1	304	6	50.66	2/55
R.J. Ratnayake	89	4	424	8	53.00	4/37
V.B. John	82.3	8	393	7	56.14	2/35
D.S. de Silva	70	5	339	6	56.50	1/29
A. Ranatunga	17	1	109	1	109.00	1/34
J.R. Ratnayeke	33	–	213	1	213.00	1/69
G. de Silva	28.2	1	148	0	—	

Also bowled: P.A. de Silva 2–0–15–0

SRI LANKA CATCHES

12–S.A.R. Silva (ct 10/st 2); 2–L.R.D. Mendis, P.A. de Silva and R.S. Madugalle; 1–S. Wettimuny, D.S.B.P. Kuruppu, R.L. Dias, A.L.F. de Mel, R.J. Ratnayake, D.S. de Silva, V.B. John, U.S.H. Karnain, A. Ranatunga and sub

Benson and Hedges World Series – Averages

AUSTRALIA BATTING

	M	Inns	NOs	Runs	HS	Av	100s	50s
A.R. Border	13	12	3	590	127*	65.55	2	4
D.M.J. Jones	8	7	3	204	99*	51.00		2
G.M. Wood	13	12	3	413	104*	45.88	1	2
S.B. Smith	6	6	1	213	73*	42.60		3
W.B. Phillips	11	10	2	336	75*	42.00		4
K.C. Wessels	13	11		312	82	28.36		2
D.C. Boon	8	7		194	55	27.71		1
G.M. Ritchie	3	3	1	49	30*	24.50		
S.P. O'Donnell	13	10	2	184	69	23.00		1
A.M.J. Hilditch	3	3		69	27	23.00		
G.F. Lawson	12	8	4	66	18*	16.50		
R.M. Hogg	12	4	3	15	6*	15.00		
M.J. Bennett	5	2	1	9	6*	9.00		
C.J. McDermott	11	5		34	19	6.80		
R.J. McCurdy	6	2		13	12	6.50		
S.J. Rixon	2	2	1	5	3	5.00		

Played in one match: R.B. Kerr 4; C.G. Rackemann, R.G. Holland and T.M. Alderman did not bat

WEST INDIES BATTING

	M	Inns	NOs	Runs	HS	Av	100s	50s
C.H. Lloyd	11	8	4	329	89*	82.25		3
I.V.A. Richards	13	11	1	651	103*	65.10	1	5
C.G. Greenidge	7	7	1	364	110*	60.66	1	2
D.L. Haynes	12	12	2	514	123*	51.40	1	3
M.D. Marshall	12	5	4	48	43	48.00		
A.L. Logie	12	12	5	280	72	40.00		2
R.B. Richardson	11	11	2	277	57*	30.77		3
P.J. Dujon	13	7	3	121	39*	30.25		
H.A. Gomes	10	9	1	214	101	26.75	1	
M.A. Holding	12	2	1	3	2*	3.00		

Also played: J. Garner 27 (12 matches); T.R.O. Payne 20; W.W. Davis 8* (11 matches); E.A.E. Baptiste, C.A. Walsh (4 matches) and R.A. Harper did not bat

AUSTRALIA BOWLING

	Overs	Mds	Runs	Wkts	Av	Best
R.J. McCurdy	49.4	6	212	10	21.20	3/19
K.C. Wessels	27.5	—	166	6	27.66	2/16
C.J. McDermott	103.1	6	482	15	32.13	3/30
R.M. Hogg	110.2	7	490	15	32.66	4/47
G.F. Lawson	112	12	400	12	33.33	2/5
S.P. O'Donnell	114.3	5	523	14	37.35	2/19
M.J. Bennett	38	4	176	2	88.00	1/23

Also bowled: A.R. Border 4–0–34–0; D.C. Boon 2.4–0–13–0; R.G. Holland 10–0–50–0; C.G. Rackemann 10–0–50–1; T.M. Alderman 10–0–41–1

WEST INDIES BOWLING

	Overs	Mds	Runs	Wkts	Av	Best
J. Garner	110	21	341	16	21.31	3/17
M.A. Holding	120	8	443	16	27.68	5/26
W.W. Davis	106	10	432	13	33.23	3/21
I.V.A. Richards	120	3	543	13	41.76	3/38
M.D. Marshall	110	10	428	10	42.80	2/29
C.A. Walsh	40	2	198	4	49.50	2/52
H.A. Gomes	16	—	92	1	92.00	1/42

Also bowled: E.A.E. Baptiste 9–0–73–1; C.H. Lloyd 0.1–0–0–1; R.A. Harper 10–0–31–1; A.L. Logie 1–0–10–0; R.B. Richardson 1–0–1–0; D.L. Haynes 5–0–24–0

AUSTRALIA CATCHES

14–W.B. Phillips (ct 12/st 2); 7–A.R. Border and K.C. Wessels; 3–D.C. Boon, R.M. Hogg, S.J. Rixon, G.M. Wood and S.P. O'Donnell; 2–S.B. Smith; 1–M.J. Bennett, D.M.J. Jones, T.M. Alderman and sub

WEST INDIES CATCHES

23–P.J. Dujon (ct 20/st 3); 8–I.V.A. Richards; 5–A.L. Logie; 4–J. Garner; 3–C.G. Greenidge and M.A. Holding; 2–R.B. Richardson and sub; 1–D.L. Haynes, E.A.E. Baptiste, H.A. Gomes and T.R.O. Payne

14 February 1985

at Sydney

England XI 149 for 8
Sydney Metropolitan XI 145 for 9 (P. Clark 55)

England XI won by 4 runs

In their warm-up for the World Championship of Cricket, the England XI gave a very disappointing display.

McDonald's Cup Final
NEW SOUTH WALES *v.* SOUTH AUSTRALIA

The domestic limited-over competition once more suffered a set-back when its final was scheduled for the eve of the World Championship of Cricket and played the day before Australia met England. Both sides were deprived of leading players who were on international duty and what should have been a grand occasion was relegated to a minor supporting role in a heavily congested season.

After losing Seabrook at 12, New South Wales completely dominated the game. Wellham hit a brisk fifty and Dyson and Clifford added 130 for the third wicket. Imran Khan hit ferociously and the New South Wales total of 278 always looked too formidable for South Australia who lost wickets steadily.

Dirk Wellham was named Man of the Match.

Benson and Hedges World Championship of Cricket

First One-Day International
AUSTRALIA *v.* ENGLAND

'The Greatest Show on Turf', as it was called by the Australian media, arranged to celebrate the 150th anniversary of the founding of the state of Victoria began with a day–night match between the oldest adversaries in the competition. England perplexed many by their team selection. Pocock and French had returned to England after the tour of India and of the fourteen remaining players, Foster, Moxon and Robinson were omitted. The selection of Agnew ahead of Foster and the selection of Cowdrey ahead of anybody was as hard to understand as it was to defend. Agnew's qualities are not ones of economy and Cowdrey is floundering at international level.

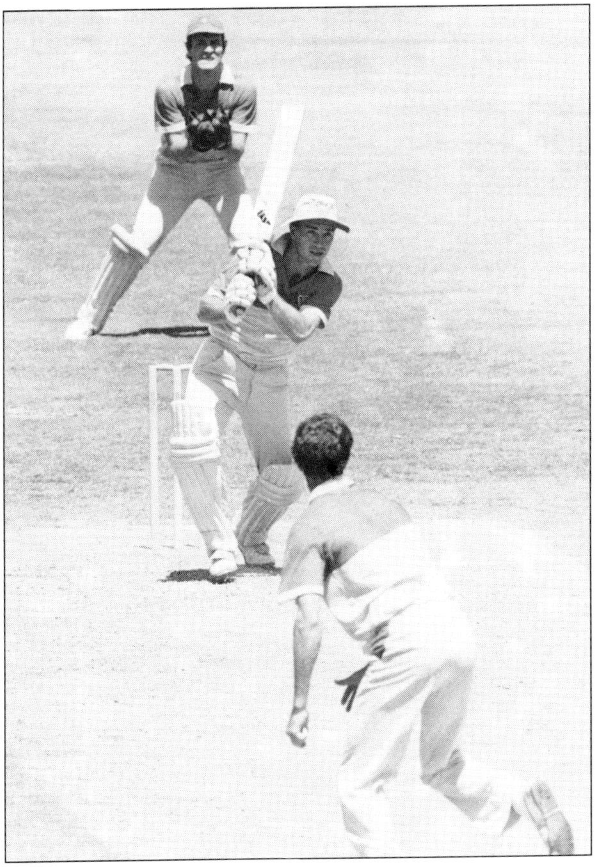

The McDonald's Cup Final. Greg Matthews hits out and New South Wales move to a formidable score. Kelly is behind the stumps. (Adrian Murrell)

Gower won the toss and England batted. The phlegmatic Downton acquitted himself well. He looked safe and his scoring rate was only marginally slower than Fowler's. They gave England a sound start with 61 in 17 overs, but then three wickets fell quickly. Fowler hit the ball firmly back to McDermott. Downton scooped a short ball to long leg and Gower lazily pulled the ball into the hands of mid-wicket.

Lamb and Gatting now gave the innings the substance and impetus that had been hoped for. In 15 overs of assured batting they added 82. A big England total looked most probable and then once more three wickets fell quickly and the innings fell apart.

Lamb pulled the ball high to mid-wicket where Kerr raced round the boundary to take a splendid catch. Cowdrey, playing across the line, his feet in a tangle, was lbw first ball. Gatting, so positive in his approach but strangely subdued in his stroke play, hit O'Donnell firmly into the hands of short mid-wicket. The Australian fielding had not been good and chances, one straightforward one at slip off Fowler, had been missed, but their bowling, generally below top pace, was accurate.

Marks and, in particular, Edmonds tried to hustle the score along, but the final score was now doomed to be a moderate one.

Cowans and Agnew provided Wessels with the ideal width

McDONALD'S CUP FINAL – NEW SOUTH WALES *v.* SOUTH AUSTRALIA
16 February 1985 at Sydney

NEW SOUTH WALES

J. Dyson	c Kelly, b Hilditch	79
W.J.S. Seabrook	c Kelly, b Carmichael	5
D.M. Wellham†	c Kelly, b Prior	51
P.S. Clifford	b Carmichael	69
Imran Khan	c Hookes, b Prior	36
G.R.J. Matthews	run out	10
G.C. Dyer*	c O'Connor, b Prior	4
T.M. Chappell	not out	8
P.H. Marks	not out	7
M.J. Bennett		
D.R. Gilbert		
Extras	b 6, w 2, nb 1	9
(50 overs)	(for 7 wickets)	278

	O	M	R	W
Brinsley	3	—	15	—
Carmichael	10	—	57	2
Hookes	3	—	23	—
Hilditch	10	—	51	1
Prior	10	—	53	3
Johnston	10	1	47	—
Wundke	4	—	26	—

FALL OF WICKETS
1- 12, 2- 75, 3- 205, 4- 220, 5- 234, 6- 248, 7- 264

SOUTH AUSTRALIA

A.M.J. Hilditch	b Matthews	33
G.A. Bishop	c Dyer, b Gilbert	10
D.W. Hookes†	c Clifford, b Chappell	16
M.D. Haysman	b Gilbert	44
D.F. O'Connor	c Marks, b Matthews	3
S. Wundke	c Marks, b Imran	31
P. Brinsley	st Dyer, b Matthews	1
D.J. Kelly*	c Clifford, b Marks	30
D.A.H. Johnston	run out	1
I.R. Carmichael	not out	6
W. Prior	b Marks	0
Extras	b 5, lb 6, w 4	15
(45.5 overs)		190

	O	M	R	W
Imran Khan	7	—	20	1
Gilbert	8	—	34	2
Marks	7.5	1	30	2
Chappell	6	—	28	1
Matthews	9	1	29	3
Bennett	8	—	38	—

FALL OF WICKETS
1- 20, 2- 45, 3- 74, 4- 80, 5- 135, 6- 140, 7- 166, 8- 167, 9- 189

New South Wales won by 88 runs

FIRST ONE-DAY INTERNATIONAL – AUSTRALIA *v.* ENGLAND
17 February 1985 at Melbourne

ENGLAND		
G. Fowler	c and b McDermott	26
P.R. Downton*	c McCurdy, b McDermott	27
D.I. Gower†	c Alderman, b McCurdy	6
A.J. Lamb	c Kerr, b Lawson	53
M.W. Gatting	c Alderman, b O'Donnell	34
C.S. Cowdrey	lbw, b McDermott	0
V.J. Marks	b Lawson	24
P.H. Edmonds	b Lawson	20
R.M. Ellison	not out	2
J.P. Agnew	not out	2
N.G. Cowans		
Extras	b 3, lb 12, nb 5	20
(49 overs)	(for 8 wickets)	214

	O	M	R	W
Lawson	10	3	31	3
Alderman	10	—	48	—
McDermott	10	—	39	3
McCurdy	10	1	42	1
O'Donnell	9	—	39	1

FALL OF WICKETS
1- 61, 2- 66, 3- 77, 4- 159, 5- 159, 6- 166, 7- 200, 8- 211

AUSTRALIA		
K.C. Wessels	c Gatting, b Ellison	39
R.B. Kerr	not out	87
K.J. Hughes	run out	0
A.R. Border†	c Cowans, b Marks	1
D.M.J. Jones	not out	78
W.B. Phillips*		
S.P. O'Donnell		
G.F. Lawson		
C.J. McDermott		
R.J. McCurdy		
T.M. Alderman		
Extras	b 1, lb 3, nb 6	10
(45.2 overs)	(for 3 wickets)	215

	O	M	R	W
Cowans	10	—	52	—
Ellison	10	4	34	1
Agnew	8	—	59	—
Marks	7.2	—	33	1
Edmonds	10	—	33	—

FALL OF WICKETS
1- 57, 2- 57, 3- 58

Australia won by 7 wickets

to employ his favourite cut and in 14 overs he raced to 39 out of 57. Ellison gave him greater problems of line and length and in attempting another cut, he was superbly caught at slip by Gatting, diving to his left and holding the ball one-handed.

The Australians had lost Smith out of their party through injury and with Wood and Hogg also injured, the party of fourteen was reduced to twelve, and it was Faulkner who was named as twelfth man. Kim Hughes came in and was cheered all the way to the wicket, but his nightmare continued. He drove Ellison to the off and ran. There was stop and start and he was run out by half the length of the pitch for 0. Border swept at Marks' first ball and gave Cowans an easy catch at deep square-leg. When Jones joined Kerr Australia were 58 for 3.

The two young batsmen took a little time to adjust to the situation, but confidence grew with every over. Kerr's quickness of reflex and presence of mind was illustrated when he chopped down on a ball which was bounding towards his stumps until he kicked it away.

Edmonds alone of the bowlers maintained a consistent length, for Ellison, after a very good beginning, erred, as did Marks. Marks conceded 12 runs in an over and Cowans, who replaced him, conceded 9. When Agnew returned Jones hit him massively for 16 in an over. The contest had now been decided and the two eager young players rushed Australia to victory with an unbroken partnership of 157 which brought them to their target with 22 balls to spare.

Jones' 78 came off 94 balls, but Kerr, rightly, was named Man of the Match, having survived the storm and taken a fine catch. 82,494 people watched the game. Australia rejoiced. England reflected on strange selections and on opposition which had a little more substance than they had met in India.

Benson and Hedges World Championship of Cricket

Second One-Day International
INDIA *v.* PAKISTAN

Since their triumph in the World Cup at Lord's in 1983 India's successes had been very limited, but they played some of their best cricket for a considerable number of matches to beat Pakistan convincingly.

Pakistan welcomed the return of Imran Khan and batted when they won the toss. There was a missed catch by Viswanath, but he held Mohsin off Binny at 8 and thereafter the Indian fielding was excellent in every department. The bowling was commendably accurate and the Pakistani batsmen could never begin to accelerate. Madan Lal produced a spell which made all wonder why he had not appeared in the series against England, so restricting and troubling to the batsmen was he. Gavaskar introduced the leg-spin of Sivaramakrishnan in the 18th over and this was the testing time for India and for the outstanding young bowler.

Sivaramakrishnan's first three overs cost 19 runs, but in his fourth over he caught and bowled Zaheer and in his eighth he accounted for Qasim Umar in the same manner. Ultimately the leg-spinner's spell was a testing and crucial one. He was well supported by Shastri who allowed no frivolities with his unerring length and low trajectory.

The Pakistan innings could still gain no momentum. Mudassar was run out by Kapil Dev's fine throw from deep third man. Imran skied to mid-off and Rashid was well caught by Amarnath at long-on. Binny bowled tidily and Pakistan's 183 looked moderate.

It became more formidable when Imran, relishing the return to international cricket and bowling with his old fire if not his old pace, had Shastri taken at slip in the first over. Srikkanth fell the same way and Vengsarkar was caught in the gully first ball, a fine catch by Mudassar.

The World Championship of Cricket begins. Prime Minister Bob Hawke talks to Allan Border and David Gower before the toss is made. (Adrian Murrell)

Azharuddin came in at the fall of the first wicket to withstand Imran's early onslaught. He, too, was on trial. The glories of his Test debut against England were being measured against different opposition. Again he triumphed. In a

SECOND ONE-DAY INTERNATIONAL – INDIA *v.* PAKISTAN
20 February 1985 at Melbourne

PAKISTAN

Mohsin Khan	c Viswanath, b Binny	3
Qasim Umar	c and b Sivaramakrishnan	57
Zaheer Abbas	c and b Sivaramakrishnan	25
Javed Miandad†	c Sivaramakrishnan, b Binny	17
Rameez Raja	c Shastri, b Kapil Dev	29
Imran Khan	c Madan Lal, b Kapil Dev	14
Mudassar Nazar	run out	6
Tahir Naqqash	c Amarnath, b Madan Lal	0
Rashid Khan	c Shastri, b Binny	17
Anil Dalpat*	c Kapil Dev, b Binny	9
Wasim Akram	not out	0
Extras	lb 3, w 2, nb 10	6
(49.2 overs)		183

	O	M	R	W
Kapil Dev	9	1	31	2
Binny	8.2	3	35	4
Madan Lal	9	2	27	1
Amarnath	3	—	11	—
Sivaramakrishnan	10	—	49	2
Shastri	10	1	27	—

FALL OF WICKETS
1- 8, 2- 73, 3- 98, 4- 119, 5- 144, 6- 151, 7- 158, 8- 156, 9- 183

INDIA

R.J. Shastri	c Javed, b Imran	2
K. Srikkanth	c Mohsin, b Imran	12
M. Azharuddin	not out	93
D.B. Vengsarkar	c Mudassar, b Imran	0
S.M. Gavaskar†	lbw, b Mudassar	54
M.B. Amarnath	not out	11
R.N. Kapil Dev		
R.M.H. Binny		
U.S. Madan Lal		
S. Viswanath*		
L. Sivaramakrishnan		
Extras	lb 9, w 3	12
(45.5 overs)	(for 4 wickets)	184

	O	M	R	W
Imran Khan	10	1	27	3
Wasim Akram	8.5	—	38	—
Rashid Khan	7	—	38	—
Tahir Naqqash	10	—	34	—
Mudassar Nazar	10	—	38	1

FALL OF WICKETS
1- 2, 2- 27, 3- 27, 4- 159

India won by 6 wickets

stand of quality, he and Gavaskar added 132. He paced his innings to the needs of his side, beginning with solidity and ending by whipping the ball away on both sides of the wicket. His captain, too, was at his best until lbw to Mudassar, but by then victory was assured and was accomplished with 25 balls and 6 wickets to spare.

The attendance was 6,956 as opposed to the crowd of above 80,000 which had watched England and Australia in the first game. It was a figure on which to ponder.

16 February 1985

at Hastings

Sri Lankans 327 for 9 (S.A.R. Silva 100, A. Ranatunga 61, J.R. Ratnayeke 59, R.S. Madugalle 56, L. Slocombe 4 for 96)
Mornington Peninsula 177 (M.D. Vonhagt 4 for 45)

Sri Lankans won by 150 runs

19 February 1985

at Ballarat

England XI 268 for 5 (A.J. Lamb 95)
Victoria 264 (D.F. Whatmore 99, P. King 52, V.J. Marks 5 for 42)

England XI won by 4 runs

A disastrous practice match for England in that they lost Robinson with a broken finger and Cowdrey with a fractured wrist.

21 February 1985

at Bendigo

England XI 276 (P.R. Downton 111, M.D. Moxon 95)
Victorian II XI 253 for 4 (J.M. Wiener 107, V. Richardson 60)

England XI won by 23 runs

Downton and Moxon added 187 in 29 overs for the second wicket. Weiner and Richardson put on 116 in 31 overs for the first wicket for the home side.

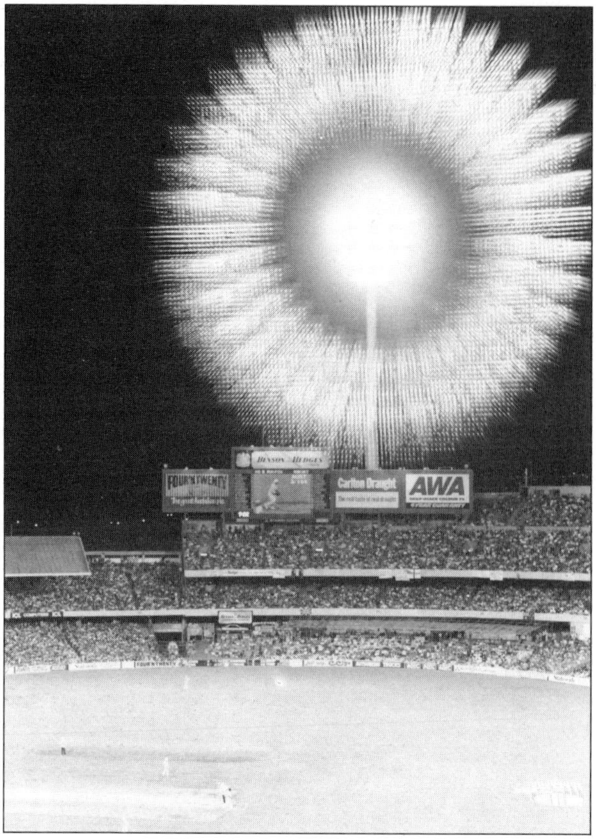

ABOVE: *The Mini World Cup comes alight. Sydney at night. (Adrian Murrell)*

Viswanath appeals as Mudassar, walking away, is run out. India v. Pakistan at Melbourne, 20 February 1985. (Adrian Murrell)

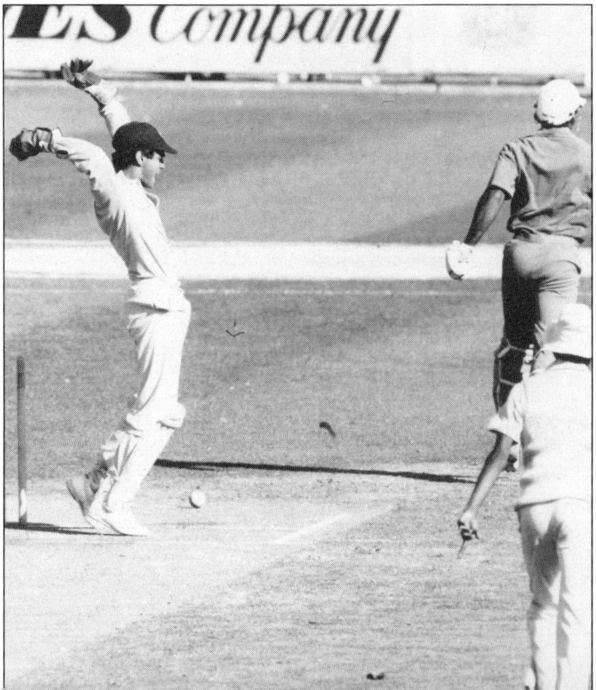

Benson and Hedges World Championship of Cricket

Third One-Day International
NEW ZEALAND *v.* WEST INDIES

The second scheduled match in the competition had to be postponed from the Tuesday until the Thursday because of rain, and rain again halted play after 18.4 overs so that the sides took one point each. Howarth and Wright defended stubbornly against the speed of Marshall and Garner for the first twelve overs at the end of which Howarth fell. Reid began liberally against Davis who accounted for Wright before the rain returned.

The attendance of 7,499 was disappointingly low for the second day running.

Benson and Hedges World Championship of Cricket

Fourth One-Day International
NEW ZEALAND *v.* SRI LANKA

New Zealand became the first side to reach the semi-finals of

THIRD ONE-DAY INTERNATIONAL – NEW ZEALAND *v.* WEST INDIES
21 February 1985 at Sydney

NEW ZEALAND				WEST INDIES
G.P. Howarth†	c Dujon, b Garner	8		D.L. Haynes
J.G. Wright	c Logie, b Davis	22		R.B. Richardson
J.F. Reid	not out	22		H.A. Gomes
M.D. Crowe	not out	0		I.V.A. Richards
J.J. Crowe				C.H. Lloyd†
J.V. Coney				A.L. Logie
I.D.S. Smith*				P.J. Dujon*
R.J. Hadlee				M.D. Marshall
M.C. Sneeden				M.A. Holding
B.L. Cairns				J. Garner
E.J. Chatfield				W.W. Davis
Extras	lb 1, nb 4	5		
(18.4 overs)	(for 2 wickets)	57		

	O	M	R	W
Garner	6	3	11	1
Marshall	6	1	13	—
Davis	3.4	—	23	1
Holding	3	—	9	—

FALL OF WICKETS
1- 21, 2- 57

Match abandoned

FOURTH ONE-DAY INTERNATIONAL – NEW ZEALAND *v.* SRI LANKA
23 February 1985 at Melbourne

NEW ZEALAND		
G.P. Howarth†	c Madugalle, b John	11
J.G. Wright	b John	4
J.F. Reid	c Dias, b Karnain	62
M.D. Crowe	run out	22
P.E. McEwan	b John	27
J.V. Coney	c D.S. de Silva, b Karnain	21
R.J. Hadlee	c de Mel, b Ranatunga	9
I.D.S. Smith*	b R.J. Ratnayake	22
B.L. Cairns	c de Mel, b R.J. Ratnayake	25
M.C. Snedden	b R.J. Ratnayake	7
E.J. Chatfield	not out	2
Extras	lb 6, w 5	11
(49.4 overs)		223

	O	M	R	W
John	10	1	29	3
de Mel	10	—	48	—
R.J. Ratnayake	8.5	1	40	3
D.S. de Silva	5	—	25	—
Karnain	9.5	—	50	2
Ranatunga	6	—	25	1

FALL OF WICKETS
1- 11, 2- 21, 3- 64, 4- 100, 5- 145, 6- 161, 7- 170, 8- 213, 9- 216

SRI LANKA		
S.A.R. Silva*	c M.D. Crowe, b Chatfield	33
J.R. Ratnayeke	run out	8
R.S. Madugalle	lbw, b Coney	8
R.L. Dias	c Smith, b Coney	9
L.R.D. Mendis†	c and b Hadlee	7
A. Ranatunga	c Wright, b Coney	34
U.S.H. Karnain	lbw, b Hadlee	0
A.L.F. de Mel	run out	27
R.J. Ratnayake	c Hadlee, b Coney	1
D.S. de Silva	not out	24
V.B. John	c Chatfield, b Cairns	11
Extras	lb 9, nb 1	10
(42.4 overs)		172

	O	M	R	W
Cairns	8.4	1	25	1
Hadlee	6	1	23	2
Chatfield	10	3	25	1
Snedden	8	—	44	—
Coney	10	—	46	4

FALL OF WICKETS
1- 26, 2- 48, 3- 60, 4- 67, 5- 75, 6- 75, 7- 118, 8- 125, 9- 143

New Zealand won by 51 runs

the competition, but not before they had some moments of anxiety against Sri Lanka. Put in to bat, New Zealand lost both openers to John with only 21 scored, and it was John Reid's defiant innings which halted further progress by the Sri Lankans who bowled with more accuracy than they had shown in the World Series triangular tournament. Their fielding also showed improvement from the depths that it had reached in that tournament.

Reid's innings won him the Man of the Match award, and there were sound, if unspectacular contributions from the rest of the New Zealand order which took the side to 223. Nevertheless, this looked to be a score within Sri Lanka's reach and their openers hustled eagerly and confidently. The flow was halted when Ratnayeke was run out and with Madugalle, Dias and Mendis going cheaply, Sri Lanka's hopes quickly drained away.

Benson and Hedges World Championship of Cricket

Fifth One-Day International
AUSTRALIA *v.* PAKISTAN

Put in to bat, Pakistan responded with an opening stand of 141 in 29 overs by the reunited Mudassar and Mohsin. Beginning with a sedate 32 in the first ten overs, they took 64 off the next ten and the inexperience and limitations of Australia's bowling were clearly exposed. McDermott and McCurdy were clouted over the top of the fielders by Mudassar and the introduction of Wessels' gentle pace brought sixteen runs in two overs.

Australia gained some encouragement when three wickets fell for five runs, but Imran Khan hit 32 off 27 balls at the end to lift Pakistan to 262, not as many as they might have hoped for after their exciting start, but still a formidable score.

It grew immense when Wasim Akram, the eighteen-year old left-arm quick bowler, took the first five Australian wickets in 28 deliveries for 13 runs. It virtually ended the contest. He yorked Kerr, clipped Wessels' off-stump and forced Jones to play on in his first three overs. Border was then forced onto the back foot and dislodged a bail and the unhappy Hughes was too cramped on an ambitiously early pull. Hughes left the ground to catch a plane to Perth almost immediately, an act which caused comment although it was later disclosed that his ticket had been booked for him by the Australian manager.

At 42 for 5, Phillips and O'Donnell came together and played so well as to mock what had gone before. In 13 overs, they added 79 and it was some relief to Pakistan when Phillips drove rashly at Tahir and Javed held a diving catch. Lawson also batted well as Simon O'Donnell continued to impress with his clean hitting, but the target was now far distant and Pakistan moved to an unexpected victory which they thoroughly deserved.

The attendance was 19,224, a quarter of the number that had watched on the previous Sunday. It was a fine day and Australia, with a chance of reaching the semi-final, were playing, but this was the 23rd one-day international to be played in Australia inside two months.

22, 23, 24 and 25 February 1985

at Adelaide

South Australia 404 (M.D. Haysman 157, D.W. Hookes 83) and 103 for 6
Western Australia 191 (M.W. McPhee 60) and 459 (M.R.J. Veletta 143, G. Shipperd 129, G.R. Marsh 67)

Match drawn
South Australia 4 pts, Western Australia 0 pts

at Devonport

Victoria 390 (M.D. Taylor 67, D.F. Whatmore 64, P.D. King 65, G.N. Yallop 51, M.P. Tame 4 for 138) and 58 for 4
Tasmania 196 (M. Ray 65, R.J. Bright 5 for 41) and 333 (G.W. Goodman 89, D.C. Boon 78, S.L. Saunders 69, R. McCarthy 4 for 80, S.P. Davis 4 for 101)

Match drawn
Victoria 4 pts, Tasmania 0 pts

at Sydney

Queensland 156 (G.M. Ritchie 59) and 151 (B.A. Courtice 50, G.R.J. Matthews 5 for 32, D.R. Gilbert 4 for 42)
New South Wales 368 (J. Dyson 93, G.R.J. Matthews 87)

New South Wales won by an innings and 61 runs
New South Wales 16 pts, Queensland 0 pts

FIFTH ONE-DAY INTERNATIONAL – AUSTRALIA *v.* PAKISTAN
24 February 1985 at Melbourne

PAKISTAN			
	Mudassar Nazar	c McDermott, b O'Donnell	69
	Mohsin Khan	b Alderman	81
	Qasim Umar	b O'Donnell	31
	Javed Miandad†	b McCurdy	19
	Zaheer Abbas	b Lawson	3
	Imran Khan	not out	32
	Rameez Raja	c Alderman, b Lawson	3
	Tahir Naqqash	not out	5
	Rashi Khan		
	Anil Dalpat*		
	Wasim Akram		
	Extras	lb 8, w 9, nb 2	19
	(50 overs)	(for 6 wickets)	262

	O	M	R	W
Lawson	10	2	45	2
Alderman	10	—	42	1
McDermott	8	—	51	—
McCurdy	10	—	58	1
O'Donnell	10	1	42	2
Wessels	2	—	16	—

FALL OF WICKETS
1- 141, 2- 190, 3- 190, 4- 195, 5- 224, 6- 229

AUSTRALIA			
	K.C. Wessels	b Wasim Akram	10
	R.B. Kerr	b Wasim Akram	2
	D.M.J. Jones	b Wasim Akram	11
	A.R. Border†	hit wkt, b Wasim Akram	11
	K.J. Hughes	c Tahir, b Wasim Akram	1
	W.B. Phillips*	c Javed, b Tahir	44
	S.P. O'Donnell	not out	74
	G.F. Lawson	c Rameez, b Mudassar	27
	C.J. McDermott	run out	4
	R.J. McCurdy	run out	1
	T.M. Alderman	b Imran	2
	Extras	b 2, lb 9, w 2	13
	(42.3 overs)		200

	O	M	R	W
Imran Khan	6.3	—	24	1
Wasim Akram	8	1	21	5
Rashid Khan	10	—	51	—
Zaheer Abbas	3	—	16	—
Tahir Naqqash	7	—	37	1
Mudassar Nazar	8	—	40	1

FALL OF WICKETS
1- 4, 2- 15, 3- 30, 4- 37, 5- 42, 6- 121, 7- 178, 8- 183, 9- 187

Pakistan won by 62 runs

Career bests with bat and ball by Greg Matthews and the spin trio of Holland, Bennett and Matthews inspired New South Wales to overwhelm Queensland in Sydney. The win took New South Wales and Queensland into the Sheffield Shield Final and emphasised once more how much the northern state had missed their Test players. At full strength they had won all four games with maximum points; without Border, Wessels and McDermott they had picked up only 8 points in 5 matches.

The clash at the other end of the table saw Victoria introduce two new players to first-class cricket, Jordan and McCarthy. McCarthy took 4 wickets in the second innings, but Victoria were thwarted by a late innings from Saunders and the match was drawn. Tasmania lost their last 9 wickets for 97 runs in their first innings as Ray Bright produced his best bowling for some time.

Haysman again batted in top form for South Australia and shared a 4th wicket partnership of 138 with Hookes. Western Australia lost their last 9 wickets for 94 runs and were forced to follow-on. McPhee fell to Prior without a run scored and then Veletta and Shipperd put on 248, Veletta once again emphasising his promise and Shipperd the fact that he has remained under-rated for several season. South Australia found the task of scoring 247 in 3 hours beyond their capabilities, Hogan producing a particularly accurate spell.

28 February 1985

at Sydney (Manly Oval)

England XI 111
New South Wales II XI 115 for 4
New South Wales II XI won by 6 wickets

Benson and Hedges World Championship of Cricket

Sixth One-Day International
ENGLAND *v.* INDIA

The triumphs on the Indian sub-continent seemed in the long distant past when India outplayed England at Sydney and so ended their interest in the competition. Mathematically, England retained a chance of qualifying for the semi-finals, but only the wildest of optimists could believe in the possibility of them being in the last four.

India were given a rousing start by Srikkanth who launched into Cowans and Ellison with gusto. After 10 overs, India were 52 for 0 and Srikkanth was 41 not out. A direct hit on the stumps from long-leg by Cowans brought the end of Srikkanth, but he had hit 57 off 53 balls with ten fours and lifted India to an anticipation of prosperity. Azharuddin and Vengsarkar built soundly on his work without ever suggesting that they could maintain his rate of scoring. Kapil Dev hit fiercely, but briefly, and Gavaskar batted well, but the accurate bowling of Edmonds and Foster had frustrated India in their attempt to build a score that was out of England's reach and Gower's men left the field content that they had restricted their opponents to 235 when a score of 280 or so had looked ominously possible.

Gavaskar looks over his shoulder, but his partner, Azharuddin, not in picture, is safely home. (Adrian Murrell)

SIXTH ONE-DAY INTERNATIONAL – ENGLAND *v.* INDIA
26 February 1985 at Sydney

INDIA

R.J. Shastri	c Fowler, b Ellison	13
K. Srikkanth	run out	57
M. Azharuddin	c and b Cowans	45
D.B. Vengsarkar	run out	43
R.N. Kapil Dev	c Downton, b Cowans	29
S.M. Gavaskar†	not out	30
M.B. Amarnath	c Lamb, b Cowans	6
R.M.H. Binny	c Marks, b Foster	2
U.S. Madan Lal	c Downton, b Foster	0
S. Viswanath*	run out	8
L. Sivaramakrishnan		
Extras	lb 2	2
(50 overs)	(for 9 wickets)	235

	O	M	R	W
Cowans	10	—	59	3
Ellison	10	1	46	1
Foster	10	—	33	2
Edmonds	10	1	38	—
Marks	10	—	57	—

FALL OF WICKETS
1- 67, 2- 74, 3- 147, 4- 183, 5- 197, 6- 216, 7- 220, 8- 220, 9- 235

ENGLAND

G. Fowler	c Viswanath, b Binny	26
M.D. Moxon	c and b Sivaramakrishnan	48
D.I. Gower†	c Vengsarkar, b Sivaramakrishnan	25
A.J. Lamb	b Sivaramakrishnan	13
M.W. Gatting	c Viswanath, b Shastri	7
P.R. Downton*	c Shastri, b Kapil Dev	9
V.J. Marks	st Viswanath, b Shastri	2
P.H. Edmonds	st Viswanath, b Shastri	5
R.M. Ellison	c Viswanath, b Madan Lal	1
N.A. Foster	c Srikkanth, b Madan Lal	1
N.G. Cowans	not out	3
Extras	b 3, lb 4, w 1, nb 1	9
(41.4 overs)		149

	O	M	R	W
Kapil Dev	7	—	21	1
Binny	8	—	33	1
Madan Lal	6.4	—	19	2
Sivaramakrishnan	10	—	39	3
Shastri	10	2	30	3

FALL OF WICKETS
1- 41, 2- 94, 3- 113, 4- 126, 5- 126, 6- 130, 7- 142, 8- 144, 9- 144

India won by 86 runs

Fowler and Moxon began with good sense without ever suggesting permanence or solidity, but the singles they accumulated provided a suggested foundation for a winning score. Kapil Dev was mean and menacing and Moxon was uneasy, but he survived. At 41, Fowler swung on the leg-side at Binny and skied the ball to the wicket-keeper. Gower played with calm and confidence, content to take the singles which were offered in plenty, particularly when Sivaramakrishnan bowled to a field not ideal to the context of the match. It was the spinners, however, who were to assert India's authority and England's ineptitude.

Moxon swatted Shastri's first ball to mid-wicket where Gavaskar made a hash of the catch, jumping late and getting only one hand to the ball. For a time this depressed India and their fielding and bowling erred for the only time in the match. Moxon was lucky on two other occasions, both of Sivaramakrishnan who missed a caught and bowled and saw a stumping chance go begging. In the 24th over, with England at 94 for 1 and well placed to achieve their target, Gower hit a full toss from Sivaramakrishnan from outside the off-stump into the hands of Vengsarkar on the mid-wicket boundary. It was a bad shot and one that was totally out of context with what had gone before.

It proved to be the turning point of the match. Moxon's luck ran out and he drove the ball back hard to Sivaramakrishnan. Lamb looked bemused by the young leg-spinner and played one of the worst shots that could have been seen in an international. Sweeping, he had his off stump clipped. Without addition, Gatting cut at Shastri who was turning the ball more than Sivaramakrishnan and was caught behind. The left-arm bowler then beat Marks through the air and Viswanath stumped the batsman very smartly. Edmonds was more comprehensively stumped and Downton slashed Kapil Dev to gully. It was total disintegration and the eager Indians swept to success, leaving the impression that they had outplayed England in every department of the game.

Benson and Hedges World Championship of Cricket

Seventh One-Day International
WEST INDIES *v.* SRI LANKA

Rain in the early part of the day reduced the match by three overs an innings and Sri Lanka elected to bat first when they won the toss. They struggled against the pace of Marshall, Garner and Holding whose bowling just short of a length kept the Sri Lankan batsmen on the back foot and frustrated their stroke play. Only 18 runs came in the first 12 overs. Dias played two exciting hooks for 4, but he fell when he attempted to cut a ball that was too close to him and although Ratnayeke battled bravely, the Sri Lankan innings crumbled as batsmen attempted to play shots against restrictive bowling.

There was never any doubt that West Indies would get the required runs, but they suffered two major setbacks. Richardson was hit on the side of the head by a ball from de Mel in the third over and Gomes was hit in the mouth by a ball from Rumesh Ratnayake in the eleventh over and lost two teeth as well as needing stitches in his upper lip. Wes Hall, the West Indian manager, reported that Richardson was likely to be fit for the semi-final, but he was less hopeful about Gomes.

Group B – Final Positions

	P	*W*	*L*	*D*	*Pts*	*Sc Rate*
West Indies	2	1	–	1	3	5.87
New Zealand	2	1	–	1	3	4.07
Sri Lanka	2	–	2	–	0	3.16

SEVENTH ONE-DAY INTERNATIONAL – WEST INDIES *v.* SRI LANKA

27 February 1985 at Melbourne

SRI LANKA			
	S.A.R. Silva*	c Haynes, b Garner	4
	J.R. Ratnayake	c Haynes, b Holding	50
	R.L. Dias	c Dujon, b Davis	16
	A. Ranatunga	b Richards	1
	L.R.D. Mendis†	run out	1
	R.S. Madugalle	not out	36
	D.S. de Silva	c and b Richards	5
	U.S.H. Karnain	c and b Richards	1
	A.L.F. de Mel	not out	15
	R.J. Ratnayake		
	V.B. John		
	Extras	b 1, lb 4, w 1	6
	(47 overs)	(for 7 wickets)	135

	O	M	R	W
Marshall	10	1	26	—
Garner	10	3	16	1
Davis	9	—	35	1
Holding	9	1	26	1
Richards	9	—	27	3

FALL OF WICKETS
1- 7, 2- 52, 3- 53, 4- 57, 5- 86, 6- 102, 7- 106

WEST INDIES			
	D.L. Haynes	b de Mel	36
	R.B. Richardson	retired hurt	11
	H.A. Gomes	retired hurt	20
	I.V.A. Richards	c de Mel, b R.J. Ratnayake	12
	C.H. Lloyd†	not out	14
	A.L. Logie	not out	29
	P.J. Dujon*		
	M.D. Marshall		
	M.A. Holding		
	J. Garner		
	W.W. Davis		
	Extras	b 1, lb 7, w 2, nb 4	14
	(23.1 overs)	(for 2 wickets)	136

	O	M	R	W
de Mel	8	—	47	1
John	7	—	39	—
R.J. Ratnayake	7	—	29	1
Ranatunga	1	—	13	—

FALL OF WICKETS
1- 86, 2- 90

West Indies won by 8 wickets

1, 2, 3 and 4 March 1985

at Sydney

New South Wales 326 (G.R.J. Matthews 103, S.R. Waugh 94, R.J. Bright 5 for 112) and 201 for 3 dec (D.M. Wellham 81, J. Dyson 54)
Victoria 259 (G.N. Yallop 147, D.R. Gilbert 5 for 70) and 243 (J.D. Siddons 75, M.J. Bennett 6 for 57)

New South Wales won by 25 runs
New South Wales 16 pts, Victoria 0 pts

at Adelaide

South Australia 210 (R.J. Inverarity 55, J.N. Maguire 5 for 62) and 363 (D.J. Kelly 100 not out, D.F. O'Connor 57)

A seagull audience for Sri Lanka at Melbourne. (Adrian Murrell)

Queensland 378 (G.S. Trimble 76, A.B. Henschell 73, T.V. Hohns 72 not out, T.J. Barsby 72, R.J. Inverarity 7 for 86) and 183 (C.B. Smart 54, T.B.A. May 6 for 24)

South Australia won by 12 runs
South Australia 12 pts, Queensland 4 pts

at Hobart

Tasmania 307 for 5 dec (D.C. Boon 147, M. Ray 53) and 83 for 4
Western Australia 158 for 2 dec (M.W. McPhee 52, G.R. Marsh 51 not out)

Match drawn
Tasmania 4 pts, Western Australia 0 pts

The match in Hobart was ruined by rain, but there was time enough for David Boon to hit his third century of the season and be named as Sheffield Shield player of the year, a title for which he must have been challenged strongly by Peter Clifford of New South Wales.

New South Wales fought a thrilling game with Victoria for whom Graham Yallop showed that his rehabilitation was complete. New South Wales were 91 for 4 when Waugh and Matthews came together. Matthews hit a maiden century and Waugh a career best as they added 178. Gilbert had his best spell of the season and Victoria trailed by 67 on the first innings. Wellham and Dyson hit sparklingly in a second wicket stand of 125 and Wellham declared shortly before the end of the third day. Victoria were 16 for 0 at the close in search of 269. Siddons, coming in at 78 for 4, gave them hope with his best innings for the state and at 235 for 6, Victoria were in sight of victory, but the last 4 wickets fell for 8 runs and Murray Bennett, with his career best 6 for 57, won the game for the home side.

Queensland took the first innings points thanks to solid batting in the middle order and the bowling of John Maguire. They seemed to be heading for victory when South Australia ended the third day at 251 for 7, a lead of only 83. Next morning, wicket-keeper Kelly reached a maiden hundred in fine style out of 169 and Queensland were left a little stunned and asked to make 196 to win. At 133 for 3, victory seemed assured, but the spin of May who turned in the best bowling performance of his career saw the last 7 wickets fall for 50 and South Australia snatch a win by 12 runs.

Sheffield Shield – Final Table

	P	*W*	*L*	*D*	*1st Inns lead*	*Pts*
New South Wales	10	4	–	6	8	80
Queensland	10	4	3	3	7	76
South Australia	10	4	4	2	3	60
Western Australia	10	2	1	7	4	42
Victoria	10	–	4	6	4	18
Tasmania	10	–	2	8	3	12

(Victoria and Western Australia include two points each for no result on first innings of match drawn)

ABOVE: *Greg Matthews. A key figure in New South Wales' double triumph. He finished the season with a career best 5 for 32 and a maiden century. (Adrian Murrell)*

Australia v. Pakistan, 24 February. Wasim Akram, 5 for 21, has just dismissed Allan Border. (Adrian Murrell)

EIGHTH ONE-DAY INTERNATIONAL – ENGLAND *v.* PAKISTAN
2 March 1985 at Melbourne

PAKISTAN			
	Mudassar Nazar	c Foster, b Edmonds	77
	Mohsin Khan	c Moxon, b Ellison	9
	Rameez Raja	c Moxon, b Marks	21
	Javed Miandad†	c Downton, b Foster	11
	Imran Khan	b Ellison	35
	Saleem Malik	c Gatting, b Foster	8
	Qasim Umar	b Cowans	12
	Tahir Naqqash	not out	21
	Anil Dalpat*	b Ellison	8
	Azeem Hafeez	not out	0
	Wasim Akram		
	Extras	b 5, lb 4, w 2	11
	(50 overs)	(for 8 wickets)	213

	O	M	R	W
Cowans	10	—	52	1
Ellison	10	—	42	3
Foster	10	—	56	2
Marks	10	2	25	1
Edmonds	10	1	29	1

FALL OF WICKETS
1- 37, 2- 93, 3- 114, 4- 126, 5- 144, 6- 181, 7- 183, 8- 212

ENGLAND			
	G. Fowler	c Anil, b Imran	0
	D.I. Gower†	c Tahir, b Imran	27
	A.J. Lamb	c Wasim Akram, b Azeem	81
	M.W. Gatting	c Mudassar, b Tahir	11
	P.R. Downton*	run out	6
	R.M. Ellison	c Anil, b Tahir	6
	V.J. Marks	run out	1
	M.D. Moxon	c Imran, b Azeem	3
	P.H. Edmonds	not out	0
	N.A. Foster	run out	1
	N.G. Cowans	b Tahir	0
	Extras	b 1, lb 7, w 1, nb 1	10
	(24.2 overs)		146

	O	M	R	W
Imran Khan	7	—	33	2
Wasim Akram	10	—	59	—
Azeem Hafeez	3	—	22	2
Tahir Naqqash	4.2	—	24	3

FALL OF WICKETS
1- 0, 2- 56, 3- 102, 4- 125, 5- 138, 6- 139, 7- 141, 8- 145, 9- 146

Pakistan won by 67 runs

Benson and Hedges World Championship of Cricket

Eighth One-Day International
ENGLAND *v.* PAKISTAN

England's last remaining hope of qualifying for the semi-finals of the competition was that India should beat Australia and that they should beat Pakistan at such a run rate that they would move into second place. In the event, they died desperately trying to achieve such a rate. It was a brave attempt, but it also underlined some of the weaknesses in batting which had become most evident in Australia.

Mudassar gave Pakistan a spirited start, but Javed could not get going and the middle order stagnated against the accurate spin of Marks and Edmonds. Imran and Tahir revitalised the innings, but the final score of 213 was well within England's capabilities. The scoring rate required demanded that they reach the target in 32.4 overs, however, and it was this that accounted for the bizarre approach.

Fowler swished wildly at the second ball and Anil Dalpat took a tumbling catch. Gower and Lamb added 56 off 61 balls before Gower again dragged across the line and was caught at long-on. Lamb played magnificently and, with a six off Imran and twelve fours, he hit 81 off 69 balls, the most exciting innings of the tournament. He was out when he hooked Azeem and Wasim Akram sprinted thirty yards to take the ball below his knees as he ran in, a fine catch. Gatting had already left, Downton stupidly run out and Ellison dropped by Javed off a simple chance before Lamb's departure in the 22nd over. Total disintegration followed. There were two run outs, one of them insane and Ellison, feet in concrete, was caught behind. Moxon swatted and Cowans was bowled first ball. Six wickets fell for 8 runs and England's tour was over.

Benson and Hedges World Championship of Cricket

Ninth One-Day International
AUSTRALIA *v.* INDIA

Having seemed assured of a place in the semi-finals after their victories over England and Pakistan, India arrived at their last match threatened by non-qualification on run rate after Pakistan's win over England the previous day. Whatever worries they may have had were not evident, however, and they completely outplayed Australia to win the group and move into the semi-final.

The beginning of the Australian innings was once again quite dreadful. Kerr played no shot and was bowled off his pads. Wood and Border drove wildly and paid the penalty. Wessels hooked impetuously and Jones cut insanely and Australia were 37 for 5 without the threatening spinners having yet taken off their sweaters. Wayne Phillips hit lustily and left one to ponder again what he might become if he were left to do the job for which Australia originally selected him, open the innings. He has the attitude of another Gooch, but he will fall between the striving after two talents if he is asked to keep wicket.

In spite of Phillips and some brave play by the tail, Australia made only 163. This was never likely to trouble India. Srikkanth and Shastri began sensibly and then Srikkanth burst into action with a series of lofted drives. They put on 124 before Man of the Match Shastri was caught behind off O'Donnell. Alderman had Azharuddin lbw second ball, the first time that the batsman had failed to reach 40 for India, but Srikkanth went gleefully on to 93 and India to the easiest of victories. Australia had played their sixteenth one-day international of the season, and must have had a sense of relief that this ridiculous itinerary had come to an end.

NINTH ONE-DAY INTERNATIONAL – AUSTRALIA *v.* INDIA
3 March 1985 at Melbourne

AUSTRALIA			
	G.M. Wood	b Binny	1
	R.B. Kerr	b Kapil Dev	4
	K.C. Wessels	c Madan Lal, b Kapil Dev	6
	A.R. Border†	b Binny	4
	D.M.J. Jones	c Viswanath, b Amarnath	12
	W.B. Phillips*	c Amarnath, b Sivaramakrishnan	60
	S.P. O'Donnell	c Amarnath, b Shastri	17
	G.F. Lawson	c and b Sivaramakrishnan	0
	R.M. Hogg	run out	22
	R.J. McCurdy	not out	13
	T.M. Alderman	b Binny	6
	Extras	b 2, lb 9, w 5, nb 2	18
	(49.3 overs)		163

	O	M	R	W
Kapil Dev	10	2	25	2
Binny	7.3	—	27	3
Madan Lal	5	—	18	—
Amarnath	7	1	16	1
Sivaramakrishnan	10	—	32	2
Shastri	10	1	34	1

FALL OF WICKETS
1- 5, 2- 5, 3- 17, 4- 17, 5- 37, 6- 85, 7- 85, 8- 134, 9- 147

INDIA			
	R.J. Shastri	c Phillips, b O'Donnell	51
	K. Srikkanth	not out	93
	M. Azharuddin	lbw, b Alderman	0
	D.B. Vengsarkar	not out	11
	S.M. Gavaskar†		
	M.B. Amarnath		
	R.N. Kapil Dev		
	R.M.H. Binny		
	U.S. Madan Lal		
	S. Viswanath*		
	L. Sivaramakrishnan		
	Extras	lb 1, w 3, nb 6	10
	(36.1 overs)	(for 2 wickets)	165

	O	M	R	W
Lawson	8	1	35	—
Hogg	6	2	16	—
McCurdy	7.1	—	30	—
Alderman	8	—	38	1
O'Donnell	7	—	45	1

FALL OF WICKETS
1- 124, 2- 125

India won by 8 wickets

Group A – Final Positions

	P	*W*	*L*	*D*	*Pts*	*Sc Rate*
India	3	3	–	–	6	4.42
Pakistan	3	2	1	–	4	4.39
Australia	3	1	2	–	2	3.98
England	3	–	3	–	0	3.41

Benson and Hedges World Championship of Cricket

Semi-Final
NEW ZEALAND *v.* INDIA

India moved into the final of the competition displaying an efficiency and commitment that had characterised their cricket since they had arrived in Australia and they emphasised the quality of their cricket to a crowd of just over 16,000.

Gavaskar won the toss and asked New Zealand to bat. His discretion brought quick reward, Wright being caught behind off the third ball of the match. In the sixth over McEwan was also caught behind and the New Zealand total was only 14. The pitch was slow and the bounce low so that stroke play was not encouraged by the conditions. New Zealand's immediate concern appeared to be for survival and Reid dug in for 35 overs to score 55 while Coney batted 21 overs for his 33.

Their caution was necessary in that Martin Crowe, on whom their hopes rested, was caught off the accurate Madan Lal after scoring 9 in as many overs. He was taken at backward cover off his first attempt to force the ball.

The impetus to the New Zealand innings was given by Lance Cairns who hit 39 in 7 overs, but the final score of 206 did not look too forbidding. Once again the Indians had bowled well and fielded well. Kapil Dev was always menacing. Madan Lal once more posed the question as to why other, lesser men had been selected ahead of him for the series against England. Binny was totally efficient and the spinners bowled with their customary accuracy and guile.

New Zealand's only hope of victory rested in their bowlers' ability to maintain a frustrating line and length and this, initially, they achieved. Srikkanth's energies were curbed when he was caught hooking in the ninth over and Azharuddin denied his range of shots by pitch and bowlers managed only eight runs off his first 43 deliveries. Six overs produced only 4 runs and India were in danger of being becalmed. Azharuddin responded by advancing down the wicket to the medium pacers and Howarth, the shrewdest of captains, erred in taking off Snedden who had reduced the batsmen to impotence.

Azharuddin fell when he skied Cairns to mid-wicket where Coney, running back, held a magnificent catch. Throughout, Shastri had batted with great good sense, scoring 53 from 84 balls and denying any hint of panic or pressure. Howarth brought back Hadlee and Shastri patted his first ball to cover. It was the 30th over and Kapil Dev came in for the decisive confrontation. In two overs Hadlee was hit for 26 runs and Kapil Dev was dropped at mid-off by Reid. New Zealand's chance had gone. Kapil Dev was at his blistering best and Vengsarkar moved into his eloquent mood. From 74 deliveries 105 runs were scored and India were once more in sight of the top of the world.

Shastri was named Man of the Match which seemed a little hard on the mighty Kapil Dev.

BENSON AND HEDGES WORLD CHAMPIONSHIP SEMI-FINAL – NEW ZEALAND *v.* INDIA
5 March 1985 at Sydney

NEW ZEALAND		
J.G. Wright	c Viswanath, b Kapil Dev	0
P.E. McEwan	c Viswanath, b Binny	9
J.F. Reid	c Kapil Dev, b Shastri	55
M.D. Crowe	c Azharuddin, b Madan Lal	9
G.P. Howarth†	run out	7
J.V. Coney	b Shastri	33
I.D.S. Smith*	c Amarnath, b Madan Lal	19
R.J. Hadlee	c Madan Lal, b Shastri	3
B.L. Cairns	c Srikkanth, b Madan Lal	39
M.C. Snedden	c Azharuddin, b Madan Lal	7
E.J. Chatfield	not out	0
Extras	lb 21, w 1, nb 3	25
(50 overs)		206

	O	M	R	W
Kapil Dev	10	1	34	1
Binny	6	—	28	1
Madan Lal	8	1	37	4
Amarnath	7	—	24	—
Sivaramakrishnan	9	—	31	—
Shastri	10	1	31	3

FALL OF WICKETS
1- 0, 2- 14, 3- 52, 4- 69, 5- 119, 6- 145, 7- 151, 8- 188, 9- 206

INDIA		
R.J. Shastri	c McEwan, b Hadlee	53
K. Srikkanth	c Reid, b Chatfield	9
M. Azharuddin	c Coney, b Cairns	24
D.B. Vengsarkar	not out	63
R.N. Kapil Dev	not out	54
S.M. Gavaskar†		
M.B. Amarnath		
S. Viswanath*		
R.M.H. Binny		
U.S. Madan Lal		
L. Sivaramakrishnan		
Extras	b 1, lb 2, nb 1	4
(43.3 overs)	(for 3 wickets)	207

	O	M	R	W
Cairns	9	—	35	1
Hadlee	8.3	3	50	1
Chatfield	10	—	38	1
Snedden	8	1	37	—
Coney	8	—	44	—

FALL OF WICKETS
1- 28, 2- 73, 3- 102

India won by 7 wickets

Benson and Hedges World Championship of Cricket

Semi-Final
WEST INDIES *v.* PAKISTAN

Against his usual custom, Lloyd decided to bat when he won the toss. This may have been influenced by the fact that his side was depleted through injuries, for Gomes was still recovering from the knock in the face he suffered against Sri Lanka and Greenidge had returned to the West Indies with an injured back.

West Indies began sedately but looked secure and then suddenly 44 for 1 became 45 for 3. Richardson had been bowled by Tahir Naqqash at 29 and the same bowler then had Haynes caught at deep square-leg and Richards caught

Rameez Raja reaches his half-century in the semi-finals. Mohsin Khan applauds. (Adrian Murrell)

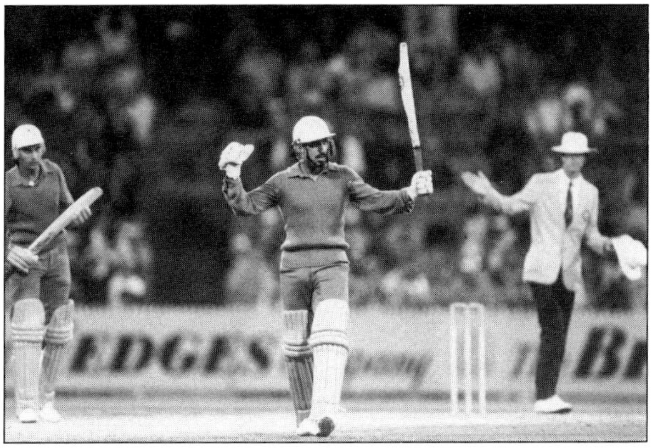

An unusual sight. A West Indian batsman struck by a bouncer. Gomes receives attention after being hit by a ball from Ratnayake. (Adrian Murrell)

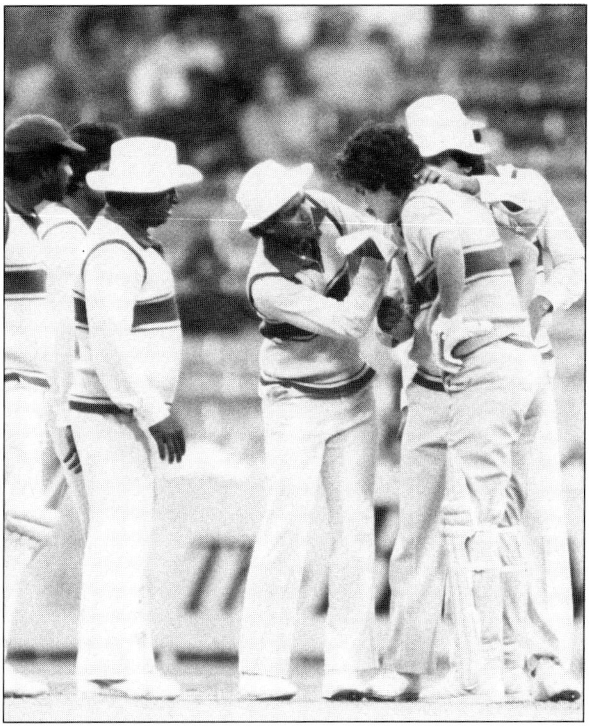

Allan Lamb lashes out during his daring innings of 81 for England against Pakistan at Melbourne. (Adrian Murrell)

behind as he prodded defensively. As long as Lloyd was at the wicket West Indies still had hopes of a winning score, but in the 33rd over he hit Mudassar straight to short extra cover and the same bowler dismissed Logie who hit a long hop comfortably to square-leg.

The West Indian batsmen had been threatened by Tahir's fine early spell and frustrated by an excellent spell of controlled leg-spin from Wasim Raja, now they succumbed to Mudassar's gentle swing. Harper alone offered positive resistance on the slow and tired wicket, but the final score of 159 was scarcely respectable and Pakistan were exultant.

They suffered an early loss in their bid for victory, Mudassar falling to Marshall at 8, but Rameez Raja played quite splendidly, getting in line to Marshall and Holding and later hooking the pace men with confidence and courage. Meanwhile, Mohsin Khan played an innings which, at another time, might have been frowned upon, but in this context was admirable. He scored only 23 off 93 balls and was not out until the 36th over when the score was 116, but he had given Pakistan the solidity needed to complement the exuberance of Rameez and Qasim who, in company with Javed, stroked his side gleefully and attractively to the final.

Benson and Hedges World Championship of Cricket

Third Place Play-Off
WEST INDIES *v.* NEW ZEALAND

In the play-off match for third place in the tournament, West Indies beat New Zealand with ease. It was an unmemorable contest.

West Indies were without Clive Lloyd who had flown to England to visit his sick wife. So Lloyd had captained West Indies for the last time when they were beaten by Pakistan in the semi-final. His record as a captain is an impressive one and one should not detract from it, but many would have liked to have seen a stronger discipline asserted over his side and a greater concern for the conduct of the game in a less hostile manner, nor, too, should it be forgotten that he played a leading role in the Packer revolution that has culminated in the pyjama game of an excessive number of one-day internationals created for the benefit of the sponsors

Allan Border falls to Roger Binny, Australia v. *India at Melbourne. (Adrian Murrell)*

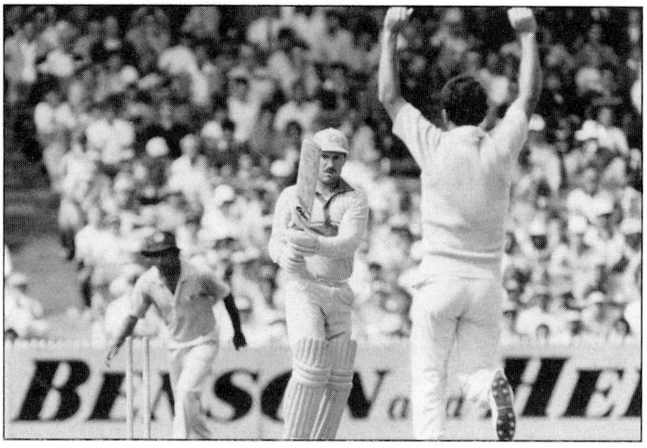

BENSON AND HEDGES WORLD CHAMPIONSHIP SEMI-FINAL – WEST INDIES *v.* PAKISTAN
6 March 1985 at Melbourne

WEST INDIES			
	D.L. Haynes	c Mudassar, b Tahir	18
	R.B. Richardson	b Tahir	13
	P.J. Dujon*	c Anil, b Wasim Raja	22
	I.V.A. Richards	c Anil, b Tahir	1
	C.H. Lloyd†	c Javed, b Mudassar	25
	A.L. Logie	c Qasim Umar, b Mudassar	8
	M.D. Marshall	c Javed, b Mudassar	10
	R.A. Harper	not out	25
	M.A. Holding	b Wasim Akram	5
	J. Garner	c Wasim Raja, b Mudassar	13
	W.W. Davis	c Javed, b Mudassar	3
	Extras	b 4, lb 7, w 4, nb 1	16
	(44.3 overs)		159

	O	M	R	W
Imran Khan	9	1	39	—
Wasim Akram	10	2	26	1
Tahir Naqqash	8	3	23	3
Wasim Raja	10	—	32	1
Mudassar Nazar	7.3	—	28	5

FALL OF WICKETS
1- 29, 2- 44, 3- 45, 4- 61, 5- 75, 6- 96, 7- 103, 8- 122, 9- 152

PAKISTAN			
	Mudassar Nazar	c Logie, b Marshall	6
	Mohsin Khan	c Dujon, b Garner	23
	Rameez Raja	c and b Harper	60
	Qasim Umar	not out	42
	Javed Miandad†	not out	10
	Imran Khan		
	Saleem Malik		
	Wasim Raja		
	Tahir Naqqash		
	Anil Dalpat*		
	Wasim Akram		
	Extras	b 3, lb 7, w 6, nb 3	19
	(46 overs)	(for 3 wickets)	160

	O	M	R	W
Marshall	9	2	25	1
Garner	8	3	19	1
Holding	8	3	19	—
Davis	7	—	35	—
Harper	10	1	38	1
Richards	4	—	14	—

FALL OF WICKETS
1- 8, 2- 97, 3- 116

Pakistan won by 7 wickets

BENSON AND HEDGES WORLD CHAMPIONSHIP THIRD PLACE PLAY-OFF – NEW ZEALAND *v.* WEST INDIES
9 March 1985 at Sydney

NEW ZEALAND			
	G.P. Howarth†	lbw, b Garner	11
	J.G. Wright	c Logie, b Garner	5
	J.F. Reid	c Dujon, b Davis	18
	M.D. Crowe	c Harper, b Holding	8
	J.J. Crowe	b Harper	1
	J.V. Coney	c Payne, b Garner	35
	I.D.S. Smith*	c Payne, b Harper	15
	B.L. Cairns	b Holding	5
	R.J. Hadlee	b Marshall	11
	J.G. Bracewell	not out	11
	E.J. Chatfield	not out	2
	Extras	b 1, lb 8, w 2, nb 5	16
	(50 overs)	(for 9 wickets)	138

	O	M	R	W
Garner	10	2	29	3
Marshall	10	1	32	1
Davis	10	—	23	1
Holding	10	1	23	2
Harper	10	1	22	2

FALL OF WICKETS
1- 14, 2- 24, 3- 45, 4- 51, 5- 52, 6- 78, 7- 83, 8- 116, 9- 127

WEST INDIES			
	D.L. Haynes	c Coney, b Hadlee	1
	R.B. Richardson	c Smith, b Hadlee	8
	T.R.O. Payne	b Chatfield	28
	A.L. Logie	not out	34
	I.V.A. Richards†	b Hadlee	51
	P.J. Dujon*	not out	9
	M.D. Marshall		
	R.A. Harper		
	M.A. Holding		
	J. Garner		
	W.W. Davis		
	Extras	lb 3, w 2, nb 3	8
	(37.2 overs)	(for 4 wickets)	139

	O	M	R	W
Hadlee	10	4	23	3
Chatfield	9	—	25	1
Bracewell	8	2	42	—
Cairns	8	—	39	—
Coney	2.2	—	7	—

FALL OF WICKETS
1- 4, 2- 24, 3- 54, 4- 126

West Indies won by 6 wickets

and the television company rather than for cricket.

Richards put New Zealand in and they were soon struggling. Coney hit 35 off 76 balls and he and Hadlee added 33 for the eighth wicket, the best stand of the innings. Hadlee began with a spell of 2 for 8 in 6 overs, but Payne and Logie stabilised the innings before Richards hit 51 off 61 deliveries.

Benson and Hedges World Championship of Cricket

The Final
INDIA *v.* PAKISTAN

Both sides were forced to make changes for the final. Roger Binny awoke with a temperature and was replaced by Chetan

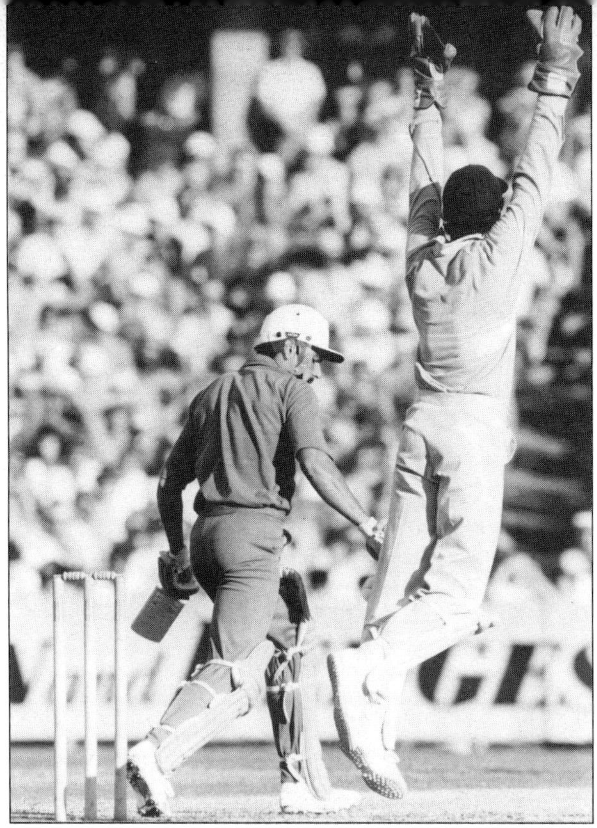

Left: *Tahir Naqqash, caught Viswanath, bowled Shastri for 10. (Adrian Murrell)*

Sharma while Wasim Akram chipped a finger at practice and gave way to Azeem Hafeez.

Javed Miandad won the toss and decided to bat. There seemed the likelihood that Mohsin and Mudassar would give Pakistan a sound start, but in the fifth over, Mohsin flicked Kapil Dev lazily to Azharuddin at square-leg. In the eleventh over Kapil Dev struck twice. Mudassar played unwisely at a very wide delivery which was swinging away and was caught behind, and Qasim was yorked first ball. Rameez was splendidly caught in the twelfth over, Srikkanth running in quickly to take the ball low, and Pakistan were in tatters at 33 for 4. The position would have been even worse had a confident appeal for a catch at the wicket against Imran been upheld at the same score.

Javed and Imran added 68 for the fifth wicket, taking no liberties with the accurate bowling, and they were not separated until the thirty-third over just after they had raised the hundred. Imran drove to cover in Sivaramakrishnan's first over and insanely started to run. He was sent back and thrown out by Gavaskar's excellent return. Javed and Saleem added 30 in 6 overs and then fell to successive deliveries. Saleem hit to cover and Javed was beaten by a leg-break and stumped. It was bowling of the highest quality and once more answered the critics who believe that only medium

BENSON AND HEDGES WORLD CHAMPIONSHIP FINAL – INDIA *v.* PAKISTAN
10 March 1985 at Melbourne

PAKISTAN				INDIA			
	Mudassar Nazar	c Viswanath, b Kapil Dev	14		R.J. Shastri	not out	63
	Mohsin Khan	c Azharuddin, b Kapil Dev	5		K. Srikkanth	c Wasim Raja, b Imran Khan	67
	Rameez Raja	c Srikkanth, b Chetan Sharma	4		M. Azharuddin	b Tahir Naqqash	25
	Qasim Umar	b Kapil Dev	0		D.B. Vengsarkar	not out	18
	Javed Miandad†	st Viswanath, b Sivaramakrishnan	48		S.M. Gavaskar†		
	Imran Khan	run out	35		M.B. Amarnath		
	Saleem Malik	c Sharma, b Sivaramakrishnan	14		R.N. Kapil Dev		
	Wasim Raja	not out	21		U.S. Madan Lal		
	Tahir Naqqash	c Viswanath, b Shastri	10		S. Viswanath*		
	Anil Dalpat*	c Shastri, b Sivaramakrishnan	0		Chetan Sharma		
	Azeem Hafeez	not out	7		L. Sivaramakrishnan		
	Extras	b 7, lb 8, w 1, nb 2	18		Extras	lb 2, w 2	4
	(50 overs)	(for 9 wickets)	176		(47.1 overs)	(for 2 wickets)	177

	O	M	R	W
Kapil Dev	9	1	23	3
Chetan Sharma	7	1	17	1
Madan Lal	6	1	15	—
Amarnath	9	—	27	—
Shastri	10	—	44	1
Sivaramakrishnan	9	—	35	3

	O	M	R	W
Imran Khan	10	3	28	1
Azeem Hafeez	10	1	29	—
Tahir Naqqash	10	2	35	1
Wasim Raja	7.1	—	42	—
Mudassar Nazar	5	—	26	—
Saleem Malik	2	—	15	—

FALL OF WICKETS
1- 17, 2- 29, 3- 29, 4- 33, 5- 101, 6- 131, 7- 131, 8- 142, 9- 145

FALL OF WICKETS
1- 103, 2- 142

Umpires: R. Isherwood and A. Crafter

India won by 8 wickets

ABOVE: *India – Champions again. (Adrian Murrell)*

LEFT: *Man of the Series Shastri hit over the top. (Adrian Murrell)*

BELOW: *Man of the Match Srikkanth in his exciting innings of 67. (Adrian Murrell)*

tedium can be effective in limited-over cricket.

Sivaramakrishnan should have had a hat-trick. He tossed the ball up to Tahir who responded by hitting high to the long-on boundary where the fielder misjudged the catch and allowed the ball to go for four. Tahir was caught behind by the lively, if not always secure, Viswanath and Sivaramakrishnan got a third wicket when Anil hit straight to extra cover. Wasim Raja and Azeem Hafeez added 31 useful runs for the last wicket and India had failed to bowl out a side for the first time in the competition although once again the standard of their attack and the safety and energy of their fielding had been a delight to watch.

Shastri and Srikkanth, a subtle blend as an opening pair and the best in the competition, began with greater caution than usual, but Srikkanth was soon into his exciting, lofted drives, twice clearing the fence. Imran bowled finely, but the Pakistan attack was a degree below the Indians and the Indian batting was several degrees above the Pakistani's. In the 29th over, Srikkanth slashed straight to cover, but by then he had made 67 and the score was 103. Not surprisingly, he won another Man of the Match award.

Azharuddin maintained the scoring rate with his wide range of shots that suggest he has so much time to spare. He

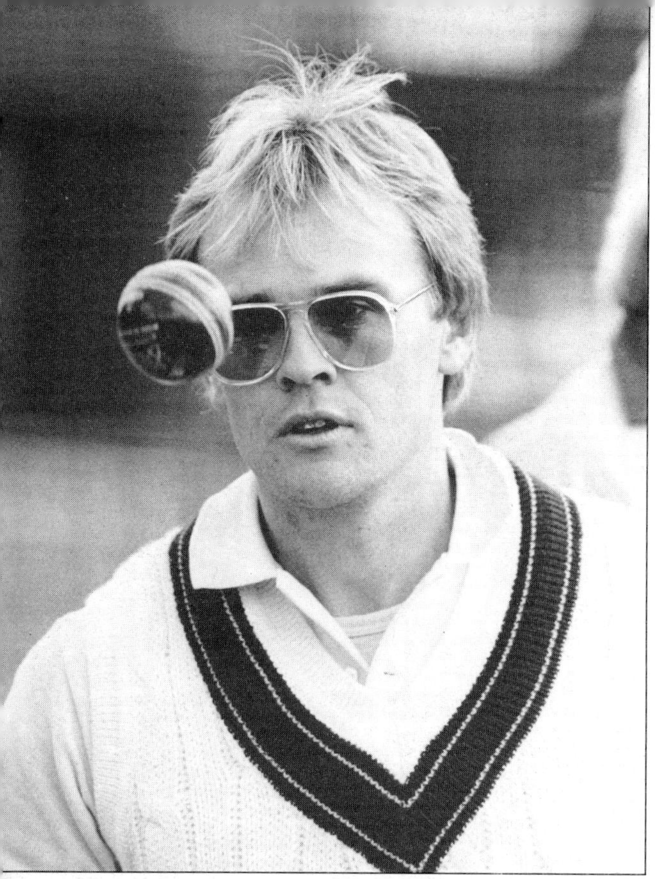

Dirk Wellham led New South Wales to their double triumph. (Adrian Murrell)

should have been caught by Anil who had an unhappy match and he was bowled playing lazily at Tahir, but India were now well in sight of victory. Shastri, a cricketer whose stature increased enormously in 1985, and the elegant Vengsarkar saw them home without fuss and with great joy.

India were by far and away the best side in the competition and to add this championship to their World Cup triumph of 1983 was a remarkable achievement. Their only regret must be that they have failed to produce this magnificent form in their own country.

Sheffield Shield Final
NEW SOUTH WALES *v.* QUEENSLAND

A long and arduous Australian season swamped by international matches came to an end with an exciting domestic final.

Queensland, in search of their first Sheffield Shield win, began uneasily against the pace of Imran Khan and Gilbert. Wessels and Border steadied the innings, but it was a splendid knock by Trevor Hohns that lifted the northern state. He and Phillips added 97 for the 7th wicket and Hohns

SHEFFIELD SHIELD FINAL – NEW SOUTH WALES *v.* QUEENSLAND
15, 16, 17, 18 and 19 March 1985 at Sydney

QUEENSLAND

	FIRST INNINGS		SECOND INNINGS	
R.B. Kerr	b Imran	9	(2) lbw, b Imran	3
B.A. Courtice	b Gilbert	5	(1) b Imran	0
K.C. Wessels	c Dyson, b Gilbert	49	c Dyson, b Holland	22
A.R. Border†	c Dyson, b Bennett	64	(5) c Dyson, b Imran	45
G.M. Ritchie	c Waugh, b Imran	20	(6) c and b Bennett	12
G.S. Trimble	c Wellham, b Bennett	38	(7) c Waugh, b Bennett	16
T.V. Hohns	st Rixon, b Holland	103	(8) c Clifford, b Bennett	2
R.B. Phillips*	c Smith, b Waugh	53	(4) c Wellham, b Imran	47
J.N. Maguire	b Imran	19	b Imran	4
C.G. Rackemann	b Imran	1	c Imran, b Bennett	3
J.R. Thomson	not out	0	not out	1
Extras	b 3, lb 5, nb 5	13	b 3, lb 2, w 1, nb 2	8
		374		163

	O	M	R	W	O	M	R	W
Imran Khan	27.3	6	66	4	19	6	34	5
Gilbert	27	6	67	2	15	5	24	—
Matthews	27	10	53	—	2	—	8	—
Waugh	12	6	15	1	6	1	21	—
Bennett	34	16	54	2	20	4	32	4
Holland	43	12	111	1	15	3	39	1

FALL OF WICKETS
1- 12, 2- 18, 3- 99, 4- 141, 5- 159, 6- 224, 7- 321, 8- 370, 9- 374
1- 0, 2- 3, 3- 41, 4- 116, 5- 129, 6- 143, 7- 154, 8- 154, 9- 160

NEW SOUTH WALES

	FIRST INNINGS		SECOND INNINGS	
J. Dyson	c Ritchie, b Rackemann	66	c Phillips, b Thomson	19
S.B. Smith	c Phillips, b Maguire	76	hit wkt, b Rackemann	7
S.J. Rixon*	c Phillips, b Maguire	0	(4) c and b Thomson	2
D.M. Wellham†	lbw, b Thomson	31	(3) b Thomson	39
P.S. Clifford	c Phillips, b Thomson	13	not out	83
G.R.J. Matthews	lbw, b Maguire	16	c Phillips b Rackemann	8
Imran Khan	c Phillips, b Maguire	7	c Border, b Rackemann	18
S.R. Waugh	c Maguire, b Thomson	71	c Phillips, b Rackemann	21
M.J. Bennett	c Phillips, b Border	10	c Border, b Rackemann	1
R.G. Holland	c Trimble, b Border	0	c Kerr, b Rackemann	10
D.R. Gilbert	not out	8	not out	8
Extras	lb 1, nb 19	20	b 3, lb 2, nb 2	7
		318	(for 9 wkts)	223

	O	M	R	W	O	M	R	W
Thomson	27.3	6	83	3	29	4	81	3
Rackemann	30	9	80	2	30.2	8	54	6
Maguire	33	6	90	3	14	2	27	—
Border	7	2	27	2				
Hohns	24	7	37	—	20	4	56	—

FALL OF WICKETS
1- 98, 2- 98, 3- 167, 4- 185, 5- 219, 6- 223, 7- 226, 8- 281, 9- 283
1- 13, 2- 53, 3- 59, 4- 76, 5- 100, 6- 140, 7- 173, 8- 175, 9- 209

New South Wales won by 1 wicket

ABOVE: *Ray Phillips. Two fifties for Queensland in the Sheffield Shield Final and the leading wicket-keeper of 1984–85. (Adrian Murrell)*

RIGHT: *David Boon, Tasmania. Sheffield Shield Player of the Year. (David Munden)*

BELOW: *David Gilbert, New South Wales. A highly successful season, with 5 for 70 and a hat-trick against Victoria in the penultimate match. (Ken Kelly)*

was finally stumped off Bob Holland, having hit 103 out of 211.

Dyson and Smith gave New South Wales a fine start and they ended the second day at 116 for 2. The home side slumped in the middle of their innings and Queensland looked set to take a substantial lead, but Waugh played a powerful innings, hitting 71 of the last 95 runs before falling to Thomson. He had batted New South Wales back into the game and Imran Khan consolidated what he had done by removing both openers before the close of the third day.

Queensland never effectively recovered. Imran's pace allied to Murray Bennett's spin shot them out for 163 and New South Wales needed 220 to win. On a wicket that was crumbling this was never going to be a formality and Rackemann produced his best bowling of the season in an effort to bring Queensland the honour which had always evaded them. It was Jeff Thomson, however, who threatened after Rackemann's initial breakthrough and New South Wales slumped to 76 for 4. Rackemann now took over and the match became a battle between him and Clifford, a most impressive young batsman. Waugh again hit to good effect in a stand of 33, but Bennett fell almost immediately and New South Wales were 45 short with only two wickets remaining. Holland gave Clifford good support until he became Rackemann's sixth victim with the score at 209.

Gilbert joined Clifford with 11 runs required, and he brought with him a useful record in that he had only been dismissed twice in 14 innings during the season. He played with great good sense and with the scores level he drove Rackemann through the covers to bring the Shield back to New South Wales and to leave Queensland disappointed for yet another season.

First Class Averages

BATTING	M	Inns	NOs	Runs	HS	Av	100s	50s
G. Shipperd	11	18	6	823	139	68.58	3	3
D.M.J. Jones	7	11	1	681	243	68.10	2	3
S.P. O'Donnell	6	8	1	398	129*	56.85	1	2
K.C. Wessels	11	19		1020	173	53.68	3	6
T.J. Barsby	5	9		461	137	51.22	2	1
R.D. Woolley	11	16	2	717	144	51.21	1	5
P.S. Clifford	12	21	3	919	143	51.05	3	4
A.M.J. Hilditch	11	19		960	184	50.52	2	5
M.D. Taylor	11	18	2	801	234*	50.06	2	3
W.J.S. Seabrook	3	4		196	165	49.00	1	
R.B. Kerr	10	18	4	623	201*	44.50	2	1
M.D. Haysman	10	19	2	744	172	43.76	2	3
G.M. Ritchie	11	15		639	136	42.60	1	5
B.F. Davison	6	10	3	295	98*	42.14		2
K. Bradshaw	7	12	2	419	121	41.90	1	2
B.A. Courtice	7	13		540	135	41.53	1	4
D.C. Boon	10	18	2	664	147	41.50	3	2
D.M. Wellham	12	21	1	829	115	41.45	2	4
J. Dyson	12	22		897	98	40.77		9
P.A. Hibbert	4	5	1	163	61	40.75		1
D.F. O'Connor	11	21	2	773	118	40.68	1	8
A.R. Border	11	19	3	645	144*	40.31	1	2
M.W. McPhee	8	13		513	135	39.46	1	4
M.R.J. Veletta	11	19	2	665	143	39.11	2	2
G.W. Goodman	10	18	1	659	123	38.76	1	5
D.F. Whatmore	3	6		228	64	38.00		2
G.M. Wood	8	15		565	141	37.66	1	3
W.M. Darling	3	5	2	113	58*	37.66		1
G.N. Yallop	7	14	1	472	147	36.30	2	2
G.R.J. Matthews	13	22	3	684	103	36.00	1	4
R.S. Hyatt	9	13	5	287	56*	35.87		2
G.R. Marsh	12	20	3	592	143*	34.82	1	4
D.J. Kelly	7	11	2	310	100*	34.44	1	1
D.W. Hookes	11	20		664	151	33.20	1	4
P. Gonella	5	8	2	199	46*	33.16		
R.B. Phillips	12	18	3	491	59	32.73		4
G.A. Bishop	11	21		685	170	32.61	1	3
S.R. Waugh	5	7		223	94	31.85		2
G.S. Trimble	10	16	2	445	90	31.78		3
K.J. Hughes	10	19	2	537	183	31.58	2	1
T.V. Hohns	12	18	1	536	103	31.52	2	2
G.W. Richardson	6	9		282	87	31.33		2
J.D. Siddons	5	9		280	75	31.11		2
M. Ray	11	20	1	576	82	30.31		5
R.J. Bennett	8	14	2	357	89	29.75		2
C.B. Smart	6	11	1	297	54	29.70		4
P.I. Faulkner	8	12	1	326	100	29.63	1	
R.J. Bright	11	15	2	384	84	29.53		1
D.J. Buckingham	8	14	1	382	78	29.38		2
A.K. Zesers	5	6	1	137	85	27.40		1
P.W. Young	3	6	1	134	55	26.80		1
Imran Khan	7	11	1	267	70	26.70		1
S.C. Clements	8	13	1	317	60	26.41		3
R.J. Zadow	6	11		288	55	26.18		1
R.J. Inverarity	10	16	2	363	69	25.92		2
S.B. Smith	9	17	1	407	76	25.43		3
S.J. Rixon	12	21	1	507	115*	25.35	1	2
C.G. Geise	4	7	1	151	84	25.16		1
A.I.C. Dodemaide	6	8		201	74	25.12		1
P.D. King	5	9	1	200	65	25.00		1
T.M. Chappell	3	6	1	115	65	23.00		1
S.L. Saunders	10	15	1	318	107	22.71	1	2
T.J. Zoehrer	8	13	1	270	69*	22.50		3
W.B. Phillips	6	12	1	238	54	21.63		1
D.B. Robinson	3	5		107	52	21.40		1
A.B. Henschell	3	6		124	73	20.66		1
M.B. Quinn	3	6		122	54	20.33		1
I.R. Carmichael	11	14	8	110	24	18.33		
P.H. Marks	8	12	1	198	75	18.00		2
W.G. Whiteside	6	8		139	57	17.37		1
G.F. Lawson	8	14	3	183	49	16.63		
M.J. Bennett	9	13	3	165	23	16.50		
T.B.A. May	6	12	2	154	26	15.40		
W.M. Clark	8	11	2	132	46*	14.66		
R.J. McCurdy	9	13	3	146	34	14.60		
K.H. MacLeay	6	8		107	52	13.37		1
T.G. Hogan	11	15	1	181	27	12.92		
J.N. Maguire	12	17	2	189	61	12.60		1
C.G. Rackemann	12	17	7	108	25*	10.80		

(Qualification – 100 runs, average 10.00)

BOWLING	Overs	Mds	Runs	Wkts	Av	Best	5/inn	10/m
Imran Khan	265.5	88	536	28	19.14	5/34	1	
M.J. Bennett	338.4	108	677	33	20.51	6/32	2	
G.F. Lawson	307.2	75	785	37	21.21	8/112	2	1
C.J. McDermott	243.3	55	779	35	22.25	6/45	1	
R.J. Inverarity	405.4	104	1016	43	23.62	7/86	2	
E.G. Spalding	100	19	308	12	25.66	4/37		
R.G. Holland	620.3	180	1522	59	25.79	9/83	2	2
J.N. Maguire	461.1	104	1273	46	27.67	6/48	3	
K.H. MacLeay	214.3	52	589	21	28.04	5/54	2	
T.M. Alderman	421	112	1247	44	28.34	6/42	3	1
C.G. Rackemann	436	99	1201	42	28.59	6/54	1	
M.P. Tame	101.3	15	353	12	29.41	5/74	1	
J.R. Thomson	326	65	1135	38	29.86	7/27	1	
R.J. Bright	515.3	163	1218	40	30.45	5/41	3	
R.J. McCurdy	358	74	1175	38	30.92	7/55	3	
A.K. Zesers	174	56	434	14	31.00	5/51	1	
W.M. Clark	287.5	77	712	21	33.90	4/70		
S.P. Davis	389.1	68	1089	32	34.03	4/101		
P.M. Clough	214.1	46	648	19	34.10	4/59		
B.A. Reid	226.4	65	581	17	34.17	4/88		
B.P. Patterson	376	51	1359	37	36.72	5/67	2	
G.R.J. Matthews	378.2	121	924	25	36.96	5/32	1	
R.L. Brown	255.4	41	1083	29	37.34	4/46		
D.R. Gilbert	403.1	89	1136	30	37.86	5/70	1	
T.B.A. May	253.5	71	711	18	39.50	6/24	1	
S.P. O'Donnell	125	20	455	11	41.36	3/84		
P.H. Marks	152	30	421	10	42.10	4/83		
T.V. Hohns	336.4	89	845	20	42.25	5/56	1	
M.G. Hughes	164.2	38	466	11	42.36	3/63		
R.M. Hogg	212.1	34	653	15	43.53	4/101		
I.R. Carmichael	431.5	114	1307	27	48.40	3/32		
T.G. Hogan	504.5	124	1333	26	51.26	5/106	1	
P.I. Faulkner	336.3	80	917	17	53.94	3/42		
S.L. Saunders	271	48	878	15	58.53	3/89		

(Qualification – 10 wickets)

LEADING WICKET-KEEPERS

56–R.B. Phillips (ct 55/st 1); 34–S.J. Rixon (ct 27/st 7); 30–M.G. Dimattina (ct 26/st 2); 28–R.D. Woolley (ct 26/st 2); 27–T.J. Zoehrer (ct 25/st 2); 24–D.J. Kelly (ct 22/st 2); 15–W.B. Phillips (ct 14/st 1); 10–G.C. Dyer (ct 8/st 2)

LEADING FIELDERS

19–J. Dyson; 16–M. Ray; 14–G.A. Bishop; 12–A.R. Border, B.A. Courtice and M.D. Haysman; 11–G.M. Ritchie and A.M.J. Hilditch; 10–M.J. Bennett, D.W. Hookes and G.R.J. Matthews

THE SHEFFIELD SHIELD SEASON 1984/85

by Frank Tyson

New South Wales' 38th triumph in the Sheffield Shield in 1984/85 underlined the biblical truth that the race is not just to the swift. Other factors invariably influence the outcome of Australia's most prestigious domestic cricket competition: attributes such as consistency and – most important of all – the ability to produce the supreme effort in moments of crisis. New South Wales' capacity to rise to the big occasion was exemplified by its final surge in the last round of the 1984/85 competition. Queensland, the breakaway leader in the early games of the Shield, required only 196 runs in the final innings of its last preliminary game to defeat South Australia and thus earn the advantage of staging the deciding match on its own Woolloongabba ground. New South Wales for its part, needing every point from its game against Victoria to afford its spinners, Bennett, Matthews and Holland the encouragement of bowling on the turning Sydney wicket, had to dismiss the Melbourne team in a day for fewer than 269 runs. Excessive batting caution and a 41-year-old South Australian by the name of John Inverarity caused Queensland to fall 12 runs short of its moderate target. New South Wales, on the other hand, staked all on a daring declaration, Imran Khan and its spinners and won by 25 runs. The latter decision, it must be added, was just as much the consequence of Victoria's conservatism as it was Wellham's adventurous captaincy. It was rumoured that Bright, the Victorian skipper, chagrined by an adverse lbw decision, instructed his last four batsmen, who had a mere 39 runs to score in 20 overs, to put up the shutters! This overcaution occasioned disaster and Victoria were all out for the addition of 13 runs in 18.5 overs. Fortune on this occasion, justly favoured the brave.

Declining gates at Sheffield Shield matches and the rapidly escalating costs of the domestic competition have caused furrowed brows around the table at Australian Cricket Board meetings in recent years. Many stratagems have been adopted to inject renewed interest into state cricket – the most recent innovation being the introduction of a play-off for the trophy between the two sides at the top of the Shield Table at the end of the home-and-away games. The 1984/85 final between New South Wales and Queensland was a promotional triumph, attracting a 24,063 crowd reminiscent of the post-war era. Small wonder that the spectators flocked to see the match, for it provided a thrilling finish, with New South Wales, set 220 runs for victory in the fourth innings, making the winning run with its last two batsmen at the crease. It was a satisfying climax to a season which, at the outset, did not promise a second successive Shield triumph to Wellham and his men.

The Sydney team won its initial encounter against South Australia in Adelaide by a gratifying 134 runs; but it was a match which promised future complications for coach, Bobby Simpson, and his selectors. Dyson struck a rich vein of form, scoring 70 in his side's first innings total of 7/447 declared. When his batting success extended to another score of 76 in the second game, it was obvious that the opener would be under the national selectors' scrutiny for the First Test against the West Indies. Clifford notched the first century of the season in this game and Matthews and Wellham contributed eighties. Like Dyson, Matthews was destined to complicate New South Wales' campaign to retain the Shield by his candidacy for an Australian cap. David Hookes' South Australians made a spirited 9/313 reply to the substantial New South Wales score, with Andrew Hilditch reaching 184 against his former team-mates. Indeed, when the expatriate Victorian fast bowler, Rod McCurdy, returned a career-best analysis of 7/55 to bundle out the Sydneysiders for only 144 in their second innings, the Adelaide men had an outside chance of victory. The 38 year-old leg-spinner, Bob Holland, quickly extinguished South Australian victory aspirations, however, with his second haul of four wickets in the game and, when the scores were tallied, it was discovered that the home side had fared no better than its opponents in their second batting attempt.

Rain and a capricious wicket made the bowlers dictators of events in the capital clash between New South Wales and Western Australia in Canberra. When, having dismissed its opponents for 156, the western team replied with 0/112, it seemed that it had sealed the issue of the match. Lawson and his fellow bowlers, Gilbert and Holland, however, struck back to claim the next 10 wickets for 59 and restrict the lead of Hughes' team to 15. Dyson's 76 and an unbeaten 49 from the pig-tailed Matthews allowed their side to close its second innings at 9/218 and challenge the Perth batsmen to score 204 for victory. Speedster, Gilbert, quickly established that the task would not be easy by claiming a wicket before the rain descended once more with the score standing at 26.

With the season three matches and three weeks old, Wellham's team were still on the trail and had yet to play a game in the familiar surrounds of the Sydney Cricket Ground. Tasmania was its next port of call and on Launceston's placid wicket it played a draw with Roger Woolley's Taswegians. Batting first, the visitors chalked up 333, with opener Steve Smith contributing 54 and the South African-born all-rounder, Phil Marks, 75. Determined not to be shown up in front of their own spectators, the Apple Islanders riposted with 313, David Boon compiling the first of two centuries which were to come his way in one memorable week and put him on the Test selectors' short list. Wellham tried to force an issue to the game by closing his second innings at 7/262, shortly after he had been dismissed for 115, but the weather once more had a say in the season's events and Tasmania were only permitted the symbolic reply of 1/93 as the game died to a close.

Still on the move, Wellham's Wanderers followed John Soule's time-honoured advice and went west turning their attention to Western Australia and Perth. Their skipper was still in fine fettle and led the way with a solid 86 when his side asked the home team to exceed 386 to gain first innings points. Clifford, Imran Khan and Marks all contributed half-centuries towards the boosting of the New South Welsh morale. That confidence was severely shaken when the home side took the points as Shipperd notched 61, Marsh 73 and wicketkeeper Zoehrer 50. The real credit for the westerners' first-innings win however, went to their numbers 10 and 11, Wayne Clark and Peter Clough, who came together with the total at 9/340 and scored the requisite 47 runs. When New South Wales batted a second time Peter Clifford recorded an unbeaten 102 and Trevor Chappell 65 in a pointless meander to 3/245. When Dirk Wellham returned to Sydney for his state's ensuing clash with South Australia, he was feeling far from confident about retaining the Sheffield Shield. His men had garnered only 4 points from their last three games and only 20 points in all from their season's efforts. This was hardly the form of potential champions!

The New South Welsh transfiguration began the moment that Wellham's men felt the homely turf of the Sydney Cricket Ground beneath their feet in late November. From this point in time, they refused to concede a point in their remaining six fixtures, three of which they won outright. It was the leg-spinner from provincial Newcastle, Bob Holland, who first set his side's feet on the final steep climb to the Shield premiership. His 9/83 in South Australia's final knock was only the second analysis of such proportions for New South Wales in 40 years and was the deciding influence in

West Indians in Australia 1984–85
First Class Matches

BATTING	v. Queensland (Brisbane) 19–22 October 1984		v. South Australia (Adelaide) 26–29 October 1984		v. Western Australia (Perth) 2–4 November 1984		First Test Match (Perth) 9–12 November 1984		v. New South Wales (Sydney) 16–19 Nov. 1984		Second Test Match (Brisbane) 23–26 November 1984		v. Victoria (Melbourne) 30 Nov.–3 Dec. 1984		Third Test Match (Adelaide) 7–11 December 1984		v. Tasmania (Hobart) 14–17 Dec. 1984		Fourth Test Match (Melbourne) 22–27 Dec. 1984		Fifth Test Match (Sydney) 30 December 1984–2 January 1985	
D.L. Haynes	10	—	7	94	15	60*	56	—	26	21	21	7	155	—	0	50			13	63	34	3
R.B. Richardson	65	—			42	50*	0	—	8	1	138	5	145	—	8	3	8	2	51	3	2	26
H.A. Gomes	18	—	16	9	—	—	127	—			13	9*	28	—	60	120*	14*	85	68	18	28	8
I.V.A. Richards	23	—	80	102	1	—	10	—	27	4	6	3*			0	42	16	11	208	0	15	58
A.L. Logie	8	—			18	—			37	6			40	—			7	134				
C.H. Lloyd	21	—	7	63	95	—	0	—	64*	47	114	—			78	6	30	49	19	34*	33	72
P.J. Dujon	5	—	10	151*	12	—	139	—			14	—	17	—	77	32			0	49*	22	8
M.D. Marshall	1	—	35	2*			21	—			57	—			9	—			55	—	0	32*
E.A.E. Baptiste	4	—	30	—					19	0							54	0				
W.W. Davis	1	—			50	—			1	11			24*	—			17*	6				
J. Garner	6*	—					17	—	2	9*	0*	—	—	—	8*	—			8	—	0	8
C.G. Greenidge			26	79	42	12	30	—	9	9	44	—	78	—	95	4			10	1	18	12
R.A. Harper			1	—					4	8			38*	—	9	26	2	11	5	—		
M.A. Holding			21	—	10	—	1	—			1	—					16	—			0	0
C.A. Walsh			0*	—	5*	—	9*	—			0	—	—	—	0	—	16	2*	18*	—	1*	4
T.R.O. Payne									4	14			18	—			2	55				
Byes				6		4	1		3		2				5			2	1	4		2
Leg-byes	5		8	7	3	2	1		8	3	6	2	8		4	2	1	4	11	9	3	12
Wides	2																					
No-balls	8		1	1	9	1	4				8		7		3	7	1	3	12	5	7	8
Total	177		242	514	302	129	416		212	133	424	26	558		356		184	364	479	186	163	253
Wickets	10		10	5	9	1	10		10	10	10	2	7		10	7	9†	9‡	10	5	10	10
Result	D		D		W		W		L		W		D		W		D		D		L	

Catches 29–P.J. Dujon (inc. one as sub)
15–R.B. Richardson (inc. two as sub)
10–T.R.O. Payne (inc. one as sub)
9–C.G. Greenidge
8–I.V.A. Richards and R.A. Harper (inc. two as sub)
7–C.H. Lloyd
† H.A. Gomes retired hurt

6–M.A. Holding
5–D.L. Haynes
4–M.D. Marshall and J. Garner (inc. one as sub)
3–H.A. Gomes (inc. one as sub)
2–C.A. Walsh
1–W.W. Davis and E.A.E. Baptiste
‡ M.A. Holding absent hurt

BOWLING	J. Garner	M.D. Marshall	W.W. Davis	H.A. Gomes	E.A.E. Baptiste	I.V.A. Richards	C.A. Walsh	M.A. Holding	R.A. Harper
v. Queensland (Brisbane)	14–8–19–4	17.1–5–37–3	23–8–58–3	10–4–16–0	12–2–39–0	1–0–3–0			
19–22 October 1984		3–2–7–1	2·4–1–3–0						
v. South Australia (Adelaide)		21–5–75–4			8–3–11–0	5–1–23–0	18–5–53–3	21.2–4–54–2	26–8–72–1
26–29 October 1984		11–2–26–0		14–3–25–1	18–7–44–2	17–7–20–1	16–4–49–1	8–2–19–0	2–0–6–0
v. Western Australia (Perth)			23–0–128–0	19–3–44–0		12–2–26–0	20–4–54–3	26–7–57–0	
2–4 November 1984			7–2–23–2				18.5–4–60–5	12–4–26–3	
First Test Match (Perth)	7–0–24–2	15–5–25–2						9.2–3–21–6	
9–12 November 1984	16–5–52–3	21–4–68–4		1–0–1–0		1–0–4–0	20–4–43–2	11.3–1–53–1	
v. New South Wales (Sydney)	19–8–38–1		26–6–72–3		22.1–5–65–3	5–0–20–0			37–11–84–1
16–19 November 1984	8–6–2–1		9–3–21–0		7–5–4–0	21–10–18–4			27.5–5–72–5
Second Test Match (Brisbane)	18.4–5–67–4	14.4–5–39–2					16–5–55–3	6.2–2–9–1	
23–26 November 1984	20–4–80–0	34–7–82–5				1–0–1–0	5–2–7–1	30–7–92–4	
v. Victoria (Melbourne)	19–3–43–0		25–3–110–1	10–3–22–0			36–6–141–4		51–12–118–1
30 Nov.–3 Dec. 1984									
Third Test Match (Adelaide)	26–5–61–2	26–8–69–5					24–8–88–2		21–4–56–1
7–11 December 1984	16–2–58–1	15.5–4–38–5					4–0–20–0		15–6–43–4
v. Tasmania (Hobart)			2–1–6–0		38.2–6–120–2	17–2–33–1	40–15–119–6	6–3–5–0	38–5–95–1
14–17 December 1984					15.5–0–67–4		16–1–38–2		
Fourth Test Match (Melbourne)	24–6–74–2	31.5–6–86–5				1–0–9–0	21–5–57–2		14–1–58–1
22–27 December 1984	19–1–49–3	20–4–36–0		2–2–0 1		6–2–7–1	18–4–44–1		22–4–54–2
Fifth Test Match (Sydney)	31–5–101–2	37–2–111–0		12–2–29–1		7–2–11–0	38.2–1–118–2	31–7–74–3	
30 Dec. 1984–2 Jan. 1985									
	237.4–58–668–25 *av.* 26.72	267.3–59 699–36 *av.* 19.41	117.4–24–421–8 *av.* 52.62	68–17–137–3 *av.* 45.66	121.2–28–350–11 *av.* 31.81	94–26–175–7 *av.* 25.00	311.1–68–946–37 *av.* 25.56	161.3–40–410–20 *av.* 20.50	253.5–56–658–17 *av.* 38.70

a R.B. Richardson 10–1–40–0, P.J. Dujon 7–3–43–1

	M	Inns	NOs	Runs	HS	Av
	10	17	1	635	155	39.68
	10	17	1	557	145	34.81
	10	15	3	621	127	51.75
	10	17	1	606	208	37.87
	5	7	—	250	134	35.71
	10	16	2	732	114	52.28
	9	13	2	536	151*	48.72
	7	9	2	212	57	30.28
	4	6	—	107	54	17.83
	5	7	2	110	50	22.00
	8	9	4	58	17	11.60
	9	15	—	469	95	31.26
	6	9	1	104	38*	13.00
	6	7	—	49	21	7.00
	9	10	6	55	18*	13.75
	3	5		93	55	18.60

A.L. Logie	C.G. Greenidge	D.L. Haynes	Byes	Leg-byes	Wides	No-balls	Total	Wkts
			1	7		25	180	10
						3	10	1
				7	1	17	295	10
	3-0-7-0			4		7	200	6
			5	3		18	317	3
			1	1		5	111	10
			4	2		7	76	10
				7		14	228	10
			3	5		10	287	10
			8	4		2	129	10
			4	1		11	175	10
			4	5		8	271	10
10-1-29-1		6-0-27-0	6	22		30	601	7a
			2	8		26	284	10
			7	7		4	173	10
			4	6		27	387	10
			1	4		2	110	6
			5	7	1	22	296	10
			6	2		9	198	8
			7	20		17	471	9
10-1-29-1 av. 29.00	3-0-7-0 —	6-0-27-0 —						

that side's victory by 112 runs. Batting first the home team compiled 370, with the ever consistent Wellham falling just 11 runs short of his second century of the summer and Clifford and wicketkeeper Rixon each contributing fifties. Paceman McCurdy showed the stamina which was to earn him an Australian cap after Christmas by taking 5/109. Hookes' batsmen failed to match their opponent's effort by 110 runs in spite of a gallant 80 from Andrew Hilditch, who throughout the season made a fetish of never failing against the state who discarded him as captain and player. Rixon opened the second New South Welsh innings and his unbeaten 115, allied to Dyson's 72 permitted Wellham to make an imaginative declaration at 4/223. Hilditch and Inverarity began the victory quest for 334 runs with a first-wicket partnership of 83 and the South Australian cause seemed far from hopeless. Then Holland struck, capturing nine of the 10 wickets to fall in the space of the next 134 runs. The personal pity of Holland's triumph was that fast bowler Lawson inadvertently bowled a straight delivery to tail-ender, Tim May, and prevented the leg-spinner from joining the elite ranks of the 10 Australians who have taken 10 wickets in one innings of a first-class match.

The preview of the Shield final between Queensland and New South Wales in Brisbane was curtailed by rain, with the visitors earning the first-innings points by 42 runs. Matthews fell a frustrating three runs short of his maiden first-class century in New South Wales' initial score of 357, with Peter Clifford outscoring the all-rounder by one. Queensland batted consistently with Courtice, Smart, Ritchie and Phillips all topping the half-century mark but being unable to extend their innings into three figures. The 'rocker' off-spinner, Matthews, rocked Thomson's batsmen with figures of 4/81 as he moved ever closer to national selection. New South Wales was 16 runs without loss in its second innings when the Queensland climate intervened once more.

Bob Holland was back on home territory for his state's clash with Tasmania. The Newcastle curator, obviously determined to avoid any accusations of preparing a wicket to suit the local bowler, outdid himself, rolling out a surface which yielded 1401 runs in four days. Tasmania fired the first shots by notching 8/409 before declaring, Saunders leading the way with 107 and Goodman and Bradshaw following the all-rounder's example with scores of 50 and 78 respectively. Not to be outbatted, Wellham replied personally with 113, only to be outscored by 30 by Clifford. With Rixon contributing 94 and Dyson 87, the home side eventually led by 110 runs on the first innings. Still the persecution of the bowlers continued as Woolley's batsmen piled on 321 runs in their second innings, Buckingham contributing 78 and Bradshaw completing a sound double with a knock of 63. Needing 212 for outright victory, the home side took the laudable positive approach which characterised the totality of its season's performances and went after the runs. Smith hit the quick-fire 62 which earned him selection in the Australian side for the Benson and Hedges/World Series Cup; but when his wicket fell, New South Wales slumped to 7/152 and reluctantly called off the hunt as they themselves became the quarry for the Tasmanian medium-pacers, Brown and Faulkner. Nonetheless, the home side approached to within 60 runs of what would have been an astonishing and commendable victory.

Queensland 1984–85
First Class Matches

BATTING	v. West Indians (Brisbane) 19–22 October, 1984		v. Victoria (Brisbane) 26–29 October 1984		v. South Australia (Brisbane) 16–19 Nov. 1984		v. Tasmania (Launceston) 30 Nov.–3 Dec. 1984		v. New South Wales (Brisbane) 7–11 Dec. 1984		v. Western Australia (Brisbane) 14–17 Dec. 1984		v. Victoria (Melbourne) 11–14 January 1985		v. Western Australia (Perth) 17–20 January 1985		v. Tasmania (Brisbane) 25–28 January 1985		v. New South Wales (Sydney) 22–25 February 1985		v. South Australia (Adelaide) 1–4 March 1985	
K.C. Wessels	0	7	60	28	64	144	4	—			137	—										
R.B. Kerr	24*	0*	106	19*	40	2	27	—	6	—	22	14*	3	41	35	11	60	201*				
A.R. Border	23	0*	0	8*	32	41	144*	—			42	—										
G.M. Ritchie	4	—	136	—	84	37	59	—	71	—	65	—					2	—	59	38	4	11
G. S. Trimble	42	—	90	—	0	67*	36	—	29	—	0	0*	15	20	8	0					76	8
T.V. Hohns	6	—	25	—	15	3	90	—	12	—	23	—	32	23	10	103	3	—	1	6	72*	7
R.B. Phillips	38*	—	0	—	16	56*	39	—	56	—	5	—	26	28*	10	22	59	—	1	4	15	16
C.J. McDermott	7	—	14	—	0	—	18	—	4*	—	30	—										
J.N. Maguire	1	—	1	—	10*	—	61	—	3	—	21	—	11	8*	34	1	10	—	5	0	0	0
C.G. Rackemann	0	—	11*	—	4*	—	17	—	2	—	0*	—	18*	—	8*	4			25*	0	15*	0
J.R. Thomson	2	—	6	—	—	—	25	—	0	—	—	—	10	—	5	0*	2*	—	4	0*	—	5*
B.A. Courtice									64	—			69	70	14	2	34	135	10	50	42	45
C.B. Smart									54	—			38	50	7	0	50	21*	20	3	0	54
T.J. Barsby													49	0	133	11	137	—	14	30	72	15
A.B. Henschell													16	12					4	0	73	19
H. Frei															26	9	6	—				
G.K. Whyte																	4	—	2	11		
Byes	1		3			1	9		7		7				9		7	3	2	5	1	1
Leg-byes	7		10	1	8	10	7		4		8	1	7	5		2	2	3	8	4	5	2
Wides							2		2				5	1	1				1		1	
No-balls	25	3	5		10	9	4		1		6		2	2	10	6	8	6			2	
Total	180	10	467	56	283	370	542		315		366	15	301	260	310	171	384	369	156	151	378	183
Wickets	10	1	10	1	8	5	10		10		9	0	10	7	10	10	10	1	10	10	8	10
Result	D		W		W		W		D		W		D		L		D		L		L	
Points	—		16		16		16		0		16		4		4		0		0		4	

Catches 56 – R.B. Phillips (ct 55/st 1)
12 – B.A. Courtice
11 – G.M. Ritchie
8 – A.R. Border
7 – T.V. Hohns, R.B. Kerr, C.B. Smart and G.S. Trimble
5 – J.N. Maguire
3 – J.R. Thomson, A.B. Henschell and C.J. McDermott
2 – T.J. Barsby and C.G. Rackemann
1 – H. Frei and K.C. Wessels

BOWLING	C.G. Rackemann	J.R. Thomson	J.N. Maguire	C.J. McDermott	T.V.Hohns	A.R. Border	K.C. Wessels	A.B. Henschell	H. Frei
v. West Indians (Brisbane)	8–1–38–1	5.1–0–48–1	15–1–48–6	14.1–3–38–2					
19–22 October 1984									
v. Victoria (Brisbane)	16–5–28–3	12–2–48–1	14.1–6–31–2	19–6–55–4	24–13–31–0				
26–29 October 1984	25.4–7–66–3	17–3–53–0	16–4–56–1	23–6–52–2	40–16–81–1	3–2–3–0			
v. South Australia (Brisbane)	14–2–43–1	10–3–52–2	17–2–64–0	13–2–59–1	25.1–9–56–5				
16–19 November 1984	21–2–63–1	17–6–68–0	19–4–59–1	26–9–36–2	23–3–90–1	7–2–24–3	5–0–25–1		
v. Tasmania (Launceston)	13–1–60–1	4–0–27–1	19–5–63–2	17–7–45–6					
30 Nov.–3 Dec. 1984	15–2–60–2	11.3–2–47–3	12–3–40–0	11–0–44–2	9–0–38–2				
v. New South Wales	31.5–5–96–1	16–2–73–3	24–7–42–2	20–8–78–4	14–2–50–0				
7–11 December 1984			2–0–8–0	2.2–1–7–0					
v. Western Australia (Brisbane)	12–1–39–1	14.5–5–27–7	8–1–25–0	15–3–35–1	12–4–25–0				
14–17 December 1984	16.3–4–57–4	13–1–37–2	11–5–28–1	14–2–57–1	14–3–37–2				
v. Victoria (Melbourne)	12·5–4–28–3	11–4–29–3	15–6–36–4						
11–14 January 1985	36–8–98–3	18–3–57–0	35–6–98–1		30–8–78–2			7–1–38–0	
v. Western Australia (Perth)	26–9–62–3	25–5–84–0	34.3–7–84–6						16–4–44–0
17–20 January 1985	13.5–2–30–2	8–1–27–1	25–3–79–3		1–0–3–0				21–8–53–1
v. Tasmania (Brisbane)		32–8–105–2	43–8–111–3		40.3–6–129–4				29–10–67–0
25–28 January 1985									
v. New South Wales (Sydney)	22–2–70–1	15–3–51–2	35–6–88–3		20–2–50–1			10–1–30–0	
22–25 February 1985									
v. South Australia (Adelaide)	26–13–46–3	20–2–71–2	29.3–13–62–5		10–3–19–0				
1–4 March 1985	38–11–77–1	20–5–67–2	40–9–134–3		30–9–05–2			4–1–8–0	
v. New South Wales (Sydney)	30–9–80–2	27.3–6–83–3	33–6–90–3		24–7–37–0	7–2–27–2			
15–19 March 1985	30.2–8–54–6	29–4–81–3	14–2–27–0		20–4–56–0				
	408–96–1095–42 *av.* 26.07	326–65–1135–38 *av.* 29.86	461.1–104–1273–46 *av.* 27.67	174.3–47–506–25 *av.* 20.24	336.4–89–845–20 *av.* 42.25	17–6–54–5 *av.* 10.80	5–0–25–1 *av.* 25.00	21–3–76–0 —	66–22–164–1 *av.* 164.00

v. New South Wales (Sydney) 15–19 March 1985		M	Inns	NOs	Runs	HS	Av
49	22	6	10	—	515	144	51.50
9	3	10	18	4	623	201*	44.50
64	45	6	10	3	399	144*	57.00
20	12	10	14	—	602	136	43.00
38	16	10	16	2	445	90	31.78
103	2	12	18	1	536	103	31.52
53	47	12	18	3	491	59	32.73
		6	6	1	73	30	14.60
19	4	12	17	2	189	61	12.60
1	3	11	15	7	108	25*	13.50
0*	1*	12	13	6	60	25	8.57
5	0	7	13	—	540	135	41.53
		6	11	1	297	54	29.70
		5	9	—	461	137	51.22
		3	6	—	124	73	20.66
		2	3	—	41	26	13.66
		2	3	—	17	11	5.66
3	3						
5	2						
	1						
5	2						
374	163						
10	10						
	L						
	—						

G.K. Whyte	B.A. Courtice	Byes	Leg-byes	Wides	No-balls	Total	Wkts
			5	2	8	177	10
			8		13	201	10
			8	1	6	319	10
			3		22	277	10
			10		23	375	9
		1	4	3	13	200	10
		8			7	237	9†
		9	9		16	357	10
			1			16	0
			5		9	156	10
		8			7	224	10
		4	4		5	101	10
		1	13	8	6	383	7
			7		27	281	10
		8	1		9	201	8
31–11–88–0			7	2	15	507	9
33–10–77–2			2	2	5	368	10
	2–1–4–0	2	6	2	7	210	10
			12	1	11	363	10
			1		19	318	10
		3	2		2	223	9
64–21–165–2 *av.* 82.50	2–1–4–0 –						

† B.F. Davison retired hurt

Four days later, the Sydneysiders journeyed south to Melbourne, where they confronted a dispirited Victorian eleven, languishing at the tail of the Shield field. There was nothing passive about the home side's batting, however, when it took strike first on a moribund wicket. Five batsmen bettered the fifty mark as Bright's team piled on 438 runs. When New South Wales replied with 265 for its first wicket, that total paled into insignificance against the background of a pitch which afforded the bowlers not one iota of encouragement. Dyson notched 97 and Seabrook, in his first innings for New South Wales, pillaged 165 runs off a totally ineffective attack in 289 balls. It was left to O'Neill to hammer home the final nail in Victoria's coffin, as he compiled a 45-run innings which earned first innings points for the Sydneysiders. Thereafter there was little point to a contest which became routine practice for the home batsmen who coasted to 4/236 against the nine bowlers employed by Wellham. Yallop, after his first innings 58, took advantage of the atmosphere of detente to display his true potential with an unbeaten 125, whilst the youthful Siddons gave a glimpse of future promise with a competent knock of 68.

In mid-February, New South Wales foreshadowed what would happen if it was afforded the luxury of contesting the deciding match of the Sheffield Shield on its native heath. Wellham's slow bowlers annihilated their Queensland opponents on a turning wicket by an innings and 61 runs. In two batting attempts the Brisbane batsmen could muster no more than 307 runs against a spin attack which significantly reaped a 15-wicket reward from the encounter. Even though they batted when the wicket was at its best, the Brisbane batsmen could only profit by 156 runs in their first innings with Matthews, Bennett and Holland each claiming three victims. The pace-oriented Queensland attack thereupon conceded 368 on an unsympathetic surface which allowed Dyson to reach 93 and Matthews 87. The trendy off-spinner went on to climax a highly satisfying match by capturing five Queensland second-innings wickets for 32 as the northern team collapsed a second time for 151, leaving the day, and foreseeably the Sheffield Shield, to New South Wales.

On the crest of a wave of success, Wellham's men entertained – if that be the right euphemism – Victoria in the final game of the season at the Sydney Cricket Ground. The destiny of the 1984/85 Sheffield Shield competition virtually hinged on this crucial encounter since, if Victoria could deny Wellham's side the game's full allocation of 16 points, the deciding match would take place at the 'Gabba where the spinning effectiveness of the New South Wales attack would be considerably blunted. Queensland needed only first innings points from its game against South Australia – plus the support of Victoria – to gain the home-ground advantage in the final. Whilst Border's team failed to maximise its opportunities in Adelaide, it did earn four points – but it was grievously let down by Victoria!

New South Wales headed the Melbourne side on the first innings by 67 runs, thanks mainly to Graeme Matthews' maiden first-class century and a splendid 94 from the bat of the youthful Waugh. Yallop's 147 constituted well over 50% of Victoria's 259 run reply: a sobering reflection on the effectiveness of the southern state's rebuilding policies of the previous two years. Gilbert, showed that he had learned much under Imran Khan's tutelage by bowling with great

Tasmania 1984–85
First Class Matches

BATTING	v. Western Australia (Perth) 19–22 October 1984		v. New South Wales (Launceston) 9–12 Nov. 1984		v. Victoria (Melbourne) 15–18 Nov. 1984		v. South Australia (Adelaide) 22–25 Nov. 1984		v. Queensland (Launceston) 30 Nov.–3 Dec. 1984		v. West Indians (Hobart) 14–17 Dec. 1984		v. South Australia (Hobart) 20–23 Dec. 1984		v. New South Wales (Newcastle) 17–20 January 1985		v. Queensland (Brisbane) 25–28 January 1985		v. Victoria (Devonport) 22–25 February 1985		v. Western Australia (Hobart) 1–4 March 1985	
M. Ray	13	8	10	38*	60	8	49	—	28	5	59	11	82	8	15	5	14	—	65	23	53	22
G.W. Goodman	57	10	16	53	7	0	30*	—			123	22	14	10	50	39	88	—	45	89	6	0
D.C. Boon	1	2	138	0*	104	—			12	1	32	1*							7	78	147	9
K. Bradshaw	16	4	0	—									0*	42	78	63	121	—	20	27	41*	7
B.F. Davison	29	98*	34	—			66	—	30	11*									5	0	5	17*
R.D. Woolley	144	61	55	—	10	—	51	—	1	93	35	22*	—	15	30	37	67	—	22	32	42*	—
S.L. Saunders	1	1	10	—	6	2*	53	—	28	24	0	13			107	0	4	—	0	69	—	—
P.I. Faulkner	30	12	13	—	27	—	40	—	0	26	23	0*			25	30	100	—				
R.S. Hyatt	16	3*	22	—	36	—	56*	—	3	6*	29	6	—	50	26*	28	6*	—				
B.P. Patterson	12	—	7*	—	2*	—	—	—	0	0	4	—	—	0			—	—	2	0	—	—
R.L. Brown	11*	—			20	—	9	—	2*	0	21*	—	—	4	—	4	5	—	6*	1*	—	—
W.S. Kirkman			2	—									—	6								
R.J. Bennett					14	14*	89	—	41	40	0	4	60	6	18	3	41	—			1	26*
D.J. Buckingham					71	17	20	—	34	16	25	24	18*	32	8	78	37	—	0	2		
M.P. Tame													—	7*	35*	12*			19	4	—	—
Byes	7	1		1	1	2	5		1	8	4	1		2	4	6			1	3	2	
Leg-byes	9	9	3	1	6		5		4		5	4		3	11	12	7		1	1	5	2
Wides					1				3					1	1	4	2			3	2	
No-balls	13	3	3		3		14		13	7	27	2	14	7	1		15		3	1	3	
Total	359	212	313	93	368	43	487		200	237	387	110	188	193	409	321	507		196	333	307	83
Wickets	10	7	10	1	10	3	8		10	9†	10	6	3	10	8	10	9		10	10	5	4
Result	D		D		D		D		L		D		L		D		D		D		D	
Points	0		0		0		4		0		—		0		0		4		0		4	

Catches 28 – R.D. Woolley (ct 26/st 2)
16 – M. Ray
8 – D.J. Buckingham
6 – D.C. Boon and R.S. Hyatt
5 – B.F. Davison, R.L. Brown, G.W. Goodman and S.L. Saunders
3 – R.J. Bennett and K. Bradshaw (two as sub)
1 – M.P. Tame, B.P. Patterson and sub (Dell)

† B.F. Davison retired hurt

BOWLING	B.P. Patterson	R.L. Brown	P.I. Faulkner	S.L. Saunders	R.S. Hyatt	M. Ray	W. Kirkman	D.C. Boon	M.P. Tame
v. Western Australia (Perth)	33.4–1–146–2	3–1–15–0	41–11–121–1	33–6–105–3	18–3–46–1	21–2–62–0			
19–22 October 1984	16–0–75–0		20.4–7–49–1	11–2–43–1					
v. New South Wales (Launceston)	26.2–4–102–3		35–8–94–1	14–5–30–1	12–4–30–3		17–4–63–2		
9–12 November 1984	22.3–3–68–4		30–7–51–1	14–0–39–0	13–4–30–0	11–2–31–1	10–3–29–0		
v. Victoria (Melbourne)	33.3–7–107–1	25–2–101–1	37–10–68–2	40–10–89–3	37–11–84–2	2–1–2–0		3–1–12–1	
15–18 November 1984									
v. South Australia (Adelaide)	17–2–58–2	15–6–46–4	22–6–53–2	9–1–72–0	13–3–52–0				
22–25 November 1984	19–3–62–2	30–6–101–2	18–3–60–0	23–4–74–1	22–3–51–1	11.5–4–28–3			
v. Queensland (Launceston)	40–5–141–3	21–2–112–3	33.5–8–107–1	18–2–56–2	13–1–51–0	7–0–34–1			
30 Nov.–3 Dec. 1984									
v. West Indians (Hobart)	17–2–67–2	13–3–72–4	17–5–42–3	1–0–2–0					
14–17 December 1984	21.2–3–74–3	10–3–29–3		20–2–104–1	20–2–77–0	21–2–74–2			
v. South Australia (Hobart)	15–2–50–1	13–2–54–0					10–3–34–0		11–0–58–1
20–23 December 1984	18.3–3–67–5	8–1–42–1			2–0–3–0		7–0–29–1		9–2–35–1
v. New South Wales (Newcastle)		25–2–112–1	37–5–103–1	29–3–99–1	15–2–37–0	27–5–76–2			25.3–3–74–5
17–20 January 1985		10–0–68–3	10–2–73–2						
v. Queensland (Brisbane)	31.1–6–93–5	31–7–105–2	24–7–63–2	13–1–39–0		9–1–33–0			
25–28 January 1985	21–4–44–0	15–3–74–0	11–1–33–0	19–2–84–0	29–6–73–1	12–2–37–0			
v. Victoria (Devonport)	30–3–123–2	22.4–2–94–2		10–3–22–2		2–1–2–0			38–7–138–4
22–25 February 1985	4–0–35–2	3–0–22–2							
v. Western Australia (Hobart)	10–3–47–0	11–1–36–1		17–7–20–0		3–2–4–0			18–3–48–1
1–4 March 1985									
	376–51– 1359–37 *av.* 36.72	255.4–41– 1083–29 *av.* 37.34	336.3–80 917–17 *av.* 53.94	271–48– 878–15 *av.* 58.53	194–39– 534–8 *av.* 66.75	126.5–22 383–9 *av.* 42.55	44–10– 155–3 *av.* 51.66	3–1– 12–1 *av.* 12.00	101.3–15– 353–12 *av.* 29.41

a D.J. Buckingham 1–0–1–0– R.D. Woolley 1–1–0–0 b H.A. Gomes retired hurt c M.A. Holding absent injured d K. Bradshaw 5–0–17–0

	M	Inns	NOs	Runs	HS	Av
	11	20	1	576	82	30.31
	10	18	1	659	123	38.76
	7	13	2	532	147	48.36
	7	12	2	419	121	41.90
	6	10	3	295	98*	42.14
	11	16	2	717	144	51.21
	10	15	1	318	107	22.71
	8	12	1	326	100	29.63
	9	13	5	287	56*	35.87
	10	9	2	27	12	3.85
	10	11	5	83	21*	13.83
	2	2	—	8	6	4.00
	8	14	2	357	89	29.75
	8	14	1	382	78	29.38
	4	5	3	77	35*	38.50

G.W. Goodman	R.J. Bennett	B.F. Davison	Byes	Leg-byes	Wides	No-balls	Total	Wkts
			5	4	1	24	504	10
			2	1		2	170	4
				14	2	8	333	10
			5	9		5	262	7
			14	13		8	491	10a
			2	6		14	289	10
	1–0–2–1		4	1		8	383	10
		7–2–25–0	9	7	2	4	542	10
				1		1	184	9b
			2	4		3	364	9c
				9		1	205	2
				4		1	180	8
			1	17		6	519	10
1–0–6–1				5			152	7
15–6–42–1			7	2		8	384	10
1–0–1–0			3	3		6	369	1d
2–0–4–0				7	1	10	390	10
			1			1	58	4
			3			4	158	2
19–6–53–2 *av.* 26.50	1–0–2–1 *av.* 2.00	7–2–25–0 —						

spirit to take 5/70 in the Victorian innings and placing a New South Wales victory within the bounds of possibility. Wellham's 81 and Dyson's 54 in the New South Wales second innings gave the home side an advantage of 268 and enabled Wellham to declare before stumps on the third day of the game. The curtain rose on the final act with Bright's men needing 252 to win and become heroes – in the eyes of Queenslanders! It fell with the Victorians cast as villains to Queenslanders and New South Welshmen alike. Wellham condemned the refusal of Victoria's last four batsmen to attempt 39 runs in the last 20 overs as disgraceful and their team's defeat by 25 runs as well deserved. More importantly Victoria had failed Queensland by handing the home-ground advantage in the final to New South Wales on a plate.

Initially that benefit was offset by Queensland batting first and accumulating a respectable total of 374. The voyage to that score, however, was not all plain sailing, for with both of its Test stars, Border and Wessels out, Queensland four itself facing a moderate score at 5/159. It was at this opportune moment that Trevor Hohns chose to compile his second Shield hundred and add 97 for the sixth wicket with 'keeper Ray Phillips. New South Wales began its riposte with a solid 98-run partnership between Dyson and Smith, but then slipped into danger with the loss of seven wickets for an additional 132 runs. The Sydneysiders' Messiah was young Steve Waugh who clubbed 71 from 109 balls to restrict the Queensland first-innings advantage to 56 runs. At this stage of the match, New South Wales was powerless to prevent Queensland's inaugural Sheffield Shield triumph – provided Border's batsmen performed with solid common sense in their second innings. But it seemed that Queensland did not know how to win. Just as it squandered its winning chances against South Australia in its penultimate match, it wasted them in this far more crucial game. Imran Khan opened up the throttle to take 5/34 and dismiss the less-than-resolute men from north of the River Tweed for 163. Thus New South Wales were confronted with the ostensibly simple task of scoring 220 for victory and the Shield and on the fourth evening had knocked off 64 of those runs for the loss of three wickets. On the succeeding day fast bowler, Carl Rackemann, made the 156 runs separating New South Wales from the premiership seem like a 1000. In a superb 30.2 overs of aggressive bowling he captured 6/54 and brought his side to the verge of tantalising triumph and New South Wales, at one stage, to the incipient disaster of 8/175. The Wondai speedster would have won the game for Border – if Peter Clifford had not hung on defiantly for the Sydneysiders, as he had on so many occasions throughout the season, to score 83 not out. With 11 runs standing between New South Wales and glory, Border gambled on the second new ball; but Rackemann, drained by his 30 over effort, could not produce the necessary head of steam and Gilbert, his side's last hope, drove him for the winning runs past mid-off. It seemed like an eternity before the devastated Rackemann could bring himself to realise what had transpired, raise himself from his haunches – to which he had sunk after the final ball – and make his dejected way back to the pavilion on the consoling arm of Allan Border. One wicket had separated Queensland from its maiden triumph in the Sheffield Shield. Just one wicket!

Queensland were undoubtedly the most deserving team in

Victoria 1984–85
First Class Matches

BATTING	v. Queensland (Brisbane) 26–29 October 1984		v. Western Australia (Melbourne) 9–12 Nov. 1984		v. Tasmania (Melbourne) 15–18 Nov. 1984		v. West Indians (Melbourne) 30 Nov.–3 Dec. 1984		v. South Australia (Melbourne) 14–17 Dec. 1984		v. Western Australia (Perth) 20–23 Dec. 1984		v. Queensland (Melbourne) 11–14 January 1985		v. South Australia (Adelaide) 17–20 January 1985		v. New South Wales (Melbourne) 25–28 January 1985		v. Tasmania (Devonport) 22–25 February 1985		v. New South Wales (Sydney) 1–4 March 1985	
P.A. Hibbert	15	42	61	—	39	—							6*	—								
M.B. Quinn	0	54											16	26	16	10						
G.N. Yallop	0	2											21	0	34	1	58	125*	51	22	147	8
D.M.J. Jones	26	34	33	—	67	—	71	—	58*	5	243	8	0	136								
M.D. Taylor	57	15	14	—	118	—	234*	—	37*	28	34	0	3	47	38	17	77	2	67	—	13	0
S.P. O'Donnell	5	54	10	—	42	—	78	—	—	38	42	129*										
A.I.C. Dodemaide	36	74	13	—	12	—	3	—	—	6	22	35										
P.A. Hyde	7	10																				
R.J. Bright	6	19	34	—	42	—	—	—	—	33	18	10*	19	40*	15	7	84	—	30	—	0	27
R.M. Hogg	28	0*			17	—																
S.P. Davis	0*	0	1*	—	15*	—			—	0	0	—	0	—	4	1*	5*	—	0*	—	1	0
G.W. Richardson			80	—	87	—	12	—	35	9	28	0			12	19						
W.G. Whiteside			24	—	7	—	57	—	—	16	0	25	0	10								
M.G. Dimattina			8*	—	10	—	1*	—	—	1	0	—	7	10*	0	8	12	—	8	—	9*	2*
M.G. Hughes			13	—			—	—	—	9*	3*	—					8	—				
D.B. Robinson							52	—	10	34	3	8										
J.D. Siddons							35	—							15	46	17	68	12	0	12	75
S.F. Graf													0	49								
P.D. King													16	37	11	20	19	—	65	2*	5	25
J.M. Wiener															31	16	19	9				
C.K. Smith															13*	1						
D.F. Whatmore																	63	11	64	26	30	34
P.W. Young																	55	12*	10	5	17	35
G. Jordan																			29	1*		
R. McCarthy																			36	—	0	2
D. Emerson																					16	32
Byes			3		14		6			16	1	7	4	1	1	2	1			1	1	
Leg-byes	8	8	13		13		22			5	4	7	4	13	6	2	12	9	7		4	2
Wides		1							1		1	1		8			1		1		1	
No-balls	13	6	3		8		30		6	10	6	1	5	6	1		7		10	1	3	1
Total	201	319	310		491		601		147	210	405	231	101	383	197	150	438	236	390	58	259	243
Wickets	10	10	9		10		7		2	10	10	6	10	6	10	10	10	4	10	4	10	10
Results	L		D		D		D		L		D		D		L		D		D		L	
Points	0		2		4		—		4		4		0		0		0		4		0	

Catches 30 – M.G. Dimattina (ct 24/st 6) 8 – J.D. Siddons 6 – D.M.J. Jones and G.W. Richardson (one as sub) 5 – S.P. Davis, M.D. Taylor and D.F. Whatmore 4 – P.A. Hibbert and R.J. Bright 3 – P.A. Hyde, G.N. Yallop, S.P. O'Donnell, W.G. Whiteside

BOWLING	R.M. Hogg	S.P. Davis	S.P. O'Donnell	R.J. Bright	A.I.C. Dodemaide	M.G. Hughes	W.G. Whiteside	J.M. Wiener	D.B. Robinson
v. Queensland (Brisbane)	32–5–94–2	30–7–80–1	22–3–84–3	31–2–133–3	19.2–3–63–1				
26–29 October 1984		6.3–0–35–0	6–0–20–1						
v. Western Australia (Melbourne)		26–2–69–3	12–1–31–0	43–15–113–2	28.2–5–70–2	32–6–84–3	7–1–12–0		
9–12 November 1984									
v. Tasmania (Melbourne)	26–6–67–1	20–3–45–0	29–10–72–2	34.4–8–60–2	35–4–90–3		9–1–25–2		
15–18 November 1984	7–0–18–1	5–1–12–1			2–0–10–1				
v. West Indians (Melbourne)			22–1–112–2	40–11–98–2	30–4–137–0	25–4–88–1	5–0–16–0		22–3–99–1
30 Nov.–3 Dec. 1984									
v. South Australia (Melbourne)		17–2–55–3		10–4–15–0	12–3–43–0	13.2–4–32–1			
14–17 December 1984		15–1–62–0	10–0–52–1	32–8–100–2	9–0–48–0	17–2–52–0	10–1–23–1		4–0–29–0
v. Western Australia (Perth)		20.2–4–38–2	12–2–38–1	29–9–62–4	21–2–65–1	26–11–69–2	1–0–2–0		
20–23 December 1984		12–2–39–2	12–3–46–1	26–9–56–3	11–3–32–0	20–3–63–3			1–0–1–0
v. Queensland (Melbourne)		30.3–4–106–4		25–11–49–0			11–4–27–0		
11–14 January 1985		27–4–79–2		35–13–60–3			5–1–12–0		
v. South Australia (Adelaide)		36–10–103–2		59–20–99–3				18–6–41–0	
17–20 January 1985									
v. New South Wales (Melbourne)		48–14–108–3		47–13–139–5		31–8–78–1		6–1–11–0	
25–28 January 1985									
v. Tasmania (Devonport)		21–3–50–2		21–10–41–5					
22–25 February 1985		30.5–6–101–4		26–11–29–1					
v. New South Wales (Sydney)		29–4–75–3		39.5–12–112–5					
1–4 March 1985		15–1–32–0		17–7–52–0					
	65–11–179–4 av. 44.75	389.1–68–1089–32 av. 34.03	125–20–455–11 av. 41.36	515.3–163–1218–40 av. 30.45	167.4–24–558–8 av. 69.75	164.2–38–466–11 av. 42.36	48–8–117–3 av. 39.00	24–7–52–0 —	27–3–129–1 av. 129.00

a D.M.J. Jones 1–0–2–0
b P.A. Hibbert 1–0–1–0
c C.K. Smith 20–3–69–2
d R. McCarthy 22–6–75–1
e R. McCarthy 22–1–80–4
G.N. Yallop 8–1–25–0
f R. McCarthy 18–6–66–2
D. Emerson 23–5–60–0

M	Inns	NOs	Runs	HS	Av
4	5	1	163	61	40.75
3	6	—	122	54	20.33
6	12	1	469	147	42.63
7	11	1	681	243	68.10
11	18	2	801	234*	50.06
6	8	1	398	129*	56.85
6	8	—	201	74	25.12
1	2	—	17	10	8.50
11	15	2	384	84	29.53
2	3	1	45	28	22.50
10	13	6	27	15*	3.85
6	9	—	282	87	31.33
6	8	—	139	57	17.37
10	13	5	76	12	9.50
5	4	2	33	13	16.50
3	5	—	107	52	21.40
5	9	—	280	75	31.11
1	2	—	49	49	24.50
5	9	1	200	65	25.00
2	4	—	75	31	18.75
1	2	1	14	13*	14.00
3	6	—	228	64	38.00
3	6	1	134	55	26.80
1	2	1	30	29	30.00
2	3	—	38	36	12.66
1	2	—	48	32	24.00

nd P.D. King — 2–A.I.C. Dodemaide and subs (Watts) — 1–M.B. Quinn, M.G. Hughes, G. Jordan, D.B. Robinson, R.J. McCurdy and D.A. Emerson

S.F. Graf	P.D. King	J.D. Siddons	Byes	Leg-byes	Wides	No-balls	Total	Wkts
			3	10		5	467	10
				1			56	1
			5	5			389	10
			1	6	1	3	368	10a
			2				43	3b
				8		7	558	7
				1		3	146	4
			6	6		7	378	5
			4	2	1	8	280	10
			2	6		3	245	9
22–7–51–2	20–5–61–3			7	5	2	301	10
16–3–40–2	20–1–64–0			5	1	2	260	7
	29–2–90–2	8–0–26–0	6	7	1	2	441	10c
	12–1–66–0	11–0–27–0	4	9	4	5	442	9
	10–4–27–2	1–0–1–0	1	1		3	196	10d
	23–3–78–1	6–1–16–0	3	1	3	1	333	10e
		3–1–10–0	1	2	1		326	10f
	15–5–52–1		8				201	3g
38–10–91–4 *av.* 22.75	129–21–438–9 *av.* 48.66	29–2–80–0 —						

g R. McCarthy 10–3–26–1
D. Emerson 14–1–31–0

the 1984/85 Sheffield Shield competition. Theirs would have been the power and the glory, if they had not been consistently crippled by national demands on their key players, Wessels, Border and McDermott who, even when they returned to the Queensland side, were rarely in first unjaded bloom of fitness. Jeff Thomson deputised for absentee skipper Allan Border during the international season and with the support of the experienced John Maguire, Trevor Hohns and Carl Rackemann bonded the northern men into a formidable cricketing machine which moved into top gear from the first day of the season. Stringing together a succession of four outright victories Queensland virtually assured itself of a place in the Shield final before the summer was six weeks old.

Border presided over Queensland's annihilation of Victoria by nine wickets in Brisbane's initial Shield game in late October. McDermott's pace and Rackemann's bounce were just too much for the under-prepared southerners on the lively 'Gabba wicket. Bright's batsmen capitulated for 201 in their first innings as McDermott and Rackemann mowed down a swathe of seven batsmen. Queensland's batsmen had outscored the touring West Indians in the preceding game and found the Victorian bowlers much less daunting than the likes of Garner, Marshall and Holding. Ritchie and Kerr reeled off fluent centuries and with Glenn, the son of former Australian representative, Sam Trimble, helping himself to 90 runs, the home side amassed 467: a lead of 266. Its pride pricked, Victoria staged a comeback in its second innings with O'Donnell and Quinn each scoring 54 and the promising Dodemaide 74 in a total of 319. The inexperience of its batsmen was still self-evident, however, in the fact that both O'Donnell and Quinn were run out after having established firm foundations for what should have been major innings. Had they lingered at the crease, Queensland would have been faced with a more substantial task than that of notching 56 for victory in its second innings: a challenge which it met and overcame for the loss of one wicket.

Still enjoying its home-ground, fine-weather advantage Border's side next accounted for South Australia by five wickets. Leg-spinner, Trevor Hohns was the major restrictive factor in confining South Australia's first innings total to 277: a score which owed its substance to 87 from opener Wayne Bishop and 53 from the left-handed Donald O'Connor. Queensland's subsequent first innings superiority of six runs was only achieved with eight wickets down and by dint of hard-won scores of 84 from Greg Ritchie and 64 from Kepler Wessels. Thereupon, South Australia threw down the gauntlet by compiling 9/375 in its second knock and asking its opponents to match all but five of that total on the last day. Wessels, Trimble and Ray Phillips accepted the challenge; Wessels was in an irresistible mood, cruising to 144 to win the game for his side by five wickets and, in the process, retaining his place in the Australian Test side.

In Launceston Queensland needed only three days to despatch Tasmania by an innings and 105 runs. The speedy Craig McDermott wrecked the first day for the home team by taking 6/45 and shooting out the locals for 200. Then Border piled on the agony by notching 144 not out and conspiring with Hohns, Ritchie and Maguire – each of them the scorers of a half-century or more – to give his side a first innings lead of 342. The third act of the Tasmanian tragedy was a mere

New South Wales 1984–85
First Class Matches

BATTING	v. South Australia (Adelaide) 19–22 October 1984		v. Western Australia (Canberra) 26–29 October 1984		v. Tasmania (Launceston) 9–12 Nov. 1984		v. West Indians (Sydney) 16–19 Nov. 1984		v. Western Australia (Perth) 23–26 Nov. 1984		v. South Australia (Sydney) 30 Nov.–3 Dec. 1984		v. Queensland (Brisbane) 7–11 Dec. 1984		v. Tasmania (Newcastle) 17–20 January 1985		v. Victoria (Melbourne) 25–28 January 1985		v. Queensland (Sydney) 22–25 February 1985		v. Victoria (Sydney) 1–4 March 1985	
S.B. Smith	27	0	19	3	54	12	33	8	27	43	7	—	0	15*	14	62						
J. Dyson	70	18	5	76			98	16			16	72			87	5	97	—	93	—	28	54
D.M. Wellham	80	3	0	23	9	115	36	29	86	3	89	1	9	—	113	7*	30	—	27	—	18	81
P.S. Clifford	125	5	15	22	27	12	24	6	51	102*	64	2	98	—	143	0	25	—	45	—	19	38*
G.G. Geise	1	84	0	11	39	15*			1	—												
G.R.J. Matthews	86	17	33	49*	6	66	2	1	11	20*	42	0	97	—	8	—	11	—	87	—	103	14*
S.J. Rixon	24	3	23	7	33	19	0	15	28	—	58	115*			94	33	0	—				
P.H. Marks	18*	12			75	2	4	7	51	—					3	8	0	—	3	—	15	—
G.F. Lawson	4*	0	30	1							17	—										
R.G. Holland	—	0	12	1	0	—	20	8			0	—			24	—	31	—	27	—	10	—
D.R. Gilbert	—	0*	0*	3*	38*	—	6	10*	21*	—	0*	—	0	—	0*	—	1*	—	1*	—	0*	—
M.J. Bennett			10	12	2	—	16*	6			19	—							22	—	19	—
T.M. Chappell					26	2			10	65			12	0*								
Imran Khan							30	9	70	—	43	23*	17	—	5	30	15	—				
M.D. O'Neill									8	—			13*	—			45*	—				
R.J. Bower													7	—								
S.R. Waugh													31	—	4	2			0	—	94	—
G.C. Dyer													39	—					43	—	2	—
W.J.S. Seabrook																	165	—	11	—	14	6
Byes			1	2		5	3	8		2	2	4	9		1		4				1	8
Leg-byes	5	1	4	6	14	9	5	4	6	8	10	6	9	1	17	5	9		2		2	
Wides	6	1			2												4		2		1	
No-balls	1		4	2	8	5	10	2	16	2	3		16		6		5		5			
Total	447	144	156	218	333	262	287	129	386	245	370	223	357	16	519	152	442		368		326	201
Wickets	7	10	10	9	10	7	10	10	10	3	10	4	10	0	10	7	9		10		10	3
Results	W		D		D		W		D		W		D		D		D		W		W	
Points	16		0		4		—		0		16		4		4		4		16		16	

Catches 22 – S.J. Rixon (ct 16/st 6) 19 – J. Dyson; 10 – G.C. Dyer (ct 8/st 2) 9 – G.R.J. Matthews; 8 – S.R. Waugh; 7 – D.M. Wellham, S.B. Smith and P.S. Clifford; 6 – M.J. Bennett; 5 – R.G. Holland, P.H. Marks and G.G. Geise (three as sub)

BOWLING	G.F. Lawson	D.R. Gilbert	P.H. Marks	R.G. Holland	G.R.J. Matthews	G.G. Geise	M.J. Bennett	T.M. Chappell	Imran Khan
v. South Australia (Adelaide)	28.4–7–42–2	23–3–73–1	19–3–43–2	37–9–86–4	19–1–57–0				
19–22 October 1984	13–3–37–3	8–1–24–2	7–3–19–1	14.2–3–48–4	3–1–9–0				
v. Western Australia (Canberra)	25–10–42–4	27–5–69–3		10–3–22–2		1–0–7–0	7–1–19–0		
26–29 October 1984	4–2–6–0	8–3–15–1				4–2–4–0			
v. Tasmania (Launceston)		27.2–7–80–3	22–3–65–1	15–4–46–0	14–2–30–0		21–8–34–2	19–5–55–3	
9–12 November 1984		8.2–1–36–1	4–1–6–0	6–1–17–0	1–0–8–0		8–0–21–0	4–3–3–0	
v West Indians (Sydney)		9.3–2–25–2		30–6–81–4			14–1–53–2		14–2–42–2
16–19 November 1984		12–0–45–0		18–3–38–3	4–1–9–0		15.3–6–32–6		5–1–6–1
v. Western Australia (Perth)		46–11–116–1	13–2–33–0		43–14–92–4	16–9–17–0		4–2–5–0	24–8–51–2
23–26 November 1984									
v. South Australia (Sydney)	23–8–30–4	19–1–70–1		27.5–10–50–2	8–1–30–0		9–1–31–0		17–6–32–2
30 Nov.–3 Dec. 1984	19–6–39–1	4–0–10–0		38.5–12–83–9	10–2–35–0		19–5–30–0		9–4–14–0
v. Queensland (Brisbane)		31–8–105–2			40–13–81–4			6–1–8–0	40–19–47–3
7–11 December 1984									
v. Tasmania (Newcastle)		16–3–52–0	25–4–83–4	50–17–102–2	21–10–68–1				33–11–78–1
17–20 January 1985		9–1–36–0	11–2–38–1	20–5–52–1	32–10–86–2				28–10–44–4
v. Victoria (Melbourne)		30–13–61–1	9–3–21–1	50–17–111–4	39–12–91–1				38.2–10–106–3
25–28 January 1985		13–4–44–1	17–5–47–0	18–7–38–2	15–3–46–0				11–5–16–1
v. Queensland (Sydney)		12–3–28–0	4–1–8–0	25–9–49–3	16.5–8–22–3		27–13–39–3		
22–25 February 1985		16–5–42–4	6–0–15–0	21–12–39–1	26–13–32–5		20–12–14–0		
v. Victoria (Sydney)		26–4–70–5	10–2–31–0	25–12–44–0	17–6–47–1		25.4–11–47–3		
1–4 March 1985		16–3–44–0	5–1–12–0	26–7–62–2	26–12–53–2		39.5–17–57–6		
v. Queensland (Sydney)		27–6–67–2		43–12–111–1	27–10–53–0		34–16–54–2		27.3–6–66–4
15–19 March 1985		15–5–24–0		15–5–39–1	2–0–8–0		20–4–32–4		19–6–34–5
	112.4–36–196–14 av. 14.00	403.1–89–1136–30 av. 37.86	152–30–421–10 av. 42.10	490–154–118–45 av. 24.84	363.5–119 857–23 av. 37.26	21–11–28–0 —	260–95–463–28 av. 16.53	33–11–71–3 av. 23.66	265.5–88–536–28 av. 19.14

a J. Dyson 5–0–15–0, P.S. Clifford 2–1–4–0, W.J.S. Seabrook 1–0–1–0

v. Queensland (Sydney) 15–19 March 1985		M	Inns	NOs	Runs	HS	Av
76	7	9	17	1	407	76	25.43
66	19	9	16	—	820	98	51.25
31	39	12	21	1	829	115	41.45
13	83*	12	21	3	919	143	51.05
		4	7	1	151	84	25.16
16	8	12	20	3	677	103	39.82
0	2	9	16	1	454	115*	30.26
		8	12	1	198	75	18.00
		3	5	1	52	30	13.00
0	10	10	13	—	143	31	11.00
8*	8*	12	15	13	96	38*	48.00
10	1	7	10	1	117	22	13.00
		3	6	1	115	65	23.00
7	18	7	11	1	267	70	26.70
		3	3	2	66	45*	66.00
		1	1	—	7	7	7.00
71	21	5	7	—	223	94	31.85
		3	3	—	84	43	28.00
		3	4	—	196	165	49.00
	3						
1	2						
19	2						
318	223						
10	9						
W							
—							

4–Imran Khan 2–T.M. Chappell (one as sub)
3–D.R. Gilbert 1–R.J. Bower

M.D. O'Neill	S.R. Waugh	R.J. Bower	Byes	Leg-byes	Wides	No-balls	Total	Wkts
			5	7	1	2	313	9
			4	3			144	10
			6	6	2	2	171	10
				1		1	26	1
				3		3	313	10
			1	1			93	1
			3	8			212	10
				3			133	10
37–15–62–1			2	9	1		387	9
			3	14	1		260	10
			7	3			221	10
	23–12–34–0	9–1–29–0	7	4	2	1	315	10
	6–2–11–0		4	11	1	1	409	8
	11–1–47–1		6	12	4		321	10
9–2–35–0			1	12	1	7	438	10
4–0–16–0				9			236	4a
			2	8	1		156	10
			5	4			151	10
	9–2–15–1		1	4	1	3	259	10
	5–1–13–0			2		1	243	10
	12–6–15–1		3	5		5	374	10
	6–1–21–0		3	2	1	2	163	10
50–17–113–1 *av.* 113.00	72–25–156–3 *av.* 52.00	9–1–29–0						

formality. The Queensland attack of Thomson, McDermott, Maguire, Rackemann and Hohns steadily eroded the home resistance and, after a stern innings of 93 from the local captain, Roger Woolley, had ended, the Banana Benders were able to catch a plane back to Brisbane, a day earlier than they had anticipated.

Border's triumphal progress suffered a minor check in early December, when rain and New South Wales combined to deny him even first-innings points in the Brisbane game against the eventual Shield champions. But Queensland were soon back on the victory trail with a ten-wicket rout of Western Australia when it visited the Sunshine State. Once again Border's players displayed the happy knack of complementing each other's efforts. In the Tasmanian game, McDermott and Border had decided the issue; against Western Australia, Wessels and Thomson were rostered on duty. Wessels' 137, competently supported by Ritchie's 65, allowed Border to declare at 9/366. Then it was Jeff Thomson's turn. His 7/27 had the Perth batsmen back in the pavilion for the first time with only 156 runs on the board. Valetta contributed 58 to this total and Geoff Marsh 55; only one of their team-mates reached double figures. Batting a second time in succession, the side from the other side of the Nullabor Plain did only slightly better, falling this time to the combined efforts of Rackemann, Thomson, Maquire, Hohns and McDermott for 224. Valetta completed a good double for Western Australia with another half-century, after which Kerr and Trimble knocked off the 15 runs required for victory with a minimum of fuss.

Queensland were foiled in their attempt to extract 16 points from Victorian hides in its next game by a combination of the determination of the burgeoning Australian batsman, Dean Jones, and the villainy of the moribund Melbourne wicket. On a pitch which was uncharacteristically lively on the first day, Courtice and the debutant Barsby did well to notch 69 and 49 respectively, thus enabling their side to reach the respectability of a first innings aggregate of 301. There was no respectability in store for the home team. Their batsmen were sped to and from the crease in the space of 101 runs by the combined efforts of the Queensland pace attack – Maguire having the best figures of 4/36. Expeditiously the Brisbane batsmen pressed home their advantage; Courtice compiled a rapid-fire 70 and Smart 50 in a second innings of 7/260 declared. When Thomson closed, setting Victoria the task of scoring 461 for an improbable victory and captured the home side's first four wickets for 187, it seemed that nothing could prevent his side completing the double over the weak southern state. One thing could – Dean Jones. Coming to the crease when the first wicket fell at 21, Jones defended tenaciously for the whole of the last day in searing heat and on a now virtually bounceless pitch. His 136 alone stood between a tireless Rackemann and the soft under-belly of the Victorian batting. The Queensland paceman's stamina was superb and he scotched for ever the often-broadcast imputation that he was injury-prone.

After being denied victory in Melbourne, the Queensland ship seemed to lose its way. In Perth its batsmen suffered their first attack of second innings collywobbles and consequently went down to defeat by two wickets against Western Australia – in spite of outscoring the home side in the first innings. The aggressive Trevor Barsby, in only his second

South Australia 1984–85
First Class Matches

BATTING	v. New South Wales (Adelaide) 19–22 October 1984		v. West Indians (Adelaide) 26–29 October 1984		v. Queensland (Brisbane) 16–19 Nov. 1984		v. Tasmania (Adelaide) 22–25 Nov. 1984		v. New South Wales (Sydney) 30 Nov.–3 Dec. 1984		v. Victoria (Melbourne) 14–17 Dec. 1984		v. Tasmania (Hobart) 20–23 Dec. 1984		v. Western Australia (Perth) 10–13 January 1985		v. Victoria (Adelaide) 17–20 January 1985		v. Western Australia (Adelaide) 22–25 February 1985		v. Queensland (Adelaide) 1–4 March, 1985	
A.M.J. Hilditch	184	56	2	49	7	41	16	86	80	47	47	88					16	—	0	—	22	34
D.F. O'Connor	10	0	51	33	53	55	0	16	42	19	59*	50	72*	24	23	52	118	—	35	2	2	57
M.D. Haysman	21	2	91	3	0	72	53	12	0	15			33*	0	172	2	34	—	157	30*	5	42
D.W. Hookes	1	12	27	24	5	79	151	4	1	15	9	62	—	35	0	73	25	—	83	6	18	34
W.B. Phillips	26	9	0	2*	32	0			20	13												
G.A. Bishop	15	6	29	18	87	43	10	170	29	11	2	10	88	60	4	25	0	—	37	14	25	2
R.J. Inverarity	10	24	17	40*			25	1	43*	36	—	—	—	0	69	0	13	—	9	17	55	4
T.B.A. May	26	1	4	14*	18	10			14	19									14	1*	23	10
R.J. McCurdy	4	13	18*	—	34	13	0	8	1	11*	—	—	—	8*	4	13	19	—				
S.D.H. Parkinson	0*	14			15	8*																
I.R. Carmichael	1*	0*	22	—	1*	—	3*	6*	11	24	—	—	—	—	8*	0*	1*	—	11	—	4	18
J.J. Benton			9	6	0	21																
D.J. Kelly							8	17			—	36*	—	2	3	0	72	—	24	22	26	100*
C.L. Harms							0	33	1	1												
A.K. Zesers							1	17			—	—	—	10*	22	2	85	—				
R.J. Zadow											0	55	2	31	47	41	42	—	14	6	13	37
W.M. Darling											25*	58*	—	5	19	6						
W. Prior																			0*	—	0*	1
Byes	5	4					2	4	3	7		6			3		6			2	2	
Leg-byes	7	3	7	4	3	10	6	1	14	3	1	6	9	4	16	4	7		10	1	6	12
Wides	1		1						1								1		2		2	1
No-Balls	2		17	7	22	23	14	8			3	7	1	1	18	3	2		8	2	7	11
Total	313	144	295	200	277	375	289	383	260	221	146	378	205	180	408	221	441		404	103	210	363
Wickets	9	10	10	6	10	9	10	10	10	10	4	5	2	8	10	10	10		10	6	10	10
Result	L		D		L		D		L		W		W		L		W		D		W	
Points	0		—		0		0		0		12		16		0		16		4		12	

Catches 24 – D.J. Kelly (ct 22/st 2)
14 – G.A. Bishop
12 – M.D. Haysman
10 – D.W. Hookes and A.M.J. Hilditch
8 – W.B. Phillips (ct 7/st 1) and D.F. O'Connor
6 – R.J. McCurdy
5 – R.J. Inverarity
4 – I.R. Carmichael and C.L. Harms (one as sub)
2 – T.B.A. May, J.J. Benton and R.J. Zadow
1 – A.K. Zesers and subs (Davis, Christensen, Parkinson and Favell)

BOWLING	R.J. McCurdy	S.D.H. Parkinson	T.B.A. May	I.R. Carmichael	R.J. Inverarity	D.W. Hookes	J.J. Benton	D.F. O'Connor	M.D. Haysman
v. New South Wales (Adelaide)	28–4–107–0	21–9–66–1	34–7–95–0	24–9–48–0	34–8–94–5	7–0–32–1			
19–22 October 1984	17.4–2–55–7	5–3–12–0	16–8–36–1	9–3–27–0	10–4–13–1				
v. West Indians (Adelaide)	14–6–39–1		20–1–87–3	15–2–72–3	5–0–18–2		4–1–18–0		
26–29 October 1984	13.2–2–75–1		5–1–21–0	23–4–85–0	24–0–105–0	12.4–0–43–0	32–2–144–2	5–0–22–1	2.4–0–5–0
v. Queensland (Brisbane)	21–5–80–3	17–3–56–1	10–2–36–1	24–6–83–2		1–0–10–1	1–0–10–0		
16–19 November 1984	5–1–18–1	10.1–1–41–0	32–8–113–1	31–6–111–2		6–2–31–1	10–1–37–0	1–0–4–0	2–0–4–0
v. Tasmania (Adelaide)	40–10–120–3			40–15–80–1	44–12–113–2	3–0–22–0			3–0–8–0
22–25 November 1984									
v. New South Wales (Sydney)	36–7–109–5		16–3–35–0	23–6–63–0	31.2–5–76–3				
30 Nov.–3 Dec. 1984	18–3–55–0		2–0–14–0	23–2–73–1	16–4–50–3				
v. Victoria (Melbourne)	15–3–44–1			5–0–23–0	11–3–28–1	2–1–2–0			
14–17 December 1984	24–5–67–2			9.3–3–31–2	23–9–34–1	14–5–38–2		2–0–2–1	
v. Tasmania (Hobart)	15–3–57–1			16–1–49–0	12–2–21–2	3–2–1–0			
20–23 December 1984	17–5–38–2			14.1–3–32–3	23–12–29–2	13–2–49–1		3–0–11–0	2–1–1–0
v. Western Australia (Perth)	23–2–84–2			19–4–72–1	28–5–83–2	12–1–49–2			8–1–28–0
10–13 January 1985	24–2–109–5			17–3–72–2		1–0–1–0			
v. Victoria (Adelaide)	25–4–66–0			16.3–6–46–2	13–3–22–2				
17–20 January 1985	22–10–52–4			5–3–6–1	24.3–6–63–4				
v. Western Australia (Adelaide)			24–8–57–3	24.4–13–41–3	24–9–56–2	4–1–7–0			
22–25 February 1985			52–22–95–2	42–15–117–3	33.5–12–75–2	2–0–13–0		3–0–15–0	5–0–18 0
v. Queensland (Adelaide)			32–10–98–1	32–9–117–0	33–8–86–7	9–1–32–0			
1–4 March 1985			10.5–1–24–6	19–1–59–1	16–2–50–2	3–1–11–0			
	358–74–1175–38 av. 30.92	53.1–16–175–2 av. 87.50	253.5–71–711–18 av. 39.50	431.5–114–1307–27 av. 48.40	405.4–104–1016–43 av. 23.62	92.4–16–341–8 av. 42.62	47–4–209–2 av. 104.50	14–0–54–2 av. 27.00	22.4–2–64–0 —

a G.A. Bishop 3.3–0–20–0
b W. Prior 12–5–24–0
c W. Prior 34–6–112–3
d W. Prior 7–1–25–0
e W. Prior 11–2–36–1

M	Inns	NOs	Runs	HS	Av
9	16	—	775	184	48.43
11	21	2	773	118	40.68
10	19	2	744	172	43.76
11	20	—	664	151	33.20
4	8	1	102	32	14.57
11	21	—	685	170	32.61
10	16	2	363	69	25.92
6	12	2	154	26	15.40
9	13	3	146	34	14.60
2	4	2	37	15	18.50
11	14	8	110	24	18.33
2	4	—	36	21	9.00
7	11	2	310	100*	34.44
2	4	—	35	33	8.75
5	6	1	137	85	27.40
6	11	—	288	55	26.18
3	5	2	113	58*	37.66
2	3	2	1	1	1.00

A.K. Zesers	C.L. Harms	A.M.J. Hilditch	Byes	Leg-byes	Wides	No-balls	Total	Wkts
				5	6	1	447	7
				1	1		144	10
				8		1	242	10
		0.2–0–1–0	6	7		1	514	5
				8		10	283	8
			1	10		9	370	5
34–9–85–1	30–10–49–1		5	5		14	487	8
	21–2–75–2		2	10		3	370	10
		5–0–21–0	4	6			223	4
8–0–50–0					1	6	147	2
13–7–17–2			16	5		10	210	10
18–6–60–0						14	188	3
12–5–28–1			2	3	1	7	193	10
30–6–85–1				8		6	409	8
12–1–33–3			3	3		3	241	10a
35–18–51–5		4–2–5–0	1	6		1	197	10
12–4–25–1			2	2			150	10
			2	4		1	191	10b
		1–1–0–0	3	11			459	10c
		8–1–14–0	1	5	1	2	378	8d
			1	2			183	10e
174–56–434–14 *av.* 31.00	51–12–124–3 *av.* 41.33	18.2–4–41–0 —						

game for his state, contributed 133 of his side's 310 run total; the next highest score in Queensland's first innings was Kerr's 35! Maguire's 6/84 analysis was equally as meritorious as Barsby's effort and gained the visitors a lead of 29 runs. This advantage, however, proved worthless when the local Test hero, paceman Terry Alderman, took charge of the game. In just under 28 overs, he carved his way through the Queensland batting, taking 6/42 and dismissing Thomson's side for 171. Hohns played a lone hand, scoring 103 of his side's final tally. Queensland's second innings collapse confronted Shipperd's batsmen with the ostensibly non-too-difficult job of scoring 201 runs for victory. Rackemann, Thomson, Frei and Maguire made them fight all of the way and eight wickets were down before the winning hit was made. Had Shipperd not played a dogged hand of 69 not out, that hit might never have been made.

Trevor Barsby completed his second first-class hundred – and his first on the 'Gabba – in only his third experience of Shield cricket. His 137 was the major contribution to Queensland's 384 total against Tasmania and was supplemented by 59 from 'keeper Ray Phillips, 60 from Kerr and 50 from Smart. Tasmania's Jamaican fast bowler, Patrick Patterson, who had bowled with great penetration in the early season, recalled some of his previous successes with a persevering performance of 5/93 on a wicket which was totally devoid of sympathy for the bowlers. This was glaringly obvious when the Apple Islanders replied with a massive 9/507 declared. Bradshaw compiled an impressive 121, Peter Faulkner a rounded maiden century, opener Goodman 88 and Woolley 67. Maguire, who had performed well in away games to take 14 wickets, was the most successful Queensland bowler, adding a further three scalps to his belt at a cost of 111 runs. The already benign wicket got even better as the match wore on – as Queensland demonstrated by beginning its second innings with a record partnership of 331 in 349 minutes between Kerr and Courtice. Courtice was finally dismissed for 135 but Kerr remained undefeated on 201 as the match was aborted in an atmosphere of frustration and fury.

For its part, Queensland continued to distance itself from the form which had produced an uninterrupted string of victories at the beginning of the season. Two batting failures in the New South Welsh spin attack led to the ignominy of an innings defeat in Sydney. Then came the nadir of Queensland's summer of discontent: the unnecessary loss in Adelaide which surrendered the vital advantage of staging the deciding game of the Shield competition against New South Wales on the 'Gabba. Thomson's men embarked upon their return game against South Australia with the assurance of a side which seemed confident of repeating its earlier five-wicket success in Brisbane. Maguire and Rackemann bundled out the home side for 210 with Maguire taking 5/62 and only Inverarity putting up any significant opposition with a solid knock of 55. Barsby, Trimble, Henschell and Hohns all contributed seventies to Queensland's subsequent reply of 9/378 declared: a score which would have been considerably greater had it not been for the evergreen John Inverarity taking 7/86 with his left-handed orthodox spinners. Even though his side trailed by 168 runs on the first innings, skipper David Hookes had not relinquished all hope of a South Australia victory. In a spirited second attempt

Western Australia 1984–85
First Class Matches

BATTING	v. Tasmania (Perth) 19–22 October 1984		v. New South Wales (Canberra) 26–29 October 1984		v. West Indians (Perth) 2–4 November 1984		v. Victoria (Melbourne) 9–12 Nov. 1984		v. New South Wales (Perth) 23–26 Nov. 1984		v. Queensland (Brisbane) 14–17 Dec. 1984		v. Victoria (Perth) 20–23 Dec. 1984		v. Sri Lankans Perth) 31 December 1984–2 January 1985		v. South Australia (Perth) 10–13 January 1985		v. Queensland (Perth) 17–20 January 1985		v. South Australia (Adelaide) 22–25 February 1985	
G.M. Wood	94	46	61	3	141	13																
M.R.J. Veletta	21	16*	49	15*	6	3	100	—	35	—	58	59	8	8			6	40	19	22	36	143
G. Shipperd	46	—	7	6*	97*	27*	17	—	61	—	6	8	131*	24			139	11	15	69*	3	129
K.J. Hughes	183	67*	18*	—	12	13					1	14					21	111	15	1		
G.R. Marsh	6	30	4	—	26*	1	20	—	73	—	55	19	0	143*	8	13	25	14	23	10	4	67
S.C. Clements	51	0	3	—	9*	9	58	—	40	—	12	33	11	12	60	19						
K.H. MacLeay	27	6	0	—	—	1	52	—	17	—	1	3										
W.D. Hill	9	—	2	—	—	7	8	—														
T.G. Hogan	11	—	7	—	—	19	2	—	11	—	8*	10	22	0			6	14	14	27	19	11
W.M. Clark	13	—	0	—	—	7	19*	—	46*	—	0	11	9	1	25	1						
T.M. Alderman	9*	—	4	—	—	4					0	0*	15	4			16	5	18	1		
M.W. McPhee							85	—	25	—			23	25	19	6	135	0	67	16	60	0
P.M. Clough							9	—	11*	—	0	21	2	0*							0	12*
R.W. Gartrell							9	—					41	13	21	3						
T.J. Zoehrer									50	—	1	31	3	4	69*	0	1	23	58	7	9	14
C.D. Matthews									6	—												
P. Gonnella															22	10	46*	12	12	28	45*	24
D. Smith															0	2						
G.E. Bush															1*	21					0	0
B.A. Reid															—	0*	—	2*	6	2*	8	23
E.G. Spalding															—	0	—	0	0*	—		
G.J. Ireland																					0	22
Byes	5	2	6		5	1	5		2			8	4	2	4			3		8	2	3
Leg-byes	4	1	6	1	3	1	5		9		5		2	6	7	2	8	3	7	1	4	11
Wides	1		2						1				1									
No-Balls	24	2	2	1	18	5					9	7	8	3	9	2	6	3	27	9	1	
Total	504	170	171	26	317	111	389		387		156	224	280	245	245	79	409	241	281	201	191	459
Wickets	10	4	10	1	3	10	10		9		10	10	10	9	7	10	8	10	10	8	10	10
Result	D		D		L		D		D		L		D		L		W		W		D	
Points	4		4		—		2		4		0		0		—		16		12		0	

Catches 27 – T.J. Zoehrer (ct 25/st 2) 9 – M.R.J. Veletta 8 – W.D. Hill 7 – T.M. Alderman and G.R. Marsh 5 – T.G. Hogan 4 – K.J. Hughes, W.M. Clark and S.C. Clements 3 – K.H. MacLeay, B.A. Reid and M.W. McPhee (one as sub)

BOWLING	T.M. Alderman	W.M. Clark	T.G. Hogan	K.H. MacLeay	S.C. Clements	P.M. Clough	R.W. Gartrell	G. Bush	E.G. Spalding
v. Tasmania (Perth)	29.1–2–110–3	37–14–70–4	46–13–104–2	26–9–59–1					
19–22 October 1984	16–1–66–1	6–0–31–0	14–0–51–1	21.3–5–54–5					
v. New South Wales (Canberra)	14.4–2–46–2	13–1–27–2	18–5–29–2	28–8–49–3					
26–29 October 1984	36–9–62–4	40–10–75–4	27–4–58–1	9–3–15–0					
v. West Indians (Perth)	19–7–52–4	18–4–80–0	12–2–52–0	22–2–115–5					
2–4 November 1984	8–1–32–0	5–1–21–0	3–0–20–0	10–2–42–1	0.2–0–8–0				
v. Victoria (Melbourne)		43–17–89–4	47.5–16–78–1	24–5–48–1		32–6–78–3	1–0–1–0		
9–12 November 1984									
v. New South Wales (Perth)		28–8–74–1	18–3–57–1	26–6–90–2		24–6–67–3			
23–26 November 1984			30–8–77–0	27–10–66–3	6–2–19–0	18–4–64–0			
v. Queensland (Brisbane)	28–8–76–3	34–5–84–3	31–5–86–1	19–2–48–0		20.1–3–57–2			
14–17 December 1984			1–0–3–0	2–0–3–0					
v. Victoria (Perth)	30–9–106–1	34.5–6–87–1	31–7–106–5			30–4–101–2			
20–23 December 1984	19–4–55–0	18–6–40–1	23–8–61–1			17–6–59–4	2–0–2–0		
v. Sri Lankans (Perth)		11–5–34–1						11–1–43–1	15–3–59–2
31 Dec. 1984–2 Jan. 1985								9–3–26–0	5–0–42–2
v. South Australia (Perth)	43.4–14–109–6		39–10–112–2						20–3–41–0
10–13 January 1985	17.1–4–50–1		25–6–92–3						13–1–37–4
v. Queensland (Perth)	34–10–102–4		31–9–72–1						14–6–35–1
17–20 January 1985	27.2–10–42–6		23–6–44–0						13–3–23–1
v. South Australia (Adelaide)			28–5–107–1			31–7–100–1		33.1–9–88–2	
22–25 February 1985			10–6–13–2			11–2–20–2		10–3–30–0	
v. Tasmania (Hobart)			31–5–79–1			21–5–71–1			13–0–65–1
1–4 March 1985			16–6–32–1			10–3–31–1			7–3–6–1
	322–81–908–35 av. 25.94	287.5–77–712–21 av. 33.90	504.5–124–1333–26 av. 51.26	214.3–52–589–21 av. 28.04	6.2–2–27–0 —	214.1–46–648–19 av. 34.10	3–0–3–0 —	63.1–16–187–3 av. 62.33	100–19–308–12 av. 25.66

a C.D. Matthews 27–7–92–3 b C.D. Matthews 3–0–6–0, M.W. McPhee 2–1–2–0 c D. Smith 6–1–29–2

v. Tasmania (Hobart) 1–4 March 1985		M	Inns	NOs	Runs	HS	Av
		3	6	—	358	141	59.66
21	—	11	19	2	665	143	39.11
27*	—	11	18	6	823	139	68.58
		6	11	2	456	183	50.66
51*	—	12	20	3	592	143*	34.82
		8	13	1	317	60	26.41
		6	8	—	107	52	13.37
		4	4	—	26	9	6.50
—	—	11	15	1	181	27	12.92
		8	11	2	132	46*	14.66
		7	11	2	76	18	8.44
52	—	8	13	—	513	135	39.46
—	—	6	8	3	55	21	11.00
		3	5	—	87	41	17.40
—	—	8	13	1	270	69*	22.50
		1	1	—	6	6	6.00
—	—	5	8	2	199	46*	33.16
		1	2	—	2	2	1.00
		2	4	1	22	21	7.33
—	—	5	6	3	41	23	13.66
—	—	4	3	1	0	0*	0.00
—	—	2	2	—	22	22	11.00
3							
3							
158							
2							
D							
0							

2–G. Shipperd, P. Gonnella and G.M. Wood

1–D. Smith, G.E. Bush, R.W. Gartell and G.J. Ireland

G. Shipperd	B.A. Reid	P. Gonnella	Byes	Leg-byes	Wides	No-balls	Total	Wkts
			7	9		13	359	10
			1	9		3	212	7
			1	4		4	156	10
			2	6		2	218	9
				3		9	302	9
			4	2		1	129	1
			3	13		3	310	9
				6		16	386	10a
1–0–1–0			2	8		2	245	3b
			7	8		6	366	9
1–0–8–0				1			15	0
			1	4	1	6	405	10
			7	7	1		231	6
	10–1–40–0	1–0–8–0		4		3	217	8c
	12.1–3–33–1		4	3	1	3	108	3
	45–14–106–2	8–2–21–0	3	16		18	408	10
	14–3–38–0			4		3	221	10
	33.3–10–88–4	2–0–4–0	9		1	10	310	10
	27–10–60–2			2		6	171	10
	35–6–90–3	2–0–9–0		10	2	8	404	10
	10–1–37–2		2	1		2	103	6
	29–12–77–2	3–1–8–0	2	5	2	3	307	5
	11–5–12–1			2			83	4
2–0–9–0 —	226.4–65–581–17 *av.* 34.17	16–3–50–0 —						

with the bat, wicketkeeper, Kelly scored 100 and Donald O'Connor 57 and South Australia were eventually able to ask Queensland to score 196 to bring the Shield final to Brisbane. Since the job did not seem too difficult, Thomson's batsmen saw no reason for undue haste and adopted a slow but sure policy. Courtice occupied the crease for 125 minutes to score 45: Smart came in at number three and agonised for 158 minutes over 54 runs. Too late Queensland realised that it now needed seven runs per over to win – and by this stage Hookes' men were patrolling the short Adelaide boundaries with the mean speed of latter-day Scrooges. The desperate Queensland batsmen panicked against the off-spin of Tim May. He snaffled 6/24 as Thomson's batsmen finally surrendered, 12 runs short of their target. Queensland's cup of misery overflowed when, subsequently, news filtered through that New South Wales had unexpectedly defeated Victoria and won the right to stage the Sheffield Shield final on the Sydney Cricket Ground: the happy hunting ground for their spinners Bennett, Holland and Matthews and the scene of Queensland's earlier defeat by an innings.

New South Wales supporters had justification to be content with their team's performance in 1984/85, for it swept the board of first-class honours by winning both the Sheffield Shield and the McDonald's Cup. Wellham's men, honed to razor-edged efficiency in the field by their coach, former Australian skipper, Bobby Simpson, and bowling and batting with predetermined purpose, were irresistible in the one-day cup games. In the preliminary rounds, they easily accounted for Western Australia and Tasmania by 14 and 90 runs respectively. They won an even more impressive seven-wicket victory in the semi-final against Victoria, before going on to annihilate South Australia by 88 runs in the game which decided the future home of the McDonald's Cup.

It was small wonder that honours came the way of Wellham's side, for, whilst it was not studded with outstanding talents, it was an efficient, balanced cricket machine, endowed with batting and bowling depth and well-supported by young and able reserves. Its top-order batsmen Clifford, Dyson and Wellham all scored more than 800 runs, whilst down the list, all-rounder Matthews was capable of scoring 684 and wicketkeeper Rixon 507. So strong was the New South Wales batting that youngsters such as Seabrook – who notched 165 in his debut against Victoria – and the promising Steven Waugh were unable to command regular places in the side. But it was in the bowling department that the Sydney team outshone every other state side in Australia. Its formidable trio of spinners, Holland, Bennett and Matthews overthrew no fewer than 117 opposing batsmen. Holland, with 59 victims to his name, was the leading wicket-taker in the country and Bennett, with 33 wickets to his credit at 20.51 runs each, one of the most economically effective. But it was the balance and versatility of the New South Wales attack which made it such a devastating strike force. Nor did it place its trust solely in its slower men and the turning Sydney wicket. It possessed big pace guns in the persons of Gilbert, Imran Khan and Lawson. Imran made a wide choice when he came to Australia to recuperate from his serious shin injury of 1983/84. The move enabled him to nurse himself back to top pace gradually: a policy which he pursued so successfully that he was firing on all cylinders when the Shield final arrived and was thus able to play a vital role in the decisive second innings of the match. Gilbert's 30 wickets in the season earned him an Esso Scholarship to England and, after the organisation of the unauthorised Australian tour to South Africa, a place in the official Australian touring team to the U.K. Lawson, even though periodically plagued by a back injury, still managed to collect 37 wickets and have himself classified by the National Trust as one of the treasures in the Australian Test side, worthy of conservation.

By comparison with New South Wales' attack, the Queensland wicket-taking engine was built solely for speed. McDermott, Maguire, Rackemann and Thomson did everything that was asked of them. The youthful McDermott claimed 35 victims, Maguire 46, Rackemann 42 and Thomson 38 in the season. But there was no variety in the boiler room to take advantage of every type of wicket. The only slow bowler worthy of note in the Queensland averages was Trevor Hohns, whose 20 wickets cost him an expensive 42.25 runs each. Wessels was the rock on which the Queensland batting reliability was founded. His 1020-run aggregate, however, was almost 400 runs more than that of his closest colleague. Ritchie, Kerr and Border each topped 600 runs and Courtice and Hohns 500, but their contributions were not in the same category as those of Wellham, Dyson and Clifford's to the New South Wales cause. One detected an air of fragility about the Brisbane team's batting which, from time to time, in isolated innings, caused it to fail inexplicably. These failures were enough to lose the northern state its first Sheffield Shield.

Even South Australia's batting appeared more substantive than Queensland's. Opener Andrew Hilditch aggregated 960 and he was well supported by offerings of 773 from Don O'Connor and 744 from Michael Haysman. Bishop and Hookes each totalled more than 600 runs for the season and, with wicketkeeper Kelly chipping in with a century at the appropriate time and he and Inverarity exceeding the 300 run mark, the Adelaide team's batting was far less fragile than it appeared to be when it set out so disastrously on the 1984/85 Sheffield Shield trail. Its bowling predicament, however, was a vastly different and more dismal story. On the evidence of figures, the most potent force in Hookes' attack was John Inverarity, whose left-handed tweakers yielded him a harvest of 43 wickets at 23.62 runs each. Even paceman Rod McCurdy's 38 victims cost him 30.92 runs per head, whilst the left-handed medium-pacer, Ian Carmichael – a man who had taken over 40 wickets in the previous season – could do no better than 27 wickets at 48.40. So desperate was South Australia's bowling plight that, towards the end of the season, the superannuated speedster, Wayne Prior, was taken out of mothballs and pressed into service. McCurdy's departure from Adelaide and the Sheffield Shield scene at the end of the season has only exacerbated the South Australian tundra scenario of fast bowling.

Western Australia underwent transplant surgery of the most painful kind in 1984/85. Fortunately there was no rejection of the new batting tissue and the Perth side can hopefully look forward to a season of healthy scores next year. McPhee, Valetta and Marsh were successful implants and each scored more than 500 runs and averaged more than 35. Hughes and Wood emulated the younger brigade's achievements, but did not fulfil the expectations which a side normally has of its senior citizens. Shipperd was the batting anchor of the Westerners. He aggregated 823 runs and topped the national averages, and, just at a time when the selectors' eyes might have been expected to have turned his way, has opted to place himself in international exile by choosing to tour South Africa. Alderman was easily the best of the Western Australian bowlers, capturing 44 wickets at a mean cost of 28.34. Wayne Clark, Hogan and MacLeay lent Alderman support although, in their individual capacities, they were not half as efficient as the veteran medium-pacer. There is hope on the horizon, however, in the achievements of speedster Reid who took 17 wickets in a handful of games, and who, with Earl Spalding, constitutes the Western state's hopes of replacing, in part, the irreplaceable Dennis Lillee.

The 1984/85 Victorian averages were just damned discouraging statistics. The two solitary bright spots were the achievements of Dean Jones and Mick Taylor. Jones accumulated 681 runs and ended the season in second place in the national averages. Taylor was studiously neglected by the Australian selectors, in spite of totalling 801 runs at a mean figure of 50.06. It was perhaps not surprising that, when the offer of an overseas tout to South Africa came Taylor's way, the scorned batsmen accepted it! Yallop, handicapped by a knee injury, did not find touch until late in the season when he scored most of his 472 runs – only to be subsequently omitted from the national team. Simon O'Donnell was more fortunate. He recorded only 398 first-class runs for the season and took 11 wickets. But these were deemed credentials enough to gain him a place in the Australian Benson and Hedges/World Series Cup side and a berth in the touring team to England. The left-handed slows of skipper Ray Bright earned him the premier place in the Victorian bowling averages: but his wickets cost him 30.45 runs each and he rarely bowled well enough to win points. The medium-pacer, Simon Davis, laboured long and hard for his 32 wickets without turning in a match-winning performance. But at least Bright and Davis outshone by far the other bowlers in their side, none of whom took more than 15 wickets. The seasonal Victorian figures have to be viewed in the light of the unstable nature of the Victorian team.

Surprising though it may seem, Test player David Boon was barely the second most prolific scorer in the Tasmanian side. He only outscored opener Goodman by five runs – although at times his first-class opposition was considerably tougher. The Tasmanian batting record was good. Skipper Woolley outshone his team-mates, including David Boon, by piling up 717 runs for the season. Boon was not far behind him with 664 as was Goodman with 659. The batting depth of the Taswegians was reflected by the fact that opener Ray notched 576 runs, Bradshaw 419 and Saunders 318. It was in the bowling sector that the island side was deficient. Jamaican speedster, Patrick Patterson was the lone hero of Tasmania's strike force. He took 37 wickets and conceded 36 runs per victim. Medium-pacer Tame was cheaper; his wickets cost him only 29 runs each – but he only took 12. Peter Faulkner captured five wickets more but at virtually twice the cost – scored a first-class hundred – and gained a place in the Australian one-day squad!

There was nothing unsubstantial or unsubstantiated, however, about the result of the Australian 1985/85 first-class season. New South Wales were demonstrably the best side in the country.

SECTION C

Consolidating Success

The season in New Zealand.
Shell Trophy. Shell Cup.
New Zealand *v.* Pakistan Test and One-Day International series.
Form Charts and Averages.
Review of the season by Don Cameron.

Jeremy Coney – the hero of Dunedin and New Zealand.
(George Herringshaw)

In common with most of the other Test playing countries, New Zealand was confronted with a surfeit of international cricket. In the early weeks of the New Zealand season, the national team would be completing a tour of Sri Lanka and Pakistan, a tour which Howarth and Hadlee had declined. The Pakistan side followed New Zealand home to engage in another three-test series and to contest four one-day internationals. Both sides would then go to Australia for the Benson and Hedges World Championship of Cricket. The New Zealand players were to return home before the semi-finals in order to play in the closing stages of the domestic competitions, and would then go back to Australia for the completion of the international tournament. From there they were to go to West Indies for the Test and one-day international series.

The hazards of such a programme must be not only in the surfeit of international cricket which players and spectators are suffering, but the devaluation that domestic competitions all over the world are suffering because so many of the leading players are scarcely participating in those tournaments. It is an annual complaint that we make in these pages, and it is echoed elsewhere, yet the warning goes unheeded. A glance at the form charts in this section will show how often a provincial side is denied its best players, often its elected captain, and therefore how often the local supporters of the game are given no glimpse of their heroes.

In spite of this, New Zealand cricket remained buoyant as the national side continued to enjoy the best period in its history.

Paul McEwan. One of the most consistent run getters in New Zealand. (Adrian Murrell)

Shell Trophy

13, 14 and 15 December 1984

at Dudley Park, Rangiora

Canterbury 88 (S.J. Maguiness 7 for 17) and 293 (V.R. Brown 104)

Wellington 192 (R.J. Hadlee 5 for 46, V.R. Brown 4 for 45) and 107 (R.J. Hadlee 4 for 36)

Canterbury won by 82 runs
Canterbury 12 pts, Wellington 4 pts

The Shell Trophy opened earlier than usual and marked the debut of Dudley Park as a Shell Trophy venue. The game itself was remarkable. Steve Maguiness, with a career best, bowled Canterbury out for 88, and then, after Wellington had slipped to 141 for 9 in reply, added 51 for the last wicket with Richard Pither whose contribution was 8 not out. Maguiness' 43 at number eleven seemed decisive in placing Wellington in a dominant position and when Canterbury were 27 for 4 in their second innings his side appeared to be coasting to victory. Vaughan Brown then hit the fourth century of his career, his 104 coming in 192 minutes with twenty fours. Asa Hart (36 not out) and Craig Thiele (49), both career bests, put on 85 for the last wicket and Wellington were set to make 190 to win. Hadlee and McNally reduced them to 5 for 5, and they never effectively recovered so that the reigning champions gained an extraordinary victory.

Shell Cup

16 December 1984

at Dudley Park, Rangiora

Canterbury 140 (G.N. Cederwall 5 for 17)
Wellington 142 for 8

Wellington (2 pts) won by 2 wickets

Runs were no easier to get in the one-day game than they had been in the Shell Trophy match and Grant Cederwall established a new record for the Cup competition with 5 for 17 in 8.3 overs as Canterbury were bowled out in 42.3 overs. Wellington struggled to victory with 8.5 overs to spare.

Shell Trophy

27, 28 and 29 December 1984

at Pukekura Park, New Plymouth

Northern Districts 331 (B.G. Cooper 91, R.D. Broughton 67) and 212 (L.M. Crocker 41, M.D. Crowe 5 for 51)
Central Districts 204 (I.D.S. Smith 51, S.M. Carrington 4 for 39) and 341 for 5 (M.D. Crowe 143, R.T. Hart 84)

Central Districts won by 5 wickets
Central Districts 12 pts, Northern Districts 4 pts

at Eden Park, Auckland

Auckland 337 (P.N. Webb 76, G.B. Troup 58, T.J. Franklin 51, R.J. Hadlee 5 for 74)
Canterbury 159 (A. Nathu 56) and 142 (G.B. Troup 6 for 53)

Auckland won by an innings and 36 runs
Auckland 16 pts, Canterbury 0 pts

28, 29 and 30 December 1984

at Molyneux Park, Alexandra

Wellington 124 and 195
Otago 111 (S.J. Maguiness 4 for 29) and 182 (E.J. Gray 5 for 43, E.J. Chatfield 4 for 56)

Wellington won by 26 runs
Wellington 16 pts, Otago 0 pts

On a comfortable wicket at New Plymouth, Northern Districts, aided by some limp fielding and bowling by Central, reached 331 in even time. The Central Districts' batting was little better than their bowling and only a breezy fifty from Ian Smith and a valuable 37 by nightwatchman Derek Stirling saw them to 204. Northern Districts went to 72 before losing a wicket in their second innings, but Martin Crowe then produced a fine spell of medium pace bowling and Central needed 340 to win. Crowe dominated the last day and his brilliant 143 gave Central an unexpected win. He and Ron Hart shared a third wicket stand of 167.

In Auckland, a fair batting display by the home side proved overwhelming for the champions who gave a shameful batting performance. Gary Troup had six wickets before injury forced him to leave the field in the second innings.

Rain made Molyneux Park a difficult wicket and neither Otago nor Wellington could reach 200 while Vance's second innings 47 was top score of the match. Maguiness had another fine match and bowled Wellington to first innings points, but Gray, with 7 wickets in the match, and 38 not out in the second innings took the individual honours and Wellington won a close, but never very exciting affair.

Shell Cup

27 December 1984

at Alexandra

Otago 64
Wellington 65 for 5

Wellington (2 pts) won by 5 wickets

30 December 1984

at Auckland

Canterbury 169 for 9
Auckland 160 (S.R. McNally 5 for 25)

Canterbury (2 pts) won by 9 runs

at Wanganui

Central Districts 289 for 8 (R.T. Hart 67, R.E. Hayward 61)
Northern Districts 201 (G.K. Robertson 5 for 36)

Central Districts (2 pts) won by 88 runs

Molyneux Park had been drenched with rain in the days preceding the match between Otago and Wellington so that the Shell Cup was a stark business, Otago scoring 64 off 38.4 overs and Wellington stumbling to victory.

At Auckland, Dempsey was bowled by the first ball of the match, but Canterbury recovered to reach 169. John Reid and Jeff Crowe came together at 33 for 2 and took the score to 70, but both fell as McNally and Thiele reduced Auckland to 75 for 5, and the home side slipped to defeat.

The best cricket of the competition to date came at Cook's Gardens, Wanganui, where Gary Robertson took the bowling honours in a match in which batsmen flourished.

Martin Crowe, 5 for 51 and 143 at New Plymouth, 27–29 December, inspired Central Districts to their only Shell Trophy victory of the season. (Sporting Pictures UK)

Shell Trophy

1, 2 and 3 January 1985

at Basin Reserve, Wellington

Auckland 242 (J.F. Reid 82, G.N. Cederwall 4 for 54) and 195 for 4 (J.J. Crowe 54)
Wellington 180 (T.D. Ritchie 52 not out, J.G. Bracewell 6 for 68) and 171 for 6

Match drawn
Auckland 4 pts, Wellington 0 pts

at Tauranga

Northern Districts 282 (B.L. Cairns 85, W.P. Fowler 51, C.M. Kuggeleijn 50)
Canterbury 284 for 6 (P.E. McEwan 88, V.R. Brown 74)

Match drawn
Canterbury 4 pts, Northern Districts 0 pts

2, 3 and 4 January 1985

at Oamaru

Otago 430 (W.K. Lees 91, N.A. Mallender 88, A.H. Jones 53, D.R. O'Sullivan 6 for 103) and 158 for 6

Central Districts 409 (T.E. Blain 129, R.T. Hart 59, P. Neutze 5 for 109)

Match drawn
Otago 4 pts, Central Districts 0 pts

Auckland were without the injured Troup and Kelly. Troup's replacement was Willie Watson who was making his first-class debut. John Reid gave the substance to the Auckland innings, but their 242 did not look formidable until John Bracewell and Martin Snedden left Wellington stunned at 69 for 7. The home side was rallied by Tim Ritchie and Grant Cederwall, but Auckland led by 62 on the first innings. Some brisk scoring allowed Snedden to declare and set Wellington to make 258, a task which they found to be too daunting.

A sluggish pitch saw Lance Cairns play the longest innings of his career and Northern Districts and Canterbury condemned to battle for first innings points alone.

Batsmen revelled in the conditions at Oamaru and Neil Mallender, who hit a career best, and Warren Lees added 88 for the eighth wicket. Tony Blain hit an attractive maiden first-class hundred and leg-spinner Peter Neutze had an impressive first-class debut.

Neil Mallender – career bests with bat and ball and a splendid season for Otago. (Adrian Murrell)

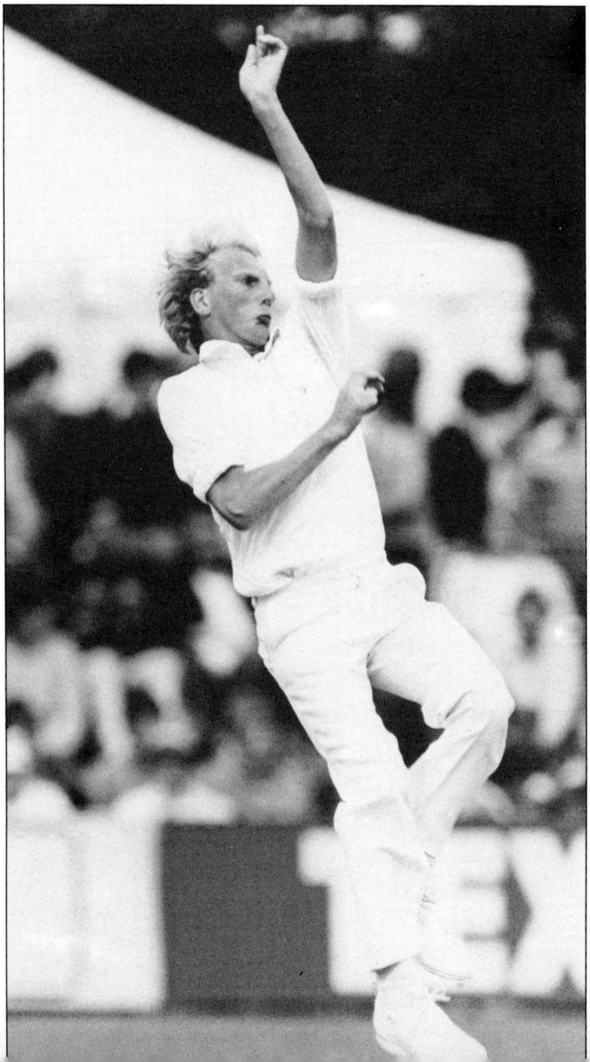

Shell Cup

1 January 1985

at Alexandra

Central Districts 193
Otago 194 for 7 (D.J. Walker 63 not out)

Otago (2 pts) won by 3 wickets

4 January 1985

at Wellington

Auckland 161 (P.N. Webb 62)
***v.* Wellington**

Match abandoned
Auckland 1 pt, Wellington 1 pt

at Tauranga

Northern Districts 115
Canterbury 118 for 4

Canterbury (2 pts) won by 6 wickets

Otago continued the inconsistent season by beating Central Districts who could not maintain their run-getting of the previous match. Derek Walker was named Man of the Match and received good support.

A moderate batting performance by Auckland cost them little for the match was ruined by rain while Canterbury beat struggling Northern Districts with 17 overs to spare.

Shell Cup

6 January 1985

at Gisborne

Otago 171 (B.R. Blair 4 for 37)
Northern Districts 174 for 7 (B.G. Cooper 50)

Northern Districts (2 pts) won by 3 wickets

at Levin

Central Districts 213 (I.D.S. Smith 70, S.J. Gillespie 4 for 55)
Auckland 216 for 5 (M.C. Snedden 79, T.J. Franklin 72 not out)

Auckland (2 pts) won by 5 wickets

Northern Districts' win over Otago, inspired by good all-round cricket from Bruce Blair and another welcome batting performance from Cooper, made it possible for any one of the six competing sides to reach the final of the tournament. Auckland won in style against Central Districts. Snedden followed his 3 wickets with 79 in an opening stand of 133 with Franklin.

Shell Trophy

7, 8 and 9 January 1985

at Harry Barker Reserve, Gisborne

Northern Districts 353 (L.M. Crocker 95, B.L. Cairns 89, B.G. Cooper 51, J.A.J. Cushen 4 for 109) and 188 for 7 dec (B.G. Cooper 60)
Otago 262 for 8 dec (S.J. McCullum 66, B.L. Cairns 4 for 39) and 121

Northern Districts won by 158 runs
Northern Districts 16 pts, Otago 0 pts

at Palmerston North

Central Districts 345 (T.E. Blain 100, G.K. Robertson 73, S.R. Tracy 4 for 97) and 322 for 3 (P.S. Briasco 104 not out, T.E. Blain 96, R.E. Hayward 65)
Auckland 348 for 4 dec (J.J. Crowe 86, A.J. Hunt 78 not out, J.G. Bracewell 54)

Match drawn
Auckland 4 pts, Central Districts 0 pts

Northern Districts gained their first win of the season and so left Otago as the only side yet to record a victory. With three rounds of matches completed, only 12 points separated five teams. The match at Gisborne saw Crocker and Cooper, at last giving indications of fulfilling his potential, batting well and Cairns, in more vigorous fashion, hitting 89 in 107 minutes, only the tenth time he had batted for as long as 100 minutes. He was named Man of the Match after a good bowling spell and he certainly played a significant role in Northern's victory.

Tony Blain gave another impressive batting display at Palmerson North, but on a fine wicket, it was batsmen who dominated. Blain came close to hitting a hundred in each innings. Scott Briasco again excited and Auckland's consistency gave them first innings points.

8, 9 and 10 January 1985

at Lancaster Park

Canterbury 309 for 4 dec (J.G. Wright 106, P.E. McEwan 73, R.T. Latham 62) and 209 for 6 dec (R.T. Latham 75, J.G. Wright 57)
Pakistanis 289 (Javed Miandad 112, Mudassar Nazar 75, G.K. MacDonald 6 for 62) and 223 for 2 (Qasim Umar 114 not out, Mohsin Khan 71)

Pakistanis won by 8 wickets

The opening match of the Pakistani tour produced some fine individual achievements. John Wright hit his first century for Canterbury and gave an exciting display punishing all the bowlers. Javed Miandad responded with an aggressive century for the tourists and he and Mudassar put on 139 for the third wicket. The remarkable achievement, however, came from off-spinner Gary MacDonald who, although long in experience at club level, was playing only his fourth game for the province. His 6 for 62 was a career best and four of them were caught and bowled. He also caught Qasim Umar so that his five catches equal the New Zealand record. He held a sixth catch in the second innings, and dropped one. Fulton misjudged his declaration and, led by a Qasim Umar century off 119 deliveries with thirteen fours, the visitors romped to victory. Qasim and Mohsin shared an opening stand of 131.

Shell Cup

11 January 1985

at Basin Reserve, Wellington

Wellington 181 (B.A. Edgar 70, E.B. McSweeney 55, W.P. Fowler 4 for 15)
Northern Districts 150 (E.J. Gray 4 for 30)

Wellington (2 pts) won by 31 runs

12 January 1985

at Auckland

Auckland 170 for 8
Otago 141 (W. Watson 7 for 23)

Auckland (2 pts) won by 29 runs

at Waimate

Canterbury 138
Central Districts 139 for 4 (R.T. Hart 54)

Central Districts (2 pts) won by 6 wickets

In the game at Auckland, which was reduced to 35 overs by the weather, Watson, the nineteen-year old seamer, shattered Shell Cup records with a devastating display of bowling. Wellington maintained their lead at the top of the table when Edgar, the forgotten man of New Zealand cricket, batted solidly, McSweeney swung lustily and Gray bowled well as did Derbyshire's Fowler. Central Districts kept up the pressure with a comfortable win at Waimate.

First One-Day International
NEW ZEALAND *v.* PAKISTAN

New Zealand crushed Pakistan in the first of the one-day internationals, outplaying the tourists in every department of the game. The weakness of the Pakistan attack was fully exploited by New Zealand in a consistent batting display

Martin Snedden. He led Auckland by example and was desparately unlucky not to captain his side to at least one honour. (George Herringshaw)

FIRST ONE-DAY INTERNATIONAL – NEW ZEALAND *v.* PAKISTAN
12 January 1985 at Napier

NEW ZEALAND

J.G. Wright	c Kamal, b Tahir	24
G.P. Howarth†	st Anil, b Iqbal Qasim	68
J.F. Reid	b Mudassar	11
M.D. Crowe	c Umar, b Tahir	32
I.D.S. Smith*	run out	14
J.J. Crowe	run out	35
J.V. Coney	not out	24
R.J. Hadlee	not out	34
B.L. Cairns		
J.G. Bracewell		
E.J. Chatfield		
Extras	b 4, lb 17, w 14	35
(50 overs)	(for 6 wickets)	277

	O	M	R	W
Azeem Hafeez	10	—	47	—
Mohsin Kamal	10	—	61	—
Tahir Naqqash	10	—	60	2
Mudassar Nazar	10	—	51	1
Iqbal Qasim	10	1	37	1

FALL OF WICKETS
1- 62, 2- 103, 3- 157, 4- 160, 5- 189, 6- 225

PAKISTAN

Mohsin Khan	b Cairns	4
Mudassar Nazar	c Smith, b Hadlee	17
Qasim Umar	c Smith, b Hadlee	0
Javed Miandad†	run out	38
Saleem Malik	run out	11
Wasim Raja	c Smith, b Chatfield	30
Tahir Naqqash	lbw, b Cairns	11
Iqbal Qasim	b Chatfield	9
Anil Dalpat*	not out	21
Azeem Hafeez	c Hadlee, b Howarth	15
Mohsin Kamal	not out	0
Extras	b 4, lb 3, w 4	11
(50 overs)	(for 9 wickets)	167

	O	M	R	W
Hadlee	8	—	30	2
Cairns	10	—	27	2
Chatfield	10	2	20	2
Coney	10	—	45	—
Bracewell	10	1	28	—
Howarth	1	—	4	1
Wright	1	—	6	—

FALL OF WICKETS
1- 24, 2- 24, 3- 26, 4- 46, 5- 91, 6- 106, 7- 125, 8- 132, 9- 161

New Zealand won by 110 runs

which was founded on a good opening partnership between Howarth and Wright and ended with an explosive attack on the bowling by Hadlee who won the individual award.

Only the slow left-arm of the experienced Iqbal Qasim, outstanding in the series in Pakistan a few weeks earlier, stemmed the flow of runs. Cairns and Hadlee undermined the Pakistan batting in a fierce opening spell and once the tourists had slumped to 26 for 3 and 46 for 4, they gave up hopes of winning the match and settled for batting practice.

Lance Cairns played two of the longest innings of his career for Northern Districts and scored 85 and 89 in successive matches at the beginning of 1985. (Adrian Murrell)

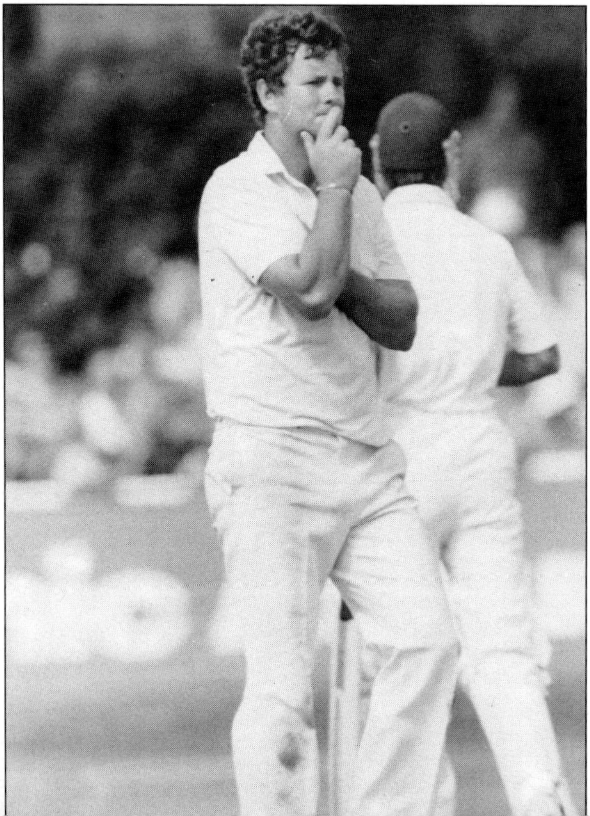

Shell Trophy

13, 14 and 15 January 1985

at Basin Reserve, Wellington

Wellington 378 (B.A. Edgar 81, J.G. Boyle 71, R.H. Vance 54, B.P. Bracewell 4 for 114) and 118 for 4 dec
Northern Districts 267 (B.G. Cooper 55, E.J. Gray 5 for 87) and 173 for 8 (B.R. Blair 63, L.M. Crocker 57, E.J. Gray 5 for 61)

Match drawn
Wellington 4 pts, Northern Districts 0 pts

at Lancaster Park, Christchurch

Canterbury 246 (R.T. Latham 95, D.R. O'Sullivan 5 for 75) and 280 (R.T. Latham 109, V.R. Brown 61, D.R. O'Sullivan 5 for 101)
Central Districts 150 (C.H. Thiele 4 for 45) and 254 (T.E. Blain 70, C.J. Smith 55 not out, V.R. Brown 4 for 88)

Canterbury won by 105 runs
Canterbury 16 pts, Central Districts 0 pts

at Eden Park, Auckland

Auckland 305 for 8 dec (M. Pringle 72, S.J. Gillespie 60, P.A. Horne 58) and 50 for 9 (N.A. Mallender 7 for 27)
Otago 377 (K.R. Rutherford 130, W.K. Lees 54 not out, W. Watson 4 for 96)

SECOND ONE-DAY INTERNATIONAL – NEW ZEALAND *v.* PAKISTAN
15 January 1985 at Hamilton

PAKISTAN			
	Mohsin Khan	c Smith, b Chatfield	49
	Wasim Raja	c Reid, b Coney	15
	Qasin Umar	b Coney	15
	Javed Miandad†	not out	90
	Saleem Malik	run out	14
	Mudassar Nazar	not out	22
	Shoaib Mohammad		
	Anil Dalpat*		
	Iqbal Qasim		
	Tahir Naqqash		
	Azeem Hafeez		
	Extras	b 1, lb 10, w 3, nb 2	16
	(50 overs)	(for 4 wickets)	221

	O	M	R	W
Cairns	10	2	56	—
Hadlee	10	3	43	—
Coney	10	1	16	2
Bracewell	10	—	51	—
Chatfield	10	—	39	1

FALL OF WICKETS
1- 32, 2- 62, 3- 131, 4- 160

NEW ZEALAND			
	G.P. Howarth†	c Anil, b Wasim Raja	5
	J.G. Wright	c Javed, b Saleem Malik	39
	J.F. Reid	b Wasim Raja	17
	M.D. Crowe	c Tahir, b Iqbal Qasim	59
	J.J. Crowe	b Azeem Hafeez	35
	J.V. Coney	not out	31
	I.D.S. Smith*	c Azeem Hafeez, b Tahir	13
	R.J. Hadlee	not out	13
	B.L. Cairns		
	J.G. Bracewell		
	E.J. Chatfield		
	Extras	lb 5, w 5	10
	(48.5 overs)	(for 6 wickets)	222

	O	M	R	W
Wasim Raja	10	—	29	2
Saleem Malik	10	1	34	1
Iqbal Qasim	10	—	58	2
Azeem Hafeez	7.5	—	36	—
Mudassar Nazar	7	—	41	—
Tahir Naqqash	4	—	19	1

FALL OF WICKETS
1- 9, 2- 36, 3- 90, 4- 154, 5- 164, 7- 191

New Zealand won by 4 wickets

Match drawn
Otago 4 pts, Auckland 0 pts

Splendid bowling by Evan Gray could not force victory for Wellington at Basin Reserve. Edgar, Boyle and Vance gave the home side a fine start and the third wicket did not fall until the score had reached 209. Northern Districts batted solidly in reply but still trailed by 111 runs. Wellington went for brisk runs in their second innings and Vance made a challenging declaration to which the visitors made a positive response, but Gray nearly tempted them to defeat.

Latham was outstanding at Christchurch and his magnificent batting took Canterbury to a convincing win and to the top of the table.

Martin Pringle scored 72 on his first-class debut for Auckland who also included Ray Hunter, making his first appearance in first-class cricket for 9 years and 2 days. He had played in two first-class games in the 1975–76 season. Auckland scored well, but Rutherford's dominant century gave Otago the points. Then, in 43 overs, Otago almost pulled off an amazing innings victory. Neil Mallender, in 22 overs, took a career best 7 for 27, and Auckland were saved only by their last pair.

Second One-Day International
NEW ZEALAND *v.* PAKISTAN

A much improved batting display by Pakistan enabled them to hold New Zealand for most of the second one-day match, but the limitations of their attack were still apparent.

RIGHT: *Geoff Howarth, another keen season with the bat, but 68 in the first one-day international at Napier and the most successful captain in New Zealand's Test history. (Mike Powell)*

Javed Miandad, captain of the Pakistani touring side and a century in the first match at Lancaster Park. (George Herringshaw)

Mohsin Khan and Wasim Raja withstood the opening attack of Cairns and Hadlee, but the advent of Coney, too rarely used in limited-over games, accounted for both Wasim Raja and Qasim Umar and cripped the run rate. A dashing innings from skipper Javed revitalised Pakistan and when Howarth was caught behind early on, the visitors seemed to take a grip on the game.

An aggressive innings from Martin Crowe with good support from first Wright and then Jeff Crowe raised the scoring rate, but when Ian Smith was dismissed at 191, New Zealand still needed 31 from just over six overs. Hadlee and Coney kept cool and Jeremy Coney lofted Azeem Hafeez to the mid-wicket boundary for the winning runs with seven balls remaining.

Shell Trophy

17, 18 and 19 January 1985

at Lancaster Park, Christchurch

Otago 383 (G.J. Dawson 79, A.H. Jones 62, R.N. Hoskin 60, T.J. Wilson 52, C.H. Thiele 4 for 112) and 162 for 7 (V.R. Brown 4 for 68)
Canterbury 203 (A.H. Jones 4 for 28, V. Johnson 4 for 59) and 366 for 8 dec (A.P. Nathu 147, V.R. Brown 71)

Match drawn
Otago 4 pts, Canterbury 0 pts

at Seddon Park, Hamilton

Northern Districts 227 (B.R. Blair 53, W. Watson 4 for 40, M.C. Snedden 4 for 78) and 157 (M.C. Snedden 4 for 21, G.B. Troup 4 for 57)
Auckland 314 for 8 dec (T.J. Franklin 181) and 74 for 4

Auckland won by 6 wickets
Auckland 16 pts, Northern Districts 0 pts

at Horton Park, Blenheim

Wellington 402 for 7 dec (T.D. Ritchie 105 not out, E.B. McSweeney 95, R.H. Vance 66) and 161 for 6 dec (B.A. Edgar 82 not out)

Trevor Franklin, 181 v. *Northern Districts, the highest score made for Auckland for 37 years. (Mark Baker)*

Central Districts 253 for 7 dec (R.T. Hart 108) and 123 for 4

Match drawn
Wellington 4 pts, Central Districts 0 pts

Auckland took over as leaders in the Championship race with a resounding win at Hamilton. After Watson and Snedden had bowled well Trevor Franklin hit the highest score of his career and the highest score made for Auckland for 37 years. Snedden and Troup, restored to fitness, bowled Northern out a second time and Auckland moved comfortably to maximum points.

Sound batting throughout the order, highlighted by a sixth wicket stand of 154 between Ritchie and McSweeney, took Wellington to a big score at Blenheim. Ron Hart hit a good hundred in reply and Hayward declared as soon as the follow-on had been avoided, but the game was destined for a draw.

Consistent batting throughout the order put Otago in a strong position in Christchurch and Jones and Johnson, in his third first-class match, forced Canterbury to follow-on. Anap Nathu hit a career best when Canterbury batted again and Vaughan Brown batted and bowled well so that the home side almost pulled off a surprise win.

First Test Match
NEW ZEALAND *v.* PAKISTAN

There was no play possible on the last day because of rain, but by that time the game already seemed destined to be drawn.

Pakistan welcomed Abdul Qadir to their party after his absence in Pakistan for treatment to his foot injury, but he had a barren first day as New Zealand ground to 220 for 4,

FIRST TEST MATCH – NEW ZEALAND *v.* PAKISTAN
18, 19, 20, 21 and 22 January 1985 at Basin Reserve, Wellington

NEW ZEALAND

	FIRST INNINGS		SECOND INNINGS	
G.P. Howarth†	run out	33	c Anil, b Hafeez	17
J.G. Wright	c Shoaib, b Hafeez	11	lbw, b Mudassar	11
J.F. Reid	b Hafeez	148	c Qadir, b Iqbal	3
M.D. Crowe	c Anil, b Iqbal	37	c Qadir, b Iqbal	33
J.J. Crowe	c Shoaib, b Iqbal	4	not out	19
J.V. Coney	b Qadir	48	not out	18
R.J. Hadlee	c Javed, b Hafeez	89		
I.D.S. Smith*	c and b Mudassar	65		
B.L. Cairns	b Hafeez	36		
S.L. Boock	c Anil, b Hafeez	0		
E.J. Chatfield	not out	3		
Extras	b 5, lb 12, nb 1	18	lb 2	2
		492	(for 4 wkts)	103

	O	M	R	W	O	M	R	W
Mudassar Nazar	29	5	80	1	6	3	13	1
Azeem Hafeez	48	12	127	5	15	3	51	1
Abdul Qadir	51	13	142	1	8	1	18	—
Iqbal Qasim	41	5	105	2	16	8	19	2
Wasim Raja	2	—	10	—				
Shoaib Mohammad	1	—	4	—				
Javed Miandad	3	1	7	—				

FALL OF WICKETS
1- 24, 2- 61, 3- 126, 4- 138, 5- 230, 6- 375, 7- 414, 8- 488, 9- 488
1- 24, 2- 30, 3- 42, 4- 73

PAKISTAN

	FIRST INNINGS	
Mudassar Nazar	c and b Boock	38
Mohsin Khan	c Wright, b Boock	40
Shoaib Mohammad	run out	7
Qasim Umar	b Boock	8
Javed Miandad†	c Smith, b Boock	30
Saleem Malik	c Cairns, b Hadlee	66
Wasim Raja	c M. Crowe, b Boock	14
Abdul Qadir	c Smith, b Hadlee	54
Anil Dalpat*	c Smith, b Chatfield	15
Iqbal Qasim	not out	27
Azeem Hafeez	c Boock, b Cairns	3
Extras	b 9, lb 9, nb 2	20
		322

	O	M	R	W
Hadlee	32	11	70	2
Cairns	27.4	5	65	1
Chatfield	25	10	52	1
Boock	45	18	117	5

FALL OF WICKETS
1- 62, 2- 85, 3- 95, 4- 102, 5- 161, 6- 187, 7- 223, 8- 288, 9- 309

Umpires: S.J. Woodward and G.C. Morris

Match drawn

Reid and Coney effecting a recovery after the first four wickets had gone for 138.

The fifth wicket stand ended at 230, but Reid batted on relentlessly taking 551 minutes over his 148. Richard Hadlee gave the innings some fillip as he prompted a record sixth wicket stand of 145 with Reid, and Cairns and Smith hit well at the close of the day. Howarth decided to bat on on the third morning, but only 7 runs were added as the last 3 wickets fell.

Pakistan began confidently, but the advent of Boock changed the situation. He had Mohsin caught at cover in his third over and in the afternoon session he bowled Qasim Umar, desperately in need of runs, and caught and bowled Mudassar after the ball had rebounded from Cairns at silly point. Shoaib was run out and Pakistan were 120 for 4 at tea.

Javed and Saleem added 59, but Javed became another Boock victim and Saleem was Hadlee's thousandth first-class wicket. Pakistan closed at 236 for 7 and New Zealand were in control.

Beginning the fourth day still needing 57 to avoid the follow-on, Pakistan were well served by Abdul Qadir and Anil Dalpat who put on 65 in 64 minutes. Iqbal Qasim also batted well and the last three Pakistan wickets added 99 runs. When New Zealand batted again their only hope of forcing a

John Reid. New Zealand's most successful batsman of 1985 and the quickest New Zealander to a thousand runs in Test cricket when he hit 158 not out against Pakistan in Auckland. (Adrian Murrell)

LEFT: *Azeem Hafeez – a fine spell for Pakistan in the First Test at Wellington. (Adrian Murrell)*

BELOW: *Richard Hadlee. One thousand wickets in first-class cricket when he had Saleem Malik caught by Lance Cairns in the First Test. (Adrian Murrell)*

victory was to score quick runs, but they were thwarted by the accuracy of Iqbal Qasim.

Shell Cup

20 January 1985

at Lancaster Park, Christchurch

Otago 228 for 8 (K.R. Rutherford 99, S.R. McNally 5 for 45)
Canterbury 210 (R.W. Fulton 55 not out, P.E. McEwan 53)

Otago (2 pts) won by 18 runs

at Nelson

Central Districts 288 (R.T. Hart 81, R.E. Hayward 55, G.N. Cederwall 5 for 32)
Wellington 123

Central Districts (2 pts) won by 105 runs

at Rotorua

Auckland 197 for 9
Northern Districts 200 for 6 (B.R. Blair 79 not out, B.G. Cooper 63)

Northern Districts (2 pts) won by 4 wickets

With Wellington already assured of a place in the final, the last round of matches began with Auckland favourites to join them. Auckland's hopes disappeared, however, when Northern Districts, using four spinners to bowl 33 of their 50 overs, outfought and outplayed them. The ball turned slowly and held up to make stroke play difficult after Auckland had got away to a good start. When Northern batted Auckland seemed to have taken a grasp on the game for Broughton, Crocker and Kuggeleijn were out with only 29 scored, but Cooper and Blair added 97 and Northern won with 10 balls to spare.

Ken Rutherford blighted Canterbury's chances with 99 off 142 deliveries, sharing an opening stand of 90 with McCullum.

Vance asked Central Districts to bat at Nelson and Ron Hart, Man of the Match, steered his side to 228. Rain reduced Wellington's target, but they were never in contention and to the surprise of many, Central Districts qualified for the final.

Shell Cup – Final Table

	P	*W*	*L*	*Ab*	*Pts*
Wellington	5	3	1	1	7
Central Districts	5	3	2		6
Auckland	5	2	2	1	5
Canterbury	5	2	3		4
Northern Districts	5	2	3		4
Otago	5	2	3		4

Bob Vance, 99 against Canterbury, and captain of Wellington as they clinched the Shell Trophy.

Second Test Match
NEW ZEALAND *v.* PAKISTAN

Howarth won the toss and asked Pakistan to bat first on a green wicket in uncertain weather which delayed the start by half an hour. Pakistan gave a first Test cap to eighteen-year old Wasim Akram and included Zaheer who had just arrived from Pakistan.

Pakistan struggled for most of the first day. Mudassar was beaten for pace and Mohsin fell in the last over before lunch when Pakistan were 58 for 2. With Chatfield accurate and Cairns and Hadlee hostile, New Zealand held a tight grip on the game and in a six-over spell in mid-afternoon, Pakistan went from 105 for 3 to 123 for 7, Chatfield capturing his wickets in one over. The majority of the wickets fell to close catches, Jeff Crowe at first slip, Coney at second and Martin Crowe at forward short-leg. Bad light ended play 105 minutes early when Pakistan were 147 for 8 and Wasim Akram yet to face a ball.

Pakistan must have regretted batting Saleem so low and he was left undefeated when Hadlee finished off the innings on the second morning. New Zealand began ferociously, Howarth and Wright taking 27 from the first three overs, but the highlight of the day was a third wicket stand of 137 between Reid and Martin Crowe which was ended in the last session when a leg-break from Abdul Qadir ran up Crowe's leg and touched the top of his bat before being caught.

Reid took ninety minutes on the third morning to reach his second successive Test century and in a few minutes he reached a thousand runs in Test cricket. It was his twentieth Test innings and no New Zealander has reached the mark quicker. Reid's 158 not out was his fifth century in twelve Tests and he has supplied the New Zealand batting with a solidity to complement its attractive stroke-players. The left-hander was forced to retire when struck by a bouncer from Azeem Hafeez when he was on 123, but he returned after having five stitches in his chin and altogether faced 318 deliveries before Howarth declared at the end of the day.

SECOND TEST MATCH – NEW ZEALAND *v.* PAKISTAN
25, 26, 27 and 28 January 1985 at Eden Park, Auckland

PAKISTAN

	FIRST INNINGS		SECOND INNINGS	
Mudassar Nazar	lbw, b Hadlee	12	b Cairns	89
Mohsin Khan	c Coney, b Cairns	26	c Coney, b Hadlee	1
Qasim Umar	c M. Crowe, b Cairns	33	c Cairns, b Chatfield	22
Zaheer Abbas	c J. Crowe, b Cairns	6	(6) c sub, b Hadlee	12
Javed Miandad†	c Smith, b Chatfield	26	c Smith, b Chatfield	1
Wasim Raja	c Smith, b Chatfield	4	(7) c Wright, b Boock	11
Abdul Qadir	run out	0	(8) lbw, b Cairns	10
Saleem Malik	not out	41	(4) c Cairns, b Chatfield	0
Anil Dalpat*	c J. Crowe, b Hadlee	7	lbw, b Cairns	6
Wasim Akram	c M. Crowe, b Hadlee	0	(11) not out	0
Azeem Hafeez	c Boock, b Hadlee	6	(10) lbw, b Cairns	17
Extras	lb 5, nb 3	8	lb 11, nb 3	14
		169		183

	O	M	R	W	O	M	R	W
Hadlee	19.5	3	60	4	17	1	66	2
Cairns	29	10	73	3	19.4	8	49	4
Chatfield	14	5	24	2	19	5	47	3
Coney	4	1	7	—				
Boock					4	1	10	1

FALL OF WICKETS
1- 33, 2- 58, 3- 93, 4- 105, 5- 111, 6- 115, 7- 123, 8- 147, 9- 151
1- 13, 2- 54, 3- 54, 4- 57, 5- 79, 6- 122, 7- 140, 8- 152, 9- 178

NEW ZEALAND

	FIRST INNINGS	
G.P. Howarth†	c Javed, b Mudassar	13
J.G. Wright	c Saleem, b Akram	66
J.F. Reid	not out	158
M.D. Crowe	c sub, b Qadir	84
S.L. Boock	c Raja, b Hafeez	10
J.J. Crowe	run out	30
J.V. Coney	c Anil, b Mudassar	25
R.J. Hadlee	c Mohsin, b Hafeez	13
I.D.S. Smith*	c Javed, b Akram	7
B.L. Cairns	b Hafeez	23
E.J. Chatfield	not out	1
Extras	b 6, lb 9, nb 6	21
	(for 9 wkts dec	451

	O	M	R	W
Azeem Hafeez	47	10	157	3
Wasim Akram	34.4	4	105	2
Mudassar Nazar	34	5	85	2
Abdul Qadir	22	5	52	1
Wasim Raja	1	—	3	—
Saleem Malik	8.2	2	34	—

FALL OF WICKETS
1- 60, 2- 108, 3- 245, 4- 278, 5- 359, 6- 366, 7- 387, 8- 411, 9- 447

Umpires: F.R. Goodall and S.J. Woodward

New Zealand won by an innings and 99 runs

On the fourth day only Mudassar Nazar offered any resistance to spirited bowling by Cairns and Chatfield and Pakistan surrendered limply to lose by an innings with more than a day to spare.

Shell Trophy

25, 26 and 27 January 1985

at Carisbrook, Dunedin

Otago 241 (K.R. Rutherford 89 not out, T.J. Wilson 55, W. Watson 4 for 41, M.C. Snedden 4 for 74) and 184 for 5 dec (K.R. Rutherford 61, A. H. Jones 58 not out, A.T.R. Hellaby 4 for 84)
Auckland 185 (A.J. Hunt 51) and 237 for 9 (T.J. Franklin 65, M.J. Greatbatch 55, T.J. Wilson 7 for 57)

Match drawn
Otago 4 pts, Auckland 0 pts

at Basin Reserve, Wellington

Canterbury 273 (A.W. Hart 70 not out, P.E. McEwan 56, E.J. Gray 4 for 107) and 263 for 7 dec (P.E. McEwan 105, E.J. Gray 5 for 115)
Wellington 314 for 9 dec (R.H. Vance 99, G.N. Cederwall 57 not out, V.R. Brown 4 for 83) and 223 for 5 (J.G. Boyle 89)

Wellington won by 5 wickets
Wellington 16 pts, Canterbury 0 pts

In the Shell Trophy leap-frog Wellington hopped into the lead with an efficient team performance over Canterbury. Gray was again an outstanding contributor with 9 wickets in the match and skipper Vance played splendidly as did Boyle in leading the race for victory at five an over. Grant Cederwall, enjoying his best season, hit 81 runs without being dismissed while for Canterbury McEwan once more displayed the form he has never quite managed for the Test side.

At Carisbrook, Ken Rutherford carried his bat through Otago's innings, the first time this had been done for a provincial side for 22 years. His effort, and Wilson's late fifty, gave Otago the advantage and Rutherford again batted well in the second innings. Lees timed his declaration perfectly and John Wilson in his second first-class match almost snatched the game after Auckland had needed only 4 to win with three wickets to fall

Bruce Edgar. Some useful innings for Wellington, but still in search of the form that made him the most prolific run scorer in New Zealand a few years ago. (Adrian Murrell)

1, 2 and 3 February 1985

at Basin Reserve, Wellington

Pakistanis 217 for 9 dec (Zaheer Abbas 92, E.J. Gray 5 for 68) and 222 for 3 dec (Rameez Raja 70 not out, Saleem Malik 61, Qasim Umar 55)
Wellington 205 for 7 dec (R.W. Ormiston 67, R.H. Vance 66) and 53 for 2

Match drawn

Shell Trophy

at Seddon Park, Hamilton

Central Districts 254 (R.T. Hart 60) and 312 for 7 dec (P.S. Briasco 76, T.E. Blain 72, C.W. Dickeson 5 for 139)
Northern Districts 322 for 9 dec (B.G. Cooper 65, B. Young 53 not out) and 165 for 7 (R.D. Broughton 51)

Match drawn
Northern Districts 4 pts, Central Districts 0 pts

In spite of three declarations, the game between Wellington and the tourists was drawn. Zaheer was in commanding form until being caught at short-leg off Gray immediately after tea. Zaheer had rallied Pakistan after Chatfield and Cederwall had exploited conditions favourable to seam bowling early on, but it was Gray who was again the most successful of the Wellington bowlers. The home side's innings was founded on a third wicket stand of 115 between Vance and Ormiston. Rameez Raja and Saleem Malik hit 101 in 75 minutes, but the declaration came too late to bring a result.

In the Shell Trophy match, a last wicket stand of 55 between Carrington and Young, undefeated, gave Northern the advantage. The exciting young batsmen, Briasco and Blain, put on a brisk 92 when Central batted again, but Northern, set to make 245 to win, faltered after being 93 without loss and hung on to draw.

Third One-Day International
NEW ZEALAND *v.* PAKISTAN

The beginning of the match tended to be overshadowed by the announcements that Zaheer had retired from county cricket, news that was not unexpected, and that Abdul Qadir was being sent back to Pakistan for disciplinary reasons. Qadir's relationship with the controllers of the game in Pakistan has been an uneasy one, but his dismissal came as a surprise. Qadir himself could offer no reason for his banishment and later stated that he was considering playing in Australia and that he would not play for Pakistan again until certain selectors had been dismissed. He named chief selector, Haseeb Ahsan, as one of them.

A 92-run second wicket partnership between left-handers Wright and Reid put New Zealand in a strong position and the later batsmen built on the firm foundations with some strong hitting. The New Zealand total of 264 looked formidable and when Mudassar, Qasim Umar and Saleem were dismissed for 22 it seemed that they were heading for a massive victory. Zaheer and Javed halted the collapse, and a thrilling seventh wicket stand of 108 between Rameez Raja and wicket-keeper Anil Dalpat gave glimpses of a Pakistan win, but the return of Hadlee ended the challenge and New Zealand took a winning 3–0 lead in the series when Iqbal Wasim was bowled with two balls remaining and Pakistan still 13 short of New Zealand's total.

Third Test Match
NEW ZEALAND *v.* PAKISTAN

As Abdul Qadir was being sent home to Pakistan Rashid Khan was arriving in New Zealand and the medium pace bowler was included in the side for the third Test. Brendon Bracewell returned for New Zealand in an attempt to re-establish a Test career and both sides relied on pace to the exclusion of spinners.

Pakistan, after losing Mudassar at 25, batted well, and a stand of 141 between Qasim and Javed for the third wicket moved them towards a very strong position. Jeremy Coney halted the advance when he had the splendid Qasim Umar

ABOVE: *Ian Smith, New Zealand's ebullient wicket-keeper. (Adrian Murrell)*

THIRD ONE-DAY INTERNATIONAL – NEW ZEALAND *v.* PAKISTAN
6 February 1985 at Lancaster Park, Christchurch

NEW ZEALAND			
G.P. Howarth†	c Anil, b Azeem	12	
J.G. Wright	c Saleem, b Tahir	65	
J.F. Reid	c Saleem, b Azeem	88	
M.D. Crowe	run out	20	
B.L. Cairns	c and b Mudassar	8	
R.J. Hadlee	c Anil, b Tahir	9	
J.V. Coney	c Iqbal, b Azeem	12	
J.J. Crowe	c Wasim Raja, b Tahir	13	
I.D.S. Smith*	not out	5	
J.G. Bracewell	not out	20	
E.J. Chatfield			
Extras	b 3, lb 5, w 4	12	
(50 overs)	(for 8 wickets)	264	

	O	M	R	W
Wasim Raja	10	1	34	—
Azeem Hafeez	10	—	56	3
Iqbal Qasim	5	—	33	—
Mudassar Nazar	10	—	56	1
Tahir Naqqash	8	—	40	3
Saleem Malik	3	—	16	—
Zaheer Abbas	4	—	21	—

FALL OF WICKETS
1- 29, 2- 121, 3- 166, 4- 177, 5- 192, 6- 216, 7- 237, 8- 241

PAKISTAN		
Mudassar Nazar	c J.J. Crowe, b Cairns	8
Qasim Umar	run out	1
Saleem Malik	b Cairns	0
Zaheer Abbas	st Smith, b Bracewell	58
Javed Miandad†	c M.D. Crowe, b Cairns	30
Rameez Raja	run out	75
Wasim Raja	c Howarth, b Chatfield	12
Anil Dalpat*	c M.D. Crowe, b Hadlee	37
Tahir Naqqash	c Howarth, b Hadlee	11
Azeem Hafeez	not out	1
Iqbal Qasim	b Hadlee	0
Extras	b 4, lb 6, w 4, nb 4	18
(49.4 overs)		251

	O	M	R	W
Cairns	10	4	39	3
Hadlee	9.4	1	32	3
Chatfield	10	—	75	1
Coney	10	—	44	—
Bracewell	10	1	51	1

FALL OF WICKETS
1- 1, 2- 1, 3- 22, 4- 103, 5- 105, 6- 129, 7- 237, 8- 250, 9- 250

New Zealand won by 13 runs

caught four short of his century. In his last three overs of the day Richard Hadlee then took 4 wickets at a personal cost of 5 runs, and Pakistan had moved from 241 for 2 to 251 for 7 in the last half hour.

There was no recovery on the second morning and Hadlee's devastating bowling had nullified the good work of Javed and Qasim. Howarth and Wright began the New Zealand reply solidly enough, but after Wright's dismissal at 41 of which he had scored 32 in 53 minutes, Howarth, Reid and Jeff Crowe were out in the space of 35 minutes and New Zealand were 92 for 4.

Martin Crowe and Coney added 57 in 97 minutes, and although Coney and Hadlee were out before the close, New Zealand ended at a happier 201 for 6. Sadly for New Zealand, the third morning produced only 19 runs for them, and they trailed by 54 on the first innings, victims of the unbounding enthusiasm of Wasim Akram.

Pakistan had increased their lead to 163 by the close of the third day, again they collapsed, to Hadlee and Cairns, after seemingly being set for a big score. Much rested on Qasim Umar who was 50 not out. He did not fail his side, taking his score to 89 as 114 runs were added on the fourth day.

Needing 278 to win, New Zealand began disastrously. Again it was young Wasim Akram who caused the problems after Wright had been taken at slip off Azeem Hafeez. Howarth and Reid edged catches off Wasim and Jeff Crowe was lbw first ball to the teenager. Coney and Martin Crowe saw New Zealand from 23 for 4 to 114 at the close, but a Pakistan victory looked a formality.

Martin Crowe and Jeremy Coney took their stand to 157 before Crowe was caught off Tahir Naqqash shortly before lunch on the last day. Hadlee stayed until the score reached 208, but he, Smith and Brendon Bracewell fell while 20 runs were scored and Lance Cairns was forced to retire hurt when hit on the head by a Wasim Akram bouncer. Cairns was later said to have a hairline fracture of the skull, but he remained padded up unless he was needed to return to the wicket. He was not. Ewen Chatfield, who had never reached 20 in a Test match nor 30 in a first-class game, helped Jeremy Coney to make the 50 runs that were needed for victory.

It was a courageous performance that brought an historic victory. Jeremy Coney, who had come to the wicket at 23 for 4, defeat a formality, stayed to hit his second hundred in Test cricket, 111 not out, and to accomplish one of the most glorious wins in Test history.

Fourth One-Day International
NEW ZEALAND *v.* PAKISTAN

Rain prevented play on the Saturday and the game was rearranged for the Sunday when rain again began to fall at lunch time and the match was abandoned.

A splendid stand of 64 between Rameez Raja and Tahir Naqqash raised Pakistan from 92 to 7. Tahir continued to hit well until the end of the innings. Earlier the accurate New Zealand seam attack had devastated the best of the Pakistan batting.

For New Zealand, who had enjoyed another triumphant home season, there was further good news. It was reported

THIRD TEST MATCH – NEW ZEALAND *v.* PAKISTAN
9, 10, 11, 13 and 14 February 1985 at Carisbrook, Dunedin

PAKISTAN

	FIRST INNINGS		SECOND INNINGS	
Mudassar Nazar	c J. Crowe, b Hadlee	18	c Coney, b Bracewell	5
Mohsin Khan	run out	39	c M. Crowe, b Hadlee	27
Qasim Umar	c J. Crowe, b Coney	96	c Smith, b Chatfield	89
Javed Miandad†	c Smith, b Hadlee	79	c Reid, b Hadlee	2
Zaheer Abbas	c Reid, b Hadlee	6	lbw, b Cairns	0
Rashid Khan	c M. Crowe, b Hadlee	0	(9) b Bracewell	37
Anil Dalpat*	b Bracewell	16	(7) b Chatfield	21
Saleem Malik	lbw, b Hadlee	0	(6) b Cairns	9
Tahir Naqqash	c Wright, b Hadlee	0	(8) run out	1
Azeem Hafeez	c Smith, b Bracewell	4	b Chatfield	7
Wasim Akram	not out	1	not out	8
Extras	b 1, lb 2, nb 12	15	b 1, lb 9, nb 7	17
		274		223

	O	M	R	W	O	M	R	W
Hadlee	24	5	51	6	26	9	59	2
B.P. Bracewell	18.2	1	81	2	14.4	2	48	2
Cairns	22	—	77	—	22	5	41	2
Chatfield	24	6	46	—	26	5	65	3
Coney	6	1	16	1				

FALL OF WICKETS
1- 25, 2- 100, 3- 241, 4- 243, 5- 245, 6- 251, 7- 251, 8- 255, 9- 273
1- 5, 2- 72, 3- 75, 4- 76, 5- 103, 6- 157, 7- 166, 8- 169, 9- 181

NEW ZEALAND

	FIRST INNINGS		SECOND INNINGS	
G.P. Howarth†	b Akram	23	c Mohsin, b Akram	17
J.G. Wright	c Umar, b Hafeez	32	c Mohsin, b Hafeez	1
J.F. Reid	b Akram	24	c Anil, b Akram	0
M.D. Crowe	c Javed, b Akram	57	c Mudassar, b Tahir	84
J.J. Crowe	lbw, b Akram	6	lbw, b Akram	0
J.V. Coney	c Anil, b Rashid	24	not out	111
R.J. Hadlee	c Anil, b Rashid	18	b Hafeez	11
I.D.S. Smith*	lbw, b Tahir	12	c Javed, b Akram	6
B.L. Cairns	c Anil, b Akram	6	retired hurt	0
B.P. Bracewell	c Rashid, b Tahir	3	c Tahir, b Akram	4
E.J. Chatfield	not out	2	not out	21
Extras	b 7, lb 5, nb 1	13	b 5, lb 6, w 1, nb 11	23
		220	(for 8 wkts)	278

	O	M	R	W	O	M	R	W
Rashid Khan	23	7	64	2	9	2	33	—
Azeem Hafeez	20	6	65	1	32	9	84	2
Wasim Akram	26	7	56	5	33	10	72	5
Tahir Naqqash	16.4	4	23	2	16.4	1	58	1
Mudassar Nazar					9	2	20	—

FALL OF WICKETS
1- 41, 2- 81, 3- 84, 4- 92, 5- 149, 6- 185, 7- 203, 8- 205, 9- 216
1- 4, 2- 5, 3- 23, 4- 23, 5- 180, 6- 208, 7- 216, 8- 228

Umpires: F.R. Goodall and G.C. Morris

New Zealand won by 2 wickets

ABOVE: *Wasim Akram. His magnificent bowling at Dunedin, 10 for 128, failed to bring his side victory. (Adrian Murrell)*

that Cairns had not suffered a hairline fracture of the skull as originally feared and that he would be fit to travel with the side to Australia. Pakistan mused on the very bad beating that they had received at the hands of the New Zealanders and there were reports that Imran Khan would bolster the side in Australia where he had been playing for New South Wales.

Shell Cup Final
WELLINGTON *v.* CENTRAL DISTRICTS

The Shell Cup had provided a season of records. Central Districts' 289 for 8 against Northern Districts at Wanganui at the end of December was the highest score yet made in the competition while Otago's 64 at Alexandra three days earlier was the lowest. The best bowling performance in the Shell Cup had twice been established and the record had ended with Willie Watson whose 7 for 23 against Auckland in Otago also included the first hat-trick ever performed in the competition. In conclusion, Central Districts reached the final of a one-day competition for the first time, and then proceeded to win it.

They outplayed Wellington, the hosts, from start to finish which came with 6.2 overs still remaining and eight Central

The heroes of Dunedin. A ninth wicket stand of 50 and a famous victory. ABOVE: *Jeremy Coney who came to the wicket at 23 for 4 and stayed to make 111 not out. (Ken Kelly)* BELOW: *Ewen Chatfield, 21 not out, his highest Test score when it was needed most. (Adrian Murrell)*

FOURTH ONE-DAY INTERNATIONAL – NEW ZEALAND *v.* PAKISTAN
17 February 1985 at Eden Park, Auckland

PAKISTAN

Mudassar Nazar	c M.D. Crowe, b Chatfield	10
Qasim Umar	c Smith, b Snedden	6
Zaheer Abbas	c Smith, b Chatfield	4
Javed Miandad†	run out	9
Rameez Raja	st Smith, b J.G. Bracewell	59
Saleem Malik	lbw, b Chatfield	7
Wasim Raja	c Howarth, b J.G. Bracewell	0
Anil Dalpat*	c J.G. Bracewell, b McEwan	3
Tahir Naqqash	c Wright, b Snedden	61
Rashid Khan	not out	8
Wasim Akram	b Hadlee	2
Extras	b 3, lb 9, w 8	20
(49.1 overs)		189

	O	M	R	W
Chatfield	10	2	20	3
Hadlee	9.1	3	24	1
Snedden	10	3	36	2
McEwan	10	—	54	1
J.G. Bracewell	10	1	43	2

FALL OF WICKETS
1-17, 2-25, 3-25, 4-61, 5-70, 6-73, 7-92, 8-156, 9-182

NEW ZEALAND

G.P. Howarth†
J.G. Wright
J.F. Reid
M.D. Crowe
P.E. McEwan
R.J. Hadlee
I.D.S. Smith*
J.G. Bracewell
M.C. Snedden
J.V. Coney
E.J. Chatfield

Match abandoned

New Zealand *v.* Pakistan – Test Match Averages

NEW ZEALAND BATTING

	M	Inns	NOs	Runs	HS	Av	100s	50s
J.F. Reid	3	5	1	333	158*	83.25	2	
J.V. Coney	3	5	2	226	111*	75.33	1	
M.D. Crowe	3	5		295	84	59.00		3
R.J. Hadlee	3	4		131	89	32.75		1
J.G. Wright	3	5		121	66	24.20		1
I.D.S. Smith	3	4		90	65	22.50		1
B.L. Cairns	3	4	1	65	36	21.66		
G.P. Howarth	3	5		103	33	20.60		
J.J. Crowe	3	5	1	59	30	14.75		
S.L. Boock	2	2		10	10	5.00		

Played in three Tests: E.J. Chatfield 3*, 1*, 2* and 21*
Played in one Test: B.P. Bracewell 3 and 4

PAKISTAN BATTING

	M	Inns	NOs	Runs	HS	Av	100s	50s
Qasim Umar	3	5		248	96	49.60		2
Mudassar Nazar	3	5		162	89	32.40		1
Saleem Malik	3	5	1	116	66	29.00		1
Javed Miandad	3	5		138	79	27.60		1
Mohsin Khan	3	5		133	40	26.60		
Abdul Qadir	2	3		64	54	21.33		1
Anil Dalpat	3	5		65	21	13.00		
Wasim Raja	2	3		29	14	9.66		
Wasim Akram	2	4	3	9	8*	9.00		
Azeem Hafeez	3	5		37	17	7.40		
Zaheer Abbas	2	4		24	12	6.00		

Played in one Test: Shoaib Mohammad 7; Izbal Qasim 27*; Rashid Khan 0 and 37; Tahir Naqqash 0 and 1

NEW ZEALAND BOWLING

	Overs	Mds	Runs	Wkts	Av	Best	5/inn
R.J. Hadlee	118.5	29	306	16	19.12	6/51	1
S.L. Boock	49	19	127	6	21.16	5/117	1
J.V. Coney	10	2	23	1	23.00	1/16	
E.J. Chatfield	108	31	234	9	26.00	3/47	
B.L. Cairns	120.2	28	305	10	30.50	4/49	
B.P. Bracewell	33	3	129	4	32.25	2/48	

PAKISTAN BOWLING

	Overs	Mds	Runs	Wkts	Av	Best	5/inn	10/m
Wasim Akram	93.4	21	233	12	19.41	5/56	2	1
Tahir Naqqash	33.2	5	81	3	27.00	2/23		
Iqbal Qasim	57	15	124	4	31.00	2/19		
Azeem Hafeez	162	40	484	12	40.33	5/127	1	
Rashid Khan	32	9	97	2	48.50	2/64		
Mudassar Nazar	78	15	198	4	49.50	2/85		
Abdul Qadir	81	19	212	2	106.00	1/52		

Also bowled: Wasim Raja 3–0–13–0; Shoaib Mohammad 1–0–4–0; Javed Miandad 3–1–7–0; Saleem Malik 8.2–2–34–0

NEW ZEALAND CATCHES
9–I.D.S. Smith; 5–M.D. Crowe; 3–J.G. Wright, J. J. Crowe, J. V. Coney, B.L. Cairns and S.L. Boock; 2–J.F. Reid; 1–sub (J.G. Bracewell)

PAKISTAN CATCHES
8–Anil Dalpat; 5–Javed Miandad; 3–Mohsin Khan; 2–Mudassar Nazar, Shoaib Mohammad and Abdul Qadir; 1–Qasim Umar, Saleem Malik, Wasim Raja, Rashid Khan, Tahir Naqqash and sub (Shoaib Mohammad)

SHELL CUP FINAL – WELLINGTON *v.* CENTRAL DISTRICTS
23 February 1985 at Basin Reserve, Wellington

WELLINGTON

B.A. Edgar	b Robertson	0
J.G. Boyle	c Blain, b Gill	0
R.H. Vance†	lbw, b Briasco	25
R.W. Ormiston	b O'Sullivan	7
E.J. Gray	run out	53
E.B. McSweeney*	run out	13
T.D. Ritchie	c and b O'Sullivan	9
G.R. Larsen	c Toynbee, b Martin	26
G.N. Cederwall	b Martin	3
S.J. Maguiness	c Briasco, b Robertson	3
K.D. James	not out	0
Extras	lb 4, w 4, nb 6	14
(48.3 overs)		153

	O	M	R	W
Robertson	7.3	2	26	2
Gill	10	2	26	1
Stirling	2	—	17	—
Briasco	10	2	25	1
O'Sullivan	10	4	20	2
Martin	9	—	35	2

FALL OF WICKETS
1-0, 2-10, 3-43, 4-43, 5-65, 6-82, 7-138, 8-149, 9-151

CENTRAL DISTRICTS

T.E. Blain*	b Gray	56
R.T. Hart	run out	28
P.S. Briasco	not out	30
G.N. Edwards	not out	28
R.E. Hayward†		
M.H. Toynbee		
G.K. Robertson		
S.J. Gill		
D.A. Stirling		
D.R. O'Sullivan		
W. Martin		
Extras	lb 8, w 4, nb 2	14
(43.4 overs)	(for 2 wickets)	156

	O	M	R	W
James	9	—	32	—
Cederwall	8	1	25	—
Gray	10	—	23	1
Larsen	10	—	43	—
Maguiness	6.4	1	25	—

FALL OF WICKETS
1-85, 2-100

Central Districts won by 8 wickets

wickets still standing. Wellington never recovered from the loss of both openers for 0, and although Gray, inevitably, fought well, the enthusiasm of the fielding and the tightness of the bowling, proved too much for the home side. Sadly, in his season of bitter disappointment, Derek Stirling erred once more and could find neither length, direction, nor pace.

A stand of 56 between Gray and Larsen provided Wellington with their one glimmer of hope, but six wickets had already fallen before these two came together. Blain and Hart put on 85 for Central's first wicket and Man of the Match Briasco finished matters.

Shell Trophy

25, 26 and 27 February 1985

at McLean Park, Napier

Central Districts 318 for 7 dec (R.T. Hart 111, T.E. Blain 60) and 245 for 2 dec (C.J. Smith 103 not out, P.S. Briasco 75)
Canterbury 292 (D.J. Hartshorn 103) and 184 for 6 (V.R. Brown 61 not out, A.P. Nathu 51)

Match drawn
Central Districts 4 pts, Canterbury 0 pts

at Eden Park, Auckland

Auckland 311 (P. Horne 72, M.J. Greatbatch 67, J.J. Crowe 61) and 211 for 5 (P. Horne 70, P.N. Webb 51 not out)
Wellington 360 (R.H. Vance 59, M.C. Snedden 4 for 89)

Match drawn
Wellington 4 pts, Auckland 0 pts

Qasim Umar. Two fine innings for 96 and 89 for Pakistan in the third Test, but still he finished on the losing side. (Adrian Murrell)

John Wright, a storming end for Canterbury. 151 not out in the victory over Northern Districts on the last afternoon of the season. (Adrian Murrell)

at Carisbrook, Dunedin

Otago 165 (A.H. Jones 59 not out, K.R. Treiber 4 for 61) and 137
Northern Districts 83 (N.A. Mallender 6 for 31) and 161 (J.A.J. Cushen 5 for 37)

Otago won by 58 runs
Otago 16 pts, Northern Districts 0 pts

Otago gained their first win of the season in a low scoring match at Carisbrook. Otago's batting was resuscitated by Andrew Jones and Neil Mallender continued his magnificent form as Northern were routed on a doubtful wicket. The home side grafted to 137 in their second innings and Northern never looked like saving the game against Mallender, Vaughan Johnson and the thirty-eight year old John Cushen.

At Eden Park, Wellington gained vital points to keep them ahead in the championship race. Auckland scored heavily at the beginning of their innings, but failed to sustain the good start that they were given. Wellington batted consistently after losing Boyle at 8, and their last 4 wickets added 121 runs. With a result out of the question, Auckland batted out time against occasional bowlers.

In Napier, there were some fine individual performances. Ron Hart made a patient 111 and Tony Blain furthered his claim for the second wicket-keeping spot on the West Indian tour. Canterbury slumped to 101 for 5, but David Hartshorn, the New Zealand under-19 all-rounder, hit a maiden first-class century, his 103 coming in 212 minutes with 11 boundaries. Central led by 26 on the first innings, the first time in the season that they had taken first innings points, and increased their domination when John Smith, with a maiden hundred, and Scott Briasco put on 146 for the second wicket. Central threatened to win when Canterbury, having reached 98 for 1, lost 5 wickets for 59 runs, but Vaughan Brown stood firm.

With one round of matches remaining, Wellington led the table with 48 points, but three other sides could beat them in the title race in one of the most exciting finishes to a domestic competition.

Shell Trophy

1, 2 and 3 March 1985

at Basin Reserve, Wellington

Otago 275 (S.J. McCullum 66, E.J. Gray 6 for 89) and 273 for 3 (K.J. Burns 111 not out, A.H. Jones 102 not out)
Wellington 204 (T.D. Ritchie 60, S.L. Boock 6 for 64)

Match drawn
Otago 4 pts, Wellington 0 pts

at Eden Park, Auckland

Central Districts 78 (W. Watson 5 for 36, G.B. Troup 4 for 28) and 265 (C.J. Smith 67, M.C. Snedden 6 for 63)
Auckland 80 for 0 dec and 190 for 9 (T.J. Franklin 81, W. Martin 4 for 59

Match drawn
Auckland 4 pts, Central Districts 0 pts

at Lancaster Park, Christchurch

Northern Districts 274 (L.M. Crocker 57, S.R. McNally 4 for 77) and 235 for 6 dec (B.R. Blair 66, B. Young 65 not out)
Canterbury 210 and 300 for 2 (J.G. Wright 151 not out, P.E. McEwan 69, V.R. Brown 61 not out)

Canterbury won by 8 wickets
Canterbury 12 pts, Northern Districts 4 pts

The exciting finale to the season did not, in fact, materialise and Wellington, not at their best, won by default. They took no points in the game against Otago, being thwarted by the slow left-arm of Boock after Gray had put them into a reasonable position. Boock sent down 47 overs and Gray 52 to underline the tenseness of the struggle. When Otago batted again, Kevin Burns and Andrew Jones hit maiden centuries and shared an unbeaten stand of 212. Burns had been recalled to the Otago side after an absence of four years, having made 0, 1, 2 and 1 in his previous two matches in 1980–81. Their stand was a fourth wicket record for Otago.

McSweeney also established a record when he finished the year with 41 dismissals so beating Ian Smith's record of 35 set up in 1980.

Auckland needed to beat Central Districts at Eden Park to win the title, but they were hampered by wet conditions and, in spite of Snedden's positive leadership, they were nearly beaten. Snedden declared as soon as first innings points had been won. Troup and Watson had done the damage in the first innings, but solid, defiant batting kept them at bay in the second, and Auckland were left to make 264 at nearly 4 an over. Franklin held the innings together, but Wayne Martin caused problems and when O'Sullivan took the ninth wicket in semi-darkness it was the last delivery of the match and possibly his last in first-class cricket.

Canterbury finished level on points with Auckland by beating Northern Districts, but once again they failed to gain first innings advantage and this cost them the title. They won the game with an inspired innings by John Wright who led his side to an improbable victory with a magnificent unbeaten 151, a fine close to the season.

Shell Trophy Final Table (1984 positions in brackets)

	P	*W*	*L*	*D*	*1st Inns Lead*	*Pts*
Wellington (3)	8	2	1	5	6	48
Canterbury (1)	8	3	2	3	2	44
Auckland (4)	8	2	–	6	5	44
Otago (5)	8	1	2	5	6	36
Northern Districts (6)	8	1	4	3	4	28
Central Districts (2)	8	1	1	6	1	16

First-Class Averages

BATTING	M	Inns	NOs	Runs	HS	Av	100s	50s
J.F. Reid	6	9	1	465	158*	58.12	2	1
A.H. Jones	8	15	4	608	102*	55.27	1	4
M.D. Crowe	6	10		541	143	54.10	1	3
T.E. Blain	8	15	1	678	129	48.42	2	4
P.E. McEwan	6	11	1	482	105	48.20	1	4
B.L. Cairns	5	6	1	239	89	47.80		2
D.J. Hartshorn	3	6	2	191	103	47.75	1	
J.G. Wright	7	12	1	495	151*	45.00	2	2
R.T. Hart	8	15		665	111	44.33	2	3
K.R. Rutherford	6	11	1	442	130	44.20	1	2
P.N. Webb	6	9	3	245	76	40.83		2
T.J. Franklin	8	14	1	522	181	40.15	1	3
R.H. Vance	9	14	1	522	99	40.15		5
C.J. Smith	6	12	3	352	103*	39.11	1	2
V.R. Brown	9	16	2	540	104	38.57	1	5
J.V. Coney	6	10	2	291	111*	36.37	1	
B.A. Edgar	7	12	1	390	82*	35.45		2
R.T. Latham	9	16		561	109	35.06	1	3
P.S. Briasco	8	15	2	451	104*	34.69	1	2
M.J. Greatbatch	5	8	1	234	67	33.42		2
R.E. Hayward	7	12	3	293	65	32.55		1
P.A. Horne	7	13	1	386	72	32.16		4
A.P. Nathu	9	17		542	147	31.88	1	2
T.D. Ritchie	9	15	4	350	105*	31.81	1	2
S.J. McCullum	8	15		469	66	31.26		2
G.N. Cederwall	8	14	6	247	57*	30.87		1
J.J. Crowe	8	12	1	337	86	30.63		1
B.G. Cooper	8	15		450	91	30.00		5
L.M. Crocker	8	15		449	95	29.93		4
B.A. Young	8	15	4	325	65*	29.54		2
W.K. Lees	8	13	2	318	91	28.90		2
A.J. Hunt	8	13	2	299	78*	27.18		2
S.J. Gill	4	5	1	107	39	26.75		
B.R. Blair	8	15		401	66	26.73		3
J.G. Boyle	9	16		459	89	26.68		2
I.D.S. Smith	8	12	1	286	65	26.00		2
C.H. Thiele	7	9	5	103	49	25.75		
M. Pringle	3	6		151	72	25.16		1
D.A. Stirling	8	11	4	171	42	24.42		
E.B. McSweeney	9	14		327	95	23.35		1
T.J. Wilson	4	7		157	55	22.42		2
G.K. Robertson	8	11	1	222	73	22.20		1
R.J. Hadlee	8	12	2	221	89	22.10		1
E.J. Gray	8	11	1	218	49	21.80		
R.D. Broughton	8	15		318	67	21.20		2
M.H. Toynbee	4	7	1	127	40*	21.16		
G.J. Dawson	6	11	1	210	79	21.00		1
P.R. Facoory	3	6		125	39	20.83		
A.W. Hart	9	12	2	206	70*	20.60		1
M.J. Child	5	10	3	142	33	20.28		
B.P. Bracewell	8	14	3	215	46	19.54		
K.D. James	6	6		117	36	19.50		
R.W. Fulton	9	16	2	268	35	19.14		
G.P. Howarth	8	14		267	39	19.07		
N.A. Mallender	8	12	1	206	88	18.72		1
C.M. Kuggeleijn	7	13		242	50	18.61		1
R.W. Ormiston	9	14	2	223	67	18.58		1
R.N. Hoskin	7	12		209	60	17.41		1
W.P. Fowler	6	11		169	51	15.36		1
J.A.J. Cushen	8	13	3	118	44	11.80		
S.J. Maguinness	9	11	1	107	43	10.70		

(Qualification – 100 runs, average 10.00)
(K.J. Burns 20 and 111* in one match)

BOWLING	Overs	Mds	Runs	Wkts	Av	Best	10/m	5/inn
T.J. Wilson	56	20	139	10	13.90	7/57		1
K. Treiber	50	13	147	10	14.70	4/61		
R.J. Hadlee	287.3	86	652	38	17.15	6/51		3
M.C. Snedden	253.3	82	533	30	17.76	6/63		1
N.A. Mallender	259.5	73	637	35	18.20	7/27		2
G.B. Troup	151	38	432	21	20.57	6/53		1
V.A. Johnson	100	28	280	13	21.53	4/59		
E.J. Gray	436	149	1044	48	21.75	6/51		3
G.K. MacDonald	155.4	33	449	20	22.45	6/62		1
W. Watson	208.1	55	546	24	22.75	5/36		1
S.L. Boock	300	133	597	26	22.96	5/117		1
B.L. Cairns	197.2	53	433	18	24.05	4/39		
J.A.J. Cushen	330.5	112	748	31	24.12	5/37		1
B.R. Blair	101	26	276	11	25.09	3/10		
C.H. Thiele	183.5	37	604	24	25.16	4/35		
A.T.R. Hellaby	98.2	21	254	10	25.40	4/84		
E.J. Chatfield	297.5	86	617	24	25.70	4/56		
G.N. Cederwall	208.2	44	618	23	26.86	4/54		
J.G. Bracewell	204.4	63	489	18	27.16	6/68		1
D.R. O'Sullivan	425.3	124	1042	38	27.42	6/103	1	3
S.J. Maguiness	330.5	117	673	24	28.04	7/17	1	1
S.R. Tracy	71.4	16	295	10	29.50	4/97		
C.W. Dickeson	273.2	88	594	20	29.70	5/39		1
B.P. Bracewell	241	37	742	24	30.90	4/114		
S.M. Carrington	177.5	39	527	17	31.00	4/39		
V.R. Brown	333	87	972	31	31.35	4/45		
G.K. Robertson	216.5	31	737	21	35.09	3/51		
K.D. James	159.1	44	456	11	41.45	2/23		
S.R. McNally	212.2	48	673	15	44.86	4/77		
D.A. Stirling	167.4	25	568	10	56.80	3/39		

(Qualification – 10 wickets)

LEADING FIELDERS

41–E.B. McSweeney (ct 31/st 10); 27–W.K. Lees (ct 24/st 3); 23–A.W. Hart (ct 17/st 6); 21–B.A. Young; 19–T.E. Blain (ct 14/st 5); 17–I.D.S. Smith; 14–R.H. Vance; 13–P.S. Briasco; 12–N.A. Scott (ct 11/st 1), S.J. Maguiness and G.K. MacDonald; 9–J.J. Crowe, J.G. Bracewell, S.J. McCullum and R.T. Latham; 8–P.J. Kelly, R.T. Hart (ct 6/st 2), G.J. Dawson and B.R. Blair.

Auckland 1984–85
First Class Matches

BATTING	v. Canterbury (Auckland) 27–29 Dec. 1984		v. Wellington (Wellington) 1–3 January 1985		v. Central Districts (Palmerston N.) 7–9 January 1985		v. Otago (Auckland) 13–15 January 1985		v. Northern Districts (Hamilton) 17–19 January 1985		v. Otago (Dunedin) 25–27 January 1985		v. Wellington (Auckland) 25–27 February 1985		v. Central Districts (Auckland) 1–3 March 1985		M	Inns	NOs	Runs	H/S	Av
T.J. Franklin	51	—	0	32	40	—	18	8	181	3	4	65	12	4	23*	81	8	14	1	522	181	40.15
P. Horne	2	—	13	31			58	4	3	6	28	29	72	70	55*	15	7	13	1	386	72	32.16
J.F. Reid	25	—	82	6											—	19	3	4	—	132	82	33.00
J.J. Crowe	14	—	21	54	86	—							61	41	—	1	5	7	—	278	86	39.71
P.N. Webb	76	—	14	40*	44*	—	11	4					5	51*	—	0	6	9	3	245	76	40.83
A.J. Hunt	16	—	24	26*	78*	—	24	2	18	2	51	2	11	6	—	9	8	13	2	299	78*	27.18
J.G. Bracewell	21	—	7	—	54	—							1	—	—	14*	5	5	1	97	54	24.25
M.C. Snedden	4	—	26	—	—	—			3	—	5	7	18	18*	—	1	7	8	1	82	26	11.71
P.J. Kelly	40*	—							36*	—	20	0*					3	4	3	96	40*	96.00
G.B. Troup	58	—							5	—	1	1	26	—	—	6	5	6	—	97	58	16.16
S.R. Tracy	6	—	33	—	—	—											3	2	—	39	33	19.50
N.A. Scott			8	—	—	—	10*	6					15	—			4	4	1	39	15	13.00
W. Watson			4*	—	—	—	—	0*	—	—	0	0	6*	—	—	—	7	5	3	10	6*	5.00
M.J. Greatbatch					29	—			22	32*	13	55	67	10	—	6	5	8	1	234	67	33.42
A.T.R. Hellaby					—	—	29	2	16	5*	6	17					4	6	1	75	29	15.00
M. Pringle							72	3	11	17	10	38					3	6	—	151	72	25.16
S.D. Adams							5	1									1	2	—	6	5	3.00
S.J. Gillespie							60	13									1	2	—	73	60	36.50
R.J. Hunter							4*	4*	—	—	28*	5*										
Byes	1		1	1	1		2	2	1	5	6	8	4	5	2							
Leg-byes	11		8	5	5		6	1	9		7	8	10	4		7						
Wides	1		1		2						1		1	1		1						
No-balls	11				9		6		9	4	5	2	2	1								
Total	337		242	195	348		305	50	314	74	185	237	311	211	80	190						
Wickets	10		10	4	4		8	9	8	4	10	9	10	5	0	8						
Result	W		D		D		D		W		D		D		D							
Points	16		4		4		0		16		0		0		4							

Catches
12 – N.A. Scott (ct 11/st 1)
9 – J.G. Bracewell
8 – P.J. Kelly
7 – A.J. Hunt
6 – J.J. Crowe
5 – W. Watson and R.J. Hunter
4 – M.C. Snedden, P. Horne, P.N. Webb and T.J. Franklin
2 – G.B. Troup, J.F. Reid, A.T.R. Hellaby, M.J. Greatbatch and subs
1 – M. Pringle, S.D. Adams and S.J. Gillespie

BOWLING	G.B. Troup	S.R. Tracy	M.C. Snedden	J.G. Bracewell	A.J. Hunt	W. Watson	R.J. Hunter	A.T.R. Hellaby	P.N. Webb
v. Canterbury (Auckland)	15–4–37–3	14–1–46–3	18–3–37–2	14–6–23–2					
27–29 December 1984	17–1–53–6	1–0–7–0	16–4–24–2	16.4–6–48–2	3–2–4–0				
v. Wellington (Wellington)		11–4–40–0	28–14–35–3	37–17–68–6		15–6–29–1			
1–3 January 1985		13–3–48–3	8–2–18–1	21–5–59–2	3–1–7–0	7–3–27–0			
v. Central Districts (Palmerston		19.4–6–97–4	6–2–25–0	30–8–80–2	4–0–8–0	25–7–90–3		12–2–37–1	
North) 7–9 January 1985		13–2–57–0	20–5–40–0	8–2–24–0	15–2–35–0	7–1–14–0		13–1–39–2	30–6–86–1
v. Otago (Auckland)					20–4–40–1	39–7–96–4	58–17–117–2	32.3–10–54–2	
13–15 January 1985									
v. Northern Districts (Hamilton)	12–1–73–1		23.5–9–78–4			20–8–40–4	8–2–20–1	3–0–10–0	
17–19 January 1985	21–7–57–4		17–9–21–4			5–2–6–0	20–8–56–2	2–0–11–0	
v. Otago (Dunedin)	23–9–57–1		28.2–6–74–4			19–4–41–4	10–3–30–0	11–2–19–1	
25–27 January 1985	6–2–21–0		9–2–20–0			21–5–53–0		24.5–6–84–4	
v. Wellington (Auckland)	28–7–68–2		40.2–13–89–4	38–10–84–1	9–4–26–1	24–6–75–1			
25–27 February 1985									
v. Central Districts (Auckland)	14–4–28–4		10–4–9–0	2–0–5–1		14.1–5–36–5			
1–3 March 1985	15–3–38–0		29–9–63–6	38–9–98–2	1–0–4–0	12–1–39–2			
	151–38–432–21 *av.* 20.57	71.4–16–295–10 *av.* 29.50	253.3–82–533–30 *av.* 17.76	204.4–63–489–18 *av.* 27.16	55–13–124–2 *av.* 62.00	208.1–55–546–24 *av.* 22.75	96–30–223–5 *av.* 44.60	98.2–21–254–10 *av.* 25.40	30–6–86–1 *av.* 86.00

a J.F. Reid 2–0–8–0 b P. Horne 1–0–1–0

REVIEW OF THE SEASON
by
DON CAMERON

If there was one phrase which re-echoed and re-echoed about New Zealand cricket during a passing fair summer it was 'uneven bounce'. It was used to describe, *ad nauseam*, the pitches on which New Zealand twice defeated and once drew with Javed Miandad's touring Pakistan team.

Earlier there had been claims of uneveness while the New Zealanders toured Pakistan, although this was directed more at the home umpires than at the quality of the pitches there.

And in the figurative sense, there was a similarly uneven bounce about the New Zealand performances in the World Championship of Cricket in Australia, in which the luck of the draw worked New Zealand into the semi-finals, but no further toward the top prize.

A few days after that expedition, in which the New Zealanders had fancied themselves as an interesting long shot to take the title, New Zealand departed for a two-month tour of West Indies and heading, one suspects, for performances of uneven quality.

When, seven or eight months ago, we looked forward to the season of cricket it was unusually promising, both in content and promise. The first engagement was a tour of Zimbabwe, a cluster of proven Test players mixed with seven or eight players hopefully on the fringe of international cricket.

From there four men joined the main party for three Tests and four one-day internationals of the tour of Pakistan. Within a month Pakistan were back in New Zealand for a similar tour, and then came the frills and spills of the WCC affair in Australia. All this leading up to the major event, the tour of West Indies.

So seven or eight months ago New Zealand seemed poised for a very healthy season. There was already the nucleus of a sound Test side and over the summer months the promise that perhaps four or five new players would be woven into the fabric.

Alas, uneveness persisted. By the time the 15 players were picked for West Indies all the budding talent of months before had produced two untried top-order batsmen, Ron Hart, of Central Districts, and Ken Rutherford of Otago, and a medium-fast bowler Derek Stirling who had charted a very uneven course during the summer and whose selection for the Caribbean was more an article of faith than a coolly logical choice.

Without the senior players, Geoff Howarth, the captain, and Richard Hadlee, the eminent opening bowler, the New Zealand team was sent to Pakistan under Jeremy Coney's captaincy, and with more hope of success than certainty. It was regarded as an especially difficult tour, and so it proved. The Test series was lost 0–2, the one-day internationals 1–3, and halfway through came an official complaint from Coney about the quality of Pakistan umpiring.

To those of us at home, knowing Coney as a man of equable temperament, any complaint about umpiring came as a surprise. In the event the Pakistan board took notice, appointed a two-man investigating committee and, some weeks after the event, released findings which stated that there had actually been umpiring errors and most of them had favoured the home side. These findings were, of course, too late to change anything, but still left the uneasy feeling that one of the old traditions of cricket, the acceptance of umpiring decisions, had been uncomfortably eroded.

The tour did have its profit for New Zealand, apart from persuading Coney himself that he did not enjoy the reins of captaincy.

John Reid, the slim, elegant and industrious left-hand batsman whose earlier brief Test career had included a home century against India and a long century against Sri Lanka at Colombo, blossomed in the heat and dust of Pakistan with a century in the second Test, and a 97 in the third. Reid had always been regarded as technically among the better New Zealand batsmen at playing spin bowling, and he came back secure in the No. 3 position formerly held by Howarth.

Stirling was another who came nobly back from Pakistan. He is a big strapping young man, about 6 ft 3 in tall, $14\frac{1}{2}$ stones in weight, and he kept charging in at the Pakistan batsmen and making their life very uncomfortable indeed. At last, everyone exclaimed, New Zealand has a ready-made new-ball partner for Hadlee.

There were minor benefits – Martin Crowe's stature as a Test batsman and occasional bowler moved up a notch, as did Ian Smith's ability as a wicket-keeper and decidedly useful batsman. Stephen Boock, the slow left-armer, joined the select group of New Zealanders who have taken seven wickets in a Test innings.

Soon afterward Pakistan were in New Zealand, and very soon rather lost. They had left behind Abdul Qadir, the leg-spinner, who arrived just before the first Test. They left behind Zaheer Abbas, the very senior batsman, who arrived just before the second Test. Worst of all, they could not entice Imran Khan away from New South Wales, and this became the sharpest loss of all, for Pakistan developed in young Wasim Akram and the doughty Azeem Hafeez a most promising new-ball attack and only needed Imran to show

J.J. Crowe	T.J. Franklin	S.J. Gillespie	Byes	Leg-byes	Wides	No-balls	Total	Wkts
			4	12		12	159	10
				6		6	142	10
			5	3		1	180	10
			2	2			171	6a
			4	4		8	345	10
10–6–20–0	3–1–5–0			2		5	322	3
		23–13–43–1	16	11	1	7	377	10
				6	1	9	227	10
				6		2	157	10
			3	17		5	241	10
			4	2			184	5
			4	13		9	360	10b
						6	78	10
			17	6	1	6	265	10
10–6–20–0	3–1–5–0	23–13–43–1						
—	—	*av.* 43.00						

Canterbury 1984–85
First Class Matches

BATTING	v. Wellington (Rangiora) 13–15 Dec. 1984		v. Auckland (Auckland) 27–29 Dec. 1984		v. Northern Districts (Tauranga) 1–3 January 1985		v. Pakistanis (Christchurch) 8–10 January 1985		v. Central Districts (Christchurch) 13–15 January 1985		v. Otago (Christchurch) 17–19 January 1985		v. Wellington (Wellington) 25–27 January 1985		v. Central Districts (Napier) 25–27 February 1985		v. Northern Districts (Christchurch) 1–3 March 1985		M	Inns	NOs	Runs	H/S	Av
R.P. Jones	5	2																	1	2	—	7	5	3.50
A.P. Nathu	23	1	56	26	40	—	21	17	49	9	23	147	6	16	39	51	14	4	9	17	—	542	147	31.88
D.A. Dempsey	13	18																	1	2	—	31	18	15.50
R.W. Fulton	0	1	0	1	24	—	7*	34*	35	5	5	16	22	34	21	33	30	—	9	16	2	268	35	19.14
R.T. Latham	4	38	8	42	0	—	62	75	95	109	20	44	28	0	21	15	0	—	9	16	—	561	109	35.06
V.R. Brown	3	104	25	4	74	—	—	2	7	61	16	71	35	16	0	61*	0	61*	9	16	2	540	104	38.57
R.J. Hadlee	13	5	19	1	14*	—	30*	0									8	—	5	8	2	90	30*	15.00
G.K. MacDonald	1	15	8*	14	3*	—	—	2	0	5	0	25*			12*	—	8*	—	8	12	5	93	25*	13.28
S.R. McNally	10	8	2	15	—	—	—	—			1	11	3	—	16	2	21	—	8	10	—	89	21	8.90
A.W. Hart	4	36*	1	9	—	—	—	—	6	2	33	4	70*	0	18	—	23	—	9	12	2	206	70*	20.60
C.H. Thiele	3*	49	2	7*			—	—	9*	2*	3*	—	28	—	0	—			7	9	5	103	49	25.75
J.G. Wright			8	4	12	—	106	57									36	151*	4	7	1	374	151*	62.33
P.E. McEwan			2	7	88	—	73	13*			17	13	56	105			39	69	6	11	1	482	105	48.20
G.C. Bateman					—	—													1	—				—
P.J. Rattray									9	20			0	5					2	4	—	34	20	8.50
R.M. Carter									11	36	23	0							2	4	—	70	36	17.50
M.W. Priest									10	4									1	2	—	14	10	7.00
S.N. Bateman									2	12					18	10*			2	4	1	42	18	14.00
D.J. Hartshorn											48	14*	5	17*	103	4			3	6	2	191	103	47.75
W.R. Eddington													1	49*					1	2	1	50	49*	50.00
D.J. Boyle															17	0			1	2	—	17	17	8.50
R.V. Masefield																	8	—	1	1	—	8	8	8.00
Byes			4		7		1		2	7	4	6	9	3	13	2	2							
Leg-byes	7	8	12	6	12		2	5	7	6	5	8	4	12	11	5	6	10						
Wides	1						3		2				2	1	2	1								
No-balls	1	8	12	6	10		4	4	2	2	5	7	4	5	1		15	5						
Total	88	293	159	142	284		309	209	246	280	203	366	273	263	292	184	210	300						
Wickets	10	10	10	10	6		4	6	10	10	10	8	10	7	10	6	10	2						
Result	W		L		D		L		W		D		L		D		W							
Points	12		0		4		—		16		0		0		0		12							

Catches 23 – A.W. Hart (ct 17/st 6)
12 – G.K. MacDonald
9 – R.T. Latham
6 – V.R. Brown and R.W. Fulton
5 – P.E. McEwan
4 – P.J. Rattray
3 – S.R. McNally, A.P. Nathu, D.A. Dempsey and D.J. Hartshorn
2 – J.G. Wright and R.M. Carter
1 – sub

BOWLING	R.J. Hadlee	C.H. Thiele	S.R. McNally	G.K. MacDonald	V.R. Brown	D.A. Dempsey	R.T. Latham	P.E. McEwan	G.C. Bateman
v. Wellington (Rangiora)	30.1–13–46–5	17–8–31–1	7–0–29–0	4–0–21–0	23–11–45–4	3–0–12–0			
13–15 December 1984	16.3–4–36–4	6–1–11–1	11–4–22–3	1–1–0–0	10–3–33–1				
v. Auckland (Auckland)	36–14–74–5	20–5–43–1	26–5–57–2	7–1–32–1	33–7–84–1		7–2–19–0	4–1–16–0	
27–29 December 1984									
v. Northern Districts (Tauranga)	35–14–53–3		30–14–54–2	29–7–58–3	16–4–52–2				24–7–55–0
1–3 January 1985									
v. Pakistan (Christchurch)	17–2–63–2	10–1–46–0	9–0–35–0	20.4–4–62–6	22–4–77–2				
8–10 January 1985	3–0–15–0	15–0–92–1	11.4–2–54–0	4–1–19–0	11–0–48–1				
v. Central Districts (Christchurch)		17–3–45–4		17–6–36–2	18–7–31–2				
13–15 January 1985		14.5–4–35–4		12–1–58–2	29–6–88–4				
v. Otago (Christchurch)		26–4–112–4	14–1–56–1	22–7–57–3	39–13–108–2				
17–19 January 1985		7–0–40–2	5–1–27–0	5–0–11–1	17–0–68–4				
v. Wellington (Wellington)		26–4–75–3	15–0–70–0		34–8–83–4		5–0–19–0	4–0–8–1	
25–27 January 1985		9–0–46–1	2–1–9–0		19–3–84–2			11–2–48–1	
v. Central Districts (Napier)		15–7–23–2	19–2–53–2	16–3–50–1	17–7–42–0				
25–27 February 1985		1–0–5–0	23–5–93–1	3–0–12–0	9–4–24–0				
v. Northern Districts (Christchurch)	19–5–43–2		24.4–7–77–4	12–1–24–1	18–3–45–2			3–0–15–0	
1–3 March 1985	12–5–16–1		15–6–37–0	3–1–9–0	18–7–60–0		31–12–75–3		
	168.4–57–346–22 *av.* 15.72	183.5–37–604–24 *av.* 25.16	212.3–48–673–15 *av.* 44.86	155.4–33–449–20 *av.* 22.45	333–87–972–31 *av.* 31.35	3–0–12–0 —	43–14–113–3 *av.* 37.66	22–3–87–2 *av.* 43.50	24–7–55–0 —

a W.R. Eddington 11–3–39–1 b R.V. Masefield 16–1–59–1 c R.V. Masefield 0–1–23–0

them the intricacies of Test-class bowling.

The Pakistanis were keen, but some of them were very new to international cricket, and it took the whole party some weeks before they adapted to the modes and methods of New Zealand cricket, especially those pitches of uneven bounce.

New Zealand meantime welcomed back Howarth and Hadlee, the latter keen and fit, the former a trifle rusty after a three-month break, and in the process of deciding whether he should bat in contact lenses or spectacles.

With Coney a reluctant captain Howarth was an essential choice as leader, but rather than interfere with an established middle-order of Reid, Martin and Jeff Crowe and Coney, Howarth was moved up to open with John Wright, which meant that Bruce Edgar, that staunch left-hand opener, was not required.

Significantly, too, the New Zealand selectors found they could do without Stirling. He had played two or three matches for Central Districts and had failed completely to recapture his control and fire of Pakistan, so the bowling fell back on the tried men, Hadlee, Lance Cairns, Ewen Chatfield Coney and the off-spinner John Bracewell.

In a trice Pakistan had been quite out-played in the first two one-day internationals, but they retained their good humour. None more so than Yawar Saeed, a member of the Pakistan selection panel and tour manager, whose opening press conference ended with the amazed query from Yawar that the subject of umpiring had not been raised.

There were times later when Yawar might have asked painful questions about two or three umpiring decisions which had gone against his team, but neither he nor Miandad would take the bait – which made one wonder all the more about Coney's sorrowful plea in Pakistan.

As the New Zealanders had been labouring and losing on dry and dusty pitches in Pakistan the word had gone about New Zealand that no-one (apart from the Pakistanis) would mind if the Tests were played on hard, grassy, seaming pitches.

Yet when the teams arrived at the Basin Reserve in Wellington – usually the fastest, bounciest pitch in New Zealand – there were smiles from the Pakistanis and frowns from the New Zealanders. Some months before the pitch had been top-dressed with the wrong type of soil. Instead of a hard and bouncy pitch it looked like something specially imported from Karachi.

Thankfully Howarth won the toss, batted first and a 572-minute vigil for 148 by Reid (plus a brilliant 89 by Hadlee and a timely 65 by Ian Smith) led New Zealand to 492. With Boock taking five wickets at the start Pakistan were 187 for six, apparently certain to follow-on, but Saleem Malik played dashing strokes for 66, Qadir held out for 54, Iqbal Qasim played a notable hand for 27 not out and Pakistan reached 322 and made New Zealand bat again.

That was virtually that, New Zealand 103 for four, with not enough time to arrange a reasonable declaration, and rain in any case wiped out the fifth and last day.

However two factors had already emerged that dictated the trend of a Test series between two teams not really at peak form. The first was the two-faced nature of the pitch, the speed and bounce both variable.

The second was Miandad's back-foot tendency in the field. New Zealand had suggested to Pakistan a 96-over day in Tests, 16 to the hour. Pakistan replied with an 84-over day, 14 to the hour. New Zealand agreed, and Miandad used the rule shrewdly. Whenever his bowlers were under pressure, which was the rule rather than the exception, Miandad slowed play down until the bare 14 overs were provided each hour.

So to Eden Park for the second Test, more grass on the pitch, nothing there for the spinners, consistent help for the seamers – and again that pesky inconsistent bounce.

Zaheer was into the Test within 24 hours of landing in Auckland, so was the 18-year-old Akram, a willowy left-arm seamer. New Zealand retained the same XI, and retained their luck, for Howarth again won the toss, but followed the Eden Park habit of putting the opposition in.

Although the pitch was not especially fast the ball moved a lot, Hadlee, Chatfield and Cairns were dominant, Pakistan were gone for 169, with only Saleem Malik, 41 not out from No. 6, appearing to bat with any confidence.

Again Reid took charge, this time with a 486-minute innings of 158 not out, along the way becoming the fastest scorer of 1000 runs in New Zealand Test history – 12 Tests and 20 innings compared with Glenn Turner's 13 Tests and 26 innings.

Reid was flanked by 66 from John Wright and a lovely, resounding 84 by Martin Crowe, New Zealand reached 451 and Pakistan, 282 behind were again in the toils of the Hadlee–Chatfield–Cairns trinity on a pitch that continued to give, in the jargon, sideways movement, and the occasional awkward bounce.

Only Mudassar Nazar, with 89 in four hours, first in and last out, could adapt, and Pakistan were gone for 183, New Zealand taking the Test by an innings and 99 runs.

On the way to the third Test in Dunedin the teams played a one-dayer at Christchurch, with Reid again the dominant batsmen with 88 of the 50-over score of 264 for eight wickets.

S.N. Bateman	M.W. Priest	D.J. Hartshorn	*Byes*	*Leg-byes*	*Wides*	*No-balls*	*Total*	*Wkts*
			5	3		11	192	10
				5		4	107	10
			1	11	1	11	337	10
			6	4		8	282	10
			3	3		6	289	10
			4	1		3	233	2
13–6–35–2				3		6	150	10
8–0–33–0	6–1–29–0		1	10		5	254	10
		13–3–40–0	6	4	3		383	10
		1–0–4–0	6	6			162	7
			17	3	2	1	314	9a
		8.2–2–28–1	5	3			223	5
11–3–37–0		28–4–103–1	2	8		3	318	7
18–4–63–1		10–1–38–0	3	7	1		245	2
						4	274	10b
			7	8			235	6c
50–13–168–3 *av.* 56.00	6–1–29–0 —	60.2–10–213–2 *av.* 106.50						

Central Districts 1984–85
First Class Matches

BATTING	v. Northern Districts (New Plymouth) 27–29 Dec. 1984		v. Otago (Ozmaru) 2–4 January 1985		v. Auckland (Palmerston N.) 7–9 January 1985		v. Canterbury (Christchurch) 13–15 January 1985		v. Wellington (Blenheim) 17–19 January 1985		v. Northern Districts (Hamilton) 1–3 February 1985		v. Canterbury (Napier) 25–27 February 1985		v. Auckland (Auckland) 1–3 March 1985		*M*	*Inns*	*NOs*	*Runs*	*H/S*	*Av*
R.T. Hart	0	84	59	—	27	26	34	47	108	38	60	6	111	7	13	45	8	15		665	111	44.33
T.E. Blain	15	25	129	—	100	96	6	70	22	4	20	72	60	49*	1	9	8	15	1	678	129	48.42
D.A. Stirling	37	—	14	—	18	—	0	42	21*	—	0	20*	2*	—	10*	7	8	11	4	171	42	24.42
P.S. Briasco	21	8	45	—	0	104*	23	11	3	36*	10	76	2	75	0	37	8	15	2	451	104*	34.69
M.D. Crowe	20	143	38	—											11	34	3	5		246	143	49.20
R.E. Hayward	1	48*	0	—	2	65	21	4	21	16*	36	35*	44	—			7	12	3	293	65	32.55
R.A. Pierce	21	13	10	—	2	—			2	15							4	6	—	63	21	10.50
I.D.S. Smith	51*	9*	27	—	46	—					12	20			11	20	5	8	1	196	51	28.00
G.K. Robertson	2	—	40*	—	73	—	5	0	7	—	39	16	40	—	0	0	8	11	1	222	73	22.20
D.R. O'Sullivan	9*	—	20	—	15*	—	5*	3	—	—	19	—	—	—	4	6	8	8	3	81	20	16.20
P.J. Visser	0	—					0	0	—	—							3	3	—	0	0	—
S.J. Gill			17	—	39	—	10	6	35*	—							4	5	1	107	39	26.75
C.J. Smith					7	24*	22	55*	19	7	18	18	2	103*	10	67	6	12	3	352	103*	39.11
M.H. Toynbee							15	0			24	34	40*	—	4	10	4	7	1	127	40*	21.16
W. Martin											0*	—	—	—	8	0*	3	3	2	8	8	8.00
G.N. Edwards													4	—			1	1	—	4	4	4.00
Byes	4				4			1			1	6	2	3		17						
Leg-byes	8	3	2		4	2	3	10	2		6	3	8	7		6						
Wides		1							2	1	2			1		1						
No-balls	15	7	8		8	5	6	5	11	6	7	6	3		6	6						
Total	204	341	409		345	322	150	254	253	123	254	312	318	245	78	265						
Wickets	10	5	10		10	3	10	10	7	4	10	7	7	2	10	10						
Result	W		D		D		L		D		D		D		D							
Points	12		0		0		0		0		0		4		0							

Catches
19 – T.E. Blain (ct 14/st 5)
13 – P.S. Briasco
8 – I.D.S. Smith and R.T. Hart (ct 6/st 2)
5 – D.A. Stirling
4 – M.H. Toynbee
3 – P.J. Visser, G.K. Robertson and W. Martin
2 – R.E. Hayward and R.A. Pierce
1 – C.J. Smith and M.D. Crowe

BOWLING	D.A. Stirling	G.K. Robertson	M.D. Crowe	P.J. Visser	D.R. O'Sullivan	R.A. Pierce	S.J. Gill	P.S. Briasco	T.E. Blain
v. Northern Districts (New	21–8–57–1	19–3–65–3	15.2–5–54–1	15–3–51–1	28–7–96–3				
Plymouth) 27–29 December 1984	10–2–31–0	12.5–0–54–3	20–6–51–5	9–4–11–1	25–7–54–1				
v. Otago (Oamaru)	18–3–74–0	26–7–97–1	14–4–40–1		55–18–103–6	11–2–44–1	10–0–47–0		
2–4 January 1985	5–0–10–1				32–15–39–3	13–5–16–1	3–0–3–0	15–3–40–0	6–4–12–1
v. Auckland (Palmerston North)	23–4–82–0	22–2–58–2			47–10–116–0	10–4–23–2	27–9–55–0	5–2–7–0	1–0–1–0
7–9 January 1985									
v. Canterbury (Christchurch)	12–5–25–1	20–5–51–3		14–3–35–0	28–7–75–5				
13–15 January 1985	6–0–28–0	7–1–24–1		3–0–14–0	37–8–101–5		4–2–10–0		
v. Wellington (Blenheim)	24–1–80–2	35–1–123–3		16–5–43–0	25–9–61–0	4–1–8–0	22–4–71–2		
17–19 January 1985	5–0–25–0	8–1–29–1		15–3–38–1	13.3–3–35–2	5–0–26–2			
v. Northern Districts (Hamilton)	14–2–50–2	21–4–99–2			37–14–80–3				
1–3 February 1985	5–0–19–0	7–0–28–0			20–5–64–3				
v. Canterbury (Napier)	11–0–39–3	24–4–46–1			34–13–72–2			1–1–0–0	
25–27 February 1985	5–0–18–0	7–2–27–0			17–1–65–3				
v. Auckland (Auckland)	5.4–0–18–0	5–1–21–0			5–2–20–0				
1–3 March 1985	3–0–12–0	3–0–15–1			22–5–61–2			17–9–19–2	
	167.4–25–568–10 *av.* 56.80	216.5–31–737–21 *av.* 35.09	49.2–15–145–7 *av.* 20.71	72–18–192–3 *av.* 64.00	425.3–124–1042–38 *av.* 27.42	43–12–117–6 *av.* 19.50	66–15–186–2 *av.* 93.00	38–15–66–2 *av.* 33.00	7–4–16–1 *av.* 16.00

a R.E. Hayward 6–2–13–0

There were signs that at last Pakistan were settling down to New Zealand conditions, for Zaheer scored 58, Miandad 30 and a lively youngster Rameez Raja, brother of Wasim, gave the New Zealanders a real fright with a blistering 75. It was not quite enough, New Zealand still had 13 runs to spare at the end, but it was a hint that Pakistan were improving, and that the grip that the New Zealand seamers had held was loosening.

It should be noted that the Lancaster Park pitch, the scene of England's inglorious innings defeat 12 months before, this time played truly and well – not that that would bring any year-old comfort to Bob Willis and his men.

Carisbrook, venue of the third Test, had not been used for an international since that pulsating one-wicket defeat of West Indies in 1980. Since then the ground and pitch had been re-laid and in a match a week before no fewer than three Auckland batsmen had suffered broken fingers or thumbs from the short-pitched fliers of Neil Mallender, Otago's itinerant professional.

So Hadlee and company flexed their fingers, and the selectors recalled Brendon Bracewell, who had started his career as a tearaway teenager in 1979, to strengthen the heavy artillery. There was some sympathy for Pakistan, who still could not get Imran to come to New Zealand, and seemed threatened with a blitz of short-pitched fliers.

Not unexpectedly Howarth, with his hat-trick of winning Test tosses, put Pakistan in again, but this time the ruse back-fired. The pitch was of modest speed and bounce, certainly not a fiery flier, and from 100 for two Qasim Umar (96) and Miandad (79) counter-attacked so bravely Pakistan reached 241 for two with 30 minutes of the first day left.

But again Pakistan faltered. Coney winkled out Umar and then Hadlee with the second new ball, smashed through with four rapid wickets, Pakistan were reduced to 251 for seven by stumps, and were gone for 274 the next morning, with Hadlee finishing with six for 51.

M.H. Toynbee	I.D.S. Smith	W. Martin	*Byes*	*Leg-byes*	*Wides*	*No-balls*	*Total*	*Wkts*
				8	1	7	331	10
			2	9	2	4	212	10
			5	20		3	430	10
	6–2–15–0		5	5		2	158	6a
			1	5	2	9	348	4
15.3–0–51–1			2	7	2	2	246	10
24.5–4–90–3			7	6		2	280	10
			4	12	2	4	402	7
			7	1		1	161	6
11–4–31–0		27–9–53–2	2	7	2		322	9
5–2–9–1	1–0–4–0	10–0–32–1		9			165	7
11–2–33–1		34–13–78–2	13	11	2	1	292	10
12–1–45–3		9–1–22–0	2	5	1		184	6
3–0–12–0		4–0–7–0	2				80	0
4–0–16–0		19–2–59–4		7	1		190	9
86.2–13– 287–9 *av.* 31.88	7–2– 19–0 —	103–25– 251–9 *av.* 27.88						

In the context of the two previous Tests this was a modest first innings total, but the pitch was still not completely trustworthy, Hafeez and Akram were quite inspired, Reid could manage only 24, Martin Crowe found a solid 57, but New Zealand were sent back for 220, and Pakistan rejoined with a first innings lead of 54.

Stung by this New Zealand swept back to attack. Mudassar went quickly and while Umar (89) batted with serene command he lost Mohsin Khan at 72, Miandad at 75, the hapless Zaheer at 76 and Malik at 103.

Rashid Khan, a replacement all-rounder, chipped in with 37 at the end but Pakistan could reach only 223 and New Zealand needed 278 to win.

Then unfolded one of the great Test cricket finishes, the balance flicking back and forth, the drama building up with every over.

For a start Pakistan were quite dominant. Hafeez removed John Wright at four, Akram had Reid out at five and, at 23 and with consecutive balls, Akram dismissed both Howarth and Jeff Crowe.

By stumps Coney and Martin Crowe had lifted New Zealand to 114 for four wickets. The next morning the New Zealanders counter-attacked. They peppered Miandad's deep-set field with fours, the score raced to 180 and there was the heady prospect that both would complete the win with unbeaten centuries.

Instead, just before lunch, Crowe was given out caught at gully – not the first hairline decision of the match – and New Zealand tip-toed through to lunch at 192 for five, Coney still there on 72.

He lost Hadlee at 208 and Smith did his best to commit suicide, and succeeded at 217 for seven, still 61 runs needed.

Out strode Cairns, all muscular menace, but for once without his helmet. Straightaway Akram let fly with a bumper, Cairns made a hash of avoiding it, it hit him on the back of the head and he went down like a pole-axed ox.

Brendon Bracewell survived until 228 for eight, Chatfield arrived, with the knowledge that Cairns might be too dizzy to bat and that only he and Coney stood between Pakistan and victory.

It was nerve-wracking, gut-wrenching cricket to watch. Chatfield patiently prodded away, picking up the occasional run, while Coney eschewed any risks and settled for singles to the widespread field. Akram came back with the second new ball, Chatfield stoically took a few on the arms and shoulders, Coney kept edging along, single after single, quite often refusing singles that would have exposed Chatfield, and they reached tea at 253 for eight, Coney 97, Chatfield 10.

By now the whole country had stopped as everyone crowded round television sets watching the tingling drama.

Tragedy for Pakistan. In the first over after tea Coney got an edge to Rashid, and Anil Dalpat, the keeper, dropped a quite reasonable chance.

So it was down to the hard work again, Coney picking up his 22nd consecutive single to 98, and then scoring a two for his hundred in 337 minutes.

Then it was back to the singles again, the cricketing equivalent of the Chinese water torture, the score edging up one at a time until Chatfield somehow managed a full-bladed whack to midwicket for a four and a score of 271.

Still the Pakistanis poured on the pressure, looking

Northern Districts 1984–85

First Class Matches

BATTING	v. Central Districts (New Plymouth) 27–29 Dec. 1984		v. Canterbury (Tauranga) 1–3 January 1985		v. Otago (Gisborne) 7–9 January 1985		v. Wellington (Wellington) 13–15 January 1985		v. Auckland (Hamilton) 17–19 January 1985		v. Central Districts (Hamilton) 1–3 February 1985		v. Otago (Dunedin) 25–27 February 1985		v. Canterbury (Christchurch) 1–3 March 1985		*M*	*Inns*	*NOs*	*Runs*	*H/S*	*Av*
L.M. Crocker	26	51	12	—	95	10	25	57	13	27	15	36	0	13	57	12	8	15	—	449	95	29.93
R.D. Broughton	67	26	9	—	21	28	35	5	26	5	15	51	4	4	12	10	8	15	—	318	67	21.20
W.P. Fowler	24	6	51	—	0	7	12	4	37	4			13	11			6	11	—	169	51	15.36
B.G. Cooper	91	8	9	—	51	60	55	3	16	2	65	25	1	19	36	9	8	15	—	450	91	30.00
G.P. Howarth	39	38	9	—	12	24					12	6			0	24	5	9	—	164	39	18.22
B.R. Blair	5	8	3	—	41	3	4	63	53	17	19	19	13	45	42	66	8	15	—	401	66	26.73
C.M. Kuggeleijn	15	6	50	—			43	2	0	7	31	1	23	27	3	34	7	13	—	242	50	18.61
B.A. Young	7	18	9	—	13	26*	32	5	26	38	53*	4*	4	1	24	65*	8	15	4	325	65*	29.54
C.M. Presland	0	22															1	2	—	22	22	11.00
B.P. Bracewell	41*	9	9	—	0	14*	27	8	21	0	29	4*			46	—	7	12	3	208	46	23.11
S.M. Carrington	0	3*	18*	—	0*	—	8*	—	0*	12	34*	—	7	4			7	10	6	86	34*	21.50
B.L. Cairns			85	—	89	—											2	2	—	174	89	87.00
C.W. Dickeson					3	13	0	0*	9	10*	5	—	4*	1	11	—	6	10	3	56	13	8.00
M.J. Child							10	8*	10	27	33	10	5	11*	28	0*	5	10	3	142	33	20.28
K.R. Treiber													1	2	0*	—	2	3	1	3	2	1.50
Byes		2	6		8	2		4			2		2	11		7						
Leg-byes	8	9	4		17		12	8	6	6	7	9	5	6	11	8						
Wides	1	2			1				1		2			2								
No-balls	7	4	8		2	1	4	6	9	2			1	4	4							
Total	331	212	282		353	188	267	173	227	157	322	165	83	161	274	235						
Wickets	10	10	10		10	7	10	8	10	10	9	7	10	10	10	6						
Result	L		D		W		D		L		D		L		L							
Points	4		0		16		0		0		4		0		4							

Catches

21 – B.A. Young
8 – B.R. Blair
6 – W.P. Fowler and M.J. Child
5 – C.M. Kuggeleijn and L.M. Crocker
3 – B.P. Bracewell, S.M. Carrington, C.W. Dickeson and B.G. Cooper
2 – R.D. Broughton
1 – B.L. Cairns

BOWLING	S.M. Carrington	B.P. Bracewell	C.M. Presland	W.P. Fowler	B.R. Blair	C.M. Kuggeleijn	B.G. Cooper	B.L. Cairns	C.W. Dickeson
v. Central Districts (New	16.5–6–39–4	17–3–59–2	12–1–67–2	5–2–6–1	4–0–21–1				
Plymouth) 27–29 December 1984	16–1–61–1	16–1–75–1	10–1–65–1	15.5–1–61–1	4–1–20–0	10–0–38–0	2–0–18–0		
v. Canterbury (Tauranga)	14–5–36–0	20–3–51–1		15–4–37–0	13–4–16–2	13–5–30–0	12–4–26–1	42–15–69–2	
1–3 January 1985									
v. Otago (Gisborne)	15–0–63–1	21–6–55–1		7–2–8–0	4–0–15–0		10–1–23–0	25–7–39–4	25–7–53–2
7–9 January 1985	8–1–39–2	8–1–32–2		3.3–2–4–2				10–3–20–2	12–1–21–2
v. Wellington (Wellington)	30–7–88–2	37–4–114–4		16–9–34–1	5–1–14–0				44–18–82–1
13–15 January 1985						20–5–48–1	18–4–53–1		1.5–0–12–1
v. Auckland (Hamilton)	20–3–52–0	36–5–67–2		16–6–33–0	11–2–34–2				38.3–13–83–3
17–19 January 1985	7–2–10–1	7–1–19–1							11–3–30–1
v. Central Districts (Hamilton)	16–2–62–1	15–3–34–3			15–7–41–1	3–0–16–0			30–10–44–2
1–3 February 1985	5–3–4–0	10–4–18–1			13–3–29–0	24–5–81–1	7–0–32–0		47–12–139–5
v. Otago (Dunedin)	16.2–4–37–3				8–2–20–1				11–5–13–1
25–27 February 1985	13.4–5–36–2				9–4–10–3				4–2–10–1
v. Canterbury (Christchurch)		15–1–67–2			8–2–21–1				18–8–38–1
1–3 March 1985		6–2–22–0			7–0–35–0	6–0–31–0	4–1–15–0		31–9–69–0
	177.5–39–527–17 *av.* 31.00	208–34–613–20 *av.* 30.65	22–2–132–3 *av.* 44.00	78.2–26–183–5 *av.* 36.60	101–26–276–11 *av.* 25.09	76–15–244–2 *av.* 122.00	53–10–167–2 *av.* 83.50	77–25–128–8 *av.* 16.00	273.2–88–594–20 *av.* 29.70

a L.M. Crocker 0.2–0–4–0 b R.D. Broughton 0.3–0–4–0

aggrieved after missing a caught-behind appeal against Chatfield at 272. Four more singles, a deathly hush over the ground and then a tumult of joy as Coney hit the two which won the match.

The margin allegedly was two wickets, but Cairns, while padded up, was frightfully groggy and would have been little use. He was immediately sent to hospital, fortunately there was no fracture, but he was only let out after four days.

So Coney, 111 not out in 385 minutes, and Chatfield, 21 from 84 balls, came back in triumph, although Glen Turner, as judge of the Man of the Match award, gave it to Akram with five wickets in each innings of his second Test.

And the whole of New Zealand began to breath again.

The Pakistanis finished with an anti-climatic one-dayer at Auckland, which New Zealand won handily.

Immediately both were off to Australia for the WCC tournament, but New Zealand were never really in contention. Their group game against West Indies was ruined by rain, they beat Sri Lanka to reach the semi-finals, but then lost to India in the semi-final, and to West Indies in the consolation final.

So the memories stayed of New Zealand's most profitable home series – a 2–0 win in the Tests, a 4–0 dominance of the one-dayers.

But already there were clouds on the horizon. Bruce Edgar, so long neglected by the national selectors but very likely the best partner available for Wright at the start of the innings, announced he would not be available for the West Indies tour as his wife Nicky was due to have their first child while the tour was on. Whether or not the selectors were concerned at that news is open to question. They seemed to have discarded Edgar in any case.

But the really shattering news came from Reid, that he would not be available for West Indies. He had been New Zealand's outstanding player of the series, 333 runs in the Tests at 83.25, 106 in the one-dayers at 35.3. With Edgar gone

M.J. Child	K.R. Treiber	G.P. Howarth	*Byes*	*Leg-byes*	*Wides*	*No-balls*	*Total*	*Wkts*
			4	8		15	204	10
				3	1	7	341	5
			7	12		10	284	6
				6	1	3	262	8
			2	3	1	2	121	10
11–3–28–2			4	14		9	378	10
			1	4		1	118	4
21–8–35–1			1	9		9	314	8
5–2–6–1			5			4	74	4a
20.4–6–50–1			1	6	2	7	254	10
1–1–0–0			6	3		6	312	7
8–2–21–1	19–3–61–4		3	10	1	1	165	10
17–9–26–0	18–8–44–3		4	7			137	10
11–3–34–1	13–2–42–3		2	6		15	210	10
21–3–81–1		8–1–33–0		10		5	300	2b
115.4–37–281–8 *av.* 35.12	50–13–147–10 *av.* 14.70	8–1–33–0 —						

Reid was the only New Zealand batsman with the technique and patience to play the really long innings.

The selectors were not amused, and tried various ways of having Reid change his mind.

But Reid is something out of the ordinary in these days of the professional money-gathering cricketer. In a rather old-fashioned amateur spirit Reid maintained that he had three priorities in life – his wife and two young children first, his work as a secondary school geography master at Waitakere College second, and playing cricket distinctly third.

The basic reason Reid was not available, he said, was that he was not enjoying the constant grind of cricket; that it was not contributing to his ideas of quality of life.

So suddenly New Zealand lost the under-pinning of their batting structure, a batsman who in 13 Tests had scored five centuries and, best of all, had become the backbone of the batting. It should be noted that Reid has scored his centuries against Pakistan (three), India and Sri Lanka, and that on the selectors' whim he has not been chosen to play against Australia, West Indies or England.

Reid may return next summer, another hectic merry-go-round of a three-Test tour to Australia, the WSC–Benson and Hedges one-dayers in Australia, and then Australia back in New Zealand for a three-Test tour – followed later in the year by a half-tour of England.

But all that will depend on Reid's feelings at the time. His priorities will remain the same: family first, teaching second, cricket third.

So New Zealand went off to West Indies without two of their most solid batsmen, Reid and Edgar, with a speculative bowling attack, and very much with a question mark over the form of their captain Howarth.

Howarth would be first to admit that, at 33 going on 34, his time as a free-scoring and consistent Test batsman is running out, but he remains a first-rate captain. He was never really in batting form this summer, and his placing as an opener with Wright was very much a compromise. The idea would not have been entertained against, say, the Australian new-ball attack, and hopefully Howarth will not have to open in the West Indies.

Wright had only modest success this summer, by his own high standards, 121 runs in three Tests, top scores 66, average 24.20. It cannot have helped his composure that Howarth, of uncertain staying power, should have opened with him.

There must also be a question mark about the batting of Jeff Crowe, who did not score above 30 in the Tests against Pakistan. Crowe does have time on his side, but if Howarth is to remain in the test team Crowe may be the batsman who has to make way.

On the other hand Martin Crowe, 295 runs at 59 against Pakistan, is making steady progress upward. He is a batsman of real, if sometimes moody, promise. The pity is that a back injury has persuaded Crowe that he should not bowl for a year. He, and to a certain extent Hadlee, are the only ranking all-rounders in the New Zealand side, and with Crowe able to bowl New Zealand have much stronger selection options for both Tests and one-dayers.

So the New Zealand batting for the immediate future will rest very heavily on the shoulders of Wright, Coney and Martin Crowe, while the younger Hart promises to develop into the mould set by Edgar and more recently Reid.

Otago 1984–85
First Class Matches

BATTING

BATTING	v. Wellington (Alexandra) 28–30 Dec. 1984		v. Central Districts (Oamara) 2–4 January 1985		v. Northern Districts (Gisborne) 7–9 January 1985		v. Auckland (Auckland) 13–15 January 1985		v. Canterbury (Christchurch) 17–19 January 1985		v. Auckland (Dunedin) 25–27 January 1985		v. Northern Districts (Dunedin) 25–27 February 1985		v. Wellington (Wellington) 1–3 March 1985		*M*	*Inns*	*NOs*	*Runs*	*H/S*	*Av*
P.R. Facoory	2	19	38	18	39	9											3	6	—	125	39	20.83
S.J. McCullum	11	42	45	27	66	17	28	—	38	28	18	22	19	37	66	5	8	15	—	469	66	31.26
R.N. Hoskin	17	2	23	24	16	0	29	—	60	24	5	3			6	—	7	12	—	209	60	17.41
G.J. Dawson	7	27	7	30*	9	12	33	—	79	0	5	1					6	11	1	210	79	21.00
A.H. Jones	16	31	53	12	44	25	28	—	62	43*	4	58*	59*	30	41	102*	8	15	4	608	102*	55.27
D.J. Walker	14	1	9	5			1	—									3	5	—	30	14	6.00
W.K. Lees	22	10	91	20*	1	21	54*	—	20	15	12	—	23	3	26	—	8	13	2	318	91	28.90
N.A. Mallender	6	17	88	—	24*	5	6	—	10	0	9	—	1	0	40	—	8	12	1	206	88	18.72
V.A. Johnson	7	11					16	—	17	—			5	2			4	6	—	58	17	9.66
S.L. Boock	0	4*	3*	—	10*	7	0	—					6	9*	10	—	6	9	4	49	10*	9.80
J.A.J. Cushen	1*	1	44	10	2	8	17	—	7	4*	0	—	1	14	9*	—	8	13	3	118	44	11.80
P.S. Neutze			1	—	—	0*			3*	—							3	3	2	4	3*	4.00
K.R. Rutherford					41	9	130	—	22	29	89*	61	30	0	0	31	6	11	1	442	130	44.20
T.J. Wilson									52	7	55	33	4	0	6	—	4	7	—	157	55	22.42
S.J. Richards											19	—	0	12			2	3	—	31	19	10.33
P.W. Hills											0	—					1	1	—	0	0	0.00
S. Robinson													2	19			1	2	—	21	19	10.50
G.A. Blakely															28	6	1	2	—	34	28	17.00
K.J. Burns															20	111*	1	2	1	131	111*	131.00
Byes	1		5	5		2	16		6	6	3	4	3	4	2	12						
Leg-byes	6	17	20	5	6	3	11		4	6	17	2	10	7	12	2						
Wides	1				1	1	1		3				1		1							
No-balls			3	2	3	2	7				5		1		8	4						
Total	111	182	430	158	262	121	377		383	162	241	184	165	137	275	273						
Wickets	10	10	10	6	8	10	10		10	7	10	5	10	10	10	3						
Result	L		D		L		D		D		D		W		D							
Points	0		4		0		4		4		4		16		4							

Catches

27 – W.K. Lees (ct 24/st 3)
9 – S.J. McCullum
8 – G.J. Dawson
7 – A.H. Jones
5 – N.A. Mallender
4 – S.L. Boock
3 – P.R. Facoory, D.J. Walker, R.N. Hoskin and K.R. Rutherford
1 – J.A.J. Cushen, V.A. Johnson and S.J. Richards

BOWLING

BOWLING	N.A. Mallender	J.A.J. Cushen	V.A. Johnson	S.L. Boock	D.J. Walker	P.S. Neutze	A.H. Jones	T.J. Wilson	P.W. Hills
v. Wellington (Alexandra)	19–7–29–2	18–7–27–3	7–2–13–1	26–11–50–3					
28–30 December 1984	19.1–9–32–3	24–11–31–3	10–2–36–1	30–14–64–2	15–8–24–0				
v. Central Districts (Oamaru)	21–2–88–1	44–13–106–2		31–12–73–1	11–3–31–0	26.2–1–109–5			
2–4– January 1985									
v. Northern Districts (Gisborne)	20–2–65–2	30.1–10–109–4		46–22–85–2		7–0–35–0	13–5–34–1		
7–9 January 1985	9–0–18–2	15–2–51–2		19–5–54–3		12–0–63–0			
v. Auckland (Auckland)	30–6–87–1	39–16–92–3	18–4–52–2	29–11–57–1	6–3–9–1		1–1–0–0		
13–15 January 1985	22–13–27–7	4–0–7–0		17–12–13–2					
v. Canterbury (Christchurch)	14–4–37–0	20–6–39–1	18–5–59–4			5–0–31–0	13.5–6–28–4	2–2–0–1	
17–19 January 1985	15–2–51–3	29–8–79–1	12–3–49–1			20–4–74–0	23–8–50–2	23–10–49–1	
v. Auckland (Dunedin)	27.4–9–48–3	34–11–56–3						8–4–13–1	17–2–55–3
25–27 January 1985	14–2–51–1	22–7–72–1						16–2–57–7	9–0–41–0
v. Northern Districts (Dunedin)	16.1–9–31–6	18–5–27–3	10–4–18 1						
25–27 February 1985	21–7–39–2	25.4–12–37–5	25–8–53–3	6–3–10–0				4–2–5–0	
v. Wellington (Wellington)	11.5–1–34–2	8–4–15–0		47–24–64–6			26–10–65–2	3–0–15–0	
1–3 March 1985									
	259.5–73–637–35 *av.* 18.20	330.5–112–748–31 *av.* 24.12	100–28–280–13 *av.* 21.53	251–114–470–20 *av.* 23.50	32–14–64–1 *av.* 64.00	70.2–5–312–5 *av.* 62.40	76.5–30–177–9 *av.* 19.66	56–20–139–10 *av.* 13.90	26–2–96–3 *av.* 32.00

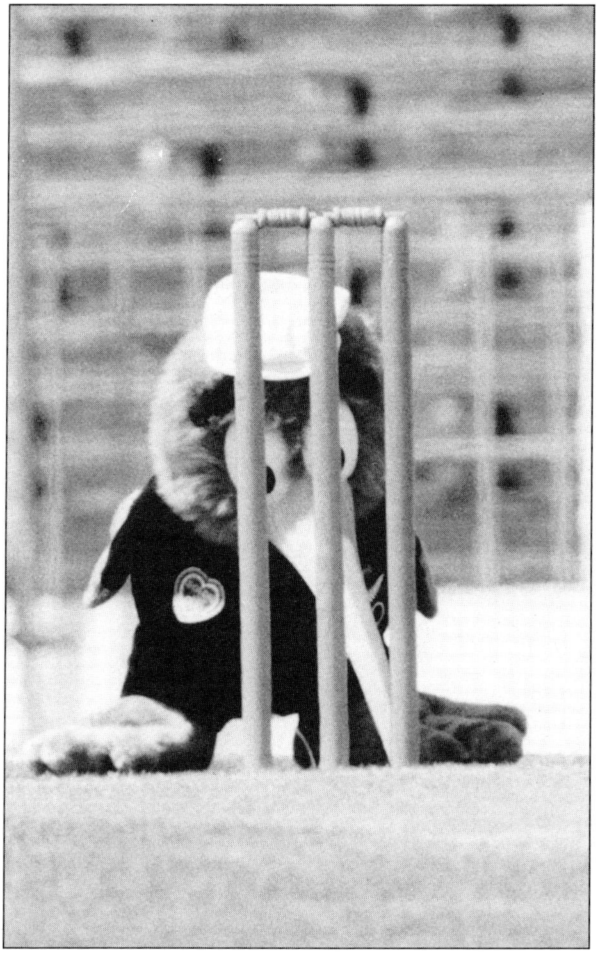

New Zealand rules OK. The Kiwi mascot is in place still. (Adrian Murrell)

Byes	Leg-byes	Wides	No-balls	Total	Wkts
	5	1	4	124	10
3	5		1	195	10
	2		8	409	10
8	17	1	2	353	10
2			1	188	7
2	6		6	305	8
2	1			50	9
4	5		5	203	10
6	8			366	8
6	7	1	5	185	10
8	8		2	237	10
2	5		1	83	10
11	6	2	4	161	10
6	5		5	204	10

The New Zealand bowling throughout the summer, and perhaps in the West Indies, was always serviceable and, when Hadlee was at his sharpest, very effective. Stirling will need to develop quickly, and New Zealand will need consistent work from the spinners, John Bracewell and Stephen Boock (both used little against Pakistan) in the Caribbean.

New Zealand may again need to look searchingly at its home first-class programme, for this still has to adjust – in terms of playing ability and public interest – to the widening demands of international cricket.

The Shell Oil company have recently signed another five-year sponsorship contract with the New Zealand Cricket Council, and this suggests that the future format will change only slightly.

At the moment there are eight series of games among the six teams in the three-day Shell Trophy contest, and a round-robin of five one-day games for the Shell Cup.

It is a fact of life that the cricketing public, so heavily bombarded these days by live broadcasts of Tests and one-day internationals, tend not to be drawn to domestic three- or one-day matches. This has especially been the case in this and last summer, when the Shell competitions have been interrupted by international matches.

The anti-climax was most noticeable this season. There were useful crowds in the early Shell series matches, and considerable interest in some of the new players emerging, such as Willie Watson, a 19-year-old seamer from Auckland, Tony Blain, a talented wicket-keeper and batsman from Central Districts, and a punishing batsman Rod Latham from Canterbury.

But once the international matches were over the Shell series finished in a whimper. And this when the results on the last day of the last match could have meant that any one of the four teams could have won the Shell Trophy.

In the event Wellington, while not playing to their best form, squeezed out with a four-point lead ahead of Auckland and Canterbury, while Central Districts at last won a Shell prize when they beat Wellington in the one-day final.

Auckland made the early running in the three-day contest, but had two bad games, home and away, against Otago. Canterbury were always within range of the leaders, and Otago came with a late rally. Central and Northern Districts were, quite frankly, disappointing in the results they produced from considerable talent.

But it was a shattering criticism of the layout of the season that the last three three-day games, all of them poised to produce a winner on the last day, should be played before only a smattering of spectators.

This season the last two series of matches were played between the New Zealand team's two brief expeditions to Australia – on the theory that the home matches would keep the New Zealand players in form.

The theory did not work. Most of the New Zealand players had been on the move since the Pakistan tour in November (and some earlier to Zimbabwe) and if they did play for their home sides they were not exactly at peak form or enthusiasm.

In recent times, too, the Shell series has been devised so that Test candidates can have match-play before, during and after the matches against whichever touring team is in New Zealand. The selectors maintain that this suits them in their choice of New Zealand teams.

Wellington 1984–85
First Class Matches

BATTING	v. Canterbury (Rangiora) 13–15 Dec. 1985		v. Otago (Alexandra) 28–30 Dec. 1984		v. Auckland (Wellington) 1–3 January 1985		v. Northern Districts (Wellington) 13–15 January 1985		v. Central Districts (Blenheim) 17–19 January 1985		v. Canterbury (Wellington) 25–27 January 1985		v. Pakistanis (Wellington) 1–3 February 1985		v. Auckland (Auckland) 25–27 February 1985		v. Otago (Wellington) 1–3 March 1985		M	Inns	NOs	Runs	H/S	Av
J.G. Boyle	42	0	9	6	18	35	71	39	46	26	31	89	16	15	5	—	11	—	9	16	—	459	89	28.68
R.H. Vance	30	1	24	47	13	—	54	—	66	9	99	31	66	23*	59	—	0	—	9	14	1	522	99	40.15
T.D. Ritchie	3	0	12	3	52*	27*	32	10	105*	0	6	20*	1	—	19	—	60	—	9	15	4	350	105*	31.81
R.W. Ormiston	15	2	1	11	11	2	28	—	16	—	4	28	67	10*	27*	—	1	—	9	14	2	223	67	18.58
D.F. Oakley	8	1											2	—					2	3	—	11	8	3.66
E.B. McSweeney	24	41	5	6	0	28	6	—	95	2	32	21	26	—	41	—	0	—	9	14	—	327	95	23.35
G.F. Larsen	0	3					26*	—	14	—			0*	—					4	5	2	43	26*	14.33
G.N. Cederwall	0	5	1*	21	44	24*	5	29	3*	26	57*	24*	1*	—			7	—	8	14	6	247	57*	30.87
R.J. Pither	8*	19*																	1	2	2	27	19*	—
K.D. James	0	22					11	—	—	—	14	—			36	—	34	—	6	6	—	117	36	19.50
S.J. Maguiness	43	4	3	8	1	—	5	2*	—	7	0	—	—	—	20	—	14	—	9	11	1	107	43	10.70
B.A. Edgar			39	6	22	25	81	32	18	82*	0	1			37	—	47	—	7	12	1	390	82*	35.45
J.V. Coney			6	32	0	7									20	—			3	5	—	65	32	13.00
E.J. Gray			6	38*	2	19	32	—	17	—	33	—	11	1	49	—	10	—	8	11	1	218	49	21.80
E.J. Chatfield			8	8	8	—							—	—	21	—			4	4	—	45	21	11.25
A.A. Griffiths											15*	—					4*	—	2	2	2	19	15*	—
Byes	5			3	5	2	4	1	4	7	17	5	3		4		6							
Leg-byes	3	5	5	5	3	2	14	4	12	1	3	3	11	2	13		5							
Wides			1						2		2	1	1											
No-balls	11	4	4	1	1		9	1	4	1	1			2	9		5							
Total	192	107	124	195	180	171	378	118	402	161	314	223	205	53	360		204							
Wickets	10	10	10	10	10	6	10	4	7	6	9	5	7	2	10		10							
Results	L		W		D		D		D		W		D		D		D							
Points	4		16		0		4		4		16		—		4		0							

Catches

41 – E.B. McSweeney (ct 31/st 10)
14 – R.H. Vance
12 – S.J. Maguiness
5 – E.J. Gray
4 – J.V. Coney, G.N. Cederwall and R.W. Ormiston
3 – J.G. Boyle and T.D. Ritchie
2 – B.A. Edgar, D.F. Oakley and A.A. Griffiths
1 – E.J. Chatfield and sub

BOWLING	K.D. James	G.N. Cederwall	S.J. Maguiness	G.R. Larsen	R.J. Pither	E.J. Chatfield	E.J. Gray	J.V. Coney	R.W. Ormiston
v. Canterbury (Rangiora)	5–0–21–0	15–7–32–2	14.2–7–17–7	4–1–11–1					
13–15 December 1984	29–8–95–2	26.4–4–65–3	31–7–82–3	11–3–23–2	6–1–20–0				
v. Otago (Alexandra)		4–1–7–1	20–9–29–4			22.5–6–37–2	12–2–31–2		
28–30 December 1984		10–1–34–1	19–5–33–0			28–9–56–4	36.5–14–43–5		
v. Auckland (Wellington)		24–9–54–4	18–5–53–1			34–11–76–0	21.4–9–30–3	10–2–20–2	
1–3 January 1985		4–0–21–0	20–8–29–1			15–3–36–0	20–5–61–2	11–2–42–1	
v. Northern Districts (Wellington)	22–4–67–2	16–4–43–1	22–11–38–0	12–7–16–1			45.3–18–87–5		
13–15 January 1985	7–3–13–0	6–0–23–0	9–0–39–3				19–5–61–5		4–0–25–0
v. Central Districts (Blenheim)	22–7–65–0	23–7–62–3	28–11–48–2	11–4–23–0			25–14–53–2		
17–19 January 1985	8–4–16–1	10–2–33–2	3–2–4–0	2–1–8–0			9–5–22–1		4–1–27–0
v. Canterbury (Wellington)	14.1–4–23–2	13–2–37–1	16–5–44–0				29–6–107–4		
25–27 January 1985	5–0–30–0	7–0–28–1	22–10–40–0				45–14–115–5		
v. Pakistanis (Wellington)		9–0–42–1	16–4–42–0	2–1–1–0		27–5–60–3	29–8–68–5		
1–3 February 1985		16–3–56–0	19–3–68–0	6–2–7–1		18–5–17–2	4–1–12–0		6–0–37–0
v. Auckland (Auckland)	20–5–51–2		36.3–9–72–3			40–15–85–3	19–7–70–0	10–5–19–0	
25–27 February 1985	6–1–22–0		4–0–7–0			5–1–16–1	18–2–70–3	15–4–44–1	2–0–15–0
v. Otago (Wellington)	14–5–39–1	12.4–2–40–2	16–10–17–0				52–22–89–6		
1–3 March 1985	7–3–14–1	12–2–41–1	17–11–11–0				51–17–125–0		3–1–10–0
	159.1–44–456–11 av. 41.45	208.2–44–618–23 av. 26.86	330.5–117–673–24 av. 28.04	48–19–89–5 av. 17.80	6–1–20–0 —	189.5–55–383–15 av. 25.53	436–149–1044–48 av. 21.75	46–13–125–4 av. 31.25	19–2–114–0 —

a R.H. Vance 3–2–4–0
b E.B. McSweeney 1–0–8–0
c R.H. Vance 1–0–6–0
J.G. Boyle 1–0–5–0
d R.H. Vance 3–2–1–0
e R.H. Vance 1–0–4–0

Youthful enthusiasm for New Zealand's success.

A.A. Griffiths	B.A. Edgar	T.D. Ritchie	*Byes*	*Leg-byes*	*Wides*	*No-balls*	*Total*	*Wkts*
				7	1	1	88	10
				8		8	293	10
			1	6	1		111	10
				17			182	10
			1	8	1		242	10
			1	5			195	4
				12		4	267	10a
			4	8		6	173	8
				2	2	11	253	7
	2–1–1–0	2–1–4–0				6	123	4b
18–5–49–3			9	4	2	4	273	10
18–7–35–1			3	12	1	5	263	7
			2	2		2	217	9
		3–0–22–0		3		6	222	3
			4	10	1	2	311	10
	5–1–15–0	1–0–2–0	5	4	1	1		c
35–5–75–1			2	12	1	8	275	10d
17.3–3–54–0			12	2		4	273	3e
88.3–20–213–5 *av.* 42.60	7–2–18–0 —	6–1–28–0 —						

Unfortunately that theory has not turned to fact, either. Once in the international mood the players seem to find difficulty in playing to their full ability at home first-class level.

The solution seems to be, then, that the NZCC must organise the Shell series starting earlier in December, and finishing before or during whichever international tour is taking place in New Zealand.

That at least would give the public an uninterrupted view of the Shell matches through to their conclusion. For, as other countries have found, once the cricket public start to turn on their television sets for the major matches, it is very difficult to lure them back to minor games.

Pakistan in New Zealand 1985
First Class Matches

BATTING	v. Canterbury (Christchurch) 8–10 January 1985		First Test Match (Wellington) 18–22 January 1985		Second Test Match (Auckland) 25–28 January		v. Wellington (Wellington) 1–3 February 1985		Third Test Match (Dunedin) 9–14 February 1985		M	Inns	NOs	Runs	H/S	Av
Mudassar Nazar	75	—	38	—	12	89			18	5	4	6	—	237	89	39.50
Mohsin Khan	1	71	40	—	26	1	12	27	39	27	5	9	—	244	71	27.11
Qasim Umar	27	114*	8	—	33	22	20	55	96	89	5	9	1	464	114*	58.00
Javed Miandad	112	17	30	—	26	1			79	2	4	7	—	267	112	38.14
Saleem Malik	22	23*	66	—	41*	0	7	61	0	9	5	9	2	229	66	32.71
Rameez Raja	4	—					7	70*			2	3	1	81	70*	40.50
Wasim Raja	8	—	14	—	4	11	19	0*			4	6	1	56	19	11.20
Anil Dalpat	8	—	15	—	7	6	4	—	16	21	5	7	—	77	21	11.00
Tahir Naqqash	14	—					20	—	0	1	3	4	—	35	20	8.75
Wasim Akram	6*	—			0	0*			1*	8*	3	5	4	15	8*	15.00
Mohsin Kamal	0	—					8*	—			2	2	1	8	8*	8.00
Shoaib Mohammad			7	—							1	1	—	7	7	7.00
Abdul Qadir			54	—	0	10	6	—			3	4	—	70	54	17.50
Iqbal Qasim			27*	—			16*	—			2	2	2	43	27*	—
Azeem Hafeez			3	—	6	17			4	7	3	5	—	37	17	7.40
Zaheer Abbas					6	12	92	—	6	0	3	5	—	116	92	23.20
Rashid Khan									0	37	1	2	—	37	37	18.50
Byes	3	4	9				2		1	1						
Leg-byes	3	1	9		5	11	2	3	2	9						
Wides																
No-balls	6	3	2		3	3	2	6	12	7						
Total	289	233	322		169	183	217	222	274	223						
Wickets	10	2	10		10	10	9	3	10	10						
Result	W		D		L		D		L							

Catches
11 – Anil Dalpat (ct 10/st 1)
5 – Javed Miandad
4 – Qasim Umar
3 – Abdul Qadir and Mohsin Khan
2 – Rameez Raja, Mudassar Nazar, Tahir Naqqash and Shoaib Mohammad
1 – Iqbal Qasim, Saleem Malik, Rashid Khan, Wasim Akram, Wasim Raja, Mohsin Kamal and sub

BOWLING	W. Akram	M. Kamal	T. Naqqash	M. Nazar	W. Raja	S. Makik	J. Miandad	A. Qadir	I. Qasim
v. Canterbury (Christchurch) 8–10 January	14–3–39–0	12–1–78–1	16–1–65–1	8–1–32–0	11–1–50–1	5–0–26–0	4–0–16–1		
	15–6–30–0	13.4–1–66–2	13–3–36–0	20–0–45–1	7.3–0–27–3	0.2–0–0–0			
First Test Match (Wellington) 18–22 January				29–5–80–1	2–0–10–0		3–1–7–0	51–13–142–1	41–5–105–2
				6–3–13–1				8–1–18–0	16–8–19–2
Second Test Match (Auckland) 25–28 January	34.4–4–105–2			34–5–85–2	1–0–3–0	8.2–2–34–0		22–5–52–1	
v. Wellington (Wellington) 1–3 February		9–1–28–2	13–4–24–0		3–2–2–2			28–7–71–3	28–6–66–0
		6–1–20–0	8–3–11–2			3–2–5–0		3–2–2–0	5–4–1–0
Third Test Match (Dunedin) 9–14 February	26–7–56–5		16.4–4–23–2						
	33–10–72–5		16.4–1–58–1	9–2–20–0					
	122.4–30–302–12 *av.* 25.16	40.4–4–192–5 *av.* 38.40	83.2–16–217–6 *av.* 36.16	106–16–275–5 *av.* 55.00	24.3–3–92–6 *av.* 15.33	16.4–4–65–0 —	7–1–23–1 *av.* 23.00	112–28–285–5 *av.* 57.00	90–23–191–4 *av.* 47.75

a Shoaib Mohammad 1–0–4–0 b Rameez Raja 2–1–4–0

A. Hafeez	R. Khan	Q. Umar	*Byes*	*Leg-byes*	*Wides*	*No-balls*	*Total*	*Wkts*
			1	2	3	4	309	4
				5		4	209	6
48–12–127–5			5	12		1	492	10a
15–3–51–1				2			103	4
47–10–157–3			6	9		6	451	9
			3	11	1		205	7
		4–1–8–0		2		2	53	2b
20–6–65–1	23–7–64–2		7	5		1	220	10
32–9–84–2	9–2–33–0		5	6	1	11	278	8
162–40–484–12 *av.* 40.33	32–9–97–2 *av.* 48.50	4–1–8–0 —						

SECTION D

Meagre Fare

The season in Sri Lanka.
One-Day series *v.* New Zealand.
The visit of the Pakistan under-23 side.
Other first-class matches.

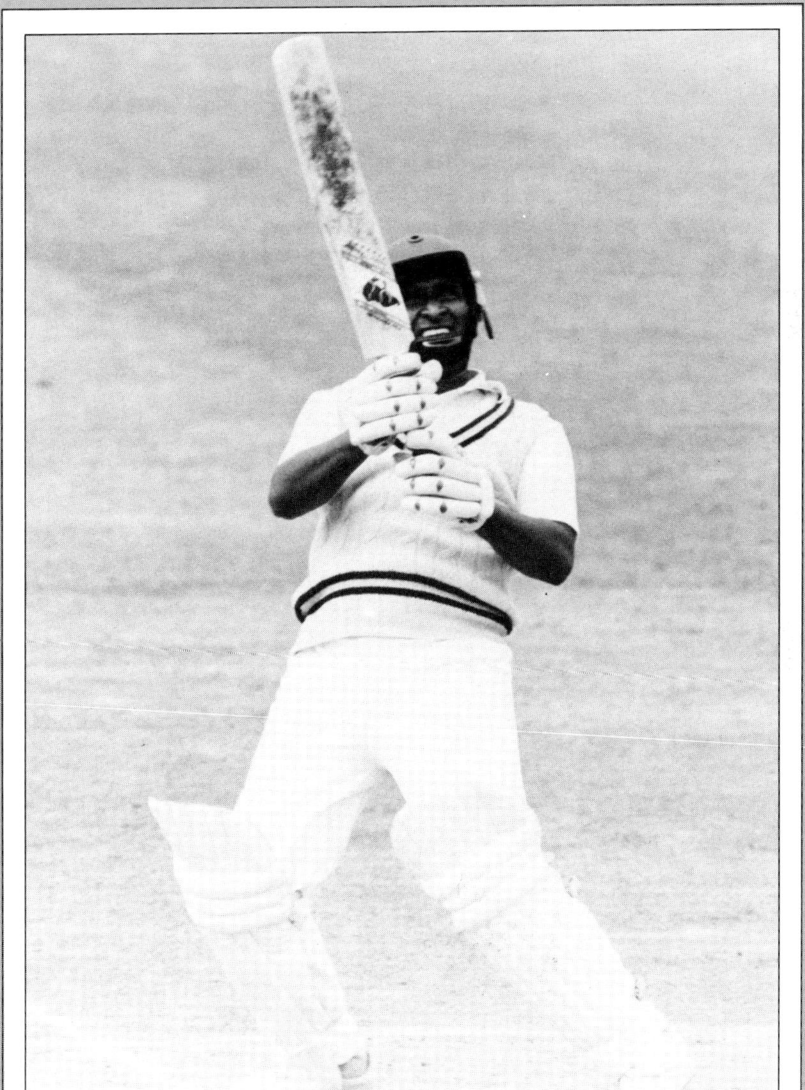

Duleep Mendis, captain of Sri Lanka.
(Adrian Murrell)

Following their fine showing in the Test match at Lord's, Sri Lanka returned home in high spirits, but with no prospect of being able to flex their muscles in the Test arena again in the immediate future. Indeed, with the one-day competitions in Australia occupying the months of January, February and half of March, it was apparent that the leading Sri Lankan players would be spending little time in their own country during the season so that the two-match limited-over series with New Zealand was avidly anticipated.

First One-Day International
SRI LANKA *v.* NEW ZEALAND

With neither Howarth nor Hadlee available for the tour, Coney led New Zealand for the first time and chose to bat on an easy paced pitch when he won the toss. Some tight bowling and eager fielding restricted New Zealand to a meagre 171 from their 45 overs, a total which would have been even more moderate but for the steadiness of Jeff Crowe.

In their turn, Sri Lanka struggled. Wettimuny was out of touch and although Silva and Madugalle promised substance, Coney and Chatfield brought about a decline which saw four wickets fall for 36. Roy Dias provided the necessary

ABOVE: *Vinothen John who bowled steadily in the one-day internationals against New Zealand. (Adrian Murrell)*

stability and the exciting young Aravinda de Silva hit a brisk fifty to win the match.

Second One-Day International
SRI LANKA *v.* NEW ZEALAND

Sri Lanka again fielded the side which had served so nobly in the Test match at Lord's. New Zealand, who again won the toss, included the members of their party who had not played in the first match.

Martin Crowe dismissed both opening batsmen and with

LEFT: *Aravinda de Silva, the most exciting young talent in Sri Lanka. (Adrian Murrell)*

FIRST ONE-DAY INTERNATIONAL – SRI LANKA *v.* NEW ZEALAND
3 November 1984 at Colombo

NEW ZEALAND			
	J. G. Wright	c Silva, b John	11
	B.A. Edgar	c Silva, b Ratnayeke	6
	M.D. Crowe	b Ranatunga	23
	J.F. Reid	c Ratnayeke, b de Mel	21
	J.J. Crowe	not out	57
	J.V. Coney†	c P.A. de Silva, b John	24
	B.L. Cairns	c P.A. de Silva, b John	4
	I.D.S. Smith*	not out	5
	M.C. Snedden		
	S.L. Boock		
	E.J. Chatfield		
	Extras	b 1, lb 14, w 3, nb 2	20
	(45 overs)	(for 6 wickets)	171

	O	M	R	W
de Mel	9	3	26	1
John	9	2	37	3
Ratnayeke	9	—	40	1
Ranatunga	9	—	23	1
D.S. de Silva	9	1	25	—

FALL OF WICKETS
1- 20, 2- 36, 3- 58, 4- 84, 5- 124, 6- 133

SRI LANKA			
	S. Wettimuny	c Edgar, b Cairns	1
	S.A.R. Silva*	c Boock, b Chatfield	21
	R.S. Madugalle	c Wright, b Chatfield	31
	A. Ranatunga	c Reid, b Coney	9
	R.L. Dias	c Wright, b Boock	34
	L.R.D. Mendis†	c J. Crowe, b Coney	3
	P.A. de Silva	not out	50
	A.L.F. de Mel	not out	15
	D.S. de Silva		
	J.R. Ratnayeke		
	V.B. John		
	Extras	b 3, lb 5, nb 2	10
	(39.4 overs)	(for 6 wickets)	174

	O	M	R	W
Snedden	6	1	30	—
Cairns	6.4	2	37	1
Chatfield	9	—	34	2
Boock	9	—	29	1
Coney	4	—	16	2
M.D. Crowe	5	—	18	—

FALL OF WICKETS
1- 13, 2- 43, 3- 62, 4- 73, 5- 79, 8- 144

Sri Lanka won by 4 wickets

Madugalle disastrously run out for 0, Sri Lanka had no foundation to their innings. They continued to struggle on a pitch which presented few difficulties and their final total of 144 was never likely to give New Zealand the slightest trouble.

There was a ray of hope for the home side when de Mel bowled Wright and had McEwan caught with only 19 scored, but Reid and Martin Crowe soon began to hit the ball firmly, and Crowe, who had a fine match, hit his 52 off only 57 deliveries to win the match.

SECOND ONE-DAY INTERNATIONAL – SRI LANKA *v.* NEW ZEALAND
4 November 1984 at Colombo

SRI LANKA			
	S. Wettimuny	b M.D. Crowe	3
	S.A.R. Silva*	c Smith, b M.D. Crowe	9
	R.S. Madugalle	run out	0
	R.L. Dias	st Smith, b Coney	10
	L.R.D. Mendis†	c Snedden, b Stirling	13
	A. Ranatunga	run out	15
	P.A. de Silva	run out	15
	A.L.F. de Mel	c Reid, b Stirling	15
	D.S. de Silva	b Chatfield	13
	J.R. Ratnayeke	not out	8
	V.B. John	not out	0
	Extras	b 3, lb 6, w 1, nb 3	13
	(41 overs)	(for 9 wickets)	114

	O	M	R	W
Chatfield	9	2	17	1
Snedden	7	2	14	—
M.D. Crowe	9	3	17	2
Stirling	9	1	28	2
Coney	4	—	7	1
McEwan	3	—	18	—

FALL OF WICKETS
1- 12, 2- 12, 3- 22, 4- 35, 5- 47, 6- 66, 7- 91, 8- 91, 9- 114

NEW ZEALAND			
	J.G. Wright	b de Mel	6
	P.E. McEwan	c P.A. de Silva, b de Mel	9
	J.F. Reid	c Dias, b Ranatunga	34
	M.D. Crowe	not out	52
	J.J. Crowe	not out	7
	J.V. Coney†		
	E.J. Gray		
	I.D.S. Smith*		
	D.A. Stirling		
	M.C. Snedden		
	E.J. Chatfield		
	Extras	lb 3, w 5, nb 2	10
	(31.4 overs)	(for 3 wickets)	118

	O	M	R	W
de Mel	7	3	23	2
John	9	2	37	—
Ratnayeke	6	1	9	—
D.S. de Silva	4	1	14	—
Ranatunga	5.4	1	25	1

FALL OF WICKETS
1- 15, 2- 19, 3- 98

New Zealand won by 7 wickets

7, 8 and 9 November 1984

at Colombo

President's XI 298 for 9 dec (P.A. de Silva 105) and 134 for 7 (M.D. Vonhagt 53, P.I. Pocock 4 for 57)
England XI 273 for 9 dec (M.W. Gatting 97, D.I. Gower 86, A.J. Lamb 53)

Match drawn

The tragic events in India brought the unexpected bonus to the Sri Lankan season of a brief visit by the England party who were desperately in need of practice. The first of two hastily arranged matches was against the President's XI and the opening day was made memorable by a splendid maiden century from the nineteen-year old Aravinda de Silva. He was hit on the cheek by the second ball he received, from Foster, and at lunch, when the home side were 54 for 3, he was 28 not out and went to hospital for an examination. He returned immediately after lunch and attacked the bowling in a gloriously exciting manner, his second fifty coming off 37 balls. He and Madugalle added 99 in 25 overs for the fourth wicket. On the second day England lost both openers quickly, but Gatting and Gower gave reassurance with a stand of 166 in 32 overs. The game was always destined for a draw, but the spin of Pocock and Edmonds impressed on the last day.

Ranatunga who led Sri Lanka under-23 side against the Pakistan tourists. (Adrian Murrell)

10 November 1984

at Colombo

Sri Lankan XI 178 for 5 (38 overs)
England XI

Match abandoned

Heavy rain ended England's short venture in Sri Lanka after the Sri Lankan XI had batted steadily in the one-day match.

The second half of the Sri Lankan season saw a tour by a Pakistani under-23 side under the management of Khan Mohammad. Saleem Malik was named as captain and the rest of the party was Rameez Raja, Azeem Hafeez, Wasim Akram, Manzoor Elahi, Mohsin Kamal, Akram Raza, Ijaz Ahmed, Shahid Anwar, Asif Mujtaba, Moin-ul-Atiq, Ameer Akbar Babar, Zulqarnian, Tanvir Ali, Haafiz Shahid Yaqoob and Ghaffer Kazmi.

The tour had been eagerly awaited by the Pakistanis who were anxious to test the strength of their emerging talent, but they returned bitterly disappointed, particularly at the attitude and behaviour of some of their players. As the new Pakistan cricket magazine, *Cricket Star*, reported, 'Most of the Pakistanis questioned the decisions when the ball didn't hit the stumps or there was a lofted catch. This does not augur well for the future considering that these players are only 23 years old or less.'

9 and 10 May 1985

Nondescripts Ground, Colombo

President of Sri Lankan Cricket Board's Colts XI 000 for 0 (R. Mahanama 97 not out)
Pakistan u-23 301 for 7 (Saleem Malik 113 not out, Rameez Raja 56)

Match drawn

Both sides used this match for batting practice. The Colts XI occupying the first day and the tourists the second. Saleem Malik gave an exhilarating display with 4 sixes and 7 fours in his 113 not out.

11 May 1985

at P. Saravanamutu Stadium, Colombo

Sri Lanka u-23 191 for 9 (S. Warnakulasuriya 82 not out)
Pakistan u-23 193 for 6 (Saleem Malik 56)

Pakistan u-23 won by 4 wickets

Saleem Malik was named Man of the Match as Pakistan won the first of the 45-over contests with an over to spare in spite of some good bowling by Rumesh Ratnayake who took 3 for 45.

Amal Silva, attacking batsman and improving wicket-keeper. (Ken Kelly)

13, 14, 15 and 16 May 1985

at Asgiriya Stadium, Kandy

Pakistan u-23 331 for 8 dec (Saleem Malik 140 not out, Manzoor Elahi 58, R.J. Ratnayake 5 for 12) and 45 for 2
Sri Lanka u-23 346 for 9 dec (R. Jurangpathy 102, P.A. de Silva 92)
Match drawn

The first of the *Test* matches was marred by rain and by some cross talk between Pakistan players and umpires. Saleem Malik hit another fine century, but was overshadowed by the performance of Roshan Jurangpathy who was making his first-class debut at the age of 17 years, 11 months and 12 days. The first player from the Malay community to appear in a first-class game in Sri Lanka, Jurangpathy became the youngest player to score a century on his debut in Sri Lanka. There was some fine bowling by Rumesh Ratnayake, but Sri Lanka were struggling at 48 for 4 until skipper Ranatunge and the brilliant Aravinda de Silva put on 107, and Jurangpathy and Rumesh Ratnayake added 101 for the eighth wicket.

22 May 1985

at P. Savaranamutu Stadium, Colombo

Pakistan u-23 159
Sri Lankan u-23 163 for 6
Sri Lanka u-23 won by 4 wickets

The second four day match was abandoned without a ball being bowled and a one-day game was played as a compensation. The home side won with 5.1 overs to spare. Gurusinghe hit 42 not out and Jurangpathy was named Man of the Match; he hit 36.

25 May 1985

---

at Sinhalese Sports Club, Colombo

Sri Lanka u-23 99
Pakistan u-23 101 for 1 (Ijaz Ahmed 79 not out)

Pakistan u-23 won by 9 wickets

The match was reduced to 26 overs by rain, but Sri Lanka batted badly and were out in 24.4 overs. Mahanama, 21 not out, and Jurangpathy, 20, were the only batsmen to profit. Ijaz Ahmed dominated the reply and victory came in 17.1 overs.

26 May 1985

---

at Sinhalese Sports Club, Colombo

Pakistan u-23 161 (A. Ranatunge 4 for 25)
Sri Lanka u-23 159

Pakistan u-23 won by 2 runs

Again rain reduced the number of overs, this time to 27. Rameez Raja, Man of the Match, hit a brisk 47, but Pakistan also owed much to Mohsin Kamal whose 3 for 24 snatched victory, but Sri Lanka panicked at the close and an insane run out contributed to their downfall.

28, 29, 30 and 31 May 1985

---

at P. Savaranamutu Stadium, Colombo

Sri Lanka u-23 344 (A. Gurusinghe 106, H. Tillekeratne 67, P.A. de Silva 66, Tanver Ali for for 98)
Pakistan u-23 147 (R.J. Ratnayake 6 for 60, R. Jurangpathy 4 for 44) and 183 (Manzoor Elahi 57, R. Jurangpathy 4 for 59)

Sri Lanka u-23 won by an innings and 14 runs

This match was shifted from Galle to Colombo because the ground was waterlogged. Sri Lanka won the match comfortably after recovering from 45 for 4 through the efforts of Aravinda de Silva and the three schoolboys, Gurusinghe, Thillakeratne and Jurangpathy. Jurangpathy also had a fine match with his off-spin, taking 8 for 103. He and Rumesh Ratnayake, who had match figures of 9 for 130, took 8 Pakistani wickets for 58 before lunch on the third day, and another 9 wickets fell before the close of play as the visitors followed-on. Only a last wicket stand of 21 in 57 minutes saved Pakistan from total humiliation. The partners were Mohsin Kamal and Azeem Hafeez, and Azeem partnered Shahid Anwar in a last wicket stand of 44 in 100 minutes in the second innings which could not, however, stave off defeat. Left-arm spinner Tanvir Ali bowled a mammoth spell and was by far the most impressive of the Pakistani bowlers, and it was surprising that he was not given more opportunity on the tour.

Sadly, in this match, Ijaz Ahmed, on being given out, knocked all three stumps over and made rude gestures to umpires and players all the way back to the pavilion. One had hoped for better from a player on the threshold of a Test career.

So the Sri Lankan season ended although the Test series with India and a possible first victory was eagerly awaited. The tour was due to take place in late August and September. There is much exciting young talent in Sri Lanka, but it will never realise its full potential if future seasons are as fragmentary as this one and if consistently stronger opposition is provided.

SECTION E

Going It Alone

The season in South Africa.
The Castle Currie Cup. The Castle Bowl.
The Benson & Hedges Trophy. The Nissan Shield. Averages.
Another Rebel Tour, Chris Harte tells the story of the gathering of the Australian party to tour South Africa in 1985–86.

Statistics supplied by Peter Sichel.

Clive Rice, captain of Transvaal, winners of every competition. (George Herringshaw)

For the first time in four years a South African season began without the prospect of a visit from a side from another country so that it seemed that all interest and energies would be centred on the Castle Currie Cup and Castle Bowl.

Once again Transvaal seemed likely to dominate the South African year. Clive Rice, their skipper, maintained that they were the best provincial side in the world, a view that results would support, but it was expected that they would be strongly challenged by Western Province, under an enthusiastic new leader, the twenty-four year old Adrian Kuiper, and by Natal who had remained unbeaten since Paddy Clift had become captain mid-way through the 1983–84 season. As Natal were to be reinforced by the services of Collis King and Hartley Alleyne, their prospects looked good. Northern Transvaal, on the other hand, lost Dave Richardson, who returned to Eastern Province.

4, 5 and 6 October 1984

at Port Elizabeth (U.P.E. Ground)

Eastern Province 287 for 5 dec (D. Callaghan 171, P.G. Amm 53) and 305 for 6 (G.S. Cowley 145 not out, D. Callaghan 55)
South African Defence Force 534 for 6 dec (M.B. Logan 172, J. Commins 116 not out, D.J. Richardson 67, S. Koch 67)

Match drawn

The opening game of the season provided a fine opportunity for batsmen to display their talents. Callaghan and Commins made maiden centuries and opposing skippers, Gavin Cowley and Mark Logan, hit career bests.

ABOVE: *Alan Kourie began Transvaal's golden year with 7 for 94 against Northern Transvaal and was outstanding as bowler, batsman and fielder. (Adrian Murrell)*

Protea Cup

10 October 1984

at Johannesburg

Western Province 174 (A.P. Kuiper 55)
Transvaal 176 for 8 (J. Cook 70)

Transvaal won by 2 wickets

Firestone Challenge

13 October 1984

at Johannesburg

Western Province 247 for 6 (S.F.A. Bacchus 91, P.N. Kirsten 51)
Eastern Province 229 (D.H. Howell 68)

Western Province won by 18 runs

Two early season challenge matches produced some good cricket and gave Bacchus the chance to show that he could prove a worthy successor to Gooch for Western Province.

BELOW: *Dave Richardson hits out. The Eastern Province wicket-keeper/batsman was engaged in national service and had a moderate season. Kevin McKenzie (Transvaal) is the fielder. (Argus)*

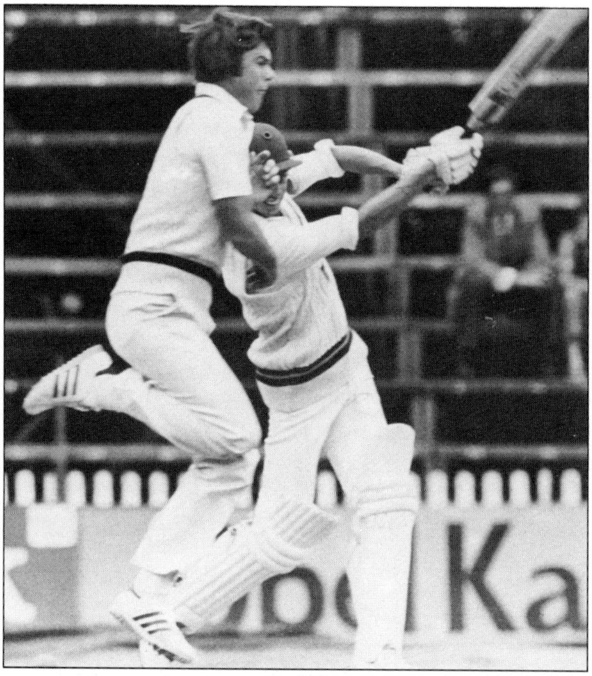

Benson and Hedges Trophy

17 October 1984

at Port Elizabeth

Impalas 200 (D.J. Cullinan 80, D.J. Brickett 5 for 40)
Eastern Province 203 for 6 (D.J. Callaghan 51 not out)

Eastern Province (2 pts) won by 4 wickets

The Benson and Hedges Trophy began with the new contestants Impalas, a mixture of players from Border, Boland,

Orange Free State and Griqualand West, taking on Eastern Province. The day–night match went in favour of the home side for whom Callaghan was again impressive.

Nissan Shield – Round One

20 October 1984

at East London

Eastern Province 122
Border 128 for 4 (R.C. Ontong 56 not out)

Border won by 6 wickets

at Bloemfontain

Orange Free State 251 for 8 (C.J. van Heerden 96)
Natal 257 for 1 (B.J. Whitfield 109 not out, R.M. Bentley 109 not out)

Natal won by 9 wickets

at Kimberley

Northern Transvaal 222 (P.J.A. Visagie 55)
Griqualand West 170

Northern Transvaal won by 52 runs

The first round of the Nissan Shield, the premier limited-over knock-out competition, produced one of the great shocks in the history of the tournament, originally sponsored by Gillette. Some steady bowling by Thomas and Ontong, the Glamorgan pair, ably supported by Gary Gower frustrated Eastern Province to 122 in 51.4 overs. The Castle Bowl side lost 3 for 36, including Trotman, in reply, but Gower and Ontong added 63 and Ontong went on to lead his side to an historic victory.

Elsewhere there was less sensation. Carl van Heerden's 96 was unavailing for Orange Free State against Natal for whom Whitfield and Bentley added an unbroken 201 for the second wicket, a record for the competition.

Collis King. Some bold hitting for Natal, but an inconsistent season. (Adrian Murrell)

Benson and Hedges Trophy

31 October 1984

at Pretoria

Western Province 224 for 9 (G.L. Ackermann 4 for 36)
Northern Transvaal 214

Western Province (2 pts) won by 10 runs

At 168 for 7, Northern Transvaal seemed well beaten, but Jones and Weidemann gave hope.

Nissan Shield – Round Two

3 November 1984

at Stellenbosch

Northern Transvaal 230 for 4 (N.T. Day 93 not out, K.D. Verdoorn 86)
Boland 125 (E.O. Simons 6 for 36)

Northern Transvaal won by 105 runs

at Cape Town

Western Province 'B' 138 (A.P. Kuiper 4 for 14)
Western Province 139 for 3

Western Province won by 7 wickets

Semi-Final – First Leg

at Johannesburg

Natal 246 for 7 (C.L. King 76)
Transvaal 249 for 4 (S.J. Cook 88, H.R. Fotheringham 51)

Transvaal won by 6 wickets

There were no surprises in the second round of the Nissan Shield. A third wicket stand of 131 between Day and Verdoorn, and fine fast-medium bowling by Eric Simons dashed Boland's hopes at Stellenbosch. At Cape Town, the senior side had no frights against Western Province 'B'. In the third round, or 'semi-finals' stage, Collis King and Paddy Clift lifted Natal with some fierce hitting, but an opening stand of 142 between Cook and Fotheringham set Transvaal on the road to an easy win.

Benson and Hedges Trophy

7 November 1984

at Johannesburg

Impalas 79
Transvaal 82 for 5

Transvaal (2 pts) won by 5 wickets

9 November 1984

Eastern Province 191
Natal 152 (W.K. Watson 4 for 14)

Eastern Province (2 pts) won by 39 runs

Castle Currie Cup

9, 10 and 12 November 1984

at Pretoria

Transvaal 408 for 8 dec (R.G. Pollock 114, C.E.B. Rice 102 not out, S.J. Cook 52) and 67 for 5
Northern Transvaal 232 (M. Yachad 124, A.J. Kourie 7 for 94) and 241 (A. Geringer 70)

Transvaal won by 5 wickets
Transvaal 20 pts, Northern Transvaal 5 pts

Castle Bowl

9, 10 and 11 November 1984

at Johannesburg

Northern Transvaal 'B' 155 (C.R. Norris 5 for 48) and 189 (C.R. Norris 4 for 15)
Transvaal 'B' 240 (H.A. Page 57, G.R. Grobler 4 for 80) and 105 for 6 (G.R. Grobler 4 for 58)

Transvaal 'B' won by 4 wickets
Transvaal 'B' 17 pts, Northern Transvaal 'B' 4 pts

The two first-class competitions began with a double for Transvaal. Their 'B' side always had command of the game at Wanderers with left-arm medium Craig Norris having splendid match figures of 9 for 63. In the senior match at Pretoria, the might of Transvaal was once more revealed. Cook and Fotheringham gave them a sound start and then Graeme Pollock hit his 60th century, his 114 coming in 143 minutes with twenty fours. Rice bolstered his side to a commanding total and Northern Transvaal, in spite of Yachad's 124 out of 195 for 6, fell to the slow left-arm of Alan Kourie and were forced to follow-on. At 83 for 6, they appeared to be heading for an innings defeat, but Anton Geringer, on his Currie Cup debut, hit 70 and shared a last wicket stand of 67 in 59 minutes with Eric Simons who then took 3 wickets as Transvaal scored the required runs at 5 an over.

Benson and Hedges Trophy

14 November 1984

at Green Point, Cape Town

Eastern Province 212 for 6 (P. Willey 109 not out)
Western Province 152

Eastern Province (2 pts) won by 60 runs

16 November 1984

Transvaal 209 (C.E.B. Rice 72, G.R. Grobler 4 for 37)
Northern Transvaal 182 (I.F.N. Weideman 60 not out)

Transvaal (2 pts) won by 27 runs

Going in at 35 for 2, Peter Willey hit a pugnacious century which led Eastern Province to their third Benson and Hedges win in as many matches. Transvaal also maintained their one hundred per cent record so that these two sides looked set for the final even though there was much of the tournament still to be played.

Alvin Kallicharran led Orange Free State by example and both he and his side enjoyed memorable seasons. (Adrian Murrell)

Nissan Shield

Semi-Final – Second Leg

18 November 1984

at Durban

Transvaal 250 for 5 (R.G. Pollock 74, K.A. McKenzie 67)
Natal 174 (B.J. Whitfield 72, A.J. Kourie 4 for 45)

Transvaal won by 76 runs

A third wicket stand of 137 between Pollock and McKenzie put the game out of Natal's reach and helped Transvaal to complete the double. The last 5 Natal wickets fell for 9 runs.

Castle Currie Cup

16, 17 and 18 November 1984

at Cape Town

Western Province 313 for 9 dec (A.P. Kuiper 87, P.H. Rayner 64, E.A. Moseley 4 for 33) and 45 for 5 (E.A. Moseley 4 for 13)
Eastern Province 133 and 221 (G.S. Cowley 56, G.S. le Roux 4 for 49)

Western Province won by 5 wickets
Western Province 21 pts, Eastern Province 4 pts

Castle Bowl

17, 18 and 19 November 1984

at Kimberley

Griqualand West 302 (M.J.P. Ford 77, M.N. Kellow 76) and 251 (G.P. van Rensburg 64)
Natal 'B' 294 (D.A. Scott 72, M.J. Pearse 51, G.N. Lister-James 50, G.P. van Rensburg 4 for 46) and 32 for 1

Match drawn
Griqualand West 6 pts, Natal 'B' 5 pts

at East London

Eastern Province 'B' 185 (I. Foulkes 5 for 50) and 244 (M.W. Rushmere 83, R.C. Ontong 4 for 71)
Border 283 (D.J. Cullinan 70, R.C. Ontong 55, G.L. Hayes 55, M.K. van Vuuren 4 for 59) and 147 for 3 (D.J. Cullinan 60 not out)

Border won by 7 wickets
Border 19 pts, Eastern Province 'B' 3 pts

Western Province had a most convincing start to their Currie Cup programme when they beat Eastern Province in two days at Newlands. The home side recovered from the depths of 53 for 3 through the efforts of Paul Rayner and new skipper Adrian Kuiper, but their total did not look too formidable a one. The combined attack of Jefferies, le Roux and Hobson totally demolished the visitors, however, who lost their last 9 wickets for 96 runs. They were saved from the indignity of an innings defeat by skipper Cowley and Moseley had a blistering seven-over spell before Western Province clinched victory.

In the Castle Bowl there was a somewhat uninspiring drawn game at Kimberley, but at East London, Rodney Ontong, who had maintained that Border could win the competition, led his side to a fine win and there were two excellent innings by 17-year old Darryl Cullinan, one of the

ABOVE: *Graeme Pollock, nearing retirement, but still a force for Transvaal and one of the world's great batsmen. (Argus)*

most exciting batting prospects to have emerged in the Republic for some years.

Castle Bowl

21, 22 and 23 November 1984

at Bloemfontein

Orange Free State 327 (C.J. van Heerden 74, A.I. Kallicharran 69, M.D. Makin 6 for 36) and 239 (M.D. Makin 6 for 99)
Natal 'B' 280 (D.A. Scott 67, A.C. Hudson 50, G.N. Lister-James 50, C.J.P.G. van Zyl 4 for 76) and 232 (P.H. Williams 89, C.J.P.G. van Zyl 5 for 56)

Orange Free State won by 54 runs
Orange Free State 16 pts, Natal 'B' 7 pts

22, 23 and 24 November 1984

at Cape Town

Western Province 'B' 175 (G.J. Parsons 4 for 65) and 297 (T.A. Clarke 82, I.M. Wingreen 72, P.D. Swart 61, G.J. Parsons 5 for 106)
Boland 173 (J. During 4 for 37) and 204 (G.J. Parsons 76)

Western Province 'B' won by 95 runs
Western Province 'B' 16 pts, Boland 5 pts

23, 24 and 25 November 1984

at Uitenhage

Northern Transvaal 'B' 274 (W. Kirsh 119, C.P.L. de Lange 58, K.G. Bauermeister 5 for 40) and 214 for 2 (V.F. du Preez 117)
Eastern Province 'B' 433 (M.W. Rushmere 114, D.G. Emslie 84, A.V. Birrell 55, M.B. Billson 54, G.L. Ackermann 6 for 137)

Match drawn
Eastern Province 'B' 6 pts, Northern Transvaal 'B' 5 pts

Castle Currie Cup

23, 24 and 26 November 1984

at Pretoria

Natal 170 (G. Grobler 4 for 32, E.O. Simons 4 for 43) and 245 (D. Bestall 96 not out, G. Grobler 5 for 65)
Northern Transvaal 293 (M. Yachad 97, N.T. Day 69, K.R. Cooper 5 for 80) and 126 for 4

Northern Transvaal won by 6 wickets
Northern Transvaal 20 pts, Natal 5 pts

24, 25 and 26 November 1984

at Johannesburg

Eastern Province 124 (I.K. Daniell 60, S.T. Clarke 5 for 29, A.J. Kourie 4 for 34) and 136
Transvaal 403 for 9 dec (C.E.B. Rice 121, S.J. Cook 107, A.J. Kourie 78)

Transvaal won by an innings and 143 runs
Transvaal 22 pts, Eastern Province 3 pts

Transvaal swept aside Eastern Province with contemptuous ease to assert their dominance in the Currie Cup. Ian Daniell alone offered any resistance to Sylvester Clarke and Alan Kourie. Jim Cook, with eighteen fours in his 107, and Clive Rice added 113 for Transvaal's fourth wicket and Rice and Kourie added 114 for the sixth so that Rice was able to declare at an impregnable total. Eastern Province succumbed limply for a second time.

At Pretoria, Northern Transvaal gained their first home win in the Currie Cup for twenty-three years and gave a most encouraging performance. The medium pace combination of Grobler, left-arm, and Simons, right-arm, was too much for Natal and Mandy Yachad and Noel Day then steered the home side to a comfortable lead in spite of Cooper's efforts. Darryl Bestall batted bravely and there was some fierce hitting by Robin Smith, but the home side were not to be denied. Noel Day established a provincial record with nine catches behind the stumps.

In the Castle Bowl at Uitenhage, both sides enjoyed batting practice and there were maiden centuries for Kirsh and Rushmere. At Newlands, a magnificent all-round performance by Gordon Parsons of Leicestershire could not save Boland from defeat. Makin was in the same position at Bloemfontein where he took a career best 12 for 135, but Alvin Kallicharran led the home side to a positive victory.

BELOW: *Faoud Bacchus hit a brisk century for Western Province in the Benson and Hedges Trophy match against Natal, but he proved a disappointing replacement for Graham Gooch. (George Herringshaw)*

Benson and Hedges Trophy

28 November 1984

at Pietermaritzburg

Western Province 275 for 5 (S.F.A. Bacchus 132, P.N. Kirsten 52)
Natal 124 (G.S. le Roux 4 for 20)

Western Province (2 pts) won by 151 runs

Nissan Shield

Semi-Finals – First Leg

1 December 1984

at East London

Border 199 (N.P. Minnaar 60, R.C. Ontong 60, H.A. Page 4 for 35)
Transvaal 203 for 6 (K.A. McKenzie 77 not out)

Transvaal won by 4 wickets

at Pretoria

Western Province 246 for 7 (P.N. Kirsten 105, R.F. Pienaar 50)
Northern Transvaal 177

Western Province won by 69 runs

The first leg of the semi-finals produced no surprises although Border died bravely, losing with only ten balls to spare.

Benson and Hedges Trophy

7 December 1984

at Pretoria

Northern Transvaal 236 for 6 (N.T. Day 66 not out)
Impalas 129

Northern Transvaal (2 pts) won by 107 runs

8, 9 and 10 December 1984

at Johannesburg

South African Universities 269 (G.J. Turner 66, R.F. Pienaar 54) and 150 (P.G. Amm 75)
Transvaal 221 (S.J. Cook 76, C.J. van Heerden 4 for 62) and 200 for 5 (M.S. Venter 64 not out)

Transvaal won by 5 wickets

Transvaal, including many 'B' team players in their side, were 95 for 6 in their first innings, but were rallied by acting skipper Jim Cook, batting at number seven. Jennings took nine catches behind the wicket.

Neal Radford enjoyed a fine season as a vital part of Transvaal's pace attack. (Sporting Pictures UK Ltd)

Laurie Potter, Griqualand West, had career best performances with bat and ball. (Adrian Murrell)

Benson and Hedges Trophy

12 December 1984

at Johannesburg

Transvaal 236 for 6 (S.J. Cook 60)
Natal 217

Transvaal (2 pts) won by 19 runs

The third win in the competition for Transvaal and the third defeat for Natal was a closer affair than the divergence between top and bottom of the table would suggest. Rice, Pollock and Cook gave the Transvaal innings substance, but Natal fought back well through Collis King and skipper Paddy Clift. They were eventually thwarted by the bowling of Clarke and Kourie. This win left Transvaal level at the top of the table with Eastern Province. Western Province, with 4 points, were in third place.

Castle Currie Cup

14, 15 and 16 December 1984

at Johannesburg

Transvaal 154 (S.J. Cook 80, E.O. Simons 4 for 34, A.M. Ferreira 4 for 26) and 210 (G. Grobler 4 for 70)
Northern Transvaal 161 (S.T. Clarke 5 for 38) and 148 (N.T. Day 55, S.T. Clarke 4 for 45)

Transvaal won by 55 runs
Transvaal 15 pts, Northern Transvaal 5 pts

14, 15 and 17 December 1984

at Port Elizabeth

Eastern Province 299 (M. Michau 71, P. Willey 56, P.B. Clift 4 for 52) and 184 for 8 dec (M. Michau 103, J.K. Lever 4 for 58, P.B. Clift 4 for 46)
Natal 257 (R.A. Smith 69, T.G. Shaw 6 for 42) and 131 for 7 (R.M. Bentley 61 not out, M.K. van Vuuren 4 for 45)

Match drawn
Eastern Province 6 pts, Natal 4 pts

Castle Bowl

13, 14 and 15 December 1984

at Durban

Border 308 for 7 dec (I. Foulkes 132 not out, R.C. Ontong 60) and 258 for 8 dec (D.J. Cullinan 100)
Natal 'B' 276 for 7 dec (P.H. Williams 79) and 152 for 5

Match drawn
Natal 'B' 8 pts, Border 7 pts

14, 15 and 17 December 1984

at Bloemfontein

Orange Free State 166 (A.I. Kallicharran 90, C.D. Mitchley 4 for 55) and 372 (J.J. Strydom 88, B.M. Osborne 58, A.M. Green 57, A.I. Kallicharran 53)
Transvaal 'B' 189 (B. Roberts 63, C.J.P.G. van Zyl 5 for 38) and 194 (C.J.P.G. van Zyl 7 for 71)

Orange Free State won by 155 runs
Orange Free State 15 pts, Transvaal 'B' 6 pts

at Stellenbosch

Griqualand West 305 (P.W. Romaines 85, K.C. Dugmore 67, L. Potter 65, O. Henry 4 for 92) and 148 (O. Henry 4 for 41, G.J. Parsons 4 for 46)

Gordon Parsons was one of the outstanding cricketers of the season. He was second in the first-class bowling averages, took a career best 9 for 72 for Boland against Transvaal 'B' at Johannesburg and was the most successful bowler in the Castle Bowl. He also averaged 24.37 with the bat and no English player enjoyed such a fine season. (Adrian Murrell)

Boland 284 for 8 dec (S.A. Jones 87, L. Potter 4 for 63) and 171 for 3 (B. Munnik 82 not out, D.P. le Roux 65)

Boland won by 7 wickets
Boland 13 pts, Griqualand West 6 pts

The medium pace attack of Simons and Ferreira gave the first indication that Transvaal were not invincible. Eighteen wickets fell on the first day and only Jim Cook came to terms with a difficult and lively wicket. Clarke and Radford bowled Transvaal back into the game, but a spirited ninth wicket stand between Visagie and Simons snatched a narrow lead for the visitors. Transvaal were 55 for 5 in their second innings and looked beaten, but the tail wagged furiously. In need of 204 to win, Northern Transvaal never recovered from 85 for 8 in spite of the brave efforts of Weidemann and Simons.

Consistent scoring was the feature at Port Elizabeth where Michau hit a maiden hundred and Shaw had career best bowling figures.

There were some fine individual performances at Durban where Ivor Foulkes and Rodney Ontong shared a fourth wicket stand of 148 for Border and Darryl Cullinan hit his second first-class century. Gordon Parsons was again in fine form for Boland and this time, in harness with Omar Henry, he brought his side victory. Laurie Potter and Paul Romaines began the match with a stand of 93 and Potter later took four wickets.

Alvin Kallicharran roused Orange Free State from despair and led them to a fine win at the Ramblers. His own first innings, coming in at 5 for 2, was masterly, but it was consistent batting application of the home side batsmen in the second innings and the inspired fast medium bowling of Cornelius van Zyl who took ten wickets in a match for the first time and had career best figures in the second innings that brought Orange Free State victory and took them to the top of the embryo Bowl table.

Peter Kirsten – centuries in successive matches for Western Province. (Argus)

Benson and Hedges Trophy

19 December 1984

at Durban

Natal 307 for 3 (B.J. Whitfield 101, R.A. Smith 98)
Impalas 181 (R.C. Ontong 51)

Natal (2 pts) won by 126 runs

21 December 1984

at Cape Town

Western Province 175
Transvaal 176 for 4 (S.J. Cook 60, R.G. Pollock 52 not out)

Transvaal (2 pts) won by 6 wickets

Castle Currie Cup

26, 27 and 28 December 1984

at Johannesburg

Natal 241 (M.B. Logan 66, R.A. Smith 53) and 170 (A.J. Kourie 5 for 69)
Transvaal 207 (R.G. Pollock 93, P.B. Clift 4 for 55) and 205 for 4 (S.J. Cook 76)

Transvaal won by 6 wickets
Transvaal 17 pts, Natal 8 pts

at Port Elizabeth

Western Province 167 (R.F. Pienaar 61, E.A. Moseley 4 for 48) and 250 (S.T. Jefferies 71, P.H. Rayner 69, A.P. Kuiper 55, E.A. Moseley 5 for 48, K.G. Bauermeister 4 for 66)
Eastern Province 420 for 5 dec (R.L.S. Armitage 100 not out, I.K. Daniell 95, P.G. Amm 74, D.J. Richardson 63)

Eastern Province won by an innings and 3 runs
Eastern Province 17 pts, Western Province 1 pt

Castle Bowl

26, 27 and 28 December 1984

at Pietermaritzburg

Transvaal 'B' 223 (B.M. McMillan 65, P.H. Williams 4 for 19, P.E. Smith 4 for 50) and 161 (N.R. Boonzaaier 52, P.E. Smith 4 for 51)
Natal 'B' 135 (M.J. Pearse 51, C.D. Mitchley 5 for 50) and 130

Transvaal 'B' won by 119 runs
Transvaal 'B' 17 pts, Natal 'B' 5 pts

at East London

Western Province 'B' 176 (G.J. Turner 51, E.N. Trotman 5 for 30) and 237 (G.D. Tullis 56, J.G. Thomas 5 for 68)
Border 305 (I.L. Howell 64, E.N. Trotman 59, M.B. Minnaar 5 for 92) and 109 for 3

Border won by 7 wickets
Border 17 pts, Western Province 'B' 3 pts

Transvaal won their fourth successive victory in the Currie Cup and looked unassailable at the head of the log, but Natal gave them their biggest fright of the season. Robin Smith and Whitfield gave Natal a good start with a stand of 98, but they then slumped to 126 for 6 against the varied Transvaal attack. They were lifted by Logan, but 241 remained a disappointing total. It became larger as Transvaal struggled against Lever and Clift. They would have been routed but for a magnificent 93 in 169 minutes by Graeme Pollock. He hit thirteen fours. Natal led by 34 on the first innings, but Kourie's spin restored the balance in favour of Transvaal who moved to victory without any further worries.

Transvaal's victory gained even more worth by the astonishing result at Port Elizabeth where second favourites Western Province, badly missing Gooch and McEwan, neither of whom was available for the season, were trounced by an innings. They were totally outplayed and there were unhappy consequences when Jefferies was reported for misconduct on the field. Ezra Moseley brought about their downfall with the ball and Ian Daniell and Philip Amm gave the foundation to Eastern Province's mighty score with an opening stand of 162. Robert Armitage hit his fourth first-class hundred, Richardson hit fiercely in a stand of 108 and the visitors were only saved from complete humiliation by the middle order efforts of Rayner, Pienaar, Kuiper and Jefferies.

In the Bowl matches, Transvaal 'B' kept up the challenge at the top with a convincing win in a low scoring match in which Cyril Mitchley starred with his medium pace. Remarkably, in East London, Trotman, who had been used as wicket-keeper, was given the new ball and put Border on the way to a comfortable win. There was resolute batting throughout Border's innings and, under Ontong, they played convincingly as a team.

Castle Bowl

31 December 1984, 1 and 2 January 1985

at Pretoria

Border 139 (P.A. Robinson 4 for 31) and 194 (G.C.G. Fraser 78 not out, J. van Duyker 4 for 40)
Northern Transvaal 'B' 257 (W. Kirsh 64, G.W. Jones 51) and 77 for 0

Northern Transvaal 'B' won by 10 wickets
Northern Transvaal 'B' 19 pts, Border 5 pts

Border's hopes of winning the Bowl received a severe setback with this second defeat. Jones, Ackermann and Robinson boosted Northern with some aggressive batting at the end of their first innings.

Castle Currie Cup

31 December 1984, 1 and 2 January 1985

at Durban

Northern Transvaal 193 (A.M. Ferreira 52) and 295 (M. Yachad 60, A.M. Ferreira 57, L.J. Barnard 55, T.J. Packer 5 for 90)
Natal 420 for 9 dec (T.R. Madsen 111, B.J. Whitfield 76, C.L. King 75, E.O. Simons 4 for 74) and 69 for 2

Natal won by 8 wickets
Natal 18 pts, Northern Transvaal 3 pts

1, 2 and 3 January 1985

at Cape Town

Transvaal 227 (C.E.B. Rice 62, C.R. Norris 55, D. Norman 4 for 53) and 275 for 8 dec (C.E.B. Rice 57, K.A. McKenzie 55)
Western Province 232 (S.F.A. Bacchus 59, S.T. Clarke 5 for 41) and 255 (P.N. Kirstan 80, A.P. Kuiper 68, A.J. Kourie 4 for 62, S.T. Clarke 4 for 106)

Transvaal won by 15 runs
Transvaal 18 pts, Western Province 8 pts

Natal gained ample revenge for their defeat in Pretoria with a comfortable win over Northern Transvaal in Durban. The visitors batted poorly and were indebted to a seventh wicket stand of 61 between Ferreira and Visagie for their innings having any substance. Whitfield held Natal's innings together and King hit lustily before wicket-keeper Trevor Madsen hit his maiden century. Packer and Lever encountered more resistance when the visitors batted again, but the result was never in doubt.

The annual New Year encounter between Transvaal and Western Province maintained the tradition of splendid cricket that has always been a feature of these matches. It was sullied only on the last day when Jennings and Kourie chose to show dissent and were disciplined. Transvaal struggled initially against Norman and Jefferies and they were revived only by a fourth wicket stand of 107 between Norris and Rice. It was apparent that the great side was ageing and form was becoming a little less predictable. Western Province looked set for a big lead as Bacchus, Rayner and Kirsten savaged Kourie's spin and took their side to 164 for 2. Then Sylvester Clarke broke through and he and Norris destroyed the middle order so that the expected big lead ended at a paltry five. Transvaal batted with more conviction in their second innings and Rice and McKenzie added 105 for the sixth wicket. Asked to make 271 to win, Western Province soon lost Bacchus, but a ferocious stand of 116 in an hour for the fifth wicket raised hopes. They hit Clarke for 65 off 6 overs. Then Kourie dismissed both batsmen and the target always remained just out of reach, the last four wickets falling for 7 runs. Richard Ryall took eight catches and made two stumpings to equal Jennings' record and Jennings, as well as his disciplinary problem, seemed very much under threat as South Africa's number one wicket-keeper. Large crowds watched all three days play.

Nissan Shield

Semi-Finals – Second Leg

5 January 1985

at Johannesburg

Transvaal 258 for 5 (C.E.B. Rice 95, S.J. Cook 86)
Border 206 (R.C. Ontong 72, H.A. Page 4 for 17)

Transvaal won by 52 runs

at Cape Town

Western Province 218 (L. Seeff 52, A. Geringer 5 for 38)
Northern Transvaal 211 (A. Geringer 67, S.T. Jefferies 4 for 24)

Western Province won by 7 runs

Transvaal and Western Province completed doubles in the semi-finals to leave no ambiguities as to who was to contest the Nissan Shield Final. Rice and Cook dominated to take Transvaal to a comfortable win in a high scoring match in Johannesburg while the game at Newlands provided a closer finish. It was Steve Jefferies' bowling which proved decisive.

Sylvester Clarke (Transvaal) – the most feared bowler in South Africa, 58 wickets at less than 13 runs apiece. (Adrian Murrell)

Castle Bowl

10, 11 and 12 January 1985

at Kimberley

Griqualand West 209 (W.M. van der Merwe 5 for 54) and 233 (L.M. Phillips 82 not out)
Orange Free State 242 (A.I. Kallicharran 110, R.A. le Roux 66, G.P. van Rensburg 6 for 91) and 201 for 3 (R.A. le Roux 89 not out, A.I. Kallicharran 81 not out)

Orange Free State won by 7 wickets
Orange Free State 18 pts, Griqualand West 7 pts

12, 13 and 14 January 1985

at Pietermaritzburg

Natal 'B' 234 (M.J. Pearse 55, J. Havenga 4 for 60) and 275 for 4 dec (M.D. Mellor 124 not out)
Eastern Province 'B' 148 (D.H. Howell 59, C.M. Lister-James 4 for 55) and 173 for 4 (D.H. Howell 52)

Match drawn
Natal 'B' 8 pts, Eastern Province 'B' 5 pts

at Johannesburg

Boland 168 (C.D. Mitchley 4 for 46) and 198 (L.L. Roberts 54, G.J. Parsons 51, B.M. McMillan 4 for 53)
Transvaal 'B' 183 (B. Roberts 55, G.J. Parsons 9 for 72) and 184 for 8

Transvaal 'B' won by 2 wickets
Transvaal 'B' 16 pts, Boland 5 pts

Orange Free State won their third match in succession and asserted their challenge to Transvaal 'B' at the top of the Castle Bowl, trailing them by 7 points with a game in hand. Free State's victory owed everything to skipper Alvin Kallicharran. Coming in at 58 for 3 in the first innings after Gert van Rensburg's medium pace had disturbed the earlier batsmen, he shared a stand of 100 with Raymond le Roux and went on to complete a fine century. In the second innings, Free State, having been set 201 at 4 an over, had lost Green, Osborne and van Heerden for 71 when Kallicharran again joined le Roux. This time they added 130 and won the match.

At Pietermaritzburg, Natal 'B' failed to force home the advantage of Mellor's hundred and a first innings lead of 86, but at Wanderers, Transvaal 'B' snatched victory when all seemed lost and thwarted a wonderful all-round performance by Gordon Parsons. The home side were saved by Roberts and Mitchley after Parsons had reduced them to 40 for 5. In spite of Parsons taking a career best 9 for 72, they took a first innings lead of 15. Nor had the Leicestershire player finished. Boland were 98 for 8 in their second innings, but he and Roberts, who hit a maiden fifty on his first-class debut, added 51. Needing 184 to win, the home side went from 112 for 3 to 170 for 8 against Parsons and Traut, but McBride and Kerr won the match with a stand of 14 which were made amid great excitement.

Castle Currie Cup

11, 12 and 13 January 1985

at Port Elizabeth

Transvaal 379 (H.R. Fotheringham 184, S.J. Cook 77) and 171 for 6 dec (R.G. Pollock 53)
Eastern Province 234 (P.G. Amm 53, S.T. Clarke 5 for 52) and 109 for 8 (H.A. Page 4 for 12)

Match drawn
Transvaal 8 pts, Eastern Province 6 pts

12, 13 and 14 January 1985

at Cape Town

Western Province 295 (P.N. Kirsten 52, H.L. Alleyne 5 for 103) and 198 for 2 (P.H. Rayner 69 not out, S.F.A. Bacchus 65)
Natal 392 (D. Bestall 134 not out, C.L. King 94, B.J. Whitfield 57, R.M. Bentley 50, D.L. Hobson 5 for 92)

Match drawn
Natal 10 pts, Western Province 6 pts

Transvaal failed to win for the first time in the season when they were thwarted by a stubborn innings from Philip Amm. Transvaal's first innings was dominated by a career best from Henry Fotheringham. Eastern Province, 103 for 8 in reply, seemed destined for the follow-on and a possible innings defeat after Sylvester Clarke had torn apart their middle order. Amm and Ezra Moseley added 61 for the ninth wicket, and Moseley and Michael van Vuuren put on 70 for the last wicket. Transvaal still led by 145 and Rice delayed his declaration too long, for there was little chance that Eastern Province would score the 317 that was asked. Page's left-arm medium pace caused problems and they were 67 for 7 before Amm found reliable partners in Bauermeister and Moseley.

The highlight of a somewhat tedious draw at Newlands was Natal's fourth wicket stand of 144 between Bestall and Collis King. The draw left both sides wondering if they would make the semi-final stage of the Currie Cup for only 12 points separated the four sides below Transvaal.

Castle Bowl

17, 18 and 19 January 1985

at Pietersburg

Boland 121 (P.A. Robinson 5 for 61, I.F.N. Weideman 4 for 52) and 193 for 4 (N.M. Lambrechts 58)
Northern Transvaal 'B' 269 (V.F. du Preez 74)

Match drawn
Northern Transvaal 'B' 7 pts, Boland 3 pts

18, 19 and 20 January 1985

at Johannesburg

Transvaal 'B' 374 for 7 dec (B. Roberts 90, K.J. Rule 68, N.R. Boonzaaier 52 not out, G.W. Johnson 50, B.A. Matthews 4 for 58) and 53 for 0
Western Province 'B' 222 (I.M. Wingreen 62, C.D. Mitchley 4 for 40, J.J. Hooper 4 for 65) and 203 (I.M. Wingreen 83, A.G. Elgar 62, K.J. Kerr 5 for 36)

Transvaal 'B' won by 10 wickets
Transvaal 'B' 18 pts, Western Province 'B' 3 pts

Weather frustrated Northern Transvaal 'B' after they had bowled out Boland in 21.4 overs although their batting, runs coming at little more than 2 an over, did not help their cause.

Transvaal 'B' overwhelmed Western Province 'B' with a consistent batting performance in which Bruce Roberts hit a career best. The visitors were well served by openers Allan Elgar and Ivan Wingreen who shared stands of 104 and 139 only to see the remaining batsmen flounder. Transvaal extended their lead in the competition to 25 points so putting the onus on Orange Free State and Border to win their outstanding matches.

Castle Currie Cup

18, 19 and 20 January 1985

at Cape Town

Northern Transvaal 169 (L.J. Barnard 54, S.T. Jefferies 4 for 39) and 219 (S.T. Jefferies 4 for 61)
Western Province 408 for 8 dec (P.N. Kirstan 126 not out, L. Seeff 71, A.P. Kuiper 64, W.F. Morris 4 for 97)

Western Province won by an innings and 20 runs
Western Province 19 pts, Northern Transvaal 2 pts

19, 20 and 21 January 1985

at Durban

Natal 225 and 175 (R.M. Bentley 75, A.J. Kourie 5 for 61)
Transvaal 421 (C.E.B. Rice 126, K.A. McKenzie 115, A.J. Kourie 54 not out)

Transvaal won by an innings and 21 runs
Transvaal 23 pts, Natal 6 pts

Transvaal, assured of first place in the Currie Cup log, and Western Province gained innings victories which placed them ahead of the other challengers. Western Province's victory left Northern Transvaal and Eastern Province vying for the fourth semi-final place. The bowling of Jefferies and Hobson was too much for Northern Transvaal whose attack was punished by Kirsten, Seeff and Kuiper.

In Durban, pace in the first innings and spin in the second was the undoing of Natal. The home side were well in the game, however, for, having made 225, they had Transvaal at 78 for the loss of Cook, Norris, Fotheringham and Pollock. Then Clive Rice was joined by Kevin McKenzie and they shared a partnership of 237 which made Transvaal immune from defeat and established the platform for victory.

Castle Bowl

24 and 25 January 1985

at Welkom

Northern Transvaal 'B' 118 and 172 (S. Vercueil 59 not out, C.J.P.G. van Zyl 8 for 84)
Orange Free State 300 (W.M. van der Merwe 96, A.I. Kallicharran 62)

Orange Free State won by an innings and 10 runs
Orange Free State 21 pts, Northern Transvaal 'B' 5 pts

25, 26 and 27 January 1985

at Constantia

Western Province 'B' 335 (D. Rundle 110, A.G. Elgar 97, J. Havenga 5 for 88) and 263 for 9 dec
Eastern Province 'B' 275 for 4 dec (T.B. Reid 120 not out, A.V. Birrell 82) and 326 for 4 (M.W. Rushmere 119 not out, T.B. Reid 111)

Eastern Province 'B' won by 6 wickets
Eastern Province 'B' 19 pts, Western Province 'B' 7 pts

26, 27 and 28 January 1985

at East London

Griqualand West 232 (P.W. Romaines 55) and 288 for 6 dec (L. Potter 165 not out, M.N. Kellow 50)
Border 227 for 8 dec (E.N. Trotman 65, A.P. Beukes 4 for 50) and 296 for 5 (E.N. Trotman 102, D.J. Cullinan 71)

Border won by 5 wickets
Border 15 pts, Griqualand West 5 pts

Orange Free State emphasised their challenge for the Castle Bowl with their fourth win in as many matches. They beat Northern Transvaal 'B' inside two days and moved to within four points of Transvaal 'B' with a game in hand. A good all round attack disposed of Northern Transvaal 'B' in 38 overs, but Free State slipped to 57 for 4 and 144 for 6. Left-hander Willem van der Merwe then hit a career best blistering 96 and the last two wickets added 98 runs. Free State's heroics had not finished yet for Cornelius van Zyl took a career best 8 for 84, equalling the state record for most wickets in an innings.

Border won an exciting match of fluctuating fortunes in East London and held third place in the table. Griqualand West took a narrow first innings lead which was nullified when they slipped to 23 for 3 in their second innings. Kent's Laurie Potter then hit a career best 165 not out and Beukes was able to declare and set Border to make 294 at nearly five an over. Minaar went at 18, but Trotman and Cullinan put on 156 brisk runs for the second wicket. They fell at 174 and 182, but skipper Ontong maintained the necessary scoring rate and, aided by Foulkes and Hayes, saw his side home.

Elgar and Wingreen again proved their reliability as an opening pair when they began the match in Constantia with a stand of 96. Rundle's maiden first-class century provided the

Graham Johnson, captain of Transvaal 'B' who won the Castle Bowl. (Simon Miles, Allsport)

middle innings solidity and Western, with Zimbabwe's Duncan Fletcher in their side for the first time, reached an impressive total. Eastern replied with an opening stand of 63 and a second wicket stand of 135 as Terry Reid hit a career best. Emslie declared 60 runs in arrears in an effort to force a result, but Minaar offered a stiff target when, after a solid batting display throughout the order, he asked Eastern to make 324 at $4\frac{1}{2}$ an over. They lost 3 wickets for 99 runs when Reid was joined by Mark Rushmere. They added 173, a provincial 'B' record, and Reid hit his second century of the match. Rushmere hit his second hundred in three matches and a career best as he carried his bat to give Eastern Province 'B' a memorable victory.

Castle Currie Cup

25, 26 and 28 January 1985

at Pretoria

Northern Transvaal 235 (T.G. Shaw 4 for 51) and 265 for 5 dec (M. Yachad 90, W. Kirsh 89)
Eastern Province 161 (E.O. Simons 6 for 26) and 113 (A.M. Ferreira 6 for 23)

Northern Transvaal won by 226 runs
Northern Transvaal 16 pts, Eastern Province 4 pts

26, 27 and 28 January 1985

at Durban

Natal 228 (T.R. Madsen 54, G.S. le Roux 4 for 46, D.L. Hobson 4 for 54) and 245 for 6 dec (B.J. Whitfield 96 not out)
Western Province 280 (P.N. Kirsten 133, T.J. Packer 4 for 75, H.L. Alleyne 4 for 83) and 46 for 1

Match drawn
Western Province 8 pts, Natal 5 pts

Peter Kirsten scored his second hundred in successive matches in an otherwise rather laboured draw in Durban. The other noteworthy performance of the match was Whitfield's 96 not out in 92 overs when Natal batted again. Richie Ryall again emphasised his challenge to Jennings' title as South Africa's leading wicket-keeper with six catches and two stumpings in the match and another fine display behind the stumps.

In a low scoring game in Pretoria Northern Transvaal were bowled to victory by Simons and Ferreira, and therefore almost certainly into a place in the semi-finals of the Cup. The only batsmen to excel were Mandy Yachad and William Kirsh who began Northern Transvaal's second innings with a match-winning stand of 157.

Benson and Hedges Trophy

30 January 1985

at Cape Town

Western Province 166 (S.F.A. Bacchus 53, P.N. Kirsten 50, C.J. van Heerden 5 for 19)
Impalas 112

Western Province (2 pts) won by 54 runs

Van Heerden's bowling performance was the best for Impalas in the competition.

Nissan Shield Final
TRANSVAAL *v.* WESTERN PROVINCE

The Nissan Shield Final has now become one of the outstanding events of the South African season and a capacity crowd assembled at the Wanderers eagerly anticipating a keen contest between the two strongest sides in the competition. They must have been a little disappointed for, although there was some fine bowling by Page and some excellent batting by Cook and Fotheringham, the match was very one-sided and Transvaal ran out easy winners.

When Kuiper won the toss he had anticipated, and hoped, that his side would make 280 on a good wicket. His hopes were encouraged by some loose bowling from Clarke who was completely unable to find his line and bowled three wides in his opening over. The batsmen failed to capitalise on Clarke's extravagancies, however, and even though Radford was far from impressive, only 25 runs came in the first 10 overs for the loss of Bacchus who faced 26 balls for his 3 runs. He was a victim of Page's bowling and it was Page who blighted the Western innings, keeping the batsmen on the front foot on the line of the off stump, and removing Rayner and Kirsten as well as Bacchus in the space of 26 deliveries.

Kirsten had looked in good form hitting Mitchley for

Clive Rice not only led Transvaal to triumph in every competition, but took his 330th wicket in the Currie Cup when he bowled Anton Ferreira in the final. (David Munden)

NISSAN SHIELD FINAL – TRANSVAAL *v.* WESTERN PROVINCE
2 February 1985 at Wanderers, Johannesburg

WESTERN PROVINCE			
	S.F.A. Bacchus	c Jennings, b Page	3
	P.H. Rayner	c Jennings, b Page	11
	L. Seeff	c Pollock, b Mitchley	67
	P.N. Kirsten	c Jennings, b Page	11
	R.F. Pienaar	lbw, b Kourie	17
	S.T. Jefferies	c Clarke, b Kourie	18
	A.P. Kuiper†	c Jennings, b Mitchley	11
	A.G. Elgar	c Pollock, b Clarke	18
	G.S. le Roux	not out	24
	R.J. Ryall*	not out	2
	D. Norman		
	Extras	lb 5, w 7, nb 6	18
	(55 overs)	(for 8 wickets)	200

	O	M	R	W
Clarke	11	3	18	1
Radford	11	—	43	—
Page	11	2	48	3
Mitchley	11	—	42	2
Kourie	11	1	44	2

FALL OF WICKETS
1- 21, 2- 25, 3- 44, 4- 86, 5- 118, 6- 144, 7- 170, 8- 173

TRANSVAAL			
	S.J. Cook	c Ryall, b le Roux	85
	H.R. Fotheringham	not out	103
	C.E.B. Rice†	not out	3
	R.G. Pollock		
	K.A. McKenzie		
	A.J. Kourie		
	H.A. Page		
	R.V. Jennings*		
	S.T. Clarke		
	N.V. Radford		
	C.D. Mitchley		
	Extras	b 7, lb 2, w 2	11
	(46 overs)	(for 1 wicket)	202

	O	M	R	W
le Roux	11	2	47	1
Jefferies	1	—	6	—
Kuiper	9	—	46	—
Kirsten	9	2	28	—
Norman	11	—	50	—
Pienaar	2	—	4	—
Elgar	3	—	12	—

FALL OF WICKET
1- 171

Umpires: D.H. Bezuidenhout and O.R. Schoof

Transvaal won by 9 wickets

successive boundaries, but once he fell to the Page–Jennings combination, the Western Province innings lost all authority and Rice was able to employ attacking fields even for his spinners.

With a total of 200 to defend, Western Province needed an early break-through, but after 10 overs Transvaal were 47 for 0 and the contest over. Additionally, Stephen Jefferies had broken down and retired from the attack after one over and Garth le Roux had been savaged for 17 in his opening spell of four overs, a rate of scoring greater than Transvaal needed throughout their innings.

That the game continued as a spectacle was due entirely to the sparkling batting of Jimmy Cook and Henry Fotheringham. Kuiper was forced to use occasional spinners Roy Pienaar and Allan Elgar as replacements for Jefferies, and Fotheringham, in particular, thrived against all the spinners.

Cook was out in the thirty-seventh over after sharing an opening stand of 171. It is possible that Transvaal could have won with some 15 overs to spare, but Rice nursed Fotheringham to his century which came off the last ball of the forty-sixth over of the match and gave Transvaal victory by 9 wickets with 9 overs to spare, a most emphatic win.

All the honours went to Transvaal. Sylvester Clarke, rather luckily, won the individual bowling award, Ray Jennings was named as the outstanding fielder and Henry Fotheringham the best batsman. Western Province, chastened, were left feeling that perhaps they needed a more professional approach in preparation for such a game as this.

Castle Bowl

7, 8 and 9 February 1985

at Port Elizabeth

Eastern Province 'B' 346 for 8 dec (I.K. Daniell 101, M.B. Billson 94, C.J.P.G. van Zyl 4 for 74) and 113 for 3
Orange Free State 184 (A.M. Green 64, R.L.S. Armitage 4 for 50, D. Ferrant 4 for 35) and 273 (A.I. Kallicharran 63, B.M. Osborne 61, W.M. van der Merwe 58)

Eastern Province 'B' won by 7 wickets
Eastern Province 'B' 20 pts, Orange Free State 4 pts

8, 9 and 11 February 1985

at Stellenbosch

Boland 275 for 8 dec (D.P. le Roux 70, O. Henry 50) and 216 for 7 dec (D.P. le Roux 71, K.J. Barnett 59)
Natal 'B' 194 and 221 (D.K. Pearse 58, O. Henry 4 for 64)

Boland won by 76 runs
Boland 19 pts, Natal 'B' 5 pts

Orange Free State's ambitions in the Castle Bowl received a severe setback at the Union Cricket Club ground in Port Elizabeth. The home side lost both openers for 31, but Ian Daniell equalled his career best score and provided the middle order with necessary substance. Coming in at number six, Mark Billson put the Free State attack to total disarray with a hard hit career best 94. He had fine support from wicket-keeper Tullis and Eastern reached an impressive 346 before Emslie declared on Billson's dismissal. A good innings by Allan Green could not save Free State from avoiding the follow-on, Ferrant and Armitage doing the damage. Six wickets were lost before the arrears were cleared, but a late fifty from van der Merwe at least set Eastern Province a reasonable target. The points obtained in this match brought Orange Free State level with Transvaal 'B', but the defeat virtually cost them the title.

At Stellenbosch, a second innings opening stand of 104 between Kim Barnett and Darryl le Roux consolidated Boland's first innings advantage and good all-round cricket by Omar Henry played a significant part in their victory.

Castle Currie Cup

8, 9 and 11 February 1985

at Pretoria

Northern Transvaal 140 (N.T. Day 51, D. Norman 5 for 38) and 205 for 7 dec (L.J. Barnard 65, A.P. Kuiper 4 for 55)
Western Province 104 (E.O. Simons 4 for 26, A.M. Ferreira 4 for 32) and 93 for 6 (L. Seeff 52)

Match drawn
Northern Transvaal 5 pts, Western Province 5 pts

9, 10 and 11 February 1985

at Durban

Eastern Province 213 for 4 dec (T.B. Reid 56, M.D. Makin 4 for 81)
Natal 5 for 0

Match drawn
No points

Rain reduced play to only a few hours on the last day at Durban. Western Province engaged in a dogged, rain-interrupted draw at Berea Park. Northern batted slowly, but they gained a first innings advantage thanks again to Simons and Ferreira. More stubborn batting on a difficult wicket gave them a further advantage and Western Province were grateful for rain in the end. The draw and sharing of points gave Northern the chance of gaining a home draw in the semi-finals from their last match.

Castle Bowl

14, 15 and 16 February 1985

at Pretoria

Northern Transvaal 'B' 156 (P.L. Symcox 63, P.A. Koen 4 for 31, R.R. Lawrenson 4 for 32) and 163 (D.B. Rundle 4 for 37)
Western Province 'B' 131 (G.L. Ackermann 5 for 42) and 180 (G.L. Ackermann 7 for 69)

Northern Transvaal 'B' won by 8 runs
Northern Transvaal 'B' 15 pts, Western Province 'B' 5 pts

15, 16 and 17 February 1985

at Kimberley

Transvaal 'B' 328 for 8 dec (P.L. Selsick 183, C.R. Norris 74, L. Potter 4 for 88)
Griqualand West 120 (P.W. Romaines 53, J.J. Hooper 5 for 29) and 205 (K.J. Kerr 5 for 35)

Transvaal 'B' won by an innings and 3 runs
Transvaal 'B' 22 pts, Griqualand West 4 pts

Transvaal 'B' finished their Castle Bowl campaign with a commanding victory at Kimberley which left Orange Free State the hardest of tasks in attempting to deprive them of the title. Peter Selsick's mighty maiden first-class hundred and his opening stand of 165 with Craig Norris set the tone of Transvaal's dominance and Griqualand West offered little resistance in their first innings and only some late defiance in the second.

At Berea Park, Northern Transvaal 'B' won one of the most exciting games of the season. They were 83 for 7 in their first innings and were salvaged by Patrick Symcox. Gerald Ackermann then bowled them to a 25-run lead, ably assisted by van Duyker. Bowlers continued to dominate as Northern, 84 for 5, reached 163 in their second innings so leaving Western Province 'B' to make 189 for victory. Once again Ackermann was the hero returning a career best 7 for 69. Western recovered from 48 for 4 to 156 for 8, but when the ninth wicket fell they were still 12 short of victory, and Ackermann caught and bowled the defiant Knowles 3 runs later to give his side victory.

Castle Currie Cup

15, 16 and 17 February 1985

at Johannesburg

Western Province 150 (L. Seeff 73) and 148 (A.J. Kourie 4 for 40, H.A. Page 4 for 56)
Transvaal 369 for 6 dec (H.R. Fotheringham 80, C.E.B. Rice 67, R.G. Pollock 52)

Transvaal won by an innings and 71 runs
Transvaal 21 pts, Western Province 3 pts

at Port Elizabeth

Northern Transvaal 239 (N.T. Day 84, L.J. Barnard 52) and 84 for 7 (M. Yachad 53)
Eastern Province 83 (I.F.N. Weideman 6 for 43) and 239 (G.S. Cowley 87, W.F. Morris 5 for 83)

Northern Transvaal won by 3 wickets
Northern Transvaal 16 pts, Eastern Province 2 pts

Transvaal completed the Currie Cup league fixtures in convincing fashion as they totally outplayed Western Province, considered to be their strongest rivals. In spite of Seeff's brave innings, Western Province were always struggling against the Transvaal pace attack. The home side, in contrast, gave a consistent batting display to take a lead of 219. Western floundered again and their last six wickets fell for the addition of 31 runs.

A hard earned win, threatened only by last day nerves, took Northern Transvaal above Western Province in the table and gave them home advantage in the semi-final. Their innings was founded on the middle order batting of Day and Barnard, but it was the remarkable bowling of Izak Weideman which shattered Eastern Province. The medium pacer had a career best 6 for 43 as the home side were shot out for 83. Following-on, they were 102 for 6, but skipper Gavin Cowley played a brave knock and Northern had to bat again. They had ample time in which to get the 84 that they needed, but they panicked against the off-spin of Peter Willey and the slow left-arm of Timothy Shaw on a wearing wicket. It took them 54 overs and the loss of 7 wickets to get the runs with only opener Mandy Yachad showing common sense and nerve.

Currie Cup Log

	P	W	L	D	Pts
Transvaal	8	7	—	1	144
Northern Transvaal	8	3	4	1	72
Western Province	8	2	3	3	71
Natal	8	1	3	4	56
Eastern Province	8	1	4	3	42

Currie Cup Semi-Finals

22, 23, 25 and 26 February 1985

at Pretoria

Western Province 325 (A.P. Kuiper 86, L. Seeff 76, S.F.A. Bacchus 58, E.O. Simons 4 for 62) and 160
Northern Transvaal 371 (M. Yachad 120, E.O. Simons 58, A. Geringer 56, L.J. Barnard 51) and 120 for 2 (M. Yachad 62)
Northern Transvaal won by 8 wickets

23, 24 and 25 February 1985

at Johannesburg

Natal 308 for 9 dec (B.J. Whitfield 90, M.B. Logan 81, A.J. Kourie 4 for 115) and 139 (H.A. Page 5 for 31, A.J. Kourie 4 for 53)
Transvaal 451 for 6 dec (S.J. Cook 140, H.R. Fotheringham 100, R.G. Pollock 84, M.S. Venter 53)
Transvaal won by an innings and 4 runs

The resurgence of Northern Transvaal continued and a confident display against Western Province took them into the Currie Cup Final. The visitors were never entirely happy on the first day and owed much to skipper Adrian Kuiper who shared a sixth wicket stand of 104 with Turner to lift his side to a respectable score. Northern Transvaal were well served again by Mandy Yachad who put on 120 with skipper Barnard for the second wicket. It looked as if their efforts had been in vain when the middle order batted inconsistently, but Simons at number eight, enjoying a splendid season, hit a maiden fifty and took his side to a useful first innings lead. He then took 3 wickets as Western Province slumped to 86 for 6. They never effectively recovered and Northern Transvaal swept into the final scoring the runs they needed at 5 an over.

In Johannesburg, Natal got off to a fine start as Whitfield and Logan put on 158 for the first wicket. The later batsmen failed to build on this and the last 8 wickets fell for 82 runs. That formidable opening pair, Cook and Fotheringham, then dominated the match with an opening stand of 232. Venter and Pollock built on this and Transvaal took a lead of 143 before Rice declared. A dispirited Natal side had little left to offer and succumbed to the pace of Page and the spin of Kourie to go down by an innings.

Castle Bowl

28 February, 1 and 2 March 1985

at Cape Town

Orange Free State 471 (R.J. East 163 not out, A.M. Green 84, A.I. Kallicharran 79, B.A. Matthews 4 for 109) and 54 for 4
Western Province 'B' 280 (A.G. Elgar 94, V.M. van der Merwe 4 for 41, C.J.P.G. van Zyl 4 for 62) and 310 (I.M. Wingreen 62, R.P. Richardson 52 not out, C.J.P.G. van Zyl 5 for 82)
Match drawn
Orange Free State 13 pts, Western Province 'B' 7 pts

1, 2 and 3 March 1985

at Cradock

Griqualand West 176 and 294 for 2 (P.W. Romaines 170 not out, L. Potter 62 not out)
Eastern Province 'B' 436 for 7 dec (M.B. Billson 91, M.W. Rushmere 82, R.L.S. Armitage 76, D.G. Emslie 70, M.K. van Vuuren 60)
Match drawn
Eastern Province 'B' 8 pts, Griqualand West 3 pts

1, 2 and 4 March 1985

at Stellenbosch

Boland 201 (D.P. le Roux 57, I.L. Howell 6 for 60) and 111 for 3 dec (D.P. le Roux 64)
Border 4 for 0 dec and 67
Boland won by 241 runs
Boland 12 pts, Border 5 pts

Orange Free State failed in a most courageous attempt to win the Castle Bowl, thwarted in the end by the Western Province tail. Needing to score heavily and quickly, Orange Free State took *eight* batting points as they reached 471 at 4.6 an over. It was heady stuff. They were given a fine start by Allan Green who hit his highest score in South Africa, but their chief hero was Robert East who summoned his renowned hitting powers to reach a fiercely struck 163 not out. He received fine support from Kallicharran, van der Merwe and van Zyl. It was the last two who were mainly instrumental in bowling out the home side for 280, opening batsman Elgar providing the biggest obstacle to their success. Western Province 'B' followed-on 191 in arrears and when they lost their first six second innings wickets for 185 it seemed that Orange Free State would win and gain the ten points that they needed for the title. The seventh wicket went down at 226, but the last three wickets, thanks mainly to Richardson and Koen, added 84 and used up vital time so that Free State were denied victory and the title. Eventually, they needed 120 to win at nearly ten an over which was a little too much even for their enthusiasm.

The bat dominated at Standard C.C. ground, Cradock. After both openers had gone for 65, Eastern Province 'B' saw the next five of their batsmen reach fifty. In Griqualand West's second innings Paul Romaines hit his highest score in South Africa and shared a stand of 120, undefeated, with Laurie Potter.

Weather ruined the match at Oude Libertas, but Rodney Ontong breathed life back into the game when he declared after Kim Barnett had bowled one ball. Jones declared in turn and set Border to make 309 to win. It proved far too great a task. Border collapsed in 32.3 overs and only number nine Ian Howell, who had earlier taken a career best 6 for 6, reached double figures.

There was encouraging news to offset the disappointments suffered by Orange Free State and Border in that both associations were to be admitted to the Currie Cup competition in 1985–86.

Castle Bowl Log

	P	W	L	D	Pts
Transvaal 'B'	6	5	1	—	96
Orange Free State	6	4	1	1	87
Border	6	3	2	1	68
Eastern Province 'B'	6	2	1	3	61
Boland	6	3	2	1	57
Northern Transvaal 'B'	6	2	2	2	55
Western Province 'B'	6	1	4	1	47
Natal 'B'	6	—	3	3	38
Griqualand West	6	—	4	2	31

Benson and Hedges Trophy

1 March 1985

at Durban

Natal 164 for 7
Northern Transvaal 168 for 6

Northern Transvaal (2 pts) won by 4 wickets

Northern Transvaal's victory, achieved mainly because of Geringer's 32 not out, brought them a realistic chance of reaching the final against Transvaal if they could beat Eastern Province in their last match.

Castle Currie Cup Final
TRANSVAAL *v.* NORTHERN TRANSVAAL

To many people the wicket which was prepared for the Currie Cup Final, which should have been the height of the South African season, was a disgrace. Former South African Test batsman Jackie McGlew stated, after watching two overs, that Rice would be able to declare at about 120 and win the match.

It was Transvaal that had first use of the fiery pitch and they owed much to the splendid opening batting of Cook and Fotheringham. François Weideman, medium pace, and Eric Simons forced both openers to play four out of six deliveries off their chests, but with admirable technique and application, the Transvaal pair coped with the conditions and put on 55, a decisive contribution to the winning of the match.

Transvaal moved past 100 before they lost their third wicket, but 4 wickets fell while 8 runs were scored and the home crowd celebrated. Their joy was short-lived. Kourie and Jennings added a rumbustious 69, the biggest stand of the match, and Jennings and Page added 37. In taking 6 for 57, Eric Simons crowned his year by passing 50 wickets.

Northern Transvaal soon found that the feared Sylvester Clarke and Hugh Page, the fastest and most improved white bowler in South African cricket, relished the lively pitch. Kirsh alone offered any hope, but it was brief. Having scored only 232, Transvaal still found they were able to enforce the follow-on and had added celebration when Anton Ferreira, offering no shot, was bowled by Clive Rice to give the Transvaal captain his 330th wicket in Currie Cup cricket.

Anton Ferreira. His fine all-round form was a feature of Northern Transvaal's cricket and one of the main reasons that they enjoyed their most successful season for many years. (Ken Kelly)

CASTLE CURRIE CUP FINAL – NORTHERN TRANSVAAL *v.* TRANSVAAL
8 and 9 March 1985 at Berea Park, Pretoria

TRANSVAAL

	FIRST INNINGS	
S.J. Cook	lbw, b Ferreira	26
H.R. Fotheringham	c Morris, b Weideman	40
M.S. Venter	c Geringer, b Simons	23
R.G. Pollock	b Weideman	9
C.E.B. Rice†	b Simons	0
K.A. McKenzie	c Day, b Simons	1
A.J. Kourie	lbw, b Simons	28
R.V. Jennings*	run out	50
H.A. Page	b Simons	26
S.T. Clarke	c Day, b Simons	11
N.V. Radford	not out	1
Extras	lb 7, w 3, nb 7	17
		232

	O	M	R	W
Simons	24.5	6	57	6
Weideman	28	8	71	2
Ferreira	19	6	31	1
Ackermann	12	2	36	—
Morris	7	2	20	—

FALL OF WICKETS
1- 55, 2- 96, 3- 101, 4- 101, 5- 109, 6- 109, 7- 178, 8- 215, 9- 219

NORTHERN TRANSVAAL

	FIRST INNINGS		SECOND INNINGS	
M. Yachad	c Page, b Clarke	4	lbw, b Rice	7
W. Kirsh	b Clarke	24	c Fotheringham, b Page	20
L.J. Barnard†	b Page	0	c Jennings, b Page	0
N.T. Day*	b Clarke	0	c Pollock, b Clarke	30
C.P.L. de Lange	c Jennings, b Clarke	10	lbw, b Page	0
A. Geringer	b Clarke	1	c Jennings, b Kourie	23
A.M. Ferreira	b Rice	8	b Kourie	37
E.O. Simons	c Jennings, b Page	0	c Jennings, b Kourie	6
W.F. Morris	c Venter, b Page	4	c Jennings, b Page	0
I.F.N. Weideman	not out	0	lbw, b Rice	37
G.L. Ackermann	lbw, b Page	0	not out	0
Extras	lb 6, w 3, nb 1	10	b 1, lb 3, w 1, nb 1	6
		61		166

	O	M	R	W	O	M	R	W
Clarke	11	5	8	5	12	3	34	1
Page	7.4	1	14	4	18	4	67	4
Radford	6	—	21	—	8	2	20	—
Rice	3	2	8	1	6.2	4	10	2
Kourie					8	2	29	3

FALL OF WICKETS
1- 10, 2- 16, 3- 18, 4- 31, 5- 40, 6- 49, 7- 49, 8- 61, 9- 61
1- 31, 2- 31, 3- 31, 4- 31, 5- 79, 6- 118, 7- 127, 8- 128, 9- 130

Umpires: D.A. Sansom and D.H. Bezuidenhout

Transvaal won by an innings and 5 runs

BENSON AND HEDGES TROPHY FINAL – TRANSVAAL *v.* NORTHERN TRANSVAAL
29 March 1985 at Wanderers, Johannesburg

NORTHERN TRANSVAAL

M. Yachad	b Kourie	34
W. Kirsh	lbw, b Page	28
L.J. Barnard†	b Radford	19
N.T. Day*	b Rice	17
K.D. Verdoorn	b Radford	15
A. Geringer	b Rice	2
A.M. Ferreira	run out	13
E.O. Simons	run out	0
W.F. Morris	c Venter, b Page	5
I.F.N. Weideman	lbw, b Page	7
G. Grobler	not out	10
Extras	b 3, lb 14, w 9	26
(43.1 overs)		176

	O	M	R	W
Clarke	8	3	19	—
Radford	9	—	37	2
Kourie	9	—	29	1
Rice	9	1	32	2
Page	8.1	—	33	3

FALL OF WICKETS
1- 72, 2- 80, 3- 114, 4- 133, 5- 137, 6- 139, 7- 140, 8- 157, 9- 158

TRANSVAAL

S.J. Cook	c Yachad, b Weideman	2
H.R. Fotheringham	st Day, b Morris	42
M.S. Venter	not out	53
R.G. Pollock	lbw, b Grobler	0
C.E.B. Rice†	not out	55
K.A. McKenzie		
A.J. Kourie		
R.V. Jennings*		
H.A. Page		
S.T. Clarke		
N.V. Radford		
Extras	lb 13, w 7, nb 7	27
(36.2 overs)	(for 3 wickets)	179

	O	M	R	W
Simons	6.2	2	19	—
Weideman	8	—	51	1
Grobler	8	2	27	1
Morris	9	—	40	1
Ferreira	5	—	29	—

FALL OF WICKETS
1- 23, 2- 68, 3- 71

Umpires: D.D. Schoof and D.A. Sansom

Transvaal won by 7 wickets

It seemed that the match might go into a third day when the home side offered stiffer resistance in their second innings. Geringer and Ferreira put on 39 for the sixth wicket and Weideman hit lustily at the close, but the might of Transvaal and the pitch had long decided the issue.

Benson and Hedges Trophy

15 March 1985

at Johannesburg

Eastern Province 177 (D.J. Richardson 57)
Transvaal 181 for 7

Transvaal (2 pts) won by 3 wickets

20 March 1985

at Pretoria

Eastern Province 181 (P. Willey 88)
Northern Transvaal 182 for 9

Northern Transvaal (2 pts) won by 1 wicket

Transvaal's continued dominance was shown with their fifth win in five matches in the floodlit competition. Northern Transvaal earned the right to meet them in the final with a thrilling win over Eastern Province. They owed much to Day who made 47 and especially to Verdoorn who was not out 46 at the end.

Benson and Hedges Trophy Log

	P	*W*	*L*	*Pts*
Transvaal	5	5	—	10
Northern Transvaal	5	3	2	6
Eastern Province	5	3	2	6
Western Province	5	3	2	6
Natal	5	1	4	2
Impalas	5	—	5	0

Benson and Hedges Trophy Final
TRANSVAAL *v.* NORTHERN TRANSVAAL

Transvaal completed a clean sweep when they won the Benson and Hedges Floodlit Trophy by 7 wickets with 8.4 overs to spare. This made them champions in each of the four domestic competitions.

After Yachad and Kirsh had given the visitors a sound start there was little significant resistance. Transvaal lost 3 for 71, including Pollock for a duck, but thereafter Venter and Rice were in total command.

First Class Averages

BATTING	M	Inns	NOs	Runs	HS	Av	100s	50s
M.B. Billson	4	6	2	289	94	72.25		3
A.I. Kallicharran	6	11	2	263	110	69.22	1	7
D.J. Cullinan	4	8	2	345	100	59.00	1	3
G.S. Cowley	9	14	6	459	145*	57.37	1	2
M.W. Rushmere	8	12	3	498	119*	55.33	2	2
T.B. Reid	5	9	1	399	120*	49.87	2	1
S.J. Cook	11	16		782	140	48.87	2	5
C.E.B. Rice	10	15	2	629	126	48.38	3	3
L. Potter	6	12	2	462	165*	46.20	1	2
M.D. Logan	8	13	1	553	172	46.08	1	2
P.L. Selsick	5	9	1	342	183	42.75	1	
I. Foulkes	6	11	3	342	132*	42.75	1	
P.N. Kirsten	8	14	2	511	133	42.58	2	2
P.W. Romaines	6	12	1	462	170*	42.00	1	3
M.D. Mellor	5	8	2	237	124*	39.50	1	
R.J. East	6	10	2	313	163*	39.12	1	
D.G. Emslie	7	9	2	273	84	39.00		2
D. Bestall	9	15	3	468	134*	39.00	1	1
W. Kirsh	7	13	1	466	119	38.83	1	2
L.M. Phillips	4	7	2	190	82*	38.00		1
A.J. Kourie	10	14	4	379	78	37.90		2
R.G. Pollock	10	15		567	114	37.80	1	4
G.N. Lister-James	4	5	1	151	50	37.75		2
G.C.G. Fraser	6	8	3	188	78*	37.60		1
M. Yachad	10	20		751	124	37.55	2	5
F.W. Swarbrook	4	8	2	220	49*	37.33		
I.M. Wingreen	6	11		405	83	36.81		4
H.R. Fotheringham	10	15		549	184	36.60	2	1
D.P. Le Roux	6	12		434	71	36.16		5
C.L. King	7	10		361	94	36.10		2
M. Michau	7	12	1	396	103	36.00	1	1
B. Roberts	6	10		357	90	35.70		3
A.G. Elgar	7	14		496	97	35.42		3
K.A. McKenzie	10	15	4	384	115	34.90	1	1
W.M. van der Merwe	5	7		242	96	34.57		2
B.J. Whitfield	9	16	2	465	96*	33.21		4
T.R. Madsen	9	14	1	415	111	31.92	1	1
A.P. Kuiper	9	15		477	87	31.80		4
D.J. Callaghan	8	15	2	412	171	31.69	1	1
L. Seeff	9	17	1	505	76	31.56		4
A.M. Green	6	11		344	84	31.27		3
M.J. Pearse	6	11	2	281	55	31.22		3
S.A. Jones	5	9	3	186	87	31.00		1
M.S. Venter	10	16	2	426	64*	30.42		2
R.C. Ontong	6	11	1	298	60	29.80		2
E.O. Simons	11	17	7	298	58	29.80		1
E.N. Trotman	6	11		326	102	29.63	1	2
P.H. Rayner	10	19	2	501	69*	29.47		3
A.V. Birrell	6	10		290	82	29.00		2
P.G. Amm	9	15	1	404	75	28.85		4
I.K. Daniell	8	15		432	101	28.80	1	2
R.A. le Roux	6	11	1	287	89*	28.70		2
D.B. Rundle	5	10		286	110	28.60	1	
P.H. Williams	5	9		257	89	28.55		2
S. Vercueil	6	9	1	220	59*	27.50		1
D.A. Scott	8	14	1	357	72	27.46		2
G.J. Turner	8	16		438	66	27.37		2
L.J. Barnard	10	20	1	517	65	27.21		5
K.C. Dugmore	2	4		108	67	27.00		1
R.M. Bentley	9	15	2	350	73	26.92		3
D.K. Pearse	6	10	2	208	58	26.00		1
B.M. Osborne	6	11	1	256	61	25.60		2
K.J. Barnett	6	12		303	59	25.25		1
S.T. Jefferies	6	8		201	71	25.12		1
N.M. Lambrechts	6	11		273	58	24.81		1
R.L.S. Armitage	8	13	1	297	100*	24.75	1	1
D.J. Richardson	9	15		371	67	24.73		2
N.T. Day	10	20	3	415	84	24.41		4
G.J. Parsons	6	9	1	195	76	24.37		2
D.L. Howell	7	13		316	59	24.30		2
G.L. Hayes	5	8	1	170	55	24.28		1
J.B. Munnik	4	8	1	170	82*	24.28		1
M.J.P. Ford	4	8		194	77	24.25		1
A.M. Ferreira	10	19	3	381	57	23.81		2
V.F. du Preez	7	13		304	117	23.38	1	1
G.W. Johnson	5	7	1	136	50	22.66		1
R.F. Pienaar	9	15		340	61	22.66		2
P.J. Allan	4	7	1	134	28*	22.33		
M.J.D. Doherty	5	9		201	48	22.33		
N.R. Boonzaaier	7	12	1	237	52*	21.54		2
A.C. Hudson	6	12		258	50	21.50		1
H.A. Page	11	13	3	215	57	21.50		1
P.L. Symcox	6	9		193	63	21.44		1

G.S. le Roux	7	11	4	147	48*	21.00	
R.V. Jennings	11	15	4	225	50	20.45	1
T.A. Clarke	3	6		121	82	20.16	1
I.L. Howell	6	8		161	64	20.12	1
A. Geringer	11	19		379	70	19.94	2
M.K. van Vuuren	9	11	4	139	60	19.85	1
M.N. Kellow	4	8		158	76	19.75	2
C.R. Norris	8	14		273	74	19.50	2
A.P. Beukes	6	12	1	214	48	19.45	
C.D. Mitchley	7	10		193	46	19.30	
S.F.A. Bacchus	9	17		324	65	19.05	3
S. Nackerdien	6	11	4	132	33*	18.85	
R.A. Smith	9	15		280	69	18.66	1
C.P.L. de Lange	9	15	1	260	58	18.57	1
K.J. Rule	6	10		185	68	18.50	1
P.A. Robinson	4	6		109	43	18.16	
O. Henry	6	9		163	50	18.11	1
L.J. Wenzler	6	9	1	142	35	17.75	
W.G. Kruger	3	6		105	39	17.50	
P.D. Swart	3	6		104	61	17.33	1
M. Bacher	5	8	1	120	47*	17.14	
K.D. Robinson	6	11	1	165	36	16.50	
P.J.A. Visagie	6	12		193	38	16.08	
J.J. Strydom	7	12		186	88	15.50	1
G.P. van Rensburg	6	10	2	123	64	15.37	1
M.B. Minaar	6	12	5	105	27*	15.00	
G.D. Tullis	6	12		174	56	14.50	1
C.J. van Heerden	7	12		171	74	14.25	1
N.P. Minaar	5	10		142	38	14.20	
P.B. Clift	7	12	1	154	39*	14.00	
I.F.N. Weideman	10	14	2	139	37	11.58	
E.A. Moseley	9	12	2	115	40	11.50	
C. van Rensburg	6	11	1	114	29	11.40	
B.M. McMillan	6	10		113	65	11.30	1
W.F. Morris	8	13	2	123	29	11.18	
K.D. Verdoorn	7	14		153	34	10.92	
P. Willey	7	11		119	56	10.81	1

(Qualification: 100 runs, average 10.00)
(Also batted: J.B. Commins (South African Defence Force) 116 not out)

BOWLING	Overs	Mds	Runs	Wkts	Av	Best	10/m	5/in
S.T. Clarke	329.4	88	738	58	12.72	5/8	1	6
G.J. Parsons	195.3	53	515	39	13.20	9/72	1	2
C.J.P.G. van Zyl	232.4	40	676	50	13.52	8/84	2	5
K.J. Kerr	114.3	43	246	18	13.66	5/35		2
C.R. Norris	90.1	15	288	20	14.40	5/48		1
H.A. Page	263.2	74	775	50	15.50	5/61		1
J.J. Hooper	141	24	460	28	16.42	5/29		1
E.O. Simons	309.4	68	859	51	16.84	6/26		2
E.N. Trotman	64.1	16	170	10	17.00	5/30		1
G.L. Ackermann	154.4	16	482	27	17.85	7/69	1	3
I.L. Howell	129.5	47	255	14	18.21	6/60		1
C.D. Mitchley	214	42	652	35	18.62	5/50		1
K.D. Robinson	139.3	30	347	18	19.27	4/33		
T.G. Shaw	202.4	64	446	23	19.39	6/42		1
E.A. Moseley	291.3	90	665	34	19.55	5/48		1
D.B. Rundle	74	14	216	11	19.63	4/37		
J.C. van Duyker	77.4	9	236	12	19.66	4/40		
P.A. Robinson	78.4	12	259	13	19.92	5/61		1
A.J. Kourie	365.3	89	1009	50	20.18	7/94		3
I. Foulkes	112.5	29	263	13	20.23	5/50		1
P.E. Smith	118.5	20	305	15	20.33	4/50		
O. Henry	174.2	45	460	22	20.90	4/41		
M.D. Makin	177.3	44	511	23	22.21	6/36	1	2
G.S. le Roux	204.5	33	608	27	22.51	4/46		
R.R. Lawrenson	88	15	273	12	22.75	4/32		
W.F. Morris	177.4	59	435	19	22.89	5/83		1
B.M. McMillan	148.3	33	477	20	23.85	4/53		
B.D.C. Logan	72	13	240	10	24.00	3/44		
G. Grobler	230.3	35	725	30	24.16	5/65		1
D. Norman	224.1	46	633	26	24.34	5/38		1
A.M. Ferreira	278.3	77	710	29	24.48	6/23		1
J. Havenga	85	16	246	10	24.60	5/88		1
B.A. Matthews	223.1	41	592	24	24.66	4/58		
P.B. Clift	234	53	618	25	24.72	4/46		
J.G. Thomas	209.2	37	612	24	25.50	5/68		1
N.V. Radford	280.2	56	817	32	25.53	3/31		
K.G. Bauermeister	119	17	413	16	25.81	5/40		1
S.T. Jefferies	192	29	529	20	26.45	4/39		
W.M. van der Merwe	148.2	25	437	16	27.31	5/54		1
H.L. Alleyne	134.3	16	529	19	27.84	5/103		1
I.F.N. Weideman	258	60	771	27	28.55	6/43		1
D.K. Pearse	174.4	56	372	13	28.61	3/54		
R.L.S. Armitage	127.1	31	290	10	29.00	4/50		
M.K. van Vuuren	263	65	697	24	29.04	4/45		
C.J. van Heerden	116.5	23	408	14	29.14	4/62		
D. Ferrant	125	33	322	11	29.27	4/35		
J.K. Lever	179	52	432	14	30.85	4/58		
G.P. van Rensburg	162.1	22	557	18	30.94	6/91		1
T.J. Packer	198.3	41	665	21	31.66	5/90		1
B.T. Player	91.4	17	324	10	32.40	2/37		
A.P. Kuiper	139	24	361	11	32.81	4/55		
C. Wulfsohn	137	21	438	13	33.69	3/67		
D.L. Hobson	263	52	916	27	33.92	5/92		1
L. Potter	191.3	40	516	15	34.40	4/63		
J. Pieterse	122.5	31	379	11	34.45	3/89		
P. Willey	164	53	363	10	36.30	3/25		
R.C. Ontong	242.2	83	505	13	38.84	4/71		
A.P. Beukes	162.1	33	466	11	42.36	4/50		
A.V. Birrell	176.3	29	645	15	43.00	3/57		

(Qualification – 10 wickets)

LEADING FIELDERS

55–R.V. Jennings (ct 49/st 6); 46–N.T. Day; 40–R.J. Ryall (ct 34/st 6); 28–R.J. East (ct 27/st 1), B. McBride, and D.J. Richardson (ct 24/st 4); 27–T.R. Madsen (ct 26/st 1); 22–D.P. le Roux (ct 19/st 3); 21–A.J. Kourie; 17–P.A. Tullis (ct 14/st 3); 14–G.D. Tullis (ct 13/st 1) and M.J. Pearse (ct 13/st 1); 13–S. Vercueil; 12–A. Geringer; 11–S.F.A. Bacchus, K.J. Kerr, L.M. Phillips (ct 9/st 2), C.E.B. Rice, and M.S. Venter; 10–R.A. le Roux and P.L. Symcox

Another Rebel Tour

As the South African season drew to its close the news broke that an Australian side including several Test players was to tour the Republic in 1985–86. Once again the cricket world was in turmoil and three of the players who had been selected to tour England with the Australian party in 1985, Alderman, McCurdy and Rixon, withdrew from the side rather than give the undertaking that they would not tour South Africa. Here, *Chris Harte*, cricket historian and author based in Adelaide, relates the events which brought about another *rebel* tour of South Africa.

The Advertiser on Saturday, 13 April 1985, was the first newspaper to break to the sporting world the names of the Australian cricketers signed for an unauthorised tour of South Africa.

Those named included Wayne Phillips and Rod McCurdy, of SA, NSW's Steve Rixon, Dirk Wellham, Murray Bennett and John Dyson, WA's Terry Alderman and Graeme Wood, Queensland's Carl Rackemann and John Maguire, and Victoria's Graham Yallop and Rodney Hogg.

But the story did not begin then. It began almost three years ago in London. At the time of the International Cricket Council conference at Lord's in 1982, former South African captain Dr Ali Bacher, now the managing director of the Transvaal Cricket Council, approached Barbadian and Surrey fast bowler Sylvester Clarke to play for Transvaal.

Clarke eventually contacted former Barbados fast bowler Gregory Armstrong and four months later planning got under way for the first of the two West Indies tours of the republic.

The South African negotiators were forced to use code names for each player and used public phone boxes for communications with the West Indies contacts.

At the 11th hour the South African Cricket Union was forced to abort the tour due to a leak by someone close to the SACU administrators to an Australian journalist.

But arrangements were quickly reinstated and the rearranging of tickets and travel routes begun.

On 12 January 1983, the 'rebel' West Indian team arrived at Johannesburg's Jan Smuts Airport and the visiting captain, Lawrence Rowe, declared: 'We're professionals and we've come here to do a job.'

While the negotiations with the West Indians had been starting and failing, before starting again, moves were afoot in Australia.

In my book on the last England tour of Australia in 1982–83 I have described the happenings on a daily basis.

For 21 November 1982, the second day of the NSW versus England match I wrote: *The morning's cricket had been dull and uninteresting. Bill O'Reilly was still holding forth about the lack of patrons at the ground.*

Rumours had then started to circulate about another rebel tour of South Africa in the offing. A local reporter said former Australian and NSW opening batsman Bruce Francis was organising something along these lines, but we did not know what it was.

Speculation then ceased when the NSW Cricket Association issued a Press release about the provision of a boundary rope.

So, was something in the wind at that time? Two days later, I wrote:

As the England team flew north, two events were happening affecting cricket. One concerned Kim Hughes; the other Dennis Lillee.

Kim Hughes, when approached for comment by a Tasmanian journalist in Devonport, admitted that he had been approached the previous week, in Sydney during the day–night McDonald's Cup match against NSW, concerning his interest in going to play cricket in South Africa. Hughes stated that former Australian and NSW batsman Bruce Francis had asked about South Africa, but Hughes had said that he was not interested – for obvious reasons.

Reports coming from London suggested that a joint Australian–West Indian team was being formed for an eight-week tour, worth $180,000 to each player. The names of the West Indian players were common knowledge – but who were the Australians? And who was doing the attempted signing? Francis? Or someone else?

The someone else turned out to be Hugh Tayfield, the 53-year-old former Springbok off-spinner who was in Australia supposedly writing on the Test series for the 'Johannesburg Star' newspaper.

Armed with a cheque book and rumoured to be backed by a giant engineering concern, Tayfield was authorised to pay any Test player up to $100,000 for a five-week South African tour.

The Australian Cricket Board acted quickly. It told PBL Marketing, the board's promoter, to get its solicitors to send a letter to Francis telling him the ACB had Australia's top 25 players under contract, and that an undertaking was sought from Francis that he would not attempt to induce any player to breach his contract.

Phil Ridings, as ACB chairman, then issued a strongly worded statement saying that any player who breached his ACB contract could expect the breach to be viewed most seriously by the board.

Most certainly legal action would be considered, and this immediately stopped three of the provisionally signed-up players from continuing their discussions any further with either Tayfield or Francis.

Success, however, had not eluded either man, for they had signatures already on contracts. Test players of very recent vintage had signed. Batsmen, pace bowlers, spin bowlers – even a wicketkeeper. But would the proposed tour ever eventuate?

The Department of Foreign Affairs in Canberra prepared a brief for its Minister. The ACB discussed the matter with the department, with the Federal Government washing its hands of the problem. It belonged, it said, to the ACB.

Ridings could not help but be concerned at one of Francis's comments. For it started to publicise the certain 'arrangements' made for the spontaneous criticism of South Africa during the current season.

Francis had said he had approached Kim Hughes to seek his personal views after Greg Chappell and Rodney Marsh had made recent unsolicited critical remarks against South Africa.

Ridings, in his statement, also had added that several players, including captain Greg Chappell and vice-captain Kim Hughes, had stated repeatedly that 'they do not wish to become involved with any tour of South Africa that would threaten the stability of cricket relations between the seven Test match countries'.

The headlines and awkward comments about South Africa lasted one day. Something far more important in the eyes of Australia's cricketing public had arisen.

Dennis Lillee's knee was crook.

And that was it for the season.

The West Indian team in South Africa had proved to be a success with huge crowds, of all racial origins, turning up for the matches.

After the tour, a meeting was held in Cape Town to discuss the possibility of signing an Australian team for the following season, when the West Indies would return, for a triangular tournament.

The Australian team headed for London in early June, 1983, for the third World Cup in England over $2\frac{1}{2}$ hectic weeks.

On 29 and 30 June, just after the World Cup final, the International Cricket Conference held its annual meeting. As in 1982 the South African delegation was not given a hearing.

'To such an extent,' said Wisden, 'did the question of South Africa, and of past and future "rebel" tours to that country, dominate the conference that the atmosphere surrounding it was more that of a political convention than a cricket meeting.'

A fortnight later, the MCC membership at a special general meeting, voted 6604 to 4344 against sending a team to South Africa.

While all this had been going on, the cricketers mostly were back in their own countries. The Australians, however, had had a most interesting visit to London. Most of the team had been approached by South African representatives while the tournament had been on, and vice-captain David Hookes had been told he could captain a team to South Africa.

Within 24 hours of the offer, Adelaide journalist Trevor

Gill had reported the fact in the afternoon newspaper *The News*. And as Gill was Hookes's ghost writer, one can only but surmise as to his source.

Rumours flew around in late June, 1983, that the Australian Government had offered its nation's cricketers a retainer or compensation to stay away from South Africa.

So what was going on? Was the Australian team approached or had the leaked story ruined a potential tour? Or had the money not been enough?

As the then president of the South African Cricket Union, Joe Pamensky, said: 'As far as I am concerned the players that have refused so far have done so primarily because the package has not been attractive enough to them.'

His then deputy, Geoff Dakin, went even further when he said: 'We have not spoken to the Australian players; let me make it quite clear. But if the Australians came to us and wanted a tour, or rather if they responded to our want for a tour, we would have a package that we would pay to the Australian cricket administration, and they would distribute money to the players after the tour is over.'

Mr Dakin continued: 'Because we can't deal with your administration, we get hold of an agent, he talks to players for us, and we say, "This is the sum of money available; the identical sum of money which would have been available to the administration."

'But instead of Australian cricket benefiting to the extent that the players would get a portion, the administration would get a portion which would go towards the betterment of Australian cricket; we pay it all to the players. So the players are really on the gravy train.'

So the planning went into hibernation. Or did it?

After returning in May, 1984, from its tour of the West Indies, the Australian team had a three-month break until the short tour of India which started in late September. Just before the tour started, the team was instructed to go to Canberra for four days for a general training, fitness and a 'getting-to-know-each-other' session.

It was in Canberra that the first meeting of the players took place to discuss the possibility of a South African tour. The subject was discussed at some length, quite ironically as it happened, for the players' course at the Institute of Sport also was to teach the cricketers 'to ignore outside pressures which have made its record overseas particularly poor in recent years'.

Only a fortnight before the Canberra meeting, the ACB had concluded its annual general meeting in Melbourne by formally approving a new contract system for the international players.

Under the system 16 players were given the 'security' they had sought – a 12-month contract from 1 October 1984. The players had been retained in three categories ranging from around $11,000 to $4000.

Those on the top level were Hughes, Allan Border, Geoff Lawson, Rodney Hogg and Kepler Wessels. Five others were put on a second tier, and another six on a third tier.

The South African representative, Francis, made it quite clear to the players what the offer comprised. Two tours, each of around three months duration. For their troubles, the players would each get $200,000 – tax-free.

One Australian player said afterwards: 'You work that out. $200,000 really means around $350,000 gross. That would take me between 10 and 12 years to earn If I stayed at the top in Australian cricket.

'Look what happened to Terry Alderman with his shoulder. It could happen to me tomorrow. I'm just totally tired of the pressures of cricket. PBL Marketing treat us like sheep, and herd us around at their whim and fancy. No thanks, I couldn't stand another 12 years of all that nonsense.'

Arrangements were made with the players who had agreed to take part in a South African tour for their contracts to be signed outside Australia.

Francis had obtained Queen's Counsel advice that this was the best course to take. The players' contracts with the ACB would expire on 30 September 1985, and with PBL Marketing on 31 October 1985. The unauthorised tour could then take place after that date.

Kim Hughes and his team flew off to India to record a 3–0 success in the tournament to celebrate the golden jubilee of the Ranji Trophy, India's principal cricket competition.

After the final match, Mike Coward wrote in the *Sydney Morning Herald*: 'To a man, the Australian players care about Hughes and his future in the game. They believe he is the right man to lead Australia and plan to give him unconditional support.'

Stirring stuff. But not correct, for on the way home from India a number of players stopped off in Singapore for a few days.

They met up with other Australian players and their legal representatives to discuss the South African arrangements.

Dr Ali Bacher was present at these discussions, which included one private meeting with the solicitor of a player (who is an England tourist and whose name has never been mentioned in a South Africa context) who valued his client's services at $600,000.

The meeting failed to conclude with a contract and the solicitor enjoyed two days holiday before flying back to Australia empty-handed.

The players signed a document giving power of attorney to a third party. This person then signed contracts on the players' behalf – contracts that were drawn up by lawyers from South Africa, England and the US who had expertise in sports agreements.

Bacher was then going to give the players an advance payment of $5000. Bruce Francis disagreed. He argued the point that $5000 could be returned easily if anyone had a change of heart.

Pay them $25,000, he urged, for that would be a much more binding commitment.

Bacher eventually agreed.

On his return to Australia, Francis had a telephone call from Dirk Wellham. The NSW captain wanted his money urgently. Francis went to a bank on the Gold Coast, drew a cheque and drove immediately to Wellham to hand over the money.

Other players also wanted their advance. It appeared that some were spending quite well.

But why give power of attorney to an agent to sign contracts in Singapore? The answer would appear to be legal and somewhat complex.

It could be argued that signing outside Australia's legal jurisdiction meant no Australian court could be used by either the ACB or the Australian Government to try to invalidate the contracts.

But could the Australian players be stopped from leaving the country? No, said the leading Sydney QC. In his opinion, he added: 'On what grounds and under what legislative power could the Government invoke such an order of restraint?'

Soon after the players arrived home, other top cricketers were aware of the situation. Some were approached; some refused, most notably senior players Allan Border and Geoff Lawson.

Australia continued its disastrous season. Kim Hughes resigned the captaincy; Allan Border took over.

The signed players began to think, especially those who had a large amount of money tied up in the ACB's provident fund, known officially as the 'Retirement Benefits Payments Scheme'. Each player contributed a percentage of his earnings towards an eventual payout, with the ACB contributing an equal share.

Once a player had accrued 30 'credits', then the payout monies rose on an involved actuarial basis. A player with fewer than 30 credits had his money refunded – with interest. Each Test match accrued one credit, and each one-day international was worth a quarter of a credit.

The players who were being considered for a South African tour and who would be affected by having more than 30 credits were John Dyson, Rodney Hogg, Graeme Wood and Graham Yallop.

A table of credits would look like this:

	Tests played	*One-day intern. credits*	*Total*
Dyson	30 +	$7\frac{1}{4}$ =	$37\frac{1}{4}$
Hogg	38 +	$17\frac{3}{4}$ =	$55\frac{3}{4}$
Wood	48 +	$18\frac{3}{4}$ =	$66\frac{3}{4}$
Yallop	39 +	$7\frac{1}{2}$ =	$46\frac{1}{2}$

Hogg had already worked this out. He went to see Australian team manager Bob Merriman about his theoretical payout figure.

Merriman, a commissioner of the Australian Conciliation and Arbitration Commission on 18 months leave of absence from his post, was versed enough in Australian law to give Hogg the answer he needed.

Merriman allegedly told Hogg that, if the fast bowler was considering going to South Africa, he need not worry about getting a full and proper payout from the scheme.

The players had been worried because it had been generally assumed that the ACB would veto any payout should a player take part in any match without ACB approval.

Clause 10 of the ACB Player Contract said no player could play in any match outside Australia without the board's permission.

The argument, so the ACB felt, was that breaching of this clause would give the board the right to withhold payment. Merriman obviously disagreed with this line of thinking.

Merriman would have been surprised how quickly his comments spread around Australian cricketing circles. Within a few days it was common knowledge among most first-class cricketers.

Another point relevant to the players' decision to sign for a South African tour was the ACB Player Contract foisted on them just before the short trip to India.

Any average lawyer could have driven a horse and cart through the loopholes in the contract and the players were well aware of this.

After the rebellion before the tour of the West Indies in February 1984, when all but two of the tourists had refused until the last minute to sign the contracts placed before them, the revision contract was valid up to 30 September 1985.

The $15,000 fee for the England tour, from 30 April 1985, to 4 September 1985, was considered by one prominent player as 'a joke'.

The players concerned wanted to go on the tour because it was considered to be the highlight of any career.

As another touring player said: 'Just consider the contract in the light of reality. All the board will provide is our travel, bed and breakfast. We have to pay for meals.

'We can't make money on the side by doing any writing or broadcasting, or even officially make any comment whatever.

'Even any photos we take on tour have to be copyrighted to the ACB.

'If we fall ill or suffer any injury the board will only pay us a proportion of the tour fee.

'Look at it honestly. After paying tax, we are left with around two-thirds of the money. Take off general living expenses and what are we left with? Around $6000 to $7000 by my calculations.

'$15,000 is all we get – gross. Even the West Indies board – who claim that they are always poverty stricken – pay their players $40,000 a tour.

'And you wonder why I've signed for South Africa?'

Other than the ACB contract's expiration at the end of September, 1985, another fact to influence the players was that their compulsory contracts with PBL Marketing ran only until 31 October 1985. The players felt that they would be free of all restraints.

But would they?

Clause 10 of their contract, which has been referred to before, states inter-alia:

... that the Player undertakes and agrees with (the) ACB that he shall during the term of the Agreement and the Further Term not play in a cricket match ... unless it is a match contracted by (the) ACB ... or approved by (the) ACB and further undertakes and agrees with (the) ACB that he shall not without the prior permission of (the) ACB which may be granted or withheld upon such terms and conditions as (the) ACB in its absolute discretion may decide, play cricket outside Australia.

Would it not be possible for the board to argue that the further term so stated – and forming the last half of Part 3 of the schedule to the contract – further bound the players from 1 October 1985 to 30 September 1986?

'No,' said the players. They had taken legal advice and the opinion sent them to Section 3.3 of the main contract.

Headed, 'Guarantee by ACB', the section refers to: 'the player ... is available and fit for selection for matches to be played by the team during the further term ...' and continues to talk about payments.

The opinion given to the players was that all they needed to do was to make themselves unavailable for selection.

Q(uod) E(rat) D(emonstrandum) said 'the intelligent player'.

The stage was set for Australia's biggest cricket confrontation since the World Series Cricket plans were announced to the world on 9 May 1977.

The plan was simple: Wait until the Australian touring team was in England in May 1985, then leak details of the planned South African tour to the media.

The players involved in the unofficial tour could not be recalled to Australia, went the scenario, and therefore pressure would be put on the International Cricket Conference to admit the South African delegates to its June meeting this year.

The South Africans argued, with good reason, that everything that had been asked of them 15 years previously had now been met. Cricket was fully multiracial in the republic and if the ICC would not give the South Africans a fair hearing then they would go their own way and buy international teams for their cricket-starved fans.

It was not so much the South Africans chasing the players; it was the players chasing South Africa. During the World Cup tournament in England in 1983 the whole Pakistan team, less only Imran Khan, was offered on a plate to the South African delegation. The offer was politely declined – for the present.

The plan for the Australian 'rebels', like all good plans, had a flaw. The players' South African tour contracts had a clause which stated unequivocally that to speak about the tour would cost the players financially.

But the players spoke among themselves. Dressing rooms around Australia fairly hummed with the story.

In late October, word reached the Adelaide Oval Press box that something concerning South Africa was happening, but as with previous rumours it was mentally filed.

The big break came in late January, when someone in South Africa who should have known better decided to telephone Adelaide.

At 1.30 a.m. on 30 January, my telephone rang. Had I heard of an impending tour of South Africa by an Australian team?

Twice before, this person had raised the possibility with me, only this time he appeared more certain of his facts.

Later that day, a number of phone calls left me with the distinct impression something was going on.

The matter was discussed with *The Advertiser* cricket writer Alan Shiell, and the evening was spent putting together the article that 'broke' the story.

It speculated on the possible dates for a tour, and also threw in a few names of players known to have been spoken to by South African representatives.

Australian Cricket Board chairman Fred Bennett denied any knowledge of such a tour when rung late that night at his Sydney home.

As the next day wore on, a number of cricketers were being asked questions. Australian captain Allan Border said: 'I haven't heard any of these so-called rumours and as far as I am concerned the whole thing is undiluted rubbish. I'm not concerned because I don't think it exists.'

From Perth, Rod Marsh said: 'I haven't had any sort of approach.'

Kim Hughes said: 'Despite all these rumours, only once has anyone even suggested I speak to them about South Africa.' Hughes was referring to Bruce Francis's approach in November, 1982.

In Johannesburg, South African Cricket Union vice-president Joe Pamensky was angry. Who had leaked the story?

He soon found out from an unwise statement attributed from Sydney, and not long afterwards gave my telephone caller – in his words during a later conversation – 'the biggest payout that I've had in my life'.

The SACU brought in its professional consultant, former Test captain Dr Ali Bacher, who said: 'There is no foundation to these reports. It is not the first time there have been rumours of a tour but they are not true.'

Over the following weeks, a story started to unfold with snippets of news arriving from various sources. Then two fortunate phone calls helped to put the pieces of the jigsaw into place.

The first came from a South African cricket official on holiday in Australia. He was unaware of the newspaper articles. Gently questioned on the possibility of a tour, it having been put to him on a matter-of-fact basis, the official disclosed who the proposed tour sponsors would be and where the team would practice after its arrival in Johannesburg.

The second phone call was pure luck and more positive. In every situation there is a weak link, and in this instance it happened to be some of the players' wives. They had been talking among themselves with the occasional interloper around.

One such interloper related a whole conversation concerning a certain player who had signed a contract to play in South Africa.

The time now was ripe for another push to see who could be drawn into making more comment.

The player, when approached, had been reluctant to say too much. Urged on by a close friend, the player had finally admitted he knew the risks he was taking. He knew he would be banned from cricket in Australia but was prepared to accept the consequences.

He added that he was sick of cricket, especially after the season that PBL Marketing had devised for the players. 'They're burning us out,' he said. 'And they couldn't care less. Even when you add our prizemoney to the basic fee, it's all just not worth it.'

On 21 March, *The Advertiser* ran another story. It was the sole story, for no other newspaper picked it up. Maybe they just did not believe a 'rebel' tour was possible.

The team to tour England had been announced. At least seven of the 17 players were going to use the tour as their swansong, because they had signed for South Africa. One fast bowler had been greeted by his State coach with the comment: 'Well done. You'll have a good tour, I'm sure. Then no doubt you'll be enjoying Johannesburg.'

The player was stunned. How on earth did his coach know?

More than his State coach knew. Officials and administrators of the ACB also knew. Whether they closed their eyes to the situation in those early months is not known, yet ACB chief executive David Richards and general manager Graham Halbish had enjoyed a lengthy convivial lunch in

Melbourne with Bruce Francis, the rebel tours' chief organiser.

One can only presume the subject of South Africa was broached.

ACB chairman Bennett also may have been aware of the situation. His company, Cricket Sports Sales Pty Ltd, of North Rocks, NSW, employed a couple of good local cricketers. One of them, who had just broken into the NSW team, made enquiries about the possibility of a contract to tour South Africa with 'the team'. It was a clumsy effort and the individual concerned was sent packing. Was the board aware or was this just an attempt to see if anything was in the offing?

The Federal Government always was concerned that a tour of this nature might take place. It had been warned in March, 1983, that unless it reappraised its official attitude to South Africa and its people, it could expect the worst.

Francis, in a personal letter to the Prime Minister, Mr Hawke, had stated: '... in England we have the present situation of many national sporting associations refusing to accept the Commonwealth Games' Code of Conduct (on South Africa). Additionally, we have the heavy pressure for normalisation with the MCC. The momentum, in my view, is irreversible and one far better gently guided by enlightened government policy than allowed to develop into an outright and undisciplined rebellion which inconsistent, hypocritical government policies would inevitably provoke.'

In November, 1984, Francis fired off a lengthy letter to Sir Nicholas Shehadie, president of the Australian Rugby Football Union. Again a warning was given, especially as more than 300 copies of the letter were sent to various sporting bodies. The first chink in the armour for the South African tourists came in early February. Murray Bennett wanted out.

As one of his colleagues said at the time: 'He (Bennett) really has been depressed recently. He lives miles north of Sydney in an old fibro home and just needs to improve himself. I really do feel sorry for him.'

Bennett had thought long and hard over his South African contract. He made his decision and contacted Francis.

Bennett told Francis he wanted to be released from his contract and that he would not tour South Africa. Bennett said he would take the consequences even if it meant stepping out of cricket.

Francis thought this over then gave Bennett his reply. If, said Francis, the SACU agreed to release him from his contract, and if the other signed players unanimously agreed he could opt out, then maybe an arrangement could be accommodated. 'It's up to you,' Bennett was told.

Francis spoke to all the other players, Bennett spoke to one. 'No way,' said the players, and Bennett was informed of their feelings.

The Australian team selected to play in two matches in the oil-rich emirate of Sharjah on the coast of the Persian Gulf arrived there on 22 March and returned to Australia on 4 April. A number of administrators had gone with the team, returning just before Easter – too late to send out any contracts to the players for the tour of England. Certain players, because of their South African contracts, would find the ACB contracts somewhat awkward to sign without omitting a number of sections.

Was this the lull before the storm?

The storm broke with a vengeance on 13 April, when an *Advertiser* scoop named the players who had signed for the South African tour. For days it had been a matter of when to tell the story.

On 10 April, Jim Maxwell, an Australian Broadcasting Corporation cricket commentator in Sydney, went to the NSW Cricketer of the Year award dinner.

Maxwell found out the details of the South African venture from a slightly emotional Test cricketer later that night, and broadcast the fact on radio the following day.

Later that night ACB chairman Fred Bennett said: 'The ACB is aware of the latest rumours on a possible tour of South Africa by Australian players.

'The ACB has continually monitored the situation, and we are alert to the fact that there appears to be some strength behind the latest rumours.

'The board is deeply concerned about individuals or organisations attempting to undermine Australian cricket by hiring our players.

'It is impossible to comment further at this stage because the board has no official confirmation, and nobody has produced a list of players who have allegedly entered into any contracts to play in South Africa.'

That was the bait needed, and *The Advertiser* published a list of names that included Wayne Phillips and Rod McCurdy, of SA, NSW's Murray Bennett, Dirk Wellham, John Dyson and Steve Rixon, Queensland's John Maguire and Carl Rackeman, WA's Graeme Wood and Terry Alderman, and Victoria's Rodney Hogg and Graham Yallop.

Kepler Wessels, Queensland's South African-born batsman, also was named. But this was incorrect because Wessels had decided not to sign a South African contract because of some personal disagreement with Dr Ali Bacher, of the South African Cricket Union.

There would be two tours from mid-November to late-January, worth $200,000 each to the players – tax-free. And should the Australian Government decide to penalise the players, the SACU would pay all the penalties. So that was the offer – $100,000 a season in the pocket.

The Government acted predictably with the Minister for Sport, Tourism and Recreation, Mr Brown, making various threats. He called on the ACB to punish any cricketer who accepted South African contracts.

These statements were just what Bruce Francis wanted to hear.

Francis's reaction was to say: 'This call for punitive action must be the most obnoxious request ever put by an Australian government to a sports association.

'Mr Brown has loaded the gun for someone else to fire, but he would appear to be extremely hasty in his desire to have someone pull the trigger. Bluntly put, it would seem that Mr Brown is asking the cricket board to be his hit man.'

After that outburst, and despite many media requests for face-to-face debates, the Minister refused to discuss the matter with Francis.

In South Africa, the three main protagonists, SACU president Geoff Dakin, vice-president Joe Pamensky and cricket consultant Ali Bacher, were keeping a close eye on the situation developing in Australia.

Two days after the story broke Dakin said: 'Our policy is to have more tours because they are essential to the welfare of

South Africa. But we cannot compromise any player or any nation by divulging their names.'

On Tuesday, 16 April, the day before the ACB's scheduled three-day meeting in Perth, news filtered through to the Australian media that the board would get the players chosen for the England tour to sign statutory declarations stipulating that they would not tour South Africa.

The following day Bennett confirmed that the players had until the following Tuesday, 23 April, to sign a statutory declaration.

'In the event that any player is unable or unwilling to complete this declaration and the appropriate contract, he will be regarded as ineligible for this tour and the selectors will be directed to select a replacement player,' Mr Bennett said.

But the real drama was unfolding behind the scenes. Media magnate Kerry Packer was acutely aware his television station, Channel 9, had spent considerable money in organising coverage of the England series for Australian viewers. The best three players signed for South Africa – Wellham, Wood and Phillips – would have to be lured back into the fold.

At 3.30 that Wednesday afternoon, John Dyson, Steve Smith and Dirk Wellham were in Bruce Francis's flat in Sydney's eastern suburbs. They were discussing aspects of the tour.

Wellham's employer, the managing director of Lion Insurance, former England captain Tony Greig, managed to get a message to him: 'Kerry wants to see you.' By 5.30 p.m. Wellham had announced to Francis that he was withdrawing from his South African commitment.

In Adelaide, Wayne Phillips received a phone call. Within a few minutes he, too, was out of the unauthorised tour.

In Perth, another Packer employee, Austin Robertson, was frantically trying to find Graeme Wood. The offer to Wood, who accepted, was the same as to the other two and was believed to include the payment of lawyers' and legal fees if the SACU decided to sue for breach of contract.

News quickly reached Johannesburg of these moves and the SACU acted promptly in getting its solicitors to send a telex to Packer, Greig, Robertson and PBL Marketing managing director Lynton Taylor threatening them with court action if they attempted to get the three players to breach their contracts.

Wellham already had received legal advice that he could not sign the statutory declaration but could give the ACB a verbal assurance instead.

In Canberra, the Prime Minister, Mr Hawke, told Parliament: 'If they (the players) have signed contracts (with South Africa) the Government will be ready to assist should there be any legal action against them for the breaking of such contracts.'

Mr Hawke also had made it known that the Australian taxation authorities would look 'extraordinarily closely' at any financial arrangements made by the 'rebel' cricketers to ensure that payment of tax in Australia was not avoided.

With various moves taking place behind the scenes, the ACB let it be known it was satisfied with having Wellham, Wood and Phillips back. Murray Bennett was a bonus. The rest were 'dead wood' and it was an excellent opportunity to have a 'clean-out of Australian cricket'.

Allan Border lent his thoughts to the matter. At times, more a shop steward than Australia's captain and supposed establishment figure, he said the Australian Government's stance on the question of sporting ties with South Africa was 'a bit hypocritical'.

'I would love to play South Africa; they are a great cricket country, but unfortunately politics dominates and sportsmen suffer,' Border said.

In Johannesburg, a SACU board meeting had finished, with president Dakin telling reporters: 'The tour is on. For some time I have had in my hands signed contracts of 12 Australian players – with two optional members also.'

Mr Dakin then expressed his disappointment at the four Australian players who had renegaded on their contracts, and hinted that they 'may have to pay the price of the contract'.

As the time drew closer for the players to sign their statutory declarations, the pace of discussions between the lawyers working for the ACB, the players and the Packer organisation gained momentum.

A breakthrough was made at the 11th hour when the ACB agreed not to force the issue of the signed South African contracts. Because it was too late on Tuesday, 23 April, to retype the declaration, Wood, Wellham and Phillips signed the telex paper on which the final declaration was sent to them.

The ACB then knew who had not signed the declaration: McCurdy, Alderman and Rixon.

At 9.55 on the morning of 24 April, the ACB informed Queensland fast bowler John Maguire he was a replacement for the England tour. The board also selected Ray Phillips and Carl Rackemann.

At 10.05 a.m., Maguire's lawyers informed the ACB that their client, although willing to go to England, had signed for the South African tour and would be unable to sign the statutory declaration.

At 10.10 a.m., the ACB withdrew Maguire's invitation. Within an hour, Rackemann also had received an invitation, which also was withdrawn.

At 10.30 a.m., in the Cricketers' Club of NSW, Fred Bennett held a Press conference. He announced the three replacements for McCurdy, Alderman and Rixon, knowing full well that two had withdrawn. Then a rider was added that Jeff Thomson and Dave Gilbert would go to England if Maguire and Rackemann would not sign their statutory declarations.

The gathering finished with the hint of action to be taken by the ACB against Francis and the SACU.

Two other things, one public and one private, then started to happen.

The previous day, the Packer organisation had contacted five of Australia's most promising young players – each individually chosen by Kerry Packer. Each was offered a three-year, $45,000 contract to allow PBL Marketing to be his sole manager and general factotum. They were NSW's Steve Waugh and Peter Clifford, Queensland's Robbie Kerr, Victoria's Dean Jones and WA's Mike Veletta.

The first year's money was paid over so quickly that by the time Mr Bennett had finished his Press conference, Peter Clifford was showing off his brand-new car to his family.

In Brisbane, Allan Border was most unhappy. For being

disloyal to Australian cricket, and then being re-admitted to the fold, Wayne Phillips, Wellham and Wood had benefited financially. Then there were five young players getting money for doing nothing. If Kerry Packer could spend his money buying eight cricketers, where would it end.?

A shop steward to the end, Border had to look after his loyal players, who were going to get only $15,000 each for the Ashes tour.

Border discussed the matter with Test selector Greg Chappell. By the following day Chappell knew a serious problem was in the making, for Border had said he would not only resign as Australia's captain but also would not tour.

Chappell telephoned Fred Bennett and they arranged an early meeting in Brisbane on Friday, 26 April.

There the matter was thrashed out, and Border called a Press conference.

Border, sitting with Chappell, told of sweetness and light although admitting he had considered resigning as captain.

Meanwhile, Francis was a busy man. Ever since his name had been linked to the South African tour, his telephones had not stopped ringing.

In his own words: 'You would not believe the number of top-class cricketers who have spoken to me about South Africa.'

Francis had replaced the four defectors easily and had other players in reserve.

Both tours would go ahead.

But as a postscript to this whole episode, there are some matters which need to be cleared up.

Obviously names cannot be mentioned because of the breaking of confidences, not can certain other information be printed because it would not do any good to Australian cricket.

However, I am very certain on one point: there is a very serious leak in the highest echelons of Australian cricket to those with South African sympathies.

The speed at which information was leaked, sometimes before events happened, leaves me with no other conclusion.

SECTION F

Impressive Progress

The season in Zimbabwe.
The Young New Zealanders tour.
The English Counties team's tour.
Full score cards of all major matches.

Statistics and data by John R. Ward.

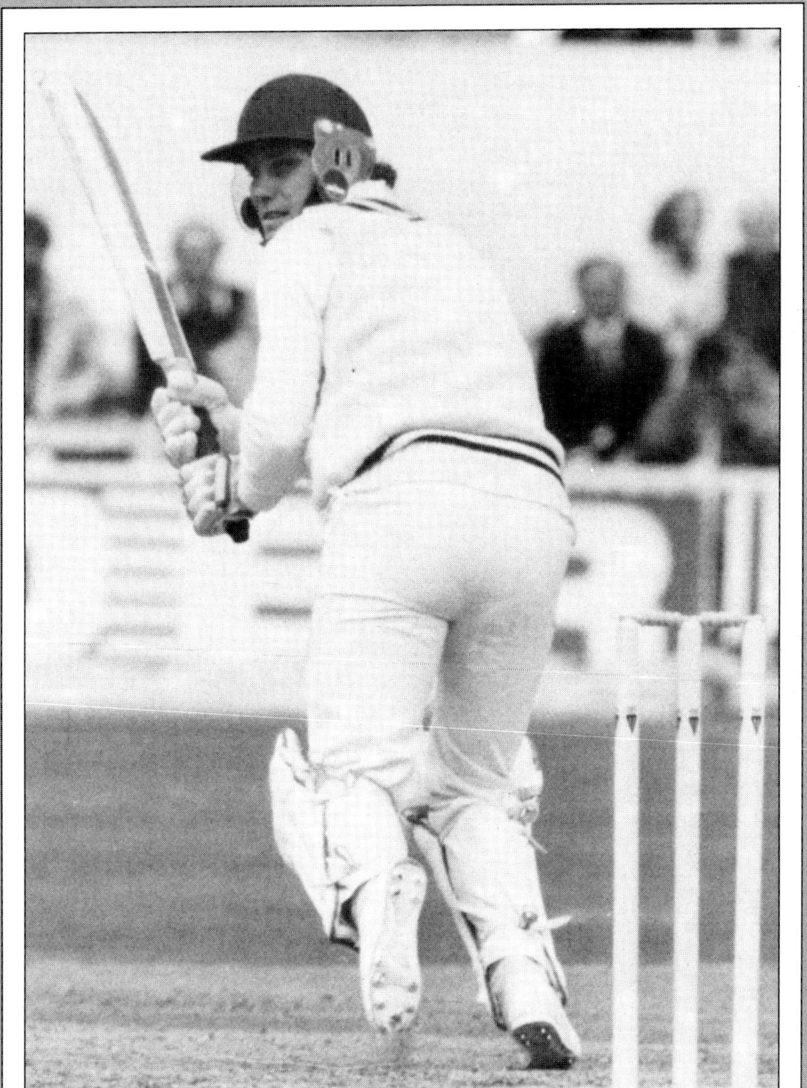

Andy Pycroft, captain of Zimbabwe.
(Ken Kelly)

After the successes of recent years, Zimbabwean cricket was faced with its most exciting and significant season since Independence. The Young New Zealand side, led by Jeff Crowe, included six players with Test experience. They were confronted with what was probably the most intense and exhausting itinerary accorded to a touring side in Zimbabwe.

In the second part of the season, an English Counties side, under the management of Mike Vockins, was to tour Zimbabwe, and that side included four players who had played in the Test series against West Indies in 1984.

The Zimbabwe Cricket Union, under its president, Alwyn Pichanick, deserves great credit for arranging its ambitious programme, and local centres enjoyed an improvement in both the quality and quantity of the cricket with which they were presented.

It had been recognised that, in the past, Zimbabwe cricketers were lacking practice and experience in first-class matches and it was pleasing to note that the number of three-day games was increased, but, as the pitches were easy-paced, it might be wise to increase the first-class games to four days in future.

No praise can be too high for the Young New Zealand side, managed by Ken Deas, which provided the pre-Christmas cricket in Zimbabwe. The team was a blend of young players who had just broken into the Test team and of less mature players who were striving to establish themselves. They were popular and respected wherever they went, approachable and friendly off the field, hard and determined on the field, but never violating the courtesies of the game. John Bracewell was one of three players to win a place in the New Zealand side to tour Pakistan on the strength of his performances in Zimbabwe, the other two were Stirling and Snedden. Crocker and Martin Crowe were original selections for the side, but both withdrew and were replaced by the experienced McEwan and Edgar.

Traicos, who had led Zimbabwe in 1983–84, gave way to Pycroft as captain, a move which seemed hard on the veteran off-spinner and on vice-captain Dave Houghton, but the selectors were obviously looking to the I.C.C. Trophy in 1986 and to the next World Cup.

3 October 1984

at Harare South Country Club

Young New Zealanders 234 for 5 (T.J. Franklin 56)
Zimbabwe Country Districts 196 (G.A. Hick 56, G.A. Paterson 52, K.R. Rutherford 4 for 24, D.A. Stirling 4 for 38)

Young New Zealanders won by 38 runs

Cricket among the farming community remains strong and the Country Districts side, with eight players who had had first-class experience, looked as if they might surprise the

FIRST INTERNATIONAL – ZIMBABWE *v.* YOUNG NEW ZEALAND

5, 6 and 8 October 1984 at Harare Sports Club

YOUNG NEW ZEALAND

	FIRST INNINGS	
T.J. Franklin	not out	153
B.A. Edgar	c Brown, b Duers	2
K.R. Rutherford	c Brown, b Rawson	1
J.J. Crowe†	c Houghton, b Duers	5
V.R. Brown	c Paterson, b Duers	1
P.E. McEwan	c Pycroft, b Duers	0
E.B. McSweeney*	c Butchart, b Traicos	29
M.C. Snedden	c Butchart, b Hick	47
J.G. Bracewell	c Houghton, b Rawson	27
D.A. Stirling	c and b Traicos	32
S.R. Tracy	c Butchart, b Fletcher	1
Extras	b 4, lb 7, nb 2	13
		311

	O	M	R	W
Rawson	32	8	87	2
Duers	25	5	82	4
Butchart	4	—	25	—
Traicos	32	10	70	2
Hick	15	6	23	1
Fletcher	5.2	1	13	1

FALL OF WICKETS
1- 8, 2- 9, 3- 18, 4- 20, 5- 20, 6- 79, 7- 161, 8- 227, 9- 308

Umpires: D.J. Arnott and B. McLachlan

Match drawn

ZIMBABWE

	FIRST INNINGS		SECOND INNINGS	
R.D. Brown	c sub (Hoskin), b Snedden	45	c McEwan, b Brown	6
K.G. Walton	c McSweeney, b Snedden	3	lbw, b Snedden	37
G.A. Hick	c and b Snedden	8	c sub (Hoskin), b Brown	23
A.J. Pycroft†	c Bracewell, b Stirling	21	b Tracy	88
D.L. Houghton*	c McSweeney, b Snedden	21	c Rutherford, b Brown	84
D.A.G. Fletcher	c McEwan, b Snedden	5	not out	32
G.A. Paterson	c McSweeney, b Snedden	0	b Tracy	0
I.P. Butchart	c McSweeney, b Snedden	18	not out	22
P.W.E. Rawson	c McSweeney, b Snedden	5		
A.J. Traicos	c sub (Hoskin), b Bracewell	3		
K.G. Duers	not out	4		
Extras	lb 1, nb 8	9	b 1, lb 6, nb 5	12
		142	(for 6 wkts)	304

	O	M	R	W	O	M	R	W
Stirling	8	—	32	1	15	4	61	—
Tracy	2	1	4	—	14	5	33	2
Snedden	21.3	2	73	8	17	5	30	1
Bracewell	16	4	32	1	24	5	83	—
Brown					20	8	43	3
Rutherford					2		27	—

FALL OF WICKETS
1- 33, 2- 45, 3- 74, 4- 90, 5- 99, 6- 99, 7- 114, 8- 127, 9- 138
1- 20, 2- 61, 3- 86, 4- 240, 5- 273, 6- 273

FIRST ONE-DAY INTERNATIONAL – ZIMBABWE v. YOUNG NEW ZEALAND
7 October 1984 at Harare Sports Club

ZIMBABWE		
R.D. Brown	run out	11
G.A. Paterson	run out	14
G.A. Hick	b Snedden	6
A.J. Pycroft†	c Crowe, b Snedden	5
D.L. Houghton*	c McSweeney, b McEwan	31
D.A.G. Fletcher	run out	23
K.M. Curran	b Stirling	11
I.P. Butchart	b Stirling	7
P.W.E. Rawson	not out	31
A.J. Traicos	c Robertson, b Stirling	15
K.G. Duers	not out	2
Extras	lb 12, w 6, nb 1	19
(50 overs)	(for 9 wickets)	175

	O	M	R	W
Stirling	10	—	46	3
Bracewell	10	2	16	—
Snedden	10	4	22	2
Robertson	5	—	23	—
Brown	8	1	29	—
McEwan	7	1	27	1

FALL OF WICKETS
1-29, 2-31, 3-42, 4-42, 5-103, 6-103, 7-116, 8-127, 9-162

YOUNG NEW ZEALAND		
B.A. Edgar	c Rawson, b Duers	1
P.S. Briasco	run out	32
J.J. Crowe†	c Curran, b Fletcher	21
P.E. McEwan	run out	9
R.N. Hoskin	c Houghton, b Butchart	8
G.K. Robertson	c Butchart, b Traicos	4
V.R. Brown	run out	0
E.B. McSweeney*	c Traicos, b Butchart	1
M.C. Snedden	b Fletcher	25
J.G. Bracewell	not out	35
D.A. Stirling	b Butchart	15
Extras	b 6, lb 13, nb 5	24
(50 overs)		175

	O	M	R	W
Rawson	8	2	30	—
Duers	6	2	18	1
Fletcher	8	1	24	2
Traicos	10	3	19	1
Butchart	10	2	43	3
Hick	8	—	22	—

FALL OF WICKETS
1-5, 2-43, 3-60, 4-75, 5-83, 6-83, 7-83, 8-86, 9-151

Zimbabwe won on losing fewer wickets

tourists when Hick and Paterson added 100 for the second wicket, but the middle order succumbed to the unlikely medium-pace of Rutherford.

First International
ZIMBABWE v. YOUNG NEW ZEALAND

Pycroft won the toss and asked New Zealand to bat. Kevin Duers, a medium-pace bowler from Bulawayo who came into the side as a late replacement for the injured Curran, responded to his captain's decision with an exciting display. Showing accuracy and ability to move the ball late, he had a sensational first-class debut, taking 4 for 5 in 6 overs.

Zimbabwe were thwarted by the New Zealanders later batsmen who gave the redoubtable Franklin the support he deserved. Carrying his bat through an innings for the first time, Franklin reached a career best in 306 minutes, only to miss most of the rest of the match with a groin strain.

On the second afternoon, Zimbabwe floundered against Martin Snedden who moved the ball at a brisk pace to have seven of his eight victims caught in the arc behind the wicket. He recorded a career best and Zimbabwe followed-on 169 in arrears and finished the day at 20 for 1, bad light ending play early.

The home side showed more resolution in their second innings and owed much to Pycroft and Houghton who added 154 for the fourth wicket. Houghton, in sight of his maiden first-class hundred, fell to a rash shot to mid-wicket which he must have regretted and Pycroft was bowled by a beautiful back-break from Tracy, but they had made the game safe.

Trevor Franklin drives Traicos during his innings of 153 not out in the First International at Harare. (Bob Nixon)

First One-Day International
ZIMBABWE v. YOUNG NEW ZEALAND

John Bracewell, used to open the bowling with his accurate off-spinners, caused the home side to struggle and only stands of 61 for the fifth wicket between Houghton and Fletcher and 35 for the ninth wicket between Rawson and Traicos led them to a total of 175 which still looked far from adequate.

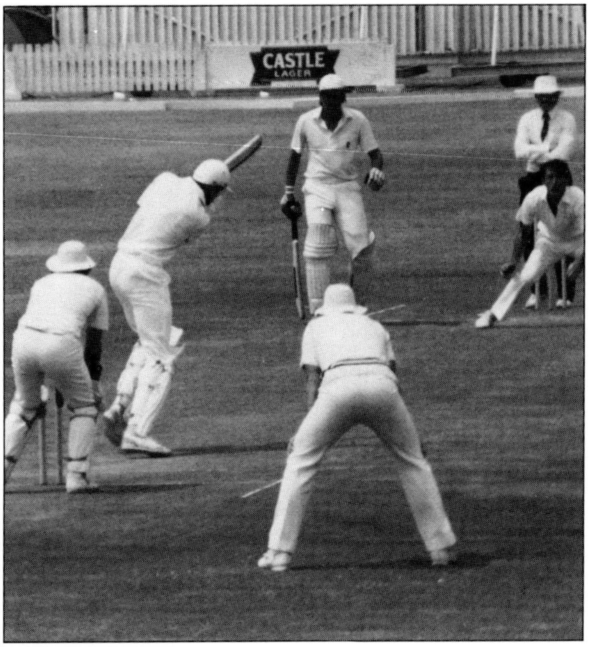

New Zealand batted in poor light and never found run-getting easy. A dreadful middle order collapse which saw 6 wickets fall for 26 runs seemed to have doomed the visitors to defeat, but the last three batsmen fought back magnificently. The batsmen hit furiously and the fielders found it difficult to sight the ball. With one ball remaining, the scores were level. Had there been an appeal against the light, the tourists would have won on the faster scoring rate, but Stirling stayed and was yorked by Butchart so that Zimbabwe won on having lost fewer wickets.

10 October 1984

at Kwekwe Sports Club

Young New Zealanders 188 (K.R. Rutherford 85, A.H. Omarshah 4 for 22)
Young Zimbabwe 189 for 7 (A.H. Omarshah 63)
Young Zimbabwe won by 3 wickets

A fine all-round performance by Ali Omarshah who had had a lean time since the World Cup led the home side to a good win.

Second International
ZIMBABWE *v.* YOUNG NEW ZEALAND

Electing this time to bat when he won the toss, Pycroft saw his side make another very poor start. It was the captain himself in company with Houghton who rescued the side, adding 118 for the fourth wicket. Fletcher then played quite magnificently and seemed in sight of a maiden first-class century in a long and distinguished career, but he chose to bat recklessly and was twice dropped before falling to Bracewell.

Pycroft declared before the close of the first day and although Franklin went early on the second morning, Bruce Edgar took total command to reach the first double century of his career. The visitors batted on into the third morning and the game seemed certain to be drawn, but Zimbabwe collapsed miserably before Stirling and Snedden. Pycroft provided the solitary light in a dismal batting display, but the crucial wicket was that of Hick who was run out after a confident and cautious start.

Young New Zealand had 8 overs in which to score 56 for victory. They needed only 6.3 and to add to Zimbabwe's problems, Butchart split his hand.

Martin Snedden bowls to Ian Butchart. Bracewell, Jeff Crowe and McSweeney are the eager fielders behind the wicket. Snedden had a career best 8 for 73 in the First International. (Bob Nixon)

Butchart bowls to Edgar who hit 203 in the Second International at Bulawayo. (Bob Nixon)

Second One-Day International
ZIMBABWE *v.* YOUNG NEW ZEALAND

Overnight rain delayed the start and reduced the match to 40 overs. Jeff Crowe played his first significant innings of the tour, but the visitors' total, although commendable, did not look unbeatable. Zimbabwe, however, chose to give a wretched batting display, losing their first six wickets for 33. As they were to crumple again the following day, the last day of the three-day game, it was a very dismal time for Zimbabwean cricket.

17 October 1984

at Hwange C.C.

Young Zimbabwe 208 (C.A.T. Hodgson 60, G.K. Robertson 4 for 48)
Young New Zealanders 209 for 9
Young New Zealanders won by 1 wicket

Craig Hodgson, out of form and favour for two years, made a significant contribution to the home side's score and a ninth wicket stand of 62 between Meman and Jarvis enabled them to reach respectability. Snedden, who was captaining the side, and Tracy scored the 12 runs needed for victory after they had come together for the last wicket.

SECOND INTERNATIONAL – ZIMBABWE *v.* YOUNG NEW ZEALAND

12, 13 and 15 October 1984 at Bulawayo Athletic Club

ZIMBABWE

	FIRST INNINGS		SECOND INNINGS	
G.A. Paterson	c McSweeney, b Snedden	17	c Rutherford b Stirling	0
K.G. Walton	c Crowe, b Tracy	7	c Rutherford, b Stirling	33
R.D. Brown	c Rutherford, b Tracy	3	b Stirling	0
A.J. Pycroft†	c and b Snedden	74	lbw, b Snedden	56
D.L. Houghton*	c Snedden, b Brown	54	c Snedden, b Stirling	20
G.A. Hick	c Bracewell, b Brown	0	run out	30
D.A.G. Fletcher	c Rutherford, b Bracewell	93	c McSweeney, b Snedden	2
I.P. Butchart	c Rutherford, b Bracewell	29	c Franklin, b Snedden	14
P.W.E. Rawson	b Bracewell	10	b Brown	1
A.J. Traicos	not out	12	c McEwan, b Snedden	2
K.G. Duers			not out	4
Extras	lb 7, nb 11	18	b 2, lb 1, nb 2	5
	(for 9 wkts dec)	317		167

	O	M	R	W	O	M	R	W
Stirling	14	4	43	—	13	3	66	4
Tracy	11	—	42	2	5	1	14	—
Snedden	23	3	70	2	16	9	26	4
Brown	18	2	75	2	13	4	28	1
McEwan	1	—	5	—				
Bracewell	16.5	2	75	3	10	2	30	—

FALL OF WICKETS

1- 27, 2- 30, 3- 35, 4- 153, 5- 165, 6- 167, 7- 251, 8- 277, 9- 317

1- 0, 2- 2, 3- 72, 4- 99, 5- 143, 6- 143, 7- 146, 8- 149, 9- 158

YOUNG NEW ZEALAND

	FIRST INNINGS		SECOND INNINGS	
T.J. Franklin	c Traicos, b Duers	13	run out	5
B.A. Edgar	b Butchart	203	b Fletcher	3
K.R. Rutherford	c Houghton, b Duers	27		
P.E. McEwan	c Pycroft, b Butchart	69	(3) not out	35
J.J. Crowe†	c Houghton, b Duers	33	(4) not out	9
V.R. Brown	not out	67		
J.G. Bracewell	c Walton, b Duers	6		
D.A. Stirling	b Duers	1		
E.B. McSweeny*				
M.C. Snedden				
S.R. Tracy				
Extras	lb 9, w1	10	lb 4	4
	(for 7 wkts dec)	429	(for 2 wkts)	56

	O	M	R	W	O	M	R	W
Rawson	32	6	112	—	1.1	—	9	—
Duers	34.1	6	108	5				
Fletcher	11	3	29	—	3	—	25	1
Traicos	26	3	92	—				
Butchart	16	—	47	2	2.2	—	18	—
Hick	7	—	32	—				

FALL OF WICKETS

1- 33, 2- 69, 3- 203, 4- 290, 5- 411, 6- 426, 7- 429

1- 3, 2- 36

Young New Zealand won by 8 wickets

SECOND ONE-DAY INTERNATIONAL – ZIMBABWE *v.* YOUNG NEW ZEALAND

14 October 1984 at Bulawayo Athletic Club

YOUNG NEW ZEALAND

T.J. Franklin	c Brown, b Traicos	37
P.S. Briasco	c Houghton, b Rawson	13
J.J. Crowe†	run out	53
P.E. McEwan	c Rawson, b Butchart	7
R.N. Hoskin	c Brown, b Fletcher	13
V.R. Brown	c and b Fletcher	10
E.B. McSweeney*	b Fletcher	17
J.G. Bracewell	c Houghton, b Butchart	16
M.C. Snedden	not out	9
D.A. Stirling	not out	9
S.R. Tracy		
Extras	lb 7, w 4	11
(40 overs)	(for 8 wickets)	195

	O	M	R	W
Rawson	8	—	33	1
Duers	3	—	19	—
Traicos	8	—	35	1
Butchart	7	1	27	2
Fletcher	8	—	46	3
Hick	6	—	28	—

FALL OF WICKETS

1- 40, 2- 66, 3- 78, 4- 112, 5- 124, 6- 147, 7- 170, 8- 178

ZIMBABWE

R.D. Brown	st McSweeney, b Bracewell	2
G.A. Paterson	c Tracy, b Stirling	1
K.M. Curran	lbw, b Stirling	1
A.J. Pycroft†	c Snedden, b McEwan	26
D.L. Houghton*	c Crowe, b Stirling	14
D.A.G. Fletcher	c Brown, b Stirling	0
G.A. Hick	c and b Bracewell	2
I.P. Butchart	lbw, b Snedden	17
P.W.E. Rawson	c Briasco, b McEwan	7
A.J. Traicos	not out	14
K.G. Duers	c McSweeney, b Tracy	3
Extras	b 2, lb 4, w 2	8
		95

	O	M	R	W
Stirling	8	2	10	4
Bracewell	8	2	27	2
Tracy	6.4	—	20	1
Snedden	8	4	20	1
McEwan	4	—	12	2

FALL OF WICKETS

1- 3, 2- 3, 3- 6, 4- 24, 5- 24, 6- 33, 7- 67, 8- 69, 9- 80

Young New Zealand won by 100 runs

THIRD INTERNATIONAL – ZIMBABWE *v.* YOUNG NEW ZEALAND
19, 20 and 22 October 1984 at Harare Sports Club

YOUNG NEW ZEALAND

	FIRST INNINGS	
B.A. Edgar	c Rawson, b Curran	41
T.J. Franklin	c Houghton, b Duers	9
P.S. Briasco	c Traicos, b Hick	89
P.E. McEwan	c Hick, b Rawson	153
J.J. Crowe†	b Fletcher	2
V.R. Brown	not out	85
E.B. McSweeney*	c Duers, b Curran	34
J.G. Bracewell	c Brown, b Curran	10
M.C. Snedden	lbw, b Traicos	6
G.K. Robertson	c Omarshah, b Hick	21
D.A. Stirling	st Houghton, b Traicos	33
Extras	lb 8, w 2, nb 6	16
		499

	O	M	R	W
Rawson	23	2	105	1
Duers	18	4	62	1
Curran	19	6	82	3
Traicos	28.5	9	80	2
Omarshah	8	2	30	—
Fletcher	16	5	43	1
Hick	22	2	89	2

FALL OF WICKETS
1- 22, 2- 65, 3- 256, 4- 277, 5- 316, 6- 378, 7- 395, 8- 416, 9- 455

ZIMBABWE

	FIRST INNINGS		SECOND INNINGS	
K.G. Walton	c McSweeney b Robertson	23	lbw, b Robertson	2
A.H. Omarshah	c McSweeney, b Robertson	0	b Snedden	33
R.D. Brown	c McSweeney, b Stirling	0	not out	124
D.L. Houghton*	c McEwan, b Bracewell	33	(5) lbw, b Snedden	2
G.A. Hick	lbw, b Bracewell	95	(6) lbw, b Brown	22
D.A.G. Fletcher	c and b Bracewell	10	(7) not out	47
K.M. Curran	c Crowe, b Bracewell	0		
P.W.E. Rawson	c Crowe, b Bracewell	14		
A.J. Traicos	c Crowe, b Bracewell	5		
K.G. Duers	not out	1		
A.J. Pycroft†	absent ill	—	(4) c Bracewell, b Brown	24
Extras	b 2, lb 12, nb 7	21	b 1, lb 9, nb 7	17
		202	(for 5 wkts)	271

	O	M	R	W	O	M	R	W
Stirling	9	2	46	1	7.1	1	20	—
Robertson	12	2	47	2	10	—	40	1
Snedden	8	—	23	—	19	3	58	2
Bracewell	15.1	5	48	6	27	4	72	—
Brown	3	—	24	—	25	6	71	2

FALL OF WICKETS
1- 4, 2- 5, 3- 58, 4- 66, 5- 88, 6- 99, 7- 171, 8- 191, 9- 202
1- 5, 2- 65, 3- 121, 4- 131, 5- 196

Umpires: I.D. Robinson and D.B. Arnott (B. McLoughlin on days 2 and 3)

Match drawn

Third International
ZIMBABWE *v.* YOUNG NEW ZEALAND

After Crowe had won the toss Young New Zealand batted until mid-afternoon on the second day to reach the highest total recorded against Zimbabwe for 17 years. The innings was founded on a partnership of high quality between Briasco and McEwan, and McEwan became the third batsman in successive matches to take 150 off the Zimbabwe attack. It was the sixth century of his career. Brown played solidly and there was some enterprising play from Robertson and Stirling at the close.

Pycroft was taken ill with a severe bout of 'flu on the first afternoon and was unable to bat. Traicos relieved him as captain. The Zimbabwe innings was a disaster against Bracewell's off-spin, but Hick was a shining exception. In his first major innings in his own country, he hit 95 in under two hours and was especially able in his cutting. He was out swinging injudiciously across the line when joined by last man Duers.

ABOVE: *Franklin is caught Houghton, bowled Duers for 9 in the Third International, Zimbabwe v Young New Zealand. (Bob Nixon)*

LEFT: *Rawson bowls to McEwan during his innings of 153 in the Third International. (Bob Nixon)*

THIRD ONE-DAY INTERNATIONAL – ZIMBABWE *v.* YOUNG NEW ZEALAND
21 October 1984 at Harare Sports Club

ZIMBABWE			
	K.G. Walton	c Tracy, b Bracewell	24
	A.H. Omarshah	c Tracy, b Bracewell	16
	D.A.G. Fletcher	c McSweeney, b Bracewell	27
	D.L. Houghton*	not out	119
	G.A. Hick	c McSweeney, b Tracy	61
	G.A. Paterson	not out	9
	C.A.T. Hodgson		
	I.P. Butchart		
	P.W.E. Rawson		
	A.J. Traicos†		
	K.G. Duers		
	Extras	b 4, lb 9, w 5, nb 5	23
	(50 overs)	(for 4 wickets)	279

	O	M	R	W
Stirling	10	—	39	—
Robertson	5	—	34	—
Bracewell	10	1	30	3
Snedden	10	1	60	—
Tracy	10	1	66	1
McEwan	3	—	19	—
Brown	2	—	18	—

FALL OF WICKETS
1- 33, 2- 77, 3- 77, 4- 245

YOUNG NEW ZEALAND			
	T.J. Franklin	c Fletcher, b Rawson	5
	B.A. Edgar	c Houghton, b Duers	6
	J.J. Crowe†	c Rawson, b Duers	11
	P.E. McEwan	c Houghton, b Duers	0
	V.R. Brown	b Butchart	31
	E.B. McSweeney*	c Rawson, b Duers	0
	J.G. Bracewell	b Butchart	59
	M.C. Snedden	c Fletcher, b Butchart	3
	G.K. Robertson	b Butchart	3
	D.A. Stirling	not out	5
	S.R. Tracy	c Hick, b Butchart	8
	Extras	lb 6, w 2, nb 2	10
	(38 overs)		141

	O	M	R	W
Rawson	7	—	23	1
Duers	10	1	29	4
Fletcher	4	—	18	—
Butchart	9	—	41	5
Traicos	8	—	24	—

FALL OF WICKETS
1- 6, 2- 19, 3- 19, 4- 41, 5- 42, 6- 94, 7- 109, 8- 118, 9- 133

Zimbabwe won by 138 runs

Following-on, Zimbabwe were saved by the revival of Robin Brown whose return to form after a long period in the doldrums was marked by the fourth century of his career which he reached off 217 deliveries. In all, he batted for 244 minutes and hit twelve fours. Pycroft, who has played in every one of Zimbabwe's matches since Independence, was out for 24, the first time he had failed to reach 30 in the twenty-six matches played since that time.

Third One-Day International
ZIMBABWE *v.* YOUNG NEW ZEALAND

With Pycroft unwell, John Traicos took over the captaincy and called out the team early in the morning for concentrated practice. Walton, Omarshah and Fletcher gave the innings a useful start and then Houghton batted quite magnificently sharing a partnership of 168 with the impressive Hick.

Confronted by a formidable total, Young New Zealand suffered at the hands of Duers who again showed his ability to lay waste the beginning of an innings. Bracewell batted doggedly, but Iain Butchart romped through the tail to round off Zimbabwe's best day of the season against the New Zealanders.

Fourth One-Day International
ZIMBABWE *v.* YOUNG NEW ZEALAND

After their splendid performance in the third one-day international Zimbabwe gave a disappointingly lethargic performance in the fourth and final match of the series which the visitors won easily and so drew level at two matches each.

Hick, 95 in the Third International, his first major innings at the top level. (Ken Kelly)

FOURTH ONE-DAY INTERNATIONAL – ZIMBABWE *v.* YOUNG NEW ZEALAND
24 October 1984 at Mutare Sports Club

ZIMBABWE			
	K.G. Walton	b Tracy	50
	A.H. Omarshah	b Bracewell	7
	D.A.G. Fletcher	b Bracewell	1
	A.J. Pycroft†	b Tracy	49
	D.L. Houghton*	run out	15
	G.A. Hick	run out	0
	C.A.T. Hodgson	lbw, b Tracy	6
	I.P. Butchart	lbw, b Tracy	3
	P.W.E. Rawson	c Crowe, b Stirling	14
	A.J. Traicos	c Edgar, b Stirling	3
	K.G. Duers	not out	4
	Extras	b 2, lb 10, nb 1	13
	(48.4 overs)		165

	O	M	R	W
Stirling	8.4	—	24	2
Bracewell	10	2	15	2
Snedden	7	1	24	—
McEwan	5	—	25	—
Brown	10	2	29	—
Tracy	8	—	36	4

FALL OF WICKETS
1- 28, 2- 46, 3- 90, 4- 114, 5- 114, 6- 140, 7- 142, 8- 147, 9- 158

YOUNG NEW ZEALAND			
	T.J. Franklin	lbw, b Duers	71
	B.A. Edgar	c and b Hick	27
	K.R. Rutherford	not out	55
	P.E. McEwan	not out	12
	J.J. Crowe†		
	R.N. Hoskin*		
	V.R. Brown		
	J.G. Bracewell		
	M.C. Snedden		
	D.A. Stirling		
	S.R. Tracy		
	Extras	b 1, lb 1, w 1, nb 1	4
	(42.2 overs)	(for 2 wickets)	169

	O	M	R	W
Rawson	6	—	33	—
Duers	6	—	33	1
Hick	10	—	32	1
Traicos	10	—	21	—
Omarshah	5	—	17	—
Butchart	5	—	27	—
Hodgson	0.2	—	4	—

FALL OF WICKETS
1- 72, 2- 141

Young New Zealand won by 8 wickets

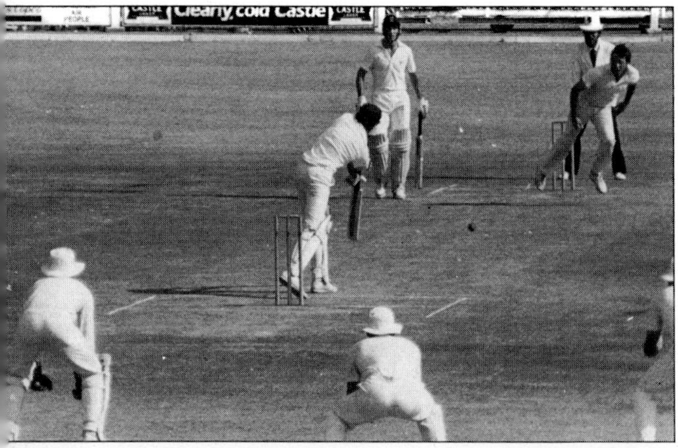

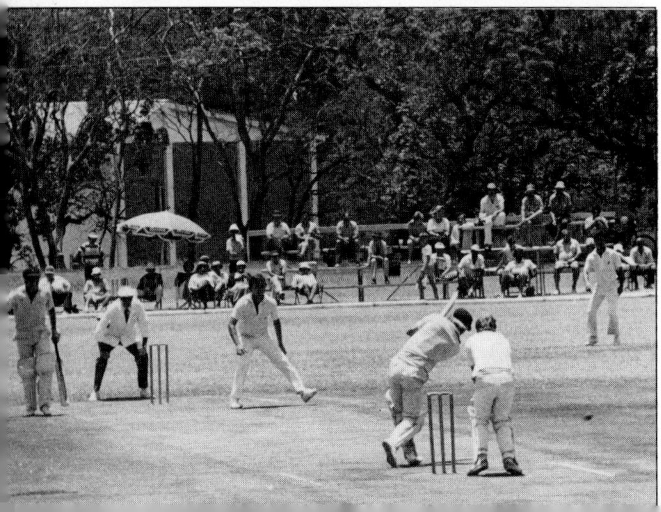

Kevin Walton hit a thoroughly deserved fifty and Pycroft again batted well, but two run outs in the middle order brought about a collapse which was compounded by Tracy.

The tourists batted soundly and it was gratifying for them that two of their less experienced players, Franklin and Rutherford, should show such authority.

Fourth International
ZIMBABWE *v.* YOUNG NEW ZEALAND

Two-one down in the series, Zimbabwe batted well but had little hope of bowling out the tourists on a placid pitch. Young New Zealand were handicapped when Brown pulled a muscle in the second over of the match and was unable to bowl. Brown, who kept wicket in the second innings, Houghton and Hick, now firmly established as Zimbabwe's brightest hope for the future, all batted encouragingly, but the fireworks came from Butchart. He retired hurt at 14 with the score at 321 for 6 after being hit on the chin by a bumper from Stirling. He returned the following morning at the fall of the seventh wicket and hit four sixes, three of them off successive deliveries from Bracewell, as he ran to his highest first-class score.

Zimbabwe declared at lunch on the second day and Jeff Crowe and McEwan added 133 in a sparkling stand which

ABOVE: *Snedden bowls to Brown, one of the great successes of the series against Young New Zealand. (Bob Nixon)*

LEFT: *Vaughan Brown bowls to Hodgson in the beautiful setting of Mutare Sports Club. (Bob Nixon)*

FOURTH INTERNATIONAL – ZIMBABWE *v.* YOUNG NEW ZEALAND

26, 27 and 28 October 1984 at Harare Sports Club

ZIMBABWE

	FIRST INNINGS		SECOND INNINGS	
K.G. Walton	c Hoskin b Robertson	10	c McSweeney, b Stirling	14
A.H. Omarshah	run out	42	c Briasco, b Stirling	0
R.D. Brown	c Hoskin, b Bracewell	73	(7) not out	16
A.J. Pycroft†	c McSweeney, b Robertson	31	(5) lbw, b Snedden	2
D.L. Houghton*	c Bracewell, b Snedden	53	(4) c McEwan, b Snedden	0
G.A. Hick	c McSweeney b Robertson	88	(3) not out	38
D.A.G. Fletcher	c Hoskin, b Bracewell	23		
I.P. Butchart	c Crowe, b Snedden	71	(6) lbw, b Stirling	0
A.J. Traicos	not out	37		
P.W.E. Rawson	c sub (Tracy), b Bracewell	13		
K.G. Duers				
Extras	b 8, lb 6, w 2, nb 22	38	lb 5, nb 6	11
	(for 9 wkts dec)	479	(for 5 wkts dec)	81

YOUNG NEW ZEALAND

	FIRST INNINGS		SECOND INNINGS	
J.J. Crowe†	lbw, b Duers	88		
B.A. Edgar	c Houghton, b Duers	17		
P.S. Briasco	c Fletcher, b Duers	0		
P.E. McEwan	b Hick	90	(5) not out	17
R.N. Hoskin	b Duers	5	(6) not out	2
V.R. Brown	c Rawson, b Duers	17		
E.B. McSweeney*	c Houghton, b Duers	9	(4) c Pycroft, b Traicos	0
J.G. Bracewell	c Houghton, b Duers	75		
M.C. Snedden	c Duers, b Hick	28	(3) c Brown, b Traicos	12
D.A. Stirling	not out	26	(2) c and b Hick	45
G.K. Robertson	c Rawson, b Duers	0	(1) c Brown, b Rawson	14
Extras	lb 2, w 4, nb 3	9	lb 9	9
		364	(for 4 wkts)	99

	O	M	R	W	O	M	R	W
Stirling	23	2	78	—	12	2	40	3
Robertson	20	1	113	3	3	—	20	—
Snedden	41	12	102	2	9	2	16	2
Bracewell	39	6	172	3				

	O	M	R	W	O	M	R	W
Rawson	17	3	71	—	6	—	29	1
Duers	25.5	4	102	8	4	—	30	—
Fletcher	4	1	19	—				
Butchart	9	2	41	—				
Traicos	15	2	43	—	4	—	18	2
Hick	17	—	86	2	2	—	13	1

FALL OF WICKETS (Zimbabwe)
1- 38, 2- 84, 3- 140, 4- 220, 5- 238, 6- 305, 7- 357, 452, 8- 479
1- 3, 2- 45, 3- 46, 4- 48, 5- 56

FALL OF WICKETS (Young New Zealand)
1- 35, 2- 43, 3- 176, 4- 195, 5- 206, 6- 233, 7- 236, 8- 297, 9- 364
1- 26, 2- 59, 3- 69, 4- 95

Umpires: I.D. Robinson and B. McLaughlin

Match drawn

The Young New Zealand innings ends in the Fourth International. Robertson is caught at slip by Rawson off Duers. (Bob Nixon)

RIGHT: *Hick slashes Robertson through the off side during his innings of 88 in the Fourth International. (Bob Nixon)*

Zimbabwe *v.* Young New Zealand – Averages

ZIMBABWE BATTING

	M	Inns	NOs	Runs	HS	Av	100s	50s
R.D. Brown	4	8	2	267	124*	44.50	1	1
G.A. Hick	4	8	1	304	95	43.43		2
D.A.G. Fletcher	4	7	2	212	93	42.40		1
A.J. Pycroft	4	7		296	88	42.28		3
D.L. Houghton	4	8		267	84	33.37		3
I.P. Butchart	3	6	1	154	71	30.80		1
A.J. Traicos	4	5	2	59	37*	19.66		
A.H. Omarshah	2	4		75	42	18.75		
K.G. Walton	4	8		129	37	16.12		
P.W.E. Rawson	4	5		43	14	8.60		
G.A. Paterson	2	4		17	17	4.25		

Played in four matches: K.G. Duers 4*, 1* and 4*
Played in one match: K.M. Curran 0

YOUNG NEW ZEALAND BATTING

	M	Inns	NOs	Runs	HS	Av	100s	50s
P.E. McEwan	4	6	2	364	153	91.00	1	2
V.R. Brown	4	4	2	170	85*	85.00		2
T.J. Franklin	3	4	1	180	153*	60.00	1	
B.A. Edgar	4	5		266	203	53.20	1	
P.S. Briasco	2	2		89	89	44.50		1
J.J. Crowe	4	5	1	137	88	34.25		1
D.A. Stirling	4	5	1	137	45	34.25		
J.G. Bracewell	4	4		118	75	29.50		1
M.C. Snedden	4	4		93	47	23.25		
E.B. McSweeney	4	4		72	34	18.00		
K.R. Rutherford	2	2		28	27	14.00		
G.K. Robertson	2	3		35	21	11.66		

Also batted: S.R. Tracy 1 (two matches); R.N. Hoskin 5 and 2* (one match)

ZIMBABWE BOWLING

	Overs	Mds	Runs	Wkts	Av	Best	5/inn
K.G. Duers	107	19	384	18	21.33	8/102	2
K.M. Curran	19	6	82	3	27.33	3/82	
G.A. Hick	63	8	243	6	40.50	2/86	
D.A.G. Fletcher	39	10	129	3	43.00	1/13	
A.J. Traicos	105.5	24	303	6	50.50	2/18	
I.P. Butchart	31.2	2	131	2	65.50	2/47	
P.W.E. Rawson	111.1	19	413	4	103.25	2/87	

Also bowled: A.H. Omarshah 8–2–30–0

YOUNG NEW ZEALAND BOWLING

	Overs	Mds	Runs	Wkts	Av	Best	5/inn
M.C. Snedden	154.3	36	418	21	19.90	8/73	1
S.R. Tracy	32	7	93	4	23.25	2/33	
V.R. Brown	79	20	241	8	30.12	3/43	
G.K. Robertson	45	3	220	6	36.66	3/113	
J.G. Bracewell	148	28	512	13	39.38	6/48	1
D.A. Stirling	101.1	18	386	9	42.88	4/66	

Also bowled: K.R. Rutherford 2–0–27–0; P.E. McEwan 1–0–5–0

ZIMBABWE CATCHES

9–D.L. Houghton (ct 8/st 1); 5–R.D. Brown; 3–A.J. Pycroft, I.P. Butchart, A.J. Traicos and P.W.E. Rawson; 2–G.A. Hick and K.G. Duers; 1–D.A.G. Fletcher, A.H. Omarshah, K.G. Walton and G.A. Paterson

NEW ZEALAND CATCHES

13–E.B. McSweeney; 6–K.R. Rutherford; 5–P.E. McEwan, J.J. Crowe and J.G. Bracewell; 4–M.C. Snedden; 3–R.N. Hoskin; 1–T.J. Franklin and P.S. Briasco

McEwan dominated. There was a minor collapse on the last morning which gave Zimbabwe hope of victory, but Bracewell, who had suffered badly with his off-spinners, Snedden and Stirling prevented further joy for the home side.

The game ended with some light-hearted hitting. After the match Duncan Fletcher announced his retirement although he was to play for Western Province B in South Africa later in the season after he had emigrated. Fletcher, once the greatest of Zimbabwe's cricketers who has played a most significant part in the advance of cricket in the country in recent years, left with a career record of 4079 runs, average 23.85, 216 wickets at 27.65 runs a piece, and 75 catches.

While saying goodbye to the old, Zimbabwe welcomed the arrival of the new as twenty-four year old medium-pacer Kevin Duers became only the sixth bowler to take 8 wickets in an innings for Zimbabwe. The feat has been achieved seven times, Joe Partridge having done it twice.

The second half of the Zimbabwe season saw the tour by an English Counties XI under the management of Mike Vockins, the Worcestershire secretary. The English side was led by Mark Nicholas, the new Hampshire skipper, and contained four players with Test experience. Don Oslear also travelled with the side and stood in all the major matches, local umpires benefitting from his vast experience.

The Zimbabwe Cricket Union had approached the T.C.C.B. and asked for an England B side to make the tour, but the idea did not meet with approval and it was due to the efforts of Mike Vockins, a splendid and popular manager of a popular team, that the Counties side tour went ahead.

The team suffered a number of strains and minor injuries, but they never made this an excuse for their failures on the field. Nicholas led the side well and in a positive manner, but only Chris Broad and Paul Terry batted with professional consistency. Sadly, Andy Lloyd failed to find form with the bat or in the field and clearly he was still suffering from the effects of the blow he received in his one Test innings.

Neil Williams and Nick Cook looked the best of the bowlers, but the fielding generally was of a poor standard.

There was some disappointment that many of the Zimbabwe players did not apply the lessons that they should have learned from the tour by the Young New Zealanders. Kevin Walton was very unlucky to be dropped after his gritty showing in the first part of the season, but it was good to see Grant Paterson produce his league form in first-class cricket. Middle-order Districts batsman Andy Waller was the great success. His previous experience was limited to a one-day match against the Young Indians last season, but, although like Butchart a nervous starter, also like Butchart, he showed that he could hit the ball very hard.

Unfortunately, Kevin Curran, a much talented all-rounder, did not play in this series and his replacement was Denis Streak who, at the age of 35, returned to first-class cricket after an absence of nine years.

13 February 1985

at Harare South Country Club

English Counties XI 211 for 6 (B.C. Broad 111 not out)
Zimbabwe Country Districts 162 (G.A. Hick 53)
English Counties XI won by 49 runs

A fifty-over game in which Chris Broad quickly made his presence felt with an unbeaten century. Hick, one of only three local players with first-class experience, was the only Zimbabwe player to make 20.

First International Match
ZIMBABWE *v.* ENGLISH COUNTIES XI

Pycroft won the toss and asked the visitors to bat. His decision looked a good one as Rawson, Duers and Butchart troubled the early batsmen, but Chris Broad gave the innings solidity and the later batsmen, Neil Williams in particular, flourished and the tourists batted into the second morning.

Zimbabwe were given a sound start and then enterprising batting from Waller, Butchart and Rawson prompted Pycroft to declare 76 runs in arrears in order to get the Counties batting again before the close. Richard Williams was unable to bowl because of a back strain and Broad's leg strain brought Terry in as Lloyd's partner.

They survived until the close and next day they sought brisk runs in an effort to bring a declaration. Terry was impressive, but he only dominated in the later stages of his innings.

Nicholas' declaration left Zimbabwe just over three hours in which to make 255, an undaunting task. All that was required was to play to their normal limited-over standard, instead they chose to swat wildly and lost wickets to indiscreet strokes, Pycroft apart who was beaten by Cook's arm ball. There was some brisk hitting and hope from

Zimbabwe v English Counties at Harare. Traicos bowls to skipper Nicholas with the field clustered close. (Bob Nixon)

Butchart, but it was Houghton who fought a lone battle until caught at silly point with only 200 balls remaining.

Cook and Richard Williams bowled splendidly to close set fields and Neil Williams tormented the tail.

First One-Day International
ZIMBABWE *v.* ENGLISH COUNTIES

A consistent batting performance took Zimbabwe to a creditable total although no batsman reached fifty. Broad and Terry responded with a challenging opening partnership which looked likely to set up a win for the tourists but, after

FIRST INTERNATIONAL – ZIMBABWE *v.* ENGLISH COUNTIES XI
15, 16 and 18 February 1985 at Harare Sports Club

ENGLISH COUNTIES XI

	FIRST INNINGS		SECOND INNINGS	
B.C. Broad	c Pycroft, b Streak	64	(6) not out	26
T.A. Lloyd	b Duers	7	(1) c Pycroft, b Streak	50
M.C.J. Nicholas†	c Butchart, b Rawson	6	b Traicos	0
V.P. Terry	lbw, b Butchart	15	(2) not out	80
R.G. Williams	b Rawson	38	(4) c Hick, b Streak	0
P. Bainbridge	c and b Rawson	46	(5) b Butchart	17
T.M. Tremlett	c Houghton, b Hick	22		
N.F. Williams	not out	62		
R.J. Parks*	c Houghton, b Butchart	8		
P.G. Newman	c Rawson, b Traicos	8		
N.G.B. Cook	c Streak, b Rawson	10		
Extras	b 1, lb 5, w 1, nb 2	9	lb 2, w 1, nb 2	5
		295	(for 4 wkts dec)	178

	O	M	R	W	O	M	R	W
Rawson	29.5	5	92	4	9	2	32	—
Duers	20	1	67	1	8	2	21	—
Butchart	20	4	50	2	3	—	18	1
Traicos	27	8	50	1	12	1	49	1
Hick	9	2	18	1	6	2	27	—
Streak	5	—	12	1	14	3	29	2

FALL OF WICKETS
1- 10, 2- 39, 3- 65, 4- 139, 5- 149, 6- 201, 7- 206, 8- 249, 9- 270
1- 86, 2- 89, 3- 90, 4- 129

Umpires: D.G. Oslear and D.B. Arnott

English Counties XI won by 117 runs

ZIMBABWE

	FIRST INNINGS		SECOND INNINGS	
R.D. Brown	c Parks, b N. Williams	28	c R. Williams, b Cook	15
G.A. Paterson	c sub, b Tremlett	14	b Cook	27
G.A. Hick	c Parks, b Newman	42	lbw, b Cook	6
A.J. Pycroft†	c sub, b Cook	0	(5) lbw, b Cook	0
D.L. Houghton*	b Newman	11	(4) c Bainbridge, b R. Williams	55
A.C. Waller	not out	60	st Parks, b R. Williams	0
I.P. Butchart	c Tremlett, b Cook	33	c Nicholas, b R. Williams	23
P.W.E. Rawson	c Lloyd, b Tremlett	20	lbw, b Cook	4
D.H. Streak			c Cook, b N. Williams	2
A.J. Traicos			c Parks, b N. Williams	0
K.G. Duers			not out	0
Extras	lb 5, nb 6	11	lb 2, nb 3	5
	(for 7 wkts dec)	219		137

	O	M	R	W	O	M	R	W
N.F. Williams	20	7	54	1	9	2	28	2
Newman	9	2	30	2	4	—	17	—
Tremlett	14.1	1	51	2	3	1	10	—
Cook	30	8	48	2	21	8	41	5
Bainbridge	5	—	31	—				
R.G. Williams					14.4	2	39	3

FALL OF WICKETS
1- 30, 2- 67, 3- 68, 4- 96, 5- 103, 6- 156, 7- 219
1- 34, 2- 47, 3- 54, 4- 54, 5- 59, 6- 114, 7- 119, 8- 135, 9- 135

Christ Broad, one of the outstanding successes of the tour, cuts Hick for four. (Bob Nixon)

Nicholas, the later batting fell apart against the combination of Butchart's medium pace and Hick's off-spin. Neil Williams made some lusty hits, but the issue had long since been decided.

20 February 1985

at Kwekwe

English Counties XI 214 for 5 (B.C. Broad 78)
Zimbabwe B 177

English Counties XI won by 37 runs

The home side's bowlers, Jarvis and Meman in particular, did well to restrict the visitors for whom Broad was again outstanding. Newman and Tremlett, however, soon had the B side in disarray and only Houghton, being given experience as captain, rallied the side with a knock of 35.

22, 23 and 25 February 1985

at Bulawayo

English Counties XI 338 (P. Bainbridge 147 not out, M.C.J. Nicholas 91) and 260 for 5 dec (V.P. Terry 135 not out, D.B. d'Oliveira 50)
Zimbabwe B 331 (M.P. Jarvis 58, E.A. Brandes 56, K.G. Walton 54, A.H. Omarshah 50, R.G. Williams 4 for 86) and 138 (R.G. Williams 7 for 49)

English Counties XI won by 129 runs

This match was accorded first-class status. Nicholas batted superbly after Terry had gone for 0. He shared a stand of 101 with Lloyd, who hit 24, and Phil Bainbridge later hit a career best and rallied the visitors at a time when they appeared to be failing. Only Newman, in a stand of 80 for the ninth wicket, gave him support. Zimbabwe B were given a fine start by Omarshah and Walton, Omarshah attacked in fine style, and Walton was second out at 130. The middle-order fell apart and the innings appeared dead at 207 for 8. Pace bowlers and genuine tail-enders, Malcolm Jarvis and Eddo Brandes, then launched a violent attack on the bowling and added 87.

A fine century by Paul Terry re-established English Counties' authority on the last day and, as the seniors had done a week earlier, the home side disintegrated in their second innings. Richard Williams did the damage and returned career best figures with his off-breaks.

Second One-Day International
ZIMBABWE *v.* ENGLISH COUNTIES

Excellent batting by Nicholas and Terry put the tourists into a strong position. They added 128 for the third wicket and

FIRST ONE-DAY INTERNATIONAL – ZIMBABWE *v.* ENGLISH COUNTIES XI
17 February 1985 at Harare Sports Club

ZIMBABWE			
	G.A. Paterson	c Davis, b Tremlett	35
	K.G. Walton	c Terry, b Monkhouse	26
	G.A. Hick	c Broad, b Cook	41
	A.J. Pycroft†	c and b Tremlett	30
	D.L. Houghton*	c Broad, b N.F. Williams	47
	A.C. Waller	b Davis	18
	I.P. Butchart	c Tremlett, b Davis	6
	P.W.E. Rawson	not out	17
	D.H. Streak	c Nicholas, b Davis	0
	A.J. Traicos	not out	1
	K.G. Duers		
	Extras	lb 7, w 3, nb 1	11
	(50 overs)	(for 8 wickets)	232

	O	M	R	W
N.F. Williams	10	2	62	1
Davis	10	—	40	3
Tremlett	10	—	28	2
Monkhouse	7	—	31	1
Cook	10	2	41	1
Bainbridge	3	—	23	—

FALL OF WICKETS
1- 62, 2- 72, 3- 122, 4- 152, 5- 207, 6- 209, 7- 216, 8- 217

ENGLISH COUNTIES XI			
	B.C. Broad	c Pycroft, b Hick	52
	V.P. Terry	st Houghton, b Hick	28
	M.C.J. Nicholas†	c Waller, b Hick	23
	P. Bainbridge	c Houghton, b Butchart	0
	D.B. d'Oliveira	run out	7
	N.F. Williams	c Rawson, b Butchart	28
	T.M. Tremlett	c Duers, b Butchart	7
	R.J. Parks*	c Hick, b Butchart	0
	G. Monkhouse	not out	7
	N.G.B. Cook	b Butchart	2
	M.R. Davis	not out	4
	Extras	b 2, lb 10, w 3, nb 3	18
	(50 overs)	(for 9 wickets)	176

	O	M	R	W
Rawson	10	1	37	—
Duers	10	3	32	—
Traicos	10	1	33	—
Butchart	10	1	31	5
Hick	10	—	31	3

FALL OF WICKETS
1- 88, 2- 95, 3- 98, 4- 112, 5- 142, 6- 156, 7- 157, 8- 163, 9- 167

Zimbabwe won by 56 runs

took their side to a formidable score. Brown and Paterson responded for Zimbabwe with an excellent opening partnership, but the middle-order failed to maintain the momentum. Fifty runs were needed from the last five overs and the match seemed lost, but Waller and Butchart, who had played themselves in sensibly, launched a violent attack and neither Cook nor Neil Williams could halt them. The winning hit, a huge six by Andy Waller, came with 7 balls remaining. It was a memorable victory.

27 February 1985

at Hwange

Zimbabwe B 184 for 8 (G. Monkhouse 5 for 44)
English Counties XI 186 for 3 (B.C. Broad 115)
English Counties XI won by 7 wickets

Only Robertson and Houghton offered any real resistance to the bowling of Monkhouse and a tidy visitors' attack. Chris Broad then totally dominated the Zimbabwe bowling as the Counties ran to an easy win with 9.1 overs to spare.

Paterson drives Cook for six, too rare a sight for Zimbabwe eyes. (Box Nixon)

Second International Match
ZIMBABWE *v.* ENGLISH COUNTIES XI

Nicholas elected to bat when he won the toss and Broad and Terry, who survived a difficult slip chance at 18, began with a confident stand of 130. Terry, who had a fine tour, showed exactly why he had won a Test cap against West Indies. His defence was sound and his range of shots exciting. There seemed no possibility of his being dismissed until Pycroft, having run from slip to third man, hit the stumps with a direct throw. Terry's dismissal heralded a startling collapse, the last 7 wickets falling for 15 runs. It was Duers who did most of the damage.

With Neil Williams taking three middle-order wickets in 4 balls and the last 3 wickets in 5 balls, Zimbabwe were shot out for 178, a most disappointing display. Paterson and Houghton alone escaped from the debacle with any credit. Paterson, dropped at the wicket first ball, played an innings of sense and maturity and reached a maiden first-class fifty

SECOND ONE-DAY INTERNATIONAL – ZIMBABWE *v.* ENGLISH COUNTIES XI
24 February 1985 at Bulawayo Athletics Club

ENGLISH COUNTIES XI

P.C. Broad	c Pycroft, b Butchart	36
T.A. Lloyd	run out	4
M.C.J. Nicholas†	c Butchart, b Streak	73
V.P. Terry	c Hick, b Duers	77
P. Bainbridge	c Rawson, b Butchart	16
R.G. Williams	c Hick, b Duers	19
N.F. Williams	run out	18
T.N. Tremlett	run out	0
R.J. Parks*	not out	0
M.R. Davis		
N.G.B. Cook		
Extras	b 2, lb 4, w 2, nb 1	9
(50 overs)	(for 8 wickets)	252

	O	M	R	W
Rawson	8	2	24	—
Duers	10	1	60	2
Butchart	9	—	35	2
Traicos	10	—	33	—
Hick	7	—	55	—
Streak	6	—	39	1

FALL OF WICKETS
1- 15, 2- 60, 3- 188, 4- 198, 5- 226, 6- 245, 7- 251, 8- 252

ZIMBABWE

R.D. Brown	st Parks, b Cook	80
G.A. Paterson	c Parks, b Nicholas	39
G.A. Hick	c and b R.G. Williams	10
A.J. Pycroft†	c R.G. Williams, b Nicholas	13
D.L. Houghton*	b R.G. Williams	4
A.C. Waller	not out	56
I.P. Butchart	c Broad, b N.F. Williams	38
P.W.E. Rawson	not out	1
D.H. Streak		
A.J. Traicos		
K.G. Duers		
Extras	b 1, lb 15, nb 1	17
(48.5 overs)	(for 6 wickets)	258

	O	M	R	W
N.F. Williams	9.5	—	53	1
Davis	4	—	25	—
Cook	10	—	61	1
R.G. Williams	10	2	29	2
Tremlett	5	—	15	—
Nicholas	8	—	41	2
Bainbridge	2	—	18	—

FALL OF WICKETS
1- 96, 2- 109, 3- 140, 4- 155, 5- 164, 6- 251

Zimbabwe won by 4 wickets

SECOND INTERNATIONAL – ZIMBABWE *v.* ENGLISH COUNTIES XI

1, 2 and 4 March 1985 at Harare Sports Club

ENGLISH COUNTIES XI

	FIRST INNINGS		SECOND INNINGS	
B.C. Broad	c Houghton, b Rawson	59	lbw, b Rawson	0
V.P. Terry	run out	129	b Rawson	53
M.C.J. Nicholas†	c Hick, b Traicos	38	c Houghton, b Rawson	95
D.B. d'Oliveira	lbw, b Rawson	22	(5) lbw, b Rawson	6
P. Bainbridge	c Rawson, b Traicos	0	(4) st Houghton, b Traicos	9
R.G. Williams	b Duers	15	not out	8
N.F. Williams	not out	13		
G. Monkhouse	c Houghton, b Duers	0		
R.J. Parks*	c Houghton, b Duers	0		
P.G. Newman	c Hick, b Duers	1		
N.G.B. Cook	c Houghton, b Rawson	0		
Extras	b 2, lb 2, w 4, nb 3	11	lb 1, nb 2	3
		288	(for 5 wkts dec)	174

	O	M	R	W	O	M	R	W
Rawson	26.5	7	80	3	23.4	2	70	4
Duers	19	5	49	4	7	—	34	—
Butchart	14	2	48	—	11	2	19	—
Traicos	29	8	64	2	23	5	48	1
Streak	6	1	19	—	2	1	2	—
Hick	4	—	24	—				

FALL OF WICKETS
1- 130, 2- 207, 3- 249, 4- 273, 5- 273, 6- 273, 7- 273, 8- 284, 9- 287
1- 0, 2- 103, 3- 118, 4- 142, 5- 174

ZIMBABWE

	FIRST INNINGS		SECOND INNINGS	
R.D. Brown	c Parks, b N. Williams	11	lbw, b N. Williams	4
G.A. Paterson	lbw, b Cook	76	b Newman	12
G.A. Hick	st Parks, b Cook	14	c and b N. Williams	23
A.J. Pycroft†	c Bainbridge, b N. Williams	12	c Parks, b N. Williams	4
D.L. Houghton*	not out	26	c Parks, b Monkhouse	84
A.C. Waller	c Terry, b N. Williams	0	b Cook	75
I.P. Butchart	c Terry, b N. Williams	0	not out	49
P.W.E. Rawson	c Parks, b Monkhouse	17	c Cook, b Monkhouse	0
D.H. Streak	b N. Williams	2	not out	21
A.J. Traicos	c Parks, b N. Williams	0		
K.G. Duers	b N. Williams	0		
Extras	lb 1, nb 19	20	b 3, lb 6, nb 7	16
		178	(for 7 wkts)	288

	O	M	R	W	O	M	R	W
N.F. Williams	18	3	55	7	13	—	64	3
Newman	9	—	37	—	5	—	36	1
Monkhouse	13	4	33	1	10	—	60	2
Cook	16	4	34	2	23.3	6	76	1
R.G. Williams	6	2	18	—	6	—	34	—
Nicholas					2	—	9	—

FALL OF WICKETS
1- 40, 2- 85, 3- 123, 4- 132, 5- 132, 6- 132, 7- 171, 8- 178, 9- 178
1- 16, 2- 20, 3- 45, 4- 50, 5- 213, 6- 213, 7- 214

Umpires: D.G. Oslear and K. Kanjee

Zimbabwe won by 3 wickets

although he has been a prolific scorer in the league. When he fell to Cook, Houghton found himself again in the role of saviour, but could only watch frustrated as wickets tumbled at the other end.

Zimbabwe received a lift when Rawson, bowling with greater fire than he had done in the first innings, had Broad lbw second ball, but Terry was again in good form and the Counties closed the second day at 75 for 1. Rawson bowled well on the final morning, but Terry and Nicholas took the Englishmen to a commanding position. When Rawson had Nicholas caught behind Counties declared and Zimbabwe were set to make 285 in a minimum of 52 overs.

The spectre of defeat haunted them again and at 50 for 4 the match was following a familiar pattern. Houghton and Waller had other ideas and played Cook's slow left-arm spin with caution. Nicholas attempted to buy wickets and the batsmen got on top, but at the beginning of the final twenty overs, Zimbabwe still needed more than 7 an over and the most that they could hope for seemed to be a draw. Houghton and Waller attacked successfully and suddenly there were hopes of a famous victory, but both were denied the centuries they richly deserved. Rawson was also out so that 3 wickets fell in the space of 3 overs. With 10 overs left, 71 runs were needed and only 3 wickets remained so that the Counties seemed poised for victory.

Denis Streak had done little in the series, but now he played with great heart and maturity. He gave Butchart both support and confidence. He pushed for ones and twos and Butchart began to hit fiercely. With two overs left 16 were needed. Neil Williams bowled and 5 runs were scrambled from the first 4 balls. Butchart then decided it was time to act. He hooked Williams for six and pulled the next ball for four. The scores were level.

Cook bowled the last over and Streak played the first two deliveries firmly, but defensively. The third he hit past point

D'Oliveira is caught by Houghton off Hick at Harare. (Bob Nixon)

and it raced to the boundary. There are no pitch invasions in Zimbabwe although there is some gentle barracking. The players were allowed to leave the field unmolested, but not unappreciated. The crowd stood and roared its approval at what many saw as Zimbabwe's finest achievement on the cricket field.

Third One-Day International
ZIMBABWE *v.* ENGLISH COUNTIES XI

The English innings was rescued from complete humiliation only by a gem of an innings from Damian d'Oliveira, and there was intelligent support later from Tim Tremlett and Monkhouse. The Counties' meagre total was never likely to worry Zimbabwe and Brown and Paterson gave the confident start that was necessary for the home side to clinch the one-day series with ease.

6 March 1985

at Mutare

English Counties XI 259 for 9 (B.C. Broad 76, M.C.J. Nicholas 56)
Zimbabwe B 184 (C.A.T. Hodgson 68)
English Counties XI won by 71 runs

A second wicket partnership of 119 between Broad and Nicholas provided the substance for the Counties innings. The B side put up a brave fight with Houghton and Hodgson, both victims of Tremlett, putting on 96 for the fourth wicket.

Brown, caught Parks, bowled Williams 28, First International. (Bob Nixon)

Fourth One-Day International
ZIMBABWE *v.* ENGLISH COUNTIES XI

With Hick in a responsible vein, but unable to accelerate later in his innings, Zimbabwe were taken past 200 only by Peter Rawson's last flourish, and it was Rawson who was the hero when he dismissed Broad first ball. Terry again looked impressive, and at 106 for 3 the Counties looked well set although lagging behind the clock. Sustained pressure by Zimbabwe in the field frustrated the Counties and brought

THIRD ONE-DAY INTERNATIONAL – ZIMBABWE *v.* ENGLISH COUNTIES XI
3 March 1985 at Harare Sports Club

ENGLISH COUNTIES XI

B.C. Broad	c Brown, b Rawson	12
T.A. Lloyd	c Brown, b Rawson	0
M.C.J. Nicholas†	c Houghton, b Rawson	0
V.P. Terry	c Butchart, b Duers	0
D.B. d'Oliveira	c Butchart, b Rawson	63
R.G. Williams	run out	6
N.F. Williams	c and b Hick	3
T.M. Tremlett	not out	35
G. Monkhouse	c Waller, b Rawson	19
R.J. Parks*	not out	6
N.G.B. Cook		
Extras	w 3, nb 2	5
(50 overs)	(for 8 wickets)	149

	O	M	R	W
Rawson	10	1	33	5
Duers	10	3	20	1
Traicos	10	3	13	—
Butchart	10	4	41	—
Hick	8	1	24	1
Streak	2	—	18	—

FALL OF WICKETS
1- 3, 2- 7, 3- 10, 4- 19, 5- 29, 6- 40, 7- 111, 8- 134

ZIMBABWE

R.D. Brown	b d'Oliveira	75
G.A. Paterson	c Tremlett, b Cook	31
G.A. Hick	c N.F. Williams, b Tremlett	6
A.J. Pycroft†	not out	23
D.L. Houghton*	not out	5
A.C. Waller		
I.P. Butchart		
P.W.E. Rawson		
D.H. Streak		
A.J. Traicos		
K.G. Duers		
Extras	b 3, w 2, nb 5	10
(46.4 overs)	(for 3 wickets)	150

	O	M	R	W
N.F. Williams	10	2	32	—
Tremlett	8	1	28	1
R.G. Williams	9	1	28	—
Cook	10	1	31	1
d'Oliveira	8	2	24	1
Broad	0.4	—	4	—

FALL OF WICKETS
1- 78, 2- 97, 3- 143

Zimbabwe won by 7 wickets

FOURTH ONE-DAY INTERNATIONAL – ZIMBABWE *v.* ENGLISH COUNTIES XI
9 March 1985 at Harare Sports Club

ZIMBABWE

R.D. Brown	b Cook	49
G.A. Paterson	b Nicholas	30
G.A. Hick	not out	61
D.L. Houghton*	c Terry, b N.F. Williams	11
A.J. Pycroft†	c and b N.F. Williams	17
A.C. Waller	b Nicholas	7
I.P. Butchart	c Parks, b Nicholas	5
P.W.E. Rawson	not out	14
A.H. Omarshah		
A.J. Traicos		
K.G. Duers		
Extras	lb 5, w 3	8
(50 overs)	(for 6 wickets)	202

	O	M	R	W
N.F. Williams	10	3	25	2
Davis	8	—	41	—
Tremlett	9	—	32	—
d'Oliveira	9	1	38	—
Cook	8	—	36	1
Nicholas	6	1	25	3

FALL OF WICKETS
1- 68, 2- 96, 3- 113, 4- 145, 5- 166, 6- 173

ENGLISH COUNTIES XI

B.C. Broad	c Houghton, b Rawson	0
T.A. Lloyd	run out	7
M.C.J. Nicholas†	c Brown, b Duers	39
V.P. Terry	c Paterson, b Traicos	48
P. Bainbridge	lbw, b Butchart	20
D.B. d'Oliveira	c Traicos, b Hick	4
N.F. Williams	c Houghton, b Butchart	3
T.M. Tremlett	c Omarshah, b Traicos	2
R.J. Parks*	c Hick, b Rawson	4
M.R. Davis	not out	23
N.G.B. Cook	not out	11
Extras	lb 5, w 5, nb 2	12
(50 overs)	(for 9 wickets)	173

	O	M	R	W
Rawson	10	2	24	2
Duers	10	—	41	1
Traicos	10	3	25	2
Butchart	10	3	41	2
Hick	10	—	37	1

FALL OF WICKETS
1- 0, 2- 30, 3- 67, 4- 106, 5- 121, 6- 129, 7- 129, 8- 136, 9- 139

Zimbabwe won by 29 runs

about a middle-order collapse. Omarshah's magnificent catch, a diving effort at long leg to dismiss Tremlett, was symbolic of Zimbabwe's excellence in the field and the Counties were able to reduce the margin of defeat only through a light-hearted last wicket stand between Davis and Cook.

Fifth One-Day International
ZIMBABWE *v.* ENGLISH COUNTIES XI

Zimbabwe completed a 5–0 whitewash in the one-day series, giving a relaxed performance in celebration of the announcement of the side to tour England. The opening partnership

FIFTH ONE-DAY INTERNATIONAL – ZIMBABWE *v.* ENGLISH COUNTIES XI
10 March 1985 at Harare Sports Club

ZIMBABWE

R.D. Brown	c Parks, b Tremlett	3
G.A. Paterson	c Parks, b Tremlett	0
G.A. Hick	c Terry, b N.F. Williams	14
D.L. Houghton*	c Bainbridge, b Monkhouse	76
A.H. Omarshah	st Parks, b d'Oliveira	40
A.J. Pycroft†	c Cook, b Nicholas	53
A.C. Waller	run out	15
I.P. Butchart	c Parks, b Tremlett	3
P.W.E. Rawson	not out	16
A.J. Traicos	run out	4
K.G. Duers	not out	0
Extras	b 3, lb 7, w 3, nb 6	19
(50 overs)	(for 9 wickets)	243

	O	M	R	W
N.F. Williams	10	—	39	1
Tremlett	10	—	40	3
Monkhouse	10	—	48	1
Nicholas	7	—	40	1
Cook	8	—	44	—
d'Oliveira	5	—	22	1

FALL OF WICKETS
1- 2, 2- 8, 3- 28, 4- 103, 5- 179, 6- 217, 7- 222, 8- 223, 9- 241

ENGLISH COUNTIES XI

B.C. Broad	c Houghton, b Duers	28
V.P. Terry	c and b Hick	12
M.C.J. Nicholas†	b Hick	42
P. Bainbridge	c Omarshah, b Hick	9
D.B. d'Oliveira	c Brown, b Hick	4
R.G. Williams	b Butchart	8
N.F. Williams	b Butchart	17
T.M. Tremlett	b Traicos	26
G. Monkhouse	b Butchart	1
N.G.B. Cook	c Traicos, b Waller	2
R.J. Parks*	not out	3
Extras	b 4, lb 3, w 8	15
(50 overs)		167

	O	M	R	W
Rawson	8	2	23	—
Duers	10	2	36	1
Hick	10	—	32	4
Butchart	9	—	30	3
Traicos	10	1	36	1
Waller	0.4	—	3	1

FALL OF WICKETS
5?, 2- 51, 3- 61, 4- 85, 5- 112, 6- 115, 7- 151, 8- 160, 9- 162

Zimbabwe won by 76 runs

failed, but an attacking innings by Omarshah and another splendid effort by Houghton asserted Zimbabwe's authority. Pycroft played well and his side once again made a good score. Zimbabwe again fielded outstandingly and took some fine catches. Once more the Counties' middle-order collapsed and although Williams and Tremlett batted encouragingly, there was little doubt as to what the result would be.

It was a disappointment for the English side, but they left behind them a feeling of warmth and friendship. As John Traicos said, 'It was a pleasure to play against them.'

First Class Averages

BATTING	M	Inns	NOs	Runs	HS	Av	100s	50s
A.C. Waller	2	4	1	135	75	45.00		2
D.A.G. Fletcher	4	7	2	212	93	42.40		1
D.L. Houghton	7	14	1	483	84	37.15		5
G.A. Hick	6	12	1	389	95	35.36		2
R.D. Brown	6	12	2	325	124*	32.50	1	1
I.P. Butchart	5	10	2	259	71	32.37		1
A.J. Pycroft	6	11		312	88	28.36		3
A.H. Omarshah	3	6		152	50	25.33		1
K.G. Walton	5	10		209	54	20.90		1
G.A. Paterson	4	8		146	76	18.25		1
A.J. Traicos	6	7	2	59	37*	11.80		

(Qualification – 50 runs, average 10.00)
(E.A. Brandes 56 and 2; M.P. Jarvis 58 and 6*)

BOWLING	Overs	Mds	Runs	Wkts	Av	Best	5/inn
K.G. Duers	161	27	555	23	24.13	8/102	2
G.A. Hick	82	12	312	7	44.57	2/86	
P.W.E. Rawson	200.3	35	687	15	45.80	4/70	
A.J. Traicos	196.5	46	514	11	46.72	2/18	
I.P. Butchart	79.2	10	266	5	53.20	2/47	

(Qualification – 5 wickets)

LEADING FIELDERS
20–D.L. Houghton (ct 18/st 2); 6–P.W.E. Rawson; 5–R.D. Brown, G.A. Hick and A.J. Pycroft; 4–I.P. Butchart; 3–A.J. Traicos and A.H. Omarshah

Neil Williams drives off the back foot. He enjoyed a good tour. (Bob Nixon)

Butchart slashes Tremlett through the covers. (Bob Nixon)

SECTION G

Never-Ending Season

The season in Pakistan.
Pakistan *v.* India, Tests and One-Day Internationals.
Pakistan *v.* New Zealand, Tests and One-Day Internationals.
BCCP Patron's Trophy. The Quaid-e-Azam Trophy.
PACO Pentagular Tournament. Averages.
The Four Nations Tournament in Sharjah.

Spectators. (Adrian Murrell)

Each year in these pages we make the plea that the international programme should be drastically cut, for it is strangling domestic competitions all over the world and if they continue to be devalued, the ultimate casualty will be the game of first-class cricket. The plea goes unheeded as each year the international programme grows bigger and bigger and the appearances of the top cricketers in Shell Shield, Quaid-e-Azam Trophy, Sheffield Shield and the rest become fewer and fewer. The season that confronted a leading Pakistan cricketer was even more daunting than it had been in 1983–84. The visit of the Indian side for the Test and one-day series was to be followed by a visit from the New Zealanders who would be playing three Tests and four one-day internationals. A Pakistan side would then travel to New Zealand for return series before moving on to Australia for the Benson and Hedges World Championship of Cricket. That would be followed by the Four Nations Tournament in Sharjah. Somewhere in the midst of this hectic programme, the Pakistan Board hoped to play the BCCP Patron's Trophy, the Quaid-e-Azam Trophy and the PACO Pentagular Championship. The programme was completed, but in some cases matches were postponed for a month and other games were played when a Championship has already been decided.

1, 2 and 3 September 1984

at National Stadium, Karachi

Punjab Governor's XI 157 (Naved Anjum 59, Masood Anwar 51, Shahid Mahboob 4 for 49, Azeem Hafeez 4 for 50) and 118 (Naved Anjum 55, Azeem Hafeez 4 for 24)
Sind Governor's XI 379 for 9 dec (Sagheer Abbas 94, Sajid Ali 83, Shaukat Mirza 81, Tahir Naqqash 4 for 119)

Sind Governor's XI won by an innings and 104 runs

The match was scheduled for four days, but it ended in two and a half. Azeem and Shahid bowled out the Punjab XI by mid-afternoon and Sind had taken a 23-run lead for the loss of only 2 wickets by the close. Sajid and Shaukat Mirza put on 146 for the second wicket, and Sagheer and Sultan Rana 105 for the fourth. Azeem and Shahid quickly bowled out Punjab again, returning match figures of 8 for 74 and 7 for 76 respectively.

12, 13, 14 and 15 September 1984

at Qaddafi Stadium, Lahore

Sind Governor's XI 276 (Iqbal Sikander 65, Shoaib Mohammed 64, Tahir Naqqash 6 for 72) and 121 for 5 (Tahir Naqqash 4 for 35)
Punjab Governor's XI 376 for 9 dec (Rameez Raja 172, Rashid Khan 6 for 116)

Match drawn

The match was dominated by skipper Rameez Raja of Punjab who enhanced his Test claims with an innings of 172 out of 255 scored while he was at the wicket and by Tahir Naqqash, the underrated medium pace bowler, who had match figures of 10 for 107.

First One-Day International
PAKISTAN *v.* INDIA

Put in to bat, Pakistan made a sedate start before losing both openers in quick succession. Zaheer increased the rate of scoring and had sound support from Javed, but it was the two young players, Naved and Manzoor, who produced the brightest cricket of the day. Naved hit the only six of the match and was brilliantly caught by Amarnath, high above his head on the boundary, when he tried to hit another. Manzoor, later named Man of the Match in what was his debut in international cricket, was out on the penultimate ball of the innings, which, at 199, ended a little disappointingly.

It seemed that India would win quickly, particularly as Tahir was most erratic at the start, and 21 runs came from the first three overs. Once Tahir discovered length and direction the character of the match changed and India began to struggle. Gavaskar and Binny batted sensibly, but three wickets fell for 9 runs, all to reckless shots and the back of the innings was broken. There was to be no recovery and Pakistan swept to a joyful, if unexpected victory.

14 October 1984

at Pindi Club Ground, Rawalpindi

Indian XI 260 for 2 (D.B. Vengsarkar 88 not out, S.M. Patil 72 not out, A.D. Gaekwad 63)
Pakistan XI 203 for 8 (Maninder Singh 4 for 41)

Indian XI won by 57 runs

The spirit of this 'Charity' match was sustained throughout. Gaekwad brought up the visitors' 100 with a six out of the ground and Patil reached his fifty with a six. Later Manzoor Elahi hit three sixes in his 34, but Pakistan could never match the required rate.

FIRST ONE-DAY INTERNATIONAL – PAKISTAN *v.* INDIA
12 October 1984 at Ayub Stadium, Quetta

PAKISTAN		
Mohsin Khan	lbw, b Sharma	13
Saadat Ali	c Khanna, b Sandhu	12
Zaheer Abbas †	c and b Maninder	55
Javed Miandad	run out	25
Naved Anjum	c Amarnath, b Kapil Dev	30
Manzoor Elahi	b Kapil Dev	36
Ashraf Ali*	c Maninder, b Kapil Dev	6
Mudassar Nazar	not out	7
Tahir Naqqash	not out	0
Rashid Khan		
Tauseef Ahmed		
Extras	lb 12, w 3	15
(40 overs)	(for 7 wickets)	199

	O	M	R	W
Kapil Dev	8	—	36	3
Chetan Sharma	7	—	42	1
Sandhu	7	—	35	1
Madan Lal	5	—	20	—
Maninder Singh	5	—	24	1
Shastri	8	—	30	—

FALL OF WICKETS
1- 27, 2- 39, 3- 113, 4- 122, 5- 165, 6- 174, 7- 199

INDIA		
R.J. Shastri	lbw, b Tahir	6
S.C. Khanna*	lbw, b Tahir	31
R.M.H. Binny	c Javed, b Mudassar	19
S.M. Gavaskar†	st Ashraf, b Tauseef	25
S.M. Patil	c Ashraf, b Naved	11
R.N. Kapil Dev	b Manzoor	0
M.B. Amarnath	b Manzoor	5
C. Sharma	not out	20
U.S. Madan Lal	run out	6
B.S. Sandhu	b Naved	7
Maninder Singh	b Rashid	4
Extras	b 2, lb 10, w 5, nb 2	19
(37.1 overs)		153

	O	M	R	W
Tahir Naqqash	6	—	35	2
Rashid Khan	6.1	1	20	1
Mudassar Nazar	8	2	14	1
Tauseef Ahmed	8	—	27	1
Manzoor Elahi	4	—	18	2
Naved Anjum	5	—	27	2

FALL OF WICKETS
1- 33, 2- 42, 3- 83, 4- 91, 5- 92, 6- 110, 7- 114, 8- 123, 9- 136

Pakistan won by 46 runs

LEFT: *Rameez Raja, 172 for Punjab Governor's XI at Lahore in September. One of Pakistan's most exciting young cricketers. (Adrian Murrell)*

BELOW: *Sunil Gavaskar played his hundredth Test match for India* v. *Pakistan at Lahore, October, 1984. (Adrian Murrell)*

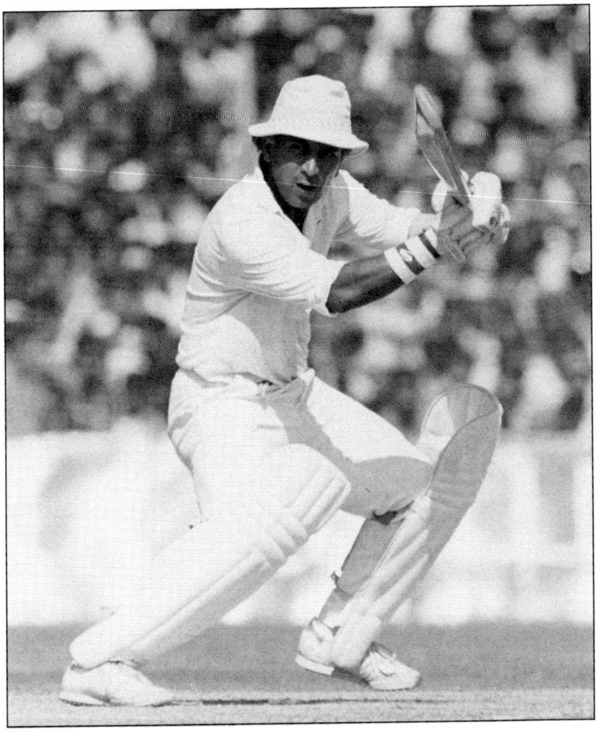

First Test Match
PAKISTAN *v.* INDIA

The annual series between Pakistan and India began, predictably, with a draw although for much of the match, it looked as if India would be beaten.

Zaheer won the toss and Pakistan batted. The selection of Wasim Raja had caused much debate and hostility while India gave a first cap to Chetan Sharma. Sharma could hardly have begun better, for, with his fifth delivery in Test cricket, he beat Mohsin with an inswinger and bowled him. In his seventh over, he had Mudassar taken at slip and in his third spell, he had Javed also taken at slip. Zaheer and Saleem steadied a faltering innings and Pakistan ended the first day on 211 for 5.

On the second day Pakistan took complete command of the game. Zaheer Abbas had taken 176 minutes to reach fifty and, having lost Wasim Raja without addition to the overnight score, he continued slowly until lunch, but after the interval, he and Ashraf attacked the bowling to add 64 in an hour. Zaheer reached his sixth Test century against India and his partnership was 142 for the seventh wicket with Ashraf Ali was a record for the series. Pakistan finished at 428 for 9 and Zaheer declared overnight.

Gavaskar, playing his hundredth Test match and having been reinstated as captain, lost Gaekwad in Jalal-ud-Din's second over, but thereafter the batsmen seemed untroubled. In his first over after lunch, however, Azeem Hafeez had Gavaskar caught and this heralded an Indian collapse during which 8 wickets fell for 23 runs. The Pakistan hero was the fast-medium left-arm bowler Azeem Hafeez who returned his best figures in Test cricket and bowled most impressively to take six wickets on a pitch which gave him no assistance. Sadly the day was marred by the reactions of Indian players,

FIRST TEST MATCH – PAKISTAN *v.* INDIA
17, 18, 19, 21 and 22 October 1984 at Qaddafi Stadium, Lahore

PAKISTAN

	FIRST INNINGS	
Mohsin Khan	b Sharma	4
Mudassar Nazar	c Gavaskar, b Sharma	15
Qasim Umar	c Amarnath, b Shastri	46
Javed Miandad	c Amarnath, b Sharma	34
Zaheer Abbas†	not out	168
Saleem Malik	c and b Shastri	45
Wasim Raja	c Amarnath, b Kapil Dev	3
Ashraf Ali*	c Gavaskar, b Gaekwad	65
Tauseef Ahmed	c Gavaskar, b Maninder	10
Jalal-ud-Din	lbw, b Shastri	17
Azeem Hafeez	not out	17
Extras	lb 7, w 1, nb 11	19
	(for 9 wkts dec)	428

	O	M	R	W
Kapil Dev	30	4	104	1
Chetan Sharma	29	2	94	3
Binny	8	1	20	—
Maninder Singh	40	10	90	1
Shastri	46	13	90	3
Amarnath	4	—	19	—
Gaekwad	1	—	4	1

FALL OF WICKETS
1- 6, 2- 54, 3- 100, 4- 110, 5- 195, 6- 212, 7- 354, 8- 394, 9- 397

INDIA

	FIRST INNINGS		SECOND INNINGS	
S.M. Gavaskar†	c Saleem, b Azeem	48	lbw, b Jalal-ud-Din	37
A.D. Gaekwad	b Jalal-ud-Din	4	c Saleem, b Tauseef	60
D.B. Vengsarkar	c Ashraf, b Azeem	41	c Mudassar, b Azeem	28
M.B. Amarnath	b Raja	36	not out	101
S.M. Patil	c Saleem, b Azeem	0	b Jalal-ud-Din	7
R.J. Shastri	lbw, b Azeem	0	lbw, b Saleem	71
R.N. Kapil Dev	lbw, b Azeem	3	(8) not out	33
R.M.H. Binny	lbw, b Mudassar	0	(7) lbw, b Raja	13
S.M.H. Kirmani*	c sub (Rameez), b Mudassar	2		
C. Sharma	b Azeem	4		
Maninder Singh	not out	4		
Extras	b 2, lb 7, w 1, nb 4	14	b 6, lb 7, w 4, nb 4	21
		156		371

	O	M	R	W	O	M	R	W
Jalal-ud-Din	17	5	41	1	24	3	61	2
Azeem Hafeez	23	7	46	6	43	12	114	1
Mudassar Nazar	16	2	31	2	14	3	34	—
Tauseef Ahmed	13	3	19	—	50	19	93	1
Wasim Raja	5.3	—	10	1	19	4	46	1
Saleem Malik					5	2	6	1
Javed Miandad					1	—	4	—

FALL OF WICKETS
1- 7, 2- 94, 3- 112, 4- 114, 5- 114, 6- 119, 7- 120, 8- 130, 9- 135
1- 85, 2- 114, 3- 147, 4- 164, 5- 290, 6- 315

Umpires: Shakoor Rana and Khizar Hayat

Match drawn

SECOND TEST MATCH – PAKISTAN *v.* INDIA
24, 25, 26, 28 and 29 October 1984 at Iqbal Stadium, Faisalabad

INDIA

	FIRST INNINGS	
S.M. Gavaskar†	c Umar, b Qadir	35
A.D. Gaekwad	c and b Manzoor	74
D.B. Vengsarkar	c Mohsin, b Qadir	5
M.B. Amarnath	hit wkt, b Azeem	37
S.M. Patil	c Zaheer, b Mudassar	127
R.J. Shastri	c Ashraf, b Qadir	139
R.N. Kapil Dev	c Manzoor, b Azeem	16
U.S. Madan Lal	c Ashraf, b Azeem	6
S.M.H. Kirmani*	c sub (Shoaib), b Azeem	6
S.N. Yadav	c Saleem, b Qadir	29
C. Sharma	not out	18
Extras	b 1, lb 6, nb 7	14
		500

	O	M	R	W
Jalal-ud-Din	34	5	103	—
Azeem Hafeez	44	9	137	4
Mudassar Nazar	25	5	74	1
Abdul Qadir	38	8	104	4
Manzoor Elahi	21	3	74	1
Saleem Malik	1	—	1	—

FALL OF WICKETS
1- 88, 2- 100, 3- 143, 4- 170, 5- 370, 6- 412, 7- 420, 8- 441, 9- 461

PAKISTAN

	FIRST INNINGS	
Mohsin Khan	c Gavaskar, b Sharma	59
Mudassar Nazar	c Kirmani, b Yadav	199
Qasim Umar	c Yadav, b Gaekwad	210
Javed Miandad	st Kirmani, b Shastri	16
Zaheer Abbas†	c Kirmani, b Madan Lal	26
Saleem Malik	not out	102
Manzoor Elahi	run out	26
Ashraf Ali*	not out	9
Abdul Qadir		
Jalal-ud-Din		
Azeem Hafeez		
Extras	b 7, lb 6, w 1, nb 13	27
	(for 6 wickets)	674

	O	M	R	W
Kapil Dev	5	—	22	—
Chetan Sharma	32	—	139	1
Madan Lal	27	—	94	1
Shastri	50	17	99	1
Yadav	75	18	196	1
Gaekwad	27	5	75	1
Amarnath	8.5	—	36	—

FALL OF WICKETS
1- 141, 2- 391, 3- 430, 4- 494, 5- 608, 6- 650

Umpires: Amanullah Khan and Mehboob Shah

Match drawn

SECOND ONE-DAY INTERNATIONAL – PAKISTAN v. INDIA
31 October 1984 at Jinnah Stadium, Sialkot

INDIA				
	A.D. Gaekwad	b Mudassar	12	
	G.A.H.M. Parkar	b Mudassar	20	
	D.B. Vengsarkar	not out	94	
	S.M. Patil	b Tauseef	59	
	R.J. Shastri	not out	6	
	M.B. Amarnath†			
	R.M.H. Binny			
	S.M.H. Kirmani*			
	U.S. Madan Lal			
	B.S. Sandhu			
	Maninder Singh			
	Extras	lb 9, w 6, nb 4	19	
	(40 overs)	(for 3 wickets)	210	

	O	M	R	W
Rashid Khan	8	—	43	—
Tahir Naqqash	8	—	55	—
Mudassar Nazar	8	1	27	2
Manzoor Elahi	8	3	24	—
Naved Anjum	1	—	10	—
Tauseef Ahmed	7	—	42	1

FALL OF WICKETS
1- 35, 2- 53, 3- 196

PAKISTAN
Saadat Ali
Sajid Ali†
Zaheer Abbas
Javed Miandad
Naved Anjum
Manzoor Elahi
Mudassar Nazar
Ashraf Ali*
Tahir Naqqash
Tauseef Ahmed
Rashid Khan

Match abandoned

Kapil Dev in particular, to umpiring decisions. India followed-on 272 runs in arrears.

India's only hope of escaping defeat was to bat out two days, a feat which they accomplished thanks to some stubborn batting from Gaekwad and, above all, Amarnath and Shastri, who added 126 for the fifth wicket. Mohinder Amarnath was splendid and after the horrors of the previous season his century marked his rehabilitation in Test cricket.

Qasim Umar, his first Test double century at Faisalabad in the second Test against India. (Adrian Murrell)

Second Test Match
PAKISTAN v. INDIA

The New Zealanders had already expressed their unwillingness to play at Faisalabad and after five days of Test cricket between India and Pakistan it was easy to see why. Abdul Qadir and Manzoor Elahi, who was making his Test debut, were brought into the Pakistan side for Wasim Raja and Tauseef Ahmed, and some thought that Ashraf, who had missed vital chances at Lahore, was lucky to retain his place. Binny and Maninder Singh gave way to Madan Lal and Yadav in the Indian side.

Patil and Shastri put on 200 for India's fifth wicket, their stand spanning the first and second days. Patil hit fourteen fours before mishooking to Zaheer and Shastri was ninth out when he edged a Qadir googly to Ashraf. The match now developed into a contest of batting records on a pitch that was so docile as to destroy all bowlers. In five days only 16 wickets fell, a record. 1174 runs were scored. Mudassar Nazar and Qasim Umar put on a record 250 for Pakistan's second wicket, Qasim hitting his first double century in a Test match and Mudassar being the first batsman to be out on 199 in a Test.

Saleem Malik became the fifth batsman in the match to hit a century at 3.55 on the last afternoon after which, mercifully, a halt was called, Pakistan having made their highest ever score in Test cricket.

Second One-Day International
PAKISTAN v. INDIA

The Indian tour of Pakistan came to an abrupt and sad end when the second one-day international was abandoned as

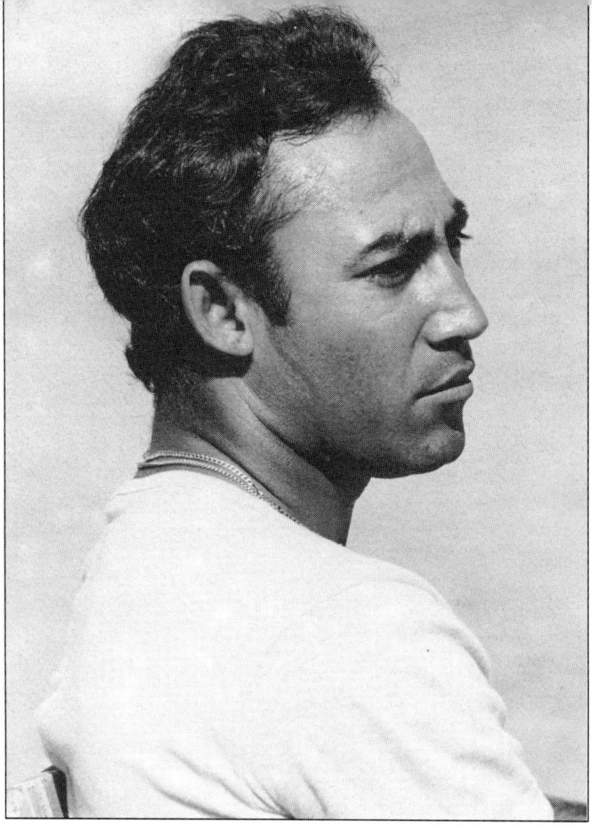

Mudassar relaxes after his 199 against India at Faisalabad. He and Qasim Umar shared a second wicket stand of 250 for the second wicket, a record. (Adrian Murrell)

news reached Sialkot of the tragic death of Mrs Gandhi. The Indians had batted well with Vengsarkar reaching his highest score in a limited-over international.

B.C.C.P. PATRON'S TROPHY

Contested among seventeen teams, divided into four groups, this competition served as the zonal cricket championship of Pakistan. For the first time in several years a Lahore team failed to reach the semi-final stage of a national tournament, but despite the fact that departmental and commercial organisations have decimated the resources of the cities and zones by luring the best cricketers to their own ranks, the resurgence of the major cricketing nurseries of Karachi and Lahore was one of the most heartening aspects of the season.

It is interesting to note that so congested was the season that the Wills One-Day Knock-Out Tournament could not be played, and two of the matches in Group A the B.C.C.P. Patron's Trophy were not played.

Group A
8 and 9 October 1984

at Bakhtiari Youth Centre, Karachi

Karachi Whites 328 for 2 (Mohammad Aslam 142 not out, Ijaz Faqih 125 not out)
Sukkur 61 (Iqbal Qasim 5 for 6) and 53 (Ijaz Faqih 5 for 29)

Karachi Whites won by an innings and 214 runs

The match was over before lunch on the second day, a reflection of the gap between the standard of the two sides. Mohammad Aslam and Ijaz Faqih added 245 before the innings was closed when the allotted 75 overs had been reached. Skipper Iqbal Qasim had match figures of 8 for 12 in 15.1 overs.

12, 13 and 14 October 1984

at Niaz Stadium, Hyderabad

Sukkur 213 (Aftab Soomro 54, Ghulam Hussain 5 for 56) and 302 for 8 (Naimatullah 85, Arshad Ali 69, Ghulam Hussain 7 for 128)
Hyderabad 267 for 5 (Meer Haider 96, Zulfiqar 69)

Match drawn

A rather laboured match in which honours went to spinner Ghulam Hussain. In Sukkur's second innings Arshas Ali and Naimatullah put on 109 for the third wicket.

20 and 21 October 1984

at Bakhtiari Youth Centre, Karachi

Karachi Whites 369 for 6 (Ijaz Faqih 124 not out, Sajid Ali 101)
Quetta 66 and 75 (Iqbal Qasim 5 for 26, Ijaz Faqih 4 for 26)

Karachi Whites won by an innings and 228 runs

Again Karachi Whites won with a day and a half to spare as they totally outplayed much weaker opposition.

29, 30 and 31 October 1984

at Bakhtiari Youth Centre, Karachi

Karachi Whites 351 for 5 (Mohammad Aslam 164, Moin-ul-Ataq 112) and 243 for 3 dec (Zafar Ali 139 not out)
Hyderabad 117 (Haaris A. Khan 4 for 14) and 107 (Iqbal Qasim 5 for 25)

Karachi Whites won by 370 runs

Karachi Whites, for whom Mohammad Aslam and Moin-ul-Atiq shared an opening stand of 245, decided not to enforce the follow-on. Iqbal Qasim felt it better to give some of his later order batsmen some practice. Zafar Ali, promoted to number one, responded with a century and shared an opening stand of 129 with Azeem Ahmed. They usually batted at numbers seven and eight. Karachi Whites, having won all three of their matches, qualified for the semi-finals. Hyderabad gained a walk-over against Quetta who, in their turn, gained a walk-over against Sukkur.

Group B
8, 9 and 10 October 1984

at Bahawal Stadium, Bahawalpur

Bahawalpur 287 for 6 (Farooq Shera 93, Qasim Shera 72, Azhar Abbas 67) and 93 for 2
Lahore City Whites 91 (Mohammad Altaf 5 for 26, Qasim Shera 4 for 26) and 285 (Shahid Anwar 109, Maqsood Raza 58, Mohammad Altaf 5 for 80, Abdur Rahim 4 for 112)

Bahawalpur won by 8 wickets

at Sahiwal Stadium, Sahiwal

Multan 243 for 9 (Ijaz Ahmed 76) and 311 for 9 dec (Humayun Muzammil 53, Zahid Ahmed 5 for 94)
Karachi Blues 280 for 5 (Asif Mutjaba 94, Aftab Baloch 68, Rizwan-uz-Zaman 59) and 168 for 5 (Rizwan-uz-Zaman 100 not out)

Match drawn

Bahawalpur enforced the follow-on only to see Lahore City Whites fight back well with Shahid Anwar and Skipper Maqsoos Raza putting on 150 for the second wicket after Dastgir Butt had gone for 0. The middle order failed to consolidate their efforts, however, and the home side was left with a comparatively easy task.

Batsmen always dominated at Sahiwal and as the match petered to a draw the main interest was in a fluent century by the talented Rizwan.

12, 13 and 14 October 1984

at Sahiwal Stadium, Sahiwal

Karachi Blues 232 (Asif Mujtaba 66, Rizwan-uz-Zaman 64, Nasir J. Charlie 6 for 64) and 332 (Rizwan-uz-Zaman 166, Asif Mujtaba 55, Haseeb-ul-Hasan 50, Zulfiqar Butt 5 for 110)
Lahore City Whites 225 for 9 (Nadeem Ahmed 77, Shahid Anwar 60, Rizwan-uz-Zaman 4 for 29) and 175 (Javed Qayyum 70, Akhlaq Qureshi 50, Tanvir Ali 5 for 66)

Karachi Blues won by 164 runs

at Bahawal Stadium, Bahawalpur

Multan 192 (Ijaz Ahmed 100 not out, Akram Chaudhri 5 for 37) and 273 (Humayun Muzammil 90 not out, Masood Anwar 72)
Bahawalpur 265 for 9 (Farooq Shera 101 not out, Azhar Abbas 61, Masood Anwar 4 for 81) and 65 for 0

Match drawn

A splendid game at Sahiwal saw Karachi Blues triumph mainly due to a magnificent innings of 166 by Rizwan-uz-Zaman, the young batsman who was taken to Australia with the Pakistani side in 1981 when still raw, but has since been forgotten. Set to make 340 to win, Lahore City Whites collapsed to 50 for 5 against Tanvir. They were rallied by a century stand between Akhlaq and Javed, but they fell to Sultan Kamdar in quick succession and Karachi ran to an easy victory.

A lack of enterprise doomed the match at Bahawal. Multan were 6 for 3 when Ijaz Ahmed came to the wicket and hit a brave century. Bahawalpur were pegged back, but Farooq Shera hit 101 out of the last 145 runs to give them a useful lead. Without the injured Mohammad Ayub and losing Mohammed Javed, the other opener, without a run scored, Multan batted solidly at the second attempt to ensure a draw.

16, 17 and 18 October 1984

at Bahawal Stadium, Bahawalpur

Bahawalpur 244 for 7 (Farooq Shera 112 not out, Azhar Abbas 52) and 188 for 9 (Mohammad Altaf 52 not out, Aqeel Qureshi 5 for 87)
Karachi Blues 258 for 5 (Asif Mujtaba 58, Rizwan-uz-Zaman 57, Aftab Baloch 52 not out)

Match drawn

at MCC Ground, Multan

Multan 309 for 9 (Ijaz Ahmed 117, Naved Mushtaq 55) and 239 for 8 dec (Zakir Hussain 80, Islam-ul-Haq 65, Azhar Saeed 4 for 70)
Lahore City Whites 223 (Nadeem Ahmed 78, Masood Anwar 6 for 94) and 255 for 7 (Shahid Anwar 69, Maqsood Raza 65 not out, Ashfaq Ahmed 51, Masoos Anwar 5 for 107)

Match drawn

With these last two matches in Group B drawn, it meant that

Iqbal Qasim in devastating form for Karachi Whites in the Patron's Trophy. (Adrian Murrell)

Wasim Raja, good all-round cricket for Lahore City Blues in the Patron's Trophy. (Adrian Murrell)

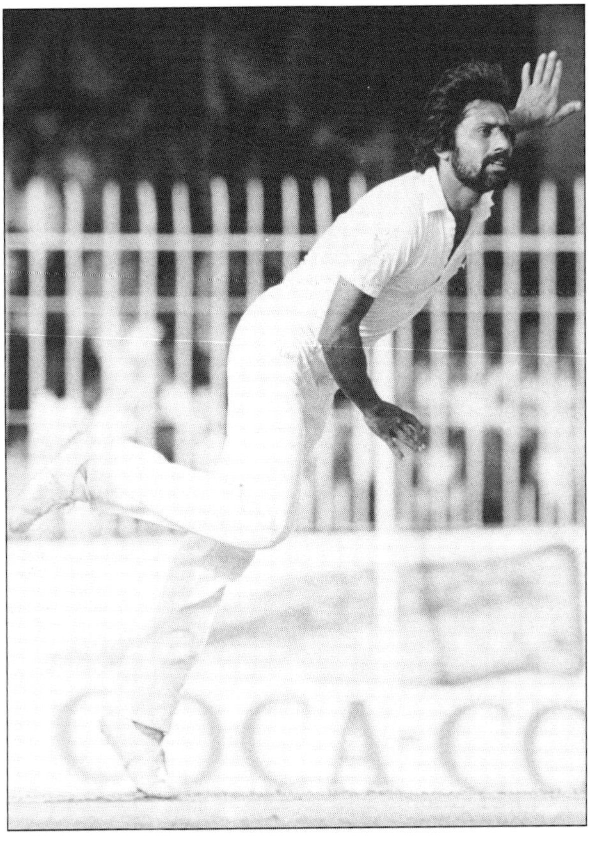

four of the six games in this section had ended without a definite result. There was never much chance of a result at Bahawalpur after the home side had taken 81 overs to reach 188 in their second innings. Farooq Shera hit his second century in successive innings and brought his total of runs in the competition to 314 at an average of 157.

Chasing a target of 326, Lahore City Whites were given a fine start by Ashfaq Ahmed and Shahid Anwar who put on 115, but 5 wickets fell for 76 and only Maqsood's patience saved the match.

Karachi Blues qualified for the semi-finals with Bahawalpur, the only other winners, in second place.

Group C
1, 2, and 3 October 1984

at Sargodha Stadium, Sargodha

Sargodha 258 for 7 (Arshad Pervez 116 not out, Saleem Cheema 50, Akhtar Hussain 4 for 88) and 183 for 8 dec
Faisalabad 156 (Ghulam Abbas 4 for 55, Shakeel Cheema 4 for 57) and 143 (Wasim Haider 51 not out, Aziz-ur-Rehman 7 for 45)

Sargodha won by 142 runs

at Jinnah Park, Sialkot

Gujranwala 259 for 8 (Tahir Mahmood 55, Shahid Tanvir 4 for 75) and 178 for 4 dec (Mansoor Khan 70, Tahir Mahmood 55)
Lahore Division 200 for 7 (M. Ashraf Ali 94) and 99 (Sajid Bashir 4 for 15)

Gujranwala won by 138 runs

A remarkable spell of bowling by Aziz-ur-Rehman who spun out 7 of the last 8 Faisalabad batsmen brought victory to Sargodha. Faisalabad lost their last 8 wickets for 92 runs.

There was an even more remarkable collapse at Sialkot where, on a crumbling wicket, Lahore Division lost their last 9 wickets for 68 runs.

8, 9 and 10 October 1984

at LCCA Ground, Lahore

Lahore Division 199 (Shahid Tanvir 95, Asim Butt 4 for 35) and 176 (Waqar Ali 57, Asim Butt 5 for 53)
Lahore City Blues 195 and 181 for 3 (Mohsin Riaz 76 not out, Aamer Malik 72)

Lahore City Blues won by 7 wickets

at Bagh-e-Jinnah Ground, Faisalabad

Gujranwala 197 (Ijaz Ahmed 83, Tanvir Afzal 6 for 80) and 206 (Tahir Mahmood 56, Tanvir Afzal 5 for 86)
Faisalabad 301 for 7 (Mohammad Ashraf 140) and 104 for 5 (Shakir Ali 60 not out)

Faisalabad won by 5 wickets

Of the five sides in Section C, only Lahore Division were left without a victory after two rounds of matches. They slumped to close rivals Lahore City Blues in a low scoring contest. Asim Butt's spin was a dominant factor for the Blues who were left the whole of the last day in which to score 181. They won by mid-afternoon, Mohsin Riaz and Aamer Malik putting on 137 for the second wicket.

Faisalabad had a somewhat harder struggle and produced two heroes, Tanvir Afzal, who had match figures of 11 for 166 in 50 overs of spin, and wicket-keeper opening batsman Mohammad Ashraf who hit a fine century and had five dismissals.

12, 13 and 14 October 1984

at LCCA Ground, Lahore

Faisalabad 282 for 4 (Suja-ud-Din 114, Mohammad Ashraf 101 not out) and 132 (Arshad Butt 4 for 35)
Lahore City Blues 194 (Wasim Raja 78, Tanvir Afzal 4 for 66) and 221 for 7 (Mohsin Riaz 80, Pervez J. Mir 54, Tanvir Afzal 5 for 111)

Lahore City Blues won by 3 wickets

at Sargodha Stadium, Sargodha

Sargodha 312 (Mohammad Aslam 167, Ijaz Ahmed 4 for 50) and 228 for 9 dec (Mohammad Aslam 88, Saleem Cheema 65, Ijaz Ahmed 4 for 73)
Gujranwala 188 (Aziz-ur-Rehman 6 for 70) and 333 (Tahir Mahmood 108, Yahya Khan 56 not out, Aziz-ur-Rehman 5 for 74)

Sargodha won by 19 runs

Two splendid matches saw considerable changes of fortune. Mohammad Ashraf and Shuja-ud-Din began the match at Lahore with a stand of 186, and Faisalabad led by 88 on the first innings when the home side were all out in 65.4 overs. Arshad Butt and Wasim Raja then bowled Lahore City Blues back into contention and with 221 needed to win, the City Blues finished the second day on 35 for 0. Moeez Butt went early next morning, but Mohsin Riaz and Pervez J. Mir added 71 and although Aamer Malik Malik and Wasim Raja went cheaply, the later batsmen kept their heads and the game was won.

Two magnificent innings by Mohammad Aslam seemed to have put Sargodha in total command and Arsgad Pervez declared, leaving Gujranwala to make 353, a daunting task. The result appeared to be a formality when Gujranwala slipped to 181 for 7, but Yahya Khan joined Tahir Mahmood in a stand of 49. Tahir's fine innings came to an end when he was caught behind, but Yahya found a belligerent partner in Mohammad Imtiaz and they added 82. When Imtiaz was caught Gujranwala were still 41 short of victory with only one wicket standing. Shajjad Bashir gave Yahya brave support, and most of the strike, but at 333 he became Aziz's eleventh victim of the match and Sargodha won by 19 runs. It was a significant victory and proved to be decisive in giving them a place in the semi-finals.

16 and 17 October 1984

at Sargodha Stadium, Sargodha

Lahore Division 152 (Sarfraz Azeem 62, Aziz-ur-Rehman 4 for 34) and 162 (Shahid Tanvir 97, Ghulam Abbas 7 for 66)
Sargodha 358 for 3 (Tasnim Abidi 131, Arshad Pervez 76 not out, Saleem Cheema 67)

Sargodha won by an innings and 44 runs

A third win in three matches for Sargodha was accomplished inside two days. Tasnim and Saleem Cheema had an opening stand of 165 for the victors.

20, 21 and 22 October 1984

at Jinnah Park, Sialkot

Faisalabad 209 (Mohammad Ashraf 100, Gauhar Butt 5 for 30) and 193 (Bilal Ahmed 54)
Lahore Division 177 (Tanvir Afzal 4 for 68, Humayun Farkhan 4 for 78) and 110 (Humayun 4 for 25)

Faisalabad won by 115 runs

In a low scoring match, Lahore Division slumped to 17 for 4 and 73 for 8 in their second innings and were only lifted to three figures by some brave hitting from Anis Ahmed and Aqib Javed.

30, 31 October and 1 November 1984

at LCCA Ground, Lahore

Gujranwala 257 (Ijaz Ahmed 74, Sajid Bashir 55, Akram Raza 6 for 97, Mazhar Hussain 4 for 24) and 325 (Ijaz Ahmed 75, Yahya Khan 63, Tahir Mahmood 61)
Lahore City Blues 298 for 9 (Mohsin Riaz 78, Pervez J. Mir 74) and 75 for 4

Match drawn

Gujranwala closed the second day at 54 for 1 and quickly lost Jahanzeb Burki on the last morning, but Lahore City Blues failure to effect a significant breakthrough after this cost them the chance of victory and, as it transpired, a place in the semi-finals.

3, 4 and 5 November 1984

at LCCA Ground, Lahore

Lahore City Blues 226 for 9 (Pervez J. Mir 50, Aziz-ur-Rehman 4 for 71, Ghulam Abbas 4 for 79) and 188 for 5 dec (Abdul Qadir 72, Pervez J. Mir 69 not out)
Sargodha 174 (Mohammad Aslam 75, Asim Butt 4 for 38, Abdul Qadir 4 for 62) and 132 (Abdul Qadir 9 for 59)

Lahore City Blues won by 108 runs

Led by Sarfraz Nawaz and with Abdul Qadir in the side, Lahore City Blues trounced Sargodha and gained some consolation for the fact that Sargodha had just beaten Lahore Division for the place in the semi-finals. The match was dominated by Abdul Qadir. Leading by 52 on the first innings, City Blues were 52 for 4 when he joined Pervez J. Mir in the second innings. They added 127 of which Qadir scored 72. Then, with Sargodha asked to make 241 to win, he took 9 for 59 in 28 overs of immaculately controlled and inventive leg-spin. Few spin bowlers in the world have ever excited so much pleasure, or so much controversy.

Group D
1 and 2 October 1984

at Pakistan Ordanance Factories Oval, Wah Cantt

Dera lamail Khan 90 (Naeem Ahmed 5 for 12, Nasim Piracha 4 for 44) and 57 (Naeem Ahmed 5 for 12, Aziz Ahmed 4 for 20)
Rawalpindi 251 for 4 dec (Masood Anwar 86, Majid J. Khan 78 not out)

Rawalpindi won by an innings and 104 runs

at Peshawar University Hostel, Peshawar

Hazara 138 (Ijaz Butt 69, Farrukh Zaman 4 for 56) and 131 (Wasim Fazal 50, Aamer Mirza 6 for 29)
Peshawar 270 for 8 (Nasim Fazal)

Peshawar won by an innings and 1 run

The two opening matches in Group D both ended inside two days. The weak and lowly-rated Dera Ismail Khan side were predictably outclassed by Rawalpindi, captained by the veteran Majid Khan while Peshawar had a surprisingly easy win over Hazara.

8 and 9 October 1984

at CMT & SD Ground, Rawalpindi

Rawalpindi 345 for 5 (Masood Anwar 186, Tariq Javed 73, Sabih Azhar 52 not out)
Hazara 150 and 142 (Farrukh 57, Raja Afaq 5 for 52)

Rawalpindi won by an innings and 53 runs

at Peshawar University Hostel, Peshawar

Dera Ismail Khan 69 (Farrukh Zaman 4 for 8) and 101 (Farrukh Zaman 4 for 26)
Peshawar 195 (Qazi Shafiq 52, Jamal A. Nasir 4 for 64)

Peshwar won by an innings and 25 runs

So uneven was the competition in this group and so weak two of the sides that the second round of matches again ended inside two days. At Rawalpindi, Masood Anwar reached 105 before lunch on the first day. He was the only Pakistani batsman to achieve this feat during the season. He and Tariq Javed shared a first wicket stand of 189. Hazara had two players absent ill in their second innings.

12 and 13 October 1984

at University Ground, Peshawar

Hazara 115 and 124 (Jamal A. Nasir 4 for 45)
Dera Ismail Khan 124 (Asif Aslam 4 for 47) and 98 (Imran Khaliq 6 for 28)

Hazara won by 17 runs

The ineptitude of the batsmen of two very weak sides brought this game to a close in two days.

16, 17 and 18 October

at Pakistan Ordnance Factories, Wah Cantt

Rawalpindi 225 for 6 dec (Masood Anwar 88, Tariq Javed 84, Iqbal Butt 5 for 98) and 226 for 5 dec (Tariq Javed 100)
Peshawar 97 (Mohammad Riaz 5 for 10) and 105 (Mohammad Riaz 4 for 41)

Rawalpindi won by 249 runs

In the only match in the group that lasted three days, and even then ended before lunch on the last day, Rawalpindi dominated and beat the only other side in the group of any strength to reach the semi-finals. An opening stand of 159 between Masood Anwar and Tariq Javed was the foundation of Rawalpindi's victory and Majid declared with 9 balls of his side's 75 overs remaining. His decision brought quick benefits for Peshawar closed the day at 92 for 7 and added only 5 more runs the next morning. A brisk hundred by Tariq Javed brought another declaration and Peshawar closed the second day in total disarray at 61 for 7. Aftab Ahmed and Maazullah Khan offered some resistance on the last morning.

Semi-Finals
7, 8, 9 and 10 November

at Bagh-e-Jinnah Ground, Lahore

Rawalpindi 277 (Mujahid H. Mir 51 not out, Aziz-ur-Rehman 4 for 60) and 222 (Raja Afaq 60)
Sargodha 214 (Arshad Pervez 115, Aziz Ahmed 6 for 62) and 253 (Arshad Pervez 110, Raja Afaq 6 for 68)

Rawalpindi won by 32 runs

A fine game ended on the last afternoon when Sargodha, having been set to make 286 to win and finished the previous evening on 38 for 0, were beaten by 32 runs. Arshad Pervez hit a century in each innings, a feat which was accomplished five times in the season, but still finished on the losing side. Rawalpindi, without Majid Khan, were bowled out in 84.4 overs on the first day, and Sargodha reached 17 for 0 before the close. They began the second day disastrously, losing both openers for the addition of one run. It was Arshad who rallied them, but they ended 63 runs in arrears and Rawalpindi had increased their lead by 19 before the close. It was a dour third day with Rawalpindi building patiently against tight bowling, but their slowness proved to be justified when, in spite of Arshad's innings, they snatched victory on the last day. Sargodha reached 250 for 5, seemingly set for victory, but Arshad's dismissal heralded a dreadful collapse which saw the last 5 wickets fall for 3 runs and Rawalpindi grasp an amazing win.

11, 12, 13 and 14 November 1984

at National Stadium, Karachi

Karachi Whites 300 for 9 (Moin-ul-Atiq 101) and 254 (Mohammad Aslam 87, Tanvir Ali 6 for 85)
Karachi Blues 251 for 8 (Rizwan-uz-Zaman 59, Iqbal Qasim 4 for 88) and 99 (Ijaz Faqih 6 for 44, Iqbal Qasim 4 for 18)

Karachi Whites won by 204 runs

The second semi-final saw Karachi Whites win a big victory over their third local rivals who collapsed to lose their last 9 wickets for 45 runs on the last morning. The Whites innings occupied the first day, and on the second, the Blues fell 49 runs short of their opponent's total in their 85 overs. There seemed no indication that the Karachi Whites would gain such an overwhelming victory when the Blues ended the third day needing 274 more runs for victory with 9 wickets in hand. It was the combined wiles of Ijaz Faqih's off-spin and Iqbal Wasim's slow left-arm which brought them to disaster on the final morning.

The Final

When a match is scheduled to be played over five days and ends in two it cannot be anything but a great disappointment. Rawalpindi had played in the qualifying competition, but they failed to do themselves justice in the final, suffering one of those wretched matches that come to all sides. Undoubtedly, as later events proved, Karachi Whites were the better side, and a very good side, but the difference between the two sides was not as great as the margin of victory would suggest.

Rawalpindi won the toss and there were no early alarms as Masood and Shahid began confidently enough, but pace bowler Rashid Khan achieved a breakthrough with three quick wickets and Rawalpindi never effectively recovered, the later batsmen struggling against Ijaz Faqih's off-spin. By the close Karachi Whites had taken total command, having reached 132 for 2.

They failed to improve on this as much as had been expected on the second morning when Rawalpindi fought back through Sabih, but their own batting again failed, and this time it was the slow left-arm of Zahid Ahmed which troubled them. No batsman was able to play a substantial innings and Karachi Whites moved to an easy victory.

BCCP PATRON'S TROPHY FINAL – KARACHI WHITES *v.* RAWALPINDI
17 and 18 November 1984 at National Stadium, Karachi

RAWALPINDI

	FIRST INNINGS		SECOND INNINGS	
Masood Anwar†	c Moin, b Rashid	10	lbw, b Zahid	30
Shahid Gulrez	b Ijaz	24	run out	11
Rafat Ijaz	c Pervez, b Rashid	0	b Ijaz	0
Sabih Azhar	c Tehsin, b Rashid	11	(6) c and b Zahid	0
Mujahid H. Mir	c Moin, b Ijaz	18	(4) lbw, b Zahid	13
Raja Afaq	b Ijaz	1	(5)c Tehsin, b Ijaz	23
Hamid A. Shah	lbw, b Zahid	5	c Rashid, b Zahid	17
Nadim Piracha	c Moin, b Ijaz	2	(10) not out	14
Asif Faridi	b Ijaz	14	c Ijaz, b Zahid	1
Shahid Munir*	not out	17	(8) c Rashid, b Ijaz	10
Ahmer Doshi	st Pervez, b Ijaz	0	c Nadeem, b Zahid	0
Extras	b 10, lb 6, nb 8	24	b 4, lb 5, w 1, nb 2	12
		126		132

	O	M	R	W	O	M	R	W
Rashid Khan	12	4	38	3	6	—	26	—
Humayun Khan	3	1	18	—	2	—	17	—
Ijaz Faqih	14.2	2	36	6	19	6	35	3
Zahid Ahmed	6	2	19	1	16.2	3	45	6

FALL OF WICKETS
1- 34, 2- 40, 3- 41, 4 65, 5- 79, 6- 80, 7- 83, 8- 87, 9- 111
1- 28, 2- 29, 3- 53, 4- 58, 5- 58, 6- 93, 7- 110, 8- 113, 9- 121

KARACHI WHITES

	FIRST INNINGS		SECOND INNINGS	
Mohammad Aslam	lbw, b Asif	75	not out	5
Moin-ul-Atiq	b Ahmer	34	not out	6
Zafar Ali	lbw, b Afaq	48		
Ijaz Faqih†	c and b Afaq	6		
Saeed Azad	c Rafat, b Ahmer	23		
Zahid Ahmed	b Sabih	19		
Tehsin Ahmed	c Hamid, b Sabih	11		
Nadeem Moosa	run out	7		
Rashid Khan	b Sabih	3		
Pervez-ul-Hasan*	not out	0		
Humayun Khan	b Sabih	1		
Extras	b 1, lb 6, w 1, nb 8	16	b 6	6
		243	(for no wicket)	17

	O	M	R	W	O	M	R	W
Asif Faridi	16	2	55	1	2	—	3	—
Nasim Piracha	3	—	22	—	1	—	2	—
Hamid A. Shah	2	—	8	—				
Raja Afaq	31	6	78	2				
Ahmer Doshi	21	6	53	2				
Sabih Azhar	7.3	2	20	4				
Shahid Gulrez					1	—	6	—

FALL OF WICKETS
1- 90, 2- 132, 3- 150, 4- 186, 5- 207, 6- 223, 7- 236, 8- 242, 9- 242

Umpires: Khizar Hayat and Saleem Badar

Karachi Whites won by 10 wickets

FIRST ONE-DAY INTERNATIONAL – PAKISTAN *v.* NEW ZEALAND
12 November 1984 at Shahi Bagh Stadium, Peshawar

PAKISTAN

Saadat Ali	c Cairns, b Chatfield	1
Sajid Ali	c J.J. Crowe, b Cairns	16
Zaheer Abbas†	lbw, b Cairns	13
Javed Miandad	not out	80
Naved Anjum	c M.D. Crowe, b Stirling	29
Manzoor Elahi	c Stirling, b Snedden	15
Mudassar Nazar	not out	17
Sarfraz Nawaz		
Anil Dalpat*		
Tauseef Ahmed		
Zakir Khan		
Extras	b 2, lb 8, w 8, nb 2	20
(39 overs)	(for 5 wickets)	191

	O	M	R	W
Stirling	8	—	32	1
Cairns	8	—	38	2
Chatfield	7	—	38	1
M.D. Crowe	8	—	37	—
Snedden	8	—	36	1

FALL OF WICKETS
1- 14, 2- 27, 3- 38, 4- 87, 5- 123

NEW ZEALAND

J.G. Wright	lbw, b Manzoor	8
J.J. Crowe	c Anil, b Zakir	8
M.D. Crowe	c Anil, b Zakir	8
P.E. McEwan	lbw, b Zakir	3
J.F. Reid	c Javed, b Zakir	14
J.V. Coney†	c and b Mudassar	23
I.D.S. Smith	c Sajid, b Mudassar	59
M.C. Snedden	c Anil, b Mudassar	1
B.L. Cairns	c Zaheer, b Tauseef	7
D.A. Stirling	run out	2
E.J. Chatfield	not out	1
Extras	lb 4, w 7	11
(36.2 overs)		145

	O	M	R	W
Zakir Khan	8	2	19	4
Manzoor Elahi	8	1	27	1
Sarfraz Nawaz	4	1	18	—
Naved Anjum	3	—	13	—
Tauseef Ahmed	7	—	30	1
Mudassar Nazar	6.2	—	34	3

FALL OF WICKETS
1- 19, 2- 19, 3- 22, 4- 39, 5- 44, 6- 99, 7- 103, 8- 113, 9- 142

Pakistan won by 46 runs

8, 9 and 10 November 1984

at Pindi Club Ground, Rawalpindi

New Zealanders 234 (M. D. Crowe 71, B. A. Edgar 60, Waseem Akram 7 for 50) and 261 for 6 dec (J. G. Wright 93, B. A. Edgar 71, M. D. Crowe 50 not out)
BCCP Patron's XI 229 for 7 dec (Shoaib Mohammad 108 not out) and 30 for 1
Match drawn

The opening day of the New Zealand tour produced some fine cricket. Seventeen-year old pace bowler Waseem Akram had a most impressive day with seven good wickets and Martin Crowe, in flamboyant style with thirteen fours, and Bruce Edgar, patiently, added 100 for the second wicket. Thereafter the match deteriorated with Shoaib taking 280 minutes over his innings and the last day being reduced to batting practice.

First One-Day International
PAKISTAN *v.* NEW ZEALAND

Coney won the toss and asked Pakistan to bat. His decision seemed to be the right one when Chatfield and Cairns took the first three wickets for 38, but Javed Miandad rallied the home side with a fine innings. His 80 not out included two mighty sixes and four fours and he was almost solely responsible for Pakistan reaching 191 in the given two hours.

In the conditions New Zealand's task of scroring at 4.89 an over was never likely to be easy and it became worse when Zakir Khan had the Crowe brothers caught behind, McEwan lbw and Reid caught, a performance which rightly earned him the Man of the Match award. New Zealand never recovered from 44 for 5 although Smith hit a brave fifty.

Javed Miandad kneels and muses. He hit a century in each innings in the second Test match against New Zealand. (Adrian Murrell)

First Test Match
PAKISTAN *v.* NEW ZEALAND

The retirement from Test cricket of Sarfraz Nawaz and the suspicion that the pitch would aid the spinners from the first day led Pakistan to enter the match with only one front-line pace bowler, Azeem Hafeez, but, as it transpired, after Coney had won the toss, it was Mudassar Nazar, an unlikely

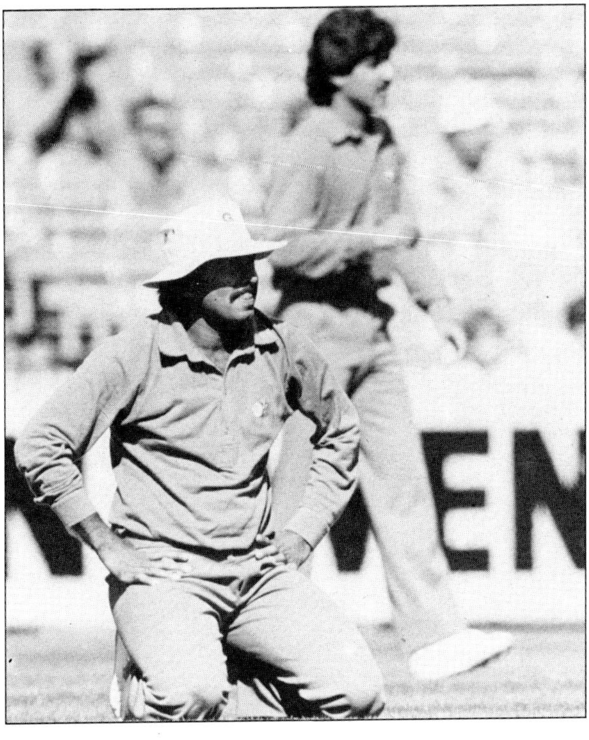

FIRST TEST MATCH – PAKISTAN *v.* NEW ZEALAND
16, 17, 18, 19 and 20 November 1984 at Qaddafi Stadium, Lahore

NEW ZEALAND

	FIRST INNINGS		SECOND INNINGS	
J.J. Crowe	c Anil, b Mudassar	0	(5) c Anil, b Iqbal	43
B.A. Edgar	b Mudassar	3	lbw, b Azeem	26
M.D. Crowe	c Umar, b Qadir	55	c sub (Rameez), b Iqbal	33
J.G. Wright	c Anil, b Azeem	1	(1) run out	65
J.F. Reid	lbw, b Mudassar	2	(4) b Qadir	6
J.V. Coney†	c Mohsin, b Iqbal	7	c Anil, b Azeem	26
E.J. Gray	c sub (Rameez), b Iqbal	12	(8) c Mudassar, b Qadir	6
I.D.S. Smith*	c Iqbal, b Azeem	41	(9) not out	11
D.A. Stirling	b Iqbal	16	(10) c Anil, b Iqbal	10
S.L. Boock	c Javed, b Iqbal	13	(7) c Javed, b Qadir	0
E.J. Chatfield	not out	6	c Umar, b Iqbal	0
Extras	b 1	1	b 8, lb 2, w 1, nb 4	15
		157		241

	O	M	R	W	O	M	R	W
Mudassar Nazar	11	5	8	3	10	1	30	—
Azeem Hafeez	18	9	40	2	13	5	37	2
Abdul Qadir	21	6	58	1	26	4	82	3
Iqbal Qasim	22.4	10	41	4	29.5	10	65	4
Tauseef Ahmed	2	—	9	—	4	—	17	—

FALL OF WICKETS
1- 0, 2- 11, 3- 28, 4- 31, 5- 50, 6- 76, 7- 120, 8- 124, 9- 146
1- 66, 2- 123, 3- 138, 4- 140, 5- 208, 6- 209, 7- 220, 8- 220, 9- 235

PAKISTAN

	FIRST INNINGS		SECOND INNINGS	
Mudassar Nazar	c Reid, b Stirling	26	b Boock	16
Mohsin Khan	c Reid, b Gray	58	c and b Gray	38
Qasim Umar	c J. Crowe, b Boock	13	lbw, b Stirling	20
Javed Miandad	c Reid, b Gray	11	not out	48
Zaheer Abbas†	c M. Crowe, b Boock	43	c Smith, b Gray	31
Saleem Malik	lbw, b Stirling	10	not out	24
Abdul Qadir	c Coney, b Chatfield	14		
Anil Dalpat*	b M. Crowe	1		
Iqbal Qasim	c Coney, b Chatfield	22		
Azeem Hafeez	c Boock, b Chatfield	11		
Tauseef Ahmed	not out	0		
Extras	nb 2	2	lb 4	4
		221		181

	O	M	R	W	O	M	R	W
Stirling	27	7	71	2	15.1	2	60	1
M. Crowe	7	1	21	1				
Gray	8	1	19	2	18	—	45	2
Chatfield	28.2	7	57	3	13	7	12	—
Boock	24	7	53	2	17	2	56	1
Coney					2	1	4	—

FALL OF WICKETS
1- 54, 2- 84, 3- 103, 4- 114, 5- 144, 6- 165, 7- 188, 8- 189, 9- 212
1- 33, 2- 77, 3- 77, 4- 138

Umpires: Mahboab Shah and Shakeel Khan

Pakistan won by 6 wickets

SECOND ONE-DAY INTERNATIONAL PAKISTAN *v.* NEW ZEALAND
23 November 1984 at Iqbal Stadium, Faisalabad

PAKISTAN

Saleem Malik	b Snedden	41
Mohsin Khan	b M.D. Crowe	0
Zaheer Abbas†	c Stirling, b Snedden	25
Javed Miandad	run out	20
Manzoor Elahi	not out	39
Mudassar Nazar	lbw, b M.D. Crowe	10
Shoaib Mohammad	not out	10
Anil Dalpat*		
Zakir Khan		
Waseem Akram		
Tauseef Ahmed		
Extras	lb 7, w 4, nb 1	12
(20 overs)	(for 5 wickets)	157

	O	M	R	W
M.D. Crowe	4	—	17	2
Coney	2	—	10	—
Cairns	4	—	25	—
Chatfield	2	—	25	—
Snedden	4	—	41	2
Stirling	4	—	32	—

FALL OF WICKETS
1- 3, 2- 67, 3- 81, 4- 105, 5- 128

NEW ZEALAND

J.G. Wright	b Mudassar	55
J.J. Crowe	lbw, b Zakir	7
M.D. Crowe	c Zaheer, b Mudassar	19
P.E. McEwan	lbw, b Mudassar	7
B.L. Cairns	c Saleem, b Mudassar	10
J.G. Bracewell	not out	16
I.D.S. Smith*	run out	4
D.A. Stirling	run out	1
J.V. Coney†	not out	17
M.C. Snedden		
E.J. Chatfield		
Extras	b 2, lb 7, w 7	16
(20 overs)	(for 7 wickets)	152

	O	M	R	W
Waseem Akram	4	—	31	—
Zakir Khan	4	—	28	1
Manzoor Elahi	4	—	31	—
Mudassar Nazar	4	—	27	4
Tauseef Ahmed	4	—	26	—

FALL OF WICKETS
1- 20, 2- 61, 3- 78, 4- 106, 5- 112, 6- 127, 7- 132

Pakistan won by 5 runs

opening bowler, who caused problems for the New Zealanders. With his third ball he had Jeff Crowe caught behind and his three wickets in eleven overs for 8 runs destroyed the heart of the New Zealand batting so that they were 50 for 5 at lunch.

Iqbal Qasim, a late inclusion in the side who was destined to be Man of the Match, continued the New Zealand decline in the afternoon and although there was a late rally, inspired by Smith, the visitors were all out before the close for 157.

Mudassar and Mohsin took their overnight 26 to an opening stand of 54 before Mudassar fell to Stirling who was making his debut in Test cricket. Mohsin batted dourly to become top-score and Pakistan closed a dull second day at 189 for 7. Boock and Gray had applied the restraint on the Pakistan innings, but it was Chatfield who ended it on the third morning after Iqbal Qasim had scored some valuable runs.

John Wright, reverting to opener, was hit on the head, but battled on to hit a six and four fours before he was run out. The third day closed with New Zealand on 212 for 6 and the match in the balance, but, with the wicket improving, Iqbal Qasim turned the game in favour of Pakistan on the fourth morning when the visitors were bowled out in less than an hour.

Pakistan had a target of 178 in ten hours and laboured to 153 for 4 by the close of the day. Their one moment of apprehension had been when Mohsin and Qasim Umar were out to successive deliveries, but Javed and Zaheer batted with patience and Zaheer passed 5,000 runs in Test cricket, the first Pakistani to achieve this feat.

In Stirling's first over on the last day, Saleem Malik hit 13 runs and Pakistan had won within 18 minutes.

Second One-Day International
PAKISTAN *v.* NEW ZEALAND

Showers in the morning caused the match to be reduced to a twenty-over contest so that Coney followed a customary policy when he asked Pakistan to bat after he had won the toss. Mohsin fell in the first over, but Saleem Malik played a sparkling innings with a six and four fours and won the individual award. He was out in the ninth over when the score was 67. Javed and Zaheer kept the score moving, but it was an impressive knock from the highly promising Manzoor Elahi which helped raise Pakistan to a creditable 157.

A second wicket partnership of 41 between John Wright and Martin Crowe took the score to 61 in ten overs at which point Mudassar joined the attack and dismissed Crowe. In his fourth over Mudassar, having accounted for McEwan and Cairns earlier, bowled Wright to complete a fine spell.

New Zealand began the last over needing 23 to win. Victory for Pakistan seemed certain, but after a single to Bracewell, Coney hit four successive fours so that six were needed off the last ball to tie the score. Coney swung at Waseem Akram, but he could manage only a single.

Second Test Match
PAKISTAN *v.* NEW ZEALAND

Pakistan won the series when they beat New Zealand by 7 wickets at Hyderabad, but once more it was the umpires who drew more attention than the cricketers who seem to accept no responsibility for dubious decisions even though an appeal has required a decision in the first place.

This was the thousandth Test match. It took 97 years to play the first 750; it has taken 10 to play the last 250. The golden-egg laying goose must be close to extinction, yet none will listen to the death cry. On the brighter side, it was appropriate that Pakistan and New Zealand should contest the thousandth match for they have given much to Test cricket in the past few years and their achievements are among the most notable.

SECOND TEST MATCH – PAKISTAN *v.* NEW ZEALAND
25, 26, 27 and 29 November 1984 at Hyderabad

NEW ZEALAND

	FIRST INNINGS		SECOND INNINGS	
J.G. Wright	c Anil, b Iqbal	18	c Anil, b Iqbal	22
B.A. Edgar	c Saleem, b Qadir	11	lbw, b Mudassar	1
M.D. Crowe	b Qadir	19	(4) st Anil, b Iqbal	21
J.F. Reid	lbw, b Azeem	106	(3) lbw, b Qadir	21
J.V. Coney†	c Manzoor, b Qadir	6	b Iqbal	5
J.J. Crowe	c Saleem, b Zaheer	39	lbw, b Iqbal	57
I.D.S. Smith*	c Iqbal, b Zaheer	6	c Mudassar, b Azeem	34
E.J. Gray	lbw, b Mudassar	25	c Umar, b Iqbal	5
J.G. Bracewell	c Mudassar, b Qadir	0	c and b Qadir	0
D.A. Stirling	not out	11	b Qadir	11
S.L. Boock	lbw, b Qadir	12	not out	8
Extras	b 13, nb 1	14	b 1, lb 4, nb 3	8
		267		189

	O	M	R	W	O	M	R	W
Mudassar Nazar	7	4	14	1	5	2	8	1
Azeem Hafeez	18	4	29	1	8	3	33	1
Iqbal Qasim	33	6	80	1	24.1	7	79	5
Abdul Qadir	40.3	11	108	5	18	3	59	3
Manzoor Elahi	2	1	2	—				
Zaheer Abbas	8	1	21	2	1	—	5	—

FALL OF WICKETS
1- 30, 2- 30, 3- 74, 4- 88, 5- 150, 6- 164, 7- 237, 8- 239, 9- 243
1- 2, 2- 34, 3- 58, 4- 71, 5- 80, 6- 125, 7- 149, 8- 149, 9- 167

PAKISTAN

	FIRST INNINGS		SECOND INNINGS	
Mudassar Nazar	c M. Crowe, b Bracewell	28	c Coney, b Boock	106
Mohsin Khan	c Gray, b Boock	9	b M. Crowe	2
Qasim Umar	c Coney, b Boock	45	lbw, b M. Crowe	0
Javed Miandad	c J. Crowe, b Boock	104	not out	103
Anil Dalpat*	b Bracewell	1		
Zaheer Abbas†	st Smith, b Boock	2		
Saleem Malik	b Boock	1		
Manzoor Elahi	c J. Crowe, b Boock	19	(5) not out	4
Abdul Qadir	lbw, b Boock	11		
Iqal Qasim	c J. Crowe, b Bracewell	8		
Azeem Hafeez	not out	0		
Extras	lb 2	2	b 5, lb 7, nb 3	15
		230	(for 3 wickets)	230

	O	M	R	W	O	M	R	W
Stirling	3	1	11	—	4	—	26	—
M.D. Crowe	3	—	8	—	8	1	29	2
Coney	10	4	8	—	4	1	9	—
Boock	37	12	87	7	23.4	4	69	1
Bracewell	16.1	3	44	3	13	2	36	—
Gray	22	4	70	—	11	—	49	—

FALL OF WICKETS
1- 26, 2- 50, 3- 153, 4- 154, 5- 159, 6- 169, 7- 191, 8- 215, 9- 230
1- 14, 2- 14, 3- 226

Pakistan won by 7 wickets

Shoaib Mohammad won a place in the Test side for the third match against New Zealand, but his season was a passive one. (Adrian Murrell)

Coney won the toss, but on a wicket which gave some assistance to the spinners, New Zealand seemed to have frittered away the advantage of batting first when they lost four wickets for 88. Reid, with a mixture of caution and aggression, played the innings that was needed and was given good support by Jeff Crowe. The first day closed with New Zealand 239 for 7, but disappointingly Reid was out quickly next morning and it was only a last wicket flourish that bolstered the score.

Abdul Qadir had been New Zealand's chief tormentor and Coney quickly had his spinners in action. They were held up by Qasim Umar and Javed Miandad with a second wicket stand of 103, but in the last three overs of the second day, New Zealand took 3 wickets for 6 runs and Pakistan closed at an unpromising 159 for 5.

Wickets continued to fall on the third day, in all 13 fell in the day, 11 of them to spinners, but Javed Miandad hit his twelfth Test hundred, a splendid effort, and Pakistan came to within 37 of the New Zealand score. Stephen Boock had bowled quite beautifully with immaculate control to return his best figures in Test cricket.

Where Boock's slow left-arm had thrived, so too did the leg-spin of Abdul Qadir and the slow left-arm of Iqbal Qasim whose return to Test cricket had been remarkable. By the end of the day they had reduced New Zealand to 158 for 8. Only Smith's adventurous hitting had lifted the visitors' innings although Jeff Crowe again batted very well.

Eventually Pakistan were set to make 227 to win, but they started disastrously when Martin Crowe dismissed Mohsin and Qasim with successive deliveries. Crowe had once again been used as opening bowler with Stirling who, in spite of being punished by Mudassar, looked a bowler of pace and promise. He had kept both Cairns and Chatfield out of the side, and Cairns had been considered as New Zealand's main force before the series began.

Mudassar and Javed went on to the attack. They added 100 in 120 minutes and in 215 minutes, Mudassar had run to his hundred. He was out when the scores were level, but by then 212 had been added and Javed Miandad had become the second Pakistani batsman, after Hanif Mohammad, to score a century in each innings of a Test match. There are some who would dare to suggest that he is the best batsman Pakistan has ever produced and he is certainly a player who has been consistently undervalued outside his own country.

Third One-Day International
PAKISTAN *v.* NEW ZEALAND

New Zealand recorded their first win of the tour and gave themselves some hope of avoiding defeat in the one-day series with an emphatic victory in the third one-day international in Sialkot.

Zaheer won the toss and asked New Zealand to bat. Wright began briskly, but makeshift opener John Bracewell fell at 14. The substance of the innings came in the stand between John Reid and Martin Crowe for the third wicket. Crowe was the outstanding batsman of the game and was later named Man of the Match. His two wickets after Stirling had had Mohsin Khan lbw in the opening over tilted the game in New Zealand's favour and the home side never really recovered.

Zaheer offered hope with an aggressive knock, but once he fell to a good catch by Jeff Crowe off the bowling of Bracewell the game slipped further from their grasp and the task of scoring 54 from the last six overs well beyond them.

4, 5 and 6 December 1984

at Bahawalpur

New Zealanders 291 for 4 dec (J.V. Coney 79, E.J. Gray 56) and 152 for 3 (J.F. Reid 55 not out)
Punjab Governor's XI 189 (Shaukat Mirza 51)
Match drawn

A dull game ended in a predictable draw. Evan Gray, used as an opener, batted well and bowled well as the Governor's XI were contained, Mirza batting two hours and forty minutes for his 51. Javed Miandad's younger brother Anwar showed promise.

Fourth One-Day International
PAKISTAN *v.* NEW ZEALAND

The match began late because the stadium was unable to cope with the large rush of spectators seeking entrance and the match therefore was reduced to 35 overs.

On winning the toss, Coney elected to bat first and Wright and McEwan began very briskly, 40 coming in 8 overs before McEwan was brilliantly caught in the deep. The Crowe brothers threatened a big, fast-scoring stand but both were run out. It was left to Coney and Smith to consolidate the

THIRD ONE-DAY INTERNATIONAL – PAKISTAN *v.* NEW ZEALAND
2 December 1984 at Jinnah Park Stadium, Sialkot

NEW ZEALAND

J.G. Wright	c Saleem, b Mohsin Kamal	24
J.G. Bracewell	c Saleem, b Mohsin Kamal	1
J.F. Reid	run out	34
M.D. Crowe	b Mohsin Kamal	67
J.J. Crowe	not out	15
P.E. McEwan	st Saleem Yousuf, b Tauseef	4
B.L. Cairns	b Tauseef	0
J.V. Coney†	run out	1
I.D.S. Smith	c Saleem, b Tauseef	9
D.A. Stirling	c Saleem, b Tauseef	4
M.C. Snedden	not out	0
Extras	lb 6, w 21, nb 1	28
(36 overs)	(for 9 wickets)	187

	O	M	R	W
Mohsin Kamal	8	—	46	3
Zakir Khan	8	—	22	—
Mudassar Nazar	8	—	58	—
Manzoor Elahi	6	—	17	—
Tauseef Ahmed	6	—	38	4

FALL OF WICKETS
1- 14, 2- 47, 3- 128, 4- 156, 5- 162, 6- 166, 7- 168, 8- 178, 9- 187

PAKISTAN

Mohsin Khan	lbw, b Stirling	2
Shoaib Mohammad	lbw, b M.D. Crowe	22
Saleem Malik	b M.D. Crowe	6
Javed Miandad	c Wright, b Cairns	14
Zaheer Abbas†	c J.J. Crowe, b Bracewell	42
Manzoor Elahi	b Cairns	16
Mudassar Nazar	c Stirling, b Snedden	3
Saleem Yousuf*	lbw, b Bracewell	1
Tauseef Ahmed	not out	27
Zakir Khan	not out	8
Mohsin Kamal		
Extras	lb 6, w 3, nb 3	12
(36 overs)	(for 8 wickets)	153

	O	M	R	W
Stirling	8	—	36	1
M.D. Crowe	5	—	21	2
Cairns	6	—	30	2
Snedden	8	—	29	1
Bracewell	8	—	23	2
Coney	1	—	8	—

FALL OF WICKETS
1- 2, 2- 14, 3- 42, 4- 52, 5- 90, 6- 97, 7- 100, 8- 133

New Zealand won by 34 runs

FOURTH ONE-DAY INTERNATIONAL – PAKISTAN *v.* NEW ZEALAND
7 December 1984 at Qasim Bagh Stadium, Multan

NEW ZEALAND

J.G. Wright	b Tauseef	11
P.E. McEwan	c Saadat, b Mohsin Kamal	22
J.F. Reid	run out	10
M.D. Crowe	run out	28
J.J. Crowe	run out	13
J.V. Coney†	c Saleem, b Zaheer	34
I.D.S. Smith*	c Javed, b Saadat	41
B.L. Cairns	c Saleem, b Saadat	2
J.G. Bracewell	not out	14
D.A. Stirling	not out	1
M.C. Snedden		
Extras	b 18, lb 8, w 10, nb 1	37
(35 overs)	(for 8 wickets)	213

	O	M	R	W
Mohsin Kamal	5	—	21	1
Shahid Mahboob	4	—	18	—
Tauseef Ahmed	7	—	30	1
Mudassar Nazar	7	—	40	—
Manzoor Elahi	2	—	19	—
Saadat Ali	4	—	24	2
Zaheer Abbas	6	—	35	1

FALL OF WICKETS
1- 40, 2- 47, 3- 64, 4- 110, 5- 114, 6- 179, 7- 183, 8- 211

PAKISTAN

Saadat Ali	c Bracewell, b Stirling	6
Shoaib Mohammad	c Bracewell, b Coney	35
Zaheer Abbas†	b Bracewell	73
Javed Miandad	c Smith, b Snedden	32
Saleem Malik	c Cairns, b Snedden	28
Manzoor Elahi	c Bracewell, b Snedden	8
Mudassar Nazar	run out	1
Tauseef Ahmed	not out	15
Shahid Mahbob	lbw, b M.D. Crowe	1
Masood Iqbal*	run out	2
Mohsin Kamal	not out	5
Extras	lb 5, w 1, nb 2	8
(35 overs)	(for 9 wickets)	214

	O	M	R	W
M.D. Crowe	5	—	22	1
Stirling	7	—	44	1
Snedden	7	—	38	3
Cairns	5	—	42	—
Coney	4	—	27	1
Bracewell	7	—	36	1

FALL OF WICKETS
1- 8, 2- 80, 3- 148, 4- 154, 5- 164, 6- 169, 7- 199, 8- 203, 9- 206

Pakistan won by 1 wicket

position with a furious stand of 69 until both became the unlikely victims of the occasional off-spin of Saadat Ali and Zaheer Abbas.

New Zealand had scored at more than six runs an over, but they had been assisted by some lax bowling and moderate wicket-keeping, the Pakistani selectors chosing to blood yet another keeper in international cricket, Masood Iqbal.

Saadat Ali mishooked Stirling, but Zaheer and Shoaib added 72 good runs before Shoaib fell to Bracewell's second well-judged catch.

Javed Miandad helped Zaheer to maintain the momentum, but Zaheer's dismissal brought about a minor collapse. Saleem Malik righted matters but when he was out the game was excitingly balanced, Pakistan needing 15 to win with three overs and three wickets remaining.

The game swung in New Zealand's favour when Shahid

was lbw to Martin Crowe and Masood was run out while only 7 were scored. Pakistan needed 8 to win off the last over with the last two batsmen at the wicket.

With scampering and driving, the scores were levelled with one ball remaining. Stirling bowled to Mohsin Kamal who nudged the ball away and found Tauseef on him almost before he got into his stride. Pakistan had taken the one-day series by 3–1.

Third Test Match
PAKISTAN *v.* NEW ZEALAND

When, on the fourth afternoon, the New Zealand side became so incensed at umpire Shakoor Rana rejecting an appeal for caught behind against Javed Miandad that it seemed that they would leave the field it was the culmination of the visitors' dissatisfaction with the umpiring during the Test matches. A television recording, however, showed that umpire Rana had been quite correct in dismissing the appeal, and one hoped that players everywhere would pause and reflect.

Pakistan, who won the toss, recalled Wasim Raja and Shoaib Mohammad in place of Manzoor Elahi and Mohsin Khan. Mudassar and Shoaib created a record in opening the Pakistan innings in that they are the sons of Pakistan's first Test openers, Nazar Mohammad and Hanif Mohammad. Pakistan had little cause for celebration, however, as Stirling exploited a bouncy pitch to have the home side struggling to 134 for 5 at tea.

There had been a distinct lack of enterprise in the Pakistan batting, but Saleem and Wasim Raja whose Test career appears to have frequent rebirths batted sensibly and aggressively to take their side to 203 by the close.

They were separated quickly the next morning and at 226 for 7 Pakistan were in trouble, particularly as Abdul Qadir was struck on the foot and retired hurt. He was to return later, but he was unable to bowl in the match, a grievous blow to Pakistan for the wicket was the most suitable for him of the three in the series.

Pakistan were rescued by Anil Dalpat, who hit ten fours, and Iqbal Qasim who had had a splendid series since being called up unexpectedly for the first Test. Boock again bowled well and reached fifty wickets in Test cricket, but Pakistan's 328 was well beyond what they could have expected at tea on the first day.

New Zealand began in blazing form, fifty coming in 52 minutes, and although Edgar was run out, they were 99 for 1 at the close and John Wright had scored 81 of them. Sadly, New Zealand did not continue in the same aggressive vein on the third day after Wright had reached his century and fallen to Iqbal Qasim. Reid batted faultessly before edging to the lone slip, but his innings occupied 326 minutes. As Pakistan had lost Mudassar with a sprained ankle and their attack was reduced to two regular bowlers, New Zealand's failure to

THIRD TEST MATCH – PAKISTAN *v.* NEW ZEALAND
10, 11 12, 14 and 15 December 1984 at the National Stadium, Karachi

PAKISTAN

	FIRST INNINGS		SECOND INNINGS	
Mudassar Nazar	c Smith, b Stirling	5	c McEwan, b Stirling	0
Shoaib Mohammad	c Smith, b Stirling	31	c McEwan, b Boock	34
Qasim Umar	lbw, b Boock	45	c and b M.D. Crowe	17
Javed Miandad	c Smith, b M.D. Crowe	13	c J. Crowe, b Boock	58
Zaheer Abbas†	c Smith, b Stirling	14	c Smith, b Bracewell	3
Saleem Malik	c and b M.D. Crowe	50	not out	119
Wasim Raja	lbw, b Stirling	51	not out	60
Abdul Qadir	c Wright, b Boock	7		
Anil Dalpat*	b Boock	52		
Iqbal Qasim	not out	45		
Azeem Hafeez	lbw, b Boock	0		
Extras	b 5, lb 6, w 1, nb 3	15	b 2, lb 8, nb 7	17
		328	(for 5 wickets)	308

	O	M	R	W	O	M	R	W
Stirling	29	5	88	4	14	1	82	1
M.D. Crowe	21	4	81	2	10	3	26	1
McEwan	4	1	6	—	2	—	7	—
Boock	41	19	83	4	30	10	83	2
Coney	5	3	5	—				
Bracewell	20	5	54	—	33	11	83	1
J.J. Crowe					2	—	9	—
Wright					1	—	1	—
Reid					2	—	7	

FALL OF WICKETS
1- 14, 2- 80, 3- 92, 4- 102, 5- 124, 6- 204, 7- 226, 8- 315, 9- 319
1- 5, 2- 37, 3- 119, 4- 126, 5- 130

NEW ZEALAND

	FIRST INNINGS	
J.G. Wright	c Anil, b Iqbal	107
B.A. Edgar	run out	15
J.F. Reid	c Iqbal, b Azeem	97
M.D. Crowe	lbw, b Wasim Raja	45
J.J. Crowe	c Javed, b Azeem	62
J.V. Coney†	c and b Iqbal	16
P.E. McEwan	not out	40
I.D.S. Smith*	c Saleem, b Iqbal	0
D.A. Stirling	c Umar, b Iqbal	7
J.G. Bracewell	c Anil, b Azeem	30
S.L. Boock	c Anil, b Azeem	0
Extras	b 1, lb 5, nb 1	7
		426

	O	M	R	W
Mudassar Nazar	15.4	2	45	—
Azeem Hafeez	46.4	9	132	4
Iqbal Qasim	57	13	133	4
Wasim Raja	33	8	97	1
Zaheer Abbas	5.2	1	13	—

FALL OF WICKETS
1- 83, 2- 163, 3- 258, 4- 292, 5- 338, 6- 352, 7- 353, 8- 361, 9- 426

Umpires: Shakoor Rana and Javed Akhtar

Match drawn

Pakistan v. New Zealand – Test Match Averages

PAKISTAN BATTING

	M	Inns	NOs	Runs	HS	Av	100s	50s
Javed Miandad	3	6	2	337	104	84.25	2	1
Saleem Malik	3	5	2	204	119*	68.00	1	1
Iqbal Qasim	3	3	1	75	45*	37.50		
Mudassar Nazar	3	6		181	106	30.16	1	
Mohsin Khan	2	4		107	58	26.75		1
Qasim Umar	3	6		140	45	23.33		
Anil Dalpat	3	3		64	52	21.33		1
Zaheer Abbas	3	5		93	43	18.60		
Abdul Qadir	3	3		32	14	10.66		
Azeem Hafeez	3	3	1	11	11	5.50		

Played in one Test: Tauseef Ahmed 0*; Manzoor Elahi 19 and 4*; Shoaib Mohammad 31 and 34; Wasim Raja 51 and 60*

NEW ZEALAND BATTING

	M	Inns	NOs	Runs	HS	Av	100s	50s
J.F. Reid	3	5		232	106	46.40	1	1
J.G. Wright	3	5		213	107	42.60	1	1
J.J. Crowe	3	5		201	62	42.20		2
M.D. Crowe	3	5		173	55	34.60		1
I.D.S. Smith	3	5	1	92	41	23.00		
D.A. Stirling	3	5	1	55	16	13.75		
J.V. Coney	3	5		60	26	12.00		
E.J. Gray	2	4		48	25	12.00		
B.A. Edgar	3	5		56	26	11.20		
J.G. Bracewell	2	3		30	30	10.00		
S.L. Boock	3	5	1	29	13	7.25		

Played in one Test: E.J. Chatfield 6* and 0; P.E. McEwan 40*

PAKISTAN BOWLING

	Overs	Mds	Runs	Wkts	Av	Best
Mudassar Nazar	48.4	14	105	5	21.00	3/8
Iqbal Qasim	166.4	46	398	18	22.11	5/79
Abdul Qadir	105.3	24	307	12	25.58	5/108
Azeem Hafeez	103.4	30	271	10	27.10	4/132

Also bowled: Tauseef Ahmed 6–0–26–0; Zaheer Abbas 14.2–2–39–0; Manzoor Elahi 2–1–2–0; Wasim Raja 33–8–97–1

NEW ZEALAND BOWLING

	Overs	Mds	Runs	Wkts	Av	Best
E.J. Chatfield	41.2	14	69	3	23.00	3/57
S.L. Boock	172.4	54	431	17	25.35	7/87
M.D. Crowe	49	9	165	6	27.50	2/29
D.A. Stirling	92.1	16	338	8	42.25	4/88
E.J. Gray	59	5	183	4	45.75	2/19
J.G. Bracewell	82.1	21	217	4	54.25	3/44

Also bowled: J.V. Coney 21–9–26–0; P.E. McEwan 6–1–13–0; J.F. Reid 2–0–7–0; J.G. Wright 1–0–1–0; J.J. Crowe 2–0–9–0

PAKISTAN FIELDING

11–Anil Dalpat (ct 10/st 1); 4–Qasim Umar and Iqbal Qasim; 3–Mudassar Nazar, Javed Miandad and Saleem Malik; 2–sub (Rameez Raja); 1–Mohsin Khan, Abdul Qadir and Manzoor Elahi

NEW ZEALAND FIELDING

7–I.D.S. Smith (ct 6/st 1); 5–J.J. Crowe; 4–M.D. Crowe and J.V. Coney; 3–J.F. Reid; 2–E.J. Gray and P.E. McEwan; 1–J.G. Wright and S.L. Boock

seize the initiative cost them any chance of winning the match.

They moved to a lead of 98 and Pakistan were 77 for 2 at the end of the fourth day. New Zealand still had a chance of victory when, with 200 minutes and 20 overs remaining, Pakistan were 130 for 5. They were thwarted by Saleem Malik, one of the world's top batsmen, and Wasim Raja who added 178 delightful runs in 200 minutes. Saleem's innings was one of charm and authority and included a six and nineteen fours.

QUAID-E-AZAM TROPHY

Pakistan's premier tournament was restructured for the 1984–85 season. Just before the Championship a qualifying competition was held among some departmental teams and WAPDA won an exciting final against Agricultural Development Bank of Pakistan when they reached a target of 321 in their second innings with the last pair at the wicket.

In 1983–84, the national championship had been confined to ten teams, all belonging to government departments or commercial organisations, but restructuring for 1984–85 allowed for twelve teams to participate in two, as opposed to one, leagues, and for Lahore and Karachi to be restored as participants. One of the most encouraging aspects of the season was how well the two cities fared when one considers that they were unable to draw upon the best talent from their city clubs.

Group A
6, 7, 8 and 9 December 1984

at Niaz Stadium, Hyderabad

H.B.F.C. 243 (Sagheer Abbas 76, Tariq Alam 75 not out) and 367 (Tariq Alam 89, Ijaz Ahmed 83, Munir-ul-Haq 66, Raaes Ahmed 62, Wasim Raja 4 for 125)
National Bank 281 (Asad Rauf 85, Kazim Mehdi 4 for 87) and 189 (Raees Ahmed 5 for 59)

H.B.F.C. won by 140 runs
H.B.F.C. 17 pts, National Bank 8 pts

Trailing by 38 runs on the first innings, H.B.F.C. lost their first two second innings wickets for 20, but came back strongly. Sagheer Abbas and Ijaz Ahmed added 116 for the 5th wicket, and the score reached 346 before the 6th wicket fell. Four wickets then went down for 2 runs, but the total was already too formidable for National Bank who struggled on a crumbling wicket and were well beaten.

11, 12, 13 and 14 December 1984

at Bahawal Stadium, Bahawalpur

P.A.C.O. 194 (Shaukat Mirza 96 not out, Tariq Wahab 4 for 40) and 266 for 8 dec (Shaukat Mirza 116 not out, Ijaz Ahmed 54, Kazim Mehdi 6 for 79)
H.B.F.C. 212 (Ijaz Ahmed 61, Noor-ul-Qamar 50, Raees Ahmed 50, Arshad Nawaz 5 for 45) and 170 for 4 (Raees Ahmed 64, Tariq Alam 56 not out)

Match drawn
H.B.F.C. 8 pts, P.A.C.O. 5 pts

With the run-rate throughout the match never reaching three an over, it was not surprising that the match was drawn. Shaukat Mirza had a splendid match, scoring 212 runs without being dismissed. Set to score 249 to win, H.B.F.C. laboured to 170 for 4 in 70 overs.

23, 24, 25 and 26 December 1984

at National Stadium, Karachi

P.A.C.O. 215 (Umar Rasheed 53, Tanvir Ali 8 for 83) and 355 for 2 dec (Ijaz Ahmed 201 not out, Shaukat Mirza 132)
Karachi 234 for 6 (Moin-ul-Atiq 80) and 303 for 4 (Zafar Ali 111, Mohammas Aslam 71, Asif Mujtaba 61 not out)

Match drawn
Karachi 9 pts, P.A.C.O. 5 pts

at Bahawal Stadium, Bahawalpur

P.I.A. 181 (Rizwan-uz-Zaman 50, Raees Ahmed 4 for 58) and 272 (Hasan Jamil 92, Aftab Baloch 66, Kazim Mehdi 5 for 62)
H.B.F.C. 234 (Munir-ul-Haq 104 not out, Zahid Ahmed 7 for 68) and 223 for 3 (Munir-ul-Haq 120 not out, Raees Ahmed 50)

H.B.F.C won by 7 wickets
H.B.F.C. 17 pts, P.I.A. 5 pts

After his success for Karachi Blues in the BCCP Patron's Trophy, slow left-arm bowler Tanvir Ali, one month past his 21st birthday, continued to mystify batsmen in the Quaid-e-Azam Trophy and brought confusion to P.A.C.O. who, having reached 101 without loss, were bowled out for 215. In 35 overs of controlled spin, his 'arm' ball being particularly devastating, Tanvir Ali returned a career best 8 for 83. Karachi did not find batting an easy task and nudged their way to a 19-run lead in their 85 overs. By now, any devils that the wicket had held had vanished. Umar Rasheed was bowled at 4, but Ijaz Ahmed, with the season's only double century in domestic competition, and Shaukat Mirza added 316 for the second wicket, the only 300-stand of the year in Pakistan. Tanvir Ali's second innings figures were 0 for 107 in 29 overs. Set to make 337 to win, Karachi batted calmly and sparked by Zafar Ali and Asif Mujtaba, they came very close. The pair added 145 for the fourth wicket, but the earlier batsmen batted too slowly and the victory was denied.

Mohammad Nazir – an outstanding season as bowler and skipper for Railways. (Adrian Murrell)

H.B.F.C. always had the better of the match against Pakistan International Airlines. Munir-ul-Haq carried his bat through the innings, withstanding the threat of Zahid Ahmed who bewildered his team-mates. Trailing by 53 on the first innings, P.I.A. were in dreadful trouble at 55 for 5, but Aftab Baloch and Hasan Jamil, the captain, put on 133. H.B.F.C. found themselves facing a bigger target than they had anticipated, but Munir-ul-Haq hit his second century of what for him had been an outstanding match, and the win was achieved comfortably.

29, 30, 31 December 1984 and 1 January 1985

at Bahawal Stadium, Bahawalpur

P.I.A. 86 (Mian Fayyaz 5 for 27) and 228 (Mian Fayyaz 6 for 101)
P.A.C.O. 149 and 166 for 8 (Rashid Khan 5 for 49)

P.A.C.O. won by 2 wickets
P.A.C.O. 14 pts, P.I.A. 4 pts

There was no play on the second day because of rain and the weather was so uncertain and the wicket doubtful that Shahid Mahboob had no hesitation in asking P.I.A. to bat when he won the toss. P.I.A. struggled to survive on the turning wicket, but they could muster only 86 in 49.5 overs. P.A.C.O. closed the day on 102 for 6 and added only one run before losing a wicket on the third morning. With Qaisser Hussain retiring hurt, they gained a lead of only 63, and P.I.A.'s second innings was a much more determined affair even though they scored at less than two an over, Mian Fayyaz sending down 51 overs for his 6 for 101 and Arshad Nawaz bowling 35 overs for 49 runs. Needing 166 to win, P.A.C.O. were never at ease. Moin Mumtaz scored 48, but the 8th wicket fell at 150 and it was a sound 28 not out from Yahya Toor and stubborn defence from Arshad Nawaz that brought victory.

30, 31 December 1984, 1 and 3 January 1985

at National Stadium, Karachi

Allied Bank 315 for 4 (Athar A. Khan 154 not out, Iqtidar Ali 68) and 231 (Feroze Najamuddin 62, Zafar Ahmed 50)
Karachi 265 for 9 (Asif Mujtaba 71, Tanvir Ali 51, Jalal-ud-Din 4 for 61) and 227 for 9 (Saaed Azan 82, Jalal-ud-Din 4 for 43)

Match drawn
Allied Bank 10 pts, Karachi 6 pts

A stand of 139 between Iqtidar Ali and Athar A. Khan put Allied Bank in a good position. Karachi collapsed to 37 for 4, but rallied through consistent application by the middle order to cut the first innings deficit to 50. Asked to make 282 to win, Karachi lost 4 for 39 and were never in sight of victory and it was only the stubborn defence of Haaris A. Khan and Saleem Jaffer that saved them from defeat after the ninth wicket had fallen at 213.

4, 5, 6 and 7 January 1985

at National Stadium, Karachi

National Bank 225 (Tanvir Ali 4 for 51) and 276 (Shahid Tanvir 60, Tanvir Ali 4 for 77)

Karachi 323 for 8 (Nasir Shah 88, Asif Mujtaba 57, Haseeb-ul-Hasan 54) and 182 for 2 (Sajid Khan 76)

Karachi won by 8 wickets
Karachi 18 pts, National Bank 7 pts

5, 6, 7 and 8 January 1985

at Bahawal Stadium, Bahawalpur

Allied Bank 276 for 8 (Shoaib Habib 84 not out, Iqtidar Ali 76) and 276 (Iqtidar Ali 69, Shoaib Habi 50, Iqbal Sikander 5 for 82)
P.I.A. 213 for 9 (Hasan Jamil 56 not out) and 222 for 3 (Ferize Mehdi 104 not out)

Match drawn
Allied Bank 10 pts, P.I.A. 6 pts

Karachi gained their first win in the competition and moved to within 9 points of H.B.F.C. at the top of the table. They batted, bowled and fielded consistently and never relinquished their grip on the match at the National Stadium.

In spite of Iqbal's five second innings wickets and Feroze Mehdi's century, P.I.A. were never in contention at Bahawalpur and the game always seemed headed for a draw.

10, 11, 12 and 13 January 1985

at National Stadium, Karachi

H.B.F.C. 301 for 9 (Munir-ul-Haq 67, Rafat Alam 60, Wasim Arif 53, Tanvir Ali 6 for 122) and 282 (Munir-ul-Haq 66, Rafat Alam 54, Tanvir Ali 8 for 93)
Karachi 256 for 8 (Nasir Shah 76 not out) and 139 for 3 (Saaed Azad 60, Haseeb-ul-Hasan 52 not out)

Match drawn
H.B.F.C. 10 pts, Karachi 8 pts

Abdul Qadir (Habib Bank) Whatever his misdemeanours on the international scene, he remained a potent force in domestic cricket. (Adrian Murrell)

at Bahawal Stadium, Bahawalpur

P.A.C.O. 185 for 7 (Shoaib Habib 4 for 63) and 185 (Shaukat Mirza 74, Amin Lakhani 6 for 73)
Allied Bank 127 (Mian Fayyaz 4 for 38) and 177

P.A.C.O. won by 66 runs
P.A.C.O. 15 pts, Allied Bank 4 pts

With H.B.F.C.'s innings going into the second day because of delays due to rain, there was little chance of a result at Karachi once the Karachi batsman had suggested a sense of permanency. Once again the outstanding performer was slow left-armer Tanvir Ali who bowled 72.4 overs in the match to take 14 for 215. Karachi wicket-keeper Pervez-ul-Hasan had five catches in H.B.F.C.'s second innings, and on the last day, Karachi finished breezily, scoring at five an over at the close.

In the game at Bahawalpur, originally scheduled for mid-December, P.A.C.O. won a low scoring match. Spinner Amin Lakhani who thrust himself into reckoning for a Test place three years ago with two hat-tricks had an impressive match.

16, 17 and 18 January 1985

at Ibn-e-Qasim Bagh Stadium, Multan

H.B.F.C. 263 (Sagheer Abbas 73, Rafat Alam 60, Tariq Alam 51 not out, Jalal-ud-Din 6 for 66) and 326 (Noor-ul-Qamar 101, Wasim Arif 60, Ijaz Ahmed 56, Jalal-ud-Din 5 for 63)
Allied Bank 326 (Saleem Yousuf 67, Zafar Ahmed 55, Feroze Najamuddin 54, Athar A. Khan 53, Kazim Mehdi 4 for 52) and 265 for 8 (Iqtidar Ali 77, Shoaib Habib 67 not out, Kazim Mehdi 4 for 79)

Allied Bank won by 2 wickets
Allied Bank 18 pts, H.B.F.C. 8 pts

Wicket-keeper Saleem Yousuf of Allied Bank had three catches and three stumpings in H.B.F.C's first innings, but like all else about this match, it is a performance best forgotten. The two umpires alleged after the match that the two sides had arranged the result in order to allow Allied Bank to gain enough points to reach the semi-finals of the competition. An official inquiry found that this had, in fact, been the case. Thc two teams were expelled from the P.A.C.O. Pentagular Tournament for which, as semi-finalists in the Quaid-e-Azam, they had qualified and were debarred from all first-class cricket until the end of the 1985–86 season. This ban was later lifted when it was realised that some fifty players, employed by the two teams, would be rendered jobless. It was one of the most unhappy events in world cricket in 1984–85.

16, 17, 18 and 19 January 1985

at Bahawal Stadium, Bahawalpur

National Bank 143 (Shahid Mahboob 4 for 25, Mian Fayyaz 4 for 61) and 265 (Saleem Pervez 112, Masood Anwar 5 for 101)
P.A.C.O. 306 for 7 (Moin Mumtaz 135 not out) and 103 for 1 (Ijaz Ahmed 50 not out)

P.A.C.O. won by 9 wickets
P.A.C.O. 18 pts, National Bank 4 pts

at National Stadium, Karachi

Karachi 299 (Nasir Shah 62, Asif Mujtaba 59, Haseeb-ul-Hasan 57, Moin-ul-Stuq 52) and 350 for 6 dec (Nasir Shah 120, Asif Mujtaba 54)

P.I.A. 286 for 7 (Aftab Baloch 60 not out, Tanvir Ali 5 for 78) and 180 for 3 (Rizwan-uz-Zaman 104 not out)

Match drawn
Karachi 10 pts, P.I.A. 8 pts

The weak National Bank side was overwhelmed by P.A.C.O., the game ending before lunch on the last day. National Bank were 56 for 6 and recovered slightly through the determination of their tail-enders. P.A.C.O. lost both openers for 16, but Shaukat Mirza and Moin Mumtaz added 102 and from that time, in spite of a brave hundred from Saleem Pervez, they dominated the match.

Once again it was Karachi's failure to bowl out the opposition that was their undoing. The attack depended so heavily on Tanvir Ali that once he was blunted, there was little chance of the opposition being dismissed. Nasir Shah delayed his declaration too long and P.I.A. had no option but to bat for a draw, a task which was accomplished and embellished by a century from the highly talented Rizwan.

22, 23 and 24 January 1985

at National Stadium, Karachi

National Bank 257 (Sajid Ali 73, Shoaib Habib 5 for 63) and 165 (Jalal-ud-Din 4 for 68)
Allied Bank 296 for 9 (Talat Masood 117, Iqbal Butt 4 for 81) and 130 for 3

Allied Bank won by 7 wickets
Allied Bank 18 pts, National Bank 8 pts

National Bank gave a better account of themselves with the bat in the first innings than might have been expected, but, trailing by 39 on the first innings, they lost 4 wickets before clearing the arrears. All four wickets fell to Jalal-ud-Din, discarded as an international player, and National Bank never recovered from this blow.

2, 3, 4 and 5 February 1985

at National Stadium, Karachi

P.I.A. 273 for 7 (Rizwan-uz-Zaman 119) and 245 for 3 dec (Rizwan-uz-Zaman 121 not out, Asif Mohammad 116 not out)
National Bank 260 for 8 (Saleem Anwar 125 not out) and 158 for 3 (Sajid Ali 95, Saleem Anwar 51)

Match drawn
P.I.A. 10 pts, National Bank 8 pts

This game was to have been played at Hyderabad in December, but had to be postponed because of the non-availability. It was, in fact, being played at the same time as the final of the competition was taking place so emphasising the total disarray that had been caused by the indigestable fixture list dominated by international cricket. With a century in each innings, Rizwan-uz-Zaman capped a wonderful season, reaching a thousand runs during his second innings when he and Asif Mohammad shared an unbroken stand of 237.

Group A – Final Table

	P	W	L	D	Pts
H.B.F.C.	5	2	1	2	60
Allied Bank	5	2	1	2	60
P.A.C.O.	5	3	—	2	57
Karachi	5	1	—	4	51
National Bank	5	—	4	1	35
Pakistan Int. Airlines	5	—	2	3	33

H.B.F.C. were placed first on faster run rate

Group B
29, 30 November and 1 December 1984

at LCCA Ground, Lahore

Lahore 230 (Shahid Anwar 115, Mazhar Hussain 83 not out) and 126 (Tauseef Ahmed 5 for 63, Shahid Butt 4 for 36)
United Bank 299 for 8 (Saadat Ali 116, Mansoor Akhtar 95, Pervez J. Mir 5 for 84) and 59 for 2

United Bank won by 8 wickets
United Bank 18 pts, Lahore 7 pts

at Qaddafi Stadium, Lahore

Railways 313 for 5 (Ameer Akbar 103, Talat Mirza 63, Pervez Shah 51 not out)
Habib Bank 114 and 142 (Shahid Pervez 5 for 27)

Railways won by an innings and 57 runs
Railways 18 pts, Habib Bank 3 pts

Lahore began the competition disastrously, losing their first 5 wickets for 17 runs. A mighty stand of 177 between Shahid Anwar, who had opened and withstood the early barage of Sikhander Bakht, and Mazhar Hussain rescued them, but United Bank replied with an opening stand of 202 between Mansoor Akhtar and Saadat Ali. The United Bank spinners shot out Lahore in the second innings and the visitors moved to an easy victory with a day and a half to spare.

Railways, who were to dominate the group, overwhelmed Habib Bank, the game again ending early on the third day.

5, 6, 7 and 8 December 1984

at Qaddafi Stadium, Lahore

Muslim Commercial Bank 226 for 9 (Anwar-ul-Haq 113, Kamal Merchant 5 for 54) and 263 (Asif Ali 81 not out, Ehtesham-ud-Din 9 for 124)
United Bank 370 for 6 (Ali Zia 100, Mansoor Akhtar 65) and 121 for 2 (Shafiq Ahmed 62 not out)

United Bank won by 8 wickets
United Bank 18 pts, Muslim Commercial Bank 6 pts

A magnificent bowling performance by veteran medium pacer Ehtesham-ud-Din who was called from the Bolton League to play for Pakistan against England in 1982 was the highlight of this match. His 9 for 124 in 35.3 overs was the second best bowling performance of the season and he was the only bowler to take 9 wickets in an innings in a Quaid-e-Azam Trophy match. Ali Zia had lashed United Bank into a substantial first innings lead after Anwar-ul-Haq had played a lone hand for Muslim Commercial Bank and Ehtesham-ud-Din's bowling set up the victory which was accomplished shortly after lunch on the last day.

11, 12, 13 and 14 December 1984

at Iqbal Stadium, Faisalabad

Railways 135 (Farrukh Zaman 6 for 42) and 275 (Shahid Saaed 69)

Mansoor Akhtar – his batting for the all conquering United Bank reawakened hopes that he could yet become a Test player of world class. (George Herringshaw)

Muslim Commercial Bank 200 (Mohammad Nazir 6 for 77) and 139 (Mohammad Nazir 4 for 35)

Railways won by 71 runs
Railways 14 pts, Muslim Commercial Bank 6 pts

A reversal of fortunes in the course of the match saw Railways gain a surprisingly easy win after trailing by 65 runs on the first innings. Put in to bat, Railways floundered on a turning wicket and by the end of the first day, Muslim Commercial Bank, 116 for 3, seemed in total command. Mohammad Nazir bowled his side back into contention on the second day with his off-spin and kept the first innings deficit within bounds. Solid and determined batting throughout the order gave Railways some hope and the Bank were left to make 211 in a day and a half. The backbone of the side was broken on the third evening when 6 wickets fell for 85 runs and skipper Mohammad Nazir finished the job on the last morning.

23, 24, 25 and 26 December 1984

at LCCA Ground, Lahore

W.A.P.D.A. 322 for 7 (Akram Raza 101 not out, Tanvir Razzaq 98, Farrukh Raza 58) and 332 for 6 dec (Tanvir Razzaq 90, Mohammad Ashraf 81, Akram Raza 51 not out)
Lahore 250 (Mohammad Ishaq 86, Pervez J. Mir 54) and 406 for 5 (Shahid Anwar 137, Mohammad Ishaq 112, Aaamer Sohail 57 not out)

Lahore won by 5 wickets
Lahore 18 pts, W.A.P.D.A. 8 pts

at Pindi Club Ground, Rawalpindi

Habib Bank 321 for 2 (Anwar Miandad 118 not out, Arshad Pervez 88, Azhar Khan 68 not out) and 267 for 8 dec (Zaheer Ahmed 112 not out, Noman Sgabbir 77, Asif Ali 4 for 71)
Muslim Commercial Bank 263 for 9 (Anwar-ul-Haq 79, Azhar Khan 4 for 70) and 152 (Anwar-ul-Haq 76, Abdur Raqeeb 5 for 67)

Habib Bank won by 173 runs
Habib Bank 18 pts, Muslim Commercial Bank 5 pts

On one of the most thrilling matches of the season Lahore gained a memorable victory over W.A.P.D.A. who were making their debut in the competition. The newcomers began uncertainly and lost 3 for 35, but Farrukh Raza and Tanvir Razzaq added 122, and Akram Raza hit 101 out of the last 165 runs scored. Lahore reached 146 for 1 in reply and then collapsed to 250 all out as they strove for quick runs. W.A.P.D.A. batted strongly again and declared shortly after tea on the third day, setting Lahore to make 405 at 3.6 an over, a formidable task. Mohammad Ishaq and Shahid Anwar gave them just the start that was needed, an opening stand of 193. Mohsin Riaz hit a brisk 33 and Pervez J. Mir kept the momentum going. When the fifth wicket fell only 16 runs were needed for victory and, with Aamer Sohail in fine form, that was achieved with 23 balls to spare.

Habib Bank, with Anwar Miandad sharing century stands with Arshad Pervez and Azhar Khan, threatened to overwhelm Muslim Commercial, Habib faltered at the start of their second innings, losing 6 for 50, but wicket-keeper Zaheer Ahmed hit 112 not out and Muslim Commercial were left needing 329 to win. They had little hope and crashed to their third defeat, their batting almost entirely dependant on skipper Anwar-ul-Haq.

29, 30, 31 December 1984, 1 January 1985

at LCCA Ground, Lahore

Lahore 310 for 5 (Shahid Anwar 153 not out, Mohammad Ishaq 68)
v Muslim Commercial Bank

Match abandoned
Lahore 9 pts, Muslim Commercial Bank 8 pts

at Pindi Club Ground, Rawalpindi

W.A.P.D.A. 148 (Liaqat Ali 5 for 59) and 248 (Shahid Pervez 65, Abdur Raqeeb 5 for 61)
Habib Bank 346 for 6 dec (Azhar Khan 103, Sultan Rana 77, Tensin Javed 55 not out) and 54 for 0

Habib Bank won by 10 wickets
Habib Bank 18 pts, W.A.P.D.A. 3 pts

Mohammad Ishaq and Shahid Anwar, who hit his second century in succession, put on 151 for the first wicket at Lahore, but rain prevented any further play after 9 minutes of the final session on the first day. The teams shared the 10 points given for a win.

W.A.P.D.A. were well beaten by Habib Bank for whom Azhar Khan and Sultan Rana shared a fourth wicket stand of 117.

4 and 5 January 1985

at LCCA Ground, Lahore

Lahore 157 (Pervez J. Mir 50, Mohammad Nazir 5 for 52) and 69 (Nadeem Ghauri 5 for 24)
Railways 247 (Ameer Akbar 107, Tahir Shah 60)

Railways won by an innings and 21 runs
Railways 17 pts, Lahore 5 pts

4, 5, 6 and 7 January 1985

at Qaddafi Stadium, Lahore

W.A.P.D.A. 216 (Sajjad Akbar 84, Haafiz Shahid 64 not out, Naved Anjum 5 for 58) and 168 (Sajjad Akbar 76) not out, Naved Anjum 4 for 41)
United Bank 237 (Shafiq Ahmed 118, Imran Ali 6 for 80, Haafiz Shahid 4 for 77) and 151 for 8 (Haafiz Shahid 7 for 59)

United Bank won by 2 wickets
United Bank 17 pts, W.A.P.D.A. 6 pts

Electing to bat first in overcast conditions on a wicket which gave the spinners assistance, Lahore dragged their way to 157 all out. Bad light ended play early, but next morning Ameer Akbar and Tahir Shah added 100 for the fourth wicket, the one substantial stand of the match. Lahore batted woefully at their second attempt and were out in 32.4 overs to give Railways victory with more than two days to spare.

It was a closer contest elsewhere in Lahore where W.A.P.D.A. battled bravely. They were 49 for 6 and then Sajjad Akbar and Haafiz Shahid added 114. It was Haafiz who joined with Imran Ali to restrict United Bank's lead after skipper Shafiq Ahmed had threatened to dominate the match. W.A.P.D.A. collapsed when they battled again, 8 wickets falling for 56, but a courageous stand of 99 between Sajjad Akbar and Afzal Butt gave them a fighting chance on a wicket which was now taking spin. Needing 148 to win, United Bank battled against Haafiz Shahid who was again their tormentor. At 58 for 6, they looked beaten, but Naved Anjum and Ashraf Ali added 43. Ashraf was bowled by Haafiz and at 126, Tauseef Ahmed became Haafiz's seventh victim. Shahid Aziz now joined Naved Anjum and they hit the runs needed for victory, Naved finishing on 43 not out, a match-wining innings.

10, 11, 12 and 13 January 1985

at Qaddafi Stadium, Lahore

Railways 199 (Tauseef Ahmed 8 for 83) and 150 (Shahid Saeed 50, Tauseef Ahmed 7 for 65)
United Bank 203 for 6 (Ashraf Ali 80 not out, Shafiq Ahmed 52 not out, Shahid Pervez 4 for 54) and 132 (Mohammad Nazir 4 for 34)

Railways won by 14 runs
Railways 14 pts, United Bank 6 pts

at LCCA Ground, Lahore

Habib Bank 280 (Azhar Khan 115, Pervez J. Mir 5 for 79) and 274 (Arshad Pervez 152 not out, Agha Zahid 73)
Lahore 292 (Mohsin Riaz 71, Khalid Javed 59 not out, Abdur Raqeeb 4 for 107, Abdul Qadir 4 for 115) and 209 (Pervez J. Mir 74, Khalid Javed 60, Abdul Qadir 5 for 97)

Habib Bank won by 53 runs
Habib Bank 18 pts, Lahore 8 pts

at Gujranwala Stadium, Gujranwala

W.A.P.D.A. 135 (Farrukh Zaman 6 for 48) and 307 (Ashfaq Ahmed 58, Haafiz Zhahid 56)
Muslim Commercial Bank 217 (Nadeem Yousuf 61 not out, Haafiz Shahid 4 for 54) and 229 for 5 (Babar Basharat 68 not out)

Muslim Commercial Bank won by 5 wickets
Muslim Commercial Bank 16 pts, W.A.P.D.A. 4 pts

Railways continued their winning ways with a close victory against chief challengers United Bank. Runs were never easy to get, but the batting honours went to United Bank's skipper Shafiq Ahmed and wicket-keeper Ashraf Ali who came together at 80 for 6 and took the score to 203 by the end of the 85 overs. The individual honours of the game also went to a United Bank player, off-spinner Tauseef Ahmed, who took 15 wickets for 148 runs in the match and finished on the losing side. No man could have done more and he bowled his side into a position where they needed only 147 to win. They lost key batsmen Saadat Ali and Mansoor Akhtar on 16, but veteran Sadiq Mohammad suggested he would play a vital role until he fell to Shahid Pervez for 35. At 105 for 6, United Bank looked to be better placed, but 2 wickets fell for 3 runs and the advantage moved to Railways. They did not relinquish it again in spite of another brave innings by Ashraf Ali.

There were fluctuating fortunes at LCCA Ground too. Azhar Khan was the only Habib batsman to play with confidence in the first innings and consistent application took Lahore to a 12-run lead. This was soon nullified by Agha Zahid and Arshad Pervez who scored 164 for Habib Bank's first wicket in the second innings. Arshad carried his bat through the innings for 152. He and Munir-ul-Haq were the only batsmen to achieve this feat during the season. Needing 263 to win, Lahore tumbled to 46 for 5, but a fine stand of 144 between skipper Pervez and Khalid Javed raised hopes of the unexpected only for the last 5 wickets to fall for 19.

Once again W.A.P.D.A. found that their courageous recovery was not enough. They were 82 behind on the first innings, but batted consistently enough at the second attempt to set Muslim Commercial a target of 226. The issue was never in doubt, however, and the target was reached comfortably on the last afternoon.

16, 17 and 18 January 1985

at LCCA Ground, Lahore

Railways 267 for 8 (Abdus Sami 63)
W.A.P.D.A. 96 (Nadeem Ghauri 4 for 44) and 118 (Mohammad Nazir 6 for 44, Nadeem Ghauri 4 for 54)

Railways won by an innings and 53 runs
Railways 18 pts, W.A.P.D.A. 4 pts

at Qaddafi Stadium, Lahore

Habib Bank 152 (Arshad Pervez 84, Tauseef Ahmed 5 for 37) and 173 (Ehtesham-ud-Din 7 for 77)
United Bank 332 for 9 (Saadat Ali 169, Shafiq Ahmed 52, Liaqat Ali 6 for 110)

United Bank won by an innings and 7 runs
United Bank 18 pts, Habib Bank 5 pts

Railways and United Bank made certain of their semi-final places with innings victories inside three days. Railways' victory meant that they had won all their five matches in the group. Their spinners proved far too much for W.A.P.D.A. in a low scoring match.

United Bank won with surprising ease. They put Habib in and only Arshad was able to save something from the wreckage wrought by Tausses and bizarre running. Saadat Ali, who had not shown quite the dominance of the previous season, then played his best innings of the year in spite of good bowling by former Test pace man Liaqat. When Habib

Group B – Final Table

	P	W	L	D	Pts
Railways	5	5	—	—	81
United Bank	5	4	1	—	77
Habib Bank	5	3	2	—	62
Lahore	5	1	3	1	47
Muslim Commercial Bank	5	1	3	1	41
W.A.P.D.A.	5	—	5	—	25

Bank batted again Ehtesham-ud-Din exploited the conditions even better than Liaqat had done and at one time Habib were 98 for 7, salvaging some pride through their tail.

Semi-Finals
28, 29, 30 and 31 January 1985

at National Stadium, Karachi

United Bank 340 for 7 (Mansoor Akhtar 101, Mahmood Rasheed 81, Izhar Ahmed 4 for 102) and 272 (Kamal Merchant 72, Raaes Ahmed 4 for 100)
H.B.F.C. 164 (Sikhander Bakht 4 for 51) and 204 (Ijaz Ahmed 88, Shahid Aziz 6 for 106)

United Bank won by 244 runs

at Qaddafi Stadium, Lahore

Allied Bank 232 (Zafar Ahmed 73 not out, Iqtidar Ali 57, Mohammad Nazir 4 for 47) and 324 for 7 dec (Zafar Mehdi 94, Iqtidar Ali 62, Athar A. Khan 59)
Railways 353 for 9 (Manzoor Elahi 78 not out, Tahir Shah 76, Pervez Shah 57, Jalal-ud-Din 4 for 133) and 104 for 2 (Shahid Saeed 53 not out)

Match drawn
Railways qualified for final on first innings lead

Mansoor Akhtar played the type of innings which indicated why he had been considered a batsman of Test class only a year earlier and shared a stand of 156 with Mahmood Rasheed for the fourth wicket. This put United Bank in a mightily strong position and when Sikhander reduced H.B.F.C. to 49 for 4 the position was strengthened even more. Tauseef removed further opposition and with United Bank batting consistently in their second innings and H.B.F.C. losing Noor-ul-Qamar at 2 before the close of the third day, the last day could hold no surprises.

Railways recovered from 84 for 4 to reach 353, a lead of 121, and an impregnable position. Allied Bank batted bravely at the second attempt, but Railways were never likely to throw away the position they had earned, but finished the drawn match in high spirits, scoring at 6 an over.

The Final

The semi-finals had been delayed a week; the final was delayed 33 minutes. The delay was caused as part of the ground was flooded due to clogged gutters. The flooding also meant that the wicket had to be changed and the match was played on a rather hastily prepared track. This new wicket was at first unpredictable, with an uneven bounce that benefited the spinners.

Railways had every reason to be confident with their fine record in reaching the final and this confidence proved justified when skipper Mohammad Nazir, the veteran off-spinner, skittled out United Bank for 214. Overnight and early morning rain robbed the spectators of three hours of play on the second day, but United Bank did well to capture 4 wickets for 105 in the time available.

QUAID-E-AZAM TROPHY CHAMPIONSHIP FINAL – RAILWAYS *v.* UNITED BANK
3, 4, 5, 6 and 7 February 1985 at Qaddafi Stadium, Lahore

UNITED BANK

	FIRST INNINGS		SECOND INNINGS	
Mansoor Akhtar	c Zulqarnain, b Nadeem	28	lbw, b Manzoor	87
Saadat Ali	c Sami, b Manzoor	15	st Zulqarnain, b Nadeem	35
Shafiq Ahmed†	c Zulqarnain, b Nazir	43	c Zulqarnain, b Nadeem	115
Ali Zia	c Saaed, b Nazir	26	b Sami	81
Mahmood Rasheed	c Sami, b Nazir	1	b Manzoor	15
Naved Anjum	c Zulqarnain, b Nadeem	17	c and b Sami	159
Ashraf Ali*	c Zulqarnain, b Nazir	19	not out	59
Kamal Merchant	not out	36	not out	7
Tauseef Ahmed	b Nazir	17		
Sikhander Bakht	c Sami, b Nazir	6		
Shahid Aziz	run out	1		
Extras	lb 1, nb 4	5	b 1, lb 7, nb 3	11
		214	(for 2 wkts dec)	568

	O	M	R	W	O	M	R	W
Manzoor Elahi	9	2	31	1	29	1	112	2
Pervez Shah	6	2	14	—	17	3	69	—
Shahid Pervez	7	1	22	—				
Mohammad Nazir	33.5	8	70	6	38	6	82	—
Nadeem Ghauri	29	2	76	2	68	13	170	2
Abdus Sami					23	1	56	2
Tahir Shah					18	1	60	—
Ameer Akbar					1	—	11	—

FALL OF WICKETS
1- 25, 2- 91, 3- 99, 4- 101, 5- 130, 6- 136, 7- 162, 8- 198, 9- 204
1- 106, 2- 226, 3- 245, 4- 295, 5- 419, 6- 539

RAILWAYS

	FIRST INNINGS		SECOND INNINGS	
Talat Mirza	c Ashraf, b Sikhander	6	c Ali Zia, b Mansoor	43
Shahid Saeed	c Ashraf, b Kamal	21	c Ashraf, b Shahid	10
Abdus Sami	c Mahmood, b Tauseef	51		
Ameer Akbar	c Shafiq, b Tauseef	0	(3) not out	52
Tahir Shah	c Shafiq, b Shahid	9	(4) not out	1
Pervez Shah	c Ashraf, b Tauseef	39		
Manzoor Elahi	c sub, b Tauseef	14		
Mohammad Nazir†	b Tauseef	1		
Shahid Pervez	c Mahmood, b Tauseef	5		
Zulqarnain*	not out	2		
Nadeem Ghauri	b Tauseef	6		
Extras	lb 5, nb 2	7	b 4, lb 3, nb 2	9
		161	(for 2 wickets)	115

	O	M	R	W	O	M	R	W
Sikhander Bakht	6	—	27	1	3	1	10	—
Naved Anjum	6	3	6	—	1	1	0	—
Tauseef Ahmed	24.4	5	61	7	4	2	8	—
Kamal Merchant	9	5	16	1	2	—	9	—
Shahid Aziz	15	3	45	1	13	4	41	1
Ali Zia	1	—	1	—	11	2	26	—
Shafiq Ahmed					2	—	2	—
Mansoor Akhtar					1	—	2	1
Mahmood Rasheed					1	—	10	—

FALL OF WICKETS
1- 12, 2- 40, 3- 70, 4- 75, 5- 131, 6- 133, 7- 136, 8- 149, 9- 155
1- 32, 2- 102

Umpires: Amanullah Khan and Mian Aslam

Match drawn – United Bank won on first innings

Railways hopes of the crucial first innings lead rested on the not out pair Abdus Sami and Pervez Shah. They carried the score next morning to 131, adding 56 runs, before Sami was dismissed by Tauseef. This heralded an astounding collapse as the last six wickets fell to the off-spinner while only 30 runs were added. In effect, this decided the destiny of the Championship.

The pitch eased out with the passage of time and Shafiq Ahmed decided not to go for an outright win so killing all hopes of a positive result. Content to take the title on the first innings lead, United Bank reached a mammoth score with Naved Anjum hitting a career best and his first century in the Quaid-e-Azam Trophy. When Sahfiq, who also hit a hundred, declared at lunch time on the final day, he set Railways the task of scoring 622 in 150 minutes and 20 overs. The game was ended mercifully after one of the compulsory 20. It was the fourth time United Bank had won the title in the last eight years.

P.A.C.O. Pentagular Tournament

With Allied Bank and H.B.F.C. banned from the competition, P.A.C.O. and Habib Bank, who held third places in the group, were promoted to the Pentagular Tournament while Karachi, as winners of the Patron's Trophy, completed the contestants.

9, 10, 11 and 12 February 1985

at Qaddafi Stadium, Lahore

Railways 310 for 7 (Tahir Shah 75, Talat Mirza 61) and 228 for 6 dec (Tahir Shah 88, Munawwar Javed 51)
Karachi 253 for 9 (Nasir Shah 86) and 203 for 9 (Saeed Azad 91)

Match drawn
Railways 10 pts, Karachi 8 pts

A defiant innings by Saeed Azad and stalwart defence by the tail-enders after Karachi had slipped from 162 for 3 to 195 for 8 thwarted Railways in the opening match of the competition. Tahir Shah won the individual award.

14, 15, 16 and 17 February 1985

at Qaddafi Stadium, Lahore

P.A.C.O. 205 (Shaukat Mirza 97) and 240 (Masood Anwar 72 not out, Nadeem Moosa 4 for 50)
Karachi 288 for 4 (Saeed Azad 120, Zafar Ali 60, Nasir Shah 58) and 161 for 6 (Moin-ul-Atiq 70 not out, Shahid Mahboob 5 for 68)

Karachi won by 4 wickets
Karachi 18 pts, P.A.C.O. 4 pts

at LCCA Ground, Lahore

Habib Bank 255 for 4 (Arshad Pervez 123, Nadeem Ghauri 4 for 95) and 207 (Noman Shabir 66 not out, Nadeem Ghauri 8 for 68)
Railways 293 for 8 (Shahid Saaed 87, Ameer Akbar 63, Abdur Raqeeb 5 for 108) and 129 (Abdur Raqeeb 4 for 47)

Habib Bank won by 40 runs
Habib Bank 18 pts, Railways 6 pts

Karachi had much the better of the exchange with P.A.C.O. and looked winners from the time that Zafar Ali and Man of the Match Saeed Azad put on 73 for the second wicket, and Saaed and Nasir Shah added 114 for the third. P.A.C.O. looked well beaten when they were 140 for 8 in their second innings, but a whirlwind 72 from Masood Anwar at number 10 ensured that Karachi would have some runs to chase for victory.

Railways suffered their first defeat of the season even though they had a first innings lead of 38 and Nadeem Ghauri had the splendid match figures of 12 for 163. They collapsed in their second innings much as they had done in the Quaid-e-Azam Final, losing their last 9 wickets for 75 runs.

19, 20 and 21 February 1985

at LCCA Ground, Lahore

P.A.C.O. 282 for 9 (Moin Mumtaz 103, Yahya Toor 76 not out, Abdul Qadir 6 for 136) and 172 (Atiq-ur-Rehman 5 for 60, Abdul Qadir 5 for 69)
Habib Bank 264 for 9 (Arshad Pervez 73, Shahid Mahboob 4 for 88) and 192 for 4 (Azhar Khan 58)

Habib Bank won by 6 wickets
Habib Bank 18 pts. P.A.C.O. 8 pts

19, 20, 21 and 22 February 1985

at Qaddafi Stadium, Lahore

United Bank 373 for 8 (Mansoor Akhtar 180, Saudat Ali 75, Nadeem Moosa 4 for 118) and 312 for 5 dec (Saadat Ali 134, Shafiq Ahmed 61)
Karachi 306 for 8 (Moin-ul-Atiq 140) and 145 (Tauseef Ahmed 5 for 43, Alia Zia 4 for 37)

United Bank won by 234 runs
United Bank 18 pts, Karachi 8 pts

Defying the art of Abdul Qadir, Moin Mumtaz and Yahya Toor took P.A.C.O. from 95 for 5 to 216 before Moin was caught and bowled by the leg-spinner. Habib Bank surrendered a first innings lead of 18, but quickly seized the initiative when Qadir and Atiq bowled P.A.C.O. out for 172 in their second innings. Habib Bank had little trouble in scoring the required runs.

The impressive opening partnership of Mansoor Akhtar and Saadat Ali, named Man of the Match, scored heavily against Karachi. They put on 134 in the first innings and although Mansoor was run out cheaply in the second innings, Saadat played another fine innings, shared a second wicket stand of 146 with Shafiq, and took United Bank to an impregnable position. Moin-ul-Atiq had kept Karachi in contention with a fine century in the first innings and he was top scorer with 27 in the second, but the off-spin of Tauseef brought Karachi to defeat. He took 5 of the first 7 wickets.

24, 26 and 27 February 1985

at Qaddafi Stadium, Lahore

United Bank 237 (Ashraf Ali 54, Shahid Pervez 4 for 71) and 104 (Nadeem Ghauri 6 for 25)
Railways 139 (Shahid Butt 5 for 33, Tauseef Ahmed 5 for 52) and 175 (Shahid Butt 5 for 73)

United Bank won by 27 runs
United Bank 17 pts, Railways 4 pts

24, 26, 27 February and 1 March 1985

Karachi 258 for 9 (Saaed Azad 55, Abdul Qadir 5 for 126) and 172 (Abdul Qadir 8 for 67)
Habib Bank 225 (Tanvir Ali 8 for 87) and 209 for 4 (Anwar Miandad 64)

Habib Bank won by 6 wickets
Habib Bank 17 pts, Karachi 8 pts

These two results left both Banks with one hundred per cent records and reduced the competition to a direct contest between the two of them. Railways bowled well, but their batting appeared to have lost the confidence it had shown in the group matches in the Quaid-e-Azam Trophy and they slipped to defeat in three days.

Whatever his misdemeanours on the international field, Abdul Qadir was a potent force in domestic cricket. He won the individual award for the second successive match and spun Karachi to defeat. Tanvir Ali, in his year of wonders, took 8 for 87 in 32.2 overs to give Karachi a first innings lead, but Qadir had 13 wickets in the match and it was his bowling that proved decisive.

3, 4 and 5 March 1985

at LCCA Ground, Lahore

United Bank 318 for 9 (Alia Zia 96, Abdul Qadir 5 for 143) and 118 (Abdul Qadir 5 for 64)
Habib Bank 167 (Tauseef Ahmed 8 for 52) and 147 (Azhar Khan 57, Shahid Butt 6 for 53)

United Bank won by 122 runs
United Bank 18 pts, Habib Bank 5 pts

3, 4, 5 and 6 March 1985

at Qaddafi Stadium, Lahore

Railways 281 for 8 (Tahir Shah 80, Abdus Sami 54) and 254 for 8 dec (G.M. Ahmed 5 for 82)

Hope for the future – Saleem Malik, captain of the under-23 side that toured Sri Lanka. (Adrian Murrell)

P.A.C.O. 164 (Mohammad Nazir 7 for 62) and 259 (Ijaz Ahmed 107, Yahya Toor 63, Mohammad Nazir 5 for 89, Nadeem Ghauri 5 for 134)

Railways won by 112 runs
Railways 18 pts, P.A.C.O. 5 pts

With victory inside three days over Habib Bank, United Bank virtually assured themselves of the P.A.C.O. Pentagular Championship. Solid and consistent batting took them to a good score and there was a personal triumph for Tauseef Ahmed when Habib batted as he took 8 for 52 in 24 overs. United stumbled in their second innings to Qadir, but the result was never in doubt.

Railways gained their first victory in the competition, recapturing their early season form with skipper Mohammad Nazir taking the Man of the Match award for his 12 for 151.

7, 8 and 9 March 1985

at Qaddafi Stadium, Lahore

United Bank 326 for 4 (Alia Zia 176, Shafiq Ahmed 69) and 210 for 5 dec (Alia Zia 102 not out)
P.A.C.O. 165 (Tauseef Ahmed 7 for 67) and 119 (Tauseef Ahmed 7 for 52)

United Bank won by 252 runs
United Bank 18 pts, P.A.C.O. 3 pts

United Bank took the title in the grand manner with the fourth win in four matches in which they dropped only one point. They were the team of the season in every respect. There were two personal triumphs in the match which United dominated and won with more than a day to spare. Ali Zia hit a century in each innings and Tauseef Ahmed, with 14 and 119 in the match, took his total of wickets for the season to 83, eleven ahead of his nearest rival.

P.A.C.O. Pentagular Trophy – Final Table

	P	W	L	D	Pts
United Bank	4	4	—	—	71
Habib Bank	4	3	1	—	58
Karachi	4	1	2	1	42
Railways	4	1	2	1	38
P.A.C.O.	4	—	4	—	20

Four Nations Tournament – First Match
INDIA *v.* PAKISTAN

A capacity crowd of 12,000 saw India maintain their winning form in one-day internationals after a most uncertain start. Javed Miandad won the toss and asked India to bat. It seemed the most logical thing to do when Imran began to seam the ball mightily and Taussef's off-spinners turned prodigiously. Azharuddin alone showed any composure and once more underlined his quality with an intelligent and forceful innings as all about him floundered. Kapil Dev played some typically aggressive shots, but Imran's 6 for 14 looked to have won the match for Pakistan when India could muster only 125.

Mudassar and Mohsin began confidently, but a bizarre run out accounted for Mohsin. The pitch had now dried and

ROTHMAN TROPHY – INDIA *v.* PAKISTAN
22 March 1985 at Sharjah

INDIA			
R.J. Shastri	lbw, b Imran Khan	0	
K. Srikkanth	c Saleem Malik, b Imran	6	
M. Azharuddin	b Tauseef	47	
D.B. Vengsarkar	c Ashraf Ali, b Imran	1	
S.M. Gavaskar	c Ashraf Ali, b Imran	2	
M.B. Amarnath	b Imran Khan	5	
R.N. Kapil Dev†	b Tauseef	30	
R.M.H. Binny	c Javed, b Mudassar	8	
U.S. Madan Lal	c Ashraf Ali, b Imran	11	
S. Viswanath*	not out	3	
L. Sivaramakrishnan	c Saleem Malik, b Wasim Akram	1	
Extras	b 5, lb 4, w 2	11	
(42.4 overs)		125	

	O	M	R	W
Imran Khan	10	2	14	6
Wasim Akram	7.4	—	27	1
Tahir Naqqash	5	—	12	—
Mudassar Nazar	10	1	36	1
Tauseef Ahmed	10	—	27	2

FALL OF WICKETS
1-0, 2-12, 3-20, 4-28, 5-34, 6-80, 7-95, 8-113, 9-121

PAKISTAN		
Mudassar Nazar	c Gavaskar, b Binny	18
Mohsin Khan	run out	10
Rameez Raja	c Gavaskar, b Kapil Dev	29
Javed Miandad†	c Gavaskar, b Shastri	0
Ashraf Ali*	c Vengsarkar, b Sivaramakrishnan	0
Imran Khan	st Viswanath, b Sivaramakrishnan	0
Saleem Malik	c Gavaskar, b Shastri	17
Manzoor Elahi	c and b Madan Lal	9
Tahir Naqqash	c Viswanath, b Kapil Dev	1
Tauseef Ahmed	b Kapil Dev	0
Wasim Akram	not out	0
Extras	lb 1, w 1, nb 1	3
(32.5 overs)		87

	O	M	R	W
Kapil Dev	6.5	1	17	3
Binny	3	—	24	1
Sivaramakrishnan	7	2	16	2
Shastri	10	5	17	2
Madan Lal	6	2	12	1

FALL OF WICKETS
1-13, 2-35, 3-40, 4-41, 5-41, 6-74, 7-85, 8-87, 9-87

India won by 38 runs

neither Shastri nor Sivaramakrishnan could find any help. Nevertheless, they contrived to tear the heart out of the Pakistan innings. The Indians fielded splendidly, Gavaskar held four fine catches at first slip, and Pakistan batted as if haunted by ghosts. Rameez Raja and Saleem Malik raised hopes with a sixth wicket stand of 33, but the return of Kapil Dev soon restored India's sovereignty and brought about a win which had seemed most unlikely at the start of the day.

Four Nations Tournament – Second Match
ENGLAND *v.* AUSTRALIA

England's miserable record since their success in India continued when Australia beat them off the last ball although the margin of victory would have been greater had the Australians not panicked.

Fowler and Robinson made a good start with 47 in 9 overs.

ROTHMAN TROPHY – ENGLAND *v.* AUSTRALIA
24 March 1985 at Sharjah

ENGLAND		
G. Fowler	c Hughes, b Alderman	26
R.T. Robinson	c Rixon, b Matthews	37
M.D. Moxon	lbw, b O'Donnell	0
D.W. Randall	st Rixon, b Bennett	19
C.M. Wells	lbw, b Bennett	17
D.R. Pringle	st Rixon, b Border	4
P.H. Edmonds	not out	15
B.N. French*	c Rixon, b Border	4
R.M. Ellison	c Wessels, b Border	24
N.A. Foster	not out	5
N. Gifford†		
Extras	b 9, lb 5, w 6, nb 6	26
(50 overs)	(for 8 wickets)	177

	O	M	R	W
Alderman	7	1	36	1
McCurdy	5	—	23	—
O'Donnell	8	2	26	1
Bennett	10	2	27	2
Matthews	10	3	15	1
Border	7	—	21	3
Wessels	3	—	15	—

FALL OF WICKETS
1-47, 2-53, 3-95, 4-109, 5-123, 6-128, 7-134, 8-169

AUSTRALIA		
K.C. Wessels	b Edmonds	16
G.M. Wood	c French, b Pringle	35
D.M.J. Jones	c Moxon, b Edmonds	27
A.R. Border†	c and b Pringle	9
K.J. Hughes	c French, b Foster	14
G.R.J. Matthews	c Fowler, b Ellison	24
S.P. O'Donnell	c Moxon, b Ellison	19
S.J. Rixon*	not out	11
M.J. Bennett	run out	0
R.J. McCurdy	not out	6
T.M. Alderman		
Extras	lb 9, w 8	17
(50 overs)	(for 8 wickets)	178

	O	M	R	W
Foster	10	1	34	1
Ellison	10	1	28	2
Pringle	10	—	49	2
Edmonds	10	2	31	2
Gifford	10	1	27	—

FALL OF WICKETS
1-54, 2-64, 3-82, 4-100, 5-120, 6-151, 7-168, 8-168

Australia won by 2 wickets

ROTHMAN TROPHY – THIRD-PLACE MATCH – ENGLAND *v.* PAKISTAN
26 March 1985 at Sharjah

PAKISTAN

Mudassar Nazar	c French, b Gifford	36
Mohsin Khan	c Robinson, b Pringle	13
Rameez Raja	lbw, b Pringle	16
Javed Miandad†	c Gifford, b Edmonds	71
Saleem Malik	lbw, b Gifford	2
Imran Khan	c Pringle, b Gifford	0
Shoaib Mohammad	st French, b Gifford	3
Ashraf Ali*	not out	19
Tahir Naqqash	not out	2
Tauseef Ahmed		
Wasim Akram		
Extras	b 1, lb 9, nb 3	13
(50 overs)	(for 7 wickets)	175

	O	M	R	W
Pringle	7	1	32	2
Ellison	7	1	18	—
Edmonds	10	—	47	1
Pocock	10	1	20	—
Gifford	10	—	23	4
Bailey	6	—	25	—

FALL OF WICKETS
1- 24, 2- 43, 3- 107, 4- 113, 5- 113, 6- 125, 7- 173

ENGLAND

G. Fowler	c Javed, b Tauseef	19
R.T. Robinson	b Tahir	9
M.D. Moxon	b Shoaib	11
C.M. Wells	b Shoaib	5
R.J. Bailey	not out	41
D.R. Pringle	b Wasim Akram	13
P.H. Edmonds	c and b Shoaib	3
R.M. Ellison	b Wasim Akram	3
B.N. French*	c Shoaib, b Tahir	7
N. Gifford†	c Javed, b Imran	0
P.I. Pocock	run out	4
Extras	b 1, lb 12, w 4	17
(48.2 overs)		132

	O	M	R	W
Imran Khan	9	2	26	1
Wasim Akram	10	—	28	2
Tashir Naqqash	9.2	1	20	2
Tauseef Ahmed	10	1	25	1
Shoaib Mohammad	10	1	20	3

FALL OF WICKETS
1- 19, 2- 35, 3- 48, 4- 49, 5- 76, 6- 89, 7- 98, 8- 117, 9- 121

Pakistan won by 43 runs

Robinson played the best innings for England and was unlucky to be given out caught behind when the ball appeared to cóme off his pad. After the sound start England succumbed to the spinners, Matthews and Bennett inducing impotence and Border Claiming the spoils.

With Pringle and Foster straying in direction and Wood clouting two sixes and three fours as they fed his strong leg side, Australia. Edmonds brought some calm to England's sloppy outcricket and Australia struggled for what should have been achieved with ease. Ten runs were needed off the last 2 overs and 4 off the last three balls. The scores were level when the last ball from Ellison was lashed to Gifford at mid-off by Rixon and the batsmen completed a single, much to the delight of the Australian party and of the enthusiastic locals.

Four Nations Tournament – Play-Off Match
ENGLAND *v.* PAKISTAN

For the second time in a few weeks England ended a limited-over competition with the wooden spoon. Javed Miandad hit the first half-century of the tournament after Pakistan had been put in to bat on a wicket which gave considerable advantage to the spinners. Javed's was a fine innings, particularly as the veterans, Gifford and Pocock, bowled so well, always testing the batsmen with perfect control and teasing flight. Ashraf Ali played some useful shots and England faced a target of 176.

It quickly appeared to be beyond them. Tahir bowled Robinson in the seventh over, and Fowler fell in the fourteenth. Shoaib bowled Wells with his third ball of the tournament and Moxon shortly after. Bailey batted with confidence, promising for the future rather than for victory in this match, but England were running out of time as quickly as he was running out of partners.

Hope for the future – pace bowler Wasim Akram. (Adrian Murrell)

Four Nations Tournament – Final
INDIA *v.* AUSTRALIA

India won the Rothman Trophy for the second time in as many years and, as they had won the World Championship of Cricket and the World Cup in the space of two years, they had every right to consider themselves top of the world in the limited-over game.

A capacity crowd of 15,000 saw Australia get off to a fine start, Wessels and Wood putting on 60 in 15 overs. Then, as the day became hotter, Australia wilted. Wood ran himself out, Jones tried to run before he could walk and Wessels seemed incapable of raising the pace, so dying of frustration. Hughes was still grossly out of touch and a rest from cricket seemed the most sane cure for him. Both he and Border offered Amarnath return catches. There was no recovery and India were left with the simplest of tasks.

India began badly, but Azharuddin played some firm shots

New Zealanders in Pakistan 1984

First Class Matches

BATTING	v. BCCP Patron's XI (Rawalpindi) 8–10 Nov. 1984		First Test Match (Lahore) 16–20 Nov. 1984		Second Test Match (Hyderabad) 25–29 Nov. 1984		v. Punjab Governor's XI (Bahawalpur) 4–6 December 1984		Third Test Match (Karachi) 10–15 December 1984		M	Inns	NOs	Runs	HS	Av
J.G. Wright	3	93	1	65	18	22			107	—	4	7	—	309	107	44.14
B.A. Edgar	60	71	3	26	11	1	23	14	15	—	5	9	—	224	71	24.88
M.D. Crowe	71	50*	55	33	19	21			45	—	4	7	1	294	71	49.00
J.J. Crowe	45	3	0	43	39	57	49	—	62	—	5	8	—	298	62	37.25
J.F. Reid	1	0	2	6	106	21	13*	55*	97	—	5	9	2	301	106	43.00
E.J. Gray	25	4	12	6	25	5	56	—			4	7	—	133	56	19.00
I.D.S. Smith	11	30	41	11*	6	34			0	—	4	7	1	133	41	22.16
J.G. Bracewell	5*	—			0	0	—	20	30	—	4	5	1	55	30	13.75
B.L. Cairns	7	—					—	10*			2	2	1	17	10*	17.00
D.A. Stirling	0	—	16	10	11*	11			7	—	4	6	1	55	16	11.00
S.L. Boock	1	—	13	0	12	4*	—	—	0	—	5	6	1	30	13	6.00
J.V. Coney			7	26	6	5	79	—	16	—	4	6	—	139	79	23.16
E.J. Chatfield			6*	0			—	—			2	2	1	6	6*	6.00
P.E. McEwan							33*	44	40*	—	2	3	2	117	44	117.00
M.C. Snedden							—	—			1					—
Byes			1	8	13	1	8	4	1							
Leg-byes	3	5		2		4	9	2	5							
Wides				1			10									
No-balls	2	5		4	1	3	11	3	1							
Total	234	261	157	241	267	189	291	152	426							
Wickets	10	6	10	10	10	10	4	3	10							
Result	D		L		L		D		D							

Catches 10 – I.D.S. Smith (ct 8/st 2)
7 – J.J. Crowe
5 – M.D. Crowe
4 – J.F. Reid and J.V. Coney
3 – B. L. Cairns and E. J. Gray
2 – P.E. McEwan and M.C. Snedden
1 – J.G. Wright and S.L. Boock

BOWLING	D.A. Stirling	B.L. Cairns	J.G. Bracewell	S.L. Boock	M.D. Crowe	E.J. Gray	E.J. Chatfield	J.V. Coney	M.C. Snedden
. B.C.C.P. Patron's XI (Rawalpindi)	15.4–2–44–1	13–2–45–1	12–3–34–0	21–5–46–2	6–2–16–0	17–3–38–3			
8–10 November 1984	4–1–10–0	4–2–6–0	5–3–4–1			3–1–8–0			
First Test Match (Lahore)	27–7–71–2			24–7–53–2	7–1–21–1	8–1–19–2	28.2–7–57–3		
16–20 November 1984	15.1–2–60–1			17–2–56–1		18–0–45–2	13–7–12–0	2–1–4–0	
Second Test Match (Hyderabad)	3–1–11–0		16.1–3–44–3	37–12–87–7	3–0–8–0	22–4–70–0		10–4–8–0	
25–29 November 1984	4–0–26–0		13–2–36–0	23.4–4–69–1	8–1–29–2	11–0–49–0		. 4–1–9–0	
v. Punjab Governor's XI		6–1–24–1	18–4–39–1	28–16–24–2		11–3–24–3	10–3–24–1		11–1–52–3
(Bahawalpur) 4–6 Dec. 1984									
Third Test Match (Karachi)	29–5–88–4		20 5–54–0	41–19–83–4	21–4–81–2			5–3–5–0	
10–15 December 1984	14–1–82–1		33–11–83–1	30–10–83–2	10–3–26–1				
	111.5–19–392–9 av. 43.55	23–5–75–2 av. 37.50	117.1–31–294–6 av. 49.00	221.4–75–501–21 av. 23.85	55–11–181–6 av. 30.16	90–12–253–10 av. 25.30	51.2–17–93–4 av. 23.25	21–9–26–0 —	11–1–52–2 av. 26.0

a J.G. Wright 1–0–1–0

ROTHMAN TROPHY – FINAL – INDIA *v.* AUSTRALIA
29 March 1985 at Sharjah

AUSTRALIA			
	G.M. Wood	run out	27
	K.C. Wessels	c Gavaskar, b Madan Lal	30
	D.M.J. Jones	c Viswanath, b Madan Lal	8
	A.R. Border†	c and b Amarnath	27
	K.J. Hughes	c and b Amarnath	11
	G.R.J. Matthews	lbw, b Kapil Dev	11
	S.P. O'Donnell	run out	3
	S.J. Rixon*	run out	4
	M.J. Bennett	lbw, b Shastri	0
	R.J. McCurdy	c Vengsarkar, b Shastri	0
	C.J. McDermott	not out	0
	Extras	lb 13, w 5	18
	(42.3 overs)		139

	O	M	R	W
Kapil Dev	6	3	9	1
Binny	5	—	25	—
Madan Lal	7	—	30	2
Sivaramakrishnan	8	1	29	—
Shastri	9.3	1	14	2
Amarnath	7	1	19	2

FALL OF WICKETS
1- 60, 2- 71, 3- 78, 4- 114, 5- 115, 6- 131, 7- 138, 8- 139, 9- 139

INDIA			
	R.J. Shastri	c Rixon, b O'Donnell	9
	K. Srikkanth	lbw, b McDermott	0
	M. Azharuddin	c Jones, b McDermott	22
	D.B. Vengsarkar	b McDermott	35
	S.M. Gavaskar	run out	20
	M.B. Amarnath	not out	24
	R.N. Kapil Dev†	b Matthews	1
	R.M.H. Binny	b Matthews	2
	U.S. Madan Lal	not out	7
	S. Viswanath*		
	L. Sivaramakrishnan		
	Extras	lb 9, w 7, nb 4	20
	(39.2 overs)	(for 7 wickets)	140

	O	M	R	W
McDermott	10	—	36	3
McCurdy	4	1	10	—
O'Donnell	4	1	11	1
Bennett	10	—	35	—
Matthews	10	1	33	2
Border	1.2	—	6	—

FALL OF WICKETS
1- 2, 2- 37, 3- 41, 4- 98, 5- 103, 6- 117, 7- 120

India won by 3 wickets

and had to endure a verbal barrage from McCurdy, O'Donnell and McDermott who looked very quick and very strong. Vengsarkar and Gavaskar cemented the innings and blunted the threat of Bennett and Matthews who, however, dismissed Binny and Kapil Dev before Amarnath brought sanity and victory which was greeted with a symphony of klaxons even louder than they had been throughout the day.

First-Class Averages

Batting	M	Inns	NOs	Runs	HS	Av	100s	50s
Farooq Shera	3	4	2	314	112*	157.00	2	1
Rizwan-uz-Zaman	9	17	3	1101	166	78.64	5	5
Saleem Malik	6	8	3	361	119*	72.20	2	1
Munir-ul-Haq	5	10	3	483	120*	69.00	2	3
Javed Miandad	6	9	2	410	104	58.57	2	1
Arshad Pervez	14	27	5	1253	152*	56.95	5	4
Mohammad Aslam	5	9	0	483	167	53.66	1	2
Shahid Anwar	8	15	1	746	153*	53.28	4	2
Ijaz Faqih	8	9	2	371	125*	53.00	2	
Remeez Raja	3	5	1	212	172	53.00	1	
Tariq Alam	6	12	4	422	89	52.75		4
Tariq Javed	4	6	0	314	100	52.33	1	2
Azhar Abbas	3	5	1	207	67	51.75		3
Shoaib Mohammad	4	7	2	257	108*	51.40	1	1
Tahir Mahmood	4	8	0	405	108	50.62	1	4
Qasim Umar	5	8	0	396	210	49.50	1	
Mudassar Nazar	5	8	0	395	199	49.37	2	
Mohammad Aslam	9	15	2	637	164	49.00	2	3
Masood Anwar	7	11	0	529	186	48.09	1	3
Zaheer Abbas	5	7	1	287	168*	47.83	1	
Mohammad Ishaq	4	7	0	331	112	47.28	1	2
Shaukat Mirza	12	22	3	894	132	47.05	2	5
Ijaz Ahmed	12	23	2	983	201*	46.80	2	5

P.E. McEwan	J.J. Crowe	J.F. Reid	Byes	Leg-byes	Wides	No-balls	Total	Wkts
				6		17	229	7
			1	1		3	30	1
						2	221	10
				4			181	4
				2			230	10
			5	7		3	230	3
			1	1	4	8	189	10
4–1–6–0			5	6	1	3	328	10
2–0–7–0	2–0–9–0	2–0–7–0	2	8		7	308	5a
6–1–13–0 —	2–0–9–0 —	2–0–7–0 —						

Tauseef Ahmed, 83 wickets, the outstanding bowler of the season. (Adrian Murrell)

Anwar-ul-Haq	5	8	0	368	113	46.00	1	2
Saleem Anwar	4	8	1	313	125*	44.71	1	1
Shoaib Habib	6	9	2	313	84*	44.71		3
Ijaz Ahmed	9	17	1	710	117	44.37	2	5
Naved Anjum	10	17	3	617	159	44.07	1	2
Shafiq Ahmed	11	21	4	742	118	43.64	2	5
Noman Shabbir	6	7	2	217	77	43.40		2
Saadat Ali	11	20	1	817	169	43.00	3	1
Nasir Shah	9	17	2	639	120	42.60	1	5
Athar A. Khan	6	12	1	464	154*	42.18	1	2
Asif Mujtaba	13	22	2	842	94	42.10		9
Moin-ul-Atiq	13	24	2	919	140	41.77	3	3
Ali Zia	11	20	2	750	176	41.66	3	2
Sajid Ali	8	13	0	537	101	41.30	1	3
Zafar Ahmed	6	12	4	330	73*	41.25		3
Aftab Baloch	9	16	5	449	68	40.81		4
Mansoor Akhtar	11	21	0	857	180	40.80	2	3
Azhar Khan	8	15	1	570	115	40.71	2	3
Tahir Shah	11	18	1	666	88	39.17		5
Zaheer Ahmed	5	8	1	272	112*	38.85	1	
Pervez J. Mir	9	17	1	619	74	38.68		7
Zafar Ali	11	19	3	617	139*	38.56	2	1
Tanvir Razzaq	4	8	0	308	98	38.50		2
Wasim Raja	5	8	1	269	78	38.42		3
Mohammad Ashraf	9	18	1	647	140	38.05	3	1
Iqtidar Ali	6	12	0	449	77	37.41	6	
Ashraf Ali	14	19	5	523	80*	37.35		4
Raees Ahmed	6	12	1	404	64	36.72		4
Moin Mumtaz	9	17	2	547	135*	36.46	2	
Akram Raza	7	11	3	291	101*	36.37	1	1
Saeed Azad	12	19	0	678	120	35.68	1	5
Ameer Akbar	11	19	2	602	107	35.41	2	2
Haseeb-ul-Hasan	12	22	8	492	57	35.14		4
Haafiz Shahid	5	9	3	206	64*	34.33		2
Shahid Saeed	11	19	1	608	87	33.77		4
Sajjad Akbar	5	10	2	259	84	32.37		2
Talat Masood	6	12	0	387	117	32.25	1	
Pervez Shah	10	15	2	416	57	32.00		2
Azhar Sultan	5	9	2	223	50	31.85		1
Sagheer Abbas	8	14	0	442	94	31.57		3
Saleem Pervez	4	7	0	221	112	31.57	1	
Mohsin Riaz	9	15	1	428	80	30.57		4
Mohsin Khan	5	7	0	206	59	29.42		2
Babar Basharat	5	8	1	204	68*	29.14		1
Saleem Cheema	5	9	0	259	67	28.77		3
Shahid Tanvir	9	18	1	482	97	28.35		3
Anwar Miandad	11	20	2	481	118*	26.72	1	1
Farrukh Raza	4	8	0	208	58	26.00		1
Sultan Rana	12	19	1	461	77	25.61		1
Noor-ul-Qamar	5	9	0	224	101	24.88	1	1
Abdus Sami	10	16	0	397	63	24.81		3
Rafat Alam	5	10	1	217	60	24.11		3
Zafar Mehdi	6	10	0	241	94	24.10		1
Iqbal Sikander	7	13	3	238	65	23.80		1
Agha Zahid	8	16	1	356	73	23.73		1
Yahya Toor	9	16	3	303	76*	23.30		2
Sajid Khan	8	13	0	286	76	22.00		1
Mohammad Jamil	5	10	0	215	47	21.50		
Abdul Qadir	9	11	0	232	72	21.09		1
Talat Mirza	10	17	0	356	63	20.94		2
Masood Anwar	12	21	1	390	72*	19.50		2
Mahmood Rasheed	9	16	3	247	81	19.00		1
Tehsin Javed	9	14	2	277	55*	18.91		1
Shahid Mahboob	9	15	0	271	46	18.06		
Manzoor Elahi	10	16	2	252	78*	18.00		1
Tasnim Abidi	10	18	0	284	131	15.77	1	

(Qualification 200 runs, average 15.00)

Bowling	Overs	Mdns	Runs	Wkts	Av	Best	5/inn	10/m
Naeem Ahmed	19.2	7	24	10	2.40	5/12	2	1
Iqbal Qasim	304.3	108	606	48	12.62	5/6	4	
Jamal A. Nasir	56	15	139	11	12.63	4/45		
Ijaz Faqih	227.2	63	525	38	13.81	6/35	3	
Aziz Ahmed	108.4	37	236	17	13.88	6/62	1	
Mohammad Nazir	546.2	169	947	66	14.34	7/62	6	2
Aziz-ur-Rehman	203.3	42	522	34	15.35	7/45	3	1
Tauseef Ahmed	546.2	125	1316	83	15.85	8/52	10	3
Raja Afaq	139.3	31	309	19	16.26	6/68	2	
Wasim Akram	80.5	18	222	13	17.07	7/50	1	
Shahid Pervez	196.2	47	190	28	17.50	5/27	1	
Fareedullah	61	17	176	10	17.60	3/35		
Tanvir Afzal	173	25	513	29	17.68	6/80	3	1
Ali Zia	140.2	26	359	20	17.95	4/37		
Humayun Farkhan	149.3	35	360	20	18.00	4/25		
Tariq Wahab	95	29	234	13	18.00	4/40		
Ijaz Ahmed	49.1	4	181	10	18.10	4/50		
Tahir Naqqash	98	19	317	17	18.64	6/72	1	1
Abdul Qadir	471.5	106	1349	72	18.73	9/59	9	4
Nadeem Ghauri	385.3	83	956	50	19.12	8/68	4	1
Ghulam Abbas	226	62	518	27	19.18	7/66	1	1
Ehtesham-un-Din	145.3	32	413	21	19.66	9/124	2	
Naveed Anjum	87	14	268	13	20.61	5/58	1	
Nadeem Moosa	104.4	21	290	14	20.71	4/50		
Sabih Azhar	69.3	13	208	10	20.80	4/20		
Zahid Ahmed	178.5	37	480	23	20.86	7/68	2	
Kamal Merchant	122	45	213	10	21.30	5/54	1	
Farrukh Zaman	255.3	63	731	34	21.50	6/42	2	
Asim Butt	130.2	21	351	16	21.93	5/53	1	
Kazim Mehdi	270.3	64	747	34	21.97	6/79	2	
Azeem Hafeez	243.4	65	642	29	22.13	6/46	1	
Ghulam Hussian	81.5	12	288	13	22.15	7/128	2	1
Abdur Raqeeb	339.4	75	913	41	22.26	5/61	3	
Rashid Khan	153	30	474	21	22.57	6/110	2	
Jalal-ud-Din	245.2	48	766	33	23.21	6/66	2	1
Anwar Miandad	84.2	15	235	10	23.50	3/28		
Nasim Piracha	79	22	261	11	23.72	4/44		
Mian Fayyaz	296	88	665	28	23.75	6/101	2	1
Rizwan-uz-Zaman	200	52	456	19	24.00	4/29		
Haafiz Shahid	122.2	20	459	19	24.15	7/59	1	1
Iqbal Butt	229.3	41	701	29	24.17	5/98	1	
Masood Anwar	413.4	86	1141	47	24.27	6/94	3	1
Tanvir Ali	618.4	131	1771	72	24.59	8/83	7	1
Pervez J. Mir	231.2	39	673	27	24.92	6/65	3	
Mohammad Altaf	144.1	33	350	14	25.00	5/26	2	1
Shahid Mahboob	321.4	50	1028	39	26.35	5/68	1	
Shahid Butt	264.5	66	691	26	26.57	6/53	3	1
Shoaib Habib	203	46	483	18	26.83	5/63	1	
Raees Ahmed	182.1	20	681	25	27.24	5/59	1	
Sikander Bakht	119	26	362	13	27.84	4/51		
Nasir J. Charlie	127.5	14	446	16	27.87	6/64	1	
Pervez Shah	210.3	50	597	21	28.42	3/33		
Shakeel Cheema	136	14	435	15	29.00	4/57		
Zafar Mehdi	145.1	27	496	17	29.17	3/25		
Amin Lakhani	221	58	597	20	29.85	6/73	1	
Shahid Aziz	105.3	16	304	10	30.40	6/106	1	
Wasim Raja	190.3	37	493	16	30.81	4/125		
Liaqat Ali	114	21	433	14	30.92	6/110	2	
Arshad Nawaz	303.3	98	653	21	31.09	5/45	1	
Ikyas Khan	97	15	312	10	31.20	3/92		
Tariq Alam	129.3	25	444	13	34.15	3/42		
Saleem Jaffer	387	59	1251	35	35.74	3/41		
Akram Raza	204.4	39	612	17	36.00	6/97	1	
Haseeb-ul-Hasan	192.2	31	652	18	36.22	3/36		
Sajjad Akbar	164.5	22	460	12	38.33	3/65		
Haaris A. Khan	311.1	54	935	24	38.95	4/14		
Shahid Tanvir	282.4	31	933	23	40.56	4/75		
Afzaal Butt	166	24	595	14	42.50	3/73		
Atiq-ur-Rehman	183	22	738	17	43.41	5/60	1	
Aftab Baloch	185.4	49	438	10	43.80	2/27		
Iqbal Sikander	213	46	656	13	50.46	5/82	1	

(Qualification 10 wickets)

LEADING FIELDERS

38–Arshad Pervez (st 14/ct 24); 24–Mahmood Rasheed (st 9/ct 15); 26–Ali Zia (st 11/ct 15); 26–Shafiq Ahmed (st 11/ct15); 27–Asif Mujtaba (st 13/ct 14); 27–Moin-ul-Atiq (st 13/ct 14); 25–Sultan Rana (st 12/ct 13); 24–Saadat Ali (st 11/ct 13); 21–Abdur Raqeeb (st 9/ct 12); 22–Talat Mirza (st 10/ct 12); 23–Tahir Shah (st 11/ct 12); 20–Rizwan-uz-Zaman (st 9/ct 11); 22–Shahid Saeed (st 11/ct 11); 21–Ameer Akbar (st 11/ct 10); 22–Haseeb-ul-Hasan (st 12/ct 10); 22–Shaukat Mirza (st 12/ct 10)

SECTION H

Continuing Triumph

The season in the West Indies.
The Jones Cup. The Beaumont Cup. The Shell Shield.
The New Zealand tour, Tests and One-Day Internationals.
Form Charts and Averages.

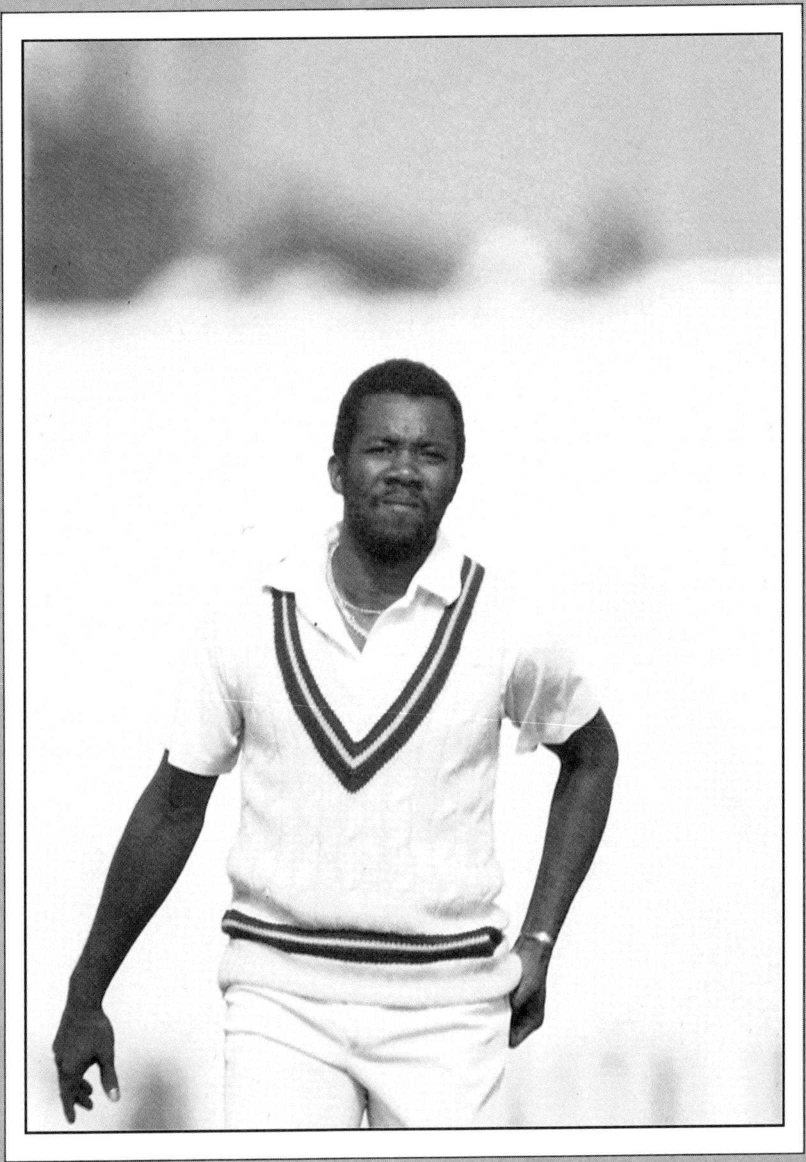

Malcolm Marshall – Fastest in the world.
(Adrian Murrell)

The West Indian Test team has now become like a circus on permanent tour. While the Shell Shield was in progress in the Caribbean the leading West Indian players, having just completed Test series against England and Australia, were engaged in the Benson and Hedges World Series and the World Championship of Cricket. They would return home only to play a Test series against New Zealand before most of them dispersed to play for English counties. This means that Dujon has not played for Jamaica since 1983 and Richards has played only once for Leeward Islands in two years. It is a pattern which is being repeated in many cricket-playing countries, and the dangers should be apparent to all.

As has become traditional, the West Indian Shell Shield season was precluded by the Jones Cup in Guyana and the Beaumont Cup in Trinidad, and both matches produced better cricket of a higher quality than they had done in the previous season.

Jones Cup

9, 10, 11 and 12 November 1984

at Albion Sports Complex, Berbice

Berbice 266 (C.B. Lambert 104, C.L. Hooper 5 for 71) and 242 (D. Persaud 55, C.L. Hooper 4 for 71)
Demerara 288 (A.A. Lyght 104) and 222 for 6

Demerara won by 4 wickets

Impressive bowling by Hooper won him a place in the Guyana side for the Shell Shield. Lambert and Lyght, the country's openers, both hit hundreds.

Beaumont Cup

3, 4 and 5 January 1985

at Guaracara Park, Point-a-Pierre

South Trinidad 160 and 154 (T. Cuffy 71)
North Trinidad 372 (K.C. Williams 91, P.V. Simmonds 71, R.A. Glasgow 65, R. Sampath 4 for 42, R. Nanan 4 for 67)

North Trinidad won by an innings and 58 runs

Two moderate batting performances by the South against a varied attack surrendered the game limply. North lost Gabriel without a run on the board, but Simmonds and Glasgow added 134 for the second wicket, and Kevin Williams, at number eight, hit a career best 91, never having previously passed fifty.

24, 25, 26 and 27 January 1985

at Sabina Park, Kingston

Trinidad and Tobago 204 (P.V. Simmonds 64, E.E. Brown 4 for 44) and 317 (P.V. Simmonds 70, K.C. Williams 62, A.G. Daley 4 for 69)
Jamaica 180 (M.C. Neita 75 not out, A.H. Gray 4 for 51) and 264 (A.B. Williams 102, A.H. Gray 6 for 76)

Trinidad and Tobago won by 77 runs
Trinidad and Tobago 16 pts, Jamaica 0 pts

The opening game in the Shell Shield saw Trinidad win with comparative comfort. Phil Simmonds alone held the visitors' batting together in the first innings, but Jamaica fared worse when Anthony Gray, 6′ 8″ tall, disturbed with a pace that suggested a new Joel Garner. Mark Neita gave stubborn resistance, but Trinidad gained a first innings lead which they extended with some consistent batting. Kevin Williams hit his best Shield score and Simmonds again batted well. Skipper Basil Williams hit a fine hundred but received little support and Gray bowled Trinidad to victory with a career best 6 for 76.

31 January, 1, 2 and 3 February 1985

at Sabina Park, Kingston

Jamaica 135 (L.C. Sebastien 4 for 49) and 320 (A.B. Williams 91, O.W. Peters 72, W.W. Lewis 59, N. Phillips 6 for 90)
Windward Islands 405 (L.D. John 137, S.J. Hinds 72, I. Cadette 56, A.G. Daley 4 for 108) and 52 for 3

Windward Islands won by 7 wickets
Windward Islands 16 pts, Jamaica 0 pts

1, 2, 3 and 4 February 1985

at Kingston Oval, Bridgetown

Barbados 384 (M.C. Worrell 105, C.A. Best 67, C.G. Butts 7 for 107) and 227 for 2 dec (C.A. Best 114 not out, T.A. Hunte 53)
Guyana 271 (C.L. Hooper 126, R.O. Estwick 5 for 83) and 220 for 7 (M.A. Harper 81, T. Mohammed 61)

Match drawn
Barbados 8 pts, Guyana 4 pts

at Queen's Park Oval, Port of Spain

Leeward Islands 204 (R.M. Otto 110) and 246 for 5 (L.L. Lawrence 93, A.L. Kelly 55)
Trinidad and Tobago 336 (P.V. Simmonds 118, A. Rajah 55, C.E.I. Bartlette 4 for 69)

Match drawn
Trinidad and Tobago 8 pts, Leeward Island 4 pts

Barbados were 187 for 7 on the opening day when wicket-keeper Mike Worrell came to the wicket. He and Dave Cumberbatch added 95 and although Daniel went quickly, Worrell then added 90 for the last wicket with Estwick. Worrell, having never before passed fifty, reached a maiden century and made it possible for the home side to take first innings points. Guyana, in their turn, floundered in reply and were 178 for 7, but, like the home side, they found a hero and a maiden centurion in Carl Hooper, a most impressive young all-rounder. Skipper Best hit a fine century when Barbados batted again, but, in spite of reducing Guyana to 50 for 4, he could not force a win, Mark Harper and Timur Mohammed sharing a stand of 107.

Jamaica collapsed on the first day at Sabina Park to the combined pace of Phillip and Collymore and the leg-spin of Sebastien. Lance John hit a career best 137 and shared a stand of 117 for the second wicket with night-watchman Ignatius Cadette. Hinds hit 72 in 113 minutes to consolidate Windward's strong position. Lewis and Ordelmo Peters began the second innings with a stand of 109, but Norbert Phillip tore the heart out of the middle order and the visitors looked set for victory inside three days until Basil Williams and Daley added 104 for the sixth wicket. Resistance ended early on the last morning and the game was over before lunch.

Two fine centuries by Ralston Otto and Philip Simmonds,

who had started the season in outstanding form, dominated the game in Port of Spain. The second Leeward innings began with a stand of 88 between Kelly and Lawrence whose stubborn knock ensured a draw.

8, 9, 10 and 11 February 1985

at Guaracara Park, Pointe-a-Pierre

Windward Islands 259 (N Phillip 81, L.D. John 50, A.H. Gray 5 for 86) and 146 (G. Mahabir 4 for 37)
Trinidad and Tobago 112 (T.Z. Kentish 4 for 20) and 295 for 6 (K.C. Williams 84 not out, P.V. Simmonds 78, R.S. Gabriel 60, T.Z. Kentish 5 for 88)
Trinidad and Tobago won by 4 wickets
Trinidad and Tobago 16 pts, Windward Islands 5 pts

at Sabina Park, Kingston

Barbados 240 (S.R. Greaves 67, M.C. Worrell 53 not out, A.G. Daley 5 for 64) and 260 (C.A. Best 147)
Jamaica 545 for 8 dec (G. Powell 110, C.A. Davidson 98, D. Dixon 75, A.B. Williams 59, A.G. Daley 50 not out)
Jamaica won by an innings and 45 runs
Jamaica 16 pts, Barbados 0 pts

BELOW RIGHT: *Anthony Gray – 10 for 127 for Trinidad against Jamaica in the first Shell Shield game of the season and a decisive factor in his side's championship year. (Tom Morris)*

BELOW: *Wayne Daniel, 7 for 33 against Leeward Islands as Barbados win their only game of the season. (Adrian Murrell)*

at Recreation Ground, St John's, Antigua

Guyana 214 (C.B. Lambert 53, T.A. Merrick 5 for 101) and 210 (T. Mohammed 80, T.A. Merrick 4 for 76)
Leeward Islands 293 (E.E. Lewis 70, C.G. Butts 5 for 113) and 132 for 9 (A.L. Kelly 52, C.G. Butts 5 for 40)

Leeward Islands won by 1 wicket
Leeward Islands 16 pts, Guyana 0 pts

Trinidad emphasised their bid to win the Shell Shield with a victory over Windward Islands inside three days. It proved to be the decisive match of the season for Windward had led by 147 runs on the first innings. On the first day they made 259, losing their last 6 wickets for 44 runs. The second day saw 18 wickets fall while 235 runs were scored. Windward added 23 to their overnight score on the third morning and Trinidad were left to make 294 to win. They had the best possible start when Simmonds and Gabriel put on 146 for the first wicket. Windward were handicapped when Collymore, their opening bowler who had been injured in the first innings but stated that he was fit to bowl in the second, retired from the match after bowling one no-ball. Nevertheless the game seemed to have swung in favour of the visitors when 5 wickets fell for 25 runs. Rajah and Kelvin Williams added 80, and Williams, bristling with confidence with the bat, hit Norbert Philip for four consecutive sixes to win the match and give Trinidad the lead in the Shell Shield.

In Kingston, Jamaica gained their first win over Barbados for fourteen years. Barbados were bowled out by Daley and

Dixon on the first day which the home side closed at 63 for 2, having lost both openers with only 8 scored. By the end of the second day they were in command. George Powell had hit a century and they were 385 for 6. The tail wagged violently on the third morning, Davidson, Daley and Dixon all hitting furiously. Barbados were 116 for 4 at the close and could hope only for a draw. It did not come. In spite of a career best from skipper Carlisle Best, Jamaica were not to be denied and the match was over 40 minutes after lunch on the final day.

Leeward Islands took maximum points against Guyana in a most exciting game which virtually ended Guyana's championship hopes. Anthony Merrick was outstanding and Leeward displayed fine team work as Butts, enjoying a

Barbados 1985
First Class Matches

BATTING	v. Guyana (Bridgetown) 1–4 February 1985		v. Jamaica (Kingston) 8–11 February 1985		v. Leeward Islands (Bridgetown) 16–19 February 1985		v. Windward Islands (Roseau) 22–25 February 1985		v. Trinidad and Tobago (Port of Spain) 1–3 March 1985		M	Inns	NOs	Runs	H/S	Av
C.A. Best	67	114*	30	147	26	18	11	—	2	22	5	9	1	437	147	54.62
A.S. Gilkes	16	40	5	3	29	13					3	6	—	106	40	17.66
T.A. Hunte	1	53	37	0	1	52	6	—	28	0	5	9	—	178	53	19.77
L.N. Reifer	8	—	0	21							2	3	—	29	21	9.66
S.R. Greaves	44	—	67	18			12	—	51	0	4	6	—	192	67	32.00
R.L. Skeete	38	—	18	13	10	12	18	—	48	36	5	8	—	193	48	24.12
N.A. Phillips	0	2*			0	21*	—	—	12	0	4	6	2	35	21*	8.75
D.A. Cumberbatch	45	—	11	19							2	3	—	75	45	25.00
M.C. Worrell	105	—	53*	1	22*	20	8*	—	0	6*	5	8	4	215	105	53.75
W.W. Daniel	5	—	3	7*	1	6*	—	—	5	3	5	7	2	30	7*	6.00
R.O. Estwick	34*	—	0	11	0	0	—	—	0	8	5	7	1	53	34*	8.83
M.A. Small			0	0							1	2	—	0	0	0.00
N. Johnson					29	98	17	—	1	11	3	5	—	156	98	52.00
G.N. Reifer					4	0	7*	—	17	0	3	5	1	28	17	7.00
N. da C. Broomes					13	0	—	—			2	2	—	13	13	6.50
E. Proverbs									16*	8	1	2	1	24	16*	24.00
Byes	7	3	2	5	2					3						
Leg-byes	6	6	7	8	1	4	1		1	7						
Wides	2		1			2										
No-balls	6	9	6	7	2	1	3		5	4						
Total	384	227	240	260	140	247	83		186	108						
Wickets	10	2	10	10	10	9	5		10	10						
Result	D		L		W		Ab.		L							
Points	8		0		16		4		0							

Catches 16 – M.C. Worrell (ct 15/st 1)
6 – C.A. Best
4 – R.O. Estwick and T.A. Hunte
3 – D.A. Cumberbatch
2 – N.A. Phillips and N. da C. Broomes
1 – A.S. Gilkes, R.L. Skeete, W.W. Daniel, N. Johnson, G.N. Reifer and sub

BOWLING	W.W. Daniel	R.O. Estwick	S.R. Greaves	N.A. Phillips	D.A. Cumberbatch	C.A. Best	R.L. Skeete	M.A. Small	T.A. Hunte
v. Guyana (Bridgetown)	16–1–65–3	17–1–83–5	10–0–41–0	8–2–25–0	11.1–0–55–1				
1–4 February	18–2–37–1	16–2–77–3	5–0–26–0	13–1–42–2	6–1–25–0	2–0–7–1	1–1–0–0		
v. Jamaica (Kingston) 8–11 February	32–3–151–3	20.2–4–60–0			27.4–2–98–1	11–2–26–1		33–3–147–3	12.4–2–36–0
v. Leeward Islands	13.4–4–33–7	12–1–52–3		5–0–14–0					
(Bridgetown) 16–19 February	22–7–65–1	23.4–2–83–5		17–3–47–2					
v. Windward Islands (Roseau) 22–25 February	22.5–5–35–5	23–5–49–1	12–1–27–2	18–1–69–2					
v. Trinidad and Tobago (Port of Spain) 1–3 March	27–4–72–2	30–6–91–3	24–3–91–2	27–3–82–3					
	151.3–26–458–22 av. 20.81	142–21–495–20 av. 24.75	51–4–185–4 av. 46.25	88–10–279–9 av. 31.00	44.5–3–178–2 av. 89.00	13–2–33–2 av. 16.50	1–1–0–0 —	33–3–147–3 av. 49.00	12.4–2–36–0 —

wonderful season with his off-breaks, nearly won the game for the visitors.

15, 16, 17 and 18 February 1985

at Arnos Vale, St Vincent

Guyana 395 (D.I. Kallicharran 88, R. Seeram 67, T. Mohammed 58) and 186 for 4 (R. Seeram 100 not out)
Windward Islands 281 (N. Phillips 80, L.C. Sebastien 57, G.E. Charles 7 for 105)

Match drawn
Guyana 8 pts, Windward Islands 4 pts

16, 17, 18 and 19 February 1985

at Kensington Oval, Bridgetown

Leeward Islands 103 (W.W. Daniel 7 for 33) and 282 (E.E. Lewis 103, A.L. Kelly 58, R.O. Estwick 5 for 83)
Barbados 140 (N.C. Guishard 5 for 49) and 247 for 9 (N. Johnson 98, T.A. Hunte 52)

Barbados won by 1 wicket
Barbados 16 pts, Leeward Islands 0 pts

Individual performances dominated in St Vincent where Ram Seeram hit a maiden first-class hundred and pace man Garfield Charles returned career best bowling figures, but the rather aimless draw blighted the Shield hopes of both sides.

Leeward Islands' defeat in Bridgetown was a severe setback to their title hopes. It was the only game in the season where they failed to gain a point and it can be said to have cost them the championship. Eighteen wickets fell on the first day. Wayne Daniel routed the visitors and Barbados stumbled against the off-breaks of Noel Guishard. Leeward Islands, 37 in arrears on the first innings, came back strongly with Enoch Lewis hitting a century and Luther Kelly batting with great determination. This time it was Estwick who did most of the damage, but the Barbadian hero was wicket-keeper Worrell with six catches. The home side needed 246 to win, never an easy task on a wicket which had always given the bowlers some encouragement, and they were 60 for 4. Nigel Johnson found an excellent partner in Terry Hunte and there were significant contributions from Phillips and Worrell. At 223 for 6, the home side looked to be moving to a comfortable victory, but three wickets fell for 14 runs. Wayne Daniel then joined Philips and the last pair won the match.

N. Da C. Broomes	G.N. Reifer	E. Proverbs	*Byes*	*Leg-byes*	*Wides*	*No-balls*	*Total*	*Wkts*
			1	1	1	8	271	10
				6	4	4	220	7
			17	10	8	7	545	8
1–0–1–0			1	2	1	1	103	10
23–2–67–1	4–1–10–0		4	6	4	10	282	10
3–0–8–0			5	6		8	199	10
	1–0–3–0	1–0–4–0		5	1	28	348	10
27–2–76–1 *av.* 76.00	5–1–13–0 —	1–0–4–0 —						

22, 23, 24 and 25 February 1985

at Warner Park, Basseterre, St Kitts

Leeward Islands 380 (E.E. Lewis 92, N.C. Guishard 63) and 71 for 2
Jamaica 131 (T.A. Merrick 4 for 43) and 319 (G. Powell 55, E. Whittingham 54, T.A. Merrick 5 for 102)

Leeward Islands won by 8 wickets
Leeward Islands 16 pts, Jamaica 0 pts

at Windsor Park, Roseau

Windward Islands 199 (L.A. Lewis 76, W.W. Daniel 5 for 35)
Barbados 83 for 5

Match abandoned
Windward Islands 4 pts, Barbados 4 pts

at Bourda, Guyana

Trinidad and Tobago 127 (D.I. Kallicharran 4 for 25) and 161 (C.L. Hooper 4 for 27, C.G. Butts 4 for 49)
Guyana 226 (G. Mahabir 6 for 62) and 63 for 0

Guyana won by 10 wickets
Guyana 16 pts, Trinidad and Tobago 0 pts

Leeward Islands trounced Jamaica and with Trinidad well beaten in Guyana, the Shell Shield moved into the last round of matches with five teams separated by only 12 points. Only Jamaica were out of contention for the trophy.

Jamaica, who had suspended Mark Neita for the remainder of the season following incidents on the field between himself and skipper Basil Williams during the game against Windward Islands, fell to Man of the Match Anthony

BELOW: *Mylton Pydanna, captain of Guyana, who had a good season behind the stumps. (Adrian Murrell)*

Merrick who had 9 for 145 in the match. They were never in contention and the game ended shortly after lunch on the last day.

The match in Roseau was ruined by rain, but Shield leaders Trinidad were overwhelmed in Bourda and the match was over in three days. Thirteen wickets fell on the first day which Guyana finished 12 runs ahead. They built on this position on the second day and Trinidad fell to the combined off-spin of Clyde Butts and Carl Hooper, a most exciting young all-rounder.

Guyana 1985
First Class Matches

BATTING	*v.* Barbados (Bridgetown) 1–4 February 1985		*v.* Leeward Islands (Antigua) 8–11 February 1985		*v.* Windward Islands (St Vincent) 15–18 February 1985		*v.* Trinidad and Tobago (Bourda) 22–24 February 1985		*v.* Jamaica (Guyana) 1–4 March 1985		*M*	*Inns*	*NOs*	*Runs*	*H/S*	*Av*
A.A. Lyght	7	10	24	23	19	0	46	29*	39	18	5	10	1	215	46	23.88
C.B. Lambert	2	3	53	16	5	8	37	32*	12	24*	5	10	2	192	53	24.00
A.F.D. Jackman	24	8	18	21	16	33			36	—	4	8	—	156	36	19.50
T. Mohammed	15	61	27	80	58	16	5	—	39	9*	5	9	1	310	80	38.75
M.A. Harper	32	81	5	26	31	15*	25	—			4	7	1	215	81	35.83
C.L. Hooper	126	0	9	10	36	—	37	—	49	—	5	7	—	267	126	38.14
D.I. Kallicharran	34	0	8	16	88	—	20	—	10	—	5	7	—	176	88	25.14
G.E. Charles	0	15*			3	—	0	—	25	—	4	5	1	43	25	10.75
M.R. Pydanna	14	28*	28	9	46	—	0	—	25*	—	5	7	2	150	46	30.00
C.G. Butts	6	—	30*	3	3*	—	7*	—	7	—	5	6	3	56	30*	18.66
R.F. Joseph	0*	—	5	1*							2	3	2	6	5	6.00
C.V. Solomon			0	0							1	2	—	0	0	0.00
R. Seeram					67	100*	25	—	31	—	3	4	1	223	100*	74.33
D.A. Hewitt							13	—	14	—	2	2	—	27	14	13.50
Byes	1		1	1	7	2			1							
Leg-byes	1	6	1	1	3	2	8	1	6	2						
Wides	1	4			1		1									
No-balls	8	4	5	3	12	10	2	1	8							
Total	271	220	214	210	395	186	226	63	302	53						
Wickets	10	7	10	10	10	4	10	0	10	1						
Result	D		L		D		W		D							
Points	4		0		8		16		8							

Catches 14 – C.B. Lambert
12 – M.R. Pydanna (ct 10/st 2)
6 – M.A. Harper
5 – C.L. Hooper, D.I. Kallicharran and G.E. Charles
4 – T. Mohammed
2 – R. Seeram
1 – A.A. Lyght, C.G. Butts, R.F. Joseph and D.A. Hewitt

BOWLING	R.F. Joseph	G.E. Charles	C.G. Butts	D.I. Kallicharran	C.L. Hooper	C.V. Solomon	M.A. Harper	A.A. Lyght	D.A. Hewitt
v. Barbados (Bridgetown)	9–0–50–0	18–2–66–2	58.4–17–107–7	29–2–92–1	14–0–56–0				
1–4 February	11–0–65–0	19–1–71–1	25–6–58–1	6–0–24–0					
v. Leeward Islands	4.5–0–27–1		41–9–113–5	28–3–44–0	21–3–79–3	5–0–25–0			
(Antigua) 8–11 February	5–0–15–2		17.5–4–40–5	16–2–38–0	3–0–13–0	4–0–24–2			
v. Windward Islands		44.1–6–105–7	38–11–74–3	19–6–40–0	5–0–20–0		9–1–26–0	2–0–4–0	
(St Vincent) 15–18 February									
v. Trinidad and Tobago		10–1–43–2	17–8–14–3	12.4–5–25–4					11–3–39–1
(Bourda) 22–24 February		5–1–16–0	20–4–49–4	9–2–37–1	8.4–3–27–4				8–1–20–1
v. Jamaica (Guyana)		6–1–13–0	36.5–8–68–2	23–6–45–5	20–0–73–3				6–1–22–0
1–4 March		16–0–62–1	49–14–92–2	37.5–4–102–3	19–4–59–2				8–2–12–0
	29.5–0–157–3 *av.* 52.33	118.1–12–376–13 *av.* 28.92	303.2–81–615–32 *av.* 19.21	175.3–35–447–14 *av.* 31.92	90.4–10–327–12 *av.* 27.25	9–0–49–2 *av.* 24.50	9–1–26–0 —	2–0–4–0 —	33–7–93–2 *av.* 46.50

a A.B. Williams absent hurt

RIGHT: *Desmond Haynes – Man of the Match in the third one-day international and the most consistent of West Indian batsmen. (Adrian Murrell)*

1, 2, 3 and 4 March 1985

at Queen's Park Oval, Port of Spain

Barbados 186 (S.R. Greaves 51, G. Mahabir 4 for 69) and 108 (G. Mahabir 4 for 39)
Trinidad and Tobago 348 (P. Moosai 110, A. Rajah 57)

Trinidad and Tobago won by an innings and 54 runs
Trinidad and Tobago 16 pts, Barbados 0 pts

at Suddie, Guyana

Jamaica 237 (A.B. Williams 53, D.I. Kallicharran 5 for 45) and 342 (W.W. Lewis 127)
Guyana 302 (A.G. Daley 4 for 63) and 53 for 1

Match drawn
Guyana 8 pts, Jamaica 4 pts

at Charlestown, Nevis

Leeward Islands 292 for 8 dec (A.L. Kelly 88, T.Z. Kentish 5 for 98) and 119 for 6 dec
Windward Islands 177 (E.T. Willett 4 for 46) and 116 for 4 (L.C. Sebastien 60 not out)

Match drawn
Leeward Islands 8 pts, Windwards 4 pts

Needing to win to take the Shell Shield for the first time in nine years, they shared the title in 1976 and last won it

Shell Shield – Final Table

	P	*W*	*L*	*D*	*NR*	*Pts*
Trinidad and Tobago (6)	5	3	1	1	—	56
Leeward Islands (4)	5	2	1	2	—	44
Guyana (2)	5	1	1	3	—	36
Windward Islands (5)	5	1	1	2	1	33
Barbados (1)	5	1	2	1	1	28
Jamaica (3)	5	1	3	1	—	20

(1984 positions in brackets)

BELOW: *Martin Crowe. At last the big Test innings. 188 at Georgetown. (Adrian Murrell)*

Byes	Leg-byes	Wides	No-balls	Total	Wkts
7	6	2	6	384	10
3	6		9	227	2
1	4		6	293	10
	2		5	132	9
9	3	1	5	281	10
4	2			127	10
1	11			161	10
4	12	1		237	10
5	10	1	1	342	9a

outright in 1971, Trinidad humbled reigning champions Barbados inside three days and so took the trophy. Kelvin Williams and Anthony Gray were a most impressive opening attack and leg-spinner Ganesh Mahabir took over after the initial burst. Prakash Moosai batted 6 hours, 15 minutes for his 110 and Kelvin and David Williams hit furiously at the close of the innings to gain a lead of 162. Trinidad's innings ended 40 minutes after lunch on the third day and they bowled out Barbados, disrupted by injury, in 155 minutes to take the match and the title. They were ably led by Ranjie Nanan and their bowlers were well supported by wicket-keeper David Williams who established a new Shield record with 24 dismissals.

With seven and a half hours lost to rain, Leeward Islands made a bold effort to beat arch rivals Windward Islands, but they were frustrated by the experienced Lockhart Sebastien.

Guyana and Jamaica played a rather tame draw, and the highlight of the match was an excellent maiden Shield hundred by opener Wayne Lewis. He batted for 4 hours, 34 minutes and hit a six and nine fours.

FIRST ONE-DAY INTERNATIONAL – WEST INDIES *v.* NEW ZEALAND
20 March 1985 at St John's, Antigua

WEST INDIES

C.G. Greenidge	c Smith, b Troup	3
D.L. Haynes	b Troup	54
R.B. Richardson	b Hadlee	3
I.V.A. Richards†	b Coney	70
A.L. Logie	c Cairns, b Coney	11
P.J. Dujon*	st Smith, b Coney	14
R.A. Harper	not out	45
E.A.E. Baptiste	b Cairns	8
M.A. Holding	b Hadlee	9
J. Garner	not out	1
W.W. Davis		
Extras	b 1, lb 6, w 3, nb 3	13
(46 overs)	(for 8 wickets)	231

	O	M	R	W
Troup	10	—	52	2
Hadlee	10	—	29	2
Chatfield	8	—	38	—
Cairns	8	—	42	1
Coney	10	—	63	3

FALL OF WICKETS
1- 4, 2- 7, 3- 134, 4- 141, 5- 160, 6- 191, 7- 208, 8- 226

NEW ZEALAND

J.G. Wright	b Holding	0
R.T. Hart	c Dujon, b Garner	3
J.J. Crowe	b Harper	53
M.D. Crowe	lbw, b Harper	41
B.L. Cairns	c Richards, b Holding	20
J.V. Coney	run out	18
R.J. Hadlee	c Harper, b Holding	2
I.D.S. Smith*	c Holding, b Garner	12
G.P. Howarth†	not out	12
G.B. Troup	not out	16
E.J. Chatfield		
Extras	b 2, lb 18, w 5, nb 6	31
(46 overs)	(for 8 wickets)	208

	O	M	R	W
Garner	10	4	26	2
Holding	10	2	33	3
Baptiste	10	1	49	—
Davis	8	—	46	—
Harper	8	—	34	2

FALL OF WICKETS
1- 5, 2- 20, 3- 111, 4- 124, 5- 151, 6- 158, 7- 173, 8- 180

West Indies won by 23 runs

SECOND ONE-DAY INTERNATIONAL – WEST INDIES *v.* NEW ZEALAND
27 March 1985 at Port of Spain, Trinidad

NEW ZEALAND

J.G. Wright	c Dujon, b Davis	5
K.R. Rutherford	c Dujon, b Davis	2
J.J. Crowe	c Richards, b Davis	0
M.D. Crowe	not out	20
J.V. Coney	not out	19
G.P. Howarth†		
I.D.S. Smith*		
R.J. Hadlee		
B.L. Cairns		
G.B. Troup		
E.J. Chatfield		
Extras	lb 1, w 1, nb 3	5
(22 overs)	(for 3 wickets)	51

	O	M	R	W
Garner	6	2	6	—
Davis	6	2	7	3
Holding	5	—	16	—
Baptiste	5	—	21	—

FALL OF WICKETS
1- 6, 2- 9, 3- 9

WEST INDIES

D.L. Haynes	b Chatfield	4
R.B. Richardson	c Smith, b Troup	3
H.A. Gomes	c Smith, b Troup	4
I.V.A. Richards†	c Cairns, b Rutherford	27
A.L. Logie	not out	8
P.J. Dujon*	not out	4
R.A. Harper		
E.A.E. Baptiste		
M.A. Holding		
J. Garner		
W.W. Davis		
Extras	lb 2, w 1, nb 2	5
(17 overs)	(for 4 wickets)	55

	O	M	R	W
Chatfield	6	—	15	1
Troup	5	1	22	2
Coney	3	1	4	—
Rutherford	3	—	12	1

FALL OF WICKETS
1- 4, 2- 11, 3- 21, 4- 51

West Indies won by 6 wickets

15, 16 and 17 March 1985

at Kingston, Jamaica

New Zealanders 267 (M.D. Crowe 118, J.J. Crowe 67, C. Butts 7 for 90) and 199 (J.G. Wright 69, M.D. Crowe 62, A.H. Gray 5 for 55, G. Mahabir 4 for 72)
Shell Award XI 316 (A.L. Kelly 132, Timur Mohammed 60) and 16 for 1

Match drawn

The New Zealand tourists, weakened by the withdrawal of John Reid from the party, drew the opening match of their West Indian tour. After Rutherford and Hart, the newcomers, had fallen for 43, the Crowe brothers added 102, but there was little else to commend in the New Zealand batting. Off-spinner Clyde Butts destroyed the middle order and the West Indian side moved into a commanding position as Kelly and Mohammed shared a third wicket stand of 123. After nine years in first-class cricket, Luther Kelly reached a maiden century, a sparkling innings, but John Bracewell and Stephen Boock, the spinners, bowled the tourists back into the game. John Wright, reverting to number one, batted well in the second innings and there was another good knock from Martin Crowe so that a draw became inevitable in spite of good bowling by the Trinidad pair, medium-pacer Anthony Gray and leg-spinner Ganesh Mahabir.

First One-Day International
WEST INDIES *v.* NEW ZEALAND

West Indies recovered from the loss of Greenidge and Richardson for 7 to beat New Zealand with surprising ease in the end. They owed much to Richards who delighted his home crowd with a steadying and forceful innings of 70 from 85 balls. He shared a partnership of 127 for the third wicket with Haynes to provide the platform for an assault on the bowling. The assault was made by Roger Harper who hit 45 off 29 deliveries with three sixes and three fours and lifted the home side to 231 from 46 overs.

Hart, in his first international, and Wright went quickly, but the Crowe brothers added 91 in 17 overs to revive New Zealand's hopes. Harper, who won the Man of the Match award, dismissed them both and Richards took a magnificent one-handed catch at extra-cover to get rid of the dangerous Cairns. He then threw out Coney with a direct hit on the stumps at the bowler's end and West Indies were assured of victory.

22, 23 and 24 March 1985

at Basseterre, St Kitts

New Zealanders 171 (J.G. Wright 101, C. Hooper 5 for 35) and 238 for 4 (K.R. Rutherford 109 not out, J.V. Coney not out)
West Indies Under-23 XI 285 (L.L. Lawrence 79, T.A. Hunte 69, D.A. Stirling 4 for 68)

Match drawn

A century by John Wright saved the tourists from total humiliation against the bowling of Merrick and Hooper. The home side fared little better and were indebted to a third wicket stand of 144 between Lawrence and Hunte. When it looked as if the New Zealanders could again be in trouble Ken Rutherford, promoted to open the innings, hit a splendid century after Merrick's fiery spell had accounted for Wright, Jeff Crowe and Hart.

ABOVE: *A Test century at Port of Spain for Gordon Greenidge was followed by illness. (Adrian Murrell)*

Second One-Day International
NEW ZEALAND *v.* WEST INDIES

A fierce opening spell by Winston Davis reduced the visitors to 13 for 3 after 12 overs. Martin Crowe and Jeremy Coney were just in the middle of repairing the innings when three hours of rain reduced the match to the twenty-overs that the New Zealanders had already faced. This handed the game to the West Indians who had little trouble in reaching the target.

First Test Match
WEST INDIES *v.* NEW ZEALAND

Two wickets in the fifth over of the first day gave New Zealand hope of victory in the first Test of the series, but, surprisingly, Hadlee, the wicket-taker, was rested after only six overs. When he returned after lunch he had Greenidge, then on 40, dropped at slip by Howarth. Greenidge prospered after this error and he and Richardson revived West Indies with a stand of 185 in $4\frac{3}{4}$ hours. They were out in successive overs in the last session of the day, Greenidge cutting at Boock just after he had reached his century and Richardson taken at slip driving at Coney's gentle outswing. Richards and Logie took the home side to 231 for 4 at the close, a most healthy position after such a poor start.

Chatfield quickly mopped up the tail on the second day and the last six wickets fell for 71 runs. New Zealand began disastrously when poor Ken Rutherford was taken at short leg for 0. Wright and Jeff Crowe added 109 with sensible batting and indicated that West Indies might find New Zealand a stronger proposition than they had done England or Australia, but 3 wickets fell for 22 and it was left to Howarth and Coney to steady the innings again before the

Jamaica 1985
First Class Matches

BATTING	v. Trinidad (Kingston) 24–27 January 1985		v. Windward Islands (Kingston) 31 Jan.–3 Feb. 1985		v. Barbados (Kingston) 8–11 February 1985		v. Leeward Islands (St Kitts) 22–25 February 1985		v. Guyana (Guyana) 1–4 March 1985		M	Inns	NOs	Runs	H/S	Av
A.B. Williams	0	102	28	91	59	—	1	45	53	—	5	8	—	379	102	47.37
W.W. Lewis	24	26	0	59	3	—	20	48	34	127	5	9	—	341	127	37.88
O.W. Peters	5	8	1	72	3	—	4	0	28	43	5	9	—	164	72	18.22
P.A. Francis	1	16	0	0	16*	—	0	28*	4	13	5	9	2	78	28*	11.14
M.C. Neita	75*	34	23	6	49	—					3	5	1	187	75*	46.75
M. Williams	3	0									1	2	—	3	3	1.50
R.C. Haynes	25	5	15	1							2	4	—	46	25	11.50
A.G. Daley	9	14	2	45*	50*	—	10	13	9	18	5	9	2	170	50*	24.28
E.E. Brown	1	27	16	2							2	4	—	46	27	11.50
K.W. McLeod	0	0									1	2	—	0	0	0.00
C.U. Thompson	21	8*									1	2	1	29	21	29.00
G. Powell			23	20	110	—	7	55	1	45	4	7	—	261	110	37.28
E.L. Wilson			8	3	—	—	7*	1	0	14*	4	6	2	33	14*	8.25
D. McKenzie			6*	3							1	2	1	9	6*	9.00
C.A. Davidson					98	—	45	36	18	17	3	5	—	214	98	42.80
J. Adams					40	—	0	14	19*	28	3	5	1	101	40	25.25
D. Dixon					75	—	17	0	21	13	3	5	—	126	75	25.20
E. Whittingham							13	54			1	2	—	67	54	33.50
T.A. Corke									33	7	1	2	—	40	33	20.00
Byes	9	7	4	2	17			1	4	5						
Leg-byes	3	15	1	6	10		5	9	12	10						
Wides			2		8		1	2	1	1						
No-balls	4	2	6	10	7		1	13		1						
Total	180	264	135	320	545		131	319	237	342						
Wickets	10	10	10	10	8		10	10	10	9†						
Result	L		L		W		L		D							
Points	0		0		16		0		4							

Catches 10 – P.A. Francis (ct 8/st 2)
4 – W.W. Lewis and O.W. Peters
3 – A.G. Daley and C.A. Davidson
2 – J. Adams and T.A. Corke
1 – M.C. Neita, R.C. Haynes, E.E. Brown, C.U. Thompson and E.L. Wilson

† A.B. Williams absent hurt

BOWLING	K.W. McLeod	A.G. Daley	C.U. Thompson	E.E. Brown	R.C. Haynes	M.C. Neita	D. McKenzie	E.L. Wilson	D. Dixon
v. Trinidad and Tobago	11–4–27–0	17.5–1–51–2	4–0–17–0	24–14–44–4	15–4–40–2	6–1–13–1			
(Kingston) 24–27 January	10–2–35–1	24.4–4–69–4	17–5–46–1	30–6–73–1	21–3–64–2	3–1–5–1			
v. Windward Islands (Kingston)		29–3–108–4		17–4–32–0	29–3–74–2	4–1–15–0	30–7–67–2	45–17–98–2	
31 January–3 February		8–0–25–3					3–0–9–0	5.2–1–11–0	
v. Barbados (Kingston)		18.5–1–64–5				1–0–8–0		21–9–48–1	20–1–81–3
8–11 February		31–8–103–3						24–5–45–2	26.5–3–80–3
v. Leeward Islands (St Kitts)		28–3–98–2						43–12–94–3	24–6–73–0
22–25 February		7 2 26–1						10.2–3–22–0	2–0–13–0
v. Guyana (Guyana)		24.2–2–63–4						30–4–90–1	16–2–48–1
1–4 March		6–0–31–1							5–1–20–0
	21–6–62–1 *av.* 62.00	194.2–24–638–29 *av.* 22.00	21–5–63–1 *av.* 63.00	71–24–149–5 *av.* 29.80	65–10–178–6 *av.* 29.66	14–3–41–2 *av.* 20.50	33–7–76–2 *av.* 38.00	178.4–51–408–9 *av.* 45.33	93.5–13–315–7 *av.* 45.00

ABOVE: *West Indian triumph. (Adrian Murrell)* BELOW: *Malcolm Marshall – 11 wickets in the third Test match and 27 wickets in the series. (George Herringshaw)*

close at 166 for 4. Next day only the pre-lunch session and nine balls after lunch were possible before rain ended play. In that time Coney was lbw and 57 runs were scored.

West Indies took command of the match on the fourth day although they were without Gordon Greenidge who was ill.

New Zealand declined from 223 for 5 at the start to 262 all out before lunch. Surviving the early loss of Richardson, West Indies batted positively and were 273 ahead with 4 wickets down at the close. They lost 4 wickets on the final morning as they went for quick runs before Richards declared and set New Zealand to make 307 to win, but with little time in which to do anything but bat for a draw. New Zealand found their own hero in Chatfield whose 6 for 73, his

J. Adams	E. Whittingham	T.A. Corke	*Byes*	*Leg-byes*	*Wides*	*No-balls*	*Total*	*Wkts*
			11	1	2	9	204	10
			16	9	2	15	317	10
			3	8		3	405	10
			6	1		3	52	3
12–1–30–0			2	7	1	6	240	10
18–7–19–1			5	8		7	260	10
9–2–26–2	27–0–72–2		5	12	2	10	380	10
5–1–9–0				1			71	2
20–3–57–2		11–1–37–1	1	6		8	302	10
				2			53	1
64–14–141–5 *av.* 28.20	27–0–72–2 *av.* 36.00	11–1–37–1 *av.* 37.00						

best performance in a Test match, brought his match figures to 10 for 124, his best match figures in a Test.

Ken Rutherford, the nineteen-year old opener, playing his first Test, was run out off the last ball of the first over so giving him a 'pair' on his debut, but he could gain encouragement from recalling that Gooch suffered the same fate on his Test debut.

Wright was lbw just before lunch and when, shortly before tea, Marshall produced a ferocious spell which accounted for the Crowe brothers and Hadlee, New Zealand faced defeat. Coney batted with his usual defiance and although falling to Marshall before the close, he had done enough, along with the most sensible Hadlee, to save the day for New Zealand.

Leeward Islands 1985
First Class Matches

BATTING	*v.* Trinidad (Port of Spain) 1–4 February 1985		*v.* Guyana (Antigua) 8–11 February 1985		*v.* Barbados (Bridgetown) 16–19 February 1985		*v.* Jamaica (St Kitts) 22–25 February 1985		*v.* Windward Islands (Nevis) 1–4 March 1985		*M*	*Inns*	*NOs*	*Runs*	*H/S*	*Av*
A.L. Kelly	7	55	47	54	8	58	35	22	88	29	5	10	—	403	88	40.30
L.L. Lawrence	31	93	36	0	12	20	25	5	14	6	5	10	—	242	93	24.20
E.E. Lewis	12	1	70	0	43	103	92	—	8	32	5	9	—	361	103	40.11
R.M. Otto	110	34	17	0	5	14	7	14*	1	20	5	10	1	222	110	24.66
V.A. Eddy	3	11	3	8							2	4	—	25	11	12.50
S.I. Williams	18	31*	31	15	0	12	12	—	6	10*	5	9	2	135	31*	19.28
N.C. Guishard	4	—	32	18	3	40	63	—	14	5*	5	8	1	179	63	25.57
C.E.I. Bartlette	2	—	0	5*	9	0					3	5	1	16	9	4.00
T.A. Merrick	3	—	24	3	0	3	0	—	48*	—	5	7	1	81	48*	13.50
E.T. Willett	1	—	7	1*	8	1*	40	—	13*	—	5	7	3	71	40	17.75
J.D. Thompson	3*	—			0*	0	23*	—	—	—	4	4	3	26	23*	26.00
U.V.C. Lawrence			15	21							1	2	—	36	21	18.00
E.A. Lewis					10	7	30	29*	48	11	3	6	1	135	48	27.00
E.A.E. Baptiste							24	—	38	0	2	3	—	64	38	21.33
Byes	1	8	1		1	4	5		4	1						
Leg-byes	4	5	4	2	2	6	12	1	8	3						
Wides	2	1			1	4	2		1							
No-balls	3	7	6	5	1	10	10		1	2						
Total	204	246	293	132	103	282	380	71	292	119						
Wickets	10	5	10	9	10	10	10	1	8	6						
Result	D		W		L		W		D							
Points	4		16		0		16		8							

Catches 9–R.M. Otto and S.I. Williams (ct 8/st 1)
8–A.L. Kelly
4–T.A. Merrick
3–E.A. Lewis, E.A.E. Baptiste, C.I.E. Bartlette and N.C. Guishard
2–L.L. Lawrence and J.D. Thompson
1–V.A. Eddy and E.T. Willett

BOWLING	T.A. Merrick	C.E.I. Bartlette	E.T. Willett	J.D. Thompson	N.C. Guishard	U.V.C. Lawrence	E.A.E. Baptiste
v. Trinidad and Tobago	27.2–1–99–3	19–1–69–4	32–10–59–1	17–5–49–0	19–3–47–1		
(Port of Spain) 1–4 February							
v. Guyana (Antigua)	22.3–2–101–5	7–0–28–1	9–4–16–1		10–3–31–2	15–4–36–1	
8–11 February	19–4–76–4	11–1–47–0	17.1–1–40–3		22–6–38–2	3–1–7–0	
v. Barbados (Bridgetown)	10–1–15–0	8–1–16–0	13–4–38–1	9–2–19–3	23.5–3–49–5		
16–19 February	9–3–24–2	3–1–13–0	19.4–2–44–0	40–9–78–3	43–11–84–3		
v. Jamaica (St Kitts)	12.4–2–43–4		12–3–17–1	12–3–24–1			12–2–42–3
22–25 February	32–4–102–5		30 14–45–2	14–1–44–0	33–8–73–1		17–3–45–2
v. Windward Islands	7–3–31–0		20.3–3–46–4	8–2–11–0	26–5–59–2		19–10–28–3
(Nevis) 1–4 March	7–1–39–0		4–3–1–0	7–1–22–0	11–5–22–1		7–1–23–3
	146.3–21–530–23– *av.* 23.04	48–4–173–5 *av.* 34.60	157.2–44–306–13 *av.* 23.53	107–23–247–7 *av.* 35.28	187.5–44–403–17 *av.* 23.70	18–5–43–1 *av.* 43.00	55–16–138–11 *av.* 12.54

FIRST TEST MATCH – WEST INDIES *v.* NEW ZEALAND
29, 30, 31 March, 2 and 3 April 1985 at Port of Spain

WEST INDIES

	FIRST INNINGS		SECOND INNINGS	
C.G. Greenidge	b Boock	100		
D.L. Haynes	c Rutherford, b Hadlee	0	(1) c M. Crowe, b Chatfield	78
H.A. Gomes	c Smith, b Hadlee	0	c and b Chatfield	25
R.B. Richardson	c Hadlee, b Coney	78	(2) c Smith, b Chatfield	3
I.V.A. Richards†	b Hadlee	57	(4) b Cairns	78
A.L. Logie	b Chatfield	24	(5) b Cairns	42
P.J. Dujon*	b Chatfield	15	(6) b Chatfield	5
M.D. Marshall	c sub, b Chatfield	0	(7) c Coney, b Chatfield	1
R.A. Harper	c Howarth, b Chatfield	0	(8) not out	11
M.A. Holding	lbw, b Hadlee	12	(9) c J. Crowe, b Chatfield	8
J. Garner	not out	0		
Extras	b 1, lb 16, nb 4	21	lb 3, nb 7	10
		307	(for 8 wkts dec)	261

	O	M	R	W	O	M	R	W
Hadlee	24.3	6	82	4	17	2	58	—
Chatfield	28	11	51	4	22	4	73	6
Cairns	26	3	93	—	19	2	70	2
Boock	19	5	47	1	14	4	57	—
Coney	9	3	17	1				

FALL OF WICKETS
1- 5, 2- 9, 3- 194, 4- 196, 5- 236, 6- 267, 7- 267, 8- 269, 9- 302
1- 10, 2- 58, 3- 172, 4- 226, 5- 239, 6- 240, 7- 241, 8- 261

NEW ZEALAND

	FIRST INNINGS		SECOND INNINGS	
J.G. Wright	c Richardson, b Harper	40	lbw, b Holding	19
K.R. Rutherford	c Haynes, b Marshall	0	run out	0
J.J. Crowe	c and b Harper	64	c Garner, b Marshall	27
M.D. Crowe	lbw, b Holding	3	c Haynes, b Marshall	2
G.P. Howarth†	c sub, b Holding	45	b Marshall	14
J.V. Coney	lbw, b Marshall	25	c Dujon, b Marshall	44
R.J. Hadlee	c Garner, b Holding	18	not out	39
I.D.S. Smith*	c Logie, b Holding	10	not out	11
B.L. Cairns	c Harper, b Garner	8		
S.L. Boock	c sub, b Garner	3		
E.J. Chatfield	not out	4		
Extras	b 12, lb 11, nb 19	42	b 17, lb 6, nb 8	31
		262	(for 6 wkts)	187

	O	M	R	W	O	M	R	W
Marshall	25	3	78	2	26	4	65	4
Garner	21.3	8	41	2	18	2	41	—
Holding	29	8	79	4	17	6	36	1
Harper	22	11	33	2	14	7	19	—
Richards	2	—	7	—	2	1	1	—
Gomes	1	—	1	—	2	1	2	—
Richardson					1	1	0	—
Logie					1	1	0	—

FALL OF WICKETS
1- 1, 2- 110, 3- 113, 4- 132, 5- 182, 6- 223, 7- 225, 8- 248, 9- 250
1- 0, 2- 40, 3- 59, 4- 76, 5- 83, 6- 158

Umpires: C.E. Cumberbatch and D.A. Archer

Match drawn

Second Test Match
WEST INDIES *v.* NEW ZEALAND

West Indies introduced off-spinner Clyde Butts to Test cricket, but it was on a wicket that was hardly likely to give him any encouragement.

Richards won the toss and West Indies, having lost Greenidge early, ground their way to 271 for 2 on the first

	Byes	*Leg-byes*	*Wides*	*No-balls*	*Total*	*Wkts*
	9	4	1	3	336	10
	1	1		5	214	10
	1	1		3	210	10
	2	1		2	140	10
		4	2	1	247	9
		5	1	1	131	10
	1	9	2	13	319	10
		2	1	4	177	10
	8	1		1	116	4

Chatfield – ten wickets in a Test match for the first time, Port of Spain. (Adrian Murrell)

day and 511 for 6 by the close of the second, which came only 25 minutes after tea because of rain.

The West Indies hero was Richie Richardson who finished the first day on 140 and was dropped at gully early on the second morning by Coney off Hadlee. He went on to make a career best in 465 minutes before being run out after a mix up with Gus Logie. Logie and Dujon added brisk runs at the end before Richards declared.

The New Zealand reply began sadly. Rutherford scored his first Test runs when he edged Garner's third ball through

Trinidad and Tobago 1985
First Class Matches

BATTING	*v.* Jamaica (Kingston) 24–27 January 1985		*v.* Leeward Islands (Port of Spain) 1–4 February 1985		*v.* Windward Islands (Port of Spain) 8–10 February 1985		*v.* Guyana (Bourda) 22–24 February 1985		*v.* Barbados (Port of Spain) 1–3 March 1985		*M*	*Inns*	*NOs*	*Runs*	*H/S*	*Av*
K.R. Bainey	7	17	19	—							2	3	—	43	19	14.33
P.V. Simmonds	64	70	118	—	5	78	24	22	9	—	5	8	—	390	118	48.75
R.A. Glasgow	17	7									1	2	—	24	17	12.00
A. Rajah	11	38	55	—	13	30	11	29	57	—	5	8	—	244	57	30.50
P.Moosai	41	32	13	—	14	7	1	1	110	—	5	8	—	219	110	27.37
R. Nanan	12	23	46	—	1	6	13	10	4	—	5	8	—	115	46	14.37
K.C. Williams	2	62	0	—	5	84*	23	38	41	—	5	8	1	255	84*	36.42
D. Williams	20	14	13	—	16	9*	3	11	49*	—	5	8	2	135	49*	22.50
A.H. Gray	0	8	14	—	18	—	1	2	26	—	5	7	—	69	26	9.85
G.S. Antoine	8	4	12*	—	1*	—	2*	5*			4	6	4	32	12*	16.00
G. Mahabir	0*	0*	7	—	0	—	4	0	0	—	5	7	2	11	7	2.20
R.S. Gabriel			22	—	14	60	28	16	4	—	4	6	—	144	60	24.00
D.C. Furlonge					11	0					1	2	—	11	11	5.50
D.I. Mohammed							11	15	2	—	2	3	—	28	15	9.33
M. Bodoe									12	—	1	1	—	12	12	12.00
Byes	11	16	9		1	2	4	1								
Leg-byes	1	9	4		4	7	2	11	5							
Wides	1	2	1						1							
No-balls	9	15	3		9	12			28							
Total	204	317	336		112	295	127	161	348							
Wickets	10	10	10		10	6	10	10	10							
Result	W		D		W		L		W							
Points	16		8		16		0		16							

Catches 23 – D. Williams (ct 19/st 4)
9 – P.V. Simmonds
7 – A. Rajah
3 – G. Mahabir
2 – R. Nanan, K.C. Williams, R.S. Gabriel and D.I. Mohammed
1 – K.R. Bainey, P. Moosai, A.H. Gray, G.S. Antoine, D.C. Furlonge, M. Bodoe and sub

BOWLING	G.S. Antoine	A.H. Gray	K.C. Williams	R. Nanan	G. Mahabir	P.V. Simmonds	M. Bodoe
v. Jamaica (Kingston)	9–0–33–1	17–1–51–4	10–1–34–1	12–1–30–2	2.5–0–6–1	2–0–14–0	
24–27 January	3–0–16–0	23–2–78–6	3–0–13–0	36–8–73–2	36–7–62–2		
v. Leeward Islands	6–0–31–1	15–4–36–2	18.3–5–38–1	24–8–40–3	28–7–54–3		
(Port of Spain) 1–4 February	12.4–1–60–2	15–1–57–0	12–1–34–0	20–8–29–0	28–5–53–3		
v. Windward Islands	9–0–60–0	21–3–86–5	15–4–30–1	15–3–24–0	18.2–3–45–3	1–0–5–0	
(Port of Spain) 8–10 February	11–2–33–3	11–1–44–2	7–0–30–1		12.3–1–37–4		
v. Guyana (Bourda)	4–0–31–1	8–0–46–0	7–0–41–0	21–6–38–3	23.3–5–62–6		
22–24 February	2–0–10–0			6–0–28–0	5.4–0–24–0		
v. Barbados (Port of Spain)		8–3–30–2	13–1–36–1	14.4–3–39–3	22–4–69–4		5–1–11–0
1–3 March		7–0–30–2	5–2–17–1	11.5–5–12–2	13–3–39–4		
	50.4–3–274–8 *av.* 34.25	125–15–458–23 *av.* 19.91	90.3–14–273–6 *av.* 45.50	160.3–42–313–15 *av.* 20.86	189.5–35–451–30 *av.* 15.03	3–0–19–0 —	5–1–11–0 —

SECOND TEST MATCH – WEST INDIES *v.* NEW ZEALAND
6, 7, 8, 10 and 11 April 1985 at Georgetown, Guyana

WEST INDIES

	FIRST INNINGS		SECOND INNINGS	
C.G. Greenidge	b Chatfield	10	c and b Coney	69
D.L. Haynes	b Hadlee	90	c Smith, b Hadlee	9
R.B. Richardson	run out	185	(4) c J. Crowe, b Cairns	60
H.A. Gomes	lbw, b Cairns	53	(5) c sub, b Rutherford	35
I.V.A. Richards†	st Smith, b Coney	40	(8) not out	7
A.L. Logie	c Howarth, b Hadlee	52	not out	41
P.J. Dujon*	not out	60	b Cairns	3
M.D. Marshall				
M.A. Holding				
J. Garner				
C. Butts			(3) c Smith, b Hadlee	9
Extras	b 1, lb 16, w 1, nb 3	21	b 7, lb 24, w 1, nb 2	34
	(for 6 wkts dec)	511	(for 6 wkts)	268

	O	M	R	W	O	M	R	W
Hadlee	25.5	5	83	2	16	3	32	2
Chatfield	30	3	122	1	16	3	43	—
Cairns	36	5	106	1	18	4	47	2
Boock	43	11	106	—	18	3	52	—
Coney	18	2	62	1	10	3	20	1
Howarth	4	1	15	—	5	4	2	—
Rutherford					9	1	38	1
Wright					3	1	2	—

FALL OF WICKETS
1- 30, 2- 221, 3- 327, 4- 394, 5- 407, 6- 511
1- 22, 2- 46, 3- 150, 4- 191, 5- 207, 6- 225

NEW ZEALAND

	FIRST INNINGS	
J.G. Wright	run out	27
K.R. Rutherford	c Dujon, b Garner	4
J.J. Crowe	b Marshall	22
M.D. Crowe	lbw, b Garner	188
G.P. Howarth†	c Haynes, b Marshall	4
J.V. Coney	c Richards, b Holding	73
R.J. Hadlee	c Dujon, b Marshall	16
I.D.S. Smith*	lbw, b Marshall	53
B.L. Cairns	b Holding	3
S.L. Boock	b Holding	0
E.J. Chatfield	not out	3
Extras	b 12, lb 2, w 6, nb 27	47
		440

	O	M	R	W
Marshall	33	3	110	4
Garner	27.4	5	72	2
Holding	28	6	89	3
Butts	47	12	113	—
Richards	8	1	22	—
Gomes	8	2	20	—

FALL OF WICKETS
1- 8, 2- 45, 3- 81, 4- 98, 5- 240, 6- 261, 7- 404, 8- 415, 9- 415

Umpires: D.J. Narine and L.H. Barker

Match drawn

Richie Richardson, a career best 185 in the second Test match at Georgetown. (Sporting Pictures UK Ltd)

	Byes	Leg-byes	Wides	No-balls	Total	Wkts
	9	3		4	180	10
	7	15		2	264	10
	1	4	2	3	204	10
	8	5	1	7	246	5
	5	4		10	259	10
		2		4	146	10
		8	1	2	226	10
		1		1	63	0
		1		5	186	10
	3	7		4	108	10

THIRD ONE-DAY INTERNATIONAL – WEST INDIES *v.* NEW ZEALAND
14 April 1985 at Berbice, Guyana

WEST INDIES

D.L. Haynes	not out	145
R.B. Richardson	c Smith, b Hadlee	7
H.A. Gomes	c Smith, b Chatfield	13
I.V.A. Richards†	c Wright, b Bracewell	51
A.L. Logie	c Troup, b Cairns	26
R.A. Harper	c Smith, b Troup	1
P.J. Dujon*	not out	4
E.A.E. Baptiste		
M.A. Holding		
J. Garner		
W.W. Davis		
Extras	lb 6, w 1, nb 5	12
(50 overs)	(for 5 wickets)	259

	O	M	R	W
Troup	7	—	28	1
Hadlee	10	1	46	1
Chatfield	10	—	35	1
J.G. Bracewell	9	—	50	1
Cairns	10	—	69	1
Coney	4	—	25	—

FALL OF WICKETS
1- 18, 2- 47, 3- 172, 4- 252, 5- 253

NEW ZEALAND

G.P. Howarth†	b Garner	3
J.G. Wright	b Garner	0
J.J. Crowe	b Davis	9
M.D. Crowe	b Holding	20
J.V. Coney	b Baptiste	11
I.D.S. Smith*	b Baptiste	1
R.J. Hadlee	b Harper	16
J.G. Bracewell	c Richards, b Gomes	15
B.L. Cairns	c Davis, b Harper	33
G.B. Troup	not out	6
E.J. Chatfield	b Gomes	6
Extras	b 2, lb 4, w 1, nb 2	9
(48.1 overs)		129

	O	M	R	W
Garner	6	2	16	2
Davis	6	3	7	1
Holding	6	—	12	1
Baptiste	7	2	18	2
Harper	10	1	35	2
Richards	10	4	23	—
Gomes	2.1	—	6	2
Logie	1	—	6	—

FALL OF WICKETS
1- 4, 2- 8, 3- 24, 4- 41, 5- 48, 6- 55, 7- 75, 8- 115, 9- 121

West Indies won by 130 runs

FOURTH ONE-DAY INTERNATIONAL – WEST INDIES *v.* NEW ZEALAND
17 April 1985 at Port of Spain, Trinidad

NEW ZEALAND

G.P. Howarth†	c Dujon, b Garner	6
J.G. Wright	c Dujon, b Garner	1
J.J. Crowe	c Richardson, b Garner	4
M.D. Crowe	b Garner	1
J.V. Coney	c Dujon, b Richards	33
I.D.S. Smith*	c and b Holding	3
R.J. Hadlee	c Richards, b Davis	41
B.L. Cairns	b Harper	12
J.G. Bracewell	run out	1
G.B. Troup	run out	4
E.J. Chatfield	not out	1
Extras	lb 3, w 2, nb 4	9
(42.3 overs)		116

	O	M	R	W
Garner	6	1	10	4
Davis	6.3	1	10	1
Baptiste	5	—	31	—
Holding	7	1	24	1
Harper	10	2	18	1
Richards	8	1	20	1

FALL OF WICKETS
1- 6, 2- 10, 3- 14, 4- 18, 5- 25, 6- 83, 7- 100, 8- 104, 9- 114

WEST INDIES

D.L. Haynes	not out	85
R.B. Richardson	not out	28
H.A. Gomes		
I.V.A. Richards†		
A.L. Logie		
P.J. Dujon*		
E.A.E. Baptiste		
R.A. Harper		
M.A. Holding		
J. Garner		
W.W. Davis		
Extras	lb 2, nb 2	4
(25.2 overs)	(for no wicket)	117

	O	M	R	W
Hadlee	6	1	18	—
Troup	8	2	30	—
Cairns	7	—	50	—
Chatfield	4	—	14	—
J.G. Bracewell	0.2	—	3	—

FALL OF WICKETS
nil

West Indies won by 10 wickets

the slips for 4. He was not so fortunate with the fifth which he touched to the wicket-keeper. Wright responded with a crisp attack on the bowling, but he was needlessly run out and when Jeff Crowe and Howarth followed, New Zealand were 98 for 4 and in great trouble.

Martin Crowe at last produced the innings that had been expected of him in Test cricket and Coney batted with his usual tenacity to wrest the initiative from West Indies with a stand which left New Zealand on 230 for 4 at the close, only 81 runs away from safety, the avoidance of the follow-on.

Coney was out with only 10 runs added on the fourth morning, but Hadlee and Smith both aided Martin Crowe in steering New Zealand to comfort. Coney and Crowe added 142 and Smith and Crowe added 143, both New Zealand records against West Indies.

Martin Crowe batted magnificently. He never offered a chance and was last out for a career best score. Greenidge was missed by Wright off Chatfield to allow the West Indies to avoid further embarrassment after the loss of Haynes, and they spent the last day indulging in batting practice.

Third One-Day International
WEST INDIES *v.* NEW ZEALAND

Put in to bat on a placid wicket, West Indies romped to 259 in their fifty overs with Desmond Haynes carrying his bat for 145, an innings rich in fine strokes. He and Richards added 125 in 25 overs before Richards fell to a catch on the mid-wicket boundary. The pair had eased pressure on their side who were 47 for 2 after Hadlee's early breakthrough and Chatfield's dismissal of Gomes. The only thing that disturbed the West Indian innings after that was a swarm of bees which also disquieted a capacity crowd of 15,000.

Within the first three overs of the New Zealand innings Garner bowled both Howarth and Wright. The next five batsmen were also bowled and New Zealand's pitiful batting was only heightened by Cairns who hit three sixes and a four.

Fourth One-Day International
WEST INDIES *v.* NEW ZEALAND

For the second time in three days West Indies overwhelmed New Zealand in a one-day international. Richards asked New Zealand to bat first on a grassy wicket and Garner proved unplayable. He made the ball rise sharply and moved it both ways so that when he retired from the attack after bowling six overs he had accounted for Howarth, Wright and the Crowe brothers at a personal cost of 10 runs. After 14 overs New Zealand were 25 for 5 and the game had been decided.

Coney and Hadlee restored some pride with a stand of 58 in 15 overs, relishing some rather loose bowling by Baptiste, but Harper's control thwarted any real recovery.

Haynes was again in bubbling form and West Indies coasted to victory.

19, 20 and 21 April 1985

at Castries, St Lucia

New Zealanders 307 for 7 dec (J.V. Coney 99, B.L. Cairns 52 not out, K.R. Rutherford 51, J.G. Bracewell 50) and 181 (K.R. Rutherford 53, C.A. Walsh 4 for 61)
President's XI 264 (R. Seeram 75 not out, T.R.O. Payne 56, D.A. Stirling 4 for 66) and 114 for 4 (C.A. Best 53 not out)
Match drawn

Recovering from the depths of 31 for 3 and 68 for 4 through the efforts of Rutherford, Coney and the hard-hitting late

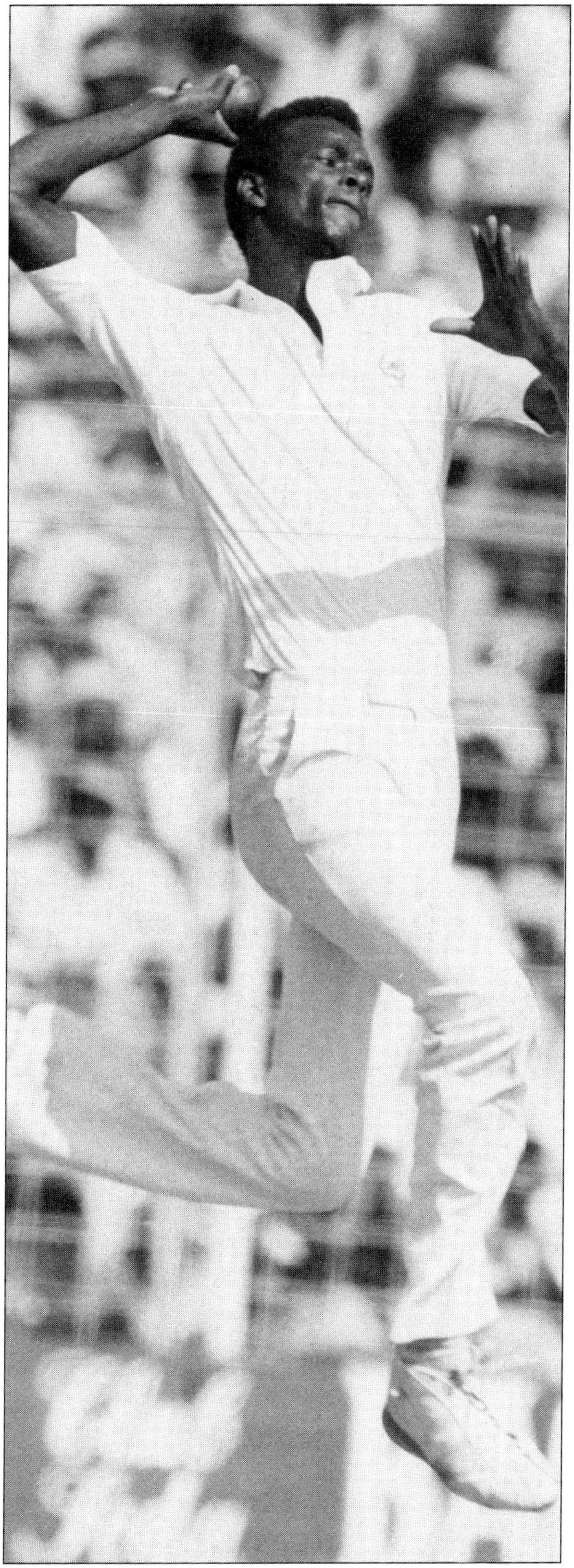

Winston Davis, an impressive return to the West Indian side. (Adrian Murrell)

order, the tourists reached a commendable score and Cairns and Stirling bowled them to a 43-run lead. Rain delayed the start on the last day and the New Zealanders were bowled out on the stroke of tea which left the home side to make 225 in two hours.

Fifth One-Day International
WEST INDIES *v.* NEW ZEALAND

A partnership of 184 in 33 overs between Gomes and Haynes established a winning position for West Indies. Haynes

Windward Islands 1985
First Class Matches

BATTING	*v.* Jamaica (Kingston) 31 Jan.–3 Feb. 1985		*v.* Trinidad and Tobago (Port of Spain) 8–10 February 1985		*v.* Guyana (St Vincent) 15–18 February 1985		*v.* Barbados (Roseau) 22–25 February 1985		*v.* Leeward Islands (Nevis) 1–4 March 1985		*M*	*Inns*	*NOs*	*Runs*	*H/S*	*Av*
L.C. Sebastien	28	15	12	31*	57	—	6	—	33	60*	5	8	2	242	60*	40.33
L.D. John	137	1	50	43	1	—	30	—	4	0	5	8	—	266	137	33.25
I. Cadette	56	0	0	2	5	—	7	—	34	—	5	7	—	104	56	14.85
L.A. Lewis	0	—	37	6	24	—	76	—	13	5	5	7	—	161	76	23.00
F.X. Maurice	17	21*	7	5							2	4	1	50	21*	16.66
J.D. Charles	6	5*	49	21	11	—	29	—	1	34	5	8	1	156	49	22.28
N. Phillip	22	—	81	4	80	—	0	—	3	—	5	6	—	190	81	31.66
D.J. Collymore	24	—	1	2							2	3	—	27	24	9.00
S.J. Hinds	72	—	3	6	2	—	5	—	14	—	5	6	—	102	72	17.00
T.Z. Kentish	29*	—	0*	20	40	—	14	—	4	—	5	6	2	107	40	26.75
J.T. Etienne	0	—	0	0							2	3	—	0	0	0.00
A.D. Texeira					31	—	6	—	36	6	3	4	—	79	36	19.75
W. Thomas					9*	—	0*	—	14*	—	3	3	3	23	14*	—
S.A.E. Murphy					3	—					1	1	—	3	3	3.00
R. Marshall							7	—	14	1*	2	3	1	22	14	11.00
Byes	3	6	5		9		5			8						
Leg-byes	8	1	4	2	3		6		2	1						
Wides					1				1							
No-balls	3	3	10	4	5		8		4	1						
Total	405	52	259	146	281		199		177	116						
Wickets	10	3	10	10	10		10		10	4						
Result	W		L		D		Ab.		D							
Points	16		5		4		4		4							

Catches 9 – I. Cadette (ct 7/st 2)
5 – J.D. Charles
4 – L.C. Sebastien
3 – N. Phillip, D.J. Collymore and T.Z. Kentish
2 – L.D. John
1 – L.A. Lewis, F.X. Maurice, S.J. Hinds, J.T. Etienne, A.D. Texeira, W. Thomas and sub

BOWLING	N. Phillip	D.J. Collymore	L.C. Sebastien	T.Z. Kentish	J.T. Etienne	S.J. Hinds	S.A.E. Murphy	W. Thomas	J.D. Charles
v. Jamaica (Kingston)	14–3–31–3	14–1–50–2	13.1–1–49–4						
31 January–3 February	28–5–90–6	26.2–4–81–2	4–1–28–0	7–3–8–0	36–12–69–2	12–1–36–0			
v. Trinidad and Tobago	13–1–35–1	16.5–4–45–3		13–4–20–4	1–0–7–0	0.1–0–0–1			
(Port of Spain) 8–10 February	21–3–87–1	0–0–1–0	1–0–9–0	33–5–88–5	9–2–40–0	12–1–61–0			
v. Guyana (St Vincent)	21–3–74–2		6–1–10–0	35–11–55–1		42–16–83–2	23–5–76–2	19.5–0–73–3	6–1–14–0
15–18 February			12–2–43–0	6–2–12–0		3–0–9–0	14–3–40–1	22–3–59–2	
v. Barbados (Roseau)	2–0–13–0			19–8–34–3		7–2–8–0		4–0–14–1	
22–25 February									
v. Leeward Islands (Nevis)	9.2–0–27–0			45–13–98–5		37–11–99–2		8–1–32–0	
1–4 March	16–1–37–1			9–0–27–2		4–1–7–0		12–2–44–2	
	124.2–16–394–14 *av.* 28.14	57.1–9–177–7 *av.* 25.28	36.1–5–139–4 *av.* 34.75	167–46–342–20 *av.* 17.10	46–14–116–2 *av.* 58.00	117.1–32–303–5 *av.* 60.60	37–8–116–3 *av.* 38.66	65.5–6–222–8 *av.* 27.75	6–1–14–0 —

FIFTH ONE-DAY INTERNATIONAL – WEST INDIES *v.* NEW ZEALAND
23 April 1985 at Bridgetown

WEST INDIES			
	D.L. Haynes	c Coney, b Chatfield	116
	R.B. Richardson	c Coney, b Chatfield	21
	H.A. Gomes	c J.J. Crowe, b Cairns	78
	I.V.A. Richards†	not out	33
	A.L. Logie	not out	11
	P.J. Dujon*		
	R.A. Harper		
	E.A.E. Baptiste		
	M.A. Holding		
	J. Garner		
	W.W. Davis		
	Extras	lb 5, w 1	6
	(49 overs)	(for 3 wickets)	265

	O	M	R	W
Troup	10	—	57	—
Hadlee	9	1	26	—
Chatfield	10	1	61	2
Cairns	10	1	63	1
Coney	10	—	53	—

FALL OF WICKETS
1- 31, 2- 215, 3- 223

NEW ZEALAND			
	J.G. Wright	c Richards, b Garner	22
	G.P. Howarth†	c Dujon, b Davis	6
	K.R. Rutherford	c Holding, b Harper	18
	M.D. Crowe	c Logie, b Davis	6
	J.V. Coney	b Baptiste	5
	J.J. Crowe	c Logie, b Harper	30
	B.L. Cairns	c Logie, b Harper	5
	I.D.S. Smith*	c Garner, b Davis	37
	R.J. Hadlee	not out	16
	G.B. Troup	not out	0
	E.J. Chatfield		
	Extras	b 2, lb 2, w 4	8
	(49 overs)	(for 8 wickets)	153

	O	M	R	W
Garner	6	2	10	1
Davis	8	—	32	3
Baptiste	7	1	11	1
Holding	6	1	10	—
Harper	10	3	38	3
Richards	8	—	31	—
Gomes	3	1	16	—
Logie	1	—	1	—

FALL OF WICKETS
1- 30, 2- 30, 3- 36, 4- 47, 5- 84, 6- 91, 7- 104, 8- 152

West Indies won by 112 runs

continued his remarkable sequence in one-day internationals by hitting two sixes and eight fours in his eighth century in this form of cricket.

New Zealand were never in contention and when Wright, Howarth and Martin Crowe were dismissed in the eleventh and twelfth overs West Indies 5–0 win in the series became inevitable.

Third Test Match
WEST INDIES *v.* NEW ZEALAND

Manager Wes Hall and skipper Viv Richards had called for grassier wickets and the Bridgetown groundsman gave them their wish. As if the assistance of the groundsman were insufficient, the gods of cricket aided the West Indians with overnight and early morning rain which delayed the start until after lunch and left the well grassed pitch sweating. Richards won the toss, asked New Zealand to bat and within three overs they were 1 for 3. More rain after tea ended play for the day when New Zealand were 18 for 3.

There was an hour and a quarter lost at the beginning of the second day, but there was no respite for New Zealand who were all out 38 minutes before tea for the lowest Test score made at Kensington Oval. Hadlee dismissed Greenidge before the break and Haynes, Richardson and Gomes were out before the close, but after Stirling had dismissed night-watchman Davis the next morning and Logie and Dujon had fallen cheaply, Richards, escaping a half-chance on the first ball of the day, and Marshall added 83 for the eighth wicket. Richards hit his nineteenth Test hundred and the game passed out of New Zealand's reach.

The day was cut short by rain and New Zealand finished on 18 for 0. After the rest day, Marshall, bowling round the wicket, scythed through the New Zealand top order. Wright batted spiritedly and Coney gave a defiant display which took his side into the last day and helped to avoid an innings defeat. Smith, forced to retire hurt after being hit on the arm, slashed a boundary on the last morning which ensured that West Indies would have to bat again, but Marshall caught and bowled him to become the first West Indian to take ten wickets in a Test against New Zealand.

Greenidge and Haynes quickly scored the required runs and West Indies had beaten New Zealand for the first time in 16 years.

L.A. Lewis	R. Marshall	*Byes*	*Leg-byes*	*Wides*	*No-balls*	*Total*	*Wkts*
		4	1	2	6	135	10
		2	6	10		320	10
		1	4		9	112	10
		2	7		12	295	6
		7	3	1	12	395	10
5–0–19–0		2	2		10	186	4
	10–4–13–1		1		3	83	5
	11–3–24–0	4	8	1	1	292	8
		1	3	2		119	6
5–0– 19–0 —	21–7– 37–1 *av.* 37.00						

Fourth Test Match
WEST INDIES *v.* NEW ZEALAND

The largest crowd at Sabina Park since its renovations in 1981 saw West Indies, who had Walsh replacing the injured

THIRD TEST MATCH – WEST INDIES *v.* NEW ZEALAND
26, 27, 28 and 30 April, 1 May at Kensington Oval, Bridgetown

NEW ZEALAND

	FIRST INNINGS		SECOND INNINGS	
G.P. Howarth†	c Greenidge, b Garner	1	(2) c Haynes, b Marshall	5
J.G. Wright	c Dujon, b Marshall	0	(1) c Richardson, b Davis	64
K.R. Rutherford	c Richards, b Marshall	0	c Holding, b Marshall	2
M.D. Crowe	hit wkt, b Holding	14	c Dujon, b Marshall	2
J.J. Crowe	c Dujon, b Davis	21	b Davis	4
J.V. Coney	c Richardson b Marshall	12	c Logie, b Marshall	83
I.D.S. Smith*	c Greenidge, b Marshall	2	c and b Marshall	26
R.J. Hadlee	c Logie, b Davis	29	c Greenidge, b Davis	3
D.A. Stirling	c Logie, b Davis	6	b Marshall	3
S.L. Boock	c Dujon, b Garner	1	c Haynes, b Marshall	22
E.J. Chatfield	not out	0	not out	4
Extras	nb	8	b 8, lb 1, w 2, nb 19	30
		94		248

	O	M	R	W	O	M	R	W
Marshall	15	3	40	4	25.3	6	80	7
Garner	15	9	14	2	19	5	56	—
Holding	7	4	12	1	1	—	2	—
Davis	10.4	4	28	3	18	—	66	3
Richards					13	3	25	—
Gomes					4	—	10	—

FALL OF WICKETS
1- 1, 2- 1, 3- 1, 4- 18, 5- 37, 6- 44, 7- 80, 8- 87, 9- 90
1- 26, 2- 35, 3- 45, 4- 60, 5- 108, 6- 141, 7- 149, 8- 226, 9- 235

WEST INDIES

	FIRST INNINGS		SECOND INNINGS	
C.G. Greenidge	c J. Crowe, b Hadlee	2	not out	4
D.L. Haynes	c Smith, b Hadlee	62	not out	5
R.B. Richardson	lbw, b M. Crowe	22		
H.A. Gomes	c J. Crowe, b M. Crowe	0		
W.W. Davis	c Smith, b Stirling	16		
I.V.A. Richards†	c M. Crowe, b Boock	105		
A.L. Logie	c J. Crowe, b Chatfield	7		
P.J. Dujon*	b Hadlee	3		
M.D. Marshall	c J. Crowe, b Chatfield	63		
J. Garner	not out	37		
M.A. Holding	c Smith, b Stirling	1		
Extras	b 2, lb 8, w 6, nb 2	18	w 1	1
		336	(for no wkt)	10

	O	M	R	W	O	M	R	W
Hadlee	26	5	86	3				
Chatfield	28	10	57	2				
Stirling	14.1	—	82	2				
M.D. Crowe	10	2	25	2				
Boock	15	1	76	1	1	1	0	—
Rutherford					0.4	—	10	—

FALL OF WICKETS
1- 12, 2- 91, 3- 91, 4- 95, 5- 142, 6- 161, 7- 174, 8- 257, 9- 327

Umpires: D.M. Archer and L.H. Barker

West Indies won by 10 wickets

LEFT: *Wes Hall, the West Indian manager, called for more grass on the wickets and was rewarded in Bridgetown and Kingston.* RIGHT: *Viv Richards. When he was named as captain of West Indies a day's holiday was called in Antigua. He remains the most dominant batsman in world cricket, 105 in the third Test match. (Adrian Murrell)*

FOURTH TEST MATCH – WEST INDIES *v.* NEW ZEALAND
4, 5, 6, 8 and 9 May, 1985 at Sabina Park, Kingston

WEST INDIES

	FIRST INNINGS		SECOND INNINGS	
C.G. Greenidge	c J. Crowe, b M. Crowe	46	not out	33
D.L. Haynes	c J. Crowe, b M. Crowe	76	not out	24
R.B. Richardson	c M. Crowe, b Coney	30		
H.A. Gomes	c Wright, b Hadlee	45		
I.V.A. Richards†	lbw, b Hadlee	23		
A.L. Logie	c M. Crowe, b Hadlee	0		
P.J. Dujon*	c Bracewell, b Troup	70		
M.D. Marshall	lbw, b Bracewell	26		
W.W. Davis	c M. Crowe, b Troup	0		
J. Garner	c M. Crowe, b Hadlee	12		
C.A. Walsh	not out	12		
Extras	b 7, lb 9, w 1, nb 6	23	b 1, lb 1	2
		363	(for no wkt)	59

	O	M	R	W	O	M	R	W
Hadlee	28.4	11	53	4	5	1	15	—
Troup	17	1	87	2	3	—	13	—
Chatfield	26	5	85	—	2	—	10	—
M.D. Crowe	10	2	30	1				
Bracewell	21	5	54	1	4	—	14	—
Coney	14	3	38	2				
Smith					3	1	5	—

FALL OF WICKETS
1- 82, 2- 144, 3- 164, 4- 207, 5- 207, 6- 273, 7- 311, 8- 311, 9- 339

Umpires: J.G. Gayle and D.M. Archer

West Indies won by 10 wickets

NEW ZEALAND

	FIRST INNINGS		SECOND INNINGS	
J.G. Wright	b Davis	53	c Dujon, b Garner	10
G.P. Howarth†	c Gomes, b Marshall	5	c Garner, b Walsh	84
J.J. Crowe	c Richardson, b Garner	2	c Marshall, b Richards	112
M.D. Crowe	c Davis, b Walsh	6	c Dujon, b Walsh	1
J.V. Coney	retired hurt	4	absent injured	—
K.R. Rutherford	c Dujon, b Marshall	1	(5) lbw, b Marshall	5
I.D.S. Smith*	b Garner	0	(6) b Marshall	9
R.J. Hadlee	c Dujon, b Davis	18	(7) c Walsh, b Marshall	14
J.G. Bracewell	not out	25	(8) c Gomes, b Marshall	27
G.B. Troup	c Marshall, b Davis	0	(9) c Richardson, b Garner	2
E.J. Chatfield	b Davis	2	(10) not out	0
Extras	b 4, lb 1, w 2, nb 15	22	b 7, lb 4, nb 8	19
		138		283

	O	M	R	W	O	M	R	W
Marshall	17	3	47	2	28.4	8	66	4
Garner	16	—	37	2	19	8	41	2
Davis	13.5	5	19	4	21	1	75	—
Walsh	9	1	30	1	16	4	45	2
Richards					14	2	34	1
Gomes					3	—	11	—
Richardson					1	1	0	—

FALL OF WICKETS
1- 11, 2- 15, 3- 37, 4- 65, 5- 68, 6- 106, 7- 113, 8- 122, 9- 138
1- 13, 2- 223, 3- 223, 4- 228, 5- 238, 6- 242, 7- 259, 8- 281, 9- 283

West Indies *v.* New Zealand – Test Match Averages

WEST INDIES BATTING

	M	Inns	NOs	Runs	HS	Av	100s	50s
R.B. Richardson	4	6		378	185	63.00	1	2
I.V.A. Richards	4	6	1	310	105	62.00	1	2
D.L. Haynes	4	8	2	344	90	57.33		4
C.G. Greenidge	4	7	2	264	100	52.80	1	1
J. Garner	4	3	2	49	37*	49.00		
A.L. Logie	4	6	1	166	52	33.20		1
P.J. Dujon	4	6	1	156	70	31.20		2
H.A. Gomes	4	6		158	53	26.33		1
M.D. Marshall	4	4		90	63	22.50		1
W.W. Davis	2	2		16	16	8.00		
M.A. Holding	3	3		21	12	7.00		

Played in one Test: R.A. Harper 0 and 11*; C.G. Butts 9; C.A. Walsh 12*

WEST INDIES BOWLING

	Overs	Mds	Runs	Wkts	Av	Best	5/inn	10/m
M.D. Marshall	170.1	30	486	27	18.00	7/80	1	1
W.W. Davis	63.3	10	188	10	18.80	4/19		
M.A. Holding	82	24	218	9	24.22	4/79		
C.A. Walsh	25	5	75	3	25.00	2/45		
R.A. Harper	36	18	52	2	26.00	2/33		
J. Garner	136.1	37	302	10	30.20	2/14		
I.V.A. Richards	39	7	89	1	89.00	1/34		
H.A. Gomes	18	3	44	0	—			

Also bowled: C.G. Butts 47–12–113–0; R.B. Richardson 2–2–0–0; A.L. Logie 1–1–0–0

WEST INDIES CATCHES
11–P.J. Dujon; 5–R.B. Richardson and D.L. Haynes; 4–A.L. Logie; 3–C.G. Greenidge, J. Garner and M.D. Marshall; 2–I.V.A. Richards, H.A. Gomes, R.A. Harper and subs (P.V. Simmonds); 1–W.W. Davis, M.A. Holding and C.A. Walsh

NEW ZEALAND BATTING

	M	Inns	NOs	Runs	HS	Av	100s	50s
J.V. Coney	4	6	1	241	83	48.20		2
J.J. Crowe	4	7		252	112	36.00	1	1
M.D. Crowe	4	7		216	188	30.85	1	
J.G. Wright	4	7		213	64	30.42		2
R.J. Hadlee	4	7	1	137	39*	22.83		
G.P. Howarth	4	7		158	84	22.57		1
I.D.S. Smith	4	7	1	111	53	18.50		1
E.J. Chatfield	4	6	5	13	4*	13.00		
S.L. Boock	3	4		26	22	6.50		
B.L. Cairns	2	2		11	8	5.50		
K.R. Rutherford	4	7		12	5	1.71		

Played in one Test: G.B. Troup 0 and 2; J.G. Bracewell 25* and 27; D.A. Stirling 6 and 3

NEW ZEALAND BOWLING

	Overs	Mds	Runs	Wkts	Av	Best	5/inn	10/m
M.D. Crowe	20	4	55	3	18.33	2/25		
R.J. Hadlee	143	33	409	15	27.26	4/53		
J.V. Coney	51	11	137	5	27.40	2/38		
E.J. Chatfield	152	36	441	13	33.92	6/74	1	1
K.R. Rutherford	9.4	1	48	1	48.00	1/38		
G.B. Troup	20	1	100	2	50.00	2/87		
B.L. Cairns	99	14	316	5	63.20	2/47		
J.G. Bracewell	25	5	68	1	68.00	1/54		
S.L. Boock	110	25	338	2	169.00	1/47		
G.P. Howarth	9	5	17	0	—			

Also bowled: D.A. Stirling 14.1–0–82–2; J.G. Wright 3–1–2–0; I.D.S. Smith 3–1–5–0

NEW ZEALAND CATCHES
8–I.D.S. Smith (ct/st 1); 7–J.J. Crowe; 6–M.D. Crowe; 2–J.V. Coney, G.P. Howarth and subs; 1–J.G. Wright, K.R. Rutherford, E.J. Chatfield and J.G. Bracewell

Holding, reach 273 for 6 on the opening day. Local favourite Jeff Dujon entertained the crowd on the second morning with some fine shots and the last four wickets produced 90 runs. New Zealand made a dreadful start in reply. Howarth was caught at cover, Jeff Crowe taken at slip and Martin Crowe mishooked to Walsh so that the visitors were 40 for 3 at tea.

New Zealand unhappiness continued. Coney broke a bone

New Zealanders in West Indies 1985

First Class Matches

BATTING	*v.* Shell Award XI (Kingston) 15–17 March 1985		*v.* West Indies U/23 (Basseterre) 22–24 March 1985		First Test Match (Port of Spain) 29 March–3 April 1985		Second Test Match (Georgetown) 6–11 April 1985		*v.* President's XI (Castries) 19–21 April 1985		Third Test Match (Bridgetown) 26 April–1 May 1985		Fourth Test Match (Kingston) 4–9 May 1985		*M*	*Inns*	*NOs*	*Runs*	*H/S*	*Av*
K.R. Rutherford	12	0	19	109*	0	0	4	—	51	53	0	2	1	5	7	13	1	256	109*	21.33
R.T. Hart	8	8	4	7					4	3					3	6	—	36	8	6.00
J.J. Crowe	67	14	4	0	64	27	22	—	3	14	21	4	2	112	7	13	—	354	112	27.23
M.D. Crowe	118	62			3	2	188	—			14	2	6	1	5	9	—	396	188	44.00
J.G. Wright	9	69	101	40	40	19	27	—	25	1	0	64	53	10	7	13	—	458	101	35.23
G.P. Howarth	0	4	8	6	45	14	4	—	0	10	1	5	5	84	7	13	—	186	84	14.30
J.G. Bracewell	0	10	1	—					50	0			25*	27	4	7	1	113	50	18.83
B.L. Cairns	21	10	11	—	8	—	3	—	52*	6					5	7	1	111	52*	18.50
D.A. Stirling	6	0	8*	—					2*	17	6	3			4	7	2	42	17	8.40
G.B. Troup	1*	8*							—	0*			0	2	3	5	3	11	8*	5.50
S.L. Boock	6	3	0	—	3	—	0	—	—	7	1	22			6	8	—	42	22	5.25
J.V. Coney			1	58*	25	44	73	—	99	48	12	83	4*	—	6	10	2	447	99	55.87
R.J. Hadlee					18	39*	16	—			29	3	18	14	4	7	1	137	39*	22.83
I.D.S. Smith					10	11*	53	—			2	26	0	9	4	7	1	111	53	18.50
E.J. Chatfield			4	—	4*	—	3*	—			0*	4*	2	0*	5	7	5	17	4*	8.50
Byes	1	3		10	12	17	12		1	8		8	4	7						
Leg-byes	12	3	3	6	11	6	2		1	7		1	1	4						
Wides							6		1			2	2							
No-balls	6	5	7	2	19	8	27		18	7	8	19	15	8						
Total	267	199	171	238	262	187	440		307	181	94	248	138	283						
Wickets	10	10	10	4	10	6	10		7	10	10	10	9†	9						
Result	D		D		D		D		D		L		L							

Catches 10 – J.J. Crowe; 8 – I.D. Smith (ct 7/st 1); 7 – M.D. Crowe; 4 – G.P. Howarth; 3 – K.R. Rutherford, J.V. Coney, J.G. Bracewell and subs; 2 – R.T. Hart and E.J. Chatfield; 1 – J.G. Wright, D.A. Stirling, G.B. Troup and S.L. Boock

† J.V. Coney retired hurt, absent hurt

BOWLING	D.A. Stirling	G.B. Troup	B.L. Cairns	S.L. Boock	J.G. Bracewell	R.J. Hadlee	E.J. Chatfield	J.V. Coney	G.P. Howarth
v. Shell Award XI (Kingston) 15–17 March	17–2–92–3	15–3–41–2 2–0–12–0	16–1–48–0 1–0–1–1	26–6–63–2	27–8–58–3				
v. West Indies U/23 (Basseterre) 22–24 March	16–4–68–4		18–4–39–2	23.1–8–35–1	25–5–59–2		27–9–52–1	1–0–6–0	
First Test Match (Port of Spain) 29 March–3 April			26–3–93–0 19–2–70–2	19–5–47–1 14–4–57–0		24.3–6–82–4 17–2–58–0	28–11–51–4 22–4–73–6	9–3–17–1	
Second Test Match (Georgetown) 6–11 April			36–5–106–1 18–4–47–2	43–11–106–0 18–3–52–0		25.5–5–83–2 16–3–32–2	30–3–122–1 16–3–43–0	18–2–62–1 10–3–20–1	4–1–15–0 5–4–2–0
v. President's XI (Castries) 19–21 April	13–1–66–4	14–4–58–1 5–0–39–0	15.5–3–45–3 11–0–47–3	12–3–34–0 6–0–22–1	11–1–38–1				
Third Test Match (Bridgetown) 26 April–1 May	14.1–0–82–2			15–1–76–1 1–1–0–0		26–5–86–3	28–10–57–2		
Fourth Test Match (Kingston) 4–9 May		17–1–87–2 3–0–13–0			21–5–54–1 4–0–14–0	28.4–11–53–4 5–1–15–0	26–5–85–0 2–0–10–0	14–3–38–2	
	60.1–8– 308–13 *av.* 23.69	56–8– 250–5 *av.* 50.00	160.1–22– 496–14 *av.* 35.42	177.1–42– 492–6 *av.* 82.00	88–19– 223–7 *av.* 31.85	143–33– 409–15 *av.* 27.26	179–45– 493–14 *av.* 35.21	52–11– 143–5 *av.* 28.60	9–5– 17–0 —

a I.D.S. Smith 3–1–5–0

in his arm when struck by a ball from Joel Garner, and Coney was later to complain about the intimidatory tactics of the West Indian fast bowlers who, he asserted, were aiming to injure. With Coney retired hurt, New Zealand were all out before lunch on the third day for 138 and forced to follow on.

Wright was out at 13 when he skied a catch to Dujon as he attempted to hook, but Jeff Crowe attacked the bowling and hit one massive six off Richards as well as four fours as he reached his fifty in ninety minutes. Howarth gave solid support and by the close New Zealand were 211 for 1 with Jeff Crowe on 108 not out, having hit six more fours and batted for 230 minutes.

They were out in successive overs on the fourth morning, their stand having realised 210, a record for New Zealand in Test cricket. A collapse followed and the visitors were 245 for 6 at lunch with Coney unable to bat. There was no recovery and West Indies moved to an easy victory and another series win.

K.R. Rutherford	J.G. Wright	M.D. Crowe	*Byes*	*Leg-byes*	*Wides*	*No-balls*	*Total*	*Wkts*
			8	6	7	5	316	10
				3		1	16	1
			14	12	5	3	285	10
			1	16		4	307	10
				3		7	261	8
			1	16	1	3	511	6
9–1–38–1	3–1–2–0		7	24	1	2	268	6
			14	9	3	5	264	10
				6	2	1	114	4
		10–2–25–2	2	8	6	2	336	10
0.4–0–10–0					1		10	0
		10–2–30–1	7	9	1	6	363	10
			1	1			59	0a
9.4–1–48–1 *av.* 48.00	3–1–2–0 —	20–4–55–3 *av.* 18.33						

First Class Averages

BATTING	M	Inns	NOs	Runs	HS	Av	100s	50s
R. Seeram	5	8	3	314	100*	62.80	1	2
I.V.A. Richards	4	6	1	310	105	62.00	1	2
D.L. Haynes	4	8	2	344	90	57.33		4
C.A. Best	7	13	3	543	147	54.30	2	2
R.B. Richardson	5	7		379	185	54.14	1	2
M.C. Worrell	5	8	4	215	105	53.75	1	1
C.G. Greenidge	4	7	2	264	100	52.80	1	1
M.C. Neita	3	5	1	187	75*	46.75		1
A.L. Kelly	6	12		535	132	44.58	1	4
K.C. Williams	6	9	1	346	91	43.25		3
C.A. Davidson	3	5		214	98	42.80		1
A.B. Williams	6	9		383	102	42.55	1	3
L.C. Sebastien	5	8	2	242	60*	40.33		2
P.V. Simmonds	8	12		474	118	39.50	1	4
T. Mohammed	7	12	1	426	80	38.72		4
W.W. Lewis	5	9		341	127	37.88	1	1
G. Powell	4	7		261	110	37.28	1	1
E.E. Lewis	6	11	1	369	103	36.90	1	1
M.A. Harper	4	7	1	215	81	35.83		1
L.D. John	5	8		266	137	33.25	1	1
A.L. Logie	4	6	1	166	52	33.20		1
A.A. Lyght	6	12	1	353	104	32.09	1	
S.R. Greaves	4	6		192	67	32.00		2
N. Phillip	5	6		190	81	31.66		2
C.L. Hooper	9	12		377	126	31.41	1	
P.J. Dujon	4	6	1	156	70	31.20		2
N. Johnson	3	5		156	98	31.20		1
A. Rajah	6	9		280	57	31.11		2
C.B. Lambert	6	12	2	309	104	30.90	1	1
L.L. Lawrence	6	11		321	93	29.18		2
E.A. Lewis	3	6	1	135	48	27.00		
T.Z. Kentish	5	6	2	107	40	26.75		
D.I. Kallicharran	6	9		239	88	26.55		1
H.A. Gomes	4	6		158	53	26.33		1
P. Moosai	6	9		235	110	26.11	1	
M.R. Pydanna	6	9	2	180	46	25.71		
N.C. Guishard	5	8	1	179	63	25.57		1
J. Adams	3	5	1	101	40	25.25		
D. Dixon	3	5		126	75	25.20		1
T.A. Hunte	6	10		247	69	24.70		3
R.L. Skeete	5	8		193	48	24.12		
L.A. Lewis	5	7		161	76	23.00		1
J.D. Charles	5	8	1	156	49	22.28		
R.M. Otto	6	12	1	238	110	21.63	1	
A.G. Daley	6	10	2	170	50*	21.25		1
A.F.D. Jackman	7	13		274	39	21.07		
R.S. Gabriel	5	7		144	60	20.57		1
S.I. Williams	5	9	2	135	31*	19.28		
O.W. Peters	5	9		164	72	18.22		1
A.S. Gilkes	3	6		106	40	17.66		
S.J. Hinds	5	6		102	72	17.00		1
R. Nanan	6	10		160	46	16.00		
D. Williams	8	12	2	159	49*	15.90		
T.A. Merrick	7	9	1	120	48*	15.00		
I. Cadette	5	7		104	56	14.85		1

(Qualification – 100 runs, average 10.00)

BOWLING	Overs	Mds	Runs	Wkts	Av	Best	5/inn	10/m
E.A.E. Baptiste	55	16	138	11	12.54	3/23		
G. Mahabir	283.2	51	708	42	16.85	6/62	1	
T.Z. Kentish	167	46	342	20	17.10	5/88	2	
M.D. Marshall	170.1	30	486	27	18.00	7/80	1	1
W.W. Davis	63.3	10	188	10	18.80	4/19		
R. Nanan	184.3	47	380	19	20.00	4/67		
W.W. Daniel	151.3	26	458	22	20.81	7/33	2	
T.A. Merrick	220.2	38	709	34	20.85	5/101	2	
A.H. Gray	240.2	39	771	36	21.41	6/78	3	1
C.G. Butts	479.2	126	991	45	22.02	7/90	4	1
C.L. Hooper	190.5	22	646	28	23.07	5/35	2	
E.T. Willett	157.2	44	306	13	23.53	4/46		
N.C. Guishard	187.5	44	403	17	23.70	5/49	1	
A.G. Daley	221.2	30	710	29	24.48	5/64	1	
R.O. Estwick	142	21	495	20	24.75	5/83	2	
N. Phillip	124.2	16	394	14	28.14	6/90	1	
J. Garner	136.1	37	302	10	30.20	2/14		
K.C. Williams	115.3	22	334	11	30.36	3/32		
G.E. Charles	134.1	13	458	14	32.71	7/105	1	
D.I. Kallicharran	221.3	42	572	16	35.75	5/45	1	

(Qualification – 10 wickets)

LEADING FIELDERS

29–D. Williams (ct 24/st 5); 16–M.C. Worrell (ct 15/st 1); 15–C.B. Lambert; 14–M.R. Pydanna (ct 11/st 3); 11–P.J. Dujon; 10–P.V. Simmonds and P.A. Francis (ct 8/st 2); 9–R.M. Otto, A. Rajah, S.I. Williams (ct 8/st 1) and I Cadette (ct 7/st 2); 8–C.L. Hooper, A.L. Kelly and C.A. Best

22 for 1.
Carlsberg
Carlsberg Lager
Probably the best lager in the world.

SECTION I

The English Season

The Britannic Assurance County Championship.
The Benson & Hedges Cup. The NatWest Trophy.
The John Player Special League. The Texaco Trophy.
The Australian tour. The Zimbabwe tour.
The Cornhill Test series – England *v.* Australia.
Form Charts for One-Day and First-Class matches.
Review of the Season by David Lemmon.
Book Reviews. Averages. *Women's Cricket* by Rachael Heyhoe-Flint.

Derbyshire v. *Lancashire at Chesterfield in May.*
(All Sport)

The success of the England side in India and the prospect of the return to Test cricket of Gooch, Emburey and the others banned for their involvement in the South African venture of 1982 had obliterated the memories of the West Indian torment of twelve months previously when the 1985 English season dawned. It was a time of optimism and joy for it was the year of the Ashes and there is nothing quite so stimulating as the contest between the game's oldest rivals.

There was an early season crisis when it was learned that several Australian players were contracted to play in South Africa later in the year. The full story of these events is told by Chris Harte in the South African section of this annual, but initially rumours and denials were strong and with the withdrawal of Rixon, Alderman and McCurdy from the Australian party as originally selected, it was considered in some quarters that the team finally to fly to England was in the nature of a second string side. Allan Border quickly dispelled such ideas. He emerged at the first press conference as a positive leader, strong and diplomatic in his dealings with the media and inspiring to his side both on and off the field. He insisted on discipline and courtesy and his inexperienced team responded eagerly. In the first few weeks of the season he set a tone that made possible a fine series played in the right spirit.

England's prelude to the season had not been without its traumas. Tavare was replaced as captain of Kent by Chris Cowdrey, a decision which to many seemed harsh. Tavare himself was deeply upset and for a time there was speculation that he would leave Kent. On the happier side Kent launched an appeal and plans for the building of a new stand and ground improvements at Canterbury, already one of the most beautiful in the country. They are a lively, friendly, hospitable county club and deserve a permanent place in the sun. In Yorkshire, an equally friendly county where they seem to treat visitors better than they treat each other, the Boycott saga continued and referendums were still being held on the eve of the season.

The season's first centurion. Julian Wyatt of Somerset in The Parks, 22 April. (Adrian Murrell)

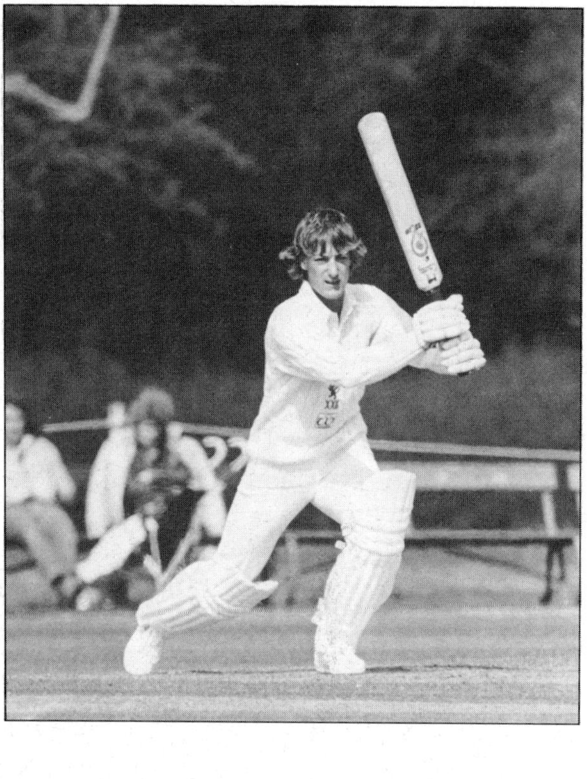

20, 22 and 23 April

at Cambridge

Essex 339 for 6 dec (G.A. Gooch 99, K.W.R. Fletcher 56 not out, K.R. Pont 55) and 327 for 4 dec (B.R. Hardie 112 not out, K.S. McEwan 110, G.A. Gooch 88)
Cambridge University 222 for 6 dec. (D.J. Fell 85, T.A. Cotterell 69 not out) and 69 for 2

Match drawn

at Oxford

Somerset 351 for 1 dec (J.G. Wyatt 145, P.M. Roebuck 123 not out, N.F.M. Popplewell 67 not out)
Oxford University 247 for 5 (J.D. Carr 115, G.J. Toogood 59)

Match drawn

A hailstorm followed by snow began the season at Oxford although on the Monday Julian Wyatt hit the season's first century and a career best as he and Peter Roebuck put on 245 for the first wicket. John Carr played finely for the university and he and Giles Toogood added 154 for the third wicket.

At Fenner's, Gooch began with 99 which brought sighs of pleasure all round, Hardie and McEwan added 158 in 115 minutes and David Fell made 85 on his first class debut. Cotterell hit a career best and Gooch hit seven sixes in a second innings flurry.

24, 25 and 26 April

at Lord's

Essex 162 (N.G. Cowans 6 for 68) and 258 for 5 (K.S. McEwan 63, K.R. Pont 62 not out)
M.C.C. 377 for 9 dec (M.C.J. Nicholas 121, M.D. Moxon 104, D.R. Pringle 4 for 70)

Match drawn

at Cambridge

Nottinghamshire 269 for 6 dec (M. Newell 74, D.W. Randall 74, A.M.G. Scott 5 for 68) and 251 for 3 dec (D.W. Randall 100, M. Newell 58, B.C. Broad 51)
Cambridge University 115 (K.E. Cooper 7 for 10) and 192 for 2 (D.J. Fell 109 not out)

Match drawn

at Oxford

Oxford University 282 (D.A. Thorne 98 not out, J.D. Carr 81, J.G. Thomas 4 for 47) and 109 for 4 (A.J.T. Miller 61)
Glamorgan 456 (Younis Ahmed 113, J.F. Steele 100, J.A. Hopkins 81)

Match drawn

The Champion County were mutilated by the pace of Norman Cowans on the opening day of the match at Lord's. The Middlesex bowler was wayward early on but returned to bring about Essex's fall from 97 for 2 to 167 all out. He had a spell of 5 for 8 in 35 balls. In reply, M.C.C. were encouraged by fluent innings from skipper Nicholas and Martyn Moxon, his first match at Lord's, who added 163 for the third wicket. Fletcher retired from the match with sinus trouble, but McEwan, Gooch, Prichard and Pont saved the match.

David Fell hit a century in his second first class match, but the outstanding performance at Fenner's was by Kevin Cooper who took 7 for 10 in 19 overs on a cold Thursday. Derek Randall then hit a century to rekindle hopes he might be remembered by the selectors.

At Oxford Carr was again in fine form and David Thorne was left unbeaten on a career best 98. Greg Thomas, an England contender, bowled well and John Steele hit his first century for Glamorgan for whom Steve Malone made his debut having previously played for Essex and Hampshire.

27, 28 and 29 April

at Chelmsford

Essex 212 (C.M. Old 6 for 68) and 293 for 6 dec (K.S. McEwan 69, A.W. Lilley 63, G.A. Gooch 61)
Warwickshire 238 (T.A. Lloyd 68, R.I.H.B. Dyer 53, N.A. Foster 4 for 73) and 178 (A.M. Ferreira 61, J.K. Lever 5 for 27, D.R. Pringle 4 for 65)

Essex won by 89 runs
Essex 22 pts, Warwickshire 6 pts

BELOW: *A fine beginning to the season for Norman Cowans, 6 for 68 for M.C.C.* v. *Essex, 24 April. Paul Prichard is the Essex batsman. (Adrian Murrell)*

RIGHT: *Kevin Cooper, 7 for 10 in 19 overs for Notts against Cambridge, 25 April. (Michael King)*

BELOW RIGHT: *Dickie Bird in chilly weather at Oxford as the English season begins in a smattering of snow. (Mark Leech)*

at Southampton

Kent 232 (M.R. Benson 61, A.P.E. Knott 55, T.M. Tremlett 5 for 66) and 344 for 2 dec (M.R. Benson 162, C.J. Tavare 102 not out, S.G. Hinks 65)
Hampshire 308 for 8 dec (R.A. Smith 88, V.P. Terry 69) and 267 for 3 (V.P. Terry 88, C.L. Smith 84)

Match drawn
Hampshire 7 pts, Kent 5 pts

at Old Trafford

Lancashire 237 (S.T. Jefferies 93, J. Abrahams 67, C.M. Wells 4 for 78)
Sussex 113 for 4 (A.P. Wells 55 not out)

Match drawn
Sussex 4 pts, Lancashire 3 pts

Mark Nicholas, captain of Hampshire. His early season form made him a strong candidate for an England place. (Sporting Pictures UK Ltd)

at Leicester

Leicestershire 170 and 45 for 0
Yorkshire 306 for 5 dec (K. Sharp 96, D.M. Moxon 60)

Match drawn
Yorkshire 8 pts, Leicestershire 3 pts

at Taunton

Somerset 312 for 8 dec (I.T. Botham 90) and 133 (I.T. Botham 50, P.M. Such 5 for 73)
Nottinghamshire 288 (R.T. Robinson 195, V.J. Marks 5 for 66, M.R. Davis 4 for 83) and 160 for 1 (B.C. Broad 56 not out, R.T. Robinson 54)

Nottinghamshire won by 9 wickets
Nottinghamshire 22 pts, Somerset 8 pts

at The Oval

Surrey 300 for 6 dec (A.R. Butcher 121, M.A. Lynch 85 not out) and 181 for 7 dec
Glamorgan 264 for 6 dec (Javed Miandad 125, R.C. Ontong 61) and 218 for 3 (J.A. Hopkins 90)

Glamorgan won by 7 wickets
Glamorgan 21 pts, Surrey 6 pts

27, 29 and 30 April

at Derby

Northamptonshire 240 for 7 dec (G. Cook 87, R.J. Finney 5 for 68) and 140 for 2 dec (G. Cook 69)
Derbyshire 0 for 0 dec and 281 (W.P. Fowler 79, K.J. Barnett 62, R.G. Williams 4 for 91)

Northamptonshire won by 99 runs
Northamptonshire 18 pts, Derbyshire 3 pts

at Lord's

Worcestershire 301 for 6 dec (R.N. Kapil Dev 100, D.B. d'Oliveira 73 not out) and 103
Middlesex 195 (W.N. Slack 72 not out, J.E. Emburey 56, P.J. Newport 5 for 57) and 211 for 2 (R.O. Butcher 80 not out, P.R. Downton 69)

Middlesex won by 8 wickets
Middlesex 19 pts, Worcestershire 8 pts

at Cambridge

Gloucestershire 265 for 2 dec (C.W.J. Athey 112 not out, P. Bainbridge 75 not out) and 114 for 3 dec (P.W. Romaines 60 not out)
Cambridge University 88 for 6 dec (J.W. Lloyds 4 for 24) and 51 for 6

Match drawn

In the first round of matches in the Britannic Assurance County Championship, Essex showed their intention of defending their title fiercely when they beat Warwickshire in positive fashion at Chelmsford. Like all matches it was played in bitterly cold weather and Essex, put in to bat, were 97 for 6 before they were roused by Lilley, Pont, East and Foster. Andy Lloyd, returning to the county scene after his injury in the Test match against West Indies twelve months earlier, and their highly promising Robin Dyer began Warwickshire's reply with a stand of 119, but the innings then subsided to Foster and Lever. Gooch, benefitting from a dropped catch at the wicket in the first over, lashed Essex into the lead and on the last morning McEwan and Lilley hit well so that Gooch was able to declare and ask the visitors to make 268 in 74 overs. They never looked like escaping defeat. Dyer fell in the first over and good bowling and rash shots ended the Warwickshire challenge, only Ferreira's lusty blows salvaging some pride.

Notts, thwarted of the title on the last afternoon of 1984, gave Essex and others indication that they too would be challenging in 1985. Ian Botham hit five sixes on the opening day and took his side to maximum points. The visitors could not match this in spite of a splendid century by Tim

Mike Garnham is caught and bowled by Simon Dennis, Leicestershire v Yorkshire, 27 April. Dennis' season was to be ruined by injury. (David Munden)

Robinson, a very fine player with the wisdom acquired in India behind him. Somerset, however, collapsed to Such and Cooper when they batted again and only avoided humiliation through another aggressive knock from Botham who was suffering from a calf injury and could not bowl. Needing 160 to win, Notts were led by Broad and Robinson who opened with 98. Randall joined Broad to complete the victory.

Another side mentioned as likely champions, Middlesex, reversed fortune and gained a fine win over Worcestershire. Kapil Dev hit 100 off 76 balls and lifted his side from 96 for 5 to maximum batting points. Although Wilf Slack carried his bat, Phil Newport bowled the visitors to a first innings lead of 106, but their strong position was nullified when they collapsed against Williams, Cowans and Emburey. In the absence of Barlow, Downton opened with Slack and the pair put on 81 for the first wicket. Gatting fell to Radford at 96, but Roland Butcher inspired a splendid victory as he hit 80 off 62 balls in 63 minutes to see his side home with 19 overs to spare.

The game at Leicester was ruined by rain and although Yorkshire could take comfort in the form of Moxon and Sharp, they were distressed by an injury to Simon Denis. The match at Old Trafford was also marred by rain, there was no play on the last day, but Steve Jefferies hit a career best 93.

Also badly hit by rain was the match at Derby, but the home side forfeited their first innings in order to force a result. Roger Finney had five wickets on the Saturday, including a spell of 3 for 4 and was awarded his county cap. Asked to make a rather ungenerous 381 in 105 overs, Derbyshire battled bravely after early lapses, but eventually they succumbed to the off-spin of Williams.

Glamorgan batted quite magnificently to force a win at The Oval. Allan Butcher scored the first championship hundred of the season on the opening day and Javed responded on the Sunday when Ontong declared 36 runs behind. Pocock declared in turn and set Glamorgan to make 218 in 42 overs. Hopkins and Alan Lewis Jones gave them a sparkling start with a stand of 96. Hopkins and Holmes continued the charge until Hopkins mis-hit to leg at 180, but

ABOVE: *David Lawrence, Gloucestershire, the most improved fast bowler in England and one of the main reasons for the transformation of cricket in Gloucestershire. (Adrian Murrell)*

BELOW LEFT: *Kapil Dev hits out during his innings of 100 off 76 balls for Worcestershire against Middlesex. (Adrian Murrell)*

BELOW: *David Smith squats and ponders as his side collapse around him in the second innings, Worcestershire and Middlesex at Lord's, 29 April. (Adrian Murrell)*

Alec Stewart of Surrey, career best 158 v *Kent at Canterbury, 2 May. (George Herringshaw)*

by then Glamorgan were cruising to victory and although Holmes left at 201, it came with 2 overs to spare.

Kent lost their last 9 wickets for 126 runs on the Saturday to confirm general belief that Hampshire would be strong challengers for the championship. Hampshire duly moved to a substantial lead the next day with Robin Smith giving evidence of why such high expectations are held of his ability. Another batsman with Test ambitions, Mark Benson responded with a career best 162. He and Hinks put on 142 for the first wicket and he and Chris Tavare added 177 for the second. Tavare reached his hundred with three sixes in four balls off Cowley and his 102 took only 117 minutes. Benson hit a six and 19 fours. Hampshire were asked to make 269 in 51 overs. Chris Smith and Paul Terry began with 167 in 37 overs. 141 were needed off the last 20 overs and 14 off Dilley's final over. Mark Nicholas needed to hit the last ball for 4, but only 2 were managed and a magnificent game was drawn.

1, 2 and 3 May

at Bristol

Lancashire 318 (P.J.W. Allott 78 not out, S.T. Jefferies 57, M. Watkinson 57, J. Stanworth 50 not out, D.V. Lawrence 5 for 79) and 165 (G.E. Sainsbury 5 for 44, D.V. Lawrence 4 for 70)
Gloucestershire 189 (P.J.W. Allott 4 for 44) and 220 (P. Bainbridge 67, S.T. Jefferies 4 for 64)

Lancashire won by 74 runs
Lancashire 24 pts, Gloucestershire 5 pts

at Canterbury

Kent 336 (C.S. Cowdrey 159, S.G. Hinks 92, D.J. Thomas 5 for 51) and 282 for 8 dec (D.G. Aslett 111, C.S. Cowdrey 95)
Surrey 445 for 9 dec (A.J. Stewart 158, M.A. Lynch 115, D.B. Pauline 56 not out, G.R. Dilley 5 for 97)

Match drawn
Surrey 8 pts, Kent 7 pts

at Trent Bridge

Essex 273 (P.J. Prichard 70, G.A. Gooch 67, C.E.B. Rice 4 for 24) and 297 for 5 dec (G.A. Gooch 202)
Nottinghamshire 227 (C.E.B. Rice 108 not out, N.A. Foster 5 for 83) and 302 for 7 (D.W. Randall 117, P. Johnson 84, J.D. Birch 68 not out)

Match drawn
Essex 7 pts, Nottinghamshire 6 pts

at Taunton

Glamorgan 387 for 7 dec (G.C. Holmes 88, Javed Miandad 85, R.C. Ontong 64, Younis Ahmed 59) and 43 for 1
Somerset 237 (I.T. Botham 112) and 191 (N.F.M. Popplewell 81)

Glamorgan won by 9 wickets
Glamorgan 24 pts, Somerset 5 pts

at Cambridge

Middlesex 369 for 4 dec (W.N. Slack 81, M.W. Gatting 80, R.O. Butcher 56, P.R. Downton 55, C.T. Radley 54 not out) and 226 for 6 dec (J.F. Sykes 126, N.F. Williams 67)
Cambridge University 231 (C.R. Andrew 66, N.F. Cowans 5 for 37, A.R.C. Fraser 4 for 48) and 0 for 0

Match drawn

at Oxford

Leicestershire 330 (M.A. Garnham 100, I.P. Butcher 95, P. Willey 57, J.D. Carr 4 for 65, J.D. Quinlan 4 for 76)
Oxford University 24 (G.P. Parsons 6 for 11) and 231

Leicestershire won by an innings and 65 runs

Glamorgan moved to the top of the embryo Britannic Assurance County Championship with their second win in as many matches. They recovered from the loss of both openers for 26 to an impressive 387 for 7 mainly because of an exciting third wicket stand of 183 between the rapidly improving Holmes and Javed. Roebuck was bowled by Thomas before the close, and on the second day Somerset slumped to 89 for 5. Botham then hit a hundred off 76 balls. There were 8 sixes and 7 fours in his innings. He failed to save Somerset from the follow-on however and the visitors ran to a comfortable win early on the third day.

Lancashire, who had had to wait until August for a Championship win in 1984, revived heroically to beat Gloucestershire at Bristol. They were 94 for 6 before Watkinson and Jefferies rallied them with a stand of 69, but it was the last wicket stand of 115 between Allott and John Stanworth who hit a maiden first-class fifty that lifted them to maximum points in spectacular fashion. Allott's career best came off 72 deliveries. Allott dismissed Stovold third ball and he and Jefferies bowled Lancashire to a lead of 129 so that even Lancashire's second innings collapse to the pace of Lawrence and the late swing of Sainsbury could not loosen their grip on the game. Phil Bainbridge who had cracked a cheekbone on the second day threatened to thwart Lancashire with the aid of a stubborn middle order, but the visitors won with 13 overs to spare.

At Canterbury there was a run feast. The match began disastrously for Kent with Benson lbw to the first ball of the match, Tavare playing on at 11 and Aslett lbw to Thomas at 16. Cowdrey and Hinks dominated the rest of the day adding 173 in 52 overs. The stand was broken when Jesty took his first wicket for his new county, that of Hinks who played quite splendidly. Chris Cowdrey reached a career best 159 with 2 sixes and 17 fours, an aggressive chanceless innings. The next day was Surrey's turn. They were 41 for 4, but Alec Stewart and Monty Lynch added 252 in 56 overs. Stewart's career best included 3 sixes and 24 fours. Lynch hit 19 fours. Kent faced defeat on the last day when they slumped to 46 for 5, but Aslett and Cowdrey, who was lbw to Allan Butcher five short of his second century of the match, added 217 and saved the match.

The meeting of the giants at Trent Bridge lived up to expectation. Fletcher won the toss and Gooch and Prichard began with a stand of 121. Six wickets fell for 65 runs, but the tail wagged well. Notts lost Robinson and Randall to Foster before the close and were only kept in contention on the second day through Rice's gritty century. Graham Gooch then took over the match. He thundered to a mighty double century with 32 fours and Notts were invited to score 344 in 82 overs. Robinson, Broad and Rice fell before lunch with only 12 scored and Essex seemed set for victory. Randall had other ideas. He and Johnson added 130 and he and Birch had another defiant stand. Randall fell at 269, but Birch, surviving the loss of two more wickets, steered Notts to safety.

There was no play on the last afternoon at Fenner's, but before then Middlesex had indulged themselves in batting practice and Cowans and the enthusiastic young Fraser had bowled admirably. The outstanding performance came in Middlesex's second innings when Williams, opening, made his top score and Sykes, batting at number three, reached a maiden century.

In the Parks Mike Garnham hit a maiden first-class century after Leicestershire had been troubled by the medium pace of Jeremy Quinlan. It was the last trouble Leicestershire endured. They bowled Oxford out in 93 minutes, 22.4 overs, on the second morning, only three batsmen scoring, and bowled them out again in the afternoon to win by an innings inside two days.

4, 5 and 7 May

at Northampton

Northamptonshire 373 for 8 dec (R.J. Bailey 101, W. Larkins 83, R.G. Williams 50) and 244 (A.C. Storie 106, C.A. Connor 4 for 62)
Hampshire 352 for 8 dec (M.C.J. Nicholas 94, R.J. Parks 52 not out) and 2 for 0

Match drawn
Northamptonshire 7 pts, Hampshire 6 pts

at Leeds

Yorkshire 304 for 9 dec (P.E. Robinson 62, A. Sidebottom 55) and 135
Middlesex 225 for 2 dec (W.N. Slack 86 not out, P.R. Downton 70) and 212 (W.N. Slack 99)

Yorkshire won by 2 runs
Yorkshire 20 pts, Middlesex 6 pts

ABOVE: *Jamie Sykes, a young all-rounder of exciting promise. (Adrian Murrell)*
BELOW: *Alastair Storie leaves the field after his maiden hundred in first-class cricket, on his debut, Northamptonshire v. Hampshire at Northampton, 7 May. (David Munden)*

Cold and wet marred both games, but at Headingley a wonderfully exciting finish resulted. Boycott was out of the Yorkshire side with a strained back and Sidebottom, opening in his stead, hit 55 as Yorkshire batted their way solidly, if unspectacularly to the 300 mark. To compensate for lost time Gatting declared 79 runs behind after some brisk scoring by Downton, in good early season form. Yorkshire lost Moxon and Blakey before the close. Blakey was making his first-class debut and kept wicket in the second innings as Bairstow was injured. He took four catches. Middlesex bowlers continued their success on the last morning and the visitors were left to make 215 in 60 overs. With Slack the dominant partner in the second innings, the Middlesex openers put on 62 before Downton was out and at 109 for 1, they needed 106 in 28 overs. Then, in 6 overs they lost 4 wickets for 14 runs. Emburey was Blakey's fourth victim and Slack, who had been the anchor man, was caught at mid-wicket with 37 needed from 5 overs and 3 wickets left. Edmonds, who had batted well, was bowled at 184 and Cowans after a lusty 12 at 205. Williams was dropped and the last over was reached with him and Daniel needing 4 to win the match. A leg-bye came from the first ball and Jarvis had Williams lbw with the second to give Yorkshire victory by 2 runs.

At Northampton the interest was in two young Northants players, Bailey and Storie, who each scored centuries. Storie was making his debut in the Championship and only came into the side when Cook was pronounced unfit half an hour before the start. Bailey, one of the most promising young batsmen in England, was awarded his county cap.

RIGHT: *John Stanworth, a most promising young wicket-keeper, whose maiden fifty in first-class cricket for Lancashire against Gloucestershire at Bristol did much to help his side to an early season victory. (Sporting Pictures UK Ltd)*

BELOW: *Alan Hill (Derbyshire). A Gold Award in the Benson and Hedges Cup and a fine start to the season before being forced out by a knee injury. (George Herringshaw)*

Benson and Hedges Cup

4 May

at Cardiff

Kent 201 for 7 (C.S. Cowdrey 54)
Glamorgan 181 (R.C. Ontong 58, E.A.E. Baptiste 5 for 30)

Kent (2 pts) won by 20 runs
(Gold Award – E.A.E. Baptiste)

at Bristol

Gloucestershire 288 for 5 (P.W. Romaines 125, A.W. Stovold 60)
Nottinghamshire 255 for 9 (D.W. Randall 62, R.T. Robinson 56)

Gloucestershire (2 pts) won by 33 runs
(Gold Award – P.W. Romaines)

at The Oval

Combined Universities 166 for 9 (A.J.T. Miller 57, T.E. Jesty 4 for 23)
Surrey 167 for 3 (D.B. Pauline 69 not out, G.S. Clinton 63)

Surrey (2 pts) won by 7 wickets
(Gold Award – T.E. Jesty)

at Worcester

Worcestershire 277 for 8 (D.M. Smith 126, T.S. Curtis 75)
Warwickshire 273 for 7 (A.I. Kallicharran 104, G.W. Humpage 62)

Worcestershire (2 pts) won by 4 runs
(Gold Award – D.M. Smith)

at Aberdeen

Derbyshire 228 for 9 (A. Hill 107 not out, B. Roberts 56, W.A. McPate 4 for 42)
Scotland 135 (O. Henry 59, R.J. Finney 5 for 40)

Derbyshire (2 pts) won by 93 runs
(Gold Award – A. Hill)

at Shrewsbury

Minor Counties 93
Somerset 94 for 3

Somerset (2 pts) won by 7 wickets
(Gold Award – M.R. Davis)

4 and 6 May

at Chelmsford

Sussex 143 (N.A. Foster 4 for 39)
Essex 144 for 5

Essex (2 pts) won by 5 wickets
(Gold Award – G.A. Gooch)

6 May

at Old Trafford

Lancashire 145 (G.J.F. Ferris 4 for 31)
Leicestershire 147 for 7 (J.C. Balderstone 58 not out, S.J. O'Shaughnessy 4 for 17)

Leicestershire (2 pts) won by 3 wickets
(Gold Award – J.C. Balderstone)

The first round of the Benson and Hedges Cup produced results in all eight matches in spite of the weather. The holders, Lancashire, could not play until the Monday and then batted miserably. They were revived from the depths of 35 for 5 by Abrahams and Watkinson, but 146 looked a meagre target for Leicestershire. That it became a formidable one was due entirely to Jack Simmons, 11 overs for 5 runs, and Steve O'Shaughnessy, 4 for 17 in his 11 overs. Throughout the traumas Balderstone, dropped when 2, remained composed and he hit Allott through mid-wicket to bring victory with 10 balls to spare.

Derbyshire and Somerset won expected victories, Alan Hill carried his bat through the Derbyshire innings, and Essex won a surprisingly easy victory over Sussex. Sussex floundered to 124 for 8 on a rain-scarred Saturday and added only 19 more on the Monday. Prichard and Gooch gave Essex a bristling start with 77 in 19 overs and although le Roux took 3 for 9 in 18 balls, the issue was never in doubt.

Derrick and Ontong rallied Glamorgan from 58 for 7, but Baptiste returned to dismiss Derrick and Ontong was run out so that Kent won comfortably.

Jesty showed further evidence that he was settled at Surrey and Paul Romaines played a dominating innings against Nottinghamshire at Bristol. He and Andy Stovold began the match with a stand of 153 and although Robinson and Randall put on 82 for Notts' second wicket, the visitors were never abreast of the required run rate.

The most exciting finish was at Worcester. Weston was out with only one run scored, but David Smith and Curtis added 174 and Smith and Kapil Dev hit 61 in 7 overs. Undismayed, Warwickshire chased the big target of 278 in eager fashion. Kallicharran and Humpage put on 156 in 24 overs. Kallicharran was finely stumped by Rhodes and Humpage was run out. Paul Smith needed to hit Kapil Dev's last ball for 4 to tie the match, but he was caught at cover.

5 May

at Arundel

Australians 261 for 6 dec (G.M. Ritchie 72, A.R. Border 65)
Lavinia, Duchess of Norfolk's XI 145 for 5 (R.D.V. Knight 63 not out)

Match drawn

The Australian tour begins in the leisurely setting of Arundel. (Adrian Murrell)

John Player Special League

at Chelmsford

Essex 148 (I.A. Greig 4 for 26)
Sussex 150 for 1 (G.D. Mendis 78 not out)

Sussex (4 pts) won by 9 wickets

at Cardiff

Glamorgan 175 for 8
Kent 138 for 6 (C.J. Tavare 67 not out)

Kent (4 pts) won on faster scoring rate

at Old Trafford

Lancashire 127 for 9
Leicestershire 8 for 1

Matched abandoned
Lancashire 2 pts, Leicestershire 2 pts

at Northampton

Hampshire 224 for 7 (D.R. Turner 65)
Northamptonshire 227 for 2 (A.J. Lamb 125 not out, R.J. Bailey 79 not out)

Northamptonshire (4 pts) won by 8 wickets

at The Oval

Surrey 304 for 6 (A.J. Stewart 86, A.R. Butcher 72)
Warwickshire 300 for 9 (A.I. Kallicharran 70)

Surrey (4 pts) won by 4 runs

at Worcester

Worcestershire 75 for 7
Somerset 45 for 0

Match abandoned
Worcestershire 2 pts, Somerset 2 pts

at Bradford

Yorkshire 132 for 9 *v* **Middlesex**

Match abandoned
Yorkshire 2 pts, Middlesex 2 pts

Rain fractured the beginning of the Sunday League programme. Three matches were abandoned and the Kent – Glamorgan game saw Kent's target reduced to 135 in 30 overs. Sussex beat Essex with great ease after Green and Mendis had put on 91 for the first wicket. Lamb and Bailey set up a John Player League third wicket record at Northampton with 207 in 32 overs. Lamb hit 4 sixes and 7 fours. There was another record at The Oval where 604 runs were scored. Alec Stewart hit 8 fours and 4 sixes in his 86 off 57 balls, but Warwickshire pursued their mammoth target courageously and Paul Smith and Ferreira hit 72 in 9 overs. Monkhouse dismissed them both in the penultimate over and Surrey gained an exciting victory.

The Australian tour began with an amiable draw in the cold against the Duchess of Norfolk's eleven. Thomson bowled with fire and Ritchie and Border impressed with the bat.

8, 9 and 10 May

at Leicester

Derbyshire 226 (A. Hill 89, N.E. Briers 4 for 29) and 279 for 3 dec (K.J. Barnett 134 not out, B. Roberts 96)
Leicestershire 301 (P. Willey 133, D.I. Gower 57, P.G. Newman 4 for 92)

Match drawn
Leicestershire 8 pts, Derbyshire 6 pts

at Lord's

Middlesex 303 for 6 dec (W.N. Slack 105, C.T. Radley 50) and 257 for 6 dec (M.W. Gatting 90, C.T. Radley 85 not out, C. Penn 4 for 63)
Kent 237 (C.S. Cowdrey 95, W.W. Daniel 4 for 32) and 124 for 1 (M.R. Benson 62 not out)

Match drawn
Middlesex 8 pts, Kent 4 pts

at The Oval

Surrey 341 (G.S. Clinton 87, A.R. Butcher 81, T.E. Jesty 75, P.J.W. Allott 6 for 71) and 191 for 7 dec (T.E. Jesty 96)
Lancashire 222 (A. Needham 5 for 42) and 77 (D.J. Thomas 4 for 20)

Surrey won by 233 runs
Surrey 24 pts, Lancashire 5 pts

at Edgbaston

Glamorgan 253 (Javed Miandad 98, R.C. Ontong 55, S. Wall 4 for 59) and 255 (Javed Miandad 52, G.C. Small 5 for 84)
Warwickshire 472 (T.A. Lloyd 160, D.L. Amiss 86, R.I.H.B. Dyer 80) and 22 for 1

Match drawn
Warwickshire 8 pts, Glamorgan 4 pts

at Worcester

Gloucestershire 270 (P. Bainbridge 83, P.J. Newport 4 for 48) and 200 (R.N. Kapil Dev 4 for 63)
Worcestershire 164 and 265 (D.B. d'Oliveira 99, P. Bainbridge 5 for 60)

Gloucestershire won by 40 runs
Gloucestershire 23 pts, Worcestershire 5 pts

at Taunton

Australians 356 for 4 dec (A.R. Border 106, D.M. Wellham 64, D.C. Boon 62 not out, W.B. Phillips 56 not out) and 316 for 6 dec (K.C. Wessels 156, S.C. Booth 4 for 98)
Somerset 314 (B.C. Rose 81 retired hurt, I.T. Botham 65, V.J. Marks 50, R.G. Holland 4 for 87) and 125 (J.R. Thomson 6 for 44)

Australians won by 233 runs

at Oxford

Hampshire 373 for 4 dec (R.A. Smith 120, C.L. Smith 110) and 252 for 2 dec (C.L. Smith 100, M.C.J. Nicholas 52 not out)
Oxford University 303 for 8 dec (D.A. Thorne 85, C.D.M. Tooley 66) and 69 for 2

Match drawn

Andy Lloyd, 160 for Warwickshire against Glamorgan at Edgbaston and a total return to fitness. (George Herringshaw)

Wayne Phillips, the Australian wicket-keeper, catches Nigel Popplewell of Somerset at Taunton and the slip cordon explodes in appeal. (David Munden)

at Cambridge

Sussex 236 for 4 dec (P.W.G. Parker 61) and 106 for 2 dec
Cambridge University 132 for 5 dec. and 127

Sussex won by 83 runs

The Australians began their tour in earnest with a fine display at Taunton and Jeff Thomson quickly refuted the idea that he was no longer to be taken seriously as an international player. On the opening day Border hit a splendid hundred. He and Wellham put on 136 in 24 overs for the third wicket and the Somerset attack was savaged. The home side was struggling at 65 for 4 before Rose and Botham launched a counter attack, but on the second day leg-spinner Bob Holland bowled beautifully having Botham stumped by substitute wicket-keeper Ray Phillips as one of his four victims. Sadly, Rose had his arm broken by a ball from McDermott and the Australians had their problems with Lawson and Wayne Phillips both unwell. Wessels reached the first hundred of the tour and on the last day Thomson routed the home side to give Australia a most satisfying start to the tour.

Centuries to Peter Willey and Kim Barnett who shared a stand of 191 with Bruce Roberts were the best aspects of a rather dour game at Leicester and Kent's negative tactics determined a draw at Lord's. Wilf Slack again provided the backbone of the Middlesex innings and on the second day it was Chris Cowdrey who saved Kent, reviving them from 88 for 5 and again missing his century by only 5 runs. Unfortunately he fell from grace on the last day when, having asked Middlesex to bat first, he refused the challenge of 324 runs in 77 overs. Hinks stayed on 11 for 35 minutes and Tavare faced 52 balls without scoring. A miserable draw resulted. Earlier Christ Penn had returned career best bowling figures.

Butcher and Clinton gave Surrey a fine start at The Oval with a stand of 167. Jesty batted well, but Allott halted the Surrey advance with 3 wickets in 5 overs. Soren Henriksen, the Danish pace bowler, made his first-class debut for Lancashire and caught and bowled Jesty. Lancashire fell to Needham on the second day and, following Jesty's 2 sixes and 11 fours, they collapsed to Thomas and Pocock on the last.

Championship leaders Glamorgan struggled at Edgbaston. Javed Miandad led them out of the despair of 1 for 2, but Wall had career best bowling figures and, having dismissed Glamorgan in 75.2 overs, Warwickshire closed at 112 for 0. Lloyd and Dyer took their stand to 186 next morning and Andy Lloyd trumpeted his full recovery with 160 in 311 minutes, an innings which included 20 fours. Left with only the prospect of trying to save the game, Glamorgan batted dourly and John Steele was in for 151 minutes for his 26. It was this innings which thwarted Warwickshire who were left 2 overs in which to make 37, a task which Ferreira, Humpage and Amiss could not accomplish.

Two counties with a new look about them, Worcestershire and Warwickshire, contested a keen match on a lively wicket. Gloucestershire batted consistently, but Worcestershire lost their last 6 first innings wickets for 44 runs. In contrast, Gloucestershire's second innings was rallied by the tail and the home side faced a formidable target of 307. At 79 for 5, they seemed doomed to an early defeat, but Damian d'Oliveira hit 3 sixes and 13 fours in an innings which lasted 101 minutes. He was lbw to Bainbridge, who had a fine all-round match, and Gloucestershire triumphed.

The Smith brothers each scored a century at Oxford and Chris Smith made two in the match to remind people that he was England's opening batsman two years ago. The University responded positively as Miller and Tooley, who made a career best, put on 100 for the second wicket.

At Cambridge, where the home side bowled well, a result was contrived in spite of the weather.

Jeff Thomson devastated the Somerset second innings – he took 6 for 44. In windy conditions captains and umpires agreed to play without bails. (Adrian Murrell)

The Australians at Worcester. (Adrian Murrell)

11, 12 and 13 May

at Worcester

Worcestershire 303 for 6 dec (P.A. Neale 108, T.S. Curtis 76) and 93 for 4
Australians 364 for 5 dec (A.R. Border 135, D.C. Boon 73 not out)

Match drawn

Phil Neale took the first century of the summer off the Australian bowling, but he was overshadowed by Allan Border who hit 6 sixes and 16 fours and became the first Australian captain to start an English tour with hundreds in his first two first-class matches. He hit 22 in one over by Illingworth and faced only 140 balls. He and Boon added 104 for the 5th wicket and Boon again remained unbeaten. No play was possible on the last day.

Benson and Hedges Cup

11 May

at Swansea

Minor Counties 76 (S.R. Barwick 4 for 11)
Glamorgan 77 for 1 (G.C. Holmes 53 not out)

Glamorgan (2 pts) won by 9 wickets
(Gold Award – S.R. Barwick)

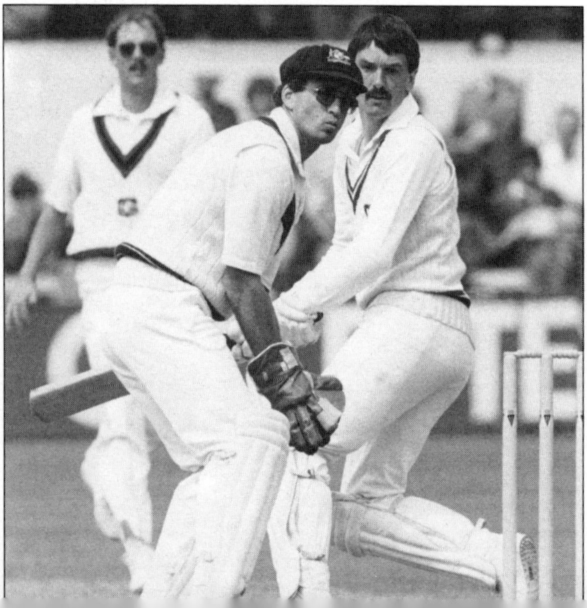

at Leicester

Yorkshire 244 for 4 (J.D. Love 90 not out)
Leicestershire 243 for 9 (I.P. Butcher 101, P. Willey 60)

Yorkshire (2 pts) won by 1 run
(Gold Award – D.L. Bairstow)

at Northampton

Gloucestershire 217 (C.W.J. Athey 77, A. Walker 4 for 46)
Northamptonshire 220 for 6 (R.G. Williams 58, R.J. Bailey 52)

Northamptonshire (2 pts) won by 4 wickets
(Gold Award – R.G. Williams)

at Hove

Surrey 170 (T.E. Jesty 61, G.S. le Roux 4 for 40)
Sussex 174 for 7 (A.P. Wells 62)

Sussex (2 pts) won by 3 wickets
(Gold Award – G.S. le Roux)

at Edgbaston

Warwickshire 282 for 4 (T.A. Lloyd 137 not out, A.I. Kallicharran 57)
Lancashire 219 (S.J. O'Shaughnessy 66)

Warwickshire (2 pts) won by 63 runs
(Gold Award – T.A. Lloyd)

at Cambridge

Combined Universities 138 for 9 (P.H. Edmonds 5 for 43)
Middlesex 139 for 1 (W.N. Slack 58 not out)

Middlesex won by 9 wickets
(Gold Award – P.H. Edmonds)

at Coatbridge

Nottinghamshire 216 for 8 (R.T. Robinson 120)
Scotland 188 for 9 (A.B. Russell 73 not out)

Nottinghamshire (2 pts) won by 28 runs
(Gold Award – R.T. Robinson)

11 and 13 May

at Canterbury

Hampshire 215 for 8
Kent 125 (C.A. Connor 4 for 27)

Hampshire (2 pts) won by 90 runs
(Gold Award – M.C.J. Nicholas)

Phil Neale, the Worcestershire skipper, took the first century of the summer off the Australian bowlers. He turns a ball to leg. Murray Bennett and wicket-keeper Ray Phillips look on. (Adrian Murrell)

Andy Lloyd continued his triumphant return with a masterly innings against a moderate Lancashire side at Edgbaston. His 137 not out was the highest made in the competition by a Warwickshire player. He and Dyer put on 119 for the first wicket and Lancashire, 53 for 5 until revived by O'Shaughnessy, Jefferies, Simmons and Maynard, were never in the hunt.

Glamorgan, with Steve Barwick winning his first Gold Award, and Middlesex gained expectedly easy victories, but Russell offered spirited resistance at number eight for Scotland. Tim Robinson's cultured batting was the decisive factor in Notts' win.

The clash between Hampshire and Kent, eagerly awaited, was frustrated by bad light on the Saturday and reduced to 43 overs on the Monday. Aslett with 49 was the only Kent batsman to offer resistance after Mark Nicholas, who took his first Gold Award, had led the Hampshire attack on the bowling.

Surrey owed much to Jesty, but it was their last two wickets which boosted them from 128 to 170. Monkhouse hit 24 and Pocock 14. Sussex were soon in trouble, losing Green and Parker for 3, but Mendis and Alan Wells added 103 and made victory possible although not without further alarms.

At Northampton, the home side paced themselves better to win with an over to spare in spite of losing Allan Lamb for 0, and the match at Leicester provided the most thrilling tie of the round. Yorkshire, with Love recalling the days when he was an England prospect and Bairstow making some typical lusty blows, reached 244. Ian Butcher held the Leicestershire reply together and reached his century, his first in the Benson and Hedges Cup, in the last over at the beginning of which 9 runs were needed. Butcher was run out

Cardigan Connor – four wickets for Hampshire in the Benson and Hedges Cup game at Canterbury. (Trevor Jones)

and Parsons needed to hit the last ball for 4 to win the match. He drove hard but Sharp dived to stop the ball on the boundary and so gave Yorkshire victory.

After two rounds Lancashire, the holders, with two defeats, looked to have joined Minor Counties, Scotland and Combined Universities in exiting from the competition.

John Player Special League

12 May

at Derby
Derbyshire 119 for 8
Northamptonshire 121 for 1 (A.J. Lamb 69 not out)
Northamptonshire (4 pts) won by 9 wickets

Allan Border on his way to his second century of the tour for the Australians at Worcester. (Ken Kelly)

at Canterbury

Kent 218 for 9 (C.J. Tavare 101, E.A.E. Baptiste 50, T.M. Tremlett 5 for 28)
Hampshire 30 for 1

Match abandoned
Kent 2 pts, Hampshire 2 pts

at Leicester

Leicestershire 223 for 5 (J.J. Whitaker 86 not out, N.E. Briers 77)
Yorkshire 224 for 3 (P.E. Robinson 78 not out, K. Sharp 73 not out)

Yorkshire (4 pts) won by 7 wickets

at Lord's

Gloucestershire 149 for 5 (C.W.J. Athey 67 not out)
Middlesex 150 for 2 (M.W. Gatting 69 not out)

Middlesex (4 pts) won by 8 wickets

at Taunton

Somerset 174 for 8 (P.M. Roebuck 74 not out)
Glamorgan 175 for 8 (J.A. Hopkins 64)

Glamorgan (4 pts) won by 2 wickets

at Hove

Sussex 194 for 6 (G.D. Mendis 70)
Surrey 173 for 2 (A.R. Butcher 67, G.S. Clinton 67)

Surrey (4 pts) won on faster scoring rate

at Edgbaston

Warwickshire 213 (D.L. Amiss 53, G.W. Humpage 53)
Lancashire 190

Warwickshire (4 pts) won by 23 runs

Dennis Amiss became the most prolific scorer in the Sunday League with 6174 runs. He shared a century stand with Humpage as Warwickshire won comfortably. Gloucestershire recovered from 29 for 4, but rain reduced their match at Lord's to 28 overs and Gatting smote Middlesex to victory.

Briers and Whitaker put on 102 for Leicestershire's fourth wicket, but Yorkshire, with Robinson making a maiden one-day fifty and sharing a stand of 138 with Sharp for the fourth wicket, won with 19 balls to spare. Northants were even more decisive winners at Derby. Chasing 120, they lost Cook for 0, but Lamb and Larkins took them to their target with 15.4 overs left.

Glamorgan won off the last ball at Taunton. Steele and Davies scored 15 in the last two overs and ran a bye off the last ball. Somerset handicapped by injuries gave a debut to Sulley, a 34-year old club cricketer.

Butcher and Clinton stroked Surrey to an easy win at Hove. Their target was reduced to 170 in 35 overs and the opening partnership realised 132.

Benson and Hedges Cup

14 May

at Taunton

Kent 293 for 6 (C.J. Tavare 143)
Somerset 191

Kent (2 pts) won by 42 runs
(Gold Award – C.J. Tavare)

Mike Gatting clips another boundary during his magnificent innings of 143 not out for Middlesex in the Benson and Hedges Cup match at Hove, 15 May. (Trevor Jones)

14 and 15 May

at Derby

Northamptonshire 88 for 6 *v* **Derbyshire**

Match abandoned
Derbyshire 1 pt, Northamptonshire 1 pt

at Bristol

Gloucestershire 184 for 8 (K.M. Curran 53 not out, P. Bainbridge 53)
Scotland 131

Gloucestershire (2 pts) won by 53 runs
(Gold Award – K.M. Curran)

at Southampton

Hampshire 294 for 9 (C.G. Greenidge 99, M.C.J. Nicholas 74, J.G. Thomas 4 for 38)
Glamorgan 178 (Javed Miandad 57, T.M. Tremlett 4 for 54)

Hampshire (2 pts) won by 116 runs
(Gold Award – C.G. Greenidge)

at The Oval

Surrey 139 (T.E. Jesty 69 not out, N.A. Foster 5 for 32)
Essex 140 for 1 (G.A. Gooch 81)

Essex (2 pts) won by 9 wickets
(Gold Award – N.A. Foster)

at Hove

Middlesex 280 for 5 (M.W. Gatting 143 not out)
Sussex 249 (C.M. Wells 55, W.W. Daniel 4 for 58)

Gordon Greenidge announces his return with an innings of 99 for Hampshire against Glamorgan in the Benson and Hedges Cup match at Southampton, 14 May. Davies is the wicket-keeper. (Adrian Murrell)

Mark Nicholas during his innings of 74 for Hampshire against Glamorgan at Southampton, 14 May. (Adrian Murrell)

Middlesex (2 pts) won by 31 runs
(Gold Award – M.W. Gatting)

15 May

at Old Trafford

Lancashire 146 (G.B. Stevenson 4 for 26)
Yorkshire 144 for 9

Lancashire (2 pts) won by 2 runs
(Gold Award – S.J. O'Shaughnessy)

at Leicester

Leicestershire 212 for 7 (J.C. Balderstone 77)
Worcestershire 195 for 7

Leicestershire (2 pts) won by 17 runs
(Gold Award – J.C. Balderstone)

A patient 77 by Chris Balderstone was the foundation of a Leicestershire victory which put them at the top of Group B. Their nearest rivals, Yorkshire, faltered in alarming style at Old Trafford. They fielded poorly and Lancashire, with Steve O'Shaughnessy making 48, were fortunate to reach 146, the match having been reduced to 32 overs. Sharp, with 45, was the only Yorkshire batsman to establish himself however and after he was run out the run rate slackened. The last over arrived with 12 runs needed and the ninth wicket pair, Jarvis and Carrick, at the wicket. Jarvis was caught off the fifth ball and Carrick needed to hit the last ball for 6 to level the scores. He swung Allott over square-leg and raised his arms in triumph only to see the ball drop just short of the boundary.

Foster routed Surrey and Gooch and Hardie, 126 for the first wicket, completed the job. Tavare's century eliminated a weakened Somerset side from the competition in the only match which could be completed on the scheduled day.

Scotland disturbed Gloucestershire who lost both openers for 15, but Kevin Curran, the Zimbabwe all-rounder, whose arrival at the county had made a vast difference to their middle order and to their attack, hit a good fifty and bowled well to take his first Gold Award and play a significant part in his side's victory.

Gordon Greenidge announced his return from West Indies with 99 off 97 deliveries which devastated Glamorgan and virtually assured Hampshire of a place in the quarter-finals. At Hove, Mike Gatting made the highest individual score for Middlesex in the competition. Sussex responded bravely after losing Mendis and Green for 43, but Edmonds and Emburey frustrated the middle order although it was Daniel who took the wickets.

16 May

at The Oval

Australians 216 for 7 (W.B. Phillips 66 not out)
Surrey 217 for 4 (G.S. Clinton 86, A.R. Butcher 64)

Surrey won by 6 wickets

Concern over a knee injury to Allan Border was ended when it was revealed that he had only minor ligament trouble which could be treated by injection. Hilditch led the side in

John Lever raises his arms in triumph as he takes one of his five wickets for 13 runs against Middlesex at Lord's, 16 May. (Mike Powell)

the 55-over game at The Oval and the Australians gave their poorest performance of the tour. Clinton and Butcher, in fine form, put on 140 for Surrey's first wicket. Australia's fielding and catching lapses aided them. The game against Notts two days earlier was abandoned without a ball being bowled.

Benson and Hedges Cup

16 May

at Southampton

Somerset 167 for 8
Hampshire 169 for 3 (R.A. Smith 63 not out, D.R. Turner 52 not out)

Hampshire (2 pts) won by 7 wickets
(Gold Award – R.J. Parks)

at Canterbury

Minor Counties 132 for 8
Kent 133 for 5

Kent (2 pts) won by 5 wickets
(Gold Award – D.L. Underwood)

at Lord's

Middlesex 73 (J.K. Lever 5 for 13)
Essex 74 for 6

Essex (2 pts) won by 4 wickets
(Gold Award – J.K. Lever)

at Northampton

Scotland 185 for 9 (W.A. Donald 59, O. Henry 54)
Northamptonshire 191 for 4 (W. Larkins 105)

Northamptonshire (2 pts) won by 6 wickets
(Gold Award – W. Larkins)

at Trent Bridge

Nottinghamshire 196 for 6 (C.E.B. Rice 73 not out)
Derbyshire 143 (P.G. Newman 56 not out, K.E. Cooper 4 for 30)

Nottinghamshire (2 pts) won by 53 runs
(Gold Award – C.E.B. Rice)

at Worcester

Lancashire 258 for 5 (S.J. O'Shaughnessy 90, J. Abrahams 57)
Worcestershire 261 for 4 (P.A. Neale 94 not out)

Worcestershire (2 pts) won by 6 wickets
(Gold Award – P.A. Neale)

at Leeds

Warwickshire 159 (G.B. Stevenson 4 for 34)
Yorkshire 165 for 3 (P. Carrick 53)

Yorkshire (2 pts) won by 7 wickets
(Gold Award – P. Carrick)

at Oxford

Sussex 241 for 7 (Imran Khan 82 not out, A.D.H. Grimes 5 for 36)
Combined Universities 133 for 6

Sussex (2 pts) won by 108 runs
(Gold Award – Imran Khan)

The penultimate round of matches in the Benson and Hedges Cup saw Hampshire and Kent clinch the qualifying places in Group D. A rather dispirited Somerset side could muster only 167 and Robin Smith and David Turner took Hampshire to victory with an unbeaten stand of 107. At Canterbury, Underwood bowled his 11 overs for 6 runs, but David Surridge gave Kent a few worries before Cowdrey struck some hard blows.

On a dreadful wicket at Lord's, Middlesex, put in to bat, sank without trace to John Lever and the Essex seam attack. Barlow was caught at short leg off the first ball of the day and only Emburey's wallops to the tavern boundary helped the score past 50. Essex lost Hardie with a bruised hand and made rather heavy weather of their task, 3 wickets falling while the last 4 runs were scored, a bonus for the Middlesex strike rate.

With Essex leading Group C unbeaten, Sussex, out of the tournament, gained small consolation at Oxford. Imran Khan received the individual award which was a little hard on Alexander Grimes who returned the best bowling figures ever recorded for the Combined Universities in the competition.

The other two groups remained very open. O'Shaughnessy and Abrahams added 128 in 20 overs after Lancashire had been 57 for 2. O'Shaughnessy was in majestic form, but both batsmen were aided by dropped catches. Lancashire's bowling could not match their batting. At times it was quite dreadful and they conceded 7 wides and 8 no-balls. Neale and d'Oliveira scored the last 98 runs in 14 overs and Worcestershire won with 11 balls to spare.

Phil Carrick became Moxon's fifth opening partner of the season and celebrated with a match-winning 53 in a stand of 111 which, following his two wickets, gave him his first Gold Award.

Wayne Larkins hit a century off 85 balls as Northants romped to victory over Scotland while at Trent Bridge, Derbyshire were 38 for 8 facing Notts' 196 when Holding joined Newman. They put on 83, a ninth wicket record for the competition, but could not save their side from defeat.

18, 19, 20 and 21 May

at Hove

Australians 321 (D.C. Boon 119, K.C. Wessels 56) and 275 for 6 dec (G.M. Ritchie 100 not out, W.B. Phillips 91)

Angus Fraser of Middlesex who bowled so well in the Benson and Hedges zonal matches. (Mike Powell)

Sussex 262 (G.D. Mendis 81, D.R. Gilbert 4 for 97) and 153 for 9
Match drawn

Boon and Wessels added 98 in 108 minutes to rescue Australia from the depths of 37 for 3, Boon confirming his most impressive start to the tour with 20 fours in his innings. Ritchie, a six and 11 fours, and Wayne Phillips, 14 fours, put on 142 for the fifth wicket in the second innings. Barclay deflected a ball from Thomson into his face and had to have seven stitches and ultimately Imran and le Roux held out for just under five overs to save the game for Sussex. Once again Australia were plagued by dropped catches.

Benson and Hedges Cup

18 May

at Chesterfield

Derbyshire 202 for 7 (K.J. Barnett 86)
Gloucestershire 55 for 2
Derbyshire (2 pts) won on faster run rate
(Gold Award – K.J. Barnett)

at Chelmsford

Essex 333 for 4 (B.R. Hardie 113, K.S. McEwan 100 not out, G.A. Gooch 89)
Combined Universities 203 for 6 (C.R. Andrew 82 not out, J.D. Carr 67)
Essex (2 pts) won by 130 runs
(Gold Award – G.A. Gooch)

at Lord's

Surrey 227 for 4 (G.S. Clinton 106 not out, A.R. Butcher 56)
Middlesex 219 (M.W. Gatting 51, A.R. Butcher 4 for 36)
Surrey (2 pts) won by 8 runs
(Gold Award – A.R. Butcher)

at Trent Bridge

Nottinghamshire 242 for 5 (B.C. Broad 70, D.W. Randall 54)
Northamptonshire 29 for 1
Match abandoned
Nottinghamshire 1 pt, Northamptonshire 1 pt

at Taunton

Glamorgan 237 (G.C. Holmes 70, Javed Miandad 57, Younis Ahmed 55)
Somerset 144 (R.C. Ontong 5 for 30)
Glamorgan (2 pts) won by 93 runs
(Gold Award – R.C. Ontong)

at Bradford

Worcestershire 214 for 9 (D.M. Smith 77, T.S. Curtis 50, A. Sidebottom 5 for 27)
Yorkshire 130 (R.K. Illingworth 4 for 36)
Worcestershire (2 pts) won by 84 runs
(Gold Award – A. Sidebottom)

at Reading

Hampshire 264 for 8 (C.G. Greenidge 123, D.R. Turner 63 not out)
Minor Counties 129 (M.C.J. Nicholas 4 for 34)
Hampshire (2 pts) won by 135 runs
(Gold Award – C.G. Greenidge)

18 and 20 May

at Edgbaston

Warwickshire 246 for 5 (A.I. Kallicharran 55, D.L. Amiss 53, G.W. Humpage 51 not out)
Leicestershire 247 for 3 (J.J. Whitaker 73 not out, P. Willey 68 not out)
Leicestershire (2 pts) won by 7 wickets
(Gold Award – J.J. Whitaker)

Being forced to leave the field in stygian gloom on Saturday evening, Gloucestershire were unable to continue their innings in wretched weather on Monday so that Derbyshire found themselves, rather fortunately, in the quarter-finals, the game at Trent Bridge having also been abandoned, but in this case with no result possible.

Worcestershire, with Smith hitting 3 sixes as he and Curtis added 109 for the second wicket, overwhelmed Yorkshire, and Leicestershire joined them as qualifiers when, on the Monday, they romped to victory at Edgbaston. Willey and Whitaker finished with an unbroken stand of 146.

Hampshire completed their programme with a hundred per cent record and Greenidge gained his second Gold Award inside a week with 123 off 131 balls with 4 sixes and 15 fours. Glamorgan gained consolation with an easy win at Taunton as the Somerset decline continued.

There were strange events at Chelmsford. Gooch and Hardie raised the hundred in 14 overs. Gooch was in powerful mood, but McEwan and Hardie batted sweetly in adding 169 for the third wicket. Fletcher joined McEwan for the last rites and, seemingly, was run out by yards on the last ball of the innings, but umpire Oslear announced later that as no appeal had been made, Fletcher was not out and McEwan was 100 not out and not 99 not out as all had believed. It mattered only to the record book. The Universities, Carr in particular, batted well in reply.

At Lord's, Middlesex were beaten by 8 runs yet found themselves in the play-offs by virtue of a superior striking rate. Surrey cursed Essex for losing only one wicket against them and for being profligate against Middlesex two days earlier. Butcher and Clinton yet again shared a century opening partnership, 101, and Butcher added the wickets of Barlow, Slack, Emburey and Edmonds for good measure.

Benson and Hedges Cup – Group Tables

GROUP A	P	W	L	Pts
Northamptonshire	4	2	—	6
Derbyshire	4	2	1	5
Nottinghamshire	4	2	1	5
Gloucestershire	4	2	2	4
Scotland	4	—	4	0
GROUP B				
Worcestershire	4	3	1	6
Leicestershire	4	3	1	6
Yorkshire	4	2	2	4
Warwickshire	4	1	3	2
Lancashire	4	1	3	2
GROUP C				
Essex	4	4	—	8
Middlesex	4	2	2	4
Surrey	4	2	2	4
Sussex	4	2	2	4
Combined Universities of Oxford & Cambridge	4	—	4	0
GROUP D				
Hampshire	4	4	—	8
Kent	4	3	1	6
Glamorgan	4	2	2	4
Somerset	4	1	3	2
Minor Counties	4	—	4	0

John Player Special League

19 May

at Southampton

Hampshire 208 for 7 (R.A. Smith 104)
Surrey 160 for 9

Hampshire (4 pts) won by 48 runs

at Old Trafford

Lancashire 220 for 6
Gloucestershire 223 for 4 (P.W. Romaines 65, B.F. Davison 57)

Gloucestershire (4 pts) won by 6 wickets

at Lord's

Middlesex 166 for 8 (G.D. Barlow 59, J.F. Steele 5 for 30)
Glamorgan 167 for 3 (J.A. Hopkins 72)

Glamorgan (4 pts) won by 7 wickets

at Trent Bridge

Nottinghamshire 186 for 3 (J.D. Birch 55 not out, B.C. Broad 54)
v **Leicestershire**

Match abandoned
Nottinghamshire 2 pts, Leicestershire 2 pts

at Scarborough

Yorkshire *v* **Derbyshire**

Match abandoned
Yorkshire 2 pts, Derbyshire 2 pts

Glamorgan asserted their early season promise when, after Barlow and Slack had put on 101 for the first wicket, Middlesex were frustrated by a Steele spell of 4 for 9 and Hopkins took them to a comfortable win. Robin Smith hit his highest Sunday League score off 94 balls with 2 sixes and 9 fours to confirm Hampshire's challenge, and the revitalised Gloucestershire were consistent and convincing in brushing aside Lancashire.

22, 23 and 24 May

at Chesterfield

Derbyshire 243 (K.J. Barnett 103, W.P. Fowler 76, P.J.W. Allott 5 for 33) and 0 for 0 dec
Lancashire 20 for 1 dec and 126 for 4 (D.W. Varey 57 not out)

Match drawn
Lancashire 4 pts, Derbyshire 2 pts

at Cardiff

Middlesex 297 for 7 dec (C.T. Radley 127, P.R. Downton 67, J.G. Thomas 4 for 61)
Glamorgan 111 (N.G. Cowans 5 for 56) and 478 for 5 dec (Younis Ahmed 177, Javed Miandad 95, T. Davies 75, G.C. Holmes 58)

Match drawn
Middlesex 7 pts, Glamorgan 2 pts

at Leicester

Nottinghamshire 301 for 3 dec (R.T. Robinson 94, D.W. Randall 89 not out, B.C. Broad 70) and 46 for 1
Leicestershire 165 for 1 dec (J.C. Balderstone 72 not out, I.P. Butcher 52)

Match drawn
Nottinghamshire 4 pts, Leicestershire 2 pts

at Northampton

Kent 270 for 9 dec (A.P.E. Knott 87 not out, R.M. Ellison 71, A. Walker 4 for 38) and 122 for 5 dec (D.J. Capel 4 for 47)
Northamptonshire 162 (W. Larkins 52, E.A.E. Baptiste 6 for 42) and 120 for 2 (R.J. Bailey 50 not out)

Match drawn
Kent 6 pts, Northamptonshire 4 pts

at Taunton

Somerset 298 (I.T. Botham 149) and 358 for 5 dec (I.V.A. Richards 186, N.F.M. Popplewell 68)
Hampshire 334 for 8 dec (K.D. James 124, T.M. Tremlett 102 not out) and 325 for 5 (C.L. Smith 121, V.P. Terry 83)

Hampshire won by 5 wickets
Hampshire 24 pts, Somerset 6 pts

at Hove

Sussex 141 (D.V. Lawrence 7 for 48) and 89 for 2
Gloucestershire 251 for 4 dec (A.W. Stovold 104, P.W. Romaines 64, D.A. Reeve 4 for 86)

Match drawn
Gloucestershire 7 pts, Sussex 1 pt

at Edgbaston

Surrey 347 for 7 dec (T.E. Jesty 126, D.B. Pauline 77, G.C. Small 5 for 66) and 235 for 3 dec (A.R. Butcher 86, G.S. Clinton 72)
Warwickshire 300 for 7 dec (G.W. Humpage 70, D.L. Amiss 57) and 285 for 6 (A.I. Kallicharran 76, R.I.H.B. Dyer 64, G.W. Humpage 55 not out, A.H. Gray 4 for 68)

Warwickshire won by 4 wickets
Warwickshire 23 pts, Surrey 7 pts

Ian Butcher catches Chris Broad for 70, Leicestershire v Nottinghamshire at Grace Road, 22 May. (David Munden)

at Sheffield

Yorkshire *v* **Essex**

Match abandoned. No points

at Lord's

Australians 377 for 6 dec (A.R. Border 125, S.P. O'Donnell 100 not out, K.C. Wessels 60) and 222 for 3 (D.M. Wellham 81 not out)
M.C.C. 291 for 2 dec (A.J. Lamb 122 not out, M.C.J. Nicholas 115 not out)

Match drawn

at Oxford

Oxford University 105 (R.K. Illingworth 6 for 9) and 183 (A.J.T. Miller 72, R.K. Illingworth 7 for 50)
Worcestershire 310 for 9 dec (M.J. Weston 97, D. A. Banks 76, D. A. Thorne 4 for 64)

Worcestershire won by an innings and 22 runs

Rain ravaged many matches. Not a ball was bowled at Sheffield and, in spite of generous declarations, the weather won at Chesterfield where Kim Barnett gave another impressive display, batting for 5 hours when his side was struggling and sharing a fifth wicket stand of 135 with Fowler.

A downpour ended play at lunch on the last day at Leicester where there had been only 38 overs possible on the first day. Robinson and Broad put on 152 for Nottinghamshire's first wicket and Butcher and Balderstone responded with 107 for Leicestershire's opening stand.

Wessels evades the cluster of fielders. (Adrian Murrell)

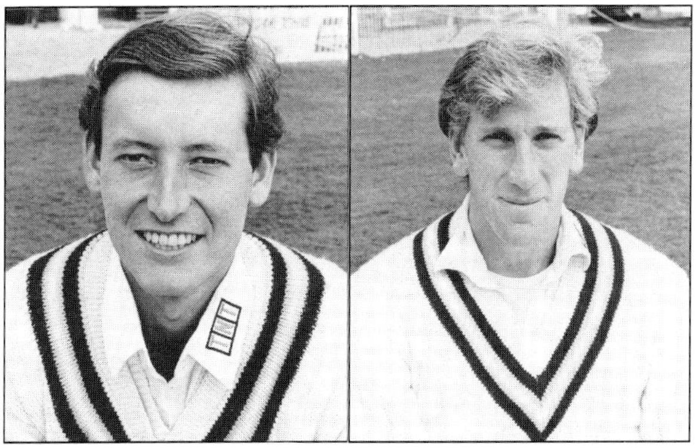

Hampshire heroes Tim Tremlett and Kevan James. Both scored maiden centuries and shared a stand of 227 for Hampshire's 8th wicket against Somerset at Taunton, a record for the county. (Trevor Jones)

David Lawrence, bowling very quickly and looking the most improved pace man in the country, routed Sussex in their first innings at Hove, but there were ten stoppages in miserable weather and although Andy Stovold and Paul Romaines asserted Gloucestershire's dominance with an opening stand of 165, the match was doomed to a draw.

Alan Knott and Richard Ellison brought about a remarkable revival in Kent's fortunes at Northampton. Kent were 112 for 8 when Knott joined Ellison at the end of a rain fractured first day. On the second morning they took their stand to 136, a ninth wicket record for any county against

Richard Illingworth (Worcestershire) 13 wickets for 59 runs at Oxford. (Mike Powell)

Northants. Baptiste then devastated the home side who slipped from 132 for 2 to 162 all out, but rain was the eventual winner.

The leaders of the Britannic Assurance County Championship, Glamorgan, suffered a terrible mauling on the first two days at Cardiff. Ontong asked Middlesex to bat first in the one hundredth county championship match to be played at Sophia Gardens. His decision seemed correct when the visitors slumped to 67 for 4, but Clive Radley hit his first century of the summer and shared a fifth wicket stand of 162 with Paul Downton. Glamorgan were shot out by Cowans, Daniel and the promising young Fraser on the second morning and followed-on 186 runs in arrears. They were saved by a mighty innings from Younis, who at one time had to retire hurt, and fine knocks from Javed and wicket-keeper Terry Davies who hit a career best. Glamorgan reached their highest second innings score in post-war cricket, but with Downton bowling 8 overs for 6 runs while Gatting kept wicket, the last day had little to commend it.

In contrast, the game at Taunton produced some memorable cricket. Put in to bat on a lively pitch, Somerset were 58 for 4, Roebuck having broken a finger and Richards having been caught off Tremlett for 0. They were soon 70 for 5 and 108 for 6, but Ian Botham took over. He equalled his own fastest century of the season, reaching three figures off 76 balls and, in all, he faced 106 balls and hit 6 sixes and 20 fours. It was astonishing stuff and left Hampshire shattered. They finished the day at 90 for 5 and descended to 107 for 7 the next morning. Tim Tremlett, the only bowler whom Botham had not been able to master, then joined Kevan James, Hampshire's new signing from Middlesex. They stayed together for 227 minutes and added 227 in 72 overs so beating the Hampshire eighth wicket record which had stood for 60 years. Both batsmen reached maiden centuries. James hit 10 fours and Tremlett sixteen. Tremlett has always promised more with the bat than he has achieved and he is a purposeful, elegant player. James' left-handed batting was a revelation, mocking his previous highest score of 34 and his number 10 and 11 spot in the Wellington batting line-up a few months earlier. It was a magnificent achievement by these two likeable young men and Hampshire, threatened with the follow-on when they came together, took a first innings lead of 36 instead. Wyatt fell before the close, but Popplewell and Richards added 112. Richards was at his regal best and hit 10 sixes and 19 fours. The 132 runs he made on the last morning came off 110 balls. It was an innings of indolent mastery, of a style that no other in the world can approach. Botham's declaration left Hampshire the improbable task of scoring 323 in 66 overs. Greenidge went at 4, but Terry and Chris Smith, at an ever increasing tempo, added 180 in 41 overs. When Botham, who had taken a marvellous slip catch to dismiss Greenidge, bowled Chris Smith Hampshire needed 72 from 12 overs; 40 were still needed from the last 5. Marks was savaged for 14 and when Garner began the last over 10 were needed. Marshall swung the first ball for 2, snicked the second through the slips for 4 and pulled an enormous 6 out of the ground next ball to win a glorious game of cricket in the best possible manner and to indicate that Hampshire had the character of which champions are made.

Surrey went to Edgbaston in an aura of controversy. Sylvester Clarke had been declared unfit for the remainder of the season so Surrey had gone to Trinidad for an instant replacement in the shape of fast bowler Gray. There was a time when counties turned to their local leagues when in need of players, but success now dominates all, and the money it brings. The rule which allows counties to sign an overseas player at a moment's notice on a year's contract is a silly one and it will bring an erosion of quality and commitment into the game. A further idiocy in the Surrey situation was that newly appointed captain Geoff Howarth would now find no place in the side as Gray had claimed the overseas player spot. Gray's debut at Edgbaston overshadowed the first-class debut of Warwickshire's Hoffman and Jesty's first hundred for Surrey. He and Pauline added 177 for the fifth wicket. Clinton and Butcher began Surrey's second innings with a partnership of 165 and the home side were eventually asked to make 283 in 50 overs. Kallicharran, with 2 sixes and 12 fours, put on 111 in 50 minutes with Robin Dyer who was more sedate but equally valuable. There were blistering efforts from Andy Lloyd and Geoff Humpage and Warwickshire romped home.

The belief that the Oxbridge sides did not deserve first-class status gained further credibility when Oxford were beaten in two days by Worcestershire. Richard Illingworth had career best figures in each innings and the first ten wicket haul of the season. In their second innings the University went from 129 for 2 to 183 all out. Miller and Hagan put on 106 for the first wicket.

Lord's witnessed some glorious batting. Allan Border hit his third century in successive matches and Simon O'Donnell hit a magnificently powerful hundred. They added 206 in 154 minutes for the sixth wicket with some scintillating batting. The next day it was England's turn as skipper Mark Nicholas and Allan Lamb put on 239 for the third wicket without being parted. There was more fine batting on the last day and

Simon O'Donnell – a glorious hundred on his debut at Lord's. (Sporting Pictures UK Ltd)

Bobby Parks dives to catch opposing wicket-keeper Davies, Hampshire v Glamorgan at Southampton, 25 May. (Adrian Murrell)

although the weather was unkind, the match excited even more interest in the forthcoming Test series.

25, 26 and 27 May

at Old Trafford

Yorkshire 205 (S.N. Hartley 52, B.P. Patterson 6 for 77) and 58 for 4
Lancashire 269 (N.H. Fairbrother 128, I. Folley 69, P.W. Jarvis 4 for 57)

Match drawn
Lancashire 7 pts, Yorkshire 6 pts

at Worcester

Warwickshire 315 for 9 dec (D.L. Amiss 100 not out, A.I. Kallicharran 63, N.V. Radford 4 for 100) and 16 for 1
Worcestershire
214 (T.S. Curtis 66, R.N. Kapil Dev 56)

Match drawn
Warwickshire 7 pts, Worcestershire 5 pts

at Derby

Australians 278 for 5 (A.R. Border 100, D.M. Wellham 77, A.M.J. Hilditch 60)
v **Derbyshire**

Match drawn

25, 27 and 28 May

at Bristol

Somerset 211 for 9
v **Gloucestershire**

Match drawn
Gloucestershire 4 pts, Somerset 2 pts

at Southampton

Glamorgan 197 (R.C. Ontong 90 not out, M.D. Marshall 4 for 57) and 176 for 8 dec
Hampshire 115 (S.J. Malone 5 for 38) and 259 for 7 (C.L. Smith 96, C.G. Greenidge 65)

Hampshire won by 3 wickets
Hampshire 20 pts, Glamorgan 5 pts

ABOVE: *Steve Malone in fine form for Glamorgan against his old county, 25 May. (George Herringshaw)*
BELOW: *Neil Fairbrother – a century in the Roses match at Old Trafford. (Sporting Pictures UK Ltd)*

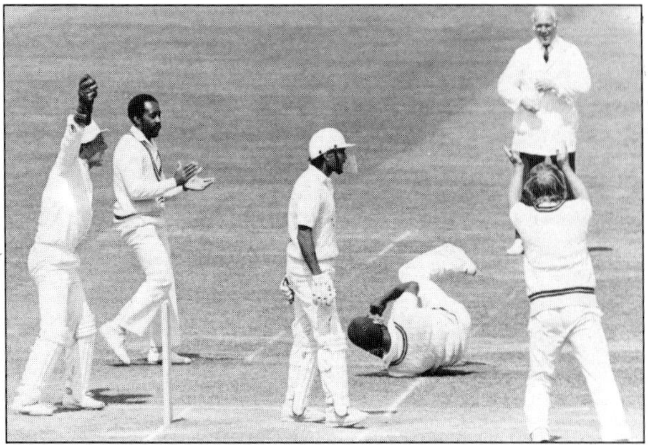

ABOVE: *Middlesex* v *Sussex at Lord's. Slack rolls over as he catches Gehan Mendis. Downton, Butcher and Radley applaud. (Adrian Murrell)*

LEFT: *Trevor Jesty – heartening success as captain of Surrey. (Tom Morris)*

at Leicester

Leicestershire 304 for 5 (J.C. Balderstone 83, J.J. Whitaker 79, D.I. Gower 52, R.A. Harper 4 for 103)
v **Northamptonshire**

Leicestershire 3 pts, Northamptonshire 1 pt

at Lord's

Sussex 132 (N.G. Cowans 5 for 44) and 180 (N.G. Cowans 4 for 18)
Middlesex 339 for 6 dec (P.R. Downton 85 not out, R.O. Butcher 70)

Middlesex won by an innings and 27 runs
Middlesex 24 pts, Sussex 2 pts

at The Oval

Essex 336 for 6 dec (D.R. Pringle 121 not out, D.E. East 69, G.A. Gooch 57, B.R. Hardie 54) and 0 for 0 dec
Surrey 10 for 0 dec and 327 for 3 (T.E. Jesty 112 not out, G.S. Clinton 106)

Surrey won by 7 wickets
Surrey 18 pts, Essex 4 pts

A wretched holiday week-end all but destroyed the cricket programme and cost counties dear. Derbyshire, expecting a bumper crowd for four days, saw their scheduled four-day match with the Australians begin at 1.40 in gloom on the Saturday and end the same day. With two days lost to rain, a one-day game was played on the Tuesday. In the first-class match, Border hit 10 fours and 5 sixes in his fourth hundred in as many matches. He and Wellham added 148 in 35 overs, Border's 100 coming off 112 balls.

There was no play after the first day at Bristol and no play on the last day at Worcester where Dennis Amiss hit the ninety-second century of his career. Harper and Wheeler made debuts for Northants at Leicester where there was no play after the first day.

Rain eventually destroyed the Roses match, but there was some fine cricket before it did. Yorkshire fell to the pace of Patterson and were 26 for 4 after his ferocious opening spell. Neil Hartley, their top scorer, also suffered a broken thumb.

Lancashire fared little better, being 25 for 3 before Fairbrother and night-watchman Folley put on 142 in 53 overs. Both batsmen hit career best scores and Fairbrother's fine innings included 15 fours. Allott had Yorkshire struggling in their second innings before the rain.

Essex began with a partnership of 114 between Gooch and Hardie and then slipped to 150 for 5. Pringle and David East shared a sparkling stand of 173 to put their side back on top, but there was no play on the second day. Fletcher was generous in leaving Surrey a day in which to make 327 to win, both captains having forfeited innings. Surrey grasped the chance eagerly. Clinton gave the early stability and Jesty, awarded his county cap and named as acting captain, hit a six and 11 fours in his 112 which came off 158 balls so that Surrey won with 21.3 overs to spare. Perplexed by the weather more than most, Essex were also handicapped by the loss of two young batsmen, Gladwin and Prichard, with an injured back and broken finger respectively.

Sussex gave two more poor batting displays at Lord's. The pace trio, Cowans, Daniel and Williams, shot them out in 42 overs on the first day which Middlesex closed at 219 for 4. There were only 30 overs possible on the second day, but Middlesex made the most of them, Downton and Emburey adding 96 in 24 overs. Sussex batted with more determination on the last day, but Cowans broke the middle order when he sent back Alan Wells, Greig and Imran in 19 balls.

The highly professional Middlesex victory took them to the top of the Britannic Assurance Championship table one point ahead of Surrey with Hampshire and Glamorgan in third and fourth places. These two counties fought out a splendid game at Southampton with Hampshire again winning an exciting victory. A doubtful wicket produced a sensational first day. Marshall and Connor shot out Glamorgan for 197 with Rodney Ontong playing an innings of heroic stature. He came to the wicket at 20 for 3, which quickly became 24 for 4, but stayed to the end to steer his side to calmer waters. He hit 12 fours and batted for $3\frac{1}{2}$ hours. Hampshire fared even worse than Glamorgan. Thomas, Barwick and Malone, revelling in success against his old county, routed them in 40.5 overs and Glamorgan had lost Derrick in their second innings before the close of a day which had seen 21 wickets fall and 316 runs scored. No play was possible on the second day, but Ontong was happy to see Holmes, Davies and Javed bat his side to a good lead and enable him to set Hampshire to make 259 off 44 overs, a stern task on a wicket which still gave occasional problems. Terry and Nicholas were out with only 13 scored, but Greenidge and Chris Smith, in glorious form, put on 166 in 27 overs of thrilling batting. Twelve overs remained when Greenidge was run out and Chris Smith followed him 3 runs later with 77 still required. Robin Smith and Marshall maintained the tempo, but when the last two balls arrived, with Tremlett and Cowley at the wicket, 8 runs were needed. The penultimate ball of the match was driven for 6 by Tim Tremlett and the last delivery by Greg Thomas was cut to third man where a misfield allowed the batsmen to scamper the two runs required.

28 May

at Derby

Derbyshire 188 for 9 (K.J. Barnett 54)
Australians 192 for 4 (K.C. Wessels 64)

Australians won by 6 wickets

The Australians won with 2.2 of their 55 overs to spare in this match arranged to compensate for the loss of the first-class match through rain. Murray Bennett strained his left ankle during net practice.

John Player Special League

26 May

at Bristol

Gloucestershire 87 for 4
Kent 88 for 3

Kent (4 pts) won by 7 wickets

at Basingstoke

Hampshire *v.* Glamorgan

Match abandoned
Hampshire 2 pts, Glamorgan 2 pts

at Leicester

Leicestershire 35 for 1
***v.* Northamptonshire**

Match abandoned
Leicestershire 2 pts, Northamptonshire 2 pts

at Lord's

Sussex 87 for 2
Middlesex 88 for 3

Middlesex (4 pts) won by 7 wickets

Alan Wells (Sussex) – a century against Glamorgan, 29 May. (George Herringshaw)

Allan Green (Sussex). Weeks of good form and well deserved maiden hundred, 31 May. (George Herringshaw)

at Trent Bridge

Nottinghamshire 100 for 4
Somerset 106 for 3

Somerset (4 pts) won by 7 wickets

at The Oval

Essex 63 for 3
***v.* Surrey**

Match abandoned
Surrey 2 pts, Essex 2 pts

There were 10-over slogs at Bristol and Lord's and a 26-over match at Trent Bridge which Somerset, with Botham hitting 40 off 22 balls, won with 5.1 overs to spare. There was dampness everywhere.

29, 30 and 31 May

at Basingstoke

Derbyshire 246 (P.G. Newman 56 not out) and 350 for 6 dec (A. Hill 120, B. Roberts 66)
Hampshire 218 (M.D. Marshall 64) and 380 for 6 (R.A. Smith 140 not out, C.L. Smith 83, V.P. Terry 61)

Hampshire won by 4 wickets
Hampshire 22 pts, Derbyshire 6 pts

at Northampton

Northamptonshire 303 (G. Cook 126, R.A. Harper 76, A.M. Ferreira 4 for 81) and 339 for 9 dec (R.G. Williams 118, D.J. Capel 63, A.C. Storie 50 not out)
Warwickshire 301 for 3 dec (A.I. Kallicharran 152 not out, D.L. Amiss 83) and 321 for 6 (D.L. Amiss 140, G.W. Humpage 123 not out, R.A. Harper 4 for 116)

Match drawn
Warwickshire 8 pts, Northamptonshire 5 pts

at Trent Bridge

Nottinghamshire 382 for 5 dec (C.E.B. Rice 171 not out, P. Johnson 118) and 162 for 4 dec (D.W. Randall 108 not out)
Leicestershire 247 (I.P. Butcher 120) and 210 for 6 (I.P. Butcher 74, E.E. Hemmings 4 for 89)

Match drawn
Nottinghamshire 7 pts, Leicestershire 4 pts

at The Oval

Surrey 255 (A.J. Stewart 77) and 402 for 6 dec (M.A. Lynch 144 not out, G.S. Clinton 80, A. Needham 73)
Middlesex 452 for 6 dec (G.D. Barlow 115, C.T. Radley 105 not out, W.N. Slack 96)

Match drawn
Middlesex 7 pts, Surrey 4 pts

at Hove

Sussex 303 for 5 dec (A.P. Wells 102, P.W.G. Parker 60) and 206 for 1 (A.M. Green 100 not out, G.D. Mendis 70)
Glamorgan 58 (D.A. Reeve 5 for 24, Imran Khan 4 for 16) and 447 (R.C. Ontong 122, S.P. Henderson 111)

Sussex won by 9 wickets
Sussex 24 pts, Glamorgan 2 pts

at Leeds

Yorkshire 383 for 4 dec (M.D. Moxon 153, R.J. Blakey 90, J.D. Love 62 not out) and 223 for 3 dec (G. Boycott 114 not out)
Somerset 257 (I.V.A. Richards 105, V.J. Marks 62) and 230 for 6 (I.V.A. Richards 53, V.J. Marks 51, P.W. Jarvis 4 for 59)

Match drawn
Yorkshire 8 pts, Somerset 4 pts

at Oxford

Kent 349 for 3 dec (D.G. Aslett 174, N.R. Taylor 120) and 202 for 2 dec (S.G. Hinks 88, M.R. Benson 55)
Oxford University 252 for 8 dec (D.A. Thorne 89, R.S. Rutnagur 66, G.R. Dilley 4 for 40) and 173 for 5 (D.A. Thorne 66)

Match drawn

Championship leaders dominated the first day's play at The Oval. Surrey reached a reasonably respectable score only through the efforts of Pat Pocock who hit 41 at the end of the innings, but Middlesex took total command when Barlow and Slack put on 225 for the first wicket with Barlow reaching his first hundred of the season. Clive Radley continued in his fine form and Middlesex declared with a lead of 197. Surrey lost Butcher at 6 and night-watchman Monkhouse was forced to retire hurt with a broken arm. Clinton and Needham batted defiantly, but at 222 for 6, Monkhouse unable to bat, and three hours remaining, Surrey faced defeat. Lynch was joined by Richards and, without hint of surrender, they batted through to the close, adding 180 with Lynch reaching his second hundred of the summer.

Middlesex's failure to bowl a side out twice again cost them the leadership which was taken over by Hampshire who gained their third magnificent win against the odds in

Blakey – a new start on the Yorkshire horizon. (Adrian Murrell)

succession. Nicholas asked Derbyshire to bat at Basingstoke and with the visitors at 128 for 8, he was well satisfied. Moir, Newman and Connor took the score to 246, however, the last pair adding 70. Hampshire were soon in trouble themselves and kept in contention only through Marshall's aggressive knock. Alan Hill batted for 5 hours and hit 15 fours to give Derbyshire a position of solidity, and, it seemed impregnability. Barnett declared and set Hampshire to make 379 in 79 overs, a daunting task. Greenidge and Terry got them off to a good start, but Nicholas went cheaply and it was a stand of 161 in 130 minutes for the fourth wicket by the Smith brothers. The target was brought to 65 from the last 10 overs, and 53 from the last 8. Tremlett played an able supporting role and ran well to give Robin Smith the strike. The younger Smith's innings occupied 169 minutes and he faced 165 balls, hitting 4 sixes and 13 fours. It was exhilarating stuff and Robin Smith won the match when he hit Miller for two sixes in the penultimate over.

Early season leaders Glamorgan faltered again, but ultimately they died bravely. Sussex gained their first batting points of the season on the first day thanks mainly to an aggressive hundred from Alan Wells. By the close Glamorgan were in total disarray at 29 for 5. The following morning Reeve and Imran finished the job they had started the evening before and Glamorgan, out for 58, followed-on 205 runs in arrears. They lost their first 4 wickets for 117, but Ontong joined Henderson in a stand of 221 which raised hopes of saving the game. Henderson hit 17 fours and Ontong 18. Sussex were left 41 overs in which to make 203. Mendis and Green gave them the necessary start, 136 in 28 overs, and Green went on to a maiden century, with a six and 12 fours off 106 balls. Glamorgan were handicapped by an injury to Thomas, but it was a splendid Sussex victory.

Leicestershire declined the challenge at Trent Bridge. Rice and Johnson put on 208 for the fourth wicket on the first day although they benefitted from some lapses in the field by Leicestershire. Butcher responded with a century for the visitors on the second day and Randall hit his third hundred of the season before a puzzlingly dour innings by Birch and the eventual draw.

There were five centuries at Northampton after the home side have been 97 for 6 on the opening day. Resurrected by Cook and Harper in their differing methods, Northants were savaged by Kallicharran and Amiss on the second day in a stand of 197. On the last morning 169 runs were scored in the two hours before lunch, Richard Williams hitting a fierce hundred. Set to make 342, Warwickshire were 30 for 3, but

Cricket at Horsham. (Michael King)

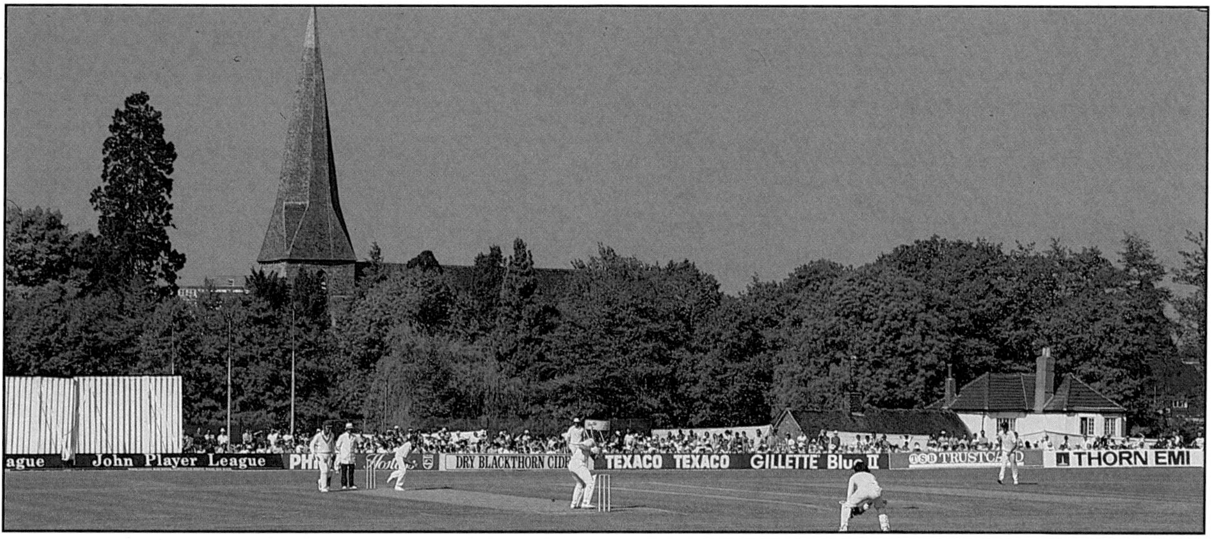

Amiss and Humpage hit glorious centuries, technically sound and excitingly positive, to add 232 in 155 minutes. It was Amiss' second hundred in a week, the ninety-third of his career. Eventually Warwickshire fell 22 short of their target after their brave effort.

Oxford University could make no such response at The Parks where batsmen flourished and Rutnagur hit a career best. Benson led Kent for the first time.

Two sides depleted by injuries fouught out a draw in the sun at Headingley. Bail made his debut for Somerset and Moxon and Blakey, with a career best, added 223 for the second wicket, a Yorkshire record against Somerset. Viv Richards hit a masterly century on the second day after the weakened Somerset side had been struggling, and this was followed by a Boycott hundred in a different vein. It was the 114th of his career and came off 189 balls. Set 350 to win, Somerset never looked likely to succeed and Yorkshire never looked to have the guile to counter Richards or the durable, eminently likeable Vic Marks.

The Texaco Trophy

The second year of Texaco's sponsorship of the one-day international series was again blessed with glorious weather and cricket that was in keeping with sun and capacity crowds. Gooch and Willey returned to the England sqead after their three years suspension and Botham was recalled to the England side after missing the tour to India.

Cricket depends much on sponsorship these days and it is well that we should remember it. There can be few sponsors as considerate, courteous and generous as Texaco. With promotion instigators Barry Ashman and Sue Ville cricket enthusiasts in the separate camps of England and Australia, the series was a joyful one and the perfect curtain raiser for the Test series ahead.

First Texaco One-Day International
ENGLAND *v.* AUSTRALIA

England selected Fowler, badly out of form, in preference to Robinson and it was the Lancastrian who was first to go. He hit a glorious shot through the covers and then, not for the first time, chased a wide delivery and was caught behind. Like Fowler, Gower had been in no sort of form and the selectors had indicated that he still had to prove himself in

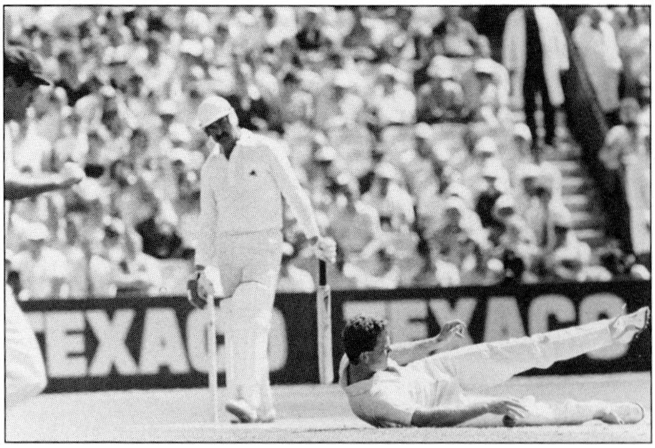

ABOVE: *Gooch returns to international cricket and McDermott slips in his delivery stride, First Texaco Trophy match, Old Trafford. (Adrian Murrell)*
RIGHT: *Botham – the power and the glory. Phillips looks on in admiration. (Adrian Murrell)*

order to retain the captaincy for the summer. He had elected to bat on a slowish wicket and had also decided that he would bat at number three, a decision which caused some debate. He was soon back in the pavilion, bowled by an excellent ball from Lawson which came back at him sharply. Lamb joined him immediately, caught behind first ball, another splendid delivery which lifted and left the batsman late. England were 27 for 3 in the ninth over.

Gooch and Botham added 116 and 28 overs. Gooch was anxious, and nervous, in re-establishing himself again in international cricket. In his three years absence his reputation had grown enormously and he was welcomed in many quarters as the returning messiah, come to put all right with English cricket. It was a role he did not relish, but he responded to the situation with strength, hard work and dignity and it was five overs into the afternoon before he was out, caught on the square-leg boundary sweeping at Holland

BELOW AND LEFT: *Botham – the downfall. He attempts to reverse sweep Matthews and is bowled, First Texaco Trophy match, Old Trafford. Peter May, chairman of selectors, banned the reverse sweep after this match. (Ken Kelly)*

INSET: *The Texaco Flag. (David Munden)*
ABOVE: *Blue skies at Old Trafford. (Adrian Murrell)*

who, in spite of Botham's attack on him, bowled with admirable control and economy.

From the point of Gooch's dismissal the England batting began to disappoint. Gatting dabbled. He played the dilettante with the reverse sweep which did not suit him and it looked as though India had been erased from his memory. Botham was quite magnificent. He hit 5 sixes and his 72, his highest score in limited-over internationals, came off 82 balls at a time when England were in dire straits, but his glory ended so grotesquely. Matthews tossed his off-breaks at the off-stump and Botham was bowled going for a wretched reverse sweep. It was poor cricket. One shudders to criticise a man who was the top scorer, Man of the Match and the most vital player in the game, but it was a violation of the aesthetic, a lapse in majesty. It certainly caused the England innings to

FIRST TEXACO ONE-DAY INTERNATIONAL – ENGLAND *v.* AUSTRALIA
30 May 1985 at Old Trafford, Manchester

ENGLAND

G.A. Gooch	c O'Donnell, b Holland	57
G. Fowler	c Phillips, b McDermott	10
D.I. Gower†	b Lawson	3
A.J. Lamb	c Phillips, b Lawson	0
I.T. Botham	b Matthews	72
M.W. Gatting	not out	31
P. Willey	b Holland	12
P.R. Downton*	c Matthews, b Lawson	11
P.H. Edmonds	c Border, b Lawson	0
P.J.W. Allott	b McDermott	2
N.G. Cowans	c and b McDermott	1
Extras	b 2, lb 7, w 2, nb 9	20
(54 overs)		219

	O	M	R	W
Lawson	10	1	26	4
McDermott	11	—	46	3
O'Donnell	11	—	44	—
Matthews	11	1	45	1
Holland	11	2	49	2

FALL OF WICKETS
1- 21, 2- 27, 3- 27, 4- 143, 5- 160, 6- 181, 7- 203, 8- 203, 9- 213

AUSTRALIA

G.M. Wood	c Downton, b Cowans	8
K.C. Wessels	c Botham, b Willey	39
D.M. Wellham	c and b Edmonds	12
A.R. Border†	c and b Allott	59
D.C. Boon	c Botham, b Gooch	12
W.B. Phillips*	c Gatting, b Cowans	28
S.P. O'Donnell	b Botham	1
G.R.J. Matthews	not out	29
G.F. Lawson	not out	14
C.J. McDermott		
R.G. Holland		
Extras	b 2, lb 12, w 4	18
(54.1 overs)	(for 7 wickets)	220

	O	M	R	W
Cowans	10.1	1	44	2
Botham	11	2	41	1
Edmonds	11	2	33	1
Allott	11	—	47	1
Willey	9	1	31	1
Gooch	2	—	10	1

FALL OF WICKETS
1- 19, 2- 52, 3- 74, 4- 118, 5- 156, 6- 157, 7- 186

Umpires: D.G.L. Evans and K.E. Palmer

Man of the Match: I.T. Botham

Australia won by 3 wickets

Border hits to leg. Boon anticipates the run. (Ken Kelly)

decline to a total well below what had looked probable. Australia soon had problems of their own. Wood was caught behind off Cowans at 15 and the ungainly Wessels should have gone the same way off Allott before the score reached 30.

Edmonds had an inhibiting effect upon the batsmen. He caught and bowled Wellham as soon as he came on and had Wessels caught at mid-wicket off his one bad ball, a full toss. Border could not quite find his usual fluency, but soon he improvised to hit 59 off 16 overs. He should have been stumped off Willey and could have been caught off Allott, but he also played some exciting shots. When he was out in the forty-fourth over Australia were still 64 short of victory, but Phillips, Matthews and Lawson batted far more sensibly than their England counterparts had done and saw Australia home with 5 balls to spare.

Gatting took a memorable catch at short third man to dismiss Phillips and earlier Matthews, whose vibrant commitment to the game and sense of fun made him a favourite with the crowd, had taken an equalling thrilling catch at backward cover to dismiss Downton. They were catches in keeping with a spirited game between the friendliest of rivals. Cricket in England was alive and well again and the talk of an Australian 'second eleven' had become muted in admiration for Border and his men.

Second Texaco One-Day International
ENGLAND *v.* AUSTRALIA

Invited to bat first on a good wicket, England, who brought in Robinson for Fowler, began well, 63 coming for the first wicket in 15 overs. Robinson fell when O'Donnell deceived him with a slower ball and quickly changed course to take a fine return catch. Poor Gower attempted a rash cut, feet firmly planted, and Phillips took a high catch. Lamb was never in touch, but he and Gooch added 65 which occupied 21 overs.

The momentum had been lost and soundly as he batted, Gooch never quite managed the power and run rate expected of him. Responsibility and expectation seemed to weigh heavily upon him and his 115 contained a six and 9 fours, a low proportion of boundaries for such a usually dominating player. His innings lasted for 159 balls, but there was enough

An inglorious end to a glorious innings – Gooch swings at McDermott and is bowled for 115. (Adrian Murrell)

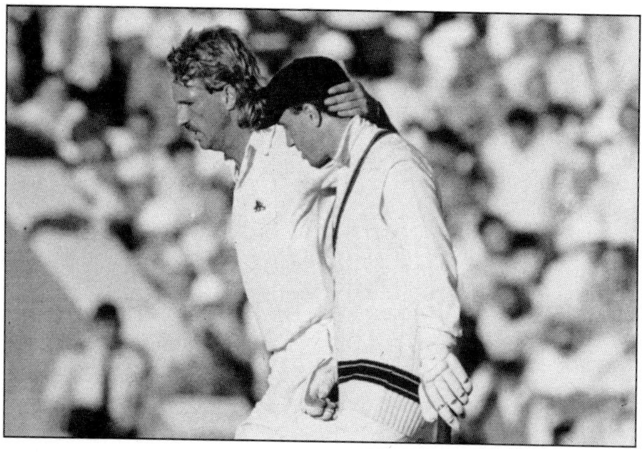

Botham congratulates Greg Matthews who has just made the winning hit to put Australia one up in the Texaco series. (Adrian Murrell)

sense of authority to suggest that the hopes that had been expressed about his return to Test cricket would be fulfilled.

He and Botham added 57 off 69 before Wellham caught Botham well at mid-on, and the restrictions on Gooch and Botham were a credit to the Australian fielding.

Gatting and Willey perished in the chase for runs and the England total was once again disappointing. It took on greater proportions when Wood was lbw in Cowans's fiery

Gower at his lowest ebb, dismissed by O'Donnell for 0 in the Second Texaco Trophy match at Edgbaston. (Adrian Murrell)

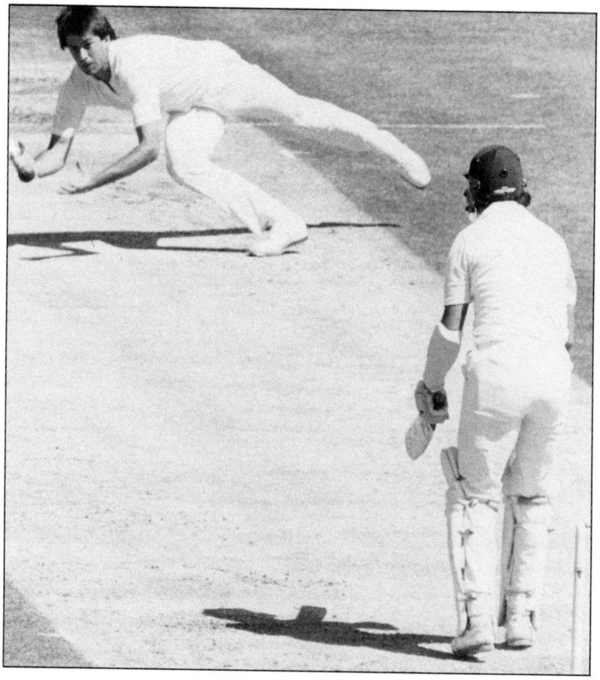

O'Donnell takes an excellent return catch to dismiss Robinson. (Adrian Murrell)

opening spell, and Wellham, never at ease, shuffled across in front to a ball from Botham.

Border now took command. What luck there was went Australia's way, but Border needs no luck. Wessels left in the thirty-fourth over, 116 for 3, and Boon perished swiping in the thirty-ninth over 21 runs later. Wayne Phillips hinted extraordinary power and adventure which could well leave a lasting memory of him in England hearts and minds, and O'Donnell played with calm and youthful authority. Thirty runs were needed from 6 overs and O'Donnell should have been run out and caught and bowled by Cowans in the fiftieth over. He finally fell to Botham by which time only 11

BELOW: *Botham and Downton combine to drop Wessels off Allott. (David Munden)*

SECOND TEXACO ONE-DAY INTERNATIONAL – ENGLAND *v.* AUSTRALIA
1 June 1985 at Edgbaston, Birmingham

ENGLAND

G.A. Gooch	b McDermott	115
R.T. Robinson	c and b O'Donnell	26
D.I. Gower†	c Phillips, b O'Donnell	0
A.J. Lamb	b Thomson	25
I.T. Botham	c Wellham, b Lawson	29
M.W. Gatting	c Lawson, b McDermott	6
P. Willey	c Phillips, b Lawson	0
P.R. Downton*	not out	16
P.H. Edmonds	not out	6
P.J.W. Allott		
N.G. Cowans		
Extras	lb 2, w 2, nb 4	8
(55 overs)	(for 7 wickets)	231

	O	M	R	W
Lawson	11	—	53	2
McDermott	11	—	56	2
O'Donnell	11	2	32	2
Thomson	11	—	47	1
Matthews	10	—	38	—
Border	1	—	3	—

FALL OF WICKETS
1- 63, 2- 69, 3- 134, 4- 193, 5- 206, 6- 208, 7- 216

AUSTRALIA

K.C. Wessels	c and b Willey	57
G.M. Wood	lbw, b Cowans	5
D.M. Wellham	lbw, b Botham	7
A.R. Border†	not out	85
D.C. Boon	b Allott	13
W.B. Phillips*	c Gatting, b Cowans	14
S.P. O'Donnell	b Botham	28
G.R.J. Matthews	not out	8
G.F. Lawson		
J.R. Thomson		
C.J. McDermott		
Extras	lb 13, w 2, nb 1	16
(54 overs)	(for 6 wickets)	233

	O	M	R	W
Botham	10	2	38	2
Cowans	11	2	42	2
Allott	10	1	40	1
Willey	11	1	38	1
Edmonds	10	—	48	—
Gooch	2	—	14	—

FALL OF WICKETS
1- 10, 2- 19, 3- 116, 4- 137, 5- 157, 6- 222

Umpires: D.J. Constant and D.R. Shepherd

Man of the Match: A.R. Border

Australia won by 4 wickets

Botham reaches wide to slash a boundary. (Varley Agency)

Greg Matthews bowling – an eager and aggressive cricketer. (Ken Kelly)

Man of the Match Allan Border. (George Herringshaw)

ABOVE: *Eager crowd at Edgbaston. (George Herringshaw)*

LEFT: *Gooch demonstrates his return to the England side, a mighty off-drive during his century at Edgbaston. (Adrian Murrell)*

BELOW LEFT: *Boon just gets home. (Adrian Murrell)*

were needed. Matthews, having stirred the crowd and enjoyed it when fielding, arrived to face 7 deliveries and smite Australia to victory and the Texaco Trophy with an over to spare.

Allan Border stood majestically undefeated, 85 not out off 123 balls, quietly proud of his inexperienced side which had performed so well.

Third Texaco One-Day International
ENGLAND *v.* AUSTRALIA

Foster for Edmonds was the change in the England line up, and Australia brought in Hilditch and Ritchie for Wessels and Wellham. Gower won the toss and decided he would like to bat second. He was soon rewarded when Foster had Hilditch lbw and Ritchie was beautifully taken at slip, left-handed, by Gooch off Botham.

Border joined Wood and again displayed his total authority. At lunch, after 31 overs, Australia were 111 for 2, a huge total beckoning. In the thirty-eighth over Lamb just

BELOW: *One of the Lord's centurions. Graeme Wood clips the ball to leg during his innings of 114. (Mark Leech)*

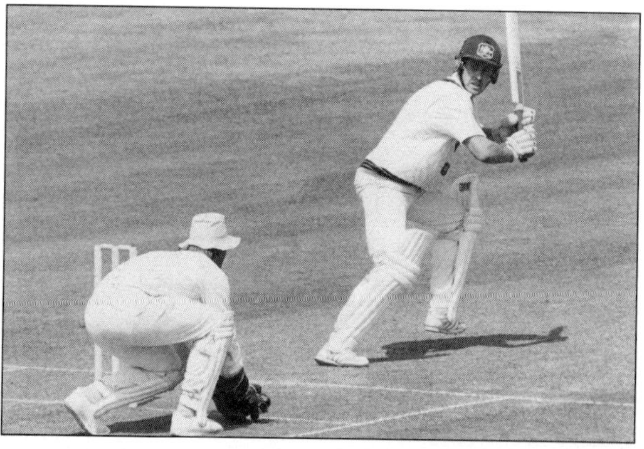

missed pulling off a spectacular catch to dismiss Wood, but Gooch, the suffering bowler, clipped Border's leg stump next ball. Boon played crisply and powerfully and Wood reached a fine hundred in the fifty-second over. He had faced 154 deliveries. He hit a six off Willey in the final over and should

Lord's and an England victory. (Adrian Murrell)

David Gower acknowledges the applause on reaching his century at Lord's. It was the curtain-raiser to a memorable summer. (Adrian Murrell)

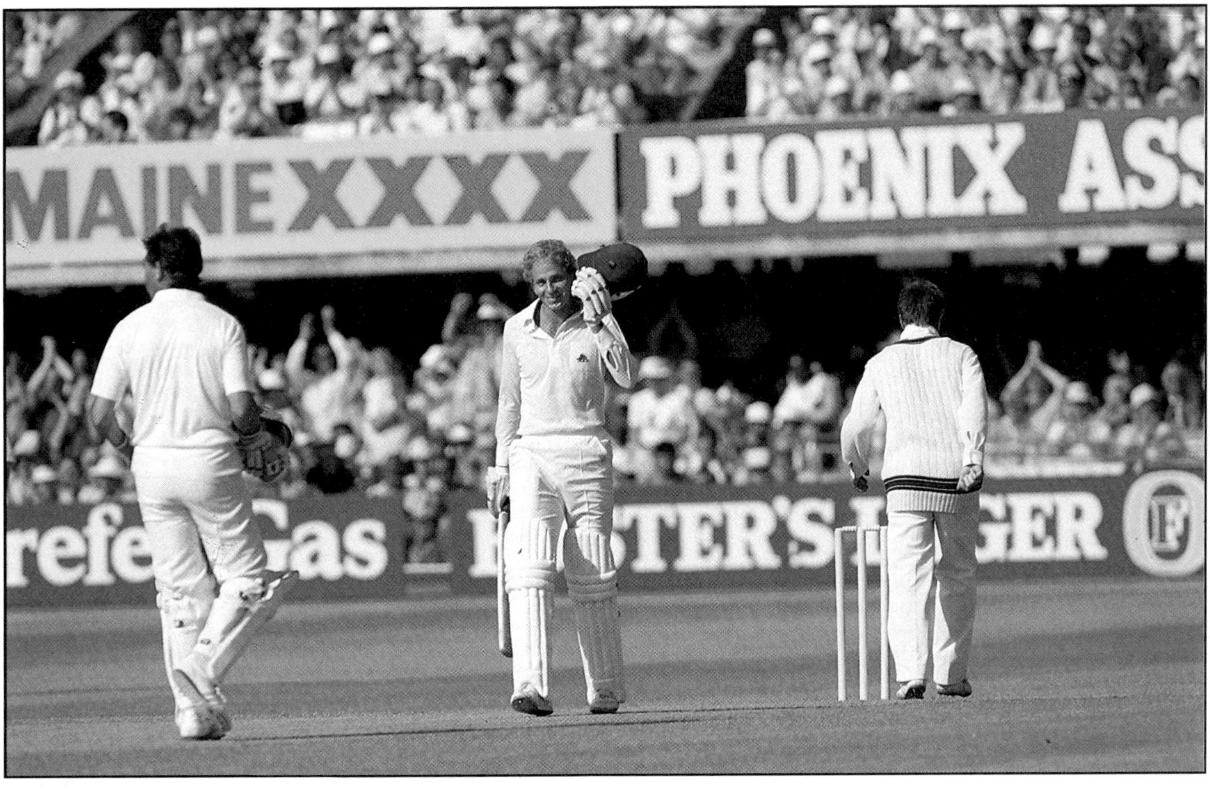

THIRD TEXACO ONE-DAY INTERNATIONAL – ENGLAND *v.* AUSTRALIA
3 June 1985 at Lord's

AUSTRALIA			
	G.M. Wood	not out	114
	A.M.J. Hilditch	lbw, b Foster	4
	G.M. Ritchie	c Gooch, b Botham	15
	A.R. Border†	b Gooch	44
	D.C. Boon	c Gower, b Willey	45
	W.B. Phillips*	run out	10
	S.P. O'Donnell	not out	0
	G.R.J. Matthews		
	G.F. Lawson		
	C.J. McDermott		
	J.R. Thomson		
	Extras	b 2, lb 13, w 6, nb 1	22
	(55 overs)	(for 5 wickets)	254

	O	M	R	W
Cowans	8	2	22	—
Foster	11	—	55	1
Botham	8	1	27	1
Allott	7	1	45	—
Gooch	11	—	46	1
Willey	10	1	44	1

FALL OF WICKETS
1- 6, 2- 47, 3- 143, 4- 228, 5- 252

ENGLAND			
	G.A. Gooch	not out	117
	R.T. Robinson	lbw, b McDermott	7
	D.I. Gower†	c Border, b McDermott	102
	A.J. Lamb	not out	9
	I.T. Botham		
	M.W. Gatting		
	P. Willey		
	P.R. Downton*		
	N.A. Foster		
	P.J.W. Allott		
	N.G. Cowans		
	Extras	b 2, lb 9, w 2, nb 9	22
	(49 overs)	(for 2 wickets)	257

	O	M	R	W
Lawson	9	—	37	—
McDermott	10	—	51	2
Thomson	8	1	50	—
O'Donnell	11	—	54	—
Matthews	10	—	49	—
Border	1	—	5	—

FALL OF WICKETS
1- 25, 2- 227

Umpires: H.D. Bird and B.J. Meyer

Man of the Match: D.I. Gower

England won by 8 wickets

have been stumped, but he, and Australia, seemed well satisfied.

When Botham had Ritchie taken at slip he became the first man to have taken 100 wickets and scored 1000 runs in limited-over internationals.

Gower had pulled off a fine running catch to dismiss Boon and soon he was partnering Gooch, who opened his account with a six off McDermott, after Robinson had fallen to the young Queenslander.

The Gooch–Gower partnership was a memorable one. It was batting of the highest quality in the summer sun. There was fluency, power and elegance and the crowd revelled in it. Gower, who was received with warmest affection and sympathy, a fact which he himself acknowledged and appreciated, hit a six and 14 fours. His hundred came off 111 balls. Gooch, who nursed Gower wisely early on and encouraged him, hit a six and 11 fours and his hundred came off 138 balls.

Their stand realised a record 202 and ended when Gower flicked loosely at McDermott. Gooch, England's Man of the Series, stayed to the end for his highest score against Australia. It was glorious stuff and a fitting end to a splendid three-match series.

ABOVE: *The vital break-through for England in the Third Texaco Trophy match at Lord's – Border is bowled by Gooch. (Mark Leech)*

BELOW: *The confidence booster – David Gower dives to take a magnificent catch to dismiss Boon. (Adrian Murrell)*

Viv Richards, 322 for Somerset against Warwickshire at Taunton, 1 June. He hit 8 sixes and 42 fours in making the highest score made in England for 36 years. (Adrian Murrell)

1, 3 and 4 June

at Derby

Gloucestershire 398 for 3 dec (C.W.J. Athey 170, P. Bainbridge 151 not out) and 291 for 4 dec (A.W. Stovold 112, C.W.J. Athey 58)
Derbyshire 381 for 5 dec (B. Roberts 100 not out, K.J. Barnett 83, R.J. Finney 82) and 82 (D.V. Lawrence 5 for 38, C.A. Walsh 5 for 44)

Gloucestershire won by 226 runs
Gloucestershire 22 pts, Derbyshire 5 pts

at Chelmsford

Essex 213 (D.E. East 54, J.P. Agnew 4 for 59) and 162 for 3 (A.W. Lilley 56 not out)
Leicestershire 392 for 7 dec (N.E. Briers 129, P.B. Clift 106, M.A. Garnham 51)

Match drawn
Leicestershire 6 pts, Essex 4 pts

at Canterbury

Kent 189 and 146 (C.J. Tavare 60)
Worcestershire 204 (D.M. Smith 64, K.B.S. Jarvis 5 for 53) and 132 for 3 (D.M. Smith 50 not out)

Worcestershire won by 7 wickets
Worcestershire 22 pts, Kent 5 pts

Bill Athey, 170 for Gloucestershire against Derbyshire at Derby, 1 June. (George Herringshaw)

Phil Bainbridge hit 151 not out for Gloucestershire at Derby and shared a third wicket stand of 305 with Bill Athey. (George Herringshaw)

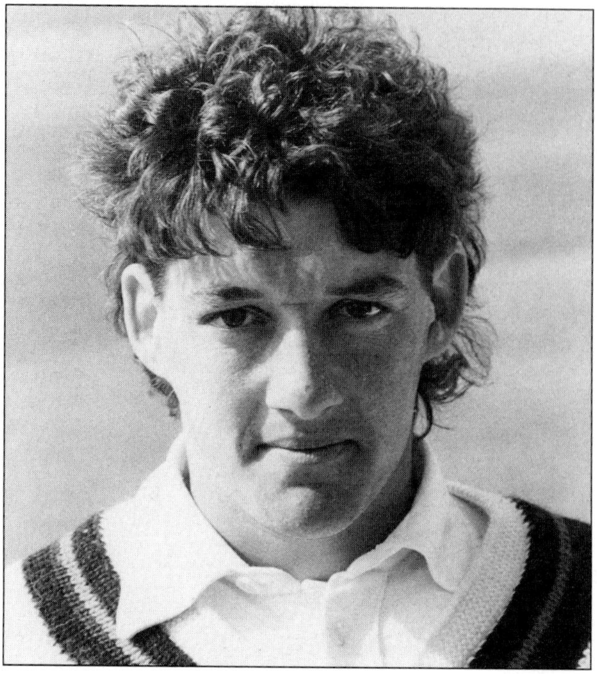

Ian Folley, 6 for 8 in 16 overs for Lancashire against Oxford University. (Sporting Pictures UK Ltd)

at Taunton

Somerset 566 for 5 dec (I.V.A. Richards 322, V.J. Marks 65, N.F.M. Popplewell 55, R.L. Ollis 55) and 226 for 5 dec (V.J. Marks 66 not out)
Warwickshire 442 for 9 dec (A.M. Ferreira 101 not out, P.A. Smith 93, D.L. Amiss 81, T.A. Lloyd 61, M.S. Turner 4 for 74) and 181 for 2 (A.I. Kallicharran 89, R.I.H.B. Dyer 63 not out)

Match drawn
Somerset 6 pts, Warwickshire 6 pts

at Horsham

Sussex 391 for 7 dec (P.W.G. Parker 105, A.M. Green 90, I.J. Gould 58 not out, C.M. Wells 56) and 281 for 6 dec (A.M. Green 106, D.J. Thomas 4 for 88)
Surrey 271 (T.E. Jesty 99) and 153 for 3 (M.A. Lynch 61 not out)

Match drawn
Sussex 8 pts, Surrey 6 pts

at Middlesbrough

Hampshire 341 for 6 dec (C.L. Smith 143 not out, R.A. Smith 63, M.D. Marshall 50) and 223 for 6 dec (C.L. Smith 68, M.D. Marshall 60)
Yorkshire 283 (G. Boycott 115, M.D. Marshall 5 for 48) and 114 for 5

Match drawn
Hampshire 7 pts, Yorkshire 4 pts

at Oxford

Lancashire 338 for 3 dec (D.W. Varey 112, D.P. Hughes 75 not out, N.H. Fairbrother 68 not out, M.R. Chadwick 63) and 223 for 2 dec (J. Abrahams 101 not out, M. Watkinson 59)
Oxford University 144 (D.A. Thorne 76, B.P. Patterson 7 for 49) and 47 (I. Folley 6 for 8)

Lancashire won by 370 runs

In the Britannic Assurance County Championship only the matches at Derby and Canterbury produced a result. On the opening day at Derby, Gloucestershire romped to 398 in 100 overs. Athey and Bainbridge came together at 65 for 2 and added 305, both batsmen reaching their highest scores in first-class cricket. Derbyshire responded in kind on the second day. Barnett gave his usual calm display of elegant batting, but Roberts with a maiden century off 116 balls and Finney with a career best added 169 for the fifth wicket to take the honours. Andy Stovold took Gloucestershire to a position of dominance on the last morning and Graveney asked the home side to make 309 on what was still a blissful pitch. Barnett was bowled by a shooter for 19 and the rest of the side succumbed abjectly to Walsh and Lawrence to be dismissed for a miserable 82 in 24 overs. The pair bowled fiercely and finely, extracting unexpected life from the pitch, but the batting was very poor. To add to Derbyshire's woe, the reliable Alan Hill suffered a knee injury which threatened to keep him out for the rest of the season.

Hampshire, the leaders, failed to force a win at Middlesbrough. The Smith brothers were again in good form, putting on 146 for the fourth wicket on the opening day. It created one of those quaint records, the highest stand by brothers against Yorkshire. Boycott, who was left out of the Sunday side, replied with 115 in 280 minutes after twice being dropped on 26. Some fierce hitting by Chris Smith, five sixes, and Malcolm Marshall enabled Nicholas to declare and set Yorkshire to make 282 in 53 overs. Five wickets had been captured and 21 ovebs remained when drizzle and gloom ended the match.

Rain ended the game at Chelmsford where Essex were

Nigel Briers – a century as Leicestershire's captain against Essex at Chelmsford. (George Herringshaw)

fortunate to survive after playing rather badly. They were 48 for 4 on the Saturday and again owed their recovery to the effervescent David East and to Derek Pringle. Fletcher also batted well. Leicestershire were 89 for 4 in reply, but acting captain Nigel Briers and Paddy Clift added 165 in 55 overs and ultimately Essex were indebted to Lilley, McEwan and the rain.

On a doubtful wicket at Canterbury Patel and Illingworth put Worcestershire in charge on the Saturday, the visitors closing at 113 for 4 after bowling out Kent for 189. Smith fell straight away on the Monday and the Worcestershire lead was disappointingly small, but their all round attack again disposed of Kent cheaply, only Tavare, Johnson and Knott offering real resistance. On a wicket that was giving the bowlers assistance Worcestershire's task was not an easy one, but night-watchman Illingworth gave Smith fine support to give them victory.

At Horsham rain ended play just as Monte Lynch promised to give a rousing climax, 48 of his 50 runs had come in boundaries. On the first day, after Mendis had gone without a run scored, Green and Parker put on 187. Sussex declared at 391 off 94 overs, skipper Gould hitting lustily at the close,

Allan Green is bowled by Peter Waterman for 90, Sussex v. *Surrey at Horsham. Green hit a century in the second innings. (Tom Morris)*

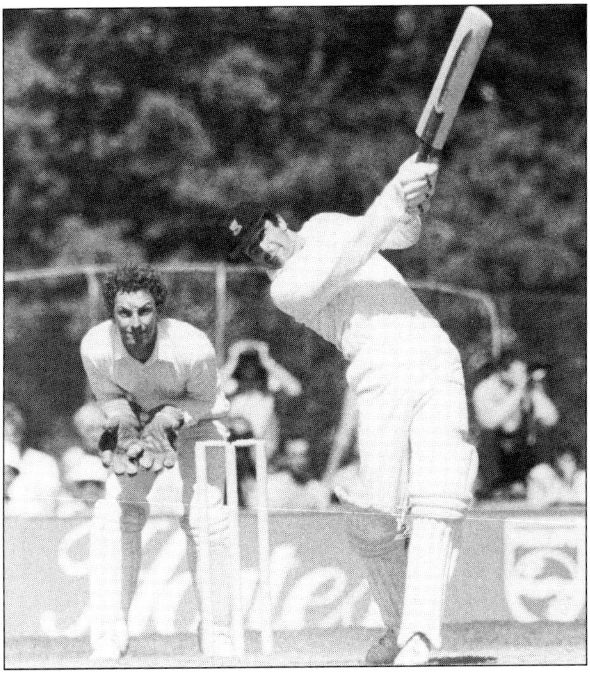

Paul Parker hits Andy Needham for his second successive six and reaches his century for Sussex against Surrey at Horsham. Richards is the wicket-keeper. (Tom Morris)

Monte Lynch gave Surrey hope of victory before the rain came. He on drives Waller with Green and Gould looking on. (Mark Leech)

and Surrey ended a miserable day at 37 for 3. On the Monday, however, Jesty brightened their outlook, being caught by Parker off Colin Wells one short of his hundred. Green hit his second century in successive matches in the final session of the day and Gould finally asked Surrey to make 402 in 85 overs. They were 59 for 3 and then came Lynch and the rain.

Lancashire enjoyed themselves at Oxford. David Varey hit his first century for Lancashire, Patterson had career best bowling figures and Folley had 6 for 8 in 16 overs. Oxford were again doleful.

Much of what happened elsewhere was totally overshadowed on the Saturday by events at Taunton. Viv Richards hit the highest score ever made for Somerset, beating Gimblett's 310 made in 1948, and the highest score made in England for 36 years. He hit 8 sixes, 42 fours, and reached 300 off 244 deliveries. Even by his standards it was breathtaking stuff. On a perfect wicket the game was always destined to be drawn once Warwickshire had countered with some enterprising batting of their own, not the least important contribution coming from Paul Smith with a championship best.

John Player Special League

2 June

at Derby

Derbyshire 223 for 9 (K.J. Barnett 69)
Gloucestershire 207 for 7 (P.W. Romaines 73)

Derbyshire (4 pts) won by 16 runs

at Chelmsford

Essex 139
Leicestershire 139 for 9

Match tied
Essex 2 pts, Leicestershire 2 pts

at Canterbury

Kent 226 for 6 (M.R. Benson 93, E.A.E. Baptiste 54 not out)
Worcestershire 191 for 9

Kent (4 pts) won by 35 runs

at Northampton

Lancashire 205 for 7 (J. Abrahams 59)
Northamptonshire 205 for 5 (G. Cook 98)

Match tied
Northamptonshire 2 pts, Lancashire 2 pts

at Taunton

Somerset 183 for 9 (I.V.A. Richards 62)
Warwickshire 187 for 3 (D.L. Amiss 78 not out, R.I.H.B. Dyer 50)

Warwickshire (4 pts) won by 7 wickets

at Horsham

Sussex 196 for 7 (Imran Khan 71)
Nottingham 197 for 8 (C.E.B. Rice 67, D.A. Reeve 4 for 32)

Nottinghamshire (4 pts) won by 2 wickets

at Middlesborough

Hampshire 257 for 6 (C.G. Greenidge 78, V.P. Terry 70)
Yorkshire 259 for 4 (K. Sharp 81 not out)

Yorkshire (4 pts) won by 6 wickets

Weather allowed all matches to go their full distance and some exciting results ensued. Kent took a two-point lead at the top of the table with a comfortable win at Canterbury. Benson hit 93 off 112 balls and Baptiste reached 50 off 36.

Northamptonshire, in second place, were involved in one of the two tied matches. Lancashire, after a slow start, reached 205 which did not seen too daunting a score for Northants, but they lost impetus after Larkins had gone for 48 and Geoff Cook was run out on the last ball of the match in going for what would have been the winning run. His consolation was his highest Sunday League score.

Essex batted poorly after Hardie and Lilley had begun with a stand of 40, but, Leicestershire, 80 for 1, chasing a small target, panicked and had five batsmen run out, the last going for the decisive run and the match was tied. With 5 overs left, Leicestershire had been 131 for 4.

Richards apart, Somerset batted poorly at Taunton and Amiss and Humpage stroked the visitors to victory with 19 balls left. Dyer hit his best score in the League and Richard Hayward, formerly of Hampshire and now captain-coach of Central Districts in New Zealand, made his debut for Somerset having been signed to compensate for injuries.

Greenidge and Terry put on 108 for Hampshire's first wicket, but Kevin Sharp, with a best in the League, saw Yorkshire to victory and joint second place with 3 balls to spare. Derbyshire were always on top against Gloucestershire, but Notts won a dramatic last ball victory at Horsham. Sussex had struggled early on, but they hit furiously at the close to reach 196. In return, Notts laboured unevenly and the last ball came with 3 needed for victory. Saxelby cut the ball to the boundary where a fumbled pick up allowed the 3 runs to be made.

5, 6 and 7 June

at Leeds

Australians 195 for 2 dec (G.M. Wood 102 not out, G.M. Ritchie 58 not out)
Yorkshire 124 for 2 (G. Boycott 52 not out)

Match drawn

Graeme Wood hit his second century in three days, but rain washed out play on the second day and limited it drastically on the third.

Benson and Hedges Cup
Quarter Finals

5 June

at Chelmsford

Derbyshire 167 for 9 (K.J. Barnett 60)
Essex 4 for 1

Match abandoned

at Southampton

Leicestershire 243 for 4 (J.C. Balderstone 60, P. Willey 56, I.P. Butcher 55)
Hampshire 239 (R.A. Smith 81)

Leicestershire won by 4 runs
(*Gold Award* – P. Willey)

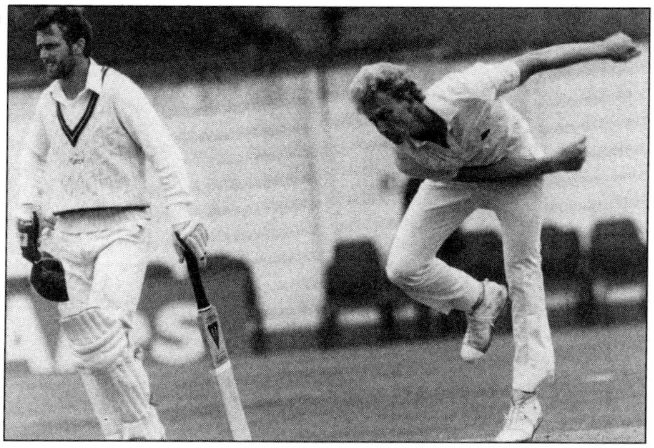

ABOVE: *Dilley bowls. Cook is the non-striking batsman. Northants* v. *Kent, Benson and Hedges Cup quarter-final ruined by rain. (Tom Morris)*

RIGHT: *Peter Willey – Gold Award in the glorious game at Southampton. (George Herringshaw)*

at Northampton

Northamptonshire 158 for 2 (G. Cook 78, W. Larkins 52)
***v.* Kent**

Match abandoned. Kent qualified for semi-finals on superior strike rate in zonal matches

5 and 7 June

---

at Worcester

Worcestershire 220 (D.M. Smith 57)
Middlesex 45 for 1

Match abandoned. Middlesex qualified for semi-finals on superior strike rate in zonal matches

7 June

---

at Chelmsford

Essex 150 for 4 (G.A. Gooch 72 not out)
Derbyshire 132 for 6

Essex won by 18 runs
(*Gold Award* – G. A. Gooch)

Wretched weather cast gloom on the Benson and Hedges Quarter Final matches and the games at Worcester and Northampton had to be abandoned leaving the home sides aggrieved in each case, but at least the system now adopted is superior to the toss of a coin used two years ago.

Derbyshire too could feel a little upset. They laboured on a fractured first day, but in the closing gloom Holding bowled Gooch with the fourth ball of his first over. Shortly afterwards play ended for the day. Rain ruled out further hopes until the Friday afternoon when a new game, 20-overs an innings, had to be started. Given a reprieve, Gooch hit fiercely and bowled economically and Essex looked winners from the moment he cut loose.

The great game of the round came at Southampton which enjoyed the only fine weather of the first day. Butcher and Balderstone began well for Leicestershire, making 104 in 28 overs after Butcher had been dropped at slip by Nicholas in Marshall's first over and Marshall himself had dropped Balderstone off Tremlett, a straightforward catch at second slip when the opener was 14. Gower fell to an airy shot, but Willey hit 56 off 65 balls and Leicestershire, having been put in, could be content with 243 although it had looked at one time that they would score more.

Hampshire, looking for inspiration from Greenidge, were disappointed. Their start was subdued and the West Indian mishooked Clift's first ball to square-leg with the score on 25. Terry followed shortly after and Chris Smith, in a rich vein of form, was insanely run out for 8. Nicholas stayed to help Robin Smith to add 64 and the last 20 overs arrived with 132 needed. Marshall and James also gave Robin Smith notable help, but it was the young South African, now qualified for England, who dominated. He batted gloriously and while he lived Hampshire were in sight of victory. He played on to Paddy Clift at 210, having hit 81 off 81 balls with a six and 8 fours and having batted with power, majesty and charm. One would be very surprised if this young man does not play Test cricket.

Nearly six overs remained when Smith was out and Hampshire, 4 wickets in hand, were only 34 short of their target, but Leicestershire tightened their grip on the game. The last over arrived with 10 needed. James' brave knock ended when he was caught at cover off the second ball and, in spite of some intelligent play by Parks, Connor skied the fifth ball to Willey who held on to put Leicestershire in the semi-finals and clinch the Gold Award, a decision not welcomed by the home supporters.

8, 10 and 11 June

---

at Ilford

Essex 281 (N.A. Foster 63, K.R. Fletcher 50, B.P. Patterson 4 for 67) and 108 for 9 dec (B.P. Patterson 6 for 45)
Lancashire 191 (J.K. Lever 5 for 66, G.A. Gooch 4 for 22) and 174 for 9 (G.A. Gooch 5 for 46)

Gooch followed his success with the bat for England with 9 wickets for 68 in Essex's match against Lancashire at Ilford. (George Herringhsaw)

Match drawn
Essex 7 pts, Lancashire 5 pts

at Abergavenny

Worcestershire 294 (P.A. Neale 77, D.M. Smith 55) and 309 for 6 (R.N. Kapil Dev 92, D.N. Patel 67, T.S. Curtis 51)
Glamorgan 250 for 0 dec (J.A. Hopkins 114 not out, G.C. Holmes 106 not out)

Match drawn
Glamorgan 7 pts, Worcestershire 3 pts

at Tunbridge Wells

Kent 163 (M.R. Benson 71, K. Saxelby 6 for 64) and 191 (K. Saxelby 4 for 49)
Nottinghamshire 198 (R.T. Robinson 90, K.B.S. Jarvis 5 for 43) and 157 for 6

Nottinghamshire won by 6 wickets
Nottinghamshire 21 pts, Kent 5 pts

at Lord's

Derbyshire 236 (J.E. Morris 99, P.H. Edmonds 6 for 87) and 221 for 3 dec (K.J. Barnett 72, I.S. Anderson 55)
Middlesex 178 (M.W. Gatting 77, O.H. Mortensen 4 for 47) and 17 for 1

Match drawn
Derbyshire 6 pts, Middlesex 5 pts

at Northampton

The Zimbabwe side which began a tour of England with a match against Oxford University. (Ken Kelly)

Northamptonshire 302 for 9 dec (R.J. Boyd-Moss 67, A.J. Lamb 65, D.J. Capel 58, Imran Khan 4 for 116) and 145 for 5 dec
Sussex 201 for 8 dec (N.A. Mallender 4 for 57) and 47 for 4

Match drawn
Northamptonshire 7 pts, Sussex 6 pts

at Bath

Gloucestershire 332 for 9 dec (J.W. Lloyds 95 not out, K.M. Curran 83, C.W.J. Athey 52, V.J. Marks 4 for 65) and 84 for 4
Somerset 243 (I.T. Botham 76 not out)

Match drawn
Gloucestershire 8 pts, Somerset 6 pts

Patrick Patterson, career best for Lancashire at Ilford, 8–11 June. Match figures of 10 for 112. (Sporting Pictures UK Ltd)

at Edgbaston

Warwickshire 127 (M.D. Marshall 6 for 50, T.M. Tremlett 4 for 42) and 198 for 7 (D.L. Amiss 57)
Hampshire 433 for 8 dec (C.G. Greenidge 204, C.L. Smith 52, N. Gifford 4 for 89)

Match drawn
Hampshire 8 pts, Warwickshire 3 pts

at Oxford

Oxford University 262 for 7 dec (D.A. Thorne 124) and 149 for 5 (R.S. Rutnagur 57)
Zimbabwe 440 (G.A. Hick 230, D.L. Houghton 104, R.S. Rutnagur 5 for 112)

Match drawn

at Cambridge

Cambridge University 142 (C.C. Ellison 51) and 161 (N.S. Taylor 7 for 44)
Surrey 156 for 8 dec (G.P. Howarth 53, A.M.G. Scott 4 for 60) and 43 for 5

Match drawn

8, 9, 10 and 11 June

at Leicester

Leicestershire 454 (D.I. Gower 135, J.C. Balderstone 134, J.R. Thomson 5 for 103) and 28 for 0
Australians 466 (W.B. Phillips 128, G.M. Ritchie 115, A.M.J. Hilditch 56, C.J. McDermott 53 not out)

Match drawn

Weather again mauled the Britannic Assurance County Championship programme and Notts, in a low-scoring game at Tunbridge Wells, were the only victors. Kevin Saxelby had best bowling figures for an innings and for a match as Kent twice failed to come to terms with a difficult wicket. By the end of the first day Tim Robinson had almost put Notts into the lead, but Jarvis cut short their hopes of domination with a fine spell on the Monday which saw the last 5 wickets fall for 14 runs. Kent promised more than they achieved in the second innings and their last 5 wickets fell for 34. Needing 157 to win, Notts lost Robinson and Cooper to Jarvis for 13 before the close, but on the last day Randall, Johnson and Birch batted with determination to bring victory.

The Championship leaders Hampshire were thwarted by the rain at Edgbaston. Marshall and Tremlett shot out Warwickshire on the opening day and Greenidge had battered them to a 63-run lead by the close of play. When Greenidge completed his fifth double century for Hampshire with 2 sixes and 26 fours in 296 minutes and Warwickshire slipped to 91 for 3 before the end of the second day it seemed the visitors were destined for an innings victory, but rain deprived them on the last day which ended at 2.30.

Middlesex, in second place, had the worst of the match with Derbyshire and only 70 minutes play was possible on the Tuesday. Edmonds, omitted by the England selectors from the side for the first Test, gave his reply with six wickets on the opening day.

On a slow, low wicket at Northampton, Sussex did not end their first innings until the last morning and ultimately they were thankful for the rain joining the wintry weather to save them from defeat. Surrey were also saved by the weather at Fenner's where, after Nicholas Taylor's career best bowling performance, they were struggling to survive when the rain came. Geoff Howarth led Surrey for the first time in the season.

Gloucestershire's hopes of advancement were blighted by rain which delayed the start on the second day until after tea. They moved to an impressive total on the Saturday and the declaration overnight left Lloyds 5 short of a century against his former county. Somerset were lifted by Botham's 76 off 47 deliveries.

Neil Foster's powerful hitting took Essex from 165 for 7 to 281 all out, but it was Lever and Gooch who bowled Essex to a first innings lead of 90. Patterson, with a career best, routed Essex on the last morning and Lancashire, needing 199 in 51 overs, looked set for victory, but Gooch had another fine spell and eventually Folley and Patterson batted through the last 5 overs in the rain to save their side from defeat.

Glamorgan tried to save their match from rain interruption at Abergavenny by declaring when both openers had reached centuries in a stand of 250 in 66.1 overs. Worcestershire, with a doctor in attendance and several players on the sick list, batted through the last day.

Geoff Lawson also reported sick at Leicester and was placed in doubt for the first Test. Gower, confidence and elegance abounding, and Balderstone put on 253 for Leicestershire's second wicket on the Saturday and Phillips and Ritchie added 177 for the Australians' fourth wicket in 42 overs. Border was out for less than a hundred for the first time in a first-class game on the tour and only 75 minutes play was possible on the last day.

Zimbabwe began their short tour in impressive fashion at Oxford. Thorne hit his maiden first-class hundred and Rutnagur had his best bowling for the University, but they were overshadowed by Hick whose 230, with a 4 sixes and 31 fours in 282 minutes, was the sixth highest maiden first-class hundred recorded in England. Houghton also hit a maiden first-class hundred and they added 277 for the fourth wicket. A delightful group of men, courteously managed by David Ellman-Brown who was adamant that his side must qualify for the next World Cup so that the large amount of money earned could be ploughed back into the game in their country, Zimbabwe deserve every encouragement and success. Their cricket is played with zest and joy.

John Player Special League

9 June

at Ilford

Lancashire 183 for 2 (C.H. Lloyd 64 not out, S.J. O'Shaughnessy 60)
Essex 91 for 3

Match abandoned
Essex 2 pts, Lancashire 2 pts

at Ebbw Vale

Glamorgan 147 for 3 (Jarved Miąndad 95 not out)
Worcestershire 125 for 9

Glamorgan (4 pts) won by 22 runs

at Lord's

Derbyshire 161 for 9 (B. Roberts 56)
Middlesex 121 for 0 (G.D. Barlow 66 not out)

Middlesex (4 pts) won on faster scoring rate

LEFT: *John Hopkins and* ABOVE: *Geoff Holmes. Their fine form was a vital factor in Glamorgan's excellent start to the year. They shared an unbroken first wicket partnership of 250 against Worcestershire at Abergavenny. (George Herringshaw)*

BELOW: *Kim Barnett (Derbyshire) – a valiant skipper and the backbone of his side's batting. (George Herringshaw)*

at Bath

Somerset 247 for 6 (N.F.M. Popplewell 58, I.V.A. Richards 56, N.A. Felton 52)
Gloucestershire 164

Somerset (4 pts) won by 83 runs

at Edgbaston

Hampshire 175 for 8
Warwickshire 176 for 5 (A.I. Kallicharran 69)

Warwickshire (4 pts) won by 5 wickets

at Sheffield

Sussex 197 for 6 (A.P. Wells 57 not out, A.M. Green 51)
Yorkshire 161 (M.D. Moxon 67, Imran Khan 4 for 15, A.C.S. Pigott 4 for 28)

Sussex (4 pts) won by 36 runs

Most matches were hit by the weather. At Ilford, Essex had only 15 of their 28 overs before the rain returned. O'Shaughnessy and Lloyd hit bravely for Lancashire and Henriksen, the Dane, bowled Gooch with the first ball of Essex's innings. Barlow and Slack relished a reduced target at Lord's and Middlesex went joint top of the table with Kent and Glamorgan who beat Worcestershire comfortably. Javed's 95 came off 71 balls in a match reduced to 21 overs.

Warwickshire and Sussex gained surprisingly comfortable wins and Somerset overwhelmed Gloucestershire but lost Trevor Gard who was concussed after a collision.

12, 13 and 14 June

at Derby

Derbyshire 256 (K.J. Barnett 109, J.G. Wright 91, C.E. Waller 7 for 61)
Sussex 250 for 7 dec (A.M. Green 68)

Match drawn
Derbyshire 5 pts, Sussex 4 pts

at Ilford

Northamptonshire 279 (A.C. Storie 81, D.J. Capel 52) and 266 for 5 dec (G. Cook 8, R.G. Williams 63, J.K. Lever 4 for 84)

Graeme Hick – a maiden first-class century, 230 for Zimbabwe against Oxford University. (Ken Kelly)

Essex 354 (B.R. Hardie 131, R.A. Harper 4 for 118) and 185 for 9 (B.R. Hardie 78 not out, N.A. Mallender 4 for 36, R.A. Harper 4 for 80)

Match drawn
Essex 8 pts, Northamptonshire 6 pts

at Bournemouth

Hampshire 184 (M.C.J. Nicholas 54, P.H. Edmonds 4 for 44) and 263 for 8 dec (V.P. Terry 57, M.D. Marshall 55)
Middlesex 183 (M.D. Marshall 5 for 68, T.M. Tremlett 4 for 30) and 166 for 8 (J.F. Sykes 52 not out)

Match drawn
Hampshire 5 pts, Middlesex 5 pts

at Tunbridge Wells

Gloucestershire 204 (P. Bainbridge 52, R.M. Ellison 4 for 46) and 199 (B.F. Davison 53, J.W. Lloyds 50, R.M. Ellison 5 for 46)
Kent 144 (K.M. Curran 5 for 42) and 200 (M.R. Benson 80, C.A. Walsh 4 for 59)

Gloucestershire won by 59 runs
Gloucestershire 22 pts, Kent 4 pts

at Hinckley

Warwickshire 16 for 0 dec and 160 (J.P. Agnew 5 for 46)
Leicestershire 15 for 1 dec and 162 for 6 (R.A. Cobb 65)

Leicestershire won by 4 wickets
Leicestershire 16 pts, Warwickshire 0 pts

at Bath

Somerset 304 for 7 dec (N.A. Felton 76, I.V.A. Richards 65, J. Simmons 4 for 78)
Lancashire 153 (D.P. Hughes 57, J. Garner 4 for 18) and 89 (V.J. Marks 8 for 17)

Somerset won by an innings and 62 runs
Somerset 22 pts, Lancashire 3 pts

at The Oval

Nottinghamshire 301 for 3 dec (D.W. Randall 106, M. Newell 59, P. Johnson 51 not out) and 265 for 4 dec (D.W. Randall 97, B.C. Broad 62, B.N. French 52 not out)
Surrey 301 for 3 dec (A. Needham 132, A.R. Butcher 126) and 166 for 4 (A.R. Butcher 97, K.E. Cooper 4 for 38)

Match drawn
Surrey 5 pts, Nottinghamshire 5 pts

at Cambridge

Worcestershire 216 for 5 dec (D.J. Humphries 62 not out, D.A. Banks 50 not out)
Cambridge University 143 for 6

Match drawn

at Oxford

Yorkshire 322 for 6 dec (S.N. Hartley 108 not out, J.D. Love 106) and 259 for 4 dec (A.A. Metcalfe 109, K. Sharp 69 not out)
Oxford University 268 for 6 dec (J.D. Carr 101, D.A. Thorne 56) and 62 for 0

Match drawn

The meeting between the two sides leading the Britannic Assurance County Championship produced a fine match at Bournemouth with an heroic rearguard action by Jamie Sykes and Simon Hughes which saved the game for Middlesex. Edmonds seemed to have bowled Middlesex into a strong position on the first day when, ably supported by

Kevin Saxelby, career best bowling figures of 10 for 115, won Notts the match at Tunbridge Wells. (George Herringshaw)

Above: *Nick Taylor. Splendid bowling for Surrey at Cambridge, but no regular place in the championship side. (Tom Morris)*

Left: *Vic Marks, a match-winning 8 for 17 won for Somerset against Lancashire at Bath, 14 June. (George Herringshaw)*

Hughes who was deputising for Cowans, he had the home side out for 184, but Marshall and Tremlett struck back for the home side and gave Hants a one-run lead. Having gained an unexpected grip on the game, Hampshire tightened it with some solid batting which saw Chris Smith become the first player to reach 1000 runs in the season. Nicholas asked Middlesex to make 265 in 63 overs, and when his bowlers had reduced them to 82 for 8 with 29 overs remaining it seemed Hampshire were certain to increase their lead at the top of the table. Sykes and Hughes batted throughout the 29 overs, however, and their stand of 84 was the highest of the match. Great credit should also be given to Tomlins who hit 36 when Marshall was at his fastest and all about him were falling. Sykes and Tomlins, like Hughes, were only in the Middlesex side because of Test calls.

Gloucestershire moved menacingly into second place with a fine win at Tunbridge Wells where Kent's agonies continued. Richard Ellison showed a return to his best form with 9 wickets, but a seventh wicket stand of 70 between Davison and Lloyds in Gloucestershire's second innings proved decisive. Kent batted like a side lacking all confidence. Benson and Aslett were the exceptions and their stand of 78 raised hopes that they might reach the 260 needed to win. The new and more aggressive Gloucestershire attack proved too much for the rest of the home side however and Lawrence, with his extra pace, Walsh, a great asset, and Curran, a positive cricketer, were emerging as one of the most impressive attacks in the country. To add to Kent's woes Chris Cowdrey was denied a hat-trick when Tavare dropped Russell at slip in the first innings.

There was no such excitement at Derby. There was a best bowling performance by Chris Waller and another century for Kim Barnett who must despair what more he has to do to gain international recognition, but Sussex are not a side noted for enterprise and the match ended tediously. At Ilford, Essex allowed Northants to make more runs than they should have done on the opening day when conditions favoured the seamers. Hardie and Gladwin, restored to fitness, put on 125 for the Essex first wicket and the home side batted briskly to take a 75-run lead. This was nullified when

Simon Hughes. He shared a stand with Sykes which saved the game for Middlesex at Bournemouth, 14 June. (Sporting Pictures UK Ltd)

Cook and emergency opener Mallender began Northants second innings with a stand of 110. Cook asked Essex to make 192 in 39 overs and they sought the target bravely. McEwan hit Harper for 3 sixes as rain began to fall, but Mallender bowled him. The last ball arrived with Essex needing 6 to win and 8 wickets down. Lever swung massively but skied the ball to the bowler, Harper. Lever had had some consolation earlier when, bowling slow spin, he had taken his 1500th first-class wicket.

Leicestershire gained their first win of the season when captains agreed on first innings closures and Agnew, Clift and Taylor skittled out Warwickshire in their second innings. Somerset also gained their first win of the season when they routed a limp Lancashire side at Bath. There were only four capped players in the Somerset side, but they eased their way doggedly to three hundred and twice bowled out Lancashire. Their hero was Vic Marks who returned the best bowling figures of his career and the best recorded in the championship so far in the season. His 8 for 17 came in 22 overs.

There was a run feast at The Oval where Randall and Butcher both came close to scoring a century in each innings. Indeed, Butcher's second innings ended when he was caught by Johnson off a shot which would otherwise have given him the fastest century of the season. His 97 came off 75 balls. In the first innings he and Needham had put on 233, including 1 run scored by Clinton before he retired hurt, for the first wicket.

Worcestershire, weakened by illness and a proposed match against Zimbabwe, gave first-class debuts to seven players at Fenner's and fielded only two capped players. At Oxford there were four centuries and Hartley and Love added 193 for the fifth wicket.

First Cornhill Test Match
ENGLAND *v.* AUSTRALIA

So enthralling had been the Ashes series of 1981 that many feared the 1985 contests could only provide a disappointment in comparison, but such fears were quickly dispelled by the excitement and individual achievements of the first match of the series.

The selection of the two sides showed a marked contrast. Australia played only four bowlers and kept faith with Hilditch who had had a poor start to the tour. England, surprisingly, omitted Foster and selected Willey who batted at number seven and did not bowl so making his selection even more confusing. The opening day was cool and overcast and a quarter of an hour was lost at tea-time, but Australia must have been well pleased to have made 284 for 6 by the close as the ball had moved considerably all day.

There was an early success for England when Wood, half forward, was lbw to Allott, but Australia lunched at 96 for 1, a fine score. England had not bowled well, but Australia, Hilditch in particular, had batted splendidly. He rarely missed a scoring opportunity, hooking Botham and Cowans for sixes and relishing the chance to square cut. His century came in the forty-fourth over out of 156. He and Wessels added 132 in 38 overs.

Wessels was brilliantly caught at slip when he slashed at Emburey and Hilditch was caught behind off Gooch who swung the ball appreciably. Boon got himself in a dreadful

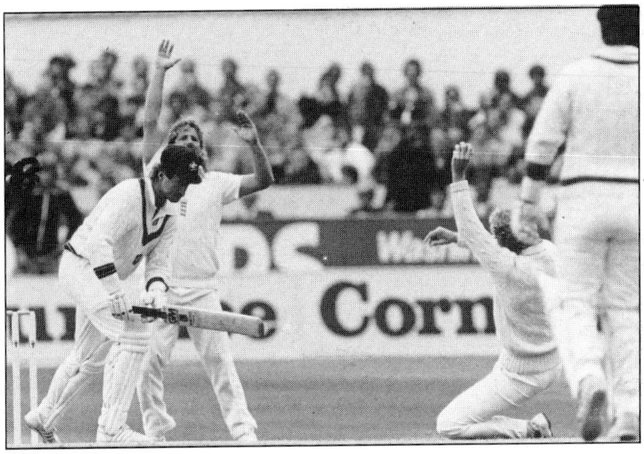

TOP: *The first wicket falls. Wood, lbw, bowled Allott for 14. (Adrian Murrell)*

MIDDLE: *Botham catches Wessels at slip off Emburey. (Adrian Murrell)*

BOTTOM: *David Gower catches Wayne Phillips off John Emburey's bowling. A vital wicket for England at the end of the first day. (Adrian Murrell)*

tangle and Border was taken low at slip, the wickets falling in successive overs, but Ritchie and Phillips began to play exciting shots. Phillips hit 30 off 35 balls and when he was caught close in shortly before the close it was, in retrospect, a decisive moment, for the next day Australia lost their last 4 wickets for 5 runs in ten deliveries.

Half the second day was lost to rain, but England ended it in a good position. Gooch was lbw playing back to McDermott and Gower was caught behind off the same

FIRST CORNHILL TEST MATCH – ENGLAND *v.* AUSTRALIA
13, 14, 15, 17 and 18 June 1985 at Headingley, Leeds

AUSTRALIA

	FIRST INNINGS		SECOND INNINGS	
G.M. Wood	lbw, b Allott	14	(2) c Lamb, b Botham	3
A.M.J. Hilditch	c Downton, b Gooch	119	(1) c Robinson, b Emburey	80
K.C. Wessels	c Botham, b Emburey	36	b Emburey	64
A.R. Border†	c Botham, b Cowans	32	c Downton, b Botham	8
D.C. Boon	lbw, b Gooch	14	b Cowans	22
G.M. Ritchie	b Botham	46	b Emburey	1
W.B. Phillips*	c Gower, b Emburey	30	c Lamb, b Botham	91
C.J. McDermott	b Botham	18	(10) c Downton, b Emburey	6
S.P. O'Donnell	lbw, b Botham	0	(8) c Downton, b Botham	24
G.F. Lawson	c Downton, b Allott	0	(9) c Downton, b Emburey	15
J.R. Thomson	not out	4	not out	2
Extras	lb 13, w 4, nb 1	18	b 4, lb 3, w 1	8
		331		324

	O	M	R	W	O	M	R	W
Cowans	20	4	78	1	13	2	50	1
Allott	22	3	74	2	17	4	57	—
Botham	29.1	8	86	3	33	7	107	4
Gooch	21	4	57	2	9	3	21	—
Emburey	6	1	23	2	43.4	14	82	5

FALL OF WICKETS
1- 23, 2- 155, 3- 201, 4- 229, 5- 229, 6- 284, 7- 326, 8- 326, 9- 327
1- 5, 2- 144, 3- 151, 4- 159, 5- 160, 6- 192, 7- 272, 8- 307, 9- 318

ENGLAND

	FIRST INNINGS		SECOND INNINGS	
G.A. Gooch	lbw, b McDermott	5	lbw, b O'Donnell	28
R.T. Robinson	c Boon, b Lawson	175	b Lawson	21
D.I. Gower†	c Phillips, b McDermott	17	c Border, b O'Donnell	5
M.W. Gatting	c Hilditch, b McDermott	53	c Phillips, b Lawson	12
A.J. Lamb	b O'Donnell	38	not out	31
I.T. Botham	b Thomson	60	b O'Donnell	12
P. Willey	c Hilditch, b Lawson	36	not out	3
P.R. Downton*	c Border, b McDermott	54		
J.E. Emburey	b Lawson	21		
P.J.W. Allott	c Boon, b Thomson	12		
N.G. Cowans	not out	22		
Extras	b 5, lb 16, w 5, nb 14	40	lb 7, w 1, nb 3	11
		533	(for 5 wickets)	123

	O	M	R	W	O	M	R	W
Lawson	26	4	117	3	16	4	51	2
McDermott	32	2	134	4	4	—	20	—
Thomson	34	3	166	2	3	—	8	—
O'Donnell	27	8	77	1	15.4	5	37	3
Border	3	—	16	—				
Wessels	3	2	2	—				

FALL OF WICKETS
1- 14, 2- 50, 3- 186, 4- 264, 5- 344, 6- 417, 7- 422, 8- 462, 9- 484
1- 44, 2- 59, 3- 71, 4- 83, 5- 110

Umpires: B.J. Meyer and K.E. Palmer

England won by 5 wickets

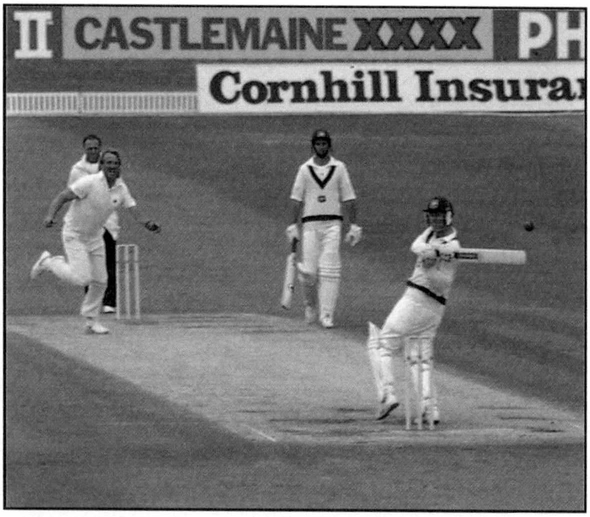

ABOVE: *Australia's hero. Andrew Hilditch hooks Botham for four. (Ken Kelly)*

RIGHT: *A star is born. Tim Robinson hooks Thomson to the boundary during his innings of 175. (Ken Kelly)*

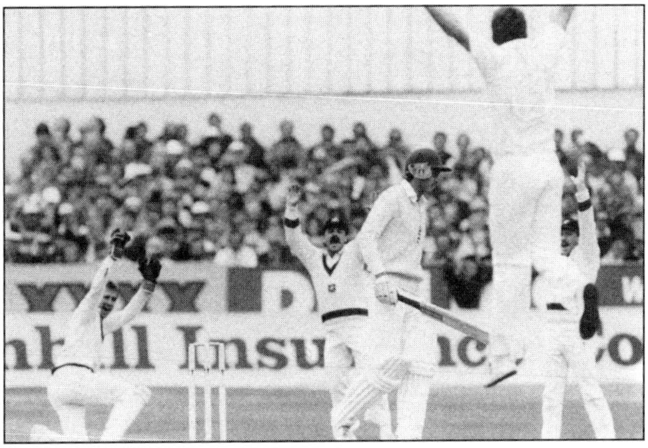

ABOVE: *Headingley – scene of the first Cornhill Test match.* TOP RIGHT: *Simon O'Donnell is lbw to Botham for 0 on his Test debut. Botham took 3 wickets in 4 balls as Australia lost their last 4 wickets for 5 runs in ten deliveries.* RIGHT: *McDermott leaps for joy as Phillips takes the catch to dismiss Gower for 17. Boon and Border join the appeal. (Adrian Murrell)* BELOW: *Wessels is bowled by Emburey for 64 and Australia began the slide to defeat.* BOTTOM: *Ritchie bowled by a grounder from Emburey. (Ken Kelly)*

bowler when he fended off a good delivery which lifted and left him. Robinson survived all alarms, including being dropped on 22. He finished the day with 66 off 76 balls and the following morning he continued in the same manner. Gatting mishooked and Lamb was beaten by O'Donnell to give the young all-rounder his first Test wicket, but Botham played an innings of glorious savagery, 60 off 51 balls, and the crowd thrilled to it.

But the day really belonged to Tim Robinson who, playing his first Test in England, hit 175 off 270 deliveries. He hit 27 fours and batted for more than $6\frac{1}{4}$ hours. His defence was confident and his strokes positive. He was rightly named Man of the Match. His innings ended when he edged low to slip where Boon took a good catch.

England began the fourth day at 484 for 9, but there was no early surrender as Downton and Cowans added 49 runs, frustrating to Australia, invaluable to England. Wood again went early, hooking impetuously, but the game seemed set for a draw as Wessels and Hilditch once again produced a substantial partnership. They had added 139 when Wessels was caught in two minds and bowled and immediately after tea Hilditch was caught sweeping. Border was unable to avoid a lifter from Botham and was given out caught behind, perhaps a little unluckily, and Ritchie had horrible luck when he was bowled by a ball which rolled along the ground. Four wickets had fallen for 16 runs and England now appeared set for victory as Australia ended the day still 12 runs in arrears.

The following morning Boon was bowled off his boot by

Fierce conflict. Downton hooks McDermott in his innings of 54. (Varley Picture Agency)

the last ball of the first over and an early finish seemed likely. Phillips now batted with sense and panache. He and O'Donnell shared a delightfully aggressive stand of 80 which suggested that the match may not yet have found its ultimate hero. Shortly before lunch O'Donnell was caught behind and the last 3 wickets fell, somewhat irresponsibly, while 52 brisk runs were added. Phillips batted admirably. He is a fine striker of the ball, eager always to score and he died as he had lived, caught at mid-wicket as he attempted to pull a four.

England needed only 123 to win and reached 44 before Robinson was beaten by Lawson. Gooch looked ill at ease and was lbw after shuffling right across his wicket. By that time Gower had been well taken at slip and when O'Donnell knocked back Botham's off stump and Gatting was well caught by Phillips doubts had begun to arise in English minds and the marvels of 1981 had passed into history replaced by contemporary heroics.

Lamb lived uncertainly, but he hit hard enough to bring victory closer. The scores were levelled by a no-ball and Willey was dropped by Border off a simple chance which would have given Thomson his 200th Test wicket. It was a sad miss for Thomson had bowled poorly in the first innings and it seemed unlikely that he would again play Test cricket.

The end of the match was disappointing, the only blight on the game. Lamb lofted the ball and as Lawson attempted to make the catch he was engulfed by invading spectators, mindless idiots who profess to love the game but who violate its majesty by their antics, physical and verbal.

15, 17 and 18 June

at Swansea

Glamorgan 173 (N.A. Foster 5 for 40) and 214 for 3 dec (G.C. Holmes 92, J.A. Hopkins 60)
Essex 79 for 3 dec and 185 for 2 (C. Gladwin 92 not out, K.S. McEwan 63 not out)

Match drawn
Essex 4 pts Glamorgan 2 pts

at Old Trafford

Derbyshire 201 (J.G. Wright 75, D.J. Makinson 5 for 60, J.Simmons 4 for 55) and 251 for 8 dec (J.G. Wright 95, J. Simmons 4 for 89)
Lancashire 240 (D.P. Hughes 68, N.H. Fairbrother 51, R.J. Finney 7 for 61) and 215 for 7 (G. Miller 6 for 110)

Lancashire won by 3 wickets
Lancashire 22 pts, Derbyshire 5 pts

at Lord's

Middlesex 257 (W.N. Slack 53, N.G.B. Cook 4 for 59) and 233 for 3 dec (W.N. Slack 109, G.D. Barlow 102)
Leicestershire 197 (W.W. Daniel 5 for 48) and 149 for 3 (I.P. Butcher 71 not out)

Match drawn
Middlesex 6 pts, Leicestershire 4 pts

at Northampton

Gloucestershire 295 for 7 dec (C.W.J. Athey 82, P. Bainbridge 67, P.W. Romaines 55) and 73 for 2
Northamptonshire 119 (G.E. Sainsbury 7 for 38) and 246 (A.C. Storie 71)

Gloucestershire won by 8 wickets
Gloucestershire 23 pts, Northamptonshire 2 pts

at Trent Bridge

Kent 258 (R.M. Ellison 98, M.R. Benson 55, K.E. Cooper 4 for 43) and 322 for 5 dec (C.J. Tavare 94 not oet, S.G. Hinks 67, D.G. Aslett 53, M.R. Benson 50)
Nottinghamshire 252 for 5 dec (J.D. Birch 60 not out, R.J. Hadlee 52 not out) and 159 for 1 (B.C. Broad 71 not out, C.E.B. Rice 71)

Match drawn
Nottinghamshire 6 pts, Kent 4 pts

Gary Sainsbury celebrates. His career best 7 for 38 took Gloucestershire to the top of the Britannic Assurance County Championship, 17 June. (George Herringshaw)

LEFT: *Worcestershire centurion – Martin Weston, 15 June. (Adrian Murrell)* RIGHT: *Worcestershire centurion – Tim Curtis, 15 June. (Adrian Murrell)*

ABOVE: *John Birch just gets home as Alan Knott breaks the wicket, Nottinghamshire v. Kent at Trent Bridge, 17 June. (David Munden)* BELOW: *Career best bowling for Derbyshire's Roger Finney, 7 for 61 v. Lancashire at Old Trafford, 17 June.* BELOW LEFT: *David Makinson, fine bowling and hard hitting in Lancashire's victory over Derbyshire at Old Trafford, 15–18 June. (George Herringshaw)*

at Hove

Sussex 257 (P.W.G. Parker 80, A.M. Green 54) and 238 for 3 dec (A.M. Green 93, G.D. Mendis 62, P.W.G. Parker 53 not out)
Hampshire 221 for 6 dec (C.G. Greenidge 56) and 123 for 7 (I.A. Greig 4 for 37)

Match drawn
Hampshire 6 pts, Sussex 5 pts

at Worcester

Worcestershire 354 for 5 dec (M.J. Weston 132, T.S. Curtis 126 not out) and 253 for 5 dec (P.A. Neale 152 not out)
Surrey 304 for 3 dec (G.S. Clinton 117, A.R. Butcher 66, A. Needham 63) and 82 for 2

Match drawn
Surrey 6 pts, Worcestershire 5 pts

at Oxford

Warwickshire 371 for 8 dec (D.L. Amiss 125, T.A. Lloyd 123, A.M. Ferreira 58 not out) and 166 for 5 dec (T.A. Lloyd 58)
Oxford University 266 for 8 dec (P.C. MacLarnon 56, D.A. Thorne 55) and 250 (G.J. Toogood 77, D.A. Thorne 68 not out)

Warwickshire won by 21 runs

15 June

at Taunton

Somerset 191 for 5 (R. Harden 56, K.G. Duers 5 for 26)
Zimbabwe 195 for 6

Zimbabwe won by 4 wickets

For the first time in the season Hampshire came close to defeat. They enjoyed a satisfactory first day when they took four bowling points and closed at 24 for 0, but they were unable to find their batting momentum on the Monday and when Green and Mendis began Sussex's second innings with a stand of 166 the match ran very much in favour of the home side. Set to score 275 in 58 overs, Hampshire floundered and were saved from defeat only by the dogged defence of Hardy, Tremlett and Maru.

They surrendered their place at the top of the table to Gloucestershire who had a fine win at Northampton where they beat the rain as well as the home side. A solid, though not exciting batting performance saw them to a good position on the Saturday and on the Monday Gary Sainsbury, who had been unable to hold a regular place in the side since the arrival of Walsh and Curran, dook a career best 7 for 38 and routed Northants. Following-on, Northants were 180 for 6 before the close and only the remarkable Storie offered serious resistance. There was no play until after lunch on the last day and then only for half-an-hour during which time Storie was out. When play resumed again only 21 overs remained and three Northants wickets still stood. These were duly captured, but to win Gloucestershire had to make 71 in 11 overs. They reached the target with 9 balls to spare and deservedly went to the top of the table.

Lancashire were the other winners, scoring 213 in 37 overs to beat Derbyshire. David Makinson returned a career best bowling performance and hit the penultimate ball of the match for a winning six. Roger Finney had also had a career best performance so that left-arm medium pace thrived throughout the match. John Wright played two fine innings, Jack Simmons bowled as well as ever and Hughes and Fairbrother shared a fourth wicket stand of 106 in Lancashire's first innings.

The game at Swansea ended in some acrimony. Essex dominated the first day, Lever and Foster exploiting overcast conditions. Only 35 minutes play was possible on the second day and after declaring at his overnight score Fletcher accused Ontong of violating an agreement that they had made that Glamorgan should set Essex to make 280 in 63 overs. Fletcher was later reprimanded for his remarks and the game descended to farce.

Ellison hit his highest score in the championship, but the game at Trent Bridge also descended to farce as Cowdrey declined to declare and set Notts a reasonable target pleading that his side was plagued by injuries. They were also plagued by dropped catches with Aslett the biggest culprit.

At Lord's, Middlesex laboured badly on the Saturday and Leicestershire collapsed to Daniel and Edmonds on the Monday, their last 6 wickets falling for 27 runs. Barlow and Slack then hit an impressive 203 for Middlesex's first wicket, their second double century partnership of the season. Leicestershire were asked to make 293 in 73 overs, but bad light, bouncers and drizzle made a draw the only possible result.

Curtis and Weston, disbanded as an opening pair, came together to add 227 for Worcestershire's fifth wicket. Weston's hundred came in just over 3 hours. Clinton and Butcher began Surrey's reply with a stand of 121. Clinton and Needham then added 106 for the second wicket. Phil Neale reached his first championship century of the season and made 152 in under four hours, but rain brought an early end to an interesting match.

Oxford University fought well against Warwickshire for whom Dennis Amiss hit the ninety-fourth hundred of his career.

John Player Special League

16 June

at Swansea

Essex 205 for 7
Glamorgan 191 (Javed Miandad 86, J.K. Lever 4 for 40)

Essex (4 pts) won by 14 runs

at Old Trafford

Derbyshire 182 for 9 (J.E. Morris 52, D.J. Makincon 4 for 28)
Lancashire 186 for 3 (G. Fowler 98 not out)

Lancashire (4 pts) won by 7 wickets

at Lord's

Middlesex 163 for 8
Leicestershire 158 for 8 (J.J. Whitaker 53)

Middlesex (4 pts) won by 5 runs

at Northampton

Gloucestershire 211 for 7 (P.W. Romaines 105)
Northamptonshire 196 (D.J. Wild 63 not out, G. Cook 51)

Gloucestershire (4 pts) won by 15 runs

at Trent Bridge

Kent 224 for 9 (M.R. Benson 90)
Nottinghamshire 182 (K.B.S. Jarvis 5 for 24)

Kent (4 pts) won by 42 runs

at Bath

Yorkshire 215 for 7 (M.D. Moxon 86, J. Garner 5 for 27)
Somerset 164

Yorkshire (4 pts) won by 51 runs

at Hove

Sussex 238 for 4 (Imran Khan 104 not out)
Hampshire 239 for 1 (C.G. Greenidge 124 not out, V.P. Terry 82)

Hampshire (4 pts) won by 9 wickets

at Worcester

Surrey 193 for 8 (M.A. Lynch 52)
Worcestershire 197 for 2 (D.B. d'Oliveira 103)

Worcestershire (4 pts) won by 8 wickets

A full and uninterrupted Sunday league programme saw Essex, the reigning champions, gain their first win of the season on a day which was dominated by batsmen. Greenidge and Terry took the honours with an opening partnership of 221. Greenidge reached his hundred off 87 balls. Romaines took only 4 balls more at Northampton and Imran, with 5 sixes and 7 fours, hit his first John Player League century off 79 balls. There was a maiden Sunday

century too for Damian d'Oliveira who shared an opening stand of 139 with Patel. Kent, with Benson in aggressive form, and Middlesex, who won a close contest at Lord's, shared top place in the table, but Yorkshire were only 2 points behind after a fine win over a very poor Somerset side. Moxon batted well to hold the innings together, but Bairstow with a blistering knock and a miraculous running catch to dismiss Marks took the honours. The most pleasing innings of the day was at Old Trafford where Graeme Fowler, an England hero only a few months ago and now out of form and forgotten, hit 98 not out in 39 overs, his highest John Player League score, to take his side to victory after they had needed 83 from the last 10 overs.

Paddy Clift receives his Gold Award and a copy of Benson and Hedges Cricket Year, 1984 *from Phil Sharpe after Leicestershire had beaten Kent in the Benson and Hedges Cup semi-final at Grace Road. (George Herringshaw)*

Benson and Hedges Cup

Semi-Finals

19 June

at Leicester

Kent 101
Leicestershire 102 for 2 (I.P. Butcher 55)

Leicestershire won by 8 wickets
(*Gold Award* – P.B. Clift)

19 and 20 June

at Chelmsford

Essex 202 for 8 (G.A. Gooch 58, J.E. Emburey 4 for 36)
Middlesex 140 (W.N. Slack 60)

Essex won by 62 runs
(*Gold Award* – J.E. Emburey)

David Gower won the toss and asked Kent to bat at Grace Road. On a damp, grassy pitch the ball moved about appreciably early on Kent sank almost without trace to the bombardment of the Leicestershire seam attack. Benson and Hinks put on 24 for Kent's first wicket, both beginning with positive shots, but Agnew dismissed them both. Tavare struggled for 11 overs for 4, Aslett took 6 overs to get off the mark and was out in the twenty-third over to make the score

John Emburey (Middlesex) – Gold Award winner at Chelmsford, but on the losing side. (Adrian Murrell)

Alan Lilley. His brilliant catch to dismiss Mike Gatting off the bowling of Stuart Turner was one of the highlights of the Benson and Hedges Cup, Chelmsford, 20 June. (Trevor Jones)

47 for 4. Baptiste and Cowdrey suggested defiant aggression, but they fell in successive overs. The innings came to a sudden end when Les Taylor took the last three wickets in his ninth over. Conditions were better when Leicestershire batted and the bowling less demanding. In 21.5 overs the target had been reached and the match ended at 4.20.

The match at Chelmsford was taken into a second day by a lunch-time thunderstorm and it produced a most memorable contest. Essex were put in to bat and prospered against some erratic bowling which was liberally peppered with no-balls. Williams struck in the sixth over when he bowled Hardie off his pads, but by then the score was 43. Prichard, playing his first game since breaking a finger, was dropped at slip first ball and responded by playing some delightful strokes until he pulled Cowans to mid-wicket at 87. McEwan followed quickly, failing to read the slow pace of the wicket and driving loosely at Cowans to be caught behind. Pringle chopped on to the steady Edmonds and when the deluge came Essex were 114 for 4 off 33 overs, Gooch on 50 not out.

The next morning when play resumed amid the sawdust 27 were added in 10 overs before Gooch cut at Emburey and was bowled. Emburey threatened a stranglehold on the Essex batting as the score slipped to 167 for 8 and Middlesex had victory in their grasp. Foster then joined David East in a pulsating stand. Emburey's figures were ruined. He had taken 4 for 18 in 8 overs, but Foster and East took 24 runs off the last two overs, 12 of them off Emburey.

The wicket was slow and run getting was not easy, but 203 did not look too formidable a target. Slack and Barlow had been in magnificent form and Essex desperately needed to break their partnership early if they were to have any chance of victory. The breakthrough came, but in an unexpected way. Barlow drove to the off and turned for a comfortable second run. Slack ignored him and turning to regain his ground, Barlow slipped and was run out by yards as Prichard's throw came over the stumps. In the post lunch session Gatting appeared in complete command, but the Essex outcricket was of the very highest quality and with the score on 63, Gatting cut Turner fiercely and Lilley, square at cover, held the ball in his left hand as he was knocked backwards by the force of the shot. It was a catch that will become part of the legend of Essex cricket. It was the turning point of the match. The Essex bowlers did not deliver a loose ball and there was the suggestion of only one slight misfield in the entire innings. Radley, fretting to break the grip, moved forward to Pringle and was bowled, 97 for 3 in the twenty-ninth over. Butcher too fell to Pringle and Downton, conscious that the demand to score more frequently was growing ball by ball, hit out at Turner only to see Hardie make a goal-keeper like dive at mid-on to hold the second miraculous catch of the innings.

Hardie ran out Edmonds with a direct throw and Slack, having batted 43 overs for his 60, cracked. He swung horrendously at Turner and was bowled. The end came swiftly. In Foster's ninth over Williams was run out by Prichard, Cowans was lbw and Daniel bowled. Emburey was named Man of the Match. It was a most controversial decision and many would have plumped for Fletcher who organised his side magnificently in one of the most thrilling displays of outcricket ever witnessed.

19, 20 and 21 June

at Swansea

Glamorgan 214 (A.L. Jones 80, I.P. Butchart 5 for 65) and 187 for 4 (S.P. Henderson 52 not out)
Zimbabwe 364 (G.A. Hick 192, G.A. Paterson 69, G.C. Holmes 4 for 49)

Match drawn

There was no play on the last day because of rain. Butchart returned career best bowling figures and Glamorgan lost their last 6 wickets for 19 runs. Hick gave another exciting batting display, just missing a second double century. He hit 3 sixes and 22 fours and added 148 in 30 overs for the second wicket with Paterson.

Tilcon Trophy
19 June

at Harrogate

Nottinghamshire 267 for 7 (B.C. Broad 60, B.N. French 58 not out)
Yorkshire 169

Nottinghamshire won by 98 runs

20 June

Gloucestershire 198 (I.R. Payne 58, P. Bainbridge 55, S. Wall 5 for 21)
Warwickshire 202 for 3 (T.A. Lloyd 70, G.J. Lord 64)

Warwickshire won by 7 wickets

Rain prevented any play in the final and the trophy was won by Warwickshire when the two sides bowled at a single stump. Warwickshire won by 5 hits to 1.

20 June

at Cambridge

Australians 265 for 8 (D.C. Boon 108)
Combined Universities 186 for 6 (P.G.P. Roebuck 75 not out, A.G. Davies 51 not out, M.J. Bennett 4 for 26)

Australians won by 79 runs

22, 23 and 24 June

at Harrogate

Worcestershire 300 for 8 dec (T.S. Curtis 72, D.B. d'Oliveira 60, A. Sidebottom 4 for 70) and 185 for 3 dec
Yorkshire 215 for 7 dec (G. Boycott 105 not out) and 124 for 3 (G. Boycott 64 not out)

Match drawn
Worcestershire 7 pts, Yorkshire 5 pts

22, 24 and 25 June

at Bristol

Gloucestershire *v.* **Sussex**

Match abandoned. No points.

Even the mightiest fall. Viv Richards is bowled by Duncan Pauline for 5 at The Oval, 22 June. (Tom Morris)

at Old Trafford

Kent 303 (M.R. Benson 102, J. Simmons 4 for 85) and 217 for 5 dec (E.A.E. Baptiste 81 not out)
Lancashire 261 for 8 dec (J. Simmons 51, D.L. Underwood 4 for 55) and 234 (J. Simmons 62 not out, G.W. Johnson 5 for 78)

Kent won by 25 runs
Kent 22 pts, Lancashire 4 pts

at Leicester

Glamorgan 197 for 9 dec (G.C. Holmes 55) and 259 for 3 dec (G.C. Holmes 112, Javed Miandad 61 not out, A.L. Jones 60)
Leicestershire 151 for 1 dec (D.I. Gower 100 not out, J.C. Balderstone 51 not out) and 265 for 9 (J.C. Balderstone 65, R.C. Ontong 4 for 66)

Match drawn
Leicestershire 3 pts, Glamorgan 1 pt

at Northampton

Northamptonshire 269 for 5 dec (A.J. Lamb 111) *v.* **Essex**

Match drawn
Northamptonshire 3 pts, Essex 2 pts

at Trent Bridge

Nottinghamshire 202 (D.W. Randall 50, W.W. Daniel 4 for 64) and 249 (R.T. Robinson 73, N.F. Williams 4 for 92)
Middlesex 437 for 8 dec (W.N. Slack 112, G.D. Barlow 81, M.W. Gatting 76, R.O. Butcher 71) and 15 for 0

Middlesex won by 10 wickets
Middlesex 24 pts, Nottinghamshire 4 pts

at The Oval

Somerset 188 (A.H. Gray 5 for 69) and 114 for 2 dec (I.T. Botham 72 not out)
Surrey 10 for 0 dec and 58 for 1

Match drawn
Surrey 4 pts, Somerset 1 pt

at Edgbaston

Warwickshire 308 for 2 dec (R.I.H.B. Dyer 109 not out, D.L. Amiss 86, T.A. Lloyd 57) and 139 for 5 dec (G.W. Humpage 76)
Zimbabwe 159 for 5 dec (A.C. Waller 56 not out) and 231 for 6 (G.A. Hick 65)

Match drawn

22, 23, 24 and 25 June

at Southampton

Hampshire 221 (V.P. Terry 60, R.G. Holland 5 for 51) and 64 for 1 dec
Australians 76 (K.D. James 6 for 22) and 154 for 7 (G.M. Ritchie 62)

Match drawn

Rain badly disrupted matches in the Britannic Assurance County Championship and Gloucestershire, without a ball bowled at Bristol, retained their place at the top. Middlesex moved into second place with a resounding win over Nottinghamshire. An all pace attack accounted for Notts in 59.4 overs on the Saturday and an opening stand of 171 between Slack and Barlow which was followed by brisk contributions from Gatting and Butcher put Middlesex in total command. Needing 235 to avoid an innings defeat, Notts were heartened by an opening stand of 111 by Broad and Robinson, but they collapsed to 167 for 9. Middlesex then became frus-

Dennis Amiss passes 40,000 runs in first-class cricket, Warwickshire v. *Zimbabwe, 22 June. (Ken Kelly)*

trated as Hadlee and Cooper, hitting the ball boldly, added 82. Cooper made a career best 46 before being bowled off stump by Cowans. The wicket fell just in time and left Middlesex to score 15 in 9 overs.

There were no heroics at Harrogate. Arnie Sidebottom celebrated his England call up and Geoff Boycott reached a fine century, the 146th of his career, but later declined the challenge to score 271 in 59 overs.

Benson and Hinks put on 152 for Kent's first wicket on the Saturday and set their side on their way to their first championship win of the season. Some aggressive all-round cricket by Jack Simmons failed to save Lancashire. He reached 50 off only 44 balls as Lancashire chased 260 in 59 overs and was undefeated on 62, but Kent won by 25 runs with 9 balls to spare.

Botham hit 5 sixes and 8 fours off motley bowling, his 72 coming off 50 balls, but rain won at The Oval and there were only 10 balls bowled before the last day at Northampton where the captains failed to agree on what would be enterprising.

Glamorgan had painful first innings progress at Leicester. They were 66 for 5 and their 197 came in 118.4 overs. John Steele batted 4 hours and faced 218 balls for his 48. In contrast, David Gower hit 100 off 112 balls with 19 fours. Holmes shared in century stands with Jones and Javed and Glamorgan were able to set Leicestershire to make 306 in the post lunch sessions on the last day. Glamorgan came close to victory, Steele missing Cook off the second ball of the last over.

Kevin Curran, the all-rounder from Zimbabwe who made a significant contribution to Gloucestershire cricket throughout the season. (David Munden)

In the match against Zimbabwe Robin Dyer, a most promising and likeable young player, hit a career best and Dennis Amiss, an older and equally likeable player, reached 40,000 runs in first-class cricket.

There were sensations at Southampton where the Australians had a terrible time on the eve of the second Test. There was no play on the Saturday and only $3\frac{1}{4}$ hours play on the Sunday. Bob Holland spun out the remaining Hampshire batsmen on the Monday. Facing a meagre 221, the Australians were routed by Kevan James, the left-arm seam bowler returning a career best 6 for 22 in 11 overs. Formerly with Middlesex, James had only 7 first-class wickets to his credit before this match, but it was a just reward for an eager and capable young cricketer. The tourists escaped the indignity of the follow-on only when last man Wayne Phillips hit 15. Bennett was the only other batsman to reach double figures. On the last day Nicholas declared and asked the visitors to make 210 in 37 overs. A spell of 3 for 12 in 11 balls by Cardigan Connor reduced them to 19 for 3, but Nicholas later persisted with spin and Bennett and McDermott, coming together at 126 for 7, survived the last 13 overs to save the match.

John Player Special League

23 June

at Swindon

Gloucestershire 126 for 5 (K.M. Curran 50)
Sussex 128 for 1 (G.D. Mendis 60 not out, P.W.G. Parker 55 not out)

Sussex (4 pts) won by 9 wickets

at Old Trafford

Kent 124 for 8 (P.J.W. Allott 4 for 28)
Lancashire 143 for 6

Lancashire (4 pts) won by 4 wickets

at Leicester

Leicestershire 177 for 5 (N.E. Briers 60)
Glamorgan 166 (Javed Miandad 62)

Leicestershire (4 pts) won by 11 runs

ABOVE: *Chris Broad, 171 for Nottinghamshire against Derbyshire at Derby, 26 June. (Sporting Pictures UK Ltd)* TOP LEFT: *Iain Anderson (Derbyshire) awarded his county cap after consistent batting. (George Herringshaw)* BELOW: *Derek Randall for whom cricket is such fun and who makes it such fun for others. He enjoyed a glorious season and many felt he should have been in the England side. (Adrian Murrell)*

Bruce Roberts hit his second century of the season for Derbyshire against Notts at Derby, 28 June. (George Herringshaw) BELOW: *Graham Barlow (George Herringshaw)* BELOW RIGHT: *Wilf Slack. (Adrian Murrell) The most prolific opening batsmen in England.*

at Luton

Essex 216 for 5 (K.S. McEwan 70, D.R. Pringle 51, G.A. Gooch 50)
Northamptonshire 217 for 4 (A.J. Lamb 82 not out, G. Cook 57)

Northamptonshire (4 pts) won by 6 wickets

at Trent Bridge

Nottinghamshire 178 for 6 (B.C. Broad 69)
Middlesex 171 (P.R. Downton 70)

Nottinghamshire (4 pts) won by 7 runs

at The Oval

Somerset 254 for 7 (I.V.A. Richards 86)
Surrey 193 for 8 (M.A. Lynch, I.V.A. Richards 4 for 39)

Somerset (4 pts) won by 61 runs

Kent lost their unbeaten record in the Sunday League, but remained equal top with Middlesex who were also beaten. Allott had 3 for 6 in his first 4 overs to wreck Kent. Gloucestershire's trip out of county to Swindon was unproductive. Mendis and Parker added 121 for Sussex's second wicket to set up an easy win. Leicestershire won narrowly and Richards, 86 off 60 balls including 23 off an over from Needham, dominated the game at The Oval. A dropped catch by Gooch in the last over at Luton cost Essex victory as Lamb continued his record of remaining not out in the John Player League.

26, 27 and 28 June

at Derby

Nottinghamshire 327 (B.C. Broad 171, C.E.B. Rice 51, P.G.

Newman 4 for 52) and 193 for 9 dec (R.J. Hadlee 54, M.A. Holding 6 for 65)
Derbyshire 264 (I.S. Anderson 95, G. Miller 52, K.E. Cooper 6 for 53) and 234 for 8 (B. Roberts 100, I.S. Anderson 70, R.J. Hadlee 4 for 44)

Match drawn
Nottinghamshire 7 pts, Derbyshire 5 pts

at Chelmsford

Kent 174 (S. Turner 4 for 36) and 184 for 5 (S.G. Hinks 94 not out)
Essex 243 (K.S. McEwan 82, P.J. Prichard 79, R.M. Ellison 6 for 61)

Match drawn
Essex 6 pts, Kent 5 pts

at Cardiff

Somerset 413 for 7 dec (I.V.A. Richards 100, N.F.M. Popplewell 84, N.A. Felton 60, P.M. Roebuck 59, R.E. Hayward 57 not out, R.C. Ontong 4 for 125) and 7 for 0
Glamorgan 289 for 9 dec (Javed Miandad 107, T. Davies 50 not out, J. Garner 5 for 46)

Match drawn
Somerset 7 pts, Glamorgan 4 pts

at Bristol

Hampshire 110 (K.M. Curran 4 for 23, D.V. Lawrence 4 for 41) and 312 for 7 dec (R.A. Smith 79, C.G. Greenidge 68)
Gloucestershire 191 (K.M. Curran 50, T.M. Tremlett 4 for 43, M.D. Marshall 4 for 57) and 53 for 4

Match drawn
Gloucestershire 5 pts, Hampshire 4 pts

at Old Trafford

Warwickshire 239 (G.W. Humpage 75, R.I.H.B. Dyer 68, D.J. Makinson 4 for 48) and 226 for 7 dec (T.A. Lloyd 62, R.I.H.B. Dyer 55, S.J. O'Shaughnessy 4 for 68)
Lancashire 207 (G. Fowler 88, A.M. Ferreira 5 for 43, G.C. Small 4 for 71) and 165 for 8 (A.M. Ferreira 5 for 41)

Match drawn
Lancashire 6 pts, Warwickshire 6 pts

at Northampton

Surrey 250 for 8 dec (G.S. Clinton 80, D.B. Pauline 50, N.A. Mallender 4 for 43) and 185 for 6 dec (R.A. Harper 4 for 55)
Northamptonshire 181 (G. Cook 70, A.H. Gray 5 for 44, P.I. Pocock 4 for 31) and 257 for 5 (W. Larkins 117)

Northamptonshire won by 5 wickets
Northamptonshire 20 pts, Surrey 6 pts

at Worcester

Worcestershire 246 and 137 (G.D. Rose 6 for 41)
Middlesex 158 for 2 dec (G.D. Barlow 103 not out) and 226 for 7 (R.O. Butcher 120, R.N. Kapil Dev 4 for 74)

Middlesex won by 3 wickets
Middlesex 21 pts, Worcestershire 2 pts

at Bradford

Yorkshire 300 for 8 dec (K. Sharp 81, D.L. Bairstow 77) and 241 for 1 dec (D.L. Bairstow 100 not out, G. Boycott 82 not out)
Leicestershire 230 for 7 dec (I.P. Butcher 82, P. Willey 60, P. Carrick 4 for 73) and 249 for 6 (J.C. Balderstone 79, I.P. Butcher 76, P. Carrick 4 for 76)

Match drawn
Yorkshire 5 pts, Leicestershire 4 pts

27 June

at Coatbridge

Zimbabwe 165 for 8 (A.J. Pycroft 54 not out)
Scotland 95 (G.A. Hick 4 for 24)

Zimbabwe won by 70 runs

The keenly anticipated clash between championship contenders Gloucestershire and Hampshire ended in stalemate after Gloucestershire had seemingly taken a firm grip on the game on the opening day. The pitch was saturated and although the sun shone, play did not begin until 4.00 pm. Put it to bat, Hampshire were 106 for 8 at the close. They were soon out the next morning, but Gloucestershire failed to take as big a lead as they had hoped. They owed much to the late flashing blades of Walsh and Russell, for only Curran and Lloyds of the earlier batsmen had offered any positivity, Curran hitting 50 off 48 balls. Trailing by 81, Hampshire soon reasserted themselves and Robin Smith batted particularly well as the Gloucestershire bowling and fielding began to lose faith in itself. Set to make 232 off 50 overs, the home side had lost 4 wickets for 53 runs in 22 overs when the rain arrived, for which, no doubt, they were thankful.

Middlesex supplanted Gloucestershire at the top of the table with a highly impressive win at Worcester. There was no play on the opening day, but Cowans, Hughes and Williams quickly disposed of Worcestershire on the second and Barlow and Slack put on a brisk hundred for the first wicket. Barlow completed his century on the last morning when Middlesex reached 158 in 45 overs and Radley declared 88 runs in arrears. Then came a remarkable bowling performance by 21-year old Graham Rose, who was deputising for the sick Wayne Daniel. In 10.5 overs he took 6 for 41 with his medium pace and Worcestershire were routed, bowled out twice in two days inside 111 overs. Middlesex needed 226 in 55 overs to win, not a simple task, but, after losing Barlow, Slack and Tomlins for 46, they were rallied by Roland Butcher and Clive Radley who added 136 for the fourth wicket. Butcher hit a six and 15 fours and his hundred came off 88 balls. It was a match-winning innings and victory came with 25 balls to spare.

At Derby, where Sharma made his championship debut for the home side, Chris Broad, so shabbily treated by the England selectors, survived missed chances and a back strain which forced him to retire for a while to reach a career best 171 after Notts had been put in to bat. Derbyshire bowled indifferently and fielded badly, but they batted a little better. Anderson had two good innings and was awarded his county cap. Holding bowled Derbyshire back into contention with his best performance in the championship and they were left to make 257 in 57 overs. They lost Barnett and Fowler for 11, but Roberts and Anderson added 154 to revive hope. Roberts, showing rapid advance as an exciting young batsman, reached his second century of the summer with a six and 16 fours off 134 balls, but the asking rate was a little too much and Derbyshire fell 23 runs short.

Another to receive his county cap was Geoff Holmes who first played for Glamorgan seven years ago. The match at Cardiff was marred by rain, but Popplewell and Roebuck put on 142 for Somerset's first wicket, and Richards and Felton 153 for the third. John Steele broke a finger trying to take a return catch from Popplewell. Glamorgan avoided the follow-on when, after Javed's hundred, the last two wickets realised 75 runs.

There was no play on the first day at Chelmsford and Kent quickly succumbed to Turner, Lever and Pringle on the second. Essex finished in a position of strength, but Ellison returned a career best on the last morning after McEwan and Prichard, playing his first innings since breaking a finger, had added 127 for the third wicket. As the game died Hinks reached a career best. Alan Knott also reminded of his continuing prowess with five catches.

Humpage and Dyer rescured Warwickshire from 41 for 3 with a stand of 112, and Graeme Fowler hit his best championship score of the season in what had been the worst period of his career. Eventually Lancashire were asked to make 259 in 60 overs and began well with Fowler and Varey putting on 53. Then Anton Ferreira struck, taking 10 wickets in a championship match for the first time and reducing Lancashire to 93 for 6. David Hughes, dropped when 6 overs remained, batted through 35 overs to save his side.

Only 30 overs were possible on the first day at Northampton, but Larkins and Cook made up for lost time on the second day with an opening stand of 70 in 12 overs. Northants were asked to make 255 in 45 overs on a worn pitch on the last afternoon and achieved a splendid victory with 14 balls to spare thanks to a scintillating 117 by Wayne Larkins. He and Bailey added 135 in 22 overs and Robin Boyd-Moss hit a rousing 42 off 23 balls which clinched the fine win.

There was some rather dour Yorkshire batting on the opening day at Bradford, but Leicestershire showed considerably more enterprise on a cheerless second day. The third day was enlivened by 100 in 94 minutes before lunch by David Bairstow. The visitors, set to make 312 in 73 overs against the raw Yorkshire attack, Carrick being the only capped bowler, started well with Butcher and Balderstone putting on 145 in 43 overs, but thereafter they lost their way and settled for a draw which left them with only Derbyshire below them in the table.

Second Cornhill Test Match
ENGLAND *v.* AUSTRALIA

Twenty-four hours before the Second Cornhill Test match was due to begin Lord's resembled a swamp, and it was only the Herculean efforts of the groundstaff, who worked throughout the night, that made it possible for the game to start on time. England brought in Foster for Cowans and Edmonds for Willey, Sidebottom being omitted from the chosen twelve, while Australia brought in leg-spinner Bob Holland for Jeff Thomson.

Border won the toss and, on a pitch which promised to give the bowlers some assistance, he asked England to bat. His decision gained early rewards when Robinson and Gooch were lbw at 26 and 51 respectively. Gooch was most unlucky to be given out by umpire Evans who was to have a nightmare match, for he seemed well outside the line of the off stump.

Gower began in imperious manner, straight driving a two and cover driving a four. Gatting also began with a flourish, but the ball was moving about significantly and he settled for

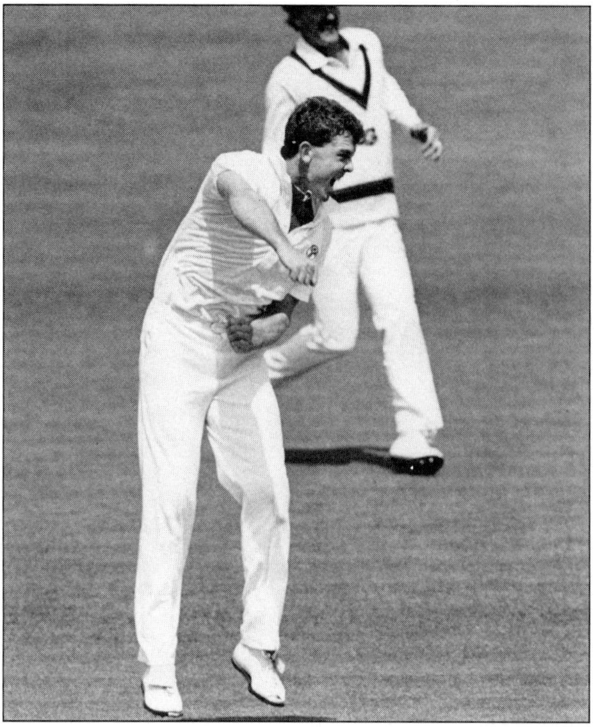

ABOVE: *Craig McDermott roars an appeal. His 6 for 70 brought about England's first innings downfall. Bob Holland, Australia's other bowling hero, is jubilant (Adrian Murrell)*
BELOW: *Allan Border – 196, the highest score of his Test career. Man of the Match. (Adrian Murrell)*

ABOVE: *Botham revives England's hopes with some powerful and controlled hitting. (Adrian Murrell)*

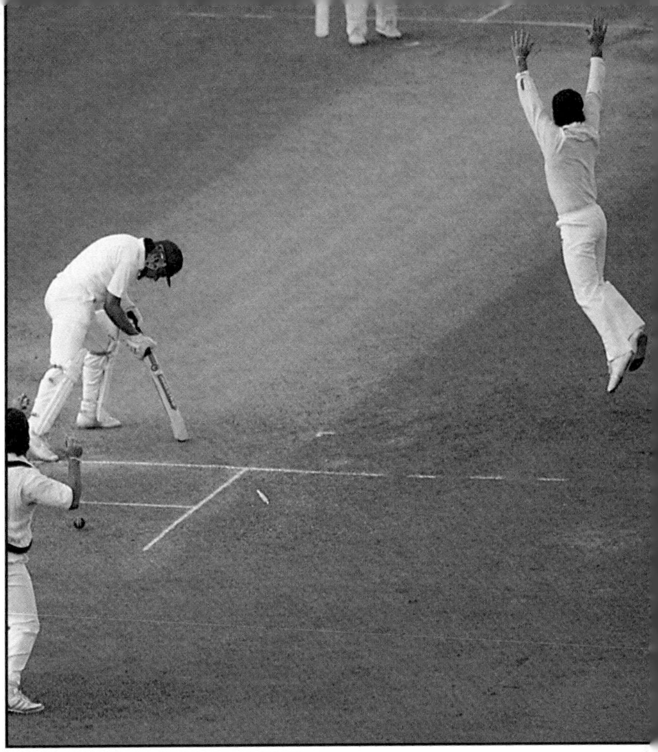

Robinson is bowled by Bob Holland late on Saturday evening and the England innings begins to crumble. (Ken Kelly)

Edmonds swings at Holland and is taken at slip by Boon. (George Herringshaw)

TOP: *Hilditch hooks. The shot was to be his undoing throughout the series. (Adrian Murrell)*

MIDDLE: *Paul Downton is caught by Boon off Holland first ball. Phillips and Wessels celebrate. (Adrian Murrell)*

BOTTOM: *Greg Ritchie drives through the off-side field during his innings of 94. He shared a stand of 216 with Allan Border. Umpire Evans is pensive. Gatting and Gower are the fielders. (Adrian Murrell)*

RIGHT: *Wessels is brilliantly run out by Gower and Australia are 63 for 4 in their second innings. (Adrian Murrell)*

accumulation. He enjoyed a little luck and then was lbw offering no stroke to a ball from Lawson which was barely outside the off stump and needed to come back only minimally to hit the wicket. It was a horrendous piece of misjudgement and echoed his errors of a year ago against West Indies on the same ground.

Lamb was not at his best, but he worked hard and, like Gatting, enjoyed some luck. He and Gower, who hit 12 fours in his fluent and attractive innings, had begun to prosper when, on the stroke of tea, Gower was taken at second slip off McDermott, by far the best of the Australian bowlers.

Botham hit from the start and in the first over after tea he drove powerfully at Lawson on the rise and was caught on the cover boundary where Ritchie had been stationed for just such a shot. Lawson had dangled the bait and Botham had bitten it. Lamb's 36-over vigil ended when he drove at a widish ball and was caught behind. Downton, Edmonds and Emburey lifted England to 273 for 8 by the close, and the next morning only 17 more runs were added. Craig McDermott took the last two wickets to give him 6 for 70, his best return in a brief, but highly impressive Test career.

Australia batted in gloomy, unfavourable conditions, and the whole day was fractured by stoppages for bad light, not all of which were easy to understand. In the fourth over Wood pulled Allott to long leg, and just after lunch Hilditch was bowled between bat and pad. Wessels played defiantly for an hour and a half before falling to Botham, somewhat dubiously, and Botham also accounted for Boon in the last over before tea. This brought together Border and Ritchie who were to play the decisive role in the match.

On 87 Border moved down the wicket to Edmonds and hit the ball hard to leg. Gatting, at short leg, caught the ball between his thighs, but as he clutched to complete the catch he threw the ball in the air and dived to try to retain it, but it fell to earth. Indeed, Border, who had begun to walk towards the pavilion, was nearly run out as the ball scurried towards Downton. By the close Border was 92 and Ritchie 46 as Australia were 183 for 4.

The English summer arrived on the Saturday and after a rather dreary pre-lunch session, the match blossomed. Border and Ritchie took their stand to 216 and it was 2.40 before Ritchie tried to turn Botham to leg and was lbw. His disappointment at not reaching his hundred was shared by many. He is a sturdy, aggressive player, especially appealing in his driving on the off and straight. Border was at his

Her Majesty the Queen is introduced to England captain David Gower by George Mann, President of M.C.C. (Adrian Murrell)

glorious best, ever eager to attack, advancing down the wicket to the slow bowlers and relishing the chance to hit the ball. He hit 22 fours in an innings which lasted $7\frac{1}{2}$ hours. He was finally well caught at slip off Botham who thus captured five wickets in a Test innings for the twenty-fifth time, yet another record to the great man.

Border's innings was one to cherish and as he left the crease he and Botham shook hands, the recognition of one giant for another. Phillips had hit 21 sweet runs in half an hour and O'Donnell hit 48 in just over the hour to suggest what a great player is in the making. There were some scatter-brained antics at the end and Australia were out with a lead of 135.

In the evening sunshine they took a vice-like grip on the game. Gooch followed a ball from McDermott that he could well have left alone and was caught down the leg-side and two runs later Robinson was bowled by Holland's top spinner. England had two night-watchmen at the crease when close of play came at a very unhappy and uneasy 37 for 2. It was very difficult to justify the use of both Emburey and Allott as numbers 3 and 4, and the criticism of the decision was compounded on the Monday morning when Allott was bowled in the first over and Emburey, after two defiant blows, chopped the ball onto his wicket.

Gower hit 5 fours, 4 of them lovely shots, and then was very well caught behind when McDermott angled the ball across his body. Lamb was again out of touch and lofted Lawson to mid-off. At 98 for 6 England faced imminent defeat.

By lunch Botham and Gatting had advanced the score to 132 for 6 and in the first over after lunch Botham hooked McDermott into the Mound Stand. He also hit 12 fours as he and Gatting, in more subdued manner, put on 131. Gatting had been very close to being lbw, not playing a shot first ball, the doubt in the umpire's mind must have been a small one and possibly influenced by harsher decisions he had given earlier, but he showed admirable restraint in his innings and both supported and balanced Botham.

Botham fell when, in attempting to drive Holland, he skied to cover. Holland had been operating from the Nursery End with commendable accuracy and now he gathered the

Border begins to walk back to the pavilion believing he has been caught by Gatting, but the fielder juggles with the ball and sees it drop to the ground. Downton and Gower can do nothing to help. (Adrian Murrell)

reward. He turned the ball across Downton to have him caught at slip first ball and Edmonds went the same way as he tried to cut, but he had stayed long enough to encourage Gatting to play some attacking shots and add 32. Foster prodded a close catch and Bob Holland finished with 5 for 68. Australia needed 127 to win.

Botham had raised the spectre of Headingley 1981 with his innings and now he tore in and bowled with great fire. In his first over he had Hilditch caught on the square leg boundary off a hook and shortly after Wood was taken in the gully off a steeply rising delivery. Botham, rampant, had become the leading wicket-taker in England Test history. The crowd bayed for more blood and Allott knocked back Ritchie's off stump. Australia were 22 for 3 and the ghost of 1981 had become clearly outlined. Border joined Wessels to take them through to the close in positive manner, but the last day began with Australia still 81 short of victory.

At 63 Wessels was magnificently run out by Gower at silly mid-off, the fielder flicking the ball back when the batsman advanced and played defensively. Boon was almost immediately bowled by Edmonds, the ball pitching on leg and hitting the off stump, and at 65 for 5, Australia were once again in trauma. Phillips responded in the grand manner, cutting and pulling vigorously, 29 in 40 minutes off 32 balls just about

ABOVE: *Andrew Hilditch is bowled by Neil Foster. Phil Edmonds is at short-leg. (Ken Kelly)*

killed England's hopes even though he did fall to Emburey, belatedly introduced into the attack.

Throughout the crises Border had remained firmly in control. There was to be no repeat of 1981 with him at the helm. O'Donnell joined him and hit a magnificent straight six

SECOND CORNHILL TEST MATCH – ENGLAND *v.* AUSTRALIA

27, 28, 29 June, 1 and 2 July 1985 at Lord's

ENGLAND

	FIRST INNINGS		SECOND INNINGS	
G.A. Gooch	lbw, b McDermott	30	c Phillips, b McDermott	17
R.T. Robinson	lbw, b McDermott	6	b Holland	12
D.I. Gower†	c Border, b McDermott	86	(5) c Phillips, b McDermott	22
M.W. Gatting	lbw, b Lawson	14	(6) not out	75
A.J. Lamb	c Phillips, b Lawson	47	(7) c Holland, b Lawson	9
I.T. Botham	c Ritchie, b Lawson	5	(8) c Border, b Holland	85
P.R. Downton*	c Wessels, b McDermott	21	(9) c Boon, b Holland	0
J.E. Emburey	lbw, b O'Donnell	33	(3) b Lawson	20
P.H. Edmonds	c Border, b McDermott	21	(10) c Boon, b Holland	1
N.A. Foster	c Wessels, b McDermott	3	(11) c Border, b Holland	0
P.J.W. Allott	not out	1	(4) b Lawson	0
Extras	b 1, lb 4, w 1, nb 17	23	b 1, lb 12, w 3, nb 4	20
		290		261

	O	M	R	W	O	M	R	W
Lawson	25	2	91	3	23	—	86	3
McDermott	29.2	5	70	6	20	2	84	2
O'Donnell	22	3	82	1	5	—	10	—
Holland	23	6	42	—	42	12	68	5

FALL OF WICKETS
1- 26, 2- 51, 3- 99, 4- 179, 5- 184, 6- 211, 7- 241, 8- 273, 9- 283
1- 32, 2- 34, 3- 38, 4- 57, 5- 77, 6- 98, 7 229, 8- 229, 9- 261

AUSTRALIA

	FIRST INNINGS		SECOND INNINGS	
G.M. Wood	c Emburey, b Allott	8	(2) c Lamb, b Botham	6
A.M.J. Hilditch	b Foster	14	(1) c Lamb, b Botham	0
K.C. Wessels	lbw, b Botham	11	run out	28
A.R. Border†	c Gooch, b Botham	196	(5) not out	41
D.C. Boon	c Downton, b Botham	4	(6) b Edmonds	1
G.M. Ritchie	lbw, b Botham	94	(4) b Allott	2
W.B. Phillips*	c Edmonds, b Botham	21	c Edmonds, b Emburey	29
S.P. O'Donnell	c Lamb, b Edmonds	48	not out	9
G.F. Lawson	not out	5		
C.J. McDermott	run out	9		
R.G. Holland	b Holland	0		
Extras	lb 10, w 1, nb 4	15	lb 11	11
		425	(for 6 wickets)	127

	O	M	R	W	O	M	R	W
Foster	23	1	83	1				
Allott	30	4	70	1	7	4	8	1
Botham	24	2	109	5	15	—	49	2
Edmonds	25.4	5	85	2	16	5	35	1
Gooch	3	1	11	—				
Emburey	19	3	57	—	8	4	24	1

FALL OF WICKETS
1- 11, 2- 24, 3- 80, 4- 101, 5- 317, 6- 347, 7- 398, 8- 414, 9- 425
1- 0, 2- 9, 3- 22, 4- 63, 5- 65, 6- 116

Umpires: H.D. Bird and D.G.L. Evans

Australia won by 4 wickets

RIGHT: *Bob Holland. The triumph of the leg-spinner, 5 for 68 at Lord's. (Adrian Murrell)*

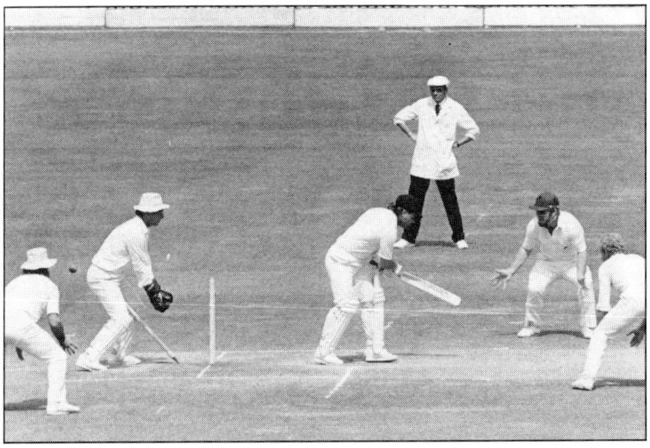

Boon is bowled by Edmonds. Australia are 65 for 5 and the ghost of the Ashes 1981 is abroad again. (Adrian Murrell)

The ghost is laid. Victory is acclaimed on the Australian balcony. (Adrian Murrell)

off Edmonds, and the pressure was gone. Border, a man for all seasons, and unquestionably man of this magnificent match, was undefeated and the series was level.

29, 30 June, 1 July

at Trent Bridge

Nottinghamshire 272 (D.W. Randall 65, D.V. Lawrence 4 for 73) and 213 for 5 dec (C.E.B. Rice 68, P. Johnson 60)
Gloucestershire 213 for 9 dec (J.W. Lloyds 88 not out) and 118 for 3 (C.W.J. Athey 54)

Match drawn
Nottinghamshire 7 pts, Gloucestershire 6 pts

at Cleethorpes

Zimbabwe 214 (L.L. de Grandhomme 59, K. Arnold 5 for 57, T.S. Smith 5 for 79) and 293 for 7 dec (A.J. Pycroft 110 not out, I.P. Butchart 82)
Minor Counties 293 for 8 dec (S.P. Atkinson 63, G.R.J. Roope 61)

Match drawn

29 June, 1 and 2 July

at Derby

Glamorgan 160 (Javed Miandad 64, M.A. Holding 5 for 33, P.G. Newman 4 for 29) and 316 (Younis Ahmed 96, G.C. Holmes 52, J. Derrick 52, P.G. Newman 4 for 94)
Derbyshire 398 (G. Miller 90, K.J. Barnett 67, P.G. Newman 52 not out, L.L. McFarlane 4 for 100) and 82 for 0

Derbyshire won by 10 wickets
Derbyshire 23 pts, Glamorgan 3 pts

at Southampton

Essex 96 (M.D. Marshall 6 for 42, T.M. Tremlett 4 for 19) and 183 (K.S. McEwan 56, T.M. Tremlett 4 for 45)
Hampshire 336 for 7 dec (J.J.E. Hardy 107 not out, C.L. Smith 59, R.J. Parks 53 not out, V.P. Terry 51)

Hampshire won by an innings and 57 runs
Hampshire 23 pts, Essex 3 pts

Jon Hardy – a match-winning century for Hampshire against Essex at Southampton, 1 July. (Trevor Jones)

at Leicester

Surrey 210 (C.J. Richards 75 not out, J.P. Agnew 6 for 86) and 224 for 9 (A. Needham 56, P. Willey 6 for 73)
Leicestershire 341 (J.J. Whitaker 109, R.A. Cobb 78, A.H. Gray 4 for 56)

Match drawn
Leicestershire 8 pts, Surrey 6 pts

at Hastings

Sussex 310 for 6 dec (G.D. Mendis 103, Imran Khan 70, C.M. Wells 69 not out) and 193 for 0 dec (G.D. Mendis 100 not out, A.M. Green 78 not out)

Cricket at Hastings. Sussex v. *Lancashire. (Adrian Murrell)*

Gehan Mendis – a century in each innings for Sussex against Lancashire at Hastings, 29 June–2 July. (George Herringshaw)

Lancashire 173 (N.H. Fairbrother 59 not out, Imran Khan 4 for 28) and 257 (J. Simmons 101, J.R.T. Barclay 5 for 99)

Sussex won by 73 runs
Sussex 23 pts, Lancashire 3 pts

at Edgbaston

Northamptonshire 142 (G.C. Small 5 for 45) and 282 (R.J. Bailey 67, D.J. Wild 55)
Warwickshire 212 (Asif Din 60, D.J. Capel 4 for 58) and 181 (R.A. Harper 4 for 47)

Northamptonshire won by 31 runs
Northamptonshire 20 pts, Warwickshire 6 pts

ABOVE RIGHT: *Norman Gifford, 6 for 20 in Warwickshire's remarkable 9-run victory over Northants in the John Player Special League, 30 June. (Adrian Murrell)*
BELOW: *Geoff Boycott (Adrian Murrell) and* BELOW RIGHT: *Martyn Moxon (Mark Leech) shared an opening stand of 351 for Yorkshire against Worcestershire at Worcester, 29 June.*

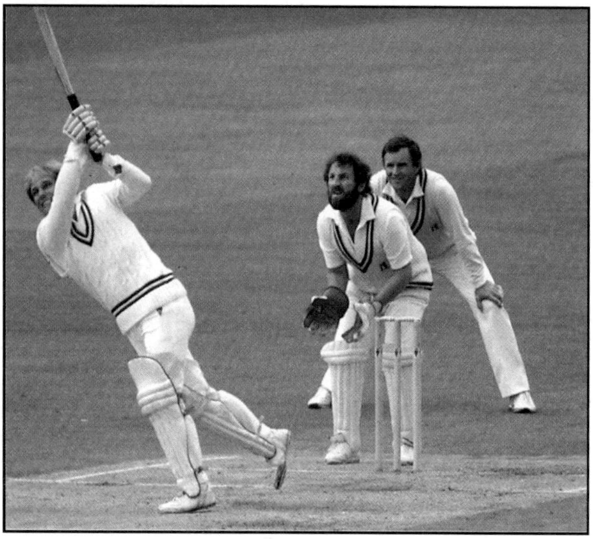

Andy Pycroft, Zimbabwe captain, 110 not out at Cleethorpes to save his side from defeat, 1 July. (Ken Kelly)

at Worcester

Yorkshire 389 for 3 dec (G. Boycott 184, M.D. Moxon 168) and 194 for 5 dec (G. Boycott 50)
Worcestershire 292 for 7 dec (S.J. Rhodes 58 not out, T.S. Curtis 51) and 291 for 8 (D.N. Patel 78, P.A. Neale 58, S.D. Fletcher 4 for 91)
Match drawn
Worcestershire 11 pts, Yorkshire 7 pts

Cricket on Goodwin Sands. Kent v. *Thanet Select XI, 1 July. Part of Kent's endeavours to raise money for the ground development at Canterbury. Underwood, Chris Cowdrey and Ellison field to Nick Dineley of Thanet. (Tom Morris)*

at Taunton

Somerset 331 for 5 dec (R.J. Harden 107, R.E. Hayward 100 not out, N.A. Felton 54) and 211 for 4 dec (N.A. Felton 74)
Cambridge University 199 (P.G.P. Roebuck 82) and 186 for 6 (C.R. Andrew 62)
Match drawn

Hampshire joined Middlesex at the top of the county championship when they outplayed the reigning champions Essex who, for the most part, gave a wretched display. Put in to bat on a green wicket under heavy cloud with Marshall and Tremlett at their best, Essex were shot out in 34.5 overs and their total was only boosted by a brave ninth wicket stand of 39 between Turner and Lever. Hampshire were soon in the lead, but then faltered against Pringle and ended Saturday on 172 for 6. On the Monday, however, Hardy, who had been dropped on 7, reached a maiden first-class hundred and shared an unbroken eighth wicket stand of 115 with Bobby Parks. There was less excuse for Essex's poor showing when they batted again, and it was the admirable Tremlett who disturbed them most and he became the first bowler in the country to reach 50 wickets.

Gloucestershire lost ground when rain blighted the second day of their match at Trent Bridge. They had been in a dreadful position when, having bowled out Notts for 272, Randall becoming the second batsman in the country to reach 1000 runs, they slumped to 58 for 6. Lloyds, with 50 off 57 balls, and Lawrence, with a career best 41, added 80 for the ninth wicket to revive them. Rice eventually asked Gloucestershire to make 273 in 50 overs, an ungenerous target in the conditions, but the visitors had a fright when 3 wickets fell for 11 runs before Athey and Bainbridge earned a draw.

No play on the first day until 3.15 at Leicester virtually doomed the match with Surrey to a draw although neither captain showed much enterprise. It was Leicestershire's tenth draw in eleven games and left them bottom of the table after Derbyshire gained their first win of the season in fine fashion.

Holding and Newman wrecked the Glamorgan innings on the opening and only a fifth wicket stand of 101 between Javed and Ontong averted total disaster. Only 10 runs behind with 8 wickets standing on the Saturday evening, Derbyshire lost two quick wickets on the Monday and laboured a little until Newman and Warner added 86 for the ninth wicket, but the basis of the innings was a stand of 88 in 28 overs between Miller, who batted with ease and assurance, and Sharma. Still one ponders why such a stylish batsman as Miller has not scored more runs. Glamorgan looked ripe for defeat in two days, but a fourth wicket stand of 119 between Younis and Holmes took the game into the third day.

Gehan Mendis scored a century in each innings for Sussex at Hastings, the first time he had accomplished this feat, and made possible an excellent victory over Lancashire. Imran Khan, who was warned for consistent short-pitched bowling at Abrahams, took 3 for 1 in 14 balls to end Lancashire's first innings, but it was John Barclay's off-spin which won the game on the last day. He had set Lancashire a reasonable target of 331 in 105 overs except that Lancashire's batsmen rarely seem capable of reaching 300. They were 60 for 5 when Jack Simmons strode in and put his colleagues to shame with a pugnacious century, the sixth of his distinguished career. His brave knock ended when Barclay held a splendid right-handed catch at slip off Pigott. It was Sussex's second win of the season and one wondered what they might have achieved had Barclay been more confident of his own abilities and not been so reluctant to bowl himself. Before this match he had bowled only 11 first-class overs in the season.

Northamptonshire gained a remarkable win at Edgbaston. They were bowled out for 142 on the Saturday which Warwickshire closed at 116 for 5. Asif Din's stubborn innings took the home side into the lead and Northants, who had lost George Sharp with a broken finger, struggled to 169 for 5. Wild, Harper and Bailey lifted them on the last day and Warwickshire were left the post lunch period in which to make 213, not a daunting task. The tenacious Robin Dyer gave the innings the substance it needed after the early loss of Andy Lloyd, but, having reached 105 for 2, seemingly on the way to an easy victory, Warwickshire lost 5 wickets for 5 runs in 6 overs. Small and Wall halted the slide with a stand of 45, but Wall was bowled by Harper with 14 overs remaining. Gifford then became rock-like in defence and it seemed that the match would be drawn until, with 4 overs remaining, the Warwickshire captain was run out and Hoffman quickly followed, caught off Harper.

The most thrilling encounter was at Worcester. A career best by Martyn Moxon and a $6\frac{1}{2}$ hour innings from Geoff Boycott took Yorkshire to a mighty position on the opening day. The openers put on 351, the first time Boycott had been in a stand of three hundred or more for Yorkshire and the highest opening stand for the county since Holmes and Sutcliffe's famous 555 at Leyton 53 years ago. Rhodes, playing against his old county, hit his first first-class fifty to help save the follow-on, and Neale declared 97 behind. Bairstow set Worcestershire to make 292 in 55 overs, a stiffer target than the one Yorkshire had refused at Harrogate a week earlier. Rhodes gave the innings brief early impetus and Neale and Patel shared a stand of 117 which made victory possible, but Pickles claimed the formidable Kapil Dev as his first championship wicket and when the last over arrived Worcestershire needed 11 for victory. Incredibly, Newport top-edged Fletcher for 6 and the last ball came with 2 needed, but Radford and Newport could manage only one so the match was drawn with Worcestershire taking 8 points as the side batting last in a drawn match with the scores level.

Zimbabwe maintained their unbeaten record when Pycroft and Butchart put on 123 for the seventh wicket in the second innings at Cleethorpes and Andrew's patience saved Cambridge University at Taunton.

John Player Special League

30 June

at Derby

Glamorgan 132 for 2 (H. Morris 53, A.L. Jones 53) *v.* **Derbyshire**

Match abandoned

Derbyshire 2 pts, Glamorgan 2 pts

at Bournemouth

Essex 161 for 9

Hampshire 162 for 2 (M.C.J. Nicholas 61 not out, R.A. Smith 61 not out)

Hampshire (4 pts) won by 8 wickets

at Canterbury

Middlesex 169 for 7 (G.D. Barlow 72)

Kent 173 for 5

Kent (4 pts) won by 4 wickets

at Leicester

Leicestershire 216 for 6 (N.E. Briers 54)

Surrey 101 for 7

Leicestershire (4 pts) won on faster scoring rate

at Hastings

Sussex 234 for 4 (Imran Khan 80, A.M. Green 70)

Lancashire 165 for 7

Sussex (4 pts) won by 69 runs

at Edgbaston

Warwickshire 142 for 9

Northamptonshire 133 for 9 (R.J. Boyd-Moss 51, N. Gifford 4 for 20)

Warwickshire (4 pts) won by 9 runs

at Worcester

Yorkshire 215 for 5 (K. Sharp 112 not out)

Worcestershire 201 for 8 (D.N. Patel 54)

Yorkshire (4 pts) won by 14 runs

Kent took a two-point lead at the top of the table when they beat Middlesex with considerable ease at Canterbury. After Barlow's good knock and an opening stand of 87 with Slack only Sykes produced the necessary aggression. He also bowled well as did Hughes, but Kent were never troubled as Tavare hit 44 brisk runs and Aslett maintained the run rate. Hampshire, who, even without the injured Greenidge, looked the best equipped side in the country for the one-day game completed a thoroughly miserable week-end for Essex who looked listless. Yorkshire moved into second place with Kevin Sharp hitting his best Sunday League score. On the Saturday Neale had asked Yorkshire to bat first and seen

TOP: *Andy Needham of Surrey is run out by Eldine Baptiste in the first round NatWest Trophy match at Canterbury. (Tom Morris)*

MIDDLE: *Nigel Felton, 112 for Somerset against Leicestershire at Taunton, 6 July. (George Herringshaw)*

Aslett is bowled by Pocock for 13, Kent v. *Surrey at The Oval. (Tom Morris)*

RIGHT: *Tavare slashes the ball through the covers as Kent move to victory over Surrey in the NatWest Trophy at Canterbury. Richards is the wicket-keeper. (Tom Morris)*

them pass 300 in 100 overs without losing a wicket, but neither Moxon nor Boycott were in the Sunday side. Imran Khan hit 80 off 62 balls at Hastings with 3 sixes and 7 fours. He and Colin Wells put on 85 in 9 overs. Lancashire were never in contention. The most remarkable victory came at Edgbaston where Warwickshire beat Northants to move into fourth place. Chasing a modest 143 in 35 overs, Northants reached 83 for 2. Norman Gifford then took 4 for 2 in 11 balls, returned his best John Player League bowling figures and snatched victory for Warwickshire by 9 runs.

NatWest Bank Trophy – First Round

3 July

at Luton

Gloucestershire 268 for 6 (C.W.J. Athey 72, A.W. Stovold 71)
Bedfordshire 127

Gloucestershire won by 141 runs
(*Man of the Match* – C.W.J. Athey)

at Birkenhead

Cheshire 159 for 7
Yorkshire 160 for 0 (M.D. Moxon 82 not out, G. Boycott 70 not out)

Yorkshire won by 10 wickets
(*Man of the Match* – M.D. Moxon)

at Derby

Derbyshire 171 (K.J. Barnett 53)
Durham 173 for 3
Durham won by 7 wickets
(*Man of the Match* – S. Greensword)

at Chelmsford

Essex 307 for 8 dec (P.J. Prichard 94, K.S. McEwan 66, D.R. Pringle 55, B.R. Hardie 51)
Oxfordshire 81 (D.R. Pringle 5 for 12)

Essex won by 226 runs
(*Man of the Match* – D.R. Pringle)

ABOVE: *Kevin Rice of Devon hit a sparkling century against Warwickshire in the first round of the NatWest Trophy and won the Man of the Match award. (Ken Kelly)* BELOW: *Clinton (Surrey) who hit a magnificent 146 against his old county in the first round of the NatWest Trophy and still finished on the losing side. Kent* v. *Surrey, Canterbury, 3 July. (Adrian Murrell)*

at Southampton

Hampshire 339 for 4 (V.P. Terry 165 not out, C.G. Greenidge 89)
Berkshire 152

Hampshire won by 187 runs
(*Man of the Match* – V.P. Terry)

at Hitchin

Worcestershire 241 for 7 (P.A. Neale 73, T.S. Curtis 63)
Hertfordshire 183 (E.P. Neal 52)

Worcestershire won by 58 runs
(*Man of the Match* – E.P. Neal)

at Canterbury

Surrey 293 for 8 (G.S. Clinton 146)
Kent 296 for 4 (S.G. Hinks 95, M.R. Benson 78, C.J. Tavare 62)

Kent won by 6 wickets
(*Man of the Match* – S.G. Hinks)

at Uxbridge

Middlesex 283 for 9 (W.N. Slack 98, R.O. Butcher 59, D. Halliwell 4 for 57)
Cumberland 152 (P.H. Edmonds 4 for 39)

Middlesex won by 131 runs
(*Man of the Match* – W.N. Slack)

at Norwich

Leicestershire 213 for 8
Norfolk 73 (L.B. Taylor 4 for 14)

Leicestershire won by 140 runs
(*Man of the Match* – L.B. Taylor)

at Trent Bridge

Nottinghamshire 243 for 7 (P. Johnson 101 not out, A.J. Webster 4 for 38)
Staffordshire 147 for 8 (G.S. Warner 51)

Nottinghamshire won by 96 runs
(*Man of the Match* – P. Johnson)

at Edinburgh

Scotland 137 (G.C. Holmes 5 for 24, J. Derrick 4 for 14)
Glamorgan 141 for 2 (A.L. Jones 60 not out)

Glamorgan won by 8 wickets
(*Man of the Match* – G.C. Holmes)

at Telford

Northamptonshire 270 for 6 (G. Cook 130, R.J. Boyd-Moss 51, A. Barnard 4 for 47)
Shropshire 170 (J. Foster 63)

Northamptonshire won by 100 runs
(*Man of the Match* – G. Cook)

at Taunton

Buckinghamshire 138 (J. Garner 5 for 18)
Somerset 139 for 3 (N.A. Felton 72 not out)

Somerset won by 7 wickets
(*Man of the Match* – J. Garner)

at Bury St Edmunds

Lancashire 233 for 6 (N.H. Fairbrother 52 not out)
Suffolk 133 for 8

Lancashire won by 100 runs
(*Man of the Match* – N.H. Fairbrother)

at Hove

Sussex 283 for 6 (P.W.G. Parker 109, C.M. Wells 76)
Ireland 39 (G.S. le Roux 5 for 7)

Sussex won by 244 runs
(*Man of the Match* – P.W.G. Parker)

at Edgbaston

Devon 221 for 7 (K.G. Rice 107)
Warwickshire 222 for 7 (A.I. Kallicharran 66, P.A. Smith 51 not out)

Warwickshire won by 3 wickets
(*Man of the Match* – K.G. Rice)

The exciting and hospitable NatWest Bank Trophy competition produced its usual quota of surprises and individual glories in the first round which admits Scotland, Ireland and thirteen of the minor counties. Busby of Oxfordshire bowled Gooch for 5, but Essex still passed 300. Cumberland fought

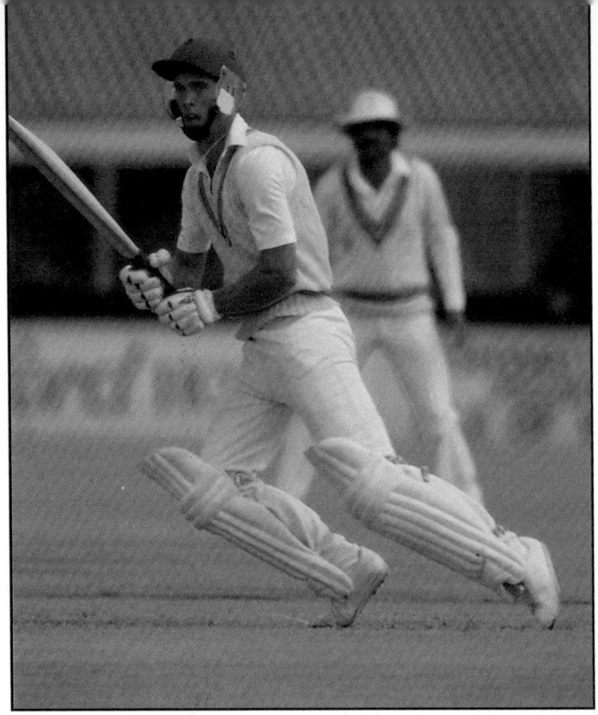

James Whitaker (Leicestershire), a rapidly maturing batsman. (David Munden)

nobly at Uxbridge, but lost the services of their leading batsman Qasim Umar who was injured. Neal hit a brave fifty at Hitchin and Nottinghamshire were brought to the brink of disaster by Webster at Trent Bridge. The Staffordshire opening bowler reduced Notts to 71 for 6, but Paul Johnson hit 100 off 135 balls to save his side.

There were some fine bowling performances. Jack Simmons bowled his 12 overs for 3 runs and Garth le Roux had a spell of 5 for 0 including the hat-trick who made the lowest score ever recorded in the competition.

At Edgbaston, Devon ran Warwickshire very close. Kevin Rice hit a magnificent century. The 20-year old Exeter player hit a six and 14 fours in his 148-minute stay and Warwickshire were struggling at 87 for 4 until first Kallicharran and then Paul Smith, Asif Din and Gladstone Small saw them to victory with 5.4 overs and 3 wickets to spare.

Durham did even better than Devon and became the first minor county to beat two first-class counties as they followed their 1973 Gillette Cup victory over Yorkshire by completely outplaying Derbyshire. Two players who had taken part in the famous victory over Yorkshire were in the Durham side on this occasion, skipper Neil Riddell and individual award winner Stephen Greensword who took 3 for 20 in 12 overs and scored a most disciplined 40 to bring Durham victory with 4.2 overs remaining. Spinner Ashok Patel played an important part when he tore the heart out of the Derbyshire middle order, taking the wickets of Barnett, Roberts and Sharma for 20 runs.

The one clash between two first-class counties produced a wonderful game at Canterbury. Surrey were given a splendid start by Clinton's chanceless innings. He faced 177 balls and hit 3 sixes and 14 fours. He and Stewart had put on 68 in 14 overs and had put Surrey into a position of great strength when Stewart was hit on the pelvic bone by a throw from the Kent substitute, Goldsmith. Stewart was forced to retire hurt and although he returned later, he did not recapture his earlier flowing form. The injury disrupted Surrey, but their total of 293 still looked large enough for victory. Clinton's marvellous innings came to an end in the penultimate over. Kent, who had opted to bat second, had a record start of 188 in 43 overs by Hinks and Benson, but Needham dismissed them both in successive overs. Aslett and Tavare maintained the momentum, but 44 were needed off the last 7 overs after

Simon Hinks sweeps Pocock for four during his maiden first-class century, Kent v. *Surrey at The Oval, 8 July. Richards is the wicket-keeper and Lynch is at slip. (Tom Morris)*

Geoff Humpage enjoyed a magnificent season for Warwickshire as wicket-keeper and batsman. (Ken Kelly)

Aslett had been dismissed and it was Tavare's powerful hitting, and improvising, which brought a fine victory.

3, 4 and 5 July

at Lord's

Cambridge University 134 (G.J. Toogood 8 for 52) and 141 for 3
Oxford University 346 for 6 dec (G.J. Toogood 149, J.D. Carr 84 not out, A.J.T. Miller 78)

Match drawn

The Varsity Match, once one of the great events of the cricket calendar, has been pushed into semi-obscurity in recent years as the standard has declined, but the 1985 game produced an outstanding individual performance before being ruined by rain. Miller won the toss and asked Cambridge to bat. Andrew and Lea scored 41 in the first hour before Miller introduced the medium pace of Giles Toogood whose bowling has been used sparingly in his 4 years at Oxford. The former Cricket Society Colt became only the second bowler this century to take 8 wickets in an innings in the Varsity match and Cambridge were routed for 134. Oxford were 60 for 1 at the close and next day took complete command as Toogood repeated his batting feat of the previous year and hit the second century of his career. He put on 150 with Miller and 146 with Carr, who looks to be one of the best players to have appeared in the match for several years. Toogood took 2 more wickets before the close, but rain ruined the last day.

6, 7, 8 and 9 July

at Chelmsford

Australians 279 (A.M.J. Hilditch 80, N. Phillip 4 for 55) and 333 (D.C. Boon 138, D.M. Wellham 63, G.A. Gooch 4 for 61, D.R. Pringle 4 for 69)
Essex 409 (B.R. Hardie 113 not out, G.A. Gooch 68, N. Phillip 50) and 169 for 8 (D.R. Gilbert 4 for 41)

Match drawn

6, 8 and 9 July

at Swansea

Nottinghamshire 321 for 6 dec (R.T. Robinson 103, E.E. Hemmings 56 not out, R.J. Hadlee 53 not out) and 230 for 2 dec (R.T. Robinson 130 not out, D.W. Randall 63 not out)
Glamorgan 272 for 9 dec (J.G. Thomas 60 not out) and 173 for 5 (Younis Ahmed 81 not out)

Match drawn
Nottinghamshire 6 pts, Glamorgan 5 pts

at Gloucester

Yorkshire 307 (D.L. Bairstow 80, P. Carrick 73) and 83 (D.V. Lawrence 5 for 50)
Gloucestershire 301 for 6 dec (P. Bainbridge 119, C.W.J. Athey 101) and 91 for 2 (A.W. Stovold 56 not out)

Gloucestershire won by 8 wickets
Gloucestershire 24 pts, Yorkshire 6 pts

at Liverpool

Lancashire 401 for 6 dec (N.H. Fairbrother 164 not out) and 115 (M.D. Marshall 4 for 45)
Hampshire 371 for 5 dec (C.L. Smith 121, M.C.J. Nicholas 61, V.P. Terry 54, I. Folley 4 for 96) and 189 for 6 (J.J.E. Hardy 54)

Hampshire won by 4 wickets
Hampshire 22 pts, Lancashire 5 pts

at Northampton

Middlesex 386 for 9 dec (G.D. Barlow 141, W.N. Slack 70, J.E. Emburey 51, D.J. Capel 4 for 84) and 283 for 4 dec (C.T. Radley 63 not out, P.R. Downton 57 not out)
Northamptonshire 244 (G. Cook 72 not out, A.J. Lamb 60, P.H. Edmonds 5 for 49) and 224 (N.A. Mallender 52 not out, P.H. Edmonds 4 for 81)

Middlesex won by 141 runs
Middlesex 24 pts, Northamptonshire 4 pts

at Taunton

Somerset 367 (N.A. Felton 112, L.B. Taylor 5 for 77) and 248 for 5 dec (N.A. Felton 58, N.F.M. Popplewell 53, I.T. Botham 50 not out)
Leicestershire 343 for 9 dec (J.J. Whitaker 105, V.J. Marks 7 for 143) and 192 for 8 (P. Willey 80, V.J. Marks 4 for 65)

Match drawn
Somerset 7 pts, Leicestershire 7 pts

at The Oval

Kent 301 (S.G. Hinks 81, P.I. Pocock 7 for 42) and 249 for 3 dec (S.G. Hinks 117, C.J. Tavare 65)
Surrey 181 (M.A. Lynch 55) and 193 (M.A. Lynch 66, G.R. Dilley 5 for 53)

Kent won by 176 runs
Kent 24 pts, Surrey 5 pts

at Hove

Sussex 405 for 3 dec (Imran Khan 117 not out, C.M. Wells 100 not out, A.M. Green 96) and 228 for 2 dec (G.D. Mendis 111 not out, A.M. Green 72)
Warwickshire 343 for 7 dec (G.W. Humpage 159, P.A. Smith 61, Imran Khan 5 for 49) and 186 for 6 (T.A. Lloyd 63)

Match drawn
Sussex 7 pts, Warwickshire 5 pts

At Worcester

Worcestershire 295 (D.N. Patel 88, D.B. d'Oliveira 63, R.J. Finney 6 for 62) and 253 for 5 dec (P.A. Neale 102)
Derbyshire 214 (A.E. Warner 50, R.N. Kapil Dev 4 for 56, N.V. Radford 4 for 78) and 336 for 7 (J.G. Wright 117, I.S. Anderson 94, R.K. Illingworth 4 for 76)

Derbyshire won by 3 wickets
Derbyshire 22 pts, Worcestershire 7 pts

Middlesex retained the leadership of the Britannic Assurance County Championship with a resounding victory at Northampton, Emburey dismissing Walker with 16 overs remain-

Knypersley, scene of the John Player Special League game Derbyshire v. *Worcestershire where Derbyshire established a league record by hitting 18 sixes. (George Herringshaw)*

ing. Once again Middlesex were indebted to a fine opening partnership as Slack and Barlow put on 134. A slump in fortune was halted by the middle order and Gatting was able to close the innings on the Saturday evening. Geoff Cook was forced to retire hurt early in the Northants innings, but he returned to steer his side out of the danger of having to follow-on after Edmonds had wreaked havoc with the middle order. Radley and Downton hit 126 in 26 overs on the last morning to make possible a lunch time declaration and although Cowans injured a hand, Daniel made quick inroads into the Northants batting before the spinners, delayed only by Mallender's lusty blows, demolished the innings.

Hampshire and Gloucestershire both maintained their challenges with good wins. Hampshire faced a target of 186 and had to call on the hobbling Greenidge to help as they faltered in their task. On the Saturday, after Graeme Fowler had been dismissed for 0, Neil Fairbrother hit a career best and Lancashire reached 401 for 6. On the Monday, Fowler sustained a severe neck injury in fielding practice and was carried from the field in great pain. The gods of cricket did not smile kindly upon him in the summer of 1985. Lancashire's plight became worse as the day wore on. Even though Greenidge had retired hurt, Hampshire reached 331 for 5, and before the close, Lancashire, with Fowler unable to bat, had slumped to 63 for 5. They never effectively recovered and Hampshire won in rather laboured manner on the last day.

Gloucestershire were much more positive. Facing Yorkshire's 307, they moved to maximum batting points on the Monday, Bainbridge and Athey sharing a third wicket stand of 213. Graveney declared as soon as the fourth point was obtained and in 22.3 overs, the Yorkshire second innings was over. David Lawrence, now strongly tipped for an England place, bowling unchanged to take 5 for 50. By the close, Gloucestershire were only 13 runs short of victory with 8 wickets in hand.

Tim Robinson hit a century in each innings to add to his growing reputation, but Younis thwarted Notts in their bid for victory.

Somerset were also thwarted at Taunton where Marks and Booth did their best to exploit a deteriorating wicket. There were impressive centuries by two young batsmen, the ever improving Whitaker of Leicestershire and Felton who flits in and out of the Somerset scene.

Another young batsman to establish himself was Simon Hinks who, after weeks of promise, reached a maiden century against Surrey at The Oval. He had hit 81 in the first innings when Pat Pocock had his best return of the season, and Surrey slumped against a Kent attack which was at last finding confidence and rhythm. Set to make 370 in 97 overs, Surrey, weakened by injuries, dissolved to Dilley and Jarvis.

There was an abundance of runs at Hove, but in the end, a furious burst from Imran nearly won the game for Sussex and it was Paul Smith and Chris Lethbridge who saved Warwickshire after they had floundered in search of 291 in 70 overs.

The outstanding performance of the round of matches was by Derbyshire who compensated for their defeat in the NatWest by a thrilling and momentous win against Worcestershire. Trailing by 81 on the first innings and savaged by Phil Neale in the second, they were asked to make 335 off 86 overs, a daunting task. Kim Barnett was out at 51, but Anderson and Wright added 193 for the second wicket. Wright was in full flow, having reached his first hundred of the summer, when he was caught and bowled by Illingworth who took three other wickets and with Kapil Dev taking wickets with successive deliveries, Derbyshire stumbled, but Roberts and Miller hit well and victory came with eight balls to spare.

Essex engaged in a fine game with the Australians which could have gone either way on the last afternoon. Gilbert bowled the Australians back into contention after they had looked likely to be beaten. Gooch had a fine match and there were splendid innings from Hardie and Boon so that a draw was a good result. At the end of the day, however, Essex, the champions, glanced at the county table and realised that they were bottom, one point behind Leicestershire.

John Player Special League

7 July

at Knypersley

Derbyshire 292 for 9 (B. Roberts 70, I.S. Anderson 52)
Worcestershire 259 for 8 (T.S. Curtis 76, P.A. Neale 54, A.E. Warner 5 for 39)

Derbyshire (4 pts) won by 33 runs

at Swansea

Glamorgan 199 (Javed Miandad 89)
Nottinghamshire 202 for 7 (R.T. Robinson 77)

Nottinghamshire (4 pts) won by 3 wickets

at Gloucester

Gloucestershire 216 for 6 (B.F. Davison 103)
Yorkshire 203 for 6 (J.D. Love 100 not out)

Gloucestershire (4 pts) won by 13 runs

at Old Trafford

Hampshire 235 for 5 (C.G. Greenidge 59 retired hurt)
Lancashire 232 (J. Abrahams 66)

Hampshire (4 pts) won by 3 runs

at Tring

Middlesex 230 for 6 (W.N. Slack 74, M.W. Gatting 54)
Northamptonshire 231 for 5 (R.J. Bailey 103 not out)

Northamptonshire (4 pts) won by 5 wickets

at Taunton

Leicestershire 176 for 6

John Birch hit 17 runs in the last over to give Notts victory at Swansea, 7 July. (David Munden)

David Bairstow is bowled by Jarvis, Kent v. Yorkshire at Maidstone, 11 July. (Tom Morris)

Somerset 133

Leicestershire (4 pts) won by 43 runs

at The Oval

Kent 222 for 7 (C.J. Tavare 84 not out)
Surrey 185 for 9 (A.R. Butcher 52)

Kent (4 pts) won by 37 runs

at Hove

Sussex 209 for 6 (Imran Khan 83, C.M. Wells 53)
Warwickshire 189 (P.A. Smith 50 not out)

Sussex (4 pts) won by 20 runs

Maiden Sunday League hundreds of Bailey and Davison were overshadowed by events at Knypersley where Derbyshire established a league record by hitting 18 sixes, Roberts, Holding and Newman each hit five. Warner had his best bowling in the league. John Birch, not always as highly valued as he deserves, hit 17 of the 18 runs scored off McFarlane's final over to give Notts victory at Swansea. Notts had needed 36 from the last two overs and Birch, 37 not out, saw that they got them. Kent's win at The Oval saw them six points clear at the head of the table with five teams clustered below them.

10, 11 and 12 July

at Southend

Essex 381 (B.R. Hardie 162, K.W.R. Fletcher 71, C.H. Dredge 5 for 95) and 181 for 6 (B.R. Hardie 66)
Somerset 315 for 4 dec (N.F.M. Popplewell 172, P.M. Roebuck 69) and 98 (J.K. Lever 6 for 49)

Essex won by 149 runs
Essex 20 pts, Somerset 5 pts

at Swansea

Glamorgan 289 for 6 dec (Javed Miandad 89, Younis Ahmed 58, R.C. Ontong 56 not out)
Leicestershire 393 for 7 (J.J. Whitaker 103, J.C. Balderstone 101, I.P. Butcher 72, M.R. Price 4 for 97)

Match drawn
Leicestershire 5 pts, Glamorgan 4 pts

at Gloucester

Gloucestershire 307 for 7 dec (C.W.J. Athey 139 not out, P. Bainbridge 58) and 170 for 9 dec (P. Bainbridge 81, P.J. Newport 5 for 18)
Worcestershire 242 (R.N. Kapil Dev 72, T.S. Curtis 62) and 125 (R.N. Kapil Dev 57, C.A. Walsh 4 for 39)

Mark Price – impressive bowling form for Glamorgan. (Sporting Pictures UK Ltd)

Gloucestershire won by 110 runs
Gloucestershire 23 pts, Worcestershire 4 pts

at Portsmouth

Sussex 327 for 8 dec (G.D. Mendis 109, I.J. Gould 51) and 209 for 5 dec (G.D. Mendis 96 not out)
Hampshire 210 (R.J. Maru 62, C.L. Smith 60) and 213 for 8 (C.L. Smith 68, J.J.E. Hardy 54)

Match drawn
Sussex 8 pts, Hampshire 5 pts

Derek Underwood, 4 for 8 in 18 overs in Kent's victory over Yorkshire at Maidstone. (Adrian Murrell)

Nigel Popplewell (Somerset) hit a career best 172 against Essex at Southend, but later announced that he was retiring at the end of the season to follow a career in law. (Sporting Pictures UK Ltd)

at Maidstone

Kent 328 (E.A.E. Baptiste 82, R.M. Ellison 64 not out, P.W. Jarvis 7 for 105) and 270 for 3 dec (C.J. Tavare 123, M.R. Benson 107)
Yorkshire 300 for 7 dec (S.N. Hartley 60) and 198 (J.D. Love 93, D.L. Underwood 4 for 8)

Kent won by 100 runs
Kent 23 pts, Yorkshire 8 pts

at Lord's

Middlesex 246 (G.D. Barlow 97, C.E.B. Rice 4 for 57) and 201 (G.D. Barlow 112, R.J. Hadlee 7 for 34)
Nottinghamshire 202 (B.C. Broad 53, N.F. Williams 5 for 71) and 249 for 5 (D.W. Randall 115, B.C. Broad 56)

Nottinghamshire won by 5 wickets
Nottinghamshire 22 pts, Middlesex 6 pts

at Northampton

Northamptonshire 334 for 7 dec (R.G. Williams 103, R.J. Bailey 81, D.J. Wild 80) and 219 for 6 dec (D.J. Capel 71, R.J. Bailey 52)
Derbyshire 264 (G. Miller 60 not out, B.J. Griffiths 4 for 37) and 162 for 6 (I.S. Anderson 51, R.G. Williams 5 for 34)

Match drawn
Northamptonshire 7 pts, Derbyshire 4 pts

at Edgbaston

Lancashire 148 (P.A. Smith 4 for 25) and 321 (M. Watkinson 87, N.H. Fairbrother 85, A.M. Ferreira 4 for 64)
Warwickshire 122 and 351 for 9 (T.A. Lloyd 91, A.I. Kallicharran 56, M. Watkinson 4 for 96)

Warwickshire won by 1 wicket
Warwickshire 20 pts, Lancashire 4 pts

10 and 11 July

at Middleton

League Cricket Conference 264 for 7 dec (D. Borthwick 65 not out) and 84 for 3 (R.C. Haynes 55 not out)
Zimbabwe 163 (A. Merrick 6 for 37) and 182 (D.L. Houghton 52)

League Cricket Conference won by 7 wickets

Gloucestershire returned to the top of the Britannic Assurance County Championship with a resounding win over Worcestershire. Bill Athey hit his second century of the week on a slow pitch which was never entirely trustworthy. Worcestershire lost their last 5 wickets for 2 runs, the last 4 for 0, after a rather dour performance brightened only by Kapil Dev's handsome strokes. Asked to make 236 to win in 61 overs, Worcestershire were soon in trouble against the pace of Lawrence and slumped to 36 for 5. There was a brief recovery, but Walsh accounted for the belligerent Kapil Dev and the tail quickly succumbed to pace.

The other leading challengers, Middlesex and Hampshire, faltered badly. The match at Lord's was finely balanced. Barlow was again in wonderful form. He and Slack began the match with a stand of 137. Barlow was out cutting, caught at second slip, five minutes, and Slack, the quiet partner, was run out without addition to the score. Middlesex, thanks to Neil Williams' career best, took a first innings lead of 44, but Richard Hadlee bowled Notts back into contention with a magnificent spell of bowling which was countered only by the dependable Barlow. Notts faced the task of making 246 in 92 overs to win the match. French was soon out, but Broad and Randall put on 173 in 44 overs to give the platform for victory. At tea, Notts needed only 56 from 40 overs and although 3 wickets fell quickly, Randall stroked them to victory, his 115 coming off 167 balls with 18 fours.

Hampshire had Sussex at 4 for 2 on the first morning, but had little success after that. A dour century from Mendis took Sussex past the 300 mark and Hampshire collapsed disastrously after Chris Smith and night-watchman Maru, with a career best, put on 115 for the second wicket. Four wickets then fell for 6 runs and Hampshire trailed by 117 on the first innings. John Barclay caused some adverse comment when he declared with Mendis, batting with brisk authority, only 4 short of his second hundred of the match. It was unfortunate in that had Mendis completed his century, he would have become only the twelfth player to have hit 5 centuries in 6 innings. Hampshire never sensed victory, but they hung on grimly to force a draw.

Rain restricted play to an innings apiece at Swansea, but James Whitaker completed his third championship hundred in four innings and Mark Price had a career best with his slow left-arm spin.

Kent's resurgence continued with a most accomplished win over Yorkshire. On the first day, Baptiste and Cowdrey put on 127 for the fifth wicket, Ellison hit well and Paul Jarvis returned a career best. Yorkshire achieved near parity on the

Trent Bridge. England v. *Australia, 1985. (Ken Kelly)*

first innings, but a violent assault on their bowling by Benson and Tavare produced 232 in 60 overs for the Kent second wicket in the second innings. Cowdrey declared at lunch on the last day and Yorkshire crumbled to Underwood who had the remarkable figures of 4 for 8 in 18 overs, 14 of which were maidens.

Richard Williams had a splendid all-round match at Northampton, but Derbyshire saved the game, and Essex sprang off the bottom with their second win of the season. On a slow wicket at Southend, Brian Hardie equalled his career best score and shared a fifth wicket stand of 158 with Keith Fletcher. Essex were blunted in their hunt for runs by the accuracy of left-arm slow bowler Stephen Booth. Somerset began with a stand of 243 between Nigel Popplewell, who hit a career best 172 off 231 balls, and Peter Roebuck, who was less conspicuous. Essex went for quick runs in their second knock and set Somerset to make 248 in 60 overs. In an amazing last afternoon, Somerset, looking a poor side, were bowled out in 39.4 overs. Lever bowled unchanged and Essex caught everything that was offered.

The most exciting happenings were at Edgbaston where both sides batted limply at the first attempt. The second innings was a reversal of the first. Lancashire were led by Watkinson and Fairbrother who made the first century stand of the match. Warwickshire were left to make 351, a hard task, but Andy Lloyd was in fine form and he and Robin Dyer put on 104 for the first wicket. The game developed fascinatingly throughout the afternoon and at tea, Warwickshire were 221 for 3. They lost five wickets quickly in the final session and Ferreira found himself, at 308 for 8, with only Pierson and Hoffman, the least experienced members of the side, to support him. He and Pierson added 18, and Hoffman offered sound defence as Ferreira, 42 not out, gave his side victory with an over to spare. Lancashire gave a debut to off-break bowler Davidson and he took the wickets of Lloyd and Kallicharran in a good spell.

Third Cornhill Test Match
ENGLAND *v.* AUSTRALIA

With Foster injured, England gave a first Test cap to Arnold Sidebottom although Agnew, in the original twelve, must have felt somewhat perplexed at being omitted. Gower had no hesitation in batting first on a bland pitch when he won the toss. From the start one realised that it would take some extraordinary event to shape the match into anything other than a draw.

Gower and Gatting – England's heroes. (George Herringshaw)
Botham just escapes being run out. (Adrian Murrell)

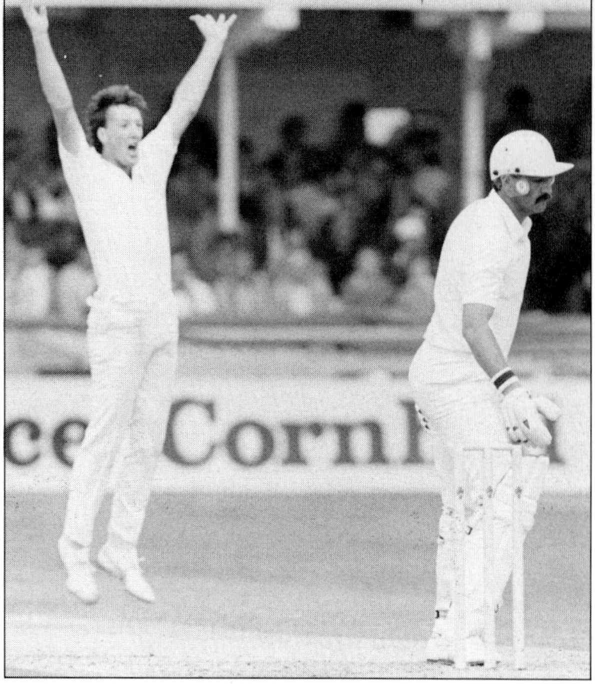

ABOVE: *Gooch falls to Lawson who took five wickets in England's first innings. (Adrian Murrell)*

LEFT: *The end of a glorious innings. Gower is caught by Phillips off O'Donnell. (Ken Kelly)*

Australia lost their chance on the first morning when, in cloudy conditions which brought a break before lunch, they failed to exploit the only help that was offered to bowlers in the course of the match. Robinson was out caught at slip off a thick edge as he pushed forward. In the post lunch period Gooch played with increasing confidence and was threatening to demolish the Australian attack when, having reached his highest score against Australia in England, he played rather loosely at Lawson and was caught in the gully.

By the time Gooch was dismissed, Gower was in total command. He has a languid grace which makes batting look the easiest thing in the world when he is timing sweetly, and the ball sped to the boundary in late afternoon with exciting regularity. Gatting gave sound support and by the close England were 279 for 2, Gower having reached his tenth Test century, his first as England's captain.

On the second day England disappointed and lost their way. Gatting and Gower failed to re-establish themselves quickly enough and only 21 runs came from the first 14 overs. Lawson helped them to find the pace again by bowling short, a failure which haunted the Australian bowlers throughout most of the summer. Gower was hitting the ball purposefully again and Gatting looked set for his first Test hundred in England when the captain drove the ball back hard down the pitch. Holland, the bowler, in attempting to stop the ball, deflected it into the stumps with Gatting out of his ground. England's third wicket pair had added 187. By lunch, Gower had also gone, caught behind off a ball that lifted and left him. His glorious innings had lasted 6 hours, 20 minutes and he had hit 17 fours.

In the afternoon England fell apart. Botham and Lamb promised a vigorous, exciting stand, but it was cut short before it could prosper. Lamb was leg before to a ball which

TOP: *Wessels is caught by Downton, bowled by Emburey for 33. (Adrian Murrell)*

MIDDLE: *Bob Holland is lbw to Arnold Sidebottom. It is the Yorkshireman's first wicket in Test cricket. (Adrian Murrell)*

BOTTOM: *Wood edges Botham short of Gooch and Emburey. (Adrian Murrell)*

The controversial dismissal of Allan Border. (Adrian Murrell)

kept low and in the next over Botham skied an intended drive to mid-off. Downton was well caught at square-leg off the first ball he faced, and Sidebottom fell to an equally good catch. Four wickets had fallen in 11 balls. Emburey and Edmonds halted the rapid decline, but Edmonds was bowled behind his legs and Allott well taken at second slip so that the last 6 wickets had fallen for 40. Lawson, who had found the right length, finished with 5 wickets, a creditable performance on a placid pitch.

Hilditch and Wood gave Australia a sound start. Hilditch raced to the forties and became becalmed and shortly before the close he fell to Allott. Next morning night-watchman Holland stayed long enough to make Wessels' entry a comfortable one and the two left-handers gave the Australian innings a sense of solidity.

At lunch, Australia were 187 for 2. Wessels touched Emburey to the keeper, but Border immediately gave the innings impetus. In 17 minutes at the crease, he faced 18 balls and hit a six and 2 fours. His end heralded a sad episode in the game. He played forward to Edmonds. The ball appeared to hit his pad and went to slip where Botham caught it and appealed for a catch. Edmonds joined in the appeal and umpire Whitehead gave Border out. It was a regrettable decision and one ponders on the commentators who, quick to slay the Indian umpires a few months earlier, were adamant that only the close-to-the-wicket fielders could know whether it was a catch or not. Television revealed quite positively that it was not a catch, but we must accept that human error in umpires is part of the game, whatever their nationality. It is not technical devices which will make their lives easier, but the attitude of players.

Boon fell to Emburey, driving the ball back chest high. Wood had reached his eighth Test century and he and Ritchie settled to a good stand. Botham responded angrily when an appeal for lbw against Ritchie was turned down. He bowled consistently short, was savaged by edges and hooks from the batsmen, incurred the wrath of umpire Whitehead and had Ritchie brilliantly caught at third man by Edmonds only to find a no-ball had been given. It was a distasteful part of the

Gråeme Wood, the backbone of Australia, 172. (Ken Kelly)

Greg Ritchie – his first Test century against England. (Ken Kelly)

BELOW: *Simon O'Donnell hits out. (Adrian Murrell)*

game and it was to have its repercussions when Botham was called before a disciplinary committee a month later.

Neither Sidebottom nor Allott was able to give a full day to England through injury and Australia closed at 366 for 5. On the Monday, the game expired. Wood and Ritchie took their stand to 161. Both reached their highest scores in Test cricket. Wood was caught at mid-wicket after batting for 10 hours. He hit 21 fours. It was a most commendable achievement by one whose place had been in doubt after a series of failures. Ritchie, strong, compact and broodingly aggressive, played some handsome shots, but the innings lost momentum. Phillips was bowled as he overbalanced playing an

Phillips is bowled as he sweeps extravagantly at Emburey. (Ken Kelly)

Jeremy Lloyds hits his first century for Gloucestershire, at Southend, 16 July. (George Herringshaw)

extravagant sweep. O'Donnell suggested class before skying Botham to the wicket-keeper who had run to square-leg. Botham took the last two wickets with successive deliveries.

Play ended early through bad light and the last day, with first Gooch and then Gower promising to entertain, concluded with Robinson showing increasing assurance and the game long since dead.

13 July

at Hove

Sussex 237 for 6 (A.P. Wells 80, N.J. Lenham 76)
Zimbabwe 238 for 5 (G.A. Paterson 95, A.H. Omarshah 52)

Zimbabwe won by 5 wickets

13, 14 and 15 July

at Chesterfield

Derbyshire 153 (J.E. Morris 53, P.B. Clift 5 for 38) and 323 (P.G. Newman 115, L.B. Taylor 5 for 86)
Leicestershire 376 (P. Willey 101, P.G. Newman 4 for 89) and 105 for 3

Leicestershire won by 7 wickets
Leicestershire 24 pts, Derbyshire 4 pts

13, 15 and 16 July

at Southend

Gloucestershire 270 (C.W.J. Athey 76, J.K. Lever 5 for 82) and 250 for 6 dec (J.W. Lloyds 101, P. Bainbridge 57 not out)
Essex 350 (D.E. East 131, K.W.R. Fletcher 78 not out, D.A. Graveney 4 for 131)

Match drawn
Essex 8 pts, Gloucestershire 6 pts

at Portsmouth

Hampshire 255 (C.L. Smith 89, P.J. Newport 5 for 89) and 211 for 6 dec (V.P. Terry 76, M.C.J. Nicholas 73 not out)
Worcestershire 249 (D.M. Smith 112, M.D. Marshall 7 for 59) and 156 for 7 (D.M. Smith 87, R.J. Maru 4 for 52)

Match drawn

Hampshire 7 pts, Worcestershire 6 pts

THIRD CORNHILL TEST MATCH – ENGLAND *v.* AUSTRALIA
11, 12, 13, 15 and 16 July 1985 at Trent Bridge, Nottingham

ENGLAND

	FIRST INNINGS		SECOND INNINGS	
G.A. Gooch	c Wessels, b Lawson	70	c Ritchie, b McDermott	48
R.T. Robinson	c Border, b Lawson	38	not out	77
D.I. Gower†	c Phillips, b O'Donnell	166	c Phillips, b McDermott	17
M.W. Gatting	run out	74	not out	35
A.J. Lamb	lbw, b Lawson	17		
I.T.Botham	c O'Donnell, b McDermott	38		
P.R. Downton*	c Ritchie, b McDermott	0		
A. Sidebottom	c O'Donnell, b Lawson	2		
J.E. Emburey	not out	16		
P.H. Edmonds	b Holland	12		
P.J.W. Allott	c Border, b Lawson	7		
Extras	b 12, w 1, nb 3	16	b 1, lb 16, nb 2	19
		456	(for 2 wickets)	196

	O	M	R	W	O	M	R	W
Lawson	39.4	10	103	5	13	4	32	—
McDermott	35	3	147	2	16	2	42	2
O'Donnell	29	4	104	1	10	2	26	—
Holland	26	3	90	1	26	9	69	—
Ritchie					1	—	10	—

FALL OF WICKETS
1- 55, 2- 171, 3- 358, 4- 365, 5- 416, 6- 416, 7- 419, 8- 419, 9- 443
1- 79, 2- 107

AUSTRALIA

	FIRST INNINGS	
G.M. Wood	c Robinson, b Botham	172
A.M.J. Hilditch	lbw, b Allott	47
R.G. Holland	lbw, b Sidebottom	10
K.C. Wessels	c Downton, b Emburey	33
A.R. Border†	c Botham, b Edmonds	23
D.C. Boon	c and b Emburey	15
G.M. Ritchie	b Edmonds	146
W.B. Phillips*	b Emburey	2
S.P. O'Donnell	c Downton, b Botham	46
G.F. Lawson	c Gooch, b Botham	18
C.J. McDermott	not out	0
Extras	b 6, lb 7, w 2, nb 12	27
		539

	O	M	R	W
Botham	34.2	3	107	3
Sidebottom	18.4	3	65	1
Allott	18	4	55	1
Edmonds	66	18	155	2
Emburey	55	15	129	3
Gooch	8.2	2	13	—
Gatting	1	—	2	—

FALL OF WICKETS
1- 87, 2- 128, 3- 205, 4- 234, 5- 263, 6- 424, 7- 437, 8- 491, 9- 539

Umpires: D.J. Constant and A.G.T. Whitehead

Match drawn

Jim Griffiths, 6 for 76, Northants v. Kent at Maidstone, 15 July. (Adrian Murrell)

Roger Harper a maiden century for Northants at Maidstone. (Sporting Pictures UK Ltd)

at Maidstone

Northamptonshire 255 (R.A. Harper 127, R.M. Ellison 7 for 87) and 247 (W. Larkins 67, R.J. Boyd-Moss 63, R.M. Ellison 4 for 77)
Kent 223 (C.S. Cowdrey 67, M.R. Benson 53, C. Penn 50, B.J. Griffiths 6 for 76) and 281 for 6 (M.R. Benson 97, E.A.E. Baptiste 58 not out)

Kent won by 4 wickets
Kent 22 pts, Northamptonshire 7 pts

at Old Trafford

Glamorgan 383 for 8 dec (Javed Miandad 164 not out) and 171 for 7 dec (A.L. Jones 75, R.C. Ontong 65 not out)
Lancashire 315 for 6 dec (J. Abrahams 77 not out, M. Watkinson 65, N.H. Fairbrother 57, S.T. Jefferies 57) and 215 for 8 (S.J. O'Shaughnessy 63, R.C. Ontong 5 for 82)

Match drawn
Lancashire 6 pts, Glamorgan 6 pts

at Lord's

Middlesex 309 (G.D. Barlow 132, S.C. Booth 4 for 88) and 225 for 5 dec (K.P. Tomlins 58, C.T. Radley 52 not out)
Somerset 345 (I.V.A. Richards 135)

Match drawn
Middlesex 7 pts, Somerset 7 pts

at Nuneaton

Warwickshire 384 for 8 dec (D.L. Amiss 117, T.A. Lloyd 94, P.A. Smith 51, K. Saxelby 5 for 73) and 238 for 5 dec (G.W. Humpage 56 not out)
Nottinghamshire 313 (C.E.B. Rice 156 not out, R.A. Pick 63, D.S. Hoffman 4 for 100) and 206 for 6 (P. Johnson 88, D.W. Randall 67)

Match drawn
Warwickshire 8 pts, Nottinghamshire 7 pts

at Sheffield

Surrey 364 (M.A. Lynch 133, G.S. Clinton 67, P.W. Jarvis 5 for 107, P. Carrick 4 for 98) and 51 for 1
Yorkshire 131 (G. Boycott 55 not out, A. H. Gray 8 for 40) and 280 (A.A. Metcalfe 77, D.L. Bairstow 65)

Surrey won by 9 wickets
Surrey 24 pts, Yorkshire 3 pts

Gloucestershire maintained their place at the top of table although they had by far the worse of a draw at Southend. Essex included new signing, medium pace bowler Topley, who had appeared for Surrey against Cambridge University earlier in the season. He bowled well to take the wickets of Athey and Curran as Gloucestershire stumbled, mainly against John Lever. It was only some fierce hitting by Lawrence and Russell that lifted the visitors to a score better than had seemed possible earlier. Essex could find no substance to their innings and were floundering at 135 for 7 when wicket-keeper David East joined skipper Keith Fletcher. The pair added 186 and East hit 2 sixes and 20 fours in a wonderfully entertaining maiden century which, with

Downton's poor form in the Test side, strengthened his claims for an England place. Fletcher sustained a back injury which was to keep him out of the Benson and Hedges Cup Final and possibly he should have declared when the Essex score reached 300, for, with Stovold unable to bat, Gloucestershire were able to hold out the next day, Lloyds scoring his first century for his new county.

Hampshire were again held. They were revived by their late middle order on the opening day and then were indebted to Malcolm Marshall who reduced Worcestershire from 145 for 2 to 249 all out with his best haul of the season. David Smith, returning after injury, hit his first century of the season, and Radford took 3 wickets before the close of the second day to leave Hampshire uneasy. They recovered on the last morning through Terry's patience and Nicholas' vigour, and made a bold declaration which asked Worcestershire to make 218 in 56 overs. Smith played another fine knock, but it was Hampshire who came closest to snatching a brave victory.

At Lord's, Middlesex were halted by Viv Richards and the weather after Barlow had hit another century to emphasise his standing as the most consistent opening batsman in the country.

Kent moved into fourth place with their second win in Maidstone week. A career best bowling performance by Richard Ellison whose form suggested a recall to the England side was imminent reduced Northants to 59 for 6 on the Saturday. Roger Harper hit a sparkling maiden hundred to rescue his side and his innings, which lasted under three hours, included 2 sixes and 20 fours. An uneven batting display saw Kent trail by 32 on the first innings, Jim Griffiths mopping up the tail in a brisk spell. Ellison again bowled well and Cowdrey snapped up 3 wickets for 5 runs on the second evening. Kent were still left the hard task of scoring 280 at 3 an over, but Benson lashed the ball about from the start and although the middle order stuttered, Aslett and Baptiste featured in a furious partnership which assured victory. Baptiste finished the match by hitting Harper for six over mid-wicket.

A maiden century by Paul Newman could not save Derbyshire at Chesterfield. They had surrendered too much on the first day and Peter Willey's hundred had put Leicestershire in total command.

Lancashire did avoid defeat at Old Trafford. Glamorgan batted into the second day. Javed Miandad, crisp, clean and authoritative, hit 14 fours in an innings which lasted $5\frac{1}{4}$ hours and Glamorgan were well on top until bold middle order batting took Lancashire to respectability. The match really came to life for the first time as Lancashire chased a target of 240. O'Shaughnessy hit 63 off 90 balls, but in the end honours were even.

There were fine hundreds for Amiss and Rice at Nuneaton, but the game ended badly for Notts who lost Rice with a broken finger, an injury that would keep him out of the NatWest Trophy match.

Surrey's increasing power and confidence took them into fifth place. They overwhelmed Yorkshire at Sheffield. Lynch pounded Surrey to a big score on the first day, the southern county profitting from dropped catches and inexperienced bowling. Surrey dropped Boycott on the Saturday evening and the opener was the only one to survive the onslaught of

Anthony Gray devastated Yorkshire at Sheffield, 15 July. He took 8 for 40, including the hat-trick. (Adrian Murrell)

Tony Gray on the Monday. The big West Indian took 8 for 40, bowling at a lively pace, and, in an after lunch spell, took 4 wickets in 5 balls, dismissing Bairstow, Jarvis and Swallow with successive deliveries to complete the hat-trick. Following-on, Yorkshire reached 133 for the loss of Boycott before the close, but 4 wickets fell for 12 runs on the last morning, and, in spite of Bairstow's brave defiance, Surrey were winners by mid-afternoon.

14 July

at Arundel

Lavinia, Duchess of Norfolk's XI 229 for 9 (N.J. Lenham 74, A.H. Omarshah 4 for 43)
Zimbabwe 220 for 3 (G.A. Paterson 88, K.G. Walton 78 not out)
Zimbabwe won by 7 wickets

John Player Special League

at Southend

Gloucestershire 184 for 7 (P.W. Romaines 60, D.R. Pringle 5 for 41)
Essex 186 for 3 (B.R. Hardie 73, K.S. McEwan 58 not out)
Essex (4 pts) won by 7 wickets

at Portsmouth

Hampshire 206 for 4 (C.L. Smith 63 not out, R.A. Smith 62)
Worcestershire 196 for 6 (T.S. Curtis 71)
Hampshire (4 pts) won by 10 runs

David Smith returned from injury to hit 112 and 87 for Worcestershire against Hampshire. He enjoyed a fine season. (Adrian Murrell)

at Maidstone

Kent 138 for 6 (C.J. Tavare 65 not out)
Northamptonshire 139 for 0 (W. Larkins 76 not out, R.J. Bailey 59 not out)
Northamptonshire (4 pts) won by 10 wickets

at Old Trafford

Lancashire 219 for 6 (C.H. Lloyd 108)
Glamorgan 219 for 5 (H. Morris 91, Javed Miandad 51)

Match tied
Lancashire 2 pts, Glamorgan 2 pts

at Lord's

Somerset 163 for 7 (B.C. Rose 53)
***v.* Middlesex**

Match abandoned
Middlesex 2 pts, Somerset 2 pts

at Edgbaston

Warwickshire 184 for 7 (D.L. Amiss 55, G.W. Humpage 51 not out)
Nottinghamshire 175 for 9 (P. Johnson 63, A.M. Ferreira 4 for 42)

Warwickshire (4 pts) won by 9 runs

at Bradford

Surrey 262 for 6 (M.A. Lynch 136)

Grant Paterson hits out during his 88 for Zimbabwe at Arundel, 14 July. (Adrian Murrell)

Yorkshire 263 for 8 (S.N. Hartley 72, K. Sharp 61, P.E. Robinson 60)

Yorkshire (4 pts) won by 2 wickets

Northants demolished Kent at Maidstone, Larkins and Bailey reaching a meagre target with 11.2 overs to spare. This win moved Northants into second place behind Kent, level with Yorkshire and Hampshire. Lynch hit 136 off 84 balls, but, in a match reduced to 36 overs, Yorkshire, well served by their first four batsmen, reached their highest score in the competition, 263, with one ball to spare. Clive Lloyd hit a thrilling hundred for Lancashire, and Glamorgan, chasing 220 to win, reached the last over needing 11. Watkinson was the bowler and Thomas and Holmes scrambled three each off the first five balls. Thomas attempted to slash the last ball, but it hit his pads and went to the third man boundary for 4 to tie the match.

17, 18 and 19 July

at The Oval

Surrey 343 for 5 dec (A. Needham 124, T.E. Jesty 100 not out) and 220 for 4 (A.J. Stewart 88 not out, T.E. Jesty 54)
Zimbabwe 226

Match Drawn

NatWest Bank Trophy – Second Round

17 July

at Chelmsford
Essex 214 (B.R. Hardie 68, G.A. Gooch 66)
Middlesex 130 (D.R. Pringle 5 for 23)

Essex won by 84 runs
(*Man of the Match* – G.A. Gooch)

at Bristol

Gloucestershire 277 for 8 (B.F. Davison 81)
Northamptonshire 240 (W. Larkins 75, G. Cook 54, K.M. Curran 4 for 34)

Gloucestershire won by 37 runs
(*Man of the Match* – K.M. Curran)

at Cardiff

Sussex 136 (J.G. Thomas 5 for 17)
Glamorgan 140 for 6

Glamorgan won by 4 wickets
(*Man of the Match* – J.G. Thomas)

at Southampton

Leicestershire 212 for 6 (P. Willey 52)
Hampshire 213 for 6 (C.G. Greenidge 67, V.P. Terry 63)

Hampshire won by 4 wickets
(*Man of the Match* – V.P. Terry)

at Canterbury

Kent 248 for 7 (M.R. Benson 78)
Durham 169

Kent won by 79 runs
(*Man of the Match* – M.R. Benson)

at Trent Bridge

Nottinghamshire 251 for 5 (R.T. Robinson 98, R.J. Hadlee 56)
Warwickshire 163 (D.L. Amiss 64, K.E. Cooper 4 for 49)

Yorkshire's top scorer Neil Hartley in action in the NatWest Trophy match against Somerset. Trevor Gard is the wicket-keeper. (Varley Picture Agency)

Robinson is bowled by Marks, NatWest Trophy Round Two, Yorkshire v. *Somerset. (Varley Picture Agency)*

LEFT: *Greg Thomas (Glamorgan), Man of the Match at Cardiff for his 5 for 17 against Sussex and regarded as an England opening bowler probable until his season was ended by injury. (Adrian Murrell)*

Nottinghamshire won by 86 runs
(*Man of the Match* – R.T. Robinson)

17 and 18 July

at Old Trafford

Worcestershire 312 for 5 (D.M. Smith 109, P.A. Neale 81)
Lancashire 298 (C.H. Lloyd 91, M. Watkinson 56, R.N. Kapil Dev 5 for 52)

Worcestershire won by 14 runs
(*Man of the Match* – C.H. Lloyd)

at Leeds

Yorkshire 208 for 8 (S.N. Hartley 69)
Somerset 209 for 6 (I.V.A. Richards 87 not out)

Somerset won by 4 wickets
(*Man of the Match* – I.V.A. Richards)

Hampshire gained ample revenge on Leicestershire for their defeat in the Benson and Hedges Cup when they won the second round NatWest Trophy match by 4 wickets with 5 balls to spare. In truth, Hampshire made hard work of the win. Leicestershire had batted in fits and starts and a target of 213 did not seem too demanding for Hampshire on a wicket which was never difficult. Greenidge and Terry began Hampshire's chase with a stand of 122, but 5 wickets fell for 29 runs and as nerves set in, Robin Smith and Cowley steered Hampshire to victory.

Greg Thomas gave a boost to his chances of an England cap with 5 for 17 in 7 overs at Cardiff. Sussex were all out in 52.3 overs and Glamorgan, after early worries, coasted to victory.

Kent were put in to bat by Durham and were given a fine start of 71 by Benson and Hinks, but Durham's failure had much to do with the catches they missed.

Fine all-round cricket by Kevin Curran was the dominant factor in Gloucestershire's victory. He shared a fifth wicket stand of 113 and, after Larkins and Cook had put on 129 for Northants' first wicket, he broke the middle order resistance.

The saddest happening was at Trent Bridge. Tim Robinson was struck on the hand in the first over and forced to retire hurt, but he returned to play a match-winning innings. Andy Lloyd was less fortunate. Hadlee's second ball broke his thumb. It was a cruel injury for a fine player who had battled back so bravely after his dreadful blow in the Edgbaston Test a year ago.

There was much comment about the match at Chelmsford after Keith Fletcher, out of the side through injury, had stated that Essex had prepared a wicket that would not aid the Middlesex pace men. There was also some controversy about Foster leaving the field on the completion of his 12 overs, as Neil Williams had done in the Benson and Hedges Final of 1983, but the umpires accepted that Foster's injury was not a legacy from a previous match, but had been sustained during the match. Gooch and Hardie put on 118 for Essex's first wicket, but Hardie could not ever master the bowling and was out in the fiftieth over. Had Edmonds and Emburey been allowed to attack to positive field placings, it is likely that Essex would have struggled to get past 150. As it was, they were asked to concentrate on containment when, in fact, the ball was turning. The general impression among the press, later rescinded, was that Essex were some 50 runs short of a winning score, but Middlesex quickly fiddled and stumbled to defeat, Pringle taking 4 for 4 in 11 balls and Downton running himself out suicidally.

Somerset had to go into a second day at Headingley, but the result never looked in doubt. The first day at Old Trafford closed with Worcestershire having run riot and reached a daunting 312. Smith hit his second century of the week and he and Neale put on 153 in 27 overs for the third wicket. Lancashire, it seemed, needed a miracle to win, and they nearly got it in the batting of Clive Lloyd. The home side were 114 for 5, but Lloyd and Watkinson put on 104. The West Indian was now batting with a runner, but he scarcely needed him as he crashed 4 sixes. He and Simmons added 52 in 7 overs. With 3 overs remaining, Lancashire needed 30 and Lloyd was brilliantly caught at mid-wicket off Kapil Dev, Neale diving far to his right. Lancashire's brave effort ended with the last ball of the fifty-ninth over.

18 July

at Jesmond

Australians 331 for 2 (D.M. Wellham 107 not out, D.C. Boon 84 not out, G.M. Wood 83
Minor Counties 206 for 7 (G.R.J. Roope 76)

Australians won by 125 runs

Boycott is lbw to Dredge, Yorkshire v. *Somerset. (Varley Picture Agency)*

at Leeds

International XI 233 for 6 (Mohsin Khan 73)
Yorkshire 200 (D.L. Bairstow 110)

International XI won by 33 runs

The Benson and Hedges Cup Final
ESSEX *v.* LEICESTERSHIRE

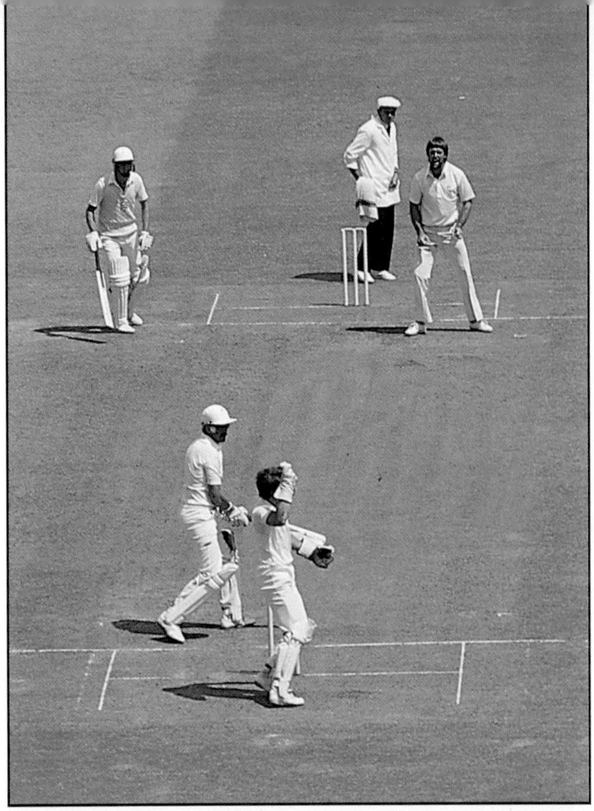

The restrictions that have been imposed in the wake of pitch invasions and soccer horrors and the unjustified limitations on the seating available to visiting members conspired to make this a low key final. The erection of the stand in front of the tavern may have created a respectability, but it has also deadened the atmosphere of the big occasion, and one hopes that there will be some rethinking. Whilst we are complaining it is also to be hoped that the ground staff can be encouraged to sell score-cards without one hand in a pocket and the other holding a cigarette. One is disturbed, too, to find that in the public area, only beer or lager can be bought. At a game

RIGHT: *Leicestershire's vital breakthrough. Gooch is bowled by Willey. (Patrick Eagar)*

BELOW: *The Essex disappointment. Lever sits with skipper Keith Fletcher who was unable to play through injury. (Patrick Eagar)*

ABOVE: *Gooch in majestic form hits square on the off. (Patrick Eagar)*

RIGHT: *As Essex press for runs, Pringle employs the reverse sweep. (Patrick Eagar)*

which is trying to attract families, it would be pleasant for a husband to be able to buy his wife a gin and tonic. It hardly seems likely that hooligans have been going on the rampage at cricket matches stimulated by gin and tonic. To the cricket.

Essex were without Fletcher and Gooch led the side. Gladwin replaced Fletcher, but, unwisely, he was not asked to open, and this left Essex without the substance of Hardie in the middle order.

Leicestershire won the toss and asked Essex to bat. Agnew began nervously and 7 came off the first over, but that rate never looked like being maintained. After 5 overs Essex had scored only 13. Gooch was broodingly defensive as if the weight of the team rested on his shoulders and it was 28 overs before he hit a four. By that time Hardie had gone, well caught above his head by Paddy Clift, the bowler, as Hardie tried to lash the ball back to the pavilion.

Prichard looked the most accomplished of players and was quickly carressing the ball to all parts of the field. Gooch should have been stumped by yards off Willey when he was on 36 in the twenty-fourth over, and it seemed that it would be a costly miss. He reached his fifty in the thirty-second over, having hit only 2 fours, and two overs later he put the hundred up with a magnificent cover drive off Willey. Next ball he was beaten and bowled.

BENSON and HEDGES CUP
1985

PRIZE STRUCTURE
£78,400 of the £400,000 Benson and Hedges sponsorship of this event will go in prize money for teams or individuals.

The breakdown is as follows:

- The Champions will win £17,000 (and hold, for one year only, the Benson and Hedges Cup)
- For the Runners-up £8,500
- For the losing Semi-finalists £4,250
- For the losing Quarter-finalists £2,125

ADDITIONAL TEAM AWARDS
The winners of all matches in the zonal stages of the Cup will receive £725.

INDIVIDUAL GOLD AWARDS
There will be a Benson and Hedges Gold Award for the outstanding individual performance at all matches throughout the Cup.

These will be:

- In the zonal matches £125
- In the Quarter-finals £200
- In the Semi-finals £275
- In the Final £550

The playing conditions and Cup records are on the reverse.

HOLDERS: LANCASHIRE COUNTY CRICKET CLUB

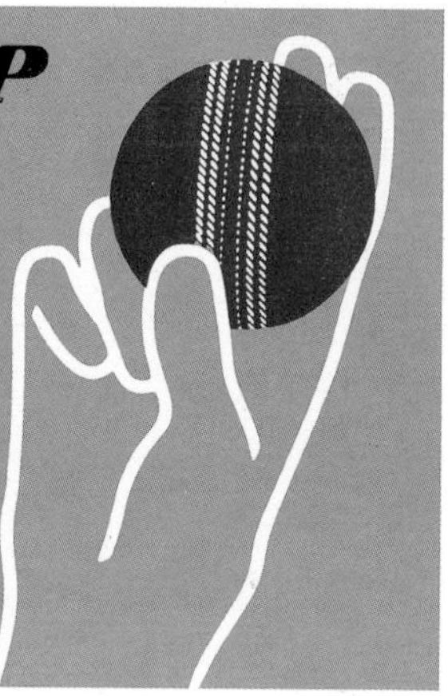

MARYLEBONE CRICKET CLUB

FINAL

20p **ESSEX v. LEICESTERSHIRE** 20p

at Lord's Ground, †Saturday, July 20th, 1985

Any alterations to teams will be announced over the public address system

ESSEX

‡1	G. A. Gooch	b Willey	57
2	B. R. Hardie	c and b Clift	25
3	P. J. Prichard	b Taylor	32
4	K. S. McEwan	c Garnham b Taylor	29
5	D. R. Pringle	c Agnew b Taylor	10
6	C. Gladwin	b Clift	14
7	A. W. Lilley	b Agnew	12
*8	D. E. East	not out	7
9	S. Turner	run out	3
10	N. A. Foster	not out	6
11	J. K. Lever		
	B 1, l-b 15, w 1, n-b 1,		18
		Total...	213

FALL OF THE WICKETS

1...71 2...101 3...147 4...163 5...164 6...191 7...195 8...198 9... 10...

Bowling Analysis	O.	M.	R.	W.	Wd.	N-b
Agnew	11	1	51	1	1	1
Taylor	11	3	26	3	...	...
Parsons	11	0	39	0	...	...
Clift	11	1	40	2	...	...
Willey	11	0	41	1	...	...
...	...	...	...	...	...	...
...	...	...	...	...	...	...

LEICESTERSHIRE

1	J. C. Balderstone	c Prichard b Pringle	12
2	I. P. Butcher	c Prichard b Turner	19
‡3	D. I. Gower	c Lilley b Foster	43
4	P. Willey	not out	86
5	J. J. Whitaker	b Gooch	1
6	N. E. Briers	l b w b Gooch	6
*7	M. A. Garnham	not out	34
8	P. B. Clift		
9	G. J. Parsons		
10	J. P. Agnew		
11	L. B. Taylor		
	B 2, l-b 9, w 2, n-b 1,		14
		Total...	215

FALL OF THE WICKETS

1...33 2...37 3...120 4...123 5...135 6... 7... 8... 9... 10...

Bowling Analysis	O.	M.	R.	W.	Wd.	N-b
Lever	11	0	50	0	...	...
Foster	11	2	32	1	...	...
Pringle	10	0	42	1	...	...
Turner	10	1	40	1	...	1
Gooch	10	1	40	2	2	...
...	...	...	...	...	...	...
...	...	...	...	...	...	...

‡Captain * Wicket-keeper

Umpires—H. D. Bird & K. E. Palmer

Scorers—C. F. Driver, G. Blackburn & E. Solomon

Toss won by—Leicestershire who elected to field

RESULT—Leicestershire won by 5 wickets

†This match is intended to be completed in one day, but three days have been allocated in case of weather interference

The playing conditions for the Benson & Hedges Cup Competition are printed on the back of this score card.

Total runs scored at end of each over:—

Essex 1	2	3	4	5	6	7	8	9	10	11	12	13	14	15	16	17	18	19	20
21	22	23	24	25	26	27	28	29	30	31	32	33	34	35	36	37	38	39	40
41	42	43	44	45	46	47	48	49	50	51	52	53	54	55					
Leicestershire 1	2	3	4	5	6	7	8	9	10	11	12	13	14	15	16	17	18	19	20
21	22	23	24	25	26	27	28	29	30	31	32	33	34	35	36	37	38	39	40
41	42	43	44	45	46	47	48	49	50	51	52	53	54	55					

Reproduced by kind permission of M.C.C.

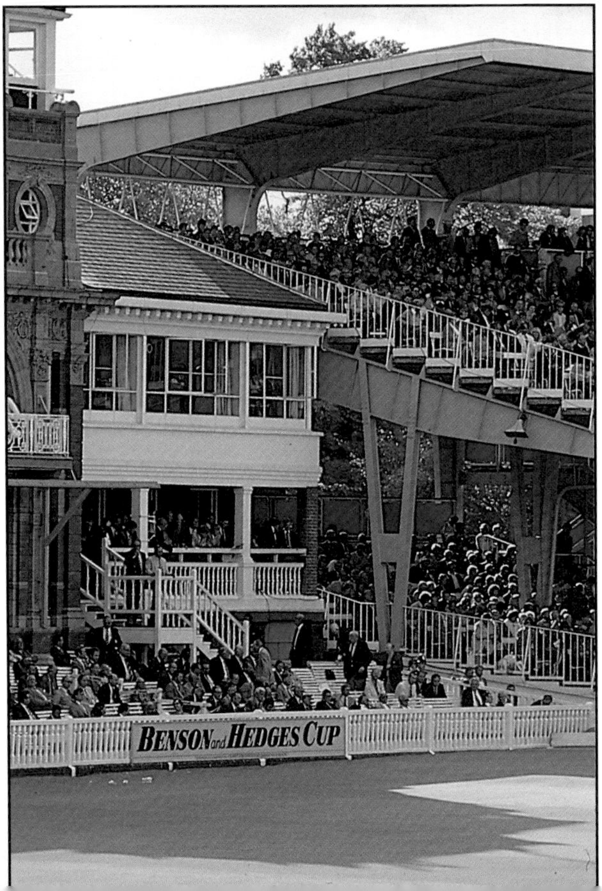

Above: *The end of the Essex innings draws near. Lilley is bowled by Agnew. (Patrick Eagar)*

Left: *Lord's on Benson and Hedges Cup Final day. (Patrick Eagar)*

At lunch, Essex were 108 for 2 off 36 overs, the platform for an advance in the afternoon. Prichard and McEwan added 39 in 7 overs after lunch and suggested that they were about to tear the Leicestershire attack apart when Prichard was bowled off his pads. Pringle helped McEwan to keep the score moving, but the forty-seventh over was, in effect, the turning point of the match. Pringle lofted Taylor to mid-on and one run later McEwan skied the ball to the wicket-keeper.

The lack of experience in the Essex middle order was apparent. Lilley and Gladwin scurried, but it was lusty hitting and furious running by Foster and East in the last over and a half that meant that Leicestershire would have to make 214 to win. It did not seem a formidable task although none had achieved such in a Benson and Hedges Final.

There was no suggestion of grandeur or confidence in the Leicestershire opening partnership, but Butcher and Balderstone nudged the runs and hinted that their side would stroll to victory.

In the thirteenth over Balderstone played a wretched shot, the ball holding up on him, and lofted a simple catch, and three overs later Butcher was beautifully caught, low at mid-on, by Prichard.

Gower played with instant majesty. Willey was initially

circumspect, but helped his captain to add a bustling 83 in 17 overs. The match just appeared to be out of Essex's reach when, shortly before tea, Gower was caught in the gully – cover area, slashing at Foster.

Gooch, who had looked the least impressive of the Essex bowlers, bowled Whitaker with the third ball after tea and for the first time Leicestershire looked as if they doubted that they could win. In the fortieth over, Briers was lbw to Gooch. Leicestershire were 135 for 5. The game was in the balance and alive for the first time.

Garnham quickly ended speculation. He had had a bad day in the field, but he prospered with the bat. Willey was now in total command and thumping the ball to all parts of the field. At this stage, Essex, usually so highly professional, were well below par. Their bowling wilted in line, length and temperament, and their fielding and field-placing fell from the usual excellent standard. Willey and Garnham did much as they pleased and Leicestershire won by a wider margin than five wickets and three overs suggests.

Willey was named Man of the Match, but the excellent

LEFT: *Gold Award winner in action. Peter Willey hits to leg as he moves Leicestershire towards victory. (Patrick Eagar)*

RIGHT: *Mike Garnham whose aggressive innings did much to bring Leicestershire the Cup drives John Lever for four. (Patrick Eagar)*

BELOW: *The final flurry. Willey and Garnham scamper a run as Lever attempts to run out Garnham. (Patrick Eagar)*

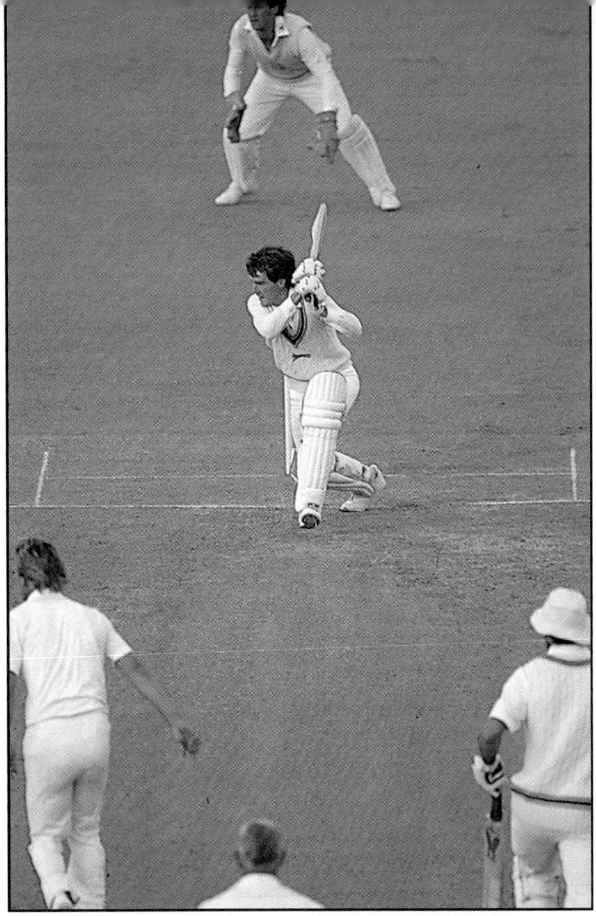

ABOVE: *Hope for Essex. Prichard catches Butcher. (Patrick Eagar)*

BELOW: *Leicestershire victorious. (Patrick Eagar)*

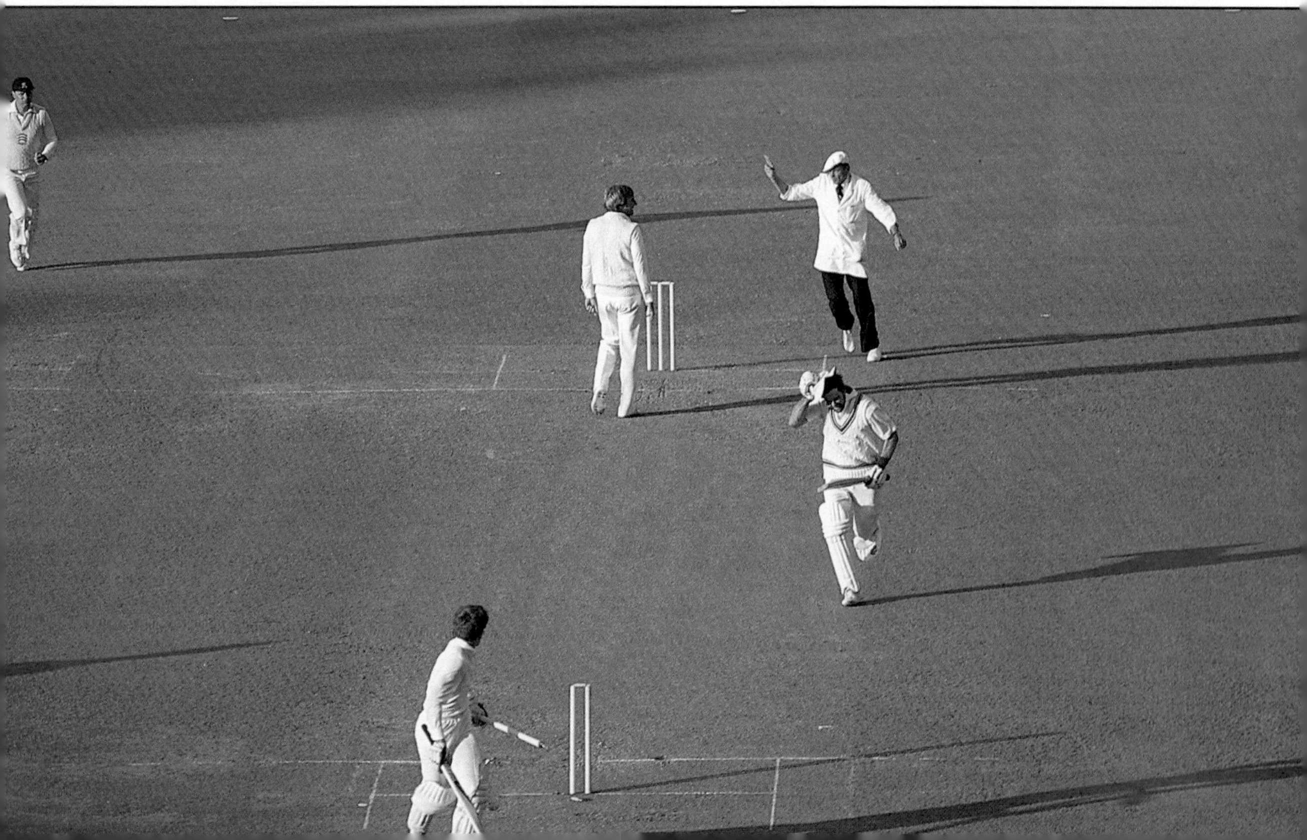

Gold Award winner Peter Willey and skipper David Gower hold the Benson and Hedges Cup. (Patrick Eagar)

Derbyshire C.C.C.
Limited-Over Matches – 1985

BATTING	v. Scotland (Aberdeen) 4 May (B.&H.)	v. Northamptonshire (Derby) 12 May (J.P.)	v. Northamptonshire (Derby) 15 May (B.&H.)	v. Nottinghamshire (Trent Bridge) 16 May (B.&H.)	v. Gloucestershire (Chesterfield) 18&20 May (B.&H.)	v. Yorkshire (Scarborough) 19 May (J.P.)	v. Gloucestershire (Derby) 2 June (J.P.)	v. Essex (Chelmsford) 5 June (B.&H.)	v. Essex (Chelmsford) 7 June (B.&H.)	v. Middlesex (Lord's) 9 June (J.P.)	v. Lancashire (Old Trafford) 16 June (J.P.)	v. Glamorgan (Derby) 30 June (J.P.)	v. Durham (Derby) 3 July (N.W.)	v. Worcestershire (Knypersley) 7 July (J.P.)	v. Somerset (Derby) 21 July (J.P.)	v. Warwickshire (Edgbaston) 28 July (J.P.)	v. Surrey (Derby) 4 August (J.P.)	v. Essex (Colchester) 11 August (J.P.)
K.J. Barnett	3	17	—	2	86		69	60	5	14	21	—	53	9	44	82*	10	18
A. Hill	107*	25	—	0	31		26											
J.E. Morris	2	2	—	9	2		44	0	5	2	52	—	12	9	10	5	0*	44
B. Roberts	56	8	—	0	48		10	36	26	56	42	—	13	70	19	42	—	8
W.P. Fowler	4	4	—	11	7*		20	10	28	22	14							
G. Miller	26	8	—	7	1*			4	—		20	—	0	17	14	38	—	0
R.J. Finney	9		—				1	5	14	1	0*	—		4		—	—	14
D.G. Moir	2	9					4			0	13							
A.E. Warner	2	15*	—	2	0		17	7	13*	5*		—	17	10	—	—	—	0
P.G. Newman	7	12*		56*	4				9	17	6	—	19	46	4*	8*	—	1
B.J.M. Maher	2*	2	—	0	—		1	5*	—	13	7	—	0	14*				
C.H. Mortensen		—	—	2	—		—	1*	—	0*	0*	—	4*	0*	—	—	—	0
M.A. Holding			—	38	3		20*	6	19*	12	0	—	27	37	2*	13	—	10
I.S. Anderson								15				—	4	52	64	11	14*	16
R.J. Sharma												—	11		8			
C. Marples															—	—	—	4*
M.A. Fell																		
A.M. Brown																		
P.E. Russell																		
J.G. Wright																		
Byes	2			3	1				1	1					2	5		1
Leg-byes	6	11		3	3		10	9	8	8	6		5	19	6	16	1	2
Wides		5		10	10			7	3	8	1		6	2	3	4		5
No-balls		1			6		1	2	1	2				3	1	1		
Total	228	119		143	202		223	167	132	161	182		171	292	177	225	25	123
Wickets	9	8		10	7		9	9	6	9	9		10	9	6	5	1	10
Result	W	L	Ab.	L	W	Ab.	W	Ab.	L	L	L	Ab.	L	W	W	W	Ab.	L
Points	2	0	1	0	2	2	4	—	—	0	0	2	—	4	4	4	2	0

Catches
9 – C. Marples (ct 8//st 1)
8 – K.J. Barnett
7 – B. Roberts
6 – P.G. Newman
5 – R.J. Finney
4 – B.J.M. Maher (ct 3/st 1), M.A. Holding, O.H. Mortensen and I.S. Anderson
3 – J.E. Morris and G. Miller
2 – M.A. Fell
1 – A. Hill, A.E. Warner, D.G. Moir, P.E. Russell and A.M. Brown

BOWLING	A.E. Warner	P.G. Newman	R.J. Finney	G. Miller	D.G. Moir	O.H. Mortensen	M.A. Holding	B. Roberts	K.J. Barnett
(B.&H.) v. Scotland (Aberdeen) 4 May	5–0–13–1	6–2–10–0	10.5–1–40–5	11–2–24–2	11–3–43–2				
(J.P.) v. Northamptonshire (Derby) 12 May	2–0–12–0	5.2–1–34–0		3–0–28–0	6–0–29–0	8–3–14–1			
(B.&H.) v. Northamptonshire (Derby) 15 May	4–0–9–1		5–0–25–1	5–1–16–2		5–0–19–1	3–0–8–1		
(B.&H.) v. Nottinghamshire (Trent Br.) 16 May	11–0–52–1	11–2–42–1		11–2–14–1		11–0–30–3	11–1–47–0		
(B.&H.) v. Glos. (Chesterfield) 18 & 20 May	6–3–10–1					10.2–1–35–1	5–1–10–0		
(J.P.) v. Yorkshire (Scarborough) 19 May									
(J.P.) v. Gloucestershire (Derby) 2 June	8–0–44–2		8–0–41–2		8–0–34–0	8–0–44–0	8–0–36–3		
(B.&H.) v. Essex (Chelmsford) 5 June						4–0–3–0	1–0–1–1		
(B.&H.) v. Essex (Chelmsford) 7 June	4–0–41–2	4–0–30–0	4–0–34–1			4–0–15–0	4–0–20–0		
(J.P.) v. Middlesex (Lord's) 9 June	5–0–41–0	4.2–0–23–0				8–1–25–0	8–1–23–0		
(J.P.) v. Lancashire (Old Trafford) 16 June		5–0–36–0	5–0–30–1	6–0–25–1	8–0–25–0	7–0–29–1	8–1–37–0		
(J.P.) v. Glamorgan (Derby) 30 June	5–0–16–0	5–0–29–1	8–0–40–0	6–0–33–0			5–3–6–1		
(N.W.) v. Durham (Derby) 3 July	12–1–46–1	12–1–25–0		9–4–15–0		10.4–2–37–1	12–2–36–1		
(J.P.) v. Worcestershire (Knypersley) 7 July	8–0–39–5	8–0–50–1	8–1–50–0			8–0–49–0	8–0–59–1		
(J.P.) v. Somerset (Derby) 21 July	6–0–27–1	7–1–28–2		6–0–33–0		7–0–45–1	7–0–36–1		
(J.P.) v. Warwickshire (Edgbaston) 28 July	6–0–44–4	6–0–39–1	6–0–58–0			6–0–39–0	6–0–37–1		
(J.P.) v. Surrey (Derby) 4 August									
(J.P.) v. Essex (Colchester) 11 August	2.2–0–10–0	7–1–33–0		7–0–37–1		4–0–21–0	7–1–21–0		
(J.P.) v. Sussex (Hove) 18 August	5–0–31–1	7–1–26–0	8–0–27–0	4–0–8–2		8–2–13–1	8–1–37–2		
(J.P.) v. Nottinghamshire (Heanor) 25 August		6–0–20–1	8–0–35–2			8–0–36–2	7–0–33–1	4–0–28–1	4–0–22–0
(J.P.) v. Kent (Folkestone) 1 September		8–0–41–1	8–0–29–1			8–0–28–1	8–3–18–2		
(Asda) v. Yorkshire (Scarborough) 4 Sept.		10–0–61–0	10–0–51–2			10–4–20–2	10–0–45–3		
(Asda) v. Lancashire (Scarborough) 6 Sept.		10–2–37–1	10–1–32–5			10–3–30–1	10–1–37–0		
(J.P.) v. Hampshire (Southampton) 8 Sept.		8–1–28–1	8–0–42–3			7.5–0–34–3	8–0–34–2		
(J.P.) v. Leicestershire (Chesterfield) 15 Sept.		8–0–16–1	8–1–18–1			8–4–10–4	8–1–17–1		
Wickets	20	11	24	9	2	23	21	1	0

v. Sussex (Hove) 18 August (J.P.)	v. Nottinghamshire (Heanor) 25 August (J.P.)	v. Kent (Folkestone) 1 September (J.P.)	v. Yorkshire (Scarborough) 4 September (Asda)	v. Lancashire (Scarborough) 6 September (Asda)	v. Hampshire (Southampton) 8 September (J.P.)	v. Leicestershire (Chesterfield) 15 September (J.P.)	Runs
10	34	13	3	0*	37	41*	631
							189
	38*	1	56	—	7	—	300
17	77*	48	24	70	3	0	673
							120
2							137
0	—	0	15*	—	14	—	77
							28
0							88
7	—	1	40	—	12	—	249
							44
0*	—	—	—	—	—	—	7
58	—	10	9	—	57	—	321
22	6	34	42	73*	31	37*	421
							19
10	—	20*	4*	—	8	—	46
0	10	21					31
	—				2*	—	2
		3*	—	—	0*	—	3
			0	27			27
		2	2				
6	9	13	7	5	8	3	
1	5	4	7	2	3	5	
3	1				4	4	
136	180	170	209	177	186	90	
10	3	8	7	2	8	1	
L	W	W	W	W	W	W	
0	4	4	—	—	4	4	

P.E. Russell	Byes	Leg-byes	Wides	No-balls	Total	Wkts
		5	2	6	135	10
		4		3	121	1
	2	9		1	88	6
	1	10	2		196	6
			3	1	55	2
	Match Abandoned					
	3	5	5	1	207	7
	Ab.		1		4	1
	1	9	1	3	150	4
	1	8	3	1	121	0
	1	3	7		186	3
		8	5		132	2
	1	12	5	2	172	3
	4	8	6		259	8
	2	5	1		176	7
		7	7	3	224	7
	Match Abandoned					
		2	3		124	1
	1	13	7	1	156	7
		5	4	4	179	8
8-1-32-3	3	10	1		161	9
10-2-22-0	2	5	3	2	206	9
10-0-26-0	1	12	4		175	7
8-0-26-0	1	14	6	3	179	10
8-3-18-2	1	7	5	1	87	9
5						

English Counties Form Charts

The statistics of all limited-over cricket matches follow in pages 380 to 419. The games covered are:

John Player League (J.P.) Tilcon Trophy (T.T.)
Benson and Hedges (B.&H.) Asda Trophy (Asda)
National Westminster Bank Trophy (N.W.)

Once again averages are not produced as it is felt that they have little relevance in limited-over cricket where batsmen often sacrifice their wickets for quick runs and bowlers are ordered to contain rather than capture wickets.
In the batting tables a blank indicates that a batsman did not *play* in a game, a dash (—) that he did not *bat*.

bowling of Les Taylor had probably been the decisive factor although some would make a claim for Garnham, confident and positive at a time when those qualitities had just seemed to evaporate.

20, 21 and 22 July

at Neath

Glamorgan 409 for 3 dec (Javed Miandad 200 not out, Younis Ahmed 118 not out)
Australians 105 for 1

Match drawn

20, 22 and 23 July

at Bristol

Zimbabwe 156 (G.E. Sainsbury 4 for 36) and 205 for 4 dec (G.A. Paterson 92)
Gloucestershire 65 for 2 dec and 299 for 3 (P.W. Romaines 114 not out, B.F. Davison 53 not out)

Gloucestershire won by 7 wickets

An unbeaten partnership of 306 in four hours by Javed and Younis was the highlight of the first day at Neath. Rain ruined the match on the second day and there was no play on the third.

The Zimbabweans' tour ended at Bristol. They were scheduled to play Leicestershire in the days following this match, but for reasons never clearly given, the Grace Road ground was not available. Their tour ended in defeat, but it was a fine game of cricket. On the Saturday, after a promising start, they fell to Sainsbury who was doing so well in his occasional outings for Gloucestershire. To beat the rain, which had washed out play on the Monday, the captains came to an agreement and, after some fine batting against the usual attack, Zimbabwe declared and left Gloucestershire to score 297 in 195 minutes. Romaines and Davison finished the task with an unbeaten stand of 104. Zaheer made a few elegant strokes, reviving happy memories in what was probably his last innings for Gloucestershire. One wishes Zimbabwe well. They are a credit to the game.

Essex C.C.C.
Limited-Over Matches – 1985

BATTING	v. Sussex (Chelmsford) 4 & 6 May (B.&H.)	v. Sussex (Chelmsford) 5 May (J.P.)	v. Surrey (The Oval) 14 & 15 May (B.&H.)	v. Middlesex (Lord's) 16 May (B.&H.)	v. C'bined Universities (Chelmsford) 18 May (B.&H.)	v. Surrey (The Oval) 26 May (J.P.)	v. Leicestershire (Chelmsford) 2 June (J.P.)	v. Derbyshire (Chelmsford) 5 June (B.&H.)	v. Derbyshire (Chelmsford) 7 June (B.&H.)	v. Lancashire (Ilford) 9 June (J.P.)	v. Glamorgan (Swansea) 16 June (J.P.)	v. Middlesex (Chelmsford) 19 & 20 June (B.&H.)	v. Northamptonshire (Luton) 23 June (J.P.)	v. Hampshire (Bournemouth) 30 June (J.P.)	v. Oxfordshire (Chelmsford) 3 July (N.W.)	v. Gloucestershire (Southend) 14 July (J.P.)	v. Middlesex (Chelmsford) 17 July (N.W.)	v. Leicestershire (Lord's) 20 July (B.&H.)	v. Kent
G.A. Gooch	46	7	81	27	89	1		0	72*	0		58	50		5		66	57	
P.J. Prichard	32	8	4*									31		14	94	33	11	32	
K.W.R. Fletcher	12*	34	—	18	0*	0*	17	—	6	—	37*	24	7*	30	15	5*			
K.S. McEwan	9	36	7*	4	100*	29	2	—	24	38*	43	3	70	24	66	58*	1	29	
D.R. Pringle	0	6	—	8	5	9*	3	—	5	18	39	2	51	40	55	2	5	10	
B.R. Hardie	27	2	43*	4*	113	20	15	—	—	—	14	14	—	0	51	73	68	25	
S. Turner	—	10*	—	1*	—	—	8	—		—		7	2*	15*		—	3	3	
A.W. Lilley	9*	4	—	1	8	—	49	0*	—	24	28	11	17		4*		17	12	
D.E. East	—	0	—	0*	—	—	2	—		—	1	12*	—	4	—	—	8	7*	
N.A. Foster	—		—	—	—			—	—		1	23*			—		0	6*	
J.K. Lever	—	14	—	—		—	1	—	—	—	—	—	—	0	—	—	1*	—	
N. Phillip		19		3	—	—	20		—	4*	23		16	4		—			
D.L. Acfield					—	—	0*			—	—		—	1*	—	—			
K.R. Pont							4				6*			19		—			
C. Gladwin								3*	29								15	14	
I.L. Pont																			
T.D. Topley																			
Byes		1							1	1					2	5		1	
Leg-byes	1	6	1	2	3		7		9	4	12	5	2	6	12	7	12	15	
Wides	1	1	3	2	12	2	8	1	1	2	1	1	1	4	3	3	5	1	
No-balls	7		1	4	3	2	3		3			11					2	1	
Total	144	148	140	74	333	63	139	4	150	91	205	202	216	161	307	186	214	213	19
Wickets	5	10	1	6	4	3	10	1	4	3	7	8	5	9	6	3	10	8	
Result	W	L	W	W	W	Ab.	Tie	Ab.	W	Ab.	W	W	L	L	W	W	W	L	W
Points	2	0	2	2	2	2	2	—	—	2	4	—	0	0	—	4	—	—	

Catches 29 – D.E. East
10 – G.A. Gooch and B.R. Hardie
8 – K.W.R. Fletcher and D.R. Pringle
7 – A.W. Lilley and P.J. Prichard
6 – K.S. McEwan
4 – N.A. Foster and J.K. Lever
2 – S. Turner and N. Phillip
1 – D.L. Acfield and sub

BOWLING	N. Phillip	J.K. Lever	G.A. Gooch	S. Turner	D.R. Pringle	N.A. Foster	D.L. Acfield	A.W. Lilley	K.R. Pont
(B.&H.) *v.* Sussex (Chelmsford) 4 & 6 May		9–1–28–1	11–3–23–2	11–2–20–1	9.2–1–21–1	11–1–39–4			
(J.P.) *v.* Sussex (Chelmsford) 5 May	8–0–27–0	8–2–15–1	6.4–0–37–0	7–1–27–0	8–1–32–0				
(B.&H.) *v.* Surrey (The Oval) 14 & 15 May		7.5–1–29–1	11–1–33–1	11–2–23–2	9–2–18–1	8–0–32–5			
(B.&H.) *v.* Middlesex (Lord's) 16 May		11–4–13–5		5–1–13–1	7–0–19–1	6.1–0–28–3			
(B.&H.) *v.* Comb. Univ. (Chelmsford) 18 May	11–2–51–1			11–1–33–0	10–0–38–2	11–1–39–2	11–2–33–0	1–0–4–1	
(J.P.) *v.* Surrey (The Oval) 26 May									
(J.P.) *v.* Leicestershire (Chelmsford) 2 June	6–0–39–0	8–1–22–1		8–3–23–0	8–2–16–0		8–3–19–3		2–0–7–0
(B.&H.) *v.* Derbyshire (Chelmsford) 5 June		11–1–41–2	11–1–29–2	11–1–35–2	11–2–27–1	11–4–26–2			
(B.&H.) *v.* Derbyshire (Chelmsford) 7 June	4–0–18–1	4–0–23–2	4–0–28–2		4–0–40–0	4–0–14–0			
(J.P.) *v.* Lancashire (Ilford) 9 June	7–0–34–0	8–1–47–1		6–0–40–0	7–0–52–1				
(J.P.) *v.* Glamorgan (Swansea) 16 June	5–0–21–1	7.3–0–40–4			8–0–33–2	8–0–35–1	6–0–32–0		5–1–18–1
(B.&H.) *v.* Middlesex (Chelmsford) 19 & 20 June		8–1–21–0	11–2–34–0	11–3–27–3	7–1–25–2	9–1–31–2			
(J.P.) *v.* Northamptonshire (Luton) 23 June	5–0–40–0	8–0–29–0	8–0–34–2	8–0–35–2	7.2–0–47–0		3–0–22–0		
(J.P.) *v.* Hants. (Bournemouth) 30 June	8–0–34–1	6.4–1–32–0		8–1–41–0	6–2–13–0				8–0–34–1
(N.W.) *v.* Oxfordshire (Chelmsford) 3 July		8–4–7–1	12–3–22–1		12–5–12–5	9.2–0–29–1	2–0–3–2		
(J.P.) *v.* Gloucestershire (Southend) 14 July	8–0–22–1	8–0–31–1		6–0–22–0	8–0–41–5		8–0–43–0		2–0–20–0
(N.W.) *v.* Middlesex (Chelmsford) 17 July		9–1–17–1	10–3–23–1	10–0–34–1	9–1–23–5	12–4–31–1			
(B.&H.) *v.* Leicestershire (Lord's) 20 July		11–0–50–0	10–1–40–2	10–1–40–1	10–0–42–1	11–2–32–1			
(J.P.) *v.* Kent (Chelmsford) 21 July	7.3–0–35–3	7–0–30–1	7–0–52–0	8–1–23–3	8–0–28–2				
(J.P.) *v.* Somerset (Taunton) 28 July			8–0–33–1	8–0–37–1	7–0–36–1		4–0–18–1		
(J.P.) *v.* Middlesex (Chelmsford) 4 August									
(N.W.) *v.* Kent (Chelmsford) 7 August		12–5–25–2	12–1–37–2	12–0–39–2	12–3–37–0	12–2–32–2			
(J.P.) *v.* Derbyshire (Colchester) 11 August		6.1–0–22–2	4–0–19–1	3–0–15–1	6–0–29–2	7–0–35–2			
(J.P.) *v.* Worcestershire (Worcester) 18 Aug.		2–0–24–0		2–0–16–2	2–0–14–0	2–0–14–0			
(N.W.) *v.* Hants. (Southampton) 21 Aug.		12–4–35–1	12–1–25–0	12–2–38–3	12–2–58–0	12–2–58–3			
(J.P.) *v.* Warwickshire (Edgbaston) 1 Sept.		8–0–44–4		8–0–50–1	7.1–0–39–3	8–0–43–1			
(N.W.) *v.* Nottinghamshire (Lord's) 7 Sept.		12–2–53–0	12–0–47–0	12–1–43–2	12–1–68–1				
(J.P.) *v.* Notts. (Trent Bridge) 8 September		7–0–35–4	6–0–29–2	8–0–45–1	8–0–50–2				
(J.P.) *v.* Yorkshire (Chelmsford) 15 September		8–0–37–0	8–0–26–3	8–0–59–0	8–0–54–1	8–1–38–0			
Wickets	8	35	22	29	39	30	6	1	2

… 28 July (J.P.)	v. Middlesex (Chelmsford) 4 August (J.P.)	v. Kent (Chelmsford) 7 & 8 August (N.W.)	v. Derbyshire (Colchester) 11 August (J.P.)	v. Worcestershire (Worcester) 18 August (J.P.)	v. Hampshire (Southampton) 21 & 22 Aug. (N.W.)	v. Warwickshire (Edgbaston) 1 September (J.P.)	v. Nottinghamshire (Lord's) 7 September (N.W.)	v. Nottinghamshire (Trent Bridge) 8 September (J.P.)	v. Yorkshire (Chelmsford) 15 September (J.P.)	*Runs*
7		43	51*		93*		91	171	12	1143
5		42	—	—	14	6	—	—	25	361
		39*	—	7*	19	2*	—	0*	7	279
4*		0	23*	22	35	118	46*	1	62	907
4		32*	—	4*	8	81*	29*	—	60	531
9		5	45	27	5	21	110	60	21	777
–		—	—	—	7*	—	—	—	7*	63
2		—	—	26	26	—	—	9*	8	281
4*		—	—	—	1	—	—	—	7	56
		—	—	—	—	—			2*	32
		—	—	—	—	—	—	—	—	16
										92
–										1
										29
										82
–				—		—	—	—		—
–										—
						5	1	2		
3		11	2	3	6	13	3	7	13	
4		2	3		6	3		2	7	
2					4	2			1	
4		174	124	89	224	251	280	252	232	
5		4	1	3	7	3	2	3	8	
W	Ab.	W	W	W	W	W	W	W	W	
4	2	—	4	4	—	4	—	4	4	

I.L. Pont	T.D. Topley	*Byes*	*Leg-byes*	*Wides*	*No-balls*	*Total*	*Wkts*
			12	4	3	143	10
			12		3	150	1
			1	3	1	140	10
				1		73	10
			5	8	6	203	6
		Match Abandoned					
			13	6	7	139	9
		Ab.	9	7	2	167	9
		1	8	3	1	132	6
		1	9	3	2	183	2
		4	8	4	2	191	10
			2	10	3	140	10
			10	1	2	217	4
			8	1	1	162	2
			8	6		81	10
		1	4	2	1	184	7
		1	1	6	2	130	10
		2	9	2	1	215	5
		1	11	6	5	180	10
5–0–18–2	8–1–26–2		5	4	1	173	9
		Match Abandoned					
			2	4		172	9
		1	2	5		123	10
2–0–15–1			5	1		88	4
			10	6	3	224	8
8–0–39–1			15	5	4	230	10
12–0–54–1			14		1	279	5
8–0–39–1		4	6	2		208	10
			17	5	2	231	7
6	2						

John Player Special League

21 July

at Derby

Somerset 176 for 7 (I.V.A Richards 51)
Derbyshire 177 for 6 (I.S. Anderson 64)

Derbyshire (4 pts) won by 4 wickets

at Chelmsford

Essex 193 for 5 (G.A. Gooch 86)
Kent 180 (L. Potter 52)

Essex (4 pts) won by 13 runs

at Leicester

Warwickshire 187 for 6 (G.J. Lord 53)
Leicestershire 175 for 1 (D.I. Gower 114 not out, N.E. Briers 51 not out)

Leicestershire (4 pts) won on faster scoring rate

at Northampton

Sussex 210 for 6 (P.W.G. Parker 85)
Northamptonshire 208

Sussex (4 pts) won by 2 runs

at Guildford

Nottinghamshire 223 for 7 (B.C. Broad 69, D.W. Randall 65)
Surrey 211 for 8 (G.S. Clinton 72, A. Needham 52 not out)

Nottinghamshire (4 pts) won by 12 runs

at Worcester

Worcestershire 197 for 9
Middlesex 175 for 8 (M.W. Gatting 68 not out)

Worcestershire (4 pts) won by 22 runs

David Gower celebrated Leicestershire's Benson and Hedges triumph in perfect fashion with a not out century and victory over Warwickshire. Essex gain consolation with a win over the leaders Kent who lost their last 6 wickets for 12 runs. The competition remained wide open with Kent holding a two-point lead, but with as many as fifteen teams in striking distance.

24, 25 and 26 July

at Chesterfield

Derbyshire 420 (K.J. Barnett 125, M.A. Holding 80, G. Miller 74 not out, P.W. Jarvis 5 for 126) and 218 for 9 dec (I.S. Anderson 62, P. Carrick 4 for 47)
Yorkshire 273 (D.L. Bairstow 113 not out, A.E. Warner 4 for 88) and 21 for 1

Match drawn
Derbyshire 8 pts, Yorkshire 6 pts

at Dartford

Essex 213 (C. Gladwin 53, D.L. Underwood 6 for 56) and 260 for 8 (G.A. Gooch 125, D.L. Underwood 4 for 80)
Kent 476 for 9 dec (C.J. Tavare 150 not out, N.R. Taylor 79, S.G. Hinks 74, M.R. Benson 64, D.L. Acfield 4 for 164)

Match drawn
Kent 8 pts, Essex 3 pts

Glamorgan C.C.C.
Limited-Over Matches – 1985

BATTING	v. Kent (Cardiff) 4 May (B.&H.)	v. Kent (Cardiff) 5 May (J.P.)	v. Minor Counties (Swansea) 11 May (B.&H.)	v. Somerset (Taunton) 12 May (J.P.)	v. Hampshire (Southampton) 14 & 15 May (B.&H.)	v. Somerset (Taunton) 18 May (B.&H.)	v. Middlesex (Lord's) 19 May (J.P.)	v. Hampshire (Basingstoke) 26 May (J.P.)	v. Worcestershire (Ebbw Vale) 9 June (J.P.)	v. Essex (Swansea) 16 June (J.P.)	v. Leicestershire (Leicester) 23 June (J.P.)	v. Derbyshire (Derby) 30 June (J.P.)	v. Scotland (Edinburgh) 3 July (N.W.)	v. Nottinghamshire (Swansea) 7 July (J.P.)	v. Lancashire (Old Trafford) 14 July (J.P.)	v. Sussex (Cardiff) 17 July (N.W.)	v. Gloucestershire (Bristol) 28 July (J.P.)	v. Worcestershire (Swansea) 7 & 8 August (N.W.)
J.A. Hopkins	8	16	18	64	5	4	72*		25	7	14			0		15	0	12
A.L. Jones	4	28									3	53	60*	0	6	21	17	6
G.C. Holmes	4	33	53*	21	36	70	8		0*	15	0	—	20	45	26*	3	25	1
Javed Miandad	14	29	—	31	57	57	32		95*	86	62	8*	21*	89	51	29	57	
Younis Ahmed	5	18	—	4	1	55	37		6	10		5*	—	5	22		20	3
J.F. Steele	0	0*	—	9*	8	0	—		—	0	9							
R.C. Ontong	58	12	—	4	19	15	—		—	17	40	—	—	34*	4	30*	12	55
J.G. Thomas	5	9	—	12	9	0	—			5	3			12	4*	2*		
J. Derrick	42	5	—	8	6	12*	—		—	8	7*	—	—	—				4
T. Davies	7	—	—	6*	6*	3	—		—	2	12	—	—	—	—	12	7*	7
S.R. Barwick	6*	—	—	—	3	1	—		—	0*	0	—	—		—	—	0	4
S.P. Henderson			1*	0	16	2	11*		12	23	11							
L.L. McFarlane									—			—	—	—		—	1*	1*
H. Morris												53	23		91	19	5	75
M.R. Price												—	—	3	—	—	11	6
S.J. Malone															—			
M.P. Maynard																		
I. Smith																		
Byes	6	4		4	1					4			2	1	4	1	4	
Leg-byes	12	14	1	7	4	7	5		8	8	5	8	7	2	9	5	6	10
Wides		7	1	5	3	10	2		1	4		5	7	7	2	1	1	4
No-balls	10		3		4	1				2			1	1		2		
Total	181	175	77	175	178	237	167		147	191	166	132	141	199	219	140	166	188
Wickets	10	8	1	8	10	10	3		3	10	10	2	2	7	5	6	9	10
Result	L	L	W	W	L	W	W	Ab.	W	L	L	Ab.	W	L	Tie	W	L	L
Points	0	0	2	4	0	2	4	2	4	0	0	2	—	0	2	—	0	—

Catches

27 – T. Davies (ct 20/st 7)
8 – G.C. Holmes
7 – J.F. Steele
6 – R.C. Ontong, Younis Ahmed and J.A. Hopkins
5 – J.G. Thomas
3 – S.R. Barwick and J. Derrick
2 – Javed Miandad, H. Morris, A.L. Jones and M.R. Price
1 – S.P. Henderson and L.L. McFarlane

BOWLING	J.G. Thomas	S.R. Barwick	R.C. Ontong	J.F. Steele	G.C. Holmes	J. Derrick	L.L. McFarlane	Younis Ahmed	M.R. Price
(B.&H.) *v.* Kent (Cardiff) 4 May	9–1–38–1	7–3–24–0	11–2–20–2	11–1–44–2	11–2–43–1	6–0–27–0			
(J.P.) *v.* Kent (Cardiff) 5 May	6–0–41–0	6–2–8–2	6.2–0–33–1	3–0–14–0	8–0–36–3				
(B.&H.) *v.* Minor Counties (Swansea) 11 May	8–2–26–3	7.1–2–11–4			11–4–26–3	6–2–8–0			
(J.P.) *v.* Somerset (Taunton) 12 May	8–0–42–1	8–0–35–2	8–1–37–2	8–0–34–2		8–1–20–1			
(B.&H.) *v.* Hants (Southampton) 14&15 May	10–1–38–4	10–0–43–2	11–0–55–0	4–0–36–0	11–0–55–1	9–2–47–1			
(B.&H.) *v.* Somerset (Taunton) 18 May	5–1–6–2	7–1–22–0	11–2–30–5	11–2–26–0	5.2–0–24–2	7–0–26–1			
(J.P.) *v.* Middlesex (Lord's) 19 May	6–0–27–1	5–0–19–0	8–0–17–0	7–0–30–5	8–0–40–1	6–1–28–0			
(J.P.) *v.* Hampshire (Basingstoke) 26 May									
(J.P.) *v.* Worcestershire (Ebbw Vale) 9 June		5–0–25–1		2–0–17–0	5–0–19–3	5–0–33–0	4–0–17–2		
(J.P.) *v.* Essex (Swansea) 16 June	8–0–41–2	4–0–17–0	8–0–34–2	4–0–23–0	8–1–42–2	8–0–36–0			
(J.P.) *v.* Leicestershire (Leicester) 23 June	8–1–32–2	8–1–10–1	8–1–38–1	8–0–30–0	7–0–44–0	1–0–12–1			
(J.P.) *v.* Derbyshire (Derby) 30 June									
(N.W.) *v.* Scotland (Edinburgh) 3 July		7–1–12–1	6–0–23–0		12–4–24–5	11–3–14–4	12–2–34–0	12–2–24–0	
(J.P.) *v.* Nottinghamshire (Swansea) 7 July	8–0–53–2		8–1–31–1		4–0–24–0	8–0–31–0	5–0–34–0		7–0–22–1
(J.P.) *v.* Lancashire (Old Trafford) 14 July	8–0–43–1	8–1–35–3	8–0–33–2		4–0–30–0				8–0–40–0
(N.W.) *v.* Sussex (Cardiff) 17 July	7–2–17–5	8–4–8–2	5–1–15–0		11.3–2–19–1		12–1–54–1		8–1–21–0
(J.P.) *v.* Gloucestershire (Bristol) 28 July		7–0–18–1	8–1–25–0		8–0–59–1		6.3–1–35–2	2–0–7–0	2–0–17–0
(N.W.) *v.* Worcestershire (Swansea) 8 August		8–0–49–2	12–2–36–0		6.3–0–20–0	12–3–27–0	9–2–32–1		7–1–22–3
(J.P.) *v.* Warwickshire (Cardiff) 11 August									
(J.P.) *v.* Northants (Wellingborough) 18 Aug.		8–0–32–1	8–0–18–1		8–0–23–3		5–1–6–0	6.3–0–20–3	4–0–17–1
(J.P.) *v.* Yorkshire (Swansea) 25 August		4–0–18–1	6–1–14–1		4–0–16–5	5–0–31–0	1–0–7–0		
(J.P.) *v.* Surrey (Cardiff) 1 September		4–1–8–0	8–0–42–0		2–0–16–0		2–0–12–0		5.4–0–30–0
(J.P.) *v.* Sussex (Cardiff) 15 September	8–1–47–1	6–0–48–1	8–3–13–1		8–0–43–1	5–0–30–0			5–0–21–0
Wickets	25	24	19	9	32	8	6	3	5

v. Warwickshire (Cardiff) 11 August (J.P.)	v. Northamptonshire (Wellingborough) 18 August (J.P.)	v. Yorkshire (Swansea) 25 August (J.P.)	v. Surrey (Cardiff) 1 September (J.P.)	v. Sussex (Cardiff) 15 September (J.P.)	Runs
	21*			10	291
			10		210
	—	27	5	21	413
	—		33		751
	—	28		0	219
					26
	—	35	0	13	348
				1	62
		1		10	103
	—	1	20	6	89
	—	1	1*	1*	17
					76
	—	0*	0*		2
	5*	7	18	45	341
	—	7	22	10	59
	—				—
		18	12	1	31
		3	2		5
				3	
	10	6	8		
		2	15		
		2			
	36	138	146	121	
	0	10	9	10	
Ab.	Ab.	W	L	L	
2	2	4	0	0	

ABOVE: *Ian Botham – a hundred off 50 balls and more sixes in a season than have been hit before. (Ken Kelly)* BELOW: *David East (Essex). A maiden first-class century was followed by a world record eight catches in an innings. (Sporting Pictures UK Ltd)*

S.J. Malone	Byes	Leg-byes	Wides	No-balls	Total	Wkts
	1	4	2		201	7
	1	5			138	6
	4	1	1	2	76	10
		6	4		174	8
	1	19	2	1	294	9
		10	6	2	144	10
		5	3		166	8
	Match Abandoned					
	1	13	2		125	9
		12	1		205	7
		11	4		177	5
	Match Abandoned					
	1	5	14	1	137	10
	2	5	1	3	202	7
4–0–32–0		6		1	219	6
		2	1	4	136	10
		7	2	2	168	4
		6	1	2	192	6
	Match Abandoned					
	1	4	4		121	10
	1	6		2	93	8
			1	1	108	0
	5	7	2		214	5
0						

Gloucestershire C.C.C.
Limited-Over Matches – 1985

BATTING	v. Nottinghamshire (Bristol) 4 May (B.&H.)	v. Nottinghamshire (Bristol) 5 May (J.P.)	v. Northamptonshire (Northampton) 11 May (B.&H.)	v. Middlesex (Lord's) 12 May (J.P.)	v. Scotland (Bristol) 14 & 15 May (B.&H.)	v. Derbyshire (Chesterfield) 18 & 20 May (B.&H.)	v. Lancashire (Old Trafford) 19 May (J.P.)	v. Kent (Bristol) 26 May (J.P.)	v. Derbyshire (Derby) 2 June (J.P.)	v. Somerset (Bath) 9 June (J.P.)	v. Northamptonshire (Northampton) 16 June (J.P.)	v. Warwickshire (Harrogate) 20 June (T.T.)	v. Sussex (Swindon) 23 June (J.P.)	v. Bedfordshire (Luton) 3 July (N.W.)	v. Yorkshire (Gloucester) 7 July (J.P.)	v. Essex (Southend) 14 July (J.P.)	v. Northamptonshire (Bristol) 17 July (N.W.)	v. Glamorgan (Bristol) 28 July (J.P.)
A.W. Stovold	60	1	11	0	9	28				6	—	27	33*	71	17			
P.W. Romaines	125	58	19	3	5	21	65	—	73	11	105	2	23	26	30	60	5	23
C.W.J. Athey	8	40	77	67*	22	2*	44	31*	44	41	8	0	1	72	21	37	44	3
B.F. Davison	38	34	41	5	5	—	57	6	28	28	18	0	8	28	103	22	81	85*
P. Bainbridge	20	3	27	12	53	0*	10*	5	7	14	41	55	0	11	20	0	7	2*
K.M. Curran	15*	46*	16	47	53*	—	32*	17	2	13	9	5	50	9	0	40	36	37
J.N. Shepherd	—	2	9	1*	1	—	—	—	11*	4								
D.A. Graveney	—	56*	0	—	3	—	—	13*	6	18	5*	6*	—	—	1*	—	12	—
R.C. Russell	—	—	0	—	0	—	—	—	—	14		17	—	—	—	3*	—	
J.W. Lloyds	—						1	4	9		4						40	7
D.V. Lawrence	—	—	0*	—	22*	—	—	—		3*	—	7	—	1*			0*	
I.R. Payne		—	2	—					13*		9*	58	—	18*	13*	4	32*	—
C.A. Walsh					—	—	—	—	—	1	0	11	—	—	—	1*	2	—
G.E. Sainsbury															—	—		—
A.J. Wright																9		
A.J. Brassington																		—
R.G.P. Ellis																		
P.H. Twizell																		
Byes	4	1	3					4	3	3	2		2	5		1	4	
Leg-byes	16	5	9	7	6		8	3	5	6	1	1	5	14	12	4	10	7
Wides	1	1	1	5	4	3	3	4	5	2	8	7	2	7	1	2	1	2
No-balls	1	2	2	2		1	3		1		1	2	2	6	1	1	3	2
Total	288	249	217	149	184	55	223	87	207	164	211	198	126	268	216	184	277	168
Wickets	5	6	10	5	8	2	4	4	7	10	7	10	5	6	6	7	8	4
Results	W	W	L	L	W	L	W	L	L	L	W	L	L	W	W	L	W	W
Points	2	4	0	0	2	0	4	0	0	0	4	—	0	—	4	0	—	4

Catches

18–R.C. Russell (ct 16/st 2)
17–C.W.J. Athey
8–D.A. Graveney
6–A.W. Stovold and P. Bainbridge
5–B.F. Davison
4–I.R. Payne
3–D.V. Lawrence, K.M. Curran, P.W. Romaines and C.A. Walsh
2–G.E. Sainsbury and subs
1–J.N. Shepherd, J.W. Lloyds, A.J. Wright, P.H. Twizell and A.J. Brassington

BOWLING	D.V. Lawrence	K.M. Curran	J.N. Shepherd	D.A. Graveney	P. Bainbridge	I.R. Payne	C.A. Walsh	G.E. Sainsbury	P.H. Twizell
(B.&H.) *v.* Nottinghamshire (Bristol) 4 May	11–0–54–1	11–1–45–3	11–1–42–2	11–0–48–1	11–0–51–1				
(J.P.) *v.* Nottinghamshire (Bristol) 5 May	8–0–47–3	8–0–56–1	8–0–43–2	8–0–37–0	4–1–19–1	4–0–24–0			
(B.&H.) *v.* Northants. (Northampton) 11 May	11–1–41–2	10.5–1–46–1	11–0–49–1	11–1–27–0	6–0–20–0	5–0–25–2			
(J.P.) *v.* Middlesex (Lord's) 12 May	5.2–0–34–0	4–0–22–0	6–0–33–1		7–0–35–0	4–1–18–1			
(B.&H.) *v.* Scotland (Bristol) 14&15 May	6–0–13–0	11–1–26–2	11–3–15–1	7–1–19–2	8–0–33–0		10.3–3–19–2		
(B.&H.) *v.* Derbyshire (Chesterfield) 18&20 May	11–1–31–0	11–1–52–2	11–0–49–2	11–2–23–1			11–0–43–2		
(J.P.) *v.* Lancashire (Old Trafford) 19 May	8–0–59–0	8–0–31–2	8–0–37–0		8–1–44–3		8–1–35–0		
(J.P.) *v.* Kent (Bristol) 26 May	2–0–20–1	1.3–0–11–0	2–0–22–1		2–0–15–0		2–0–16–1		
(J.P.) *v.* Derbyshire (Derby) 2 June		8–1–44–1	6–0–43–0	8–0–34–1	4–0–22–1	6–0–35–1	8–0–35–2		
(J.P.) *v.* Somerset (Bath) 9 June	8–0–39–1	8–0–56–1	8–0–58–0	3–0–20–0	5–0–28–2		8–0–38–2		
(J.P.) *v.* Northants. (Northampton) 16 June	8–0–44–1	7–0–28–2		6–0–34–0	2–0–18–0	6–0–39–1	8–0–28–3		
(T.T.) *v.* Warwickshire (Harrogate) 20 June	5–0–28–1	9–0–42–0		3–0–18–0	11–3–38–0	7.3–1–35–1	11–2–36–1		
(J.P.) *v.* Sussex (Swindon) 23 June	8–0–40–0	8–3–16–1			3–0–14–0	8–2–28–0	5.4–0–25–0		
(N.W.) *v.* Bedfordshire (Luton) 3 July	5–0–20–2	12–7–9–2		10–3–41–2	8–0–20–1	12–4–11–1	7–3–7–2		
(J.P.) *v.* Yorkshire (Gloucester) 7 July		4–0–22–1		7–0–28–2	5–0–42–2	8–1–27–1	8–2–38–0	8–0–31–0	
(J.P.) *v.* Essex (Southend) 14 July		7–0–37–2		7–0–31–0	2–0–15–0	6–0–30–1	8–0–34–0	6.3–0–27–0	
(N.W.) *v.* Northants. (Bristol) 17 July	9·3–1–53–2	10–0–34–4		5–0–21–0	12–2–35–2	9–0–52–0	11–1–39–0		
(J.P.) *v.* Glamorgan (Bristol) 28 July		8–2–25–4		6–0–27–1	2–0–14–1	8–0–31–1	8–0–33–0	8–0–26–1	
(N.W.) *v.* Nottinghamshire (Bristol) 8 Aug.	7–0–39–0	12–3–34–0		9–0–42–2	12–0–54–3	10–0–36–0	10–0–61–1		
(J.P.) *v.* Leicestershire (Cheltenham) 11 Aug.		2–0–11–4		2–0–12–1		2–0–23–0	2–0–12–1	2–0–17–1	
(J.P.) *v.* Warwickshire (Cheltenham) 18 Aug.		2–0–9–3				2–0–11–1	2–0–11–1	2–0–15–1	2–0–23–1
(J.P.) *v.* Hampshire (Bournemouth) 25 Aug.		3.2–0–23–0				6–0–20–0	4–0–13–1	7–1–30–1	
(J.P.) *v.* Worcs. (Moreton-in-Marsh) 8 Sept.	5–0–28–0	8–0–41–3		6–0–35–0	5–1–34–2	8–0–43–0		8–0–28–2	
(J.P.) *v.* Surrey (The Oval) 15 September		4–0–23–1		6.3–1–36–4	5–1–30–0			8–1–26–2	
Wickets	15	40	10	17	19	11	19	8	1

v. Nottinghamshire (Bristol) 8 & 9 August (N.W.)	v. Leicestershire (Cheltenham) 11 August (J.P.)	v. Warwickshire (Cheltenham) 18 August (J.P.)	v. Hampshire (Bournemouth) 25 August (J.P.)	v. Worcestershire (M'ton-in-Marsh) 8 September (J.P.)	v. Surrey (The Oval) 15 September (J.P.)	Runs
21	47*					331
		—	17	65	78	814
12	—	21	69	121*	115*	900
27		6		—	10*	631
55			1	—	—	343
36	0	48*	0	14*	14	539
						28
4	—		4*	—	—	128
14*	—	—	1*	—	—	49
20	—		3	—	—	88
1				—		34
53	0*	—	37	—		236
6*	—	—	3		—	24
—	—	—	—	—	—	—
	—	0*	8			17
						—
	21	7			—	28
		—				—
2	2		2		1	
20		2	4	10	6	
4		1	2	4	2	
2			1	3	1	
277	70	85	152	217	227	
9	1	3	8	1	2	
L	L	W	L	W	W	
—	0	4	0	4	4	

C.W.J. Athey	Byes	Leg-byes	Wides	No-balls	Total	Wkts
		15	9	1	255	9
	1	11	3	1	238	8
	3	9	1	6	220	6
		8	1		150	2
		6	6	10	131	10
	1	3	10	6	202	7
		14	12	4	220	6
		4	3		88	3
		10		1	223	9
		8	3	2	247	6
		5	3	1	196	10
	2	3	9	12	202	3
		5	3		128	1
	2	17	2		127	10
	1	14	7		203	6
	5	7	3		186	3
		6	5	8	240	10
	4	6	1		166	9
	2	19	10	2	287	8
	2				77	8
		3			72	8
		2	2	1	88	2
	1	3	2		213	9
6-0-21-2		5	6		141	10
2						

at Southport

Lancashire 278 (M. Watkinson 106, J. Abrahams 51, R.J. Doughty 4 for 56) and 145 for 7 (A.H. Gray 5 for 51)
Surrey 231 (A.J. Stewart 61, P.J.W. Allott 4 for 62)

Match drawn
Lancashire 7 pts, Surrey 6 pts

at Uxbridge

Northamptonshire 191 (R.A. Harper 97 not out, N.G. Cowans 4 for 30) and 215 (A.J. Lamb 61, P.H. Edmonds 4 for 54, W.W. Daniel 4 for 73)
Middlesex 567 for 8 dec (C.T. Radley 200, P.R. Downton 104, J.E. Emburey 68, M.W. Gatting 51, R.G. Williams 4 for 131)

Middlesex won by an innings and 161 runs
Middlesex 23 pts, Northamptonshire 3 pts

at Trent Bridge

Nottinghamshire 300 for 6 dec (R.T. Robinson 73, D.W. Randall 64, B.C. Broad 63, Imran Khan 5 for 59) and 196 for 7 dec (P. Johnson 54)
Sussex 168 (R.J. Hadlee 4 for 39) and 218 for 4 (C.M. Wells 71, Imran Khan 56 not out)

Match drawn
Nottinghamshire 7 pts, Sussex 3 pts

at Edgbaston

Somerset 207 (I.V.A. Richards 65, A.M. Ferreira 4 for 61) and 418 for 6 dec (I.T. Botham 138 not out, P.M. Roebuck 81, N.F.M. Popplewell 70, I.V.A. Richards 53, N. Gifford 4 for 128)
Warwickshire 338 (R.I.H.B. Dyer 106, P.A. Smith 62, I.T. Botham 4 for 63) and 74 for 1 (A.I. Kallicharran 51 not out)

Match drawn
Warwickshire 7 pts, Somerset 4 pts

at Hereford

Worcestershire 349 for 6 dec (D.M. Smith 102, D.B. d'Oliveira 51) and 225 (R.N. Kapil Dev 60)
Glamorgan 309 for 9 dec (Younis Ahmed 100 not out, A.L. Jones 69, G.C. Holmes 67, N.V. Radford 4 for 94) and 156 for 7

Match drawn
Worcestershire 8 pts, Glamorgan 6 pts

at Bristol

Australians 146 (K.M. Curran 5 for 35) and 410 for 3 dec (A.R. Border 130, D.M. Wellham 105, K.C. Wessels 61 not out)
Gloucestershire 181 (J.W. Lloyds 71) and 205 (C.W.J. Athey 83, K.M. Curran 58)

Australians won by 170 runs

Middlesex gained the only victory in the Britannic Assurance County Championship matches and returned to the top of the table. Northants were 93 for 7 on the opening day, but some spectacular batting by Roger Harper, who hit 8 sixes and 7 fours in his 97 off 85 balls, lifted them close to the two hundred mark. Middlesex lost their first 4 wickets for 147, but Radley and Downton took the score to 216 before the close and next day extended their stand to 289. Downton reached a maiden century and Radley hit the highest score of his career. Few men have given more to a county, or to the game itself, than Clive Radley. He is now 41 years old, but his appetite for the game is undiminished and he remains a most solidly dependable batsman. He accumulates with nudges and pushes rather than with flowing drives, but the score is ever moving and while he is at the crease or still to bat,

Hampshire C.C.C.
Limited-Over Matches – 1985

BATTING	v. Northamptonshire (Northampton) 5 May (J.P.)	v. Kent (Canterbury) 11&13 May (B.&H.)	v. Kent (Canterbury) 12 May (J.P.)	v. Glamorgan (Southampton) 14&15 May (B.&H.)	v. Somerset (Southampton) 16 May (B.&H.)	v. Minor Counties (Reading) 18 May (B.&H.)	v. Surrey (Southampton) 19 May (J.P.)	v. Glamorgan (Basingstoke) 26 May (J.P.)	v. Yorkshire (Middlesbrough) 2 June (J.P.)	v. Leicestershire (Southampton) 5 June (B.&H.)	v. Warwickshire (Edgbaston) 9 June (J.P.)	v. Sussex (Hove) 16 June (J.P.)	v. Essex (Bournemouth) 30 June (J.P.)	v. Berkshire (Southampton) 3 July (N.W.)	v. Lancashire (Old Trafford) 7 July (J.P.)	v. Worcestershire (Portsmouth) 14 July (J.P.)	v. Leicestershire (Southampton) 17 July (N.W.)	v. Somerset (Southampton) 4 August (J.P.)
V.P. Terry	24	8	16*	2	12	7	17		70	14	18	82	23	165*	45	35	63	
D.R. Turner	65	31	3	18	52*	63*	39						7			4		
M.C.J. Nicholas	38	45	—	74	18	6	7		26	41	10	8*	61*	8	26	18	16	
R.A. Smith	26	30	4*	47	63*	29	104		44	81	2	—	61*	37	12	62	24*	
C.L. Smith	1	25	—						27	8	39		—	12	47*	63*	10	
J.J.E. Hardy	10	4										—	—	1*	36	0*	1	
N.G. Cowley	24	11	—	6	—	0	6		8*	8	25	—				—	20*	
K.D. James	20*	0	—	14	—	8	1*		—	27	34	—	—	—	—	—		
T.M. Tremlett	5*	17*	—	1	—	0*	—		—	1	3*	—	—	—	—	—	—	
R.J. Parks	—	11*	—	0*	—	6	—		—	8*	3*	—	—	—	—	—	—	
C.A. Connor	—	—	—	—	—	—	—		—	0	—	—	—		—	—	—	
R.J. Maru			—															
C.G. Greenidge				99	13	123	5		78	10	23	124*		89	59*		67	
M.D. Marshall				10	—	2	14		1	25	11	—	—	—	0		1	
S.J.W. Andrew														—				
Byes				1		2				1		4		5				
Leg-byes	10	19	7	19	5	14	5		3	6	6	17	8	7	8	20	9	
Wides	1	10		2	6	4	10			4	1		1	13	2	4	1	
No-balls		4		1						5		4	1	2			1	
Total	224	215	30	294	169	264	208		257	239	175	239	162	339	235	206	213	
Wickets	7	8	1	9	3	8	7		6	10	8	1	2	4	5	4	6	
Result	L	W	Ab.	W	W	W	W	Ab.	L	L	L	W	W	W	W	W	W	Ab.
Points	0	2	2	2	2	2	4	2	0	—	0	4	4	—	4	4	—	2

Catches 33 – R.J. Parks (ct 27/st 6)
14 – R.A. Smith
10 – V.P. Terry
9 – M.C.J. Nicholas
6 – C.L. Smith
5 – T.M. Tremlett
4 – D.R. Turner, C.A. Connor and C.G. Greenidge
3 – K.D. James and M.D. Marshall
2 – N.G. Cowley
1 – J.J.E. Hardy

BOWLING	K.D. James	C.A. Connor	M.C.J. Nicholas	T.M. Tremlett	N.G. Cowley	R.J. Maru	M.D. Marshall	S.J.W. Andrew	R.A. Smith
(J.P.) v. Northants (Northampton) 5 May	8–0–25–0	7.1–0–36–2	8–0–43–0	8–0–53–0	8–0–58–0				
(B.&H.) v. Kent (Canterbury) 11&13 May	6–0–16–1	7–1–27–4	8–1–27–1	4.4–0–24–1	8–0–22–2				
(J.P.) v. Kent (Canterbury) 12 May	8–0–31–0	8–2–42–1	2–0–23–0	8–1–28–5	7–0–40–2	7–0–45–0			
(B.&H.) v. Glam. (Southampton) 14&15 May	11–0–41–1	9–0–34–1		9.1–0–54–4	9–1–26–2		8–2–18–2		
(B.&H.) v. Somerset (Southampton) 16 May	11–4–18–1	11–1–42–1	5–0–17–1	11–3–24–3	6–2–18–0		11–1–32–2		
(B.&H.) v. Minor Counties (Reading) 18 May	6–3–12–1	8.2–4–16–2	10–2–34–4	7–3–16–0	11–1–32–1		4–1–10–1		
(J.P.) v. Surrey (Southampton) 19 May	8–2–30–2	7–1–13–2		7–0–40–2	8–0–37–2		8–1–32–1		
(J.P.) v. Glamorgan (Basingstoke) 26 May									
(J.P.) v. Yorkshire (Middlesbrough) 2 June	7.3–1–44–0	8–0–55–0		8–0–55–2	8–0–54–1		8–1–39–0		
(B.&H.) v. Leics. (Southampton) 5 June	11–1–61–1	11–0–40–1		11–0–48–1	11–0–46–0		11–1–38–1		
(J.P.) v. Warwickshire (Edgbaston) 9 June	7.2–0–29–1	6–0–33–0		6–1–22–1	7–0–44–1		8–0–37–2		
(J.P.) v. Sussex (Hove) 16 June	8–0–56–0	8–0–41–1		8–0–37–1	8–0–51–1		8–0–46–0		
(J.P.) v. Essex (Bournemouth) 30 June	8–0–20–0	8–0–36–2	8–0–39–3	8–1–36–1			8–1–24–3		
(N.W.) v. Berkshire (Southampton) 3 July	12–0–31–0		12–1–39–2	7–5–2–2			3–2–1–0	10–1–28–1	2.5–0–13–2
(J.P.) v. Lancashire (Old Trafford) 7 July	8–0–41–1	8–0–37–2	8–0–53–3	8–0–51–2			8–0–37–1		
(J.P.) v. Worcestershire (Portsmouth) 14 July	8–1–20–1	8–0–37–1	8–0–47–0	8–0–58–2	8–0–26–2				
(N.W.) v. Leics. (Southampton) 17 July		12–1–49–0	12–1–40–2	12–3–44–2	12–1–28–1		12–0–45–1		
(J.P.) v. Somerset (Southampton) 4 August									
(N.W.) v. Somerset (Taunton) 7&8 August		6.2–1–14–0	9–0–40–1	9–0–33–2	6–0–41–3		9–2–17–2		
(J.P.) v. Leicestershire (Leicester) 18 August		4–0–11–0					4–0–7–1		
(N.W.) v. Essex (Southampton) 21&22 Aug.		12–0–52–3	12–0–41–2	12–1–38–0	11–0–45–1		12–1–41–0		
(J.P.) v. Glos. (Bournemouth) 25 August		8–0–32–2	8–1–27–1	8–0–43–1	8–1–26–2		8–2–18–2		
(J.P.) v. Middlesex (Southampton) 1 Sept.		8–0–25–3	8–0–22–2	6–0–32–2	8–2–24–1		7.5–0–35–1		
(J.P.) v. Derbyshire (Southampton) 8 Sept.		8–1–21–3	8–0–54–0	8–0–50–2	8–2–24–0		8–1–29–1		
(J.P.) v. Notts. (Trent Bridge) 15 Sept.		8–0–45–1	7.3–0–50–4	8–1–29–2	8–0–33–1		8–0–39–2		
Wickets	10	32	26	38	23	0	23	1	2

v. Somerset (Taunton) 7 August (N.W.)	v. Leicestershire (Leicester) 18 August (J.P.)	v. Essex (Southampton) 21 August (N.W.)	v. Gloucestershire (Bournemouth) 25 August (J.P.)	v. Middlesex (Southampton) 1 September (J.P.)	v. Derbyshire (Southampton) 8 September (J.P.)	v. Nottinghamshire (Trent Bridge) 15 September (J.P.)	Runs
105	—	7	5	55	3	19	795
38*	—	36	20*	30	34	20	460
2	—	39	—	17	3	—	463
110	—	24	—	25*	26	30	841
3	—	26	1	9*	34	—	305
	—						52
—	—	20	—	—	7	1*	136
							104
—	—	8*	—	—	17	—	52
—	—	6*	—	—	5	—	39
—	—	—	—	—	2*	—	2
							—
10	—	10	57*	2	20	122	911
2*	—	29	—	—	4	33	132
							—
3				1	1		
9		10	2	4	14	14	
7		6	2	5	6	3	
10		3	1	1	3	1	
299		224	88	149	179	243	
5		8	2	4	10	5	
W	Ab.	L	W	W	L	W	
—	2	—	4	4	0	4	

C.L. Smith	C.G. Greenidge	Byes	Leg-byes	Wides	No-balls	Total	Wkts
			12	4	1	227	2
		4	5		3	125	10
		4	5	4	1	218	9
		1	4	3	4	178	10
		1	15	13	1	167	8
		2	7	3	1	129	10
			8	2		160	9
		Match Abandoned					
			12		2	259	4
			10	3	7	243	4
			11	2		176	5
			7	1	1	238	4
			6	4		161	9
12–3–32–3			6	4	3	152	10
		1	12	7	2	232	10
		2	6	3	1	196	6
		1	5	4	1	212	6
		Match Abandoned					
		5		2	4	150	10
						18	1
	1–0–1–0		6	6	4	224	7
		2	4	2	1	152	8
		3	5	6		146	10
			8	3	4	186	8
		4	7	2	1	207	10
3	0						

Middlesex preserve hope. It is hard to imaging cricket without him. His innings included a six, a five and 26 fours. Downton hit 13 fours and the stand lasted for 340 minutes. Facing a deficit of 367, Northants were hardly likely to survive and once Lamb had fallen to Gatting, Middlesex moved to victory, but the loss of more than an hour's play on the last morning meant that Northants were able to hold out until after tea.

Deposed leaders Gloucestershire were beaten by the Australians, but thankfully their lively cricket and energetic administration was rewarded with good crowds on the first two days. Kevin Curran was the local hero as the tourists were shot out shortly after lunch, but David Lawrence was again in fiery form and although he may have allowed himself to be misled into making unwise statements to the press, he bowled fast enough and attackingly enough to be considered seriously by the Test selectors. The county, in their turn, struggled, but Lloyds batted with good sense and took them to a 35-run lead. Then Border and Wellham gave batting exhibitions of differing excellence. It was rich stuff and the Australian bowlers capitalised on it to bring victory on the last day.

Kent remained in fourth place, their chance of advancement blighted by Gooch. Essex had been rattled out by Derek Underwood, who remains a man of such charm and a bowler of such wisdom and accuracy that none minds falling to him. Tavare then led a furious assault on the Essex bowling as he hit 5 sixes and 20 fours. Essex were left with only the possibility of survival if a batsman could play a major innings. Gooch rose to the task and batted throughout most of the last day. There was a slight flutter when he fell in the final session, but David East took on the solid mantle and Kent were denied.

Rain and gloom denied Derbyshire at Chesterfield. A somewhat bizarre first day saw Kim Barnett, the gentlest of men and a batsman wrongly ignored by the England selectors, hit a fluent century in adverse conditions. In truth, the Yorkshire bowling, not for the first time, was lamentable, but in mid-innings, Paul Jarvis returned to take 4 wickets in 7 balls, including the hat-trick. Holding and Miller restored sanity with 134 in 24 overs. Inevitably, it was Bairstow who revived Yorkshire spirits, but it is doubtful whether they would have avoided defeat but for the rain and they remained bottom of the table.

Just above them were Somerset who avoided defeat when all had seemed lost. They surrendered a first innings lead of 131 after Robin Dyer and Paul Smith, two fine young players of different styles and temperaments, had batted with distinction. Somerset lost 2 wickets in clearing the arrears, but statistics took on another dimension as Botham came to bat. He hit the fastest century of the season, off 50 balls, beating his own earlier record by 26 deliveries. In all, he faced 65 balls and hit 12 mighty sixes and 13 fours. After that, the result seemed irrelevant.

Lancashire, 67 for 4, were rescued by a hard hit maiden century by Mike Watkinson, an event he had been threatening for some weeks. Eventually, the match was ruined by rain, only 10 overs being bowled on the last day.

Rain hindered progress at Trent Bridge where Sussex came back well after Notts had taken early command in dour fashion. Sussex had by far the worst of the conditions.

Kent C.C.C.
Limited-Over Matches – 1985

BATTING	v. Glamorgan (Cardiff) 4 May (B.&H.)	v. Glamorgan (Cardiff) 5 May (J.P.)	v. Hampshire (Canterbury) 11 & 13 May (B.&H.)	v. Hampshire (Canterbury) 12 May (J.P.)	v. Somerset (Taunton) 14 May (B.&H.)	v. Minor Counties (Canterbury) 16 May (B.&H.)	v. Gloucestershire (Bristol) 26 May (J.P.)	v. Worcestershire (Canterbury) 2 June (J.P.)	v. Northamptonshire (Northampton) 5 June (B.&H.)	v. Nottinghamshire (Trent Bridge) 16 June (J.P.)	v. Leicestershire (Leicester) 19 June (B.&H.)	v. Lancashire (Old Trafford) 23 June (J.P.)	v. Middlesex (Canterbury) 30 June (J.P.)	v. Surrey (Canterbury) 3 July (N.W.)	v. Surrey (The Oval) 7 July (J.P.)	v. Northamptonshire (Maidstone) 14 July (J.P.)	v. Durham (Canterbury) 17 July (N.W.)	v. Essex (Chelmsford) 21 July (J.P.)
M.R. Benson	25	4	0	21	34	21	6*	93		90	14	8	34	78	5	8	78	9
S.G. Hinks	49	26	21	0	9	4	6	21	—	14	11	0	15	95	2	13	47	11
C.J. Tavare	8	67*	12	101	143	13	32	4	—	3	4	27	44	62*	84*	65*	6	45
A.P.E. Knott	23	3	19	7	5	0*	—	5*	—	1	0	14	—	—	10	—	16	3
D.G. Aslett	7	14	49	8	3	21*	—		—	44	11	0	39	24	31	0	25	8
C.S. Cowdrey	54	1	2	5	41	49	24*	3	—	27	12	37	15*	12	38	4	19	0
E.A.E. Baptiste	4	7	3	50	43*	8	13	54*	—	1	15	18	3	0*	25	1	3	23
G.W. Johnson	14*	10*		5*	2*	—	—	—		2	13*	11*	—	—	1*	36*		
G.R. Dilley	10*		0		—	—	—	—	—	12							1*	
D.L. Underwood	—		3	2	—	—	—	—	—		2	5*	—	—	—	—	—	1
K.B.S. Jarvis	—	—	0*	—	—	—			—	0*	0	—	—	—	—	—	—	0
N.R. Taylor		—						12	—									
L. Potter		—																52
R.M. Ellison			0	5				19	—	20*	15	4	13*	—	2	5	39*	5*
C. Penn																		
G.R. Cowdrey																		
S. Marsh																		
S.N.V. Waterton																		
Byes	1	1	4	4		1		2				5		4			4	1
Leg-byes	4	5	5	5	3	4	4	8		8	3	8	3	8	13	3	6	11
Wides	2			4	3	11	3	3		2	1	5	3	8	10	3	4	6
No-Balls			3	1	7	1		2					4	5	1			5
Total	201	138	125	218	293	133	88	226		224	101	142	173	296	222	138	248	180
Wickets	7	6	10	9	6	5	3	6		9	10	8	5	4	7	6	7	10
Results	W	W	L	Ab.	W	W	W	W	Ab.	W	L	L	W	W	W	L	W	L
Points	2	4	0	2	2	2	4	4	—	4	—	0	4	—	4	0	—	0

Catches

21 – A.P.E. Knott (ct 19/st 2)
10 – E.A.E. Baptiste
8 – C.J.Tavare and S.G. Hinks
6 – G.W. Johnson
5 – D.L. Underwood and N.R. Taylor
4 – C.S. Cowdrey and M.R. Benson
3 – K.B.S. Jarvis, G.R. Dilley and S.N.V. Waterton
2 – S. Marsh, D.G. Aslett and L. Potter
1 – R.M. Ellison and G.R. Cowdrey

BOWLING	K.B.S. Jarvis	E.A.E. Baptiste	G.W. Johnson	C.S. Cowdrey	D.L. Underwood	L. Potter	R.M. Ellison	G.R. Dilley	S.G. Hinks
(B.&H.) *v.* Glamorgan (Cardiff) 4 May	9.3–3–38–3	10–0–30–5	11–1–24–0	11–0–35–1	11–2–36–0				
(J.P.) *v.* Glamorgan (Cardiff) 5 May	8–1–24–3	8–0–32–1	8–1–33–2	7–1–32–1		8–0–36–0			
(B.&H.) Hampshire (Canterbury) 11&13 May	4–0–27–0	8–0–38–1		9–0–38–3	8–2–29–1		9–0–41–1	5–0–23–1	
(J.P.) *v.* Hampshire (Canterbury) 12 May	5–0–11–0	1–0–1–0					5.1–2–11–1		
(B.&H.) *v.* Somerset (Taunton) 14 May	7.4–2–33–2	6–1–20–1	9–0–41–3	7–0–51–2	11–1–23–1			8–0–18–1	
(B.&H.) *v.* Minor Counties (Canterbury) 16 May	10–1–42–3	11–4–23–1	11–6–22–0	2–0–8–0	11–7–6–2			10–2–24–2	
(J.P.) *v.* Gloucestershire (Bristol) 26 May		2–0–14–1		2–0–15–1	2–0–12–0		2–0–18–0	2–0–21–1	
(J.P.) *v.* Worcestershire (Canterbury) 2 June		8–0–35–2		8–0–25–2	8–0–50–1		8–1–30–2	7–0–36–1	1–0–3–1
(B.&H.) *v.* Northants. (Northampton) 5 June	6–1–23–0	8–1–37–0		5–1–30–0	2–0–14–0		5–0–30–0	8–2–21–1	
(J.P.) *v.* Notts. (Trent Bridge) 16 June	6.4–1–24–5	7–0–45–2	6–2–24–1	5–0–21–1			6–0–21–1	7–0–34–0	
(B.&H.) *v.* Leicestershire (Leicester) 19 June	6–0–34–1	5–1–24–0					10.5–2–43–1		
(J.P.) *v.* Lancashire (Old Trafford) 23 June	7.2–0–32–0	8–2–17–1		8–0–34–1	8–1–28–2		7–3–16–2		
(J.P.) *v.* Middlesex (Canterbury) 30 June	8–0–40–2	8–1–27–1	8–0–21–0	1–0–7–0	8–1–30–2		7–0–30–1		
(N.W.) *v.* Surrey (Canterbury) 3 July	9–1–35–0	12–0–59–1	6–1–23–0	12–1–74–3	10–2–36–1		11–0–58–1		
(J.P.) *v.* Surrey (The Oval) 7 July	8–0–35–1	8–0–42–0		8–0–35–3	8–1–34–2		8–0–33–2		
(J.P.) *v.* Northants. (Maidstone) 24 July	5–0–18–0	6–0–26–0	2.4–0–17–0	4–0–25–0	6–0–25–0		5–0–25–0		
(N.W.) *v.* Durham (Canterbury) 17 July	11–0–56–2	12–3–22–1		7–0–16–1	12–5–26–3		7–2–13–2	10.1–1–25–1	
(J.P.) *v.* Essex (Chelmsford) 21 July	8–0–30–3	8–1–29–0		8–0–21–0	8–0–45–1		8–0–56–1		
(J.P.) *v.* Leicestershire (Leicester) 28 July									
(N.W.) *v.* Essex (Chelmsford) 9 & 8 Aug.	10–1–60–0	12–0–33–0			11–6 20–0		12–3–22–4	11.4–3–28–0	
(J.P.) *v.* Sussex (Canterbury) 11 August									
(J.P.) *v.* Yorkshire (Scarborough) 18 Aug.	8–0–37–2				8–2–13–1	8–0–30–2		8–0–24–2	
(J.P.) *v.* Derbyshire (Folkestone) 1 Sept.	8–0–41–1	5–0–27–1		6–0–39–1	8–2–20–1	6–1–9–4		7–0–19–0	
(J.P.) *v.* Warwickshire (Canterbury) 8 Sept.		6–0–52–1		8–0–60–1	8–0–44–1	4–0–21–0	8–0–61–3	6–0–32–0	
(J.P.) *v.* Somerset (Canterbury) 15 Sept.	8–1–27–1	8–0–36–2		8–0–23–2	8–0–29–0		7.5–0–23–1		
Wickets	29	22	6	23	19	6	23	10	1

v. Leicestershire (Leicester) 28 July (J.P.)	v. Essex (Chelmsford) 7 August (N.W.)	v. Sussex (Canterbury) 11 August (J.P.)	v. Yorkshire (Scarborough) 18 August (J.P.)	v. Derbyshire (Folkestone) 1 September (J.P.)	v. Warwickshire (Canterbury) 8 September (J.P.)	v. Somerset (Canterbury) 15 September (J.P.)	Runs
	22		26		12		588
	2		14	32	28	32	452
	12		7	18	59	27	843
	24		18	0			148
							284
	7		16	20	8	4	398
	0			9	60	0	340
							94
	19		3	10	10*		65
	19*		0*	3*	—	2*	37
	2*		—	1*		—	3
	51		2	13	11	21	110
			8	20	25	11	116
	8				30	6	171
			20				20
				21		20	41
					2		2
						10*	10
			1	3		1	
	2		6	10	4	7	
	4		11	1	2	1	
			1		2	1	
	172		133	161	253	143	
	9		9	9	9	8	
Ab.	L	Ab.	L	L	L	L	
2	—	0	0	0	0	0	

C. Penn	Byes	Leg-byes	Wides	No-balls	Total	Wkts
	6	12		10	181	10
	4	14	7		175	8
		19	10	4	215	8
		7			30	1
		5	2	3	191	10
	1	6	3	4	132	8
	4	3	4		87	4
		12	2		191	9
		3	6		158	2
		13	5	1	182	10
		1	1	2	102	2
		16	4		143	6
		14	1		169	7
		8	6	1	293	8
		6	7		185	9
		3	2		139	0
		11	8	1	169	10
		12	2		193	5
		Match Abandoned				
		11	2		174	4
		Match Abandoned				
8–0–41–1	8		3	5	153	9
	2	13	4		170	8
		13	7	4	284	6
		6	1		144	7
1						

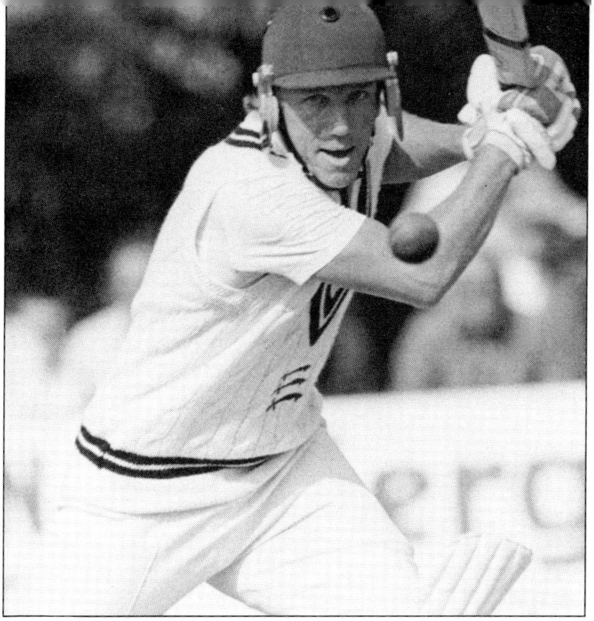

Clive Radley, the first double century of his career, Middlesex against Northants at Uxbridge. (Adrian Murrell)

Centuries sparkled at Hereford as the two left-handers, David Smith, a very fine player, strong and upright, and Younis Ahmed, immaculate of stroke, dominated. In the end, Glamorgan narrowly escaped defeat.

27, 29 and 30 July

at Bristol
Gloucestershire 416 for 6 dec (P. Bainbridge 143 not out, C.W.J. Athey 115, B.F. Davison 63, K.M. Curran 54)
Glamorgan 253 for 5 (J.A. Hopkins 70, G.C. Holmes 53)
Match drawn
Gloucestershire 6 pts, Glamorgan 5 pts

Mike Watkinson – a maiden century for Lancashire against Surrey at Southport. (David Munden)

Lancashire C.C.C.
Limited-Over Matches – 1985

BATTING	*v.* Leicestershire (Old Trafford) 5 May (J.P.)	*v.* Leicestershire (Old Trafford) 6 May (B.&H.)	*v.* Warwickshire (Edgbaston) 11 May (B.&H.)	*v.* Warwickshire (Edgbaston) 12 May (J.P.)	*v.* Yorkshire (Old Trafford) 15 May (B.&H.)	*v.* Worcestershire (Worcester) 16 May (B.&H.)	*v.* Gloucestershire (Old Trafford) 19 May (J.P.)	*v.* Northamptonshire (Northampton) 2 June (J.P.)	*v.* Essex (Ilford) 9 June (J.P.)	*v.* Derbyshire (Old Trafford) 16 June (J.P.)	*v.* Kent (Old Trafford) 23 June (J.P.)	*v.* Sussex (Hastings) 30 June (J.P.)	*v.* Suffolk (Bury St Edmunds) 3 July (N.W.)	*v.* Hampshire (Old Trafford) 14 July (J.P.)	*v.* Glamorgan (Old Trafford) 14 July (J.P.)	*v.* Worcestershire (Old Trafford) 18 July (N.W.)	*v.* Middlesex (Lord's) 28 July (J.P.)	*v.* Worcestershire (Worcester) 4 August (J.P.)
G. Fowler	11	12	9	46	29	8	35		30	98*	33	20	41	5			21	
S.J. O'Shaughnessy	23	11	66	39	48	90	20	19	60	13	13	19	14	7	42	22	13	
K.A. Hayes	3	0		2*														
N.H. Fairbrother	35	4	6	28	16		49*	10		—	2	3	52*	44	39	15	1*	
J. Abrahams	2	34	5	23	18	57	3	59	—	38*	1	6	15	66	11	15	—	
M. Watkinson	8	34	0	0	0	3		22*	—	—	34*	2	31	5	11*	56	3	
J. Simmons	16	0	33	14	3*	—	5*	0*	—	—	4*	32*	—	39	1	13	0	
P.J.W. Allott	3	1	2	1	4	—	—		—		—		—	7*			—	
J. Stanworth	2	8*																
D.J. Makinson	3*		0*	1	5	—	—	—	—	—	—		—	13	—	17	—	
B.P. Patterson	3*	15*																
J.A. Ormrod		0																
D.W. Varey			8		5	16												
S.T. Jefferies			32				35											
C. Maynard			41	4	1	22*	15	11	—	—	—	19*	0*	1	—	0	—	
C.H. Lloyd				25	8	43*		46	64*	16	17	26	30	22	108	91	13	
S. Henriksen						—	—	—	—	—				1	—	1*		
D.P. Hughes							28	20	14*	10	19	21	31				5	
M.R. Chadwick								6							0	43		
I. Folley															—			
A.N. Hayhurst																7		
Byes	6	6				2		1	1	1			4	1		1		
Leg-byes	8	14	7	6	7	9	14	10	9	3	16	10	4	12	6	9	2	
Wides	1	2	7		2	6	12	1	3	7	4	7	11	2		5	4	
No-balls	3	4	3	1		2	4		2					7	1	3		
Total	127	145	219	190	146	258	220	205	183	186	143	165	233	232	219	298	62	
Wickets	9	9	10	10	10	5	6	7	2	3	6	7	6	10	6	10	6	
Result	Ab.	L	L	L	W	L	L	Tie	Ab.	W	W	L	W	L	Tie	L	L	Ab.
Points	2	0	0	0	2	0	0	2	2	4	4	0	—	0	2	—	0	2

Catches
11 – C. Maynard (ct 9/st 2)
8 – J. Abrahams
7 – N.H. Fairbrother
6 – G. Fowler
4 – S.J. O'Shaughnessy
3 – D.J. Makinson and J. Simmons
2 – J.A. Ormrod, M. Watkinson and A.N. Hayhurst
1 – D.W. Varey, S.T. Jefferies and P.J.W. Allott

BOWLING	P.J.W. Allott	B.P. Patterson	M. Watkinson	J. Simmons	S.J. O'Shaughnessy	J. Abrahams	S.T. Jefferies	D.J. Makinson	S. Henriksen
(J.P.) *v.* Leicestershire (Old Trafford) 5 May	2–0–2–1	1.2–0–6–0							
(B.&H.) *v.* Leicestershire (Old Trafford) 6 May	9.2–1–35–0	11–1–34–1	9–1–32–1	11–8–5–1	11–5–17–4	2–0–11–0			
(B.&H.) *v.* Warwickshire (Edgbaston) 11 May	11–3–33–0		6–0–42–0	11–2–33–1	10–0–60–1		7–0–45–1	10–0–60–1	
(J.P.) *v.* Warwickshire (Edgbaston) 12 May	8–0–38–1		8–0–52–2	8–0–43–1	8–0–44–0			8–1–25–1	
(B.&H.) *v.* Yorkshire (Old Trafford) 15 May	7–0–23–1		6–0–44–2	6–0–27–0	7–0–20–3			6–0–23–1	
(B.&H.) *v.* Worcestershire (Worcester) 16 May	11–1–41–0		8.1–0–48–1	10–1–42–0	6–0–38–1			11–0–45–2	7–0–32–0
(J.P.) *v.* Glos. (Old Trafford) 19 May	7–0–36–0			5–0–19–0	5.1–0–25–0		6–0–45–1	8–1–44–2	7–0–46–1
(J.P.) *v.* Northants. (Northampton) 2 June			8–0–41–2	8–0–45–1	8–0–56–1			8–0–28–0	8–0–22–0
(J.P.) *v.* Essex (Ilford) 9 June	4–0–19–0			3–0–20–1				3–0–12–0	5–0–35–1
(J.P.) *v.* Derbyshire (Old Trafford) 16 June			8–1–38–3	8–0–37–1	8–0–55–1			8–0–28–4	8–0–18–0
(J.P.) *v.* Kent (Old Trafford) 23 June	8–2–28–4		8–2–25–1	8–2–27–2	8–0–29–0			8–1–20–1	
(J.P.) *v.* Sussex (Hastings) 30 June			8–0–42–0	8–0–58–0	8–0–43–1			8–0–46–0	8–0–40–1
(N.W.) *v.* Suffolk (Bury St Edmunds) 3 July	7–3–8–2		12–5–22–0	12–9–3–1	12–2–28–3	11–2–36–2		5–0–17–0	
(J.P.) *v.* Hampshire (Old Trafford) 7 July	8–0–55–2		7–0–35–1	8–0–39–1	3–0–24–0			7–1–31–0	7–0–43–1
(J.P.) *v.* Glamorgan (Old Trafford) 14 July			7–0–34–0	8–1–34–2	3–0–24–0			7–1–38–2	7–0–35–0
(N.W.) *v.* Worcs. (Old Trafford) 17 July			12–1–67–0	12–0–48–0	9–1–40–0			12–3–69–1	10–1–51–2
(J.P.) *v.* Middlesex (Lord's) 28 July	2–0–4–2		2–0–17–0	2–0–16–0	2–0–10–1			1.5–0–16–0	
(J.P.) *v.* Worcs. (Worcester) 4 August									
(J.P.) *v.* Yorkshire (Leeds) 11 August									
(J.P.) *v.* Notts. (Old Trafford) 18 August	6–0–28–0		5–0–35–1	4–0–13–0				6 0–27–2	
(J.P.) *v.* Somerset (Old Trafford) 25 August									
(Asda) *v.* Notts. (Scarborough) 5 Sept.	8–0–40–0		10–2–31–3	10–4–8–1	10–3–28–3		6–1–19–0	6–2–15–1	
(Asda) *v.* Derbyshire (Scarborough) 6 Sept.	9–2–35–0		7–0–24–0	10–1–31–0	4–0–17–0	1–0–5–0	7.2–0–30–1		
(J.P.) *v.* Surrey (The Oval) 8 September	8–0–33–0		6–2–19–1	8–0–41–0	8–0–22–1				
Wickets	13	1	18	13	20	2	3	18	6

a N.H. Fairbrother 7–0–30–0 b N.H. Fairbrother 2–0–15–0

v. Yorkshire (Leeds) 11 August (J.P.)	v. Nottinghamshire (Old Trafford) 18 August (J.P.)	v. Somerset (Old Trafford) 25 August (J.P.)	v. Nottinghamshire (Scarborough) 5 September (Asda)	v. Derbyshire (Scarborough) 6 September (Asda)	v. Surrey (The Oval) 8 September (J.P.)	Runs
	6		12	17	23	456
	8		0	1	29	557
			4	4		13
	26*		51	35	3	419
	—			11*	25	389
	—		4*	36*	12	261
	0		—	3	11	174
	—		—	—	—	18
						10
	12*		—			51
						18
						0
						29
			—	1		68
	—		—	—	3*	117
	46		73*	50	4	682
						2
	14				23	185
						49
						—
					12*	19
				1	1	
	6		2	12	7	
	2			4	6	
	1		1		1	
	121		147	175	160	
	5		4	7	8	
Ab.	W	Ab.	W	L	L	
2	4	2	—	—	0	

D.P. Hughes	I. Folley	A.N. Hayhurst	Byes	Leg-byes	Wides	No-balls	Total	Wkts
							8	1
				13		5	147	7
			1	8		1	282	4
				11	3		213	5
				7		2	144	9
				15	7	8	261	4
				8	3	3	223	4
			1	12	3		205	5
			1	4	2		91	3
				6	1		182	9
			5	8	5		142	8
				5		3	234	4
1–0–5–0			8	6	1		133	8
				8	2		235	5
	8–0–41–0		4	9	2		219	5
		5–0–30–0		7	5	2	312	5
				2			65	4
			Match Abandoned					
			Match Abandoned					
				12			115	5
			Match Abandoned					
				5	2	2	146	9
				5	2		177	2a
		5–0–31–0		3	3		164	2b
0	0	0						

at Leicester

Leicestershire 251 (J.J. Whitaker 73, E.A.E. Baptiste 6 for 60) and 141 for 3 dec (J.C. Balderstone 82 not out)
Kent 163 (N.R. Taylor 59 not out, S.G. Hinks 54, J.P. Agnew 9 for 70) and 128 for 6 (L.B. Taylor 4 for 42)

Match drawn
Leicestershire 7 pts, Kent 5 pts

at Uxbridge

Middlesex 318 for 4 dec (R.O. Butcher 86, M.W. Gatting 74, C.T. Radley 64 not out, M. Watkinson 4 for 71)
***v.* Lancashire**

Match drawn
Middlesex 4 pts, Lancashire 1 pt

at Worksop

Nottinghamshire 330 for 7 dec (B.C. Broad 131) and 199 for 2 dec (B.C. Broad 64)
Yorkshire 267 for 7 dec (M.D. Moxon 70) and 82 for 2 (G. Boycott 55 not out)

Match drawn
Nottinghamshire 7 pts, Yorkshire 5 pts

at Taunton

Somerset 363 for 9 dec (I.T. Botham 152, J.G. Wyatt 50, I.L. Pont 5 for 103) and 0 for 0 dec
Essex 68 for 1 dec and 296 for 3 (G.A. Gooch 173 not out)

Essex won by 7 wickets
Essex 20 pts, Somerset 4 pts

Damian d'Oliveira. Impressive form for Worcestershire. (Adrian Murrell)

Leicestershire C.C.C.
Limited-Over Matches – 1985

BATTING	v. Lancashire (Old Trafford) 5 May (J.P.)	v. Lancashire (Old Trafford) 6 May (B.&H.)	v. Yorkshire (Leicester) 11 May (B.&H.)	v. Yorkshire (Leicester) 12 May (J.P.)	v. Worcestershire (Leicester) 15 May (B.&H.)	v. Warwickshire (Edgbaston) 18 & 20 May (B.&H.)	v. Nottinghamshire (Trent Bridge) 19 May (J.P.)	v. Northamptonshire (Leicester) 26 May (J.P.)	v. Essex (Chelmsford) 2 June (J.P.)	v. Hampshire (Southampton) 5 June (B.&H.)	v. Middlesex (Lord's) 16 June (J.P.)	v. Kent (Leicester) 19 June (B.&H.)	v. Surrey (Leicester) 30 June (J.P.)	v. Glamorgan (Leicester) 23 June (J.P.)	v. Norfolk (Norwich) 3 July (N.W.)	v. Somerset (Taunton) 7 July (J.P.)	v. Hampshire (Southampton) 17 July (N.W.)	v. Essex (Lord's) 20 July (B.&H.)
D.I. Gower	6	24	0	27	37	19	—	17*		17		26*	2		41	45	12	43
N.E. Briers	0*	19	2	77	5	—	—	6*	14	—	1	—	60	54	27	9	31*	6
P. Willey	2*	1	60	2	15	68*	—	—		56		5*	40	39	17	21	52	86*
I.P. Butcher	—	14	101		25	44	—	8	41	55	25	55	2	48	12	9	31	19
J.J. Whitaker	—	0	0	86*	15	73*	—	—	1	24*	53	—	40*	0	26	16	46	1
M.A. Garnham	—	2	8	—	0*	—	—	—	22	—	41	—	10*	36	29*	6	7*	34*
P.B. Clift	—	11*	9	16	4	—	—	—	10	11*	1	—			3	27*	7	—
G.J. Parsons	—	0	25*	3*	16*	—	—	—	0	—	15	—	—	17		24*	—	—
P.A.J. de Freitas	—	—		—			—		1		8*		—	1*				
J.P. Addison	—																	
G.J.F. Ferris	—	—	0*	—	—	—	—	—							—			
J.C. Balderstone		58*	26	0	77	27			19	60	3	12			35		15	12
J.P. Agnew			1	—	—	—			4*	—	—	—	—	—	5	—	—	—
R.A. Cobb							—	—						—		—		
N.G.B. Cook								—	1		0							
L.B. Taylor									—	—	—	—	—	—	0*	—	—	—
M. Blackett													8	4*				
Byes				2	2									2			1	2
Leg-byes		13	4	5	9	11		3	13	10	6	1	11	6	8	9	5	9
Wides			2	4	7	3		1	6	3	2	1	4	7	7	8	4	2
No-balls		5	5	1		2			7	7	3	2		2	3	2	1	1
Total	8	147	243	223	212	247		35	139	243	158	102	177	216	213	176	212	215
Wickets	1	7	9	5	7	3		1	9	4	8	2	5	6	8	6	6	5
Result	Ab.	W	L	L	W	W	Ab.	Ab.	Tie	W	L	W	W	W	W	W	L	W
Points	2	2	0	0	2	2	2	2	2	—	0	—	4	4	—	4	—	—

Catches

27 – M.A. Garnham (ct 26/st 1)
8 – N.E. Briers, D.I. Gower and P. Willey
5 – L.B. Taylor and J.J. Whitaker
4 – J.P. Agnew and J.C. Balderstone
3 – P.B. Clift, I.P. Butcher and P.A.J. de Freitas
2 – N.G.B. Cook and G.J.F. Ferris
1 – M. Blackett, R.A. Cobb and sub

BOWLING	G.J.F. Ferris	G.J. Parsons	P.B. Clift	P. Willey	P.A.J. De Freitas	J.P. Agnew	L.B. Taylor	N.G.B. Cook	N.E. Briers
(J.P.) v. Lancashire (Old Trafford) 5 May	8–3–14–2	8–0–33–1	8–1–28–1	8–3–11–2	8–1–27–3				
(B.&H.) v. Lancashire (Old Trafford) 6 May	11–1–31–4	11–2–32–3	11–4–19–0	11–4–18–0	11–3–25–0				
(B.&H.) v. Yorkshire (Leicester) 11 May	11–2–63–1	11–0–44–0	11–0–55–1	11–0–35–0		11–3–34–1			
(J.P.) v. Yorkshire (Leicester) 12 May	6.5–0–33–0	8–0–42–1	5–0–51–1	8–0–24–1	2–0–25–0	7–0–41–0			
(B.&H.) v. Worcestershire (Leicester) 15 May	7–0–41–1	7–1–53–2	8–0–39–2	8–0–20–1		7–0–27–0			
(B.&H.) v. Warwick (Edgbaston) 18 & 20 May	11–0–74–0	11–1–44–3	11–4–16–1	11–0–39–0		11–1–68–1			
(J.P.) v. Notts. (Trent Bridge) 19 May	5–0–25–1	8–0–32–0	6–0–43–0	8–0–40–2	8–0–39–0				
(J.P.) v. Northants. (Leicester) 26 May									
(J.P.) v. Essex (Chelmsford) 2 June		8–0–31–0	8–1–25–3		8–0–27–3	8–1–21–2	7.2–0–28–1		
(B.&H.) v. Hampshire (Southampton) 5 June		11–1–59–0	11–2–43–2	11–0–49–1		10.5–0–38–3	11–0–43–2		
(J.P.) v. Middlesex (Lord's) 16 June		8–0–27–2	8–1–20–1		4–0–17–1	8–0–50–1	4–1–12–0	8–0–26–3	
(B.&H.) v. Kent (Leicester) 19 June		9–1–14–1	11–3–20–2	8–1–24–2		9–1–24–2	8.5–2–16–3		
(J.P.) v. Glamorgan (Leicester) 23 June		8–1–30–3		8–1–18–0	8–0–51–1	8–0–36–3	5.3–0–12–2		2–0–14–0
(J.P.) v. Surrey (Leicester) 30 June		3–0–24–1			3–0–16–1	7–2–36–2	7–1–21–2		
(N.W.) v. Norfolk (Norwich) 3 July	6–1–9–0		9–2–18–2	12–8–4–2		7–2–11–1	11–4–14–4		
(J.P.) v. Somerset (Taunton) 7 July		8–0–31–2	6–1–17–3	7–0–34–2		5–0–22–0	8–1–22–3		
(N.W.) v. Hampshire (Southampton) 17 July		11.1–3–31–1	12–2–33–1	11–0–36–1		12–0–44–1	11–0–52–1		2–0–8–1
(B.&H.) v. Essex (Lord's) 20 July		11–0–39–0	11–1–40–2	11–0–41–1		11–1–51–1	11–3–26–3		
(J.P.) v. Warwickshire (Leicester) 21 July		8–0–50–1	8–1–35–3	8–2–27–1		8–0–43–0	8–1–27–1		
(J.P.) v. Kent (Leicester) 28 July									
(J.P.) v. Glos. (Cheltenham) 11 August		1–0–14–0	2–0–10–1	1–0–6–0	2–0–10–0	2–0–16–0	2–0–12–0		
(J.P.) v. Hampshire (Leicester) 18 August									
(J.P.) v. Worcestershire (Leicester) 1 Sept.	8–0–40–3	8–0–34–0	8–0–42–0	8–0–21–2	8–0–55–3				
(J.P.) v. Sussex (Hove) 8 September		8–0–44–2	8–2–17–1	4–0–24–1	4–0–44–1	8–0–25–1	8–1–26–3		
(J.P.) v. Derbyshire (Chesterfield) 15 Sept.	3–0–21–0	5–1–15–1	5–2–11–0	2–0–9–0	2–0–4–0		4–1–13–0		1–0–6–0
Wickets	12	24	27	19	13	19	25	3	1

v. Warwickshire (Leicester) 21 July (J.P.)	v. Kent (Leicester) 28 July (J.P.)	v. Gloucestershire (Cheltenham) 11 August (J.P.)	v. Hampshire (Leicester) 18 August (J.P.)	v. Worcestershire (Leicester) 1 September (J.P.)	v. Sussex (Hove) 8 September (J.P.)	v. Derbyshire (Chesterfield) 15 September (J.P.)	Runs
114*		11			46	6	493
51*		21	13*	24	25	4	449
—		11	1*	21	20	8	525
0			3	7	3	6	508
—		13	—	46	5	0	445
—		8	—	0	28	28*	259
—		1	—	9	4	12	125
—		4	—	8	11	3	126
—		2	—	27	3	1	43
							—
				9*		4	13
				5			349
—		4*	—		13*		27
		0*	—				0
							1
—		—			6*	1*	7
			—	21*			33
3		2			1	1	
4				6	10	7	
2			1	3	3	5	
1				1	1	1	
175		77	18	187	179	87	
1		8	1	9	9	10	
W	Ab.	W	Ab.	L	L	L	
4	2	4	2	0	0	0	

D.I. Gower	I.P. Butcher	J.J. Whitaker	Byes	Leg-byes	Wides	No-balls	Total	Wkts
			6	8	1	3	127	9
			6	14	2	4	145	9
			2	11	2	5	244	4
				8	5	4	224	3
			4	11	2		195	7
				5	1	7	246	5
				7	1	1	186	3
			Match Abandoned					
				7	8	3	139	10
			1	6	4	5	239	10
			1	10	2		163	8
				3	1		101	10
				5			166	10
			1	3	1		101	7
1–0–8–0	0.3–0–6–1		1	2	1	2	73	10
			2	5	5		133	10
				9	1	1	213	6
			1	15	1	1	213	8
				5		2	187	6
			Match Abandoned					
			2				70	2
			Match Abandoned					
				3	1	2	195	8
				6	1	4	186	9
	1–0–4–0	0.2–0–4–0		3	5	4	90	1
0	1	0						

at Guildford

Hampshire 291 (C.L. Smith 58, R.A. Smith 57, N.G. Cowley 51, A.H. Gray 5 for 83)
Surrey 4 for 0

Match drawn
Surrey 4 pts, Hampshire 3 pts

at Eastbourne

Worcestershire 306 for 6 dec (D.B. d'Oliveira 139, D.M. Smith 62) and 195 for 5 dec (T.S. Curtis 54)
Sussex 177 (I.J. Gould 95, N.V. Radford 6 for 76) and 22 for 1

Match drawn
Worcestershire 8 pts, Sussex 3 pts

at Edgbaston

Derbyshire 344 for 8 (J.G. Wright 177 not out)
v. **Warwickshire**

Match drawn
Warwickshire 3 pts, Derbyshire 3 pts

27, 28, 29 and 30 July

at Northampton

Australians 404 for 5 dec (D.C. Boon 206 not out, W.B. Phillips 55, G.R.J. Matthews 51 not out)
Northamptonshire 258 for 3 (R.J. Bailey 107 not out)

Match drawn

Rain ravaged the country and blighted championship contenders. Having lost their openers for 60, Gloucestershire scored heavily on the opening day at Bristol. The Monday and much of the Tuesday was lost. There was no play after the first day at Uxbridge and very little after the first day at Guildford. Edgbaston had the last two days blank after an interesting Saturday when Derbyshire, having reached 209 for 8, were revitalised by an unbroken stand of 135 between John Wright and Roger Finney. There was also rain decimation at Northampton. David Boon continued his slaughter of county attacks and he and Greg Matthews shared an unbroken stand of 150. In the hours of the match that remained unhampered by weather, Robert Bailey hit a graceful hundred, giving evidence that, even if his season had been something of a disappointment, he was a young batsman of Test class and immense potential. The sad note from this match was that Graeme Wood suffered a broken nose and cut between the eyes after being hit by a ball from Jim Griffiths.

A majestic stand of 116 in 36 overs between Damian d'Oliveira and David Smith illuminated the first day at Eastbourne. D'Oliveira reached his career best score. Sussex struggled against Radford, in many respects the bowler of the season, and they were only saved by Ian Gould's fierce hitting. Worcestershire were thwarted by rain and Barclay was left wondering why he had asked them to bat first.

Chris Broad held together the Notts side at Worksop with two fine knocks, but here too rain was the only winner.

On the opening day at Grace Road, Leicestershire lumbered. Having moved somewhat briskly to 184, they lost their last 7 wickets for 67 runs as Baptiste found a vitality and fuller length than his colleagues. Kent closed the day at 97 for 2, both wickets having fallen to Agnew. Agnew continued to take wickets on the Monday. He quickly accounted for Hinks, Cowdrey and Baptiste. Knott joined Taylor in a brief

Middlesex C.C.C.
Limited-Over Matches – 1985

BATTING	v. Yorkshire (Bradford) 5 May (J.P.)	v. C'bined Universities (Cambridge) 11 May (B.&H.)	v. Gloucestershire (Lord's) 12 May (J.P.)	v. Sussex (Hove) 14 & 15 May (B.&H.)	v. Essex (Lord's) 16 May (B.&H.)	v. Surrey (Lord's) 18 May (B.&H.)	v. Glamorgan (Lord's) 19 May (J.P.)	v. Sussex (Lord's) 26 May (J.P.)	v. Worcestershire (Worcester) 5 & 7 June (B.&H.)	v. Derbyshire (Lord's) 9 June (J.P.)	v. Leicestershire (Lord's) 16 June (J.P.)	v. Essex (Chelmsford) 19 & 20 June (B.&H.)	v. Nottinghamshire (Trent Bridge) 23 June (J.P.)	v. Kent (Canterbury) 30 June (J.P.)	v. Cumberland (Uxbridge) 3 July (N.W.)	v. Northamptonshire (Tring) 7 July (J.P.)	v. Somerset (Lord's) 14 July (J.P.)	v. Essex (Chelmsford) 17 July (N.W.)
W.N. Slack	—	58*	3	1	11	20	35	—	20*	42*	33	60	40	25	98	74	—	32
G.D. Barlow	—	34	40	19	0	44	59	2	6	66*	15	7	0	72	35	1	—	8
M.W. Gatting	—	39*	69*	143*	1	51	16	15	7*	—		28	7		16	54		17
R.O. Butcher	—		29*	29	2	18	7	49	—	—	0	11	4	15	59	0	—	2
C.T. Radley	—	—	—	40	6	11	23*	9*	—	—	16	7	8	3	18	37	—	27
P.R. Downton	—	—	—	1	7	24	2	5*	—	—		0	70		9	23		15
J.E. Emburey	—	—	—	18*	38*	0	1	—	—	—		8*	1		2	11*		10
P.H. Edmonds	—	—	—	—	2	0	7	—	—	—	0	0	2		1*	—		0
N.F. Williams	—	—	—	—	3	29*	1	—	—	—	15	4	3	5	5	—	—	7*
N.G. Cowans								—	—	—		0	20	—	4			0
W.W. Daniel	—	—	—	—	2	8	7*	—	—	—	—	0	2*	—	7*	—		2
A.R.C. Fraser	—	—	—	—	0	2	—										—	
K.P. Tomlins		—									36			1			—	
J.F. Sykes											3			25			—	
C.P. Metson											14*			8*			—	
S.P. Hughes											18*			—		10*	—	
G.D. Rose																	—	
J.D. Carr																		
K.R. Brown																		
M. Rosebury																		
Byes		3				4			5	1	1				1			1
Leg-byes		5	8	20		1	5	5	1	8	10	2	8	14	18	17		1
Wides			1	4	1	6	3	3	2	3	2	10	5		10	2		6
No-balls				5		1			4	1		3	1	1		1		2
Total		139	150	280	73	219	166	88	45	121	163	140	171	169	293	230		130
Wickets		1	2	5	10	10	8	3	1	0	8	10	10	7	9	6		10
Results	Ab.	W	W	W	L	L	L	W	Ab.	W	W	L	L	L	W	L	Ab.	L
Points	2	2	4	2	0	0	0	4	—	4	4	—	0	0	—	0	2	—

Catches
23 – P.R. Downton (ct 14/st 9)
13 – J.E. Emburey
9 – C.T. Radley
6 – W.N. Slack and R.O. Butcher
5 – N.F. Williams
4 – M.W. Gatting, G.D. Barlow and P.H. Edmonds
3 – C.P. Metson
2 – N.G. Cowans
1 – S.P. Hughes, W.W. Daniel and A.R.C. Fraser

BOWLING	N.F. Williams	W.W. Daniel	P.H. Edmonds	A.R.C. Fraser	J.E. Emburey	M.W. Gatting	N.G. Cowans	S.P. Hughes	W.N. Slack
(J.P.) v. Yorkshire (Bradford) 5 May	6–0–23–2	8–1–25–2	8–1–22–0	7–0–46–3	8–7–9–2				
(B.&H.) v. Comb. Univ. (Cambridge) 11 May	11–2–23–1	11–3–22–2	11–2–43–5	11–1–24–0	11–4–19–1				
(J.P.) v. Gloucestershire (Lord's) 12 May	8–0–18–0	8–2–40–3		8–1–45–1	4–0–39–1				
(B.&H.) v. Sussex (Hove) 14 & 15 May	11–0–47–1	10.4–1–58–4	11–0–48–2	11–1–48–1	10–3–40–1				
(B.&H.) v. Essex (Lord's) 16 May	11–5–20–3	7–4–21–1		5–0–31–1					
(B.&H.) v. Surrey (Lord's) 18 May	11–1–62–0	11–1–53–1	11–0–40–0	11–1–30–0	11–1–33–2				
(J.P.) v. Glamorgan (Lord's) 19 May	8–1–29–2	8–1–22–0	5.2–0–26–0	8–0–31–0	8–0–48–1	1–0–6–0			
(J.P.) v. Sussex (Lord's) 26 May	2–0–25–1	2–0–15–0	2–0–19–1		2–0–11–0		2–0–15–0		
(B.&H.) v. Worcestershire (Worcester) 5 June	11–0–45–0	10–1–26–3	11–1–37–3		11–1–37–1		11–1–60–1		
(J.P.) v. Derbyshire (Derby) 9 June	8–0–38–2	6–0–25–2	8–1–37–1		8–1–25–2	2–0–16–0	8–1–11–1		
(J.P.) v. Leicestershire (Lord's) 16 June	8–0–34–1	8–2–23–3	8–1–24–1					8–0–28–1	8–0–43–1
(B.&H.) v. Essex (Chelmsford) 19 & 20 June	11–1–39–1	11–0–56–0	11–0–31–1		11–2–36–4		11–0–35–2		
(J.P.) v. Notts. (Trent Bridge) 23 June	7–0–47–2	8–0–33–0	8–1–21–2		8–1–28–1	1–0–9–0	8–2–31–0		
(J.P.) v. Kent (Canterbury) 30 June	6.5–0–47–0	8–0–26–2					7–0–34–0	8–0–31–3	
(N.W.) v. Cumberland (Uxbridge) 3 July	6–0–24–0	9–1–31–1	12–2–39–4		12–2–28–2	7.3–3–7–1	7–1–13–0		
(J.P.) v. Northamptonshire (Tring) 7 July	5.5–0–47–1	8–0–38–0	8–0–33–3		8–0–38–1			8–0–49–0	2–0–22–0
(J.P.) v. Somerset (Lord's) 14 July	8–0–34–1			6–1–21–0				7–0–38–1	
(N.W.) v. Essex (Chelmsford) 17 July	12–1–33–1	12–1–40–1	12–0–49–2		12–1–41–3		12–0–39–2		
(J.P.) v. Worcestershire (Worcester) 21 July	6–0–28–1	7–0–39–1	4–0–23–0		8–0–23–1	8–1–37–3		7–0–40–2	
(J.P.) v. Lancashire (Lord's) 28 July		2–0–10–2	2–0–15–1	2–0–15–0	2–0–11–1			2–0–9–1	
(J.P.) v. Essex (Chelmsford) 4 August									
(J.P.) v. Surrey (Lord's) 18 August	3.5–0–20–0			4–0–14–0					
(J.P.) v. Hampshire (Southampton) 1 Sept.	7.3–0–34–0			8–1–13–2				7–0–28–1	
(J.P.) v. Warwickshire (Edgbaston) 15 Sept.	8–0–38–2			8–0–28–1	8–1–25–3			7–0–22–1	
Wickets	22	28	26	9	27	4	6	10	1

A. Qasim Umar absent injured

v. Worcestershire (Worcester) 21 July (J.P.)	v. Lancashire (Lord's) 28 July (J.P.)	v. Essex (Chelmsford) 4 August (J.P.)	v. Surrey (Lord's) 18 August (J.P.)	v. Hampshire (Southampton) 1 September (J.P.)	v. Warwickshire (Edgbaston) 15 September (J.P.)	Runs
20			18	27	33	650
14	14		16	4		456
62*	22					547
13	9		43	36	8	334
0	1		9	1	1	217
31	9*				23	219
9	8*				8	114
4	—					16
0			8	5*	10*	95
						24
—	—					28
	—		7	1	0	10
						37
			10	3		41
			3	2		27
5*	—		22*	9	2	66
				30	5	35
	—		4			4
			11	14	33	58
					15	15
			2	3	4	
12	2		13	5	13	
5			12	6	5	
			1			
175	65		179	146	160	
8	4		10	10	10	
L	W	Ab.	Ab.	L	L	
0	4	2	2	0	0	

J.F. Sykes	G.D. Rose	Byes	Leg-byes	Wides	No-balls	Total	Wkts
		1	6	6	1	132	9
			7	2	3	138	9
			7	5	2	149	5
		2	6	1	7	249	10
			2	2	4	74	6
			9	1	4	227	4
			5	2		167	3
		1	1		2	87	2
		6	9	4	3	220	10
		1	8	8	2	161	9
			6	2	3	158	8
			5	1	11	202	8
		1	8	7		178	6
8–0–32–0			3	3	4	173	5
		6	4	4	3	152	9a
		1	3	1		231	5
8–0–20–1	8–0–46–1		4	4	4	163	7
			12	5	2	214	10
			7	6	2	197	9
			2	4		62	6
				Abandoned			
				1	1	34	0
8–0–22–1	7–0–47–0	1	4	5	1	149	4
	8–0–38–1	1	14	4	1	166	10
2	2						

stand, but he fell lbw and Dilley, Ellison and Underwood were all out on 145. Ellison and Underwood were out to successive deliveries so that Jarvis came in to face a hat-trick ball and a bowler who was within tantalising reach of all ten wickets. Agnew bowled a no-ball, and Jarvis blocked the remaining two deliveries. Agnew was thwarted. Jarvis hit his highest score of the season, 7, before falling to Clift. Two and a half hours were lost on the last day, but Gower, aided by some generous bowling from Kent, was able to set a challenging target which nearly brought victory. Leicestershire were held at bay by Taylor and Knott.

At Taunton, where the only outright result was achieved, there was also some conferring between the captains. The Saturday saw some sensational cricket. Ian Pont, brisk fast-medium, playing his first senior game for Essex took 5 wickets, including those of Richards and Botham. Botham hit his second century in successive innings, his hundred coming off only 68 balls. His 152 was made out of 195 from 121 deliveries. Once more he hit spectacular sixes, 4 of them, and added 16 fours before being caught at the wicket off a skier. It was one of 8 catches that David East took so equalling Wally Grout's world record and celebrating his twenty-sixth birthday. Grout's catches were made out of the full complement of 10, but Botham declared with 9 wickets down so that East's performance can be said to be the more meritorious. There was no play on the Monday and on the last day, after connivance, Essex were asked to make 296 in 90 overs. Garner was unable to bowl and Gooch made mockery of the task. He and Hardie began with a stand of 84. Prichard batted well to help add 81 and although McEwan fell for 0, Somerset enjoyed no other success as Pringle helped Gooch obtain the last 131 runs. Gooch hit 2 sixes and 21 fours in a chanceless innings which brought victory with 21 overs to spare. Essex, bottom early in the month, had climbed to seventh in the championship table. Essex kept further in the news when it was announced that Allan Border would join them in 1986 as replacement for Ken McEwan who had said that he would be remaining in South Africa.

John Player Special League

28 July

at Bristol

Glamorgan 166 for 9 (Javed Miandad 57, K.M. Curran 4 for 25)
Gloucestershire 168 for 4 (B.F. Davison 85 not out)

Gloucestershire (4 pts) won by 6 wickets

at Leicestershire

Leicestershire *v.* Kent

Match abandoned
Leicestershire 2 pts, Kent 2 pts

at Lord's

Lancashire 62 for 6
Middlesex 65 for 4

Middlesex (4 pts) won by 6 wickets

at Trent Bridge

Yorkshire 70 for 7
Nottinghamshire 73 for 4

Nottinghamshire (4 pts) won by 6 wickets

Northamptonshire C.C.C.
Limited-Over Matches – 1985

BATTING	v. Hampshire (Northampton) 5 May (J.P.)	v. Gloucestershire (Northampton) 11 May (B.&H.)	v. Derbyshire (Derby) 12 May (J.P.)	v. Derbyshire (Derby) 15 May (B.&H.)	v. Scotland (Northampton) 16 May (B.&H.)	v. Nottinghamshire (Trent Bridge) 18&20 May (B.&H.)	v. Leicestershire (Leicester) 26 May (J.P.)	v. Lancashire (Northampton) 2 June (J.P.)	v. Kent (Northampton) 5 June (B.&H.)	v. Gloucestershire (Northampton) 16 June (J.P.)	v. Essex (Luton) 23 June (J.P.)	v. Warwickshire (Edgbaston) 30 June (J.P.)	v. Shropshire (Telford) 3 July (N.W.)	v. Middlesex (Tring) 7 July (J.P.)	v. Kent (Maidstone) 14 July (J.P.)	v. Gloucestershire (Bristol) 17 July (N.W.)	v. Sussex (Northampton) 21 July (J.P.)	v. Nottinghamshire (Northampton) 4 August (J.P.)
G. Cook	1	11	0	5	6	7*	—	98	78	51	57	0	130	46	—	54	37	
W. Larkins	5	48	45*	10	105	0	—	48	52	2	38	26	34	25	75*	75	43	
A.J. Lamb	125*	0	69*	2	20	—	—		8*		82*		7	33		42	22	
R.J. Bailey	79*	52	—	25	20*	—	—	26	—	9	9	2	18*	103*	59*	8	0	
D.J. Capel	—	11	—	7	11*	—	—	3*	—	44	13	15	1*	—	—	3	0	
R.G. Williams	—	58	—	24	27	20*	—	5	11*			4	8	9*	—	8	10	
G. Sharp	—	6*	—	1*	—	—	—	—	—	4	—							
N.A. Mallender	—	—	—	—	—	—	—	—	—	3	—	4*	—	—	—	8*	—	
A. Walker	—	—	—	—	—	—	—	—	—	0	—	6*			—			
R.F. Joseph	—	—		—												6		
D.J. Wild	—	15*	—	2*			—	—		63*	5*	0	—	—	—	1	32*	
R.A. Harper			—		—	—	—	9	—	9	—	0	0	1	—		11	
B.J. Griffiths					—	—		—	—	1	—							
R.J. Boyd-Moss										1		51	51	9	—	11	21	
D. Ripley												1	—	—	—	5	11	
Byes		3		2	1			1				1	4	1				
Leg-byes	12	9	4	9				12	3	5	10	9	5	3	3	6	17	
Wides	4	1			1	1		3	6	3	1	14	11	1	2	5	4	
No-balls	1	6	3	1		1				1	2		1			8		
Total	227	220	121	88	191	29		205	158	196	217	133	270	231	139	240	208	
Wickets	2	6	1	6	4	1		5	2	10	4	9	6	5	0	10	9	
Result	W	W	W	Ab.	W	Ab.	Ab.	Tie	Ab.	L	W	L	W	W	W	L	L	Ab.
Points	4	2	4	1	2	1	2	2	—	0	4	0	—	4	4	—	0	2

Catches
13 – D. Ripley (ct 10/st 3)
10 – W. Larkins and R.A. Harper
8 – G. Sharp (ct 6/st 2)
7 – G. Cook
5 – N.A. Mallender and D.J. Wild
4 – A.J. Lamb and R. J. Bailey
3 – D.J. Capel and A. Walker
2 – R.J. Boyd-Moss
1 – B.J. Griffiths and R.G. Williams

BOWLING	N.A. Mallender	R.F. Joseph	A. Walker	R.G. Williams	D.J. Capel	W. Larkins	R.J. Bailey	R.A. Harper	B.J. Griffiths
(J.P.) *v.* Hampshire (Northampton) 5 May	5–1–31–1	4–0–21–0	8–0–50–1	8–0–35–0	8–0–35–2	7–0–42–2			
(B.&H.) *v.* Glos. (Northampton) 11 May	10–0–38–2	11–2–32–0	9.5–0–46–4	11–2–32–1	8–1–35–0		4–0–22–1		
(J.P.) *v.* Derbyshire (Derby) 12 May	8–1–25–1		8–1–28–2	8–1–15–1	8–1–21–3			8–1–19–0	
(B.&H.) *v.* Derbyshire (Derby) 15 May									
(B.&H.) *v.* Scotland (Northampton) 16 May	11–1–46–3		11–0–41–2	11–3–25–0	4–0–15–1			11–1–37–0	7–2–13–1
(B.&H.) *v.* Notts. (Trent Bridge) 18&20 May	11–0–71–1		11–1–62–1	11–1–31–0				11–0–48–3	11–2–24–0
(J.P.) *v.* Leicestershire (Leicester) 26 May	5–2–4–1		4–0–20–0			1–0–8–0			
(J.P.) *v.* Lancashire (Northampton) 2 June	8–1–32–2		8–0–39–1	8–1–33–1	3–0–22–1			7–0–46–1	6–1–22–1
(B.&H.) *v.* Kent (Northampton) 5 June									
(J.P.) *v.* Glos. (Northampton) 16 June	8–0–36–0		7–0–36–2		5–0–46–0	2–0–17–0		8–0–41–2	8–0–32–0
(J.P.) *v.* Essex (Luton) 23 June	8–0–41–1		8–0–49–2		8–0–50–2			8–2–29–0	8–1–45–0
(J.P.) *v.* Warwickshire (Edgbaston) 30 June	6–0–25–0		6–0–30–2			8–0–27–2		8–0–29–2	
(N.W.) *v.* Shropshire (Telford) 3 July	5–2–4–1			12–3–35–3	7–1–19–0		1–0–2–1	9–4–13–0	
(J.P.) *v.* Middlesex (Tring) 7 July	7–0–21–2			6–0–35–2	4–0–12–0	8–0–46–1		8–0–52–0	
(J.P.) *v.* Kent (Maidstone) 14 July	8–2–37–3		6.1–1–16–1	1.5–0–13–0	8–1–18–1	8–1–24–0		8–2–27–0	
(N.W.) *v.* Gloucestershire (Bristol) 17 July	6–0–19–1	8–0–47–0		10–0–47–1	12–0–74–2	12–3–38–2			
(J.P.) *v.* Sussex (Northampton) 21 July	8–1–35–1			3–0–19–0	6–0–43–0	8–1–25–0		7–0–32–2	
(J.P.) *v.* Notts. (Northampton) 4 August									
(J.P.) *v.* Somerset (Weston-s-Mare) 11 Aug.									
(J.P.) *v.* Glam. (Wellingborough) 18 Aug.	5–0–13–0		6–4–11–0			1–0–2–0			
(J.P.) *v.* Surrey (Guildford) 25 August	5–0–19–1		6.1–0–26–2	5–0–36–2		3–0–39–0		8–0–40–2	
(J.P.) *v.* Yorkshire (Leeds) 1 September	7–0–40–1		7–0–19–0	2–0–19–0		8–0–32–2		8–0–20–0	
(J.P.) *v.* Worcs. (Worcester) 15 Sept.	7–0–32–2		8–0–21–4	7–0–39–1		6–0–22–0		6–0–40–0	
Wickets	24	0	24	12	12	9	2	12	2

v. Somerset (Weston-s-Mare) 11 August (J.P.)	v. Glamorgan (Wellingborough) 18 August (J.P.)	v. Surrey (Guildford) 25 August (J.P.)	v. Yorkshire (Leeds) 1 September (J.P.)	v. Worcestershire (Worcester) 15 September (J.P.)	Runs
	11	—	31	54	677
	37	126	59	6	859
		132*		0	542
	7	21	32	1	471
	24		16*	26	174
	3	—	17	15	219
					11
	1*	—	—	12*	28
	4	—	—	2*	12
					6
	1	—	7	1	127
	11	13*	0	18	72
					1
	6	—	10		160
	7	—	0*	16	40
	1	4	4		
	4	7	2	8	
	4	3	3	6	
			4	2	
	121	306	185	167	
	10	2	7	9	
Ab.	Ab.	W	W	L	
2	2	4	4	0	

D.J. Wild	R.J. Boyd-Moss	A.J. Lamb	Byes	Leg-byes	Wides	No-balls	Total	Wkts
				10	1		224	7
			3	9	1	2	217	10
				11	5	1	119	8
			Match Abandoned					
			1	7	6	4	185	9
			1	5	1	2	242	5
				3	1		35	1
			1	10	1		205	7
			Match Abandoned					
			2	1	8	1	211	7
				2	1		216	5
7–1–20–2			1	10	2		142	9
8–1–33–1	12–1–47–3	0.2–0–4–1	10	3	16	1	170	10
7–0–47–1				17	2	1	230	6
				3	3		138	6
12–2–38–1			4	10	1	3	277	8
8–0–49–2				7	10		210	6
			Match Abandoned					
			Match Abandoned					
				10			36	0
8–0–44–2				9	2	1	213	10
8–1–33–4			1	17	6	1	181	8
6–0–37–0				4	7	11	195	8
13	3	1						

at Taunton

Somerset 173 for 9 (I.T. Botham 58)
Essex 174 for 5 (K.S. McEwan 54 not out)

Essex (4 pts) won by 5 wickets

at Eastbourne

Sussex 169 for 4 (Imran Khan 71, P.W.G. Parker 53)
Worcestershire 124 for 6

Sussex (4 pts) won by 45 runs

at Edgbaston

Warwickshire 224 for 7 (G.J. Lord 103, A.E. Warner 4 for 44)
Derbyshire 225 for 5 (K.J. Barnett 82 not out)

Derbyshire (4 pts) won by 5 wickets

Rain restricted the matches at Trent Bridge and Lord's and the match at Eastbourne was a 23-over affair. There were only 30 overs a side possible at Edgbaston, but runs came at 7 an over. Lord hit 103 off 88 balls but Kim Barnett steered his side to victory. Roberts and Miller made excellent contributions. Brian Davison hit 4 sixes and 8 fours as Gloucestershire won. Kevin Curran had an impressive all-round match. At Taunton, Botham hit 58 off 57 balls, but McEwan's innings and two late blows by David East off Botham took a weakened Essex side to victory.

31 July, 1 and 2 August

at Leicester

Leicestershire 327 (N.E. Briers 61, R.A. Cobb 59, M. Watkinson 5 for 109, D.J. Makinson 4 for 110) and 207 for 3 dec (R.A. Cobb 66 not out, J.J. Whitaker 66 not out)
Lancashire 278 (C.H. Lloyd 131, L.B. Taylor 4 for 52) and 81 for 8 (P.A.J. de Freitas 5 for 39)

Match drawn
Leicestershire 8 pts, Lancashire 7 pts

Javed Miandad – a brilliant double century for Glamorgan against the Australian tourists. (Mark Leech)

Nottinghamshire C.C.C.
Limited-Over Matches – 1985

BATTING	v. Gloucestershire (Bristol) 4 May (B.&H.)	v. Gloucestershire (Bristol) 5 May (J.P.)	v. Scotland (Glasgow) 11 May (B.&H.)	v. Derbyshire (Trent Bridge) 16 May (B.&H.)	v. Northamptonshire (Trent Bridge) 18 & 20 May (B.&H.)	v. Leicestershire (Trent Bridge) 19 May (J.P.)	v. Somerset (Trent Bridge) 26 May (J.P.)	v. Sussex (Horsham) 2 June (J.P.)	v. Kent (Trent Bridge) 16 June (J.P.)	v. Yorkshire (Harrogate) 19 June (T.T.)	v. Middlesex (Trent Bridge) 23 June (J.P.)	v. Staffordshire (Trent Bridge) 3 July (N.W.)	v. Glamorgan (Swansea) 7 July (J.P.)	v. Warwickshire (Edgbaston) 14 July (J.P.)	v. Warwickshire (Trent Bridge) 17 July (N.W.)	v. Surrey (Guildford) 21 July (J.P.)	v. Yorkshire (Trent Bridge) 28 July (J.P.)	v. Northamptonshire (Northampton) 4 August (J.P.)
B.C. Broad	17	28	0	1	70	54	1	24	12	60	69	2	40	23	14	69	12*	
R.T. Robinson	56	2	120	32	39	7	44*			11	15	10	77		98*	22		
D.W. Randall	62	7	7	29	54	—	9*	9	15	29	8	2	9	16	19	65	15	
C.E.B. Rice	11	7	25	73*	36	36	4	67	31	14	3	0	18	12				
P. Johnson	16	31	0	4		—	30	7	4	36	28	101*	7	63	20	6	12	
J.D. Birch	37	63	4	2	3	55*	5	49	0	5	2		39*	0				
B. N. French	4	37	8	3*	—	—	—	2	25	58*	—	49	0	6	7*	3*	19*	
E.E. Hemmings	2	7*	31	—	—	—	—	2*	6	13*		31*	1*	0	—	3	—	
K. Saxelby	2*	12*	12*	—	—	—	—	3*	0*	—		—	—	5*	—	—	—	
R.A. Pick	3*														—	—	—	
K.P. Evans	20	28			2*			18	28		0*	8		5			—	
P.M. Such		—	—															
K.E. Cooper			0*	—	—	—	—		0	—	—	—	—	4*	—	—	—	
R.J. Hadlee				39	29*	25*	—	4	42		37*	16	0	36	56	18	7	
C.D. Fraser-Darling										25	—							
S.B. Hassan															17	15	4	
D.J.R. Martindale																		
R. Evans																		
Byes		1		1	1		1	1			1		2					
Leg-byes	15	11	9	10	5	7	4	9	13	6	8	15	5	4	16	16	3	
Wides	9	3		2	1	1	1	2	5	5	7	7	1		4	3	1	
No-balls	1	1			2	1	1		1	5		2	3	1		3		
Total	225	238	216	196	242	186	100	197	182	267	178	243	202	175	251	223	73	
Wickets	9	8	8	6	5	3	4	8	10	7	6	7	7	9	5	7	4	
Results	L	L	W	W	Ab.	Ab.	L	W	L	W	W	W	W	L	W	W	W	Ab.
Points	0	0	2	2	1	2	0	4	0	—	4	—	4	0	—	4	4	2

Catches
20 – B.N. French (ct 18/st 2)
14 – D.W. Randall
12 – C.E.B. Rice
10 – R.J. Hadlee
8 – P. Johnson
6 – R.T. Robinson
5 – K. Saxelby
4 – J.D. Birch and B.C. Broad
3 – K.P. Evans
2 – K.E. Cooper, E.E. Hemmings and R.A. Pick
1 – S.B. Hassan and sub.

BOWLING	K. Saxelby	R.A. Pick	K.P. Evans	C.E.B. Rice	E.E. Hemmings	P.M. Such	K.E. Cooper	R.J. Hadlee	J.D. Birch
(B.&H.) v. Gloucestershire (Bristol) 4 May	11–0–62–2	11–0–54–0	11–0–47–1	11–1–50–1	11–0–55–0				
(J.P.) v. Gloucestershire (Bristol) 5 May	8–0–35–0		8–0–68–1	8–0–49–1	8–1–41–2	8–0–50–2			
(B.&H.) v. Scotland (Glasgow) 11 May	11–1–51–0			11–2–30–1	11–3–22–2	11–1–50–3	11–3–31–2		
(B.&H.) v. Derbyshire (Trent Bridge) 16 May	8–5–6–2			5–0–19–1	10.4–1–31–2		11–3–30–4	8–1–15–1	5–0–36–0
(B.&H.) v. Northants. (Trent Br.) 18 & 20 May	3–0–15–0						1–1–0–0	4–0–14–1	
(J.P.) v. Leicestershire (Trent Bridge) 19 May									
(J.P.) v. Somerset (Trent Bridge) 26 May	8–2–28–2			2–0–14–0			2.5–0–31–0	8–1–28–1	
(J.P.) v. Sussex (Horsham) 2 June	8–1–32–1		8–0–46–1	8–0–40–1			8–1–34–1	8–2–36–2	
(J.P.) v. Kent (Trent Bridge) 16 June	8–1–44–1		3–0–33–1	7–0–37–0	6–0–30–2		8–1–41–1	8–0–31–2	
(T.T.) v. Yorkshire (Harrogate) 19 June	8.5–1–32–2			9–1–27–1	11–0–46–2		11–4–24–3		
(J.P.) v. Middlesex (Trent Bridge) 23 June			8–1–36–3	7.4–1–35–1			8–0–24–1	8–0–23–3	
(N.W.) v. Staffordshire (Trent Bridge) 3 July	12–2–19–3		12–4–24–1	6–0–22–0	12–4–37–2		11–3–24–1	5–3–9–1	
(J.P.) v. Glamorgan (Swansea) 7 July	8–0–40–3			8–0–48–0	8–0–40–0		8–0–41–0	8–1–27–2	
(J.P.) v. Warwickshire (Edgbaston) 14 July	8–0–27–2		4–0–30–2	8–1–33–0	8–2–25–1		4–0–26–0	8–1–30–2	
(N.W.) v. Warwickshire (Trent Br.) 17 July	8–3–14–1	12–3–41–1			12–2–27–3		11.3–1–49–4	8–1–26–0	
(J.P.) v. Surrey (Guildford) 21 July	8–0–46–1	8–0–42–2			8–1–29–2		8–0–58–1	8–0–33–2	
(J.P.) v. Yorkshire (Trent Bridge) 28 July	2–0–6–3	2–0–15–1			2–0–11–0		2–0–15–0	2–0–21–1	
(J.P.) v. Northants. (Northampton) 4 Aug.									
(N.W.) v. Gloucestershire (Bristol) 8 & 9 Aug.	12–2–34–2	12–0–49–1		6–0–49–0	6–0–41–0		12–2–40–2	12–1–42–2	
(J.P.) v. Worcestershire (Trent Br.) 11 Aug.	4–0–15–1	4–0–23–2		4–0–32–0			4–0–14–1	5–0–25–0	
(J.P.) v. Lancashire (Old Trafford) 18 Aug.	3–0–10–1	3.4–0–26–0		3–0–26–0			4–0–25–1	6–1–28–3	
(N.W.) v. Worcestershire (Worcester) 21 Aug.		12–2–46–2	1–0–6–0	11–0–61–1	12–2–37–0		12–2–43–0	12–2–35–2	
(J.P.) v. Derbyshire (Heanor) 25 August		7–1–34–1		6–0–30–0	1–0–12–0		8–0–30–1	7–1–30–0	
(Asda) v. Lancashire (Scarborough) 5 Sept.	10–3–30–1	6–0–28–0			6–0–35–0	10–1–21–0	10–4–25–3		
(N.W.) v. Essex (Lord's) 7 September	12–0–73–0	8–0–36–1		7–0–38–0	12–1–54–0		9–3–27–0	12–4–48–0	
(J.P.) v. Essex (Trent Bridge) 8 Sept.		8–0–62–1	2–0–25–0	8–0–51–2	6–0–32–0		8–0–38–0	8–0–35–0	
(J.P.) v. Hampshire (Trent Bridge) 15 Sept.		8–2–43–0		8–0–43–2	8–0–48–1		8–0–49–1	8–0–46–1	
Wickets	28	12	10	12	19	5	27	26	0

a T.A. Lloyd retired hurt

v. Gloucestershire (Bristol) 8 August (N.W.)	v. Worcestershire (Trent Bridge) 11 August (J.P.)	v. Lancashire (Old Trafford) 18 August (J.P.)	v. Worcestershire (Worcester) 21/22 Aug. (N.W.)	v. Derbyshire (Heanor) 25 August (J.P.)	v. Lancashire (Scarborough) 5 September (Asda)	v. Essex (Lord's) 7 September (N.W.)	v. Essex (Trent Bridge) 8 September (J.P.)	v. Hampshire (Trent Bridge) 15 September (J.P.)	Runs
58	28	1	4	14	19	64	14	28	726
90	5		139	38	22	80	45	18	970
12	22	2	9	11	4	66	22	4	507
35	24	13	25	15		12	37	29	527
24	0	4	1	37					431
		17			5				286
14	18*	27*	11*	4	16	—	19*	18	348
3	5	—	4*	16*	29*	—	1	35	189
6*	—	—			7	—			47
6*	4*	—	—	7*	0	—	11	8*	39
			—				12		121
					2*				2
—	—	—	—	—	21	—	0	8	33
6	25	39*	18	17		22	2	18	456
				7					32
									36
					12	20*	33	7	72
								20	20
2							4	4	
19	6	12	14	5	5	14	6	7	
10	2		4	4	2		2	2	
2			4	4	2	1		1	
287	139	115	233	179	146	279	208	207	
8	7	5	6	8	9	5	10	10	
W	W	L	W	L	L	L	L	L	
—	4	0	—	0	—	—	0	0	

C.D. Fraser-Darling	P. Johnson	D.W. Randall	Byes	Leg-byes	Wides	No-balls	Total	Wkts
			4	16	1	1	288	5
			1	5	1	2	249	6
				4	1		188	9
			3	3	10		143	10
					1	1	29	1
				Match Abandoned				
				5	2		106	3
				8	5	4	196	7
				8	2		224	9
10–0–37–1				3	2	3	169	10
8–0–45–1				8	5	1	171	10
	1–0–5–0	1–0–3–0		4	3	3	147	8
			1	2	7	1	199	7
			1	12	3		184	7
				8	3	2	165	9a
				3	2	1	211	8
			1	1	1		70	7
				Match Abandoned				
			2	20	4	2	277	9
				6		1	115	6
				6	2	1	121	5
				4	5	2	232	8
2–0–24–1		2–0–3–0–		9	5	1	180	3
		0.1–0–6–0		2		1	147	4
			1	3			280	2
			2	7	2		252	3
				14	3	1	243	5
3	0	0						

at Lord's

Middlesex 289 (C.T. Radley 57, C.A. Walsh 4 for 86) and 47 for 0
Gloucestershire 351 for 8 dec (B.F. Davison 111, A.W. Stovold 92, J.D. Carr 6 for 61)

Match drawn
Gloucestershire 7 pts, Middlesex 6 pts

at The Oval

Surrey 413 for 9 dec (M.A. Lynch 145, A. Needham 138, A.M. Ferreira 4 for 85)
Warwickshire 147 (P.A. Smith 50, G. Monkhouse 4 for 46) and 63 (R.J. Doughty 6 for 33)

Surrey won by an innings and 203 runs
Surrey 24 pts, Warwickshire 3 pts

Gordon Lord, a magnificent maiden first-class century for Warwickshire, 199 against Yorkshire at Edgbaston, 3 August. (David Munden)

ABOVE: *Jon Carr, a career best 6 for 61 in the top of the table clash, Middlesex v. Gloucestershire at Lord's. (Adrian Murrell)*

ABOVE: *Philip de Freitas forced his way into the Leicestershire side and held his place with some fine medium pace bowling. (David Munden)*

at Eastbourne

Sussex 227 for 6 dec (Imran Khan 89) and 243 for 5 dec (A.M. Green 78)
Kent 200 for 3 dec (S.G. Hinks 85, M.R. Benson 80) and 162 for 1 (S.G. Hinks 99 not out)

Match drawn
Kent 4 pts, Sussex 3 pts

at Bradford

Derbyshire 199 (P. Carrick 4 for 59) and 129 (P. Carrick 6 for 46, I.G. Swallow 4 for 53)
Yorkshire 352 (D.L. Bairstow 122 not out, K.J. Barnett 6 for 115)

Yorkshire won by an innings and 24 runs
Yorkshire 22 pts, Derbyshire 3 pts

Surrey moved into fourth place in the Britannic Assurance County Championship when they annihilated Warwickshire in two days at The Oval. Needham, who opened because Clinton had fractured his right hand in practice, hit a career best 138 and Monte Lynch, who also hit a career best, shared a fourth wicket stand of 164 in 36 overs with him. It was exhilarating batting and Surrey took total command before the close when, having declared at 413, they took the wickets of Lord and Dyer for 6. Next day, Warwickshire succumbed meakly, only Paul Smith offering spirited resistance. Richard Doughty, the fast medium bowler formerly of Gloucestershire, had career best bowling figures, emphasising his value to Surrey and the impact that he had made since coming into the side. Hoffman, at number eleven, was the only Warwickshire batsman to reach double figures in the second innings.

The top of the table affair at Lord's was a grim struggle and was washed out on the last day. Stovold and Davison batted dourly to give Gloucestershire the advantage, but young Carr had 6 for 61, a career best, with his spin which was about the brightest thing in the match.

Unenterprising cricket by Leicestershire, led by Peter Willey, cost them dearly at Grace Road. Clive Lloyd's spanking hundred had brought Lancashire to near parity on the first innings, but Willey chose to bat until tea on the last day and offered Lancashire no realistic challenge. Leicestershire batted drably and then asked the visitors to make 257 in 36 overs. The bowling of Taylor and the new fast bowler de Freitas nearly brought Leicestershire an undeserved victory as Lancashire, not for the first time in the season, collapsed.

LEFT: *Phil Carrick – a match-winning 10 for 105 for Yorkshire against Derbyshire at Bradford. (Adrian Murrell)*

There was more enterprise at Eastbourne where Barclay set Kent to make 271 in 68 overs. They strove manfully in dreadful weather before play was finally abandoned and Hinks was left on 99 not out. In the first innings he and Benson put on 132 for the first wicket.

Yorkshire's second win of the season sent them galloping up the table. Derbyshire succumbed, mainly to spin, on the opening day. At 142 for 5, Yorkshire looked as if they would fare little better, but David Bairstow hit his third unbeaten century of the summer and took his side to a commanding lead. Kim Barnett, who uses his leg-spin all too rarely, kept an immaculate length and returned a career best 6 for 115 although he was not always helped by the wicket-keeper who seemed as bemused as the batsmen by such bowling. Derbyshire batted wretchedly against the Yorkshire spinners on the last day to go down by an innings.

Fourth Cornhill Test Match
ENGLAND *v.* AUSTRALIA

Wood had not recovered sufficiently from the injury he sustained at Northampton and the ebullient Matthews took his place in the Australian side. England brought in Agnew

ABOVE RIGHT: *David Boon plays the ball to leg during his innings of 61, his highest Test score. (Adrian Murrell)*

MIDDLE: *Greg Matthews is bowled by Ian Botham offering no stroke. Emburey and Gooch react. (Adrian Murrell)*

BELOW RIGHT: *Allan Border's worst shot of the summer. He is stumped by Downton off Edmonds for 8. (Adrian Murrell)*

BELOW: *First blood to England. Wessels is taken at slip by Botham off Emburey. Downton looks on. (Adrian Murrell)*

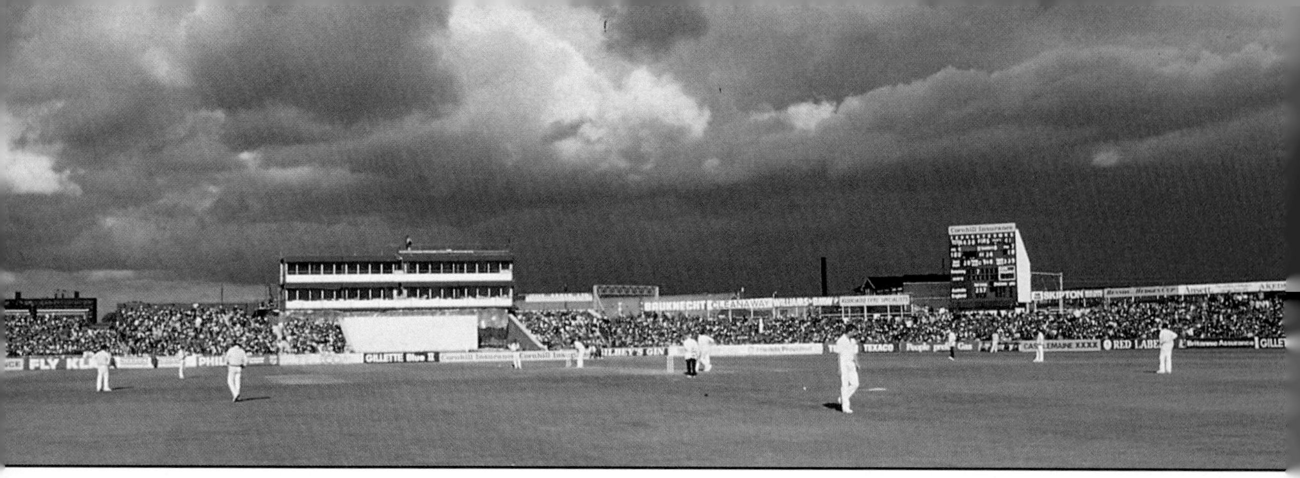

Rain clouds over Old Trafford. The blight in an enthralling series. (Adrian Murrell)

for the injured Sidebottom. Ellison was the player to stand down from the selected twelve.

Gower won the toss and asked Australia to bat on a pitch which, though damp, turned out to be nothing more demanding than a slow 'turner'. In the first session the England out-cricket was at its poorest, and after an hour, 12 overs, Australia were 57 for 0. The breakthrough came when Emburey was introduced into the attack. With a well flighted delivery he deceived Wessels who drove too soon and was taken at slip, but, 85 for 1 at lunch, Australia could be well content.

In the afternoon they began to fall apart. Hilditch pushed forward to Edmonds and Gower took a juggling catch at silly point. Border played his worst shot of the tour. He charged down the wicket at Edmonds, swung wildly and was stumped easily as he scrambled back inelegantly. In the same over Ritchie was uncertain whether to go forward or back and lofted a simple return catch. In 13 deliveries Edmonds had taken 3 for 6 and Australia were 122 for 4.

Boon had begun uncertainly, but now he produced some positive attacking shots and Phillips gave his usual accomplished display of crisp, clean hitting. They added 71, but Botham in an enlivened spell after tea, dismissed both of them. Phillips was caught behind cutting and Boon, having batted well for 191 minutes, was well taken at gully by Lamb. Lamb's brilliant fielding in any position was one of the finest features of English cricket in the season.

Matthews offered no shot and had his off stump knocked back, but O'Donnell profitted as England erred and hit 45 off 96 balls with a six and 3 fours before Edmonds returned to bowl him with his first delivery. Australia were all out in the last over of the first day for 257 and England could be well satisfied.

ABOVE: *Border ducks under a Botham bouncer as Australia save the game on the last day. (George Herringshaw)*

LEFT: *Mike Gatting cover drives during his magnificent innings of 160. Gatting's solidity gave the England batting a new dimension. (Adrian Murrell)*

McDermott's seventh and eighth wickets. He knocks back Edmonds' leg stump and uproots Allott's middle stump. (Ken Kelly)

The second day saw England move into a position of total supremacy. Robinson was well caught at slip early on, but Gooch and Gower added 121 and were threatening to tear the Australian attack to shreds when they fell in quick succession. Gooch was lbw after batting for $3\frac{1}{2}$ hours and Gower was splendidly caught just inside the boundary when he hooked at McDermott. Both Gower and Gooch benefitted from missed chances. Boon, at slip, dropped both of them and the chance offered by Gower when he was 4 was quite straightforward.

England closed at 233 for 3 and they were hampered in their progress when play could not begin until two o'clock on the Saturday. It was to end 40 minutes early, but England prospered in the time that was available. Gatting ran to his first Test century in England. He and Lamb added 156 before, in his one lax moment, Gatting drove to cover and

FOURTH CORNHILL TEST MATCH – ENGLAND *v.* AUSTRALIA
1, 2, 3, 5 and 6 August 1985 at Old Trafford, Manchester

AUSTRALIA

	FIRST INNINGS		SECOND INNINGS	
K.C. Wessels	c Botham, b Emburey	34	(3) c and b Emburey	50
A.M.J. Hilditch	c Gower, b Edmonds	49	(1) b Emburey	40
D.C. Boon	c Lamb, b Botham	61	(5) b Emburey	7
A.R. Border†	st Downton, b Edmonds	8	not out	146
G.M. Ritchie	c and b Edmonds	4	(6) b Emburey	31
W.B. Phillips*	c Downton, b Botham	36	(7) not out	39
G.R.J. Matthews	b Botham	4	(2) c and b Edmonds	17
S.P. O'Donnell	b Edmonds	45		
G.F. Lawson	c Downton, b Botham	4		
C.J. McDermott	lbw, b Emburey	0		
R.G. Holland	not out	5		
Extras	lb 3, w 1, nb 3	7	b 1, lb 6, nb 3	10
		257	(for 5 wkts)	340

	O	M	R	W	O	M	R	W
Botham	23	4	79	4	15	3	50	—
Agnew	14	—	65	—	9	2	34	—
Allott	13	1	29	—	6	2	4	—
Emburey	24	7	41	2	51	17	99	4
Edmonds	15.1	4	40	4	54	12	122	1
Gatting					4	—	14	—
Lamb					1	—	10	—

FALL OF WICKETS
1- 71, 2- 97, 3- 118, 4- 122, 5- 193, 6- 198, 7- 211, 8- 223, 9- 224
1- 38, 2- 85, 3- 126, 4- 138, 5- 213

ENGLAND

	FIRST INNINGS	
G.A. Gooch	lbw, b McDermott	74
R.T. Robinson	c Border, b McDermott	10
D.I. Gower†	c Hilditch, b McDermott	47
M.W. Gatting	c Phillips, b McDermott	160
A.J. Lamb	run out	67
I.T. Botham	c O'Donnell, b McDermott	20
P.R. Downton*	b McDermott	23
J.E. Emburey	not out	31
P.H. Edmonds	b McDermott	1
P.J.W. Allott	b McDermott	7
J.P. Agnew	not out	2
Extras	b 7, lb 16, nb 17	40
	(for 9 wkts dec)	482

	O	M	R	W
Lawson	37	7	114	—
McDermott	36	3	141	8
Holland	38	7	101	—
O'Donnell	21	6	82	—
Matthews	9	2	21	—

FALL OF WICKETS
1- 21, 2- 142, 3- 148, 4- 304, 5- 339, 6- 430, 7- 448, 8- 450, 9- 470

Umpires: H.D. Bird and D.R. Shepherd

Match drawn

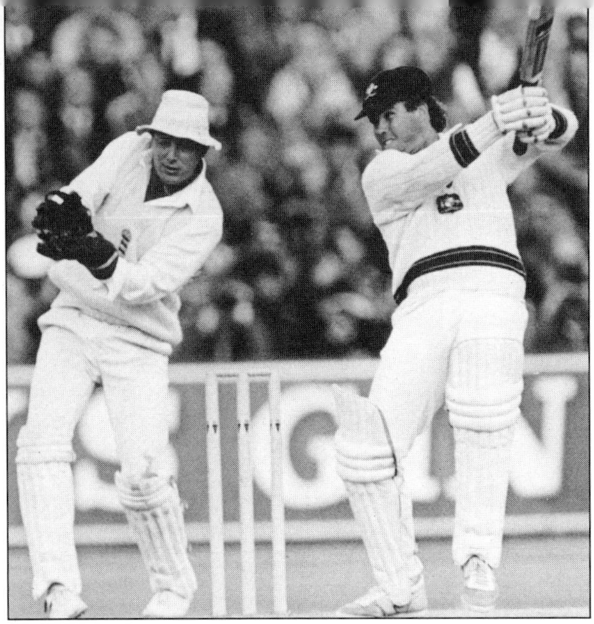

Greg Ritchie offers plucky resistance. (Adrian Murrell)

The game is saved. Border reaches his century. Gower and Emburey applaud. Wayne Phillips is the other batsman. (Ken Kelly)

called for a run which left Lamb with no hope of making his ground.

Botham was very well caught on the square-leg boundary after a few stinging blows and Gatting was caught behind swatting at McDermott. He had batted for 357 minutes,

Downton downcast after missing Border in the first over of the last day. (Adrian Murrell)

faced 266 balls and hit 21 fours. He exudes a sense of authority, and his assumption to Test standing in the last twelve months has transformed the England side.

England ended Saturday on 448 for 6 and were looking for quick runs on the Monday, but they were held back by McDermott who bowled Downton, Edmonds and Allott to finish with 8 for 141, an outstanding achievement on a wicket which gave him no assistance. It was a performance which was to win him the individual award for the match.

Australia were faced with the daunting task of scoring 225 to make England bat again. In simpler terms they had to survive for two days. Hilditch and Matthews, who opened in place of Wessels, survived until lunch. Indeed, Hilditch pulled the last ball before lunch for six, but in the first over after the break Matthews moved down the wicket to Edmonds and gave the bowler a hard return catch. Hilditch batted without apparent worries until, surprisingly, he missed a straight ball. Wessels reached an accomplished fifty and was then caught in two minds, and Boon charged down the wicket and was bowled. Border and Ritchie played out the rest of the day with fielders clustered round the bat. Australia closed at 192 for 4. Border was on 49 having been batting for three hours.

Rain restricted play to 50 overs on the last day and helped Australia to save the match, but eventually it was the tenacity of Border which kept the series level. Only 3 overs were possible before lunch and in the first of them, bowled by Botham, Border edged and could have been caught by Downton. It was a difficult chance, but Test keepers have to take difficult chances and Downton's continuing untidiness behind the stumps made it difficult to understand why he held sway before East, Parks or French.

Ritchie, after a stubborn innings, fell as Boon had done the previous day, but Phillips curbed his natural desire to attack and Border was now immovable. He batted for 346 minutes, faced 334 balls and hit 13 fours. Initially intent on unflinching defence, he only allowed himself his customary freedom when the game was safe.

3, 4 and 5 August

at Derby

Surrey 461 for 9 dec (D.M. Ward 143, A.R. Butcher 80, C.J. Richards 70, R.J. Doughty 65)
Derbyshire 186 (A.E. Warner 60, D.B. Pauline 5 for 52) and 195 (K.J. Barnett 69, G. Monkhouse 61, A.H. Gray 4 for 44)

Surrey won by an innings and 80 runs
Surrey 24 pts, Derbyshire 5 pts

at Chelmsford

Middlesex 234 (W.N. Slack 72, R.O. Butcher 61, J.K. Lever 5 for 53) and 70 for 2 dec
Essex 33 for 0 dec and 275 for 3 (K.S. McEwan 121, D.R. Pringle 69 not out)

Essex won by 7 wickets
Essex 20 pts, Middlesex 2 pts

at Bournemouth

Somerset 232 and 236 for 8 (J.G. Wyatt 100, M.D. Marshall 4 for 70)
Hampshire 346 for 2 dec (V.P. Terry 148 not out, C.D. Smith 102, C.G. Greenidge 70)

Match drawn
Hampshire 8 pts, Somerset 2 pts

at Northampton

Northamptonshire 301 for 3 dec (W. Larkins 140, G. Cook 79) and 179 for 1 dec (G. Cook 77 not out, W. Larkins 62)
Nottinghamshire 152 for 2 dec (B.C. Broad 57) and 247 for 5 (D.W. Randall 84, B.C. Broad 77, P. Johnson 61)

Match drawn
Northamptonshire 4 pts, Nottinghamshire 2 pts

at Edgbaston

Warwickshire 456 for 4 dec (G.J. Lord 199, D.L. Amiss 103 not out, A.I. Kallicharran 81)
Yorkshire 228 (P. Carrick 68 not out, G.C. Small 4 for 42) and 237 for 4 (G. Boycott 103 not out)

Match drawn
Warwickshire 8 pts, Yorkshire 3 pts

at Worcester

Lancashire 168 (P.J. Newport 4 for 35) and 165 (C.H. Lloyd 50 not out, N.V. Radford 4 for 70)
Worcestershire 264 (D.M. Smith 67, N.V. Radford 57 not out, I. Folley 4 for 39) and 70 for 3

Worcestershire won by 7 wickets
Worcestershire 23 pts, Lancashire 5 pts

at Swansea

Kent 251 for 7 dec (E.A.E. Baptiste 52) and 0 for 0 dec
Glamorgan 0 for 0 dec and 210 for 6 (R.C. Ontong 57)

Match drawn
Glamorgan 3 pts, Kent 3 pts

Surrey moved into third place in the championship with an innings victory at Derby, a victory which was illuminated by some positive cricket on the part of the visitors and two fine individual performances. When Jesty fell ill David Ward was called to Derby as replacement. Batting at number seven, he shared a seventh wicket partnership of 130 with Doughty and reached a magnificent maiden hundred in first-class cricket. He hit a six onto the pavilion roof and 21 fours. Derbyshire regretted their decision of having asked Surrey to bat as they struggled against a lively seam attack with the daunting prospect of having to score 312 to avoid the follow-on. Duncan Pauline returned a career best in the first innings and Gray, Doughty and Monkhouse were prominent in the second innings as Surrey swept to victory.

TOP: *Robin Smith – a thrilling century and the Man of the Match award as Hampshire overwhelmed Somerset at Taunton. (George Herringshaw)*

MIDDLE: *Ken McEwan led Essex to a thrilling victory over Middlesex at Chelmsford, 5 August, and completed a thousand runs for the season, a feat he has accomplished every season that he has played in England. (George Herringshaw)*

BOTTOM: *David Ward. Called late into the Surrey side for the game against Derbyshire on 3 August, he hit a brilliant maiden first-class hundred. (Adrian Murrell)*

Somerset C.C.C.
Limited-Over Matches – 1985

BATTING

BATTING	v. Minor Counties (Shrewsbury) 4 May (B.&H.)	v. Worcestershire (Worcester) 5 May (J.P.)	v. Glamorgan (Taunton) 12 May (J.P.)	v. Kent (Taunton) 14 May (B.&H.)	v. Hampshire (Southampton) 16 May (B.&H.)	v. Glamorgan (Taunton) 18 May (B.&H.)	v. Nottinghamshire (Trent Bridge) 26 May (J.P.)	v. Warwickshire (Taunton) 2 June (J.P.)	v. Gloucestershire (Bath) 9 June (J.P.)	v. Yorkshire (Bath) 16 June (J.P.)	v. Surrey (The Oval) 23 June (J.P.)	v. Buckinghamshire (Taunton) 3 July (N.W.)	v. Leicestershire (Taunton) 7 July (J.P.)	v. Middlesex (Lord's) 14 July (J.P.)	v. Yorkshire (Leeds) 17 & 18 July (N.W.)	v. Derbyshire (Derby) 21 July (J.P.)	v. Essex (Taunton) 28 July (J.P.)	v. Hampshire (Southampton) 4 August (J.P.)
P.M. Roebuck	36	—	74*	0	3	0					43	39	19	15	16	18	0	
J.G. Wyatt	2	—	13	22	8	7	—										4	
N.F.M. Popplewell	20	—	8	37	7	39	29	21	58	25	4	9	25	5	18	5	33	
B.C. Rose	18*	15*												53	1	24		
R.L. Ollis	13*	—	2	2	24	0	—	19	—	46								
I.T. Botham	—	28*	36	45	48	23	40*		7		29	—	6		37	34	58	
V.J. Marks	—	—	7	29	7	0	9*	1	0	25	26	—	7	35	4	20*	19	
T. Gard	—	—	—	1*	—	0*	—	2*	—		—	—	4	—	0*	—	11*	
G.V. Palmer	—	—	3	2	15*	3		21										
M.R. Davis	—	—	11	16	4	28	—	5	—	8	—	—	7		—	—	1	
M.S. Turner	—	—	8*	19	8*	15	—	4	7	5	—		2	—				
R.C.J. Scully			2															
R.J. Harden				7	13	11				1				0				
N.A. Felton							12	2	52	16	7	72*	4	22	25	15	3	
I.V.A. Richards							9	62	56	1	86	4	32	16	87*	51	5	
J. Garner							—	21*	16*	8	30	—			—	1	26	
R.E. Hayward								6	38*	8	10*	8*	2	5*				
S.J. Turner										8*								
C.H. Dredge												—	13*	—	—	—	3*	
J.C.M. Atkinson																		
Byes					1					1	1		2		4	2		
Leg-byes	3	1	6	5	15	10	5	16	8	8	10	1	5	4	13	5	5	
Wides	2	1	4	3	13	6	2	3	3	2	5	6	5	4	2	1	4	
No-balls				3	1	2			2	2	3			4	2		1	
Total	94	45	174	191	167	144	106	183	247	164	254	139	133	163	209	176	173	
Wickets	3	0	8	10	8	10	3	9	6	10	7	3	10	7	6	7	9	
Result	W	Ab.	L	L	L	L	W	L	W	L	W	W	L	Ab.	W	L	L	Ab.
Points	2	2	0	0	0	0	4	0	4	0	4	—	0	2	—	0	0	2

Catches

12 – T. Gard (ct 10/st 2)
9 – I.T. Botham
8 – M.R. Davis
7 – N.F.M. Popplewell (ct 5/st 2) and J. Garner
4 – N.A. Felton, C.H. Dredge and subs
3 – P.M. Roebuck, I.V.A. Richards and R.L. Ollis
2 – V.J. Marks and J.G. Wyatt
1 – B.C. Rose, G.V. Palmer, R.J. Harden and R.E. Hayward

BOWLING

BOWLING	M.R. Davis	I.T. Botham	G.V. Palmer	M.S. Turner	V.J. Marks	R.C.J. Sully	J. Garner	I.V.A. Richards	N.A. Felton
(B.&H.) v. Min. Cos. (Shrewsbury) 4 May	11–3–21–3	8.5–4–15–3	4–0–18–1	10–2–22–3	1–1–0–0				
(J.P.) v. Worcestershire (Worcester) 5 May	2–0–12–2	2–0–5–1	2–0–20–1	2–0–20–1	2–0–15–0				
(J.P.) v. Glamorgan (Taunton) 12 May	8–0–47–1	8–1–19–2	6–0–33–2	8–0–34–1	8–0–16–1	2–0–15–0			
(B.&H.) v. Kent (Taunton) 14 May	11–0–84–2	11–1–62–0	11–1–56–2	11–2–42–0	11–1–46–0				
(B.&H.) v. Hants. (Southampton) 16 May	10–2–35–2	11–3–27–0	7–0–29–1	9.5–0–53–0	9–2–20–0				
(B.&H.) v. Glamorgan (Taunton) 18 May	10–0–43–1	11–1–43–2	11–0–58–0	11–0–39–1	11–1–47–1				
(J.P.) v. Notts. (Trent Bridge) 26 May	3–0–19–0	6–0–21–0		4–1–11–0	3–0–5–0		7–0–33–2	3–0–6–2	
(J.P.) v. Warwickshire (Taunton) 2 June	8–0–41–0		2.5–0–19–0	6–0–39–0	8–0–36–0		8–1–22–1	5–0–26–0	
(J.P.) v. Gloucestershire (Bath) 9 June	8–0–32–1	6–0–28–3		8–1–36–3	8–0–28–2		5–0–21–0	2–0–10–0	
(J.P.) v. Yorkshire (Bath) 16 June	8–0–52–0			8–0–46–0	8–1–44–1		8–1–27–5	8–0–35–0	
(J.P.) v. Surrey (The Oval) 23 June	8–0–26–2	4–0–39–0		4–0–25–0	8–1–22–0		8–0–26–1	7–0–39–4	1–0–7–0
(N.W.) v. Bucks (Taunton) 3 July	9–1–31–1	8–0–21–0			12–2–32–1		8.4–2–18–5	2–0–7–1	
(J.P.) v. Leicestershire (Taunton) 7 July	8–1–28–0	8–0–37–1		5–0–34–1	8–1–21–3			4–0–19–0	
(J.P.) v. Middlesex (Lord's) 14 July									
(N.W.) v. Yorkshire (Leeds) 17 July	5–0–24–0	11–0–42–1			12–3–30–3		12–2–34–0	12–0–36–1	
(J.P.) v. Derbyshire (Derby) 21 July	6–0–29–0	5.5–0–31–3			7–1–41–1		7–2–26–1	5–0–20–0	
(J.P.) v. Essex (Taunton) 28 July	5–0–19–1	7–0–35–2			7–0–34–1		8–1–26–0	6.2–2–30–1	
(J.P.) v. Hants. (Southampton) 4 August									
(N.W.) v. Hampshire (Taunton) 7 August	12–2–57–1	12–2–57–0			3–0–20–0		12–1–50–0	9–0–49–1	
(J.P.) v. Northants. (Weston-s-Mare) 11 Aug.									
(J.P.) v. Lancashire (Old Trafford) 25 August									
(J.P.) v. Sussex (Taunton) 1 September			8–0–22–1		8–1–41–1		8–2–28–2	8–0–46–1	
(J.P.) v. Kent (Canterbury) 15 September	8–0–24–0		8–0–34–5		8–0–27–0		8–2–20–1		
Wickets	17	18	13	10	15	0	18	11	0

v. Hampshire (Taunton) 7 & 8 August (N.W.)	v. Northamptonshire (Weston-s-Mare) 11 August (J.P.)	v. Lancashire (Old Trafford) 25 August (J.P.)	v. Sussex (Taunton) 1 September (J.P.)	v. Kent (Canterbury) 15 September (J.P.)	Runs
6			34	16	319
3			0	2	61
2			74*		419
				1	112
					106
64					455
26			—	39	254
7			—	—	25
			—	8*	52
6				—	86
					68
					2
			—	20	52
9				47	286
16			66*		491
0			—	3	105
					77
					8
0*			—	1*	17
			—		—
5					
			10	6	
2			4	1	
4					
150			188	144	
10			2	7	
L	Ab.	Ab.	W	W	
—	2	2	4	4	

C.H. Dredge	Byes	Leg-byes	Wides	No-balls	Total	Wkts
	1	16	8	2	93	10
		3			75	7
	4	7	5		175	8
		3	3	7	293	6
		5	6		169	3
		7	10	1	237	10
	1	4	1	1	100	4
		4	1	1	187	3
	3	6	2		164	10
		11	1	1	215	7
		9	3		193	8
8–2–20–2	3	6	7	2	138	10
7–1–28–1		9	8	2	176	6
	Match Abandoned					
8–0–28–3	5	9	5	7	208	8
2–0–22–0	2	6	3	1	177	6
5–0–17–0		13	4	2	174	5
	Match Abandoned					
12–2–54–2	3	9	7	10	299	5
	Match Abandoned					
	Match Abandoned					
8–0–39–2	3	5	5	3	184	7
8–0–30–1	1	7	1	1	143	8
11						

Another side forced to follow-on were Yorkshire, but rain and Boycott's hundredth century for Yorkshire thwarted Warwickshire. On the Saturday, Gordon Lord, the left-handed opening batsman, hit a maiden first-class hundred. He and Kallicharran put on 206 for the second wicket and he and Amiss, who reached his ninety-sixth century, added 100 for the third. Lord was run out going for his two hundredth run. He hit 4 sixes and 29 fours in a most impressive and pugnacious display.

Endeavours and arrangements by the captains could salvage nothing from the rain-ruin at Swansea, but Radley and Fletcher came to an agreement at Chelmsford which saw Essex score an exciting, but easy, victory. Rain ended play early on the Saturday and limited it severely on the Monday. Middlesex reached 189 for 3 and then, mainly through lack of experience and good medium pace bowling, fell apart. Eventually invited to make 272 in 83 overs, Essex lost Hardie retired hurt after being hit on the helmet and Gladwin caught at the wicket. Prichard played fluently in a stand of 68, but it was McEwan and Pringle in a stand of 131 who took Essex to the brink of victory which came with 17 overs to spare. McEwan reached his first championship hundred of the season and also completed a thousand runs.

Wayne Larkins was in grand form at Northampton, but rain dashed all hopes of a result as Notts chased 329 in 71 overs. Hampshire were denied by Julian Wyatt's first championship hundred after looking set for victory at Bournemouth. Tremlett and Connor disposed of Somerset on the Saturday although the visitors recovered well from 99 for 6. On the Monday Terry and Greenidge took their opening stand to 132, and Terry and Chris Smith added 185 for the second wicket. Smith played yet another fine innings. He hit 5 sixes, one of which brought up his hundred, and 11 fours, and emphasised that he is a far better player than when he played for England two years ago. Terry was more sedate but hit 3 sixes and 14 fours. The Somerset out-cricket was pretty dreadful. The visitors lost Popplewell before the close and seemed set for defeat, but Wyatt's patience saved them and once again Hampshire were frustrated.

With Neal Radford determined to show Lancashire their error in releasing him, Worcestershire won with ease at New Road. Radford's hitting took his side to a comfortable first innings lead and then he took three quick wickets, being denied a hat-trick only because Makinson was dropped. The main consolation for Lancashire was in the bowling of Murphy, a medium-pacer from Cheshire, who was playing his second county game.

John Player Special League

4 August

at Derby

Derbyshire 25 for 1
***v.* Surrey**

Match abandoned
Derbyshire 2 pts, Surrey 2 pts

at Chelmsford

Essex *v.* Middlesex

Match abandoned
Essex 2 pts, Middlesex 2 pts

Surrey C.C.C.
Limited-Over Matches – 1985

Batting	v. Combined Univ. (The Oval) 4 May (B.&H.)	v. Warwickshire (The Oval) 5 May (J.P.)	v. Sussex (Hove) 11 May (B.&H.)		v. Essex (The Oval) 14 & 15 May (B.&H.)	v. Middlesex (Lord's) 18 May (B.&H.)	v. Hampshire (Southampton) 19 May (J.P.)	v. Essex (The Oval) 26 May (J.P.)	v. Worcestershire (Worcester) 16 June (J.P.)	v. Somerset (The Oval) 23 June (J.P.)	v. Leicestershire (Leicester) 30 June (J.P.)	v. Kent (Canterbury) 3 July (N.W.)	v. Kent (The Oval) 7 July (J.P.)	v. Yorkshire (Bradford) 14 July (J.P.)	v. Nottinghamshire (Guildford) 21 July (J.P.)	v. Derbyshire (Derby) 4 August (J.P.)	v. Middlesex (Lord's) 18 August (J.P.)	v. Northamptonshire (Guildford) 25 August (J.P.)
A.R. Butcher	1	72	24	67	13	56	8		4	12	1	18	52	11	46	—	20*	9
G.S. Clinton	63	34	5	67	4	106*	4	—	6	29	28	146		12	72		12*	13
D.B. Pauline	69*	1*	1	—	8		14	—	5	5*	10*	5	19			—	—	3
M.A. Lynch	11	43	9	—	7	6	15	—	52	58	14	31	12	136	9	—	—	55
A. Needham	8*	—				—	21		2	15	0	26	43*	23	52*	—	—	51
T.E. Jesty	—	2	61	4*	69*	27	16	—	21	8	12	1	2	18	0		—	
D.J. Thomas	—	22	7	—	4	6*	30	—	26	34		5		20		—		
C.J. Richards	—	14*	1	—	3	—	19*	—	10	10*	4	9*	3	14*	18			
G. Monkhouse	—	—	24*	—	5	—	5	—						—	5	—		
P.I. Pocock	—	—	14	—	0	—	1*	—	—		—	—	6*	—	2			
N.S. Taylor	—		2		0						—							
A.J. Stewart		86	1	22*	16	12	17	—		2	25	37			0	—	—	11
C.K. Bullen				—									10					9
P.A. Waterman						—							8		—	—		0*
D.M. Ward								—	42*	8			16	19*		—	—	9
A.H. Gray								—	—	—	2*	—	1	—	1*	—	—	
K.T. Medlycott																—		
M.A. Feltham																	—	31
R.J. Doughty																	—	10
N.J. Falkner																		
Byes		7							2		1			1				
Leg-byes	11	12	18	7	4	9	8		14	9	3	8	6	4	3			9
Wides	3	11	2	1	6	1	2		9	3	1	6	7	3	2		1	2
No-balls	1		1	5		4						1		1	1		1	1
Total	167	304	170	173	139	227	160		193	193	101	293	185	262	211		34	213
Wickets	3	6	10	2	10	4	9		8	8	7	8	9	6	8		0	10
Results	W	W	L	W	L	W	L	Ab.	L	L	L	L	L	L	L	Ab.	Ab.	L
Points	2	4	0	4	0	2	0	2	0	0	0	—	0	0	0	2	2	0

Catches

15 – C.J. Richards (ct 12/st 3)
10 – M.A. Lynch
9 – G.S. Clinton and T.E. Jesty
8 – A.J. Stewart (ct 7/st 1)
5 – D.B. Pauline
4 – A.R. Butcher
3 – D.J. Thomas
2 – A. Needham, G. Monkhouse and P.A. Waterman
1 – N.S. Taylor, D.M. Ward and R.J. Doughty

BOWLING	D.J. Thomas	N.S. Taylor	G. Monkhouse	D.B. Pauline	T.E. Jesty	P.I. Pocock	M.A. Feltham	A.R. Butcher	P.A. Waterman
(B.&H.) v. Combined Univ. (The Oval) 4 May	8–2–14–0	5–2–16–0	11–0–47–3	10–2–28–2	11–0–23–4	10–3–23–0			
(J.P.) v. Warwickshire (The Oval) 5 May	8–0–54–1		8–0–53–2	8–0–71–2	9–0–50–2	8–0–54–1			
(B.&H.) v. Sussex (Hove) 11 May	10–2–34–2	8–1–30–1	10–1–30–2	5–2–13–1	10–1–30–1	11–2–31–0			
(J.P.) v. Sussex (Hove) 12 May	8–0–22–2		8–0–58–1	8–0–40–1	2–0–10–0	8–0–25–1			
(B.&H.) v. Essex (The Oval) 14 & 15 May	11–3–28–0	5.4–0–38–0	4–0–19–0	6–0–40–0		6–1–12–1		2–1–2–0	
(B.&H.) v. Middlesex (Lord's) 18 May	10–1–37–0		10.2–0–54–1		6–0–24–1	10–0–36–3		11–1–36–4	6–0–27–0
(J.P.) v. Hampshire (Southampton) 19 May	7–0–49–1		8–0–44–3	8–0–33–0		7–0–42–2		8–0–35–1	
(J.P.) v. Essex (The Oval) 26 May	4–0–14–0		4–0–18–0	1–0–5–0		0.2–0–0–1			
(J.P.) v. Worcestershire (Worcester) 16 June	7–0–25–1			4–0–24–0	4–0–26–0	7–0–43–0		5–0–14–0	
(J.P.) v. Somerset (The Oval) 23 June	8–0–34–1			8–0–36–2	8–0–51–0			5–0–39–0	
(J.P.) v. Leicestershire (Leicester) 30 June		8–0–47–1		8–0–43–2	8–1–38–1	8–0–44–0			
(N.W.) v.Kent (Canterbury) 3 July	10–0–56–0			7–0–29–0	7–2–17–0	8–0–35–0		4–0–26–0	
(J.P.) v. Kent (The Oval) 7 July				8–1–34–0	8–0–57–2	8–0–52–2			8–0–35–0
(J.P.) v. Yorkshire (Bradford) 14 July	7–0–47–3		7–0–52–1		7–0–44–1	7–0–73–0			
(J.P.) v. Notts (Guildford) 21 July			8–0–25–1		8–0–46–1	8–0–42–0			8–0–44–1
(J.P.) v. Derbyshire (Derby) 4 August			1.2–0–7–1						2–0–17–0
(J.P.) v. Middlesex (Lord's) 18 August				8–0–36–0	0.2–0–0–1		8–0–45–1	8–0–22–4	
(J.P.) v. Northants. (Guildford) 25 August				8–0–53–1			8–0–72–1	4–0–45–0	8–1–46–0
(J.P.) v. Glamorgan (Cardiff) 1 Sept.	3–1–14–0			7–0–24–2	4–0–16–1	8–1–24–2		7–1–26–2	
(J.P.) v. Lancashire (The Oval) 8 Sept.			5–0–12–0	8–0–34–3	8–0–30–0	5–0–23–2	8–2–23–1		
(J.P.) v. Gloucestershire (The Oval) 15 Sept.			5–1–18–0		6–0–32–0	8–0–44–1	6–0–30–1		8–0–54–0
Wickets	11	2	15	16	15	16	4	11	1

a C.K. Bullen 6–0–35–0

v. Glamorgan (Cardiff) 1 September (J.P.)	v. Lancashire (The Oval) 8 September (J.P.)	v. Gloucestershire (The Oval) 15 September (J.P.)	Runs
81*			495
25*	40*		666
—	—		140
—	24	2	484
	9		250
—	14*	32	287
—			154
—	—	21	126
	—	0	39
—	—	3	26
			2
—	71*	0	300
			19
		0*	8
		5	99
—			4
			—
	—	23	54
—	—	0	10
		44	44
	3	5	
1	3	6	
1			
108	164	141	
0	2	10	
W	W	L	
4	4	0	

A.H. Gray	A. Needham	R.J. Doughty	Byes	Leg-byes	Wides	No-balls	Total	Wkts
			6	9	4	2	166	9
			3	15	5	1	300	9
			2	4	4	2	174	7
			2	2	4	1	194	6a
				1	3	1	140	1
			4	1	6	1	219	10
				5	10		208	7
8–0–26–2					2	2	63	3
7.1–0–34–0	4–0–18–1		8	5	5		197	2
8–0–30–2	3–0–53–1		1	10	5	3	254	7
8–0–36–1			2	6	7	2	216	6
11–0–66–2	11–0–55–2		4	8	8	5	296	4
8–0–31–3				13	10	1	222	7
7.5–0–39–0			1	7	3		263	8
8–0–50–2				16	3	3	223	7
				1			25	1
8–1–22–3		5–0–39–0	2	13	12	1	179	10
	4–0–33–0	8–0–46–0	4	7	3		306	2
7–0–34–2				8	15		146	9
		6–0–30–1	1	7	6	1	160	8
		7–0–42–0	1	6	2	1	227	2
17	4	1						

at Southampton

Hampshire *v.* Somerset

Match abandoned
Hampshire 2 pts, Somerset 2 pts

at Northampton

Northamptonshire *v.* Nottinghamshire

Match abandoned
Northamptonshire 2 pts, Nottinghamshire 2 pts

at Edgbaston

Warwickshire *v.* Yorkshire

Match abandoned
Warwickshire 2 pts, Yorkshire 2 pts

at Worcester

Worcestershire *v.* Lancashire

Match abandoned
Worcestershire 2 pts, Lancashire 2 pts

There was much rain.

NatWest Trophy – Quarter Finals

7 and 8 August

at Chelmsford

Kent 172 (N.R. Taylor 51)
Essex 174 for 4 (R.M. Ellison 4 for 34)

Essex won by 6 wickets
(*Man of the Match* – R.M. Ellison)

at Taunton

Hampshire 299 for 5 (R.A. Smith 110, V.P. Terry 105)
Somerset 150 (I.T. Botham 64)

Hampshire won by 149 runs
(*Man of the Match* – R.A. Smith)

at Swansea

Glamorgan 188 (H. Morris 75, R.C. Ontong 55, J.D. Inchmore 5 for 25)
Worcestershire 192 for 6 (D.M. Smith 97, D.N. Patel 54)

Worcestershire won by 4 wickets
(*Man of the Match* – J.D. Inchmore)

8 and 9 August

at Bristol

Nottinghamshire 287 for 8 (R.T. Robinson 90, B.C. Broad 58)
Gloucestershire 277 for 9 (P. Bainbridge 55, I.R. Payne 53)

Nottinghamshire won by 10 runs
(*Man of the Match* – R.T. Robinson)

It was difficult to understand why Chris Cowdrey elected to bat when he won the toss on a cloudy morning at Chelmsford. Lever quickly made him regret it when he bowled Hinks with only 5 scored. It had taken Kent 3.4 overs to open their score and they never threatened to accelerate sufficiently to put themselves in a strong enough position to win. Benson was bowled by Gooch and Tavare taken at third man by Pringle when he drove extravagantly at Turner. Cowdrey was caught behind and Baptiste went the same way first ball. Rain punctuated the play and in one session Kent came out for three overs during which they lost a wicket and gained

Sussex C.C.C.
Limited-Over Matches – 1985

BATTING

BATTING	v. Essex (Chelmsford) 4 & 6 May (B.&H.)	v. Essex (Chelmsford) 5 May (J.P.)	v. Surrey (Hove) 11 May (B.&H.)	v. Surrey (Hove) 12 May (J.P.)	v. Middlesex (Hove) 14 & 15 May (B.&H.)	v. C'bined Universities (Oxford) 16 May (B.&H.)	v. Middlesex (Lord's) 26 May (J.P.)	v. Nottinghamshire (Horsham) 2 June (J.P.)	v. Yorkshire (Sheffield) 9 June (J.P.)	v. Hampshire (Hove) 16 June (J.P.)	v. Gloucestershire (Swindon) 23 June (J.P.)	v. Lancashire (Hastings) 30 June (J.P.)	v. Ireland (Hove) 3 July (N.W.)	v. Warwickshire (Hove) 7 July (J.P.)	v. Glamorgan (Cardiff) 17 July (N.W.)	v. Northamptonshire (Northampton) 21 July (J.P.)	v. Worcestershire (Eastbourne) 28 July (J.P.)	v. Kent (Canterbury) 11 August (J.P.)
G.D. Mendis	14	78*	42	70	15	0	—	2	1	11	60*	19	3	11	28	32	18	
A.M. Green	38	45	2	36	9	10		11	51	43	5	70	6	29	1	3		
P.W.G. Parker	4	12*	0	20	48	48	23	8	25	4	55*	22	109	1	7	85	53	
A.P. Wells	21	—	62	20	38	49	42	27	57*	25	—	0*	4*	2*	6	47	7*	
C.M. Wells	1	—	19	11	55	10	—	47*	27	42*	—	35*	76	53	35	8	13	
J.R.T. Barclay	29*	—	20*	—	0	—			—	—	—	—		—	0	—	—	
I.A. Greig	0	—	1	1	31	0	—	12	7	—	—	—	8	7*	1		0*	
I.J. Gould	13	—	2*	9*	3*	18*	1*	1	10*	—				11	23*	17*	—	
G.S. Le Roux	0	—	—	18*	21	5				—	—	—	0*	—	0	1*	—	
D.A. Reeve	0	—	—		3		—	0*	—							—	—	
A.N. Jones	4	—		—			—											
Imran Khan			14		10	82*	17*	71	13	104*	—	80	38	83	28	0	71	
I.C. Waring				—				—										
C.E. Waller						—							—					
A.C.S. Pigott							—	—	—	—	—	—	—	—	—	—	—	—
C.P. Phillipson							—											
P. Moores											—	—	—					
N.J. Lenham																		
Byes			2	2	2		1						5				1	
Leg-byes	12	12	4	2	6	6	1	8	2	7	5	5	8	9	2	7	3	
Wides	4		4	4	1	7		5	1	1	3		16		1	10	2	
No-balls	3	3	2	1	7	6	2	4	3	1		3	10	3	4		1	
Total	143	150	174	194	249	241	87	196	197	238	128	234	283	209	136	210	169	
Wickets	10	1	7	6	10	7	2	7	6	4	1	4	6	6	10	6	4	
Results	L	W	W	L	L	W	L	L	W	L	W	W	W	W	L	W	W	Ab.
Points	0	4	2	0	0	2	0	0	4	0	4	4	—	4	—	4	4	2

Catches 18 – I.J. Gould (ct 16/st 2)
10 – C.M. Wells
8 – A.P. Wells
7 – G.D. Mendis and P.W.G. Parker
6 – J.R.T. Barclay
4 – A.C.S. Pigott and P. Moores
3 – Imran Khan
2 – T.A. Greig and D.A. Reeve
1 – C.P. Phillipson, A.M. Green, G.S. le Roux and A.N. Jones

BOWLING

BOWLING	C.M. Wells	G.S. Le Roux	I.A. Greig	D.A. Reeve	A.N. Jones	J.R.T. Barclay	Imran Khan	A.C. Waring	C.E. Waller
(B.&H.) *v.* Essex (Chelmsford) 4 & 6 May	2-0-16-0	11-2-39-3	11-3-29-2	6-2-22-0	3.2-0-22-0	6-1-15-0			
(J.P.) *v.* Essex (Chelmsford) 5 May	8-0-24-1	8-3-16-2	8-1-26-4	7.4-0-35-1	7-0-40-1				
(B. &H.) *v.* Surrey (Hove) 11 May	11-5-13-2	11-0-40-4	9.3-1-31-1	10-3-44-0			11-2-24-3		
(J.P.) *v.* Surrey (Hove) 12 May	6-0-21-0	6-0-30-0	7-0-45-0		4.2-0-25-1	4-0-24-1		4-0-21-0	
(B.&H.) *v.* Middlesex (Hove) 14&15 May	11-0-49-1	11-1-49-2	11-0-58-1	11-0-56-0			11-3-48-0		
(B.&H.) *v.* Combined Univ. (Oxford) 16 May	9-2-20-0	8-2-12-0	3-0-11-2			10-0-31-1	11-3-16-1		11-4-21-1
(J.P.) *v.* Middlesex (Lord's) 26 May	1.4-0-17-0		2-0-20-0	2-0-19-0			2-0-10-1		
(J.P.) *v.* Notts. (Horsham) 2 June	8-0-32-1		2-0-13-0	8-0-32-4			8-1-28-0	7-0-37-0	
(J.P.) *v.* Yorkshire (Sheffield) 9 June	8-2-17-0		4-0-30-0	8-0-41-0		2-0-15-2	8-1-15-4		
(J.P.) *v.* Hampshire (Hove) 16 June	8-0-41-0	8-1-41-0	3.5-0-29-0			3-0-27-0	8-0-34-0		
(J.P.) *v.* Glos. (Swindon) 23 June	8-0-21-0	8-0-39-2	8-1-18-0				8-2-11-3		
(J.P.) *v.* Lancashire (Hastings) 30 June	8-0-47-0	5-1-9-2	8-0-29-1			2-0-20-0	8-2-14-2		
(N.W.) *v.* Ireland (Hove) 3 July		7-4-7-5	5-1-13-0				8-3-13-1		1-1-0-1
(J.P.) *v.* Warwickshire (Hove) 7 July	8-1-16-1	6.5-0-39-1	7-0-48-2			1-0-2-1	8-1-29-2		
(N.W.) *v.* Glamorgan (Cardiff) 17 July	10-2-21-1	10.5-0-38-1	4-0-17-0				12-2-21-1		
(J.P.) *v.* Northants. (Northampton) 21 July	8-0-31-3	8-0-25-2		8-0-24-0		1-0-9-1	8-0-44-0		
(J.P.) *v.* Worcs. (Eastbourne) 28 July	5-0-16-2	4-0-17-0	1-0-2-0	5-0-26-3		1-0-15-1	5-0-15-0		
(J.P.) *v.* Kent (Canterbury) 11 August									
(J.P.) *v.* Derbyshire (Hove) 18 August	7-0-24-1	8-0-27-3	2-0-10-0	8-1-28-2			7.2-2-28-3		
(J.P.) *v.* Somerset (Taunton) 1 Sept.	8-2-21-0	6.4-0-59-0	2-0-10-0		8-1-25-0	1-0-26-0	7-0-37-1		
(J.P.) *v.* Leicestershire (Hove) 8 Sept.	8-0-29-1	8-0-38-0		8-0-31-1	8-0-33-3		8-0-37-4		
(J.P.) *v.* Glamorgan (Cardiff) 15 Sept.	8-3-18-2			8-0-26-3	8-1-32-5	6-1-24-0	7-2-18-0		
Wickets	16	27	13	14	10	7	26	0	2

v. Derbyshire (Hove) 18 August (J.P.)	v. Somerset (Taunton) 1 September (J.P.)	v. Leicestershire (Hove) 8 September (J.P.)	v. Glamorgan (Cardiff) 15 September (J.P.)	Runs
15	3	19	21	462
		7	22	388
				524
18	1	16	—	442
16	46	0	0*	494
7*	—	4*	—	60
13	6	39	3	129
11	9	28	34	190
8	30	31	54	138
—		19	—	22
	—	1*	—	5
31	67	11	66*	786
				—
				—
—				0
15*	5*			20
				—
	1*			1
1	3		5	
13	5	6	7	
7	5	1	2	
1	3	4		
156	184	186	214	
7	7	9	5	
W	L	W	W	
4	0	4	4	

A.M. Green	A.C.S. Pigott	A.P. Wells	*Byes*	*Leg-byes*	*Wides*	*No-balls*	*Total*	*Wkts*
				1	1	7	144	5
			1	6	1		148	10
				18	2	1	170	10
				7	1	5	173	2
				20	4	5	280	5
3–1–22–0					1		133	5
	2–0–17–2			5	3		88	3
	7–0–45–2		1	9	2		197	8
	6.5–0–28–4			15	3	1	161	10
	8–0–46–1		4	17		4	239	1
	5–0–30–0		2	5	2	2	126	5
	8–0–31–2	1–0–5–0		10	7		165	7
	5.4–2–4–3			2	2		39	10
	8–1–38–2		3	14	7	2	189	10
	12–1–37–2		1	5	1	2	140	6
	7–0–58–2			17	4		208	9
	2–0–25–0			8	7	1	124	6
			Match Abandoned					
	1–0–13–0			6	1	3	136	10
				10	4		188	2
			1	10	3	1	179	9
			3				121	10
0	20	0						

only a wide. It was generally grim batting. Taylor alone produced a substantial innings, but he was brilliantly run out by David East who scurried down the leg side to collect a ball off the pads and hit the stumps with his left-handed throw. Knott and Dilley batted well, but Dilley was magnificently caught at extra cover by Prichard, one-handed as he ran backwards. Underwood played some lusty shots, but the Essex out-cricket was of a very high quality and Kent never escaped from its shackles. Essex had only one over before bad light ended play and the next morning, Gooch and Prichard put on 87 for the second wicket and made winning look a formality. There was a sensation before lunch when Ellison dismissed Gooch, McEwan and Prichard in one over and Kent hoped, but Fletcher, who was missed at slip, and Pringle ended further speculation and Essex ran out easy winners.

Hampshire gave a glorious exhibition on the opening day at Taunton. They lost Greenidge, Chris Smith and Nicholas for 51 and seemed in all sorts of trouble, but the robust play of Robin Smith and the calm authority of Paul Terry brought 144 runs in 25 overs. Smith continued to dominate after Terry had been caught and bowled by Dredge and Somerset faced a most difficult task. When play ended prematurely, and controversially, due to a sinking sun causing reflections detrimental to the batsmen, Somerset, 43 for 5, were already beaten. Botham tried to prove otherwise the following morning, but no-one else had his faith.

Glamorgan, without Thomas and Javed, were put in to bat and reduced to 51 for 4 in the 24 overs that were possible on the Wednesday. Younis fell early to Inchmore the next morning, but Ontong joined Morris in a brave stand that added 102. Morris was particularly impressive, symbolic of the resurgence of cricket in Glamorgan, but 189 was not too daunting a target for Worcestershire. Barwick bowled Curtis for 0 and d'Oliveira went at 38, but David Smith and Dipak Patel added 107 and when Patel hooked Barwick into the hands of Younis at long leg only 44 were needed off 20 overs. In fact, three more wickets fell, including that of the splendidly upright Smith.

No play was possible on the Wednesday at Bristol and Robinson and Broad laid the foundation for a massive score by Notts when they began with a stand of 146. Solid batting followed and Gloucestershire faced a great struggle. They battled very bravely indeed through the middle order of Bainbridge, Curran and Payne, and by a vigorous stand of 77 in 11 overs between Davison and Bainbridge after they had been 70 for 3 after 27 overs. In 13 overs, Payne and Curran added 91, but Hadlee stemmed the flood and the home side fell just short of their target.

8 August

at Downpatrick

Australians 151 for 4 (A.R. Border 91)
***v.* Ireland**

Match abandoned

at Jesmond

England 258 for 6 (M.W. Gatting 127 not out, A.J. Lamb 60)
Rest of the World 254 for 6 (Mudassar Nazar 67, A.I. Kallicharran 56, D.W. Hookes 56, P.J.W. Allott 4 for 35)

England won by 4 wickets

Warwickshire C.C.C.
Limited-Over Matches – 1985

BATTING	*v.* Worcestershire (Worcester) 4 May (B.&H.)	*v.* Surrey (The Oval) 5 May (J.P.)	*v.* Lancashire (Edgbaston) 11 May (B.&H.)	*v.* Lancashire (Edgbaston) 12 May (J.P.)	*v.* Yorkshire (Leeds) 16 May (B.&H.)	*v.* Leicestershire (Edgbaston) 18&20 May (B.&H.)	*v.* Somerset (Taunton) 2 June (J.P.)	*v.* Hampshire (Edgbaston) 9 June (J.P.)	*v.* Gloucestershire (Harrogate) 20 June (T.T.)	*v.* Northamptonshire (Edgbaston) 30 June (J.P.)	*v.* Devon (Edgbaston) 3 July (N.W.)	*v.* Sussex (Hove) 7 July (J.P.)	*v.* Nottinghamshire (Edgbaston) 14 July (J.P.)	*v.* Nottinghamshire (Trent Bridge) 17 July (N.W.)	*v.* Leicestershire (Leicester) 21 July (J.P.)	*v.* Derbyshire (Edgbaston) 28 July (J.P.)	*v.* Yorkshire (Edgbaston) 4 August (J.P.)	*v.* Glamorgan (Cardiff) 11 August (J.P.)
T.A. Lloyd	22	24	137*	44	1	21	0		70	12	9	21	4	0*				
R.I.H.B. Dyer	9	0	40	0	4	10	50	16	4	5	18	15	1	15				
A.I. Kallicharran	104	70	57	43	33	55	33	69		44	66	0	28	27	19	9		
D.L. Amiss	12	23	16	53	35	53	78*	12	20*	7	5	25	55	64	16	21		
G.W. Humpage	62	47	8	53	10	51*	20*	4	18*	23	14	23	51*	11	28	4		
P.A. Smith	18	34	14*	5*	25	1	—	27*		3	51*	50*	3	2	28*	21		
A.M. Ferreira	5	38	—	—	27	42*	—	34*	—	2			9	18	11	38		
C.M. Old	17*	31																
G.C. Small	—	1	—	—	4	—	—	—		3	18	6	17	6*	—	3*		
N. Gifford	—	2*	—	—	0*	—	—	—	—	12*	—	12	—	2	—	—		
S. Wall	—	6*	—	—	6	—			—									
C. Lethbridge			—		0	—								4		2*		
Asif Din				1*			—	—	—	18	25	5			25	6		
D.S. Hoffman							—	—	—	0*	—	2	—	3	—	—		
G.J. Lord								1	64						53	103		
A.R.K. Pierson									—		1*	4	—					
D.A. Thorne															—			
Byes	1	3	1						2	1	2	3	1					
Leg-byes	19	15	8	11	7	5	4	11	3	10	7	14	12	8	5	7		
Wides	4	5		3	6	1	1	2	9	2	6	7	3	3		7		
No-balls		1	1		1	7	1		12			2		2	2	3		
Total	273	300	282	213	159	246	187	176	202	142	222	189	184	165	187	224		
Wickets	7	9	4	5	10	5	3	5	3	9	7	10	7	9†	6	7		
Result	L	L	W	W	L	L	W	W	W	W	W	L	W	L	L	L	Ab.	Ab.
Points	0	0	2	4	0	0	4	4	—	4	—	0	4	—	0	0	2	2

Catches 21 – G.W. Humpage (ct 14/st 7)
6 – D.L. Amiss
5 – A.I. Kallicharran, A.R.M. Pierson and G.C. Small
4 – R.I.H.B. Dyer, P.A. Smith and N. Gifford
3 – S. Wall and A.M. Ferreira
2 – D.S. Hoffman
1 – C. Lethbridge, T.A. Lloyd, D.A. Thorne and Asif Din

† T.A. Lloyd retired hurt

BOWLING	G.C. Small	C.M. Old	N. Gifford	A.M. Ferreira	S. Wall	A.I. Kallicharran	P.A. Smith	C. Lethbridge	D.S. Hoffman
(B.&H.) *v.* Worcestershire (Worcester) 4 May	11–1–47–2	10–1–41–0	11–0–31–0	10–0–72–2	8–0–45–1	5–0–32–0			
(J.P.) *v.* Surrey (The Oval) 5 May	8–0–48–0	5–0–30–0	7–0–55–3	8–0–56–0	6–0–40–0		6–0–56–3		
(B.&H.) *v.* Lancashire (Edgbaston) 11 May	8–2–18–2		11–0–48–2	10–0–48–3	11–1–31–1		7–0–30–2	5–0–37–0	
(J.P.) *v.* Lancashire (Edgbaston) 12 May	7.1–0–30–2		8–0–41–1	6–0–29–2	4–0–26–0	8–0–32–3	6–0–26–1		
(B.&H) *v.* Yorkshire (Leeds) 16 May	11–5–22–1		11–3–23–0	8–1–25–1	11–2–30–1		3–0–16–0	9–1–38–0	
(B.&H.) *v.* Leicester (Edgbaston) 18 & 20 May	11–2–35–1		11–0–36–0	10.5–1–56–2	9–2–35–0	1–0–12–0	4–0–29–0	5–0–33–0	
(J.P.) *v.* Somerset (Taunton) 2 June	8–0–26–1		8–0–40–3	8–0–50–0			8–0–33–2		8–2–18–2
(J.P.) *v.* Hampshire (Edgbaston) 9 June	8–0–41–2		8–2–19–3	8–0–46–2			4–0–22–0		8–0–41–1
(T.T.) *v.* Gloucestershire (Harrogate) 20 June			11–2–29–0	11–1–51–2	11–2–21–5				11–0–48–0
(J.P.) *v.* Northants. (Edgbaston) 30 June	8–0–30–1		8–0–20–6	8–1–29–0		1–0–7–0	3–0–14–0		7–0–23–1
(N.W.) *v.* Devon (Edgbaston) 3 July	8–0–26–0		12–1–49–2			12–0–41–3	3–0–20–0		10–0–44–0
(J.P.) *v.* Sussex (Hove) 7 July	8–0–38–3		8–0–47–1			1–0–11–0	7–0–25–2		8–0–51–0
(J.P.) *v.* Notts. (Edgbaston) 14 July	8–1–16–2		8–1–26–2	7–0–42–4			2–0–10–0		8–0–35–1
(N.W.) *v.* Notts. (Trent Bridge) 17 July	12–3–38–1		5–1–7–0	12–2–55–0			7–0–40–1	12–2–39–1	12–1–56–2
(J.P.) *v.* Leicestershire (Leicester) 21 July	5–1–24–1		4–0–21–0	6–0–39–0			4.3–0–34–0		4–0–17–0
(J.P.) *v.* Derbyshire (Edgbaston) 28 July	6–0–36–3		5–0–27–0	5.2–0–47–0			3–0–25–1	6–0–43–1	4–0–26–0
(J.P.) *v.* Yorkshire (Edgbaston) 4 August									
(J.P.) *v.* Glamorgan (Cardiff) 11 August									
(J.P.) *v.* Glos. (Cheltenham) 18 August	2–0–19–2		2–0–9–0	2–0–25–0			2–0–21–0		2–0–9–0
(J.P.) *v.* Worcs. (Worcester) 25 August			8–0–39–3	8–0–59–0	8–1–31–2		8–0–39–1		8–0–32–0
(J.P.) *v.* Essex (Edgbaston) 1 September	8–0–36–0		8–0–57–0	8–0–72–1			6–0–25–1		
(J.P.) *v.* Kent (Canterbury) 8 September	8–0–43–2		8–0–58–1	8–0–48–2			6–0–23–0		
(J.P.) *v.* Middlesex (Edgbaston) 15 Sept.	8–0–43–2		8–1–16–3	7.5–0–29–3			3–0–7–0		
Wickets	28	0	30	24	10	6	14	2	7

a Asif Din 5–0–23–1

v. Gloucestershire (Cheltenham) 18 August (J.P.)	v. Worcestershire (Worcester) 25 August (J.P.)	v. Essex (Edgbaston) 1 September (J.P.)	v. Kent (Canterbury) 8 September (J.P.)	v. Middlesex (Edgbaston) 15 September (J.P.)		Runs
	5	18	69	33		490
						187
11	1	5	97	16		787
1	27	45	9	16		593
29	24	62	27	17		586
0	17	4	12	20		335
15	0	19	20*	14		292
						48
2*		4	—	1		65
1*	16	0	—	1*		46
	2					14
						6
8		44	23	20		175
—	1*					6
0	13					234
		0	—	3		8
2	7	5*	3*	5		22
				1		
3	5	15	13	14		
	6	5	7	4		
	1	4	4	1		
72	125	230	284	166		
8	10	10	6	10		
L	L	L	W	W		
0	0	0	4	4		

Steve Barwick, 7 for 43 for Glamorgan in the rain-ruined match against Warwickshire at Cardiff. (George Herringshaw)

A.R.K. Pierson	T.A. Lloyd	D.A. Thorne	Byes	Leg-byes	Wides	No-balls	Total	Wkts
			4	5	6	1	277	8
			7	12	11		304	6
				7	7	3	219	10
				6		1	190	10
				11	8	9	165	3
				11	3	2	247	3
				16	3		183	9
				6	1		175	8
11–2–48–2				1	7	2	198	10
			1	9	14		133	9
12–2–32–0	3–1–4–1		1	4	11		221	7
8–1–28–0				9		3	209	6
7–0–42–0				4		1	175	9
				16	4		251	5
		6–0–33–0	3	4	2	1	175	1
			5	16	4	1	225	5
				Match Abandoned				
				Match Abandoned				
				2	1		85	3
			1	11	3	1	212	6
8–0–30–0		2–0–13–0	5	13	3	2	251	3
4–0–29–1		6–0–48–3		4	2	2	253	9
8–1–25–0			4	13	5		160	10a
3	1	3						

10, 11, 12 and 13 August

at Lord's

Middlesex 397 for 4 dec (W.N. Slack 201 not out, K.R. Brown 102)
Australians 396 for 6 dec (D.M. Wellham 125, W.B. Phillips 73, K.C. Wessels 56)

Match drawn

10, 12 and 13 August

at Colchester

Essex 199 (K.W.R. Fletcher 52, A.E. Warner 5 for 51) and 101 for 0 dec (A.W. Lilley 68 not out)
Derbyshire 1 for 0 dec and 263 (G Miller 105, D.L. Acfield 6 for 81)

Essex won by 36 runs
Essex 17 pts, Derbyshire 4 pts

at Cardiff

Warwickshire 220 (D.L. Amiss 77, S.R. Barwick 7 for 43)
Glamorgan 97 for 2

Match drawn
Glamorgan 4 pts, Warwickshire 2 pts

at Cheltenham

Gloucestershire 134 (L.B. Taylor 5 for 45) and 121 for 5
Leicestershire 249 (P. Willey 52)

Match drawn
Leicestershire 6 pts, Gloucestershire 4 pts

Worcestershire C.C.C.
Limited-Over Matches – 1985

BATTING	*v.* Warwickshire (Worcester) 4 May (B.&H.)	*v.* Somerset (Worcester) 5 May (J.P.)	*v.* Leicestershire (Leicester) 15 May (B.&H.)	*v.* Lancashire (Worcester) 16 May (B.&H.)	*v.* Yorkshire (Bradford) 18 May (B.&H.)	*v.* Kent (Canterbury) 2 June (J.P.)	*v.* Middlesex (Worcester) 5 & 7 June (B.&H.)	*v.* Glamorgan (Ebbw Vale) 9 June (J.P.)	*v.* Surrey (Worcester) 16 June (J.P.)	*v.* Yorkshire (Worcester) 30 June (J.P.)	*v.* Hertfordshire (Hitchin) 3 July (N.W.)	*v.* Derbyshire (Knypersley) 7 July (J.P.)	*v.* Hampshire (Portsmouth) 14 July (J.P.)	*v.* Lancashire (Old Trafford) 17 July (N.W.)	*v.* Middlesex (Worcester) 21 July (J.P.)	*v.* Sussex (Eastbourne) 28 July (J.P.)	*v.* Lancashire (Worcester) 4 August (J.P.)	*v.* Glamorgan (Swansea) 8 August (N.W.)
M.J. Weston	0	8	46	14	0	13	0	18	—	15	35	19	7	7*	11	1*		
T.S. Curtis	75	5*	21	19	50	23	39	30			63	76	71	32	16	7		0
D.M. Smith	126	25	24	41	77	7	57		18*	3				109	3	27		97
R.N. Kapil Dev	32	10	0	—	1	16	21	5		0	8	36	22	38*	22			0
D.N. Patel	3	0	3	16	1	27	13	22	47	54	4	4	13	19	15	10		54
P.A. Neale	0	2	43*	94*	35	10	33	0	—	18	73	54	4	81	5	15*		15
D.B. D'Oliveira	9	7	13	47*	7	18	6	8	103	12	31	19	6	12	45	16		7
J.D. Inchmore	0	3	1	—	16*	6*	5*	8	—				20*	—	5	—		—
N.V. Radford	13*	12*	—	—	4	8	0	13	—	30*	0*	16	—	—	14	—		—
S.J. Rhodes	3*	—	27*	—	3	41	24	3	—	13	6	4	41*	—	45*	11		6*
R.K. Illingworth	—		—	—	9*	8*	0	0*	—	—	—	3*	—	—	1*			—
P.J. Newport		—						2*	—	18*	—	10*	—			—		4*
G.A. Hick									11*							21		
D.A. Banks										13	11*							
S.M. McEwan												—						
C.L. King																		
L. Smith																		
B. Barrett																		
Byes	4		4		1		6	1	8	2	2	4	2					
Leg-byes	5	3	11	15	7	12	9	13	5	16	5	8	6	7	7	8		6
Wides	6		2	7	2	2	4	2	5	3	3	6	3	5	6	7		1
No-balls	1			8	1		3			4			1	2	2	1		2
Total	277	75	195	261	214	191	220	125	197	201	241	259	196	312	197	124		189
Wickets	8	7	7	4	9	9	10	9	2	8	7	8	6	5	9	6		6
Results	W	Ab.	L	W	W	L	Ab.	L	W	L	W	L	L	W	W	L	Ab.	W
Points	2	2	0	2	2	0	—	0	4	0	—	0	0	—	4	0	2	—

Catches

25 – S.J. Rhodes (ct 22/st 3)	4 – D.B. D'Oliveira and P. A. Neale
9 – D.M. Smith	3 – G.A. Hick
8 – D.N. Patel	2 – D.A. Banks, P.J. Newport, J.D. Inchmore and S.M. McEwan
7 – N.V. Radford	1 – R.K. Illingworth
6 – M.J. Weston	
5 – R.N. Kapil Dev	

BOWLING	R.N. Kapil Dev	N.V. Radford	J.D. Inchmore	M.J. Weston	R.K. Illingworth	D.N. Patel	P.J. Newport	D.B. D'Oliveira	S.M. McEwan
(B.&H.) *v.* Warwickshire (Worcester) 4 May	11–2–44–1	11–1–50–1	11–2–44–0	11–0–55–1	5–0–23–1	6–0–37–0			
(J.P.) *v.* Somerset (Worcester) 5 May	1.1–0–11–0	1–0–12–0	2–0–15–0				1–0–6–0		
(B.&H.) *v.* Leicestershire (Leicester) 15 May	6–1–25–1	7–0–36–0	6–0–39–1	3–0–22–1	7–0–45–1	8–0–34–1			
(B.&H.) *v.* Lancashire (Worcester) 16 May	11–0–51–0	9–3–34–1	11–1–48–0		11–1–42–0	11–0–50–3		2–0–22–0	
(B.&H.) *v.* Yorkshire (Bradford) 18 May	7–4–6–1	6–1–11–1	8–1–20–1	11–2–27–2	11–2–36–4	7.4–0–21–1			
(J.P.) *v.* Kent (Canterbury) 2 June	8–0–55–0	7–0–41–0	8–0–37–1	8–0–29–1	4–0–26–1	5–0–28–1			
(B.&H.) *v.* Middlesex (Worcester) 7 June	6–2–13–0	5–0–16–0	2–0–7–0	1–0–3–0					
(J.P.) *v.* Glamorgan (Ebbw Vale) 9 June	4–0–28–0	5–0–31–0	5–0–34–2	2–0–16–0			5–0–30–0		
(J.P.) *v.* Surrey (Worcester) 16 June		8–0–23–3	8–2–36–2	8–0–32–1	7–1–23–1	4–1–30–1	5–0–33–0		
(J.P.) *v.* Yorkshire (Worcester) 30 June	8–0–43–0	7–0–38–2		3–0–15–1	6–0–38–1	8–0–26–1	8–0–36–0		
(N.W.) *v.* Hertfordshire (Hitchin) 3 July	9–0–28–0	8–2–24–2		6.5–0–34–1	12–2–21–0	12–2–22–2	2–0–11–0	8–0–37–2	
(J.P.) *v.* Derbyshire (Knypersley) 7 July	8–0–48–2	7–0–47–2		6–0–53–2	4–0–32–2	1–0–14–0	7–0–38–0		7–0–41–0
(J.P.) *v.* Hampshire (Portsmouth) 14 July	8–0–43–0	8–1–53–2	8–1–25–1	8–0–24–1			8–0–41–0		
(N.W.) *v.* Lancashire (Old Trafford) 18 July	12–0–52–5	12–0–50–3	12–0–51–2	2–0–19–0	10–0–55–0	11–0–61–0			
(J.P.) *v.* Middlesex (Worcester) 21 July	8–0–44–1	8–2–19–3	8–0–42–0		8–1–30–3	8–2–28–1			
(J.P.) *v.* Sussex (Eastbourne) 28 July		5–0–35–1	5–0–27–0	2–0–15–0		4–0–41–0	5–0–32–2		
(J.P.) *v.* Lancashire (Worcester) 4 Aug.									
(N.W.) *v.* Glamorgan (Swansea 7 & 8 Aug.	12–1–36–2	12–4–30–0	11.5–4–25–5		10–0–41–1	4–0–14–0	10–1–32–1		
(J.P.) *v.* Notts. (Trent Bridge) 11 Aug.		3–0–14–0	4–0–15–2	5–0–31–1		1–0–9–0	4–0–29–2		4–0–35–1
(J.P.) *v.* Essex (Worcester) 18 Aug.		2–0–13–0	2–0–13–0	2–0–20–1		1.2–0–17–0	2–0–23–1		
(N.W.) *v.* Notts. (Worcester) 21 & 22 Aug.		12–2–36–1	12–1–40–1	6–0–21–0		12–0–43–2	9.2–1–43–0		
(J.P.) *v.* Warwickshire (Worcester) 25 Aug.		6.3–0–24–4	6–0–21–3			2–0–12–0	5–0–27–0		
(J.P.) *v.* Leicestershire (Leicester) 1 Sept.		8–0–53–0	8–0–41–1	8–0–18–1		8–0–33–3			8–0–36–3
(J.P.) *v.* Glos. (Moreton-in-Marsh) 8 Sept.			7–0–33–1	8–0–28–0		6–0–51–0			8–0–37–0
(J.P.) *v.* Northants. (Worcester) 15 Sept.		8–0–31–2	8–0–39–2	8–2–14–2		8–0–48–1			5–0–27–1
Wickets	13	28	25	16	15	17	6	2	5

v. Nottinghamshire (Trent Bridge) 11 August (J.P.)	v. Essex (Worcester) 18 August (J.P.)	v. Nottinghamshire (Worcester) 21 August (N.W.)	v. Warwickshire (Worcester) 25 August (J.P.)	v. Leicestershire (Leicester) 1 September (J.P.)	v. Gloucestershire (Moreton-in-Marsh) 8 September (J.P.)	v. Northamptonshire (Worcester) 15 September (J.P.)	Runs
16*	—	7	4	32	2	1	256
7	6*	92	57	1	1	4	695
36	34*	57	35			34*	810
							211
12	2	20	45	76	63	0	523
23	17	9		28	16	83	653
	15	0	3	18	17	3	422
—	—	0*	—	1*	10*	—	75
4*	—	16	18*	6*		4	158
10	—	9*	32*	6	0	2	286
							21
—	—	—	—				34
0	8		2	21	90	52	205
				0			24
—			—	—	0	—	0
		11					11
					3		3
					5*		5
			1		1		
6	5	4	11	3	3	4	
	1	5	3	1	2	7	
1		2	1	2		1	
115	88	232	212	195	213	195	
6	4	8	6	8	9	8	
L	L	L	W	W	L	W	
0	0	—	4	4	0	4	

G.A. Hick	C.L. King	B. Barrett	Byes	Leg-byes	Wides	No-balls	Total	Wkts
			1	19	4		273	7
				1	1		45	0
			2	9	7		212	7
			2	9	6	2	258	5
			1	8	2	2	130	10
			2	8	3	2	226	6
			5	1	2	4	45	1
				8	1		147	3
			2	14	9		193	8
				19	7		215	5
			6	4		5	183	10
				19	2	3	292	9
				20	4		206	4
			1	9	5	3	298	10
				12	5		175	8
2–0–15–1			1	3	2	1	169	4
				Match Abandoned				
				10	4		188	10
				6	2		139	7
				3			89	3
	8–0–36–1			14	4	4	233	6
7–0–36–2				5	6	1	125	10
				6	3	1	187	9
1–0–15–0		8–0–43–0		10	4	3	217	1
				8	6	2	167	9
3	1	0						

Chris Smith (Hampshire) one of the most consistent batsmen in the country. He was the first man to reach a thousand runs and showed a welcome return to the form which won him a place in the England side. (Sporting Pictures UK)

at Southampton

Hampshire 303 for 9 dec (M.C.J. Nicholas 94, C.L. Smith 77, G. Monkhouse 4 for 82) and 174 for 5 dec (R.A. Smith 50)
Surrey 200 for 4 dec (A.J. Stewart 71) and 107 for 4

Match drawn
Surrey 6 pts, Hampshire 5 pts

at Canterbury

Sussex 317 (N.J. Lenham 89, C.M. Wells 61, D.L. Underwood 4 for 87) and 27 for 0 dec
Kent 0 for 0 dec and 290 (C.J. Tavare 64, L. Potter 55, D.A. Reeve 5 for 70, G.S. le Roux 4 for 72)

Sussex won by 54 runs
Sussex 20 pts, Kent 3 pts

at Trent Bridge

Worcestershire 202 (K. Saxelby 4 for 47) and 225 (P.A. Neale 69, P.M. Such 4 for 74)
Nottinghamshire 322 (C.E.B. Rice 85, R.T. Robinson 82) and 98 for 7 (D.W. Randall 53, P.J. Newport 4 for 47)

Match drawn
Nottinghamshire 8 pts, Worcestershire 6 pts

at Weston-super-Mare

Somerset 409 (I.T. Botham 134, J.C.M. Atkinson 79, I.V.A. Richards 58, P.M. Roebuck 53, N.A. Mallender 5 for 83)
Northamptonshire 87 for 1

Match drawn
Somerset 4 pts, Northamptonshire 3 pts

at Leeds

Lancashire 327 for 8 dec (N.H. Fairbrother 147, P.J. Hartley 5 for 91)
Yorkshire 328 for 9 dec (M.D. Moxon 127)

Match drawn
Lancashire 7 pts, Yorkshire 5 pts

Rain ruined the contest between Middlesex and the Australians which descended to rather meaningless batting practice. Wilf Slack and Keith Brown had an opening stand of 213. Brown hit a maiden first-class hundred. Wellham battled grittily to a century.

The game at Weston-super-Mare was also ruined by rain and there was no play at all on the final day. On the Saturday

Yorkshire C.C.C.

Limited-Over Matches – 1985

BATTING	v. Middlesex (Bradford) 5 May (J.P.)	v. Leicestershire (Leicester) 11 May (B.&H.)	v. Leicestershire (Leicester) 12 May (J.P.)	v. Lancashire (Old Trafford) 15 May (B.&H.)	v. Warwickshire (Leeds) 16 May (B.&H.)	v. Worcestershire (Bradford) 18 May (B.&H.)	v. Derbyshire (Scarborough) 19 May (J.P.)	v. Hampshire (Middlesbrough) 2 June (J.P.)	v. Sussex (Sheffield) 9 June (J.P.)	v. Somerset (Bath) 16 June (J.P.)	v. Nottinghamshire (Harrogate) 19 June (T.T.)	v. Worcestershire (Worcester) 30 June (J.P.)	v. Cheshire (Birkenhead) 3 July (N.W.)	v. Gloucestershire (Gloucester) 7 July (J.P.)	v. Surrey (Bradford) 14 July (J.P.)	v. Somerset (Leeds) 17 July (N.W.)	v. Nottinghamshire (Trent Bridge) 28 July (J.P.)	v. Warwickshire (Edgbaston) 4 August (J.P.)
A. Sidebottom	0	21	—	7	—	21			1	1	12	—	—	14*				
M.D. Moxon	1	37	28	24	43	6		47	67	86	21		82*	—			12*	
K. Sharp	29	3	73*	45	24	10		81*	0	22	6	112*	—	26	61	5	16	
J.D. Love	0	90*	13	12	13*	11		46	13	37	36	7	—	100*	1			
P.E. Robinson	25	42	78*	13	—										60	0	1	
S.N. Hartley	17				4*	16		13*	7	0	2	19	—	23	72	69	15	
D.L. Bairstow	19	31*	—	10	—	15		40	38	31	11	25	—	11	5	13	9	
G.B. Stevenson	13	—	—	3	—	2						10	—	1				
P.W. Jarvis	0	—	—	3	—	20				—	5	—	—	—	6*	16	2	
S. Oldham	14*														0*	0*	—	
S.D. Fletcher	0*	—	—	0*	—			—	0*		1*	—	—	—	—	—		
P. Carrick		—	—	16*	53	5		—	6	12*	20	4*	—	1	18	16	1	
D. Byas		—	15	2														
I.G. Swallow						10*												
P.A. Booth						1		—										
A.A. Metcalfe								18	0	13		12		5	28	33	10	
C.S. Pickles								—	3	—	1	—					1*	
C. Shaw								—	7						1	6*	—	
S.J. Dennis										—								
G. Boycott											46		70*			24		
P.J. Hartley																		
Byes	1	2				1							1	1	1	5	1	
Leg-byes	6	11	8	7	11	8		12	15	11	3	19	1	14	7	9	1	
Wides	6	2	5		8	2			3	1	2	7	5	7	3	5	1	
No-balls	1	5	4	2	9	2		2	1	1	3		1			7		
Total	132	244	224	144	165	130		259	161	215	169	215	160	203	263	208	70	
Wickets	9	4	3	9	3	10		4	10	7	10	5	0	6	8	8	7	
Results	Ab.	W	W	L	W	L	Ab.	W	L	W	L	W	W	L	W	L	L	Ab.
Points	2	2	4	0	2	0	2	4	0	4	—	4	—	0	4	—	0	2

Catches 29 – D.L. Bairstow (ct 25/st 4)
9 – S.N. Hartley
6 – P.E. Robinson, K. Sharp and M.D. Moxon
5 – C.S. Pickles and S.D. Fletcher
4 – C. Shaw, P.W. Jarvis and P. Carrick
3 – J.D. Love and G.B. Stevenson
1 – I.G. Swallow and P.A. Booth

BOWLING	A. Sidebottom	P.W. Jarvis	G.B. Stevenson	P. Carrick	S.D. Fletcher	G. Boycott	P.A. Booth	C. Shaw	C.S. Pickles
(J.P.) *v.* Middlesex (Bradford) 5 May									
(B.&H.) *v.* Leicestershire (Leicester) 11 May	11–0–41–2	11–1–39–3	11–0–64–1	11–0–34–0	11–0–61–0				
(J.P.) *v.* Leicestershire (Leicester) 12 May	8–0–43–1	8–1–37–2	8–0–56–0	8–1–22–0	8–0–58–2				
(B.&H.) *v.* Lancashire (Old Trafford) 15 May	7–0–21–1	6.5–0–34–3	6–0–26–4	6–0–35–1	6–0–23–1				
(B.&H.) *v.* Warwickshire (Leeds) 16 May	11–2–21–1	10.1–2–31–3	10–1–34–4	11–1–34–2	11–0–32–0				
(B.&H.) *v.* Worcestershire (Bradford) 18 May	11–4–27–5	9–1–46–2	5–0–36–0	11–0–27–0			8–0–28–2		
(J.P.) *v.* Derbyshire (Scarborough) 19 May									
(J.P.) *v.* Hampshire (Middlesbrough) 2 June				8–0–38–1	8–0–68–2		8–0–57–1	8–0–46–2	8–0–45–0
(J.P.) *v.* Sussex (Sheffield) 9 June	8–2–29–0			8–0–39–1	8–0–43–2			8–1–47–1	8–1–37–2
(J.P.) *v.* Somerset (Bath) 16 June	7.3–2–29–2	7–0–26–3		8–0–40–0					8–0–28–2
(T.T.) *v.* Nottinghamshire (Harrogate) 19 June	3–1–15–0	11–0–39–1		11–0–40–2	11–0–67–1				11–0–64–1
(J.P.) *v.* Worcestershire (Worcester) 30 June	8–0–50–1	8–1–23–1	8–0–39–2		8–0–39–0				8–0–32–2
(N.W.) *v.* Cheshire (Birkenhead) 3 July	12–0–42–2	12–1–36–2	12–4–17–2	12–5–19–0	12–3–35–0				
(J.P.) *v.* Gloucestershire (Gloucester) 7 July	8–0–34–0	8–0–31–0	8–0–45–2	8–1–45–1	8–0–49–2				
(J.P.) *v.* Surrey (Bradford) 14 July		7–1–27–2		4–0–41–1	7–0–79–1			7–0–66–0	
(N.W.) *v.* Somerset (Leeds) 17&18 July		10–1–61–1		4–0–17–0	12–2–34–3			10.1–3–14–1	
(J.P.) *v.* Notts. (Trent Bridge) 28 July		2–0–7–2		1–0–6–0				2–0–18–1	2–0–17–0
(J.P.) *v.* Warwickshire (Edgbaston) 4 August									
(J.P.) *v.* Lancashire (Leeds) 11 August									
(J.P.) *v.* Kent (Scarborough) 18 August				3–0–10–1				8–0–40–2	8–1–21–0
(J.P.) *v.* Glamorgan (Swansea) 25 August				6–0–36–3		3–0–12–0		4–0–15–3	6–2–26–0
(J.P.) *v.* Northamptonshire (Leeds) 1 September				8–0–35–1	8–0–38–1			8–0–36–3	8–0–44–0
(Asda) *v.* Derbyshire (Scarborough) 4 Sept.				10–5–21–2	10–0–48–2	10–2–31–0			10–1–46–3
(J.P.) *v.* Essex (Chelmsford) 15 September					8–0–45–2			8–0–46–1	8–0–38–1
Wickets	15	25	15	16	19	0	3	14	11

a I.G. Swallow 11–1–42–0 b S.J. Dennis 8–0–32–1 c M.D. Moxon 8–0–36–2

v. Lancashire (Leeds) 11 August (J.P.)	v. Kent (Scarborough) 18 August (J.P.)	v. Glamorgan (Swansea) 25 August (J.P.)	v. Northamptonshire (Leeds) 1 September (J.P.)	v. Derbyshire (Scarborough) 4 September (Asda)	v. Essex (Chelmsford) 15 September (J.P.)	Runs
						77
	41	6	6	6	28	541
			12	55	114	694
	10	1	0	3	3	396
	2	2	23	29		275
	20	29	56	72	5	439
	35	3	11	13	28	348
						29
						52
	2	0*	28*	1*	1*	46
			—	—	—	1
	2	3*	2	4	15	178
						17
						10
						1
	5					124
	13*	1	8	2	6*	35
	5	—	10*		—	29
						—
		38		9	7	194
	2	0				2
	8	1	1	2		
		6	17	5	17	
	3	1	6	3	5	
	5	2	1	2	2	
	153	93	181	206	231	
	9	8	8	9	7	
Ab.	W	L	L	L	L	
2	4	0	0	—	0	

P.J. Hartley	S.N. Hartley	S. Oldham	Byes	Leg-byes	Wides	No-balls	Total	Wkts
			Match Abandoned					
				4	2	5	243	9
			2	5	4	1	223	5
				7	2		146	10
				7	6	1	159	10
			1	7	2	1	214	9a
			Match Abandoned					
				3			257	6
				2	1	3	197	6
			1	8	2	2	164	10b
				6	5	5	267	7c
			2	16	3	4	201	8
			2	8	5	6	159	7
				12	1	1	216	6
	3–0–28–1	8–0–16–1	1	4	3	1	262	6
	2–0–21–0	10–0–45–1	4	13	2	2	209	6
	0.2–0–6–0	2–0–16–1		3	1		73	4
			Match Abandoned					
			Match Abandoned					
8–1–20–1		8–0–35–3	1	6	11	1	133	9
3–0–16–0		6–0–27–2		6	2	2	138	10
		8–0–26–1	4	2	3	4	185	7
		9.1–0–54–0	2	7	7		209	7
	8–0–47–1	7.5–0–43–3		13	7	1	232	8
1	2	12						

Ian Botham hit 10 sixes in another breathtaking hundred. His total of sixes for the season rose to 74 so that he passed the record formerly held by Arthur Wellard, also of Somerset. Botham and Jonathan Atkinson, making his first-class debut, added 177 in 31 overs. Atkinson's 79 came off 91 balls

Cardiff also lost the last day's play and, indeed, only 7 balls were possible after the opening day. Rain interrupted the Roses match. Lancashire were 67 for 4 and were rescued by Neil Fairbrother who had hit a century in the first Roses match at Old Trafford. Yorkshire settled for a grim draw and the match did little to encourage the supporters of either side.

Having lost the first day at Colchester, Essex and Derbyshire contrived a result. Derbyshire asked the home side to bat first and bowled them out for 199, but the game was again interrupted and when a full day's play was possible on the Tuesday Derbyshire were asked to make 300 in 90 overs. They slumped to 68 for 4, but Geoff Miller's second first-class hundred gave them hope of victory, but he was caught by Fletcher off Acfield who bowled a mammoth spell and it was Acfield who took the vital last wicket with only 14 balls remaining. It gave Essex a third successive victory.

Gloucestershire's championship challenge was rather blunted at Cheltenham. They were put in to bat and were bowled out by Les Taylor, brought into the England side for the first time. Leicestershire took a first innings lead of 115, but rain and bad light curtailed play on the last day and Gloucestershire were happy to settle for a draw.

The other title contenders, Hampshire and Surrey, promised more than they achieved at Southampton. Rain restricted the first day to 72 overs in which Hampshire reached 211 for 4. They reached their four bonus points on the Monday and Jesty threw down a challenge by declaring 103 behind, although Surrey batted into the last morning. Nicholas asked Surrey to make 278 in 40 overs, but after the loss of both openers for 17, the visitors showed no interest in trying to get the runs.

Sussex showed more purpose and energy at the close of the match at Canterbury than they had done earlier. Benson showed imaginative captaincy and Barclay set Kent to make 345 in 96 overs. The home side went boldly for the runs and

LEFT: *Keith Brown – a maiden first-class century for Middlesex against the Australians at Lord's (Sporting Pictures UK Ltd)* RIGHT: *The rain ruined the match between Lancashire and Northants at Lytham St Annes, but there was time for David Capel to record career best bowling figures of 7 for 62. (Sporting Pictures UK Ltd)*

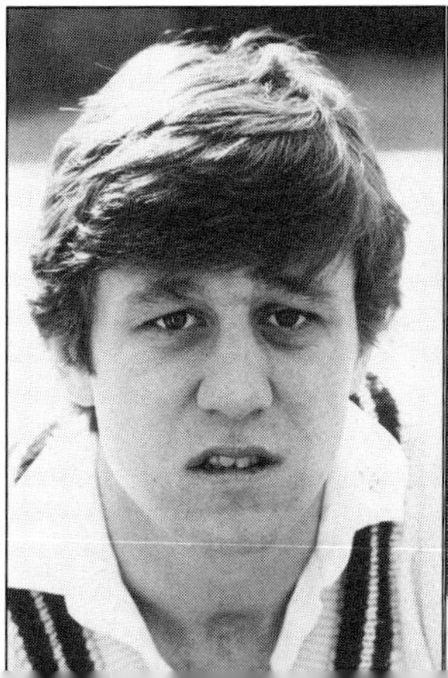

LEFT: *Nick Cook, despondent at his treatment, announces that he will be leaving Leicestershire. (David Munden)* RIGHT: *Younis Ahmed led Glamorgan to an exciting victory over Hampshire at Cardiff with a scintillating innings of 143 not out. He was awarded his county cap and has now been capped by Surrey, Worcestershire and Glamorgan. (Sporting Pictures UK Ltd)*

were 177 for 4 at tea, but Reeve bowled Knott, Penn and Dilley and Sussex snatched victory with 3.2 overs to spare. Kent's batting was inconsistent, but Taylor, Tavare and Potter, at last gaining a regular place in the Kent side, revived their hopes before Reeve struck. Neil Lenham batted with impressive calm in Sussex's first innings.

Having spent most of the match on top, Notts failed to beat Worcestershire and ended in very subdued manner. Worcestershire hung on bravely throughout the last afternoon. Radford hit 41 off 68 balls and Notts were left to make 106 in 21 overs. Robinson, Broad and Rice were out with only 6 scored and although Randall hit the boundaries necessary to maintain the rate Notts needed, the home side panicked and faded.

John Player Special League

11 August

at Colchester

Derbyshire 123
Essex 124 for 1 (G.A. Gooch 51 not out)

Essex (4 pts) won by 9 wickets

at Cardiff

Glamorgan *v.* Warwickshire

Match abandoned
Glamorgan 2 pts, Warwickshire 2 pts

at Cheltenham

Leicestershire 77 for 8 (K.M. Curran 4 for 11)
Gloucestershire 70 for 2

Leicestershire (4 pts) won by 8 wickets

at Canterbury

Kent *v.* Sussex

Match abandoned
Kent 2 pts, Sussex 2 pts

at Trent Bridge

Nottinghamshire 139 for 7
Worcestershire 115 for 6

Nottinghamshire (4 pts) won by 24 runs

at Weston-super-Mare

Somerset *v.* Northamptonshire

Match abandoned
Somerset 2 pts, Northamptonshire 2 pts

at Leeds

Yorkshire *v.* Lancashire

Match abandoned
Yorkshire 2 pts, Lancashire 2 pts

Ten overs an innings were possible at Cheltenham, 21 at Trent Bridge and 28 at Colchester. No play was possible elsewhere. Leicestershire's win took them level on points with Kent and Sussex at the head of the table. Notts and Essex moved to within two points of the leaders with their victories. Essex bowled Derbyshire out in 26.1 overs and won with 4 balls to spare, pacing their innings with great ease. Hardie and Gooch opened with a stand of 77.

14, 15 and 16 August

at Buxton
Derbyshire 25 for 3
***v.* Worcestershire**

Match drawn
Worcestershire 1 pt, Derbyshire 0 pts

at Colchester

Essex 184 (B.R. Hardie 74, G.S. le Roux 6 for 46) and 118 for 2 (P.J. Prichard 62 not out)
Sussex 380 for 8 dec (G.D. Mendis 143 not out, I.J. Gould 78, G.S. le Roux 60, D.L. Acfield 4 for 125)
Match drawn
Sussex 7 pts, Essex 3 pts

David Acfield spun Essex to victory over Derbyshire at Colchester, 13 August. (Mike Powell)

at Cardiff

Hampshire 270 for 3 dec (C.G. Greenidge 77, R.A. Smith 68, J.J.E. Hardy 64 not out) and 0 for 0 dec
Glamorgan 0 for 0 dec and 271 for 5 (Younis Ahmed 143 not out, R.C. Ontong 69)

Glamorgan won by 5 wickets
Glamorgan 17 pts, Hampshire 3 pts

at Cheltenham

Nottinghamshire 216 (J.W. Lloyds 5 for 37)
Gloucestershire 15 for 0

Match drawn
Gloucestershire 4 pts, Nottinghamshire 2 pts

at Canterbury

Warwickshire 300 for 7 dec (A.I. Kallicharran 108, R.I.H.B. Dyer 59, G.W. Humpage 52, C. Penn 4 for 71) and 138 for 6 dec
Kent 164 and 4 for 0

Match drawn
Warwickshire 8 pts, Kent 4 pts

at Lytham St Annes

Lancashire 225 (D.J. Makinson 58 not out, D.J. Capel 7 for 62)
Northamptonshire 2 for 0

Match drawn
Northamptonshire 4 pts, Lancashire 2 pts

at Weston-super-Mare

Somerset 245 (V.J. Marks 69, N.A. Felton 63, S.P. Hughes 5 for 64)
Middlesex 150 for 8 (W.N. Slack 52, R.V.J. Coombs 5 for 58)

Match drawn
Somerset 5 pts, Middlesex 5 pts

at The Oval

Surrey 120 (P.J. Hartley 4 for 43, C. Shaw 4 for 53) and 341 for 8 dec (T.E. Jesty 141 not out, M.A. Lynch 121, S.N. Hartley 4 for 51)
Yorkshire 277 (R.J. Blakey 81, J.D. Love 69, G. Monkhouse 4 for 46) and 11 for 0

Match drawn
Yorkshire 7 pts, Surrey 4 pts

Wretched weather decimated the Britannic Assurance County Championship matches. Middlesex snatched five points from the rain at Weston-super-Mare, reaching 150 in the thirty-sixth over on the last afternoon. The most interesting aspect of the match was the bowling of slow left-arm spinner Robert Coombs who took 5 for 58 on his first-class debut.

Gloucestershire bowled out Notts, but had no chance after the second day to score any runs themselves, and only 16 overs were bowled at Buxton. The consolation at Lytham where there were 6 overs on the first day, 19 on the second and 47.1 on the third was that David Capel returned the best bowling figures of his career and David Makinson made his highest score in first-class cricket.

Essex began confidently on a sluggish wicket at Colchester, but lost 6 wickets for 15 runs in mid innings. Mendis, in dour fashion, and Gould and le Roux, more brightly, put Sussex in total command. Garth le Roux had a splendid all-round match, but rain returned to effect the draw which had long looked inevitable. Sussex lost Waller with a chipped bone in his left hand.

The fast medium trio of Shaw, Peter Hartley and Oldham routed Surrey at The Oval after Bairstow had asked the home side to bat first on a damp morning. Surrey slipped to 85 for 9 and only a last wicket stand by Gray and Monkhouse took them to 120. Yorkshire took a lead of 157 with some careful batting, and they had hopes of an innings victory when Surrey slumped to 76 for 4, but Lynch and Jesty hit centuries and put on 191 to save the game.

Kallicharran hit a sparkling hundred to give Warwickshire a good position at Canterbury where 19 wickets fell on the second day. Kent, having been dismissed for 164, bowled themselves back into contention by capturing 5 Warwickshire second innings wickets for 57, but rain returned on the last day and the match had to be abandoned.

The only place where a result was achieved was Cardiff. There was no play on the first day and Hampshire reached 213 for 2 in 67 overs on the second. The visitors, led by Paul Terry in the absence of Nicholas, added another 57 in 13 overs on the last day. Glamorgan forfeited their first innings and Hampshire their second so that Glamorgan were set a target of 271 in 85 overs. They were 75 for 4 when Ontong joined Younis and the pair added 172 in 154 minutes. Ontong was caught on the long-off boundary off Cowley for 69, but Derrick hit Maru for a four and a six off successive deliveries and Glamorgan moved to their first championship win since May. Younis Ahmed was the inspiration. He hit a six and 14 fours and during the tea interval he was awarded his county cap. He had, of course, been so honoured earlier in his career by Surrey and Worcestershire.

Fifth Cornhill Test Match
ENGLAND *v.* AUSTRALIA

Heeding criticism of their selection in the first four Tests, the Australians brought in an extra bowler, Jeff Thomson, to the exclusion of a batsman, David Boon. England gave a first Test cap to Les Taylor and brought Richard Ellison into the side for the first time in the series. Allott and Agnew were omitted from the side that played at Old Trafford.

Gower won the toss and asked Australia to bat. The first

David Gower in all his glory. (Ken Kelly)

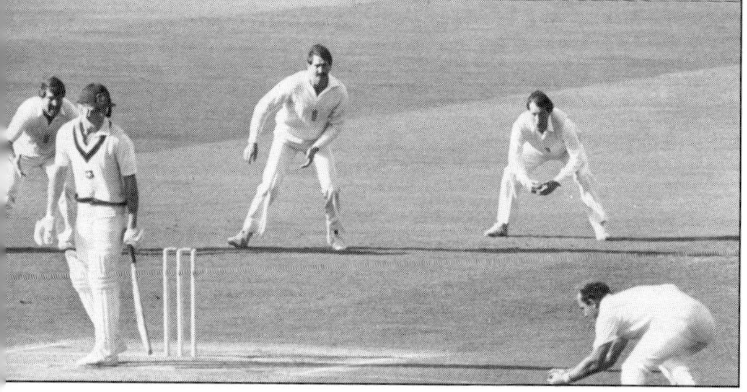

Top: *Botham bowls O'Donnell to the delight of the England fielders. (Ken Kelly)*

Middle: *Ritchie pushes forward to Emburey and is caught by Allan Lamb. England scent victory. (Ken Kelly)*

Bottom: *Botham has McDermott taken at short leg by Edmonds and England go 2–1 up in the series. (Ken Kelly)*

day gave little indication of what was to come. Rain restricted activities to two sessions, before lunch and post tea when play was extended to seven o'clock. England tended to waste the advantage of bowling first in encouraging conditions. Botham bowled too short and Taylor could find no consistent line. Australia began at a brisk rate. Wood played two handsome shots, but when he attempted to turn a lifting ball from Botham to leg he was splendidly caught at short leg by the diving Edmonds who was to give a magnificent display of aggressive cricket throughout the match. It was Edmonds who captured the next wicket, Hilditch touched a ball down the leg side shortly before lunch. When play began again in late afternoon Australia prospered. England put down three catches and Border and Wessels batted attractively to close at an impressive 181 for 2.

Richard Ellison changed the course of the game on the second morning. He achieved devastating late movement which had the Australian batsmen groping hopelessly. Border clipped him to square-leg, Wessels followed an outswinger, Ritchie was taken at second slip and Phillips slashed an indifferent delivery into the hands of cover. O'Donnell became Taylor's first Test victim and 5 wickets had gone down for 29 runs.

England were frustrated into inactivity by rain in the afternoon and when play did restart they could not recapture the zest of the pre-lunch period. Lawson and McDermott attacked and England erred. Botham was far from his best and suffered. McDermott fell to a fine diving catch by Gower at mid-off, but he and Lawson had added 58 and Thomson immediately began to hit the ball hard so that Australia closed at 335 for 8, a considerable recovery.

The Saturday belonged entirely to England who enjoyed one of the very great days in the history of the contests between the two countries. Thomson pushed the first ball of the day to Gower and mid-off. Lawson hesitated in going for the run and was beaten by the England captain's under-arm throw. Off the fifth ball of the over Holland was taken at slip. The last two wickets had fallen without a run being scored and Ellison had finished with 6 for 77, figures which in no way flattered him. His part in the match was far from over.

Gooch hit two thrilling cover drives and Robinson turned the ball off his legs to the boundary to suggest an exciting start for England, but at 38 Gooch half played at a ball from

Top: *Taylor's first Test wicket. O'Donnell is caught behind by Downton. Lamb, Botham and Emburey appeal. (Ken Kelly)*
Bottom: *Jeff Thomson's 200th Test wicket. Gooch is caught by Phillips. It was Australia's last moment of joy. (Ken Kelly)*

The controversial dismissal. Sequence shows Wayne Phillips smashing the ball against Allan Lamb. Gower catches the rebound. (Ken Kelly)

Thomson and was well caught behind as it left him late. It was Thomson's two hundredth Test wicket and it was the last piece of joy Australia was to savour in the match.

Gower and Robinson produced some of the finest batting that has been seen in a Test match in England for several years. Robinson, temperamentally at ease, was assured and delightful, particularly when hitting square either side of the wicket. Gower sent the ball rippling to the boundary with deceptively languid charm. His movement is so fluent, his timing so naturally precise, that he caresses the ball swiftly through the covers. As the sun shone Gower and Robinson produced a partnership of glory. At the end of the day, after receiving 87 overs, England were 355 for 1. Gower was not out 169, Robinson was on 140.

The stand ended on Monday morning when Robinson was bowled off his pad. He had batted quite magnificently. Few young men have ever established themselves in Test cricket so eagerly. Already within sight of a thousand runs, he had share a second wicket stand of 331 with Gower which was second only to the Hutton–Leyland stand at The Oval in 1938.

David Gower reached his highest score in first-class cricket, the second highest score ever made by an England captain against Australia and passed Denis Compton's record aggregate for a series against Australia in England. He was out when he slashed Lawson to cover, but chances

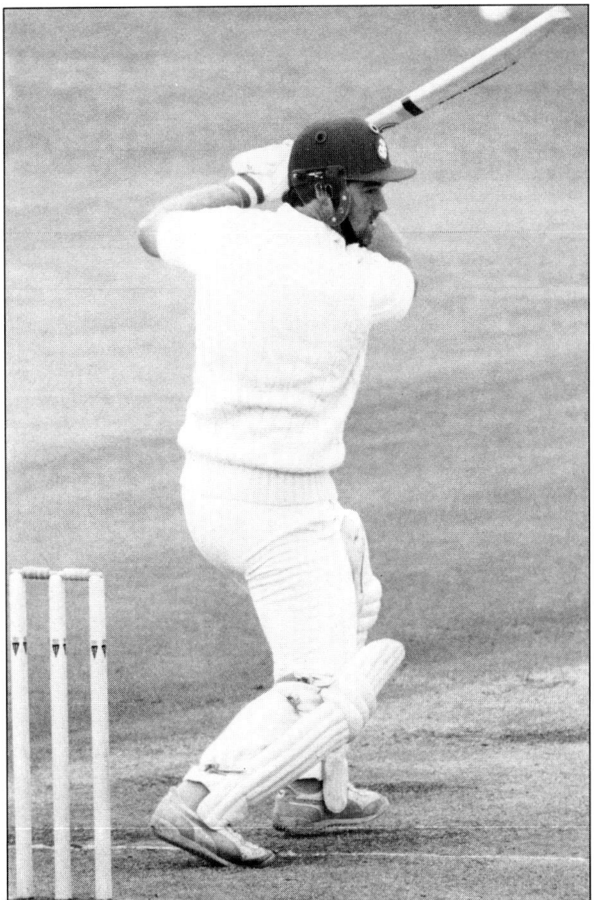

had been missed, Holland and McDermott the sufferers, as the Australian out-cricket had disintegrated.

Gatting and Lamb now took over and when Lamb was out Botham came in and hit two of the first three balls he received, from McDermott, for six. Gatting pushed to leg to reach his second century of the series, emanating solidity, belligerence and reassurance, and Gower declared. Australia, in some disarray in the field, had 95 minutes batting on the fourth evening, play again having been extended until 7.00 pm because of interruptions by rain.

Hilditch played two positive shots and then, as Botham dropped one short, he hooked into the hands of one of the two long legs that had been posted. It was a wretched shot and it heralded a period of utter misery for Australia. Wessels was dropped before he had scored, but Ellison, joining the attack at 31 for 1, quickly destroyed the backbone of the Australian batting. Wessels was deceived by an outswinger and Holland, the night-watchman, was lbw first ball. Three runs later Wood, rashly, tried to hit to leg and skied the ball to mid-off. Almost immediately Ellison captured the biggest prize of all when he moved a ball back at Border and bowled

LEFT: *Gatting rubs salt in Australian wounds. (Ken Kelly)*

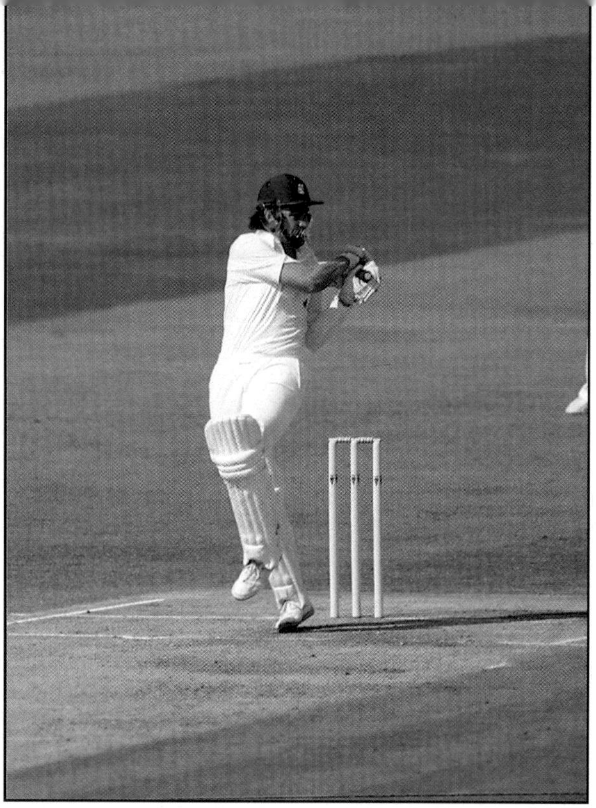

Tim Robinson in punishing mood on the leg side during his innings of 148. (Ken Kelly)

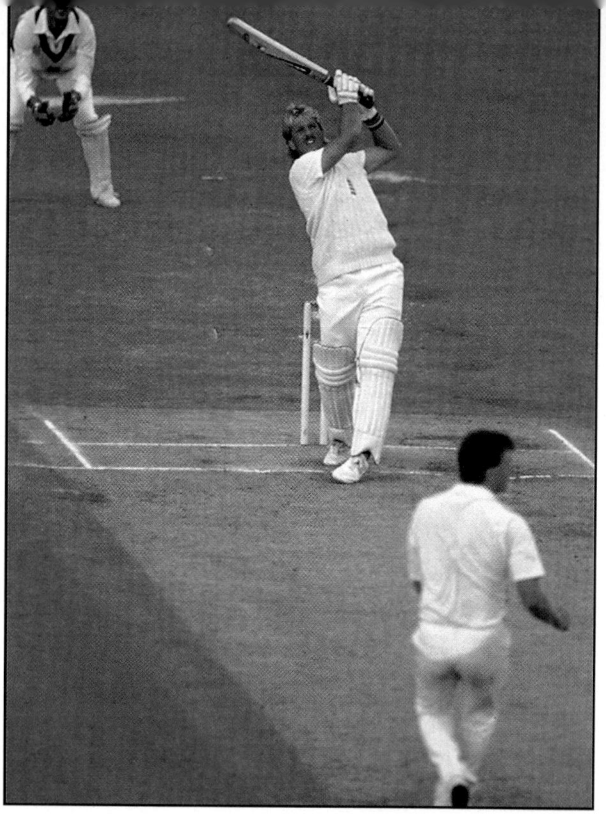

Botham hits the first ball he receives, from McDermott, for six. (Adrian Murrell)

FIFTH CORNHILL TEXT MATCH – ENGLAND *v.* AUSTRALIA
15, 16, 17, 19 and 20 August 1985 at Edgbaston, Birmingham

AUSTRALIA

	FIRST INNINGS		SECOND INNINGS	
G.M. Wood	c Edmonds, b Botham	19	(2) c Robinson, b Ellison	10
A.M.J. Hilditch	c Downton, b Edmonds	39	(1) c Ellison, b Botham	10
K.C. Wessels	c Downton, b Ellison	83	c Downton, b Ellison	10
A.R. Border†	c Edmonds, b Ellison	45	(5) b Ellison	2
G.M. Ritchie	c Botham, b Ellison	8	(6) c Lamb, b Emburey	20
W.B. Phillips*	c Robinson, b Ellison	15	(7) c Gower, b Edmonds	59
S.P. O'Donnell	c Downton, b Taylor	1	(8) b Botham	11
G.F. Lawson	run out	53	(9) c Gower, b Edmonds	3
C.J. McDermott	c Gower, b Ellison	35	(10) c Edmonds, b Botham	8
J.R. Thomson	not out	28	(11) not out	4
R.G. Holland	c Edmonds, b Ellison	0	(4) lbw, b Ellison	0
Extras	lb 4, w 1, nb 4	9	b 1, lb 3, nb 1	5
		335		142

	O	M	R	W	O	M	R	W
Botham	27	1	108	1	14.1	2	52	3
Taylor	26	5	78	1	13	4	27	—
Ellison	31.5	9	77	6	9	3	27	4
Edmonds	20	4	47	1	15	9	13	2
Emburey	9	2	21	—	13	5	19	1

FALL OF WICKETS
1- 44, 2- 92, 3- 189, 4- 191, 5- 207, 6- 208, 7- 218, 8- 276, 9- 335
1- 10, 2- 32, 4- 35, 5- 36, 6- 113, 7- 117, 8- 120, 9- 137

ENGLAND

	FIRST INNINGS	
G.A. Gooch	c Phillips, b Thomson	19
R.T. Robinson	b Lawson	148
D.I. Gower†	c Border, b Lawson	215
M.W. Gatting	not out	100
A.J. Lamb	c Wood, b McDermott	46
I.T. Botham	c Thomson, b McDermott	18
P.R. Downton*	not out	0
J.E. Emburey		
R.M. Ellison		
P.H. Edmonds		
L.B. Taylor		
Extras	b 7, lb 20, nb 22	49
	(for 5 wkts dec)	595

	O	M	R	W
Lawson	37	1	135	2
McDermott	31	2	155	2
Thomson	19	1	101	1
Holland	25	4	95	—
O'Donnell	16	3	69	—
Border	6	1	13	—

FALL OF WICKETS
1- 38, 2- 369, 3- 463, 4- 572, 5- 592

Umpires: D.J. Constant and D.R. Shepherd

England won by an innings and 118 runs

him. In 15 deliveries Ellison had taken 4 for 1. Australia were 37 for 5 and England scented victory.

The last morning was frustration for England as the rain returned. Play was due to restart at 2.30, but after two balls the players left the field in drizzle and poor light. When they returned Ritchie and Phillips played with a determination that had been lacking the previous evening. They moved to tea with assurance and seemed set to bat out the day, but the partnership was broken by a freak dismissal. Phillips slashed a ball from Edmonds down to the off side. Lamb attempted to take evasive action, but the ball hit him on the back of the leg and looped up to Gower. After consultation, the umpires ruled Phillips out. Border later voiced his displeasure at the decision.

The spinners now reassumed dominance. Ritchie pushed forward to Emburey and gave a simple catch. Lawson was also taken close in. Botham returned to finish the match. He beat and bowled O'Donnell and then, with less than 13 overs remaining, he had McDermott taken at short leg.

For England no praise can be too high. Ellison took the individual award for his fine bowling, but there had been magnificent and memorable batting by Gower and Robinson, and a punishing innings from Gatting. In all, after an uncertain start, it had been a splendid team performance and England were in sight of regaining the Ashes.

ABOVE: *The crucial wicket. Border is bowled by Ellison. (Adrian Murrell)*

BELOW: *England triumphant. (Adrian Murrell)*

Derbyshire C.C.C. First-Class Matches – Batting, 1985	v. Northamptonshire (Derby) 27–30 April	v. Leicestershire (Leicester) 8–10 May	v. Lancashire (Chesterfield) 22–24 May	v. Australians (Derby) 25–28 May	v. Hampshire (Basingstoke) 29–31 May	v. Gloucestershire (Derby) 1–4 June	v. Middlesex (Lord's) 8–11 June	v. Sussex (Derby) 12–14 June	v. Lancashire (Old Trafford) 15–18 June	v. Nottinghamshire (Derby) 26–28 June	v. Glamorgan (Derby) 29 June–2 July	v. Worcestershire (Worcester) 6–9 July	v. Northamptonshire (Northampton) 10–12 July	v. Leicestershire (Chesterfield) 13–15 July
K.J. Barnett	— 62	49 134*	103 —	— —	6 17	83 19	0 72	109 —	9 43	32 2	67 42*	27 29	44 27	20 34
A. Hill	— 4	89 33	6 —	— —	20 120	9* 10*								
J.E. Morris	— 4	20 0	1 —	— —		22 5	99 10	1 —	2 19		36 —			53 45
B. Roberts	— 41	14 96	21 —	— —	0 66	100* 2	17 39*	20 —	8 15	49 100	36 —	0 30	41 44	10 13
W.P. Fowler	— 79	6 —	76 —	— —	12 0	13 0	16 30*	16 —	6 7	1 4				
G. Miller	— 19	0 —	3 —	— —	15 46	1* 11	7 —		45 18*	52 19	90 —	6 24*	60* 4	0 0
R.J. Finney	— 5	0 —	3 —	— —	16 27*	82 1	10 —	1 —	0 3	0 4	6 —	4 6*	12 0*	0 26
D.G. Moir	— 20			— —	40 —		46 —	3 —	14 10					
B.J.M. Maher	— 9	8 —	7 —	— —	8 18*	46 1	0 —	0* —	2* 5*	0 0*	11 —	9 —	19 —	7* 0
A.E. Warner	— 16	8* —	1* —		24 —	— 12					47 —	50 0		
O.H. Mortensen	— 3*		0 —			— 0	2* —	0 —	3 —	16* —			1 —	0 2*
P.G. Newman		10 —		— —	56* —			0 —		4 2	52* —	21 10	6 8*	0 115
D.E. Malcolm		0 —												
M.A. Holding			1 —			— 13	6 —			6 17	8 —			37 12
J.G. Wright				— —	29 44			91 —	75 95			7 117	47 5	
I.S. Anderson							27 55	5 —	5 12	95 70	7 40*	36 94	0 51	2 5
R. Sharma										4 6*	26 —	35 8	15 13	10 19
P.E. Russell												3* —	2 —	
C. Marples														
M.A. Fell														
A.M. Brown														
Byes	3	9 4				6	1 4	4	4 4	1 5			5 7	7
Leg-byes	2	4 6	10		9 3	4	3 5	1	12 16	2 2	2	9 9	8 3	2 16
Wides	1		3		1 1	1 2	2 1	3	8 1	3	3	1		5
No-balls	13	9 6	8		10 8	14 6	5	2	8 3	2	7	7 8	4	12 24
Total	0 281	226 279	243 0		246 350	381 82	236 221	256	201 251	264 234	398 82	214 336	264 162	153 323
Wickets	0 10	10 3	10 0		10 6	5 10	10 3	10	10 8	10 8	10 0	10 7	10 6	10 10
Result	L	D	D	D	L	L	D	D	L	D	W	W	D	L
Points	3	6	2	—	6	5	6	5	5	5	23	22	4	4

Catches 27 – G. Miller
24 – C. Marples (ct 23/st 1)
21 – B.J.M. Maher (ct 19/st 2) and B. Roberts
16 – I.S. Anderson
13 – K.J. Barnett
7 – D.G. Moir
6 – J.G. Wright, M.A. Holding and R. Sharma
5 – J.E. Morris
4 – O.H. Mortensen and W.P. Fowler

17, 19 and 20 August

at Cheltenham

Warwickshire 127 (C.A. Walsh 7 for 51) and 211 (C.A. Walsh 6 for 77)
Gloucestershire 253 (K.M. Curran 63, J.W. Lloyds 54, G.C. Small 5 for 80) and 86 for 3

Gloucestershire won by 7 wickets
Gloucestershire 23 pts, Warwickshire 4 pts

at Old Trafford

Lancashire 334 (D.W. Varey 87, K.A. Hayes 71, N.H. Fairbrother 66) and 5 for 1
Nottinghamshire 253 for 5 dec (D.J.R. Martindale 104 not out, B.C. Broad 84)

Match drawn
Nottinghamshire 6 pts, Lancashire 5 pts

at Leicester

Hampshire 162 (P. Willey 6 for 43)
Leicestershire 106 for 5

Match drawn
Leicestershire 4 pts, Hampshire 3 pts

English Counties Form Charts

The statistics of all first-class matches are given on pages 426 to 511. The games covered are:

Britannic Assurance County Championship.
Matches against touring and representative sides.

In the batting tables a blank indicates that a batsman did not *play* in a game, a dash (—) that he did not *bat*. A dash (—) is placed in the batting averages if a player had 2 innings or less, and in the bowling figures if no wicket was taken.

v. Yorkshire (Chesterfield) 24–26 July		v. Warwickshire (Edgbaston) 27–30 July		v. Yorkshire (Bradford) 31 July–2 August		v. Surrey (Derby) 3–6 August		v. Essex (Colchester) 10–13 August		v. Worcestershire (Buxton) 14–16 August		v. Sussex (Hove) 17–20 August		v. Nottinghamshire (Trent Bridge) 24–27 August		v. Somerset (Derby) 28–30 August		v. Kent (Folkestone) 31 Aug.–3 Sept.		v. Warwickshire (Chesterfield) 11–13 September				M	Inns	NOs	Runs	H/S	Av
125	18	12	—	34	0	27	69	—	0	2	—	1	80	23	51	49	15	0	14	18	—			25	41	2	1568	134*	40.20
						0	10	—	0	7*	—	2	23											10	14	3	333	120	30.27
49	25	18	—	9	22	2	6	—	4							32	90	38	1	109*	—			18	27	1	722	109*	27.76
44	24	13	—	41	6	10	14	0*	38	13	—	7	14	1	33	1	33	33	17	4	20*			25	42	4	1128	100*	29.68
																								10	14	1	266	79	20.46
74*	13	15	—	23	11	13	5	—	105	—	—	4	18	34	9									21	31	5	744	105	28.61
3	1	44*	—	6*	0	1*	2*	—	0	—	—	13	9*	4	17	33	5*	11	3*	23	—			25	37	10	381	82	14.11
		3	—	4	38																			8	9	—	178	46	19.77
																								14	18	6	150	46	12.50
8	16	8	—	7	6	60	8	—	8	—	—	5	23	6	1									15	20	2	314	60	17.44
														1	1*	0*	—	4	—	6*	—			13	15	7	39	16*	4.87
0	0	4	—	11	2	35	18	—	34	—	—	98	6	20	11	37	9	29	1	5	—			20	29	3	604	115	23.23
																								1	1	—	0	0	0.00
80	12					0	1					67*	18			27	34	0	12	62	—			12	19	1	413	80	22.94
		177*	—	12	6			—	10	0*	—			6	76									11	16	2	797	177*	56.92
9	62	24	—	39	14	12	32	1*	39	0	—	68	7	0	3	16	26	2	2	3	13*			19	35	3	876	94	27.37
0	41*																			32	—			7	12	2	209	41*	20.90
																		0*	—					3	3	2	5	3*	5.00
8	—	—	—	1	7*	4	10	—	12*	—	—	1	4	21*	0	34	8*	3	0*	1	—			11	15	5	114	34	11.40
										—	—	21	27	0	6	19	6	12	7					5	8	—	98	27	12.25
																3	16			74	—			2	3	—	93	74	31.00
1	5	3			2	8	16		7			3	5			1	4	2	6										
10	1	10		10	11	5	2		5	2		7	4	4	5	5	6	3	3	10									
6		3		2		9				1		1			1	8	1	2		1	3								
3		10			4		2		1			14	6	5	3	7	8	8	4	6									
420	218	344		199	129	186	195	1	263	25		312	244	125	217	272	261	147	70	354	36								
10	9	8		10	10	10	10	0	10	3		10	10	10	10	10	8	10	7	9	0								
D		D		L		L		L		D		D		L		D		D		W									
8		3		3		5		4		0		8		2		7		3		24									

3 – A. Hill, A.M. Brown, R.J. Finney and subs
2 – P.G. Newman and A.E. Warner

at Lord's

Surrey 194 (N.G. Cowans 5 for 61) and 271 for 7 dec (M.A. Lynch 108, G.S. Clinton 63)
Middlesex 183 (A.H. Gray 7 for 68) and 56 for 0

Match drawn
Middlesex 5 pts, Surrey 5 pts

at Wellingborough

Northamptonshire 372 for 9 dec (R.J. Boyd-Moss 121, R.G. Williams 94, J. Derrick 4 for 60)
Glamorgan 75 for 3

Match drawn
Northamptonshire 5 pts, Glamorgan 2 pts

at Hove

Derbyshire 312 (P.G. Newman 98, I.S. Anderson 68, M.A. Holding 67 not out) and 244 (K.J. Barnett 80)
Sussex 169 (R.J. Finney 5 for 41) and 228 for 3 (Imran Khan 77 not out)

Match drawn
Derbyshire 8 pts, Sussex 5 pts

at Worcester

Essex 217 (P.J. Prichard 95, N.V. Radford 5 for 79) and 72 for 3
Worcestershire 231 (P.A. Neale 62, G.A. Hick 56, D.B. d'Oliveira 50)

Match drawn
Worcestershire 6 pts, Essex 6 pts

at Scarborough

Kent 217 (N.R. Taylor 102 not out, C. Shaw 5 for 76) and 18 for 1
Yorkshire 150 for 1 dec (G. Boycott 62 not out)

Match drawn
Yorkshire 5 pts, Kent 2 pts

Gloucestershire, the only winners in the eight Britannic Assurance County Championship matches marred by rain, moved back to the top of the table, eight points ahead of Middlesex and twenty ahead of Surrey. The London rivals clashed at Lord's. Cowans, Daniel and Hughes gave Middlesex an early advantage and Surrey, 109 for 7, were only revived by an eighth wicket stand of 56 between Doughty

Derbyshire C.C.C. First-Class Matches — Bowling, 1985	O.H. Mortenson	A.E. Warner	R.J. Finney	G. Miller	P.G. Newman	D.E. Malcolm	B. Roberts	M.A. Holding	K.J. Barnett
v. Northamptonshire (Derby) 27–30 April	18–5–60–2 14–2–38–1	16–2–74–0 11–2–27–0	21–4–68–5 6–0–25–1	16–4–33–0 13–2–50–0					
v. Leicestershire (Leicester) 8–10 May		25–3–79–3	8–5–13–0	4–2–8–0	29.3–7–92–4	17–2–82–3	4–0–20–0		
v. Lancashire (Chesterfield) 22–24 May	10–4–13–1 9–0–30–0	2–1–1–0 13–3–29–0	7–1–26–1	5–4–2–0			6–1–20–0	8–4–5–0 14–4–17–3	1–1–0–0
v. Australians (Derby) 25–28 May			14–1–52–0	39–5–125–3	7–2–27–0				
v. Hampshire (Basingstoke) 29–31 May		16–2–67–3 11–1–63–0	14–1–56–2 11–0–62–0	6–4–8–2 29–3–132–2	6.3–1–30–2 8–1–39–2				
v. Gloucestershire (Derby) 1–4 June	17–3–68–0 11–4–29–0	19–4–75–1 10–2–34–0	22–2–86–1 9–0–44–0	2–0–7–0 21–4–54–0			4–0–27–0	17–4–59–0 7–0–33–1	19–2–69–1 28–4–84–3
v. Middlesex (Lord's) 8–11 June	20–5–47–4 1.5–0–11–1		12–2–45–3	1–0–1–0				17–3–66–2	2–0–6–0
v. Sussex (Derby) 12–14 June	9–3–13–2		10–1–28–0		7–3–23–0				31–7–83–2
v. Lancashire (Old Trafford) 15–18 June	21–7–32–0 3.5–0–24–0		27.2–4–61–7 5–0–16–0	43–11–93–3 18–3–110–6					
v. Nottinghamshire (Derby) 26–28 June	24–6–73–0 10–1–57–1		22–5–70–2 11–4–28–1	13–1–50–1 5–2–14–1	23.2–7–52–4 8–4–21–0			27–6–75–2 18–5–65–6	
v. Glamorgan (Derby) 29 June–1 July		11–1–45–1 15–3–67–1	10–1–35–0 9–3–28–0	11–2–44–1	13.1–2–29–4 26–2–94–4			21–7–33–5 18.3–3–62–3	3–1–8–1
v. Worcestershire (Worcester) 6–9 July		19–3–88–3 16–2–58–0	22–4–62–6 15–4–38–1	14.5–1–33–1 10–1–41–1	15–5–37–0 19–3–72–1				
v. Northamptonshire (Northampton) 10–12 July	23–2–62–2 18–4–70–3		22–2–75–3 15.4–2–57–2	19–2–70–0 2–0–15–0	14–1–52–2 6–0–27–1				3–0–15–0
v. Leicestershire (Chesterfield) 13–15 July	21–1–95–1 4–0–28–0		23–5–77–3 2–0–4–0	4–3–5–0	31–8–89–4 10–0–35–0			30.3–3–95–2 12–2–38–3	
v. Yorkshire (Chesterfield) 24–26 July		19.5–1–88–4 2–1–2–0	12–2–33–1		18–3–74–2 4–1–6–1			22–2–56–3 6.5–4–9–0	
v. Warwickshire (Edgbaston) 27–30 July									
v. Yorkshire (Bradford) 31 July–2 August			6–3–4–0	33–9–79–0	15–5–22–1				46.3–10–115–6
v. Surrey (Derby) 3–6 August		13–3–49–0	22–5–90–3	14.3–1–79–2	17–1–80–1		2–0–22–0	16–2–70–1	15–1–52–2
v. Essex (Colchester) 10–13 August		17.4–4–51–5	6.5–3–9–0	27–6–60–3	23–4–75–2				0.1–0–0–0
v. Worcestershire (Buxton) 14–16 August									
v. Sussex (Hove) 17–20 August		5–0–10–0 3–0–19–0	20–6–41–5 12.4–2–38–0	17–3–49–1	5.3–0–21–2 15–3–52–0			21–3–78–3 13–0–59–2	3–2–6–0
v. Nottinghamshire (Trent Bridge) 24–27 August	27.3–10–49–4 4–1–11–0	23–1–87–3	18–5–55–2	18–5–42–1	24–4–70–0 3.3–1–17–0				
v. Somerset (Derby) 28–30 August	22–4–87–5		13–0–59–0		18–2–70–2			18–3–66–1	10–0–43–2
v. Kent (Folkestone) 31 August–3 September	18–6–54–2		3–0–12–0		11–4–20–1			31–4–114–3	7–2–24–0
v. Warwickshire (Chesterfield) 11–13 September	9–2–13–1 24.5–5–62–3		6–1–26–3 12–3–30–1		12.5–1–52–2 10–1–37–0		4–0–17–0	16–5–28–4 19–3–90–6	7–3–15–0
	340–75– 1026–33 *av.* 31.09	267.3–39– 1013–24 *av.* 42.20	449.3–81– 1453–53 *av.* 27.41	385.2–78– 1204–28 *av.* 43.00	400.2–76– 1315–42 *av.* 31.30	17–2– 82–3 *av.* 27.33	20–1– 106–0 —	354.5–67– 1124–50 *av.* 22.48	173.4–33– 514–17 *av.* 30.23

a J.G. Wright 6–0–42–0 b I.S. Anderson 3–1–9–0

D.G. Moir	P.E. Russell	J.E. Morris	Byes	Leg-byes	Wides	No-balls	Total	Wkts
			1	4		6	240	7
						2	140	2
			1	6	1	22	301	10
				1			20	1
				2	3	6	126	4
27–7–67–2			3	4	1	6	278	5
14–5–51–1			1	5		11	218	10
20–3–68–2				16	2	8	380	6
				7		3	398	3
			3	10	1	5	291	4
20–0–11–1			6	2			178	10
							17	1
42–12–102–3				1		6	250	7
13–1–44–0			1	9	1	1	240	10
10–0–59–0				6	4		215	7
				7	3	1	327	10
			5	3	5	2	193	9
			2	16	5	10	160	10
			4	9	1	13	316	10
	16–4–61–0		4	10	7		295	10
	16.4–4–34–2		1	9	2	2	253	5
	27–9–60–0		1	14	1	4	334	7
	5–0–21 0		8	6			219	6
			8	7	7	21	376	10
					4	5	105	3
			13	9	1	9	273	10
			4				21	1
			Match Abandoned					
58–20–114–3			6	11	2	8	352	10
			8	11	1	8	461	9
				4		5	199	10
		5.1–0–55–0	4				101	0a
			Match Abandoned					
			13	6		19	169	10
			5			11	228	3
			4	6	3	14	313	10
				2			30	0
			1	10	2	4	336	10
	25.1–5–67–2		2	7		1	300	8
			4			7	123	10
			1	4	3	11	265	10b
186–48–415–12 av. 43.08	89.5–22–243–4 av. 60.75	5.1–0–55–0 —						

Courtenay Walsh, 13 for 128 v. *Warwickshire, 17–20 August. Walsh's bowling throughout the season was one of the main reasons for the resurgence of cricket in Gloucestershire. (David Munden)*

and Monkhouse. Middlesex fared little better when they batted and finished the first day on 115 for 5. Gray ensured that there would be no recovery on the Monday and Surrey, in soggy weather, began to take command of the game. They set Middlesex to make 283 in 67 overs after Lynch had driven his way to a fine century, but rain returned at 3.00 pm on the last afternoon.

Gloucestershire's victory was achieved through some remarkable cricket on the first day and some outstanding fast bowling by Courtenay Walsh. He and Lawrence routed Warwickshire who were all out shortly after lunch, Walsh taking the last 6 wickets for 10 runs in 28 deliveries. Gloucestershire were 19 for 4 in reply, but Lloyds and Curran put on 113 and the home side reached 253 at 4.68 an over. Only 8 overs were possible on the Monday during which time Warwickshire lost both openers. The last day was cut by 34 overs, but Lawrence and Walsh again devastated

Essex C.C.C.
First-Class Matches – Batting, 1985

Essex C.C.C. First-Class Matches – Batting, 1985	v. Cambridge University (Cambridge) 20–23 April		v. M.C.C. (Lord's) 24–26 April		v. Warwickshire (Chelmsford) 27–29 April		v. Nottinghamshire (Trent Bridge) 1–3 May		v. Yorkshire (Sheffield) 22–24 May		v. Surrey (The Oval) 25–28 May		v. Leicestershire (Chelmsford) 1–4 June		v. Lacashire (Ilford) 8–11 June	
G.A. Gooch	99	88	15	41	8	61	67	202			57	—			45	19
P.J. Prichard	14	10	8	42	6	20	70	5								
K.S. McEwan	26	110	41	63	18	69	9	28			2	—	1	46*	41	6
B.R. Hardie	27	112*	31	0	13	40	5	9			54	—	4	0	4	4
A.W. Lilley	16	—			30	63					0	—	11	56*	12	10
K.R. Pont	55	—	0	62*	38	3*	10	—								
K.W.R. Fletcher	56*	—	1	—			8	5*			16	—	41	—	50	5
D.E. East	34*	2	7	39*	36	—	20	17			69	—	54	—	0	3
J.K. Lever	—	—			0	—	19*	—			—	—	2	6	3	24*
J.H. Childs	—	—	6	—							—	—	5	—		
D.L. Acfield	—	—	1*	—	2*	—	8	—			—	—	4*	—	10*	8*
D.R. Pringle			47	1	10	14	29	27*			121*	—	47	—	18	0
S. Turner			3	—									1	—		
N.A. Foster					31	—	17	—			2*	—			63	0
C. Gladwin													17	37	4	6
N. Phillip																
T.D. Topley																
I.L. Pont																
J.P. Stephenson																
Byes		1	1	4	2	5		2			3		5	1	10	9
Leg-byes	8	3	1	6	10	9	7				6		8	1	5	8
Wides	4	1			4		2	1			1		1	1	1	1
No-balls					4	9	2	1			5		12	14	15	5
Total	339	327	162	258	212	293	273	297			336		213	162	281	108
Wickets	6	4	10	5	10	6	10	5			6		10	3	10	9
Result	D		D		W		D		Ab.		L		D		D	
Points	—		—		22		7		0		4		4		7	

Essex C.C.C. First-Class Matches – Batting, 1985	v. Northamptonshire (Ilford) 12–14 June		v. Glamorgan (Swansea) 15–18 June		v. Northamptonshire (Northampton) 22–25 June		v. Kent (Chelmsford) 26–28 June		v. Hampshire (Southampton) 29 June–2 July		v. Australians (Chelmsford) 6–9 July	
G.A. Gooch					—	—					68	27
P.J. Prichard					—	—	79	—	0	1	7	4
K.S. McEwan	48	37	13*	63*	—	—	82	—	2	56	18	0
B.R. Hardie	131	78*	25	3	—	—	18	—	4	28	113*	17
A.W. Lilley	0	4	9	16							15	11
K.R. Pont	24	16					17	—	5	34		
K.W.R. Fletcher	5	8	—	—	—	—	0	—	2	8		
D.E. East	2	1	—	—	—	—	7	—	0	11	23	30*
J.K. Lever	19	3	16*	—	—	—	3	—	14*	2*		
J.H. Childs			—	—								
D.L. Acfield	10*	—	—	—	—	—	1*	—	1	4	14	—
D.R. Pringle			—	—	—	—	11	—	5	3	29	4
S. Turner	15	11					2	—	35	11		
N.A. Foster			—	—	—	—					14	15*
C. Gladwin	48	12	8	92*	—	—	8	—	25	4	5	27
N. Phillip	19	6									50	22
T.D. Topley												
I.L. Pont												
J.P. Stephenson												
Byes	20	4	1							5	12	
Leg-byes	11	5	1	4			5		2	5	8	10
Wides			5				1			2	5	
No-balls	2		1	7			9		1	9	28	2
Total	354	185	79	185			243		96	183	409	169
Wickets	10	9	3	2			10		10	10	10	8
Result	D		D		D		D		L		D	
Points	8		4		2		6		3		—	

Catches 76 – D.E. East (ct 72/st 4)
22 – B.R. Hardie
20 – G.A. Gooch
18 – D.R. Pringle
17 – K.S. McEwan
14 – P.J. Prichard
11 – K.W.R. Fletcher
9 – N.A. Foster
8 – J.K. Lever
7 – A.W. Lilley
6 – D.L. Acfield
4 – K.R. Pont and C. Gladwin

the Warwickshire batting. Walsh finished with career best match figures of 13 for 128 and 16 close catches in the two Warwickshire innings testified to the life and pace that the fast bowlers achieved. Gloucestershire needed 86 to win off 27 overs and they won with 7 overs to spare.

Hampshire's challenge was severely dampened. They were spun out by Willey on the opening day. Maru and Cowley responded, but there was no play on the last two days. A mutilated first day, dour Kent batting held together by Taylor's dogged century and a challenging declaration by Bairstow could bring no result at Scarborough where again there was no play on the last day. It was the same story at Old Trafford where a heartening stand of 155 between Varey and Kevin Hayes for the second wicket took Lancashire to a position of strength. Duncan Martindale hit a glorious maiden century for Notts on the Monday with 2 sixes and 10 fours. He and Broad put on 143 for the fourth wicket and Rice declared 81 runs behind, but the last day was lost.

Northants reached 372 on the opening day at Wellingborough thanks to a century by Robin Boyd-Moss who shared a fourth wicket stand of 134 with Richard Williams, a fine all-round cricketer who seems destined now to be denied a chance in international cricket. Only 25.4 overs were possible on the second day and only 11 balls on the last.

There was no play on the last day at Worcester where Essex had fought back to a position from which they could well have snatched victory. They were 39 for 4, but a mature innings from Paul Prichard took them to 217. In response, Worcestershire neared the Essex score with only 5 wickets down, Hick and Neale sharing a century stand, but Foster took 3 quick wickets and with Illingworth absent with bronchitis, Worcestershire's lead was cut to 14. Prichard again batted well after the splendid Radford had taken three more wickets on a pitch which was assisting the seam bowlers, but then came the rain.

Derbyshire, 50 for 5, were rallied excitingly by Newman, with his second high score of the season, and Holding. Newman and opener Anderson put on 138 for the sixth wicket and Holding and Newman added 79 for the eighth. Sussex were struggling at 42 for 3 by the close. Finney had done the early damage and Holding and Newman continued the rout on the Monday. Jones and le Roux saved the follow-on, but Derbyshire, led inevitably by Barnett, built up a formidable lead and Sussex were asked to make 388 on a wicket that was placid. They reached 228 for 3 with 34 overs remaining when rain ended the match.

v. Somerset (Southend) 10–12 July		v. Gloucestershire (Southend) 13–16 July		v. Kent (Dartford) 24–26 July		v. Somerset (Taunton) 27–30 July		v. Middlesex (Chelmsford) 3–6 August		v. Derbyshire (Colchester) 10–13 August		v. Sussex (Colchester) 14–16 August		v. Worcestershire (Worcester) 17–20 August		v. Surrey (Chelmsford) 24–27 August		v. Gloucestershire (Bristol) 28–30 August		v. Warwickshire (Edgbaston) 31 Aug.–3 Sept.		v. Essex (Lord's) 11–13 September		v. Yorkshire (Chelmsford) 14–17 September		M	Inns	NOs	Runs	H/S	Av
				17	125	19	173*			43	—					132*	94					19	145	142	—	14	23	2	1706	202	81.23
41	7	17	—	9	9	18	44	—	33	3	—	6	62*	95	35*	9	1	19	24	69*	—	0	6	6	—	21	34	4	779	95	25.96
11	20	14	—	46	14	—	0	—	121	26	—	0	6*	11	11	64	0	16	106	11	—	0	4	33	—	26	42	4	1293	121	34.02
162	66	37	—	2	24	25*	20	13*	12*	17	29*	74	28	4	6	11	13	19	35	0	—	5	48	4	—	26	45	7	1374	162	36.15
										28	68*	2	—	7	11	—	6	10	29	0	—	4	60	38	—	16	26	2	516	68*	21.50
0	7*			8	15	—	—																			10	15	3	294	62*	24.50
71	11*	78*	—			—	—	—	8*	52	—	3	—	34	—	56*	4*	16	30	2	—	13	39	66	—	23	28	7	688	78*	32.76
25	—	131	—	30	26*	—	—	—	—	2	—	42	—	7	—	—	9*	1	12	69*	—	18	100	62	—	26	32	6	889	131	34.19
7	—	8	—	10*	0			—	—	4	—	3*	—	11	—	—	—	4	18*	—	—	10*	7	—	—	23	23	9	193	24*	13.78
				3	3*																					6	4	1	17	6	5.66
0*	—	4	—	0	—	—	—	—	—	3*	—	0	—	3*	—	—	—	0*	4	—	—	2	1			25	21	11	80	14	8.00
2	14	19	—	19	15	—	45*	—	69*	0	—	3	—	1	—	5	44	0	25	4	—			23	—	23	31	4	654	121*	24.22
																										5	7	—	78	35	11.14
								—	—	12	—	3	—	15	—	—	—	11	10	—	—					14	12	2	193	63	19.30
31	41	12	—	53	8			19*	10			28	5													13	22	2	500	92*	25.00
21	7	4	—																							4	7	—	129	50	18.42
		0	—			—	—															0	9*	—	—	4	3	1	9	9*	4.50
						—	—	—	—					11	5*					—	—	11	12	9*	—	6	5	2	48	12	16.00
																		10	4							1	2	—	14	10	7.00
											4	6		1		12	9		1				7	3							
6	7	6		10	7	4	11		3	4		7	6	5	1	5	6	1	6	6		1	9	12							
4	1	1			1	2							4	6	1	1	2		2	3				1							
		19		6	13		3	1	19	5		7	5	6	2	5	12	4	4	6		9	14	14							
381	181	350		213	260	68	296	33	275	199	101	184	116	217	72	300	200	111	310	170		92	461	413							
10	6	10		10	8	1	3	0	3	10	0	10	2	10	3	4	6	10	10	5		10	10	8							
W		D		D		W		W		W		D		D		D		W		D		D		W							
20		8		3		20		20		17		3		6		7		20		5		4		24							

3–N. Phillip
1–J.H. Childs, T.D. Topley,
J.P. Stephenson and sub

John Player Special League

18 August

at Cheltenham

Gloucestershire 85 for 3
Warwickshire 72 for 8

Gloucestershire (4 pts) won by 13 runs

at Old Trafford

Nottinghamshire 115 for 5
Lancashire 121 for 5

Lancashire (4 pts) won by 5 wickets

at Leicester

Leicestershire 18 for 1
v. Hampshire

Match abandoned
Leicestershire 2 pts, Hampshire 2 pts

at Lord's

Middlesex 179 (A.R. Butcher 4 for 22)
Surrey 34 for 0

Match abandoned
Surrey 2 pts, Middlesex 2 pts

at Wellingborough

Northamptonshire 121
Glamorgan 36 for 0

Match abandoned
Glamorgan 2 pts, Northamptonshire 2 pts

at Hove

Sussex 156 for 7
Derbyshire 136 (M.A. Holding 58)

Sussex (4 pts) won by 20 runs

at Worcester

Worcestershire 88 for 4
Essex 89 for 3

Essex (4 pts) won by 7 wickets

at Scarborough

Yorkshire 153 for 9
Kent 133 for 9

Yorkshire (4 pts) won on faster scoring rate

Rain again mocked the Sunday League. Only at Hove was the full complement of overs played, and even there Derbyshire were out in 33.2 overs. Sussex's win took them two

Essex C.C.C. First-Class Matches — Bowling, 1985	J.K. Lever	K.R. Pont	G.A. Gooch	J.H. Childs	D.L. Acfield	D.R. Pringle	S. Turner	N.A. Foster	N. Phillip
v. Cambridge University (Cambridge) 20–23 April	15–6–28–2 5–4–4–0	19–9–43–2 8–3–12–0	20–6–50–1	30–10–70–1 16–8–23–0	16–6–23–0 12–4–30–1				
v. M.C.C. (Lord's) 24–26 April		12–2–38–0	11–3–41–0	21–3–58–1	22–2–65–1	33–9–70–4	35–10–97–3		
v. Warwickshire (Chelmsford) 27–29 April	23.1–3–84–3 14–5–27–5	8–2–19–1	11–5–20–2			16–7–34–0 17.5–3–65–4		20–5–73–4 16–0–85–1	
v. Nottinghamshire (Trent Bridge) 1–3 May	27.3–9–63–3 20–4–67–2		9–3–13–0 10–1–36–0		2–1–5–0 22–1–70–2	23–9–58–2 15.4–2–57–1		27–6–83–5 16–5–64–2	
v. Yorkshire (Sheffield) 22–24 May									
v. Surrey (The Oval) 25–28 May	4–2–3–0 16–1–60–1		5–2–17–0	17–1–68–1	8–2–31–0	21.4–4–70–1		4–2–6–0 16–1–74–0	
v. Leicestershire (Chelmsford) 1–4 June	26–6–82–1			48–16–96–0	30–7–75–3	31–6–71–3	19–4–54–0		
v. Lancashire (Ilford) 8–11 June	24–10–66–5 20–3–74–2		16.5–8–22–4 14–0–46–5		4–1–17–0	17–6–33–0 5–1–13–0		18–6–46–1 12–3–34–2	
v. Northamptonshire (Ilford) 12–14 June	22–3–90–3 34.4–6–84–4	15–3–43–2 5–1–18–0			25.1–4–60–2 33–5–116–1		25–3–48–2		14–2–33–1 7–1–29–0
v. Glamorgan (Swansea) 15–18 June	16–2–51–2 4–0–15–0			12–5–15–0 17–4–69–0	15–6–34–2	17–7–31–1		22–8–40–5 4–1–6–0	
v. Northamptonshire 22–25 June	13–5–36 2		22–6–61–0		25–5–57–1	18–4–52–0		22–9–53–2	
v. Kent (Chelmsford) 26–28 June	26–9–68–3 8–2–25–0	13–0–62–2			2–0–11–0 9–2–28–0	20–5–49–2 6–1–26–1	17.5–3–36–4 5–0–18–1		
v. Hampshire (Southampton) 29 June–2 July	39–9–109–2	7–2–27–0			22–7–54–1	32–6–75–3	20–5–68–1		
v. Australians (Chelmsford) 6–9 July			21–7–41–3 19.3–3–61–4		18–5–36–1 22–6–58–0	26–7–43–0 27–5–69–4		27–6–96–2 20–3–92–2	18.3–4–55–4 7–0–39–0
v. Somerset (Southend) 10–12 July	29–5–94–1 20–7–49–6	8–1–27–0			35–4–109–2 15.4–9–34–3	18–5–53–1 4–0–12–1			10–4–17–0
v. Gloucestershire (Southend) 13–16 July	28–9–82–5 25–8–63–0				23.4–6–62–1 20–3–63–0	24–4–58–2 16–7–38–2			6–1–19–0 13–2–50–1
v. Kent (Dartford) 24–26 July	14–6–28–0	9–1–64–1		36–12–129–2	42–8–164–4	30.2–8–83–2			
v. Somerset (Taunton) 27–30 July		11–0–45–1			11–1–35–0	30–2–90–3			
v. Middlesex (Chelmsford) 3–6 August	32.5–13–53–5				1–0–1–0	17–7–26–1 2–0–8–0		25–3–87–2 8–3–12–0	
v. Derbyshire (Colchester) 10–13 August	2–1–1–0 23–7–53–2				44.4–18–81–6	9–0–36–0		1–1–0–0 19–5–81–1	
v. Sussex (Colchester) 14–16 August	25–6–78–1				42–6–125–4	25–6–74–0		25–3–93–2	
v. Worcestershire (Worcester) 17–20 August	30–9–67–3				7–0–28–1	18–4–42–2		16.5–2–59–3	
v. Surrey (Chelmsford) 24–27 August	16.2–1–67–0 11–3–37–0		27–6–88–3 2–0–19–0		4–1–21–0 9.3–1–31–1	19–4–42–0 3–0–16–1		24–4–69–5 16–1–59–3	
v. Gloucestershire (Bristol) 28–30 August	16–4–59–2 12–1–27–1				20–4–64–2	19.2–3–56–3 20.2–6–42–6		32–7–79–5 8–0–20–1	
v. Warwickshire (Edgbaston) 31 August–3 September	14–4–33–1				5–1–12–1	9–3–36–1		15–3–40–3	
v. Middlesex (Lord's) 11–13 September	12–3–22–1 10–1–30–0		14–3–31–0 15.4–1–46–3		21–4–74–1				
v. Yorkshire (Chelmsford) 14–17 September	22–6–47–6 21–5–69–3		9–0–33–1			14–5–28–2			
	720.3–188– 1995–77 *av.* 25.90	115–24– 398–9 *av.* 44.22	227–54– 625–26 *av.* 24.03	197–59– 528–5 *av.* 105.60	588.4–130– 1674–41 *av.* 40.82	604.1–146– 1556–53 *av.* 29.35	121.5–25– 321–11 *av.* 29.18	413.5–87– 1351–51 *av.* 26.49	75.3–14– 242–6 *av.* 40.33

a B.R. Hardie 3–1–10–1
C. Gladwin 3–0–12–0

b R.K. Illingworth absent ill

c B.R. Hardie 3–0–25–0
K.W.R. Fletcher 4–0–35–1

D.G. Boycott absent injured

A.W. Lilley	I.L. Pont	T.D. Topley	Byes	Leg-byes	Wides	No-balls	Total	Wkts
			1	7			222	6
							69	2
			1	7		7	377	9
				8		1	238	10
				1		1	178	10
				5	1	1	227	10
			3	5	2	1	302	7
				Match Abandoned				
				1			10	0
			1	6	2	1	327	3
			2	12	1	10	392	7
				7		2	191	10
				7			174	9
				5		8	279	10
			12	7		4	266	5
				2		6	173	10
17.4–0–116–3			6	2			214	3
			2	8		2	269	5
				10		6	174	10
			1	2	1	1	184	5a
				3		5	336	7
			2	6		2	279	10
1–0–5–0			5	4	1	5	333	10
			4	11	1	2	315	4
				3			98	10
		14–4–43–2	3	3	3	3	270	10
		15–5–34–3		2	2		250	6
			1	7			476	9
	24–2–103–5	24–3–86–0		4	1	2	363	9
							0	0
	15–3–58–2		1	8	4	1	234	10
	9–0–47–1			3			70	2
							1	0
			7	5		1	263	10
			3	7	1	2	380	8
	9–1–29–0			6			231	9b
			5	10	1		302	8
11–0–63–0			9	9	4		303	6c
				5			199	10
			1	3			157	10
	5.5–0–15–4			6	2		142	10
	23–4–81–3	27.1–8–57–4	2	12	1	3	279	10
	17–5–74–3	8–1–37–1	4	5	1	1	196	7
	2–0–9–0	13–3–36–3		6	1	3	131	10
	11–0–69–1	33–7–107–2		5	1	4	278	9d
29.4–0–184–3 av. 61.33	115.5–15–485–19 av. 25.52	134.1–31–400–15 av. 26.66						

points clear at the top of the table above Essex who won the ten-over slog at Worcester with 4 balls to spare, Leicestershire who were rained off and Yorkshire who beat Kent by the smallest imaginable margin. Yorkshire's total of 153 in 40 overs looked well within Kent's reach, but rain reduced the target to 134 in 35 overs. They needed 4 from the last over bowled by Oldham and Dilley was run out by Metcalfe on the fifth ball. Knott needed two off the last ball, but he was run out going for the second run so that Yorkshire's rate of 3.825 gave them victory over Kent whose rate was 3.8. Lancashire won the 20-over game at Old Trafford with 2 balls to spare and another excellent all-round performance by Kevin Curran, 48 not out and 3 for 9, gave Gloucestershire victory in a 10-over slog.

NatWest Trophy – Semi-Finals

21 and 22 August

at Southampton

Hampshire 224 for 8
Essex 224 for 7 (G.A. Gooch 93 not out)

Essex won on losing fewer wickets with scores level
(*Man of the Match* – G.A. Gooch)

at Worcester

Worcestershire 232 for 8 (T.S. Curtis 92, D.M. Smith 57)
Nottinghamshire 233 for 6 (R.T. Robinson 139)

Nottinghamshire won by 4 wickets
(*Man of the Match* – R.T. Robinson)

The eagerly awaited conflict between Hampshire and Essex did not disappoint. Fletcher won the toss and asked Hampshire to bat on a wicket that was a little damp and on which the ball moved about considerably early on. The Essex seam attack exploited the conditions admirably and at lunch Hampshire were 92 for 3 off 39 overs. Greenidge tried one

John Inchmore dives and shouts, but Robinson's drive eludes him. Robinson's century won the match for Notts and earned him the individual award, NatWest Bank Trophy semi-final, at Worcester. (Adrian Murrell)

Glamorgan C.C.C. First-Class Matches – Batting, 1985	v. Oxford University (Oxford) 24–26 April		v. Surrey (The Oval) 27–29 April		v. Somerset (Taunton) 1–3 May		v. Warwickshire (Edgbaston) 8–10 May		v. Middlesex (Cardiff) 22–24 May		v. Hampshire (Southampton) 25–28 May		v. Sussex (Hove) 29–31 May		v. Worcestershire (Abergavenny) 8–11 June		v. Essex (Swansea) 15–18 June		v. Zimbabwe (Swansea) 19–21 June		v. Leicestershire (Leicester) 22–25 June		v. Somerset (Cardiff) 26–28 June		v. Derbyshire (Derby) 29 June–2 July		v. Nottinghamshire (Swansea) 6–9 July	
A.L. Jones	6	—	21	47	11	18*													80	5	18	60	15	—	10	13	17	0
J.A. Hopkins	81	—	9	90	8	12	0	32	9	3	3	10	13	35	114*	—	15	60	13	44	15	0	0	—				
G.C. Holmes	29	—	5	42	88	9*	0	8	1	58	11	34	1	25	106*	—	34	92	9	24	55	112	17	—	12	52	3	12
Javed Miandad	47	—	125	23*	86	—	98	52	35*	95	1	42	0	9	—	—	7	—			1	61*	107	—	64	2	1	4
Younis Ahmed	113	—	4	8*	59	—	18	32	15	177			6	35	—	—	46	44			0	—	45	—	0	96	39	81*
R.C. Ontong	16	—	61	—	64	—	55	16	3	22*	90*	15*	19	122	—	—	29	10*			5	—	5	—	29	27	31	1
J.F. Steele	100	—	15*	—	11*	—	1	26	3	—	9	1	7*	42	—	—	20	—			48	—	—	—				
J.G. Thomas	2	—	14*	—	37	—	27	19	5	—	42	17	0	29			7	—			0	—					60*	—
T. Davies	46*	—	—	—	—	—	12*	13*	0	75	0	31	4	4	—	—	4	—			38	—	50*	—	4	32	22	44*
S.J. Malone	2	—	—	—							0	—	0	0*	—	—	0	—	2	—	—	—						
L.L. McFarlane	0	—	—	—											—	—			0	—			8	—	3	0*	1*	—
J. Derrick					—	—	1	20	5	—	17	0							4	—			5	—	4	52	13	—
S.R. Barwick					—	—	0	4	4	—	5	1*	4	6	—	—	1*	—			0*	—	29	—	1*	1		
S.P. Henderson							26	10	17	27*	3	9	2	111	—	—	2	—	47*	52*								
H. Morris																			34	36					0	2	39	27
M.R. Price																			18	20*							36	—
I. Smith																			0	—					0	12		
M.L. Roberts																			0	—								
M.P. Maynard																												
P.D. North																												
S. James																												
Byes	4			3	5		2	4	8	4		6	1	3	8			6	4	4	1	14	1		2	4		
Leg-byes	10		3	5	4	1	8	12	2	8	5	3		19	18		2	2	1	1	14	7	4		16	9	6	2
Wides			1		8	2	1	1	1	2				4								1	1		5	1	2	2
No-balls			6		6	1	4	6	3	7	11	7	1	3	4		6		2	1	2	4	2		10	13	2	
Total	456		264	218	387	43	253	255	111	478	197	176	58	447	250		173	214	214	187	197	259	289		160	316	272	173
Wickets	10		6	3	7	1	10	10	10	5	10	8	10	10	0		10	3	10	4	9	3	9		10	10	9	5
Results	D		W		W		D		D		L		L		D		D		D		D		D		L		D	
Points	—		21		24		4		2		5		2		7		2		—		1		4		3		5	

Catches 49–T. Davies (ct 44/st 5), 13–Javed Miandad, 12–R.C. Ontong, 11–A.L. Jones, 10–J.F. Steele and G.C. Holmes, 8–J.A. Hopkins and subs, 6–J.G. Thomas, 4–L.L McFarlane, H. Morris S.R. Barwick

The dust flies. The ball hits the wicket. Gooch is given not out. An important decision in the NatWest Trophy semi-final at Southampton. (Patrick Eagar)

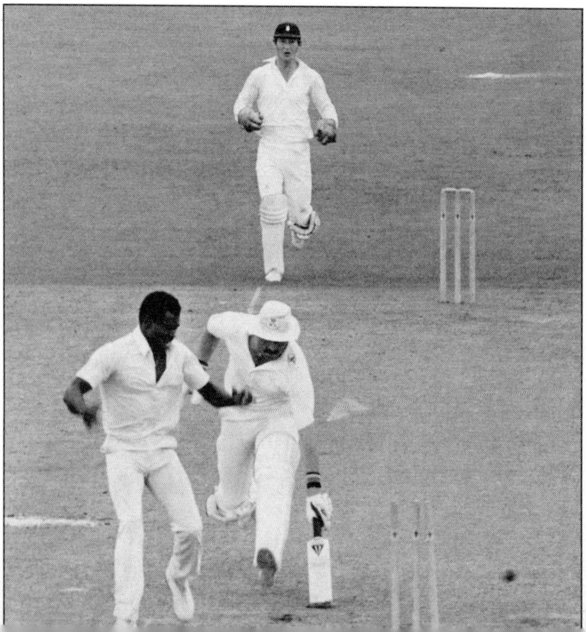

adventurous drive off Foster which fell just short of third man and was not so lucky when he attempted the shot again, Pringle taking a stinging catch at slip. Terry struggled painfully, pad more in evidence than bat, until he was lbw to Turner for 7 in the twenty-first over. It was Chris Smith, returning after injury, who threatened the Essex supremacy, but he was splendidly run out by Foster from deep square-leg when he unwisely attempted a second run. Nicholas and Robin Smith added 58 and suggested that they might take Hampshire to a useful score, but Stuart Turner, who bowled magnificently and was the outstanding bowler in the match, beat Smith and bowled him and had Nicholas lbw. On a wicket that was now easier David Turner, still one of the most attractive of batsmen, and Malcolm Marshall hit fiercely. Cowley too played some lusty blows and Hampshire's 224 was far more than had looked possible at one time in the day. They had been 117 for 5, and 130 runs had come from the last 20 overs. Essex began in brisk fashion. Connor was very ragged and Nicholas replaced him to have Hardie lbw. Prichard played confidently, but he hooked injudiciously at Nicholas, the ball plopping narrowly for 4, and, not heeding the warning, he repeated the shot and was comfortably caught on the boundary by David Turner. Gooch had been in serene mood and now, joined by

v. Leicestershire (Swansea) 10–12 July	v. Lancashire (Old Trafford) 13–16 July	v. Australians (Neath) 20–22 July	v. Worcestershire (Worcester) 24–26 July	v. Gloucestershire (Bristol) 27–30 July	v. Kent (Swansea) 3–5 August	v. Warwickshire (Cardiff) 10–13 August	v. Hampshire (Cardiff) 14–15 August	v. Northamptonshire (Wellingborough) 17–20 August	v. Yorkshire (Swansea) 24–27 August	v. Nottinghamshire (Trent Bridge) 28–30 August	v. Gloucestershire (Cardiff) 31 Aug.–3 Sept.	v. Sussex (Cardiff) 14–17 September	M	Inns	NOs	Runs	H/S	Av
8 —	34 75	24 —	69 3	0 —	— 19	38* —	— 0	3 —		35 —	— 7		19	27	2	636	80	25.44
	12 7	30 —	3 6	70 —	— 15	13 —	— 13	6 —		25 —	— 12	16* —	23	34	2	794	114*	24.81
23 —	30 0	5 —	67 2	53 —	— 10	13 —	— 18	1 —	14* 42	11 —	— 1	— —	27	40	3	1129	112	30.51
89 —	164* 1	200* —	27 5	13 —	— 22*						— 60		20	29	6	1441	200*	62.65
58 —	47 2	118* —	100* 34	12* —	— 18	28* —	— 143*	35* —	— 8				22	30	8	1421	177	64.59
56* —	38 65*	— —	7 40*	24 —	— 57	— —	— 69	— —	— 1	130 —	— 14	— —	26	30	7	1121	130	48.73
													11	12	3	283	100*	31.44
— —	4 5	— —	0 —		— —							— —	16	16	2	268	60*	19.14
10 —	29 —	— —	18 12	24* —	— 9*	— —	— —	— —	— 0	21 —	— 1*	— —	26	25	8	503	75	29.58
				— —									9	6	1	4	2	0.80
— —	— —			— —		— —	— —	— —					13	6	2	12	8	3.00
22* —						— —	— 13*	— —	0 0	4 —			14	15	2	160	52	12.30
	— —	— —	0* —	— —	— —	— —	— —	— —	— 0	1 —	— —	— —	22	15	5	57	29	5.70
													7	11	3	306	111	38.25
12 —		— —	2 35	30* —	— 38	— —	— 0	28* —	8* 62	0 —	— 8	14* —	15	18	4	375	62	26.78
— —	0 6	— —	5 8*		— 14*	— —	— —	— —	— 0	28* —	— 1	— —	14	11	4	136	28*	19.42
									— 11	4 —	— —	— —	6	5	—	27	12	5.40
													1	1	—	0	0	0.00
									— 102	58 —	— 38	— —	4	3	—	198	102	66.00
									— 0*				1	1	1	0	0*	—
												— —	1	—				—
	4 4	3	1	4		1	2		4		3							
3	14 1	9	3 5	7	1	4	8		4	9	4	1						
1	3	5	1	3					1									
7	4 5	15	8 4	13	7		5	2	1 6	3	2	1						
289	383 171	409	309 156	253	0 210	97	0 271	75	27 237	329	0 151	32						
6	8 7	3	9 7	5	0 6	2	0 5	3	1 10	10	0 8	0						
D	D	D	D	D	D	D	W	D	L	W	D	D						
4	6	—	6	5	3	4	19	2	3	24	9	0						

3 – Younis Ahmed and S.P. Henderson
2 – J. Derrick, S.J. Malone and M.R. Price
1 – M.P. Maynard

McEwan, he seemed to be stroking Essex effortlessly into the final. McEwan showed his best form and he square drove Connor to take the score to 111 at a rate well above what was required only to drive less positively at the next ball and be caught behind. Pringle joined Gooch and 20 were added. Shortly before tea Gooch was adjudged not out when Robin Smith hit the stumps as they went for an unwise single. It seemed that he was lucky to be given the benefit of the doubt. He was then on 53. At 131, Gooch ambled down the wicket for a second run after a misfield and Pringle, hesitant and unaware, sacrificed himself as his partner bore down upon him. It was insane cricket. The day had been filled with sun, but now the sky darkened and blackened. After two balls to Fletcher by Marshall, the umpires conferred and the players left the field. The rain fell and play did not start again until 1.00 pm the next day. Essex were left at 131 for 4, needing 94 more runs to win off 23.2 overs.

Much depended on Marshall and Nicholas unleashed him at Fletcher the next day. Fletcher coped superbly. When Marshall bowled short the Essex skipper twice hooked him fiercely to the boundary. He helped Gooch in a stand of 36, scoring 19 himself, blunted the Marshall threat and negotiated the most difficult period of the match for his side. He was lbw to Connor, the ball keeping low. Alan Lilley came in

Stuart Turner, the dependable, a splendidly determined all-round performance in Essex's exciting NatWest semi-final victory at Southampton. (George Herringshaw)

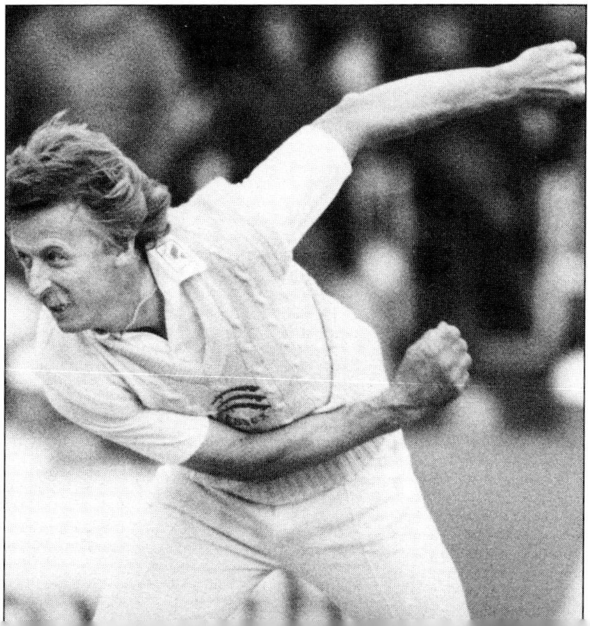

Glamorgan C.C.C. First-Class Matches — Bowling, 1985	J.G. Thomas	L.L. McFarlane	S.J. Malone	R.C. Ontong	J.F. Steele	G.C. Holmes	S.R. Barwick	J. Derrick	Younis Ahmed
v. Oxford University	22–7–47–4	14–3–28–0	20–5–55–1	19–7–38–1	30–12–75–1	12–6–27–2			
(Oxford) 24–26 April	10–0–32–0	8–1–26–0	9–2–20–2	4–1–13–1	5–3–8–0	5–2–3–1			
v. Surrey (The Oval)	19–1–72–3	9–0–43–0	20.3–4–70–0	11–0–49–1	11–3–22–0	13–2–39–2			
27–29 April	7.3–2–24–1	9–4–19–1	9–0–34–1	21–6–47–2	19–5–51–2				
v. Somerset (Taunton)	22–7–43–2			14–1–69–0	2.1–1–6–3		21–6–54–1	12–0–53–3	
1–3 May	12–0–50–1			11.5–2–36–2	10–5–17–2	12–3–25–3	12–3–33–2	10–2–23–0	
v. Warwickshire (Edgbaston)	31–2–142–3			18–3–50–1	28–2–83–0	11–2–36–0	29–6–100–2	18.4–7–55–2	
8–10 May	1–0–13–1						1–0–9–0		
v. Middlesex (Cardiff)	18.3–2–61–4			16–5–56–1	24–4–67–0	9–4–29–0	21–4–40–1	16–5–36–0	
22–24 May									
v. Hampshire (Southampton)	11–1–41–3		16–5–38–5				13.5–4–33–2		
25–28 May	17–0–96–3		5–0–26–0	7–0–51–2	2–0–24–0	2–1–5–0	7–2–26–0	3–0–20–0	
v. Sussex (Hove)	4–0–13–0		18–1–68–1	12–1–57–2	24–8–48–0	22–8–54–1	19.4–5–61–1		
29–31 May			6–0–39–0	10–1–52–1	4–0–27–0	6–1–31–0	13–0–52–0		
v. Worcestershire (Abergavenny)		25–3–81–1	9–1–38–1	24–11–48–2		12.1–3–36–3	26–4–78–1		
8–11 June		10–5–18–0	3–0–5–0	17–5–66–1	25–9–44–2		10–2–31–1		12–2–35–0
v. Essex (Swansea)	14–3–45–1			3–0–10–2	7–2–8–0		11.3–4–14–0		
15–18 June	4–1–25–1		12–1–48–0	18–7–43–1	10–5–11–0		4–2–4–0		
v. Zimbabwe (Swansea)		18–3–68–2	16.1–4–62–1			17–4–49–4		15–2–56–0	
19–21 June									
v. Leicestershire (Leicester)	9–3–31–1		3–0–20–0	2–1–5–0	5.1–1–29–0	7–1–27–0	8–1–39–0		
22–25 June	18–3–72–2		6–0–25–0	24–5–66–4	6–0–37–1	5–1–24–0	12–2–30–1		
v. Somerset (Cardiff)		20–3–78–1		37–9–125–4	2.5–0–24–0	14.1–4–42–0	22–4–62–1	20.3–1–81–1	
26–28 June		2–0–5–0					1–0–2–0		
v. Derbyshire (Derby)		22–3–100–4		21.4–7–38–1		26–5–89–2	28–3–91–2	32–6–78–1	
29 June–2 July		6–0–34–0					8–2–23–0		4–2–8–0
v. Nottinghamshire (Swansea)	20–2–76–1	16–5–42–2		15–4–38–0		9–1–31–0		21–2–69–1	
6–9 July	10–1–48–2	10–1–35–0		14–4–49–0		8–2–15–0		6–0–33–0	
v. Leicestershire (Swansea)	20.2–6–57–0	20–2–95–1		31–8–66–2		9–2–27–0		9–1–27–0	12–8–9–0
10–12 July									
v. Lancashire (Old Trafford)	16–3–39–3	11–1–61–1		36.5–9–116–2			18–2–61–0		
13–16 July	13.5–1–58–1			18–1–82–5			13–3–63–2		
v. Australians (Neath)	10–4–49–1						9.4–1–31–0		7–3–20–0
20–22 July									
v. Worcestershire (Worcester)	15–3–66–0			20–6–55–0		19–2–62–1	15–2–52–2		12–0–39–1
24–26 July	2.2–0–4–1			12–3–35–2		19–2–63–1	27–4–79–3		0.4–0–2–0
v. Gloucestershire (Bristol)		20–0–115–0	21.3–0–106–1	10–2–26–1		23–3–96–1	17–5–41–2		12–3–27–0
27–30 July									
v. Kent (Swansea)	8–2–28–0			20–6–39–1		25–11–49–3	17–4–45–1		15–4–38–1
3–5 August									
v. Warwickshire (Cardiff)		9–1–42–1		13–3–42–1		11–2–32–0	20.5–6–43–7	15–1–47–1	
10–13 August									
v. Hampshire (Cardiff)		14–5–49–1		13–5–39–0		9–2–20–0	10–1–36–0	15–3–37–1	
14–16 August									
v. Northamptonshire		16–2–69–1		25–7–68–2		14–3–47–0	15–6–32–1	21–7–60–4	
(Wellingborough) 17–20 August									
v. Yorkshire (Swansea)				29–5–91–5		3–0–22–0	11–3–25–0		
24–27 August									
v. Nottinghamshire				15–6–39–5		14–5–32–1	17.1–3–44–3	12–2–31–0	
(Trent Bridge) 28–30 August				18.3–3–67–8			6–2–11–0		
v. Gloucestershire (Cardiff)				5–1–6–1		11–3–29–2	9–0–31–0		
31 August–3 September									
v. Sussex (Cardiff)									
14–17 September									
	335.3–54–1232–39 *av.* 31.58	249–52–1008–16 *av.* 63.00	174.1–23–654–13 *av.* 50.30	585.5–145–1777–64 *av.* 27.76	215.1–60–581–11 *av.* 52.81	347.2–85–1041–27 *av.* 38.55	474.4–96–1377–36 *av.* 38.25	226.1–39–706–14 *av.* 50.42	74.4–22–178–2 *av.* 89.00

a J.A. Hopkins 2–1–9–0; S.P. Henderson 8–2–31–0
b J. A. Hopkins 4–0–13–0
c H. Morris 3–0–32–1
d P.D. North 27–7–60–1
e A.L. Jones 1–0–24–0; M.P. Maynard 0.1–0–4–0

Javed Miandad	I. Smith	M.R. Price	*Byes*	*Leg-byes*	*Wides*	*No-balls*	*Total*	*Wkts*
			8	4		5	282	10
			4	3		1	109	4
				5	1	1	300	6
			4	2	1		181	7
			5	7	2	3	237	10
			1	6		1	191	10
				6	1	4	472	8
					2		22	1
			6	2	2	4	297	7
				3	1	14	115	10
			5	6		7	259	7
			1	1	1	4	303	5
			1	4	1		206	1
			8	5		4	294	10
12–0–67–2			2	1	2	5	309	6a
			1	1	5	1	79	3
12–2–37–0				4		7	185	2b
	6–1–37–0	19–4–81–1	5	6		7	364	10
							151	1
			6	5			265	9
			3	16		1	431	7
						2	7	0
				2	3	7	398	10
	1.4–0–17–0						82	0
		27–5–62–1		3	4	11	321	6
		7–0–47–0		3	1	9	230	2
		52–20–97–4	8	7	2	13	393	7
		12–3–32–0	5	1	2	3	315	6
			8	4		1	215	8
			5		2	2	105	1
		21–6–57–1	12	6	1	4	349	6
		10.1–1–39–2	1	2	1	1	225	10
			4	1	6	2	416	6
3.3–0–16–1			3	1		5	251	7c
							0	0
			9	5		8	220	10
		19–2–82–1	4	3		4	270	3
							0	0
		24–4–80–1	4	12		3	372	9
	13–4–33–0	35.3–10–61–3	4	2	4		298	9d
	12–3–39–1	1–0–4–0	4	5		2	198	10
	4–0–10–0	20–6–27–2		5	5		120	10
	8–3–18–0	11–1–28–1	3	8	3		151	4e
			Match Abandoned					
27.3–2	44.4–11–	258.4–62–						
120–3	154–1	697–17						
av. 40.00	*av.* 154.00	*av.* 41.00						

LEFT: *Rajesh Maru. His slow left-arm bowling brought another dimension to Hampshire's cricket. (Trevor Jones)* RIGHT: *Matthew Maynard – one of the most exciting debuts in cricket history, Glamorgan* v. *Yorkshire, Swansea, 27 August. (Sporting Pictures UK Ltd)*

and played a furious knock that mocked the required run rate. He and Gooch added 41 off 9 overs so that when Lilley was caught on the boundary for 26 Essex needed only 17 runs in 4 overs. Gooch had adopted the anchor role and Essex were happy to negotiate Marshall's last over, an excellent maiden, without loss so that Nicholas' decision to give the fifty-sixth over to Connor meant that Hampshire would have to use one untried bowler as Cowley still had three of his quota left. In the fifty-seventh over, David East was marvellously caught on the boundary by Robin Smith, an outstanding fielder, and the match was in the balance and the excitement great. Connor bowled the fifty-eighth over and Turner and Gooch scored 3. This meant that Essex had to score 9 from the last two overs. Gooch took a single off Cowley's first ball and the off-spinner then tied Turner down with four full-length deliveries, supporting them well with excellent fielding to his own bowling. The Hampshire crowd roared their approval of every delivery, but off the last ball of the over Stuart Turner moved down the wicket to hit a glorious six over long-on. It was, in effect, the winning hit. Greenidge bowled the last over, an anti-climax, and started with a wide which levelled the scores. The batsmen crossed and Turner played out the moderate over to give Essex victory. Gooch was named Man of the Match for his cool and calculated innings, but there were several heroes as Essex reached their first 60-over final and Hampshire once again were disappointed.

Like the game at Southampton, the one at Worcester was left in an interesting position when play ended early on the first day. Notts were left requiring 96 from 14 overs which did not seem too easy a task as Broad, Randall, Rice and Johnson had all gone, but Tim Robinson produced another memorable innings and his side moved into the final with 4 balls to spare. Worcestershire did themselves, and cricket, a disservice in their team-selection. With Kapil Dev in Sri Lanka, they had the choice of Hick, who had been playing admirably, or Ellcock as an overseas player to include. They chose neither, electing to play instead Collis King who, although no longer on the staff, had had his registration retained by the county. It is doubtful if such a selection did much for team harmony at such a late stage in the compe-

Gloucestershire C.C.C. First-Class Matches – Batting, 1985	v. Cambridge University (Cambridge) 27–30 April		v. Lancashire (Bristol) 1–3 May		v. Worcestershire (Worcester) 8—10 May		v. Sussex (Hove) 22–24 May		v. Somerset (Bristol) 25–28 May		v. Derbyshire (Derby) 1–4 June		v. Somerset (Bath) 8–11 June		v. Kent (Tunbridge Wells) 12–14 June	
A.W. Stovold	9	5	2	7	28	19	104	—	—	—	20	112	0	2	20	1
P.W. Romaines	62	60*	18	7	4	12	64	—	—	—	32	5	2	22*	5	6
C.W.J. Athey	112*	—	24	15	30	27			—	—	170	58	52	2	6	26
P. Bainbridge	75*	—	3	67	83	0	27	—	—	—	151*	36*	0	17	52	5
B.F. Davison	—	29	40	11	35	23	29*	—	—	—	15*	47	43	26	15	53
K.M. Curran	—	2	46	39	0	33	11*	—	—	—	—	14*	83	—	43	10
J.W. Lloyds	—	13*	33	35	9	15			—	—	—	—	95*	6*	0	50
D.A. Graveney	—	—	6	27	35	0	—	—	—	—	—	—	0	—	2	8
R.C. Russell	—	—	1	0	9	24	—	—	—	—	—	—	0	—	28	19
D.V. Lawrence	—	—	7	6*	15	14	—	—	—	—	—	—	8	—	27	4
G.E. Sainsbury	—	—	1*	1	0*	8*										
A.J. Wright							3	—								
J.N. Shepherd							—	—								
C.A. Walsh							—	—	—	—	—	—	33*	—	1*	11*
A.J. Brassington																
Zaheer Abbas																
I.R. Payne																
P.H. Twizell																
R.G.P. Ellis																
Byes	3		2		4	7						3	11	9		
Leg-byes	1	5	4	2	11	10	7				7	10	5		3	2
Wides	1				2	5						1				3
No-balls	2		2	3	5	3	6				3	5			2	1
Total	262	114	189	220	270	200	251				398	291	332	84	204	199
Wickets	2	3	10	10	10	10	4				3	4	9	4	10	10
Result	D		L		W		D		D		W		D		W	
Points	—		5		23		7		4		22		8		22	

Gloucestershire C.C.C. First-Class Matches – Batting, 1985	v. Northamptonshire (Northampton) 15–18 June		v. Sussex (Bristol) 22–25 June		v. Hampshire (Bristol) 26–28 June		v. Nottinghamshire (Trent Bridge) 29 June–1 July		v. Yorkshire (Gloucester) 6–9 July		v. Worcestershire (Gloucester) 10–12 July	
A.W. Stovold	31	8			14	17	7	2	39	56*	6	7
P.W. Romaines	55	30			2	7	8	1	11	9		
C.W.J. Athey	82	12*			8	13	9	54	101	13*	139*	6
P. Bainbridge	67	—			2	3*	4	56*	119	4*	58	81
B.F. Davison	2	22*			0	9*	32	1*	12*	—	29	13
K.M. Curran	28	—			50	2	10	—	0	—	0	15*
J.W. Lloyds	20	—			23	—	88*	—	1	—	0	0
D.A. Graveney	—	—			3*	—			0*	—	—	1
R.C. Russell	0*	—			34	—	7	—	—	—	22	3
D.V. Lawrence	—	—			2	—	41	—	—	—	12*	0
G.E. Sainsbury	—	—					1	—				
A.J. Wright											20	33
J.N. Shepherd												
C.A. Walsh					37	—	0*	—	—	5	—	—
A.J. Brassington												
Zaheer Abbas												
I.R. Payne												
P.H. Twizell												
R.G.P. Ellis												
Byes	1				6		2				7	
Leg-byes	8	1			3		3	4	6	3	12	9
Wides												
No-balls	1				7	2	1		12	1	2	2
Total	295	73			191	53	213	118	301	91	307	170
Wickets	7	2			10	4	9	3	6	2	7	9
Result	W		Ab.		D		D		W		W	
Points	23		0		5		6		24		23	

Catches 65 – R.C. Russell (ct 60/st 5); 26 – C.W.J. Athey; 24 – J.W. Lloyds; 20 – A.W. Stovold; 17 – D.A. Graveney; 11 – D.V. Lawrence; 10 – P.W. Romaines and P. Bainbridge; 9 – B.F. Davison; 8 – K.M. Curran; 7 – A.J. Brassington; 4 – C.A. Walsh and I.R. Payne

tition and King's contribution to the match turned out to be moderate in the extreme, his one over on the Thursday conceding 12 runs and giving the Notts innings the impetus it needed.

Notts captured d'Oliveira in Hadlee's first over and Curtis was put down at slip by Rice, the simplest of chances, in Hadlee's next over. Smith, as ever, was in powerful form, and he and Curtis added 112 in 38 overs. It was an excellent platform from which to assault the bowling, but the pitch was sluggish and after Smith was bowled nothing went quite as well for Worcestershire as they might have hoped. King, out of practice, fretted, swung and ran himself out after scoring 11 off 23 balls. Curtis, having played well, advanced down the wicket and skied a catch to Pick, the bowler. Too much was asked of Patel and Neale too soon and the total of 232 was below expectations. It took on greater proportions when the low bounce accounted for Broad and Randall lbw. Rice played quietly and 59 were added before he was caught behind and Johnson, less happy against spin than pace, attempted to cut Patel and was bowled.

Hadlee stayed with Robinson, 75 not out, until the close at 137 for 4 off 46 overs. Hadlee never quite found his attacking mastery and he was caught and bowled by Patel for 18, but Robinson was in such magnificent form that the prospect of scoring nearly 7 an over did not seem too immense. When Hadlee was out at 175 French came in to give good support with pushes for singles which gave Robinson the strike. The England opener flowed to his century, cruelly exposing the limited bowling resources that Worcestershire had in support of Radford and Inchmore. From the last 5 overs, Notts needed 28 and it seemed that Robinson would be there at the finish as he clipped the ball off his legs or drove sweetly through the off side. Off the last ball of the 59th over, French swung Radford high to square-leg where d'Oliveira dropped a straightforward chance, but he gathered the ball and threw in immediately to run out Robinson after the batsmen had contemplated momentarily a second run. Robinson had faced 173 balls and hit 13 fours. It was his second outstanding century in five days. Newport bowled the last over and the second ball, a full-length delivery, found the edge of Hemmings' bat and skidded off for four and a Notts victory.

21, 22 and 23 August

at Ayr

Scotland 138 for 6 dec

M.C.C. 101 for 2 (D. Lloyd 51 not out)

Match drawn

v. Essex (Southend) 13–16 July		v. Zimbabwe (Bristol) 20–23 July		v. Australians (Bristol) 24–26 July		v. Glamorgan (Bristol) 27–30 July		v. Middlesex (Lord's) 31 July–2 August		v. Leicestershire (Cheltenham) 10–13 August		v. Nottinghamshire (Cheltenham) 14–16 August		v. Warwickshire (Cheltenham) 17–20 August		v. Hampshire (Bournemouth) 24–27 August		v. Essex (Bristol) 28–30 August		v. Glamorgan (Cardiff) 31 Aug.–3 Sept.		v. Northamptonshire (Bristol) 4–6 September		v. Surrey (The Oval) 14–17 September		M	Inns	NOs	Runs	H/S	Av
0				16	8	10	—	92	—	20	2	10*	—	6	10	2	2	0	0							22	37	2	694	112	19.82
		2	114*	6	0	12	—	12	—									16	35	3	—	8	2*	0	35	20	34	4	667	114*	22.23
76	41			0	83	115	—	16	—	8	6	0*	—	0	18*	18	3			71*	—	8	—	4	16	23	38	7	1442	170	46.51
37	57*	20	45	23	25	143*	—	60	—	33	—					43	46	0	69	20	—	7	—	102	4*	24	38	9	1644	151*	56.68
48	12	—	53*			65	—	111	—			—	—	0	—	15	77	42	10	0	—	5	—	59	1	24	35	7	984	111	35.14
0	6	—	—	25	58	54	—	6	—	23	36	—	—	63	10	0	3	42	1	—	—	14	—	26	9	26	34	3	762	83	24.58
6	101	—	—	71	0	1	—	5	—	1	6	—	—	54	23*	34*	0	34	1	39	—	30	—	21	3	25	33	6	818	101	30.29
1	—			23	4*	3*	—	6*	—	0	—	—	—	29*	—	3	2*	12	12*	—	—	53*	14*	19	3*	25	25	11	266	53*	19.00
28*	6			—	—					1	—	—	—	17	—	5	5	0	7	—	—	20	—	17*	0*	23	23	4	253	34	13.31
24	1*			1	0	—	—	13	—	14	8	—	—	9	—	1	0	22*	0	4*	—	26	—	0	—	25	26	5	259	41	12.33
		—	—																							6	5	3	11	8*	5.50
29	22	40*	23	4	9					0	47*	5*	—	7	7	0	0									9	16	3	249	47*	19.15
																										1	—				—
9	—			2*	4	—	—	0	—	0*	—	—	—	31	—	8	4	7	16	—	—	9	—	12	—	21	18	6	189	37	15.75
		0*	—			—	—	3*	—																	3	2	2	3	3*	—
		—	38																							1	1	—	38	38	38.00
		—	—							27	10*	—	—	11	—			19	2	—	—	37	—			7	6	1	106	37	21.20
		—	—																							1	—				—
																								3	20	1	2	—	23	20	11.50
3			18		5	4		13						1	5		4		1	3		3		2	1						
3	2	3	7	2	6	1		7		1	2			7	8	3	4	5	3	8		3		2	5						
3	2				2	6								1	5	3	1			3				2	1						
3			1	8	1	2		7		6	4			17		5	6					5		8	3						
270	250	65	299	181	205	416		351		134	121	15		253	86	140	157	199	157	151	0	228	16	277	101						
10	6	2	3	9†	9	6		9		10	5	0		10	3	10	10	10	10	4	0	10	0	10	6						
D		W		L		D		D		D		D		W		L		L		D		D		D							
6		—		—		6		7		4		4		23		4		5		1		2		7							

† R.C. Russell absent hurt

2 – A.J. Wright, R.G.P. Ellis and G.E. Sainsbury
1 – Zaheer Abbas

24, 25, 26 and 27 August

at Canterbury

Kent 333 (L. Potter 58, G.R. Cowdrey 51) and 126 (C.J. McDermott 5 for 18, M.J. Bennett 4 for 39)
Australians 364 (G.M. Ritchie 155, A.R. Border 103, K.C. Wessels 51, E.A.E. Baptiste 4 for 89) and 99 for 3
Australians won by 7 wickets

24, 26 and 27 August

at Chelmsford

Surrey 302 for 8 dec (G.S. Clinton 81, R.J. Doughty 61 not out, N.A. Foster 5 for 69) and 303 for 6 dec (A. Needham 92 not out, M.A. Lynch 68)
Essex 300 for 4 dec (G.A. Gooch 132, K.S. McEwan 64, K.W.R. Fletcher 56 not out) and 200 for 6 (G.A. Gooch 94)
Match drawn
Essex 7 pts, Surrey 5 pts

at Swansea

Yorkshire 298 for 9 dec (P. Carrick 92, G. Boycott 64, P.E. Robinson 54, R.C. Ontong 5 for 91) and 0 for 0 dec
Glamorgan 27 for 1 and 237 (M.P. Maynard 102, H. Morris 62, P. Carrick 7 for 99)
Yorkshire won by 34 runs
Yorkshire 18 pts, Glamorgan 3 pts

at Bournemouth

Gloucestershire 140 (S.J.W. Andrew 6 for 43) and 157 (B.F. Davison 77, R.J. Maru 5 for 16, M.D. Marshall 4 for 38)
Hampshire 197 (D.V. Lawrence 5 for 78) and 102 for 3 (M.C.J. Nicholas 71 not out)
Hampshire won by 7 wickets
Hampshire 17 pts, Gloucestershire 4 pts

Gloucestershire C.C.C. First-Class Matches — Bowling, 1985	D.V. Lawrence	K.M. Curran	G.E. Sainsbury	J.W. Lloyds	D.A. Graveney	P. Bainbridge	C.A. Walsh	J.N. Shepherd	C.W.J. Athey
v. Cambridge University (Cambridge) 27–30 April	8–3–18–1 8–3–11–2	8–4–11–0 5–2–5–1	7–3–17–1 3–1–6–0	19–8–24–4 15–8–14–2	14–6–14–0 16–10–12–1				
v. Lancashire (Bristol) 1–3 May	28–6–79–5 22.5–6–70–4	26–10–82–3 16–4–47–1	21.4–6–79–1 20–7–44–5	4–1–19–0	18–5–50–1				
v. Worcestershire (Worcester) 8–10 May	12.4–1–64–3 15.3–1–92–2	12–4–27–2 22–4–62–0	16–7–37–2 17–7–47–3			16–3–34–2 17–4–60–5			
v. Sussex (Hove) 22–24 May	17–2–48–7 6.4–0–19–0	6.5–2–13–0 9–3–19–2				9–4–9–2 4–2–7–0	5.1–0–22–0 10–4–26–0	12–3–31–0 2–0–10–0	
v. Somerset (Bristol) 25–28 May	22–3–76–3	10–1–36–2		3–1–4–0	11–3–22–3	9–2–30–1	15–3–38–0		
v. Derbyshire (Derby) 1–4 June	13.2–1–70–0 12–1–38–5	7–0–42–0		15–2–75–2	34–8–94–2		23–2–84–1 12–2–44–5		1–0–6–0
v. Somerset (Bath) 8–11 June	10–1–79–0	15–5–52–3		5–2–12–1	8.1–3–25–3		19–3–65–2		
v. Kent (Tunbridge Wells) 12–14 June	13–1–48–1 13.5–2–51–3	18.2–3–42–5 8–0–52–0				5–2–7–1 8–2–32–1	19–5–43–3 24–1–59–4		
v. Northamptonshire (Northampton) 15–18 June	5–0–16–0 14–2–61–3	 23–5–60–3	17.2–8–38–7 24–5–69–0	 9–4–18–1	17–4–35–3 21.4–13–27–3	4–0–22–0 5–2–7–0			 2–2–0–0
v. Sussex (Bristol) 22–25 June									
v. Hampshire (Bristol) 26–28 June	13–3–41–4 15–2–51–1	18–9–23–4 13–2–56–0		 8–1–52–0		 21–3–72–1	15–3–44–2 23–6–62–2		 2.1–0–3–3
v. Nottinghamshire (Trent Bridge) 29 June–1 July	17–0–73–4 16–1–68–1	17–4–54–2 2–1–4–0	8–0–36–0 14–5–30–3	1–0–1–0		14–2–34–1 7–1–33–0	22–12–62–3 8–1–47–0		 5–0–27–1
v. Yorkshire (Gloucester) 6–9 July	13–1–60–2 11.3–1–50–5	17–1–48–1 6–0–18–2			20–6–41–3	14–5–36–0	21–4–78–3 5–1–15–2		8–1–34–1
v. Worcestershire (Gloucester) 10–12 July	6–2–28–1 8–1–11–2	3–0–14–0 8–1–42–2		21–3–62–1 4–1–16–0	40–16–62–3 9–5–17–2	10–4–13–1	16–4–52–3 12.4–2–39–4		
v. Essex (Southend) 13–16 July	17–2–79–1	10–0–40–3		4–0–10–0	43–14–131–4	19–5–32–0	18–7–46–2		1–0–6–0
v. Zimbabwe (Bristol) 20–23 July		18.3–7–37–3	17–8–36–4 13–2–42–1	2–1–4–0		 7–1–27–1			
v. Australians (Bristol) 24–26 July	12–1–52–3 16–0–89–0	12–4–35–5 12–0–43–0		 13–0–83–0	 20–1–100–2	3–0–17–0 8–0–34–0	11–2–33–2 9–0–37–1		
v. Glamorgan (Bristol) 27–30 July	13–1–42–0	11–2–43–0			6–3–21–0	11–2–28–2	19–1–72–2		8–1–36–1
v. Middlesex 31 July–2 August	17–2–50–1 5.2–0–24–0	6–1–16–0		19–3–41–2 1–0–8–0	40–16–71–3	5–1–13–0	28.3–5–86–4 4–2–9–0		
v. Leicestershire (Cheltenham) 10–13 August	9.3–0–38–2	19–2–55–2					26–6–82–3		
v. Nottinghamshire (Cheltenham) 14–16 August	10–1–45–1	12–4–29–2		12.1–3–37–5	20–4–46–0		18–8–42–2		
v. Warwickshire (Cheltenham) 17–20 August	11–2–34–3 24.2–2–95–3	5–0–28–0 5–2–30–1					15.5–3–51–7 24–6–77–6		
v. Hampshire (Bournemouth) 24–27 August	19.2–2–78–5 7–0–32–0	17–3–44–2 6–1–22–0			 2–0–7–0	4–1–23–1	22–9–44–1 10.2–2–37–3		
v. Essex (Bristol) 28–30 August	6–1–24–1 27–2–93–3	8.1–0–13–4 14–1–49–1		 8–1–25–0	 32–6–91–4		20–9–51–5 17–6–37–2		
v. Glamorgan (Cardiff) 31 August–3 September		10–3–30–1		6–1–29–2	10–0–45–1		11–3–40–3		
v. Northamptonshire (Bristol) 4–6 September	8–2–30–1	16–5–37–0			15–6–46–3		27–6–72–4		
v. Surrey (The Oval) 14–17 September	14–3–29–1 7–1–37–1	17–3–51–4 1–0–8–0		8–1–17–1 3–1–24–0	9–3–28–0 5–1–28–0		23–3–79–4 7–1–31–0		 14–2–77–2
	544.5–66– 2093–85 *av.* 24.62	469.5–103– 1419–61 *av.* 23.26	178–59– 481–27 *av.* 17.81	180.1–42– 575–21 *av.* 27.38	410.5–133– 1013–41 *av.* 24.70	200–46– 570–19 *av.* 30.00	560.3–132– 1706–85 *av.* 20.07	14–3– 41–0 —	41.1–6– 189–8 *av.* 23.62

a T. Gard absent hurt   b M.D. Moxon absent injured   c R.G.P. Ellis 3–1–7–1

I.R. Payne	P.H. Twizell	P.W. Romaines	Byes	Leg-byes	Wides	No-balls	Total	Wkts
			3	1			88	6
				3			51	6
			3	6			318	10
				4	2	6	165	10
				2	1	9	164	10
				5		14	266	10
			9	9	1	21	141	10
			7	1		5	89	2
				5	1	2	211	9
			6	4	1	14	381	5
					2	6	82	10
			8	2	6	8	243	9a
				4	3	4	144	10
			1	5		11	200	10
			1	7	1	1	119	10
			1	3	1	1	246	10
			Match Abandoned					
				2	1	4	110	10
			2	14		7	312	7
			4	8	4	8	272	10
			1	3	2	6	213	5
				10	1	4	307	10
						8	83	9b
			2	9		1	242	10
					4	2	125	10
				6	1	19	350	10
17–4–43–1	13–4–33–0			3			156	10
8–0–59–0	15–2–65–2		1	11			205	4
			4	5		11	146	10
			15	9	1	10	410	3
			4	7	3	13	253	5
			5	7	5	12	289	10
			4	2			47	0
24–7–68–3			1	5	4	14	249	10
3–1–7–0			5	5		4	216	10
			4	10		1	127	10
2–0–7–0				2	7	9	211	10
				8		7	197	10
				4		3	102	3
6–1–22–0				1		4	111	10
4–0–8–0			1	6	2	4	310	10
							0	0
			3	4		2	151	8
							0	0
				3		6	188	9
				1	1	8	205	10
		10–0–42–3		4	2	2	258	7c
64–13–214–4 *av.* 53.50	28–6–98–2 *av.* 49.00	10–0–42–3 *av.* 14.00						

at Old Trafford

Somerset 329 for 4 dec (I.V.A. Richards 120, P.M. Roebuck 88, I.T. Botham 76 not out) and 0 for 0 dec
Lancashire 0 for 0 dec and 330 for 4 (M.R. Chadwick 132, K.A. Hayes 117)

Lancashire won by 6 wickets
Lancashire 17 pts, Somerset 4 pts

at Northampton

Northamptonshire 210 (R.G. Williams 96, P. Willey 5 for 64) and 243 for 7 (R.J. Bailey 99 not out, P.B. Clift 4 for 54)
Leicestershire 343 (P. Willey 147, R.A. Harper 5 for 94)

Match drawn
Leicestershire 5 pts, Northamptonshire 4 pts

at Trent Bridge

Nottinghamshire 313 (D.W. Randall 94, R.T. Robinson 52, D.J.R. Martindale 52, O.H. Mortensen 4 for 49) and 30 for 0
Derbyshire 125 (R.A. Pick 4 for 51) and 217 (J.G. Wright 76, K.J. Barnett 51, E.E. Hemmings 4 for 79)

Nottinghamshire won by 10 wickets
Nottinghamshire 23 pts, Derbyshire 2 pts

at Hove

Sussex 287 (A.M. Green 89, G.D. Mendis 72, J.E. Emburey 6 for 35) and 207 for 5 dec (D.A. Reeve 56)
Middlesex 203 for 4 dec (R.O. Butcher 60 not out, W.N. Slack 50) and 188 (R.O. Butcher 58 not out, M.W. Gatting 51, D.A. Reeve 4 for 64)

Sussex won by 103 runs
Sussex 20 pts, Middlesex 6 pts

at Edgbaston

Worcestershire 115 (G.C. Small 5 for 24) and 318 for 4 dec (P.A. Neale 92 not out, G.A. Hick 62)
Warwickshire 94 (N.V. Radford 6 for 45, J.D. Inchmore 4 for 42) and 154

Worcestershire won by 185 runs
Worcestershire 20 pts, Warwickshire 4 pts

Captains forfeited innings in an attempt to gain a result in spite of the wet weather and some thrilling finishes and outstanding individual performances were achieved. There was no need to contrive anything at Bournemouth, however, where a green wicket and dampness prompted Mark Nicholas to put Gloucestershire in after a delayed start. His judgement proved correct as the championship leaders finished the day at 89 for 5 off 54 tense overs. On the Monday, Stephen Andrew, aided by the variable bounce, finished with the best figures of his career and deprived Gloucestershire of a batting point. Hampshire found the going as hard as the visitors had done and they struggled to 123 for 7 against Lawrence, Walsh and Curran, an exciting and enthusiastic cricketer. Marshall and Parks then found courage which no others had mustered and added 55 in 9 overs. Crucially, Hampshire gained a lead of 57 and dismissed Stovold,

Hampshire C.C.C.
First-Class Matches – Batting, 1985

	v. Kent (Southampton) 27–29 April		v. Northamptonshire (Northampton) 4–7 May		v. Oxford University (Oxford) 8–10 May		v. Somerset (Taunton) 22–24 May		v. Glamorgan (Southampton) 25–28 May		v. Derbyshire (Basingstoke) 29–31 May		v. Yorkshire (Middlesbrough) 1–4 June	
V.P. Terry	69	88	8	—			3	83	4	0	6	61	9	14
C.L. Smith	18	84	6	—	110	100	16	121	29*	96	45	83	143*	68
M.C.J. Nicholas	12	33*	94	—	0	52*			6	4	0	4	12	11
J.J.E. Hardy	0	21*	45	—	43	48								
R.A. Smith	85	23	14	—	120	40*	5	33	2	35	12	140*	63	30
D.R. Turner	44	—			49*	—	38	8						
N.G. Cowley	8	—	8	—			0	—	14	9*			19	4*
K.D. James	33*	—			43*	—	124	7*	2	4	0	3		
T.M. Tremlett	23	—	33*	—			102*	—	1	10*	15	13*	12*	10*
R.J. Parks	3*	—	52*	—			—	—	18	—	10*	—	—	—
C.A. Connor	—	—	36	—	—	—	—	—	9	—	0	—	—	—
R.J. Maru			32	0*	—	—					32	—	—	—
S.J.W. Andrew			—	2*	—	—								
C.F.E. Goldie					—	—								
I.J. Chivers					—	—								
C.G. Greenidge							12	2	0	65	17	42	26	22
M.D. Marshall							24	49*	12	18	64	8	50	60
Byes		2	5		2	9	1	12		5	1			
Leg-byes	6	8	12		5	3	7	10	3	6	5	16	1	4
Wides		1					2		1			2		
No-balls	7	7	7		1				14	7	11	8	6	
Total	308	267	352	2	373	252	334	325	115	259	218	380	341	223
Wickets	8	3	8	0	4	2	7	5	10	7	10	6	6	6
Result	D		D		D		W		W		W		D	
Points	7		6		—		24		20		22		7	

	v. Warwickshire (Edgbaston) 8–11 June		v. Middlesex (Bournemouth) 12–14 June		v. Sussex (Hove) 15–18 June		v. Australians (Southampton) 22–25 June		v. Gloucestershire (Bristol) 26–28 June		v. Essex (Southampton) 29 June–2 July		v. Lancashire (Liverpool) 6–9 July	
V.P. Terry	5	—	25	57	36	4	60	—	1	34	51	—	54	19
C.L. Smith	52	—	4	40			29	41*	1	24	59	—	121	4
M.C.J. Nicholas	28	—	54	10	23	29	17	5	0	32	13	—	61	41
J.J.E. Hardy					27	20	27	—	4	42	107*	—	12	54
R.A. Smith	36	—	8	45	47	24	5	17*	19	79	11	—	44*	9
D.R. Turner											0	—		
N.G. Cowley	29*	—	19	21*			11	—						
K.D. James							8	—						
T.M. Tremlett	4	—	6	12	—	21*			14	2*	26	—	—	7*
R.J. Parks	26	—	17	4	0*	5	33	—	1	—	53*	—	3*	—
C.A. Connor	—	—	2*	—	—	—	4*	—	0	—				
R.J. Maru	13*	—	5	—	—	1*	4	—	2	—	—	—	—	—
S.J.W. Andrew					—	—	1*	—			—	—	—	—
C.F.E. Goldie														
I.J. Chivers														
C.G. Greenidge	204	—	21	1	56	9			43	68			13*	22*
M.D. Marshall	10	—	15	55	13	0			18	8	8	—	15	24
Byes	1		1	7	4	1	6	1		2				2
Leg-byes	14		1	2	7	5	2		2	14	3		7	6
Wides	2				2	2	2		1					
No-balls	9		6	9	6	2	12		4	7	5		1	1
Total	433		184	263	221	123	221	64	110	312	336		331	189
Wickets	8		10	8	6	7	9†	1	10	7	7		5	6
Result	D		D		D		D		D		W		W	
Points	8		5		6		—		4		23		22	

Catches 62 – R.J. Parks (ct 58/st 4); 34 – V.P. Terry; 19 – M.C.J. Nicholas; 16 – C.G. Greenidge; 15 – R.J. Maru; 14 – R.A. Smith; 12 – C.L. Smith; 10 – M.D. Marshall; 8 – C.A. Connor; 6 – K.D. James; 5 – T.M. Tremlett and S.J.W. Andrew

Wright and Athey for 6. Bainbridge and Davison batted out the day and extended their stand to 121 on the last morning, but the last 7 wickets fell for 30 runs, 5 of them to the slow left-arm of Maru who conceded only 16 runs in 12 overs and Hampshire were left to make 101 to win. They were 19 for 2 when Nicholas came to the wicket and immediately attacked the bowling. In 68 minutes he scored 71 off 68 balls and took his side to within 17 points of Gloucestershire.

Middlesex lost the chance of going top when they collapsed on the last afternoon against Sussex. The home side had begun at a vigorous pace but stuttered when Emburey and Edmonds joined the attack. Anxious to force victory, Gatting 84 behind and Sussex, propped up by nightwatchman Reeve, set the visitors to make 292 off 58 overs. Middlesex started well enough and were 115 for 2, but Reeve bowled Gatting and thereafter they capitulated miserably, the last 6 wickets falling for 26 runs.

Surrey, in fourth place, met the reigning champions Essex at Chelmsford. Having been bottom at the beginning of July, Essex had moved to within 47 points of the leaders and still had an outside chance of retaining their title. The game contained much fine cricket, but it ended very disappointingly. After a delayed start, Fletcher asked Surrey to bat, but the visitors scored briskly until Foster and Gooch engineered a mid-order collapse which left Surrey on 207 for 7 at the close. Doughty was missed early on Monday morning and celebrated with big hitting as he and Pocock added an unbeaten 92 for the ninth wicket. Surrey took their four batting points and Doughty quickly sent back Hardie and Prichard, but Gooch and McEwan added 108 with some glorious stroke-play. Gooch, at his commanding best, also added 120 in 24 overs with Fletcher and Essex reaching 300 after 61 overs of scintillating batting. Surrey were fed runs on the last morning to encourage a declaration which came after lunch leaving Essex to make 306 off 59 overs. Again Doughty struck, Prichard and McEwan falling in the same over. Essex were 31 for 3, but Gooch, who had been on the field for the entire match, was joined by Pringle in an exciting stand. They added 100 in 18 overs and Pringle then hooked Gray for 2 sixes in an over which produced 20 runs. The partnership had realised 145 when both batsmen fell. Gooch was bowled by Pocock and Pringle chased a wide ball from Butcher. Sadly, Fletcher decided to call off the chase which was rather mean spirited as he had invited Surrey to bat first.

v. Sussex (Portsmouth) 10–12 July		v. Worcestershire (Portsmouth) 13–16 July		v. Surrey (Guildford) 27–30 July		v. Somerset (Bournemouth) 3–6 August		v. Surrey (Southampton) 10–13 August		v. Glamorgan (Cardiff) 14–16 August		v. Leicestershire (Leicester) 17–20 August		v. Gloucestershire (Bournemouth) 24–27 August		v. Leicestershire (Bournemouth) 28–30 August		v. Kent (Folkestone) 4–6 September		v. Northamptonshire (Southampton) 11–13 September		v. Nottinghamshire (Trent Bridge) 14–17 September			M	Inns	NOs	Runs	H/S	Av
12	1	13	76	13	—	148*	—	24	1	28	—	10	—	17	13	3	—	5	67	7	25	128*	2		25	41	2	1284	148*	32.92
60	68	89	10	58	—	102	—	77	—					41	4	18	—	121	9*	19	2	22	6		23	39	4	2000	143*	57.14
5	19	16	73*	5	—	—	—	94	—			1	—	4	71*	146	—	36	2	33	13	40	84		24	39	4	1183	146	33.80
0	54	10	0					40	38	64*	—	15	—	10	—					8	—	45*	8		16	25	4	742	107*	35.33
19	15	2	28	57	—	6*	—	2	50	68	—	40	—	6	0*	134*	—	48	1	10	55*	7	39		26	44	8	1533	140*	42.58
20	11									22*	—	10	—												7	9	2	202	49*	28.85
				51	—	—	—			—	—	20	—					0	—						13	14	4	213	51	21.30
		42	—													2*	—								8	11	4	268	124	38.28
11	2*	29	4*	10	—	—	—	5	18*	—	—	0	—	6	—	—	—	15*	—	13	—	—	26		24	29	14	450	102*	30.00
3*	11	20	—	0	—	—	—	11	40*	—	—	3	—	33	—	—	—	2	—	17*	—	—	12		25	24	9	377	53*	25.13
		0*	—	12	—	—	—	2*	—	—	—														17	9	4	65	36	13.00
62	6*	1	0	15*	—	—	—	11*	—	—	—	0*	—	0	—	—	—	2	—	24*	—	—	17*		23	19	9	227	62	22.70
0	—													6*	—	—	—	—	—	—	—	—	0*		12	4	3	9	6*	9.00
																									1	—				—
																									1	—				—
				29	—	70	—	2	6	77	—	10	—	18	7	6	—	84	50	143	68	3	40		19	32	2	1236	204	41.20
4	9	14	0	22	—	—	—	8	17	—	—	36	—	41	—	43	—	5	15	14	66*	—	23		22	33	2	768	66*	24.77
			5							4		4				6		1	1	1	7									
8	7	11	1	9		10		9	2	3		9		8	4	4		8	6	9	6	4	7							
1	1	2		1		2		5	1							9						1	1							
5	9	6	14	9		8		13	1	4		4		7	3			6	5	2	2	2	3							
210	213	255	211	291		346		303	174	270	0	162		197	102	371		333	156	300	244	252	268							
10	8	10	6	10		2		9	5	3	0	10		10	3	5		9	5	8	4	4	9							
D		D		D		D		D		L		D		W		W		D		L		D								
5		7		3		8		5		3		3		21		24		8		8		7								

†S.J.W. Andrew retired hurt

4 – J.J.E. Hardy, N.G. Cowley and subs

2 – D.R. Turner and C.F.E. Goldie (ct 1/st 1)

There were heroics at Swansea where a barren first day led to Yorkshire forfeiting their second innings and asking Glamorgan to make 272. Thanks to Morris and Holmes they reached 119 for 2, but then lost 5 wickets for 17 runs as Phil Carrick, who had a splendid match, produced a devastating spell. Matthew Maynard, playing his first innings in first-class cricket, stood firm amid the shambles around him. He made 102 out of the 117 scored while he was at the wicket, scoring all of the last 71 runs. He hit 5 sixes and 13 fours and reached his hundred with three successive sixes off Carrick before steering the same bowler to short third man. It was an amazing display by a 19-year old on his debut, but, having scored all of the 52 added for the last wicket, he was out with Glamorgan 35 runs short of their target.

Two innings were forfeited at Old Trafford after a blank first day and another brilliant hundred by Viv Richards. Asked to make 330, Lancashire owed all to Mark Chadwick and Kevin Hayes who hit maiden championship centuries and put on 176 in 48 overs for the second wicket.

There were no such fireworks at Northampton where two of the least enterprising counties played a sombre draw. Peter Willey had a good all-round match against his old county. Richard Williams alone defied him on the first day and Robert Bailey saved his side on the last.

Ole Mortensen returned to form for Derbyshire, which was welcome, for he is such a happy and enthusiastic cricketer. He ended on the losing side, however, as Randall and Robinson continued their impressive scoring records and the frail Derbyshire batting collapsed to the medium pace of Pick and the spin of Hemmings.

Worcestershire rose from the dead to beat Warwickshire in the local derby at Edgbaston. Put in to bat, they succumbed to Gladstone Small and were 19 for 5. They recovered to reach 115 which was enough to give them a first innings lead after Radford and Inchmore had shattered Warwickshire on the Monday. Geoff Humpage, 44 not out, and Andy Lloyd, 22, were the only batsmen to reach double figures. Smith, who retired after being hit on the thumb, Neale, the eager Hick and the impressive Rhodes batted Worcestershire into a strong position, and Neale, unselfishly sacrificing a century, asked Warwickshire to make 340 in 89 overs. They never looked capable of the task, falling to a blend of pace and spin.

Brian Luckhurst came out of retirement to play for Kent against the Australians. Graham Johnson had been told that

Hampshire C.C.C. First-Class Matches — Bowling, 1985	C.A. Connor	K.D. James	T.M. Tremlett	N.G. Cowley	M.C.J. Nicholas	C.L. Smith	S.J.W. Andrew	R.J. Maru	I.J. Chivers
v. Kent (Southampton) 27–29 April	26–6–83–1 16–1–64–0	14–1–62–1 19–2–77–0	24–5–66–5 13–5–24–0	7.4–1–17–3 22–1–96–1	 8–1–28–0	 9–0–50–1			
v. Northamptonshire (Northampton) 4–7 May	25–3–97–1 27–7–62–4		24–5–74–2 16–7–30–1	16–3–32–2 23–10–33–1	6–3–13–0	 4–3–5–0	11–1–61–0 24–4–67–2	26–6–94–3 27.3–9–43–2	
v. Oxford University (Oxford) 8–10 May	23–3–63–1 7–2–21–0	23.4–15–24–2 12–8–14–0				4–0–26–0	19–4–56–2 7–3–21–0	29–10–62–3 6–3–4–1	15–2–67–0 7–3–5–1
v. Somerset (Taunton) 22–24 May	18–5–68–1 14–2–67–1	13–1–64–0 11–0–81–0	15–5–36–3 14–4–43–2	5.4–1–39–2 15–2–80–0		 4–1–28–1			
v. Glamorgan (Southampton) 25–28 May	19–2–70–3 12–4–18–0	4–1–26–0 11–2–45–2	12–3–21–1 18–2–53–3	4–0–7–0 2–2–0–0	4–0–11–1	 5–1–6–0			
v. Derbyshire (Basingstoke) 29–31 May	15.4–5–40–3 22–3–98–1	19–5–67–1 18–2–63–1	18–6–30–3 19–7–43–0		 4–0–23–0			6–0–43–0 33–13–81–1	
v. Yorkshire (Middlesbrough) 1–4 June	9–2–29–0 3–0–8–0		17–4–35–1 7–0–25–1	21–3–90–1 13–6–21–3		 1–0–4–0		22.2–6–65–3 19.1–8–45–1	
v. Warwickshire (Edgbaston) 8–11 June	13–6–28–0 17–2–44–1		15–1–42–4 23–4–69–2	 4.2–2–6–0				 7–3–6–0	
v. Middlesex (Bournemouth) 12–14 June	12–2–36–0 7–3–17–1		19.3–30–4 7–3–15–1	9–3–28–0 6–3–12–0				13–8–10–1 23–7–63–3	
v. Sussex (Hove) 15–18 June	24.1–4–79–3 15–2–47–0		25–5–70–2 10–2–23–1		 4–0–14–0		14–4–39–2 9–2–39–0	24–1–32–3 23–4–68–2	
v. Australians (Southampton) 22–25 June	16–2–46–2 4–0–27–3	11–2–22–6 5–1–26–0		 13–4–49–1		 1–0–2–0		4.5–3–7–2 13–3–41–3	
v. Gloucestershire (Bristol) 26–28 June	19–3–63–1 3–0–12–0		16.4–4–43–4 6–3–14–2					6–1–19–1 8–3–19–2	
v. Essex (Southampton) 29 June–2 July			10–2–19–4 21–6–45–4		 1–0–10–0		8–0–33–0 13–1–49–1	 12–7–15–2	
v. Lancashire (Liverpool) 6–9 July			21–4–77–1 3–0–11–0		16–4–50–0	5–1–16–1	15–0–79–2 6–1–15–1	25–2–117–0 9.2–2–38–3	
v. Sussex (Portsmouth) 10–12 July			22–4–58–1 19–4–43–0		3–0–18–0 9–2–31–0		20–6–63–1 26–3–94–3	30–6–113–1 10–2–20–0	
v. Worcestershire (Portsmouth) 13–16 July	21–5–49–0 3–1–5–0	 5–1–15–1	18–7–47–0 9–2–27–0		9–1–35–1	2–0–3–0 6–0–34–0		21–9–33–2 18.5–7–52–4	
v. Surrey (Guildford) 27–30 July	1–0–4–0								
v. Somerset (Bournemouth) 3–6 August	23–3–61–3 22–6–49–1		26–9–60–3 23–7–42–2	6.1–1–13–1 7–0–14–0	 7–3–13–1	2–0–4–0		12–2–39–2 24–10–31–0	
v. Surrey (Southampton) 10–13 August	22–5–79–3 4–0–8–1		8–2–28–0 3–1–4–0		5–0–13–0			18.4–2–49–0 15–2–58–0	
v. Glamorgan (Cardiff) 14–16 August	 8–1–25–0		 10–3–33–0	 15–1–53–3				 30–2–112–1	
v. Leicestershire (Leicester) 17–20 August			6–2–11–0	20–6–34–2				22–8–41–3	
v. Gloucestershire (Bournemouth) 24–27 August			19–3–47–2 11–1–42–0		7–3–13–0 4–0–22–0		20–8–43–6 7–1–31–1	2–0–3–0 12–4–16–5	
v. Leicestershire (Bournemouth) 28–30 August		8–2–31–1 4–0–18–0	13–5–42–5 21–8–35–0				5–2–11–1 23–5–58–4	 23.4–12–45–4	
v. Kent (Folkestone) 4–6 September			15–6–19–1 11–2–24–1	25–6–51–3 13–5–24–2			9–1–35–1 6–1–15–1	27–2–101–1 17–4–66–2	
v. Northamptonshire (Southampton) 11–13 Sept.			24.4–11–53–4 6–2–13–0		3–0–9–0 10–2–22–2	 5–0–34–0	18–5–73–1 7–1–19–0	32–11–88–1 21–1–114–5	
v. Nottinghamshire (Trent Bridge) 14–17 Sept.			25–5–53–4 2–1–1–1		9–2–31–0 10–0–80–1	 18–0–85–1	14–0–73–0 3–0–18–1	27.3–4–66–5 1–0–4–1	
	470.5–90– 1467–53 *av.* 41.91	177.4–43– 635–15 *av.* 42.33	665.5–180– 1620–75 *av.* 21.60	247.5–60– 699–25 *av.* 27.96	119–21– 436–6 *av.* 72.66	66–6– 297–4 *av.* 74.25	284–53– 992–30 *av.* 33.06	701.5–187– 1923–73 *av.* 26.34	22–5– 72–1 *av.* 72.00

a G. Fowler, absent injured b R.A. Cobb, retired hurt

M.D. Marshall	R.A. Smith	C.G. Greenidge	Byes	Leg-byes	Wides	No-balls	Total	Wkts
				4	1	2	232	10
			1	4		10	344	2
				2		4	373	8
	1–1–0–0			4		2	244	10
			1	4		8	303	8
				4			69	2
22–4–81–3			4	6	2	5	298	10
13–0–50–1				9	1	8	358	5
21.2–4–57–4				5		11	197	10
12–3–33–1	4–0–12–1		6	3		7	176	8
19–5–57–2				9	1	10	246	10
16–5–39–3				3	1	8	350	6
20–8–48–5			8	8		11	273	10
6–3–8–0				3	1		114	5
20–6–50–6				7	1	3	127	10
24–7–68–3			1	4		6	198	7
26–9–68–5				11		2	183	10
24–7–59–3					4	2	166	8
15–7–28–0			5	4		4	257	10
10–0–22–0		4–1–16–0	9		1	4	238	3
				1	2	6	76	10
	1–0–4–0		2	3		5	154	7
20–3–57–4			6	3		7	191	10
5–1–8–0						2	53	4
16.5–5–42–6				2		1	96	10
21–7–54–3			5	5	2	9	183	10
17–1–48–2			2	12		13	401	6
15–4–45–4			1	5	2	7	115	9a
25–5–70–3			4	1	2	2	327	8
2–1–10–0			4	7	2	3	209	5
30.3–12–59–7			2	21	1	4	249	10
14–7–29–2				4			166	7
							4	0
24–6–51–1				4	2	5	232	10
33–10–70–4	1–0–3–0		6	8	4	13	236	8
7–1–20–1	1–0–4–0		1	6	1	8	200	4
7–0–23–1	12–7–11–2		2	1	1	1	107	4
							0	0
20–6–36–1	0.4–0–2–0		2	8		5	271	5
4–1–11–0			6	3			106	5
23–10–31–2				3	3	5	140	10
20–6–38–4			4	4	1	6	157	10
15.2–8–12–3				4	2	3	100	10
23–11–53–1			1	5	1	14	215	9b
24.3–5–46–3			2	5		6	259	10
14.4–3–31–1			11	1	1		172	7
28–6–75–4			2	4	7	5	304	10
11–2–31–1				8		2	241	9
24–4–62–1			5	7		3	297	10
	7–0–40–1		5	1	2	1	234	6
692.3–193–1680–95 *av.* 17.68	27.4–8–76–4 *av.* 19.00	4–1–16–0 —						

his contract was not to be renewed and had refused to play in the match, a refusal which caused his contract to be terminated immediately. It was a sad end to the career of one who has graced the game and given good service to Kent in a golden period in their history. Kent recovered well to reach 333, but their bowlers were put to the sword as Border and Ritchie hit masterful centuries. In their second innings, Kent collapsed to McDermott, who bowled with great hostility. Luckhurst defended bravely at the end, but the tourists gained a welcome victory on the eve of the last Test.

Kent C.C.C. First-Class Matches – Batting, 1985	v. Hampshire (Southampton) 27–29 April		v. Surrey (Canterbury) 1–3 May		v. Middlesex (Lord's) 8–10 May		v. Northamptonshire (Northampton) 22–24 May		v. Oxford University (Oxford) 29–31 May		v. Worcestershire (Canterbury) 1–4 June		v. Nottinghamshire (Tunbridge Wells) 8–11 June	
M.R. Benson	61	162	0	11	10	62*	24	30	—	55	6	1	71	4
S.G. Hinks	39	65	92	6	13	35	35	1	10	88	21	2	15	42
C.J. Tavare	7	102*	1	13	13	18*	0	32			8	60	17	14
D.G. Aslett	0	—	2	111	12	—	4	40	174	—			2	49
C.S. Cowdrey	25	—	159	95	95	—	5	1			38	1	31	21
G.W. Johnson	8	—	6	7*	28	—	5	—	12	27*	30*	20		
A.P.E. Knott	55	—	2	0	18	—	87*	—			0	35	2	15
C. Penn	1	—			20*	—								
G.R. Dilley	24	0*	31	0			5*	—	—	—	7	1	0*	0*
D.L. Underwood	5	—	16*	4*	0	—					7	13*	3*	0
K.B.S. Jarvis	0*	—	6	—	5	—			—	—	2	0	0	0
N.R. Taylor			2	13					120*	—	16	2		
E.A.E. Baptiste					15	—	18	1*	19*	—	41	3	5	0
L. Potter							3	—	—	—				
R.M. Ellison							71	—	—	23*			6	41
S.N.V. Waterton									—	—				
S. Marsh														
G.R. Cowdrey														
B.W. Luckhurst														
Byes		1	4	9		6	2		8	5	3	3		1
Leg-byes	4	4	7	6	4		8	7	6	4	8	1	9	
Wides	1		1	1	1	2		9					1	
No-balls	2	10	7	6	3	1	3	1			2	4	1	4
Total	232	344	336	282	237	124	270	122	349	202	189	146	163	191
Wickets	10	2	10	8	10	1	9	5	3	2	10	10	9†	10
Result	D		D		D		D		D		L		L	
Points	5		7		4		6		—		5		5	

Kent C.C.C. First-Class Matches – Batting, 1985	v. Gloucestershire (Tunbridge Wells) 12–14 June		v. Nottinghamshire (Trent Bridge) 15–18 June		v. Lancashire (Old Trafford) 22–25 June		v. Essex (Chelmsford) 26–28 June		v. Surrey (The Oval) 6–9 July		v. Yorkshire (Maidstone) 10–12 July		v. Northamptonshire (Maidstone) 13–16 July	
M.R. Benson	0	80	55	50	102	4	7	7	4	18	12	107	53	97
S.G. Hinks	12	1	7	67	44	18	0	94*	81	117	18	11	16	14
C.J. Tavare	34	4	11	94*	49	21	21	10	43	65	28	123		
D.G. Aslett	0	30	26	53	11	38	40	16	13	28*			5	41
C.S. Cowdrey	29	13	10	5	6	39	4	4	19	6*	48	14*	67	7
G.W. Johnson	18	16			6	—	10	—			29	—	12	3*
A.P.E. Knott	11	10*	0	20*	5	—	0	—	2	—			7*	—
C. Penn													50	—
G.R. Dilley			13	—					14	—	1	—		
D.L. Underwood	2	11	13	—	6	—	12*	—	12*	—	1	—	1	—
K.B.S. Jarvis	0*	0	0*	—	0*	—	6	—	0	—	4	—		
N.R. Taylor													5	43
E.A.E. Baptiste	3	0	11	24	43	81*	47	42	41	—	82	3*	0	58*
L. Potter														
R.M. Ellison	24	18	98	—	12	8*	11	6*	34	—	64*	—	1	2
S.N.V. Waterton														
S. Marsh											25	—		
G.R. Cowdrey														
B.W. Luckhurst														
Byes		1	4	3	4	1		1	4	8	5			8
Leg-byes	4	5	4	5	12	3	10	2	17	4	4	9	3	5
Wides	3		1	1		1		1	5		3	1		
No-balls	4	11	5		3	3	6	1	12	3	4	2	3	5
Total	144	200	258	322	303	217	174	184	301	249	328	270	223	281
Wickets	10	10	10	5	10	5	10	5	10	3	10	3	10	6
Result	L		D		W		D		W		W		W	
Points	4		4		22		5		24		23		22	

Catches 54–A.P.E. Knott (ct 53/st 1)
23–S.G. Hinks
20–C.S. Cowdrey and C.J. Tavare
15–M.R. Benson
12–E.A.E. Baptiste and S. Marsh (ct 10/st 2)
10–L. Potter
9–C. Penn
8–S.N.V. Waterton (ct 6/st 2)
7–D.L. Underwood

John Player Special League

25 August

at Heanor

Nottinghamshire 179 for 8
Derbyshire 180 for 3 (B. Roberts 77 not out)

Derbyshire (4 pts) won by 7 wickets

at Swansea

Glamorgan 137
Yorkshire 93 for 8 (G.C. Holmes 5 for 16)

Glamorgan (4 pts) won on faster scoring rate

at Bournemouth

Gloucestershire 152 for 8 (C.W.J. Athey 69)
Hampshire 88 for 2 (C.G. Greenidge 57 not out)

Hampshire (4 pts) won on faster scoring rate

at Old Trafford

Lancashire *v.* Somerset

Match abandoned
Lancashire 2 pts, Somerset 2 pts

at Guildford

Northamptonshire 306 for 2 (A.J. Lamb 132 not out, W. Larkins 126)
Surrey 213 (M.A. Lynch 55, A. Needham 51)

Northamptonshire (4 pts) won by 93 runs

at Worcester

Worcestershire 212 for 6 (T.S. Curtis 57)
Warwickshire 125 (N.V. Radford 4 for 24)

Worcestershire (4 pts) won on faster scoring rate

Curtailed matches again dominated. Holmes effected a remarkable collapse in the Yorkshire batting and Greenidge maintained Hampshire's challenge with a thunderous innings at Bournemouth. Northamptonshire moved level with Sussex at the top of the table with an amazing display of hitting at Guildford. The game was originally scheduled for The Oval, but preparations for the Test match made it more appropriate to shift the venue. A weakened Surrey attack was brutally savaged by Larkins and Lamb who put on 176 in 20 overs for the second wicket. Larkins faced 110 balls and hit 8 sixes and 5 fours while Lamb faced only 85 deliveries and hit 4 sixes and 14 fours. Surrey replied with spirit, but they were never likely to come near the huge Northants total.

v. Essex (Dartford) 24–26 July		v. Leicestershire (Leicester) 27–30 July		v. Sussex (Eastbourne) 31 July–2 August		v. Glamorgan (Swansea) 3–5 August		v. Sussex (Canterbury) 10–13 August		v. Warwickshire (Canterbury) 14–16 August		v. Yorkshire (Scarborough) 17–20 August		v. Australians (Canterbury) 24–27 August		v. Worcestershire (Worcester) 28–30 August		v. Derbyshire (Folkestone) 31 Aug.–3 Sept.		v. Hampshire (Folkestone) 4–6 September		v. Somerset (Canterbury) 14–17 September		M	Inns	NOs	Runs	H/S	Av
64	—	5	12	80	22	35	—	—	26	13	4*	17	6*			39	44	4	—	27	10			24	43	3	1501	162	37.52
74	—	54	41	85	99*	36	—	—	15	5	0*	9	0	15	0	31	44	24	—	16	14	5	5	26	48	3	1536	117	34.13
150*	—	1	8	8	38*	9	—	—	64	21	—	22	—			27	21	33	—	8	3	14	10*	23	40	6	1225	150*	36.02
														24	13									13	23	1	732	174	33.27
		0	0									0	—	35	9	12	28*	62	—	131	39	12	9	20	36	3	1079	159	32.69
																								11	16	4	237	30*	19.75
1	—	15	36*	—	—			—	29	10	—	18	—			1	—							19	24	5	379	87*	19.94
				—	—	4*	—	—	27	0	—	0	—											8	7	2	102	50	20.40
5	—	0	—	—	—			—	0	15	—	15	—			4	—	18*	—					17	19	5	153	31	10.92
6	—	0	—	—	—	—	—	—	4*	0	—	1	—	3	0	0*	—	—	—	4*	—	—	—	24	25	9	126	16*	7.87
—	—	7	—	—	—			—	4	0*	—	7	—									—	—	19	18	5	41	7	3.15
79	—	59*	20*	17*	—	33	—	—	41	39	—	102*	5*	5	3	100	11*	25	—	7	18	24	54	16	25	7	843	120*	46.83
47	—	5	0	—	—	52	—	—	5	40	—			45	11	6	11	71	—	19	68	45	10	23	36	5	972	82	31.35
29	—			3*	—	11	—	—	55	3	—	15	—	58	28	15	—	4	—	11	6*	4	0	12	15	2	245	58	18.84
13	—	0	4			33	—							29	27					10	0*	0	1*	16	25	6	536	98	28.21
						—	—											16*	—			6*	—	3	2	2	22	16*	—
														31*	0					3	—			3	4	1	59	31*	19.66
						29*	—							51	4	53	—	33	—	10	1	20*	41	6	9	2	242	53	34.57
														1	9*									1	2	1	10	9*	10.00
1			5	4		3				4			6	4	4			2		2	11								
7		4	1	2	2	1			9			5	1	6	8	9	10	7		5	1		1						
		2	1						4			2		2	1	1					1								
		11		1	1	5			7	14		4		24	9	1	1	1		6		1	1						
476		163	128	200	162	251	0	0	290	164	4	217	18	333	126	299	170	300		259	172	131	132						
9		10	6	3	1	7	0	0	10	10	0	10	1	10	10	10	4	8		10	7	7	6						
D		D		D		D		L		D		D		L		L		D		D		D							
8		5		4		3		3		4		2		—		4		8		5		4							

† G.R. Dilley retired hurt

6 – G.W. Johnson and N.R. Taylor
5 – D.G. Aslett, G.R. Cowdrey and K.B.S. Jarvis
3 – R.M. Ellison
2 – subs
1 – G.R. Dilley

28, 29 and 30 August

at Derby

Derbyshire 272 and 261 for 8 dec (J.E. Morris 90, V.J. Marks 5 for 69)
Somerset 336 (I.V.A. Richards 123, J.G. Wyatt 90, O.H. Mortensen 5 for 87)

Match drawn
Somerset 8 pts, Derbyshire 7 pts

at Bristol

Essex 111 (C.A. Walsh 5 for 51, K.M. Curran 4 for 13) and 310 (K.S. McEwan 106, D.A. Graveney 4 for 91)
Gloucestershire 199 (N.A. Foster 5 for 79) and 157 (P. Bainbridge 69, D.R. Pringle 6 for 42)

Essex won by 65 runs
Essex 20 pts, Gloucestershire 5 pts

at Bournemouth

Leicestershire 100 (T.M. Tremlett 5 for 42) and 215 (J.J. Whitaker 65, R.J. Maru 4 for 45, S.J.W. Andrew 4 for 58)
Hampshire 371 for 5 dec (M.C.J. Nicholas 146, R.A. Smith 134 not out, P.A.J. de Freitas 4 for 80)

Hampshire won by an innings and 56 runs
Hampshire 24 pts, Leicestershire 1 pt

at Trent Bridge

Nottinghamshire 198 (C.E.B. Rice 63, R.C. Ontong 5 for 39) and 120 (R.C. Ontong 8 for 67)
Glamorgan 329 (R.C. Ontong 130, M.P. Maynard 58, E.E. Hemmings 5 for 115)

Glamorgan won by an innings and 11 runs
Glamorgan 24 pts, Nottinghamshire 4 pts

at Hove

Yorkshire 307 (M.D. Moxon 70, J.R.T. Barclay 6 for 78) and 293 for 4 dec (P.E. Robinson 79, J.D. Love 78 not out)
Sussex 323 for 4 dec (G.D. Mendis 123, P.W.G. Parker 76, A.M. Green 54) and 268 for 8 (G.S. le Roux 61, P.J. Hartley 4 for 97, P. Carrick 4 for 99)

Match drawn
Sussex 7 pts, Yorkshire 4 pts

at Worcester

Kent 299 (N.R. Taylor 100, G.R. Cowdrey 53, J.D. Inchmore 4 for 50) and 170 for 4 dec
Worcestershire 200 for 3 dec (D.N. Patel 62 not out) and 273 for 5 (T.S. Curtis 97 not out, M.J. Weston 76)

Worcestershire won by 5 wickets
Worcestershire 22 pts, Kent 4 pts

Kent First-Class Matches — Bowling, 1983	G.R. Dilley	K.B.S. Jarvis	C. Penn	C.S. Cowdrey	D.L. Underwood	G.W. Johnson	S.G. Hinks	E.A.E. Baptiste	R.M. Ellison
v. Hampshire (Southampton) 27–29 April	21–3–71–0 12–0–53–1	29–6–99–3 10–0–48–1	15.3–5–44–1 4–0–27–0	9.3–4–24–1 14–0–84–1	31–15–41–2 6–1–28–0	8–1–23–0 5–2–17–0			
v. Surrey (Canterbury) 1–3 May	24–4–97–5	22–7–62–1		13–0–58–0	16–3–57–0	30–2–142–3	5–0–18–0		
v. Middlesex (Lord's) 8–10 May		21–2–73–1 23–5–83–2	17–3–57–0 16.1–1–63–4	25–4–69–2 5–1–21–0	14–7–43–3 7–0–35–0	4–0–8–0		23–5–55–0 19–5–41–0	
v. Northamptonshire (Northampton) 22–24 May	11–4–27–0 5–1–13–0			12–2–36–1 5–1–12–0		7–1–16–0		19.3–5–42–6 5–0–26–1	15–4–37–1 6–1–17–1
v. Oxford University (Oxford) 29–31 May	22.1–8–40–4 5–1–4–1	17–4–38–0				24–4–58–0 17–4–34–2		7–3–15–0	20–11–26–1 3–2–1–0
v. Worcestershire (Canterbury) 1–4 June	3–1–6–1	22–5–53–5 13–1–35–1		10.4–0–41–2 4–0–17–0	34–12–75–2 19–8–29–1	8–4–16–0 8–0–25–0		2–0–4–0 5–1–17–1	
v. Nottinghamshire (Tunbridge Wells) 8–11 June	9–0–31–0 12–3–32–1	22.1–8–43–5 16–3–42–2		6–1–24–0	7–0–23–0 2–2–0–0			14–4–44–3 12–1–37–0	10–0–28–0 12.5–4–33–3
v. Gloucestershire (Tunbridge Wells) 12–14 June		17–6–46–3 11–1–41–1		14–3–53–2 19–3–52–1	4–1–18–0 1–0–1–0			12–0–38–1 21–5–57–3	19.4–6–46–4 21.2–7–46–5
v. Nottinghamshire (Trent Bridge) 15–18 June	18–5–60–1	15–0–66–0 5–0–27–0			7.4–1–33–0 5–0–25–1		5–0–26–0	19–2–48–2 4–0–23–0	14–3–36–2
v. Lancashire (Old Trafford) 22–25 June		16–3–52–2 9–2–29–3			35–15–55–4 20–2–93–2	24–3–67–1 19.3–3–78–5		20–7–42–1 4–1–14–0	9–1–26–0 5–1–17–0
v. Essex (Chelmsford) 26–28 June		25–6–76–3		5–1–20–0	3–1–6–0		6–0–18–1	20–4–57–0	31.2–8–61–6
v. Surrey (The Oval) 6–9 July	19–5–49–3 13–2–53–5	18–5–53–2 12.3–5–54–3		7–1–14–0	1–1–0–0 15–8–22–1			11.2–0–42–2 9–3–26–1	5–0–20–1 6–1–29–0
v. Yorkshire (Maidstone) 10–12 July	17–4–47–2 10–2–41–0	23–4–72–2 11–2–49–2			13–8–17–1 18–14–8–4	2–0–17–0		24–3–101–1 7–0–33–0	13–2–43–1 13.3–5–43–2
v. Northamptonshire (Maidstone) 13–16 July			5–0–23–0 12–2–42–1	11–0–56–1 4–0–5–3	9–2–22–0 24–11–48–1			11–2–58–2 21–6–68–1	27.3–6–87–7 24.4–6–77–4
v. Essex (Dartford) 24–26 July	16–5–41–0 23–6–58–2	18–2–59–3 11–3–36–0			22.1–6–56–6 48–18–80–4			13–3–32–1 10–4–21–0	5–1–15–0 13.5–3–29–1
v. Leicestershire (Leicester) 27–30 July	10–0–47–1 3–0–4–0	18–2–71–0 2–0–17–1			4–1–11–0			22–6–60–6	18.4–4–58–3
v. Sussex (Eastbourne) 31 July–2 August	8–1–31–0	18–7–42–1 10–1–31–0	6–0–18–1 12–1–41–2		28–11–45–1 22–7–43–0			26–0–86–3 8–3–21–1	
v. Glamorgan (Swansea) 3–5 August			5–0–26–0		18–3–80–0			15–2–47–3	7–0–27–1
v. Sussex (Canterbury) 10–13 August	12–1–42–0	27–5–71–1	13–2–44–0		35–6–87–4			5–1–11–1	
v. Warwickshire (Canterbury) 14–16 August	16–3–64–2 20–6–52–2	23–6–66–0 21–6–66–3	14–2–71–4 5–1–10–1		22–9–46–1 4–2–4–0			14–2–47–0	
v. Yorkshire (Scarborough) 17–20 August	3–0–9–0	8–3–18–0			23–8–41–1		5–0–10–0		
v. Australians (Canterbury) 24–27 August				4–1–19–0 6–1–16–1	31–6–71–2		12–1–48–0	27–7–89–4 10–0–36–2	15–2–43–3
v. Worcestershire (Worcester) 28–30 August	9–2–19–0 10.1–0–50–1			10–0–36–0 7–2–14–0	29–10–66–3 23–7–75–2			13–2–53–0 9–2–49–1	
v. Derbyshire (Folkestone) 31 August–3 September	12–4–19–0 5–0–15–0			4–1–19–0	33–17–34–4 37–28–23–3			16–3–48–4 10–6–10–1	
v. Hampshire (Folkestone) 4–6– September				15–3–66–0	34–11–76–3 18–3–76–2			17–4–44–1 19.1–7–40–3	14–6–35–0 4–1–12–0
v. Somerset (Canterbury) 14–17 September		12–3–40–0 5–2–16–0			27.2–10–44–4 25.5–8–69–4			24–6–54–2 7–1–25–0	22–8–41–2
	348.2–71– 1075–32 *av.* 33.59	530.4–115– 1674–51 *av.* 32.82	124.4–17– 466–14 *av.* 33.28	210.1–29– 756–15 *av.* 50.40	776–283– 1706–67 *av.* 26.89	156.3–24 501–11 *av.* 45.54	33–1– 120–1 *av.* 120.00	554.3–116– 1661–58 *av.* 28.63	356.2–93– 933 48 *av.* 19.43

a B.J. Griffiths, absent hurt b M.R. Benson 4–0–31–0 c M.R. Benson 10–0–69–0
d M.R. Benson 3–0–17–0 e M.R. Benson 0.3–0–4–1 f M.R. Benson 2.5–0–17–0

L. Potter	D.G. Aslett	N.R. Taylor	*Byes*	*Leg-byes*	*Wides*	*No-balls*	*Total*	*Wkts*
				6		7	308	8
			2	8	1	7	267	3
			3	8		13	445	9
				6	3	10	303	6
			1	5	1	4	257	6
8–2–17–1				3	1	1	162	9a
8–1–31–0				5		3	120	2
15–3–57–2	1–1–0–0			18	4	3	252	8
15–4–34–0	8–0–44–1	12–1–52–1		4			173	5
			4	5		4	204	10
			7	2	1	2	132	3
				5	4	1	198	10
				13	1	4	157	6
				3		2	204	10
			2		3	1	199	10
			5	4	1	2	252	5
	6–0–25–0		1	1	2		159	1b
			3	16		13	261	8
			1	2		3	234	10
				5	1	9	243	10
			3		1	4	181	10
				9	1		193	10
			10	10		3	300	7
			1	6	1	3	198	10
			1	8	3	2	255	10
			1	6	2	5	247	10
				10		6	213	10
15–5–29–1				7	1	13	260	8
				4	2	3	251	10
		11–0–50–2		1	1	1	141	3c
			1	4	1	3	227	6
18–2–70–1		5–0–16–1	1	3		4	243	5d
							0	0
5–0–29–2				1		7	210	6
13–1–46–3		3–0–7–0	1	4		7	317	10e
		3–0–9–0		1			27	0
			1	5		10	300	7
			4	2		6	138	6
20–4–66–0			4	2		4	150	1
19–3–90–1			1	3	1	4	364	10
6–0–37–0	2.1–0–9–0			1		1	99	3
8–2–23–0			1	2		5	200	3
15–2–63–1		4–1–16–0		6	1	2	273	5
14–7–22–2			2	3	2	8	147	10
30.4–22–13–3		1–1–0–0	6	3		4	70	7
25–5–87–4		5–1–16–0	1	8		6	333	9
7–2–21–0			1	6		5	156	5
2–1–1–0		12–4–20–2		11	1		211	10
15–1–36–0		8–1–34–0	8	1		1	189	4
258.4–67–772–21 *av.* 36.76	17.1–1–78–1 *av.* 78.00	64–9–220–6 *av.* 36.66						

Hampshire ended a glorious week with an innings victory over Leicestershire which took them to the top of the Britannic Assurance County Championship two points ahead of Gloucestershire. Under lowering cloud Nicholas won the toss and asked the visitors to bat on a green wicket. His pace attack, Tremlett and Marshall in particular, brought havoc to the Leicestershire batsmen and bowled them out for 100 a quarter of an hour after lunch. The lively medium pace of de Freitas accounted for Greenidge, Terry and Chris Smith with only 32 scored so that by 3.15 on the first day, 13 wickets had fallen. No more were to fall that day as Nicholas and Robin Smith scored 150 off the last 56 overs. Nicholas reached his first championship hundred of the season, a fluent, purposeful innings which was an inspiration to his side in difficult conditions. Robin Smith ran to an equally accomplished century the next day and his stand with Nicholas was extended to 259 in 82 overs. Although the wicket no longer favoured the bowlers, the Hampshire attack reduced Leicestershire to 180 for 5 before the close, Maru again playing an important part. With Cobb having broken a bone in his foot, the visitors offered little resistance on the last morning and the final honours went to Andrew and Maru.

In contrast to Hampshire's week of glory, Gloucestershire endured a week of woe. Having fallen to Hampshire, they returned to Bristol only to be beaten by Essex. Like Hampshire, Gloucestershire had the advantage of putting their opponents in on a green and uneven wicket. An all pace attack shot Essex out in 40.1 overs and, although they lost their first 4 wickets for 57, Gloucestershire had no more alarms before the close by which time they were 5 runs ahead. On the second day their batsmen disappointed and wilted against Foster and Pringle who denied them a second bonus point for batting. Essex lost Hardie, Prichard and debutant Stephenson before the arrears were cleared, but Ken McEwan struck a serene and rich vein and the match began to veer away from the home side. McEwan was out to the first ball of the last day, but there was still much resolution in the Essex batting and eventually Gloucestershire had to make 223 to win. This was not a difficult task, but in the absence of Athey, who had been called to The Oval as a stand-by for Botham, they made a terrible mess of it. Two wickets in 2 overs after lunch set them back, but at tea, they were 95 for 3, requiring 128 off 40 overs. After tea they disintegrated to Pringle and some excellent Essex out-cricket and lost their place at the top of the table.

Viv Richards hit his seventh century of the season, his hundred coming off 80 balls, but Morris steered Derbyshire to a draw on a dour last day.

The match at Hove was also drawn. Yorkshire got off to a slow start and although there was later acceleration, they just missed the fourth batting point. John Barclay was their main tormentor, returning his best championship bowling figures. Mendis and Green began Sussex's reply with a stand of 104. Parker then joined Mendis in a partnership of 135, and Mendis reached his sixth century of the season. The pre-lunch session on the last day was farcical. Mendis and Gould bowled 8 overs of donkey drops from which 140 runs were scored in an attempt to elicit a declaration. When it came Sussex were asked to make 278 in 53 overs. They made a bold bid, with le Roux particularly aggressive and Parker, Reeve

Lancashire C.C.C. First-Class Matches – Batting, 1985	v. Sussex (Old Trafford) 27–29 April		v. Gloucestershire (Bristol) 1–3 May		v. Surrey (The Oval) 8–10 May		v. Derbyshire (Chesterfield) 22–24 May		v. Yorkshire (Old Trafford) 25–27 May		v. Oxford University (Oxford) 1–4 June		v. Essex (Ilford) 8–11 June		v. Somerset (Bath) 12–14 June		v. Derbyshire (Old Trafford) 15–18 June		v. Kent (Old Trafford) 22–25 June		v. Warwickshire (Old Trafford) 26–28 June		v. Sussex (Hastings) 29 June–2 July		v. Hampshire (Liverpool) 6–9 July		v. Warwickshire (Edgbaston) 10–12 July	
G. Fowler	10	—	30	0	19	5			4	—			24	12	14	4	21	34	0	18	88	36	23	20	0	—		
J.A. Ormrod	5	—	4	2	23	16	4	0																				
S.J. O'Shaughnessy	1	—	2	40*	16	0	2*	0	4	—			5	33	9	0	24	4			2	11					7	12
N.H. Fairbrother	8	—	0	24	48	3	—	27	128	—	68*	—	41	0	5	3	51	44	28	45	1	14	59*	23	164*	0	5	85
J. Abrahams	67	—	29	26	8	5	—	18*	21	—	—	101*	33	1	14	0	8	41	37	44	36	0	29	0	42	10	1	16
M.A. Watkinson	5	—	57	14	15	9					—	59			7	0					4	11	13	31	35	11	16	87
J. Simmons	28	—	2	8	6	4	—	—	4	—			10	4	6	0	4	21*	51	62*			0	101	49	2		
S.T. Jefferies	93	—	57	24	29	8																						
J. Stanworth	1	—	50*	0	0	0																						
I. Folley	0	—	0	0					69	—	—	—	9	19*	38	5	8*	—	2	0	0	18	6	0	—	6	1	26*
P.J.W. Allott	8*	—	78	15	29	19	—	—	6*	—			15*	3					8*	20					—	15		
S. Henriksen					10*	0*																						
D.W. Varey							13*	57*	6	—	112	—	26	48	1	33	39	14	41	12	16	14	5	10	33	0	34	32
D.P. Hughes							—	13	0	—	75*	—	17	39	57	23	68	20	27	3	8	43*	13	3				
C. Maynard							—	—	7	—	—	26*	0	3	0	15	0	16	3	18	12	0	0	34	7*	20	6	3
B.P. Patterson							—	—	3	—	—	—	2	5*	0*	0*	0	—	—	0	1	—	0	1*			3*	0
D.J. Makinson							—	—			—	—					5	11*	32*	6	24*	4*	0	11	—	12*	36	27
M.R. Chadwick											63	—															4	13
R.G. Watson											—	18																
C.H. Lloyd																									44	24		
I.C. Davidson																											13	0
K.A. Hayes																												
A.J. Murphy																												
A.N. Hayhurst																												
Byes			3		5				1		10	7			2	4	1		3	1		4	5	10	2	1	6	4
Leg-byes	4		6	4	4	1	1	2	6		9	4	7	7			9	6	16	2	6	6	10	7	12	5	10	13
Wides				6	10	5		3			1	8				1	1	4			3		3	5		2		1
No-balls	7			2		2		6	10				2			1	1		13	3	6	4	7	1	13	7	6	2
Total	237		318	165	222	77	20	126	269		338	223	191	174	153	89	240	215	261	234	207	165	173	257	401	115	148	321
Wickets	10		10	10	10	10	1	4	10		2	2	10	9	10	10	10	7	8	10	10	8	10	10	6	9†	10	10
Results	D		W		L		D		D		W		D		L		W		L		D		L		L		L	
Points	3		24		5		4		7		—		5		3		22		4		6		3		5		4	

Catches 50 – C. Maynard (ct 42/st 8); 18 – J. Simmons; 15 – J. Abrahams; 12 – N.H. Fairbrother; 10 – S.J. O'Shaughnessy; 9 – J. Stanworth (ct 6/st 3) and D.P. Hughes; 8 – I. Folley; 6 – M.R. Chadwick and M. Watkinson; 5 – D.W. Varey

and Imran carrying injuries, but they failed by 10 runs.

Worcestershire did reach the target of 270 in 62 overs which Kent set them at New Road and so gained their second win of the week. The first day was ruined by rain and only 53 overs were possible. Neil Taylor confirmed his fine late season form with his third century of the season and Graham Cowdrey reached a maiden championship half-century. Neale declared 99 runs in arrears, and Kent, having set the target, persisted with the spinners so that Worcestershire received an extra 7 overs. Curtis played the anchor role. Hick and Neale gave early impetus to the innings while Weston scored 76 at more than a run a minute to provide the late burst and victory came with 5 balls to spare.

A gloomy, disjointed first day at Trent Bridge saw Notts struggle. Rodney Ontong put his side in total command on the second day as he followed his 5 wickets with an impressive century. He shared a fifth wicket stand of 122 with Matthew Maynard who gave his second mature and exciting display of the week in what was only his second first-class innings. The young batsman hit 10 boundaries and reached his fifty off 89 balls. Ontong's innings, too, was full of enterprise and authority as he hit a six and 14 fours. The Glamorgan captain's virtuoso performance continued into the last day when he took a career best 8 for 67 with his off-breaks and sent Notts to a crashing defeat. A century and 13 for 106 in the match was a remarkable achievement by Rodney Ontong and gave further optimism for Glamorgan's future.

Off the field, Ian Botham received a strong reprimand for his behaviour in the third Test match at Trent Bridge and David Bairstow was banned for four Sunday League matches, the sentence suspended for two years, for remarks made to umpires Constant and Oslear.

Sixth Cornhill Test Match
ENGLAND *v.* AUSTRALIA

Not surprisingly, England fielded the side which had won at Edgbaston while Australia made three changes, not all of them wise, Bennett, Wellham and Gilbert, making his international debut, coming in for Holland, O'Donnell and Thomson.

Gower won the toss and England batted first on a pitch which looked as if it might give the bowlers some assistance in the first session. Once again the Australian bowlers failed to exploit conditions which might have helped them. Excited by a wicket with some pace, they tended to bowl too short. They had success in the eighth over when McDermott

v. Glamorgan (Old Trafford) 13–16 July	v. Surrey (Southport) 24–26 July	v. Middlesex (Uxbridge) 27–30 July	v. Leicestershire (Leicester) 31 July–2 August	v. Worcestershire (Worcester) 3–6 August	v. Yorkshire (Leeds) 10–13 August	v. Northamptonshire (Lytham) 14–16 August	v. Nottinghamshire (Old Trafford) 17–20 August	v. Somerset (Old Trafford) 24–27 August	v. Nottinghamshire (Trent Bridge) 31 Aug.–3 Sept.	v. Leicestershire (Old Trafford) 14–17 September			M	Inns	NOs	Runs	H/S	Av
		— —	10 13	0 4				— 15					15	24	—	404	88	16.83
													4	7	—	54	23	7.71
34 63	1 1				4 —								13	23	2	275	63	13.09
57 11	0 0	— —	13 1	42 30	147 —	19 —	66 —	— 31*	8 5	— 91			25	39	4	1395	164*	39.85
77* 29	51 1	— —	9 4	0 0	23 —	4 —	34 —	— 2*	35 11	— 65			25	39	4	932	101*	26.62
65 9	106 32	— —	14 9	19 0		12 —	0 —	— —	22* 14	— 16			19	29	1	692	106	24.71
— 11	4 39	— —	0 4*	19 0		20 —	4 —	— —	8 14*	— 0			21	30	4	485	101	18.65
57 6													4	7	—	274	93	39.14
				0 7		10 —	2 0*						6	10	2	70	50*	8.75
— —	28 —	— —		14* 4	0* —	0 —	8* —		0 0*	— 1*			21	27	8	262	69	13.78
	15* —	— —			3 —			— —	6 —	— 2			14	15	5	242	78	24.00
													1	2	2	10	10*	—
	1 47*	— —	41 20	29 34	13 —	36 —	87 3	— 22	24 26	— 31			21	34	3	960	112	30.96
					2 —								10	16	2	411	75*	29.35
— 12*	3 0	— —	7 0*		43 —			— —	0 10	— 21*			19	27	5	266	34	12.09
		— —			— —	22 —	1 —	— —	0 —				16	16	5	38	22	3.45
— 0*	12 2*		15 1	24 20	40* —	58* —	32 —						15	21	9	372	58*	31.00
9 22	32 14	— —	13 8		37 —	8 —	14 2*	— 132	18 10	— 11			12	17	1	410	132	25.62
													1	1	—	18	18	18.00
			131 16	14 50*						— 9			4	7	1	288	131	48.00
													1	2	—	13	13	6.50
5 39						22 —	71 —	— 117	1 55				5	7	—	310	117	44.28
			2* —	1 0									2	3	1	3	2*	3.00
										— 17			1	1	—	17	17	17.00
5 8	4		10 1	6	1	7	1	1	4	6			† G. Fowler absent injured					
1 4	16 4		1	5 6	5	6	10	3	3 8	8								
2	1		2	2	2			1		3								
3 1	4 5		11 3	1 2	7	1	4	6	1 1	12								
315 215	278 145		278 81	168 165	327	225	334 5	0 330	126 158	0 293								
6 8	10 7		10 8	10 10	8	10	10 1	0 4	10 7	0 9								
D	D	D	D	L	D	D	D	W	D	D								
6	7	1	7	5	7	2	5	17	4	3								

4 – P.J.W. Allott, G. Fowler and B.P. Patterson
3 – J.A. Ormrod, K.A. Hayes and C.H. Lloyd
2 – C.A. Davidson, D.J. Makinson and subs
1 – S. Henriksen

bowled Robinson with an inswinging yorker. Gower began uneasily and had a narrow escape when 2. He essayed to play McDermott to leg and the ball looped over the heads of groping slips. He also came close to hooking Gilbert into the hands of a fieldsman and edged Lawson close to slip, but these blemishes were soon obscured by what followed. Gooch had been assured from the start and as soon as Gower became less frenetic, runs flowed as sweetly as they have ever flowed from English batsmen for nearly a quarter of a century. At lunch, after 20 overs, England were 100 for 1.

In the afternoon, the over-rate remained desultory, but the run-rate was dynamic, 78 runs per 100 balls. The Australian attack was mutilated by batting in the grandest manner. Newcomers Bennett and Gilbert received a dreadful mauling. Bennett packed his leg side field and Gooch crashed him through the off. He packed his off side field and Gooch hit him mercilessly to leg. Gower reached his third century of the series off 123 balls. Five minutes later Gooch reached his first hundred against Australia and then overtook his captain and was the first to reach 150.

They had added 351 in 75 overs when Gower slashed tiredly to gully. It was the second highest partnership for any wicket against Australia and it was accomplished with a grandeur that we witness only in the greatest moments of any sport. There are those of us who will be lucky enough to say in years to come 'I saw Gooch and Gower at The Oval in 1985.'

Australia gained another, unexpected, success at the close when Gatting was taken at slip off Bennett when he pushed forward.

Perhaps because England supporters, basking in the sun and the glory of Gooch and Gower, had already claimed the Ashes, England stumbled on the second morning. Emburey hit Lawson to cover. Lamb was ill at ease and was out to a wretched hook. Botham, after some massive swipes, was caught behind, Phillips jumping high to his right. Ellison, too, was caught behind. Gooch had already gone, disappointingly early in the day when many had dreamed of Sobers' 365 being passed. He was well caught and bowled, low down, by McDermott, the most positive learner from the tour, after he had taken 11 from Lawson's first over. Downton stopped the rot and Edmonds had a slog, but England's last 9 wickets had gone down for 93 runs, and Australia, their bowlers having performed with commendable resurgence of spirits, dared to hope again. Their hopes were short-lived.

Wood was unlucky to be adjudged lbw, but he had already been dropped at slip. Hilditch, as if mesmerised, again hooked Botham into the hands of long leg. In the first over

Lancashire C.C.C. First-Class Matches — Bowling, 1985	P.J.W. Allott	S.J. Jeffries	M.A. Watkinson	S.J. O'Shaugnessy	J. Simmons	I. Folley	A.J. Murphy	J. Abrahams	B.P. Patterson
v. Sussex (Old Trafford)	13–5–22–3	11–4–36–1	6–3–10–0	11–1–31–0	5–3–8–0				
27–29 April									
v. Gloucestershire (Bristol)	19–5–44–4	13.1–0–45–3	16–5–60–2	11–3–34–1					
1–3 May	19–10–25–2	19–2–64–4	8–0–34–0	8–1–27–1	21–6–53–2	5–2–15–0			
v. Surrey (The Oval)	24.5–7–71–6	23–2–72–0	10–2–46–0	6–2–9–2	25–7–71–0			2–0–16–0	
8–10 May	17–4–50–1	13–2–53–1	11.5–5–23–2		15–2–57–3				
v. Derbyshire (Chesterfield)	25.5–9–33–5			8–0–49–0	23–8–40–2				22–2–77–3
22–24 May									
v. Yorkshire (Old Trafford)	27–10–49–1			13–2–38–1	9–2–21–0	11.2–5–12–2			25–5–77–6
25–27 May	13–8–18–3			6–3–13–1		3–1–5–0			11–4–21–0
v. Oxford University			15–5–32–3			1–0–7–0			17.4–3–49–7
(Oxford) 1–4 June			13.2–6–14–2			16–13–8–6		6–3–6–1	5–2–10–0
v. Essex (Ilford)	24–10–53–1			13–2–49–2	16–9–39–2	22–7–58–1			23.5–4–67–4
8–11 June	19–6–36–3			2–0–5–0		2–0–5–0			18.3–1–45–0
v. Somerset (Bath)			8–2–26–0	6–1–18–0	45–15–78–4	44–16–89–3			22–6–75–0
8–12 June									
v. Derbyshire (Old Trafford)				7–1–21–0	33.2–16–55–4	5–2–17–0			15–2–32–1
15–18 June				3–0–14–0	30–13–89–4	30–12–83–3		1–0–8–0	7–1–23–0
v. Kent (Old Trafford)	19.5–5–58–3				39–15–85–4	28–8–67–1			19–5–33–1
22–25 June	14–3–54–3				7–0–59–1	6–0–43–0			66–1–16–0
v. Warwickshire (Old Trafford)			22.1–6–62–3	3–0–13–0		17–3–42–1		2–0–3–0	18–5–60–2
26–28 June			15–1–54–1	13–0–68–4		4–0–16–1			10–0–49–0
v. Sussex (Hastings)			17–6–51–1		34–9–91–0	29–9–50–1			10.3–0–51–0
29 June–2 July			7–0–34–0		15–0–64–0	11–0–43–0			7–1–18–0
v. Hampshire (Liverpool)	16–3–37–0		14–1–57–0		34–5–82–1	30–5–96–4			
6–9 July	12–2–48–2		11–2–25–0		9–1–23–0	20–5–58–2			
v. Warwickshire (Edgbaston)			8.2–1–25–3	2–0–19–0					10–3–23–3
10–12 July			28–6–96–4	5–1–11–0		21–1–54–2			20–1–81–0
v. Glamorgan (Old Trafford)		25–2–79–0	22–5–55–1	10–1–38–2	18.1–4–49–1	22–2–69–1			
13–16 July		12–1–30–3	8–1–21–1	3–1–13–0	8–4–9–0	2–1–8–0		6.2–0–46–3	
v. Surrey	26–7–62–4		10–2–21–2	5–1–28–1	7.1–4–11–1	17–2–47–1			
24–26 July									
v. Middlesex (Uxbridge)	22–11–30–0		22.2–5–71–4		19–2–62–0	16–0–79–0			12–0–69–0
27–30 July									
v. Leicestershire (Leicester)			40–10–109–5		11–4–23–0		20–4–71–1		
31 July–2 August			17–4–47–0		22–1–68–0		8–4–18–1	7–2–14–0	
v. Worcestershire (Worcester)			11–2–29–1		4–1–13–0	9.5–3–39–4	20–5–84–3		
3–6 August							8.2–2–34–1		
v. Yorkshire (Leeds)	23–9–38–2			7–1–23–0		15–3–57–2		7–5–6–0	29–2–95–3
10–13 August									
v. Northamptonshire (Lytham)			0.1–0–2–0						
14–16 August									
v. Nottinghamshire			20–5–50–1		26.3–5–76–1	18.2–4–56–0			21–5–43–3
(Old Trafford) 17–20 August									
v. Somerset (Old Trafford)	16–4–58–1		21–3–52–1		18–3–95–1				15–3–61–1
24–27 August									
v. Notts. (Trent Bridge)	19.5–3–47–5		14–1–52–2		5–2–5–3				10–2–29–0
31 August–3 September	12–3–29–0		7–1–18–0		17–2–46–1	10–0–43–2			10–1–40–1
v. Leicestershire (Old Trafford)	21–4–65–1		17–4–52–0		27–12–55–2	41–10–120–4			
14–17 September									
	402.4–128–927–49 *av.* 18.91	116.1–13–379–12 *av.* 31.58	420.1–94–1228–29 *av.* 31.48	142–21–521–15 *av.* 34.73	543.1–155–1427–37 *av.* 38.56	456.3–113–1286–41 *av.* 31.36	56.2–15–207–6 *av.* 34.50	31.2–10–99–4 *av.* 24.75	364.3–59–1144–41 *av.* 27.90

a S. Henriksen 12–1–44–1
b I.C. Davidson 10–3–24–2
c M.R. Chadwick 5–0–20–0
d A.N. Hayhurst 13–4–37–3

D.J. Makinson	D.P. Hughes	N.H. Fairbrother	*Byes*	*Leg-byes*	*Wides*	*No-balls*	*Total*	*Wkts*
				6		1	113	4
			2	4		2	189	10
				2		3	220	10
			4	8		1	341	10a
			2	6		4	191	7
9–1–34–0	2–2–0–0			10	3	8	243	10
			2	6	4	9	205	10
			1			1	58	4
13–2–45–0			1	10		12	144	10
7–4–5–1			1	3		2	47	10
			10	5	1	15	281	10
			9	8	1	5	108	9
				18	1	1	304	7
29–7–60–5			4	12	8	8	201	10
10–2–14–1			4	16	1	3	251	8
11–2–44–0			4	12		3	303	10
10–2–41–2			1	3	1	3	217	5
25–10–48–4			4	7	1	10	239	10
9–1–24–0			1	14	2	6	226	7
20–3–61–3				6	3	9	310	6
12–3–24–0			4	6		5	193	0
17–4–52–0				7		1	331	5
8–1–27–2			2	6		1	189	6
10–1–44–3			4	7	3	3	122	10
25–4–59–1			8	18	3	8	351	9b
25–3–75–0			4	14	3	4	383	8
3–0–16–0		2–1–3–0	4	1		5	171	7c
16–1–61–1				1	1		231	10
			7			8	318	4
25.3–1–110–4		4–2–5–0	1	8	11	5	327	10
22–7–53–2			4	3		4	207	3
24–2–81–2			3	15	2	5	264	10
7–2–29–0		2–0–3–1		4	1		70	3
22–4–56–1	19–10–26–1	7–4–9–0	6	12	3	25	328	9
							2	0
6–3–16–0			4	8		9	253	5
		11–0–55–0	2	6	1	8	329	4
							0	0
				7	1	1	140	10
			1	7	1	4	184	4
				7			336	10d
							0	0
365.3–70–1079–32 *av.* 33.71	21–12–26–1 *av.* 26.00	26–7–75–1 *av.* 75.00						

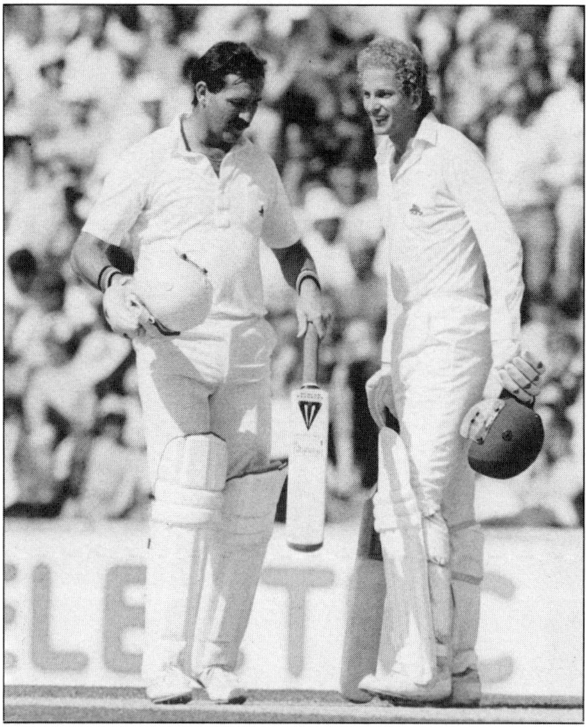

The two centurions, Gooch and Gower, who shared a second wicket stand of 351 in 75 overs. (Adrian Murrell)

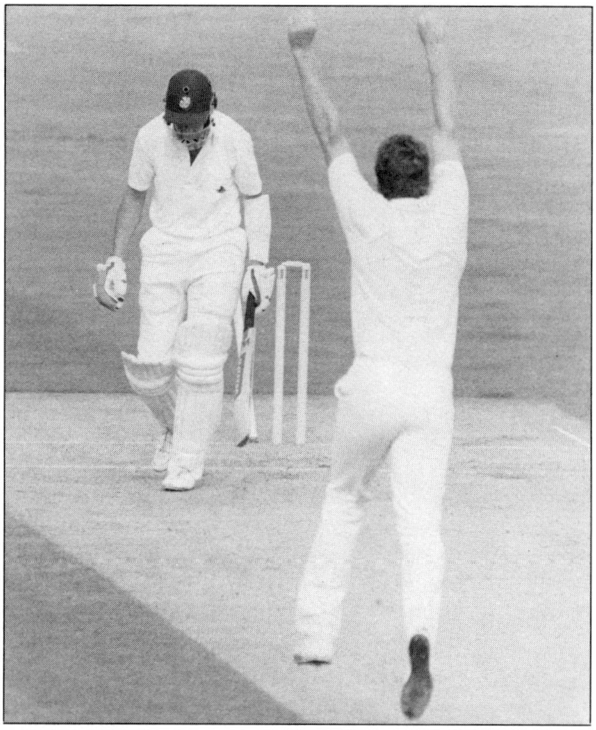

ABOVE: *Early success for Australia but little joy afterwards. Robinson is yorked by McDermott. (Adrian Murrell)*

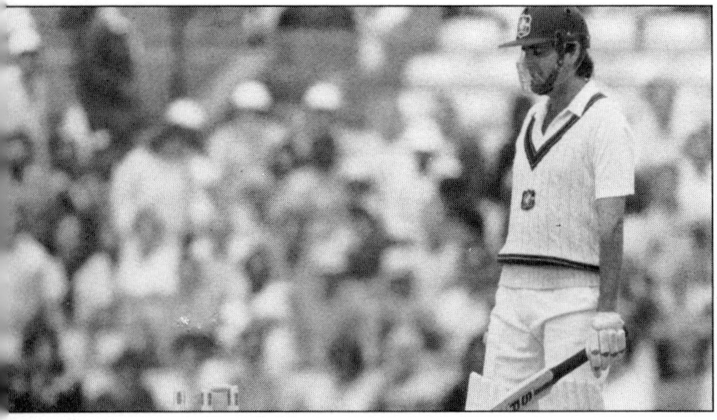

ABOVE: *Gilbert chops on to Botham and Australia must follow-on. (Ken Kelly)*

BELOW: *Majestic Gooch. (Adrian Murrell)*

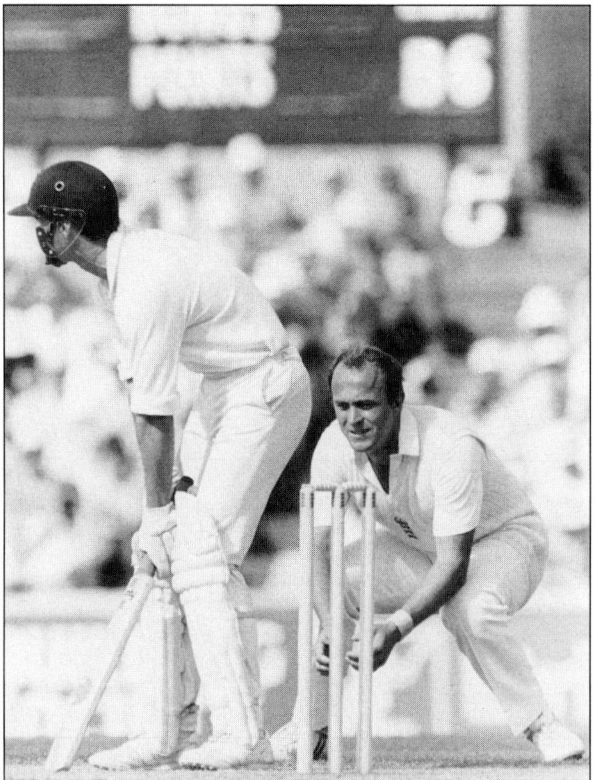

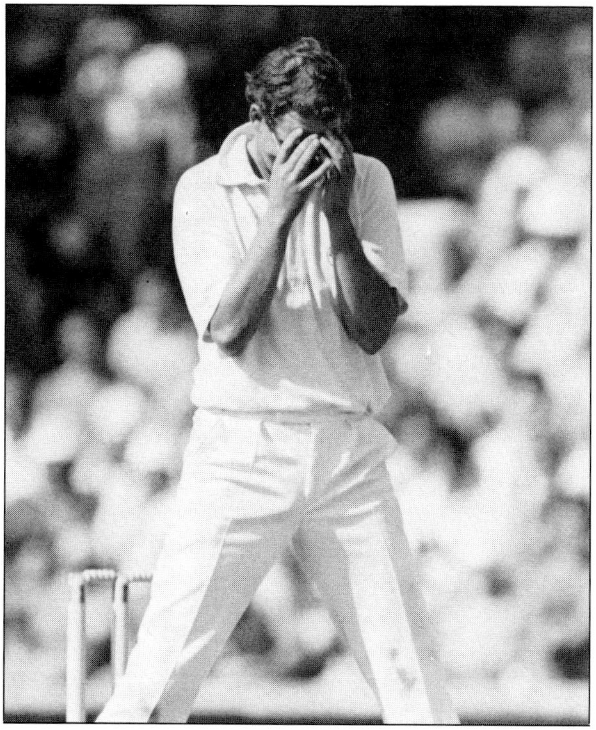

Murray Bennett holds his head in despair as he is savaged by Gooch and Gower. (Adrian Murrell)

LEFT BELOW: *England on the attack. Edmonds close at short leg. (Adrian Murrell)*

Phillips is caught by Downton off Botham and Australian resistance crumbles. (Adrian Murrell)

after tea Wessels was beaten by a clever ball from Emburey which drifted in to him and Wellham, after 45 had been added, flirted once too often outside the off stump to Ellison and was caught behind. Now came the prize catch as Edmonds beat Border through the air and saw the Australian captain play on. Edmonds struck again when Phillips unwisely cut at a ball which turned in to him and was bowled. Australia closed at 145 for 6 and an innings defeat threatened them.

Bennett and Ritchie, technically better equipped than all but Border, withstood the early onslaught on Saturday morning, but Bennett was caught at cover when Ellison joined the attack. Lawson was wonderfully caught by Botham. The batsman had made one fierce drive and drove again at Taylor. The ball flew off the outside edge and Botham, at slip, leapt and held the ball in his right hand as he twisted in mid-air. He is an unquenchable cricketer and such is his outstanding ability that there is no game on which he does not leave his indelible mark in one capacity or another. Ritchie's one flaw in a fine innings was to run out McDermott, beaten by Robinson's solid throw. Gilbert was bowled by Botham and Australia, 223 runs in arrears, were asked to follow-on.

There was debate as to whether or not Gower should have enforced the follow-on, but with the weather uncertain, the afternoon was lost to rain, he had no other choice, and he was soon justified. Wood chopped a ball from Botham onto his stumps and Hilditch, curbing his tendency to hook his way to disaster, played a dreadful loose drive at Taylor and scooped to cover. Wessels groped at Botham and Downton took a diving catch, his best of the series. Wellham, anticipating swing, was beaten by Ellison's straight ball and Australia lived through Sunday at 62 for 4.

The end came before lunch on Monday. Border was dropped by Downton second ball of the day. The Australian captain turned the ball down the leg side waist high and Downton had the ball in his hand as he dived, but he let it slip before he hit the ground. It mattered little. Ritchie never settled and it was no surprise when he edged Ellison to the keeper. Phillips also fell to a catch behind off an injudicious shot and the heart had gone out of Australia.

Border reached another admirable fifty and then was caught at slip off an Ellison outswinger. He received a standing ovation as he walked back to the pavilion, for no captain could have done more in an attempt to lead and inspire an inexperienced side, and a side too in which the more experienced had done less than Australia could have hoped. Lawson gave Downton his fourth catch of the innings and McDermott fell to another stunning catch by Botham, diving to his left at second slip. The end came when Taylor took a simple return catch from Bennett. England had won the series 3–1 and regained the Ashes.

Gooch was named Man of the Match; Gower Man of the Series. Three months earlier, Gower's position had seemed

SIXTH CORNHILL TEST MATCH – ENGLAND *v.* AUSTRALIA
29, 30, 31 August and 2 September 1985 at The Oval

ENGLAND

	FIRST INNINGS	
G.A. Gooch	c and b McDermott	196
R.T. Robinson	b McDermott	3
D.I. Gower†	c Bennett, b McDermott	157
M.W. Gatting	c Border, b Bennett	4
J.E. Emburey	c Wellham, b Lawson	9
A.J. Lamb	c McDermott, b Lawson	1
I.T. Botham	c Phillips, b Lawson	12
P.R. Downton*	b McDermott	16
R.M. Ellison	c Phillips, b Gilbert	3
P.H. Edmonds	lbw, b Lawson	12
L.B. Taylor	not out	1
Extras	b 13, lb 11, nb 26	50
		464

	O	M	R	W
Lawson	29.2	6	101	4
McDermott	31	2	108	4
Gilbert	21	2	96	1
Bennett	32	8	111	1
Border	2	—	8	—
Wessels	3	—	16	—

FALL OF WICKETS
1- 20, 2- 371, 3- 376, 4- 403, 5- 405, 6- 418, 7- 425, 8- 447, 9- 452

AUSTRALIA

	FIRST INNINGS		SECOND INNINGS	
G.M. Wood	lbw, b Botham	22	(2) b Botham	6
A.M.J. Hilditch	c Gooch, b Botham	17	(1) c Gower, b Taylor	9
K.C. Wessels	b Emburey	12	c Downton, b Botham	7
A.R. Border†	b Edmonds	38	c Botham, b Ellison	58
D.M. Wellham	c Downton, b Ellison	13	lbw, b Ellison	5
G.M. Ritchie	not out	64	c Downton, b Ellison	6
W.B. Phillips*	b Edmonds	18	c Downton, b Botham	10
M.J. Bennett	c Robinson, b Ellison	12	c and b Taylor	11
G.F. Lawson	c Botham, b Taylor	14	c Downton, b Ellison	7
C.J. McDermott	run out	25	c Botham, b Ellison	2
D.R. Gilbert	b Botham	1	not out	0
Extras	lb 3, w 2	5	b 4, nb 4	8
		241		129

	O	M	R	W	O	M	R	W
Botham	20	3	64	3	17	3	44	3
Taylor	13	1	39	1	11.3	1	34	2
Ellison	18	5	35	2	17	3	46	5
Emburey	19	7	48	1	1	—	1	—
Edmonds	14	2	52	2				

FALL OF WICKETS
1- 35, 2- 52, 3- 56, 4- 101, 5- 109, 6- 144, 7- 171, 8- 192, 9- 235
1- 13, 2- 16, 3- 37, 4- 51, 5- 71, 6- 96, 7- 114, 8- 127, 9- 129

Umpires: H.D. Bird and K.E. Palmer

England won by an innings and 94 runs

Cornhill Test Match Averages – England *v.* Australia

ENGLAND BATTING

	M	Inns	NOs	Runs	HS	Av	100s	50s
M.W. Gatting	6	9	3	527	160	87.83	2	3
D.I. Gower	6	9		732	215	81.33	2	1
R.T. Robinson	6	9	1	490	175	61.25	2	1
G.A. Gooch	6	9		487	196	54.11	1	2
A.J. Lamb	6	8	1	256	67	36.57		1
J.E. Emburey	6	6	2	130	33	32.50		
I.T. Botham	6	8		250	85	31.25		2
P.R. Downton	6	7	1	114	54	19.00		1
P.H. Edmonds	5	5		47	21	9.40		
P.J.W. Allott	4	5	1	27	12	6.75		

Played in two Tests: L.B. Taylor 1*; R.M. Ellison 3
Played in one Test: P. Willey 36 and 3*; N.G. Cowans 22*; N.A. Foster 3 and 0; A. Sidebottom 2; J.P. Agnew 2*

AUSTRALIA BATTING

	M	Inns	NOs	Runs	HS	Av	100s	50s
A.R. Border	6	11	2	597	196	66.33	2	1
G.M. Ritchie	6	11	1	422	146	42.20	1	2
A.M.J. Hilditch	6	11		424	119	38.54	1	1
W.B. Phillips	6	11	1	350	91	35.00		2
K.C. Wessels	6	11		368	83	33.45		3
G.M. Wood	5	9		260	172	28.88	1	
S.P. O'Donnell	5	8	1	184	48	26.28		
D.C. Boon	4	7		124	61	17.71		1
G.F. Lawson	6	9	1	119	53	14.87		1
C.J. McDermott	6	9	1	103	35	12.87		
R.G. Holland	4	5	1	15	10	3.75		

Played in two Tests: J.R. Thomson 28*, 4*, 4* and 2*
Played in one Test: G.R.J. Matthews 4 and 17; D.M. Wellham 13 and 5; D.R. Gilbert 1 and 0*; M.J. Bennett 12 and 11

ENGLAND BOWLING

	Overs	Mds	Runs	Wkts	Av	Best	5/inn
R.M. Ellison	75.5	20	185	17	10.88	6/77	2
I.T. Botham	251.4	36	855	31	27.58	5/109	1
J.E. Emburey	248.4	75	544	19	28.63	5/82	1
P.H. Edmonds	225.5	59	549	15	36.60	4/40	
L.B. Taylor	63.3	11	178	4	44.50	2/34	
G.A. Gooch	41.2	10	102	2	51.00	2/57	
P.J.W. Allott	113	22	297	5	59.40	2/74	

Also bowled: N.G. Cowans 33–6–128–2; N.A. Foster 23–1–83–1; M.W. Gatting 5–0–16–0; A. Sidebottom 18.4–3–65–1; J.P. Agnew 23–2–99–0; A.J. Lamb 1–0–10–0

AUSTRALIA BOWLING

	Overs	Mds	Runs	Wkts	Av	Best	5/inn
C.J. McDermott	234.2	21	901	30	30.03	8/141	2
G.F. Lawson	246	38	830	22	37.72	5/103	1
R.G. Holland	172	41	465	6	77.50	5/68	1
S.P. O'Donnell	145.4	31	487	6	81.16	3/37	
J.R. Thomson	56	4	275	3	91.66	2/166	
K.C. Wessels	6	2	18	0	—		
A.R. Border	11	1	37	0	—		

Also bowled: G.R.J. Matthews 9–2–21–0; G.M. Ritchie 1–0–10–0; M.J. Bennett 32–8–111–1; D.R. Gilbert 21–2–96–1

ENGLAND CATCHES

20–P.R. Downton (ct 19/st 1); 8–I.T. Botham and P.H. Edmonds; 7–A.J. Lamb; 6–D.I. Gower; 5–R.T. Robinson; 4–G.A. Gooch; 3–J.E. Emburey; 1–R.M. Ellison and L.B. Taylor

AUSTRALIA CATCHES

11–A.R. Border and W.B. Phillips; 4–D.C. Boon; 3–A.M.J. Hilditch, S.P. O'Donnell, G.M. Ritchie and K.C. Wessels; 2–C.J. McDermott; 1–M.J. Bennett, R.G. Holland, J.R. Thomson, G.M. Wood and D.M. Wellham

The England side that regained the Ashes – l to r (back) *Downton, Emburey, Ellison, Taylor, Edmonds, Robinson and Bernard Thomas (physiotherapist who retired after this series)* (front) *Lamb, Gatting, Gower, Botham and Gooch. (Adrian Murrell)*

BELOW: *The end of Australian hopes. Allan Border, a valiant captain and outstanding batsman, becomes another victim of the ebullient Ellison. (Adrian Murrell)*

David Gower – Man of the Series. (Adrian Murrell)

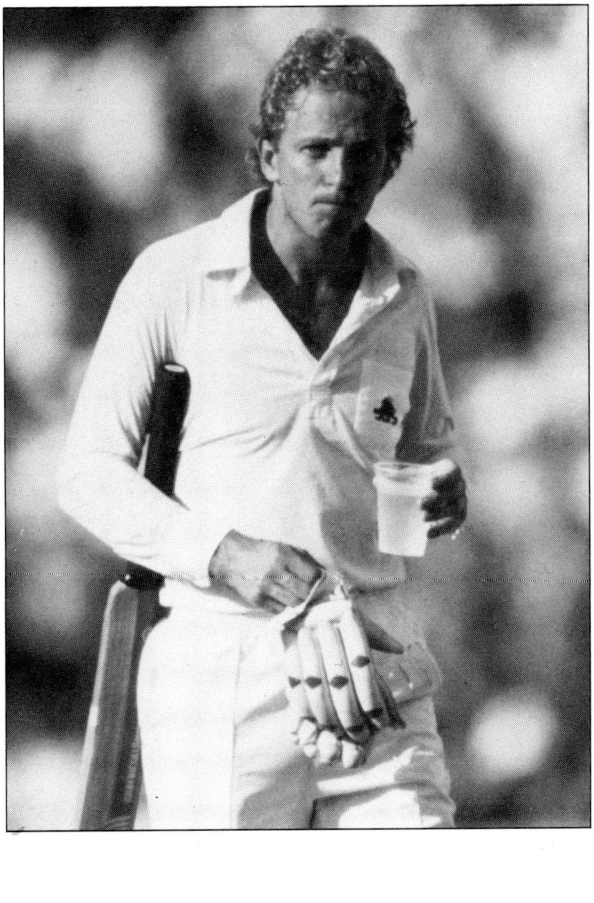

Australians in England 1985
First Class Matches

BATTING	v. Somerset (Taunton) 8–10 May		v. Worcester (Worcester) 11–13 May		v. Sussex (Hove) 18–21 May		v. M.C.C. (Lord's) 22–24 May		v. Derbyshire (Derby) 25–28 May		v. Yorkshire (Leeds) 5–7 June	
K.C. Wessels	41	156			56	18	60	—				
A.M.J. Hilditch	20	46	7	—	8	0	14	21	60	—	18	—
D.M. Wellham	64	26*					0	81*	77	—	8	—
A.R. Border	106	—	135	—			125	—	100	—		
D.C. Boon	62*	21*	73*	—	119	21			10*	—	—	—
W.B. Phillips	56*	—			33	91			0*	—		
G.R.J. Matthews	—	22	23*	—	19	1			1	—		
G.F. Lawson	—	—	—	—			—	—				
C.J. McDermott	—	0	—	—					—	—	—	—
J.R. Thomson	—	7			3	—	—	—				
R.G. Holland	—	35			4	—			—	—	—	—
R.B. Phillips			39	—			0*	—			—	—
G.M. Ritchie			21	—	16	100*	22	47			58*	—
M.J. Bennett			—	—			—	12*	—	—	—	—
D.R. Gilbert			—	—	7	—			—	—	—	—
G.M. Wood			34	—	8	18	33	48	16	—	102*	—
S.P. O'Donnell					37*	15*	110*	—			—	—
Byes			10		1	4			3			
Leg-byes	7	2	9		4	2	8	2	4		4	
Wides			1						1		3	
No-balls		1	12		6	5	15	11	6		2	
Total	356	316	364		321	275	377	222	278		195	
Wickets	4	6	5		10	6	6	3	5		2	
Results	W		D		D		D		D		D	

BATTING	v. Leicestershire (Leicester) 8–11 June		First Test Match (Leeds) 13–18 June		v. Hampshire (Southampton) 22–25 June		Second Test Match (Lord's) 27 June–2 July		v. Essex (Chelmsford) 6–9 July	
K.C. Wessels	2	—	36	64	6	6	11	28	23	0
A.M.J. Hilditch	56	—	119	80			14	0	80	35
D.M. Wellham									10	63
A.R. Border	25	—	32	8	8	21	196	41*		
D.C. Boon	39	—	14	22	0	0	4	1	21	138
W.B. Phillips	128	—	30	91	15	22	21	29		
G.R.J. Matthews	26	—							5	6
G.F. Lawson	—	—	0	15	6	0	5*	—		
C.J. McDermott	53*	—	18	6	5	17*	9	—		
J.R. Thomson	2	—	4*	2*					1	21*
R.G. Holland	5	—			0	—	0	—		
R.B. Phillips									28	9
G.M. Ritchie	115	—	46	1	3	62	94	2		
M.J. Bennett					13	16*			23	0
D.R. Gilbert					6*	—			6*	7
G.M. Wood			14	3	5	0	8	6	33	8
S.P. O'Donnell			0	24			48	9*	39	31
Byes	4			4		2			2	5
Leg-byes	4		13	3	1	3	10	11	6	4
Wides			4	1	2		1			1
No-balls	7		1		6	5	4		2	5
Total	466		331	324	76	154	425	127	279	333
Wickets	9		10		10	7	10	6	10	10
Results	D		L		D		W		D	

Catches 21 – W.B. Phillips (ct 20/st 1)
13 – R.B. Phillips and A.R. Border
12 – D.C. Boon
9 – K.C. Wessels and subs (ct 7/st 2)
7 – G.M. Wood, G.M. Ritchie and A.M.J. Hilditch

LEFT: *The lion is rampant; the kangaroo about to fall. (Ken Kelly)*

RIGHT: *The sweet smell of success. (Adrian Murrell)*

uncertain and many were calling for his head and criticising his technique. Now he had a record 732 runs to his credit in the series and was received with an acclaim which had previously been reserved for the likes of Percy Chapman and Len Hutton. It had been a summer of wretched weather, but the cricket had brightened even the dullest day. Botham had hit only two fifties for England, but he had bowled fast and well and he had caught magnificently. Gooch had returned and re-established himself. Edmonds was wonderfully aggressive. Robinson looked set for a decade as England's opener. Cowans and Foster should have been better treated, for lesser men had replaced them, but this was a well balanced England side and none who saw them will forget the cricket that they played in 1985.

31 August, 2 and 3 September

at Cardiff

Gloucestershire 151 for 4 dec (C.W.J. Athey 71 not out) and 0 for 0 dec
Glamorgan 0 for 0 dec and 151 for 8 (Javed Miandad 60)
Match drawn
Glamorgan 9 pts, Gloucestershire 1 pt

Third Test Match (Trent Bridge) 11–16 July		v. Glamorgan (Neath) 20–22 July		v. Gloucestershire (Bristol) 24–26 July		v. Northamptonshire (Northampton) 27–30 July		Fourth Test Match (Old Trafford) 1–6 August		v. Middlesex (Lord's) 10–13 August		Fifth Test Match (Edgbaston) 15–20 August		v. Kent (Canterbury) 24–27 August		Sixth Test Match (The Oval) 29 August–2 Sept.		M	Inns	NOs	Runs	HS	Av
33	—			0	61*	1	—	34	50	56	—	83	10	51	—	12	7	16	26	1	905	156	36.20
47	—	15	—			0	—	49	40			39	10	16	9	17	9	17	27	—	829	119	30.70
		43*	—	10	105					125*	—			1	38	13	5	10	16	4	669	125*	55.75
23	—			5	130			8	146*			45	2	103	—	38	58	14	21	2	1355	196	71.31
15	—	—	—			206*	—	61	7	4	—							15	20	5	838	206*	55.86
2	—			22	48	55	—	36	39*	73	—	15	59			18	10	14	22	3	893	128	47.00
		—	—	41*	—	51*	—	4	17									10	12	3	216	51*	24.00
18	—			0	—			4	—	29*	—	53	3			14	7	13	13	2	154	53	14.00
0*	—	—	—			—	—	0	—	—	—	35	8	5	—	25	2	16	14	3	183	53*	16.63
		—	—	10	—					—	—	28*	4*	0*	—			11	11	6	82	28*	16.40
10	—			0	—	—	—	5*	—	—	—	0	0					13	10	1	59	35	6.55
		—	—	23	—									8	23*			7	7	2	130	39	26.00
146	—	—	—			49	—	4	31	27	—	8	20	155	—	64*	6	16	23	3	1097	155	54.85
		—	—			—	—			7	—			8	9*	12	11	11	10	3	111	23	15.85
		—	—	12	—									0	—	1	0*	10	8	3	39	12	7.80
172	—	38*	—			20*	—			42	—	19	10	8	18	22	6	16	25	3	691	172	31.40
46	—			3	31*	8	—	45	—			1	11					11	16	5	448	100*	40.72
6		5		4	15	2			1	10			1	1			4						
7				5	9	10		3	6	5		4	3	3	1	3							
2		2			1	2		1		5		1		1		2							
12		2		11	10			3	3	13		4	1	4	1		4						
539		105		146	410	404		257	340	396		335	142	364	99	241	129						
10		1		10	3	5		10	5	6		10	10	10	3	10	10						
D		D		W		D		D		D		L		W		L							

6 – M.J. Bennett
5 – S.P. O'Donnell and R.G. Holland
3 – G.R.J. Matthews
2 – C.J. McDermott, J.R. Thomson and D.R. Gilbert
1 – G.F. Lawson and D.M. Wellham

Australians in England 1985
First Class Matches

BOWLING	J.R. Thomson	G.F. Lawson	R.G. Holland	C.J. McDermott	G.R.J. Matthews	D.R. Gilbert	M.J. Bennett	S.P. O'Donnell	A.M.J. Hilditch
v. Somerset (Taunton)	17–3–75–2	8–2–31–1	29.3–11–87–4	11–1–71–1	9–0–42–0				
8–10 May	14–1–44–6		17.1–5–30–2	12–2–46–1					
v. Worcestershire (Worcester)		13–1–65–0		13–3–39–2	23.5–8–55–2	19–1–90–0	19–8–43–2		
11–13 May		7–3–11–3		2–0–22–0		14.2–2–49–1	6–2–10–0		
v. Sussex (Hove)	13.3–4–50–0		23–5–49–2		11–3–38–2	32–6–97–4		14–4–25–1	
18–21 May	7–1–31–1		20–10–37–4		11–2–36–2	7–2–15–1		9–0–27–1	
v. M.C.C. (Lord's)	14–1–65–1	17–1–66–1					15–1–53–0	16–3–77–0	3–0–19–0
22–24 May									
v. Derbyshire (Derby)									
25–28 May									
v. Yorkshire (Leeds)				15–2–49–1		12–3–36–0	8–3–14–1	5–1–17–0	
5–7 June									
v. Leicestershire (Leicester)	24–6–103–5	15–0–71–0	32–4–112–1	28–3–87–3	16.5–3–67–1				
8–11 June			2–0–5–0						
First Test Match (Leeds)	34–3–166–2	26–4–117–3		32–2–134–4				27–8–77–1	
13–18 June	3–0–8–0	16–4–51–2		4–0–20–0				15.4–5–37–3	
v. Hampshire (Southampton)		9–5–10–1	22–8–51–5	12.2–1–39–2		14–5–35–0	33–11–78–1		
22–25 June		2–2–0–0							
Second Test Match		25–2–91–3	23–6–42–0	29.2–5–70–6				22–3–82–1	
(Lord's) 27 June–2 July		23–0–86–3	32–12–68–5	20–2–84–2				5–0–10–0	
v. Essex (Chelmsford)	24–2–93–3				15.4–1–76–3	23–2–90–3	26–4–72–1	15–1–58–0	
6–9 July	16–2–46–2				19–7–42–2	21–9–41–4	4–2–8–0	4–0–22–0	
Third Test Match		39.4–10–103–5	26–3–90–1	35–3–147–2				29–4–104–1	
(Trent Bridge) 11–16 July		13–4–32–0	26–9–69–0	16–2–42–2				10–2–26–0	
v. Glamorgan (Neath)	12–1–53–0			14–4–55–0	21–3–83–0	18–0–99–0	25.4–5–101–3		
20–22 July									
v. Gloucestershire (Bristol)	10–1–36–2	10–0–42–3	8–2–26–1			16–1–63–1		8–1–12–2	
24–26 July	9–2–38–3		13.2–2–56–3		10–2–32–0	13–1–55–2		10–5–13–1	
v. Northamptonshire			7–3–12–0	19–3–70–2	13.2–3–29–0		14–3–43–0	16–1–81–1	
(Northampton) 27–30 July									
Fourth Test Match		37–7–114–0	38–7–101–0	36–3–141–8	9–2–21–0			21–6–82–0	
(Old Trafford) 1–6 August									
v. Middlesex (Lord's)	18–4–54–0	20–8–39–0	30–3–87–1	25–3–108–1			38–5–95–2		
10–13 August									
Fifth Test Match	19–1–101–1	37–1–135–2	25–4–95–0	31–2–155–2				16–3–69–0	
(Edgbaston) 15–20 August									
v. Kent (Canterbury)	7–1–25–1			24.5–3–104–3		26–5–62–3	30–6–99–1		4–2–10–0
24–27 August				11.2–3–18–5		17–2–57–1	16–4–39–4		
Sixth Test Match (The Oval)		29.2–6–101–4		31–2–108–4		21–2–96–1	32–8–111–1		
29 August–2 September									
	241.3–33–988–29 *av.* 34.06	347–60–1165–31 *av.* 37.58	374–94–1017–29 *av.* 35.06	421.5–49–1609–51 *av.* 31.54	159.4–34–521–12 *av.* 43.41	253.2–41–885–21 *av.* 42.14	266.4–62–766–16 *av.* 47.87	242.4–47–819–12 *av.* 68.25	7–2–29–0 —

a B.C. Rose retired hurt, absent hurt b J.R.T. Barclay retired hurt c G.M. Ritchie 0.3–0–1–0 d S.J.W. Andrew retired hurt

at Folkestone

Derbyshire 147 (D.L. Underwood 4 for 34, E.A.E. Baptiste 4 for 48) and 70 for 7
Kent 300 for 8 dec (E.A.E. Baptiste 71, C.S. Cowdrey 62)

Match drawn
Kent 8 pts, Derbyshire 3 pts

at Leicester

Leicestershire 153 (P. Willey 56, N.V. Radford 4 for 55) and 167 for 9 (N.V. Radford 5 for 64)
Worcestershire 343 for 7 dec (M.J. Weston 79, D.N. Patel 69, T.S. Curtis 65)

Match drawn
Worcestershire 8 pts, Leicestershire 4 pts

at Trent Bridge

Nottinghamshire 140 (C.E.B. Rice 70, P.J.W. Allott 5 for 47) and 184 for 4 dec (D.W. Randall 50)
Lancashire 126 (R.J. Hadlee 8 for 41) and 158 for 7 (K.A. Hayes 55, E.E. Hemmings 6 for 51)

Match drawn
Nottinghamshire 4 pts, Lancashire 4 pts

at Taunton

Somerset 275 for 4 (I.V.A. Richards 112, P.M. Roebuck 60)
***v.* Sussex**

Match drawn
Somerset 3 pts, Sussex 1 pt

at Edgbaston

Warwickshire 142 (I.L. Pont 4 for 15)
Essex 170 for 5 (P.J. Prichard 69 not out, D.E. East 69 not out)

Match drawn
Essex 5 pts, Warwickshire 2 pts

K.C. Wessels	D.C. Boon	A.R. Border	Byes	Leg-byes	Wides	No-balls	Total	Wkts
			4	4		7	314	9
			4	1		5	125	9a
			6	5	2	16	303	6
				1	4	5	93	4
				3	1	19	262	9b
				7		5	153	9
			4	7	3	1	291	2
						Abandoned		
			4	4		8	124	2
			2	12	2	36	454	10
5–0–9–0	3–0–12–0			1	1		28	0c
3–2–2–0		3–0–16–0	5	16	5	14	533	10
				7	1	3	123	5
			6	2	2	12	221	9d
8–2–26–0	2–0–15–0		1				64	1e
			1	4	1	17	290	10
			1	12	3	4	261	10
			12	8	5	28	409	10
				10		2	169	8
			12		1	3	456	10
			1	16		2	196	2f
	1–0–6–0		3	9	5	15	409	3
				2		8	181	9
			5	6	2	1	205	9g
			12	11		7	258	3
			7	16		17	482	9
3–1–4–0			4	6	2	17	397	4
		6–1–13–0	7	20		22	595	5
10–4–22–0		2–1–1–0	4	6	2	24	333	10
			4	8	1	9	126	10
3–0–16–0		2–0–8–0	13	11		26	464	10
32–9–79–0 —	6–0–33–0 —	13–2–38–0 —						

e G.M. Ritchie 5–0–22–1   f G.M. Ritchie 1–0–10–0   g R.C. Russell absent hurt

at Leeds

Northamptonshire 242 for 5 (R.J. Bailey 73 not out)
***v.* Yorkshire**

Match drawn
Yorkshire 2 pts, Northamptonshire 2 pts

Weather again blighted the county championship and denied Gloucestershire the chance of overtaking Hampshire who had no game. In what play was possible on the Saturday Gloucestershire reached 123 for 4 in 44 overs. There was no play on the Monday and on the last day, forfeitures and a declaration allowed Glamorgan 37 overs in which to make 152. Ontong was run out in going for the second run off the last ball of the match, a run which would have brought victory. As the side batting second in a match where the scores ended level, Glamorgan took 9 points. One sympathised for Gloucestershire who had bowled 6 overs beyond the minimum in an effort to force victory.

A third century in succession by Viv Richards, 112 out of 146 off 115 balls was followed by two blank days at Taunton, and there was only a little play possible on the first two days at Headingley. Essex, with Foster prominent and Pont mopping up the tail, shot out Warwickshire and then collapsed to 42 for 5 themselves. Prichard and East saved them with a fine stand.

Kent took a first innings lead of 153 over Derbyshire at Folkestone, but the visitors batted out the last day in the most tedious manner imaginable. From 84 overs they reached 70 for 7. Underwood bowled 37 overs for 23 runs and Potter 30.4 for 13. It was grim stuff, particularly as Kent batted enterprisingly in the first hour.

Radford's marvellous form continued, but Blackett and Garnham were instrumental in denying Worcestershire victory. Weston had shown particular enterprise for the visitors, but the home side's problems were increasing daily. Nick Cook had said he would be leaving the club and Garnham

Leicestershire C.C.C. First-Class Matches – Batting, 1985	v. Yorkshire (Leicester) 27–29 April		v. Oxford University (Oxford) 1–3 May		v. Derbyshire (Leicester) 8–10 May		v. Nottinghamshire (Leicester) 22–24 May		v. Northamptonshire (Leicester) 25–28 May		v. Nottinghamshire (Trent Bridge) 29–31 May		v. Essex (Chelmsford) 1–4 June		v. Australians (Leicester) 8–11 June		v. Warwickshire (Hinckley) 12–14 June		v. Middlesex (Lord's) 15–18 June		v. Glamorgan (Leicester) 22–25 June		v. Yorkshire (Bradford) 26–28 June		v. Surrey (Leicester) 29 June–2 July		v. Somerset (Taunton) 6–9 July	
I.P. Butcher	33	23*	95	—	6	—	52	—	13	—	120	74	13	—	35	19*			29	71*	0	26	82	76	6	—	38	3
J.C. Balderstone	37	13*	0	—	14	—	72*	—	83	—	18	28	10	—	134	7*	5	7	7	0	51*	65	1	79	7	—	27	36
D.I. Gower	28	—	9	—	57	—	30*	—	52	—					135	—					100*	27					4	3
P. Willey	19	—	57	—	133	—			6	—					2	—					—	41	60	10	43	—	43	80
N.E. Briers	4	—	2	—	2	—	—	—	47*	—	0	44*	129	—	13	—	—	16	45	10	—	2	0	32*	0	—	34	17
M.A. Garnham	8	—	100	—	4	—	—	—	—	—	32	11	51	—	27*	—	—	0	27	6*	—	42	33	6	32	—	1	8*
G.J. Parsons	8	—	24	—	32	—	—	—	—	—	0	—	6*	—	7	—	—	10*	5	—	—	13	1*	4	15	—		
P.B. Clift	7*	—	23	—	8	—	—	—	1*	—	22	24	106	—			—	1*	0	—							40*	0
N.G.B. Cook	0	—			5	—	—	—	—	—	18	—	9*	—	1	—	—	—	0	—	—	34*	—	—	4	—	8	8*
G.J.F. Ferris	4	—			2*	—	—	—	—	—	0*	—																
L.B. Taylor	5	—	0*	—									—	—	11	—	—	—	0*	—	—	0*	—	—	2*	—	20*	8
J.J. Whitaker			0	—	8	—	—	—	79	—	22	8	12	—	18	—	—	37	7	30*	—	4	43	19	109	—	105	19
P.A.J. de Freitas			0	—																								
R.A. Cobb							—	—			3	14	31	—			8*	65	48	13			0	12*	78	—		
M. Blackett											0	3*																
J.P. Agnew													—	—	19	—	—	—	6	—	—	0	—	—	8	—	17	—
D. Billington																	—	19										
P. Whiticase																												
Byes		4	12		1		5		9		5	1	2		2			2	1	2		6	4		6		1	3
Leg-byes	6	2	1		6		6		5		4	3	12		12	1	1	5	13	4		5	3	8	15		4	5
Wides	1	1	3		1				1		1		1		2	1												
No-balls	10	3	4		22				8		2		10		36		1		9	13			3	3	16		1	2
Total	170	46	330		301		165		304		247	210	392		454	28	15	162	197	149	151	265	230	249	341		343	192
Wickets	10	0	10		10		1		5		10	6	7		10	0	1	6	10	3	1	9	7	6	10		9	8
Result	D		W		D		D		D		D		D		D		W		D		D		D		D		D	
Points	3		—		8		2		3		4		6		—		16		4		3		4		8		7	

Catches 60 – M.A. Garnham (ct 53/st 7)
20 – I.P. Butcher
11 – R.A. Cobb
10 – J.C. Balderstone and P. Willey
9 – P.B. Clift and P. Whiticase
8 – N.G.B. Cook
7 – N.E. Briers
6 – J.J. Whitaker
5 – L.B. Taylor

had followed by announcing his retirement at the age of 25. Now a third player, Gordon Parsons, stated that he had asked that he should be released.

Nottinghamshire gained much heart from a drawn game with Lancashire. Put in to bat, they fared badly against Allott and Simmons, who had 3 for 5 in 5 overs, and were only salvaged by Rice's aggression. In their turn, Lancashire fared no better and Richard Hadlee had the best bowling figures of a great career when he finished with 8 for 41. It was to the credit of both sides that a keen contest was shaped in dreadful conditions and eventually Lancashire were asked to make 199 in 40 overs. They maintained their chase until Hemmings, with his best bowling of the season, blunted their challenge.

John Player Special League

1 September

at Cardiff

Glamorgan 146 for 9
Surrey 108 for 0 (A.R. Butcher 81 not out)
Surrey (4 pts) won on faster scoring rate

at Southampton

Middlesex 146
Hampshire 149 for 4 (V.P. Terry 55)
Hampshire (4 pts) won by 6 wickets

at Folkestone

Derbyshire 170 for 8 (L. Potter 4 for 9)
Kent 161 for 9
Derbyshire (4 pts) won by 9 runs

at Leicester

Worcestershire 195 for 8 (D.N. Patel 76)
Leicestershire 187 for 9
Worcestershire (4 pts) won by 8 runs

at Taunton

Sussex 184 for 7 (Imran Khan 67)
Somerset 188 for 2 (N.F.M. Popplewell 74 not out, I.V.A. Richards 66 not out)
Somerset (4 pts) won by 8 wickets

at Edgbaston

Essex 251 for 3 (K.S. McEwan 118, D.R. Pringle 81 not out)
Warwickshire 230 (G.W. Humpage 62, J.K. Lever 4 for 44)
Essex (4 pts) won by 21 runs

v. Glamorgan (Swansea) 10–12 July	v. Derbyshire (Chesterfield) 13–15 July	v. Kent (Leicester) 27–30 July	v. Lancashire (Leicester) 31 July–2 August	v. Gloucestershire (Cheltenham) 10–13 August	v. Hampshire (Leicester) 17–20 August	v. Northamptonshire (Northampton) 24–27 August	v. Hampshire (Bournemouth) 28–30 August	v. Worcestershire (Leicester) 31 Aug.–3 Sept.	v. Middlesex (Leicester) 4–6 September	v. Sussex (Hove) 7–10 September	v. Lancashire (Old Trafford) 14–17 September		M	Inns	NOs	Runs	H/S	Av
72 —	0 4	17 8	33 1	21 —	41 —	9 —	38 29	0 6	11 0	6 4	78 —		25	39	3	1192	120	33.11
101 —	49 20	34 82*	20 26	34 —	10 —		2 20	7 28	19 14	28 31	45 —		25	40	5	1271	134	36.31
		27 24		4 —		4 —			49 18	2 128	18 —		14	19	2	719	135	42.29
20 —	101 48*	47 18*	11 37	52 —	7 —	147 —	5 20	56 35	9 0	74* 34	38 —		21	30	3	1253	147	46.40
36 —	0 —	6 —	61 —		8* —	7 —	5 3	45 0	0 8				23	29	4	576	129	23.04
18* —		0 —	9 —	6 —	— —	40 —	3 10	3 41			24 —		23	26	4	542	100	24.63
			29 —				11* 5				0 —		16	16	4	170	32	14.16
4* —	31 —	21 —	23 —	29 —	— —	0 —	7 0	13 7	30 34	0 14	50 —		22	26	5	495	106	23.57
5 —		3 —			5* —	45 —	0 7						18	16	4	152	45	12.66
— —	0* —							0* 0*	1 0		22* —		10	9	6	29	22*	9.66
— —	0 —	6 —	20 —	4 —		1* —			1* 5*	0 5			18	17	8	88	20*	9.77
103 —	42 16*	73 —	7 66*	17 —	0 —	43 —	0 65	15 4	7 89	18 0	18 —		25	34	3	1103	109	35.58
			30* —	29* —	— —		17 2*	0 9	11 11	0 7	1 —		9	12	3	117	30*	13.00
4 —	27 8		59 66*	24 —	26 —	18 —	3 33*			3 23	35 —		16	23	4	601	78	31.63
								10 28*					2	4	2	41	28*	20.50
	36	8* 6		5 —	— —	2 —		1 1		0 10*			14	14	2	119	36	9.91
	36 —												2	2	—	55	36	27.50
	47 —								15 0	32 55*			3	5	1	149	55*	37.25
8	8		1 4	1	6	6	1											
7	7	4 1	8 3	5	3	17	4 5	2 1	5 3	2 4	7							
2	7 4	2 1	11	4			2 1			1								
13	21 5	3 1	5 4	14		4	3 14	1 7	3	6 10								
393	376 105	251 141	327 207	249	106	343	100 215	153 167	158 185	171 326	336 0							
7	10 3	10 3	10 3	10	5	10	10 9†	10 9	10 10	10 9	10 0							
D	W	D	D	D	D	D	L	D	L	L	D							
5	24	7	8	6	4	5	1	4	5	5	3							

† R.A. Cobb retired hurt

4 – subs
3 – D.I. Gower and J.P. Agnew
1 – D. Billington and P.A.J. de Freitas

at Leeds

Yorkshire 181 for 8 (S.N. Hartley 56, D.J. Wild 4 for 33)
Northamptonshire 185 for 7 (W. Larkins 59)
Northamptonshire (4 pts) won by 3 wickets

On what was believed to be his farewell match before concentrating on the Law as his profession, Nigel Popplewell hit 74 not out and set the foundation for the defeat of Sussex, but it was Viv Richards who administered the death blows to the league leaders. He hit 66 off 31 balls, with 3 sixes and 8 fours. He took 26 off an over from Barclay and finished the match by hitting le Roux for four successive fours. The defeat cost Sussex dearly. Northants won off the last ball in a rather nervous game at Headingley in which Duncan Wild had his best bowling return in the competition and so moved to the top of the table. Hampshire easily beat Middlesex, however, and Essex, with McEwan and Pringle in glorious form, beat Warwickshire so that both these sides moved to within two points of Northants with a game in hand. McEwan and Pringle hit 190 off 26 overs for the fourth wicket, Ferreira was a great sufferer, and when Essex bowled Stuart Turner dismissed Kallicharran, his three hundredth wicket in the competition. Elsewhere Leicestershire's challenge faded as Worcestershire emphasised their growing strength and Kent, once leaders, slipped further down the table with some limp batting against Derbyshire. Surrey won after rain reduced their target at Cardiff, but they remained bottom of the league.

4, 5 and 6 September

at Bristol

Gloucestershire 228 (D.A. Graveney 53 not out) and 16 for 0 dec
Northamptonshire 0 for 0 dec and 188 for 9 (C.A Walsh 4 for 72)
Match drawn
Northamptonshire 4 pts, Gloucestershire 2 pts

at Folkestone

Hampshire 333 for 9 dec (C.L. Smith 121, C.G. Greenidge 84, L. Potter 4 for 87) and 156 for 5 dec (V.P. Terry 67, C.G. Greenidge 50)
Kent 259 (C.S. Cowdrey 131) and 172 for 7 (E.A.E. Baptiste 68)
Match drawn
Hampshire 8 pts, Kent 5 pts

at Leicester

Leicestershire 158 (N.G. Cowans 6 for 31) and 185 (J.J. Whitaker 89, W.W. Daniel 7 for 62)
Middlesex 298 (C.T. Radley 87) and 49 for 0
Middlesex won by 10 wickets
Middlesex 23 pts, Leicestershire 5 pts

Leicestershire C.C.C. First-Class Matches — Bowling, 1985	G.J.F. Ferris	L.B. Taylor	G.J. Parsons	P.B. Clift	N.G.B. Cook	N.E. Briers	P.A.J. de Freitas	P. Willey	J.C. Balderstone
v. Yorkshire (Leicester) 27–29 April	28–6–95–2	14–3–45–0	21–4–60–1	18–3–52–2	12–3–27–0	4–0–19–0			
v. Oxford University (Oxford) 1–3 May		8–5–10–1 7–2–14–2	11–5–11–6 11–3–42–1	 18–4–39–2			3.4–2–3–3 22–7–81–3	 17.4–6–49–2	
v. Derbyshire (Leicester) 8–10 May	20.1–5–59–2 20–4–52–0		24–5–72–1	26–9–53–3 33–12–69–1	 29–12–50–0	12–1–29–4 16.5–3–56–1		 21–9–33–0	 1–0–9–0
v. Nottinghamshire (Leicester) 22–24 May	24–1–108–0 5–1–17–0		26–5–76–1	17–8–25–0 7.1–1–14–0	13–5–33–1	11–2–48–1 6–2–12–1			
v. Northamptonshire (Leicester) 25–28 May									
v. Nottinghamshire (Trent Bridge) 29–31 May	15–4–64–1 9–0–44–0		24–7–68–0 13–0–40–1	29–8–100–1 13–2–29–1	37–5–120–3 20–8–43–2	3–0–22–0			
v. Essex (Chelmsford) 1–4 June		17–2–47–3 11–3–26–1	14–1–49–1 9–1–28–0	17.4–6–36–2 6–1–31–0	5–3–9–0 8–4–18–0				
v. Australians (Leicester) 8–11 June		16–3–72–1	28–6–88–2		29–9–87–1			18–3–67–2	
v. Warwickshire (Hinckley) 12–14 June		3–3–0–0 18–3–51–2	1–0–2–0 9–2–25–0	2–0–2–0 19–12–25–3	 2–1–1–0				
v. Middlesex (Lord's) 15–18 June		17–3–45–3 8–3–12–0	16–7–22–0 17–3–55–1	19–5–31–1 16–3–45–1	35–12–59–4 23–5–66–1	2–0–9–0			
v. Glamorgan (Leicester) 22–25 June		31.4–11–33–3 18–5–57–0	23–5–50–0 9–3–21–0		33–15–46–1 23.2–7–67–1	7–3–10–1 7.1–1–29–0		 8–1–31–0	 1–0–1–1
v. Yorkshire (Bradford) 26–28 June		25.4–12–59–1 8–4–14–0	30–8–61–1 2.2–0–17–0		35–9–82–2 19–2–71–1	 3–0–24–0		10–2–23–1 12–0–50–0	
v. Surrey (Leicester) 29 June–2 July		24–7–49–2 7–3–13–0	13–1–56–2		4–2–9–0 33–16–64–0			2–2–0–0 41–14–73–6	 7–2–17–0
v. Somerset (Taunton) 6–9 July		28–4–77–5 7–2–13–0		23–3–86–1 10–1–47–3	19.5–4–77–3 23–7–73–1			10–1–32–0 23–6–60–1	
v. Glamorgan (Swansea) 10–12 July	21.3–3–76–2	17–3–22–0		18–3–51–2	28–10–79–1			17–3–58–0	
v. Derbyshire (Chesterfield) 13–15 July	8.5–0–36–1 19–2–76–1	13–3–33–1 35–6–86–5		16–5–38–5 22–10–40–1				1–1–0–1 11–7–19–1	
v. Kent (Leicester) 27–30 July		12–4–27–0 15–6–42–4		21.4–7–61–1 7–1–25–0	 5–2–6–0			1–0–1–0 2–1–1–0	
v. Lancashire (Leicester) 31 July–2 August		27.3–5–52–4 10.5–3–12–3	20–5–58–2	29–10–64–2		 12–5–28–0	23–5–71–1 13–3–39–5	6–2–23–1	
v. Gloucestershire (Cheltenham) 10–13 August		17.4–3–45–5 16–5–34–2		14–3–33–2			14–4–20–1 12–2–36–0	 2–1–9–0	
v. Hampshire (Leicester) 17–20 August				7–3–17–0	23–7–45–2		9–5–12–1	19.1–4–43–6	
v. Northamptonshire (Northampton) 24–27 August		7–2–30–0 4–2–9–0		16–4–28–1 30–7–54–4	31–9–47–3 47–25–67–2			34–15–64–5 19–4–44–1	
v. Hampshire (Bournemouth) 28–30 August			20–2–78–0	24–10–52–0	19–3–86–1	4–1–17–0	27–3–80–4	12–2–48–0	
v. Worcestershire (Leicester) 31 August–3 September	21–1–91–1			20–1–75–0			22–0–93–3	28–8–56–2	
v. Middlesex (Leicester) 4–6 September	25–1–84–3	30–4–68–3		21–7–50–2 5–1–12–0			18.1–3–54–1 6–1–12–0	6–0–24–0	 2–1–3–0
v. Sussex (Hove) 7–10 September		17–4–50–4 13–2–51–1		19–5–36–0 22–3–60–4			23–5–59–2 14.3–1–63–1	12.4–7–8–4 15–4–65–2	 3–0–29–0
v. Lancashire (Old Trafford) 14–17 September	 15–4–24–2		 15–3–31–3	 30–11–66–2			 27–2–80–2	 31–8–69–0	 1–0–9–0
	231.3–32– 826–15 *av.* 55.06	503.2–130– 1198–56 *av.* 21.39	356.2–76– 1010–23 *av.* 43.91	595.3–169– 1446–47 *av.* 30.76	556.1–186– 1332–60 *av.* 44.40	90–18– 303–8 *av.* 37.87	234.2–43– 703–27 *av.* 26.03	379.3–111– 950–35 *av.* 27.14	15–3– 68–1 *av.* 68.00

J.P. Agnew	D.I. Gower	I.P. Butcher	Byes	Leg-byes	Wides	No-balls	Total	Wkts
			4	4	2	11	306	5
						4	24	10
			4	2	1	8	231	10
			9	4		9	226	10
			4	6		6	279	3
			6	5	1	1	301	3
				3			46	1
			Match Abandoned					
			4	4	3	9	382	5
			4	2	3	3	162	4
18–4–59–4			5	8	1	12	213	10
13–2–57–2			1	1	1	14	162	3
26–2–144–3			4	4		7	466	9
3–1–11–0				1	5	1	16	0
25–7–46–5			5	7		9	160	10
18.3–2–78–2				13		5	257	10
11–0–53–0			2	2		5	235	3
22–7–43–3			1	14		2	197	9
11.5–3–32–1			14	7	1	4	259	3
30–9–73–3				2	5	4	300	8
11–1–56–0			1	8	3	2	241	1
28.1–6–86–6				10		8	210	10
17–5–49–3			2	6			224	9
19–3–85–1			5	5		7	367	10
13–3–49–0				6		1	248	5
				3	1	7	289	6
15–5–44–2				2		12	153	10
26.1–7–79–2			7	16	5	24	323	10
19–2–70–9				4	2	11	163	10
11–1–48–2			5	1	1		128	6
			10		2	11	278	10
			1	1		3	81	8
15–4–35–2				1		6	134	10
15–3–40–3				2		4	121	5
12–3–32–1			4	9		4	162	10
16–5–38–1				3		4	210	10
9–0–46–0	1–0–3–0	2–1–5–0	10	5		6	243	
			6	4	9		371	5
6–1–17–0			5	6		22	343	7
				18		15	298	10
	1.1–0–13–0							
12–1–43–0			7	6	2	25	209	10
			1	20	2	4	289	8
							0	0
			6	8	3	12		
422.4–87–1413–55 av. 25.69	2.1–0–16–0 —	2–1–5–0 —						

at The Oval

Surrey 349 for 5 dec (G.S. Clinton 123, T.E. Jesty 82, M.A. Lynch 59) and 198 for 7 dec (A.J. Stewart 81 not out, A.N. Jones 5 for 39)
Sussex 300 for 4 dec (A.M. Green 133, Imran Khan 84 not out, G.D. Mendis 50) and 249 for 7 (Imran Khan 59)

Sussex won by 3 wickets
Sussex 22 pts, Surrey 5 pts

at Worcester

Worcestershire 300 for 3 dec (G.A. Hick 174 not out, T.S. Curtis 58) and 151 for 4 dec (D.B. d'Oliveira 64, P.A. Neale 55 not out)
Somerset 157 for 3 dec (R.J. Harden 52 not out) and 170 (N.V. Radford 4 for 45)

Worcestershire won by 124 runs
Worcestershire 21 pts, Somerset 2 pts

The rain at Bristol, the defiance of Chris Cowdrey and Kent at Folkestone and the bowling of Cowans and Daniel at Leicester combined to take Middlesex to the top of the table, two points ahead of Hampshire, nine ahead of Gloucestershire.

There was no play on the first day at Bristol and none possible until 4.00 pm on the second day. Brisk hitting, a forfeiture and a declaration left Northants 66 overs in which to make 245 runs. A fine catch by Romaines at square-leg off Lawrence accounted for Cook in the first over and the visitors struggled from then on. At tea, they were 78 for 5 in 28 overs and could only hope to bat out for a draw. Capel, Harper and Ripley all fell before the score reached 150 and Gloucestershire sensed victory. Wild, who batted well for 49, and Mallender took the score to 164, but when Wild became Graveney's third victim Gloucestershire had nine overs in which to capture one wicket. As one of the batsmen was Jim Griffiths, one of the least accomplished in the game, a Gloucestershire win seemed imminent, but Griffiths, well shielded by the excellent Mallender, stood firm and the championship aspirations of the west country faded further.

Chris Smith hit his seventh century of the season at Folkestone and this, from one of the season's most prolific scorers, supplemented by rousing knocks from Gordon Greenidge, Mark Nicholas and Robin Smith took Hampshire to a position of strength. This position was consolidated the next day when Marshall made early inroads into the Kent batting and Benson was controversially run out after Taylor had collided with Maru. At 136 for 6, there was the possibility that Kent would have to follow-on, but Chris Cowdrey played his best innings of the summer. He is a batsman of character and relishes a fight. He hit hard and defended stubbornly. When the ninth wicket fell Kent were 197, but Underwood helped his captain to add 62 for the last wicket, Cowdrey scored 55 of them. Hampshire, with Terry not at his best, lacked some urgency, but set Kent to make 231 in 62 overs, a very fair demand. After 19 overs Kent were 47 for 4, but Baptiste and Chris Cowdrey added 110 in 30 overs to revive their hopes. They fell off successive deliveries and 74 were needed in 11.5 overs with 4 wickets standing, but, sadly, Kent chose to give up the chase and Hampshire were denied.

Middlesex outplayed Leicestershire at Grace Road. The game started with some sensation as Edmonds was less than pleased to be omitted from the Middlesex to accommodate another seamer. Arguably, he would have been of more value

Middlesex C.C.C.
First-Class Matches – Batting, 1985

	v. Worcestershire (Lord's) 27–30 April		v. Cambridge University (Cambridge) 1–3 May		v. Yorkshire (Leeds) 4–7 May		v. Kent (Lord's) 8–10 May		v. Glamorgan (Cardiff) 22–24 May		v. Sussex (Lord's) 25–28 May		v. Surrey (The Oval) 29–31 May	
W.N. Slack	72*	40	81	—	86*	99	105	14	19	—	23	—	96	—
P.R. Downton	16	69*	55	—	70	13	23	15	67	—	85*	—		
M.W. Gatting	12	12	80	—	40	23	11	90	13	—	40	—		
R.O. Butcher	4	80*	56	—	14*	2	35	1	23	—	70	—	29	—
C.T. Radley	6	—	54*	0*	—	4	50	85*	127	—	25	—	105*	—
K.P. Tomlins	6	—	34*	14									14	—
J.E. Emburey	56	—	—	7	—	8	22*	0	30*	—	39	—	10	—
P.H. Edmonds	0	—			—	22	6*	21*	0	—	—	—		
N.F. Williams	8	—	—	67	—	10	—	—			6*	—	32	—
N.G. Cowans	0	—	—	6	—	12	—	—	—	—	—	—		
W.W. Daniel	1	—			—	1*	—	—	—	—	—	—	—	—
J.F. Sykes			—	126									—	—
A.R.C. Fraser			—	1					—	—				
G.D. Barlow					—	0	32	20	4	—	31	—	115	—
K.R. Brown													20*	—
S.P. Hughes													—	—
C.P. Metson														
G.D. Rose														
J.D. Carr														
A.J.T. Miller														
Byes			3		1			1	6		4		12	
Leg-byes	2	3	4	5	4	11	6	5	2		11		11	
Wides	4	1			5		3	1	2		5			
No-balls	8	6	2		5	7	10	4	4				8	
Total	195	211	369	226	225	212	303	257	297		339		452	
Wickets	10	2	4	6	2	10	6	6	7		6		6	
Result	W		D		L		D		D		W		D	
Points	19		—		6		8		7		24		7	

	v. Derbyshire (Lord's) 8–11 June		v. Hampshire (Bournemouth) 12–14 June		v. Leicestershire (Lord's) 15–18 June		v. Nottinghamshire (Trent Bridge) 22–25 June		v. Worcestershire (Worcester) 26–28 June		v. Northamptonshire (Northampton) 6–9 July		v. Nottinghamshire (Lord's) 10–12 July	
W.N. Slack	0	4*	24	1	53	109	112	9*	35	0	70	12	35	8
P.R. Downton	0	—					0	—			27	57*		
M.W. Gatting	77	1*					76	—			19	24		
R.O. Butcher	11	—	4	23	24	11*	71	—	7*	120	4	35	5	34
C.T. Radley	7	—	7	5	41	3*	0	—	—	37	26	63*	22	0
K.P. Tomlins			42	36	43	1			7	15			46	15
J.E. Emburey	9	—					44	—			51	—		
P.H. Edmonds	27	—	0	3	13	—	1*	—			4*	—		
N.F. Williams	0	—	34	3	16*	—	21	—	—	1	2	—	9	11
N.G. Cowans	13	—					4*	—	—	—	0	—		
W.W. Daniel	8*	—	1	—	8	—	—	—			19*	—	0	0
J.F. Sykes			24	52*	4	—			—	24*			4	3
A.R.C. Fraser														
G.D. Barlow	18	12	11	5	31	102	81	6*	103*	9	141	17	97	112
K.R. Brown			11	2										
S.P. Hughes			12*	30*	0	—			—	—			8*	1*
C.P. Metson					6	—			—	14*			5	2
G.D. Rose									—	4				
J.D. Carr													1	1
A.J.T. Miller														
Byes	6					2	5		2		6	8	5	8
Leg-byes	2		11		13	2	19		4	2	13	2	4	2
Wides				4			1					3	4	1
No-balls			2	2	5	5	2				4	2	1	3
Total	178	17	183	166	257	235	437	15	158	226	386	223	246	201
Wickets	10	0	10	8	10	8	8	0	2	7	9	4	10	10
Result	D		D		D		W		W		W		L	
Points	5		5		6		24		21		24		6	

Catches 42 – P.R. Downton (ct 38/st 4)
27 – W.N. Slack
24 – R.O. Butcher
18 – M.W. Gatting and C.P. Metson
16 – J.E. Emburey
13 – P.H. Edmonds
11 – C.T. Radley
10 – J.F. Sykes
8 – W.W. Daniel and K.R. Brown

to the side than Emburey, particularly with his dynamic fielding, but his bowling would have been little used on a green wicket. Norman Cowans took a career best 6 for 31 to rout the home side and Radley countered the moving ball well enough to nudge Middlesex to a substantial lead. On the last day Wayne Daniel tore into the Leicestershire batting and, in spite of a most mature and accomplished innings from Whitaker, Middlesex romped to an easy victory.

A restricted first day at Worcester was compensated for by a thrilling innings from Graeme Hick who hit his first championship century for Worcestershire. He hit 2 sixes and 24 fours, faced 243 balls and passed a thousand runs for the season. He is a young batsman of immense talent. Eventually, Somerset were asked to make 295 in 66 overs, but after Radford and Inchmore had reduced them to 73 for 6 they could only lumber to defeat. By taking 4 wickets Radford brought his total for the season to 90. It was a magnificent achievement for one who had been rejected by Lancashire and Radford's bowling, lively and accurate, was the most prominent factor in the revival of Worcestershire's fortunes in 1985.

Surrey and Sussex contrived a glorious game on a batsman's paradise at The Oval. Sussex asked Surrey to bat first on a cold, overcast day on which play ended an hour early. Clinton, ever dependable, led the home side to a formidable score, but Sussex, inspired by Allan Green's career best and by some fine hitting from Mendis and Imran, raced to 300 in under 76 overs. Set to make 248 in 48 overs after Surrey, 37 for 5, had been rescued by Stewart on the last morning, Sussex lost 4 wickets for 94 runs, but Imran and le Roux hit 72 in 11 overs. Imran was superbly stumped by Richards off Monkhouse and le Roux and Alan Wells also fell, but Gould and Greig scored the last 40 off 31 balls to bring victory with 8 balls to spare. David Thomas reappeared in the Surrey side after injury had kept him out.

Asda Cricket Challenge

4 September

---

at Scarborough

Yorkshire 206 for 9 (S.N. Hartley 72, K. Sharp 55)
Derbyshire 209 for 7 (J.E. Morris 56)
Derbyshire won by 3 wickets

5 September

Nottinghamshire 146 for 9
Lancashire 147 for 4 (C.H. Lloyd 73 not out, N.H. Fairbrother 51)
Lancashire won by 6 wickets

v. Somerset (Lord's) 13–16 July		*v.* Northamptonshire (Uxbridge) 24–26 July		*v.* Lancashire (Uxbridge) 27–30 July		*v.* Gloucestershire (Lord's) 31 July–2 August		*v.* Essex (Chelmsford) 3–6 August		*v.* Australians (Lord's) 10–13 August		*v.* Somerset (Weston-s-Mare) 14–16 August		*v.* Surrey (Lord's) 17–20 August		*v.* Sussex (Hove) 24–27 August		*v.* Leicestershire (Leicester) 4–6 September		*v.* Essex (Lord's) 11–13 September		*v.* Warwickshire (Edgbaston) 14–17 September		*M*	*Inns*	*NOs*	*Runs*	*H/S*	*Av*
26	20	16	—	32	—	44	25*	72	22	201*	—	52	—	36	23*	50	29	38	13*	0	20	74	—	26	43	8	1900	201*	54.28
		104	—	19*	—					24*	—					4*	9	32	—	1	12	40	—	16	22	6	742	104	46.37
		51	—	74	—					7	—					3	51	39	—	114	83*	76	—	16	23	2	1016	114	48.38
20	28	39	—	86	—	37	—	61	31	0	—	2	—	26	—	60*	58*	1	—	77	20	1	—	26	38	6	1210	120	37.81
22	52*	200	—	64*	—	57	—	17	1*	34	—	24*	—	47*	—	35	8	87	—	21	0	12	—	26	36	11	1348	200	53.92
9	58									14	—													9	15	1	354	58	25.28
		68	—	—	—					—	—					—	0	1	—	10	16	68	—	17	17	2	439	68	29.26
		1	—	—	—					—	—					—	11			7	10	29*	—	16	16	5	155	29*	14.09
39	—	19*	—	—	—	18	—			—	—							30	—	2	4*	46	—	21	21	4	378	67	22.23
		15*	—	—	—	15	—	1	—	—	—	10	—	13	—	—	0	12	—	4	—	0	—	21	15	2	105	15*	8.07
		—	—	—	—	4	—	1*	—					0	—	—	0	2	—	0*	—	3	—	21	15	5	48	19*	4.80
14	0*					16	—	4	—			0	—	4	—									11	13	3	275	126	27.50
																								2	1	—	1	1	1.00
132	38	32	—	28	—	10	16*	20	—			32	—	9	28*	38	13							20	32	4	1343	141	47.96
										102	—	1	—	20	—			5	25*	25	20	67	—	8	11	2	298	102	33.11
0	—							16	—	—	—	5*	—	0	—	—	4	18*	—					12	11	6	94	30*	18.80
4*	—					14*	—	12	—			2	—	0	—									8	9	3	59	14*	9.83
15	—																							2	2	—	19	15	9.50
13	8					29	—	1	—					6	—									5	7	—	59	29	8.42
						16	—	15	13*															2	3	1	44	16	22.00
	6	11		7		5	4	1		4		1		2		4			4	2	4								
8	10	5				7	2	8	3	6		7		8		5	5	18	5	12	5	21							
	1					5		4		2				3	1				1	1	1								
7	4	6		8		12		1		17				9	4	4		15	1	3	1	8							
309	225	567		318		289	47	234	70	397		150		183	56	203	188	298	49	279	196	445							
10	5	8		4		10	0	10	1	4		8		10	0	4	10	10	0	10	7	10							
D		W		D		D		L		D		D		D		L		W		D		W							
7		23		4		6		2		—		5		5		6		23		7		24							

6 – K.P. Tomlins, S.P. Hughes and G.D. Barlow
5 – N.G. Cowans
3 – N.F. Williams and J.D. Carr
2 – subs

Final

6 September

Lancashire 175 for 7 (C.H. Lloyd 50, R.J. Finney 5 for 32)
Derbyshire 177 for 2 (I.S. Anderson 73 not out, B. Roberts 70)

Derbyshire won by 8 wickets

7, 9 and 10 September

at Hove

Leicestershire 171 (P. Willey 74 not out, G.S. le Roux 5 for 41) and 326 for 9 dec (D.I. Gower 128, P. Whitticase 55 not out)
Sussex 209 (N.J. Lenham 50, P. Willey 4 for 8, L.B. Taylor 4 for 50) and 289 for 8 (I.J. Gould 101, N.J. Lenham 77, P.B. Clift 4 for 60)

Sussex won by 2 wickets
Sussex 22 pts, Leicestershire 5 pts

For the second time in four days Sussex engaged in an exciting finish. Jones, le Roux and Reeve shot out Leicestershire on the Saturday, and Sussex appeared to be heading for a big lead when Mendis and the so impressive Neil Lenham took them to 100 before the second wicket fell. Willey brought about a collapse, however, and Taylor continued to bowl Leicestershire to parity on the Monday until Barclay and the aggressive Jones put on 33 for the last wicket and gave Sussex a slender lead. It became very slender as Gower produced a century of disdainful ease and declared on the last morning, asking Sussex to make 289 in 67 overs. Another fine knock by Lenham, some lusty blows by le Roux and an ebullient hundred by Ian Gould, his first for Sussex, saw them win with 3 balls to spare and two wickets in hand.

NatWest Bank Trophy Final
ESSEX *v.* NOTTINGHAMSHIRE

The miserable summer relented for the last great cricket occasion of the season. The sun burned from just after the start of this glorious final until the last ball had been bowled and the cricket was in keeping with the weather, it shone from start to finish.

Lord's was back to its bubbling best. The anaemia which had descended upon last year's NatWest Final and on the Benson and Hedges Final earlier in the year had disappeared and there was an air of excitement and expectancy from an appreciative crowd. For Essex, there were two early shocks; Neil Foster was reported to have glandular fever and was replaced by Ian Pont, promising but inexperienced, and Notts won the toss and asked them to bat at the time when

Middlesex C.C.C. First-Class Matches — Bowling, 1985	W.W. Daniel	N.G. Cowans	N.F.G. Williams	J.E. Emburey	P.H. Edmonds	M.W. Gatting	A.R.C. Fraser	J.F. Sykes	J.D. Carr
v. Worcestershire (Lord's) 27–30 April	23–2–90–3 10–1–43–1	15.4–4–74–0 7–3–15–3	26–8–68–3 10.3–4–28–3	9–2–30–0 7–1–14–3	8–2–17–0	3–0–17–0			
v. Cambridge University (Cambridge) 1–3 May		12.4–2–37–5	11–2–42–1	28–12–55–0		 1–1–0–0	24–7–48–4	16–1–35–0	
v. Yorkshire (Leeds) 4–7 May	18–1–73–2 13–4–19–3	15–3–53–1 9–3–30–3	22–4–56–1 6–0–31–2	13.5–3–47–1 17–3–28–0	26–10–44–3 5–2–16–1	5–1–9–1 2–1–4–0			
v. Kent (Lord's) 8–10 May	18–3–32–4 7–2–25–0	20–1–81–2 5–2–4–0	14–2–72–1 4–1–5–0	7–2–15–0 26–9–55–1	7–3–19–3 24–10–28–0	3–0–14–0 1–0–1–0			
v. Glamorgan (Cardiff) 22–24 May	10–1–38–2 21–6–57–0	12–1–56–5 8–1–31–0		 36–9–89–0	 41–1–106–2	 11–5–33–0	2.5–0–7–3 17–3–64–1		
v. Sussex (Lord's) 25–28 May	10–1–25–3 18–5–72–2	13–2–44–5 10–4–18–4	9–2–35–2 11–0–38–0	4–0–11–0 15–9–18–2	 15–3–28–1	6–1–14–0			
v. Surrey (The Oval) 29–31 May	13–4–33–2 11–0–25–0		16–3–82–2 16–4–70–1	11–2–44–1 41–7–103–3				4–1–19–0 16–3–71–1	
v. Derbyshire (Lord's) 8–11 June	12–5–33–1 14–2–27–1	7–3–19–0 10–1–31–1	13.4–4–43–3 11–2–27–1	26–7–50–0 34–14–59–0	32–11–87–6 37–9–67–0				
v. Hampshire (Bournemouth) 12–14 June	15–5–52–2 15–2–49–1		12–0–51–1 15–1–59–1		31–13–44–4 41–13–66–2			 22.1–6–56–1	
v. Leicestershire (Lord's) 15–18 June	16.3–3–48–5 13–2–61–2		11–1–30–1 10–1–50–0		17–5–38–3 10–3–25–0			 2–1–2–0	
v. Nottinghamshire (Trent Bridge) 22–25 June	21–5–64–4	16–4–47–2 14.2–47–4	17.4–2–57–2 21–2–92–4	 12–3–37–0	 30–8–55–2	5–1–20–1 5–2–5–0			
v. Worcestershire (Worcester) 26–28 June		19–4–71–3 6–1–11–1	15–1–50–2 12–4–34–2					5–0–21–0	
v. Northamptonshire (Northampton) 6–9 July	17–3–89–3 18–4–83–3	11–0–51–0 2–0–9–0	7–1–18–0 3–0–7–0	17–7–24–0 12.5–3–23–3	26–10–49–5 25–5–81–4	2–1–2–1			
v. Nottinghamshire (Lord's) 10–12 July	14.5–2–63–2 11–2–49–1		18–1–71–5 10–2–44–0					6–1–18–2 21–7–58–3	 15.1–5–45–1
v. Somerset (Lord's) 13–16 July			26–2–86–3					24.4–5–97–3	3–1–2–1
v. Northamptonshire (Uxbridge) 24–26 July	12–0–83–2 18.1–2–73–4	11.1–0–30–4 8–3–12–1	8–2–35–2 5–0–13–0	 27–13–41–0	8–1–37–0 23–8–54–4	 3–1–6–1			
v. Lancashire (Uxbridge) 27–30 July									
v. Gloucestershire (Lord's) 31 July–2 August	18–2–67–1	13–0–64–1	13–0–53–1					32–5–86–0	29–6–61–6
v. Essex (Chelmsford) 3–6 August	3–1–12–0 20–0–87–2	5–3–12–0 17–2–86–1						 5–0–21–0	 9–3–20–0
v. Australians (Lord's) 10–13 August		17–3–72–0	17–0–85–0	22–5–55–0	19–4–46–2	13–1–55–3			
v. Somerset (Weston-super-Mare) 14–16 August	19–2–81–3	13–1–36–1						23–10–49–1	
v. Surrey (Lord's) 17–20 August	16.2–2–47–2 16–2–61–0	15–3–61–5 16–0–70–2						6–1–13–0 9–1–29–2	3–1–6–0 6–1–20–1
v. Sussex (Hove) 24–27 August	21–2–84–1 8–1–22–0	11–2–37–0 2–0–12–0		18.2–3–35–6 22–4–46–2	37–7–97–2 29–6–74–1	 6.5–0–31–1			
v. Leicestershire (Leicester) 4–6 September	17–3–52–2 14.1–1–62–7	9.3–1–31–6 8–1–32–2	15–2–39–1 11–1–51–1	3–1–4–0 11–3–14–0					
v. Essex (Lord's) 11–13 September	9.4–0–51–1 20–2–91–2	6–2–5–1 18–3–62–2	9–4–15–5 20.3–2–73–1	 27–2–78–0	 40–7–101–4	6–0–20–2 14–2–40–1			
v. Warwickshire (Edgbaston) 14–17 September	14–3–51–3 9.3–1–37–2	10–2–26–0	13–2–43–3 3–0–16–0	21–8–47–4 33–9–64–4	3–1–10–0 27–9–63–4	2–0–6–0			
	575.1–89– 2111–79 *av.* 26.72	392.2–67– 1377–65 *av.* 21.18	462.2–67– 1669–55 *av.* 30.34	501–141– 1086–30 *av.* 36.20	561–161– 1252–53 *av.* 23.62	88.5–17– 277–11 *av.* 25.18	43.5–10– 119–8 *av.* 14.87	191.5–42– 575–13 *av.* 44.23	65.1–17– 154–9 *av.* 17.11

a P.R. Downton, 8–6–5–0
G.D. Barlow 3–0–14–0

C.T. Radley 11–3–38–2
W.N. Slack 7–1–21–0

b C.T. Radley 2–0–5–0
W.N. Slack 2–0–8–0

b K.P. Tomlins 2–0–9–0
c K.R. Brown 1–1–0–0

S.P. Hughes	R.O. Butcher	G.D. Rose	Byes	Leg-byes	Wides	No-balls	Total	Wkts
			1	4	3	4	301	6
			2	1		7	103	10
			10	4		7	231	10
							0	0
			5	17	2	4	304	9
				7	6		135	10
				4	1	3	237	10
			6		2	1	124	1
			8	2	1	3	111	10
	7–3–8–0		4	8	2	7	478	5a
				3		6	132	10
			6		1	11	180	10
13–3–58–1			3	16	4	11	255	10
14–0–79–0	5–1–13–1		10	9	2	16	402	6b
			1	3	2		236	10
	1–0–1–0		4	5	1	5	221	3
16–6–35–3			1	1		6	184	10
11–4–24–1			7	2		9	263	8
16–1–67–1			1	13		9	197	10
5–3–5–1			2	4		13	149	3
				14	1		202	10
			1	12		10	249	10
17–5–38–3		13.2–0–57–1	9		4	6	246	10
12–3–45–1		10.5–2–41–6	5	1		3	137	10
				11		9	244	10
			12	9		5	224	10
12–1–44–1			1	5		17	202	10
11–1–41–0	1–1–0–0		8	4		9	249	5
23–2–99–1		21–6–44–2		17	1	11	345	10
			4	2		6	191	10
			12	4		11	215	10
			Match Abandoned					
			13	7		7	351	9
3–0–9–0						1	33	0
14.4–1–58–0				3		19	275	3
20–1–61–1	1–0–7–0		10	5	5	13	396	6c
18.4–2–64–5			9	6	1	12	245	10
20–5–56–2			2	9		7	194	10
15–1–71–2			4	16	2	6	271	7
11–0–28–0				6		8	287	10
	4–0–17–1			5		2	207	5
6–1–27–1				5			158	10
8–3–23–0				3		3	185	10
				1		9	92	10
			7	9		14	461	10
				4		6	187	10
				4		5	184	10
266.2–43–932–24 *av.* 38.83	19–5–46–2 *av.* 23.00	45.1–8–142–9 *av.* 15.77						

the wicket and little early cloud was likely to give the bowler any assistance.

A few words should be said about Neil Foster whose illness robbed him of his chance to appear in this memorable match. He had returned from India as England's outstanding fast bowler. It is not a department in which we are at our strongest, yet he was omitted from the Test team for the first match of the series and was troubled by injury after that. He had bowled extremely well throughout August only to be laid low on the eve of the Final. It was cruel luck, but he is a young man of tremendous talent, and, with sympathetic and intelligent handling, he will serve England well for many years to come.

Notts were also without a young man of talent, Paul Johnson, and his place was taken by another gifted young man, Duncan Martindale. Martindale's batting promises the very highest quality, but is unfortunate that his fielding, as yet, is not of the standard one would have expected in one so young.

Rice's decision to ask Essex to bat seemed justified. The ball moved quite sharply early on and Gooch edged short of slip in Hadlee's opening over. There was a great deal of tension and a run was not scored until the third over. The ball beat the bat on occasions, but Gooch was playing a most responsible innings and Hardie began to throw the bat at the

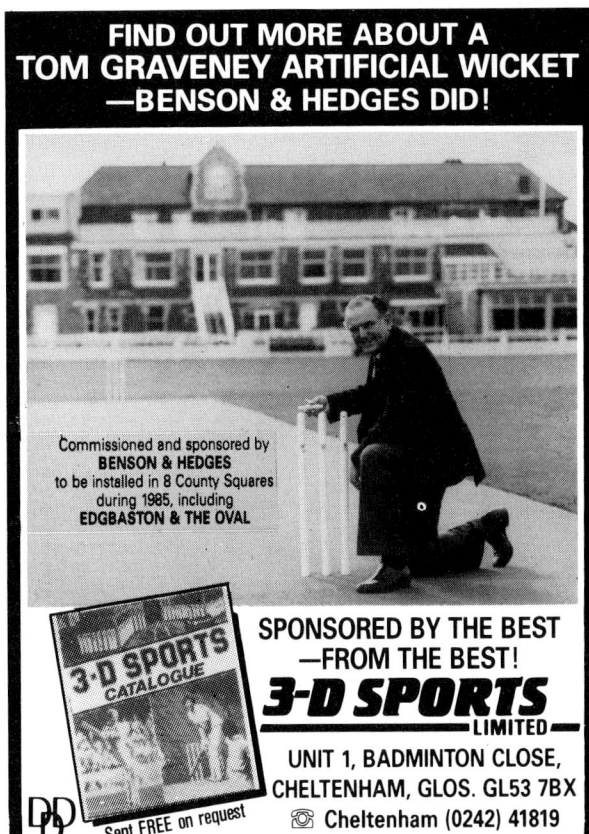

Northamptonshire C.C.C.
First-Class Matches – Batting, 1985

	v. Derbyshire (Derby) 27–30 April		v. Hampshire (Northampton) 4–7 May		v. Kent (Northampton) 22–24 May		v. Leicestershire (Leicester) 25–28 May		v. Warwickshire (Northampton) 29–31 May		v. Sussex (Northampton) 8–11 June		v. Essex (Ilford) 12–14 June	
G. Cook	87	69*			39	12	—	—	126	5	2	13	45	80
W. Larkins	46	21	83	41	52	13	—	—	45	36	41	23	11	1
R.G. Williams	3	39	50	6	1	37*	—	—	0	118	2	41	11	63
A.J. Lamb	3	9*	43	8			—	—			65	11		
R.J. Bailey	19	—	101	0	38	50*	—	—	14	6	7	18	13	38
D.J. Capel	10	—	26	16	6	—	—	—	1	63	58	14*	52	—
D.J. Wild	39*	—	34*	2	10	—	—	—	0	17				
G. Sharp	19	—	2	9	9	—	—	—	9	0	2	—	13	—
N.A. Mallender	3*	—	0	13	2	—	—	—	13	4	6	—	10	40
A. Walker	—	—	18*	11	0*	—			7*	10*	0*	—	15*	—
R.F. Joseph	—	—	—	26*										
A.C. Storie			10	106					0	50*			81	21*
R.A. Harper					0	—	—	—	76	18	38*	—	12	—
B.J. Griffiths					—	—								
M. Wheeler							—	—						
R.J. Boyd-Moss											67	22*	3	—
D. Ripley														
Byes	1								1		2			12
Leg-byes	4		2	4	3	5			7	9	9	2	5	7
Wides					1				2	1	1	1		
No-balls	6	2	4	2	1	3			2	2	2		8	4
Total	240	140	373	244	162	120			303	339	302	145	279	266
Wickets	7	2	8	10	9†	2			10	9	9	5	10	5
Results	W		D		D		D		D		D		D	
Points	18		7		4		1		5		7		6	

	v. Gloucestershire (Northampton) 15–18 June		v. Essex (Northampton) 22–25 June		v. Surrey (Northampton) 26–28 June		v. Warwickshire (Edgbaston) 29 June–2 July		v. Middlesex (Northampton) 6–9 July		v. Derbyshire (Northampton) 10–12 July		v. Kent (Maidstone) 13–16 July	
G. Cook	6	36	8	—	70	17	0	19	72*	16	3	12	1	16
W. Larkins	6	15	31	—	31	117	42	33	42	31	0	5	8	67
R.G. Williams	24	1			29	10			24	0	103	9	24	6
A.J. Lamb			111	—					60	25				
R.J. Bailey	1	16	47*	—	16	39	20	67	0	4	81	52	16	44
D.J. Capel	0	22	5*	—	11	5*	22	0	6	1	5	71	5	10
D.J. Wild							9	55			80	32*	26	7
G. Sharp	25	2	—	—	10	—	2	9*						
N.A. Mallender	0	14*	—	—	1	—	2*	10	11	52*	—	—	21*	2*
A. Walker	2*	4	—	—	0*	—	9	3	0	4				
R.F. Joseph														
A.C. Storie	4	71	45	—	6	—	2	11						
R.A. Harper	39	40	—	—	4	8*	5	34	4	6	34*	7*	127	18
B.J. Griffiths											—	—	0	0
M. Wheeler														
R.J. Boyd-Moss	2	19	10	—	0	42	17	17	4	32	5	16	0	63
D. Ripley									1	27	3*	—	13	0
Byes	1	1	2		1	7	1	3		12	1	8	1	1
Leg-byes	7	3	8		1	7	6	16	11	9	14	6	8	6
Wides	1	1					2	3			1		3	2
No-balls	1	1	2		1	5	3	2	9	5	4	1	2	5
Total	119	246	269		181	257	142	282	244	224	334	219	255	247
Wickets	10	10	5		10	5	10	10	10	10	7	6	10	10
Results	L		D		W		W		L		D		L	
Points	2		3		20		20		4		7		7	

Catches
25 – D. Ripley (ct 21/st 4)
20 – R.A. Harper
19 – G. Sharp (ct 16/st 3) and G. Cook
18 – W. Larkins
7 – A.J. Lamb
6 – A. Walker and R.J. Bailey
5 – N.A. Mallender and R.J. Boyd-Moss
4 – D.J. Capel, D.J. Wild and subs

ball in a most exciting manner. By the time Rice replaced Cooper, Essex were 55 from 19 overs and Hardie had 41 of the runs.

The Scotsman reached his fifty in the twenty-fifth over when he off-drove Pick for two, and Gooch's fifty came 9 overs later. The hundred went up in the thirtieth over and at lunch, after 38 overs, Essex were 145 for 0, Hardie and Gooch having given a thrilling display once they had founded the innings.

The tempo was increased in the afternoon; 18 runs came from the first three overs after lunch. In the forty-fourth over Hardie reached his century. It had come off 136 deliveries and included 14 fours. He has never batted better, and he batted with typical one-day panache. One delivery he would edge fiercely to the boundary through the area where once slips had been; the next would bring a flowing cover drive of full glory. All the time he batted with an infectious glee.

If Gooch was more restrained, his innings was equally valuable. He realised that much depended upon him, that his was the scalp Notts most sought to give them the psychological advantage, and he refused to surrender. Once the attack had been blunted and the fielding had shown signs of cracking, he attacked with his customary power and authority. He hit Pick into Q Stand for a memorable six and smote Saxelby through the covers for a mighty four. He should have been stumped off Hemmings when he was 70, a difficult leg-side chance, and he was finally bowled by Pick in the forty-ninth over for 91. By then he and Hardie had put on 202, a record for any wicket in the NatWest competition.

Ken McEwan came to the wicket at Lord's for the last time on a great occasion. He was given a rich ovation. Few cricketers have brought so much pleasure into the lives of others. In the fifty-first over, with the score on 203, Hardie was run out by Hemmings' fine throw. This was the danger point for Essex and the chance for Notts to claw their way back into the game, but Pringle and McEwan combined in a stand which determined that the Notts' target would be a formidable one. In the last 10 overs they added 77 runs.

Saxelby's last over, the fifty-eighth, cost him 17 runs, and 39 runs were to come in the last three overs. McEwan was badly dropped by Broad at mid-on in the fifty-sixth over, but this was the only blemish on a glorious farewell display by this gentlest of men. He cover drove Saxelby for six into the Mound Stand, a shot of genius.

v. Middlesex (Uxbridge) 24–26 July		v. Australians (Northampton) 27–30 July		v. Nottinghamshire (Northampton) 3–6 August		v. Somerset (Weston-s-Mare) 10–13 August		v. Lancashire (Lytham) 14–16 August		v. Glamorgan (Wellingborough) 17–20 August		v. Leicestershire (Northampton) 24–27 August		v. Yorkshire (Leeds) 31 Aug.–3 Sept.		v. Gloucestershire (Bristol) 4–6 September		v. Hampshire (Southampton) 11–13 September		v. Worcestershire (Worcester) 14–17 September				M	Inns	NOs	Runs	H/S	Av
4	16	24	—	79	77*	39*	—	—	—	18	—	35	4	41	—	—	0	73	36	23	72			24	38	4	1295	126	38.08
4	34	44	—	140	62	29	—	—	—	11	—	31	48	25	—	—	39	0	48	163	15			25	40	—	1534	163	38.35
7	29	35*	—	10*	—	—	—	—	—	94	—	96	7	0	—	—	1							21	31	3	880	118	31.42
5	61	—	—			—	—					4	32					0	60	22*	6			12	17	2	525	111	35.00
36	6	107*	—	30*	—	—	—	—	—	13	—	6	99*	73*	—	—	8	0	23	1*	52			25	37	7	1161	107*	38.70
		—	—	—	—			—	—	25*	-	2	3	35*	—	—	15	81	0	—	29*			23	30	6	599	81	24.95
10	23*					—	—	—	—	41	—	8	1	10	—	—	49	17	25	—	30			17	22	4	525	80	29.16
																								11	13	1	111	25	9.25
0	10			—	—	—	—	—	—	0	—	2*	—	—	—	—	43*	4	4					23	25	8	267	52*	15.70
																				—	—			12	14	8	83	18*	13.83
																								2	1	1	26	26*	—
																								7	12	2	407	106	40.70
97*	0	—	—	—	—	—	—	—	—	30	—	8	15*	—	—	—	9	76	27*	—	2			23	26	7	734	127	38.63
1	0	—	—	—	—	—	—	2*	—	0*	—			—	—	—	1*	12	1*	—	—			13	9	4	17	12	3.40
		—	—																					2	—				—
11	4	18	—	35	36*	19*	—	—	—	121	—	1	13	31	—	—	14	10	6	121	7			20	31	3	766	121	27.35
4	5	—	—	—	—	—	—	0*	—	0	—	10	—	—	—	—	0	13*	1	—	6*			14	14	4	83	27	8.30
4	12	12		1						4			10	4				2		3				† B.J. Griffiths absent injured					
2	4	11		4						12		3	5	14			3	4	8	4	5								
					1													7		1									
6	11	7		2	3					3		4	6	9			6	5	2	11	7								
191	215	258		301	179	87		2		372		210	243	242		0	188	304	241	349	231								
10	10	3		3	1	1		0		9		10	7	5		0	9	10	9	3	7								
L		D		D		D		D		D		D		D		D		W		W									
2		—		4		3		4		5		4		2		4		23		21									

3 – R.G. Williams and A.C. Storie
2 – B.J. Griffiths

Faced by a daunting task, Notts showed no sign of panic or dismay. Robinson and Broad began in workmanlike fashion. Like their Essex counterparts they played themselves in and then began to accumulate quickly. Broad, deserving of a place in the side to go to the West Indies, clipped the ball smartly to leg and showed an eagerness to score. The Essex bowling was tight without being menacing and special mention should be made of Ian Pont who bowled briskly, beating Robinson three times in his opening spell, and with no sign of nerves. At tea, after 35 overs, Notts were 124 for 0 and Essex's huge total looked far less daunting.

It was perhaps when the need to accelerate more became necessary that the difference between the two sides began to show. The Essex bowling was steadier and their fielding far better, and where McEwan had prospered, Rice failed. Broad was run out by Ian Pont's long throw when he turned for a second run. It was unwise, but he was beaten by an excellent piece of fielding. Only ten runs had been added when Robinson lofted Turner to the square-leg boundary and Hardie took the catch. Rice could not produce the impetus that was needed and he clipped the admirable Turner to mid-wicket where Hardie again took the catch.

Northamptonshire C.C.C. First-Class Matches — Bowling, 1985	N.A. Mallender	R.F. Joseph	A. Walker	R.G. Williams	D.J. Capel	R.J. Bailey	B.J. Griffiths	R.A. Harper	R.J. Boyd-Moss
v. Derbyshire (Derby) 27–30 April	14–0–48–3	16–2–70–1	13–5–29–1	32.1–8–91–4	9–2–22–0	3–0–16–0			
v. Hampshire (Northampton) 4–7 May	20–3–69–2	22–3–73–3	16–0–53–2	19.4–5–64–0	21–6–76–1				
v. Kent (Northampton) 22–24 May	32–4–91–2 8–1–24–0		20–5–38–4	2–0–7–0	13–2–35–0 10.3–1–47–4		28–9–45–3	17–4–44–0 10–0–44–1	
v. Leicestershire (Leicester) 25–28 May	17–2–45–1			16–5–34–0	20–3–67–0			44–13–103–4	
v. Warwickshire (Northampton) 29–31 May	15–4–33–0 12–2–51–1		13–2–28–0 11.3–0–54–0	13–4–48–0 13–3–42–0	13–2–51–1 8–2–24–1			29.2–10–74–1 29–3–116–4	
v. Sussex (Northampton) 8–11 June	22–3–57–4 6–1–10–1		21–6–42–3 4–4–0–1	2–0–3–0 3–3–0–1	9–4–19–0 2–1–4–0			17.2–5–39–1 6–1–32–0	
v. Essex (Ilford) 12–14 June	26–6–46–3 9–0–36–4		21–5–72–1 10–0–45–1	9–1–29–1 3–0–15–0	17–1–58–1			37–6–118–4 17–0–80–4	
v. Gloucestershire (Northampton) 15–18 June	13.1–7–19–2 5–0–45–1		16–4–47–0 4.3–0–27–1		9–2–16–0			26–5–71–1	13–2–48–3
v. Essex (Northampton) 22–25 June									
v. Surrey (Northampton) 26–28 June	21.3–7–43–4 8–1–31–0		15–5–36–1 1–1–43–1	12–4–22–0	8–2–30–0 9–1–44–1			35–9–63–2 11–4–55–4	11–3–38–1 1–1–0–0
v. Warwickshire (Edgbaston) 29 June–2 July	24–7–55–0 20–6–36–3		23.3–9–59–3 14–2–55–2		24–4–58–4 4–1–21–0			17–0–21–2 26.2–9–47–4	 1–0–7–0
v. Middlesex (Northampton) 6–9 July	26–7–79–3 15–3–43–2		9–0–50–0	8–2–30–1 5–0–28–0	23–2–84–4 23–4–71–2			37–12–77–0 12–3–38–0	4–1–16–0 7–0–33–0
v. Derbyshire (Northampton) 10–12 July	24.4–6–62–1 10–2–30–0			14–4–32–1 20–6–34–5	8–2–23–0		17–7–37–4 4–1–15–0	39–12–76–3 20–5–65–0	10–4–21–1 2–0–8–1
v. Kent (Maidstone) 13–16 July	11–1–54–1			 19–3–61–2	10–1–26–1 13–3–38–0		30.1–2–76–6 14–4–52–1	15–0–64–2 38.3–6–108–1	
v. Middlesex (Uxbridge) 24–26 July	27–5–90–0			42–10–131–4			26–5–95–2	38–14–87–1	8–1–39–0
v. Australians (Northampton) 27–30 July				21–5–66–1	22–0–107–1		25–5–72–1	11–3–27–0	
v. Nottinghamshire (Northampton) 3–6 August	9–2–29–0 12–0–47–1			5.3–1–24–1 8–0–51–2			17–5–33–1 8–0–49–0	6–0–21–0 21.1–0–89–1	
v. Somerset (Weston-super-Mare) 10–13 August	26.2–5–83–5			1–0–7–0			29–4–127–3	24–4–52–1	
v. Lancashire (Lytham) 14–16 August	16–4–28–1			12–2–80–1	20–5–62–7		20–8–35–1	3–2–1–0	
v. Glamorgan (Wellingborough) 17–20 August	6–0–17–1						13.3–5–43–2	8–2–15–0	
v. Leicestershire (Northampton) 24–27 August	22–5–56–1			23–7–59–0	15–1–67–2			45–13–94–5	30.3–10–44–2
v. Yorkshire (Leeds) 31 August–3 September									
v. Gloucestershire (Bristol) 4–6 September	14–1–48–1			9–2–21–0	10–4–21–2		14–4–36–3	23–7–75–2 2–0–4–0	4.1–0–21–2 2–0–12–0
v. Hampshire (Southampton) 11–13 September	10–0–45–0 5–2–29–0				21–3–72–2 14–4–34–2		27–11–64–4 12–3–44–0	29–9–78–2 24–3–76–2	3–2–3–0 1–0–2–0
v. Worcestershire (Worcester) 14–17 September			19–1–70–1 10.1–2–38–1		10–0–63–1 19–0–59–4		19–1–73–1 10–2–22–0	12–2–44–0 16–8–25–4	28–6–88–0
	506.4–97– 1479–48 *av.* 30.81	38–5– 143–4 *av.* 35.75	251.4–51– 786–23 *av.* 34.17	312.2–75– 979–24 *av.* 40.79	384.3–63– 1299–41 *av.* 31.68	3–0– 16–0 —	313.4–76– 918–32 *av.* 28.68	745.4–183– 2023–56 *av.* 36.12	125.4–30– 380–10 *av.* 38.00

a G. Sharp 1–0–2–0
A.J. Lamb 1–1–0–0
b M. Wheeler 14–3–30–0
c A.J. Lamb 2–0–7–0
M. Wheeler 20–0–87–1
d G. Cook 1–0–6–0

W. Larkins	D.J. Wild	A.C. Storie	*Byes*	*Leg-byes*	*Wides*	*No-balls*	*Total*	*Wkts*
							0	0
			3	2	1	13	281	10
			5	12		7	352	8
							2	0a
			2	8		3	270	9
				7	9	1	122	5
9–6–11–0			9	5	1	8	304	5b
	15–1–58–1		2	7		1	301	3
	3–0–18–0		10	6			321	6
13–4–34–0				7		2	201	8
				1			47	4
			20	11		2	354	10
			4	5			185	9
13–4–34–1		18–6–51–0	1	8		1	295	7
				1			73	2
			Match Abandoned					
			10	8			250	8
			3	9	4		185	6
1–0–4–0			5	10	1	2	212	10
3–0–11–0			2	2			181	10
5–0–31–0			6	13		4	386	9
			8	2	3	2	223	4
			5	8		4	264	10
			7	3			162	6
				3		3	223	10
2–0–4–0	4–1–7–0		6	5		5	281	6
14–1–47–0	11.5–1–62–1		11	5		6	567	8
6–0–26–0			2	10		2	404	5c
	10–2–38–0			7	3		152	2
			4	7		1	247	5
17–1–82–0	7–0–47–0		3	8		2	409	10
			7	6		1	225	10d
						2	75	3
			6	17		4	343	10
			Match Abandoned					
			3	3		5	228	10
							16	0
	8–1–28–0		1	9		2	300	8
	10–0–46–0		7	6		2	244	4
	11–1–36–0		5	13		10	392	3
	3–0–28–0		8	4	5	10	184	10
83–16–284–1 *av.* 284.00	82.5–7–368–2 *av.* 184.00	18–6–51–0 —						

Hadlee was the hope and the threat. He hit a six over long on with nonchalant ease and the two hundred was posted. He drove Pont classically and mightily to the long off boundary and then next ball, after a reassuring chat with Fletcher, Pont knocked back Hadlee's leg stump.

Randall and Martindale batted admirably, but the asking rate became greater every over in spite of some fine shots and brisk running and when the last over was reached Notts needed 18 to win and, seemingly, victory was with Essex. Rarely can there have been a more dramatic over at Lord's. Pringle bowled at leg stump with a gap on the off-side Tavern boundary. Randall stepped outside leg stump and hit him through the off for 2. He repeated the shot next ball and reached the boundary and then another 2 came from the third ball. Ten runs were now needed from three balls, still a mighty task, but Randall again crashed the ball to the Tavern boundary and the fifth ball was superbly driven past long off for 4 so that Notts needed only 2 off the last ball. For most of the day Essex had been in command, but now, with one ball remaining, Notts, through the impish virtuosity of Derek Randall, had seized the advantage.

Fletcher regrouped his field, calmed his bowler who, in all truth, had not bowled badly, and Pringle moved in to bowl the last ball. Again Randall moved down the wicket and, in retrospect, he may have done better to have stayed his ground for the ball was wide down the leg-side and may well have been signalled a wide, but Randall had charged and, caught with the ball on his toes as he tried to whip it away to leg, he clipped it to mid-wicket where Paul Prichard took a comfortable catch. Essex had won by one run.

Brian Hardie was rightly named Man-of-the-Match, but none who were privileged to see it will ever forget Derek Randall's heroic innings. He was one who was sent into this

ABOVE: *Clive Rice, the Notts captain, bowls. Fellow South African Ken McEwan is the non striking batsman. It was McEwan's last appearance in a big match at Lord's. He played a gloriously exciting innings, and, in Rice's words, 'put the match just out of our reach'. (Ken Kelly)* RIGHT: *NatWest Trophy Final scoreboard.* BELOW: *The first Notts wicket falls. Ian Pont's throw is fast and accurate and David East whips off the bails as Chris Broad just fails to get home. (Ken Kelly)* BOTTOM RIGHT: *Keith Fletcher holds the NatWest Trophy. In seven seasons he has led Essex to victory in each of the four competitions, a unique record. (All Sport)*

National Westminster Bank Trophy 1985

The County winning the Trophy will receive a prize of £17,000, the losing Finalist £8,500, the losing Semi-finalists £4,250 each and the losing Quarter-finalists £2,125 each.

MARYLEBONE CRICKET CLUB

NatWest Bank Trophy Final

20p ESSEX v. NOTTINGHAMSHIRE 20p

at Lord's Ground, †Saturday, September 7th, 1985

ESSEX

1 G. A. Gooch	b Pick	91
2 B. R. Hardie	run out	110
3 K. S. McEwan	not out	46
4 D. R. Pringle	not out	29
5 P. J. Prichard		
‡6 K. W. R. Fletcher		
7 A. W. Lilley		
*8 D. E. East		
9 S. Turner		
10 I. L. Pont		
11 J. K. Lever		
B 1, l-b 3, w , n-b ,		4
	Total...	280

FALL OF THE WICKETS

1...202 2...203 3... 4... 5... 6... 7... 8... 9... 10...

Bowling Analysis	O.	M.	R.	W.	Wd.	N-b
Hadlee	12	4	48	0	...	...
Cooper	9	3	27	0	...	...
Saxelby	12	0	73	0	...	...
Rice	7	0	38	0	...	...
Pick	8	0	36	1	...	...
Hemmings	12	1	54	0	...	...

NOTTINGHAMSHIRE

1 B. C. Broad	run out	64
2 R. T. Robinson	c Hardie b Turner	80
‡3 C. E. B. Rice	c Hardie b Turner	12
4 D. W. Randall	c Prichard b Pringle	66
5 R. J. Hadlee	b Pont	22
6 D. J. R. Martindale	not out	20
*7 B. N. French		
8 E. E. Hemmings		
9 R. A. Pick		
10 K. Saxelby		
11 K. E. Cooper		
B , l-b 14 , w , n-b 1,		15
	Total...	279

FALL OF THE WICKETS

1...143 2...153 3...173 4...214 5...279 6 7... 8... 9... 10...

Bowling Analysis	O.	M.	R.	W.	Wd.	N-b
Lever	12	2	53	0	...	...
Pont	12	0	54	1	...	1
Turner	12	1	43	2	...	...
Gooch	12	0	47	0	...	...
Pringle	12	1	68	1	...	...

Any alterations to teams will be announced over the public address system

RULES—1 The Match will consist of one innings per side and each innings is limited to 60 overs.
2 No one bowler may bowl more than 12 overs in an innings.
3 Hours of play: 10.30 a.m. to 7.10 p.m. In certain circumstances the Umpires may order extra time.

Luncheon Interval 12.45 p.m.—1.25 p.m. Tea Interval will be 20 minutes and will normally be taken at 4.30 p.m.

‡Captain *Wicket-keeper

Umpires—D. J. Constant & B. J. Meyer Scorers—C. F. Driver, L. Beaumont & E. Solomon

†This match is intended to be completed in one day, but three days have been allocated in case of weather interference

Nottinghamshire won the toss and elected to field

Essex won by 1 run

Total runs scored at end of each over:

First Innings	1	2	3	4	5	6	7	8	9	10	11	12	13	14	15	16	17	18	19	20
	21	22	23	24	25	26	27	28	29	30	31	32	33	34	35	36	37	38	39	40
	41	42	43	44	45	46	47	48	49	50	51	52	53	54	55	56	57	58	59	60
Second Innings	1	2	3	4	5	6	7	8	9	10	11	12	13	14	15	16	17	18	19	20
	21	22	23	24	25	26	27	28	29	30	31	32	33	34	35	36	37	38	39	40
	41	42	43	44	45	46	47	48	49	50	51	52	53	54	55	56	57	58	59	60

Nottinghamshire C.C.C.
First-Class Matches – Batting, 1985

	v. Cambridge University (Cambridge) 24–26 April		v. Somerset (Taunton) 27–29 April		v. Essex (Trent Bridge) 1–3 May		v. Leicestershire (Leicester) 22–24 May		v. Leicestershire (Trent Bridge) 29–31 May		v. Kent (Tunbridge Wells) 8–11 June		v. Surrey (The Oval) 12–14 June	
B.C. Broad	29	51	27	56*	18	7	70	8	10	11	0	11	30	62
M. Newell	74	58							4	0			59	3
D.W. Randall	74	100*	18	32*	0	117	89*	10*	48	108*	26	40	106	97
P. Johnson	20	23	0	—	31	84	1	—	118	9*	23	40	51*	—
J.D. Birch	5	12*	38	—	31	68*	—	—	2	18	4	25*	—	36*
K.P. Evans	13	—												
C.W. Scott	39*	—					—	—						
R.A. Pick	10*	—	15	—	16	13								
K. Saxelby	—	—	0	—	2	0*	—	—			10	—	—	—
K.E. Cooper	—	—	17*	—	1	—	—	—	—	—	3	0	—	—
J.A. Afford	—	—												
R.T. Robinson			105	54	5	1	94	25*			90	0		
C.E.B. Rice			27	—	108*	0	34*	—	171*	—	28	5	41*	—
B.N. French			18	—	4	1			—	4	1*	—	—	52*
P.M. Such			8	—	4	—			—	—				
R.J. Hadlee							—	—	9*	—	3	18*	—	8
E.E. Hemmings							—	—	—	—	0	—	—	—
C.D. Fraser-Darling														
S.B. Hassan														
D.J.R. Martindale														
Byes	1		1	7		3	6		4	4			2	
Leg-byes	3	7	8	4	5	5	5	3	4	2	5	13	4	3
Wides			2	1	1	2	1		3	3	4	1	3	
No-balls	1		4	6	1	1	5		9	3	1	4	5	4
Total	269	251	288	160	227	302	301	46	382	162	198	157	301	265
Wickets	6	3	10	1	10	7	3	1	5	4	10	6	3	4
Result	D		W		D		D		D		W		D	
Points	—		22		6		4		7		21		5	

	v. Kent (Trent Bridge) 15–18 June		v. Middlesex (Trent Bridge) 22–25 June		v. Derbyshire (Derby) 26–28 June		v. Gloucestershire (Trent Bridge) 29 June–1 July		v. Glamorgan (Swansea) 6–9 July		v. Middlesex (Lord's) 10–12 July		v. Warwickshire (Nuneaton) 13–16 July	
B.C. Broad	43	71*	27	40	171	11	35	7	37	—	53	56	25	13
M. Newell	0	—			18	1	9	15						
D.W. Randall	37	13*	50	3	5	23	65	9	16	63*	45	115	6	67
P. Johnson	11	—	1	1	2	0	16	60	1	—	32	12	2	88
J.D. Birch	60*	—	0	4	0	23	23	16*			1	5		
K.P. Evans														
C.W. Scott														
R.A. Pick													63	4*
K. Saxelby	—	—	1	10			10	—	—	—	1	—	0	—
K.E. Cooper	—	—	12	46	0	6	5*	—	—	—	0	—	23	—
J.A. Afford														
R.T. Robinson			18	73					103	130*				
C.E.B. Rice	37	71	12	14	51	13	46	68	27	—	0	22*	156*	0*
B.N. French	—	—	28*	0	44	11	28	—	10	12	16	9	6	0
P.M. Such					0*	0*			—	—	0	—		
R.J. Hadlee	52*	—	27	28*	8	54	0	26*	53*	—	21*	9*	14	1
E.E. Hemmings	—	—	11	7	17	36*	11	—	56*	12	10	—	6	4
C.D. Fraser-Darling													2	23*
S.B. Hassan														
D.J.R. Martindale														
Byes	5	1		1		5	4	1	3		1	8	2	
Leg-byes	4	1	14	12	7	3	8	3		3	5	4	5	2
Wides	1		1		3	5	4	2	4	1			1	3
No-balls	2	2		10	1	2	8	0	11	9	17	9	2	1
Total	252	159	202	249	327	193	272	213	321	230	202	249	313	206
Wickets	5	1	10	10	10	9	10	5	6	2	10	5	10	6
Result	D		L		D		D		D		W		D	
Points	6		4		7		7		6		22		7	

Catches 69 – B.N. French (ct 62/st 7); 24 – D.W. Randall; 20 – C.E.B. Rice; 18 – R.J. Hadlee; 15 – B.C. Broad; 13 – P. Johnson; 8 – R.T. Robinson; 7 – P.M. Such and E.E. Hemmings; 6 – D.J.R. Martindale; 5 – C.W. Scott and J.D. Birch; 4 – N. Newell, K.E. Cooper, S.B. Hassan, C.D. Fraser-Darling and subs

world to bring fun to the rest of us. Cricket will be a sorrier game when he is no longer part of it.

Hardie, Randall, Gooch, McEwan, Hadlee, Cooper, Turner, East, a fine performance behind the stumps, it was a game of heroes which was a credit to all who played in it and made it one of the very great occasions. In the sober dawn one could reflect that, having won nothing for the first 103 years of their existence, Essex had now won all four trophies in the space of seven years, and that all the triumphs had been achieved under the leadership of Keith Fletcher. It is a feat unparalleled in cricket history.

8, 9 and 10 September

at Scarborough

D.B. Close's XI 226 for 5 dec (M.W. Gatting 88, M.D. Moxon 51) and 137 for 8 dec
Rest of the World XI 162 (J.E. Emburey 4 for 47, P.H. Edmonds 4 for 48) and 171 (Sadiq Mohammad 65, P.H. Edmonds 4 for 59)

D.B. Close's XI won by 30 runs

John Player Special League

8 September

at Moreton-in-Marsh

Worcestershire 213 for 9 (G.A. Hick 90, D.N. Patel 63)
Gloucestershire 217 for 1 (C.W.J. Athey 121 not out, P.W. Romaines 65)

Gloucestershire (4 pts) won by 9 wickets

at Southampton

Derbyshire 186 for 8 (M.A. Holding 57)
Hampshire 179

Derbyshire (4 pts) won by 7 runs

at Canterbury

Warwickshire 284 for 6 (A.I. Kallicharran 97, T.A. Lloyd 69)
Kent 253 for 9 (E.A.E. Baptiste 60, C.J. Tavare 59)

Warwickshire (4 pts) won by 31 runs

at Trent Bridge

Essex 252 for 3 (G.A. Gooch 171, B.R. Hardie 60)
Nottinghamshire 208 (J.K. Lever 4 for 35)

Essex (4 pts) won by 44 runs

v. Sussex (Trent Bridge) 24–26 July		v. Yorkshire (Worksop) 27–30 July		v. Northamptonshire (Northampton) 3–6 August		v. Worcestershire (Trent Bridge) 10–13 August		v. Gloucestershire (Cheltenham) 14–16 August		v. Lancashire (Old Trafford) 17–20 August		v. Derbyshire (Trent Bridge) 24–27 August		v. Glamorgan (Trent Bridge) 28–30 August		v. Lancashire (Trent Bridge) 31 Aug.–3 Sept.		v. Yorkshire (Scarborough) 11–13 September		v. Hampshire (Trent Bridge) 14–17 September		M	Inns	NOs	Runs	H/S	Av
63	14	131	64	57	77	3	0	48	—	84	—	13	17*	5	32	15	32	50	72	25	5	25	47	3	1786	171	40.59
														44	24							7	13	—	309	74	23.76
64	18	38	48	45	84	0	53	41	—	2	—	94	—	32	0	21	50	0	73	48	58	25	47	7	2151	117	53.77
23	54	13	47*	23*	61	48	5	12	—	18	—	3	—									21	34	4	933	118	31.10
														22	3	0	13*					14	23	7	409	68*	25.56
								11	—	0	—											3	3	—	24	13	8.00
																						2	1	1	39	39*	—
—	4			—	—			18	—	—	—	9	—	8	17*	1	—	—	17*	10	45*	13	15	5	250	63	25.00
—	5*	—	—	—	—	29*	3*	7	—	—	—											18	13	4	78	29*	8.66
		—	—	—	—	7	—	10*	—	—	—	4	—					—	4*	1	—	22	16	4	139	46	11.58
—	—															2	—					3	1	—	2	2	2.00
73	—					82	2					52	11*					118	19	51	1	11	21	3	1107	130*	61.50
						85	0	6	—	5	—			63	9	70	41*	39	24	101	20	20	33	8	1394	171*	55.76
7*	40	19	—	—	—	3	11	7	—	19*	—	32*	—	0	12	3	2*	5*	15	2	11	23	33	8	432	52*	17.28
		—	—			0	—	0	—			5	—	0*	0	0*	—	—	—	1*	—	14	12	5	18	8	2.57
4	12*	47	—	—	4	2	4					15	—			4	22	73*	3	0	71*	19	29	11	592	73*	32.88
27*	0	6*	—	—	—	30	13*			—	—	7	—	9	4	2	—	—	10	19	—	21	22	5	297	56*	17.47
														0	8							2	4	1	33	23*	11.00
22	34	30	—	17*	6																	3	5	1	109	34	27.25
		18	27*	—	3*			42	—	104*	—	52	—	4	1	13	11	4	0	24	14	9	14	3	317	104*	28.81
1	4	8			4	4	1	5		4		4		4			1	1	7	5	5						
8	5	14	11	7	7	18	6	5		8		6	2	5	5	7	7	6	6	7	1						
4		2		3		2						3			5	1	1	1	1		2						
4	6	4	2		1	9		4		9		14		2		1	4	4	5	3	1						
300	196	330	199	152	247	322	98	216		253		313	30	198	120	140	184	301	256	297	234						
6	7	7	2	2	5	10	7	10		5		10	0	10	10	10	4	5	8	10	6						
D		D		D		D		D		D		W		L		D		D		D							
7		7		2		8		2		6		23		4		4		8		4							

3–R.A. Pick
2–J.A. Afford
1–K. Saxelby and K.P. Evans

at The Oval

Lancashire 160 for 8
Surrey 164 for 2 (A.J. Stewart 71 not out)
Surrey (4 pts) won by 8 wickets

at Hove

Sussex 186 for 9
Leicestershire 179 for 9 (Imran Khan 4 for 37)
Sussex (4 pts) won by 7 runs

The John Player League reached an exciting climax as Essex faced Notts for the second time in the week-end. Having established a record opening partnership for the NatWest Competition the previous day, Gooch and Hardie set up a new record for the Sunday league when they began the match at Trent Bridge with a stand of 239. In contrast to the Saturday, Hardie played the supporting role as Gooch hit 171 off 135 balls with 3 sixes and 18 fours. He then took the wickets of Hadlee and Rice as Essex blunted a brave Notts challenge to match their mammoth total.

This win left Essex two points clear at the top of the table with one round of matches to play. Sussex re-established their challenge with a narrow win over Leicestershire who fell apart after a promising start. Kent's claims on the title were completely extinguished when Andy Lloyd and Alvin Kallicharran added 120 for Warwickshire's second wicket at Canterbury. Tavare and Baptiste responded bravely for Kent, but they had no real hopes of reaching their target.

Paul Romaines and Bill Athey put on 186 for Gloucestershire's first wicket and the home side sailed to victory with 7 overs to spare at Moreton-in-Marsh. Earlier Hick had again demonstrated his considerable talent and his colleague in the Zimbabwe side, Kevin Curran, had taken 3 wickets to maintain his excellent run in the Sunday league. Worcestershire's defeat left them at the bottom as Surrey won at The Oval.

For Hampshire, a season which had promised so much threatened to end disappointingly. At Southampton, Derbyshire were struggling against Marshall and Connor, but Holding hit 57 off 33 balls and lifted them to 186. Hampshire started briskly enough, but no batsmen could establish himself and a frugal spell from coach Russell frustrated them. Chris Smith held the key, but he was bowled by the accurate Mortensen who blighted the hopes of the home side

Nottinghamshire C.C.C. First-Class Matches — Bowling, 1985	K.E. Cooper	K. Saxeley	R.A. Pick	K.P. Evans	J.A. Afford	B.C. Broad	C.E.B. Rice	P.M. Such	R.J. Hadler
v. Cambridge University	19–14–10–7	15–5–26–1	13–6–37–1	13–3–26–1	3–2–1–0				
(Cambridge) 24–26 April	9–5–4–1	10–3–26–0	10–2–38–0	8–4–5–0		6–1–18–1			
v. Somerset (Taunton)	25–5–119–1	23–7–49–1	25–5–79–3				18–6–38–3	10–5–12–0	
27–29 April	18–10–17–3	6–0–25–0	5–0–16–0					18.2–5–73–5	
v. Essex Trent Bridge)	23–13–21–1	15–4–67–0	19–4–72–2				16–7–24–4	18.5–3–82–3	
1–3 May	5–0–33–0	11–1–62–1	17–2–103–1				6–3–18–1	20–1–79–2	
v. Leicestershire (Leicester)	13–4–36–0	15–3–45–0							5–1–9–0
22–24 May									
v. Leicestershire (Trent Bridge)	19.3–7–39–3						5–1–12–1	27–8–74–3	19–5–37–1
29–31 May	7–1–20–0						2–1–1–0	24–8–64–1	11–3–32–1
v. Kent (Tunbridge Wells)	15–4–42–1	23–6–64–6					5–3–3–1		15–3–23–1
8–11 June	14–1–44–2	19.1–5–49–4					10–2–32–0		17–2–45–2
v. Surrey (The Oval)	17–2–65–0	13–4–50–0					13–4–36–0		11–4–19–0
12–14 June	9–1–38–4	10–0–72–0							5–0–26–0
v. Kent (Trent Bridge)	30.3–14–43–4	26–5–91–1					24–8–57–0		24–8–36–3
15–18 June	6–1–13–0	7–0–39–0				4–1–16–1	2–1–1–0		5–1–9–0
v. Middlesex (Trent Bridge)	31–3–105–2	3–0–13–0					28–9–92–1		26–5–78–1
22–25 June	1–0–5–0					1.1–0–3–0			
v. Derbyshire (Derby)	28–12–53–6						12–4–38–2	15–5–32–0	13–5–28–0
26–28 June	11–4–27–0						11–1–60–3	6–1–32–0	17.5–5–44–4
v. Gloucestershire (Trent Bridge)	14–4–37–2	17–7–45–2					11–2–40–3		19–7–59–2
29 June–1 July	8–3–16–0	9–3–21–0							8–3–16–2
v. Glamorgan (Swansea)	23–5–56–3	27–7–56–2					12–2–36–1	13–5–40–1	19–4–39–2
6–9 July	11–4–28–1	15–1–54–2						13–4–35–1	11–3–22–1
v. Middlesex (Lord's)	22–9–67–2	16–6–41–0					21–4–57–4		15–6–31–0
10–12 July	23–3–88–2	7–0–30–0					9–3–16–0	4–1–8–0	21.3–8–34–7
v. Warwickshire (Nuneaton	13–1–60–1	24–8–73–5	16–2–82–1				8–0–36–0		7–3–14–0
13–16 July		3–0–11–0	3–0–11–1						4–1–5–0
v. Sussex (Trent Bridge)		10.5–3–27–2	7–2–21–1		6–1–25–1				18–3–39–4
24–26 July		11–2–36–0	6–1–23–0		10–2–37–1				15–3–36–2
v. Yorkshire (Worksop)	19–6–59–0	23–4–68–3						14–5–24–2	25–8–60–2
27–30 July	7–3–8–0							12–2–25–0	9–2–9–2
v. Northamptonshire	24.5–7–78–1	16–3–66–1	15–3–58–0						9–0–23–0
(Northampton) 3–6 August	11–5–22–0	10–0–67–1	8–0–62–0						
v. Worcestershire	12–2–29–1	22–8–47–4					7–1–19–0	24–6–44–1	16–4–45–2
(Trent Bridge) 10–13 August	17–7–26–3	6–2–16–0						38–12–74–4	4–2–3–0
v. Gloucestershire (Cheltenham)		4–2–9–0	4–0–6–0						
14–16 August									
v. Lancashire (Old Trafford)	20–7–50–3	12–3–40–0	25.4–8–64–3	9–1–38–0			17–3–60–0		
17–20 August			6–2–5–1				5–5–0–0		
v. Derbyshire (Trent Bridge)	16.4–4–36–2		12–3–51–4					5–0–22–0	2.2–2–2–1
24–27 August	10–4–16–0		12–1–46–1			4–1–20–0		24–11–45–3	7–4–6–2
v. Glamorgan (Trent Bridge			17.2–5–54–2				15–3–28–1	31–4–99–2	
28–30 August									
v. Lancashire (Trent Bridge)			7–0–15–0		3–0–10–0		7–4–8–0	24–1–32–2	29.3–16–41–8
31 August–2 September			8–1–31–0		3–0–4–0		1–0–3–0	6–1–23–0	10–0–34–1
v. Yorkshire (Scarborough)	12–4–22–1		9–1–29–0				5–3–10–0	22–5–53–1	17.4–3–52–4
11–13 September	15–4–40–1		18–2–82–1			0.2–0–1–1	6–2–11–0	15–1–83–0	11–4–14–1
v. Hampshire (Trent Bridge)	11–3–16–0		15–1–67–2				8–0–43–0	10–1–47–0	15–5–36–1
14–17 September	14–1–78–3		12–1–44–2					11–0–50–1	12–3–20–2
	604.3–187– 1566–61 *av.* 25.67	429–102– 1385–36 *av.* 38.47	290–52– 1096–26 *av.* 42.15	30–8– 69–1 *av.* 69.00	25–5– 77–2 *av.* 38.50	15.3–3– 58–3 *av.* 19.33	284–82– 779–25 *av.* 31.16	405.1–95– 1152–32 *av.* 36.00	473.5–136 1026–59 *av.* 17.38

a M. Newell 3–0–24–0
J.D. Birch 12–3–33–0
b G.R.Dilley retired hurt

c M. Newell 9–2–38–1
J.D. Birch 5–0–14–0
d C.D. Fraser-Darling 11–3–51–0, 4–0–13–0

e D.J.R. Martindale 2–0–8–0
f D.B. d'Oliveira retired hurt
g C.D. Fraser-Darling 4–0–24–0

E.E. Hemmings	P. Johnson	D.W. Randall	Byes	Leg-byes	Wides	No-balls	Total	Wkts
			2	13	1		115	10
	3–1–23–0			21			192	2a
				17		1	314	8
				2	1		133	10
				7	2	2	273	10
			2		1	1	297	5
20–5–64–1			5	6			165	1
36–15–76–2			5	4	1	1	247	10
32–8–89–4			1	3			210	6
12–2–22–0				9	1	1	163	9b
10–2–20–1			1			4	191	10
29–5–119–2			2	10		2	301	3
3–0–30–0							166	4
14–3–23–1			4	4	1	5	258	10
4–0–12–0	20–2–112–1	12–2–60–2	3	5	1		322	5c
34–6–125–4			5	19	1	2	437	8
		1–0–7–0					15	0
41.2–10–110–2			1	2		2	264	10
11–1–64–0			5	2	3		234	8
14–5–27–0			2	3		1	213	9
11–1–61–1				4			118	3
12–3–39–0				6	2	2	272	9
13–5–32–0				2	2		173	5
18.2–3–41–3			5	4	4	1	246	10
12–4–15–0			8	2	1	3	201	10
21–5–56–1			2	10	1	2	384	8d
14–0–71–1	1–0–12–0	13–0–103–3	5	7	2	4	238	5
25–5–51–2				5	1		168	10
21–3–80–1			6				218	4
19–7–38–0			13	5		3	267	7
8–1–19–0	2–1–5–0	1–0–2–0	4	2		3	82	2e
30–10–71–1			1	4		2	301	3
8–0–28–0					1	3	179	1
5–0–12–0				6	1	1	202	9f
39–12–93–3			9	4		1	225	10
							15	0
27–9–71–3			1	10		4	334	10
							5	1
7.2–2–10–2				4		5	125	10
37.3–15–79–4				5	1	3	217	10
35–7–115–5				9		3	329	10g
4–0–17–0				3		1	126	10
12–0–51–6			4	8		1	158	7
28–6–95–4				1			262	10
22–7–69–0		1–0–2–0	1	3		4	306	4
12–3–39–1				4	1	2	252	4
15–1–69–0				7	1	3	268	9
716.3–170–2103–55 *av.* 38.23	26–4–152–1 *av.* 152.00	28–2–174–5 *av.* 34.80						

with admirable bowling at the end. Derbyshire fielded well and Marples brought off a spectacular catch behind the wicket when he held Nicholas off Holding as he dived down the leg side and took the ball one-handed.

So the competition went into its last round with Essex on 40 points, Northants and Sussex on 38, and Hampshire on 36.

11, 12, and 13 September

at Chesterfield

Derbyshire 354 for 9 dec (J.E. Morris 109 not out, A.M. Brown 74, M.A. Holding 62, P.A. Smith 4 for 121) and 36 for 0
Warwickshire 123 (M.A. Holding 4 for 28) and 265 (Asif Din 89, M.A. Holding 6 for 90)

Derbyshire won by 10 wickets
Derbyshire 24 pts, Warwickshire 3 pts

at Southampton

Hampshire 300 for 8 dec (C.G. Greenidge 143, B.J. Griffiths 4 for 64) and 244 for 4 dec (C.G. Greenidge 68, M.D. Marshall 66 not out, R.A. Smith 55 not out)
Northamptonshire 304 (D.J. Capel 81, R.A. Harper 76, G. Cook 73, T.M. Tremlett 4 for 53, M.D. Marshall 4 for 75) and 241 for 9 (A.J. Lamb 60, R.J. Maru 5 for 114)

Northamptonshire won by 1 wicket
Northamptonshire 23 pts, Hampshire 8 pts

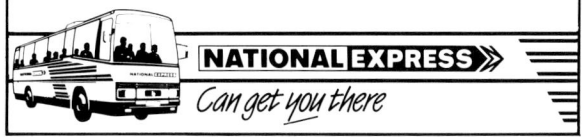

Somerset C.C.C. First-Class Matches – Batting, 1985	v. Oxford University (Oxford) 20–23 April		v. Nottinghamshire (Taunton) 27–29 April		v. Glamorgan (Taunton) 1–3 May		v. Australians (Taunton) 8–10 May		v. Hampshire (Taunton) 22–24 May		v. Gloucestershire (Bristol) 25–28 May		v. Yorkshire (Leeds) 29–31 May		v. Warwickshire (Taunton) 1–4 June		v. Gloucestershire (Bath) 8–11 June		v. Lancashire (Bath) 12–14 June		v. Surrey (The Oval) 22–25 June		v. Glamorgan (Cardiff) 26–28 June		v. Cambridge University (Taunton) 29 June–2 July		v. Leicestershire (Taunton) 6–9 July	
P.M. Roebuck	123*	—	12	36	2	26	13	33*	18	—											34	0	59	2*	28	—	21	49
J.G. Wyatt	145	—	28	18	45	19			7	13	46	—													25	26		
N.F.M. Popplewell	67*	—	2	13	5	81	25	0	28	68	31	—	10	11	55	27	44	—	39	—	30	35	84	3*			24	53
R.L. Ollis	—	—	44	0	38	14	11	4	4	34	8	—	5*	37	55	0	19	—	9	—			—	—	0	39		
I.T. Botham	—	—	90	50	112	3	65	4	149	19	5	—					76*	—			32	72*					48	50*
V.J. Marks	—	—	10	3	9*	18	50	48	17	1*	0	—	62	51	65	66*	1	—	27	—	2	—	39	—			20	8
G.V. Palmer	—	—	45*	0	0	0							11	17*													15	—
T. Gard	—	—	1	1	1	0	30	0	9	—	30	—	0	0*	—	47	—	—			15	—	—	—	—	34*		
M.S. Turner	—	—					9	0	17	19*	13*	—	5	—	17*	24*					0*	—	6	—	—	—	18	15*
S.C. Booth	—	—					4*	5					1	—	—	—	10	—	—	—					—	—	17*	—
M.R. Davis	—	—	21*	1	0	21	11	4	18*	—	7	—			25*	—	14	—	40*	—	11	—	—	—	—	26		
B.C. Rose			43	7	8	0	81*	—																				
A.P. Jones			—	1*	0	1*																						
R.J. Harden							0	17											10	—					107	2*		
I.V.A. Richards									0	186	26	—	105	53	322	—	27	—	65	—	5	—	100	—			47	—
J. Garner									14	—	8*	—	2	—	—	—	1	—	—	—	7	—	6	—				
N.A. Felton											29	—	28	31	0	45	15	—	76	—	21	—	60	—	54	74	112	58
P.A.C. Bail													4	9	8*	0												
R.E. Hayward																	12	—	9	—	2	—	57*	—	100*	—	28	8
S.J. Turner																			9*	—								
C.H. Dredge																									5*	—	0	—
J.C.M. Atkinson																												
S.A.R. Ferguson																												
R.V.J. Coombs																												
Byes					5	1	4	4	4				5	4	1		8				5	4	3		1	4	5	
Leg-byes	5		17	2	7	6	4	1	6	9	5		10	8	9	13	2		18		10	3	16		7	4	5	6
Wides				1	2				2	1	1			3	1		6		1		1				2			
No-balls	11		1		3	1	7	5	5	8	2		9	6	8	4	8		1		13		1	2	2	2	7	1
Total	351		314	133	237	191	314	125	298	358	211		257	230	566	226	243		304		188	114	431	7	331	211	367	248
Wickets	1		8	10	10	10	9†	9	10	5	9		10	6	5	5	9‡		7		10	2	7	0	5	4	10	5
Result	D		L		L		L		L		D		D		D		D		W		D		D		D		D	
Points	—		8		5		—		6		2		4		6		6		22		1		7		—		7	

Catches 38 – T. Gard (ct 31/st 7)
13 – S.C. Booth
10 – N.F.M. Popplewell and P.M. Roebuck
9 – I.T. Botham and I.V.A. Richards
8 – M.R. Davis, R.J. Harden, V.J. Marks and subs
7 – J.G. Wyatt and C.H. Dredge
6 – R.L. Ollis
5 – S.J. Turner (ct 3/st 2)

v. Essex (Southend) 10–12 July	v. Middlesex (Lord's) 13–16 July	v. Warwickshire (Edgbaston) 24–26 July	v. Essex (Taunton) 27–30 July	v. Hampshire (Bournemouth) 3–6 August	v. Northamptonshire (Weston-s-Mare) 10–13 August	v. Middlesex (Weston-s-Mare) 14–16 August	v. Lancashire (Old Trafford) 24–27 August	v. Derbyshire (Derby) 28–30 August	v. Sussex (Taunton) 31 Aug.–3 Sept.	v. Worcestershire (Worcester) 4–6 September	v. Worcestershire (Taunton) 11–13 September	v. Kent (Canterbury) 14–17 September	M	Inns	NOs	Runs	H/S	Av
69 12	11 —	40 81	17 —	6 46	53 —	0 —	88 —	9 —	60 —	45* 28	85 132*	17 —	22	33	5	1255	132*	44.82
5 7			50 —	29 100	16 —	42 —	5 —	90 —	35 —	1 0	2 19	4 39	17	26	—	816	145	31.38
172 6	25 —	4 70	27 —	15 10									18	30	2	1064	172	38.00
— 0							4 —	0 —					15	20	1	326	55	17.10
		5 138*	152 —		134 —		76* —						13	19	5	1280	152	91.42
24* 34	0 —	6 8*	17 —	13 9	0 —	69 —	— —	8 —	— —	— 49	82 —	46 23	26	34	5	885	82	30.51
				38 0				1 —		— 29	23* —		9	12	3	179	45*	19.88
— 1	9 —	7 16	27* —	26 11*	11 —	0 —	— —	0 —	— —	— —	0 —	3 —	25	25	4	279	47	13.28
													10	12	6	143	24*	23.83
— 4*	9 —	28 —											11	8	3	78	28	15.60
— 28	35 —	1 —	7 —	33* 3*								9 —	18	20	6	315	40*	22.50
		16 14										12 15	5	9	1	196	81*	24.50
					1 —								3	4	2	3	1*	1.50
	29 —			46 11	10 —	0 —	19* —	3 —	20* —	52* 3	4 33*		12	17	5	366	107	30.50
	135 —	65 53	5 —		58 —	8 —	120 —	123 —	112 —	44 0	52 125		19	24	—	1836	322	76.50
			4* —				— —	14* —	— —	— 22	1 —	13 —	15	11	3	92	22	11.50
14 3	16 —	10 8	49 —	2 8	9 —	63 —					4 25	84 24	18	27	—	922	112	34.14
									21 —	4 1		2 78*	5	9	2	127	78*	18.14
13* 0	38 —			4 7									9	12	3	278	100*	30.88
													1	1	1	9	9*	—
— 0	9* —	10* —	1 —	9 —	25* —	2* —	— —	31 —	— —	— 21*	3 —	8* —	15	13	7	124	31	20.66
					79 —	25 —	— —	40 —	19* —	— 4			6	5	1	167	79	41.75
						8 —							1	1	—	8	8	8.00
						0 —			— —		0 —	1 —	4	3	—	1	1	0.33
4		4 10		6	3	9	2	1			6 9	8						
11 3	17	3 18	4	4 8	8	6	6	10	4	4 8	16 2	11 1						
1	1	7 2	1	2 4		1	1	2	1		1	1						
2	11	1	2	5 13	2	12	8	4	3	7 5	1 7	1						
315 98	345	207 418	363 0	232 236	409	245	329 0	336	275	157 170	280 352	211 189						
4 10	10	10 6	9 0	10 8	10	10	4 0	10	4	3 9‡	10 3	10 4						
L	D	D	L	D	D	D	L	D	D	L	D	D						
5	7	4	4	2	4	5	4	8	3	2	4	5						

† B.C. Rose retired hurt, absent hurt
‡ T. Gard, absent hurt

4 – J. Garner
3 – N.A. Felton and R.E. Hayward
2 – G.V. Palmer, M.S. Turner and B.C. Rose
2 – A.P. Jones

at Lord's

Essex 92 (N.F. Williams 5 for 15) and 461 (G.A. Gooch 145, D.E. East 100, A.W. Lilley 60, P.H. Edmonds 4 for 101)
Middlesex 279 (M.W. Gatting 114, R.O. Butcher 77, T.D. Topley 4 for 57) and 196 for 7 (M.W. Gatting 83 not out)

Match drawn
Middlesex 7 pts, Essex 4 pts

at Taunton

Somerset 280 (P.M. Roebuck 85, V.J. Marks 82, I.V.A. Richards 52, N.V. Radford 4 for 59) and 352 for 3 dec (P.M. Roebuck 132 not out, I.V.A. Richards 123)
Worcestershire 466 for 7 dec (D.B. d'Oliveira 113, T.S. Curtis 83, D.M. Smith 61, R.V.J. Coombs 4 for 99)

Match drawn
Worcestershire 8 pts, Somerset 4 pts

at Scarborough

Yorkshire 262 (G. Boycott 76, R.J. Hadlee 4 for 52, E.E. Hemmings 4 for 95) and 306 for 4 dec (G. Boycott 125 not out, J.D. Love 79, M.D. Moxon 65)
Nottinghamshire 301 for 5 dec (R.T. Robinson 118, R.J. Hadlee 73 not out, B.C. Broad 50) and 256 for 8 (D.W. Randall 73, B.C. Broad 72, P.J. Hartley 5 for 75)

Match drawn
Nottinghamshire 8 pts, Yorkshire 5 pts

Derbyshire won their last championship match of the season in convincing style. A century from the promising John Morris and a pugnacious 74 from Andrew Brown in his second first-class match gave the win its foundation and the bowling of Holding and Mortensen finished the work. At Scarborough, Boycott was defiant and Robinson continued to accumulate runs. Notts were asked to make 268 in 54 overs and Broad and Randall shared a second wicket stand of 116 which set them on the way, but Peter Hartley, with 3 wickets in 2 overs, thwarted them.

A century by Damian d'Oliveira highlighted the second day's events at Taunton, but there was more impressive left-arm spin from Coombs. Roebuck, doggedly, hit his highest score of the season and Richards, entertainingly, denied Worcestershire on the last day. It was Richards' ninth hundred of the season.

Somerset C.C.C. First-Class Matches — Bowling, 1985	M.R. Davis	M.S. Turner	S.C. Booth	N.F.M. Popplewell	V.J. Marks	I.T. Botham	G.V. Palmer	J. Garner	I.V.A. Richards
v. Oxford University (Oxford) 20–23 April	21–7–35–1	8.1–2–20–2	19–7–62–1	6.5–1–41–0	14–7–16–1	6–1–13–0	20–6–56–0		
v. Nottinghamshire (Taunton) 27–29 April	24.5–3–83–4 9–1–30–0				23–5–66–5 18–4–52–0	7–1–22–0	10–0–46–0 7–1–28–0		
v. Glamorgan (Taunton) 1–3 May	20.3–2–61–3 5–0–14–0			9–0–46–0	26–6–109–1 4–2–7–0	18–1–45–1 2–1–4–0	20–2–97–2		
v. Australians (Taunton) 8–10 May	14–2–71–0 7–0–32–0	15–0–85–0 11–1–58–0	11–1–57–0 28–2–98–4	3–0–21–0	25–4–87–2 28–6–110–2	12–3–28–2 6–2–16–0			
v. Hampshire (Taunton) 22–24 May	15–3–53–0 11–1–37–0	21–4–46–1 4–0–22–0			17.3–3–64–1 17–1–105–1	15–2–69–1 13–0–60–2		22–7–39–3 12–3–45–2	20–8–55–2 8–1–34–0
v. Gloucestershire (Bristol) 25–28 May									
v. Yorkshire (Leeds) 29–31 May		19–5–83–1 22–4–72–1	21–7–64–0	1–0–4–0	28–1–105–1 12–2–38–1		13–3–58–1 16–1–65–1	16.5–5–29–1 11–2–27–0	7–1–21–0 10–3–14–0
v. Warwickshire (Taunton) 1–4 June	23.4–1–115–1 9–2–19–0	22.4–2–74–4 1–0–9–0	13–3–59–0 21–4–72–0		25–3–97–2 16–1–56–1			20–3–59–0 6–2–16–1	12–4–31–1
v. Gloucestershire (Bath) 8–11 June	11–1–57–1 8–3–17–2		4–0–10–0 10–5–13–0		17–5–65–4 12–5–24–1	16–2–54–1		28–7–68–3 7–2–21–1	27–7–62–0
v. Lancashire (Bath) 12–14 June	6–3–19–0 6–1–16–0		15–4–44–2 10.5–1–36–2		30–11–56–3 22–15–17–8			14.4–8–18–4 8–3–16–0	10–4–14–1
v. Surrey (The Oval) 22–25 June	2–1–4–0 7–0–21–0					 0.4–0–2–1		2–1–6–0 7–1–30–0	
v. Glamorgan (Cardiff) 26–28 June	23–7–58–1	19–4–52–1			35–11–88–1			27.4–11–46–5	10–1–40–1
v. Cambridge University (Taunton) 29 June–2 July	17–4–50–2 9–2–32–2	16–2–49–2 14–3–33–1	27–11–50–3 36–18–52–1						
v. Leicestershire (Taunton) 6–9 July		10–2–37–0 3–1–8–0	27–9–89–1 17–3–63–2		49–11–143–7 27–8–65–4	3–1–2–0 12–5–32–1			6–0–17–0
v. Essex (Southend) 10–12 July	15–1–77–0 3–0–14–0		42.3–17–86–3 18–1–70–3		41–9–117–2 18–0–69–3				
v. Middlesex (Lord's) 13–16 July	23–2–65–2 9–1–44–0		29–8–88–4 22–8–38–1		17.3–5–44–2 28–9–49–1				15–4–32–1 14–3–34–1
v. Warwickshire (Edgbaston) 24–26 July	14–2–56–1 3–1–3–1		23–3–72–1 2–0–15–0		40–13–91–2 12.4–5–22–0	22–7–63–4 8–1–32–0			8–2–26–0
v. Essex (Taunton) 27–30 July	 16–2–65–0			 2–0–11–0	 18–2–48–0	 8–0–61–0		1–1–0–0	
v. Hampshire (Bournemouth) 3–6 August	20–3–67–1			6–1–34–0	25–5–100–1		19–3–74–0		
v. Northamptonshire (Weston-super-Mare) 10–13 August						1–0–4–0			5–1–8–0
v. Middlesex (Weston-super-Mare) 14–16 August					6–0–36–3				
v. Lancashire (Old Trafford) 24–27 August					 43–10–125–2	 5–1–14–0		 15–4–24–1	 8–0–30–0
v. Derbyshire (Derby) 28–30 August					5–0–25–2 34–14–69–5		17–1–53–2 16–1–61–1	18–2–51–3 13–3–35–0	11–4–20–0
v. Sussex (Taunton) 31 August–3 September									
v. Worcestershire (Worcester) 4–6 September					20–3–63–1 8–0–46–1		11–0–61–0 8–0–48–0	19–3–56–0 8–2–23–2	
v. Worcestershire (Taunton) 11–13 September					28–6–87–1		10–1–36–0	18–2–76–1	12–5–56–0
v. Kent (Canterbury) 14–17 September	8–2–21–1 6–3–13–1				4–1–6–0 19–4–54–0			12–1–34–3 9–4–10–1	
	366–61– 1249–24 *av.* 52.04	185.5–30– 648–13 *av.* 49.84	396.2–112– 1138–28 *av.* 40.64	27.5–2– 157–0 —	812.4–197– 2421–72 *av.* 33.62	154.4–28– 521–13 *av.* 40.07	167–19– 683–7 *av.* 97.57	295.1–77– 739–31 *av.* 23.83	183–48– 494–7 *av.* 70.57

a A.P. Jones 14–2–62–1
12–2–39–1
b A.P. Jones 5–0–20–0
c A.P. Jones 2–0–9–1
B.C. Rose 1–0–8–0
d P.A.C. Bail 2–0–4–0
e J.G.Wyatt 1–0–1–0
f R.J. Harden 4–3–4–1
R.L. Ollis 4–1–8–0
f P.M. Roebuck 9–3–19–0
g P.M. Roebuck 1–0–4–0
h R.J. Harden 4.3–1–4–1
i P.M. Roebuck 6–0–24–0
J.G. Wyatt 6–0–40–1
j J.G. Wyatt 3–0–18–0

C.H. Dredge	J.C.M. Atkinson	R.V.J. Coombs	Byes	Leg-byes	Wides	No-balls	Total	Wkts
			4			6	247	5
			1	8	2	4	288	10a
			7	4	1	6	160	1
			5	4	8	6	387	7b
				1	2	1	43	1c
				7			356	4
				2		1	316	6
			1	7	2		384	8
			12	10			325	5
			Match Abandoned					
			4	5	3	4	383	4
				7	2	3	223	3
			1	6	1	3	442	9
				5	1	2	181	2d
			11	5			332	9
			9				84	4
			2				153	10
			4		1	1	89	10
18.4–8–36–3							10	0
13–4–30–1				5			58	1
15–1–50–1			1	4	1	2	289	9
3–0–12–0								
23–2–95–5			11	2	2	1	199	10e
3–0–21–0			2	6	2	1	186	6f
25–4–72–1			1	4		1	343	9
12–4–40–1			3	5		2	192	8g
11–4–21–1				6	4		381	10
				7	1		181	6
				8		7	309	10
			6	10	1	4	225	5h
			5	4	4		338	10
			2				74	1
				4	2		68	1i
22–0–82–3				11		3	296	3j
27–13–44–0				10	2	8	346	2k
14–1–41–1	5–1–22–0						87	1l
7–2–12–0	9–0–36–0	14–1–58–5	1	7			150	8
							0	0
18–2–79–0	15.5–2–54–1		1	3	1	6	330	4
29–10–63–3	11–2–54–0		1	5	8	7	272	10
14–5–42–1	14–3–36–1		4	6	1	8	261	8m
			Match Abandoned					
25–7–65–2	9–0–44–0			11	1	14	300	3
10–2–23–1	1.1–1–4–0		6	1		8	151	4
22–3–88–1		38–12–99–4	13	11	1	13	466	7
6–1–13–0		18–3–57–3				1	131	7
		23–11–54–4		1		1	132	6n
317.4–73–929–25 av. 37.16	65–9–250–2 av. 125.00	93–27–268–16 av. 16.75						

R.J. Harden 2–0–17–0 n P.A.C. Bail 2–2–0–0
A.P. Jones 4–0–12–0
n R.J. Harden 2–1–8–0

The significant events, however, were at Lord's and Southampton. Fletcher chose to bat first at Lord's and with Gooch not coming until number six, scarred by his ernest talk with the TCCB, Essex wilted to the bowling of Neil Williams and were out for their lowest score of the season. Slack fell to Lever's first ball, but thereafter Gatting took control. He and Butcher put on 158 and Middlesex closed the day at 236 for 3. On the second day they faded badly against Topley and Ian Pont and Gooch's commanding hundred and Alan Lilley's brisk 60 halted the Middlesex advance. Gooch became the first player in the season to reach 2000 runs. He was also the only batsman to score 1000 runs in one-day cricket. On the last day Middlesex suffered further frustration when David East, whose praises we are not tired of singing, for here is a wicket-keeper batsman to whom England should turn, hit a thumping century, his second of the season. He reached three figures with a hook for six off Daniel into the Mound Stand which was being denuded of its seats. Asked to make 275 in 51 overs, Middlesex slumped to 196 for 7 and it was Essex who came closer to victory in this remarkable match. Over the last two days Middlesex looked far from at ease with themselves and one wondered if Gatting's enthusiasm could rekindle the spirit of some of his team.

There was great drama at Southampton. Greenidge, who had had an indifferent season, hit a fine hundred and Hampshire took maximum batting points, but although they also took maximum bowling points, they trailed by 4 on the first innings, Capel and Harper holding them at bay with a seventh wicket stand of 121. Nicholas had to give his bowlers a chance to win the match and set the visitors to make 241 in 60 overs, a generous offer, particularly as he used spin, Maru and Chris Smith for a considerable time. Lamb gave his side a chance of victory, but he fell to Marshall, superbly caught at slip by Chris Smith, and Maru dented the middle order. From 4 overs, Northants needed 27, and it was at this point that Lamb became the seventh batsman out. Ripley was run out and Mallender well caught on the boundary by Tremlett so that Griffiths joined Harper with 7 needed. For the second time one of first-class cricket's rabbits, Jim Griffiths, thwarted championship contenders. He scrambled a single and Roger Harper hit Maru for six off the last ball of the match to give Northants victory. This left Middlesex one point ahead of Hampshire and 16 ahead of Gloucestershire with only one round of matches remaining.

John Player Special League

15 September

at Chesterfield

Leicestershire 87 for 9 (O.H. Mortensen 4 for 10)
Derbyshire 90 for 1

Derbyshire (4 pts) won by 9 wickets

at Chelmsford

Yorkshire 231 for 7 (K. Sharp 114)
Essex 232 for 8 (K.S. McEwan 62, D.R. Pringle 60)

Essex (4 pts) won by 2 wickets

Surrey C.C.C. First-Class Matches – Batting, 1985	v. Glamorgan (The Oval) 27–29 April		v. Kent (Canterbury) 1–3 May		v. Lancashire (The Oval) 8–10 May		v. Warwickshire (Edgbaston) 22–24 May		v. Essex (The Oval) 25–28 May		v. Middlesex (The Oval) 29–31 May		v. Sussex (Horsham) 1–4 June		v. Cambridge University (Cambridge) 8–11 June		v. Nottinghamshire (The Oval) 12–14 June		v. Worcestershire (Worcester) 15–18 June		v. Somerset (The Oval) 22–25 June		v. Northamptonshire (Northampton) 26–28 June		v. Leicestershire (Leicester) 29 June–2 July		v. Kent (The Oval) 6–9 July	
A.R. Butcher	121	35	16	—	81	21	10	86	—	25	1	3	8	28	39	0	126	97	66	10	6*	37	0	27	33	41	39	4
G.S. Clinton	39	26	3	—	87	3	21	72	4*	106	0	80	17	0			1*	22	117	46*	4*	16*	80	49	49	11		
A.J. Stewart	10	12	158	—	14	14	0	42*	—	43	77	2	39	28	0	2	—	—			—	0*	3	12	1	42		
T.E. Jesty	1	40	3	—	75	96	126	4	—	112*	0	4	99	28*			—	—	28*	17*	—	—	5	36*	0	14	9	9
M.A. Lynch	85*	10	115	—	0	11	45	24*	—	31*	31	144*	27	61*			13	10	11*	—	—	—	34	0	0	21	55	66
D.B. Pauline	20	20	56*	—			77	—							5	13			—	—	—	—	50	10*	8	3	20	30
C.J. Richards	0	11*	38	—	3	32	15*	—	5*	—	38	44*	20*	—			15*	0*	—	—	—	—	26*	—	75*	11	15	26
D.J. Thomas	17*	20	2	—	15	2*			—	—	12	9	1	—			—	4	—	—	—	—	25*	4				
G. Monkhouse	—	—			10*	0	12*	—	—	—	8*	6*																
N.S. Taylor	—	—	21*	—	0	—							18	—	6	—									6	5*	0	1*
P.I. Pocock	—	—	6	—	0	—	—	—	—	—	41	—	0	—			—	—	—	—	—	—	9	—	1	2*	0	12
A. Needham			3	—	43	—	25	—	—	—	12	73	35	—	15	14*	132	33*	63	1	—	—	0	31	18	56	0	1
A.H. Gray							—	—	—	—	1	—					—	—	—	—	—	—	—	—	1	10	0	0
P.A. Waterman													0	—	—	—	—	—	—	—								
D.M. Ward															17	6											23*	18
G.P. Howarth															53	2												
K.T. Medlycott															3	3*												
T.D. Topley															6*	—												
C.K. Bullen															—	—											12	16
R.J. Doughty																												
A. Davies																												
M.A. Feltham																												
Byes		4	3		4	2		6		1	3	10		4	4		2		1				10	3		2	3	
Leg-byes	5	2	8		8	6	13		1	6	16	9	6	2	2	2	10		13	5		5	8	9	10	6		9
Wides	1	1					1			2	4	2			3					1				4			1	1
No-balls	1		13		1	4	2	1		1	11	16	1	2	3	1	2		5	2					8		4	
Total	300	181	445		341	191	347	235	10	327	255	402	271	153	156	43	302	166	304	82	10	58	250	185	210	224	181	193
Wickets	6	7	9		10	7	7	3	0	3	10	6	10	3	8	5	3	4	3	2	0	1	8	6	10	9	10	10
Result	L		D		W		L		W		D		D		D		D		D		D		L		D		L	
Points	6		8		24		7		18		4		6		—		5		6		4		6		6		5	

Catches 45 – C.J. Richards (ct 38/st 7); 36 – M.A. Lynch; 29 – A.J. Stewart (ct 28/st 1); 19 – T.E. Jesty; 13 – G.S. Clinton; 12 – A. Needham; 11 – A.R. Butcher; 8 – G. Monkhouse and R.J. Doughty; 4 – D.B. Pauline and subs; 3 – A.H. Gray and A. Davies

at Cardiff

Sussex 214 for 5 (Imran Khan 66 not out, G.S. le Roux 54)
Glamorgan 121 (A.N. Jones 5 for 32)

Sussex (4 pts) won by 93 runs

at Canterbury

Kent 143 for 8 (G.V. Palmer 5 for 34)
Somerset 144 for 7

Somerset (4 pts) won by 3 wickets

at Trent Bridge

Hampshire 243 for 5 (C.G. Greenidge 122)
Nottinghamshire 207 (M.C.J. Nicholas 4 for 50)

Hampshire (4 pts) won by 36 runs

at The Oval

Gloucestershire 227 for 2 (C.W.J. Athey 115 not out, P.W. Romaines 78)
Surrey 141 (D.A. Graveney 4 for 36)

Gloucestershire (4 pts) won by 86 runs

at Edgbaston

Warwickshire 166
Middlesex 160

Warwickshire (4 pts) won by 6 runs

at Worcester

Worcestershire 195 for 8 (P.A. Neale 83, G.A. Hick 52, A. Walker 4 for 21)
Northamptonshire 167 for 9 (G. Cook 54)

Worcestershire (4 pts) won on faster scoring rate

Hampshire's win at Trent Bridge put them into third place in the table and, with Ole Mortensen in excellent form, Derbyshire crushed Leicestershire to finish a creditable fourth and give them heart for 1986, but before the last round of matches began only Essex, Sussex and Northants could win the title.

Northants had Worcestershire at 13 for 3, but Hick, Neale and Smith effected a recovery and after rain had reduced the visitors' target they faded away, never truly righting themselves after being 13 for 3 in their turn. A bleak day at Cardiff saw a few people watch le Roux hit the fastest televised fifty, Jones give further evidence of his prowess as a quick bowler and Sussex win with ease. This win would have given Sussex the league title had Essex lost at Chelmsford where a mighty match took place.

Fletcher won the toss and asked Yorkshire to bat. Boycott was run out by East's splendid recovery at 14 and Gooch bowled Moxon and Love and had Neil Hartley caught to give him 3 for 26 in his 8 overs and reduce Yorkshire to 80 for

v. Yorkshire (Sheffield) 13–16 July		v. Zimbabwe (The Oval) 17–19 July		v. Lancashire (Southport) 24–26 July		v. Hampshire (Guildford) 27–30 July		v. Warwickshire (The Oval) 31 July–2 August		v. Derbyshire (Derby) 3–6 August		v. Hampshire (Southampton) 10–13 August		v. Yorkshire (The Oval) 14–16 August		v. Middlesex (Lord's) 17–20 August		v. Essex (Chelmsford) 24–27 August		v. Sussex (The Oval) 4–6 September		v. Gloucestershire (The Oval) 14–17 September		M	Inns	NOs	Runs	H/S	Av
21	24*	19	14	17	—	4*	—	27	—	80	—	40	1	12	0	13	12	38	39	28	5	46	7	26	46	3	1407	126	32.72
67	6			21	—	0*	—									0	63	81	—	123	11			18	32	6	1225	123	47.11
		33	88*	61	—	—	—	1	—	0	—	71	44	7	20	44	6	5	42	0	81*	1	6	23	36	4	1009	158	31.53
3	—	100*	54	2	—	—	—	26	—			1	23*	3	141*	7	27	17	—	82	5	7	12	24	36	8	1216	144*	43.42
133	—	27	15	31	—	—	—	145	—	1	—	47*	19	4	121	26	108	1	68	59	1	4	110	25	39	7	1714	145	53.56
								10	—	6	—			15	17			21	11					13	18	2	392	77	24.50
19	—			37	—	—	—	7	—	70	—	—	—			0	9*			12*	42	56	39*	22	27	12	665	75*	44.33
																				—	5			11	12	3	116	25*	12.88
0*	—	—	—	1	—	—	—	—	—	29	—	—	—	15*	7	47	—			—	35*	30	3*	16	14	8	203	47	33.83
																								7	8	3	57	21	11.40
10	—	—	—	6	—	—	—			10*	—	—	—	13	0*	8*	3*	35*	—	—	—	27	—	24	18	6	183	41	15.25
27	19*	124	38	31	—	—	—	138	—	29	—	2	13	15	16	6	10	19	92*	25*	1	0	63	25	37	5	1223	138	38.21
8	—			0*	—	—	—	5	—	—	—	—	—	20	—	3	—	—	—	—	—			19	10	1	48	20	5.33
		—	—																			1*	—	6	2	1	1	1*	1.00
35	—									143	—	23*	2*	7	5									6	10	3	279	143	39.85
		0	3*																					2	4	1	58	53	19.33
								5	—															2	3	1	11	5	5.50
																								1	1	1	6	6*	—
																						19	6	3	4	—	53	19	13.25
19	—	—	—	22	—	—	—	33*	—	65	—	—	—	2	0	22	5	61*	2			4	4	11	12	2	239	65	23.90
		26*	—																					1	1	1	26	26*	—
																		8	27					1	2	—	35	27	17.50
4		2	2							8		1	2	5	5	2	4	5	9	1	3								
9	2	11	5	1				2		11		6	1	1	6	9	16	10	9	10	4	1	4						
		1	1	1				1		1		1	1				2	1	4	2	1	1	2						
9								13		8		8	1	1	3	7	6			7	4	8	2						
364	51	343	220	231		4		413		461		200	107	120	341	194	271	302	303	349	198	205	258						
10	1	5	4	10		0		9		9		4	4	10	8	10	7	8	6	5	7	10	7						
W		D		D		D		W		W		D		D		D		D		L		D							
24		—		6		4		24		24		6		4		5		5		5		6							

2 – D.J. Thomas, P.I. Pocock, C.K. Bullen, D.M. Ward and P.A. Waterman

1 – N.S. Taylor and T.D. Topley

4. There followed a most thrilling innings by Kevin Sharp. He hit the ball hard and cleanly to all parts of the ground and left one bemused as to why he does not score more runs in the championship. From the last ten overs Yorkshire made 90 overs and Essex faced a daunting 231. Sharp's 114 had come from only 106 balls. Gooch and Hardie began firmly, but Gooch lofted a simple catch to mid-on and Hardie was caught behind in the fifteenth over with the score on 53. A capacity crowd on a sunny afternoon cheered Ken McEwan all the way to the wicket and, on his last Sunday League appearance, the South African responded with 62 off 67 deliveries, a glorious knock full of shots of charm, including a six off the ball before he was out, caught on the long on boundary. Pringle played an aggressive and responsible innings, his 60 coming off 54 balls, but when he was out it looked as if Essex would fail. Prichard, batting low in the Sunday side, and Turner needed to score 30 from the last 4 overs. Prichard played a marvellous innings. He never strayed from the orthodox and one cover drive off Oldham was breathtaking. The penultimate over was bowled by Fletcher. Prichard drove three firm twos and then late cut excitingly for 4. The last ball was down the leg side and in the flurry went for 4 leg-byes. Essex needed 3 from the last over to be bowled by Oldham. Turner, the old campaigner in at

John Player Special League Final Table

	P	W	L	T	Nr	Pts
Essex (1)	16	9	3	1	3	44
Sussex (3)	16	10	5	0	1	42
Hampshire (9)	16	8	4	0	4	40
Derbyshire (17)	16	8	5	0	3	38
Northants (12)	16	7	4	1	4	38
Gloucs (13)	16	8	8	0	0	32
Warwicks (7)	16	7	7	0	2	32
Yorkshire (13)	16	6	6	0	4	32
Leics (13)	16	5	5	1	5	32
Kent (9)	16	6	7	0	3	30
Somerset (13)	16	5	6	0	5	30
Notts (2)	16	6	8	0	2	28
Middlesex (5)	16	5	7	0	4	28
Glamorgan (9)	16	4	7	1	4	26
Lancashire (4)	16	3	6	2	5	26
Worcs (7)	16	5	9	0	2	24
Surrey (8)	16	4	9	0	3	22

1984 positions in brackets

Surrey C.C.C. First-Class Matches — Bowling, 1985	D.J. Thomas	N.S. Taylor	G. Monkhouse	T.E. Jesty	P.I. Pocock	D.B. Pauline	A. Needham	A.R. Butcher	R.J. Doughty
v. Glamorgan (The Oval) 27–29 April	20–6–53–1 18–1–104–2	20–4–57–3 6–1–25–0	25–5–75–1	5–1–27–0 2–0–20–0	14–4–32–1 14–0–61–1	2.1–0–17–0			
v. Kent (Canterbury) 1–3 May	25.2–7–51–5 16–3–40–2	19–6–69–1 2.2–0–6–0		11–2–31–1 12–3–32–2	26–2–89–0 20–4–59–1	4–0–18–0 13.4–1–50–2	17–1–67–3 13–0–40–0	14–3–40–1	
v. Lancashire (The Oval) 8–10 May	12–3–44–1 9–1–20–4	15–2–57–2 1–0–2–0	9–1–24–2 8–0–22–1		22–8–46–0 5–1–17–3		17–6–42–5 6.2–1–15–2		
v. Warwickshire (Edgbaston) 22–24 May			11–2–47–0 5–0–24–0	7–0–36–1	26–6–65–0 19.1–2–108–2	7–3–14–0 4–0–18–0	19–3–52–3 8–1–48–0	7–1–20–0 1–0–10–0	
v. Essex (The Oval) 25–28 May	19–3–51–0		24–3–90–2	12–3–37–1	16–4–32–1		10–3–29–0	4–1–16–0	
v. Middlesex (The Oval) 29–31 May	31–4–106–1		26–6–43–2	3–0–6–1	41–13–110–2		38–2–110–0	4–1–14–0	
v. Sussex (Horsham) 1–4 June	19–5–53–1 19–2–88–4	12–2–64–1 6–0–34–0		17–6–60–1 8–1–22–0	18–2–73–1 19–2–74–1		10–4–47–1 3–1–5–0	4–0–18–0	
v. Cambridge University (Cambridge) 8–11 June		9.3–2–19–2 19.1–4–44–7				3–2–7–1	12–4–12–0	8–3–10–0	
v. Nottinghamshire (The Oval) 12–14 June	20–3–54–0 13–2–49–0			3–0–21–0	17–2–54–2 12–5–15–0		9–1–31–0 30–11–49–2	15–3–35–1 31–4–93–1	
v. Worcestershire (Worcester) 15–18 June	21–4–55–1 21–5–59–3				18–4–56–0 1–0–5–0	18–3–71–2 10–1–46–2	11–2–22–0 8–1–38–0	7–1–38–2	
v. Somerset (The Oval) 22–25 June	20–4–55–2					16–3–42–3		7–4–7–0	
v. Northamptonshire (Northampton) 26–28 June	10–0–42–1 8–0–46–2				16.4–6–31–4 17.4–1–78–1		11–1–44–0 6–0–45–0	1–0–18–0	
v. Leicestershire (Leicester) 29 June–2 July		17–0–78–0		4–0–23–1	11.4–2–38–2	10–2–40–0	31–8–69–2	8–4–16–0	
v. Kent (The Oval) 6–9 July		16–1–89–1 6–0–35–1		6–2–19–1 7.5–0–30–0	24.5–9–42–7 14–3–50–0	19–1–66–0 3.1–2–2–0	1–1–0–0 10–1–47–0	6–0–13–0	
v. Yorkshire (Sheffield) 13–16 July			7–2–14–0 20–6–46–1	9–3–21–1 8–1–50–2	20–10–22–1		2–0–12–0		17–4–40–1 24.3–7–75–3
v. Zimbabwe (The Oval) 17–19 July			12.5–2–48–3		12–4–24–1		13–5–27–1		16–1–61–3
v. Lancashire (Southport) 24–26 July			22–3–61–2 6–3–12–0		21–6–53–1 4–1–15–0		11.2–1–24–1 13–6–13–0	1–0–1–0	17–4–56–4 13–1–49–2
v. Hampshire (Guildford) 27–30 July			18–3–51–0	8–3–18–0	22–3–61–3				15–2–69–2
v. Warwickshire (The Oval) 31 July–2 August			16–3–46–4 2–1–6–0	0.3–0–0–1		2–0–21–0			7–1–32–2 9.4–4–33–6
v. Derbyshire (Derby) 3–6 August			12–5–20–1 30.5–9–61–5		2–1–3–0 7–2–6–0	19.4–7–52–5 7–4–9–0	3–3–0–0	4–2–5–0	8–2–30–1 11–0–52–1
v. Hampshire (Southampton) 10–13 August			33–5–82–4	11–2–34–1	8–0–20–0			12–2–43–3	18–2–75–1
v. Yorkshire (The Oval) 14–16 August			24–8–46–4 3–1–2–0		23–8–45–1	8–2–24–1	7–1–22–0		16–2–58–1 2–0–8–0
v. Middlesex (Lord's) 17–20 August			18–1–46–1		3–0–12–0			12–3–26–1	7–2–21–1 4.4–0–27–0
v. Essex (Chelmsford) 24–27 August					13–1–37–2 16–6–24–1	12–2–52–0 3–0–18–0	3–1–8–0	6–1–15–1	11–0–73–2 8–1–30–2
v. Sussex (The Oval) 4–6 September	12–1–47–1 8–0–38–1		19–5–51–2 12–2–47–2	8–0–29–0	6.4–0–34–0 15–1–75–3		12–3–44–1	5–1–11–0	
v. Gloucestershire (The Oval) 14–17 September			12–1–61–0 8–1–43–3	2–1–1–0	23–5–57–4 7.4–3–9–2		15–2–55–2 2–2–0–0		14–3–52–1 5–0–26–1
	321.2–54– 1055–32 *av.* 32.96	149–22– 579–18 *av.* 32.16	383.4–78– 1068–40 *av.* 26.70	144.2–28– 517–14 *av.* 36.92	576.2–131– 1632–48 *av.* 34.00	161.4–33– 567–16 *av.* 35.43	351.4–76– 1017–23 *av.* 44.21	157–34– 449–10 *av.* 44.90	223.5–36– 867–34 *av.* 25.50

a T.D. Topley 13–3–42–2, 14–3–22–0
C.K. Bullen 21–10–36–2
K.T. Medleycott 10–5–17–1, 14–7–22–0

b A.J. Stewart 2–0–19–0
G.S. Clinton 6–0–46–0
C.J. Richards 8–1–42–2

c C.K. Bullen 7–1–39–0
d J.D. Love absent hurt
e A.J. Stewart 4–0–24–0

e C.J. Richards 19–1–78–2
f M.A. Feltham 9–1–56–0, 2–0–18–0

A.H. Gray	P.A. Waterman	M.A. Lynch	*Byes*	*Leg-byes*	*Wides*	*No-balls*	*Total*	*Wkts*
				3	1	6	264	6
			3	5			218	3
			4	7	1	7	336	10
		1–1–0–0	9	6	1	6	282	8
			5	4	10		222	10
				1	5	2	77	10
16–4–54–2			10	2	2	2	300	7
12–0–68–4				9	1		285	6
16–1–72–2			3	6	1	5	336	6
9–1–40–0			12	11		8	452	6
	14–2–69–2		3	4		3	391	7
	9–2–47–1		4	7	1	4	281	6
	14–6–22–3			6	2	4	142	10a
	16–5–18–2		16	10	1	11	161	10
12–0–50–0	11–0–50–0		2	4	3	5	301	3
12–4–29–1	3–1–8–0	2–0–19–0		3		4	265	4
19–2–77–0	9–2–24–0		4	7	1	7	354	5
19–5–67–0	8–2–22–0		4	12	5	2	253	5
20.2–4–69–5			5	10	1	13	188	10
			4	3			114	2b
15–3–44–5			1	1		1	181	10
11–1–74–2			7	7		5	257	5
21–5–56–4			6	15		16	341	10
23–4–51–1			4	17	5	12	301	10
17–4–34–2			8	4		3	249	3c
17.4–6–40–8			2	2	2	1	131	10
19–5–79–2			1	7	2	1	280	9d
	16–3–58–2		4	4	2	1	228	10
22–4–64–2			4	16	1	4	278	10
14–2–51–5				4		5	145	7
24.1–5–83–5				9	1	9	291	10
14–4–43–3				5		3	147	10
8–1–24–3					3		63	10
20–5–68–3			8	5	9		186	10
21–6–44–4			16	2		2	195	10
29.4–4–83–3				9	5	13	303	9
		3–0–27–0		2	1	1	174	5e
23.3–5–68–3			5	9		2	277	10
				1			11	0
26–7–68–7			2	8	3	9	183	10
5–0–29–0					1	4	56	0
16–0–65–0			12	5	1	5	300	4f
17–6–72–2			9	6	2	12	200	6
13–0–74–0			4	6	1	2	300	4
11.4–0–76–1			1	12		1	249	7
	13–2–47–2		2	2	2	8	277	10
	2–0–17–0		1	5	1	3	101	6
524–98–1816–79 *av.* 22.98	115–25–382–12 *av.* 31.83	6–1–46–0 —						

the kill, took a single off the first ball, but Prichard, in his only sign of nerves, gave a simple catch off the second. Foster, nervously, was twice beaten as he essayed wild shots, but a chat with Turner calmed him and the fifth ball was placed through mid wicket for the winning runs. Essex had retained their title and finished the season with the remarkable record of having won two of the limited-over competitions and finished runners-up in the third, the Benson and Hedges Cup.

14, 16 and 17 September

at Chelmsford

Yorkshire 131 (J.D. Love 61, J.K. Lever 6 for 47) and 278 (M.D. Moxon 88, S.N. Hartley 52)
Essex 413 for 8 dec (G.A. Gooch 142, K.W.R. Fletcher 66, D.E. East 62)

Essex won by an innings and 4 runs
Essex 24 pts, Yorkshire 3 pts

at Cardiff

Glamorgan 32 for 0
v. **Sussex**

Match drawn
No points

at Canterbury

Somerset 211 (N.A. Felton 84, D.L. Underwood 4 for 44) and 189 for 4 dec (P.A.C. Bail 78 not out, D.L. Underwood 4 for 69)
Kent 131 for 7 dec and 132 for 6 (N.R. Taylor 54, R.V.J. Coombs 4 for 54)

Match drawn
Somerset 5 pts, Kent 4 pts

at Old Trafford

Leicestershire 336 (I.P. Butcher 78, P.B. Clift 50, I. Folley 4 for 120) and 0 for 0 dec
Lancashire 0 for 0 dec and 293 for 9 (N.H. Fairbrother 91, J. Abrahams 65)

Match drawn
Lancashire 3 pts, Leicestershire 3 pts

at Trent Bridge

Nottinghamshire 297 (C.E.B. Rice 101, R.T. Robinson 51, R.J. Maru 5 for 66, T.M. Tremlett 4 for 53) and 234 for 6 dec (R.J. Hadlee 71 not out, D.W., Randall 58)
Hampshire 252 for 4 dec (V.P. Terry 128 not out) and 268 for 9 (M.C.J. Nicholas 84)

Match drawn
Hampshire 7 pts, Nottinghamshire 4 pts

at The Oval

Surrey 205 (C.J. Richards 56, C.A. Walsh 4 for 79) and 258 for 7 dec (M.A. Lynch 110, A. Needham 63)
Gloucestershire 277 (P. Bainbridge 102, B.F. Davison 59, P.I. Pocock 4 for 57) and 101 for 6

Match drawn
Gloucestershire 7 pts, Surrey 6 pts

at Edgbaston

Warwickshire 187 (R.I.H.B. Dyer 52, J.E. Emburey 4 for 47) and 184 (P.H. Edmonds 4 for 63, J.E. Emburey 4 for 64)
Middlesex 445 (M.W Gatting 76, W.N. Slack 74, J.E. Emburey 68, K.R. Brown 67, N. Gifford 5 for 128)

Middlesex won by an innings and 74 runs
Middlesex 24 pts, Warwickshire 3 pts

Sussex C.C.C.
First-Class Matches – Batting, 1985

	v. Lancashire (Old Trafford) 27–29 April		v. Cambridge University (Cambridge) 8–10 May		v. Australians (Hove) 18–21 May		v. Gloucestershire (Hove) 22–24 May		v. Middlesex (Lord's) 25–28 May		v. Glamorgan (Hove) 29–31 May		v. Surrey (Horsham) 1–4 June	
G.D. Mendis	0	—	23	41*	81	7	45	16	5	33	17	70	0	46
A.M. Green	11	—	42	1	27	29	1	17	2	38	45	100*	90	106
P.W.G. Parker	0	—	61	39	26	12	6	36*	9	1	60	30*	105	14
Imran Khan	36*	—			0	44*			11	1	44*	—		
C.M. Wells	4	—	45*	—	38	0	7	—	2	42	11	—	56	4
A.P. Wells	55*	—	45	18*	0	5	0	7*	1	16	102	—	11	43
J.R.T. Barclay	—	—	9*	—	37*	19	27	—						
I.A. Greig	—	—	—	—	8	15	8	—	12	11	17*	—	43	34*
I.J. Gould	—	—	—	—	0	2	0	—	46*	17	—	—	58*	15*
G.S. Le Roux	—	—			20	0*								
C.E. Waller	—	—			2*	8	1*	—	4	0	—	—	—	—
A.C.S. Pigott			—	—							—	—	—	—
A.N. Jones			—	—			5	—	8	3*				
D.A. Reeve			—	—			1	—	23	0	—	—	11*	—
D.K. Standing													7	3
P. Moores														
N.J. Lenham														
I.C. Waring														
Byes			6	4			9	7			1	1	3	4
Leg-byes	6		5	3	3	7	9	1	3	6	1	4	4	7
Wides					1		1			1	1	1		1
No-balls	1				19	5	21	5	6	11	4		3	4
Total	113		236	106	262	153	141	89	132	180	303	206	391	281
Wickets	4		4	2	9†	9	10	2	10	10	5	1	7	6
Result	D		W		D		D		L		W		D	
Points	4		—		—		1		2		24		8	

	v. Northamptonshire (Northampton) 8–11 June		v. Derbyshire (Derby) 12–14 June		v. Hampshire (Hove) 15–18 June		v. Gloucestershire (Bristol) 22–25 June		v. Lancashire (Hastings) 29 June–2 July		v. Warwickshire (Hove) 6–9 July		v. Hampshire (Portsmouth) 10–12 July	
G.D. Mendis	13	1	41	—	11	62			103	100*	21	111*	109	96*
A.M. Green	8	2	68	—	54	93			8	78*	96	72	0	44
P.W.G. Parker	5	13*	17	—	80	53*			1	—	44	33	0	7
Imran Khan	38	18			7	—			70	—	117*	—		
C.M. Wells	48	0*	18	—	1	1*			69*	—	100*	—	49	24
A.P. Wells	5	12	32	—	14	15			0	—	—	—	33	3
J.R.T. Barclay	37*	—	29	—	14	—			—	—	—	—	0	—
I.A. Greig					13	—			40	—	—	—	22	8*
I.J. Gould	26	—	5*	—	10	—					—	—	51	11
G.S. Le Roux			29	—	32*	—			1*	—	—	—	33*	—
C.E. Waller	—	—	—	—	8	—							—	—
A.C.S. Pigott	10*	—	—	—					—	—	—	—		
A.N. Jones													21*	—
D.A. Reeve	2	—	4*	—										
D.K. Standing														
P. Moores									—	—				
N.J. Lenham														
I.C. Waring														
Byes					5	9				4	1		4	4
Leg-byes	7	1	1		4				6	6	9	7	1	7
Wides						1			3		2	2	2	2
No-balls	2		6		4	4			9	5	15	3	2	3
Total	201	47	250		257	238			310	193	405	228	327	209
Wickets	8	4	7		10	3			6	0	3	2	8	5
Result	D		D		D		Ab.		W		D		D	
Points	6		4		5		0		23		7		8	

Catches 40–I.J. Gould (ct 36/st 4)
16–A.M. Green
14–P.W.G. Parker
13–I.A. Greig and J.R.T. Barclay
12–A.P. Wells
11–subs
8–G.D. Mendis and D.A. Reeve
7–A.C.S. Pigott and C.M. Wells
4–N.J. Lenham
2–C.E. Waller
1–P. Moores, G.S. Le Rou[x] and A.N. Jones

at Worcester

Worcestershire 392 for 3 dec (G.A. Hick 128, D.M. Smith 104 not out, P.A. Neale 72 not out, T.S. Curtis 55) and 184 (R.A. Harper 4 for 25, D.J. Capel 4 for 59)

Northamptonshire 349 for 3 dec (W. Larkins 163, R.J. Boyd-Moss 121) and 231 for 7 (G. Cook 72, R.J. Bailey 52, N.V. Radford 4 for 68)

Northamptonshire won by 3 wickets
Northamptonshire 21 pts, Worcestershire 5 pts

If the Britannic Assurance County Championship did not reach quite the exciting climax that it had reached in 1984, it was still not decided until the last afternoon when Middlesex swamped a limp Warwickshire side to take the title. Over the last three days of the season, in spite of the brave efforts of Hampshire and Gloucestershire, it never seemed likely that Middlesex would be denied. They shot out Warwickshire on the Saturday and began to score runs quickly. Gatting led the charge and there was a violent assault by Emburey which took their first innings advantage to 258. Gatting left his bowlers a day in which to bowl out the home side for a second time and although Dyer and Lloyd offered early resistance, wickets began to fall regularly. Edmonds extracted considerable turn to bowl Dyer and Kallicharran was stumped floundering against Emburey. Lloyd was taken close in and good bowling and bad shots soon accounted for the other batsmen.

Gatting worked hard to bring his men to the title. It cannot be an easy job to fuse together such diverse talents and temperaments. Having said this, one had considerable sympathy for Hampshire and Gloucestershire. Hampshire played an exciting draw at Trent Bridge in a bold bid to take the points that would have given them the championship had Middlesex lost and Gloucestershire, after early successes at The Oval, were again blighted by the weather. Bainbridge scored an heroic century and then was forced to retire hurt in the second innings after being hit on the head as Gloucestershire chased a forlorn task. To all who saw them, however, they left a happy memory of the best cricket that any Gloucestershire side has played for many years.

Hick gave another impressive display for Worcestershire and Smith helped his cause and those who advocated that he should be taken to the West Indies, but Larkins and Boyd-Moss put on 255 for Northants' second wicket and eventually the visitors were victorious. The hero of the match, if not

v. Nottinghamshire (Trent Bridge) 24–26 July		v. Worcestershire (Eastbourne) 27–30 July		v. Kent (Eastbourne) 31 July–2 August		v. Kent (Canterbury) 10–13 August		v. Essex (Colchester) 14–16 August		v. Derbyshire (Hove) 17–20 August		v. Middlesex (Hove) 24–27 August		v. Yorkshire (Hove) 28–30 August		v. Somerset (Taunton) 31 Aug.–3 Sept.		v. Surrey (The Oval) 4–6 September		v. Leicestershire (Hove) 7–10 September		v. Glamorgan (Cardiff) 14–17 September			*M*	*Inns*	*NOs*	*Runs*	*H/S*	*Av*
42	41	13	0	29	11	27	22*	143*	—	7	16	72	19	123	6	—	—	50	46	33	4	—	—		25	43	6	1756	143*	47.45
3	4	1	10*	24	78	21	4*	46	—	4	37	89	38	54	39	—	—	133	16	4	9	—	—		25	43	4	1646	133	42.20
40	33	7	—											76	10										16	28	4	818	105	34.08
22	56*			89	30					9	77*			39*	39			84*	59			—	—		14	21	8	890	117*	68.46
15	71	3	—	39	42	61	—	4	—	11	33*	32	35	4	46	—	—	6	0	1	1	—	—		25	36	6	923	100*	30.76
6	7*			1	19*	36	—	18	—	24	—	13	9*			—	—	9*	14	6	21	—	—		23	33	7	600	102	23.07
1	—	14	—	8*	—	9	—	5	—	23	—	5	—	—	—	—	—	—	—	12*	8*	—	—		22	17	6	257	37*	23.36
												3	—			—	—	—	28*	0	2				15	16	4	264	43	22.00
5	—	95	—	10*	19*	20	—	78	—	0	—	5	4*	—	8	—	—	—	30*	0	101	—	—		24	25	8	616	101	36.23
8	—	20	—	—	—	22	—	60	—	20	—	14	—	—	61	—	—	—	40	27	34				18	16	4	421	61	35.08
8	—	0	—	—	—	6*	—	—	—							—	—								16	9	3	37	8	6.16
		0*	—			0	—																		9	3	2	10	10*	10.00
								5*	—	9*	—	0	—	—	6*	—	—	—	—	26	—	—	—		12	9	5	83	26	20.75
12*	—	4	—	—	—	14	—	7	—	13	—	8*	56	—	—					10	5*	—	—		17	15	5	170	56	17.00
																									1	2	—	10	7	5.00
																									1	—				—
		6	7*	18	36	89	—	1	—	11	49	32	39	10*	41	—	—	5	2	50	77	—	—		11	16	2	473	89	33.78
																						—	—		1	—				—
		1	2	1	1	1		3		13	5			1	4			4	1	7	1				† J.R.T. Barclay, retired hurt					
5	6	12	3	4	3	4	1	7		6		6	5	5	8			6	12	6	20									
1				3				5						2				1		2	2									
		1		3	4	7		2		19	11	8	2	9				2	1	25	4									
168	218	177	22	227	243	317	27	380		169	228	287	207	323	268			300	249	209	289									
10	4	10	1	6	5	10	0	8		10	3	10	5	4	8			4	7	10	8									
D		D		D		W		D		D		W		D		D		W		W										
3		3		3		20		7		5		20		7		1		22		22										

the season, was Neal Radford who took his total of wickets to 101, a magnificent achievement.

Lancashire and Leicestershire, denied any play on the Monday, contrived an exciting end to the season, but the match at Old Trafford was drawn. Rain again blanketed Cardiff and Somerset finished bottom after drawing at Canterbury where they gained some encouragement from the career best of Bail and the continued outstanding achievements of spinner Coombs.

At Chelmsford, Fletcher stood down as Essex's captain and celebrated his final appearance in that position with an innings win over Yorkshire. Lever returned his career best on the Saturday and Gooch hammered another thrilling hundred on the Monday when East and Fletcher himself also hit lustily. With Boycott absent with a broken thumb, Yorkshire failed to avert an innings defeat although Moxon showed spirit as did Bairstow, inevitably, and Hartley. This win took Essex to fourth place in the table and completed an outstanding season for them, the last under Fletcher's captaincy. Gooch has a hard task in following him, for Fletcher ranks with Sellers, Surridge and Robins as one of the very greatest captains in the history of county cricket.

Britannic Assurance County Championship Final Table

					Bonus pts		
	P	*W*	*L*	*D*	*Bt*	*Bl*	*Pts*
Middx (3)	24	8	4	12	61	85	274
Hants (15)	24	7	2	15	66	78	256
Glos (17)	24	7	3	14	51	78	241
Essex (1)	24	7	2	15	42	70	224
Worcs (10)	24	5	6	13	65	68	221
Surrey (8)	24	5	5	14	62	76	218
Sussex (6)	24	6	1	17	52	57	205
Notts (2)	24	6	1	17	52	57	205
Kent (5)	24	4	5	15	51	71	186
Northants (11)	24	5	4	15	52	51	183
Yorks (14)	24	3	4	17	58	59	165
Derby (11)	24	3	9	12	46	69	163
Glamorgan (13)	24	4	4	16	41	50	163
Lancs (16)	24	3	7	14	44	67	159
Warwicks (9)	24	2	8	14	47	74	153
Leics (4)	24	2	3	19	48	65	145
Somerset (7)	24	1	7	16	70	45	131

1984 positions in brackets.

Worcestershire and Glamorgan records include eight points for drawn matches in which scores finished level.

Sussex C.C.C. First-Class Matches — Bowling, 1985	Imran Khan	G.S. Le Roux	C.M. Wells	I.A. Greig	A.C.S. Pigott	A.N. Jones	D.A Reeve	J.R.T. Barclay	C.E. Waller
v. Lancashire (Old Trafford) 27–29 April	22–7–49–0	19–6–28–1	32–11–76–4	25–3–80–5					
v. Cambridge University (Cambridge) 8–10 May			8–4–17–0 10–5–16–2	11–4–21–0 13–4–26–3	9–4–10–1 9–4–11–1	8–3–12–0 7–1–22–0	16–4–31–2 8.4–2–16–1	20–9–25–2 10–5–19–3	
v. Australians (Hove) 18–21 May	21.2–10–55–3 12–5–33–0	10–2–19–1	20–5–73–1 12–2–35–1	12–2–43–1 14–4–47–1				18–2–65–2	33–9–61–1 30–9–66–2
v. Gloucestershire (Hove) 22–24 May			18–6–27–0	12–2–44–0		20–2–75–0	29.2–6–86–4		5–2–12–0
v. Middlesex (Lord's)	19–3–67–1		24–5–54–3	18–2–60–0		11–1–55–1	17–5–64–1		8–1–24–0
v. Glamorgan (Hove) 29–31 May	12–5–16–4 31.5–10–75–2		 14–4–50–0	 26–7–65–0	6–1–17–1 26–6–65–2		9–4–24–5 29–6–107–3		 18–3–43–0
v. Surrey (Horsham) 1–4 June			12–1–33–2 7–1–19–0	9–3–41–1 3–0–26–0	17.5–3–94–3 9–0–43–2		24–8–49–3 10–4–34–1		14–3–48–0 5–1–17–0
v. Northamptonshire (Northampton) 8–11 June	30–2–116–4		22–10–36–2 14.5–3–56–2		7–1–25–1 6–1–26–0		19–6–57–2 8–1–37–1		20.2–4–57–0 12–4–24–2
v. Derbyshire (Derby) 12–14 June		18–5–25–1	16–7–36–1		16–3–56–1		17–4–45–0	11–4–24–0	34.3–15–61–7
v. Hampshire (Hove) 15–18 June	16–8–28–2 16.4–7–25–3	16–1–64–0 11–3–19–0	16–4–46–1 5–1–12–0	14–3–46–2 14–4–37–4					22–10–26–1 13–5–24–0
v. Gloucestershire (Bristol) 22–25 June									
v. Lancashire (Hastings) 29 June–2 July	19.4–7–28–4 17–3–49–2	17–3–42–2 10–2–34–0	7–2–19–1	 5–0–23–0	12–4–39–0 9.3–5–22–3			12–4–30–2 30–3–99–5	
v. Warwickshire (Hove) 6–9 July	19.1–2–49–5 21–8–42–3	14–3–41–0 14–4–23–1	19–5–68–0 13–4–30–2	16–4–49–1 2–0–11–0	15–1–60–1 12–2–37–0			16–1–64–0 5–0–33–0	
v. Hampshire (Portsmouth) 10–12 July		18–5–52–3 21.5–5–51–3	9.5–5–16–2 16–7–31–1	16–5–44–1 15–4–43–3		21–4–63–3 17–3–50–1		 1–0–4–0	8–3–27–0 12–5–27–0
v. Nottinghamshire (Trent Bridge) 24–26 July	26–5–59–5 19–1–50–3	17–0–58–1 10–3–12–0	11–1–41–0 5–0–24–1				22–2–64–0 9–0–45–2	5–3–8–0	31–12–61–0 14–3–56–1
v. Worcestershire (Eastbourne) 27–30 July		17–3–53–2 8–2–21–0	18–3–63–1 12–7–14–0		20.5–3–102–3 5–0–14–0		22–8–66–0 23–2–83–1	1–1–0–0 1–0–2–2	18–9–12–0 14.3–2–56–2
v. Kent (Eastbourne) 31 July–2 August	7–3–8–0 11–3–17–0	8–1–32–0 4–0–16–0	6–1–22–0 3–2–13–0				8–0–37–0 11–2–41–0	21–5–57–1 7–0–40–0	23–6–31–1 9–2–33–1
v. Kent (Canterbury) 10–13 August		17.4–1–72–4	11–4–34–0		4.3–1–12–0		32–11–70–5	8–2–29–0	19.3–4–64–1
v. Essex (Colchester) 14–16 August		15.4–4–46–6 9.2–1–34–1				15–2–42–1 5–0–29–0	6–1–25–0 2–0–7–0	17–3–36–2 8–0–30–1	9–2–22–1
v. Derbyshire (Hove) 17–20 August	22–3–61–3 14–6–38–3	15–2–50–3	16–3–43–1 21–3–74–3			8–0–45–0 10–1–32–0	29–7–87–3 17.5–5–51–3	3–0–16–0 15–2–40–1	
v. Middlesex (Hove) 24–27 August		5–2–16–0 10–0–39–2	13–0–43–0 10–2–27–2	7–0–37–1		7–3–33–0 5–0–29–1	15–6–30–2 15–1–64–4	11–1–35–1 4–0–24–0	
v. Yorkshire (Hove) 28–30 August	18.3–7–33–2	17–3–47–1 11–1–38–1	15–2–29–1 14–3–30–1			14–3–46–0 11–2–31–0	22–6–54–0 4–1–3–0	19–1–78–6 14.4–1–42–1	
v. Somerset (Taunton) 31 August–3 September		12–2–36–0	18–4–58–0	25–5–70–2		17–2–57–1		6–1–20–0	9–3–30–0
v. Surrey (The Oval) 4–6 September	28–5–98–2 12–1–34–0	13–2–34–0 17–3–41–2	14–5–33–1 7–2–32–0	23–1–99–0 3–1–19–0		15–0–60–2 16–4–39–5		5–2–14–0 4–0–17–0	
v. Leicestershire (Hove) 7–10 September		14.5–2–41–5 12–1–48–0	11–3–30–1 20–5–56–1			10–0–41–2 23–4–77–3	20–2–53–2 26–3–83–3	1–0–4–0 27–5–58–2	
v. Glamorgan (Cardiff) 14–17 September	7–3–10–0					6–2–10–0	5–0–11–0		
	422.1–114– 1040–51 *av.* 20.39	402.2–72– 1132–40 *av.* 28.30	510.4–142– 1416–38 *av.* 37.26	283–58– 931–25 *av.* 37.24	184.4–39– 633–19 *av.* 33.31	246–37– 848–20 *av.* 42.40	475.5–107– 1424–48 *av.* 29.66	300.4–55– 913–31 *av.* 29.45	381.5–117– 882–20 *av.* 44.10

a I.J. Gould 4–0–75–0

A.M. Green	P.W.G. Parker	G.D. Mendis	*Byes*	*Leg-byes*	*Wides*	*No-balls*	*Total*	*Wkts*
				4		7	237	10
			7	9			132	5
			9	8			127	10
			1	4		6	321	10
21.3–4–76–1	1–0–12–0		4	2		5	275	6
				7		6	251	4
			4	11		5	339	6
			1			1	58	10
13–5–20–2			3	19	4	3	447	10
				6		1	271	10
2–0–8–0			4	2		2	153	3
			2	9	1	2	302	9
				2	1		145	5
1–0–4–0			4	1	3	2	256	10
			4	7	2	6	221	6
			1	5	2	2	123	7
				Match Abandoned				
			5	10	3	7	173	10
3–0–13–0			10	7	5	1	257	10
			1	11		2	343	7
			4	6	1		186	6
				8	1	5	210	10
				7	1	9	213	8
			1	8	4	4	300	6
			4	5		6	196	7
			4	6		7	306	6
				5		1	195	5
3–0–7–0			4	2		1	200	3
				2		1	162	1
							0	0
				9	4	7	290	10
			6	7		7	184	10
2–0–10–0				6	4	5	116	2
			3	7	1	14	312	10
			5	4		6	244	10
			4	5		4	203	4
				5			188	10
			5	15	1	15	307	10
4–1–6–0		4–0–65–1	2	1		7	293	4a
				4	1	3	275	4
			1	10	2	7	349	5
4–0–9–0			3	4	1	4	198	7
				2		6	171	10
				4	1	10	326	9
				1		1	32	0
53.3–10–153–3 *av.* 51.00	1–0–12–0 —	4–0–65–1 *av.* 65.00						

Review of the Season

By David Lennon

After the battering received at the hands of the West Indies in 1984, the summer of 1985 came as a tonic to followers of English cricket. The wonderful cricket that we had seen at county level in 1984 was at last transmitted to the Test arena and Gower and his men flourished in one of the most entertaining series that one has seen for many years. Elsewhere Tony Lewis remarks on the weakness of the Australian side, but, accepting that, England's performances were still heartening and one has never seen a series contested in a better spirit. It was revivifying, and for that, Allan Border and David Gower must take much of the credit. Border came to play entertaining cricket and to see that his team behaved in the right manner. He achieved both those goals although, at the end of the tour, his men looked very tired and jaded. They should have learned much and one will see more of O'Donnell, McDermott, Boon and the other young men.

Border will be returning to England in 1986 to join Essex who were the outstanding team of the season. They won two of the four titles, finished second in a third and were fourth in the other. It was a remarkable achievement, particularly when one considers that at the beginning of July they were at the bottom of the County Championship and only two points off the bottom of the John Player League. In Fletcher they had an outstanding captain and in Gooch, when not on Test duty, one of the most forceful and exciting batsmen the world has seen, but, generally, there was a feeling that Essex played most of the season well below their best. Lilley, Gladwin and Prichard, the last a young player of exceptional talent, all failed to produce quite what was hoped. Pringle has still to realise his full potential and Foster was troubled by injury and illness. Both of these players could re-establish themselves in the England side next year which leaves the Essex bowling a bit thin although John Lever shows little sign of wear if some of tear. East was an inspirational wicket-keeper and ferocious batsman and Hardie was the ever dependable as batsman and short leg.

Middlesex were a team of talents, but, as indicated earlier, Gatting needed all his powers of leadership to harness them. Barlow and Slack were a fine opening pair; Edmonds, especially, and Emburey were excellent spinners. No other county could boast a spinner to compare with them. The pace men, Cowans, shabbily treated by the England selectors, Williams, Hughes and Daniel were a great strength although their bowling was not always as intelligent as it should have been. If one has to select one player, however, as the key to Middlesex's strength, it must be Clive Radley. He is the perfect county performer, consistent and unflappable. He saw Middlesex through some sticky patches. It is worth remembering that the champions managed only two wins in their last nine matches and that the basis of their success came in what was achieved by the end of July.

Hampshire came so close and narrowly failed. Temperament, as much as anything, is their weakness. They have not yet learned to believe in success. Marshall and Tremlett were outstanding and Maru surprised his critics, but, in spite of

Warwickshire C.C.C. First-Class Matches – Batting, 1985	*v.* Essex (Chelmsford) 27–29 April		*v.* Glamorgan (Edgbaston) 8–10 May		*v.* Surrey (Edgbaston) 22–24 May		*v.* Worcestershire (Worcester) 25–27 May		*v.* Northamptonshire (Northampton) 29–31 May		*v.* Somerset (Taunton) 1–4 June		*v.* Hampshire (Edgbaston) 8–11 June		*v.* Leicestershire (Hinckley) 12–14 June	
T.A. Lloyd	68	32	160	—	34	46	13	8*	28	0	61	7			8*	6
R.I.H.B. Dyer	53	0	80	—	48	64	45	0	10	4	33	63*	0	4	1*	9
K.D. Smith	4	9	42	—									16	27		
A.I. Kallicharran	12	32			6	76	63	—	152*	11	36	89	0	5	—	36
D.L. Amiss	10	5	86	2*	57	0	100*	—	83	140	81	14*	15	57	—	14
G.W. Humpage	0	0	40	0	70	55*	0	—	18*	123*			14	45	—	3
P.A. Smith	37	0	3	—	31	5	9	—	—	24	93	—	24	11	—	16
A.M. Ferreira	0	61	4	18*	36*	19	43	—	—	1	101*	—	36	22	—	17
C.M. Old	41	19	—	—	0	10*	7	—								
G.C. Small	1	1	26	—	2*	—	0	—	—	2*	3	—	9*	13*	—	25
N. Gifford	3*	17*	—	—	—	—	8	—	—	—	0*	—	0	—	—	6*
S. Wall			20*	—					—	—	1	—	0	3*	—	7
D.S. Hoffman					—	—	13*	4*	—	—	0	—	2	—	—	0
G.A. Tedstone											22	—				
W. Morton																
A.R.K. Pierson																
G.J. Lord																
T.A. Munton																
Asif Din																
C. Lethbridge																
S. Monkhouse																
D.A. Thorne																
Byes					10				2	10	1			1		5
Leg-byes	8	1	6		2	9	5	2	7	6	6	5	7	4	1	7
Wides			1	2	2	1	2	1			1	1	1		5	
No-balls	1	1	4		2		7	1	1		3	2	3	6	1	9
Total	238	178	472	22	300	285	315	16	301	321	442	181	127	198	16	160
Wickets	10	10	8	1	7	6	9	1	3	6	9	2	10	7	0	10
Result	L		D		W		D		D		D		D		L	
Points	6		8		23		7		8		6		3		0	

Warwickshire C.C.C. First-Class Matches – Batting, 1985	*v.* Oxford University (Oxford) 15–18 June		*v.* Zimbabwe (Edgbaston) 22–25 June		*v.* Lancashire (Old Trafford) 26–28 June		*v.* Northamptonshire (Edgbaston) 29 June–2 July		*v.* Sussex (Hove) 6–9 July		*v.* Lancashire (Edgbaston) 10–12 July	
T.A. Lloyd	123	58	57	3	6	62	14	0	15	63	10	91
R.I.H.B. Dyer	2	12	109*	7	68	55	44	44	8	38	1	28
K.D. Smith	0	21*			0	1						
A.I. Kallicharran									2	6	3	56
D.L. Amiss	125	0	86	18*	12	0	28	36	31	22	1	31
G.W. Humpage	13	29	45*	76	75	31	15	23	159	10	0	25
P.A. Smith	29	3					4	3	61	14*	48	15
A.M. Ferreira	58*	32*	—	22	4	10	1	0			14	42*
C.M. Old												
G.C. Small					6	0	27	31*	—	—	15	7
N. Gifford					1*	—	1	11	—	—	4	3
S. Wall	3	—	—	—	28	1*	0	28				
D.S. Hoffman	—	—	—	—			0*	1	—	—	0	5*
G.A. Tedstone												
W. Morton	3	—	—	—								
A.R.K. Pierson	3*	—	—	2*	2	—					9*	11
G.J. Lord			—	8								
T.A. Munton			—	—								
Asif Din					15	43*	60	0	38*	0		
C. Lethbridge									15	22*		
S. Monkhouse												
D.A. Thorne												
Byes		5	2	3	4	1	5	2	1	4	4	8
Leg-byes	1	4	9		7	14	10	2	11	6	7	18
Wides	1				1	2	1			1	3	3
No-balls	10	2			10	6	2		2		3	8
Total	371	166	308	139	239	226	212	181	343	186	122	351
Wickets	8	5	2	5	10	7	10	10	7	6	10	9
Result	W		D		D		L		D		W	
Points	—		—		6		6		5		20	

Catches 80 – G.W. Humpage (ct 76/st 4)
24 – D.L. Amiss
19 – R.I.H.B. Dyer
14 – A.M. Ferreira
9 – P.A. Smith and N. Gifford
7 – G.C. Small
6 – A.I. Kallicharran
5 – T.A. Lloyd and S. Wall
3 – A.R.K. Pierson, D.S. Hoffman and W. Morton

the impressive batting, the county seems short of championship talent because they still lack sufficient depth in their bowling resources.

For Gloucestershire, the tale was different. They were lacking some substance in batting and with Romaines and Stovold off form, more and more responsibility was placed on Athey and Bainbridge. Curran, the discovery of the season, if such a term can be applied to a Zimbabwe international, was an all-rounder of highest quality. He gave fine support to pace men Walsh and Lawrence and we saw a rejuvenated Gloucestershire whose title hopes really vanished when they lost to Hampshire and Essex in the same week. Third place was, perhaps, less than they deserved, but it was some consolation for David Graveney who had weathered a winter storm to lead his side to new heights and had achieved much himself.

Kim Barnett's leadership of Derbyshire promises to take them to a new era although the batting will need more stability and there were signs of a revival under Ontong at Glamorgan. Thomas and Maynard will be closely scrutinised next year as will the reshaped Yorkshire attack. Things are beginning to settle in the White Rose county and if consistency could be achieved, they might even challenge the leaders again. Lancashire suffered key players out of form all season and will hope for better next year. Watkinson and Makinson could be the hopes for future glory.

One wonders what Lancashire supporters feel when they look at the record of Neal Radford whom the county rejected and allowed to go to Worcestershire. He bowled quite magnificently and, for many, was the cricketer of the year. There was a new look about Worcestershire. Hick is an exciting player and D'Oliveira is rich in promise although I wish he were not being asked to open. Whether there is quite enough substance in either the batting or the bowling to take the county to honours is doubtful.

Nottinghamshire failed to live up to the hopes forwarded the previous season. Robinson is a wonderful player and he and Broad a fine opening pair. Randall, the Britannic Assurance Player of the Year, rightly so, smiled runs and joy wherever he went. Johnson, until his illness, looked promising and Martindale made an impressive start. At Lord's, in the NatWest Final, in spite of Randall's marvellous innings, their weaknesses were exposed – below par fielding and a lack of real support bowling for the incomparable Hadlee.

Surrey flattered to deceive, but there is a lot of batting talent at The Oval. It could be argued that Gray was a better

v. Nottinghamshire (Nuneaton) 13–16 July	v. Somerset (Edgbaston) 24–26 July	v. Derbyshire (Edgbaston) 27–30 July	v. Surrey (The Oval) 31 July–2 August	v. Yorkshire (Edgbaston) 3–6 August	v. Glamorgan (Cardiff) 10–13 August	v. Kent (Canterbury) 14–16 August	v. Gloucestershire (Cheltenham) 17–20 August	v. Worcestershire (Edgbaston) 24–27 August	v. Essex (Edgbaston) 31 Aug.–3 Sept.	v. Derbyshire (Chesterfield) 11–13 September	v. Middlesex (Edgbaston) 14–17 September	*M*	*Inns*	*NOs*	*Runs*	*H/S*	*Av*
94 17								22 44	9 —	11 0	32 28	18	34	2	1230	160	38.43
2 49	106 4	— —	2 2	10 —	0 —	59 8	9 10	2 10	26 —	6 27	52 28	26	46	3	1242	109*	28.88
												5	9	1	120	42	15.00
8 38	48 51*	— —	23 7	81 —	0 —	108 1	34 20	7 12	5 —	6 0	18 0	21	35	2	1052	152*	31.87
117 25	14 —	— —	4 3	103* —	77 —	2 3	14 45	2 27	1 —	3 16	6 39	26	44	5	1555	140	39.87
29 56*	33 —	— —	27 7	31 —	36 —	52 34	0 45	44* 1	49 —	2 36	1 8	25	42	6	1360	159	37.77
51 9	62 —	— —	50 4	9* —	34 —	1 22	38 8	3 12	28* —	2 31	1 20	24	37	3	815	93	23.97
32 26*	4 —	— —	0 0	— —	3 —	34* 41*	4 34*	1 22	10 —	0 17	34 2	25	38	10	805	101*	28.75
				— —	33 —	12* —						7	7	2	122	41	24.40
5 —				— —	6 —	— —	7* 10	0 21*	2 —	25 15	26* 0	21	27	8	285	31*	15.00
17* —	0 —	— —	26 4	— —	1* —	— —	4 0	7 0	0 —	4 11*	0 4	24	25	8	132	26	7.76
								0 3		9* 4	4 17*	12	16	5	128	28	11.63
— —	0 —	— —	0 12					0 2	0 —			17	15	4	39	13*	3.54
												1	1	—	22	22	22.00
												2	1	—	3	3	3.00
14* —	2* —	— —	3 9*	— —	4 —	9 17*	2 3					12	14	7	90	17*	12.85
	9 17*	— —	2 7	199 —	4 —	7 0	0 18					8	11	1	271	199	27.10
												1	—				—
									4 —	44 89	3 29	6	11	2	325	89	36.11
	47 —	— —										3	3	1	84	47	42.00
			2* 5									1	2	1	7	5	7.00
							0 0					1	2	—	0	0	0.00
2 5	5 2			1	9	1 4	4			4 1							
10 7	4		5	14	5	5 2	10 2	3	6	4	4 4						
1 2	4		3	1			7	1	2	3							
2 4			3	7	8	10 6	1 9	2		7 11	6 5						
384 238	338 74		147 63	456	220	300 138	127 211	94 154	142	123 265	187 184						
8 5	10 1		10 10	4	10	7 6	10 10	10 10	10	10 10	10 10						
D	D	D	L	D	D	D	L	L	D	L	L						
8	7	3	3	8	2	8	4	4	2	3	3						

2 – G.A. Tedstone (ct 1/st 1)
and Asif Din
1 – C.M. Old, K.D. Smith and sub

acquisition for them than Clarke. The sadness that one felt at Surrey, however, was at the decline and departure of Geoff Howarth. He has been a great Test captain and the fates have not smiled on him kindly.

Sussex were a bitter disappointment and one hopes that with a revitalised administration and committee, they may offer a stronger challenge and come in from the cold where they seem to lurk alone at the moment. The same could really be said of Northants whose bowling resources are limited and still seem one of the most unenterprising of counties.

Warwickshire and Leicestershire, in spite of a great triumph in the Benson and Hedges Cup, had poor seasons. Three leading players left Leicestershire at the end of the season and the winter may be a time for a self-examination in the Leicestershire camp. As Gower was away on Test duty, the team responsibility fell mainly on Willey and it may be questioned whether or not he is the best man for the job although his own performances were excellent. His play in the Benson and Hedges Final was, indeed, match winning.

Kent had a poor time except for a brief mid season period and there is fear that so much of what seemed exciting young talent will fail to flourish. Simon Hinks was impressive, but there is not too much strength in bowling on the horizon.

For a side whose captain hit more sixes than anyone has ever done in a season and averaged 91, and who had, in Viv Richards, the batsman who topped the first-class averages, Somerset were an enigmatic disaster. At times, they looked absolutely dreadful and it was no surprise that they finished bottom of the championship. Garner was not quite himself and Davis, as well as being injured, had a very disappointing season. In spin there was hope. Coombs, in three matches, returned splendid figures and Vic Marks carried the burden on the side with his usual cheefulness.

Cricketers had much to contend with for the weather was awful, but from the rain they still shaped an exciting summer of cricket. At Test level and at county level, it was played in the best possible spirit, and when one reads of, and sees, the disasters and obscenities that beset the world every day, we should be thankful that there are still men in white flannels who bring us as much pleasure and happiness as they did in the summer of 1985.

Warwickshire C.C.C. First-Class Matches — Bowling, 1985	G.C. Small	C.M. Old	A.M. Ferreira	P.A. Smith	N. Gifford	S. Wall	D.S. Hoffman	T.A. Lloyd	Asif Din
v. Essex (Chelmsford)	17–1–56–3	19.2–6–68–6	18–3–76–1						
27–29 April	20–2–56–2	21–5–78–1	17–0–80–1	7.5–0–60–1	2–0–5–1				
v. Glamorgan (Edgbaston)	15–4–44–2	7–4–15–1	19–3–66–2	8–0–47–1	6–2–12–0	20.2–5–59–4			
8–10 May	31–8–84–5		26.1–5–77–3	10–3–31–0	8–5–5–0	20–4–42–2			
v. Surrey (Edgbaston)	22–1–66–5	23–4–81–1	22–2–89–1		19–10–33–0		14–0–65–0		
22–24 May	5–0–17–0	7–0–32–0	14–3–57–0	1–0–8–0	10–2–28–0		6–1–25–0	14–1–62–3	
v. Worcestershire (Worcester)	20–6–53–3	17–6–35–2	20.5–5–55–2		11–6–19–2		10–2–37–1		
25–27 May									
v. Northamptonshire	18–4–68–1		20.5–2–81–4		33–16–68–1	14–0–67–2	6–1–11–1		
(Northampton) 29–31 May	11–2–39–1		8–4–18–0	6–0–34–3	32–5–99–3	15–0–71–0	15–1–68–1	1–0–1–0	
v. Somerset (Taunton)	16–3–70–1		23–0–121–2	11–0–73–0	18–1–135–1	18–3–72–0	14–0–85–1		
1–4 June	8–0–31–2			9–1–43–0		5–2–7–1	2–0–12–0	16–0–64–1	
v. Hampshire (Edgbaston)	18–3–84–0		11–2–68–1	13–1–55–1	34–9–89–4	9–1–37–1	25–3–85–1		
8–11 June									
v. Leicestershire (Hinckley)						5–2–11–0	5.1–2–3–1		
12–14 June	15–3–56–1		16.4–0–54–3		21–7–30–1		4–0–15–1		
v. Oxford University			19–2–40–1	3–0–13–0		18–2–49–2	11–5–24–1		
(Oxford) 15–18 June			14–3–37–2			15–1–63–3	16–6–22–1		
v. Zimbabwe (Edgbaston)			7–4–3–1			11–3–29–2	6–2–15–0		
22–25 June			9–2–48–2			14–2–42–3	6.3–1–18–0		
v. Lancashire (Old Trafford)	23–6–71–4		29.4–10–43–5		15–5–28–1	21–1–44–0			
26–28 June	12–2–49–0		17–6–41–5		19–11–23–3	7–1–34–0			2–1–4–0
v. Northamptonshire	15.3–2–45–5		17–3–53–3		1–0–1–0	11–3–36–2			
(Edgbaston) 29 June–2 July	23–2–65–1		12–4–20–3	8–0–48–0	34–7–69–3	5–0–21–0	14–1–38–2		1.2–0–2–1
v. Sussex (Hove)	16–3–68–0			17–2–68–2	30–9–90–0		17–5–74–0		2–1–1–0
6–9 July	12–3–47–0			5–1–25–0	11–3–33–1		14–1–69–1		
v. Lancashire (Edgbaston)	17–6–38–2		21–3–35–3	11–2–25–4	6–2–4–0		10–1–30–1		
10–12 July	30–6–82–3		24–7–64–4	5–1–24–0	29–14–52–2		22–7–52–1		
v. Nottinghamshire (Nuneaton)	24–0–78–3		20–1–80–1	2–0–10–0	19.2–4–38–2		20–2–100–4		
13–16 July	9–3–24–1		8–1–50–0		20–4–67–3		11–3–53–2		
v. Somerset (Edgbaston)			24–10–61–4	9–2–19–0	1.5–0–5–1		16–2–53–3		
24–26 July			9–4–15–0	7–2–33–0	42–20–128–4		5–0–33–0		
v. Derbyshire (Edgbaston)			18–3–54–1	14–1–66–1	36–11–81–2		16–4–30–2		
27–30 July									
v. Surrey (The Oval)			18–1–85–4	13–1–69–1	25–6–74–1		19–1–77–2		
31 July–2 August									
v. Yorkshire (Edgbaston)	17.5–2–42–4	12–2–40–1	18–3–54–2	15–1–77–3	2–1–9–0				
3–6 August	19–2–47–0	29–6–69–1	19–4–58–0	10–2–30–2	9–2–23–1				
v. Glamorgan (Cardiff)	11.1–3–19–1	12–3–30–0	9–2–27–1		9–4–14–0				
10–13 August									
v. Kent (Canterbury)	8–0–20–2	5–1–18–0	19–3–56–3	6–1–27–1	10.4–3–26–3				
14–16 August	1–0–1–0			0.3–0–3–0					
v. Gloucestershire (Cheltenham)	21–3–80–5		22–1–85–3	11–1–80–2					
17–20 August	9–4–20–1		9–0–27–2	1–0–12–0	1–0–14–0				
v. Worcestershire (Edgbaston)	15–7–24–5		14.2–4–40–3			15–5–34–2	5–2–11–0		
24–27 August	25–4–97–2		29–6–83–1		15–5–28–0	19–2–57–0	10–2–34–1		
v. Essex (Edgbaston)	18–5–67–3		14–4–43–0	5–0–23–0	7–4–10–0		7–0–21–1		
31 August–3 September									
v. Derbyshire (Chesterfield)	22–8–46–0		4–0–16–0	25–2–121–4	27–2–73–1	29–4–88–4			
11–13 September			4–3–13–0			4.5–0–23–0			
v. Middlesex (Edgbaston)	28–5–96–1		29–7–94–3	4–0–19–0	48–8–128–5	25–3–87–0			
14–17 September									
	592.3–113–1850–69 *av.* 26.81	152.2–37–466–13 *av.* 35.84	673.3–130–2167–77 *av.* 28.14	237.2–24–1143–26 *av.* 43.96	611.5–188–1541–46 *av.* 33.50	301.1–44–973–28 *av.* 34.75	326.4–55–1160–29 *av.* 40.00	31–1–127–4 *av.* 31.75	5.2–2–7–1 *av.* 7.00

a A.I. Kallicharran 11.4–0–56–0

b T.A. Munton 7–0–16–0
G.T. Lord 5–0–19–0

c T.A. Munton 2–0–19–0
d S. Monkhouse 17–2–61–1

W. Morton	A.R.K. Pierson	C. Lethbridge	*Byes*	*Leg-byes*	*Wides*	*No-balls*	*Total*	*Wkts*
			2	10	4	4	212	10
			5	9		9	293	6
			2	8	1	4	253	10
			4	12	1	6	255	10
				13	1	2	347	7
			6			1	235	3
			3	12	6	2	214	10
			1	7	2	2	303	10
				9	1	2	339	9
			1	9	1	8	566	5
				13		4	226	5a
			1	14	2	9	433	8
				1		1	15	1
			2	5			162	6
36–7–98–2	20–7–33–2		3	6	12		266	8
5–0–21–0	21–1–92–3		9	6	2	4	250	10
5–0–40–0	11–2–33–1		1	3	1		159	5b
	14–1–89–1		9	6		1	231	6c
	6–2–15–0			6	3	6	207	10
	3–1–4–0		4	6		4	165	8
			1	6	2	3	142	10
			3	16	3	2	282	10
		19–2–94–1	1	9	2	15	405	3
		11–0–47–0		7	2	3	228	2
			6	10		6	148	10
	6–0–30–0		4	13	1	2	321	10
			2	5	1	2	313	10
	2–0–10–0			2	3	1	206	6
		19–4–62–2	4	3	7	1	207	10
	34–8–164–1	4–0–17–0	10	18	2		418	6
	24–7–57–0	12–1–43–2	3	10	3	10	344	8
	9–0–45–0			2	1	13	413	9d
				6		18	228	10
			4	6		12	237	4
	2–1–2–0		1	4			97	2
	3–0–13–0			4		14	164	10
							4	0
			1	7	1	17	253	10
			5	8	5		86	3
				6		1	115	10
				19	1	2	318	4
				6	3	6	170	5
				10	1	6	354	9
					3		36	0
				21		8	445	10
46–7–159–2 *av.* 79.50	155–30–587–8 *av.* 73.37	65–7–263–5 *av.* 52.60						

First-Class Averages

BATTING	M	Inns	NOs	Runs	HS	Av	100s	50s
I.V.A. Richards	19	24		1836	322	76.50	9	6
G. Boycott	20	34	12	1657	184	75.31	6	9
G.A. Gooch	21	33	2	2208	202	71.22	7	9
I.T. Botham	19	27	5	1530	152	69.54	5	9
Imran Khan	14	21	8	890	117*	68.46	1	6
M.P. Maynard	4	3		198	102	66.00	1	1
Younis Ahmed	22	30	8	1421	177	64.59	5	4
Javed Miandad	20	29	6	1441	200*	62.65	4	8
R.T. Robinson	18	31	4	1619	175	59.96	6	9
C.L. Smith	23	39	4	2000	143*	57.14	7	10
J.G. Wright	11	16	2	797	177*	56.92	2	4
M.W. Gatting	23	34	5	1650	160	56.89	3	13
P. Bainbridge	24	38	9	1644	151*	56.68	4	11
C.E.B. Rice	20	33	8	1394	171*	55.76	4	6
D.I. Gower	21	29	2	1477	215	54.70	6	3
W.N. Slack	26	43	8	1900	201*	54.28	4	11
D.W. Randall	25	47	7	2151	117	53.77	5	14
M.A. Lynch	25	39	7	1714	145	53.66	7	6
C.T. Radley	27	38	12	1375	200	52.88	3	8
G.A. Hick	17	25	1	1265	230	52.70	4	3
D.A. Thorne	12	20	3	849	124	49.94	1	8
R.C. Ontong	26	30	7	1121	130	48.73	2	8
C.H. Lloyd	4	7	1	288	131	48.00	1	1
G.D. Barlow	20	32	4	1343	141	47.96	6	2
G.D. Mendis	25	43	6	1756	143*	47.45	6	6
D.L. Bairstow	26	35	10	1181	122*	47.24	3	3
G.S. Clinton	18	32	6	1225	123	47.11	3	7
N.R. Taylor	16	25	7	843	120*	46.83	3	3
C.W.J. Athey	24	38	7	1442	170	46.51	5	7
D.M. Smith	19	28	4	1113	112	46.37	3	7
P. Willey	23	32	4	1292	147	46.14	3	6
P.M. Roebuck	22	23	5	1255	132*	44.82	2	7
C.J. Richards	22	27	12	665	75*	44.33		3
K.A. Hayes	5	7		310	117	44.28	1	2
P.A. Neale	25	42	10	1411	152*	44.09	3	7
T.E. Jesty	24	36	8	1216	141*	43.42	4	5
R.N. Kapil Dev	12	21	2	816	100	42.94	1	5
R.A. Smith	26	44	8	1533	140*	42.58	3	6
A.M. Green	25	43	4	1646	133	42.20	3	10
J.C.M. Atkinson	6	5	1	167	79	41.75		1
M.D. Moxon	23	36	1	1447	168	41.34	4	6
C.G. Greenidge	19	32	2	1236	204	41.20	2	8
A.J. Lamb	19	26	4	903	122*	41.04	2	5
J.D. Love	21	28	5	937	106	40.73	1	6
A.C. Storie	7	12	2	407	106	40.70	1	3
B.C. Broad	25	47	3	1786	171	40.59	2	14
K.J. Barnett	26	41	2	1568	134*	40.20	4	7
D.L. Amiss	26	44	5	1555	140	39.87	5	7
N.H. Fairbrother	25	39	4	1395	164*	39.85	3	7
D.M. Ward	6	10	3	279	143	39.85	1	
M.C.J. Nicholas	26	41	5	1419	146	39.41	3	8
D.A. Banks	6	7	2	196	76	39.20		2
S.T. Jefferies	4	7		274	93	39.14		3
P.R. Downton	22	29	7	856	104	38.90	1	7
R.J. Bailey	26	38	7	1194	107*	38.51	2	7
T.A. Lloyd	18	34	2	1230	160	38.43	2	8
W. Larkins	25	40		1534	163	38.43	3	4
K.D James	8	11	4	268	124	38.28	1	
S.P. Henderson	7	11	3	306	111	38.25	1	1
A. Needham	25	37	5	1223	138	38.21	3	5
G. Cook	24	38	4	1295	126	38.08	1	9
N.F.M. Popplewell	18	30	2	1064	172	38.00	1	7
R.O. Butcher	26	38	6	1210	120	37.81	1	9
G.W. Humpage	25	42	6	1360	159	37.77	2	6
M.R. Benson	24	43	3	1501	162	37.52	3	11
P. Whiticase	3	5	1	149	55*	37.25		1
R.A. Harper	24	28	7	763	127	36.33	1	3
J.C. Balderstone	25	40	5	1271	134	36.31	2	6
I.J. Gould	24	25	8	616	101	36.23	1	4
G.J. Toogood	9	15	1	507	149	36.21	1	2
B.R. Hardie	26	45	7	1374	162	36.15	4	4
T.A. Cotterell	9	12	4	289	69*	36.12		1
Asif Din	6	11	2	325	89	36.11		2

BATTING	M	Inns	NOs	Runs	HS	Av	100s	50s
C.J. Tavare	23	40	6	1225	150*	36.02	3	4
J.J. Whitaker	25	34	3	1103	109	35.58	3	5
J.J.E. Hardy	16	25	4	742	107*	35.33	1	3
B.F. Davison	24	35	7	984	111	35.14	1	5
G.S. le Roux	18	16	4	421	61	35.08		2
G.R. Cowdrey	6	9	2	242	53	34.57		2
D.E. East	26	32	6	889	131	34.19	2	4
N.A. Felton	18	27		922	112	34.14	1	7
S.G. Hinks	26	48	3	1536	117	34.13	1	10
P.W.G. Parker	16	28	4	818	105	34.08	1	5
K.S. McEwan	26	42	4	1293	121	34.02	3	6
G. Monkhouse	16	14	8	203	47	33.83		
N.J. Lenham	11	16	2	473	89	33.78		3
D.G. Aslett	13	23	1	732	174	33.27	2	1
K.R. Brown	8	11	2	298	102	33.11	1	1
I.P. Butcher	25	39	3	1192	120	33.11	1	8
V.P. Terry	25	41	2	1284	148*	32.92	2	10
R.J. Hadlee	19	29	11	592	73*	32.88		5
K.W.R. Fletcher	23	28	7	688	78*	32.76		7
A.R. Butcher	26	46	3	1407	126	32.72	2	5
C.S. Cowdrey	20	36	3	1079	159	32.69	2	4
A.I. Kallicharran	21	35	2	1052	152*	31.87	2	6
T.S. Curtis	26	45	2	1365	126*	31.74	1	12
R.A. Cobb	16	23	4	601	78	31.63		4
A.J.T. Millier	12	20	4	506	78	31.62		3
J.D. Carr	11	16	1	474	115	31.60	2	2
A.J. Stewart	23	36	4	1009	158	31.53	1	5
J.F. Steele	11	12	3	283	100*	31.44	1	
R.G. Williams	21	31	3	880	118	31.42	2	4
J.G. Wyatt	17	26		816	145	31.38	2	2
E.A.E. Baptiste	23	36	5	972	82	31.35		6
P. Johnson	21	34	4	933	118	31.10	1	6
D.J. Makinson	15	21	9	372	58*	31.00		1
D.W. Varey	21	34	3	960	112	30.96	1	2
C.M. Wells	26	37	6	960	100*	30.96	1	3
R.E. Hayward	9	12	3	278	100*	30.88	1	1
S.N. Hartley	17	20	2	554	108*	30.77	1	3
G.C. Holmes	27	40	3	1129	112	30.51	2	7
V.J. Marks	26	34	5	885	82	30.51		7
R.J. Harden	12	17	5	366	107	30.50	1	1
J.W. Lloyds	25	33	6	818	101	30.29	1	5
A. Hill	10	14	3	333	120	30.27	1	1
P.E. Robinson	13	16	1	450	79	30.00		3
T.M. Tremlett	24	29	14	450	102*	30.00	1	
B. Roberts	25	42	4	1128	100*	29.68	2	1
D.B. d'Oliveira	26	44	2	1244	139	29.61	2	6
T. Davies	26	25	8	503	75	29.58		2
D.P. Hughes	10	16	2	411	75*	29.35		3
D.J. Wild	17	22	4	525	80	29.16		2
M.J. Weston	19	30	1	845	132	29.13	1	3
R.I.H.B. Dyer	26	46	3	1242	109*	28.88	2	8
D.R. Turner	7	9	2	202	49*	28.85		
D.J.R. Martindale	9	14	3	317	104*	28.81	1	1
A.M. Ferreira	25	38	10	805	101*	28.75	1	2
G. Miller	21	31	5	744	105	28.61	1	4
P.G.P. Roebuck	9	15	3	343	82	28.58		1
J.E. Morris	18	27	1	722	109*	27.76	1	3
J.E. Emburey	25	25	4	581	68	27.66		4
J.F. Sykes	11	13	3	275	126	27.50	1	1
I.S. Anderson	19	35	3	876	94	27.37		7
R.J. Boyd-Moss	20	31	3	766	121	27.35	2	2
S.B. Hassan	3	5	1	109	34	27.25		
G.J. Lord	8	11	1	271	199	27.10	1	
R.M. Ellison	20	26	6	539	98	26.95		3
H. Morris	15	18	4	375	62	26.78		1
D.N. Patel	26	42	3	1042	88	26.71		5
J. Abrahams	25	39	4	932	101*	26.62	1	4
P.J. Prichard	21	34	4	779	95	25.96		5
R.J. Blakey	13	22	2	518	90	25.90		2
M.R. Chadwick	12	17	1	410	132	25.62	1	1
S.J. Rhodes	26	34	13	538	58*	25.61		1
J.D. Birch	14	23	7	409	68*	25.56		2
A.L. Jones	19	27	2	636	80	25.44		4
K.P. Tomlins	9	15	1	354	58	25.28		1
R.J. Parks	25	24	9	377	53*	25.13		2

BATTING	M	Inns	NOs	Runs	HS	Av	100s	50s
C. Gladwin	13	22	2	500	92*	25.00		2
R.A. Pick	13	15	5	250	63	25.00		1
K. Sharp	19	34	4	750	96	25.00		3
D.J. Capel	23	30	6	599	81	24.95		4
J.A. Hopkins	23	34	2	794	114*	24.81	1	3
M.D. Marshall	22	33	2	768	66*	24.77		5
M.A. Watkinson	19	29	1	692	106	24.71	1	4
M.A. Garnham	23	26	4	542	100	24.63	1	1
K.M. Curran	26	34	3	762	83	24.58		5
D.B. Pauline	13	18	2	392	77	24.50		3
K.R. Pont	10	15	3	294	62*	24.50		2
A. Sidebottom	11	11	3	196	55	24.50		1
B.C. Rose	5	9	1	196	81*	24.50		1
C.M. Old	7	7	2	122	41	24.40		
D.R. Pringle	23	31	4	654	121*	24.22	1	1
P.A. Smith	24	37	3	815	93	23.97		5
R.J. Doughty	11	12	2	239	65	23.90		2
M.S. Turner	10	12	6	143	24*	23.83		
M. Newell	7	13		309	74	23.76		2
P.B. Clift	22	26	5	495	106	23.57	1	1
P. Carrick	24	25	2	540	92	23.47		3
J.R.T. Barclay	22	17	6	257	37*	23.36		
P.G. Newman	20	29	3	604	115	23.23	1	3
A.P. Wells	23	33	7	600	102	23.07	1	1
N.E. Briers	23	29	4	576	129	23.04	1	1
M.A. Holding	12	19	1	413	80	22.94		3
A.E. Lea	8	15	2	298	47*	22.92		
R.J. Maru	23	19	9	227	62	22.70		1
M.R. Davis	18	20	6	315	40*	22.50		
W.R. Bristowe	5	8	1	156	42*	22.28		
P.W. Romaines	20	34	4	667	114*	22.23	1	4
N.F. Williams	22	21	4	378	67	22.23		1
D.J. Fell	9	16	1	332	109*	22.13	1	1
I.A. Greig	15	16	4	264	43	22.00		
A.W. Lilley	16	26	2	526	68*	21.50		3
A.A. Metcalfe	6	12		257	109	21.41	1	1
N.G. Cowley	13	14	4	213	51	21.30		1
I.R. Payne	7	6	1	106	37	21.20		
P.J. Newport	18	26	10	338	36	21.12		
R. Sharma	7	12	2	209	41*	20.90		
C.H. Dredge	15	13	7	124	31	20.66		
W.P. Fowler	10	14	1	266	79	20.46		2
C. Penn	8	7	2	102	50	20.40		1
A.P.E. Knott	19	24	5	379	87*	19.94		2
G.V. Palmer	9	12	3	179	43*	19.88		
P.J. Hartley	12	11	3	159	35	19.87		
A.W. Stovold	22	37	2	694	112	1982	2	2
D.G. Moir	8	9		178	46	19.77		
G.W. Johnson	11	16	4	237	30*	19.75		
M.R. Price	14	11	4	136	36	19.42		
A.J. Wright	9	16	3	249	47*	19.15		
J.G. Thomas	16	16	2	268	60*	19.14		1
D.A. Graveney	25	25	11	266	53*	19.00		1
R.S. Rutnagur	11	15	2	246	66	18.92		2
L. Potter	12	15	2	245	58	18.84		2
P.C. MacLarnon	7	10	1	168	56	18.66		1
J. Simmons	21	30	4	485	101	18.65	1	2
N. Phillip	4	7		129	50	18.42		1
P.A.C. Bail	5	9	2	127	78*	18.14		1
P.J.W. Allott	19	21	6	272	78	18.13		1
C.R. Andrew	8	15	1	253	66	18.07		2
S.R. Gorman	9	15	5	177	43	17.70		
E.E. Hemmings	21	22	5	297	56*	17.47		1
A.E. Warner	15	20	2	314	60	17.44		2
G. Fowler	16	25		428	88	17.12		1
R.L. Ollis	15	20	1	325	55	17.10		1
N.V. Radford	24	25	7	306	57*	17.00		1
D.A. Reeve	17	15	5	170	56	17.00		1
B.N. French	25	34	8	439	52*	16.88		1
D.A. Hagan	5	10	1	148	46	16.44		
N.A. Foster	15	14	2	197	63	16.41		1
C.D.M. Tooley	11	16		257	66	16.06		1
C.A. Walsh	21	18	6	189	37	15.75		
N.A. Mallender	24	25	8	267	52*	15.70		1
P.I. Pocock	24	18	6	183	41	15.25		

BATTING	M	Inns	NOs	Runs	HS	Av	100s	50s
G.C. Small	21	27	8	285	31*	15.00		
K.D. Smith	5	9	1	120	42	15.00		
J.D. Inchmore	16	9	2	100	24	14.28		
G.J. Parsons	16	16	4	170	32	14.16		
R.J. Finney	25	37	10	381	82	14.11		1
I. Folley	21	27	8	262	69	13.78		1
J.K. Lever	23	23	9	193	24*	13.78		
R.K. Illingworth	20	20	8	165	39*	13.75		
R.C. Russell	23	23	4	253	34	13.31		
T. Gard	25	25	4	279	47	13.28		
S.J. O'Shaughnessy	13	23	2	275	63	13.09		
P.H. Edmonds	23	23	6	221	29*	13.00		
P.A.J. de Freitas	9	12	3	117	30*	13.00		
D.J. Thomas	12	12	3	116	25*	12.88		
N.G.B. Cook	18	16	4	152	45	12.66		
B.J.M. Maher	14	18	6	150	46	12.50		
D.V. Lawrence	25	26	5	259	41	12.33		
J. Derrick	14	15	2	160	52	12.30		
T. Patel	9	17	4	159	47	12.23		
C. Maynard	19	27	5	266	43	12.09		
S. Wall	12	16	5	128	28	11.63		
K.E. Cooper	22	16	4	139	46	11.58		
C. Marples	11	15	5	114	34	11.40		
A.G. Davies	9	13	2	124	43*	11.27		
I.G. Swallow	10	11	2	101	25*	11.22		
G.R. Dilley	17	19	5	153	31	10.92		
P.W. Jarvis	14	16	2	151	28	10.78		
N.G. Cowans	24	17	4	130	22*	10.00		

(Qualification – 100 runs, average 10.00)

BOWLING	Overs	Mds	Runs	Wkts	Av	Best	5/inn	10/m
R.V.J. Coombs	93	27	268	16	16.75	5/58	1	
R.M. Ellison	432.1	113	1118	65	17.20	7/87	5	2
R.J. Hadlee	473.5	136	1026	59	17.38	8/41	2	
M.D. Marshall	692.3	193	1680	95	17.68	7/59	5	
G.E. Sainsbury	178	59	481	27	17.81	7/38	2	
C.A. Walsh	560.3	132	1706	85	20.07	7/51	4	1
Imran Khan	422.1	114	1040	51	20.39	5/49	2	
T.M. Tremlett	665.5	180	1620	75	21.60	5/42	2	
R.N. Kapil Dev	304.5	83	805	37	21.75	4/56		
M.A. Holding	354.5	67	1124	50	22.28	6/65	3	1
P.J.W. Allott	559.2	167	1328	58	22.89	6/71	3	
L.B. Taylor	566.5	141	1376	60	22.93	5/45	3	
N.G. Cowans	474.2	85	1676	73	22.95	6/31	6	
A.H. Gray	524	98	1816	79	22.98	8/40	6	1
K.M. Curran	469.5	103	1419	61	23.26	5/35	2	
J. Garner	295.1	77	739	31	23.83	5/46	1	
D.V. Lawrence	544.5	66	2093	85	24.62	7/48	5	
N.V. Radford	779.4	130	2493	101	24.68	6/45	4	
D.A. Graveney	410.5	133	1013	41	24.70	4/91		
R.J. Doughty	223.5	36	867	34	25.50	6/33	1	
I.L. Pont	115.5	15	485	19	25.52	5/103	1	
P.H. Edmonds	850.1	242	1942	76	25.55	6/87	2	
J.D. Inchmore	338.5	72	844	33	25.57	4/42		
K.E. Cooper	604.3	187	1566	61	25.67	7/10	2	
J.K. Lever	720.3	188	1995	77	25.90	6/47	6	
P.A.J. de Freitas	234.2	43	703	27	26.03	5/39	1	
R.J. Maru	701.5	187	1923	73	26.34	5/16	3	
P.J. Newport	362.2	57	1214	46	26.39	5/18	3	
M.W. Gatting	93.3	17	393	11	26.63	3/55		
G.A. Gooch	284.2	66	773	29	26.65	5/46	1	
G. Monkhouse	383.4	78	1068	40	26.70	5/61	1	
W.W. Daniel	575.1	89	2111	79	26.72	7/62	2	
G.C. Small	592.3	113	1850	69	26.81	5/24	5	
D.L. Underwood	807	290	1802	67	26.89	6/56	1	1
T.D. Topley	161.1	37	464	17	27.29	4/57		
J.W. Lloyds	180.1	42	575	21	27.38	5/37	1	
R.J. Finney	449.3	81	1453	53	27.41	7/61	4	
J.P. Agnew	445.4	89	1512	55	27.49	9/70	3	1
N.A. Foster	436.5	88	1434	52	27.57	5/40	4	
R.C. Ontong	585.5	145	1777	64	27.76	8/67	4	1
B.P. Patterson	364.3	59	1144	41	27.90	7/49	3	1
N.G. Cowley	247.5	60	699	25	27.96	3/17		
A.M. Ferreira	673.3	130	2167	77	28.14	5/41	2	1

BOWLING	Overs	Mds	Runs	Wkts	Av	Best	10/m	5/in
P. Willey	399.3	115	1017	36	28.25	6/43	3	
R.K. Illingworth	406.5	113	1046	37	28.27	7/50	2	1
G.S. le Roux	402.2	72	1132	40	28.30	6/46	2	
E.A.E. Baptiste	554.3	116	1661	58	28.63	6/42	2	
B.J. Griffiths	313.4	76	918	32	28.68	6/76	1	
S. Turner	121.5	25	321	11	29.18	4/36		
D.R. Pringle	604.1	146	1556	53	29.35	6/42	1	
J.E. Emburey	797.1	230	1737	59	29.44	6/35	2	
J.R.T. Barclay	300.4	55	913	31	29.45	6/78	2	
P. Carrick	712.3	185	1923	65	29.58	7/99	2	1
D.A. Reeve	475.5	107	1424	48	29.66	5/24	2	
P. Bainbridge	200	46	570	19	30.00	5/60	1	
P.W. Jarvis	371.5	53	1330	44	30.22	7/105	3	
K.J. Barnett	173.4	33	514	17	30.23	6/115	1	
N.F. Williams	490.2	69	1784	58	30.75	5/15	2	
P.B. Clift	595.3	169	1446	47	30.76	5/38	1	
O.H. Mortensen	340	75	1026	33	31.09	5/87	1	
C.E.B. Rice	284	82	779	25	31.16	4/24		
I.T. Botham	406.2	64	1376	44	31.27	5/109	1	
N.A. Mallender	521.4	98	1533	49	31.28	5/83	1	
P.G. Newman	400.2	76	1315	42	31.30	4/29		
I. Folley	456.3	113	1286	41	31.36	6/8	1	
M. Watkinson	420.1	94	1228	39	31.48	5/109	1	
J.G. Thomas	335.3	54	1232	39	31.58	4/47		
S.T. Jefferies	116.1	13	379	12	31.58	4/64		
D.J. Capel	384.3	63	1229	41	31.68	7/62	1	
P.A. Waterman	115	25	382	12	31.83	3/22		
N.S. Taylor	149	22	579	18	32.16	7/44	1	
K.B.S. Jarvis	530.4	115	1674	51	32.82	5/43	2	
S.J.W. Andrew	284	53	992	30	33.06	6/43	1	
C. Penn	124.4	17	466	14	33.28	4/63		
A.C.S. Pigott	184.4	39	633	19	33.31	3/22		
N. Gifford	611.5	188	1541	46	33.50	5/128	1	
G.R. Dilley	348.2	71	1075	32	33.59	5/53	2	
V.J. Marks	812.4	197	2421	72	33.62	8/17	4	2
D.J. Makinson	365.3	70	1079	32	33.71	5/60	1	
P.I. Pocock	576.2	131	1632	48	34.00	7/42	1	
A. Walker	251.4	51	786	23	34.17	4/38		
S.J. O'Shaughnessy	142	21	521	15	34.73	4/68		
S. Wall	301.1	44	973	28	34.75	4/59		
A.M.G. Scott	243.3	34	879	25	35.16	5/68	1	
A. Sidebottom	268.4	28	916	26	35.23	4/70		
D.B. Pauline	161.4	33	567	16	35.43	5/52	1	
C.M. Old	152.2	37	466	13	35.84	6/68	1	
P.M. Such	405.1	95	1152	32	36.00	5/73	1	
J.D. Carr	249.1	65	616	17	36.23	6/61	1	
R.A. Harper	772.3	187	2107	53	36.32	5/94	1	
D.N. Patel	442	117	1244	34	36.58	3/33		
L. Potter	258.4	67	772	21	36.76	4/87		
T.E. Jesty	144.2	28	517	14	36.92	2/32		
D.J. Thomas	354.4	62	1186	32	37.06	5/51	1	
C.H. Dredge	317.4	73	929	25	37.16	5/95	1	
I.A. Greig	283	58	931	25	37.24	5/80	1	
P.J. Hartley	315.5	40	1175	31	37.90	5/75	2	
R.J. Boyd-Moss	125.4	30	380	10	38.00	3/48		
S.R. Barwick	473.4	96	1375	36	38.19	7/43	1	
E.E. Hemmings	716.3	170	2103	55	38.23	6/51	2	
C.M. Wells	527.4	144	1457	38	38.34	4/76		
G.J. Toogood	209.2	44	691	18	38.38	8/52	1	1
K. Saxelby	429	102	1385	36	38.47	6/64	2	1
G.C. Holmes	347.3	85	1041	27	38.55	4/49		
J. Simmons	543.1	155	1457	37	38.56	4/55		
S.P. Hughes	266.2	43	932	24	38.83	5/64	1	
S.M. McEwan	177	29	635	16	39.68	3/47		
D.S. Hoffman	326.4	55	1160	29	40.00	4/100		
C. Shaw	417	95	1286	32	40.18	5/76	1	
S.C. Booth	396.2	112	1138	28	40.64	4/88		
R.G. Williams	312.2	75	979	24	40.79	5/34	1	
D.L. Acfield	588.4	130	1674	41	40.82	6/81	1	
M.J. Weston	273.5	72	777	19	40.89	3/37		
M.R. Price	258.4	62	697	17	41.00	4/97		
C.A. Connor	470.5	90	1467	35	41.91	4/62		
R.A. Pick	290	52	1096	26	42.15	4/51		
A.E. Warner	267.3	39	1013	24	42.20	5/51	1	

BOWLING	Overs	Mds	Runs	Wkts	Av	Best	10/m	5/in
K.D. James	177.4	43	635	15	42.33	6/22	1	
A.N. Jones	246	37	848	20	42.40	5/39	1	
G. Miller	385.2	78	1204	28	43.00	6/110	1	
D.G. Moir	186	48	517	12	43.08	3/102		
G.J. Parsons	356.2	76	1010	23	43.91	6/11	1	
P.A. Smith	237.2	24	1143	26	43.96	4/25		
C.E. Waller	381.5	117	882	20	44.10	7/61	1	
A. Needham	351.4	76	1017	23	44.21	5/42	1	
J.F. Sykes	191.5	42	575	13	44.23	3/58		
N.G.B. Cook	556.1	186	1332	30	44.40	4/59		
A.R. Butcher	157	34	449	10	44.90	3/43		
C.C. Ellison	223.5	58	591	13	45.46	3/76		
G.W. Johnson	156.3	24	501	11	45.54	5/78	1	
S.D. Fletcher	345.5	51	1253	26	48.19	4/91		
R.S. Rutnagar	189	25	728	15	48.53	5/112	1	
M.S. Turner	185.5	30	648	13	49.84	4/74		
S.J. Malone	174.1	23	654	13	50.30	5/38	1	
C.S. Cowdrey	210.1	29	756	15	50.40	3/5		
J. Derrick	226.1	39	706	14	50.42	4/60		
D.A. Thorne	176.1	34	664	13	51.07	4/64		
M.R. Davis	366	61	1249	24	52.04	4/83		
J.F. Steele	215.1	60	581	11	52.81	3/6		
G.J.F. Ferris	231.3	32	826	15	55.06	3/84		
I.G. Shallow	225	46	670	12	55.83	4/53		
M.P. Lawrence	341.5	65	1154	20	57.70	3/99		
L.L. McFarlane	257	42	1003	16	62.68	4/100		
J.D. Quinlan	189	37	635	10	63.50	4/76		
T.A. Cotterell	232.4	54	742	11	67.45	3/53		

(Qualification – 10 wickets)

LEADING FIELDERS

80 – G.W. Humpage (ct 76/st 4)
76 – D.E. East (ct 72/st 4)
73 – B.N. French (ct 66/st 7)
65 – R.C. Russell (ct 60/st 5)
62 – P.R. Downton (ct 57/st 5) and R.J. Parks (ct 58/st 4)
60 – M.A. Garnham (ct 53/st 7)
58 – D.L. Bairstow (ct 45/st 13)
57 – S.J. Rhodes (ct 54/st 3)
54 – A.P.E. Knott (ct 53/st 1)
50 – C. Maynard (ct 42/st 8)
49 – T. Davies (ct 44/st 5)
45 – C.J. Richards (ct 38/st 7)
40 – I.J. Gould (ct 36/st 4)
38 – T. Gard (ct 31/st 7)
36 – M.A. Lynch
34 – V.P. Terry
29 – A.J. Stewart (ct 28/st 1)
27 – G. Miller and W.N. Slack
26 – C.W.J. Athey
25 – G.A. Gooch and D. Ripley (ct 21/st 4)
24 – J.W. Lloyds, D.L. Amiss, D.W. Randall, R.O. Butcher and C. Marples (ct 23/st 1)
23 – S.G. Hinks
22 – B.R. Hardie, R.A. Harper, J.E. Emburey and P.H. Edmonds
21 – B. Roberts, B.J.M. Maher (ct 19/st 2) and D.B. d'Oliveira
20 – C.S. Cowdrey, I.P. Butcher, C.E.B. Rice and C.J. Tavare

SILK CUT CHALLENGE

World All-Rounders Tournament

20 and 21 September

at Arundel

Final positions –

1	C.E.B. Rice (South Africa)	243 pts
2	Imran Khan (Pakistan)	222 pts
3	R.J. Hadlee (New Zealand)	148 pts
4	I.V.A. Richards (West Indies)	92 pts
5	I.T. Botham (England)	38 pts
6	S.P. O'Donnell (Australia)	–5 pts
7	G.A. Gooch (England)	–63 pts

Women's Cricket
RACHAEL HEYHOE-FLINT

England's tour of Australia started with high hopes, with a splendid press call at Lord's and British Airways reception at the Westmoreland Hotel.

The England team had never lost a Test match since 1951 – but sadly apart from a superb win in the second Test in Adelaide and finishing very much on top in the first Test at Perth, England's overall record made extremely average reading. They lost their 24 year old unbeaten Test run in Gosford N.S.W. in the fourth encounter, were defeated again in the fifth in Bendigo Victoria – thus losing a series against any country for the first time in 36 years (Australia beat them 1–0 with two draws in 1949). In addition the three-match One Day International series resulted in a clean sweep for Australia.

Several factors contributed to England's downfall – some connected with the logistics of the tour and others just sheer facts of cricket life.

For the first time in the 50 year history between the two countries, the Tests were extended to four days and the series from 3 to 5 matches. A glance back over the match details in the previous 8 series between the two countries – which produced five wins for England, three for Australia and 16 draws – shows that many of those three day matches would have produced results had they been of four days duration.

Secondly, the tour was fairly compacted, for in the 61 days in Australia there were 33 days cricket, 11 days travelling or moving from private billets into hotels, and innumerable receptions and functions. This type of frenetic activity for a cricket touring team is inevitable but it was noticeable that after the half-way point of the tour was reached (when England were leading 2–1 in the Tests) the early spark and life in the fielding, bowling and batting had disappeared.

Early indications showed that England might encounter stronger opposition than in the last tour to Australia in 1968/69, for they lost the first two One Day games *v.* Western Australia but won the third one – but even at this early stage of the tour there was a frailty in England's middle order batting. The first Test in Perth however almost produced a win for England; Jackie Court's first innings 90 out of 290 was described by the press as unorthodox but effective. At the end of the second day, Australia looked well set on 196 for 4 but they were dismissed for 251 with Avril Starling picking up 3–40 to hasten the closure. The three top scorers for Australia, Peta Verco (36), Denise Emerson, Terry Alderman's sister with 84, and Jill Kennare (56) gave warning for future high scores.

A magnificent century by Janette Brittin (112) after early morning net coaching by Peter Carlstein, the ex-South African cricketer and now coach at the W.A.C.A. ground, enabled England to declare at 242 for 9, which left Australia a target of 281. Despite a fine 103 by Jill Kennare – also a lacrosse international – Australia were 209–8 which included 3 run outs and two wickets apiece for Avril Starling and

Helen Stother. Sharon Tredrea, Australia's captain who bowled faster than any other woman in the world, injured her achilles tendon in the Perth Test and was ruled out of the rest of the series. What disappointment for Australia – murmurs of relief from England – and Test veteran at 39, Raelee Thomspon, who had taken 6 wickets in the match, took on the captaincy.

The second Test at the attractive Adelaide Oval produced a remarkable win for England. They were dismissed for 91 in their first innings, mainly due to a fine spell of 4–22 by Karen Price, brought into this Test in place of the tall left arm seamer Denise Martin (WA). Denise Emerson's 121 helped Australia to an all out total of 262 – a lead of 171. England battled on the third day and part of the fourth to 296 all out with eight reaching double figures – including a belligerent 70 from Chris Watmough after her 68 minute duck in the first innings and a half century from Kent's wicketkeeper June Edney.

So Australia needed 126 to win with time-a-plenty, but what a shock followed – Australia slumped to 6 wickets for 5 runs with Starling and left arm spinner Gill McConway who shared the new ball wreaking havoc. Karen Price and Lyn Fullston lifted Australia to 73 but the sixth wicket saw the former depart for 51 brilliantly caught by Hodges off Starling. Finally Australia folded at 120 just five runs short with Starling 5–36 and McConway's 3–35 the crucial figures – and so on Christmas Eve England had won their first Test against Australia since 1963 – a splendid seasonal gift.

The Gabba in Brisbane hosted the third Test but a tame draw emerged with batting outweighing penetrative bowling. Jan Southgate top scorer in England's 275 with Test debutante Lyn Larsen – a leg spinner taking 4–33. Larsen also notched a fifty in her first innings to be matched by 59 from Lyndsay Reeler, another N.S.W. debutante in the series but Emerson stole the thunder with a graceful 84 in Australia's 326–9 declared. England safely overcame the deficit of 151 and were 204–7 at stumps – the major disappointment was the dismissal of Carole Hodges on 95 by Larsen for she richly deserved her century.

The fourth Test brought a disaster for England at the attractive Gosford ground north of Sydney. England won the toss for the fourth time and chose to field hoping that tidal fluctuation would cause a lot of early movement of the ball. It was a gamble which failed and Australia made 232–8 declared where the ever-consistent Emerson made yet another 50 – in fact Terry Alderman, out of favour with the men's selectors, was being referred to as the brother of Test cricketer Denise Emerson, such was the impact she was making in the media.

England were all out for 140 – Denise Martin, recalled for this match in place of the injured Price, bowled her left arm medium fast seamers splendidly and took 4–24 off 19 overs – Brittin made 45 but England collapsed from 66 for 0 wicket to 93 for 5, lost four wickets at 103, but Jan Aspinall 28 not out and Starling saved a bit of face with a last wicket stand of 37. England did well to restrict the opposition's scoring in the second innings to 153–9 declared, once again Starling proved most penetrative with 4–57 but despite a heroic 65 by Brittin in 315 minutes (she was eighth out at 120) and a stubborn 27 by Court for a fourth wicket stand of 54 – the target of 245 proved too great – and Australia were home by 117 runs. England lost their last 6 wickets for 26 runs. 'Lefty' Fullston captured 4–53 off 25 overs to spearhead Australia's first Test win over England for 33 years. It was a gamble to put Australia in, with England one up in the series, and the move was not really necessary, but it was a collective decision. Australia however, who had yet to bat first in any previous Test, were delighted to be given the chance – and they made the most of it.

So it came to the final Test at Bendigo – 100 miles north of Melbourne. The series was poised at 1–1; enormous media exposure had prevailed throughout the Tour and the stage was set for a grand finale, with radio, television and the sports press homing in on the town where women's cricket started in 1874, in the heart of the gold mining region. The townsfolk turned out in their thousands and there was a real carnival atmosphere, with the team being taken on 'a lap of honour' of the town by tram car, the day before the match.

Bendigo Oval hosted the 1962 MCC Team and the current groundsman, Ron Salter, bowled and toiled as Ken Barrington and Colin Cowdrey stuck memorable centuries. This England team were tired; they had just come through a non-stop spell of travelling and playing in Canberra and Sydney after the fourth Test but they felt they could lift themselves for the final onslaught; they made their first change in the Tests bringing in Jane Powell for her second Test appeareance – and her identical twin sister Jill who played for England in 1979 but who now lives in and plays for Western Australia, was in the crowd with proud parents who came out from England to support the Tour.

England won the toss (again). Australia had brought in Karen Reed (W.A.) for Wendy Napier (Victoria) into the middle over. England batted tentatively on the first day as though occupation of the crease was uppermost rather than run-gathering; and they were all out at 196; the only innings of fluency were from Hodges and Southgate but Australia's wily captain Thompson revelled in the batsmen's negative approach and beguiled the batsmen into giving her five wickets for 33 runs off 28 overs, her Test career best analysis, and she admitted she was lucky.

England battled throughout the second day in the hot sun, in front of a splendid crowd in 1,800 who filled the grassy banks. Jill Kennare back in form produced a marvellous 104, Emerson and Verco each reached the 40s and Australia went through to an hour in to the third day declaring at 285–8 – a lead of 89.

Two tragic run outs for Australia's first two wickets at 48 and 54 saw Brittin and Hodges back in the pavilion and the English struggle was on; by the close they led by just 51 runs with 5 wickets remaining.

Drama the next morning – 3 Australians and 2 English were ill with stomach upsets – and the Australians fielded three substitutes but even this could not help England's cause. Debbie Wilson, Australia's 19 year old pace hope was in fiery mood and felled Jackie Court with a bouncer whom she eventually bowled for a brave 41. Helen Stother at number 9 scored 20 – her highest of the tour but the close came at 204 – with three wickets each to Wilson and off spinner Verco. Australia had to make 116 to win off the remaining 59 overs (110 overs per day) and after a slow start they were home by 7 wickets with ten overs to spare after Kennare (one of the ill players) thrashed a quickfire 42 –

Worcestershire C.C.C. First-Class Matches – Batting, 1985	v. Middlesex (Lord's) 27–30 April		v. Gloucestershire (Worcester) 8–10 May		v. Australians (Worcester) 11–13 May		v. Oxford University (Oxford) 22–24 May		v. Warwickshire (Worcester) 25–27 May		v. Kent (Canterbury) 1–4 June		v. Glamorgan (Abergavenny) 8–11 June		v. Cambridge University (Cambridge) 12–14 June		v. Surrey (Worcester) 15–18 June		v. Yorkshire (Harrogate) 22–24 June		v. Middlesex (Worcester) 26–28 June		v. Yorkshire (Worcester) 29 June–2 July		v. Derbyshire (Worcester) 6–9 July		v. Gloucestershire (Gloucester) 10–12 July	
T.S. Curtis	8	5	3	24	76	10	0	—	66	—	0	15	30	51			126*	13	72	35	1	7	51	17	22	10	62	6
M.J. Weston	44	0	47	10	11	31	97	—	10	—	0	7	16	36			132	33	8	—	5	0	12	26	0	47	17	4
D.M. Smith	9	28	15	11	0	—			10	—	64	50*	55	—			49	—										
D.N. Patel	19	24	15	2	30	4	2	—	3	—	4	—	0	67			25	29	45	30*	48	6	32	78	88	43	9	4
P.A. Neale	8	2	19	21	108	13*			5	—	42	—	77	—			0	152*	38	36	18	12	4	58	46	102	46	4
D.B. D'Oliveira	73*	0	14	99	0	11	33	—	5	—	0	—	5	31			0	1	60	34	28	1	0	37	63	34	5	15
R.N. Kapil Dev	100	33	9	23					56	—	17	—	22	92					24	40*	49	38	44	9	16	3*	72	57
P.J. Newport	28*	1	18	23	29*	14*	18	—									3*	2*			6	18	23*	7*	0	—	0	5
S.J. Rhodes	—	0	9*	18	20*	—	0	—	7	—	37*	9	32*	7			—	0	3	—	46*	28	58*	20	0	—	19*	8
R.K. Illingworth	—	0*	3	6*	—	—	36	—	5	—	2	39*	6	15*			—	—	0	—	13	1	—	—	1	—	0	6
N.V. Radford	—	0	0	10	—	—			9	—	2	—	16	0*			—	—	4*	—	7	16*	—	10*	38	—	0	10
J.D. Inchmore					—	—			15*	—	23	—	18	—			—	—	—	—								
G.A. Hick							3	—																				
D.A. Banks							76	—							50*	—			21*	—	6	1	30	12				
S. Kimber							14*	—							—	—												
S.M. McEwan							13*	—																	0*	—	0	0*
H. Patel															39	—												
L. Smith															28	—												
M. Hussain															4	—												
P. Bent															14	—												
S.R. Lampitt															0	—												
D.J. Humphries															62*	—												
M. Scothern															—	—												
A.P. Pridgeon															—	—												
B. Barrett															—	—												
R.M. Ellcock																												
Byes	1	2			6		7		3		4	7	8	2	4		4	4		1	9	5	1		4	1	2	
Leg-byes	4	1	2	5	5	1	11		12		5	2	5	1	4		7	12	5	1	4	1	14	9	10	9	9	
Wides	3		1		2	4			6			1		2	4		1	5	2	1			1		7	2		4
No-balls	4	7	9	14	16	5			2		4	2	4	5	7		7	2	18	7	6	3	22	8		2	1	2
Total	301	103	164	266	303	93	310		214		204	132	294	309	216		354	253	300	185	246	137	292	291	295	253	242	125
Wickets	6	10	10	10	6	4	9		10		10	3	10	6	5		5	5	8	3	10	10	7	8	10	5	10	10
Result	L		L		D		W		D		W		D		D		D		D		L		D		L		L	
Points	8		5		—		—		5		22		3		—		5		7		2		11		7		4	

Catches 57 – S.J. Rhodes (ct 54/st 3), 21 – D.B. D'Oliveira, 18 – D.N. Patel, 11 – R.N. Kapil Dev, T.S. Curtis and D.M. Smith, 8 – R.K. Illingworth, 6 – G.A. Hick, 5 – P.A. Neale, 4 – N.V. Radford, J.D. Inchmore and M.J. Weston

including 6 boundaries – which earned her the real gold nugget pendant Player of the Match award.

The series went to Australia but the all round feeling of England's players was that they lost to a better all round side. A new trophy, the Peden/Archdale trophy, was inaugurated in honour of the first two captains in 1934 – Margaret Penden (Australia) and Betty Archdale.

Australia's cricket has boomed over the last ten years and Melbourne alone boasts 90 teams (England altogether only has 60!). Cricket for girls in schools is now growing; Junior (Kanga) Cricket is being promoted jointly for boys and girls; the Government is giving great financial backing; sponsors and the media are clamouring to support women's cricket. The Golden Jubilee Series between the two countries was marked by a splendid dinner at the Melbourne Cricket Ground – and six of the 1934/35 Australian team were present – and what marvellous characters they were.

Janette Brittin won the Benson and Hedges Player of the Series for her 42.90 innings average, four wickets and three catches but in her acceptance speech she praised Denise Emerson's higher total of runs (453) and average of 50.33.

The outlook for Australian Women's cricket is exciting; England must now return and rebuild and develop in preparation for the visit by India in 1986 and Australia in 1987.

Immediately after the England *v* Australia series, the Australia Women's Cricket Council hosted a three match One Day International Series against New Zealand for the Shell Trophy, in Melbourne.

Australia's veteran captain against England–Raelee Thompson had announced her retirement – and Sharon Tredrea for whom Thompson assumed the mantle after Tredrea's unfortunate calf injury in Perth) was still not fit. Thus Denise Alderman was chosen as captain against the Kiwis and her side included five uncappped players to gain experience. New Zealand were led by 22 year old Debbie Hockley who was so impressive on the tour of England in the summer of 1984. Australia won the series 2–1 and once again Emerson showed her class as one of the world's most consistent run-getters, finishing with an average of 51.33.

England's domestic summer saw the retirement of Sussex's Jan Southgate, England captain for just two years; Chris Watmough Surrey's captain and pugnacious bat who made her England debut in 1968 and made 16 Test and 34 One Day

v. Hampshire (Portsmouth) 13–16 July		v. Glamorgan (Worcester) 24–26 July		v. Sussex (Eastbourne) 27–30 July		v. Lancashire (Worcester) 3–6 August		v. Nottinghamshire (Trent Bridge) 10–13 August		v. Derbyshire (Buxton) 14–16 August		v. Essex (Worcester) 17–20 August		v. Warwickshire (Edgbaston) 24–27 August		v. Kent (Worcester) 28–30 August		v. Leicestershire (Leicester) 31 Aug.–3 Sept.		v. Somerset (Worcester) 4–6 September		v. Somerset (Taunton) 11–13 September		v. Northamptonshire (Worcester) 14–17 September		M	Inns	NOs	Runs	H/S	Av
6	8	41	3	4	54	0	33	43	20	—	—	15	—	7	5	12	97*	65	—	58	0	83	—	55	46	26	45	2	1365	126*	31.74
26	10															—	76	79	—	—	14*	40	—	—	7	19	30	1	845	132	29.13
112	87	102	32	62	34	67	15*	15	2	—	—	8	—	2	42*			48	—	0	—	61	—	104*	29	19	28	4	1113	112	46.37
38	0	45	24	29	0*	8	0	5	39	—	—	11	—	4	27	62*	4	69	—	—	1	41	—	—	28	26	42	3	1042	88	26.71
12	20	10	6	25	7*	3	3*	37	69	—	—	62	—	5	92*	35*	36	0	—	37*	55*	9	—	72*	5	25	42	10	1411	152*	44.09
10	31	51	7	139	49	30	14	8*	4	—	—	50	—	4	38	48	0	9	—	5	64	113	—	5	16	26	44	2	1244	139	29.61
		24	60			28	—			—	—															12	21	2	816	100	42.94
3	0*	12*	36	4*	—	5	—	24	14	—	—	17	—	28	—	—	—									18	26	10	338	36	21.12
3	6*	41*	39	4	—	8	—	10	6	—	—	1	—	15	30*	—	4*	13*	—	—	—	33*	—	—	4	26	34	13	538	58*	25.61
0*	—	—	0*	—	—	9	—	17*	6*	—	—	—	—													20	20	8	165	39*	13.75
8	0	—	8	—	—	57*	—	10	41	—	—	0	—	34	—			6*	—	—	—	10*	—	—	10	24	25	7	306	57*	17.00
		—	5	—	10	24	—					5*	—	0	—	—	—	—	—	—	—	—	—	—	0	16	9	2	100	24	14.28
				22	35			20	10	—	—	56	—	2	62	35	47	21	—	174*	2	38	—	128	12	11	16	1	667	174*	44.46
																—	—									6	7	2	196	76	39.20
																										2	1	1	14	14*	—
								5	0					7*	—	—	—	—	—	—	—	—	—	—	0*	10	8	5	25	13*	8.33
																										1	1	—	39	39	39.00
																										1	1	—	28	28	28.00
																										1	1	—	4	4	4.00
																										1	1	—	14	14	14.00
																										1	1	—	0	0	0.00
																										1	1	1	62	62*	—
																										1	—				—
																										1	—				—
																										1	—				—
3	—																									1	1	—	3	3	3.00
2		12	1	4		3			9							1		5			6	13		5	8	† D.B. D'Oliveira, retired hurt					
21	4	6	2	6	5	15	4	6	4			6		6	19	2	6	6		11	1	11		13	4	‡ R.K. Illingworth, absent ill					
1		1	1			2	1	1							1		1			1		1			5						
4		4	1	7	1	5		1	1					1	2	5	2	22		14	8	13		10	10						
249	166	349	225	306	195	264	70	202	225			231		115	318	200	273	343		300	151	466		392	184						
10	7	6	10	6	5	10	3	9†	10			9‡		10	4	3	5	7		3	4	7		3	10						
D		D		D		W		D		D		D		W		W		D		W		D		L							
6		8		8		23		6		1		6		20		22		8		21		8		5							

2 – D.A. Banks
D.J. Humphries and
P.J. Newport

1 – S.M. McEwan
S. Kimber and sub

Internationals appearances and Shirley Hodges wicket-keeper from 1968 to 1983 whose span of service is unrivalled by any other keeper in world women's cricket.

Hodges who made her debut for Sussex in 1960, played 44 times for England – 14 Tests, one two-day game against India and 29 One Day Internationals.

On the 1968–69 tour of Australia and New Zealand Hodges claimed 54 victims and playing against the West Indies at Canterbury in 1979 equalled the world record of 5 catches in one innings. In her One Day appearances Hodges did not concede one bye in 11 out of 29 games and in all those internationals only let a total of 36 byes go through.

Looking to the future, England host two series in successive summers. In 1986 India tour for the first time ever and will play three Four Day Tests and three One Day Internationals; in 1987 Australia are England's visitors and this tour marks 50 years of Test cricket between the two countries in England; it is dearly hoped that England will play one of the three One Day games at Lord's – they have only played one match there since the formation of the governing body in 1926 – and that was in 1976 when again Australia were the visiting team.

In 1988 Australia will stage the Fourth World Cup. Two interesting footnotes are that at the International Women's Cricket Council meeting in Melbourne in January 1985 Ireland and Denmark were admitted as full members; also it was agreed that in future all women cricketers would be referred to as batsmen (and no longer batswomen or batsperson!).

Book Reviews

All books that have been received by the editor are reviewed on the following pages.

GROWING UP WITH CRICKET. *Alan Gibson*: George Allen & Unwin: 179 pp, £8.95

In the last chapter of this book Alan Gibson writes that it has been said of him that he tells about *a day at the cricket*. It is an apt description of Gibson's reports in *The Times* and it is why they are so enchanting. On days when the batsmen bat and the bowlers bowl, which is more often than most of us like to tell, Alan Gibson still finds joy in reflecting on the English summer, the British Rail timetable, the bar and the barmaid. It is this essential humanity in his writing, founded upon the belief that cricket is neither the only thing nor the most important thing in life, that lifts Gibson above the rest of us mere mortals. He writes with ease and charm. His learning rests lightly, as it should on a cultured man, and the whole book throbs with a delight in living and being at the cricket even though cricket seems to have ceased to have given as much joy over the past twenty-five years as it once did. There is much in this book, about Hutton and cricket in the West, that Gibson has said before, but it still makes captivating reading and his three pages about Wally Hammond tell us more about that tortured man than a complete biography which was published last year managed to do. Perhaps the book becomes a little incestuous towards the end. Many would argue that there is more better cricket writing outside *The Times* now than there is in it. Woodcock remains a majestic wise master, but there are also writers like Matthew Engel, Scyld Berry and Michael Carey who represent wit, perception and compassion and deserve our notice. I suppose ultimately *Growing Up With Cricket* is not about cricket at all. It is about cricketers and men, which is what all good cricket books should be about. 'Sometimes,' writes Alan Gibson, 'I am glad of the chance to escape from a dull match to the bar, especially at Bristol when the Glorious Redheaded Imperturbable Pamela (known by the acronym of GRIP) is presiding. But the game still has its moments, and I look forward to a few more yet.' So do we Alan and we want to share them with you.

IT NEVER RAINS. *Peter Roebuck*: Unwin Paperbacks: 151 pp, £2.50
This is the paperback edition of the diary of the season which we reviewed last year. The book has been very well received in many quarters.

TEST MATCH SPECIAL TWO. *edited Peter Baxter*: Unwin Paperbacks: 233 pp, £1.95
This is the paperback edition of the book which was reviewed last year in *Benson and Hedges Cricket Year*.

CRICKET'S UNHOLY TRINITY. *David Foot*: Stanley Paul: 188 pp, £8.95
A sensitive and lucid writer, David Foot has chosen to follow his biography of Harold Gimblett with this study of three of the most complex and controversial personalities of cricket between the wars. MacBryan, Parker and Parkin, the chosen three, do not lie easily together and one is left considering whether there really is a common denominator in these three players. The study of Charlie Parker, the Gloucestershire left-arm spinner, dwarfs the other two. It is apparent that Parker is the player closest to David Foot's heart and he is also the player whose career and rejection by the Test selectors makes him the most interesting subject. Parker's off-field clashes with Pelham Warner and his opinion of Hammond the social climber give substance to the study and leave one regretting that he has not been the subject of a full-length biography by David Foot. Parkin, on the other hand, has been well documented and the essay in this book adds nothing to what we already knew. MacBryan is a surprising inclusion and one remains unconvinced that he deserves a place in this company. He lived to a ripe age, gave words of wisdom to those who visited him and felt aggrieved at his lack of recognition, but we are still left with only a shadowy hint of the man and his achievements.

Having said this, one must recommend the book unreservedly. Anything by David Foot is worth reading and the study of Parker alone is worth the money.

CRICKET TIES. *Vic Lewis*: Ebury Press: 112 pp, £5.95
From his personal collection of nearly 3000 ties from cricket clubs and societies throughout the world, Vic Lewis has selected 280 which are set down in an attractive manner. Naturally the ties are illustrated in full colour with interesting comments about each club or society. It is a fascinating book and will give happy hours of browsing and reference. It is good value and one looks forward to a second volume which will perhaps place emphasis on smaller clubs with less pretentious aspirations than many included here.

THE COURAGE BOOK OF SPORTING HEROES, 1884–1984. *edited by Chris Rhys*: Stanley Paul: 221 pp, £5.95
This is a collection of one hundred brief, readable biographies of outstanding sportsmen of the past one hundred years, from Fred Archer and W.G. Grace to David Bryant and Eric Bristow. It is an interesting selection in which cricket is well represented with Botham, Bradman, Compton, Fry, Grace, Hobbs, Hutton, Larwood, Lillee, Marsh, Pollock, Sobers and Trueman. The selection, by its omissions, arouses debate and controversy, and I would rather the 'heroes' were arranged chronologically than alphabetically, but the book is good reading and good fun, very well illustrated, and, thanks to sponsorship, excellent value. Chris Rhys, with BBC colleagues, has done a fine job. The panel of selection is named as Beaumont, Compton, Cooper, Hemery and Charlton, but one suspects that other brains have been at work too.

BILL BEAUMONT'S SPORTING YEAR. *Bill Beaumont*: Stanley Paul: 160 pp, £9.95
This book looks at sixteen sporting occasions in 1984. Cricket is represented by the Lord's Test match. Beaumont begins with a very brief history of Lord's, and he begins his report of the match on the Friday when he arrived. There is a break to talk about the BBC commentary team, quotes from Hutton, Johnston, Bailey and others. It is all rather naïve and cannot be considered a serious contribution to cricket (or sporting) literature, but I am sure many will take pleasure in it.

JOHN EDWARD SHILTON'S BOOK.*Robert Brooke*: Association of Cricket Statisticians: 64 pp, £2.25
A fervent Warwickshire man and an equally fervent pursuer of statistical accuracy, Robert Brooke has produced a delightful biography of a little known all-rounder who played for Warwickshire from 1884–95. It is a fascinating, sad tale, sensitively researched and positively written. It is a credit to author and subject and deserves the widest public and success.

THE LORD TAVERNER'S CRICKET QUIZ BOOK. *compiled by Graham* Tarrant: David & Charles: 92 pp, £3.95
I have not been too enamoured of the publications bearing the Lord's Taverners' seal of approval in recent years. Obviously the association does good work and has a captive market so one would have hoped for more worthy publications. One is pleased to report that at last they have achieved this with the best cricket quiz book to be issued. Beware of it. It is addictive. Hours one should spend working are spent trying to find out who was the soccer international who took a wicket with his first ball in first-class cricket in his one and only county match, or which two Australian bowlers dismissed Bradman for a 'duck' in the 1931–32 domestic season. This book is a delight. It is excellent value and deserves to bring every success to Lord's Taverners and the work that, thankfully, they do.

ARCHIE'S LAST STAND. *David Kynaston*: Queen Anne Press; 176 pp, £9.95
This is undoubtedly the specialist book of the year, dealing as it does with the M.C.C.'s tour of Australia and New Zealand in 1922–23. Like Kynaston's earlier book, *Bobby Abel*, it is well researched and well written although 22 pages of score-cards and statistics would suggest that the matter discovered proved to be thinner than anticipated. The pictorial content is poor, but this is a difficult period for which to find good quality photographic evidence, and the book is expensive. It does not further our knowledge of MacLaren or the game of cricket very greatly, but it is a commendable publishing venture which deserves our support, and the product is worth any ten ghosted autobiographies from elsewhere.

ENGLAND V. AUSTRALIA, A PICTORIAL HISTORY OF THE TEST MATCHES SINCE 1877. *David Frith*: Collins Willow: 336 pp, £17.95
This is the fifth edition of a famous and justly highly-praised book.

David Frith's efforts in assembling a pictorial record of cricket are well known, and this book will remain as a monument to his scholarship and endeavour. As always, he is meticulous in detail. There are 1100 pictures, including early engravings, and the comment is lucid and perceptive. No serious student or lover of the game can be without this book.

MIDDLESEX C.C.C. REVIEW, 1984–85. *edited by Alvan Seth-Smith*: Middlesex C.C.C.: 144 pp, £3.50
In five years the Middlesex Year Book, under lively and intelligent editorship, has reached a very high standard in both content and organisation. The statistics and score-cards are neatly presented and there is a splendid pictorial record of the season. These are supported by some interesting articles, notably Norman de Mesquita on Clive Radley and Viveca Dutt, organiser of coach trips to Middlesex away matches for the past seven years, on 'I Was There'. Naturally, the concern is Middlesex, but the editor is quick to picture and praise Gooch for his memorable century at Lord's in 1984 and to commend Hadlee for his wonderful all-round performances. It is a publication which is highly recommended.

IRISH CRICKET ANNUAL. *edited by Gerard Siggins*: Irish Cricket Magazine, 41 Longbridge Road, Sandymount, Dublin 4: 62 pp, £2
When so much emphasis is placed upon Test cricket and the stars how refreshing it is to pick up a book that concerns itself with the prosperity of cricket in a country which has no yearnings for Test status. If not the most attractive piece of design, this book is nevertheless a splendid effort. There are reports on and scores of the international matches, league tables, averages, and the coverage of youth and women's cricket in full. This is a labour of love and enthusiasm, and it is the efforts of such people as Gerard Siggins which keep the game alive in all parts of the world. The book does a great service to Irish cricket in particular and to cricket at grass roots level as a whole. May it prosper.

WISDEN CRICKETER'S ALMANACK, 1985: *edited by John Woodcock*: John Wisden: 1280 pp, £11.95
The publication of *Wisden* each April is still a most significant event in the cricket calendar. Since he succeeded to the editorship John Woodcock has done much to re-establish standards and discipline and the book remains supreme as a work of reference. It was good to note that the editor echoed the words written in *Benson and Hedges Cricket Year* last November regarding the West Indian fast bowling tactics, particularly in the number of bouncers to which Pat Pocock was subjected at The Oval. There is also a fine piece on George Headley by Jim Swanton and a delightful essay, *Forty Years On*, by the gentle and cultured Murray Hedgcock. John Woodcock has done so much and is so respected in the game that one hopes that in the next few years he will reconsider the Five Cricketers of the Year, a section which now appears to be struggling. It is hard to break with tradition, but a reassessment of this section is necessary. One would hope too that there could be a revitalisation of the picture content of this eminent publication.

PLAYFAIR CRICKET ANNUAL 1985. *edited by Gordon Ross*: Queen Anne Press: 256 pp, £1.75
The last work of the late Gordon Ross, *Playfair 1985*, sponsored again by NatWest Bank, maintains the high standard of its predecessors and is unquestionably the most useful pocket book on cricket that has ever been published. In praising Gordon Ross for his organisation and editorship, which will be hard to replace, one should mention that the bulk of the work is done by Brian Croudy and Brian Heald, together with Barry McCaully, and it is they who should take most of the credit for this splendid, indispensable, little book.

THE CRICKETERS' WHO'S WHO 1985. *compiled and edited by Iain Sproat*: Queen Anne Press: 544 pp, £7.95
It is rather surprising that the publishers of *Playfair* have given refuge to Iain Sproat's Who's Who, particularly as, in its new format, it is almost a duplicate of the smaller, cheaper book with players arranged under counties now rather than alphabetically. The organisation, too, leads to much repetition and waste of space. Is it really necessary, for example, to list 50 wickets in a season–0; 5 wickets in an innings–0; 10 wickets in a match–0, for someone who has never bowled in first-class cricket? It is a neat and attractive book, but the statistics leave one with a sense of doubt. A comparison with *Playfair*, from the same publishing stable, shows many discrepancies, and my money would be on *Playfair*.

STANDING UP, STANDING BACK. *Bob Taylor*: Collins Willow: 172 pp, £8.95
Bob Taylor's farewell to cricket came with this autobiography and the difficulties which his collaborator Pat Murphy encountered are readily apparent, what do you say of a man who played cricket for two decades and was a nice bloke. There are revelations about a lack of commitment to net practice on the part of some Test players and assessment of other wicket-keepers although Taylor's opinion of Rodney Marsh seems to have changed since the present writer spoke to him last. Taylor is a self-effacing and pleasant person and perhaps the book has just those qualities.

THE TRENT BRIDGE BATTERY: THE STORY OF THE SPORTING GUNNS. *Basil Haynes and John Lucas*: Collins Willow (in association with Gunn and Moore): 208 pp, £12.00
This was eagerly awaited and proved to be a little disappointing. It reads rather dourly and one feels that the Nottinghamshire cricketers deserved a little more fun. The research, the history, weigh heavily and the men themselves emerge only in glimpses. It was certainly a very necessary book, but the gap has not been totally filled by its publication. What could be beneficial is for the authors, having done so much work in preparing this volume, to concentrate their efforts on a biography of George Gunn alone. He is a man who deserves fuller treatment, one of the great characters of cricket.

100 YEARS AT SOUTHAMPTON. *edited and published by Mark Nicholas*: 75 pp, £3.00
The brainchild and work of skipper Mark Nicholas, this booklet, which comes with a fascinating cassette featuring John Arlott on Hampshire cricket, is a magnificent achievement. Well supported by advertisers, and with Wiggins Homes sponsoring the cassette, Mark Nicholas has attracted some good contributors and the result is a delightful panorama of Hampshire cricket, and some glimpses at the world beyond. Arlott's cassette is the great man at his best, his lovely warm voice reflecting on the characters of Hampshire that he has known and loved, and who have loved him in return.

CORFU AND CRICKET. *edited by Ivo Tennant*: Anglo-Corfiot Cricket Association: 48 pp, £2.00
An attractive little book and a fine publication, *Corfu and Cricket* traces the history of cricket on the island and supplements it with enjoyable reminiscences from those who have played there. The standard is consistently high and the whole publication lively and highly enjoyable. The profits from the sale of the book will go towards the provision of coaching for young Corfiot cricketers. This in itself should prompt people to buy the book, but it is such a delightful little publication that it should be part of any cricket library. It may be obtained from The Hon. Secretary of A.C.C.A., 15 St Peter's Square, London W6 9AB. The price with postage is £2.20.

CRICKET'S GOLDEN SUMMER: PAINTINGS IN A GARDEN. *Gerry Wright, with a commentary by David Frith*: Pavilion Books; 64 pp, £9.95
As a great admirer of the paintings of Gerry Wright, I found this among the most disappointing books of the year. Essentially it should be an art book, but there is no mention of art in the commentary and the standard of colour reproduction is very poor,

Worcestershire C.C.C. First-Class Matches — Bowling, 1985	R.N. Kapil Dev	N.V. Radford	P.J. Newport	M.J. Weston	R.K. Illingworth	D.N. Patel	J.D. Inchmore	D.B. D'Oliveira	S.M. McEwan
v. Middlesex (Lord's)	13–4–35–2	17–3–43–3	19.4–5–57–5	6–2–19–0	12–4–31–0	3–0–8–0			
27–30 April		15–2–65–1	12–2–48–1	7–2–20–0	7.4–1–42–0	4–0–33–0			
v. Gloucestershire (Worcester)	20–6–74–2	25–6–68–3	11.4–2–48–4	19–7–49–1	4–1–16–0				
8–10 May	25–7–63–4	24–5–57–3		26–12–58–2		3.4–1–5–1			
v. Australians (Worcester)		15–0–77–1	12–0–72–0	4–1–16–0	16–7–47–0	20–2–90–1	18–6–38–3	1–0–5–0	
11–13 May									
v. Oxford University			9–0–29–0	10–5–15–2	13.4–7–9–6	12–5–18–2			4–0–14–0
(Oxford) 22–24 May			7–0–24–0		32.3–10–50–7	29–9–52–3		6–1–20–0	5–1–10–0
v. Warwickshire (Worcester)	23–5–50–1	28–3–110–4		14–1–36–2	13–4–28–0	18–8–35–2	17–3–51–0		
25–27 May	4–1–6–0	3–0–8–1							
v. Kent (Canterbury)	9.5–3–22–3	10–4–28–1			16–5–50–3	18–4–49–3	9–3–29–1		
1–4 June	15–4–30–2	8.4–1–26–3			20–5–39–2	15–2–45–3	2–1–2–0		
v. Glamorgan (Abergavenny)	7–1–29–0	11–1–50–0		14.1–3–41–0	12–2–40–0	16–1–46–0	6–0–18–0		
8–11 June									
v. Cambridge University									
(Cambridge) 12–14 June									
v. Surrey (Worcester)		19–3–63–1	9–1–42–0	2–1–13–0	17–1–67–1	18–2–74–1	13–2–31–0		
15–18 June		7–0–30–1	7–3–8–0	9–3–18–0			5–0–21–0		
v. Yorkshire (Harrogate)	19–12–15–3	23.1–4–59–2		10–5–30–1	30–9–49–1	9–1–39–0	1.5–0–6–0		
22–24 June	8–3–14–1	8–3–20–0			19–9–29–2	8–1–30–0		7–0–23–0	
v. Middlesex (Worcester)	6–0–30–0	11–0–39–0	9–2–32–0	2–0–10–0	7–2–31–1	10–5–10–1			
26–28 June	16–0–74–4	11–0–50–2	4–2–20–0	4–1–26–0	15.5–1–54–1				
v. Yorkshire (Worcester)	22–5–54–1	24.5–5–84–1	23–3–73–0	20–2–67–1	23–2–84–0			1–0–6–0	
29 June–2 July	14–3–58–3	18–1–74–1	9–3–23–1	6–0–23–0					
v. Derbyshire (Worcester)	26–9–56–4	24–3–78–4	6–0–33–0		3–1–5–0	2–1–4–0			10–3–29–2
6–9 July	13–3–51–2	17–3–73–0	7–3–16–0		17.4–2–76–4	23–3–85–0			7–2–26–1
v. Gloucestershire (Gloucester)	8–1–18–0	16–4–40–1	20–3–47–2		26–8–55–2	29–9–77–0			15–3–51–1
10–12 July	15–3–36–2	7–1–22–1	9.1–2–18–5		27–12–48–1	8–1–37–0			
v. Hampshire (Portsmouth)		26–5–59–2	22–0–89–5	8–2–33–1	10–5–23–1	6–3–6–1			
13–16 July		18–1–67–3	14–2–54–3		10–3–27–0				
v. Glamorgan (Worcester)	4–0–18–0	24.5–3–94–4	15–2–57–1		15–4–41–0	22–7–57–2	15–2–39–1		
24–26 July		18.4–5–53–2	12–0–44–2		6–1–10–0	7–3–10–0	11–3–33–2		
v. Sussex (Eastbourne)		21–4–76–6	14–2–46–1		8.3–3–19–3		14–4–23–0		
27–30 July		5–2–10–1					4–1–7–0		
v. Lancashire (Worcester)	19–7–42–3	21–3–63–2	17.5–2–35–4		3–2–5–0	5–2–9–0	11–5–9–1		
3–6 August	18–6–30–1	23–6–70–4	16–4–25–3				17–3–28–2		
v. Nottinghamshire (Trent		23–1–78–1	21–1–93–2		12–0–37–2	17.1–4–54–3			12–2–38–2
Bridge) 10–13 August		9.5–1–33–2	10–0–47–4		1–0–11–0				
v. Derbyshire (Buston)		8–5–4–2	8–2–19–1						
14–16 August									
v. Essex (Worcester)		26–1–79–5	15–4–48–1		9–2–23–0	18.1–5–38–3	15–5–18–1		
17–20 August		14–4–37–3	5–1–18–0			3–1–5–0	5–1–11–0		
v. Warwickshire (Edgbaston)		16.5–3–45–6	2–1–1–0			1–0–3–0	17–3–42–4		
24–27 August		12–3–34–0	9–4–29–1			18–7–33–3	20–5–35–3		7–0–22–1
v. Kent (Worcester)			7–1–19–0	22–7–37–3		14–2–58–0	20–3–50–4	1–0–1–1	17–1–63–1
28–30 August				7–0–32–0		11–1–38–2	11–2–35–1		7–1–27–0
v. Leicestershire (Leicester)		14.1–3–55–4		19–7–23–2			13–4–26–1		18–5–47–3
31 August–3 September		23–4–64–5		3–0–14–0		20–14–16–2	12–3–34–0		10–2–27–1
v. Somerset (Worcester)		11–2–43–0				8–3–19–0	11–3–40–2		7–2–23–1
4–6 September		17–6–45–4		5.4–1–34–2		5–2–9–0	12–1–41–3		8–1–33–0
v. Somerset (Taunton)		22.5–5–59–4		14–4–28–0		7–0–35–0	20–3–48–2		16–3–54–2
11–13 September		27–3–68–1		23–6–67–1		6–2–27–1	11–5–21–0		14–1–77–0
v. Northamptonshire (Worcester)		30–3–125–2		19–0–68–1		11–1–41–0	11–1–49–0		9–1–59–0
14–17 September		24.5–5–68–4				17–5–49–0	17–0–59–2		11–1–35–1
	304.5–83–805–37 *av.* 21.75	779.4–130–2493–101 *av.* 24.68	362.2–57–1214–46 *av.* 26.39	273.5–72–777–19 *av.* 40.89	406.5–113–1046–37 *av.* 28.27	442–117–1244–34 *av.* 36.58	338.5–72–844–33 *av.* 25.57	16–1–55–1 *av.* 55.00	177–29–635–16 *av.* 39.68

a A.P. Pridgeon 9–2–14–1
M. Scothern 16–6–42–1
B. Barrett 18–7–40–1
S.R. Lampitt 1–0–1–0
b T. Gard absent injured

R.M. Ellcock	G.A. Hick		Byes	Leg-byes	Wides	No-balls	Total	Wkts
				2	4	8	195	10
				3	1	6	211	2
			4	11	2	5	270	10
			7	10	5	3	200	10
			10	9	1	12	364	5
7–1–18–0				2	1	1	105	10
2–0–14–0		1–1–0–0	6	7	1	4	183	10
				5	2	7	315	9
				2	1	1	16	1
			3	8		2	189	10
			3	1		4	146	10
			8	18		4	250	0
11–1–40–3			4	2		1	143	6a
			1	13		5	304	3
				5	1	2	82	2
			7	10	1	3	215	7
			1	7			124	3
			2	4			158	2
				2			226	7
				21		2	389	3
			1	15		2	194	5
				9		7	214	10
				9	1	8	336	7
			7	12		2	307	7
				9		2	170	9
	14–0–34–0			11	2	6	255	10
	14–0–57–0		5	1		14	211	6
				3		8	309	9
			1	5	1	4	156	7
			1	12		1	177	10
			2	3			22	1
				5		1	168	10
			6	6	2	2	165	10
			4	18	2	9	322	10
			1	6			98	7
				2	1		25	3
		2–0–5–0	1	5	6	6	217	10
				1	1	2	72	3
				3	1	2	94	10
		5–4–1–1					154	10
		19–5–62–0		9	1	1	299	10
		4–0–28–1		10		1	170	4
				2		1	153	10
		4–2–11–1		1		7	167	9
		6–0–28–0		4		7	157	3
				8		5	170	9b
		10–2–34–2	6	16	1	1	280	10
		21–3–81–0	9	2		7	352	3
			3	4	1	11	349	3
		3–0–15–0		5		7	231	7
20–2–72–3 av. 24.00	28–0–91–0 —	75–17–265–5 av. 53.00						

failing to bring out the exciting brush work of the artist. When one considers the standard achieved in such publications as *Say Goodbye, you may never see them again* and *Miss Carter Wore Pink* one is left saddened that Gerry Wright could not have been given a better monument, and one that would have made some comment on him as an artist. As the text stands, the comment is purely biographical and could just as well have been applied to photographs.

OUT OF THE WILDERNESS: GRAHAM GOOCH. *Collins Willow*: 153 pp, £8.95
Ghosted by Alan Lee, this book is Gooch's explanation for his South African venture. The first part of the book which concerns the subterfuge that went in to the band of English cricketers making the trip as the South African Breweries side makes very interesting reading although the author is naïve if he believes that his explanation of what happened makes the venture acceptable. Few of those who took part come out with much credit, for it is a story of friends deceived and words betrayed. It is, however, good that the details of what happened are given here and the stories of secret meetings in hotels and the reaction of wife and parents makes fascinating telling. This story, of course, is the reason for the book, but, unfortunately, the book has to be padded to give us the required number of pages and we are led through Gooch's three years at Essex when he played no international cricket. Any who watched Essex at this time will find it hard to relate this narrative to what they saw. It is really quite dreadful and Essex and Gooch's colleagues are deserving of better. Read the first sixty pages and then close the book.

THE DICTIONARY OF CRICKET. *Michael Rundell*: George Allen & Unwin; 272 pp, £12.95
Certainly one of the great cricket publishing events of the year was the issuing of this book. It is precisely what it says, a dictionary of cricketing terms. It is beautifully researched and the examples that Michael Rundell selects are most apposite. The book is very well produced and here we have a publication in which the harmony between author, subject and designer has given us something which no student or lover of the game can afford to be without.

LEARN CRICKET WITH VIV RICHARDS. *Stanley Paul*: 96 pp, £5.95
For his latest offering Viv Richards has turned again to David Foot for help and is better for it. This is a clear, well illustrated guide to the rudiments of the game which will give both pleasure and instruction to young people.

DOUBLE CENTURY: 200 YEARS OF CRICKET IN THE TIMES. *Edited Marcus Williams*: Collins Willow; 621 pp, £17.50
Marcus Williams has followed his collection of cricketing letters to *The Times* with this selection of cricket writings from the same newspaper. Whereas *The Times* has declined in standards in various ways over the past decade, John Woodcock and his band have striven to halt any slide in standard on the cricket page. Some of the intrusions onto that page in the past season have suggested that their efforts are not entirely successful, but the match reports are still better than most. Marcus Williams' selection is strong on the past, less satisfying on the immediate past. Perhaps at the insistence of the publisher, there is an emphasis on the scandals in cricket at the expense of match reports, and supporters of Essex and Somerset, having waited for over a century, must wonder where 1979 went to. That said, the book has its gems and reveals the humour and vitality of the compiler. In an Ashes victory year it is good to read that *The Times* of 19 August, 1926, deviated from its usual sobriety with an opening sentence 'We have won!'

ESSEX COUNTY CRICKET CLUB 1985 HANDBOOK. *Edited Peter Edwards*: Essex C.C.C.: 224 pp, £3.00
The tireless Peter Edwards whose success in running the Essex club off the field mirrors the success of the players on it seems to produce a bigger and better handbook every year. It is packed with inform-

Yorkshire C.C.C.
First-Class Matches – Batting, 1985

	v. Leicestershire (Leicester) 27–29 April		*v.* Middlesex (Leeds) 4–7 May		*v.* Essex (Sheffield) 22–24 May		*v.* Lancashire (Old Trafford) 25–27 May		*v.* Somerset (Leeds) 29–31 May		*v.* Worcestershire (Worcester) 29 June–2 July		*v.* Gloucestershire (Gloucester) 6–9 July	
G. Boycott	4	—							20	114*	115	25	52*	—
M.D. Moxon	60	—	10	2			7	4	153	16	25	31		
K. Sharp	96	—	15	20			8	0	42	44	19	2	24	—
J.D. Love	44	—	33	4			3	16*	62*	30*	1	5	1*	—
P.E. Robinson	42	—	62	19										
D.L. Bairstow	24*	—	26	33*			27	0*	—	—	47	16*	—	—
A. Sidebottom	15*	—	55	23			35	—	—	—				
P. Carrick	—	—	14	1			7	—	—	—	0	13*	—	—
G.B. Stevenson	—	—	14*	6										
P.W. Jarvis	—	—	13	10			28	1	—	—	0	—		
S.J. Dennis	—	—												
R.J. Blakey			32	4			1	35	90	7	43	18	31	—
S.D. Fletcher			2*	0			15*	—	—	—	0*	—	—	—
S.N. Hartley							52	—					—	—
I.G. Swallow							1	—						
P.A. Booth									—	—	0	—	—	—
S. Oldham											6	—		
C.S. Pickles													—	—
C. Shaw													—	—
A.A. Metcalfe														
P.J. Hartley														
Byes	4		5				2	1	4		8		4	
Leg-byes	4		17	7			6		5	7	8	3	4	
Wides	2		2	6			4		3	2		1		
No-balls	11		4				9	1	4	3	11		8	
Total	306		304	135			205	58	383	223	283	114	124	
Wickets	5		9	10			10	4	4	3	10	5	2	
Result	D		W		Ab.		D		D		D		D	
Points	8		20		0		6		8		4		—	

	v. Kent (Maidstone) 10–12 July		*v.* Surrey (Sheffield) 13–16 July		*v.* Derbyshire (Chesterfield) 24–26 July		*v.* Nottinghamshire (Worksop) 27–30 July		*v.* Derbyshire (Bradford) 31 July–2 August		*v.* Warwickshire (Edgbaston) 3–6 August		*v.* Lancashire (Leeds) 10–13 August	
G. Boycott	15	45	105*	64*	4	82*	184	50	24	10	25	9	55*	29
M.D. Moxon	25	7	11	3	33	45	168	—	31	—				
K. Sharp	17	69*	4	27*	81	—	9*	4	23	9	36	10	0	30
J.D. Love	106	—	4	—	23	—	—	48	1	18	19	93	0	—
P.E. Robinson														
D.L. Bairstow	8*	7	13	5	77	100*	—	49*	80	11	29	42	0	65
A. Sidebottom	—	3*	26	—			—	0*	24	12				
P. Carrick			11	—	17	—	—	21	73	2	45	0	20	7
G.B. Stevenson									21	8	35*	15		
P.W. Jarvis			—	—					0	0	25*	9	1	11
S.J. Dennis	—	—												
R.J. Blakey			0	17	5	—								
S.D. Fletcher	—	—	—	—	—	—	—	—	1*	2*	—	0*		
S.N. Hartley	108*	—									60	9	27	5
I.G. Swallow			20*	—	7	—							0	3
P.A. Booth	4	—												
S. Oldham														
C.S. Pickles					31*	—	—	—						
C. Shaw					11*	—	—	—			—	0	1	9*
A.A. Metcalfe	23	109					5	4	14	3	3	0	7	77
P.J. Hartley													13	33
Byes	4	6	7	1		1		1			10	1	2	1
Leg-byes	6	7	10	7	2	8	21	15	10		10	6	2	7
Wides	2	3	1		5	3			1			1	2	2
No-balls	4	3	3		4	2	2	2	4	8	3	3	1	1
Total	322	259	215	124	300	241	389	194	307	83	300	198	131	280
Wickets	6	4	7	3	8	1	3	5	10	9†	7	10	10	9‡
Result	D		D		D		D		L		L		L	
Points	—		5		5		7		6		8		3	

Catches 56 – D.L. Bairstow (ct 44/st 12); 16 – P. Carrick; 14 – K. Sharp; 12 – R.J. Blakey; 10 – G. Boycott; 9 – M.D. Moxon and subs; 8 – J.D. Love and S.N. Hartley; 6 – P.W. Jarvis; 5 – C. Shaw; 4 – I.G. Swallow; 3 – S.D. Fletcher and C.S. Pickles

ation and has all the statistics that could be desired. It reflects the energy and enthusiasm of the club and at £3.00, free to members, it is one of the bargains of the year.

THE PAVILION LIBRARY. Classics of Cricket Literature reissued in limp cover. Each book priced at £4.95. Published by Pavilion Books. This is a splendid series which has started with six excellent publications, attractively presented.

BRIGHTLY FADES THE DON. *Jack Fingleton*: 261 pp is a fine account of Bradman's last tour of England as captain of the 1948 Australian side. It remains one of the very best books written on a Test series and is also a balanced assessment of Bradman by one who played with him.

ODD MEN IN: A GALLERY OF CRICKET ECCENTRICS. *A.A. Thomson*: 184 pp is a delightful book on some of the odd characters of cricket by one of the great writers on the game. It is a very wise choice as one of the first six in this series, for it has become less accessible than many lesser books and this reissue does a notable service to readers and collectors.

CRICKET CRISIS. *Jack Fingleton*: 313 pp was reissued last year by Pavilion in hard-back and now takes its place among the select six. It deals primarily with the *Bodyline Series*.

CRUSOE ON CRICKET: THE WRITINGS OF R.C. ROBERTSON-GLASGOW: 320 pp. This, for me, is the pick of the collection. Few men have ever written as well on the game as 'Crusoe' and this selection does him full justice. A wonderful book and a wonderful bargain.

CRICKET COUNTRY. *Edmund Blunden*: 224 pp. A justly famous book by a poet of distinction, *Cricket Country*, first published in 1944, evokes all that is good and true in the game, and if much of which Blunden writes has vanished with the years, there is, thankfully, a prevailing spirit which the poet's tongue has caught and which, in later days, still reassures us.

CRICKET ARCHIVE. *Benny Green*: 257 pp. This was first published eight years ago as *Cricket addicts Archive*. Benny Green has made some alterations and additions to what I considered to be the best anthology that I had read when it was first published and it is to be hoped that this reissue meets with the success that it deserves.

FELSTED SCHOOL AUSTRALIAN TOUR 1985.*edited Mark Surridge*: Felsted School: 68 pp

It is customary for schools and clubs who undertake tours to issue a brochure as part of their fund-raising activities. I think, in the case of Felsted School, the brochure was issued as a way of saying thank you to those who contributed to make the trip to Australia by the cricket team possible. The energies of tour manager and cricket master Mark Surridge have not only brought about the tour but have

v. Surrey (The Oval) 14–16 August	*v.* Kent (Scarborough) 17–20 August	*v.* Glamorgan (Swansea) 24–27 August	*v.* Sussex (Hove) 28–30 August	*v.* Northamptonshire (Leeds) 31 Aug.–3 Sept.	*v.* Nottinghamshire (Scarborough) 11–13 September	*v.* Essex (Chelmsford) 14–17 September	*v.* Hampshire (Middlesbrough) 1–4 June	*v.* Australians (Leeds) 5–7 June	*v.* Oxford University (Oxford) 12–14 June	*v.* Worcestershire (Harrogate) 22–25 June	*v.* Leicestershire (Bradford) 26–28 June		*M*	*Inns*	*NOs*	*Runs*	*H/S*	*Av*
19 4*	0 55*	7 —	38 103*			62* —	64 —	43 11*	— —	76 125*	19 —		21	34	12	1657	184	75.31
	70 0	43 —	5 26	127 —	10 10*	43 —	31 —	70 20	— —	15 65	2 88		21	33	1	1256	168	39.25
21 3*	48 0	37 —	21 3	0 —	1 —								19	34	4	723	96	25.82
				27 —	69 —	— —	14 —	46 78*	— —	36 79	61 16		21	28	5	937	106	40.73
36 —	46 18*	39 —	0 0	20 —	18 —	— —	54 —	15 79	— —		0 2		13	16	1	450	79	30.00
113* —	35 —	122* —	21 49*	28 —	13 —	— —	9 —	29 —	— —	6 25	8 46		25	33	10	1163	122*	50.56
1 —													9	10	3	194	55	27.71
21 —	4 —	33 —	68* —	0 —	36 —	— —	92 —	2 —	— —	41 —	6 6		24	25	2	540	92	23.47
													4	6	2	99	35*	24.75
0 —	8* —	18 —	5 —	22 —									14	16	2	151	28	10.78
													2	—				—
					81 0*	35* —	7 —	3 48	— —	12 4	14 31		13	22	2	518	90	25.90
									— —	3* —	0 13		14	10	7	36	15*	12.00
0 4*	10 —	7 —	8 34	19 —	22 —	— —	4 —	49 47	— —	37 —	0 52		17	20	2	554	108*	30.77
	25* —	17 —	2 —	9 —			10 —			7 —			10	11	2	101	25*	11.22
													3	2	—	4	4	2.00
					2* —								2	2	1	8	6	8.00
12 —						— —		9 —					6	3	1	52	31*	26.00
12 —	— —	0 —	1 —	9* —	1 —	— —	— —	0 —	— —	5 —	6* 2*		17	13	5	57	12	7.12
6 6													6	12	—	257	109	21.41
	— —	1 —	35 —	21* —	8 —	— —	3* —	5* —	— —	23 —	5 12		12	11	3	159	35	19.87
13 4	13 4	6	4	6	5	4	4	5 2		1								
9	5 2	11	6 6	12	9 1	2	2	15 1		1 3	6 5							
1		2		3			4	1			1 1							
9	3 3	9	18 12	25	2	4		15 7		4	3 4							
273 21	267 82	352	228 237	328	277 11	150	298 0	307 293		262 306	131 278							
10 1	7 2	10	10 4	9	10 0	1	9 0	10 4		10 4	10 9†							
D	D	W	D	D	D	D	W	D	D	D	L							
6	5	22	3	5	7	5	18	4	2	5	3							

† M.D. Moxon, absent injured
‡ J.D. Love, absent injured
§ G. Boycott, absent injured

2 – P.E. Robinson and P.A. Booth

1 – S.J. Dennis, G.B. Stevenson, A.A. Metcalfe, A. Sidebottom, S. Oldham and P.J. Hartley

resulted in a brochure which, in every respect, is quite simply the best that I have seen. Contributors include Peter May, Ted Dexter, Colin Cowdrey, Colin Ingleby-Mackenzie and John Inverarity. The cover design, back and front, are watercolours by D.F. Plested, a most talented artist. Well done, Felsted, the brochure alone is something of which to be proud.

KENT COUNTY ANNUAL 1985. 208 pp, £1.50
The Kent handbook is compact and informative. With a book review section and some excellent photographs of Kent cricket, the annual covers every aspect of the game. It is neatly and tidily produced and is not only an indispensable companion to every Kent follower, and indeed to all followers of the game, but a publication which is a great credit to the club.

KEN MCEWAN. *David Lemmon*: George Allen & Unwin: 142 pp, £8.95
It is not correct for an author to offer criticism of his own book, but shortly after the book was published Ken McEwan decided that he would retire from first-class cricket in England. In conversation he said that he could see no future in driving up and down the motorways of this country with no prospect of ever being able to play Test cricket. Those who have been lucky to have known him and to have seen him play will feel the loss acutely. I am proud to have been his biographer and to have been part of his life.

CRICKET REFLECTIONS: FIVE DECADES OF CRICKET PHOTOGRAPHS. *The photographs of Ken Kelly; Text by David Lemmon*: David & Charles: 192 pp, £14.95
Ken Kelly took his first cricket photographs in 1938 and this splendid volume is a monument to one of the world's great cricket photographers and one who pioneered many of the techniques in common use today. It is a fascinating pictorial record of cricket of five decades with some of the finest photos ever taken at county and Test level. The book, too, is rich in characters.

FRED TRUEMAN'S YORKSHIRE. *Fred Trueman and Don Mosey*: Stanley Paul: 161 pp, £9.95
This is part travel book, part reminiscence, part discussion book. It is an elegant and highly readable book with, inevitably, amusing anecdote. It is not really a cricket book, and perhaps it is all the better for that.

CAUGHT SHORT OF THE BOUNDARY. *Henry Blofield*: Stanley Paul: 108 pp, £6.95
The publishers describe this book as 'not so much a cricketing book, more an absolute scandal'. The words are theirs. The stories are a little tired. 'Blowers as a miner's flying picket, my dear old thing.' Henry is a most likeable man. I wish he had given a little more time and thought to this book.

THE YOUNG CRICKETERS' YEARBOOK. *edited Gordon Ross*: Queen Anne Press: 159 pp, £4.95

Yorkshire C.C.C. First-Class Matches — Bowling, 1985	A. Sidebottom	P.W. Jarvis	G.B. Stevenson	S.D. Fletcher	P. Carrick	K. Sharp	I.G. Swallow	M.D. Moxon	S.N. Hartley
v. Leicestershire (Leicester) 27–29 April	16–3–52–2 4.4–3–5–0	13–4–36–2 4–1–9–0	13–2–39–3 3–0–13–0						
v. Middlesex (Leeds) 4–7 May	15–4–34–0 21–3–47–3	11–1–45–0 11.2–1–51–3	7–0–24–0 12–1–40–1	10–1–42–0 7–0–30–1	26–8–55–2 8–1–33–1	5–0–20–0			
v. Essex (Sheffield) 22–24 May									
v. Lancashire (Old Trafford) 25–27 May	10–1–34–2	26.1–5–57–4		17–8–50–2	22–5–55–2		17–4–50–0	2–0–16–0	
v. Somerset (Leeds) 29–31 May	18.1–2–48–3	18–3–65–2 20–7–59–4		11.5–0–62–1 16–0–53–2	22–7–36–2 22–1–74–0	 9–4–11–0			
v. Hampshire (Middlesborough) 1–4 June		3–0–13–0		25–4–100–1 11–3–44–1	43–12–102–3 36–8–99–3	 8–4–15–1		6–0–16–1	
v. Australians (Leeds) 5–7 June				13–2–48–1	3–1–9–0				12.5–4–38–0
v. Oxford University (Oxford) 8–14 June	13.4–3–59–1 6–1–14–0			9–1–20–1		5–1–14–0 4–2–15–0		2–0–10–0 7–3–12–0	9–2–39–0
v. Worcestershire (Harrogate) 22–25 June	26.3–6–70–4 11–0–48–1	10–0–39–0		23–1–90–1 11–0–62–1	12–5–23–1 9–5–14–0		15–4–56–1 11–1–32–0	3–0–17–1 7–1–27–1	
v. Leicestershire (Bradford) 26–28 June				14–1–56–1 20–5–72–0	26–5–73–4 26–3–76–4		15–1–48–1 15–1–51–1		
v. Worcestershire (Worcester) 29 June–2 July	20–2–76–3 17–1–88–2			19–8–39–3 19–1–91–4	19–8–22–0 5–0–22–1				
v. Gloucestershire (Gloucester) 6–9 July	18–1–57–1 4–1–14–0	21–3–67–1 10–1–47–0	16.4–2–74–1 6–1–13–1	8–1–26–0	27–9–67–3	1–0–4–0 2–0–6–0			
v. Kent (Maidstone) 10–12 July		26.4–3–105–7 16–0–60–1	15–4–49–0	17–4–45–0 17–2–70–0	23–7–67–2 24–2–79–2				
v. Surrey (Sheffield) 13–16 July		26.4–4–107–5 7–2–15–0			31–5–98–4		14–2–50–1		 3–0–14–0
v. Derbyshire (Chesterfield) 24–26 July	22–1–94–1	32–2–126–5 20–6–68–3			9–3–18–0 12.4–4–47–4				 10–1–35–1
v. Nottinghamshire (Worksop) 27–30 July		24–2–89–3 4–1–10–0			16–4–33–0		15–3–38–0	 5–0–35–1	 16.4–5–63–1
v. Derbyshire (Bradford) 31 July–2 August		16–2–40–1 6–1–9–0			39.4–16–59–4 35.1–17–46–6		14–4–40–2 32–13–53–4		
v. Warwickshire (Edgbaston) 3–6 August		23–2–119–2			11–0–68–0		18–4–71–0		
v. Lancashire (Leeds) 10–13 August		23–2–94–0			14–4–38–0		8–1–21–0		
v. Surrey (The Oval) 14–16 August					 15–3–76–0	 1–0–4–0		 4–0–20–0	5–2–5–0 12–0–51–4
v. Kent (Scarborough) 17–20 August					9–5–15–0 1–0–1–0				6–2–12–0
v. Glamorgan (Swansea) 24–27 August					6–3–4–0 34–8–99–7		7–1–16–0 29–4–104–2		
v. Sussex (Hove) 28–30 August					30–7–77–0 22–0–99–4				4–0–17–1
v. Northamptonshire (Leeds) 31 August–3 September				24–4–62–3					12–0–50–1
v. Nottinghamshire (Scarborough) 11–13 September				18–4–50–2 10–0–49–0	40–14–106–2 20–2–87–3		15–3–40–0		
v. Essex (Chelmsford) 14–17 September				26–1–92–1	14–2–46–1				6–0–25–1
	223–32– 740–23 *av.* 32.17	371.5–53– 1330–44 *av.* 30.22	72.4–10– 252–6 *av.* 42.00	345.5–51– 1253–26 *av.* 48.19	712.3–185– 1923–65 *av.* 29.58	35–11– 89–1 *av.* 89.00	225–46– 670–12 *av.* 55.83	36–4– 153–4 *av.* 38.25	96.3–16– 349–9 *av.* 38.77

a S.J. Dennis 16–2–37–2, 4.2–0–13–0
b P.A. Booth 11.1–4–31–1, 18–8–21–0
c P.A. Booth 32–9–76–1, 19–8–61–1
c S.Oldham 8–1–33–0
d P.A. Booth 29–7–86–3, 8–4–13–0
S.J. Dennis 13–2–36–1
e A.A. Metcalfe 3–0–4–0
f J.D. Love 1–0–8–1
g G. Boycott 5–1–15–0
h G. Boycott 1–0–3–0
i S.Oldham 12–4–13–2, 19–5–56–2
j G. Boycott 4–1–11–0

C.S. Pickles	P.J. Hartley	C. Shaw	*Byes*	*Leg-byes*	*Wides*	*No-balls*	*Total*	*Wkts*
				6	1	10	170	10a
			4	2	1	3	46	0
			1	4	5	6	255	2
				11		7	212	10
			Match Abandoned					
			1	6		10	269	10
			5	10		9	257	10b
			4	8	3	6	230	6
				1		6	341	6c
				4			223	6
14–6–40–1		19–5–56–0		4	3	2	195	2
			1	3		4	268	6d
				4	1	3	62	0e
				5	2	18	300	8
			1	1	1	7	185	3
6–3–16–0		10–1–30–1	4	3		3	230	7
5–1–16–0		7–0–26–0		8		3	249	6
27–6–70–0		27–8–70–1	1	14	1	22	292	7
4–0–27–1		10–3–54–0		9		8	291	8
				6		12	301	6
				3		1	91	2f
		17–2–53–1	5	4	3	4	329	10
		11–1–52–0		9	1	2	270	3
	18–2–62–0	13–4–34–0	4	9		9	364	10
	2–0–9–0	5–2–11–1		2			51	1
22–2–91–2		26–5–80–2	1	10	6	3	420	10
7–0–25–0		7–2–22–1	5	1			218	9g
	22–2–71–1	24.2–3–77–3	8	14	2	4	330	7
	7–0–32–0	8–0–48–0		11		2	199	2
	11–2–23–1	10–2–27–2		10	2		199	10
	2–0–5–0		2	11		4	129	10h
	27–1–122–1	20–4–61–0	1	14	1	7	456	4
	30–6–91–5	29–8–77–3	1	5	2	7	327	8
	16.5–4–43–4	19–6–53–4	5	1		1	120	10i
	21–4–85–2	7–0–38–0	5	6		3	341	8
22–11–31–2	30–6–78–3	40.3–13–76–5		5	2	4	217	10
	5–1–6–0	4–1–4–1	6	1			18	1
	1–1–0–1	2–1–3–0	4			1	27	1
	7–2–11–0	9–3–19–1		4	1	6	237	10
19.3–1–69–0	24–1–100–2	22–7–43–1	1	5	2	9	323	4j
	19–1–97–4	12–0–60–0	4	8			268	8
	18–4–60–0	19–3–52–1	4	14		9	242	5
	16–2–60–0	11–2–38–1	1	6	1	4	301	5
	15–1–75–5	9–2–32–0	7	6	1	5	256	8
	24–0–145–2	19.1–7–90–3	3	12	1	14	413	8
–30–	315.5–40–	417–95–						
6	1175–31	1286–32						
.16	*av.* 37.90	*av.* 40.18						

If this began with the idea of becoming a young person's annual, something was lost on the way. The original conception of a record of junior cricket became mutilated and ultimately obscured and what we are left with is a mixture of records, articles and advice. One doubts whether we will see a second edition.

BODYLINE. *Philip Derriman*: Collins/Sydney Morning Herald: 160 pp, £9.95
This is a pictorial record of the much documented series and there is good comment by Philip Derriman. It is Australian in origin, which gives it value, and is a worthy addition to the growing canon on the series.

THE JOY OF CRICKET. *edited John Bright-Holmes*: Unwin Paperbacks: 290 pp, £3.95
This is the paperback edition of the anthology which was published last year. It is a pleasant selection although it hardly seems distinctive enough to warrant a paperback edition.

THE BODYLINE CONTROVERSY. *Laurence Le Quesne*: Unwin Paperbacks: 317 pp, £2.50
This is the best book to have been spawned by the anniversary of the Bodyline series. It was published in hardback form in 1983 and the paperback edition of this scholarly and eminently readable work must be considered one of the snips of the year. It is certainly tremendous value and anyone interested in Test cricket should acquire it immediately. It is fascinating reading.

PERCY CHAPMAN. *David Lemmon*: Queen Anne Press: 162 pp, £9.95
This is the first biography of the England captain who regained the Ashes in 1926 and became a national hero. He rejected by the selectors in 1930 and died a sad death after he had become an alcoholic.

LAMB'S TALES. *Allan Lamb and Peter Smith*: George Allen & Unwin: 180 pp, £8.95
This book tends to be rather episodic and misses the essential serious ingredient of a discussion on Lamb's decision to become English, the point being dealt with rather tritely. There is the view put forward by the authors that, in spite of his achievements, Lamb has not really been accepted by the English cricketing authorities and public. His *fun* personality has still to cement itself on the people of this country. Perhaps, on the evidence of this book, we are seeking a little more substance.

MARKS OUT OF XI. *Vic Marks*: George Allen & Unwin. 157 pp, £8.95
Tour books have not been too popular in recent years and understandably so, but to dismiss this book as just another tour book would be a great injustice. It is alive. It is fun and it has the scent of authenticity. Vic Marks is a man of charm, humour and intelligence. All those qualities are to be found in this delightful account of last winter's tour, seen mainly from the point of view of the diary of one who spent most of his time as twelfth man. Of the professional cricketers at present trying their hands as writers, Vic Marks would seem to be by far the most proficient. There is a throb of humanity here which encompasses more than cricket.

MAKING OF A FAST BOWLER. *Anwar Shaikh*: Shri Shaikh: 436/1, Salisbury Park, Vijay Apartments, Bldg No 1, Flat No 5, Pune 411.001
One is sometimes sceptical of instructional books, but this appears to be a thoroughly honest and worthwhile manual. Anwar Shaikh played for 13 years in the Ranji Trophy and took 150 wickets. He also played in the Duleep Trophy and he has studied and practised the art of fast bowling. To see a book dedicated to one aspect of cricket technique is rare, but it is this which gives the book its strength. It is full, simple, straightforward and obviously the work of one who is totally committed to the game and to fast bowling in

particular. This is a highly recommended contribution to cricket instruction from India.

LANGLEY CRICKET CLUB. *Edited Clive Smith*
This neat little brochure was produced to mark the centenary of Langley Cricket Club. Langley is a charming village in North Essex and celebrated its centenary with a variety of activities. The booklet is an admirable souvenir for a great occasion.

NEXT MAN IN. *Gerald Brodribb*: Pelham Books: 261 pp, £9.95
This is a reissue of the book first published twenty years ago which is a light look at the laws and customs of the game. It is a fascinating study which has been meticulously reasearched and makes enthralling reading. On Law 19, Boundaries, for example, we read that P.A. Perrin hit the greatest number of boundaries in an innings, and his 343 not out is detailed. We are told, too, that Ridley, Hill and Hibbert all hit centuries without scoring a boundary. If you do not possess this book, rush to buy it. It is essential in any cricket library.

ARLOTT ON CRICKET. *Edited David Rayvern Allen*: Collins Willow: 308 pp, £10.95
David Rayvern Allen continues his gathering of Arlott's work with this volume which concentrates entirely on cricket. Any collection of this kind must offer us some pieces which are less memorable than others and the editor has, perhaps, tended to search for pieces from handbooks and brochures which are not among the great man's best writings. Even if we accept that, however, this remains an important volume and one for which we should be grateful.

GUBBY ALLEN, MAN OF CRICKET. *E.W. Swanton*: Stanley Paul: 311 pp, £12.95
The one reservation that one has about this most important biography is that the author is too close to the subject and that, on occasions, the two become blurred. Swanton brushes aside any criticism of Allen and this, surely, obscures a truth. The selection of Allen for England *was* violently opposed in several quarters. Allen's work as an administrator *has been* criticised by E.M. Wellings among others. There are those who say that the only reason that Allen did not bowl 'bodyline' was because he was no accurate enough. These views may be wrong, but they cannot be dismissed as the nonsense of the gutter press. Once we accept that the book has a bias towards its subject, rather than a sympathy, we are confronted by an engaging study of cricket over the last sixty years. Swanton's knowledge of the game in that time, as well as his knowledge of Allen, make this an indispensable volume for any who are interested in the game. The writing is of high quality and the value of the book lies in more than a notation of one of the game's leading players and administrators.

LASTING THE PACE. *Bob Willis*: Collins Willow: 183 pp, £9.95
Again ghosted by Alan Lee, Bob Willis offers us yet another book of memoirs; presumably, as he has retired, this is meant to be the definitive work. It is solid and interesting, but it follows too quickly upon the heels of the others to give us any fresh insights or outstanding revelations.

ONE TEST AFTER ANOTHER. *Henry Blofield*: Stanley Paul: 172 pp, £8.95
This is a look at the changing face of international cricket over the past few years with special note on the development of one-day cricket and the surfeit of international matches in Australia. As a great globe-trotter, Henry Blofield is in an excellent position to comment on these matters.

THE BEST JOB IN THE WORLD. *Don Mosey*: Pelham Books: 199 pp, £9.95
There is a tendency for books by people in the media about the media to become rather incestuous, and this book has its share with the inevitable stories about Fred and Johnners. Mosey has led a rich life and this is revealed with warmth in the book which is readable and mostly enjoyable. He does, however, perpetuate the myth that the cricket reporter's job is the best in the world and there are not too many in the tents on the county grounds around the country, fighting for telephones, who would agree with him.

MEMOIRS OF A TWELFTH MAN. *Anthony Couch*: Unwin Paperbacks: 140 pp, £1.95
A gentle, humorous and whimsical look at cricket on the village green, this book was published in hardback last year and now, thankfully, is brought to us in a cheap edition. There is fun for everyone here.

AT THE DOUBLE. *Richard Hadlee*: Stanley Paul: 166 pp, £7.95
It was inevitable that Richard Hadlee's great double achievement of 1984 should be celebrated with a book and this offering, in collaboration with Tony Francis, is a simple and straightforward account of a great all-rounder. It is an uncomplicated book and easy reading.

R.E.S. WYATT FIGHTING CRICKETER. *Gerald Pawle*: George Allen & Unwin: 278 pp £12.95
Another very important biography, Gerald Pawle's book is a finely detailed account of the life of one of cricket's less charismatic characters, but one whose life has spanned a great period in the history of the game. Wyatt was an unfortunate captain of England, a member of Jardine's side in Australia and, as the title suggests, a tenacious batsman at Test and county level. There is, at times, something of a dourness in the story that Pawle tells, but, in essence, that is the man about whom he is writing. One must congratulate author and publisher in giving us this valuable book.

AN INDEX TO WISDEN CRICKETER'S ALMANACK, 1864–1984. *Compiled by Derek Barnard*: Queen Anne Press: 645 pp, £17.50
This is a useful, but not exhaustive, index to the cricketer's bible which has been compiled by Derek Barnard, a Kent schoolmaster. It is very much a labour of love and is particularly useful in listing the articles that have appeared in *Wisden* over a period of 120 years, but I must admit that, at the price, I had expected something a little grander and more substantial. Having said that, I find the book of great use. In a second one can determine where to find an obituary, a book review or a comment on a player's retirement. Well done, Mr Barnard.

THE WISDEN BOOK OF TEST CRICKET, 1877 TO 1984. *Compiled and edited by Bill Frindall: Queen Anne Press: 1104 pp, £29.50*
This enlarged, revised edition supercedes Frindall's first volume, which went to 1978, and the pioneer work done by Roy Webber. It seemed that it would be impossible to improve on the 1978 edition and that all that could be done would be to bring it up to date. This is not the case, for this volume is tighter and fuller than that published six years ago. There is now a players' register and the comments on the Tests are more substantial and pertinent. This is an indispensable record of Test cricket from the first meeting between England and Australia at Melbourne in 1877 to Sri Lanka's debut at Lord's in 1984. It is very expensive, but no serious student of the game can afford to be without it.

THE JOURNAL OF THE CRICKET SOCIETY. *Edited C.W. Porter*: T[illegible] Cricket Society
The least publicised, but certainly among the most erudit[illegible] journals, *The Cricket Society Journal*, now in its twelfth volume[illegible] fascinating collection of records, remininiscences, opinions, re[illegible] statistical data, history and eccentricity. The spring edition[illegible] tained contributions from Sir Donald Bradman, Bob Willis, [illegible] Lodge, Chris Harte, Terence Prittie and Jim Coldham. It is se[illegible] to members of The Cricket Society which, in itself, is reason e[illegible] for becoming a member. A consistent and splendid achiever[illegible]